McDougal Littell

THE LANGUAGE OF
LITERATURE

ANNOTATED TEACHER'S EDITION

GRADE
7

ISBN: 0-395-73709-5

Printed in the United States of America.

5 6 7 8 9 - **DWO** - 01 00 99

Table of Contents

Telling Our Story

What Is *The Language of Literature?*

Is it a literature anthology? an integrated language arts series? a new approach to teaching and learning? *The Language of Literature* is all of these things—and much, much more.

CLASSIC STORIES, FRESH VOICES, AND NEW PERSPECTIVES

The powerful mix of selections in *The Language of Literature* reflects the exciting nature of our own society:

- Classic and contemporary literature
- Multicultural perspectives
- A mix of genres
- Authentic readings in a variety of media.

A PROGRAM, NOT A BOOK

The Language of Literature is not simply an anthology with a collection of "extras." It is a seamlessly integrated program that links a student book to comprehensive lesson support; mini-lessons in writing, language, and communication; innovative technology; and access for students with special needs.

AN INTEGRATED APPROACH TO LANGUAGE

The selections in *The Language of Literature* become the springboard to a rich mix of language experiences:

- Writing workshops
- Grammar and vocabulary instruction
- Oral communication activities
- Critical viewing and listening
- Research skills
- Visual and media literacy

A WAY TO MAKE STUDENTS CARE

A strong student-centered approach acknowledges the differences among readers and the experiences they bring to a literary selection or writing experience. Responding options, multimodal activities, access materials for all students, and strategies for using media and technology ensure that students learn in a way that matches their individual learning styles.

A NEW WAY OF SEEING

A striking art program is only the beginning of the series' attention to visual and media literacy. Special activities and features throughout the program teach students that reading literature can be the first step toward reading the people and the world around them.

A SPRINGBOARD TO THE WORLD

Every prereading page, response section, and writing workshop provides meaningful activities and thoughtful connections that link the literature to students' own lives, to other curriculum areas, to their family and community, to other cultures, and to the situations and issues they confront every day in the "real world."

A PARTNER IN TECHNOLOGY

A rich videodisc treasury of images, audio and electronic libraries, Internet connections, and the unique Writing Coach software all support the literature and activities in this series. In addition, lessons in the pupil book model the use of technology to access information, network with others, and produce creative multimedia projects.

A WAY TO CONNECT AND REFLECT

Perhaps most importantly, *The Language of Literature* provides a way for students to connect the literature to the often confusing situations they encounter on the pathway from childhood to adulthood. The thoughtfully chosen selections, carefully crafted themes, and rich variety of learning options connect to students' lives and allow them to reflect on how universal certain experiences are.

Program Authors and Consultants

Arthur N. Applebee Professor of Education, State University of New York at Albany; Director, Center for the Learning and Teaching of Literature; Senior Fellow, Center for Writing and Literacy

Andrea B. Bermúdez Professor of Studies in Language and Culture; Director, Research Center for Language and Culture; Chair, Foundations and Professional Studies, University of Houston-Clear Lake

Sheridan Blau Senior Lecturer in English and Education and former Director of Composition, University of California at Santa Barbara; Director, South Coast Writing Project; Director, Literature Institute for Teachers; Vice President, National Council of Teachers of English

Rebekah Caplan Coordinator, English Language Arts K-12, Oakland Unified School District, Oakland, California; Teacher-Consultant, Bay Area Writing Project, University of California at Berkeley; served on the California State English Assessment Development Team for Language Arts

Franchelle S. Dorn Professor of Drama, Howard University, Washington, D.C.; Adjunct Professor, Graduate School of Opera, University of Maryland, College Park, Maryland; Co-founder of The Shakespeare Acting Conservatory, Washington, D.C.

Peter Elbow Professor of English, University of Massachusetts at Amherst; Fellow, Bard Center for Writing and Thinking

Susan Hynds Professor and Director of English Education, Syracuse University, Syracuse, New York

Judith A. Langer Professor of Education, State University of New York at Albany; Co-director, Center for the Learning and Teaching of Literature; Senior Fellow, Center for Writing and Literacy

James Marshall Professor of English and English Education, University of Iowa, Iowa City

Overview

Core Components

The Language of Literature is a seamlessly integrated program that provides teachers with a common-sense system for teaching literature, language, and communication skills. The components described on these pages—the core elements of the program—provide teachers and students with all of the materials they need in a flexible, customizable format. (For more information on each element, please see pages T10 to T25.)

ANNOTATED TEACHER'S EDITION

This comprehensive book provides all of the material you require for a successful teaching experience.

- Unit Content Overview and Planning Charts
- Student Projects
- Professional Enrichment Pages
- Family and Community Involvement
- Annotations for Literature Selections and Writing Workshops
- Bar Codes to LaserLinks
- Recommended Resources

PUPIL EDITION

A rich mix of classic, contemporary and multicultural literature is the starting point from which your class begins its exploration of a world of ideas and experiences. Writing Workshops in each unit continue this exploration, moving students from the literature to interactions with real-world communication and technology.

Selected titles in Spanish & English

LITERATURE CONNECTIONS

Unique to *The Language of Literature,* these stand-alone books allow you to decide which plays and novels to include in your literature class. Each longer work is accompanied by several related readings that extend the subject or theme.

SourceBook Provides you with all the information and student support materials you will need to present fresh and effective lessons.

Spanish Editions Selected titles are also available in Spanish, with corresponding Spanish SourceBook pages.

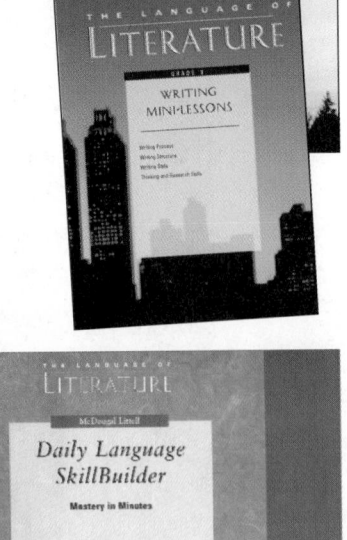

Resource Materials

UNIT RESOURCE BOOK
Organized by unit and selection, these copymasters provide you with a variety of ways to build and reinforce student skills in reading comprehension, spelling, vocabulary, and writing.

GRAMMAR MINI-LESSONS WRITING MINI-LESSONS
These transparency packs allow teachers to identify areas where students need help, and to teach exactly what is needed when it is needed. Corresponding grammar exercise sheets ensure that students get the practice they need on key areas of language and usage.

DAILY LANGUAGE SKILLBUILDER
Through daily, literature-based exercises, this product integrates the teaching of grammar, proofreading, and punctuation skills.

Integrated Technology

 LASERLINKS
A treasury of full-motion video, photographs, and fine art, this videodisc provides the following program support:

- Selection Support: Historical and Cultural Background
- Author Interviews
- Writing Springboards
- Visual Vocabulary
- Art Galleries
- Storytelling
- Spanish Audio Track

 WRITING COACH
A comprehensive word-processing program with a unique, multi-column format and on-line writing support, the Writing Coach is a powerful tool for collaborative writing, peer response, and evaluation.

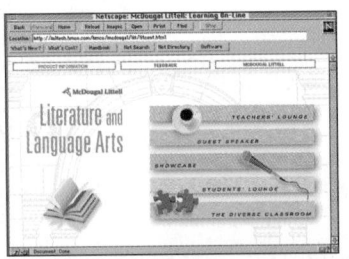

INTERNET CONNECTIONS
Program-related information can be accessed through the McDougal Littell home page at http://www.hmco.com/mcdougal

AUDIO LIBRARY
These tapes contain professional recordings of nearly every selection in the anthology. The performances can be used to enhance the literature or to provide support for less-proficient readers.

TEST GENERATOR
Use this software to customize your own selection tests from hundreds of available questions.

Assessment Package

TEACHER'S GUIDE TO ASSESSMENT AND PORTFOLIO USE This guide describes the types and uses of assessment and includes guidesheets, assessment forms, and checklists.

FORMAL ASSESSMENT This booklet contains selection and unit tests, writing assessment materials, and standardized test practice.

ALTERNATIVE ASSESSMENT With these materials—modeled on the authentic assessment materials used in many states and districts across the country—you can evaluate the processes students use as they read and write, as well as the products they create.

Access for Students Acquiring English

TEACHER'S SOURCEBOOK FOR LANGUAGE DEVELOPMENT A teacher handbook that includes teaching strategies and techniques.

TRANSLATIONS IN SPANISH A separate anthology that includes Spanish translations of one selection per unit.

RELATED READINGS Literature that is tied thematically to *The Language of Literature* units. Available in Spanish, Vietnamese, Cantonese, Cambodian, and Hmong.

SELECTION SUMMARIES Summaries of the literature in five languages: Spanish, Vietnamese, Cantonese, Cambodian, and Hmong.

READING AND WRITING SUPPORT Practice activities that support every literature selection and guidesheets for Writing Workshops.

.FAMILY AND COMMUNITY INVOLVEMENT Available in six languages, these pages allow students to extend unit activities outside the classroom.

LITERATURE CONNECTIONS Spanish translations of selected titles for grades 6-12.

AUDIO LIBRARY These professional recordings may be used as support for Students Acquiring English.

LASERLINKS A separate Spanish audio track and Spanish captions allow students full access to the resources on these videodiscs.

The Literature Lesson: Pupil Edition

Each literature lesson is divided into three sections: Previewing, the literature selection itself, and Responding Options. This student-centered lesson offers a wide range and choice of activities.

PREVIEWING

Personal Connection Helps students explore prior experience and knowledge about topics covered in the selection.

Historical (Biographical, Cultural, Literary, Geographical, Scientific, etc.) Connection Provides important background information relevant to the selection.

Reading Connection Presents direct instruction in a reading skill designed to improve comprehension of the selection.

Writing Connection Serves as an alternative to the Reading Connection. Allows students to explore selection-related topics through writing.

Graphic Organizer Helps students explore new topics and structure their thinking.

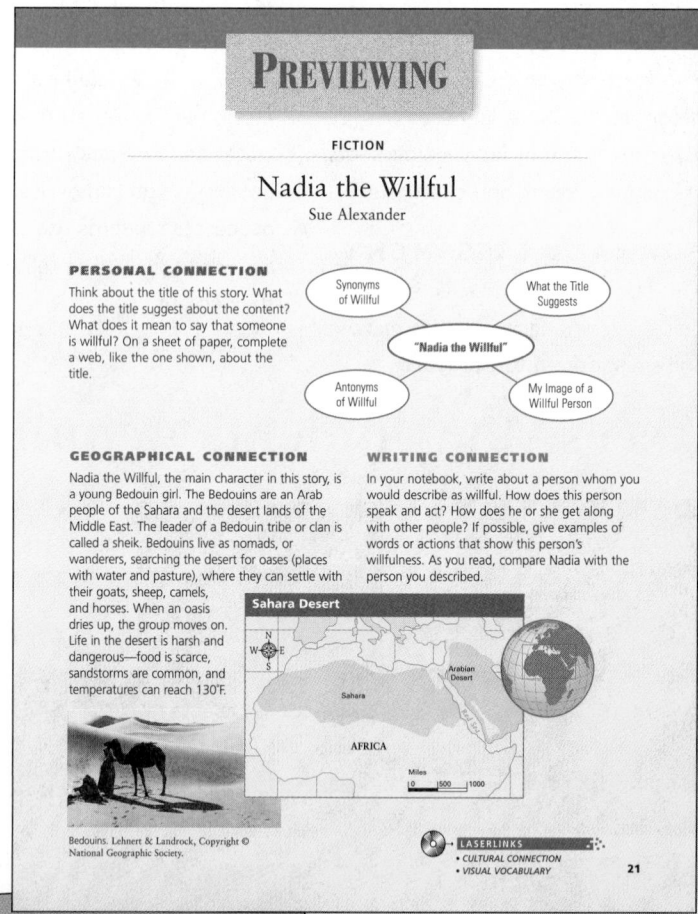

THE SELECTION

The finest literature offerings. Represented are traditional and contemporary pieces, familiar and new voices.

Natural and thematic connections. Selections are organized thematically and, where appropriate, chronologically.

Attractive, engaging design. Helps entice and motivate students.

Active reading questions. Provided as appropriate within selections to help students with comprehension of more challenging pieces.

Nadia the Willful
by Sue Alexander

In the land of the drifting sands where the Bedouin move their tents to follow the fertile grasses, there lived a girl whose stubbornness and flashing temper caused her to be known throughout the desert as Nadia the Willful.

Nadia's father, the sheik Tarik, whose kindness and graciousness caused his name to be praised in every tent, did not know what to do with his willful daughter.

Only Hamed, the eldest of Nadia's six brothers and Tarik's favorite son, could calm Nadia's temper when it flashed.

RESPONDING OPTIONS

FROM PERSONAL RESPONSE TO CRITICAL ANALYSIS

REFLECT
1. What were your thoughts about Nadia as you finished reading? Write about her in your notebook.

RETHINK
2. Think about the word web and notebook entry about willfulness that you made for the Personal Connection on page 21. In your opinion, does Nadia deserve to be called willful? Explain.

3. How does Nadia change across time, and why?

4. Nadia's father promises to punish anyone who speaks Hamed's name. Why do you think Nadia is able to change her father's mind?
   Consider
   • Nadia's character
   • the effect of grief on her father

RELATE
5. Read "Primer Lesson" on page 27. What connections do you see between Sandburg's warning about "proud words" and Nadia the Willful?

6. Nadia and Tarik have different ways of reacting to death. Do their actions bring to mind any feelings or experiences of grief and death that you know about or have read about?

LITERARY CONCEPTS

The **setting** of a story is the time and place in which the events of the story happen. Skim the story and make a list of details about the setting. What role does the setting play in this story? How important is the setting?

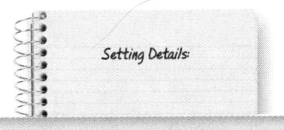

Setting Details:

ANOTHER PATHWAY

Cooperative Learning
What if this story were told by Nadia or by Tarik? With a small group, choose what you consider the most important section of the story. Then rewrite that section, telling it from either Nadia's or Tarik's point of view. Share your version with the class.

QUICKWRITES

1. Compose a **narrative poem** that tells the events of this story. (For a description of narrative poetry, see page 104.)

2. Prepare a **character sketch** that would help an actor playing Tarik in a film version of "Nadia the Willful" to understand Tarik's character.

3. Imagine you are the set designer for the film version of the story. Write a **memo** to the director, describing the setting that you want to create. In your memo use details that you gathered for the Literary Concepts activity.

📁 **PORTFOLIO** Save your writing. You may want to use it later as a springboard to a piece for your portfolio.

ALTERNATIVE ACTIVITIES

Make a desert **diorama.** Cut a small square opening in one side of a shoebox. Using sand, sandpaper, paint, and other materials, create the setting of the story inside the shoebox. Then make paper figures of the characters and their animals to position within the scene. View the scene from the top or through the opening.

ACROSS THE CURRICULUM

🧪 **Science** Find out how deserts and oases form and change. Present your information to the class in an oral report.

WORDS TO KNOW

Review the Words to Know in the boxes at the bottom of the selection pages. Write the word most closely related to the idea of each sentence.

1. The sheik was angered by the theft of the horses and commanded that anyone found stealing a horse be put to death.

2. The marketplace was packed with every imaginable item—blankets, saddles, robes of woven cloth, and even wooden toys for children.

3. Looking out at the horizon, Hamed sat and thought of the extraordinary size of the hot and silent desert.

4. They camped at the oasis, all of the families of the tribe sleeping in tents and cooking food for one another over open fires.

5. There was no way he could survive in the desert alone, but he had no choice because the tribe would not let him live among them any longer.

SUE ALEXANDER

At the age of eight, Sue Alexander began writing stories for her friends. She says, "At that time I was small for my age (I still am) and very clumsy. So clumsy, in fact, that none of my classmates wanted me on their teams at recess time." One day Alexander spent recess time telling a made-up story to someone else who was not playing. Before her story was finished, all the rest of the class had come to listen. This incident sparked her love of storytelling. Alexander says she would not tra[...] any other profession because writi[...]

1933–

sense of fun and her need to share. Her fantasy stories all begin the same way—with how she feels about something. She writes for young people because she likes to excite their imaginations.

Alexander's short stories have been published in *My Weekly Reader* and other magazines for younger readers. The book publication of *Nadia the Willful* won many honors, including one from the American Library Association in 1983.

28 UNIT ONE PART 1: SEIZING THE MOMENT

RESPONDING OPTIONS

From Personal Response to Critical Analysis Invites student-centered discussion with the response-based approach made famous by McDougal Littell. Includes questions that help students relate the literature to their own lives.

Another Pathway Offers an alternative to typical classroom discussion. Generates full exploration of major issues in the selection.

Literary Concepts Introduces or reviews major literary terms and applies them to the selection just read.

Quickwrites Give students several innovative ways of responding to what they have read through writing.

Alternative Activities Offer opportunities to respond to their reading through multimodal activities.

Words to Know Reinforces vocabulary introduced in the selection with motivating exercises.

Author Biography Makes the authors come to life with interesting, student-friendly information. Includes listings of other works by the authors.

ADDITIONAL RESPONDING OPTIONS

Critic's Corner Gives critical commentary on an author or piece of literature and asks students to respond.

Literary Links Asks students to make connection between selection just read and another selection read at an earlier point in the book.

The Writer's Style Asks students to engage in analysis of style by focusing on stylistic traits of author being studied.

Across the Curriculum Provides cross-curricular activities that invite students to go beyond the selection to investigate new areas of study.

Art Connection Asks students to reflect on a work of fine art included in the selection.

The Literature Lesson: Resource Materials

The literature in the Pupil's Edition is reinforced and extended by the following teaching tools for students' own use.

UNIT RESOURCE BOOK

Worksheets and tests provide support for all literature selections.

- **Strategic Reading: Literature Worksheets** reinforce reading strategies and extend the understanding of literary elements.

- **Reading SkillBuilders**

- **Vocabulary SkillBuilders**

- **Spelling SkillBuilders**

- **Selection and Unit Tests** stimulate higher order thinking skills as they assess understanding of selections, literary terms, and language skills.

- **Family and Community Involvement Worksheets** connect unit themes to students' world. A separate booklet provides these same worksheets in five languages: Spanish, Vietnamese, Cantonese, Cambodian, and Hmong.

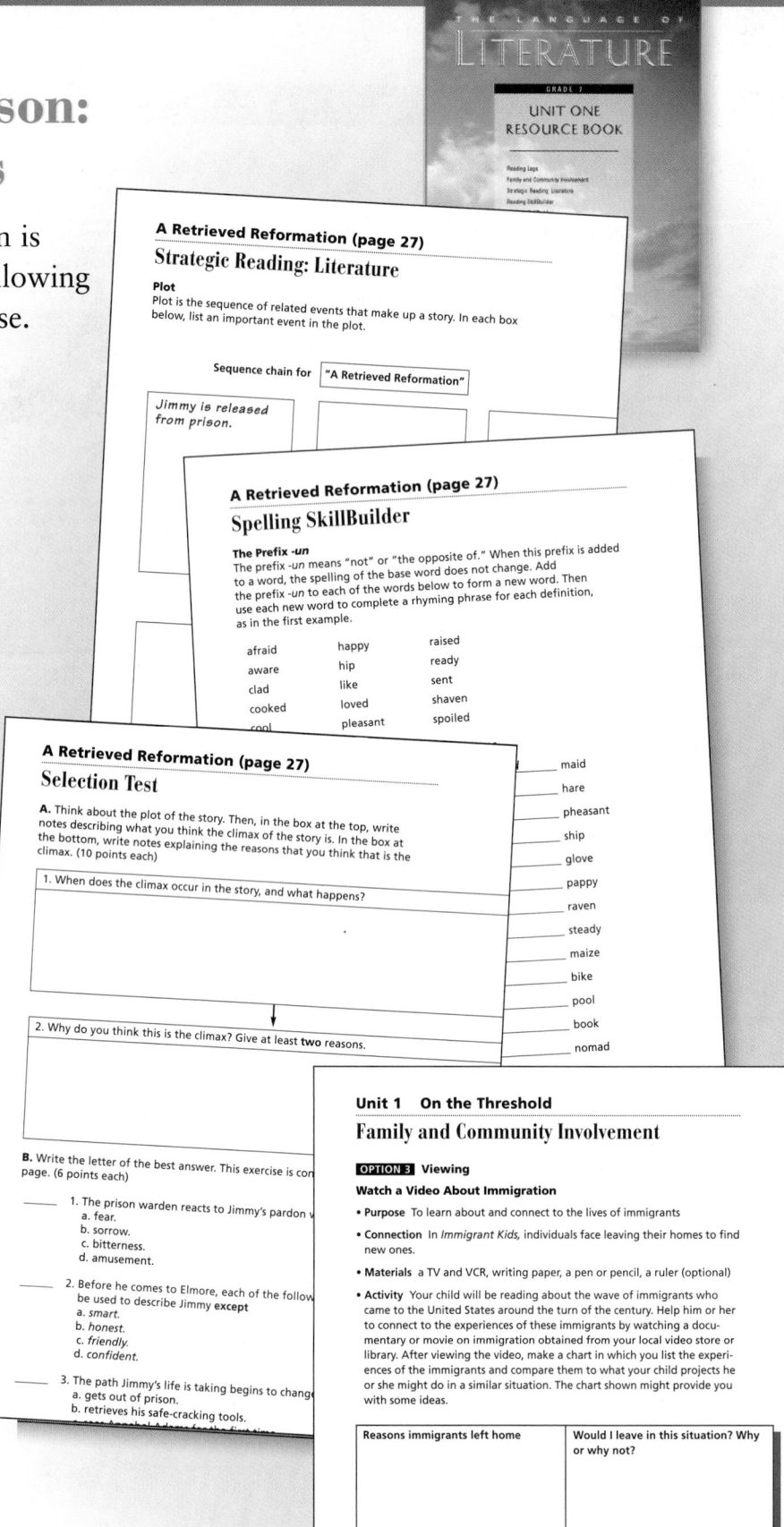

A Retrieved Reformation (page 27)

Strategic Reading: Literature

Plot
Plot is the sequence of related events that make up a story. In each box below, list an important event in the plot.

Sequence chain for "A Retrieved Reformation"

Jimmy is released from prison.

A Retrieved Reformation (page 27)

Spelling SkillBuilder

The Prefix -un
The prefix -un means "not" or "the opposite of." When this prefix is added to a word, the spelling of the base word does not change. Add the prefix -un to each of the words below to form a new word. Then use each new word to complete a rhyming phrase for each definition, as in the first example.

afraid   happy   raised
aware   hip   ready
clad   like   sent
cooked   loved   shaven
cool   pleasant spoiled

maid
hare
pheasant
ship
glove
pappy
raven
steady
maize
bike
pool
book
nomad

A Retrieved Reformation (page 27)

Selection Test

A. Think about the plot of the story. Then, in the box at the top, write notes describing what you think the climax of the story is. In the box at the bottom, write notes explaining the reasons that you think that is the climax. (10 points each)

1. When does the climax occur in the story, and what happens?

2. Why do you think this is the climax? Give at least **two** reasons.

B. Write the letter of the best answer. This exercise is con_____ page. (6 points each)

_____ 1. The prison warden reacts to Jimmy's pardon w
a. fear.
b. sorrow.
c. bitterness.
d. amusement.

_____ 2. Before he comes to Elmore, each of the follow be used to describe Jimmy **except**
a. *smart.*
b. *honest.*
c. *friendly.*
d. *confident.*

_____ 3. The path Jimmy's life is taking begins to change
a. gets out of prison.
b. retrieves his safe-cracking tools.

Unit 1   On the Threshold

Family and Community Involvement

OPTION 3   Viewing

Watch a Video About Immigration

- **Purpose** To learn about and connect to the lives of immigrants

- **Connection** In *Immigrant Kids*, individuals face leaving their homes to find new ones.

- **Materials** a TV and VCR, writing paper, a pen or pencil, a ruler (optional)

- **Activity** Your child will be reading about the wave of immigrants who came to the United States around the turn of the century. Help him or her to connect to the experiences of these immigrants by watching a documentary or movie on immigration obtained from your local video store or library. After viewing the video, make a chart in which you list the experiences of the immigrants and compare them to what your child projects he or she might do in a similar situation. The chart shown might provide you with some ideas.

Reasons immigrants left home	Would I leave in this situation? Why or why not?
Hardships faced by immigrants	What strategies would I use to cope with such hardships?
Cultural traditions/possessions saved by immigrants	What things have been passed on to me? What would I take or pass on?

LASERLINKS

A Level One videodisc program that enhances the literature curriculum, develops visual literacy, and helps students explore and interact with the literature.

- Provides historical and cultural background to strengthen interdisciplinary connections

- Helps build students' vocabulary through the Visual Vocabulary feature

- Contains author interviews

- Includes images to stimulate writing

- Presents storyteller in action

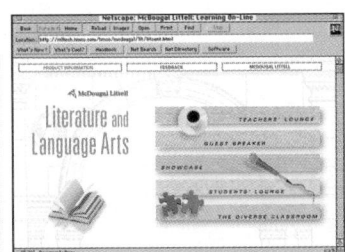

AUDIO LIBRARY

Recordings of almost all selections in each anthology. Provides easy listening, enhances and enriches students' literary experience, and helps students develop strategies for critical listening.

INTERNET CONNECTIONS

The following resources can be accessed through the McDougal Littell home page at http://www.hmco.com/mcdougal

- Literature selection support

- Links to professional materials and organizations

- Teacher discussion groups and bulletin boards

The Writing Workshops: Pupil Edition

Paired writing workshops in each unit offer students two distinct ways to respond to the literature and make "real world" connections.

WRITING ABOUT LITERATURE
This workshop appears as a set of three related lessons.

- **The Writer's Style** lesson focuses on a writing skill such as sentence variety or elaboration. Literary excerpts and a real-world model show the technique in context.

- **The Guided Assignment** invites students to explore the literature through both creative and analytical writing.

- **Complete Writing Process.** Provides advice for each stage of the writing process, from prewriting to publication and reflection.

- **Student models.** Illustrate the process and choices of another student writer.

- **Peer response questions and Standards for Evaluation.** Help students assess and revise their writing.

- **Skills Instruction.** Grammar in Context and Grammar Skillbuilders teach grammar concepts that relate to the writing.

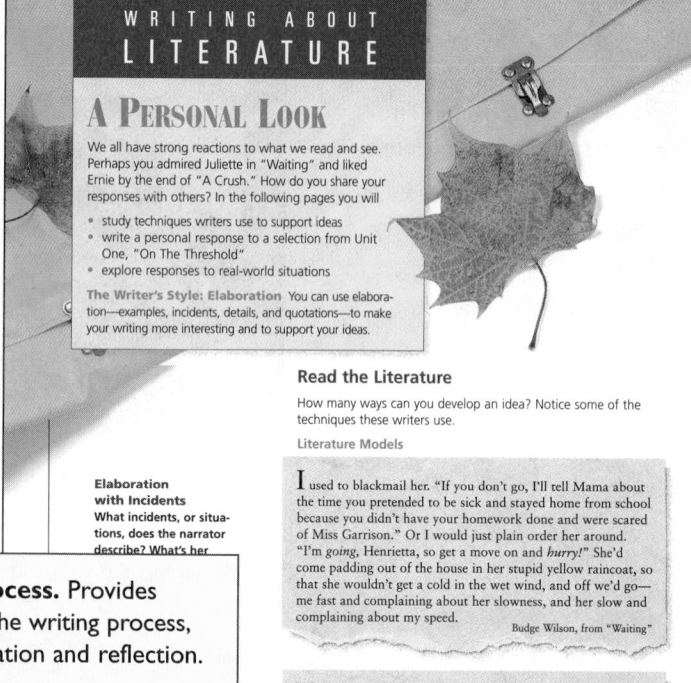

WRITING ABOUT
LITERATURE

A PERSONAL LOOK

We all have strong reactions to what we read and see. Perhaps you admired Juliette in "Waiting" and liked Ernie by the end of "A Crush." How do you share your responses with others? In the following pages you will

- study techniques writers use to support ideas
- write a personal response to a selection from Unit One, "On The Threshold"
- explore responses to real-world situations

The Writer's Style: Elaboration You can use elaboration—examples, incidents, details, and quotations—to make your writing more interesting and to support your ideas.

Elaboration with Incidents
What incidents, or situations, does the narrator describe? What's her

Read the Literature

How many ways can you develop an idea? Notice some of the techniques these writers use.

Literature Models

I used to blackmail her. "If you don't go, I'll tell Mama about the time you pretended to be sick and stayed home from school because you didn't have your homework done and were scared of Miss Garrison." Or I would just plain order her around. "I'm *going*, Henrietta, so get a move on and *hurry!*" She'd come padding out of the house in her stupid yellow raincoat, so that she wouldn't get a cold in the wet wind, and off we'd go—me fast and complaining about her slowness, and her slow and complaining about my speed.

Budge Wilson, from "Waiting"

They lived, the two of them, in tiny dark rooms always illuminated by the glow of a television set, Ernie's bags of Oreos and Nutter Butters littering the floor, his baseball cards scattered across the sofa, his heavy winter coat thrown over the arm of a chair so he could wear it whenever he wanted, and his box of Burpee seed packages sitting in the middle of the kitchen table.

Cynthia Rylant, from "A Crush"

WRITING ABOUT LITERATURE

Analysis

The plot is a series of events in a story. By studying and analyzing the events, characters, and dialogue in a story, you will be able to better understand what makes the story interesting and effective. Analyzing a story situation can also help you understand the situations that you observe in your life.

GUIDED ASSIGNMENT
Write a Plot Analysis On the next few pages, you will look closely at a key event from one of the stories you've just read. Then you'll have a chance to describe how that event was important to the story.

❶ Prewrite and Explore

In a plot analysis, you look closely at one part of a story—the events that occur—and write about how and why these events make the story interesting. Jot down stories you enjoyed and a key event you remember from each.

CHOOSING A STORY AND EVENT

These questions might help you choose a story and event to write about.

- Which story has the most surprising or interesting turn of events?
- Which event in the story is the most exciting? Why?
- What caused this event to happen? How does this event affect what happens later?

GATHERING INFORMATIO

Remember that writers someti logue to describe events in a s key information about events in the conversations the chara

Also, a story map like the one can help you think about even tion and how they help to tell

Student's Story Map

Grammar in Context

Prepositional Phrases A prepositional phrase is a group of words that begins with a preposition and ends with an object. Prepositional phrases help a writer elaborate an idea by adding precision, clarity, and details. They are often used in descriptions and to clarify when or how things happen.

In a clearing
There stood a tall tree stump that we used as a stage.

Tanya chose songs for us to sing. She sang the lead

vocals, and I practiced backup. Then *After a week* we invited our

families to a short concert.

Look at the example above.

- The first sentence has two prepositional phrases: "In a clearing" (the preposition is *in*; its object is *clearing*) and "as a stage" (the preposition is *as*; its object is *stage*).
- The last sentence has two prepositional phrases, "After a week" and "to a short concert." Identify each preposition and its object.

For more information about prepositions, see page 890 of the Grammar Handbook.

SkillBuilder

GRAMMAR FROM WRITING

Placing Prepositional Phrases
Sometimes you can move a prepositional phrase without changing a sentence's meaning.

Tanya couldn't bully me anymore after the move.

After the move, Tanya couldn't bully me anymore.

Sometimes the placement of a prepositional phrase can make the sentence unclear.

Unclear *In the tall reeds, I watched the little birds.*

Clear *I watched the little birds in the tall reeds.*

In the first example above, note how the phrase *In the tall reeds* seems to modify *I.* The phrase should be placed closer to *birds,* the word it modifies.

APPLYING WHAT YOU'VE LEARNED
Write each sentence so that its meaning is clearer.

READING THE WORLD

WHAT HAPPENS NEXT?

If you think about it, everyday life is a lot like a collection of stories. There are interesting characters, surprising plot twists, and different conversations.

View In your notebook, describe what you see in the picture.

Interpret What's going on? Why is this man doing this? What problem might he have? What will happen next?

Discuss In a group, discuss who the man might be and why this scene might not end up as you expect. Record your thoughts and the group's ideas in your notebook. You can use the SkillBuilder on this page to help you make a prediction.

SkillBuilder

CRITICAL THINKING

Predicting Outcomes

You make predictions every day, though you may not know it. For example, when you look out the window, see dark clouds, and then grab an umbrella as you go out the door, you're predicting that it might rain. When you make a prediction, you use obvious clues, information from a reliable source, or knowledge from experience to guess what might happen in the future.

What kinds of clues help you predict what may happen next in the picture on this page? Maybe something like this happened to you, and that experience tells you how to predict an outcome. What specific information in the picture helps you make your prediction? Making predictions gets you involved in a situation and can help you relate your experiences to the world.

APPLYING WHAT YOU'VE LEARNED

Write a short dialogue in which you talk to the man in the picture and give him some advice. You could tell him your predictions or maybe ask a question. How will he respond? Share your dialogue with a classmate and try reading it aloud.

READING THE WORLD **317**

■ **Reading the World** builds visual literacy and shows students how the same skills they have just used to analyze and write about literature can also be used to observe, interpret, and understand the world around them.

WRITING FROM EXPERIENCE

The second writing workshop invites students to extend the unit theme by creating products for real purposes and real audiences in situations they encounter in the world around them.

Primary source materials. Magazine and newspaper articles, photographs, charts, and graphs provide a springboard to writing while building critical thinking and media literacy skills.

Oral communication and research skills. Used during prewriting as students gather information. Students are also encouraged to use technology—from CD-ROMs to on-line services—to access information.

Alternative forms of publishing. Visual, oral, and electronic products are suggested and modeled.

WRITING FROM EXPERIENCE

WRITING A REPORT

What gives people the will to succeed? The selections in Unit Four, "Meeting Challenges," focus on characters who made extraordinary efforts to achieve a goal. What did they do to outsmart an enemy, win a sporting event, or solve a mystery?

GUIDED ASSIGNMENT

Write a Report of Information Writing a report about someone who has achieved a major goal not only can help you learn about the person but might help you achieve some goals of your own. The ideas on the following pages will help you shape information about a topic into a report.

1 Exploring Beyond the News

What challenges are represented in the materials on these pages? Often articles, pictures, or maps tell you only a small part of a person's story. To learn more, you have to do research. What else would you like to know about each topic? What kinds of sources would you use to learn more?

Brainstorm and Record Ideas

What examples of people meeting challenges have you heard or read about? In a group, brainstorm some general categories, such as

- scientific achievement
- sports
- personal triumphs
- historical events
- breakthroughs in medicine

Then discuss specific examples from each category. Where might you find information about stories that grab your interest or inspire you? Discuss your ideas with your group and record them in your notebook.

Newspaper Article

Rule-Breaking Teacher Helps Students Succeed

What makes a public school teacher quit after 14 years on the job to open her own school? How does she help "unteachable" students succeed when others can't?

In 1975, Marva Collins became frustrated with the Chicago school system's failure to teach inner-city kids. So she started her own school with $5,000 of her own money, at one point teaching out of her home. Because no one had heard of her school, she advertised by word of mouth. By working one-on-one with her students and using strict discipline, she helped them succeed. Test scores of Collins's students drastically improved, and many later succeeded in college.

Today, Collins is known as one of the country's leading educators, and her West Side Preparatory School is nationally known.

"I just feel good when I see children who develop in class right in front of me, seeing kids who were written off as failures come in here and achieve," she says.

Kids Deal with Loss at Camp Courage

How can scaling a wall help a child deal with the death of a loved one? The counselors at Camp Courage say that working with a partner to climb a steep wall can teach kids that people need one another when facing difficult challenges—whether the challenge is scaling a wall or dealing with the loss of a family member. The camp is one of about 50 in the country that work to meet the needs of bereaved youth.

"These kids are doing the most courageous thing that anybody can do, and that's dealing with loss," said Glenna Waxler, director of the program.

Newspaper Article

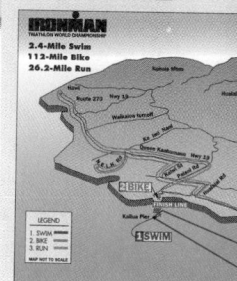

Map
This map shows the course of the Ironman Triathlon, which is held on the island of Hawaii. How do you think people prepare for the event?

3 QuickWrite

Take a few minutes to write about the people you discussed in your group. What challenges did they face? What qualities did each person need to succeed? List questions you'd ask to understand each person better.

Decision Point Choose one person whose story interests you the most. This is the person you'll research and write about.

UNIT FOUR: MEETING CHALLENGES

SCOPE AND SEQUENCE OF WRITING INSTRUCTION

The writing workshops in *The Language of Literature* grow in sophistication as your students do, providing a rich variety of writing assignments that become more challenging in every grade. In the following chart, blue dots indicate the Writing About Literature workshops, and red dots indicate the Writing from Experience workshops. The number following each assignment represents the unit in which it appears.

Writing Strands	Grade 6	Grade 7	Grade 8
Firsthand and Expressive	• Personal Response / 1* • Anecdote / 1	• Personal Response / 1 • First Hand Narrative / 1	• First Hand Narrative / 1 • Personal Response / 4
Narrative and Literary	• Character Sketch / 2 • Fill in the Blanks / 4 • Writing in Kind: Poem / 5	• Short Story / 2 • Creative Response: Extending story / 4 • Writing in Kind: Fable / 6	• Creative Response: Change Story Element / 1 • Short Story / 2 • Creative Response: Scene from play / 6
Informative Exposition	• Interpretive: Analyze passage / 2 • Analysis: Plot devices / 3 • Problem-solution / 3 • Compare/contrast / 4 • Critical: Evaluating the message / 6	• Analysis: Imagery / 2 • Interpretive: Answering big question / 3 • Definition: Abstract idea / 3 • Critical: Review (poetry) / 5 • Compare-contrast / 6	• Interpretive: Finding the message / 2 • Critical: Evaluating ideas / 3 • Problem-solution / 3 • Eye-witness / 4 • Analysis: Poetry / 5
Persuasion	• Opinion / 5	• Opinion / 5	• Persuasive essay / 5
Report	• I-Search / 6	• Report / 4	• Report / 6

* Denotes unit number

Writing and Language: Resource Materials

MINI-LESSONS

The unique mini-lesson transparency packs in *The Language of Literature* allow you to decide what your students need to learn and when they need to learn it.

- **Writing Mini-Lessons.** Cover skills ranging from unity and coherence to voice and style.

- **Grammar Mini-Lessons with Copy Masters.** Provide instruction on the most common usage problems faced by writers.

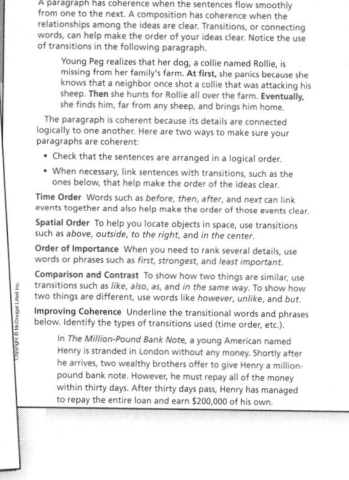

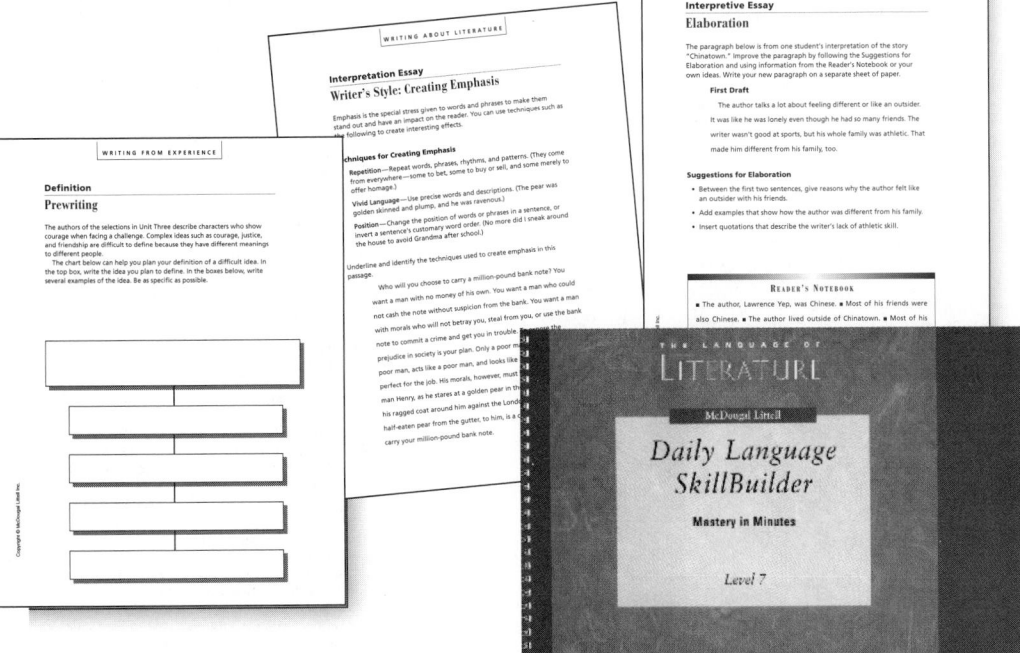

UNIT RESOURCE BOOK

In addition to support for the literature selections, the Unit Resource Book provides comprehensive practice and support for each stage of the writing process. Copymasters include the following:

Writer's Style Worksheet
Prewriting Worksheet
Elaboration Practice
Peer Response Guide
Revising and Proofreading Practice
Complete Student Model
Rubrics for Evaluation

DAILY LANGUAGE SKILLBUILDER
Through daily exercises, this product integrates grammar, proofreading, and punctuation skills with literature-based content

WRITING COACH
Collaborative Writing Software
This interactive, multimedia writing program on CD-ROM guides students through the writing process in a collaborative environment.

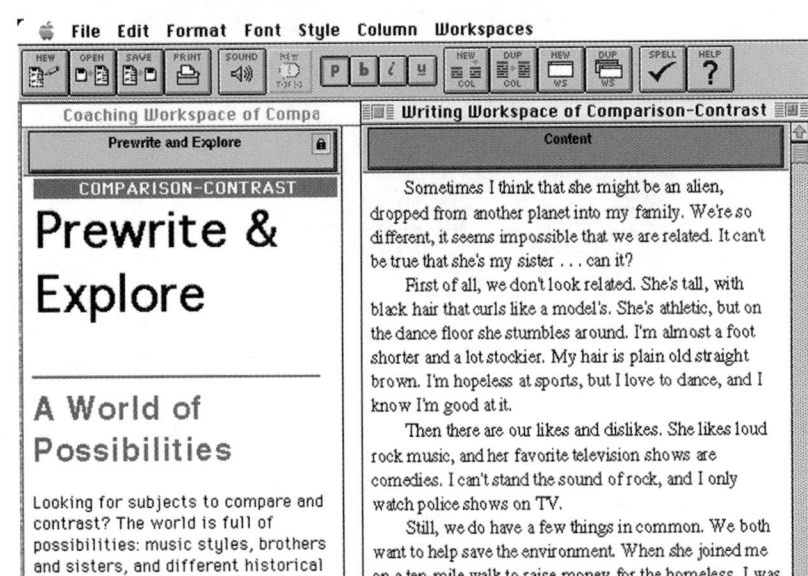

Special Features of the Pupil Edition

This book contains a wealth of special features to help enrich each student's learning experience.

WHAT DO YOU THINK?

Motivating activities at the beginning of each unit part that help introduce students to the theme they are about to encounter in the next grouping of selections.

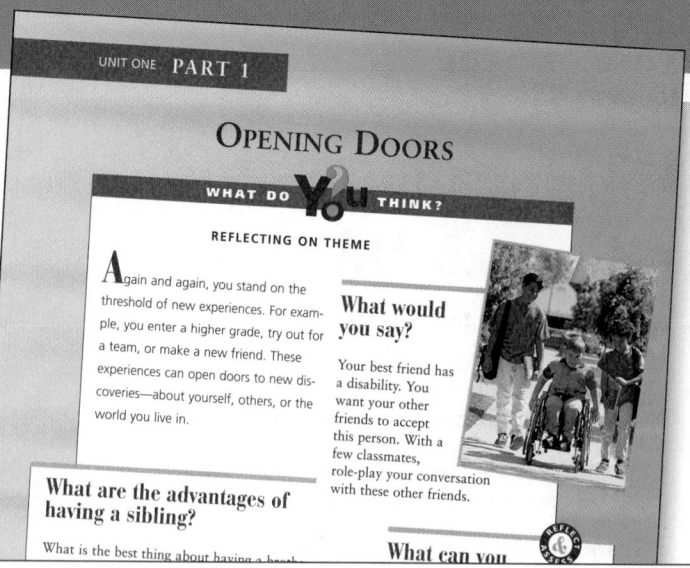

STRATEGIES FOR READING

Shows students how active readers read—what they think about as they read and how they make connections between the text and real-world experiences. Model provides thoughts and comments of two students engaged in the following active reading strategies:

- Question
- Connect
- Predict
- Clarify
- Evaluate

FOCUS ON FICTION

FOCUS ON FICTION/ NONFICTION/POETRY/DRAMA

Helps introduce and reinforce basic knowledge of literary elements. Also includes strategies used when reading a particular genre. Feature provides students with a strong foundation for the reading of literature.

Across Time and Place

The Oral Tradition

"I feel the energy of the earth coming up through my feet and all these thousands of ancestors around me. I am not just a separate voice crying out. I have a responsibility to the earth and to my ancestors to tell the truth. The truth is where I'm moved in my heart."

Brenda Wong Aoki

Brenda Wong Aoki lives in California, where she keeps the ancient traditions of her ancestors alive through storytelling.

668   669

THE ORAL TRADITION

Celebrates storytelling in an entire unit devoted to folk tales from around the world. The featured storyteller also appears on LaserLinks. Activity-based response options throughout the unit tie to other curriculum areas.

REFLECT & ASSESS

UNIT THREE: STEPPING FORWARD

As you read the selections in this unit, you probably thought deeply about what it means to step forward. Now is a good time for you to reflect on what you have learned in this unit. Choose one of the options in each of the following sections to assess how your thinking has evolved.

REFLECTING ON THEME

OPTION 1 **Making Connections** Jot down the messages about stepping forward that you got from the selections you read in this unit. Then choose two or more messages that you think young people might take to heart as words to live by. Write a paragraph or two, explaining your choices.

Consider . . .
- the challenges that the characters in the selections face
- the challenges that young people face today
- the messages that might inspire young people the most

OPTION 2 **Writing a Dialogue** Choose a character from a selection in Part 2, and imagine that character in the situation of one of the characters in Part 1. How do you think the character from

Part 2 would respond to the situation? What do you think he or she might learn about showing courage? Write a dialogue between the two characters to explore your ideas.

OPTION 3 **Holding a Panel Discussion** Work with a small group of classmates to select three or more characters whom you consider good role models for young people today. Then hold a panel discussion to explore reasons why you chose those characters over all the others. Cite examples from the selections and from your own experience to support your ideas.

Self-Assessment: Which selection influenced your thinking the most? Which influenced your thinking the least? Write a paragraph or two to explore these questions.

REVIEWING LITERARY CONCEPTS

OPTION 1 **Examining Ch**

REFLECT & ASSESS

Features end-of-unit activities that help students review and reflect upon what they have learned in the course of a unit. Includes options for:

- Reflecting on Theme
- Reviewing Literary Concepts
- Portfolio Building

① The Writing Process

The writing process consists of four stages: prewriting, drafting, revising and editing, and publishing and reflecting. As the graphic to the right shows, these stages are not steps that you must complete in a set order. Rather, you may return to any one at any time in your writing process, using feedback from your readers along the way.

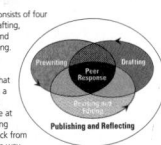

1.1 Prewriting

In the prewriting stage, you explore your ideas and discover what you want to write about.

Choosing a Topic

Ideas for writing can come from just about anywhere: experiences, memories, conversations, dreams, or imaginings. The following techniques can help you to generate ideas for writing and to choose a writing topic you care about.

Personal Techniques

Make a list of people, places, and activities that have had an effect on you.

Ask who, what, when, where, and why about an important event.

Ask what-if questions about everyday life.

Browse through magazines, newspapers, and on-line bulletin boards for ideas.

Sharing Techniques

With a group, brainstorm a topic by trying to come up with as many ideas as you can. Do not stop to evaluate your ideas for at least five minutes.

Writing Techniques

Use a word or picture as a starting point for freewriting.

Freewrite for a short time and then circle the ideas you would like to explore.

Pick a topic and list all the related ideas that occur to you.

Graphic Techniques

Create a time line of memorable events in your life.

Make a cluster diagram of subtopics related to a general topic.

Determining Your Purpose

At some time during your writing process, you need to consider your purpose, or general reason, for writing. For example, your purpose may be one of the following: to express yourself, to entertain, to explain, to describe, to analyze, or to persuade. To clarify your purpose, ask yourself questions like these:

- Why did I choose to write about my topic?
- What aspects of the topic mean the most to me?
- What do I want others to think or feel after they read my writing?

Identifying Your Audience

Knowing who will read your writing can help you clarify your purpose, focus your topic, and choose the details and tone that will best communicate your ideas. As you think about your readers, ask yourself questions like these:

- What does my audience already know about my topic?
- What will they be most interested in?
- What language is most appropriate for this audience?

1.2 Drafting

In the drafting stage, you put your ideas on paper and allow them to develop and change as you write.

There's no right or wrong way to draft. Sometimes you might be adventuresome and just dive right into your writing. At other times, you might draft slowly, planning carefully beforehand. You can combine aspects of these approaches to suit yourself and your

LINK TO LITERATURE

Inspiration for your writing can come from everyday events. Shirley Jackson's story "Charles," on page 593—a humorous account of a child's difficult but amusing introduction to kindergarten—is based on her own experience as a parent.

LINK TO LITERATURE

Roald Dahl—the author of *Boy: Tales of Childhood*, on page 473—understood the importance of identifying his audience. According to Dahl, "Children are a great discipline because they are highly critical . . . And if you think a child is getting bored, you must think up something that jolts it [the child] back. Something that tickles."

STUDENT HANDBOOKS

- **Reading Terms and Literary Concepts**
- **Writing Handbook**
- **Multimedia Handbook**
- **Grammar Handbook**

The Teacher's Edition

Unit Support

Special pages in the Teacher's Edition provide professional enrichment and help you plan your lessons, organize necessary materials, and carry out unit-related projects.

SKILLS TRACE

Allows you to see at a glance the scope and sequence of reading, writing, speaking, listening, viewing, study, research, grammar, spelling, and literary skills taught within each part of a unit. Also tracks the teaching of vocabulary words and the type and frequency of multimodal activities.

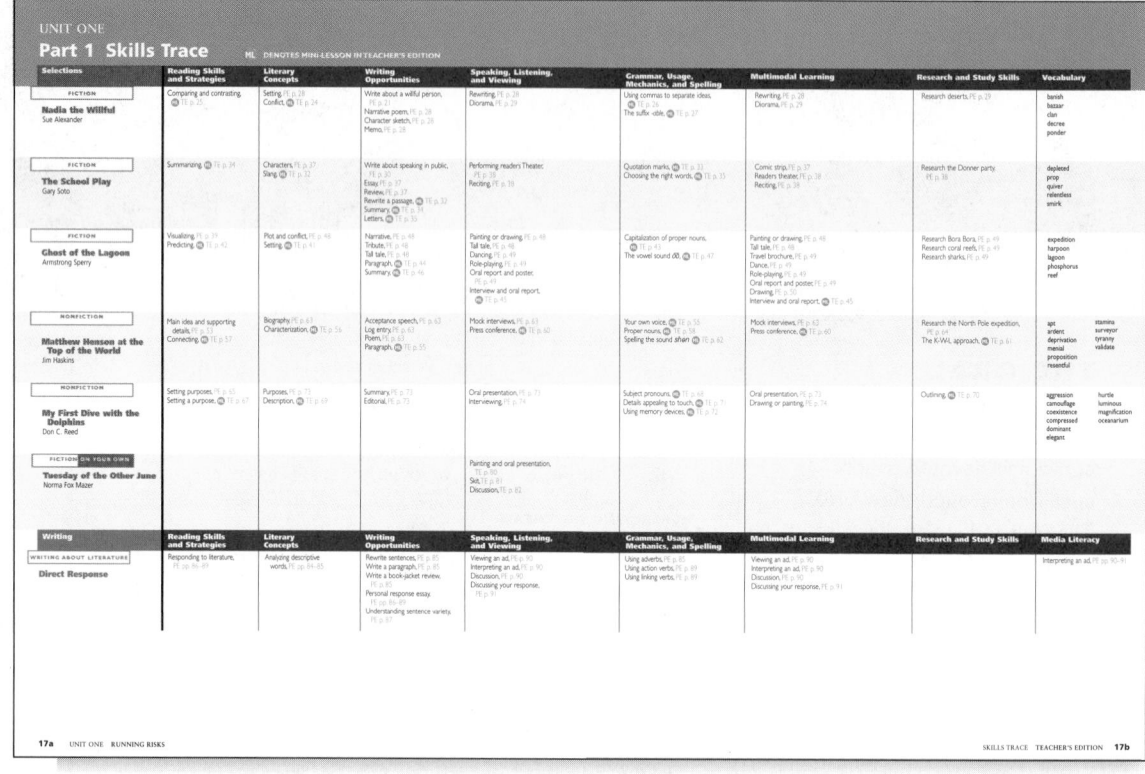

RECOMMENDED RESOURCES

Invaluable listings of unit-specific resources for both you and your students. Includes titles of novels and plays, cross-curricular readings, and media resources. Helps you extend and enrich the curriculum and enrich yourself professionally as well.

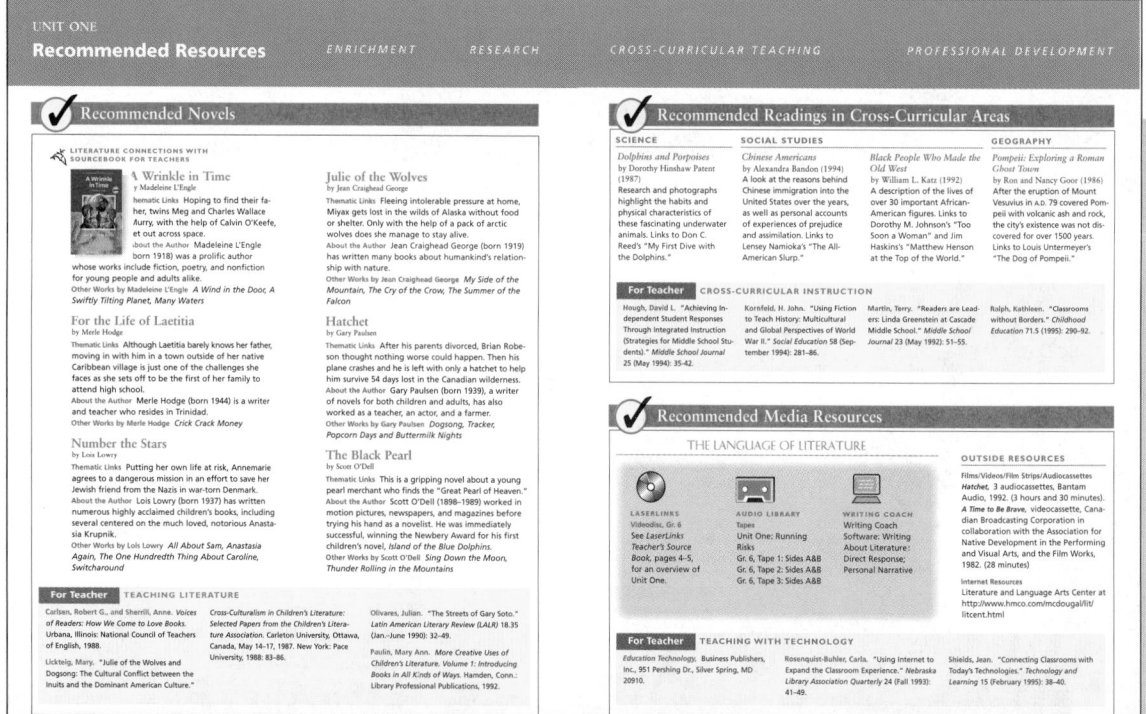

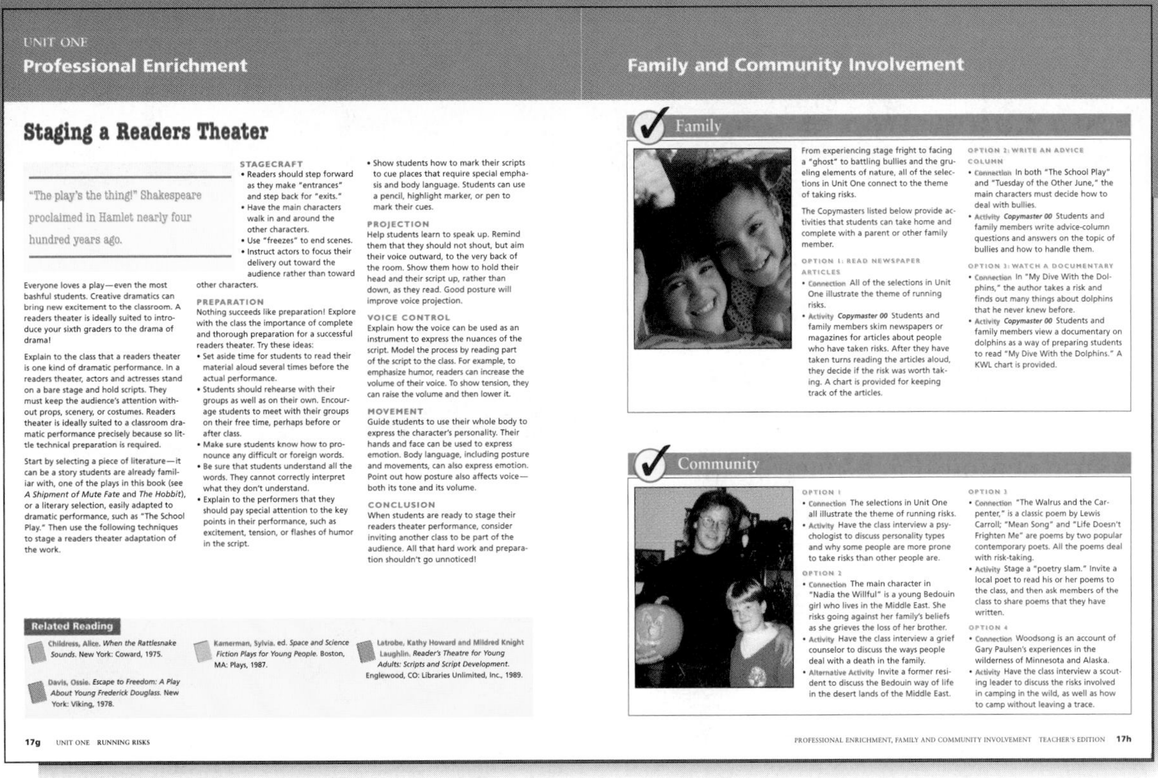

UNIT ONE

Professional Enrichment

Staging a Readers Theater

"The play's the thing!" Shakespeare proclaimed in Hamlet nearly four hundred years ago.

Everyone loves a play—even the most bashful students. Creative dramatics can bring new excitement to the classroom. A readers theater is ideally suited to introduce your sixth graders to the drama of drama!

Explain to the class that a readers theater is one kind of dramatic performance. In a readers theater, actors and actresses stand on a bare stage and hold scripts. They must keep the audience's attention without props, scenery, or costumes. Readers theater is ideally suited to a classroom dramatic performance precisely because so little technical preparation is required.

Start by selecting a piece of literature—it can be a story students are already familiar with, one of the plays in this book (see *A Shipment of Mute Fate* and *The Hobbit*), or a literary selection, easily adapted to dramatic performance, such as "The School Play." Then use the following techniques to stage a readers theater adaptation of the work.

STAGECRAFT

- Readers should step forward as they make "entrances" and step back for "exits."
- Have the main characters walk in and around the other characters.
- Use "freezes" to end scenes.
- Instruct actors to focus their delivery out toward the audience rather than toward other characters.

PREPARATION

Nothing succeeds like preparation! Explore with the class the importance of complete and thorough preparation for a successful readers theater. Try these ideas:

- Set aside time for students to read their material aloud several times before the actual performance.
- Students should rehearse with their groups as well as on their own. Encourage students to meet with their groups on their free time, perhaps before or after class.
- Make sure students know how to pronounce any difficult or foreign words.
- Be sure that students understand all the words. They cannot correctly interpret what they don't understand.
- Explain to the performers that they should pay special attention to the key points in their performance, such as excitement, tension, or flashes of humor in the script.
- Show students how to mark their scripts to cue places that require special emphasis and body language. Students can use a pencil, highlight marker, or pen to mark their cues.

PROJECTION

Help students learn to speak up. Remind them that they should not shout, but aim their voice outward, to the very back of the room. Show them how to hold their head and their script up, rather than down, as they read. Good posture will improve voice projection.

VOICE CONTROL

Explain how the voice can be used as an instrument to express the nuances of the script. Model the process by reading part of the script to the class. For example, to emphasize humor, readers can increase the volume of their voice. To show tension, they can raise the volume and then lower it.

MOVEMENT

Guide students to use their whole body to express the character's personality. Their hands and face can be used to express emotion. Body language, including posture and movements, can also express emotion. Point out how posture also affects voice—both its tone and its volume.

CONCLUSION

When students are ready to stage their readers theater performance, consider inviting another class to be part of the audience. All that hard work and preparation shouldn't go unnoticed!

Related Reading

Childress, Alice. *When the Rattlesnake Sounds*. New York: Coward, 1975.

Davis, Ossie. *Escape to Freedom: A Play About Young Frederick Douglass*. New York: Viking, 1978.

Kamerman, Sylvia. ed. *Space and Science Fiction Plays for Young People*. Boston, MA: Plays, 1987.

Latrobe, Kathy Howard and Mildred Knight Laughlin. *Reader's Theatre for Young Adults: Scripts and Script Development*. Englewood, CO: Libraries Unlimited, Inc., 1989.

17g UNIT ONE RUNNING RISKS

Family and Community Involvement

Family

From experiencing stage fright to facing a "ghost" to battling bullies and the grueling elements of nature, all of the selections in Unit One connect to the theme of taking risks.

The Copymasters listed below provide activities that students can take home and complete with a parent or other family member.

OPTION 1: READ NEWSPAPER ARTICLES

- Connection All of the selections in Unit One illustrate the theme of running risks.
- Activity *Copymaster 00* Students and family members skim newspapers or magazines for articles about people who have taken risks. After they have taken turns reading the articles aloud, they decide if the risk was worth taking. A chart is provided for keeping track of the articles.

OPTION 2: WRITE AN ADVICE COLUMN

- Connection In both "The School Play" and "Tuesday of the Other June," the main characters must decide how to deal with bullies.
- Activity *Copymaster 00* Students and family members write advice-column questions and answers on the topic of bullies and how to handle them.

OPTION 3: WATCH A DOCUMENTARY

- Connection In "My Dive With the Dolphins," the author takes a risk and finds out many things about dolphins that he never knew before.
- Activity *Copymaster 00* Students and family members view a documentary on dolphins as a way of preparing students to read "My Dive With the Dolphins." A KWL chart is provided.

Community

OPTION 1

- Connection The selections in Unit One all illustrate the theme of running risks.
- Activity Have the class interview a psychologist to discuss personality types and why some people are more prone to take risks than other people are.

OPTION 2

- Connection The main character in "Nadia the Willful" is a young Bedouin girl who lives in the Middle East. She risks going against her family's beliefs as she grieves the loss of her brother.
- Activity Have the class interview a grief counselor to discuss the ways people deal with a death in the family.
- Alternative Activity Invite a former resident to discuss the Bedouin way of life in the desert lands of the Middle East.

OPTION 3

- Connection "The Walrus and the Carpenter," is a classic poem by Lewis Carroll; "Mean Song" and "Life Doesn't Frighten Me" are poems by two popular contemporary poets. All the poems deal with risk-taking.
- Activity Stage a "poetry slam." Invite a local poet to read his or her poems to the class, and then ask members of the class to share poems that they have written.

OPTION 4

- Connection Woodsong is an account of Gary Paulsen's experiences in the wilderness of Minnesota and Alaska.
- Activity Have the class interview a scouting leader to discuss the risks involved in camping in the wild, as well as how to camp without leaving a trace.

PROFESSIONAL ENRICHMENT, FAMILY AND COMMUNITY INVOLVEMENT TEACHER'S EDITION 17h

PROFESSIONAL ENRICHMENT

Articles that give practical ideasfor teaching literature and writing. Topics relate to unit content.

FAMILY AND COMMUNITY INVOLVEMENT

Activities designed to involve parents and other family members and to foster students' interaction with other people in their communities. Corresponding worksheets are provided.

COOPERATIVE PROJECT

Content-related projects for teachers interested in cooperative learning. Includes suggestions for how to assign and manage the projects and tells how connections might be made to other curriculum areas. Two different projects are included for each unit.

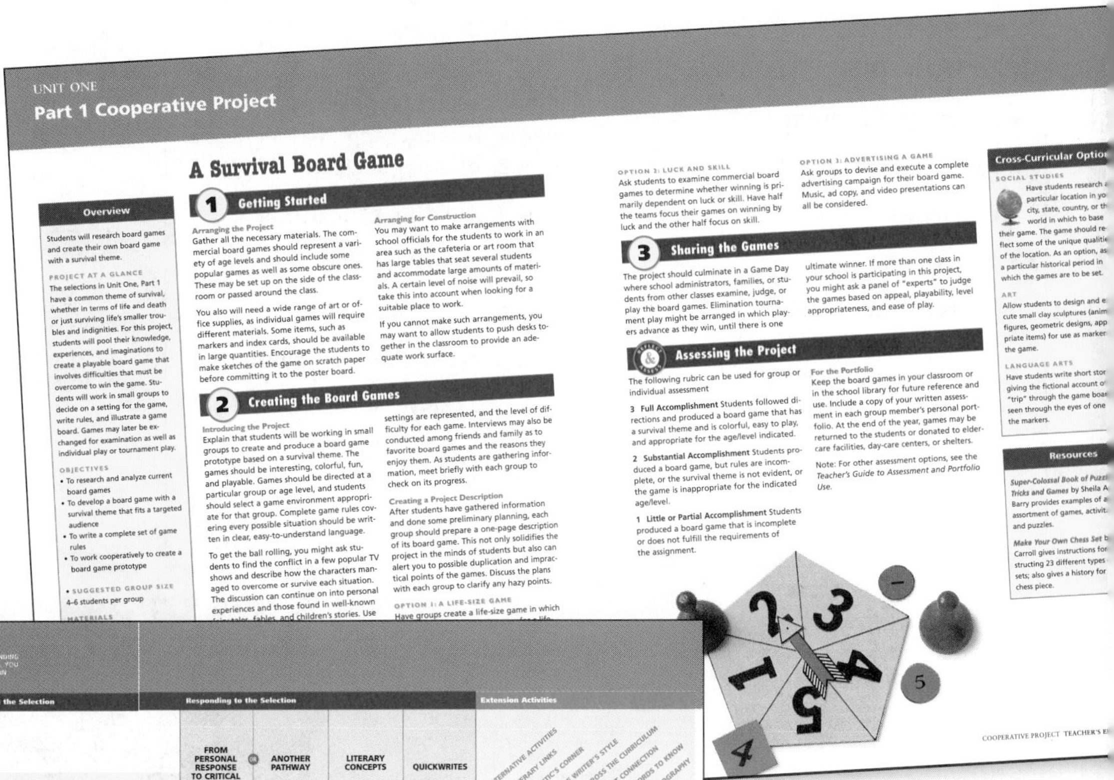

UNIT ONE

Part 1 Cooperative Project

A Survival Board Game

Overview

Students will research board games and create their own board game with a survival theme.

PROJECT AT A GLANCE

The selections in Unit One, Part 1 have a common theme of survival, whether in terms of life and death or just surviving life's smaller troubles and indignities. For this project, students will pool their knowledge, experiences, and imaginations to create a playable board game that involves difficulties that must be overcome to win the game. Students will work in small groups to decide on a setting for the game, write rules, and illustrate a game board. Games may later be exchanged for examination as well as individual play or tournament play.

OBJECTIVES

- To research and analyze current board games
- To develop a board game with a survival theme that fits a targeted audience
- To write a complete set of game rules
- To work cooperatively to create a board game prototype

• SUGGESTED GROUP SIZE

4–6 students per group

MATERIALS

1 Getting Started

Arranging the Project

Gather all the necessary materials. The commercial board games should represent a variety of age levels and should include some popular games as well as some obscure ones. These may be set up on the side of the classroom or passed around the class.

You also will need a wide range of art or office supplies, as individual games will require different materials. Some items, such as markers and index cards, should be available in large quantities. Encourage the students to make sketches of the game on scratch paper before committing it to the poster board.

Arranging for Construction

You may want to make arrangements with school officials for the students to work in an area such as the cafeteria or art room that has large tables that seat several students and accommodate large amounts of materials. A certain level of noise will prevail, so take this into account when looking for a suitable place to work.

If you cannot make such arrangements, you may want to allow students to push desks together in the classroom to provide an adequate work surface.

2 Creating the Board Games

Introducing the Project

Explain that students will be working in small groups to create and produce a board game prototype based on a survival theme. The games should be interesting, colorful, fun, and playable. Games should be directed at a particular group or age level, and students should select a game environment appropriate for that group. Complete game rules covering every possible situation should be written in clear, easy-to-understand language.

To get the ball rolling, you might ask students to find the conflict in a few popular TV shows and describe how the characters managed to overcome or survive each situation. The discussion can continue on into personal experiences and those found in well-known fairy tales, fables, and children's stories. Use

settings are represented, and the level of difficulty for each game. Interviews may also be conducted among friends and family as to favorite board games and the reasons they enjoy them. As students are gathering information, meet briefly with each group to check on its progress.

Creating a Project Description

After students have gathered information and done some preliminary planning, each group should prepare a one-page description of its board game. This not only solidifies the project in the minds of students but also can alert you to possible duplication and impractical points of the games. Discuss the plans with each group to clarify any hazy points.

OPTION 1: A LIFE-SIZE GAME

Have groups create a life-size game in which

OPTION 2: LUCK AND SKILL

Ask students to examine commercial board games to determine whether winning is primarily dependent on luck or skill. Have half the teams focus their games on winning by luck and the other half focus on skill.

OPTION 3: ADVERTISING A GAME

Ask groups to devise and execute a complete advertising campaign for their board game. Music, ad copy, and video presentations can all be considered.

3 Sharing the Games

The project should culminate in a Game Day where school administrators, families, or students from other classes examine, judge, or play the board games. Elimination tournament play might be arranged in which players advance as they win, until there is one ultimate winner. If more than one class in your school is participating in this project, you might ask a panel of "experts" to judge the games based on appeal, playability, level appropriateness, and ease of play.

Assessing the Project

The following rubric can be used for group or individual assessment

3 **Full Accomplishment** Students followed directions and produced a board game that has a survival theme and is colorful, easy to play, and appropriate for the age/level indicated.

2 **Substantial Accomplishment** Students produced a board game, but rules are incomplete, or the survival theme is not evident, or the game is inappropriate for the indicated age/level.

1 **Little or Partial Accomplishment** Students produced a board game that is incomplete or does not fulfill the requirements of the assignment.

For the Portfolio

Keep the board games in your classroom or in the school library for future reference and use. Include a copy of your written assessment in each group member's personal portfolio. At the end of the year, games may be returned to the students or donated to elder-care facilities, day-care centers, or shelters.

Note: For other assessment options, see the *Teacher's Guide to Assessment and Portfolio Use.*

Cross-Curricular Optio

SOCIAL STUDIES

Have students research a particular location in yo city, state, country, or th world in which to base their game. The game should reflect some of the unique qualitie of the location. As an option, as a particular historical period in which the games are to be set.

ART

Allow students to design and e cute small clay sculptures (anim figures, geometric designs, app priate items) for use as marker the game.

LANGUAGE ARTS

Have students write short stor giving the fictional account o "trip" through the game boar seen through the eyes of one the markers.

Resources

Super-Colossal Book of Puzz Tricks and Games by Sheila A Barry provides examples of a assortment of games, activit and puzzles.

Make Your Own Chess Set b Carroll gives instructions for structing 23 different types sets; also gives a history for chess piece.

COOPERATIVE PROJECT TEACHER'S E

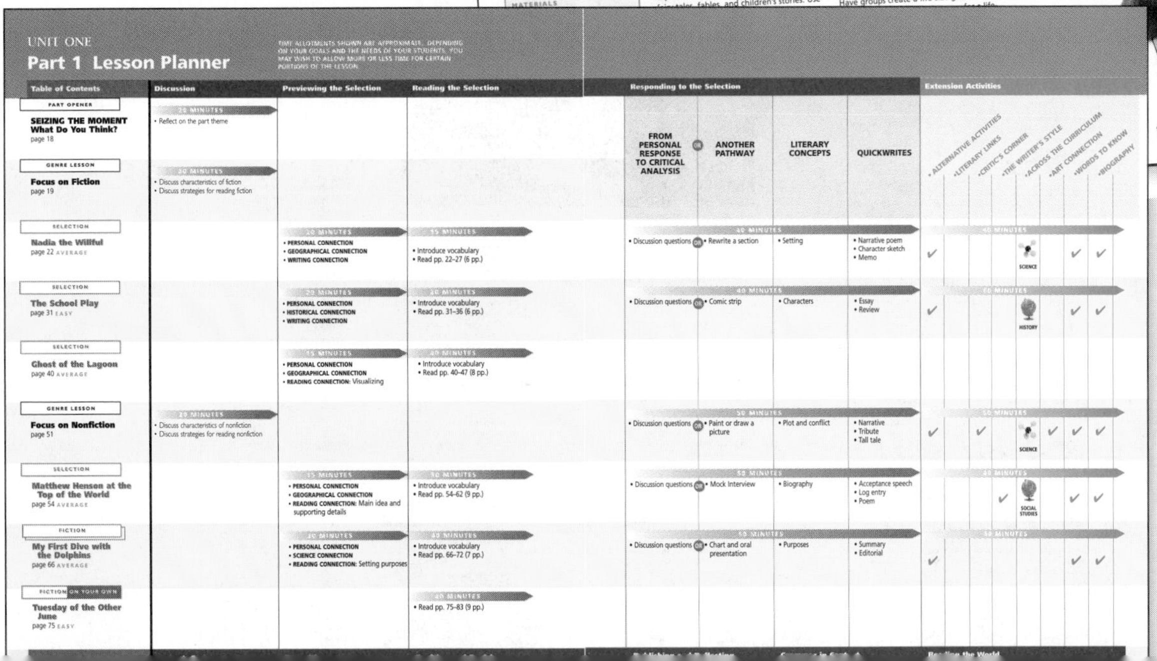

UNIT ONE

Part 1 Lesson Planner

TIME ALLOTMENTS SHOWN ARE APPROXIMATE, DEPENDING ON YOUR GOALS AND THE NEEDS OF YOUR STUDENTS. YOU MAY WISH TO ALLOW MORE OR LESS TIME FOR CERTAIN PORTIONS OF THE LESSON.

Table of Contents	Discussion	Previewing the Selection	Reading the Selection	Responding to the Selection: From Personal Response to Critical Analysis	OR Another Pathway	Literary Concepts	Quickwrites	Extension Activities: Alternative Activities	Literary Links	Critic's Corner	The Writer's Style	Across the Curriculum	Art Connection	Words to Know	Biography
PART OPENER **SEIZING THE MOMENT What Do You Think?** page 18	[illegible] MINUTES • Reflect on the part theme														
GENRE LESSON **Focus on Fiction** page 19	[illegible] MINUTES • Discuss characteristics of fiction • Discuss strategies for reading fiction														
SELECTION **Nadia the Willful** page 22 AVERAGE		[illegible] MINUTES • PERSONAL CONNECTION • GEOGRAPHICAL CONNECTION • WRITING CONNECTION	[illegible] MINUTES • Introduce vocabulary • Read pp. 22–27 (6 pp.)	[illegible] MINUTES • Discussion questions	• Rewrite a section	• Setting	• Narrative poem • Character sketch • Memo	[illegible] MINUTES ✓				SCIENCE		✓	✓
SELECTION **The School Play** page 31 EASY		[illegible] MINUTES • PERSONAL CONNECTION • HISTORICAL CONNECTION • WRITING CONNECTION	[illegible] MINUTES • Introduce vocabulary • Read pp. 31–36 (6 pp.)	[illegible] MINUTES • Discussion questions	• Comic strip	• Characters	• Essay • Review	[illegible] MINUTES ✓				HISTORY		✓	✓
SELECTION **Ghost of the Lagoon** page 40 AVERAGE		[illegible] MINUTES • PERSONAL CONNECTION • GEOGRAPHICAL CONNECTION • READING CONNECTION: Visualizing	[illegible] MINUTES • Introduce vocabulary • Read pp. 40–47 (8 pp.)												
GENRE LESSON **Focus on Nonfiction** page 51	[illegible] MINUTES • Discuss characteristics of nonfiction • Discuss strategies for reading nonfiction			[illegible] MINUTES • Discussion questions	• Paint or draw a picture	• Plot and conflict	• Narrative • Tribute • Tall tale	[illegible] MINUTES ✓		✓		SCIENCE	✓	✓	✓
SELECTION **Matthew Henson at the Top of the World** page 54 AVERAGE		[illegible] MINUTES • PERSONAL CONNECTION • GEOGRAPHICAL CONNECTION • READING CONNECTION: Main idea and supporting details	[illegible] MINUTES • Introduce vocabulary • Read pp. 54–62 (9 pp.)	[illegible] MINUTES • Discussion questions	• Mock Interview	• Biography	• Acceptance speech • Log entry • Poem	[illegible] MINUTES			✓	SOCIAL STUDIES		✓	✓
FICTION **My First Dive with the Dolphins** page 66 AVERAGE		[illegible] MINUTES • PERSONAL CONNECTION • SCIENCE CONNECTION • READING CONNECTION: Setting purposes	[illegible] MINUTES • Introduce vocabulary • Read pp. 66–72 (7 pp.)	[illegible] MINUTES • Discussion questions	• Chart and oral presentation	• Purposes	• Summary • Editorial	[illegible] MINUTES ✓						✓	✓
FICTION ON YOUR OWN **Tuesday of the Other June** page 75 EASY			[illegible] MINUTES • Read pp. 75–83 (9 pp.)												

LESSON PLANNER

Helps you plan your lessons by indicating approximate length of time for each task. Allows you to accommodate a variety of classroom situations and needs.

Selection and Writing Workshop Support

The Annotated Teacher's Edition of *The Language of Literature* is a professional sourcebook designed to promote effective and efficient teaching. Each page contains features that allow you take students into, through, and beyond the literature.

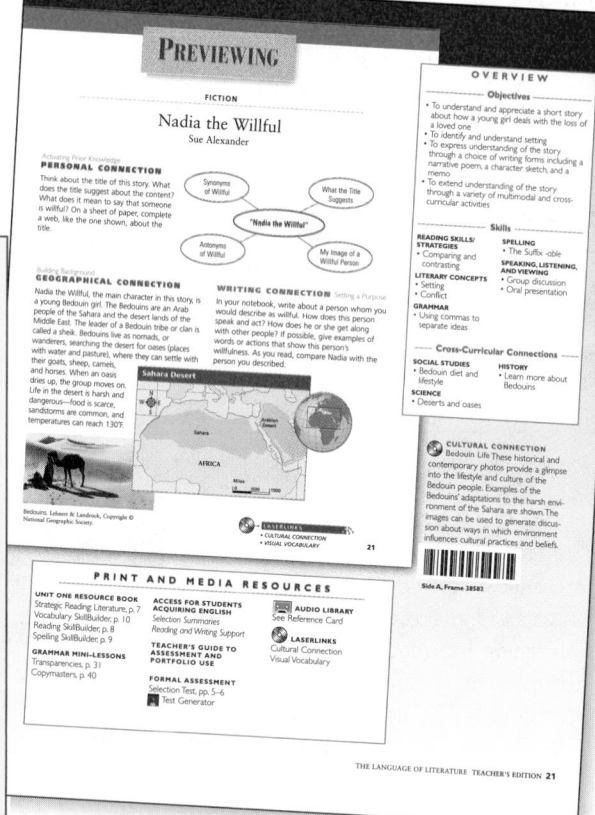

SELECTION ANNOTATIONS

Notes on literary concepts and critical thinking skills appear with each selection and its corresponding activity pages. Also included are the following features.

- **Overview** Lists objectives, key skills, and cross-curricular connections
- **Print and Media Resources**
- **Selection Summary**
- **LaserLinks bar codes**
- **Words To Know**
- **Art Notes**
- **Customizing for**
  - multiple learning styles
  - students acquiring English
  - gifted and talented students
  - less-proficient readers

- **Activities** Suggestions for whole class, small group, and individual activities
- **Mini-Lessons** Provided for grammar, spelling, reading, genre, writing, and a number of other subjects.
- **Active Reading Questions**
- **Comprehension Check**
- **Assessment Options**
- **Links Across the Curriculum**
- **Links to *The Writer's Craft***
- **Activity Support and Answer Keys**

WORKSHOP ANNOTATIONS

The Teacher's Edition notes for the Writing Workshops provide support similar to that provided for each literary selection. In addition, Writing Workshops contain the following:

- **Writing Springboards** Provides writing ideas from LaserLinks.

- **Modeling** Gives suggestions for using both literary models and student writing models.

- **SkillBuilder Mini-Lesson Support**

- **Visual and Media Literacy Features**

- **Research Skills**

- **Oral Communication**

- **Rubrics**

- **Standards for Evaluation**

Assessment Resources

The Language of Literature provides you with material that allows you to customize assessment to best fit the activities and structure of your particular classroom. With options for formal, informal, and alternative assessment, these resources provide you with all the support you need.

TEACHER'S GUIDE TO ASSESSMENT AND PORTFOLIO USE

This Teacher's Guide

■ provides information on different types and forms of assessment: formal selection and unit tests, portfolio building, authentic assessment, reading notebooks, self-assessment, group and project assessment, and more.

■ helps you decide which assessment types you wish to use and explains how to implement those approaches

■ provides forms and checklists that can be used to give shape to assessment choices

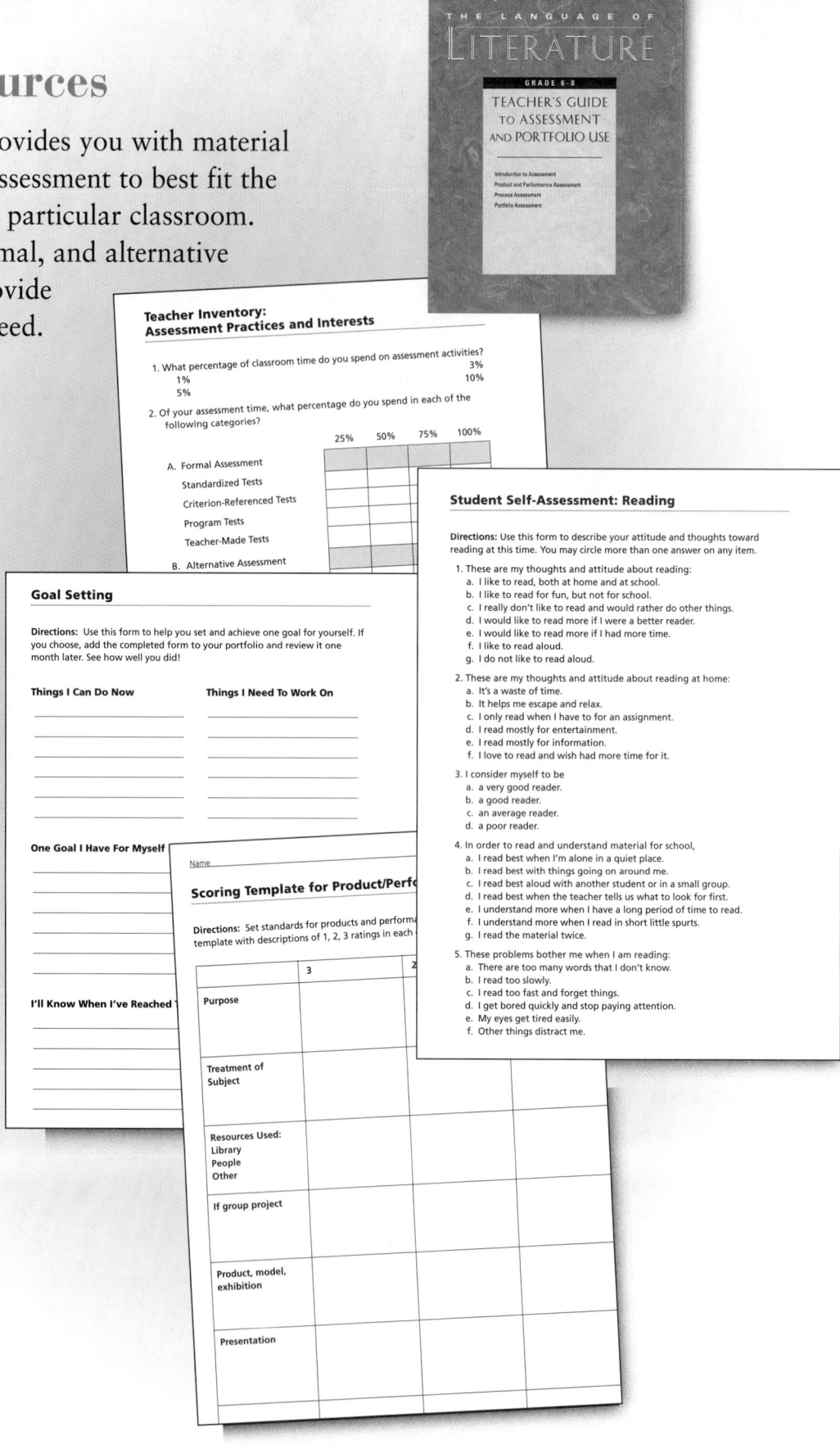

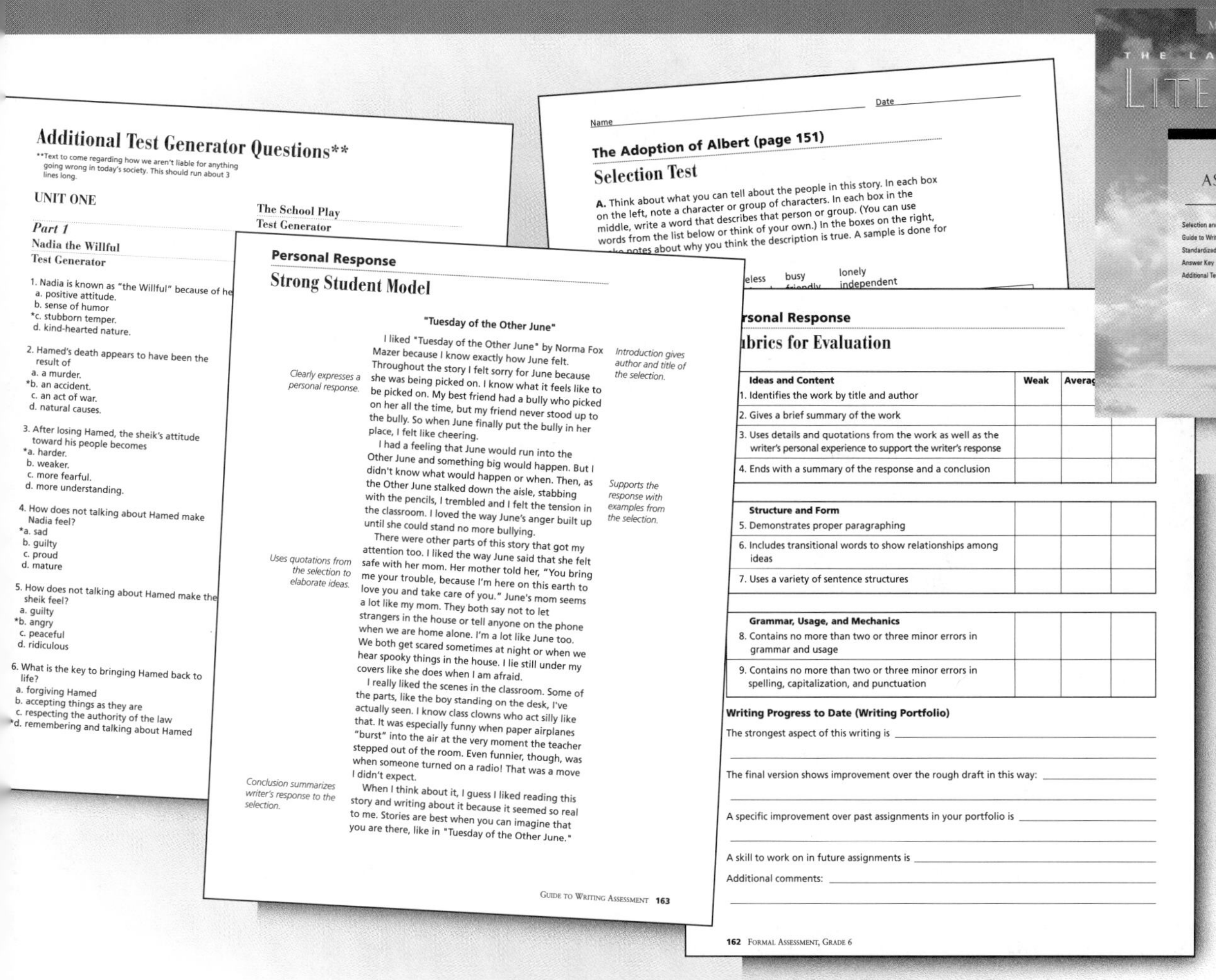

Additional Test Generator Questions**

**Text to come regarding how we aren't liable for anything going wrong in today's society. This should run about 3 lines long.

UNIT ONE

Part 1
Nadia the Willful
Test Generator

The School Play
Test Generator

1. Nadia is known as "the Willful" because of her
   a. positive attitude.
   b. sense of humor
   *c. stubborn temper.
   d. kind-hearted nature.

2. Hamed's death appears to have been the result of
   a. a murder.
   *b. an accident.
   c. an act of war.
   d. natural causes.

3. After losing Hamed, the sheik's attitude toward his people becomes
   *a. harder.
   b. weaker.
   c. more fearful.
   d. more understanding.

4. How does not talking about Hamed make Nadia feel?
   *a. sad
   b. guilty
   c. proud
   d. mature

5. How does not talking about Hamed make the sheik feel?
   a. guilty
   *b. angry
   c. peaceful
   d. ridiculous

6. What is the key to bringing Hamed back to life?
   a. forgiving Hamed
   b. accepting things as they are
   c. respecting the authority of the law
   *d. remembering and talking about Hamed

Name _____ Date _____

The Adoption of Albert (page 151)

Selection Test

A. Think about what you can tell about the people in this story. In each box on the left, note a character or group of characters. In each box in the middle, write a word that describes that person or group. (You can use words from the list below or think of your own.) In the boxes on the right, take notes about why you think the description is true. A sample is done for...

...less   busy   lonely
...   friendly   independent

Personal Response

Strong Student Model

Clearly expresses a personal response.

Uses quotations from the selection to elaborate ideas.

Conclusion summarizes writer's response to the selection.

"Tuesday of the Other June"

I liked "Tuesday of the Other June" by Norma Fox Mazer because I know exactly how June felt. Throughout the story I felt sorry for June because she was being picked on. I know what it feels like to be picked on. My best friend had a bully who picked on her all the time, but my friend never stood up to the bully. So when June finally put the bully in her place, I felt like cheering.

I had a feeling that June would run into the Other June and something big would happen. But I didn't know what would happen or when. Then, as the Other June stalked down the aisle, stabbing with the pencils, I trembled and I felt the tension in the classroom. I loved the way June's anger built up until she could stand no more bullying.

There were other parts of this story that got my attention too. I liked the way June said that she felt safe with her mom. Her mother told me, "You bring me your trouble, because I'm here on this earth to love you and take care of you." June's mom seems a lot like my mom. They both say not to let strangers in the house or tell anyone on the phone when we are home alone. I'm a lot like June too. We both get scared sometimes at night or when we hear spooky things in the house. I lie still under my covers like she does when I am afraid.

I really liked the scenes in the classroom. Some of the parts, like the boy standing on the desk, I've actually seen. I know class clowns who act silly like that. It was especially funny when paper airplanes "burst" into the air at the very moment the teacher stepped out of the room. Even funnier, though, was when someone turned on a radio! That was a move I didn't expect.

When I think about it, I guess I liked reading this story and writing about it because it seemed so real to me. Stories are best when you can imagine that you are there, like in "Tuesday of the Other June."

Introduction gives author and title of the selection.

Supports the response with examples from the selection.

GUIDE TO WRITING ASSESSMENT **163**

Personal Response

Rubrics for Evaluation

Ideas and Content	Weak	Average
1. Identifies the work by title and author		
2. Gives a brief summary of the work		
3. Uses details and quotations from the work as well as the writer's personal experience to support the writer's response		
4. Ends with a summary of the response and a conclusion		

Structure and Form		
5. Demonstrates proper paragraphing		
6. Includes transitional words to show relationships among ideas		
7. Uses a variety of sentence structures		

Grammar, Usage, and Mechanics		
8. Contains no more than two or three minor errors in grammar and usage		
9. Contains no more than two or three minor errors in spelling, capitalization, and punctuation		

Writing Progress to Date (Writing Portfolio)

The strongest aspect of this writing is _____

The final version shows improvement over the rough draft in this way: _____

A specific improvement over past assignments in your portfolio is _____

A skill to work on in future assignments is _____

Additional comments: _____

162 FORMAL ASSESSMENT, GRADE 6

FORMAL ASSESSMENT

The formal assessment booklet contains everything you will need for efficient assessment of students' skills in reading literature and in writing.

- Selection and Unit Tests
- Writing Prompts
- Scoring rubrics and sample papers
- Standardized Test Practice

A test generator is also available to help you customize assessment.

ALTERNATIVE ASSESSMENT

These assessments integrate all of the language arts processes and are modeled on authentic assessment materials used in many states across the country.

- **Unit Integrated Assessments** are completed over two days and are based on the On Your Own selections in the student book. Prereading activities and post-reading response and discussion lead to in-depth writing options.

- The **End-of-Year Integrated Assessment** includes a reader and a Student Response Booklet. It is completed over several days and requires students to respond to three or more related selections.

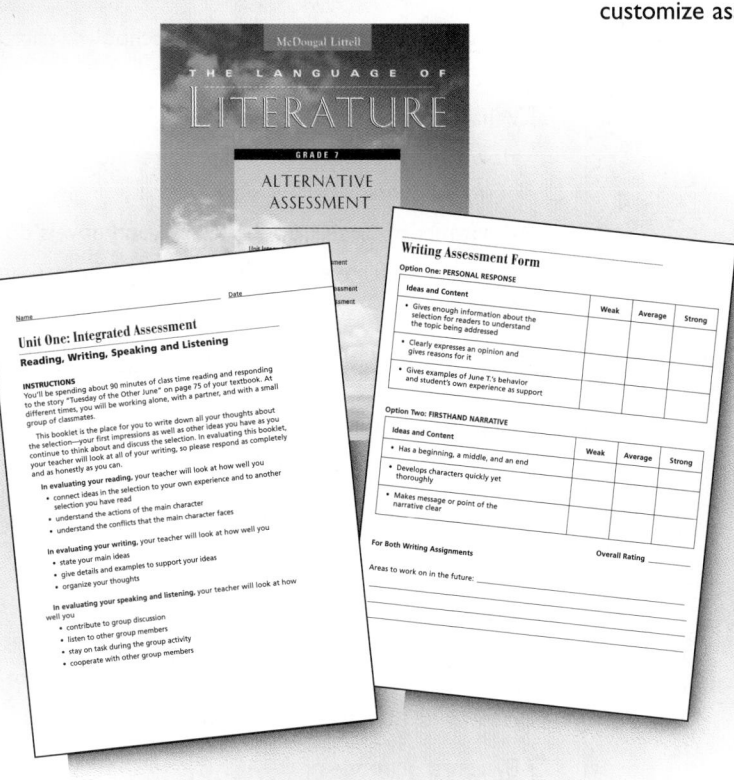

Name _____ Date _____

Unit One: Integrated Assessment
Reading, Writing, Speaking and Listening

INSTRUCTIONS
You'll be spending about 90 minutes of class time reading and responding to the story "Tuesday of the Other June" on page 75 of your textbook. At different times, you will be working alone, with a partner, and with a small group of classmates.

This booklet is the place for you to write down all your thoughts about the selection—your first impressions as well as other ideas you have as you continue to think about and discuss the selection. In evaluating this booklet, your teacher will look at all of your writing, so please respond as completely and as honestly as you can.

In evaluating your reading, your teacher will look at how well you
- connect ideas in the selection to your own experience and to another selection you have read
- understand the actions of the main character
- understand the conflicts that the main character faces

In evaluating your writing, your teacher will look at how well you
- state your main ideas
- give details and examples to support your ideas
- organize your thoughts

In evaluating your speaking and listening, your teacher will look at how well you
- contribute to group discussion
- listen to other group members
- stay on task during the group activity
- cooperate with other group members

Writing Assessment Form

Option One: PERSONAL RESPONSE

Ideas and Content	Weak	Average	Strong
Gives enough information about the selection for readers to understand the topic being addressed			
Clearly expresses an opinion and gives reasons for it			
Gives examples of June T.'s behavior and student's own experience as support			

Option Two: FIRSTHAND NARRATIVE

Ideas and Content	Weak	Average	Strong
Has a beginning, a middle, and an end			
Develops characters quickly yet thoroughly			
Makes message or point of the narrative clear			

For Both Writing Assignments   Overall Rating _____

Areas to work on in the future: _____

Advice from the Experts

Planning
YOUR YEAR

Every new school year requires much planning. The information and advice on these pages comes from the consultants on *The Language of Literature* and is designed to help you bring some of your plans into focus. (You may want to copy the pages and keep them in your lesson planner for easy reference.) As you begin your planning, here's a list of questions to consider. Their answers and some additional information can be found on the pages cited.

Developing a Classroom Profile   See pages T28–T29.

✔ **Who are my students?**

☐ What can I learn about my students from previous teachers, students, records, and portfolios—and how can I best use this information?

☐ What are my students' preferred learning styles, and how can I best accommodate them?

☐ If I have students who are not proficient in English, what will their needs be?

☐ Are there any other special needs represented in my class?

☐ What adjustments do I need to make due to tracking, mainstreaming, and other situations?

Planning My Instruction   See pages T30–T31.

✔ **What do I want to teach?**

☐ What are the requirements of my school, district, and state?

☐ What are my personal preferences?

☐ What are my students' preferences?

☐ How can I use both classic literature and young-adult literature to reflect the needs and interests of my students?

☐ What mix of stories, poetry, essays, and novels do I want to teach?

☐ How can I effectively combine writing, language, and communication skills?

☐ Do I want to teach a research paper and/or other longer projects?

✔ **How much collaborating do I want to do with other teachers?**

☐ To plan thematic units and/or projects

☐ To coordinate instruction

✔ **What mix of instructional styles do I want to use?**

☐ Lectures

☐ Cooperative/collaborative work

☐ Writing workshops/peer response groups

✔ **How will I organize the content?**

☐ By genre or mode

☐ By theme

Setting Up My Classroom

See pages T32–T33.

✔ **How will I organize my classroom?**

- ☐ In rows of desks
- ☐ With tables and chairs
- ☐ In paired-seating arrangements
- ☐ In cooperative learning groups
- ☐ In stations or centers

Taking Advantage of Technology

See pages T34–T35.

✔ **How large a role will technology play in my classroom?**

- ☐ What technological resources do I have at my disposal?
- ☐ For what purpose or purposes do I want to use them?
- ☐ How can I best set up my classroom or use a lab to take advantage of these resources?

Preparing for Assessment

See pages T36–T38.

✔ **What types of assessment do I want to use or prepare for?**

Do I want to use one or more of the following:

- ☐ Portfolios, journals, and/or logs
- ☐ Process assessment
- ☐ Product assessment
- ☐ Peer and self-assessment
- ☐ My own observations
- ☐ Tests from *The Language of Literature*
- ☐ District- or state-mandated tests
- ☐ Standardized tests

Planning Connections

See pages T39–T40.

✔ **What kinds of connections do I want to make outside the classroom?**

- ☐ To other curriculum areas
- ☐ To other classrooms or schools
- ☐ To my students' parents
- ☐ To the community
- ☐ To the world

DEVELOPING A
Classroom
PROFILE

UNDERSTANDING LEARNING STYLES

Your students are all unique. They have different sets of characteristics, abilities, and needs. It should not be surprising, therefore, to learn that they have different learning styles as well. This theory gained acceptance in the early 1980s, due in large part to the research of Harvard psychologist Howard Gardner. Gardner recognizes seven types of intelligences: linguistic, logical-mathematical, spatial, musical, bodily-kinesthetic, interpersonal, and intrapersonal. He claims that everyone has all seven of these intelligences, but in different proportions.

Understanding your students' intelligences, or learning styles, will help you teach them more effectively. How can you tell which learning style or styles your students favor? As you consider each of your students, asking yourself these questions will help.

Does the student . . .	Then he or she is mostly a . . .	So try these activities and assignments:
☐ Have good verbal skills? think in words? have highly developed auditory skills? like to read and write?	**Linguistic Learner**	Creative writing; essays; debates and speeches; oral reports; dramatic readings and performances; storytelling; joke, pun, and riddle telling
☐ Think conceptually? think and reason in a highly abstract and logical way?	**Logical-Mathematical Learner**	Graphic organizers; charts, graphs, and time lines; coded messages; prediction exercises; models; computer projects; science experiments
☐ Think in visual images and pictures? enjoy drawing, designing, building, daydreaming, inventing?	**Spatial Learner**	Drawings and paintings; comic strips; maps and flow charts; dioramas, displays, and murals; collages; drawing games; photography activities
☐ Have a sensitivity to music, nonverbal sounds, and rhythm? enjoy singing, playing, and listening to and moving to music?	**Musical Learner**	Interpretive dances; musical plays and compositions; rap songs, jingles, and melodies; rhyming games; playing a musical instrument
☐ Process knowledge through bodily sensations? have exceptional fine-motor coordination? communicate through body language?	**Bodily-Kinesthetic Learner**	Demonstration speeches; experiments; using gestures, facial expressions, and pantomime; impersonations; role-playing
☐ Understand other people? organize, communicate, and socialize well?	**Interpersonal Learner**	Discussions; cooperative and collaborative projects; peer coaching; conducting interviews; simulation activities; human graphs
☐ Prefer working alone? seem intuitive, independent, private, and self-motivated?	**Intrapersonal Learner**	Response journals, dialogue journals, learning logs; observations; photo essays; autobiographical stories; written reports

A PROFILE OF THE STUDENT ACQUIRING ENGLISH

Culturally and linguistically diverse students bring to the classroom a wealth of experiences that can enrich the learning environment of all your students. Developing multicultural sensitivity involves (a) acceptance of each student's circumstances, (b) a genuine search for information about his or her background and prior knowledge, (c) an updated bank of teaching strategies, and (d) a desire to find the best options for each student.

The Student Acquiring English

- ☐ generally focuses attention on style, not content
- ☐ is often unaware of learning strategies that could facilitate comprehension
- ☐ may become disorderly and disobedient due to an inability to relate to the learning environment
- ☐ often does not make eye contact when addressing others
- ☐ may seem to have difficulty meeting deadlines
- ☐ may not seem to understand classroom "rules"
- ☐ generally shows a different speaking and listening style
- ☐ may organize thoughts in a pattern that does not correspond to the expected linear-sequential pattern characteristic of standard English communication
- ☐ may exhibit an external locus of control, seeming overly dependent on teachers or peers for validation of responses

Common Problem Areas

The following problem areas pose special challenges to students acquiring English as they try to read and understand information.

Vocabulary Difficulty

If the student has no prior experience with the words appearing in a selection, the normal links between certain concepts and their labels will not occur. Problems often arise when a selection contains the following:

- ☐ low frequency words
- ☐ idiomatic or dialectal expressions
- ☐ jargon

Unfamiliar Content

The student may misunderstand the message in what he or she is reading if not given the proper context. This often happens as a result of the following:

- ☐ a lack of prior experience with the context
- ☐ ideas expressed in an unfamiliar or abstract way
- ☐ ideas expressed being of an unfamiliar culture

Grammatical Features of the Selection

Comprehension problems arise when the student encounters the following:

- ☐ dialectal forms
- ☐ outdated grammatical forms
- ☐ unusual word order

Effective Teaching and Learning Strategies

These instructional strategies have been shown to be successful when used with students acquiring English.

Cognitive Mapping

- ☐ Many SAE students, however, may organize and categorize information differently than English speakers would. Instruction in cognitive mapping can enable students to integrate previous experience with new knowledge.

An Integrated Approach

- ☐ The integrated approach to learning is particularly successful with students acquiring English. Students learn about reading and writing while listening, they learn about writing from reading, and they gain insights into reading from writing. Any strategy or approach based on dissecting language and mutually exclusive components jeopardizes second-language acquisition by not drawing on the prior knowledge and strengths of the learner.

Cooperative Learning

- ☐ Cooperative learning is a generic term that refers to a variety of approaches to integrating students into group activities where each participant is responsible for contributing to group outcomes and products. Cooperative learning strategies significantly improve students' achievement and productivity for a wide range of subjects and grade levels. This approach also improves self-esteem and respect for others. For more detailed information, see the *Teacher's SourceBook for Language Development*.

Planning
YOUR
INSTRUCTION

Just as your students all have their own preferred learning styles, you have your own preferred teaching styles. Understanding when and where your most comfortable style really works—and when another method would reach your goals and the goals of your students more effectively—will help you plan just the right type of instruction for every situation.

Here are some questions to ask yourself as you make decisions about your instruction:

- ☐ What is my objective for the lesson . . . today, this week, this month, this term?

- ☐ What is my time frame . . . 45 minutes, 90 minutes, three class periods, longer?

- ☐ Who are my students (refer to your classroom profiles, pages T28 and T29)?

- ☐ What teaching styles am I most comfortable with?

- ☐ What additional teaching techniques would be effective with these students and this material?

Consider these options . . .

WHOLE-CLASS INSTRUCTION

Lecture

EXAMPLES:

- ☐ Introducing a new unit of study
- ☐ Providing instruction for a project
- ☐ Introducing grammatical principles or definitions of literary elements

Teacher-led Discussion

EXAMPLES:

- ☐ Exploring students' ideas about and responses to literature selections and themes
- ☐ Examining complex issues and problems

Viewing

EXAMPLES:

- ☐ Viewing a filmstrip or a videotape
- ☐ Watching demonstrations, performances, and project presentations

COLLABORATIVE LEARNING

Pairs or Partners

EXAMPLES:

- ☐ Sharing responses to literature
- ☐ Interviewing and reciprocal questioning
- ☐ Brainstorming for project or writing ideas
- ☐ Peer tutoring
- ☐ Writing workshops

Small Groups (3-8 students)

EXAMPLES:

- ☐ Discussing literature or other topics
- ☐ Planning and problem-solving activities
- ☐ Writing workshops
- ☐ Cooperative work on reports, projects, and presentations
- ☐ Cooperative planning and producing of larger projects such as plays, panel discussions or debates, and videotapes

INDEPENDENT LEARNING

Students Working Individually

EXAMPLES:

- ☐ Independent reading and writing
- ☐ Drawing, painting, and collages
- ☐ Listening to audiotapes

☐ Developing critical listening and note-taking skills ☐ Providing unknown historical or cultural background ☐ Introducing new concepts or skills	☐ Lectures appeal to linguistic learners with highly developed auditory skills. Other students may tune you out because this style lacks interactivity. ☐ Lectures are most effective if no longer than 20 minutes. Research shows that immediately after a 10-minute presentation, average adult listeners retain less than 50% of what they hear—and 48 hours later, they recall only 25%.
☐ Developing critical listening, responding, and conversational skills ☐ Introducing or reviewing skills	☐ Not all students are comfortable speaking in front of their peers. Highly verbal students can drown out students who favor other learning styles. ☐ When you lead the discussion, students may tend to direct their comments to you rather than to other students. Encourage students to speak directly to one another as well as to you.
☐ Supporting and improving visual literacy ☐ Developing evaluative skills ☐ Encouraging appreciation for music, art, and various kinds of performances	☐ Although viewing is a comfortable activity for most students, it's essentially passive. You'll want to choose occasions carefully. ☐ To help students remain focused, agree on goals ahead of time and provide standards and forms for evaluating what students are watching.
☐ Reinforcing cooperative learning skills ☐ Providing support for students acquiring English ☐ Encouraging peer feedback for writing	☐ It's important to cultivate a classroom atmosphere of support and trust so that pair interactions are effective and productive. ☐ You may want to pair students differently for different purposes. Strong students may be paired with weaker students, native English speakers with students acquiring English, talkative students with more reserved students, and so on.
☐ Developing problem-solving skills ☐ Encouraging peer feedback for writing ☐ Reinforcing cooperative learning skills ☐ Providing opportunities for students to explore various points of view ☐ Improving social skills and promoting self-esteem in students of all abilities	☐ Some students will lean too hard on other members of the group. Both groups and individual students need to be accountable. ☐ Some students can get lost in the shuffle of a larger group. Individual students should have specific responsibilities. ☐ Group size can be determined by the task. Small groups are appropriate for sharing personal writing and receiving individual attention; larger groups are effective when the task is large or complex. ☐ The "jigsaw" method may be useful for groups working on complex tasks. The group divides the assignment into pieces and assigns each student a piece. Then students work together to meld the pieces into a coherent whole.
☐ Providing opportunities for reflection and self-assessment ☐ Providing support for students acquiring English	☐ Individual learning tasks require a quiet classroom atmosphere. Highly developed interpersonal learners may distract other students. ☐ Using independent learning too frequently can hinder students' development of collaborative and cooperative skills.

Setting Up
YOUR CLASSROOM

Are you planning to try some new instructional approaches this year? If so, you also may want to consider some new classroom setups. Moving away from the traditional arrangement of desks in rows will provide you and your students a welcome change—and will be more conducive to different teaching and learning situations. Here are a few pointers:

The ideal literature classroom is a literary community where students … have room to respond, interpret, think critically, and contrast their ideas with those of other readers.

Judith Langer
and Arthur Applebee
Professors of Education,
State University of New York
at Albany

If you teach in the same room all day, the ideas on these pages will provide ways to set up your room for a variety of purposes.

If you switch rooms, team teach, or share your room, you can find an arrangement that best meets everyone's needs. Some options:

☐ One arrangement that works for everyone

☐ Different classrooms for different purposes

☐ A resource room or common area that could be used for specific types of activities

Before you arrange your classroom, draw a scale floor plan of it. Then add furniture and design a setting that will best accommodate your instructional plans.

When you have your floor plan firmed up, post lists of procedures in the different areas of your classroom. Encourage students to add new procedures as needs arise in the future.

Don't be afraid to experiment with different arrangements throughout the year. You may find that some arrangements work better than others for specific projects or assignments.

A LOOK AT THREE CLASSROOM SETUPS
Lectures and Demonstrations

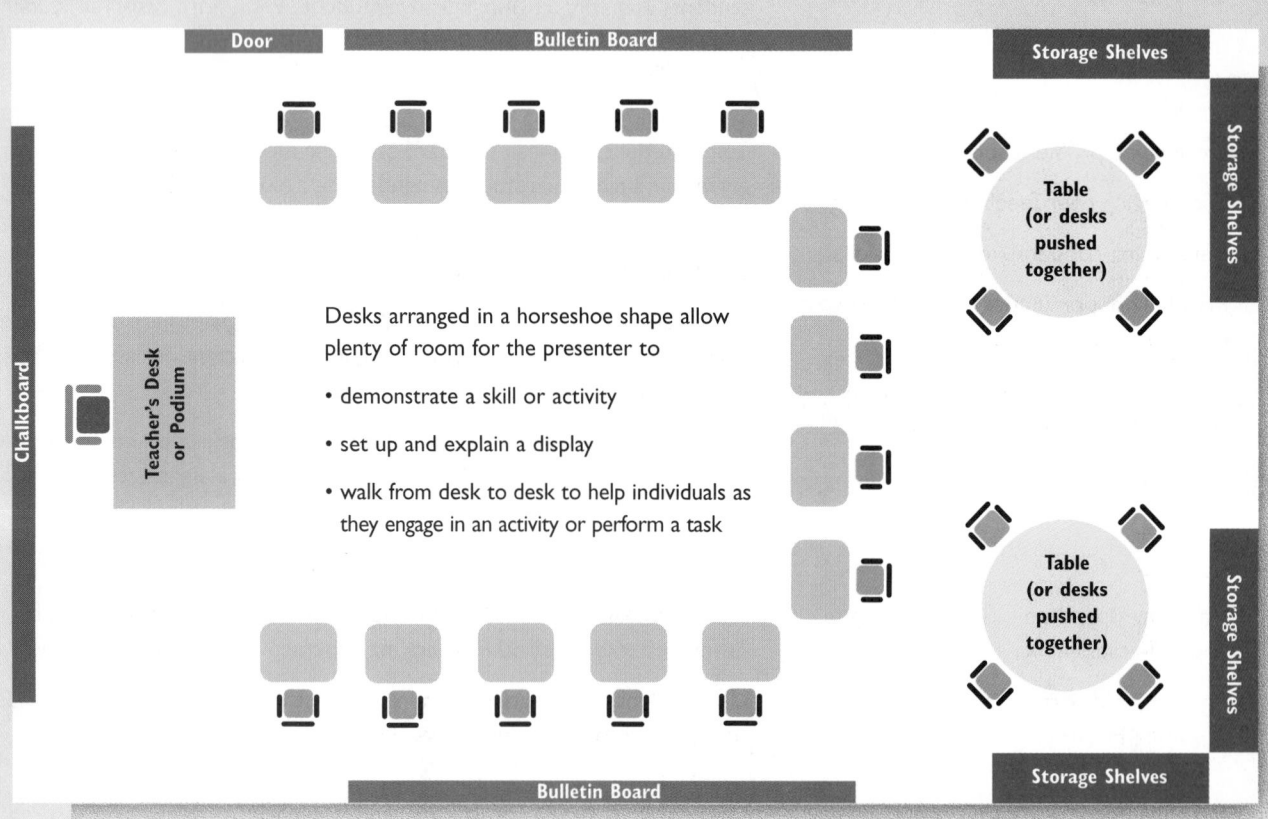

Desks arranged in a horseshoe shape allow plenty of room for the presenter to

• demonstrate a skill or activity

• set up and explain a display

• walk from desk to desk to help individuals as they engage in an activity or perform a task

Peer Tutoring & Cooperative Learning

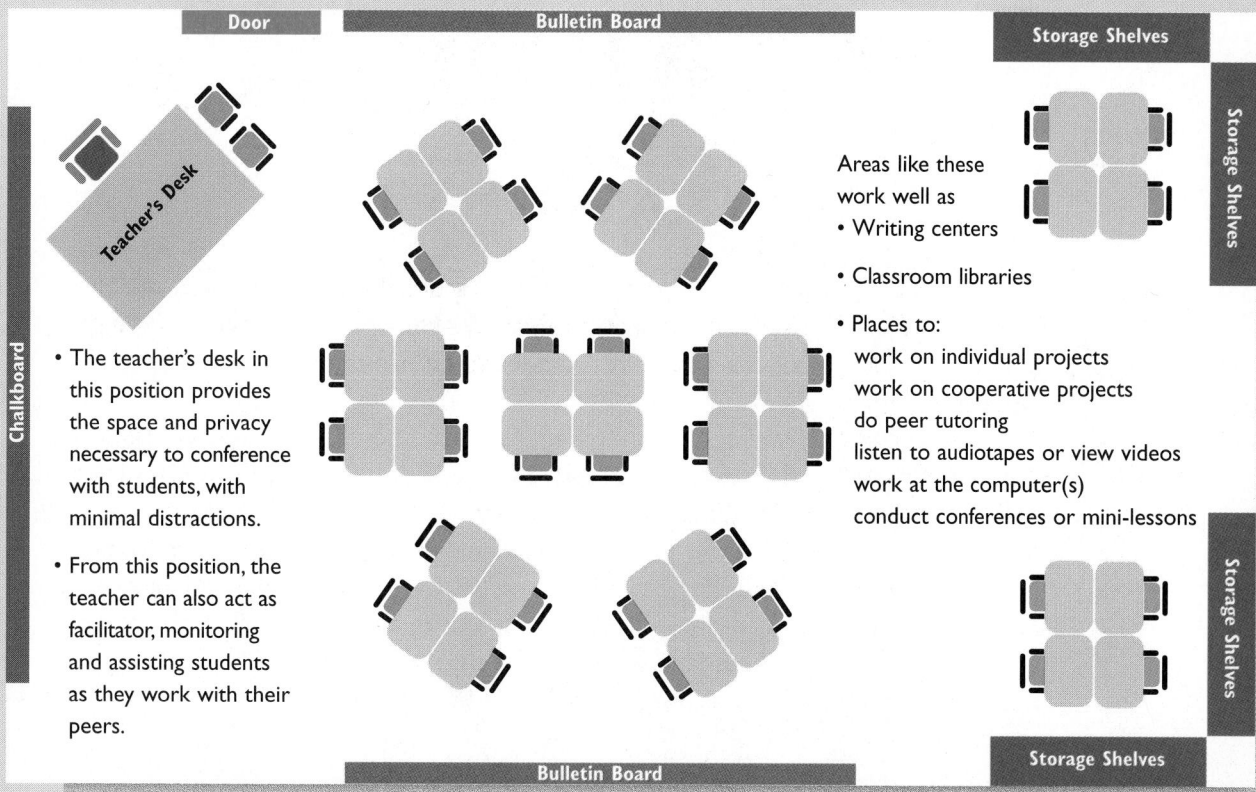

- The teacher's desk in this position provides the space and privacy necessary to conference with students, with minimal distractions.

- From this position, the teacher can also act as facilitator, monitoring and assisting students as they work with their peers.

Areas like these work well as
- Writing centers

- Classroom libraries

- Places to:
  work on individual projects
  work on cooperative projects
  do peer tutoring
  listen to audiotapes or view videos
  work at the computer(s)
  conduct conferences or mini-lessons

Work Stations

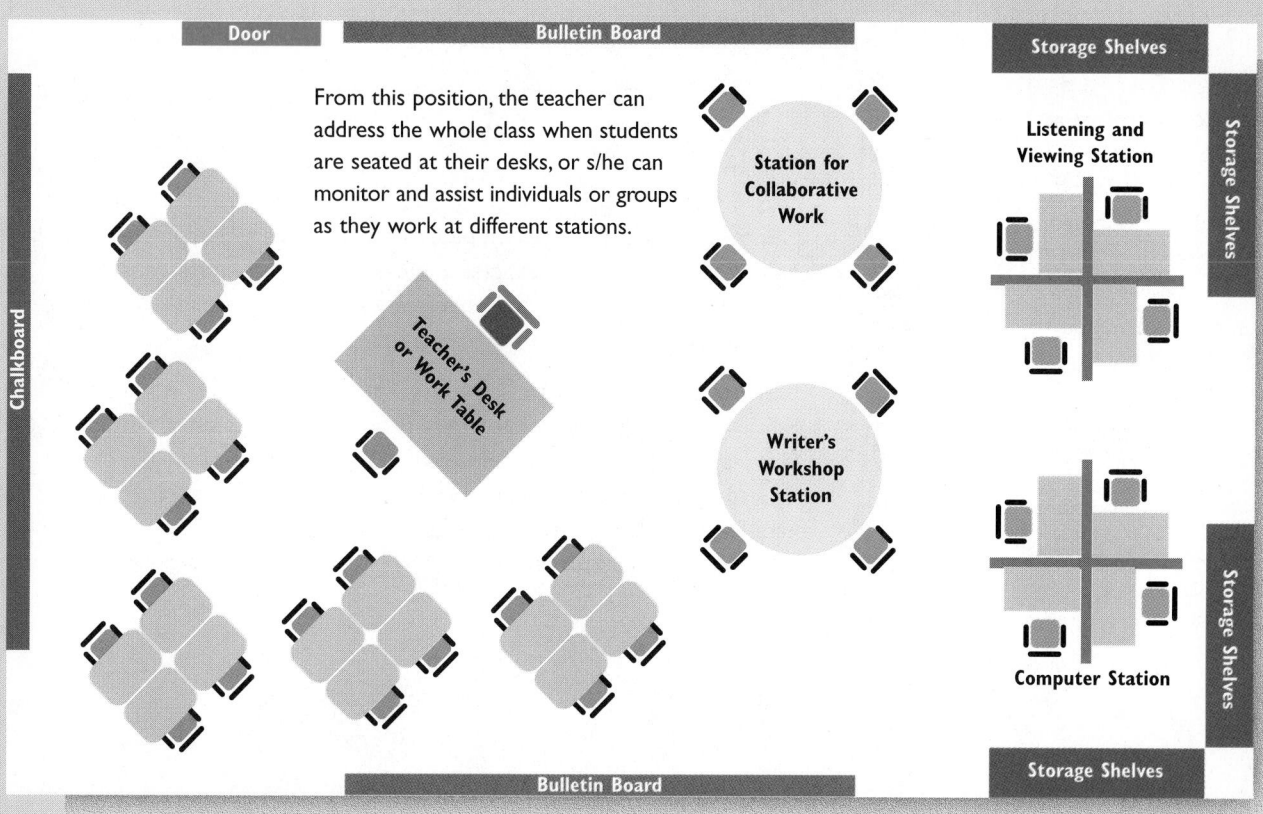

From this position, the teacher can address the whole class when students are seated at their desks, or s/he can monitor and assist individuals or groups as they work at different stations.

NEW
Technology
AND THE
ENGLISH CLASSROOM

Technology enables students to become active participants in their own learning.

Jeffrey N. Golub
Assistant Professor of English Education, University of South Florida, Tampa

The idea of using technology as part of your instructional plan is not simply the latest passing fad. Instead, it reflects continuing revelations about what is worth knowing and how students learn. For this reason, it promises to change the nature of classroom instruction.

Why is technology so important? Primarily because the use of computers is not a "spectator sport." Rather, computers require users to do the work themselves instead of passively sitting back and watching or listening to someone else—typically a teacher—dispense information. Thus, using technology enables students to become active participants in their own learning. Similarly, the teacher's role changes to that of a "designer" and "director"—one who *designs* innovative and worthwhile instructional activities and then *directs* students as they work through these activities.

Let's look for a moment at how technology is being used in English classrooms across the country.

Bringing Literature to Life

Teachers are always striving to make connections between literature and students' lives by providing "real-world" relevance in the form of historical and biographical information, cross-curricular ties, and connections to current issues. Recordings and films have always been the primary resources used to achieve this goal, but more recent technology—such as laser discs and CD-ROMs—is providing teachers with new worlds of information to draw from.

Taking the Fear Out of Writing

In probably their most familiar function, computers offer terrific opportunities for writing because (1) they provide students with more efficient and effective means of drafting, revising, editing, and publishing their writing efforts, and (2) they allow new kinds of opportunities for peer response, collaboration, and sharing.

More Enthusiastic Writers Research has shown repeatedly that students tend to be more fluent and less inhibited when they work at computers: the many editing features and on-line resources make revision easy. In addition, publishing programs allow students to create products far more exciting than words on paper have ever been. Computers can also make portfolio building simpler and cleaner: journal entries, drafts and revisions, and finished products are easy to store, categorize, and retrieve on computers or disks.

Easier Collaboration. If you have access to a writing lab, you will find that, with readily available software programs and by networking, or linking, the computers, students can be more easily encouraged to collaborate on their planning and writing efforts. When students can compose and comment on-screen they often become much more articulate and less reserved.

Making Connections

One of the most commonly heard complaints among teachers is that they seldom have a chance to network with each other and share ideas. Through the wonders of the Internet, this problem has all but disappeared. Education sites exist where teachers can find information ranging from developments in state assessments to projects that have worked well in other classrooms. Through the Internet, teachers can also set up classroom exchanges with other schools across the country, allow their students to go on electronic field trips, and plan interactions between the class and famous authors, scientists, and other professionals.

Developing Information Literacy

The use of technology in the English classroom enables teachers to help their students develop what will become one of the most basic skills needed for the 21st century—media and information literacy. Students need to learn how to access information from a wide variety of both print and electronic sources; how to select appropriate information from the vast array of available resources; how to analyze and evaluate information that they read, see, and hear daily; and how to communicate their conclusions and insights clearly, completely, ethically, and persuasively. In particular, the growth of telecommunications opportunities in the form of information webs presents students with the opportunity to actively seek pertinent information and to engage in the processes of selection, analysis, and evaluation.

Conclusion   These are just some of the ways in which technology can make learning happen for your students. But they help demonstrate that, if used creatively, technology can bring new excitement and levels of success to any English classroom—even while helping us achieve the same goals we have always had: to make our students solid readers, thinkers, and communicators.

Technology	Uses in the English Classroom	The Language of Literature
Videodisc A 12-inch disc, used with a videodisc player, that can store thousands of still images as well as full-motion video. Images can be accessed immediately through the use of bar codes.	• To provide background information and cross-curricular connections for selection enrichment • For presenting real-world situations and images that can be used as writing springboards • To bring movies, archival material, and recordings of live performances into the classroom • To teach visual literacy	**LASERLINKS** Support for lessons in the student book, including • Author and Selection Background • Visual Vocabulary • Professional Storyteller • Writing Springboards
Floppy Disks and CD-ROM's Both are information storage devices that can hold text, still images, and full-motion video. Compact discs, however, are able to store encyclopedic amounts of information.	• As sources of additional or enhanced selections • As a reference tool: encyclopedias, atlases, and almanacs are all available in CD-ROM form • For writing: publishing software, image banks, and word processing programs all enhance student writing	**THE ELECTRONIC LIBRARY** Additional classic selections to expand program options **WRITING COACH** Special word-processing program with on-line writing tips and handbooks, multiple text columns for revision and peer response, and a multimedia Idea Generator
Internet/ World Wide Web/ On-line Services A connected system of on-line computer networks through which mail and data can be transferred.	• To obtain additional information on a selection, author, or topic • To teach information-access skills • To gather professional materials, project ideas, research articles • To network with other teachers and set up classroom exchanges • To interact with authors, public figures, scientists, and other professionals	**THE MCDOUGAL LITTELL HOME PAGE** Can be accessed on the World Wide Web at http://www.hmco.com/mcdougal and contains the following resources: • Internet links for specific selections in *The Language of Literature* • Teacher discussion groups/ bulletin boards • Links to professional organizations • Guest speakers

PREPARING FOR
Assessment

The word *assessment* conjures up many different images and raises just as many questions in teachers' minds. Although assessment options are often categorized as either formal or alternative, assessment activities usually embrace qualities of both kinds. Most teachers use a combination of many types of assessment in determining what a student knows or is able to do. The overview on these three pages will introduce you to the types of assessment used in *The Language of Literature* and will help you decide which ones you might want to try with your students this year. (For teacher resources and information on implementing these types of assessment, see the following three booklets: *Teacher's Guide to Assessment and Portfolio Use, Formal Assessment,* and *Alternative Assessment.*)

WHAT TYPES OF ASSESSMENT ARE THERE?

PURPOSES

Usually paper-and-pencil tests; helps teachers

- measure students' achievement against students in their own class, district, state, or country
- report students' achievement to parents and administrators
- make appropriate instructional and grouping decisions

FORMATS

Test formats are commonly

- true-false
- standardized
- multiple choice
- norm-referenced
- matching
- criterion-referenced
- essay
- objective

FORMAL
Asks "What do you know?"

TYPES OF ASSESSMENT

ALTERNATIVE
Asks "What can you do?"

PURPOSES

Usually tasks that emulate real-life situations; helps teachers

- get a broad picture of each student as a problem solver, critical thinker, and acquirer of knowledge
- measure student growth over time

TASKS

Tasks are commonly
- authentic
- products or performances
- processes

WHAT FORMS CAN ALTERNATIVE ASSESSMENT TAKE?

For more information on implementing these types of assessment, see the *Teacher's Guide to Assessment and Portfolio Use.*

✔ Product and Performance Assessment

- Requires students to produce tangible products or create performances that demonstrate their understanding of skills and concepts

- Focuses teacher's attention on the end product rather than the processes, behaviors, or strategies students used to create them

- Is based on judgment and observation guided by criteria

TYPES OF EVALUATION CRITERIA USED
Can include rubrics, formal scales and checklists, and peer and self-evaluations

POSSIBLE PRODUCTS

- scripts, dialogues
- audiotapes, videotapes
- charts, maps, graphs
- games, puzzles
- puppet shows
- plays, skits, talent shows
- interviews, debates
- role-playing
- dances
- mock trials

- cooking or sports demonstrations
- recipes, menus
- children's books
- museum exhibits
- research papers
- inventions
- book or movie reviews
- questionnaires, surveys

- print or TV ads
- poems, riddles, jokes
- time capsules
- awards
- oral histories
- murals, collages
- computer programs
- scale models, dioramas
- essays, editorials
- family trees

✔ Process Assessment

- Requires students to demonstrate or share their processes, behaviors, strategies, and critical thinking abilities as they work to understand skills and concepts

- Focuses teacher's attention on student processes, behaviors, and strategies rather than the final results

- Is based on judgment and observation guided by criteria

TYPES OF EVALUATION CRITERIA USED
Can include rubrics, formal scales and checklists, anecdotal records, observations, and self- and peer evaluations

POSSIBLE PROCESSES
While the evaluator observes students' abilities to apply higher-order thinking skills during certain processes, he or she focuses on the following:

- the use of reading strategies to develop interpretations of a text
- behavior during peer review
- evidence of investment in a task
- the ability to work in a collaborative group

- drafts created while writing an essay
- the ability to participate in class discussions
- the use of conferences to refine work
- evolving personal criteria and standards

✔ Portfolio Assessment

- Is a purposeful collection of student work that exhibits overall efforts, progress, and achievement over time in one or more areas of the curriculum

- Is a combination of process and product assessment, with a strong measure of self-evaluation and self-reflection

TYPES OF EVALUATION CRITERIA USED
Can include inventories, conference notes, rubrics, formal scales and checklists, anecdotal records, observations, and peer evaluations

POSSIBLE PRODUCTS TO INCLUDE IN THE PORTFOLIO

- interest inventories
- outlines
- written assignments
- videotapes
- reading records
- audiotapes
- performance plans
- photographs
- logs

- sketches or drawings
- journal entries
- works in progress
- textbook tasks
- research findings
- reports
- book reports or reviews
- project evaluations
- standardized tests

HOW CAN I PREPARE MY STUDENTS FOR THESE TYPES OF ASSESSMENT?

A major difference between formal assessment and alternative assessment is what you choose to assess and how you choose to assess it. Alternative assessment is a natural outgrowth and extension of classroom practices. Therefore, it is important to establish an effective learning—and testing—environment right away. Following are a few pointers to help you get started.

✔ **Establish an environment based on trust.**

Because alternative assessment makes students much more in charge of their own learning, and much more responsible for demonstrating their learning in a variety of ways, it is important to establish a classroom environment that is based on trust. Many of the activities students will be engaging in will be unfamiliar to them—and to you. Let them see that you are right in there with them, taking risks and trying new experiences. Help them understand that it's all right to try and fail—even seemingly unsuccessful experiences bring about growth and learning.

✔ **Establish a tone of reflection and self-evaluation.**

At the beginning of the year, ask your students to write letters describing themselves as readers, writers, and classroom participants. Also have them describe what they hope to accomplish during the coming year. Have them keep their letters in their notebooks, journals, or portfolios; encourage them to reread the letters regularly. Reflecting on their performance will help them acknowledge and evaluate their growth over the year. It will also help them see that learning and evaluating are ongoing and ever-changing processes.

✔ **Help your students set goals and make commitments.**

In order to grow as learners, your students must become actively involved in setting goals and making commitments. Their goals can be for a day, a week, a project, or the year; but whatever their duration, encourage students to consider their strengths and limitations so that the goals they set will be realistic.

✔ **Help students view assessment in a new light.**

One of the best things you can do for your students is help them break away from the notion that a "test" is something to study for the night before and then to forget. Help them see that alternative assessment involves a demonstration of what they know at a particular moment, but that what they know is bound to keep changing as new knowledge builds on old.

✔ **Help your students discover their individual learning styles and preferences.**

Chances are, most of your students are not fully aware of their own learning styles and preferences. Why not help them recognize which tasks and situations suit them best and help them learn more effectively? (See page T28.) After all, the better your students understand themselves, the better you'll understand how to teach and assess them.

✔ **Encourage peer review as a regular part of the assessment process.**

Sometimes it's easier for students to "get inside the minds" of their peers. And sometimes it's easier for them to take instruction or criticism from their peers. This is an excellent strategy, as long as growth and learning are taking place.

✔ **Help your students learn to operate independently of you.**

As students get comfortable with their learning environment, they'll probably want to do more and more without your help. Try to provide as many opportunities as possible for them to develop into independent learners— you'll be doing one of the best things you can do to prepare them for life in the real world!

✔ **Improve and increase your own assessment tools.**

As an evaluator, your goal should be to get as broad a view as possible of each of your students. Increasing your ability to provide situations in which you can observe your students will help you get more complete pictures of them. It will also help you learn more about yourself!

MAKING
Connections

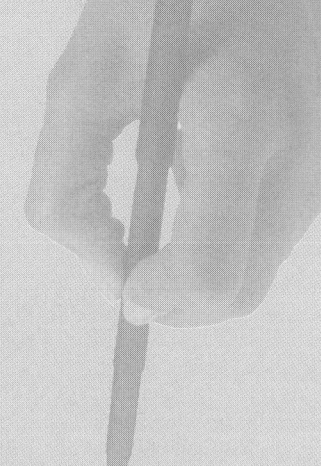

The Language of Literature bases all of its instruction on a "connected" approach to learning. On every page—from the Previewing pages to the Writing Workshops and Reading the World feature—students are encouraged to find the links between the literature, other subject areas, their own lives, and the world around them.

Of course, there are always more connections to be made, and certain themes and selections are particularly rich with possibilities. When you identify a selection or idea that you feel might have particular interest for your students, you may want to involve the class, as well as other teachers, in expanding the lesson into a more customized exploration. The following chart describes one way to accomplish this.

STEP 1 ▶ **What Will We Explore?**

As a class, or in small groups, have students ask questions such as the following:

• What really excited me or fascinated me about this selection?

• What questions did I have as I read this?

• What didn't I understand?

• What would I like to find out more about?

• What people, experiences, issues, or situations did this remind me of that might be interesting to explore?

TIP: Clustering, discussion, brainstorming, freewriting, and notebooks and logs are among the methods that can be used to generate ideas.

STEP 2 ▶ **What Skills or Information Will We Need?**

Once the questions are in place, have students identify the skills needed to find the answers. For example, the story "The Circuit" might prompt questions about the life of the migrant worker. Will students need certain map-reading or geographical skills to learn the answers? Would information about farming or economics be important?

STEP 3 ▶ **What Resources Will We Use?**

At this point, students can be encouraged to plan the kinds of resources they might use to continue their exploration. Remind them of the following possibilities:

• print resources

• interviews

• surveys and questionnaires

• CD-ROM

• the Internet and other on-line resources

TIP: This is also the point at which you might collaborate with other teachers to take advantage of team teaching and block scheduling to coordinate overlapping topics. Classroom exchanges within or between schools may also be useful to arrange at this point. Technology can provide exciting options for networking as well.

STEP 4 ▶ **How Will the Results Be Shared?**

The methods for sharing information will be as varied as the projects themselves. Following are just a few of the possibilities students might consider:

• essays	• paintings
• photo journals	• music
• dramas	• multimedia
• videos	• panel
• speeches	• fairs
• oral histories	• community program

See page T40 for an example of the explorations generated from the selection "The Moustache."

A SAMPLE PLANNING MAP

Below is an example of the different explorations that were generated from one story by a teacher following the approach outlined on page T39.

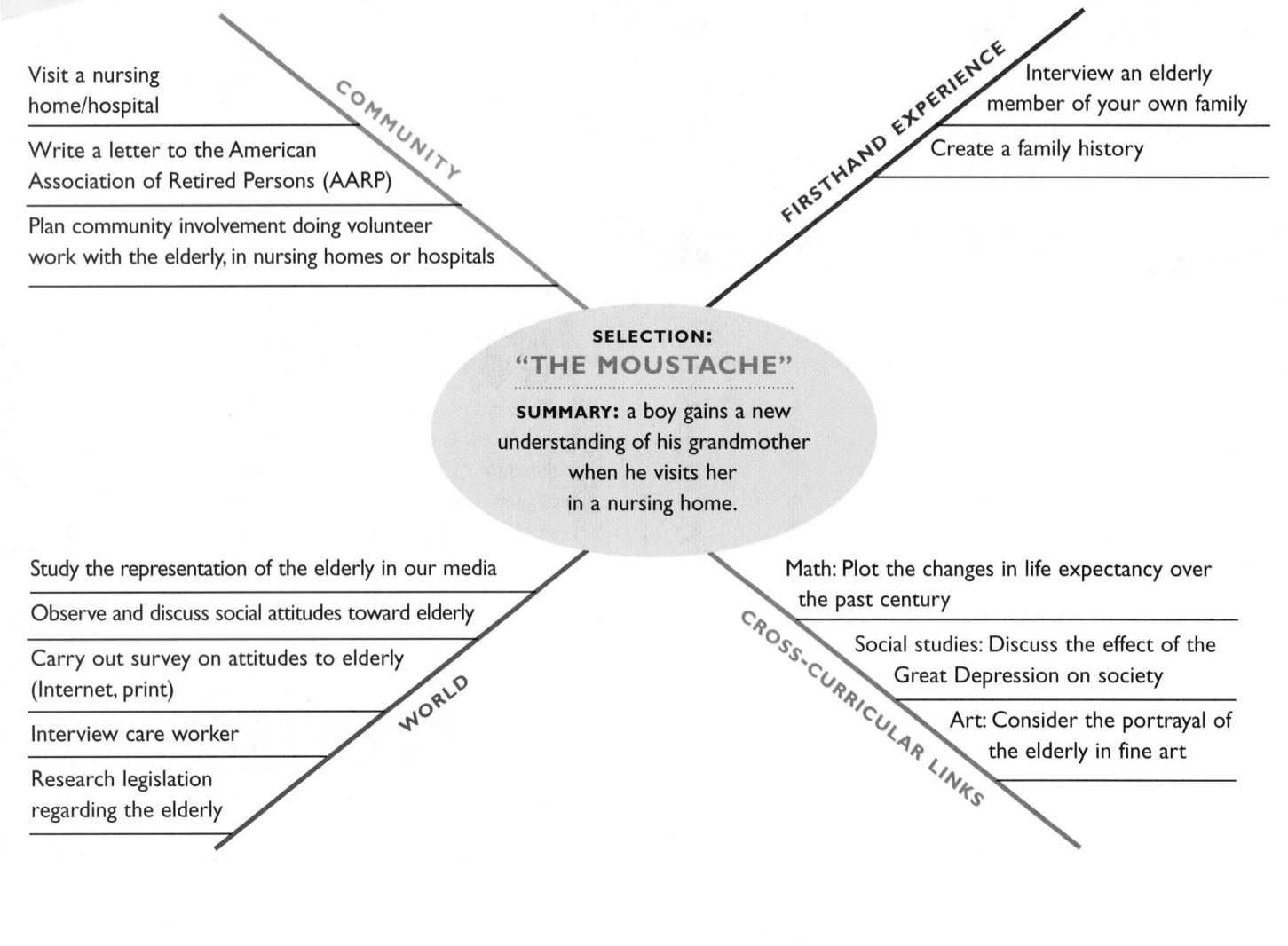

COMMUNITY

Visit a nursing home/hospital

Write a letter to the American Association of Retired Persons (AARP)

Plan community involvement doing volunteer work with the elderly, in nursing homes or hospitals

FIRSTHAND EXPERIENCE

Interview an elderly member of your own family

Create a family history

SELECTION:
"THE MOUSTACHE"

SUMMARY: a boy gains a new understanding of his grandmother when he visits her in a nursing home.

WORLD

Study the representation of the elderly in our media

Observe and discuss social attitudes toward elderly

Carry out survey on attitudes to elderly (Internet, print)

Interview care worker

Research legislation regarding the elderly

CROSS-CURRICULAR LINKS

Math: Plot the changes in life expectancy over the past century

Social studies: Discuss the effect of the Great Depression on society

Art: Consider the portrayal of the elderly in fine art

McDougal Littell

THE LANGUAGE OF
LITERATURE

McDougal Littell

THE LANGUAGE OF
LITERATURE

Arthur N. Applebee

Andrea B. Bermúdez

Sheridan Blau

Rebekah Caplan

Franchelle Dorn

Peter Elbow

Susan Hynds

Judith A. Langer

James Marshall

 McDougal Littell
A HOUGHTON MIFFLIN COMPANY

Evanston, Illinois ▪ Boston ▪ Dallas

Acknowledgments

Unit One

Estate of MacKinlay Kantor: "A Man Who Had No Eyes," from *Author's Choice: 40 Stories* by MacKinlay Kantor. By permission of Tim Kantor and Layne K. Shroder, children of the deceased author.

Orchard Books: "A Crush," from *A Couple of Kooks and Other Stories About Love;* Copyright © 1990 by Cynthia Rylant. Used by permission of Orchard Books, New York.

New Directions Publishing Corp.: "No, the human heart," from *One Hundred Poems from the Japanese* by Ki No Tsurayuki, translated by Kenneth Rexroth. By permission of New Directions Publishing Corp. All Rights Reserved.

Philomel Books and Stoddart Publishing: "Waiting," from *The Leaving and Other Stories* by Budge Wilson; Text copyright © 1990 by Budge Wilson. Reprinted by permission of Philomel Books, a division of Putnam Publishing Group, and by permission of Stoddart Publishing Co. Limited, Don Mills, Ontario.

Dutton Children's Books: Excerpt from *Immigrant Kids* by Russell Freedman; Copyright © 1980 by Russell Freedman. Used by permission of Dutton Children's Books, a division of Penguin Books USA Inc.

Continued on page 907

Cover Art

Background photo: Clouds, Copyright © 1988 David Bartruff/FPG. **Moon and astronaut:** Courtesy of NASA. **Baseball batter:** Detail of *Baseball Scene of Bastter, Catcher, and Umpire* (1915), Joseph Christian Leyendecker. Photo courtesy of the Archives of the American Illustrators Gallery, New York City. Copyright © 1995 ARTShows and Products of Holderness 03245. **Fox:** Detail of illustration reprinted from *Red Fox Running* by Eve Bunting. Illustration copyright © 1993 by Wendell Minor, published by Clarion Books. **People rising from field:** Illustration by Michael Steirnagle. **Book:** Photo by Alan Shortall. **Frame:** Photo by Sharon Hoogstraten.

ISBN 0-395-73702-8

1 2 3 4 5 6 7 8 9 – RRD – 01 00 99 98 97 96

Senior Consultants

The senior consultants guided the conceptual development for *The Language of Literature* series. They participated actively in shaping prototype materials for major components, and they reviewed completed prototypes and/or completed units to ensure consistency with current research and the philosophy of the series.

Arthur N. Applebee Professor of Education, State University of New York at Albany; Director, Center for the Learning and Teaching of Literature; Senior Fellow, Center for Writing and Literacy

Andrea B. Bermúdez Professor of Studies in Language and Culture; Director, Research Center for Language and Culture; Chair, Foundations and Professional Studies, University of Houston-Clear Lake

Sheridan Blau Senior Lecturer in English and Education and former Director of Composition, University of California at Santa Barbara; Director, South Coast Writing Project; Director, Literature Institute for Teachers; Vice President, National Council of Teachers of English

Rebekah Caplan Coordinator, English Language Arts K-12, Oakland Unified School District, Oakland, California; Teacher-Consultant, Bay Area Writing Project, University of California at Berkeley; served on the California State English Assessment Development Team for Language Arts

Franchelle Dorn Professor of Drama, Howard University, Washington, D.C.; Adjunct Professor, Graduate School of Opera, University of Maryland, College Park, Maryland; Co-founder of The Shakespeare Acting Conservatory, Washington, D.C.

Peter Elbow Professor of English, University of Massachusetts at Amherst; Fellow, Bard Center for Writing and Thinking

Susan Hynds Professor and Director of English Education, Syracuse University, Syracuse, New York

Judith A. Langer Professor of Education, State University of New York at Albany; Co-director, Center for the Learning and Teaching of Literature; Senior Fellow, Center for Writing and Literacy

James Marshall Professor of English and English Education, University of Iowa, Iowa City

Contributing Consultants

Tommy Boley Associate Professor of English, University of Texas at El Paso

Jeffrey N. Golub Assistant Professor of English Education, University of South Florida, Tampa

William L. McBride Reading and Curriculum Specialist; former middle and high school English instructor

Multicultural Advisory Board

The multicultural advisors reviewed literature selections for appropriate content and made suggestions for teaching lessons in a multicultural classroom.

Dr. Joyce M. Bell, Chairperson, English Department, Townview Magnet Center, Dallas, Texas

Dr. Eugenia W. Collier, author; lecturer; Chairperson, Department of English and Language Arts; teacher of Creative Writing and American Literature, Morgan State University, Maryland

Kathleen S. Fowler, President, Palm Beach County Council of Teachers of English, Boca Raton Middle School, Boca Raton, Florida

Noreen M. Rodriguez, Trainer for Hillsborough County School District's Staff Development Division, independent consultant, Gaither High School, Tampa, Florida

Michelle Dixon Thompson, Seabreeze High School, Daytona Beach, Florida

Teacher Review Panels

The following educators provided ongoing review during the development of the tables of contents, lesson design, and key components of the program.

CALIFORNIA
Steve Bass, 8th Grade Team Leader, Meadowbrook Middle School, Ponway Unified School District

Cynthia Brickey, 8th Grade Academic Block Teacher, Kastner Intermediate School, Clovis Unified School District

Karen Buxton, English Department Chairperson, Winston Churchill Middle School, San Juan School District

continued on page 915

Manuscript Reviewers

The following educators reviewed prototype lessons and tables of contents during the development of *The Language of Literature* program.

William A. Battaglia, Herman Intermediate School, San Jose, California

Hugh Delle Broadway, McCullough High School, The Woodlands, Texas

Robert M. Bucan, National Mine Middle School, Ishpeming, Michigan

Ann E. Clayton, Department Chair for Language Arts, Rockway Middle School, Miami, Florida

Linda C. Dahl, National Mine Middle School, Ishpeming, Michigan

Shirley Herzog, Reading Department Coordinator, Fairfield Middle School, Fairfield, Ohio

continued on page 916

Student Board

The student board members read and evaluated selections to assess their appeal for seventh-grade students.

Tommy Bartsch, Schimelpfenig Middle School, Plano, Texas

Tai-Ling Bloomfield, Mears Jr. High/Alyeska Central School, Anchorage, Alaska

Gabriel Bonilla, George Washington Carver Middle School, Coconut Grove, Florida

Christopher Bradrick, Theodore Schor Middle School, Piscataway, New Jersey

Eric de Armas, George Washington Carver Middle School, Coconut Grove, Florida

Christel Fowler, W. I. Stevenson Middle School, Houston, Texas

Ashley Barnett Green, Cooper Intermediate School, Fairfax County, Virginia

Stephanie Hicks, Grant Sawyer School, Las Vegas, Nevada

David C. Hsu, Foothill Middle School, Walnut Creek, California

Chrissy Kennedy, Foothill Middle School, Walnut Creek, California

Tony Liberati, Hampton Middle School, Allison Park, Pennsylvania

Danae Lowe, Kenilworth Jr. High School, Petaluma, California

Leslie Michelle Martinez, Sam Houston Jr. High School, Irving, Texas

Michael F. Regula, Old Trail School, Bath, Ohio

Scott Stanley Terrill, Swartz Creek Middle School, Swartz Creek, Michigan

The Language of Literature

Literature Connections

Each hardback volume contains

- **Novel or Play**

- **Related Readings**—poems, stories, plays, and articles that provide new perspectives on the longer works

- **Teacher's SourceBook** filled with background information and activities

Additional Literature Connections such as:

Roll of Thunder, Hear My Cry
by Mildred D. Taylor
and Related Readings

from **Growing Up in the Great Depression** / NONFICTION
Richard Wormser

Depression / POEM
Isabel Joshlin Glaser

The Stolen Party / SHORT STORY
Liliana Heker, translated by Alberto Manguel

from **Black Women in White America: A Documentary History** / AUTOBIOGRAPHIES
edited by Gerda Lerner

Incident / POEM
Countee Cullen

Equal Opportunity / POEM
Jim Wong-Chu

The Clearing / SHORT STORY
Jesse Stuart

The Five-Dollar Dive / SHORT STORY
Yvonne Nelson Perry

Across Five Aprils
Irene Hunt

The Call of the Wild*
Jack London

The Clay Marble
Minfong Ho

The Contender
Robert Lipsyte

The Diary of Anne Frank
Frances Goodrich and Albert Hackett

Dogsong
Gary Paulsen

Dragonwings
Laurence Yep

The Giver
Lois Lowry

The Glory Field
Walter Dean Myers

The House of Dies Drear
Virginia Hamilton

I, Juan de Pareja*
Elizabeth Borton de Treviño

Johnny Tremain
Esther Forbes

Maniac Magee
Jerry Spinelli

Nothing but the Truth
Avi

Roll of Thunder, Hear My Cry*
Mildred D. Taylor

So Far from the Bamboo Grove
Yoko Kawashima Watkins

Tuck Everlasting*
Natalie Babbitt

Where the Red Fern Grows
Wilson Rawls

The Witch of Blackbird Pond
Elizabeth George Speare

A Wrinkle in Time
Madeleine L'Engle

*A Spanish version is also available.

Part 1 Opening Doors

Part 2 Letting Others In

WRITING FROM EXPERIENCE | Firsthand and Expressive Writing

Guided Assignment: Write about a Personal Experience 128
Prewriting: Planning Your Story
Drafting: Starting to Write
Revising and Publishing: Polishing Your Narrative
SKILLBUILDERS: Classifying Details, Showing, Not Telling;
Using Verb Tenses Consistently

UNIT REVIEW: REFLECT & ASSESS 136

ACROSS TIME AND PLACE: The Oral Tradition

For more stories related to the unit theme,
see page 674.

Part 1 Learning the Hard Way

WRITING ABOUT LITERATURE   Analysis

Part 2 Making Choices

xiii

Part 1   Showing Courage

WRITING ABOUT LITERATURE   Interpretation

Part 2 A Change of Heart

WRITING FROM EXPERIENCE   Informative Exposition

Part 1 The Will to Win

Part 2　High Stakes

xvii

Part 1 Appearances to the Contrary

WRITING ABOUT LITERATURE Criticism

Part 2 Mysterious Circumstances

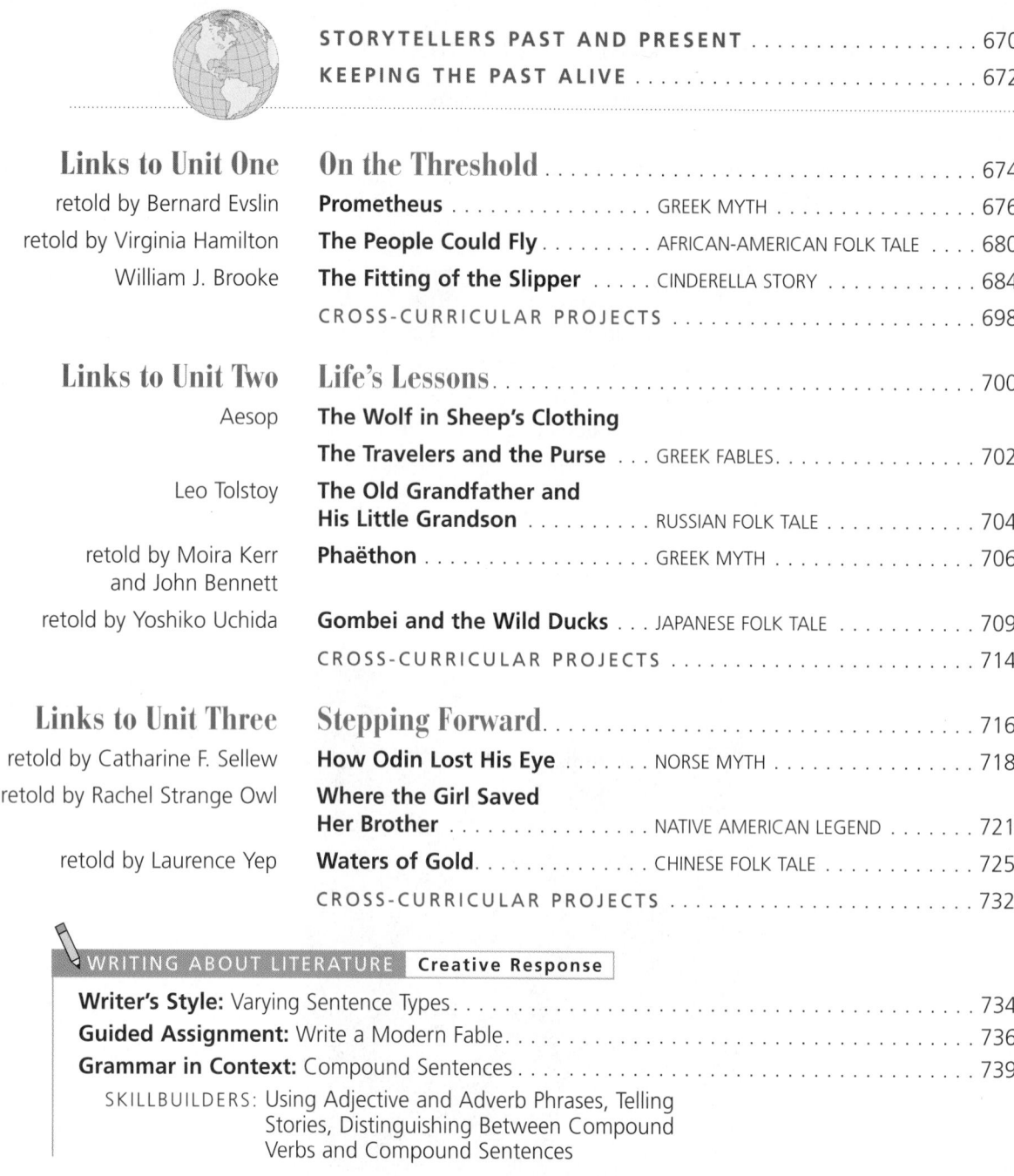

xx

WRITING FROM EXPERIENCE   **Informative Exposition**

Guided Assignment: Write a Compare-and-Contrast Essay 786

Prewriting: Sorting Through Your Ideas

Drafting: Putting Ideas on Paper

Revising and Publishing: Adding the Final Touches

SKILLBUILDERS: Analyzing Story Elements, Writing an Effective
Introduction, Using Irregular Comparatives and Superlatives

UNIT REVIEW: REFLECT AND ASSESS 794

Selections by Genre, Writing Workshops

The Oral Tradition

Myths, Legends, Folk Tales, and Fables

Writing About Literature

Writing from Experience

Visual Literacy: Reading the World

LEARNING THE LANGUAGE OF LITERATURE

Objectives

This section is designed to help students realize that their experience with the literature in this book will challenge them to discover new ways of reading, learning, and knowing. This section has the following purposes:

- To involve students in an activity that will help them think about the reading of literature in new ways
- To help students discover that literature is a way to connect to their own lives and to the world around them
- To introduce students to the parts of the book
- To familiarize students with the tools that promote learning, such as a portfolio, a reading log, and a notebook
- To provide a model that shows real students using reading strategies to become involved with literature

How Do You See It?

How many squares are in the painting? You can count each small square, but will that give you the right answer? Look at the image carefully and creatively, and you will find many, many more squares.

LOOK AGAIN

In small groups, count how many squares the figure contains. Here are some ideas about how to proceed.

1. Draw a copy of the figure on a separate piece of paper.

2. Decide as a group how you'll accomplish the task of counting all of the squares.

3. Choose one person in your group to be the recorder.

4. Count the squares. Consider how you'll know when you have counted them all.

5. When your group is satisfied with its answer, compare the number of squares you found with the number other groups found.

6. If other groups have answers that are different from yours, can your group convince the other groups that you counted all the squares accurately?

7. Can your class agree on how many squares the figure contains?

CONNECT TO LITERATURE

The number of squares you find in the painting depends on the strategies you use to count them. The ideas you find in a piece of literature depend on the strategies you use when you read. Turn the page to find out how reading literature can sharpen your thinking skills.

Look Again

Students may need help understanding that there are other squares in this painting besides the small squares. If students are having difficulty finding more squares, tell them that any group of small squares with the same number of squares on each side makes up another larger square. For example, a group of four small squares forms a larger square, and so on.

Connect to Literature

Encourage students to understand the reason for this activity by stressing the idea that reading literature involves using strategies—just as counting the number of squares does. Tell students that, just as they did when counting the squares in the painting, they should try different approaches and strategies when reading literature. Their goal should be to go beyond the obvious and experience things in new ways.

How Does Literature Broaden Your View?

When you read literature, you're free to follow your imagination as far it will take you. You might be surprised at what you find! This year, you will see some of the ways that reading can lead you to new discoveries . . .

IT OPENS UP THE WORLD

A girl in prehistoric Wales defies her clan to rescue her best friend, a kind Chinese woman discovers waters of gold, and a relay team of dogsleds braves the frozen Alaskan wilderness. The **literature selections** you'll read this year will show you worlds you may only have imagined. For a taste of what's in store, skim through "The Medicine Bag" on page 286.

IT REFLECTS YOUR SELF

Just as a mirror shows how you look on the outside, literature can reflect who you are on the inside. Most of the selections in this book begin with a **Previewing** page. This page taps into what you know about a topic and gives you important background information. For example, on page 531 you'll explore first impressions, an important aspect of the story "The Smallest Dragonboy." The **Responding** pages after a selection help you build your own ideas and interpretations. To see some responding activities, turn to page 548.

You may wish to have students read these two pages on their own, with a partner, or as a class. Encourage students to turn to the specific pages and to look at the examples suggested. Also suggest that they write down any comments or questions they think of while reading. After students have read the two pages, discuss the questions they have recorded and ask them if their expectations about the reading of literature have changed. (For further information about each of the book sections that are mentioned, please turn to pages T-10, T-11, T-14, and T-15 at the front of this Teacher's Edition.)

IT CHALLENGES YOU

Do you think two friends can face each other in a boxing tournament and remain friends? It's up to you to decide, as you'll see when you explore the **Writing About Literature** workshops. In the workshop on page 312 you will examine and extend your response to a story. You will also find opportunities to connect unit themes to your own situations and challenges. For example, the literature in Unit Three explores the ideas of courage and change. In that unit's **Writing from Experience** workshop, on page 372, you will come up with your own definition of an idea.

IT MAKES YOU WONDER

Do you recognize anything familiar in this painting? Trying to understand literature can be just as puzzling. As you read, you might wonder what a certain story or poem has to do with you. But if you give yourself time, you'll begin to find connections. The **Reading the World** feature will help you use the skills you have learned while studying literature to better understand the world around you. For example, the lesson on page 452 shows you how to use visual clues to interpret a puzzling scene.

Zero Through Nine (1961), Jasper Johns. Tate Gallery, London/Art Resource, New York. Copyright © 1996 Jasper Johns/Licensed by VAGA, New York.

LEARNING THE LANGUAGE OF LITERATURE   **3**

How Do You Find the Answers?

When literature shows you new ideas and experiences, you're bound to have questions about what you see. Finding the answers becomes easy when you take the time to explore your options.

Portfolio

MULTIPLE PATHWAYS

Do you learn best working on your own or with others? Would you choose writing, talking, acting, or drawing? This book offers you a variety of options and lets you take charge of your own learning experiences, no matter where your strengths lie. In addition, you'll be given opportunities to collaborate with classmates to share ideas, improve your writing, and make connections to other subject areas. Perhaps you'll use a computer in the process. Technological tools such as the LaserLinks and the Writing Coach offer you more ways to personalize how you learn.

PORTFOLIO

Many artists, photographers, designers, and writers keep certain pieces of their work in a portfolio that they show to others. This year, you, too, will be collecting your work in a portfolio. Your portfolio may include writing samples, records of activities, and artwork. You probably won't put all your work in your portfolio—just carefully chosen pieces. Discuss with your teacher the kind of portfolio you'll be keeping this year. You will find suggestions for how to use your portfolio throughout this book.

Reading Log

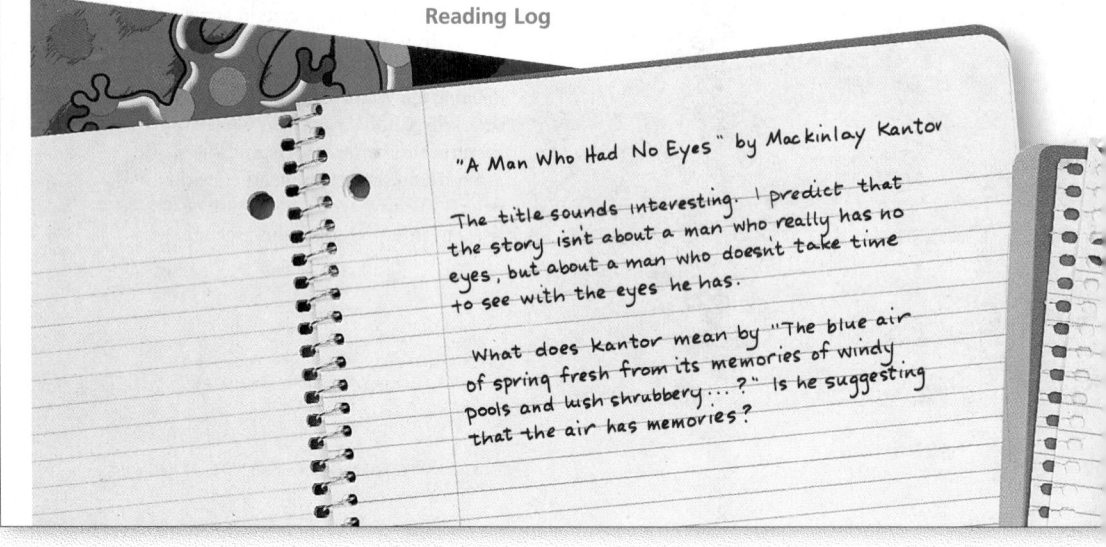

"A Man Who Had No Eyes" by Mackinlay Kantor

The title sounds interesting. I predict that the story isn't about a man who really has no eyes, but about a man who doesn't take time to see with the eyes he has.

What does Kantor mean by "The blue air of spring fresh from its memories of windy pools and lush shrubbery....?" Is he suggesting that the air has memories?

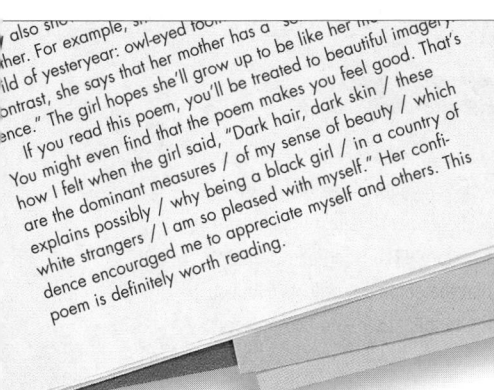

also sho... her. For example, s... ild of yesteryear: owl-eyed fool... ontrast, she says that her mother has a s... ence." The girl hopes she'll grow up to be like her m... If you read this poem, you'll be treated to beautiful imagery. You might even find that the poem makes you feel good. That's how I felt when the girl said, "Dark hair, dark skin / these are the dominant measures / of my sense of beauty / which explains possibly / why being a black girl / in a country of white strangers / I am so pleased with myself. " Her confidence encouraged me to appreciate myself and others. This poem is definitely worth reading.

NOTEBOOK

Choose any type of notebook and use it only for your study of literature. Divide the notebook into three sections. In the first section, jot down ideas, describe personal experiences, take notes, and express your thoughts before, while, and after you read a selection. You may also include any charts, diagrams, and drawings that help you connect reading to your life. The second section is for your reading log, which is described below. Use the third section as a writer's notebook to record ideas and inspirations that you might use later in your writing assignments.

READING LOG

Your reading log is for a special kind of response to literature—your direct comments as you read a selection. The reading strategies detailed at the right will help you think about what you read. In your reading log experiment with recording comments as you read. You will find opportunities to use your reading log throughout this book.

Notebook

"A Man Who Had No Eyes" by Mackinlay Kantor
Idea for a paper: how Mr. Parsons and
Mr. Markwardt are alike and different

Mr. Parsons
sells insurance
glad to be alive
generous
kind

Mr. Markwardt
begs and peddles
bitter
selfish and greedy
blind

Strategies for Reading

To get the most out of literature, you have to do more than sit back and read the words. You must think about what you read. The strategies below describe the kinds of thinking that active readers do. You may already be using some of these strategies.

QUESTION

While you read, question what's happening. Searching for reasons behind events and characters' actions can help you get more involved in what you read. Make notes about confusing words or statements, but don't worry if you don't understand everything. As you read further, you may begin to see things more clearly.

CONNECT

Connect personally with what you're reading. Think of similarities between the descriptions in the selection and what you have personally experienced, heard about, or read about.

PREDICT

Try to figure out what will happen next and how the selection might end. Then read on to see if you made good guesses.

CLARIFY

Stop occasionally to review what you understand so far, and expect to have your understanding change and develop as you read on. Also, watch for answers to questions you had earlier.

EVALUATE

Form opinions about what you read, both while you're reading and after you've finished. Make judgments about the characters and develop your own ideas about events.

Now turn the page to see how two student readers put these strategies to work.

LEARNING THE LANGUAGE OF LITERATURE **5**

Reading Strategies

Ask volunteers to recall a story that involved them deeply. Ask them to describe what it was like to read a story actively. Tell students that when they read actively they probably use some of the strategies described on this page. Explain that these strategies help readers get more pleasure and understanding from what they read and that using these strategies can make reading easier and more enjoyable.

Invite students to read aloud and discuss the descriptions of the strategies for reading on this page. Ask students to share occasions when they have used these strategies. Explain that the model they are about to read shows the comments that two students made as they were reading a story for the first time. Stress that these readers' comments are not "right" answers but rather examples of strategies at work.

READING MODEL

Objectives

This model can be used in different ways.

- You may wish to have students cover the sidebar notes and read "A Man Who Had No Eyes" as they practice recording their responses in a reading log. Afterwards, students can compare their responses with their classmates' and the student readers' to discover that readers respond to the same selection in individual ways.

- You might read the selection aloud, pausing to have students record their responses. You may wish to read aloud and have students take turns reading the comments of Jeremiah and Claire.

A Unfamiliar words and phrases can be stumbling blocks to a reader's understanding of a selection. Often the meaning of an unfamiliar word or phrase can be inferred from context clues. Jeremiah isn't sure what "furtive" means, and he notes his question. However, he moves along, knowing that he can come back later to figure out the meaning of this word if he needs to do so in order to understand the story. While questions about the meaning of words and phrases often don't need to be answered immediately, students should learn to judge whether they are making sense of the story as a whole and to recognize when vocabulary help is essential to their understanding.

B Readers often come upon situations in stories that remind them of personal experiences and concerns. Such prior knowledge can add depth and richness to a reader's response to a selection. Here, Claire connects the selection to her own experience. In addition, she pauses to clarify her understanding of the two characters, Mr. Parsons and the blind man.

Alongside the story "A Man Who Had No Eyes" are transcripts of the spoken comments that two seventh-grade students, Jeremiah Kaye and Claire Rhee, made while reading it. Jeremiah's and Claire's comments reflect the kinds of thinking that active readers do as they read a story. (The label following each comment identifies the reading strategies that the comment reflects.) As you will note, these readers responded differently to this story—no two readers think about or relate to a literary work in exactly the same way.

To get the most from this model, read the story first, jotting down your own responses in your reading log. Then read Jeremiah's and Claire's responses and compare them with your own.

A MAN WHO HAD NO EYES

by MacKinlay Kantor

Detail of *Unfinished Portrait of Tadeusz Lempicki.*

A *Jeremiah:* "the cautious, half-furtive effort of the sightless"—What does furtive *mean? I've never come across this word.*
QUESTIONING

B *Claire:* Mr. Parsons and the blind man are really different. He is rich and the beggar is poor. This reminds me of a time when I met a man who had lost one of his legs.
CLARIFYING, CONNECTING

A beggar was coming down the avenue just as Mr. Parsons emerged from his hotel.

He was a blind beggar, carrying the traditional battered cane and thumping his way before him with the cautious, half-furtive effort of the sightless. He was a shaggy, thick-necked fellow; his coat was greasy about the lapels and pockets, and his hand splayed over the cane's crook with a futile sort of clinging. He wore a black pouch slung over his shoulder. Apparently he had something to sell.

The air was rich with spring; sun was warm and yellowed on the asphalt. Mr. Parsons, standing there in front of his hotel and noting the *clack-clack* approach of the sightless man, felt a sudden and foolish sort of pity for all blind creatures.

6 READING MODEL

And, thought Mr. Parsons, he was very glad to be alive. A few years ago he had been little more than a skilled laborer; now he was successful, respected, admired. . . . Insurance. . . . And he had done it alone, unaided, struggling beneath handicaps. . . . And he was still young. The blue air of spring, fresh from its memories of windy pools and lush shrubbery, could thrill him with eagerness.

He took a step forward just as the tap-tapping blind man passed him by. Quickly the shabby fellow turned.

"Listen, guv'nor. Just a minute of your time."

Mr. Parsons said, "It's late. I have an appointment. Do you want me to give you something?"

"I ain't no beggar, guv'nor. You bet I ain't. I got a handy little article here"—he fumbled until he could press a small object into Mr. Parsons's hand—"that I sell. One buck. Best cigarette lighter made."

Mr. Parsons stood there, somewhat annoyed and embarrassed. He was a handsome figure with his immaculate gray suit and gray hat and Malacca stick. Of course the man with the cigarette lighters could not see him. . . . "But I don't smoke," he said.

"Listen. I bet you know plenty people who smoke. Nice little present," wheedled the man. "And, mister, you wouldn't mind helping a poor guy out?" He clung to Mr. Parsons's sleeve.

Mr. Parsons sighed and felt in his vest pocket. He brought out two half dollars and pressed them into the man's hand. "Certainly. I'll help you out. As you say, I can give it to someone. Maybe the elevator boy would—" He hesitated, not wishing to be boorish and inquisitive, even with a blind peddler. "Have you lost your sight entirely?"

The shabby man pocketed the two half dollars. "Fourteen years, guv'nor." Then he added with an insane sort of pride: "Westbury, sir. I was one of 'em."

"Westbury," repeated Mr. Parsons. "Ah, yes. The chemical explosion. . . . The papers haven't mentioned it for years. But at the time it was supposed to be one of the greatest disasters in—"

"They've all forgot about it." The fellow shifted his feet wearily. "I tell you, guv'nor, a man who was in it don't forget about it. Last thing I ever saw was C shop going up in one grand smudge, and that damn gas pouring in at all the busted windows."

Mr. Parsons coughed. But the blind peddler was caught up with the train of his one dramatic reminiscence. And, also, he was thinking that there might be more half dollars in Mr. Parsons's pocket.

"Just think about it, guv'nor. There was a hundred and eight people killed, about two hundred injured, and over fifty of them lost their eyes. Blind as bats—" He groped forward until his dirty

---

C *Jeremiah:* ". . . very glad to be alive"—is Mr. Parson's thinking about himself or the beggar? **QUESTIONING**

C Jeremiah questions whether a phrase refers to Mr. Parsons or to the blind man. He notes his question and continues reading. Students should learn to read ahead to see if their questions are answered later in the selection. If not, they can return to their questions to figure out the answers.

D *Claire:* How did he know that this guy was rich? Because I thought he couldn't see. How did he know? **CLARIFYING, QUESTIONING**

D Claire attempts to clarify an event in the story based on what she has just read, but this procedure also raises a question in her mind. However, Claire notes her question and continues reading. Students should be aware that readers often use more than one strategy to enrich their understanding of characters and events in a story.

E *Jeremiah:* ". . . and felt in his vest pocket." Mr. Parsons doesn't seem to want to give the beggar anything. Maybe he feels he has to give something so that he looks good in public. **EVALUATING**

E The opinions that readers form when evaluating a character in a story are usually based on personal judgments. Jeremiah makes a judgment about Mr. Parsons's conduct and suggests a reason to explain his actions.

F *Jeremiah:* ". . .Westbury, sir. I was one of 'em."—What happened at Westbury? What does the beggar mean by "one of 'em"? **QUESTIONING**

F Jeremiah questions what the blind man means. As he did earlier, he notes his question and continues reading. As he reads ahead, he will look for information to answer this question.

G *Claire:* He sounds like a beggar, especially when he says, "guv'nor." **CONNECTING, CLARIFYING**

G Claire clarifies her understanding of the blind man by visualizing this character on the basis of the writer's description of him, what he says to Mr. Parsons, and perhaps her own familiarity with similar characters. By paying careful attention to the ways in which a writer presents a character, a reader can clarify his or her understanding.

Unfinished Portrait of Tadeusz Lempicki **by Tamara de Lempicka** Tamara de Lempicka often depicted well-dressed figures from society in her paintings. Her ability to convey the physical presence of figures—like the one rendered in this painting—distinguishes her work.

Reading the Art *What kind of man do you think is represented in this painting? What details in the painting help to support your impression? How does the style of the painting also help to create this impression?*

Unfinished Portrait of Tadeusz Lempicki (about 1928), Tamara de Lempicka. Oil on canvas, 126 cm × 82 cm, Musée National d'Art Moderne, Centre National d'Art et de Culture Georges Pompidou, Paris. Copyright © 1996 Artists Rights Society (ARS), New York/SPADEM, Paris.

8   READING MODEL

hand rested against Mr. Parsons's coat. "I tell you, sir, there wasn't nothing worse than that in the war. If I had lost my eyes in the war, okay. I would have been well took care of. But I was just a workman, working for what was in it. And I got it. You're damn right I got it, while the capitalists were making their dough! They was insured, don't worry about that. They—"

"Insured," repeated his listener. "Yes. That's what I sell—"

"You want to know how I lost my eyes?" cried the man. "Well, here it is!" His words fell with the bitter and studied drama of a story often told, and told for money. "I was there in C shop, last of all the folks rushing out. Out in the air there was a chance, even with buildings exploding right and left. A lot of guys made it safe out the door and got away. And just when I was about there, crawling along between those big vats, a guy behind me grabs my leg. He says, 'Let me past, you—!' Maybe he was nuts. I dunno. I try to forgive him in my heart, guv'nor. But he was bigger than me. He hauls me back and climbs right over me! Tramples me into the dirt. And he gets out, and I lie there with all that poison gas pouring down on all sides of me, and flame and stuff. . . ." He swallowed—a studied sob—and stood dumbly expectant. He could imagine the next words: *Tough luck, my man. Damned tough. Now, I want to*—"That's the story, guv'nor."

The spring wind shrilled past them, damp and quivering.

"Not quite," said Mr. Parsons.

The blind peddler shivered crazily. "Not quite? What do you mean, you—?"

"The story is true," Mr. Parsons said, "except that it was the other way around."

"Other way around?" He croaked unamiably. "Say, guv'nor—"

"I was in C shop," said Mr. Parsons. "It was the other way around. You were the fellow who hauled back on me and climbed over me. You were bigger than I was, Markwardt."

The blind man stood for a long time, swallowing hoarsely. He gulped: "Parsons. By God. By God! I thought you—" And then he screamed fiendishly: "Yes. Maybe so. Maybe so. But I'm blind! I'm blind, and you've been standing here letting me spout to you, and laughing at me every minute! I'm blind!"

People in the street turned to stare at him.

"You got away, but I'm blind! Do you hear? I'm—"

"Well," said Mr. Parsons, "don't make such a row about it, Markwardt. . . . So am I."

Jeremiah: "That's what I sell"
—So Mr. Parsons sells insurance.
CLARIFYING

(H)

Jeremiah: ". . . and flame and stuff"
—Now I feel sorry for the beggar. He probably lost everything when he lost his eyesight. I can picture him in the past—middle class, with a house, a wife, a family.
EVALUATING

(I)

Claire: He's making a big deal out of being blind. Helen Keller was blind. It just matters how you take it. You can't just go crying about it. It's just going to come harder for you.
EVALUATING, PREDICTING

(J)

Claire: The respected man states that he's blind too. They got blind in C shop. Interesting how one man turns into a beggar. The other man gets respected.
CLARIFYING, QUESTIONING

(K)

A MAN WHO HAD NO EYES   **9**

(H) Jeremiah uses details in the passage to make inferences about Mr. Parsons's occupation. Readers must often make inferences in order to clarify their understanding of the characters in a selection.

(I) At this point in the story, Jeremiah evaluates the circumstances of the blind man's life based on details from the passage. His comment about the blind man also indicates his growing involvement in the story. Students should be encouraged to form opinions about what they read in order to develop their own ideas about characters and events.

(J) Claire's comment indicates that she has formed an opinion of the blind man's character. In addition, she compares him with someone that she has read about and makes a judgment about his response to his handicap, thus enriching her understanding of his behavior.

(K) Claire clarifies and develops her understanding of the characters in the story based on what she has read. She forms her own interpretations of the characters and events in the story.

BIOGRAPHY

MCKINLAY KANTOR

MacKinlay Kantor (1904–1977) was encouraged to write by his mother, a newspaper editor. However, it was years before Kantor found a successful market for his work in the "pulps," cheap popular magazines. Often paid only a penny a word, Kantor quickly produced stories with surprise endings and dramatic climaxes. He also wrote murder mysteries. In 1956, Kantor won the Pulitzer Prize for *Andersonville*, a novel about the conditions in a Civil War prison camp in the South. Kantor's last historical novel, *Valley Forge*, was published in 1975 in honor of the nation's bicentennial.

UNIT THEME

Unit One

On the Threshold In this unit, students will read selections that present characters who are on the threshold of new experiences. The unit contains two parts: Part 1, "Opening Doors," and Part 2, "Letting Others In." Selections in both parts contribute to the unit theme by exploring situations that lead to new experiences and the challenges that new relationships may bring.

Part 1

Opening Doors Selections in Part 1 center on characters who open the doors to new experiences, such as the safecracker in "A Retrieved Reformation" who falls in love and wants to lead an honest life.

Part 2

Letting Others In Selections in Part 2 explore what happens when characters let others into their lives, such as the narrator in "The War of the Wall" who is forced to deal with a stranger in the neighborhood.

Links to Unit Six

The Oral Tradition Unit Six, "Across Time and Place," contains literature that connects with the theme of Unit One. You may wish to begin or end Unit One by using the following selections from Unit Six that relate to the theme "On the Threshold":

- "Prometheus," p. 676
- "The People Could Fly," p. 680
- "The Fitting of the Slipper," p. 684

ON THE

THRESHOLD

You whose day it is,

make it beautiful.

Get out your rainbow,

make it beautiful.

—NOOTKA TRIBE

A NATIVE-AMERICAN PEOPLE INHABITING PARTS OF BRITISH COLUMBIA AND WASHINGTON

Three Barge Fireworks (1987), Terrie Hancock Mangat. Reverse appliqué, piecing, strip piecing, embroidery, beading, painting, appliqué on assorted fabrics, 6′ × 9′, collection of Esther Saalfeld Hancock. Photo by Terrie Hancock Mangat.

10

To help students explore the connections between the art, the quotation, and the unit theme, have them consider the following questions:

1. What kinds of images and ideas come to mind when you hear the phrase "on the threshold"? *(Possible response: A threshold is a doorway or passage into a new place. "On the threshold" means that someone is at the point of beginning something new or entering a new stage in his or her life.)*

2. In what ways do you think the quotation reflects the idea of being on the threshold? *(Possible response: The quotation expresses the idea that the start of each day is like a new beginning and that we must take advantage of the possibilities of each new day to make it the best it can be.)*

3. Do you think fireworks are a good illustration of the theme "On the Threshold"? Why or why not? *(Possible response: Yes, because fireworks are usually used to celebrate events that mark a new beginning, such as the Chinese New Year or the Fourth of July)*

4. What kinds of stories do you expect to read in this unit? *(Possible responses: This unit will contain stories about people who have new experiences and who make a new start in life. Some of the stories will be about the ways in which people change because of what they learn from new experiences they have.)*

5. In what ways do the unit theme, the quotation, and the art connect to your own experiences? Recall a time when you stood at the brink of a new experience. How did you feel? What did you learn from the experience? *(Responses will vary.)*

Art Note

Three Barge Fireworks by **Terrie Hancock Mangat** The American artist Terrie Hancock Mangat creates personalized quilts that are full of life. She has been embroidering since the age of 11. Mangat likes to embroider without a preconceived plan, letting her ideas unfold as she works.

Reading the Art *What impressions does this artwork create for you?*

Part 1 Skills Trace

ML   DENOTES MINI-LESSON IN TEACHER'S EDITION

Selections	Reading Skills and Strategies	Literary Concepts	Writing Opportunities	Speaking, Listening, and Viewing
FICTION **A Crush** Cynthia Rylant	Static and dynamic characters, PE p. 15 Question, **ML** TE p. 17	First- and third-person points of view, PE p. 24 Simile and metaphor, **ML** TE p. 21	Summary, PE p. 24 Short story, PE p. 24 Personal narrative, PE p. 24	Rank characters, PE p. 24 Role-playing, PE p. 25 Choosing/composing music, PE p. 25 Panel discussion, PE p. 25
FICTION **A Retrieved Reformation** O. Henry	Understanding motive, PE p. 27 Evaluating, **ML** TE p. 31	Plot, PE p. 35 Climax, PE p. 35 Point of View, **ML** TE p. 29	Newspaper article, PE p. 35 Report, PE p. 35 Explanatory paragraph, PE p. 35 Script, PE p. 36 Show, don't tell, **ML** TE p. 33	Mock trial, PE p. 35 Performing a scene, PE p. 36
FICTION **Waiting** Budge Wilson	Contrasting characters, PE p. 37 Connecting, **ML** TE p. 40	Characters, PE p. 51 Plot, **ML** TE p.39	Character sketches, PE p. 50 Journal entry, PE p. 50 Letter, PE p. 50	Retelling an event, PE p. 50 Performing, PE p. 51 Multimedia, PE p. 51 Interviewing, **ML** TE p. 45 Drama performance, **ML** TE p. 46
NONFICTION *from* **Immigrant Kids** Russell Freedman	Setting a purpose for reading, PE p. 55; **ML** TE p. 57	Informative nonfiction, primary sources, secondary sources, PE p. 61 Conflict, **ML** TE p. 58	Journal entries, PE p. 61 Pro or con statement, PE p. 61 Writing letters, PE p. 61 Transcript, PE p. 62	Interview, PE p. 62
NONFICTION *from* **The Autobiography of Malcolm X** Malcolm X with Alex Haley		Autobiography, PE p. 68 Point of view, TE p. 65	Write about an influential book, PE p. 63 Write a speech, PE p. 68 Poem, PE p. 68 Personal memoir, PE p. 68 Letter, PE p. 68 Personal dictionary, PE p. 68	Deliver a speech, PE p. 68 Sharing a dictionary study, PE p. 69
FICTION ON YOUR OWN **The Scholarship Jacket** Marta Salinas			Dialogue journal, TE p. 70 Writing a speech, TE p. 72	Paired reading, TE p. 70 Group reading, TE p. 70 Deliver a speech, TE p. 72

Writing	Reading Skills and Strategies	Literary Concepts	Writing Opportunities	Speaking, Listening, and Viewing
WRITING ABOUT LITERATURE **Direct Response**	Responding to literature, PE pp. 76–79	Elaboration, PE pp. 74–75	Revise a QuickWrite, PE p. 75 Write sentences and a story, PE p. 75 Write a statement, PE p. 75 Personal response essay, PE pp. 76–79 Organizing a personal response essay, PE p. 77	Using sensory language aloud, PE p. 75 Viewing a wall, PE p. 81 Interpreting a wall, PE p. 81 Discussion, PE p. 81 Discussing responses, PE p. 81

Grammar, Usage, Mechanics, and Spelling	Multimodal Learning	Research and Study Skills	Vocabulary
Compound sentences, (ML) TE p. 18 Suffixes -ness and -ly, (ML) TE p.23	Drawing "before" and "after" pictures, PE p. 25 Role-playing, PE p. 25 Choosing/composing music, PE p. 25 Panel discussion, PE p. 25 Child development chart, PE p. 25	Research the Special Olympics, PE p. 25 Research the stages of child development, PE p. 25	cherish discreetly impaled suitor swarthy
Subject-verb agreement: The pronoun you, (ML) TE p. 30 The prefix un-, (ML) TE p. 34	Mock trial, PE p. 35 Drawing a portrait, PE p. 36 Performing a scene, PE p. 36	Research the criminal justice system, PE p. 36	assiduously rehabilitate balk retribution compulsory unobtrusively elusive unperceived eminent virtuous
Choosing the right verb (let/leave, lie/lay, sit/set), (ML) TE p. 41 Words ending in -ance/-ant, (ML) TE p.49	Performing, PE p. 51 Drawing portraits, PE p. 51 Multimedia, PE p. 51 Interviewing, (ML) TE p. 45 Drama performance, (ML) TE p. 46	Research growing up during WWII, PE p. 51 SQ3R, (ML) TE p. 43	apathy quarantine arresting saunter dominant stupefying flamboyant submissive infuriatingly vigor
Plural and possessive nouns, (ML) TE p. 59 Prefixes (in-, im-) and base words, (ML) TE p. 60	Drawing a map, PE p. 62 Sketching a person, PE p. 62 Family tree, PE p. 62 Interview, PE p. 62	Research immigration routes, PE p. 62	din fervent impoverished indomitable teeming
Kinds of sentences, (ML) TE p. 66 Different a sounds, (ML) TE p. 67	Delivering a speech, PE p. 68 Drawing a mural, PE p. 69 Dictionary study, PE p. 69 Creating a poster, PE p. 69 Making a map, PE p. 69		articulate emulate feign painstaking rehabilitation
	Paired reading, TE p. 70 Group reading, TE p. 70 Deliver a speech, TE p. 72		

Grammar, Usage, Mechanics, and Spelling	Multimodal Learning	Research and Study Skills	Media Literacy
Punctuating quotations, PE p. 75 Placing prepositional phrases, PE p. 79	Using sensory language aloud, PE p. 75 Viewing a wall, PE p. 81 Interpreting a wall, PE pp. 80–81 Discussion, PE p. 81 Discussing responses, PE p. 81	Synthesizing personal responses, PE p. 81	Interpreting a wall, PE pp. 80–81

Part 2 Skills Trace

ML DENOTES MINI-LESSON IN TEACHER'S EDITION

Selections	Reading Skills and Strategies	Literary Concepts	Writing Opportunities	Speaking, Listening, and Viewing
FICTION **The War of the Wall** Toni Cade Bambara	Dialect, PE p. 83 Questioning, **ML** TE p. 86	Conflict, PE p. 93 Point of view, PE p. 93; **ML** TE p. 85	Description, PE p. 92 Letter, PE p. 92 Speech, PE p. 92 Newspaper article, PE p. 92 Personal narrative, PE p. 92 Dialogue, **ML** TE p. 87	Sharing a letter, PE p. 92 Role-playing, PE p. 93 Oral report, PE p. 93 Exhibit your flag, PE p. 93 Listening to music, **ML** TE p. 90
FICTION **Last Cover** Paul Annixter	Context clues, PE p. 95; **ML** TE p. 98	Setting, PE p. 106 Conflict, PE p. 106; **ML** TE p. 97	Advertising flyer, PE p. 106 Dialogue, PE p. 106 Describing audience, **ML** TE p. 104	Readers Theater presentation, PE p. 106 Conflict list, **ML** TE p. 97 Retelling, TE p. 101 Storytelling, **ML** TE p. 102
POETRY **The Pasture** **A Time to Talk** Robert Frost	Oral reading, PE p. 110	Imagery, **ML** TE p. 111 Rhyme, PE p. 113	Poem, PE p. 113 Recipe, PE p. 113 Travel brochure, PE p. 114	Oral reading, PE p. 110; **ML** TE p. 111 Illustrated book, PE p. 113 Choral reading, PE p. 114 Role-playing, **ML** TE p. 112
POETRY **There Is No Word for Goodbye** Mary TallMountain **Graduation Morning** Pat Mora	Understanding cultural contexts, PE p. 115	Imagery, PE p. 119 Figurative language, **ML** TE p. 118	Thoughts on crossroads, PE p. 115 Thesaurus entry, PE p. 119 Graduation card, PE p. 119 Poem or character sketch, PE p. 119 Rewriting poems, **ML** TE p. 118	Comparison diagram, PE p. 119 Oral reading, PE p. 120; **ML** TE p. 116 Playing music, PE p. 120 Oral report, PE p. 120 Interviews, TE p. 117
NONFICTION **Homeless** Anna Quindlen	Author's purpose, PE p. 121 Evaluating, **ML** TE p. 123	Essay, PE p. 126 Point of view, **ML** TE p. 124	Letter, PE p. 126 Editorial, PE p. 126 Definition, PE p. 126 Opinions, **ML** TE p. 123 Paragraph on homelessness, **ML** TE p. 124	Letter, PE p. 126 Drawing or sculpture, PE p. 127 Interview, PE p. 127 Speech, PE p. 127

Writing	Reading Skills and Strategies	Literary Concepts	Writing Opportunities	Speaking, Listening, and Viewing
WRITING FROM EXPERIENCE **Firsthand and Expressive Writing**	Classifying details, PE p. 131	Dialogue, PE p. 133	Writing about a personal experience, PE pp. 128–35 Drafting, PE pp. 132–33 Showing, not telling, PE p. 133 Revising and publishing, PE pp. 134–35	Interviewing, PE p. 131 Storytelling, PE p. 131 Monologue, PE p. 135 Video or dramatic skit, PE p. 135

Grammar, Usage, Mechanics, and Spelling	Multimodal Learning	Research and Study Skills	Vocabulary	
Pronoun case: Compound structure, (ML) TE p. 88 Different *k* sounds, (ML) TE p. 91	Design a flag, PE p. 93 Role-playing, PE p. 93 Oral report, PE p. 93 Listening to music, (ML) TE p. 90	Research the wall of respect movement, PE p. 93	beckon drawl inscription liberation scheme	
Verb tenses, (ML) TE p. 99 Different spellings of *c*, (ML) TE p. 105	Readers Theater presentation, PE p. 106 Create a poster, PE p. 107 Retelling, TE p. 101 Storytelling, (ML) TE p. 102	Research red foxes, PE p. 107 Reference books, (ML) TE p. 100	bleak confound essence harried intricate	invalid passive sanction sanctuary wily
	Oral reading, TE p. 110; (ML) TE p. 111 Illustrated book, PE p. 113 Choral reading, PE p. 114 Photo or picture essay, PE p. 114 Travel brochure, PE p. 114 Role-playing, TE p. 112	Research New England, PE p. 114		
	Comparison diagram, PE p. 119 Oral reading, PE p. 120; (ML) TE p. 116 Playing music, PE p. 120 Oral report, PE p. 120 Interviews, TE p. 117	Research Athabaskan culture, PE p. 120		
Subject-verb agreement, (ML) TE p. 125	Drawing or sculpture, PE p. 127 Interview, PE p. 127 Speech, PE p. 127	Research real estate, PE p. 127	compassionate crux enfeebled legacy rummage	

Grammar, Usage, Mechanics, and Spelling	Multimodal Learning	Research and Study Skills	Media Literacy
Showing, not telling, PE p. 133 Using verb tenses consistently, PE p. 135	Analyzing a letter, PE p. 128 Interpreting a cartoon, PE p. 129 Analyzing a contest notice, PE p. 129 Using family and personal memorabilia, PE pp. 130–31 Interviewing, PE p. 131 Storytelling, PE p. 131 Monologue, PE p. 135 Video or dramatic skit, PE p. 135	Research memory gaps, PE pp. 130–31	Analyzing a letter, PE p. 128 Interpreting a cartoon, PE p. 129 Analyzing a contest notice, PE p. 129 Using family and personal memorabilia, PE pp. 130–31

✓ Recommended Novels

LITERATURE CONNECTIONS WITH SOURCEBOOK FOR TEACHERS  SPANISH VERSION AVAILABLE

Tuck Everlasting
by Natalie Babbitt

Thematic Links When young Winnie Foster meets a family who lives forever, she learns to understand and value the natural cycle of life and death.

About the Author Natalie Babbitt (born 1932) began her career as an illustrator and then began writing books in which realistic young people learn to deal with their fears through elements of fantasy.

Other Works by Natalie Babbitt *The Eyes of the Amaryllis, Kneeknock Rise, The Search for Delicious*

The Secret Garden
by Frances Hodgson Burnett

Thematic Links In this classic tale, a young girl, orphaned and sent to live with a reclusive uncle, searches for a sense of belonging.

About the Author Frances Hodgson Burnett (1849–1924) began writing for publication at age 17, which led to an illustrious career as a novelist and children's writer.

Other Works by Frances Hodgson Burnett *That Lass o' Lowrie's, Little Saint Elizabeth and Other Stories, Editha's Burglar: A Story for Children*

Understood Betsy
by Dorothy Canfield

Thematic Links A young girl faces a fearful new way of life when she goes to live in the wilds of Vermont.

About the Author Of living in Vermont, Dorothy Canfield (1879–1958) once said: "Living in the country is like being married to humanity for better or worse, not just being on speaking terms with it, as one is in the city."

Other Works by Dorothy Canfield *Bent Twig, Our Independence and the Constitution*

Come by Here
by Olivia Coolidge

Thematic Links An African-American girl discovers the difference between visiting relatives and living with them.

About the Author Olivia Coolidge (born 1908) taught English in the United States, Germany, and England and has written young-adult biographies.

Other Works by Olivia Coolidge *Tom Paine, Revolutionary; Gandhi; The Apprenticeship of Abraham Lincoln*

Bridge to Terabithia
by Katherine Paterson

Thematic Links A young boy becomes a close friend of a new girl in his school and is distraught after her accidental death.

About the Author Katherine Paterson (born 1932) has won numerous awards for her novels for young people. According to Paterson, the three major influences in her life that affected her writing are her experiences in Japan and China, growing up in the American South, and her strong religious beliefs.

Other Works by Katherine Paterson *Of Nightingales That Weep, The Master Puppeteer, Jacob Have I Loved, The Great Gilly Hopkins*

Dancing Carl
by Gary Paulsen

Thematic Links This story focuses on two boys and their friendship with a WWII veteran broken by his wartime experiences.

About the Author Gary Paulsen (born 1939) is an accomplished writer in many genres. His young-adult books are usually set in wilderness areas and feature teenagers who attain self-awareness through their experiences in nature.

Other Works by Gary Paulsen *The Golden Stick, The Crossing, The River, Harris and Me: A Summer Remembered, Hatchet*

For Teacher TEACHING LITERATURE

Beach, Richard, and James Marshall. *Teaching Literature in the Secondary School.* Orlando: Harcourt, 1991.

Graves, Donald H. *A Fresh Look at Writing.* New York: Heinemann, 1994.

Sears, Peter. "Revising the Line: A Simple Exercise." *Teachers and Writers* #25.1 (Sept.- Oct. 1993): 9–11.

Recommended Readings in Cross-Curricular Areas

SOCIAL STUDIES

Malcolm X: By Any Means Necessary
by Walter Dean Myers (1993)

The life and legacy of Malcolm X. Links to Malcolm X's (with Alex Haley) *The Autobiography of Malcolm X.*

New Kids on the Block: Oral Histories of Immigrant Teens
by Janet Bode (1989)

Oral histories of immigrant teens from many countries. Links to Russell Freedman's *Immigrant Kids.*

No Place to Be: Voices of Homeless Children
by Judith Berck (1992)

Thirty children tell their experiences of homeless life. Links to Anna Quindlen's "Homeless."

ART

Spraycan Art
by Henry Chalfant and James Prigoff (1987)

Photographs of graffiti in the 1980s, an international look. Links to Toni Cade Bambara's "The War of the Wall."

For Teacher · CROSS-CURRICULAR INSTRUCTION

Gross, Daniel D., and Timothy D. Gross. "Tagging: Changing Visual Patterns and the Rhetorical Implications of a New Form of Graffiti." *ETC: A Review of General Semantics* #50.3 (Fall 1993): 251–64.

Blackside, Inc., staff and Robert Lavelle, eds. *America's New War on Poverty: A Reader for Action.* Companion to the Public Television Series *America's War on Poverty.* KQED, 1994.

Murphy, Don, and Jennifer Radtke, eds. *Malcolm X in Context: A Study Guide to the Man and His Times.* School Voices Press, 1992.

Teaching for Change: Anti-Racist, Multicultural Curricula, Critical Teaching. Network of Educators on the Americas, 1993.

Recommended Media Resources

THE LANGUAGE OF LITERATURE

LASERLINKS
Videodisc, Gr. 7
See *LaserLinks Teacher's Source Book,* pages 4–5, for overview of Unit One.

AUDIO LIBRARY
Tapes
Unit One: On the Threshold
Gr. 7, Tape 1: Sides A & B
Gr. 7, Tape 2: Sides A & B

WRITING COACH
Writing Coach Software: Writing About Literature: Direct Response; Personal Narrative

OUTSIDE RESOURCES

Films/Videos/Film Strips/Audiocassettes
Shadow Children, videocassette, The Cinema Guild, 1991. (30 min.)
The Secret Garden, videocassette, MGM/UA Home Entertainment. (100 min.)
O. Henry Short Stories. Two sound cassettes. Literary Listening Library.
Tracker. Read by Frank Muller. Two sound cassettes. (120 min.) Recorded Books, 1994/1984.

Internet Resources
Literature and Language Arts Center at http://www.hmco.com/mcdougal/lit/litcent.html

For Teacher · TEACHING WITH TECHNOLOGY

Fulton, Kathleen. "Teaching Matters: The Role of Technology in Education." *Ed Tech Review* (Fall–Winter 1993): 510.

Pea, Roy D., and Louis M. Gomez, "Distributed Multimedia Learning Environments: Why and How?" *Interactive Learning Environments* #2.2 (June 1992): 73–109.

Rutkowski, Kathleen M., ed. *NetTEACH News.* 13102 Weather Vane Way, Herndon, VA 22071; e-mail address: kmr@chaos.com

Professional Enrichment

Getting Your Students to Love Poetry—Again

It's literature class. You ask your students to take out their books and turn to the poem on page 34. "All right! Poetry! Our favorite!" they respond as they eagerly search for the page.

Has this ever happened to you? Probably not. Not if you teach seventh graders, anyway. For by the time they are in seventh grade, your students have probably grown to dislike poetry.

WHAT CAN YOU DO TO TURN THINGS AROUND?

Perhaps the first thing to do is to consider why many students turn off to poetry in the first place. We know that most young children love nursery rhymes. Before they even know what the words mean, they delight in their sounds, their rhythms, and their rhyming patterns. Then as children grow older, they begin to relate to the words—and to the thoughts, feelings, and experiences that the words express. As children's sophistication develops even further, they begin to relate to the poet as a writer. They appreciate his or her ability to efficiently and succinctly put words together to create powerful messages and craft beautiful pictures.

So far so good, right? So what goes wrong? Poet Eve Merriam believes that the trouble begins when children are made to feel dumb because they don't catch on to every nuance of meaning or sound that their teacher sees in a poem. Consequently, the experience of reading and enjoying poetry for its own sake turns into the act of dissecting poetry and trying to come up with one correct interpretation of it, which is usually the teacher's. In her book *In the Middle: Writing, Reading, and Learning with Adolescents*, Nancie Atwell recalls, "A couple of years ago, when I was still glibly presenting neat explications, a kid looked at the poem . . . and asked, 'Couldn't you just mark the lines with the hidden meanings?'" Is it any wonder that students get turned off?

GETTING THE JOY BACK

Following are some suggestions for helping your seventh graders enjoy poetry again—or, perhaps, for the first time.

- Provide students with a wide variety of poems and allow them to choose from among them.
- Introduce the poetry of writers whose prose works students already know and love. This will help generate interest and enthusiasm before students begin reading.
- Encourage students to read for pleasure first and literary analysis second.
- Instruct students to ignore the line breaks and look for the punctuation as they read. Poetry students of all ages have been confounded by stopping at the end of every line and losing the meaning.
- Set aside time for your students to read poetry aloud, especially if they have written it themselves. There is no better way to get the most out of a poem than to hear it read by the person who wrote it.
- If you must prepare questions to go with a poem, make them open-ended and in no way suggestive or right or wrong answers. (Poet Paul Janeczko says he doesn't want to encourage the idea that poetry is inaccessible. Instead of thinking of poems as puzzles, he wants teachers to think of them as "language experiences.")
- Don't save poetry reading or writing for special times. Do it often throughout the year so your students get to feel comfortable with it.

Related Reading

Abrahamson, R. F. (1987). "Books for Adolescents: Of Poetry and Teenagers: An Interview with Poetry Anthologist Paul Janeczko," *Journal of Reading* 30, pp. 562–566.

Atwell, N. (1987). *In the Middle: Writing, Reading, and Learning with Adolescents*. Portsmouth, NH: Boynton/Cook Publishers.

Donelson, K. L., & Nilsen, A. P. (1989). *Literature for Today's Young Adults.* Glenview, IL: Scott, Foresman and Company.

Family and Community Involvement

Family

Whether they describe the trials of first love, learning to read, meeting new people, or losing a home, the selections in Unit One all involve people standing on the threshold of new experiences. Through the following activities, your students, their families, and other community members can connect and explore thresholds that promise new relationships, ideas, events, and emotions.

The following Copymasters for Unit One provide activities that students can take home and complete with a parent or other family member.

OPTION 1: DRAW A POSTER
- **Connection** All of the selections in Unit One illustrate the theme of standing on the threshold.
- **Activity** *Copymaster, page 4* Students and family members decide on a personal threshold and illustrate that threshold in a poster.

OPTION 2: WRITE A "HOW TO" BOOKLET
- **Connection** In *The Autobiography of Malcolm X*, Malcolm takes action to improve his reading skills and vocabulary.
- **Activity** *Copymaster, page 5* Students and family members discuss the process of learning to read; they then write a booklet explaining how to teach someone to read.

OPTION 3: VIEW A VIDEO
- **Connection** In *Immigrant Kids,* individuals face leaving their homes to find new ones.
- **Activity** *Copymaster, page 6* Students and family members watch a documentary or movie about the lives of immigrants. After watching the video, they compare the immigrants' experiences to what they predict they might do in a similar situation.

Community

OPTION 1
- **Connection** The selections in Unit One all illustrate the theme of standing on the threshold.
- **Activity** Have the class poll community leaders about the most important thresholds of their lives and how their lives changed as a result.

OPTION 2
- **Connection** After serving a prison sentence, the main character of "A Retrieved Reformation" stands at the threshold of a true reformation.
- **Activity** Have the class interview a law enforcement officer or prison professional to discuss what life in prison is like and what is involved in the effort to reform prisoners.

OPTION 3
- **Connection** In "Homeless," Anna Quindlen introduces her readers to the plight of the homeless.
- **Activity** Invite a volunteer from a homeless shelter to discuss with the class his or her experiences.

A Dramatization

Students explore the topic of personal identity by working in small groups to produce and perform original skits for an audience.

PROJECT AT A GLANCE
The selections in Unit One, Part 1 deal with acceptance and self-acceptance in finding a personal identity. For this project, students will write and act in skits that show a person coming to grips with his or her individual identity. Skits may be humorous or serious. All skits will be performed in front of a live audience and should be complete with costumes, scenery, and props (insofar as they are practical). This project might be coordinated with a schoolwide Talent Day, or the skits might be scheduled for a time when families can be invited to watch.

OBJECTIVES
- To explore the theme of identity through characters in a dramatic script
- To plan, prepare, and present an original skit
- To develop listening and viewing skills by watching and evaluating the performances of others

SUGGESTED GROUP SIZE
4–6 students per group

MATERIALS
Some groups may need art materials. In general, groups should be responsible for their own props. Those groups needing specific school supplies should submit written requests in advance of the time they will be needed.

 **Getting Started**

Arranging the Project
You might want to invite your school's drama teacher or a volunteer from a local theater group to a few of each group's rehearsals. Such a person may be able to help students make their skits funnier or more dramatic and can offer helpful suggestions from a theatrical point of view regarding blocking, line reading, or gestures. Be sure that this person understands the purpose of the project and is willing to work to enhance the skits.

Have in mind the level of performance you expect from students. This project can be adapted to suit the needs and circumstances of your class, as well as any time constraints.

Performances may range from a simple dramatic reading to a full-blown production with lights, costumes, and sound effects.

Arranging the Performances
Make arrangements with the school administration for the location of the final performances. If you have access to an auditorium and stage, schedule time for each group to hold at least one private dress rehearsal. If the skits are to take place in the classroom, you might want to arrange for side screens or curtains where students can go "off stage" during performances. In the classroom, be sure the audience gives the actors as much space as possible.

 **Creating the Dramatizations**

Introducing the Project
Explain that students will be working in small groups to plan, write, and act out skits that explore the topic of personal identity. You might begin with a discussion of any popular TV shows students are familiar with that deal with personal identity, self-worth, and self-image. Ask students to point out some of the elements that make the shows funny, dramatic, or sad. Students might put themselves in a character's place and tell how they feel before, during, and after the main event of the episode. They also might describe how understanding was finally achieved. Students should keep this discussion in mind when deciding on a topic and creating a script.

Discuss all that is needed in a theatrical production, too. Students need to be aware of the work that takes place off-stage, as well as the "stardom" of the actors out front. You also may want to remind students that skits should follow the general format of exposition (the introduction, or "stage setting" background information), conflict (the problem to be overcome), and the resolution (what finally happens).

Group Investigations
Divide students into groups of four to six. Each group should brainstorm ideas about the focus of their skit. When they have developed an idea for the skit, individual assignments can be made within the group. Encourage everyone to contribute to the writing and to act in the skit, as well as perform another behind-the-scenes duty such as stage manager, director, or prop person.

Students should familiarize themselves with the general format of writing for the theater, noting that some stage directions are included and some are left to the actors' and directors' personal interpretation. Entrances, exits, and movements vital to the advancement of the plot should be indicated in the scripts.

Creating a Project Description
After students have done some preliminary planning, they should submit a brief scenario of their intended skit. This should include a list and description of all characters, as well as a plot summary. Meet with each group to discuss the scenario before allowing students to begin the actual writing of the skit. Attend two or more rehearsals for the skit to offer advice and note progress and any difficulties that the group is encountering.

OPTION 1: TELEVISION SHOW SPIN OFFS
Groups can base their skits on existing television shows. This will give them established characters and a locale around which to center their writing.

OPTION 2: VIDEOTAPED PERFORMANCES
If you cannot schedule a large block of time when all skits can be performed, groups can videotape their skits (preferably in front of an audience) and submit them for review. Tapes can be shown and critiqued in class as time allows.

OPTION 3: IMPROVISATION For especially creative students who can "think on their feet," improvisation may offer a real challenge. Ask each group to submit a brief scenario, then assign the scenarios at random to another group. They should take only a few minutes to discuss the plot among themselves before beginning a performance. This project will require some juggling of schedules, so be prepared for a certain amount of confusion. Encourage students in the audience to act as they would like their own audience to act.

 ## 3 Sharing the Skits

This project lends itself to everything from private classroom performances to a school-wide performance. You may even want to schedule an evening show and sell tickets to other students, parents, teachers, and school officials. This would give students experience in advertising, sales, and general management. (Proceeds could be donated to a charity or used for another class project.) Check with the school administration before taking such steps.

 ## Assessing the Project

The following rubric can be used for group or individual assessment.

3 Full Accomplishment Students followed directions and produced a skit that shows a character's search for personal identity.

2 Substantial Accomplishment Students produced a skit, but the script is incomplete or does not show a character's search for personal identity.

1 Little or Partial Accomplishment Students' script and skit are incomplete or do not fulfill the requirements of the assignment.

For the Portfolio
Keep a master copy of each group's script in your classroom or the school library for future reference. Include a copy of your written assessment in each student's portfolio. If you have videotaped the skits, the tapes may be handed over to teachers at the next grade level at the end of the year.

Note: For other assessment options, see the *Teacher's Guide to Assessment and Portfolio Use.*

Cross-Curricular Options

MUSIC
Encourage students to include music in their skits. This could range from a character bursting into song (as in old Hollywood musicals) to an opera. Setting new lyrics to familiar tunes will give students a stepping-off place, yet will allow them to be creative. You might also allow them to include currently popular songs as background music during the skit.

ART
Students can paint a "set" on an old sheet for use as a backdrop or scenery.

HEALTH AND SAFETY
Ask students to center their skits on a person who is disabled. Skits can show obstacles that the person must overcome, as well as the treatment he or she receives by others. Students can interview disabled people to find out more about their day-to-day activities and challenges.

Resources

Behind the Scenes: The Unseen People Who Make Theater Work by Walter Williamson discusses careers of 10 key theater personnel, such as costume designers and electricians.

Junior Broadway: How to Produce Musicals with Children 9 to 13 by Beverly B. Ross and Jean P. Durgin gives helpful ideas for both children and adults and outlines the steps of a musical performance.

UNIT ONE
Part 1 Lesson Planner

TIME ALLOTMENTS SHOWN ARE APPROXIMATE. DEPENDING ON YOUR GOALS AND THE NEEDS OF YOUR STUDENTS, YOU MAY WISH TO ALLOW MORE OR LESS TIME FOR CERTAIN PORTIONS OF THE LESSON.

Table of Contents	Discussion	Previewing the Selection	Reading the Selection
PART OPENER **OPENING DOORS** **What Do You Think?** page 12	**20 MINUTES** • Reflect on the part theme		
GENRE LESSON **Focus on Fiction** page 13	**20 MINUTES** • Discuss characteristics of fiction • Discuss strategies for reading fiction		
SELECTION **A Crush** page 16 EASY		**10 MINUTES** • **PERSONAL CONNECTION** • **BACKGROUND CONNECTION** • **READING CONNECTION:** Static and dynamic characters	**20 MINUTES** • Introduce vocabulary • Read pp. 16–22 (7 pp.)
SELECTION **A Retrieved Reformation** page 28 CHALLENGING		**20 MINUTES** • **PERSONAL CONNECTION** • **LANGUAGE CONNECTION** • **READING CONNECTION:** Motive	**40 MINUTES** • Introduce vocabulary • Read pp. 28–34 (7 pp.)
SELECTION **Waiting** page 38 CHALLENGING		**20 MINUTES** • **PERSONAL CONNECTION** • **SCIENCE CONNECTION** • **READING CONNECTION:** Contrasting characters	**50 MINUTES** • Introduce vocabulary • Read pp. 38–49 (12 pp.)
GENRE LESSON **Focus on Nonfiction** page 53	**20 MINUTES** • Discuss characteristics of nonfiction • Discuss strategies for reading nonfiction		
SELECTION *from* **Immigrant Kids** page 56 EASY		**20 MINUTES** • **PERSONAL CONNECTION** • **HISTORICAL CONNECTION** • **READING CONNECTION:** Setting purposes for reading	**15 MINUTES** • Introduce vocabulary • Read pp. 56–60 (5 pp.)
SELECTION *from* **The Autobiography of Malcolm X** page 64 EASY		**20 MINUTES** • **PERSONAL CONNECTION** • **HISTORICAL CONNECTION** • **WRITING CONNECTION**	**15 MINUTES** • Introduce vocabulary • Read pp. 64–67 (4 pp.)
FICTION ON YOUR OWN **The Scholarship Jacket** page 70 AVERAGE			**15 MINUTES** • Read pp. 70–73 (4 pp.)

Writing	Writer's Style	Prewriting	Drafting and Revising
WRITING ABOUT LITERATURE **Direct Response**	**25 MINUTES**	**25 MINUTES**	**80 MINUTES**

Time estimates assume in-class work. You may wish to assign some of these stages as homework.

FROM PERSONAL RESPONSE TO CRITICAL ANALYSIS	OR ANOTHER PATHWAY	LITERARY CONCEPTS	QUICKWRITES	ALTERNATIVE ACTIVITIES	LITERARY LINKS	CRITIC'S CORNER	THE WRITER'S STYLE	ACROSS THE CURRICULUM	ART CONNECTION	WORDS TO KNOW	BIOGRAPHY
40 MINUTES				**40 MINUTES**							
• Discussion questions	OR • Ranking static and dynamic characters	• First- and third-person point of view	• Summary • Short story • Personal Narrative	✔		✔		HEALTH	✔	✔	✔
60 MINUTES				**20 MINUTES**							
• Discussion questions	OR • Mock trial	• Plot and climax	• Article • Report • Explanatory paragraph	✔	✔			SOCIAL STUDIES		✔	✔
50 MINUTES				**40 MINUTES**							
• Discussion questions	OR • Retelling	• Characters	• Character sketches • Journal entry • Letter	✔		✔		SOCIAL STUDIES	✔	✔	✔
20 MINUTES				**20 MINUTES**							
• Discussion questions	OR • Letter	• Informative nonfiction • Primary sources • Secondary sources	• Journal entries • Pro or con statement	✔	✔			SOCIAL STUDIES		✔	✔
20 MINUTES				**20 MINUTES**							
• Discussion questions	OR • Speech	• Autobiography	• Poem • Personal memoir • Letter • Personal dictionary	✔	✔			ART		✔	✔

Publishing and Reflecting	Grammar in Context	Reading the World
30 MINUTES	**10 MINUTES**	**25 MINUTES**

WHAT DO YOU THINK?

Objectives

The activities on this page can be used to
• introduce the Part 1 theme, "Opening Doors," since each activity is connected to one or more of the selections in Part 1
• create materials for students' personal portfolios that they can later reconsider or revise
• build an understanding of theme that students can review and revise as they progress through the unit

What would you say?
Remind students that disabilities can be mental and/or physical. To help students plan their role-playing, ask them how people with disabilities are sometimes treated and how students would wish to have their disabled friends treated. (See "A Crush," p. 15.)

What are the advantages of having a sibling?
Encourage students to include, if a sibling happens to be a twin, the additional advantages of having a twin. Help students establish general categories for the responses so that the results can be graphed more easily. (See "Waiting," p. 37.)

What can you do to help?
Have students consider possible language and cultural differences that their guide could address. Ask them to imagine that they are newcomers, and have them include the information they would most want to know. (See "Immigrant Kids," p. 55.)

What have you discovered about yourself?
To spark ideas, students can make a web around the word discoveries, using the suggestions given and ideas of their own. (See "A Retrieved Reformation," p. 27; "Song of Myself," p. 49; and the excerpt from The Autobiography of Malcolm X, p. 63.)

OPENING DOORS

WHAT DO YOU THINK?

REFLECTING ON THEME

Again and again, you stand on the threshold of new experiences. For example, you enter a higher grade, try out for a team, or make a new friend. These experiences can open doors to new discoveries—about yourself, others, or the world you live in.

What would you say?

Your best friend has a disability. You want your other friends to accept this person. With a few classmates, role-play your conversation with these other friends.

What are the advantages of having a sibling?

What is the best thing about having a brother or sister? Survey your classmates to gather their responses to this question, and create a pie graph or a bar graph to display the results.

What can you do to help?

A student from another country will enter your class next week. With a small group, discuss what your class might do to help this student adjust to school. Then create a video called *A Video Guide for New Students*. Include a tour of the school that shows the location of the lunchroom, the principal's office, and other important places.

What have you discovered about yourself?

What doors of discovery have you opened during the past year? In your notebook, briefly describe a learning experience of your own and tell what you discovered about yourself, others, or the world around you. Later, you will have a chance to compare your discoveries with the ones that the characters in this unit make.

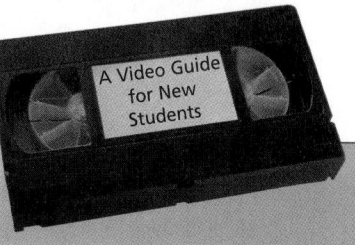

A Video Guide for New Students

12 UNIT ONE PART 1: OPENING DOORS

Cross-Curricular Connections

Social Studies Have students pretend that they are anthropologists from another planet, sent to visit Earth. Ask them to write a report that describes the experiences they've had and the discoveries they've made since landing on Earth. Their reports should address these questions:
• What are Earth people like?
• How do they treat one another?
• How do they treat their planet?
• What things do they value?
• What activities do they enjoy?
Encourage students to share their reports with their classmates.

COMMUNITY OUTREACH

To broaden students' horizons, set up a community mentoring project. Invite members of the community to address how community service can help "open doors." If possible, have groups of students work with mentors to learn more about the personal discoveries that can come from helping others in their community.

FOCUS ON FICTION

Whenever you read a made-up story, you are reading a work of fiction. **Fiction** is writing that comes from an author's imagination. Although the author makes the story up, he or she might base it on real events.

Fiction writers write short stories and novels. A **short story** usually revolves around a single idea or event and is short enough to be read at one sitting. A **novel** is much longer and more complex. Both novels and short stories contain four basic elements: **character, setting, plot,** and **theme.**

CHARACTER Characters are the people, animals, or imaginary creatures that take part in the action of a story. Usually, a short story centers on events in the life of one person or animal. That person or creature is the **main character.** Generally, there are also one or more **minor characters** in the story. Minor characters sometimes provide part of the background for the story. More often, however, minor characters interact with the main character and with one another. Their words and actions help to move the plot along.

SETTING The setting is the time and place in which the action of the story happens. The time may be in the past, the present, or the future; in daytime or at night; in any season. The place where the action of the story occurs may be real or imaginary. A story may be set on a farm, in a city, on a bus, or on a fictitious planet.

PLOT The sequence of events in a story is called the plot. The plot is the writer's blueprint for what happens, when it happens, and to whom it happens. One event causes another, which causes another, and so on until the end of the story.

Generally, a plot is built around a **conflict**—a problem or struggle involving two or more opposing forces. Conflicts can range from life-or-death struggles to disagreements between friends or relatives.

Although the development of each plot is different, traditional works of fiction generally follow a pattern that includes the following stages:

Exposition Exposition sets the stage for the story. Characters are introduced, the setting is described, and the conflict begins to unfold.

Complications As the story continues, the plot gets more complex. While the characters struggle

FOCUS ON FICTION **13**

FOCUS ON FICTION

This feature defines *fiction* and explains the terms used to discuss it. It also introduces students to the conventions of the genre and suggests strategies for reading fiction. The terms introduced here are treated in depth in the lessons that accompany the fiction selections in this book.

——————— **Objectives** ———————

• To understand and appreciate fiction
• To understand the elements of fiction: character, setting, plot, and theme
• To learn effective strategies for reading fiction

Teaching Strategies:
ELEMENTS OF FICTION

Character Write several letters of the alphabet on the board and invite students to brainstorm a fictional character for each letter. The characters can be drawn from books, movies, and television. The letter can begin the character's first or last name. Then have students write a capital *M* next to each main character and a lower case *m* next to each minor character.

Setting Invite the class to describe the setting of a familiar story such as "Robin Hood" or "Snow White."

Plot Draw on the chalkboard the plot diagram shown and use it to explain a standard plot development.

Then invite students to use the diagram to identify the parts in the plot of a well-known novel such as *The Secret Garden* or a short story the entire class has read.

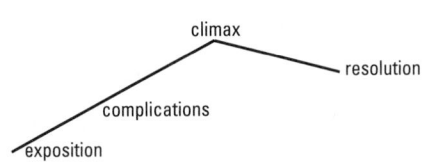

Theme Invite students to name some stories they have read on their own and to explain the message about life that they discovered in each one. Then have students use the three suggestions on this page to uncover the theme in a story that everyone in the class has read.

Reading Strategies: MODELING

Invite volunteers to read aloud the Strategies for Reading Fiction. Tell students to use these strategies as they read "A Crush" on page 15 and other short stories in this book. Then model the strategies as students read "A Crush." You may wish to use the model provided or create your own.

- **Preview** *"From the title I think this story is about someone's crush on someone else. Since there are pictures of flowers, maybe the person sends flowers as a sign of affection."*

- **Visualize** *"I see a busy small-town hardware store and sunny little garden where Ernie grows his flowers."*

- **Make Connections** *"I once had a crush on someone, but I was too shy to say anything to the person."*

- **Question** *"Why does Ernie bring Dolores flowers? Will he tell her he is the one leaving the flowers?"*

- **Predict** *"I think Dolores will find out who is bringing her the flowers."*

- **Build** *"I think Ernie is afraid to tell Dolores how he feels because he's afraid she'll reject him ."*

- **Evaluate** *"I think Rylant's descriptions of the characters are interesting, but I feel sorry for Ernie because he doesn't know how Dolores feels about him. I would have liked a happier ending."*

- **Discuss** Set up small groups for sharing and discussion. Have each group member prepare a question or an opinion for the group to discuss, such as discussing how they feel about the story's ending.

---

to find solutions to the conflict, suspense and a feeling of excitement and energy build.

Climax The climax is the point of greatest interest or suspense in the story. It is the turning point, when the action reaches a peak and the outcome of the conflict is decided. The climax may occur because of a decision the characters reach or because of a discovery or an event that changes the situation. The climax usually results in a change in the characters or a solution to the problem.

Resolution The resolution occurs at the conclusion of the story. Loose ends are tied up, and the story ends.

THEME The theme of a story is the main message the writer wishes to share with the reader. This message might be a lesson about life or a belief about people and their actions. Most themes are not stated directly; they are like hidden messages that the reader must decode. Often you will find that as you discuss literature, different readers will discover different themes in the same story. The following suggestions will help you uncover a theme:

- Review what happened to the main character. Did he or she change during the story? What did he or she learn about life?

- Skim the story for key phrases and sentences—statements that go beyond the action of the story to say something important about life or people.

- Think about the title of the story. Does it have a special meaning that could lead you to the main idea of the work?

STRATEGIES FOR READING FICTION

To really "get inside" a story, try the following strategies:

- **Preview** the story before you read it by looking at the title and the pictures, perhaps even skimming through the pages.

- Try to **visualize** the setting and the characters while you read. Can you picture the place in your mind? Can you "see" the characters and the action?

- **Make connections** as you read. Do any of the characters have thoughts or experiences that you have had? Does the story remind you of an event or a person you have heard of or read about?

- **Question** events, characters, and ideas in the story. "Why doesn't he just come out and tell her how he feels?" "Why are these children doing such a hurtful thing?" Asking good questions is at the heart of good reading.

- Stop occasionally and **predict** what might happen next or how the story might end.

- Continually **build** on what you're learning about the characters and events in the story. Let your thoughts change and grow as you learn more.

- **Evaluate** the story as you read. Think about your feelings toward the characters and their actions. Also consider how well the author is telling his or her story.

- When you have finished reading, **discuss** the story with someone else.

Remember, a story never tells you everything; it leaves room for you to formulate your own thoughts and ideas. After you read a story, you are left with first impressions, but you need to be able to elaborate and explain them on the basis of the story itself, your own experiences, and other stories you have read.

FICTION

A Crush
Cynthia Rylant

PERSONAL CONNECTION
Activating Prior Knowledge

One of the characters in "A Crush" is a person with mental retardation. What impressions do you have of people with this disability? How do other people sometimes react to people with mental retardation? What is being done to help mentally retarded people reach their potential? Jot down your ideas in your notebook and then share them with a small group of classmates.

Building Background

BACKGROUND CONNECTION

Mentally retarded people are classified by the degree of their disability as mildly, moderately, severely, or profoundly retarded. In the past, many people with mental retardation were hidden away at home or placed in institutions that offered no educational opportunities. Some were even treated as criminals. Today, however, many of them live and work within their communities as productive citizens. While some can live on their own, most live with their families or in group homes, where they can receive special care and can benefit from the interactions of group living.

People in group home at table.
Copyright © Charles Gupton/Tony Stone Images.

Active Reading/Setting a Purpose

READING CONNECTION

Static and Dynamic Characters In this story, some characters change and grow, while others remain the same. Characters who change little, if at all, are called **static characters.** Characters who change significantly are called **dynamic characters.** As you read "A Crush," think about which characters are static and which are dynamic. After you read, copy the chart shown into your notebook. Then review the story, fill in each dynamic character's name, and complete the chart.

Dynamic Character	How Did He or She Change?	What Caused the Change?

• BACKGROUND CONNECTION

A CRUSH **15**

OVERVIEW
─ Objectives ─

- To understand and appreciate a short story that deals with a mentally retarded man's first crush
- To understand static and dynamic characters
- To identify and understand first-person and third-person points of view
- To express understanding of the story through a choice of writing forms, including a summary, a short story, and a personal narrative
- To extend understanding of the story through a variety of multimodal and cross-curricular activities

─ Skills ─

READING SKILLS/ STRATEGIES
- Static and dynamic characters
- Questioning

THE WRITER'S STYLE
- Denotation and connotation

GRAMMAR
- Compound sentences

LITERARY CONCEPTS
- First-person and third-person points of view
- Figurative language: simile/metaphor

GENRE STUDY
- Fiction: short story

SPELLING
- Suffixes -ness and -ly

SPEAKING, LISTENING, AND VIEWING
- Role-playing

─ Cross-Curricular Connections ─

SCIENCE
- Seeds

GEOGRAPHY
- Regional crops

HEALTH
- Child development

MATH
- Census counting

 BACKGROUND CONNECTION
Mental Disability It is estimated that 19 percent of all U.S. adults suffer from some form of mental or emotional problem. Group-home settings, like those shown here, provide interactions and experiences that help integrate some mentally disabled people into their community. You might use these images to initiate a discussion of community attitudes toward the mentally handicapped.

Side A, Frame 49201

PRINT AND MEDIA RESOURCES

UNIT ONE RESOURCE BOOK
Strategic Reading: Literature, p. 7
Vocabulary SkillBuilder, p. 10
Reading SkillBuilder, p. 8
Spelling SkillBuilder, p. 9

GRAMMAR MINI–LESSONS
Transparencies, p. 28
Copymasters, p. 37

WRITING MINI–LESSONS
Transparencies, p. 37

ACCESS FOR STUDENTS ACQUIRING ENGLISH
Selection Summaries
Reading and Writing Support

TEACHER'S GUIDE TO ASSESSMENT AND PORTFOLIO USE

FORMAL ASSESSMENT
Selection Test, pp. 5–6
 Test Generator

AUDIO LIBRARY
See Reference Card

LASERLINKS
Background Connection
Author Background
Art Gallery

SUMMARY

Ernie, a mentally retarded man, transforms his life and the lives of several others when he falls in love with Dolores, an employee at Stan's Hardware. Once a week, Ernie secretly leaves a bouquet of homegrown flowers at the door of the hardware store. No one knows where the flowers come from or whom they are for, but they make store-owner Dick Wilcox feel appreciated, and he becomes more social. They also make Dolores feel appreciated, and she begins to dress more attractively.

Thematic Link: *Opening Doors* By reaching out to others, Ernie opens new doors for himself and for those around him.

CUSTOMIZING FOR
Students Acquiring English

- Use **ACCESS FOR STUDENTS ACQUIRING ENGLISH**, *Reading and Writing Support*.

- This story takes place in a small town in the United States. Students may need background information on hardware stores, the Lion's Club, the Confederate flag, and Big Boy restaurants.

ⓘ Funeral customs vary from culture to culture and do not always involve the display of flowers. Make sure that students understand the reference here.

STRATEGIC READING FOR
Less-Proficient Readers

Set a Purpose Spark interest in the story by pointing out the title and asking students how they would act if they had a crush on someone. Would they reveal it? If so, how? Then invite students to read the selection to see whether the person with the crush reveals his or her feelings.

Use **UNIT ONE RESOURCE BOOK**, p. 7, for guidance in reading the selection.

A Crush
by Cynthia Rylant

ⓘ

When the windows of Stan's Hardware started filling up with flowers, everyone in town knew something had happened. Excess flowers usually mean death, but since these were all real flowers bearing the aroma of nature instead of floral preservative, and since they stood bunched in clear Mason jars instead of <u>impaled</u> on Styrofoam crosses, everyone knew nobody had died. So they all figured somebody had a crush and kept quiet.

There wasn't really a Stan of Stan's Hardware. Dick Wilcox was the owner, and since he'd never liked his own name, he gave his store half the name of his childhood hero, Stan Laurel in the movies. Dick had been married for twenty-seven years. Once, his wife, Helen, had dropped a German chocolate cake on his head at a Lion's Club dance, so Dick and Helen were not likely candidates for the honest expression of the flowers in those clear Mason jars lining the windows of Stan's Hardware, and speculation had to move on to Dolores.

Dolores was the assistant manager at Stan's and had worked there for twenty years, since high school. She knew the store like a mother knows her baby, so Dick—who had trouble keeping up with things like prices and new brands of drywall compound—tried to keep himself busy in the back and give Dolores the run of the floor. This worked fine because the carpenters and plumbers and painters in town trusted Dolores and took her advice to heart. They also liked her tattoo.

WORDS
TO
KNOW

impaled (ĭm-pāld') *adj.* pierced with a sharp point **impale** *v.*

16

WORDS TO KNOW

cherish (chĕr'ĭsh) *v.* to hold dear; treasure (p. 18)
discreetly (dĭ-skrēt'lē) *adv.* in a polite way; tactfully (p. 21)
impaled (ĭm-pāld') *adj.* pierced with a sharp point **impale** *v.* (p. 16)

suitor (sōō'tər) *n.* a man seeking a woman's love (p. 17)
swarthy (swôr'thē) *adj.* having darkish skin (p. 17)

Dolores was the only woman in town with a tattoo. On the days she went sleeveless, one could see it on the taut brown skin of her upper arm: "Howl at the Moon." The picture was of a baying coyote, which must have been a dark gray in its early days but which had faded to the color of the spackling paste Dolores stocked in the third aisle. Nobody had gotten out of Dolores the true story behind the tattoo. Some of the men who came in liked to show off their own, and they'd roll up their sleeves or pull open their shirts, exhibiting bald eagles and rattlesnakes and Confederate flags, and they'd try to coax out of Dolores the history of her coyote. All of the men had gotten their tattoos when they were in the service, drunk on weekend leave and full of the spitfire of young soldiers. Dolores had never been in the service, and she'd never seen weekend leave, and there wasn't a tattoo parlor anywhere near. They couldn't figure why or where any half-sober woman would have a howling coyote ground into the soft skin of her upper arm. But Dolores wasn't telling.

That the flowers in Stan's front window had anything to do with Dolores seemed completely improbable. As far as anyone knew, Dolores had never been in love, nor had anyone ever been in love with her. Some believed it was the tattoo, of course, or the fine dark hair coating Dolores's upper lip which kept <u>suitors</u> away. Some felt it was because Dolores was just more of a man than most of the men in town, and fellows couldn't figure out how to court someone who knew more about the carburetor of a car or the back side of a washing machine than they did. Others

thought Dolores simply didn't want love. This was a popular theory among the women in town who sold Avon and Mary Kay cosmetics. Whenever one of them ran into the hardware for a package of light bulbs or some batteries, she would mentally pluck every one of the black hairs above Dolores's lip. Then she'd wash that grease out of Dolores's hair, give her a good blunt cut, dress her in a decent silk-blend blouse with a nice Liz Claiborne skirt from the Sports line, and, finally, tone down that <u>swarthy</u>, longshoreman look of Dolores's with a concealing beige foundation,[1] some frosted peach lipstick, and a good gray liner for the eyes.

Dolores simply didn't want love, the Avon lady would think as she walked back to her car carrying her little bag of batteries. If she did, she'd fix herself up.

The man who was in love with Dolores and who brought her zinnias and cornflowers and nasturtiums and marigolds and asters and four-o'clocks in clear Mason jars did not know any of this. He did not know that men showed Dolores their tattoos. He did not know that Dolores understood how to use and to sell a belt sander. He did not know that Dolores needed some concealing beige foundation so she could get someone to love her. The man who brought flowers to Dolores on Wednesdays when the hardware opened its doors at 7:00 A.M. didn't care who Dolores had ever been or what anyone had ever thought of her. He loved her, and he wanted to bring her flowers.

---

1. **concealing beige foundation:** a cosmetic that covers skin flaws.

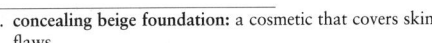

Dolores was the only woman in town with a tattoo.

| WORDS TO KNOW | **suitor** (sōō'tər) *n.* a man seeking a woman's love
swarthy (swôr'thē) *adj.* having darkish skin |

17

③

②

C

D Ask students, Who is narrating, or telling, this story—a character within the story or someone outside the story? *(someone outside)* Ask them how can they tell. *(Instead of using the pronoun I to tell the story, the narrator uses the pronouns* he, she, *and* they *to explain what happens.)*

Literary Concept:
CHARACTERIZATION

E Invite students to draw conclusions about Ernie's character from what they have read so far. *(Possible response: He is childlike, shy, loving, and sensitive.)*

Critical Thinking:
MAKING JUDGMENTS

F Ask students to state what they think Ernie's life was like when he lived with his mother. *(Possible response: Ernie's life was limited and devoid of new and exciting experiences.)*

Linking to Science

G In 1954 a mining engineer found the oldest known living seed buried in frozen silt in the Yukon. When scientists planted the 10,000-year-old seed, it produced a lupine—a plant in the pea family—that was identical to a modern lupine plant. Ask students why scientists and vendors generally store seeds under cold, dry conditions. *(to extend the life of the seeds and ensure that they will eventually sprout)*

CUSTOMIZING FOR
Multiple Learning Styles

H **Musical Learners** Challenge students sensitive to music and nonverbal sounds to compose a melody that conveys how Ernie might feel about the changes in his life, including his mother's death and his new life in the group home.

D Ernie had lived in this town all of his life and had never before met Dolores. He was thirty-three years old, and for thirty-one of those years he had lived at home with his mother in a small dark house on the edge of town near Beckwith's Orchards. Ernie had been a beautiful baby, with a shock of shining black hair and large blue eyes and a round, wise face. But as he had grown, it had become **E** clearer and clearer that though he was indeed a perfectly beautiful child, his mind had not developed with the same perfection. Ernie would not be able to speak in sentences until he was six years old. He would not be able to count the apples in a bowl until he was eight. By the time he was ten, he could sing a simple song. At age twelve, he understood what a joke was. And when he was twenty, something he saw on television made him cry.

Ernie's mother kept him in the house with her because it was easier, so Ernie knew nothing of **F** the world except this house. They lived, the two of them, in tiny dark rooms always illuminated by the glow of a television set, Ernie's bags of Oreos and Nutter Butters littering the floor, his baseball cards scattered across the sofa, his heavy winter coat thrown over the arm of a chair so he could wear it whenever he wanted, and his box of Burpee seed packages sitting in the middle of the kitchen table.

These Ernie cherished. The seeds had been delivered to his home by mistake. One day a woman wearing a brown uniform had pulled up in a brown truck, walked quickly to the front porch of Ernie's house, set a box down, and with a couple of toots of her horn, driven off again. Ernie had watched her through the curtains and, when she was gone, had ventured onto the porch and shyly, cautiously, picked up the box. His mother checked it when he carried it inside. The box didn't have their name on it,

but the brown truck was gone, so whatever was in the box was theirs to keep. Ernie pulled off the heavy tape, his fingers trembling, and found inside the box more little packages of seeds than he could count. He lifted them out, one by one, and examined the beautiful photographs of flowers on each. His mother was not interested, had returned to the television, but Ernie sat down at the kitchen table and quietly looked at each package for a long time, his fingers running across the slick paper and outlining the shapes of zinnias and cornflowers and nasturtiums and marigolds and asters and four-o'clocks, his eyes drawing up their colors.

Two months later Ernie's mother died. A neighbor found her at the mailbox beside the road. People from the county courthouse came out to get Ernie, and as they ushered him from the home he would never see again, he picked up the box of seed packages from his kitchen table and passed through the doorway.

Eventually Ernie was moved to a large white house near the main street of town. This house was called a group home, because in it lived a group of people who, like Ernie, could not live on their own. There were six of them. Each had his own room. When Ernie was shown the room that would be his, he put the box of Burpee seeds—which he had kept with him since his mother's death—on the little table beside the bed, and then he sat down on the bed and cried.

Ernie cried every day for nearly a month. And then he stopped. He dried his tears, and he learned how to bake refrigerator biscuits and how to dust mop and what to do if the indoor plants looked brown.

Ernie loved watering the indoor plants, and it

WORDS
TO
KNOW

cherish (chĕr′ĭsh) *v.* to hold dear; treasure

18

COMPOUND SENTENCES A compound sentence consists of two or more simple sentences joined together. The parts of a compound sentence are joined by a comma and a coordinating conjunction *(and, but, or)* or by a semicolon.

Application Have students turn each of the following pairs of simple sentences into a compound sentence by adding a comma and a coordinating conjunction or a semicolon. The page on which each compound sentence appears in the story is given in parentheses so students can see how the author chose to punctuate it.

1. Jack tried to explain to Ernie that the seeds would grow into vegetables. Ernie could not believe this until he saw it come true. (p. 20)
2. He thought more deeply about them. He could not carry them to the garden. (p. 20)
3. It was 6:00 A.M. The building was still dark. (p. 22)

Reteaching/Reinforcement
• Grammar Handbook, anthology pp. 879–880
• *Grammar Mini-Lessons* copymasters p. 37, transparencies p. 28

The Writer's Craft

Compound Sentences, pp. 556–557

Illustration by Patty Dryden. Copyright © Patty Dryden.

Mini-Lesson  Genre Study

FICTION On the board, draw the web shown here, and use it to explain that a **short story** is a kind of fiction with the following characteristics:
- It can generally be read in one sitting.
- It usually focuses on one or two main characters.
- The characters usually face a single problem or conflict.

Application Have students copy the web into their notebooks. Direct them to refer to it as they look for the characteristics of a short story in "A Crush."

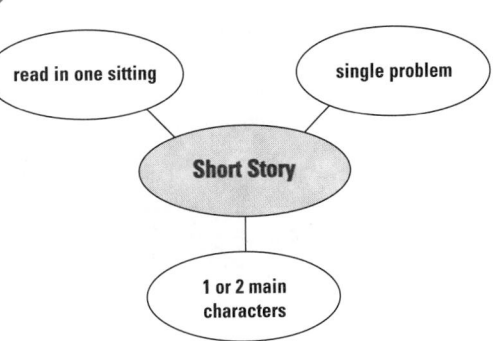

read in one sitting

single problem

Short Story

1 or 2 main characters

I Ask students why Ernie is afraid to enter the garden. Guide students by reading the following:

Think-Aloud Model *Why is Ernie so afraid to enter the garden? I know that he always stayed inside with his mother. When he did go out on his mother's porch to get the box of seeds, though, he ventured—that's the word the author uses, as if Ernie's going outside was an adventure. Boy, if he was afraid of just going out on the porch of his house, then going into the garden of the group home must frighten him even more.*

Literary Concept:
CHARACTERIZATION

J Ask students what evidence they have seen that Ernie is a dynamic character capable of change. *(Possible response: He starts to adjust to the world outside the group home, as indicated by his actions in the restaurant.)*

STRATEGIC READING FOR
Less-Proficient Readers

K Have students identify the person sending flowers to Dolores. *(Ernie)*
Making Inferences

Set a Purpose Have students read on to find out how Dolores and others react to the flowers.

---

was this pleasure which finally drew him outside. One of the young men who worked at the group home—a college student named Jack—grew a large garden in the back of the house. It was full of tomato vines and the large yellow blossoms of healthy squash. During his first summer at the house, Ernie would stand at the kitchen window, watching Jack and sometimes a resident of the home move among the vegetables. Ernie was curious but too afraid to go into the garden.

Then one day when Ernie was watching through the window, he noticed that Jack was ripping open several slick little packages and emptying them into the ground. Ernie panicked and ran to his room. But the box of Burpee seeds was still there on his table, untouched. He grabbed it, slid it under his bed, then went back through the house and out into the garden as if he had done this every day of his life.

He stood beside Jack, watching him empty seed packages into the soft black soil, and as the packages were emptied, Ernie asked for them, holding out his hand, his eyes on the photographs of red radishes and purple eggplant. Jack handed the empty packages over with a smile and with that gesture became Ernie's first friend.

Jack tried to explain to Ernie that the seeds would grow into vegetables, but Ernie could not believe this until he saw it come true. And when it did, he looked all the more intently at the packages of zinnias and cornflowers and the rest hidden beneath his bed. He thought more deeply about them, but he could not carry them to the garden. He could not let the garden have his seeds.

Love is such a mystery.

That was the first year in the large white house.

The second year, Ernie saw Dolores, and after that he thought of nothing else but her and of the photographs of flowers beneath his bed.

Jack had decided to take Ernie downtown for breakfast every Wednesday morning to ease him into the world outside that of the group home. They left very early, at 5:45 A.M., so there would be few people and almost no traffic to frighten Ernie and make him beg for his room. Jack and Ernie drove to the Big Boy restaurant which sat across the street from Stan's Hardware. There they ate eggs and bacon and French toast among those whose work demanded rising before the sun: bus drivers, policemen, nurses, mill workers. Their first time in the Big Boy, Ernie was too nervous to eat. The second time, he could eat, but he couldn't look up. The third time, he not only ate everything on his plate, but he lifted his head and he looked out the window of the Big Boy restaurant toward Stan's Hardware across the street. There he saw a dark-haired woman in jeans and a black T-shirt unlocking the front door of the building, and that was the moment Ernie started loving Dolores and thinking about giving up his seeds to the soft black soil of Jack's garden.

Love is such a mystery, and when it strikes the heart of one as mysterious as Ernie himself, it can hardly be spoken of. Ernie could not explain to Jack why he went directly to his room later that morning, pulled the box of Burpee seeds from under his bed, then grabbed Jack's hand in the kitchen and walked with him to the garden, where Ernie had come to believe things would grow. Ernie

---

Mini-Lesson   **The Writer's Style**

Word	Denotation	Connotation
crush		
love		
home		
friend		

DENOTATION AND CONNOTATION
Explain that denotation is the dictionary definition of a word, whereas connotation refers to the suggestions and associations that go along with a word, stretching well beyond its dictionary meaning. For example, the word *mother* denotes, or is defined as, "a female parent." For many people, however, the word also connotes, or suggests, images of love, warmth, and security.

Application Have students complete a chart like the one shown, filling in the denotation and the connotation of each of these words from "A Crush":

Reteaching/Reinforcement
• *Writing Mini-Lessons* transparencies, p. 37

The Writer's Craft
Denotation and Connotation, p. 310

***Sweet Peas* by Julia Jordan** The subtle interplay of light, color, and space makes this picture seem as though it were created from watercolors rather than acrylics. Notice how the artist shows water in the jar.

Reading the Art *What mood does this picture create? What does the artist do to create this feeling?*

Active Reading: CLARIFYING

 Ask students why Ernie watches Dolores. *(Possible response: He is in love with her and is fascinated by her.)*

Linking to Geography

 Geographic location determines when seeds should be planted. In the northeastern United States, for example, peas are traditionally planted on March 15; tomatoes, beans, and other warm-weather crops are planted after May 30. Invite students to make a chart showing when common vegetable and flower seeds should be planted in their region. They can use gardening books and seed catalogs as reference materials.

Sweetpeas (1992), Julia Jordan. Acrylic on paper, private collection. Photo by James Hart.

handed the packets of seeds one by one to Jack, who stood in silent admiration of the lovely photographs before asking Ernie several times, "Are you sure you want to plant these?" Ernie was sure. It didn't take him very long, and when the seeds all lay under the moist black earth, Ernie carried his empty packages inside the house and spent the rest of the day spreading them across his bed in different arrangements.

That was in June. For the next several Wednesdays at 7:00 A.M. Ernie watched every movement of the dark-haired woman behind the lighted windows of Stan's Hardware. Jack watched Ernie watch Dolores and <u>discreetly</u> said nothing.

When Ernie's flowers began growing in July, Ernie spent most of his time in the garden. He would watch the garden for hours, as if he expected it suddenly to move or to impress him

WORDS TO KNOW **discreetly** (dĭ-skrēt′lē) *adv.* in a polite way; tactfully

21

Mini-Lesson   **Literary Concepts**

REVIEWING FIGURATIVE LANGUAGE: SIMILE/METAPHOR Remind students that figurative language goes beyond the dictionary meanings of words to create fresh and original descriptions. In a figurative expression, the words are not literally true, and one thing may be described in terms of another. Two of the most common forms of figurative expressions are similes and metaphors. A simile is a comparison of two unlike things that have some quality in common. A simile usually makes this comparison by using such words as *like* or *as*. A metaphor also compares two things, but it does so directly, without using *like* or *as*.

Application Have students work in pairs to find the following figures of speech in the story and to tell whether each is a simile or a metaphor:
1. Page 16: She knew the store like a mother knows her baby. *(simile)*
2. Page 20: Love is such a mystery. *(metaphor)*

④ Students may question the use of *come up* in this sentence. They are probably more familiar with the phrase *come on* in reference to lights.

Literary Concept:
FIGURATIVE LANGUAGE

Ⓝ, Ⓞ Ask students to locate the two figures of speech on this page. *(The fragile green stems of his flowers stood uncertainly in the soil, like baby colts on their first legs; [the flowers] looked as big and bright as their pictures on the empty packages.)* Have students tell whether the figures of speech are similes or metaphors, and then have them explain what two things each one compares.

STRATEGIC READING FOR
Less-Proficient Readers

Ⓟ Have students explain how Dick and Dolores react to the flowers. *(Dick starts spending more time with customers; Dolores starts wearing blouses and jewelry.)* **Summarizing**

• Would students say that Dolores and Dick are static or dynamic characters? Why? *(dynamic; they change and grow throughout the story)*

CUSTOMIZING FOR
Gifted and Talented Students

Ask students to suggest what they think the flowers symbolize throughout this story. Do they symbolize the same thing at the beginning as they do at the end? *(Possible response: At the beginning of the story, the flowers symbolize death, but by the end, they symbolize life because they rekindle happiness and possibility in several characters' lives.)*

Ⓝ with a quick trick. The fragile green stems of his flowers stood uncertainly in the soil, like baby colts on their first legs, but the young plants performed no magic for Ernie's eyes. They saved their shows for the middle of the night and next day surprised Ernie with tender small blooms in all the colors the photographs had promised.

Ⓞ The flowers grew fast and hardy, and one early Wednesday morning when they looked as big and bright as their pictures on the empty packages, Ernie pulled a glass canning jar off a dusty shelf in the basement of his house. He washed the jar, half filled it with water, then carried it to the garden, where he placed in it one of every kind of flower he had grown. He met Jack at the car and rode off to the Big Boy with the jar of flowers held tight between his small hands. Jack told him it was a beautiful bouquet.

When they reached the door of the Big Boy, Ernie stopped and pulled at Jack's arm, pointing to the building across the street. "OK," Jack said, and he led Ernie to the front door of Stan's Hardware. It was 6:00 A.M., and the building was still dark. Ernie set the clear Mason jar full of flowers under the sign that read "Closed," then he smiled at Jack and followed him back across the street to get breakfast.

When Dolores arrived at seven and picked up the jar of zinnias and cornflowers and nasturtiums and marigolds and asters and four-o'clocks, Ernie and Jack were watching her from a booth in the Big Boy. Each had a wide smile on his face as Dolores put her nose to the flowers. Ernie giggled. They watched the ④ lights of the hardware store come up and saw

Dolores place the clear Mason jar on the ledge of the front window. They drove home still smiling.

All the rest of that summer Ernie left a jar of flowers every Wednesday morning at the front door of Stan's Hardware. Ⓟ Neither Dick Wilcox nor Dolores could figure out why the flowers kept coming, and each of them assumed somebody had a crush on the other. But the flowers had an effect on them anyway. Dick started spending more time out on the floor making conversation with the customers, while Dolores stopped wearing T-shirts to work and instead wore crisp white blouses with the sleeves rolled back off her wrists. Occasionally she put on a bracelet.

By summer's end Jack and Ernie had become very good friends, and when the flowers in the garden behind their house began to wither, and Ernie's face began to grow gray as he watched them, Jack brought home one bright day in late September a great long box. Ernie followed Jack as he carried it down to the basement and watched as Jack pulled a long glass tube from the box and attached this tube to the wall above a table. When Jack plugged in the tube's electric cord, a soft lavender light washed the room.

"Sunshine," said Jack.

Then he went back to his car for a smaller box. He carried this down to the basement, where Ernie still stood staring at the strange light. Jack handed Ernie the small box, and when Ernie opened it, he found more little packages of seeds than he could count, with new kinds of photographs on the slick paper.

"Violets," Jack said, pointing to one of them.

Then he and Ernie went outside to get some dirt. ❖

COMPREHENSION CHECK

1. At the beginning of the story, why does it seem unlikely that the flowers are for Dolores? *(She isn't very feminine, and she has never seemed interested in love.)*

2. What are Ernie's most cherished possessions? *(his seed packets)*

3. How does Ernie show his love for Dolores? *(He leaves flowers for her outside the hardware store.)*

4. How do the flowers affect Dolores and Dick? *(Possible responses: Both try new things; both seem to become happier.)*

Assessment ✓ **Option**

INFORMAL ASSESSMENT

Summarizing You can informally assess students' understanding of the story and their ability to summarize by inviting them to create a comic strip of the story and to fill in dialogue balloons to summarize the plot. Direct students to use as many panels as they need—but no fewer than six—to introduce the characters and explain the plot. Students can draw the characters or use stick figures as representations.

Rubric

3 Full Accomplishment Students completely, accurately, and concisely summarize the main events in the plot. The comic strip is well conceived and executed.

2 Substantial Accomplishment Students describe most of the important events in the story. The summary may be either sketchy or overly long.

1 Little or Partial Accomplishment Students are unable to summarize the plot accurately; important events are misplaced or omitted.

LITERARY INSIGHT

No, The Human Heart
by Ki No Tsurayuki

No, the human heart
Is unknowable.
But in my birthplace
The flowers still smell
The same as always.

Hito wa isa
Kokoro mo shirazu
Furusato wa
Hana zo mukashi no
Ka ni nioikeru

Mini-Lesson Spelling

SPELLING WITH SUFFIXES Tell students that when a suffix beginning with a consonant (*-ness, -ly*) is added to a word ending in a consonant and *y,* the *y* is usually changed to *i,* as shown in these examples:

swarthy   +   ness   =   swarthiness

swarthy   +   ly   =   swarthily

Application Have students write the new word that is formed when the suffix is added.

1. happy + ness
2. easy + ly
3. costly + ness
4. greedy + ly
5. icy + ly
6. clumsy + ness
7. hearty + ly
8. lazy + ness
9. heavy + ness
10. busy + ly

Ask students to look for more words that fit this pattern, in their own writing and in things that they read, and to add those words to their personal word lists.

Reteaching/Reinforcement
• *Unit One Resource Book,* p. 9

From Personal Response to Critical Analysis

1. Encourage students to use specific details from the story to explain their thoughts.
2. Possible response: To Ernie, love means doing something nice for someone without expecting anything in return.
3. Possible responses: She might be shocked or embarrassed and wish that Ernie were someone else; she might understand and appreciate Ernie's feelings and be kind to him, since she seems to treat people well.
4. Possible response: Jack is patient, gentle, concerned, and respectful of Ernie's feelings.
5. Possible response: Because Ernie does not know Dolores or how she feels about him, he can't know her heart.
6. Possible response: Work with mentally retarded people and you will see that they can be kind, gentle, and considerate neighbors.

Another Pathway

Cooperative Learning Assign students roles such as direction-giver, recorder, turn-taking monitor, and loudness monitor to ensure that all students contribute and that no one dominates the discussion. These roles also will help create independence among group members.

Rubric

3 Full Accomplishment Students rank the characters correctly and give ample details from the story to show how each character changes.

2 Substantial Accomplishment Students rank the characters correctly but overlook or don't support some of the characters' changes.

1 Little or Partial Accomplishment Students do not rank the characters accurately and cannot support their rankings with details from the story.

RESPONDING
OPTIONS

FROM PERSONAL RESPONSE TO CRITICAL ANALYSIS

REFLECT 1. What thoughts do you have after finishing this story? Write them in your notebook.

RETHINK 2. How would you explain what love means to Ernie?

3. How do you think Dolores would react if she were to find out who is sending her the flowers? Explain your opinion.
Consider

Close Textual Reading
• what you know about her character
• the differences between Dolores and Ernie
• how people sometimes react to those with mental retardation

4. What qualities does Jack have that make him a good friend to Ernie?

5. Reread the Insight poem on page 23. How would you relate this poem to Ernie's situation?

RELATE 6. In some communities, individuals have protested against group homes for people with mental retardation. After reading this story, what advice would you give people who do not want mentally retarded people as neighbors?

ANOTHER PATHWAY

Get together in a small group and rank each character—Ernie, Jack, Dolores, and Dick Wilcox—according to which one changes the most. Use the chart you created for the Reading Connection on page 15 and share your rankings with the class.

QUICKWRITES

1. Suppose that Jack is working in the group home as part of his college studies. Write a **summary** that he might include in a report that tells what he has learned from Ernie.

2. Everyone in town is curious about Dolores's tattoo. Write a **short story** that explains how, when, where, and why she got her coyote tattoo.

3. Write a **personal narrative** about a time when you or someone you know had a crush on someone. Your narrative can be humorous or serious.

📁 *PORTFOLIO Save your writing. You may want to use it later as a springboard to a piece for your portfolio.*

LITERARY CONCEPTS

When planning a story, a writer must decide who will narrate, or tell, the story—and from what point of view. In the **first-person point of view,** the narrator is a character in the story. He or she speaks directly to the reader and uses pronouns such as *I, me,* and *we.* In the **third-person point of view,** the narrator is someone outside the story. He or she uses pronouns such as *he, she,* and *they.*

From which point of view has Rylant written "A Crush"? Why do you think she chose this point of view?

Literary Concepts

Possible response: Rylant wrote "A Crush" in the third-person point of view; she did this in order to reveal the perspectives of all the characters and to show how all of them were affected by the flowers.

Application Invite students to work together in small groups to rewrite a few paragraphs from the story in the first-person point of view. From the paragraphs they choose, students should select the character that will be the narrator. When students are finished writing, have each group read its paragraphs aloud. The rest of the class should analyze the effects that changing the point of view has on the paragraphs.

QuickWrites

1. Urge students to begin by outlining their summary. Students can then add facts and examples from the story to flesh out the outline.

2. Have students construct a story map or other graphic organizer as they brainstorm details about the characters, plot, and setting.

3. Remind students to use the first-person point of view in their narrative. If necessary, have them review what they learned about point of view in Literary Concepts.

 **The Writer's Craft**

Short Story, pp. 78–85

ALTERNATIVE ACTIVITIES

1. What if Dolores decided to give herself a new look? Draw or paint **"before" and "after" pictures** of her similar to those sometimes found in popular women's magazines.

2. What do you think would happen if Dolores and Ernie were finally to meet? Using what you know about each character, role-play the **scene.**

3. Imagine you are turning this story into a movie. Choose a piece of **music** to use as the movie's theme. Play it for the class and explain why you chose it.

4. Work in small groups to find out more about programs for mentally retarded people. Research the Special Olympics to find out who started the games, when and why they were started, and how students can get involved. Consider how Ernie might have benefited from this program. Share your findings in a **panel discussion.**

Special Olympics Gold Medal

ART CONNECTION

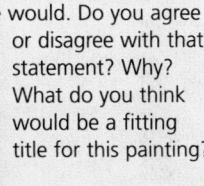

Someone once looked at Patty Dryden's painting on page 19 and said that the flowers tell us more about the man than his face would. Do you agree or disagree with that statement? Why? What do you think would be a fitting title for this painting?

Detail of illustration by Patty Dryden.
Copyright © Patty Dryden.

ACROSS THE CURRICULUM

Health Rylant says that Ernie did not speak in sentences until he was six and did not count until he was eight. Research the major stages in normal child development. For example, when do normal children usually learn to utter words, to roll over, and to walk? Display your findings on a **chart.**

CRITIC'S CORNER

According to Eric de Armas, a seventh-grade member of our student board, the main message of this story is that "everybody is equal, and nobody should be discriminated against because of something they cannot help." How would you express the main message of this story?

A CRUSH **25**

Health *Cooperative Learning* Arrange students in groups of four or five to complete their research. You may want to have group members divide up the reference material, with each student checking one source. In addition, you may wish to use role cards to help students practice the social skills they need for effective group work.

The major stages of child development are

- toddler (18 months–3 years)
- preschooler (3–5 years)
- child in the early school years (5–8 years)
- preteen (8–13 years)

During the toddler stage, children should be able to feed themselves, walk, run, and stack blocks. The average 18-month-old has a vocabulary of 10 to 20 words; the average 3-year-old knows 900 words.

ADDITIONAL SUGGESTION

Math *Census Counting* Today, about 3 percent of the people in the United States are classified as mentally retarded. According to the most recent census, there are 248,709,873 people in the United States. Have students use these figures to calculate how many Americans are classified as mentally retarded. Students may round the population statistic. *(about 7.5 million)*

Art Connection

Some students may say that the flowers hidden behind the man's back show that he intends to surprise someone and that his face wouldn't reveal that information. Other students might say that his face would tell us how he feels about the person who is to receive the flowers.

Alternative Activities

1. Suggest that students look in magazines such as *Redbook, McCalls,* and *Ladies' Home Journal* for "before" and "after" photographs of women who have had makeovers.

2. Guide students to prepare a script for their role-playing, including rough dialogue, gestures, and props. You may wish to videotape the role-playing so performers can watch themselves afterward.

3. Encourage students to consider a wide variety of musical styles, such as folk, classical, blues, jazz, and pop. Be sure that students select music that is appropriate for the classroom setting.

4. Students can find information about the Special Olympics in a recent encyclopedia or almanac. There are also many newspaper and magazine articles on the program. Encourage students to interview special-education teachers as well.

Exercise A

1. suitor   4. cherish
2. swarthy   5. impaled
3. discreetly

Exercise B

1. A   4. A
2. S   5. S
3. A

Reteaching/Reinforcement
• *Unit One Resource Book,* p. 10

CYNTHIA RYLANT

Cynthia Rylant was friendly and coop-erative as a young child, but in middle school she says she became *"erratic, like a spring somebody pulled tight and BOING let go flying across the room."* Love was a major influence: "I was completely boy-crazy and can't count the number of boys I had mad crushes on," she recalls. It was a very happy time in her life, although she believes she drove her mother "out of her mind!"

AUTHOR BACKGROUND
Cynthia Rylant In this interview, Cynthia Rylant tells about her life as an author

Side A, Frame 634

ART GALLERY
Still Lifes Flowers have inspired artists for centuries. Although today some artists choose the camera over the paintbrush, the inspiration is the same. These photos may lead to a discussion about how nature inspires cre-ativity and emotion.

Side A, Frame 49204

WORDS TO KNOW

EXERCISE A Review the Words to Know in the boxes at the bottom of the selection pages. On your paper, write the word that best completes each sentence.

1. Ernie was in love with Dolores and wished to be her ____.
2. Dolores had dark hair, dark eyes, and a ____ complexion.
3. Although Jack knew about Ernie's crush, he ____ kept it to himself.
4. Perhaps Ernie thought Dolores would ____ the flowers as much as he did.
5. Ernie's empty seed packets, ____ on stakes in the garden, showed which flowers he had planted in each row.

EXERCISE B Decide if the following pairs of words are synonyms or antonyms. Write *S* for synonyms or *A* for antonyms.
1. cherish—dislike
2. impaled—pierced
3. discreetly—carelessly
4. suitor—enemy
5. swarthy—dark

CYNTHIA RYLANT

In Kent, Ohio, where Cynthia Rylant lives, a strange small man sometimes brings flowers in Mason jars to waitresses at a little diner. That man became the inspira-tion for Ernie. Beside the diner is a hard-ware store. "That's where my imagination found Dolores," said Rylant, who claims that she enjoys taking "people who don't get any attention in the world and mak-ing them really valuable in my fiction—making them absolutely shine with their beauty."

Rylant grew up in the mountains of West Virginia. She lived with her grandparents for four years while her mother studied nursing. Her grand-father was a coal miner, and the family lived in a small house with no plumbing. When Rylant's

1954–

mother finished school, she found an apartment in which Rylant says she "felt rich" because "the whole place had run-ning water and an indoor bathroom."

Rylant wrote her first book, *When I Was Young in the Mountains,* in one night. Nevertheless, she says, "It took me about seven years to feel like a writer." Rylant has achieved success in many forms of writing: picture books for children, novels for young adults, short stories, and poetry. Her book *Missing May* was awarded the Newbery Medal in 1992.

OTHER WORKS *A Couple of Kooks and Other Stories About Love, A Fine White Dust, A Kindness, A Blue-Eyed Daisy, Waiting to Waltz: A Childhood*

Extended Reading

LASERLINKS
• *AUTHOR BACKGROUND*
• *ART GALLERY*

WHAT DO YOU THINK?

Reflecting on Theme

Have students recall the conversations they role-played in which they tried to get their friends to accept someone who is "differ-ent." Ask students, now that they have read "A Crush," whether there is anything they would add to those conversations. Invite volunteers to role-play new conversations based on any new ideas or knowledge they gained from reading this story.

PREVIEWING

FICTION

A Retrieved Reformation
O. Henry

PERSONAL CONNECTION Activating Prior Knowledge

In small groups, brainstorm a list of several characters in books or films who change for the better or for the worse. How do you account for the change in each of these characters? What do you think are the most powerful motives for change in real people? Share your ideas with your group.

List of characters

books: Colin in The Secret Garden

films:

LANGUAGE CONNECTION

Slang words and expressions come and go. For example, the slang word *rip-off*, which is often heard today, was not in use when your parents were teenagers. "A Retrieved Reformation" contains slang words and expressions that were popular around the turn of the century, when O. Henry was writing. Examples include *stir*, meaning "prison"; *get sent up*, meaning "to be sent to prison"; *cracksman*, meaning "someone who opens safes illegally"; and *rogue-catcher*, meaning "a person who captures criminals." Usually, the context of the story will provide enough clues for you to figure out the meaning of these words and expressions. If not, refer to a dictionary or a specialized slang dictionary.

READING CONNECTION Active Reading/Setting a Purpose

Understanding Motive In "A Retrieved Reformation," Jimmy Valentine, the main character, changes. As you read, think about what causes Jimmy to change. After you have read the story, create a before-and-after diagram like the one shown. Write down Jimmy's motive for change, and then list qualities that he shows before and after his change.

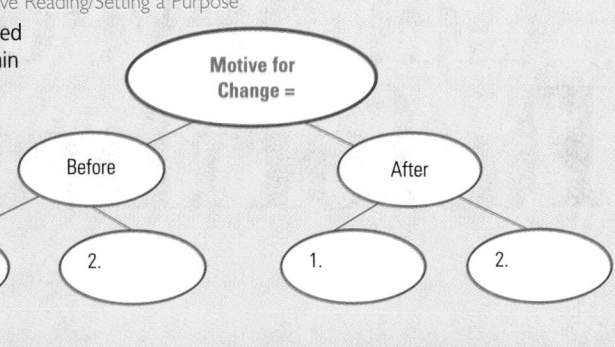

Motive for Change =

Before

After

1.   2.

1.   2.

LASERLINKS
• HISTORICAL CONNECTION

27

OVERVIEW

Objectives

- To understand and appreciate a classic in the short story genre about a character who undergoes a great change
- To understand motive
- To study plot and climax
- To express understanding of the story through a choice of writing forms, including an article, a report, and a paragraph
- To extend understanding of the story through a variety of multimodal and cross-curricular activities

Skills

READING SKILLS/STRATEGIES
- Evaluating

LITERARY CONCEPTS
- Plot
- Point of view

GENRE STUDY
- Fiction: short story

THE WRITER'S STYLE
- Show, don't tell

GRAMMAR
- Subject-verb agreement: the pronoun *you*

SPELLING
- The prefix *un-*

SPEAKING, LISTENING, AND VIEWING
- Mock trial

Cross-Curricular Connections

SOCIAL STUDIES
- Criminal justice system
- Egg creams

HISTORY
- The term *drummer*

MATH
- Computing interest

 **HISTORICAL CONNECTION**
Small-Town America The setting of this story is a small U.S. town in the late 1800s. These photos will help your students visualize the setting and understand the small-town life of the time. You might want to discuss the social values that influence the change in Jimmy Valentine, the story's main character.

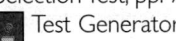

Side A, Frame 49213

PRINT AND MEDIA RESOURCES

UNIT ONE RESOURCE BOOK
Strategic Reading: Literature, p. 13
Vocabulary SkillBuilder, p. 16
Reading SkillBuilder, p. 14
Spelling SkillBuilder, p. 15

GRAMMAR MINI–LESSONS
Transparencies, p. 4
Copymasters, p. 4

WRITING MINI–LESSONS
Transparencies, p. 46

ACCESS FOR STUDENTS ACQUIRING ENGLISH
Selection Summaries
Reading and Writing Support

FORMAL ASSESSMENT
Selection Test, pp. 7–8
Test Generator

AUDIO LIBRARY
See Reference Card

LASERLINKS
Historical Connection

Jimmy Valentine, an expert safecracker, receives a pardon and leaves prison. He resumes his career as a safecracker, burglarizing three banks. Then he arrives in Elmore and falls in love with Annabel Adams, the daughter of the local banker. Concealing his past, Jimmy changes his name to Ralph D. Spencer, opens a shoe business, and begins to live honestly. Annabel falls in love with him. Two weeks before they are to be married, detective Ben Price arrives in Elmore, pursuing Jimmy for the robberies he committed after leaving prison. As Price looks on, Annabel's young niece Agatha is accidentally locked inside a bank vault. Jimmy uses his safecracking tools to open the vault, freeing the child and revealing his identity. Price pretends not to know Jimmy and walks away, refusing to arrest him.

Thematic Link: *Opening Doors* Jimmy Valentine opens the door to a new life after he falls in love and decides to reform.

Art Note

***Portrait of Prince Eristoff* by Tamara de Lempicka** In this painting, the figure's immediate physical presence is striking. The elongated limbs, immobile pose, contrasting tones, and lack of distracting background details help achieve this effect. The figure in this portrait is a nobleman, as are most of the figures in de Lempicka's work.

Reading the Art *What details suggest that the subject of the painting is concerned about his appearance?*

CUSTOMIZING FOR
Students Acquiring English

- Use **ACCESS FOR STUDENTS ACQUIRING ENGLISH,** *Reading and Writing Support.*

- Students acquiring English may find much of the vocabulary in this story difficult. Encourage them to look for cognates, or English words that are similar in spelling and meaning to words in the languages they know. For example, speakers of Romance languages may recognize and understand the word *reformation* in the title. Other cognates in the story include *pardon, represent, community,* and *combination.*

Portrait of Prince Eristoff (1925), Tamara de Lempicka. Private collection, New York. Copyright © SPADEM.

A Retrieved Reformation

by O. Henry

WORDS TO KNOW

assiduously (ə-sĭj′ōō-əs-lē) *adv.* in a steady and hard-working way (p. 29)
balk (bôk) *v.* to refuse to move or act (p. 29)
compulsory (kəm-pŭl′sə-rē) *adj.* that which must be done; required (p. 29)
elusive (ĭ-lōō′sĭv) *adj.* escaping from capture as by daring, cleverness, or skill (p. 30)
eminent (em′ə-nənt) *adj.* better than most others; very famous (p. 29)

rehabilitate (rē′hə-bĭl′ə-tāt′) *v.* to restore to useful life, as through therapy and education (p. 29)
retribution (rĕt′rə-byōō′shən) *n.* punishment for bad behavior (p. 30)
unobtrusively (ŭn′-əb-trōō′-sĭv-lē) *adv.* in a way that attracts little or no attention (p. 32)
unperceived (ŭn′pər-sēvd′) *adj.* not seen (p. 33)
virtuous (vûr′chōō-əs) *adj.* morally good; honorable (p. 29)

A guard came to the prison shoe shop, where Jimmy Valentine was <u>assiduously</u> stitching uppers, and escorted him to the front office. There the warden handed Jimmy his pardon, which had been signed that morning by the governor. Jimmy took it in a tired kind of way. He had served nearly ten months of a four-year sentence. He had expected to stay only about three months, at the longest. When a man with as many friends on the outside as Jimmy Valentine had is received in the "stir" it is hardly worthwhile to cut his hair.

"Now, Valentine," said the warden, "you'll go out in the morning. Brace up, and make a man of yourself. You're not a bad fellow at heart. Stop cracking safes, and live straight."

"Me?" said Jimmy, in surprise. "Why, I never cracked a safe in my life."

"Oh, no," laughed the warden. "Of course not. Let's see, now. How was it you happened to get sent up on that Springfield job? Was it because you wouldn't prove an alibi for fear of compromising somebody in extremely high-toned society? Or was it simply a case of a mean old jury that had it in for you? It's always one or the other with you innocent victims."

"Me?" said Jimmy, still blankly <u>virtuous</u>. "Why, warden, I never was in Springfield in my life!"

"Take him back, Cronin," smiled the warden, "and fix him up with outgoing clothes. Unlock him at seven in the morning, and let him come to the bull-pen. Better think over my advice, Valentine."

At a quarter past seven on the next morning Jimmy stood in the warden's outer office. He had on a suit of the villainously fitting, ready-made clothes and a pair of the stiff, squeaky shoes that the state furnishes to its discharged <u>compulsory</u> guests.

The clerk handed him a railroad ticket and the five-dollar bill with which the law expected him to <u>rehabilitate</u> himself into good citizenship and prosperity. The warden gave him a cigar, and shook hands. Valentine, 9762, was chronicled on the books "Pardoned by Governor," and Mr. James Valentine walked out into the sunshine.

Disregarding the song of the birds, the waving green trees, and the smell of the flowers, Jimmy headed straight for a restaurant. There he tasted the first sweet joys of liberty in the shape of a broiled chicken and a bottle of white wine—followed by a cigar a grade better than the one the warden had given him. From there he proceeded leisurely to the depot. He tossed a quarter into the hat of a blind man sitting by the door, and boarded his train. Three hours set him down in a little town near the state line. He went to the café of one Mike Dolan and shook hands with Mike, who was alone behind the bar.

"Sorry we couldn't make it sooner, Jimmy, me boy," said Mike. "But we had that protest from Springfield to buck against, and the governor nearly <u>balked</u>. Feeling all right?"

"Fine," said Jimmy. "Got my key?"

He got his key and went upstairs, unlocking the door of a room at the rear. Everything was just as he had left it. There on the floor was still Ben Price's collar-button that had been torn from that <u>eminent</u> detective's shirt-band when they had overpowered Jimmy to arrest him.

Pulling out from the wall a folding-bed, Jimmy slid back a panel in the wall and dragged out a dust-covered suitcase. He

WORDS TO KNOW

assiduously (ə-sĭj′ōō-əs-lē) *adv.* in a steady and hard-working way
virtuous (vûr′chōō-əs) *adj.* morally good; honorable
compulsory (kəm-pŭl′sə-rē) *adj.* that which must be done; required
rehabilitate (rē′hə-bĭl′ĭ-tāt′) *v.* to restore to useful life, as through therapy and education
balk (bôk) *v.* to refuse to move or act
eminent (ĕm′ə-nənt) *adj.* better than most others; very famous

29

Set a Purpose Have students, in pairs, role-play the dialogue between the warden and Jimmy on page 29. Then have them review the ideas about motives for change that they recorded for the Personal Connection. Ask students to predict what the story might be about.

Use **UNIT ONE RESOURCE BOOK**, p. 13, for guidance in reading the selection.

CUSTOMIZING FOR
Gifted and Talented Students

Have students analyze O. Henry's use of *irony*, a contrast between what is expected and what actually happens. Ask students to identify examples of irony in the plot and to explain each example.

Possible responses:

Page 29—Inmates in the prison are described as "compulsory guests."

Page 31—Applying the skills he acquired in prison, Jimmy opens a shoe store, which turns out to be a success.

Page 34—Jimmy saves Agatha's life by using his skills as a safecracker.

Literary Concept: PLOT

A Ask students to think about why O. Henry begins the story with the warden's assessment of Jimmy's character. *(Possible response: Although Jimmy is introduced to the reader as a criminal, the warden's assessment makes the reader wonder whether Jimmy might somehow change.)*

CUSTOMIZING FOR
Multiple Learning Styles

B **Bodily-Kinesthetic Learners** Invite students to pantomime Jimmy's actions, using gestures, posture, and facial expressions to communicate his feelings.

CUSTOMIZING FOR
Students Acquiring English

1 Help students understand that the phrase *discharged compulsory guests* refers to people who have served time in jail and have later been released.

2 Make sure students understand that *one* as used here means "a person named."

Mini-Lesson **Literary Concepts**

REVIEWING POINT OF VIEW Remind students that point of view is the perspective from which a story is told. The most common points of view are the first-person and the third-person. In the first-person point of view, the narrator is one of the characters in the story and uses first-person pronouns such as *I, me,* and *we*. The reader sees the events in the story and the other characters only

through the eyes of the narrator. In the third-person point of view, the narrator, who is not a character in the story, relates the events using third-person pronouns such as *he, she,* and *it*.

Application Have students, in pairs, reread the first paragraph of "A Retrieved Reformation" and identify the clues that suggest the point of view.

Active Reading: PREDICT

C Have students predict what might happen in the plot based on Jimmy's actions here. You can use the following model to show how to make predictions:

Think-Aloud Model *I wonder why Jimmy is taking out his carefully hidden burglary tools. His fond gaze at the tools and his pride in them suggest that he is going to use them again. I predict that he hasn't changed and that he's going to return to a life of crime.*

CUSTOMIZING FOR
Students Acquiring English

3 Students may be puzzled by the use of this blank. Explain that it is used to suggest that the story is true and that the author did not wish to provide the real name of the establishment.

Linking to Social Studies

D "Seltzer-and-milk" is a variation on an egg cream, a drink similar to a milk shake, made with chocolate syrup, milk, and soda water. This drink was once very popular in urban areas.

Critical Thinking: ANALYZING

E Ask students what these details about the robberies suggest about Jimmy's character and his skill as a thief. *(Possible response: Jimmy is a cool, professional, skilled thief who appears to feel no remorse for his thefts.)*

STRATEGIC READING FOR
Less-Proficient Readers

F Invite students to return to their purpose for reading. Have students explain whether or not they think Jimmy has changed.

• Who is Ben Price, and why is he following Jimmy? *(Price is a detective who wants to catch Jimmy and return him to jail.)* **Summarizing**

Set a Purpose Have students read on to find out what makes Jimmy change in Elmore.

---

opened this and gazed fondly at the finest set of burglar's tools in the East. It was a complete set, made of specially tempered steel, the latest designs in drills, punches, braces and bits, jimmies, clamps, and augers, with two or three novelties invented by Jimmy himself, in which he took pride. Over nine hundred dollars they had cost him to have made at _____, a place where they make such things for the profession.

In half an hour Jimmy went downstairs and through the café. He was now dressed in tasteful and well-fitting clothes, and carried his dusted and cleaned suitcase in his hand.

"Got anything on?" asked Mike Dolan, genially.

"Me?" said Jimmy, in a puzzled tone. "I don't understand. I'm representing the New York Amalgamated Short Snap Biscuit Cracker and Frazzled Wheat Company."

This statement delighted Mike to such an extent that Jimmy had to take a seltzer-and-milk on the spot. He never touched "hard" drinks.

A week after the release of Valentine, 9762, there was a neat job of safe-burglary done in Richmond, Indiana, with no clue to the author. A scant eight hundred dollars was all that was secured. Two weeks after that a patented, improved, burglar-proof safe in Logansport was opened like a cheese to the tune of fifteen hundred dollars, currency; securities and silver untouched. That began to interest the rogue catchers. Then an old-fashioned bank safe in Jefferson City became active and threw out of its crater an eruption of banknotes amounting to five thousand dollars. The losses were now high enough to bring the matter up into Ben Price's class of work. By comparing notes, a remarkable similarity in the methods of the burglaries was noticed. Ben Price investigated the scenes of the robberies, and was heard to remark:

"That's Dandy Jim Valentine's autograph. He's resumed business. Look at that combination knob—jerked out as easy as pulling up a radish in wet weather. He's got the only clamps that can do it. And look how clean those tumblers were punched out! Jimmy never has to drill but one hole. Yes, I guess I want Mr. Valentine. He'll do his bit next time without any short-time or clemency foolishness."

Ben Price knew Jimmy's habits. He had learned them while working up the Springfield case. Long jumps, quick get-aways, no confederates,[1] and a taste for good society—these ways had helped Mr. Valentine to become noted as a successful dodger of <u>retribution</u>. It was given out that Ben Price had taken up the trail of the <u>elusive</u> cracksman, and other people with burglar-proof safes felt more at ease.

One afternoon Jimmy Valentine and his suitcase climbed out of the mailhack in Elmore, a little town five miles off the railroad down in the blackjack country of Arkansas. Jimmy, looking like an athletic young senior just home from college, went down the board sidewalk toward the hotel.

A young lady crossed the street, passed him at the corner, and entered a door over which

---

1. **confederates** (kən-fĕd′ər-ĭts): accomplices or associates in crime.

WORDS TO KNOW **retribution** (rĕt′rə-byōō′shən) *n.* punishment for bad behavior
elusive (ĭ-lōō′sĭv) *adj.* escaping from capture as by daring, cleverness, or skill

30

Mini-Lesson ✎ **Grammar**

SUBJECT-VERB AGREEMENT: THE PRONOUN YOU Remind students that a verb must agree with its subject in number (singular or plural). Explain that the pronoun *you* has the same form in the singular and the plural and takes the plural form of a verb even when it refers to a single person. Write the following examples on the board, and invite volunteers to explain how they fit this rule:

Singular Ben, you *catch* Jimmy Valentine.

Plural Detectives, you *give* Ben some help.

Application Ask students to find several sentences in the story that have *you* as a subject and to analyze them to see if the pronoun is singular or plural. Have students record their findings on a chart like the one on the left.

Reteaching/Reinforcement
• Grammar Handbook, anthology pp. 853–854
• *Grammar Mini-Lessons* copymasters p. 4, transparencies p. 4

 The Writer's Craft

The Pronoun *you*, p. 579

was the sign "The Elmore Bank." Jimmy Valentine looked into her eyes, forgot what he was, and became another man. She lowered her eyes and colored slightly. Young men of Jimmy's style and looks were scarce in Elmore.

Jimmy collared a boy that was loafing on the steps of the bank as if he were one of the stockholders, and began to ask him questions about the town, feeding him dimes at intervals. By and by the young lady came out, looking royally unconscious of the young man with the suitcase, and went her way.

"Isn't that young lady Miss Polly Simpson?" asked Jimmy, with specious guile.[2]

"Naw," said the boy. "She's Annabel Adams. Her pa owns this bank. What'd you come to Elmore for? Is that a gold watch-chain? I'm going to get a bulldog. Got any more dimes?"

Jimmy went to the Planters' Hotel, registered as Ralph D. Spencer, and engaged a room. He leaned on the desk and declared his platform to the clerk. He said he had come to Elmore to look for a location to go into business. How was the shoe business, now, in the town? He had thought of the shoe business. Was there an opening?

The clerk was impressed by the clothes and manner of Jimmy. He, himself, was something of a pattern of fashion to the thinly gilded youth of Elmore, but he now perceived his shortcomings. While trying to figure out Jimmy's manner of tying his four-in-hand[3] he cordially gave information.

Yes, there ought to be a good opening in the shoe line. There wasn't an exclusive shoe store in the place. The dry-goods and general stores handled them. Business in all lines was fairly good. Hoped Mr. Spencer would decide to locate in Elmore. He would find it a pleasant town to live in, and the people very sociable.

Mr. Spencer thought he would stop over in the town a few days and look over the situation. No, the clerk needn't call the boy. He would carry up his suitcase, himself; it was rather heavy.

Mr. Ralph Spencer, the phoenix[4] that arose from Jimmy Valentine's ashes—ashes left by the flame of a sudden and alterative attack of love—remained in Elmore, and prospered. He opened a shoe store and secured a good run of trade.

Socially he was also a success and made many friends. And he accomplished the wish of his heart. He met Miss Annabel Adams, and became more and more captivated by her charms.

At the end of a year the situation of Mr. Ralph Spencer was this: he had won the respect of the community, his shoe store was flourishing, and he and Annabel were engaged to be married in two weeks. Mr. Adams, the typical, plodding, country banker, approved of Spencer. Annabel's pride in him almost equaled her affection. He was as much at home in the family of Mr. Adams and that of Annabel's married sister as if he were already a member.

One day Jimmy sat down in his room and wrote this letter, which he mailed to the safe address of one of his old friends in St. Louis:

DEAR OLD PAL:

I want you to be at Sullivan's place, in Little Rock, next Wednesday night, at nine o'clock. I want you to wind up some little matters for me. And, also, I want to make you a present

---

2. **specious guile** (spē′shəs gīl): innocent charm masking real slyness.

3. **four-in-hand:** a necktie tied in the usual way, that is, in a slipknot with the ends left hanging.

4. **phoenix** (fē′nĭks): a mythological bird that lived for over 500 years and then burned itself to death, only to rise out of its own ashes to live another long life. The phoenix is a symbol of immortality.

A RETRIEVED REFORMATION **31**

Reteaching/Reinforcement
• *Unit One Resource Book,* p. 14

Mini-Lesson — Reading Skills/Strategies

EVALUATING Remind students that evaluating is the process of judging the worth of something or someone. A work of literature and its elements may be evaluated by standards such as entertainment, believability, originality, and emotional power. Emphasize that if a character's motives are not believable, changes in character will seem unlikely. As a result, the plot will seem improbable.

Application Encourage students to evaluate and record, in a chart like the one shown, the changes and motives for each character. Ask students if the changes and motives are believable.

Character	Changes	Motive	Believable?
Jimmy Valentine	settles in Elmore	love	
Ben Price			
Annabel Adams			

Active Reading: CLARIFY

G Ask students what happens to Jimmy when he looks into the young lady's eyes. (*Possible response: He falls in love at first sight.*)

CUSTOMIZING FOR
Students Acquiring English

4 Students should be able to infer from the context that *naw* means "no." Model the correct pronunciation and intonation.

5 Explain that the idiom *stop over* means "stay somewhere between two parts of a trip."

Critical Thinking: SYNTHESIZING

H Ask students to explain why Jimmy wants to open a shoe business. If necessary, have students reread the first paragraph on page 29. (*Jimmy learned to make shoes in prison.*)

Literary Concept: POINT OF VIEW

I Ask students to identify the point of view used in this passage and to explain what the narrator suggests about Jimmy's motivation for staying in Elmore. (*Possible response: The point of view is third-person. The narrator suggests that Jimmy is hoping that Miss Annabel Adams will fall in love with him.*)

CUSTOMIZING FOR
Multiple Learning Styles

J Spatial or Graphic Learners Invite students to design the wedding invitation for "Ralph" and Annabel.

STRATEGIC READING FOR
Less-Proficient Readers

K Discuss with students how love has made Jimmy change and become an honest man.

• Who is Annabel Adams? (*the banker's daughter*) **Noting Relevant Details**

• What is Jimmy's new name? (*Ralph D. Spencer*) **Noting Relevant Details**

• Why does Jimmy change his name? (*Possible response: to start a new life*) **Drawing Conclusions**

Set a Purpose Have students read on to find out if Jimmy really has changed.

L Ask students to explain why the third-person point of view is an effective way of presenting Ben Price's arrival. *(Possible response: The third-person narrator tells what Ben Price is saying only to himself, and the reader can infer from what Ben says that he has come to Elmore to arrest Jimmy.)*

Critical Thinking:
MAKING JUDGMENTS

M Ask students to evaluate the conclusion that Jimmy has reached. *(Possible response: Jimmy reaches the wrong conclusion in deciding that he can safely venture out. Little does he know that Ben Price has tracked him down in Elmore.)*

Linking to History

N Explain to students that *drummer* was once a common term for a commercial traveler, or a salesman. O. Henry's audience at the time he published the story may have picked up an additional meaning in the slang term: burglars were also called *drummers* because they "screwed drums" (stole from houses).

STRATEGIC READING FOR
Less-Proficient Readers

O Explore what details suggest that Jimmy has really changed.

• What is Jimmy going to do with his burglary tools? *(give them to Billy)*

Summarizing

• In what ways has Jimmy's life become more stable? *(He is settled in one town, he is to be married, and he has an established, legitimate business.)*

Using Context Clues

Set a Purpose Have students read on to find out what happens at the Elmore Bank.

---

of my kit of tools. I know you'll be glad to get them—you couldn't duplicate the lot for a thousand dollars. Say, Billy, I've quit the old business—a year ago. I've got a nice store. I'm making an honest living, and I'm going to marry the finest girl on earth two weeks from now. It's the only life, Billy—the straight one. I wouldn't touch a dollar of another man's money now for a million. After I get married I'm going to sell out and go West, where there won't be so much danger of having old scores brought up against me. I tell you, Billy, she's an angel. She believes in me; and I wouldn't do another crooked thing for the whole world. Be sure to be at Sully's, for I must see you. I'll bring along the tools with me.

> **" I wouldn't do another crooked thing for the whole world."**

Your old friend,
JIMMY.

L On the Monday night after Jimmy wrote this letter, Ben Price jogged <u>unobtrusively</u> into Elmore in a livery buggy. He lounged about town in his quiet way until he found out what he wanted to know. From the drugstore across the street from Spencer's shoe store he got a good look at Ralph D. Spencer.

"Going to marry the banker's daughter are you, Jimmy?" said Ben to himself, softly. "Well, I don't know!"

The next morning Jimmy took breakfast at **M** the Adamses. He was going to Little Rock that day to order his wedding suit and buy something nice for Annabel. That would be the first time he had left town since he came to Elmore.

It had been more than a year now since those last professional "jobs," and he thought he could safely venture out. **M**

After breakfast quite a family party went down together—Mr. Adams, Annabel, Jimmy, and Annabel's married sister with her two little girls, aged five and nine. They came by the hotel where Jimmy still boarded, and he ran up to his room and brought along his suitcase. Then they went on to the bank. There stood Jimmy's horse and buggy and Dolph Gibson, who was going to drive him over to the railroad station.

All went inside the high, carved oak railings into the banking room—Jimmy included, for Mr. Adams's future son-in-law was welcome anywhere. The clerks were pleased to be greeted by the good-looking, agreeable young man who was going to marry Miss Annabel. Jimmy set his suitcase down. Annabel, whose heart was bubbling with happiness and lively youth, put on Jimmy's hat and picked up the suitcase. "Wouldn't I make a nice drummer?" said **N** Annabel. "My! Ralph, how heavy it is. Feels like it was full of gold bricks."

"Lot of nickel-plated shoehorns in there," said Jimmy, coolly, "that I'm going to return. Thought I'd save express charges by taking them up. I'm getting awfully economical." **O**

The Elmore Bank had just put in a new safe and vault. Mr. Adams was very proud of it, and insisted on an inspection by everyone. The vault was a small one, but it had a new patented door. It fastened with three solid steel bolts thrown simultaneously with a single handle, and had a time lock. Mr. Adams beamingly explained

WORDS
TO
KNOW

unobtrusively (ŭn′əb-trōō′sĭv-lē) *adv.* in a way that attracts little or no attention

32

A s s e s s m e n t Options

INFORMAL ASSESSMENT Evaluate how well students understand the story by having them create a story map tracing the setting, characters, and plot in "A Retrieved Reformation." Guide students to look back through the story for details to use in filling in their story maps.

Rubric

3 Full Accomplishment Students include all relevant details about the setting, characters, and plot. The map shows a clear understanding of the climax and resolution of the plot.

2 Substantial Accomplishment Students include most of the important details about setting, character, and plot. Extraneous details may be included.

1 Little or Partial Accomplishment Students are unable to summarize accurately the setting, characters, or plot. Key events are not included.

its workings to Mr. Spencer, who showed a courteous but not too intelligent interest. The two children, May and Agatha, were delighted by the shining metal and funny clock and knobs.

While they were thus engaged Ben Price sauntered in and leaned on his elbow, looking casually inside between the railings. He told the teller that he didn't want anything; he was just waiting for a man he knew.

Suddenly there was a scream or two from the women, and a commotion. Unperceived by the elders, May, the nine-year-old girl, in a spirit of play, had shut Agatha in the vault. She had then shot the bolts and turned the knob of the combination as she had seen Mr. Adams do.

The old banker sprang to the handle and tugged at it for a moment. "The door can't be opened," he groaned. "The clock hasn't been wound nor the combination set."

Agatha's mother screamed again, hysterically.

"Hush!" said Mr. Adams, raising his trembling hand. "All be quiet for a moment. Agatha!" he called as loudly as he could. "Listen to me." During the following silence they could just hear the faint sound of the child wildly shrieking in the dark vault in a panic of terror.

"My precious darling!" wailed the mother. "She will die of fright! Open the door! Oh, break it open! Can't you men do something?"

Copyright © Gary Kelley.

| WORDS TO KNOW | **unperceived** (ŭn′pər-sēvd′) *adj.* not seen |

33

Literary Concept: PLOT

P Explain that writers sometimes foreshadow—or provide hints about—events that occur later in the plot. Have students speculate about what the details in this passage might foreshadow. *(Possible response: The children's delight in seeing the "shining metal and funny clock and knobs" suggests they will play with the safe—and perhaps lock themselves in.)*

Active Reading: PREDICT

Q Invite students to predict what they think will happen next, based on what they know about Jimmy. *(Possible responses: Jimmy will open the safe to save Agatha. He won't open the safe because it will give away his identity.)*

Mini-Lesson   **The Writer's Style**

SHOW, DON'T TELL Explain to students that writers often show, rather than tell, something they want to convey to readers. Trace how O. Henry uses physical descriptions, character traits, and specific incidents to show how Jimmy Valentine changes over the course of the story. Then turn to the final paragraphs of the story. Trace how O. Henry resolves the plot by showing rather than telling. Be sure that students understand that Ben never explains why he decides to let Jimmy go free; the reader must infer Ben's reasons from the dialogue and details.

Application Have students write a sequel to the story that explains what happens to Jimmy, Ben, and Annabel. Guide students in using the elaboration techniques described in this mini-lesson.

Reteaching/Reinforcement
• Writing Handbook, anthology p. 821
• *Writing Mini-Lessons* transparencies, p. 46

 **The Writer's Craft**

Show Not Tell, pp. 262–265

Gifted and Talented Students

Have students find out how money is safeguarded in modern banks. In addition to using vaults, how do banks protect themselves against robbery? *(Possible response: Security measures include video cameras, hidden alarm buttons, guards, and automatic locks.)*

Literary Concept: PLOT

R Invite students to explain why they think Jimmy asks for Annabel's rose. *(Possible response: He thinks that he will reveal his identity and lose her love when he opens the vault, so he asks for something to remember her by.)*

Critical Thinking: SPECULATING

S Discuss with students whether they think Annabel will still marry Jimmy after she finds out about his past. *(Possible responses: yes, because Jimmy is no longer a criminal; no, because he lied about whom he really was)*

STRATEGIC READING FOR

Less-Proficient Readers

T Summarize the events that take place at the Elmore Bank. *(Annabel's niece accidentally gets locked in a safe, and Jimmy uses his skills to get her out.)*
Summarizing

• Who shouts "Ralph!" after Jimmy leaves the bank? *(Annabel)* **Making Inferences**

• What does Ben do when Jimmy turns himself in? *(Ben pretends that he doesn't know Jimmy.)* **Summarizing**

COMPREHENSION CHECK

1. Why was Jimmy in jail? *(for cracking safes)*
2. What business does Jimmy start in Elmore? *(a shoe business)*
3. How does Agatha get locked in the safe? *(While playing, her sister locks her in.)*
4. How does Agatha get out of the safe? *(Jimmy opens the safe and frees her.)*

"There isn't a man nearer than Little Rock who can open that door," said Mr. Adams, in a shaky voice. "My God! Spencer, what shall we do? That child—she can't stand it long in there. There isn't enough air, and, besides, she'll go into convulsions from fright."

Agatha's mother, frantic now, beat the door of the vault with her hands. Somebody wildly suggested dynamite. Annabel turned to Jimmy, her large eyes full of anguish, but not yet despairing. To a woman nothing seems quite impossible to the powers of the man she worships.

"Can't you do something, Ralph—try, won't you?"

He looked at her with a queer, soft smile on his lips and in his keen eyes.

R "Annabel," he said, "give me that rose you are wearing, will you?"

Hardly believing that she had heard him aright, she unpinned the bud from the bosom of her dress, and placed it in his hand. Jimmy stuffed it into his vest pocket, threw off his coat and pulled up his shirt sleeves. With that act Ralph D. Spencer passed away and Jimmy Valentine took his place.

"Get away from the door, all of you," he commanded, shortly.

He set his suitcase on the table, and opened it out flat. From that time on he seemed to be unconscious of the presence of any one else. He laid out the shining, queer implements swiftly and orderly, whistling softly to himself as he always did when at work. In a deep silence and immovable, the others watched him as if under a spell.

In a minute Jimmy's pet drill was biting smoothly into the steel door. In ten minutes—breaking his own burglarious record—he threw back the bolts and opened the door.

Agatha, almost collapsed, but safe, was gathered into her mother's arms.

Jimmy Valentine put on his coat, and walked outside the railings toward the front door. As he went he thought he heard a faraway voice that he once knew call "Ralph!" But he never hesitated.

At the door a big man stood somewhat in his way.

"Hello, Ben!" said Jimmy, still with his strange smile. "Got around at last, have you? Well, let's go. I don't know that it makes much difference, now."

And then Ben Price acted rather strangely.

"Guess you're mistaken, Mr. Spencer," he said. "Don't believe I recognize you. Your buggy's waiting for you, ain't it?"

And Ben Price turned and strolled down the street. ❖

Mini-Lesson ⒯Ⓜ Spelling

THE PREFIX *UN-* Tell students that the prefix *un-* means "not" or "the opposite of." When this prefix is added to a base word, the spelling of the base word does not change.

un + obtrusive = unobtrusive

un + friendly = unfriendly

Application Ask students to add the prefix *un-* to each of the following words and to tell the meaning of the new word.

1. noticed
2. likely
3. afraid
4. tie
5. just
6. caring
7. marked
8. natural
9. tamed
10. sure

Ask students to look for more words that fit this pattern and to add them to their personal word lists.

Reteaching/Reinforcement

• *Unit One Resource Book,* p. 15

RESPONDING
OPTIONS

FROM PERSONAL RESPONSE TO CRITICAL ANALYSIS

Multimodal Learning

REFLECT

1. How did you react to the ending of this story? Briefly describe your reactions in your notebook and share them with a partner.

RETHINK

2. Why do you think Ben Price lets Jimmy go free?

3. How do you think Jimmy will explain his actions to Annabel?

4. What is your opinion of Jimmy Valentine?

   Consider   Close Textural Reading
   - his history and what the warden says about Jimmy's character
   - the before-and-after diagram you created
   - what Jimmy risks in opening the vault

5. Both Ben Price and Jimmy Valentine make important decisions in this story. Which decision do you think took more courage, and why?

RELATE

6. Jimmy opens the door to a new way of life after falling in love with Annabel. Do you think love is powerful enough to produce permanent change in people? In exploring this issue, recall the motives for change you identified for the Personal Connection on page 27.

7. In some stories, the characters' actions and decisions seem to control what happens. In other stories, forces such as fate seem to be in charge. In "A Retrieved Reformation," do the characters control what happens, or does fate? Use examples to explain your opinion.

ANOTHER PATHWAY

Cooperative Learning
Imagine that Jimmy Valentine is arrested at the end of this story. Hold a **mock trial** in which one side argues that Jimmy should be returned to prison and the other side contends that he should be pardoned. One student should role-play Jimmy as he testifies in his own behalf.

QUICKWRITES

1. Write an **article** for the *Elmore Daily News* that narrates Agatha's rescue.

2. Imagine that you are Ben Price. Write a **report** to your supervisor explaining why you have closed the case on Jimmy Valentine.

3. Look up the words *retrieve* and *reformation* in a dictionary. Then in a **paragraph** explain whether "A Retrieved Reformation" is the best title for this story.

📁 **PORTFOLIO** *Save your writing. You may want to use it later as a springboard to a piece for your portfolio.*

LITERARY CONCEPTS

The **plot** is the sequence of events in a story. In "A Retrieved Reformation," the plot begins when Jimmy receives his pardon and ends when Ben Price lets Jimmy go free. The **climax** of a plot is the point of greatest interest in a story, the turning point of the action. In most stories, the climax occurs near the end of the plot. What event do you think is the climax in "A Retrieved Reformation"? Explain your answer.

---

1. Accept all reasonable responses.
2. Possible responses: Some students may say that Ben feels that Jimmy will never again commit crimes. Other students may say that Ben feels that Jimmy has earned the right to go free.
3. Possible responses: Some students may say that Jimmy will tell the truth about his past. Other students may say that Jimmy will try to conceal his criminal past by claiming that he learned a few safecracking tricks from a friend.
4. Students who admire Jimmy might describe him as self-sacrificing, intelligent, brave, noble, and hard-working; students who don't admire Jimmy might say he is dishonest because he never told Annabel the truth about his past.
5. Students who think Jimmy showed more courage could argue that Jimmy was risking his freedom and happiness when he decided to rescue Agatha from the vault. Students who think Ben's decision took more courage could argue that he might be sacrificing his career as a detective in refusing to arrest a criminal.
6. Students who agree may cite Jimmy's major life changes. Those who disagree may cite real-life stories of people unwilling to make major life changes for love.
7. Possible responses: Fate gave Jimmy an opportunity to redeem himself when Agatha was locked in the vault. Jimmy, however, made the decision to act on this opportunity.

Another Pathway

Cooperative Learning Have students form groups of eight or nine. Each student should be assigned one of the following roles: Jimmy, a defense lawyer, a prosecutor, three members of the jury, and witnesses who are characters from the story. Jury members should be prepared to explain the reasons for their decision.

Rubric

3 Full Accomplishment Groups conduct a mock trial successfully from beginning to end, presenting both sides of the argument clearly.

2 Substantial Accomplishment Groups are moderately successful in conducting the trial and in presenting both sides of the argument.

1 Little or Partial Accomplishment Groups have difficulty conducting the trial and presenting both sides of the argument clearly.

Literary Concepts

Have students get together in small groups to discuss the following questions. One student should serve as recorder for the group.

- What part of the story did you find the most interesting? Why?
- What is the main issue in the story?
- When is this issue resolved?

When students are finished, have them compare their answers with those of at least one other group.

QuickWrites

1. Remind students that the lead, or first paragraph, in their news article should include the five *W*'s and *H*—who, what, when, where, why, and how.
2. Guide students to select words and create sentences that explain Ben's reasons without endangering his position on the police force.
3. Have students reread the story, especially the ending, as they formulate their responses. Invite students who don't think the title is the best to suggest other titles they think would be more suitable.

 The Writer's Craft

Feature Article, pp. 208–210

Possible response: Jimmy Valentine changes by becoming honest and self-sacrificing. Ernie becomes more outgoing and confident.

Across the Curriculum

Social Studies *Cooperative Learning*
Students can work in groups of four or five to find out about the criminal justice system. Suggest they contact the state attorney general as well as using on-line services for answers to the questions posed in the activity. Have each group select one member who will make sure that all information is correct.

ADDITIONAL SUGGESTION

Math *Money in the Bank!*
Banks provide a variety of services, including savings and checking accounts, loans, and safe-deposit boxes. Have students work in pairs to find out how much money they will have earned in ten years if they deposit $1,000 in an account in which interest is compounded annually at 5 percent.

Words to Know

1. True	6. False
2. False	7. True
3. True	8. False
4. False	9. True
5. False	10. False

Reteaching
• *Unit One Resource Book*, p. 16

O. HENRY
(WILLIAM SYDNEY PORTER)

During his three years in the Ohio State Penitentiary, William Sydney Porter met many of the men whose lives he would later re-create in his stories, including the safecracker he named Jimmy Valentine. "A Retrieved Reformation" was adapted into the hit play *Alias Jimmy Valentine*, which sparked a series of "crook plays" and gangster films.

Multimodal Learning

ALTERNATIVE ACTIVITIES

1. Research men's fashions in the late 1800s. Then draw or paint a **portrait** of Jimmy, showing how you imagine he might have dressed.
2. Create a **script** based on the scene in the bank. Cast at least six students to act out the script. Rehearse and perform the scene in class.

ACROSS THE CURRICULUM

Social Studies Research the criminal justice system in your state. Look for answers to questions such as the following:
• What percentage of criminals are repeat offenders?
• What programs exist to help ex-convicts change their lives?

Record your findings on a chart to display in class. If you have access to an encyclopedia program or an on-line service, you might use a computer to start your research.

LITERARY LINKS

Review "A Crush" on page 16. Then compare how Ernie and Jimmy Valentine change after each of them falls in love.

O. HENRY

1862–1910

"O. Henry" is the pen name of William Sydney Porter. At the age of 20, Porter moved from Greensboro, North Carolina, to Texas to work as a ranch hand. He was a rather unusual cowboy, sometimes carrying a small dictionary in one pocket and a book of poems in the other. Later, he worked as a journalist and started his own weekly newspaper. When the publication failed, he took a job as a bank teller. When a shortage of money was discovered, Porter was accused of stealing funds. Although he may have been acquitted of any wrongdoing, he fled to Central America to avoid facing a trial. When he returned two years later to visit his dying wife, he was arrested and then imprisoned.

Porter spent three years in jail. While serving his sentence, he wrote about 20 short stories under his pen name. After his release, he moved to New York and turned out stories at an amazing rate, often one a week. His stories are known for their surprise endings and for their warm portrayals of common people, some of whom are victims of fate.

OTHER WORKS "The Ransom of Red Chief," "The Gift of the Magi," "After Twenty Years"

Extended Reading

On your paper, write *True* if the statement is true. Write *False* if the statement is false.

1. A prison sentence is common **retribution** for a serious crime.
2. A police officer can refuse to carry out a **compulsory** assignment.
3. A **virtuous** person shows concern for others.
4. An **unperceived** crime is one observed by several eyewitnesses.
5. Lazy people work **assiduously**.
6. An **eminent** detective is likely to be new to the job.
7. To **rehabilitate** a criminal means to restore the person to honest ways.
8. You will attract much attention by entering a room **unobtrusively.**
9. Most thieves would not **balk** at stealing jewels.
10. An **elusive** criminal is easy to catch.

Alternative Activities

1. Suggest that students check biographies of Porter and refer to books about the history of clothing, costumes, and fashion.
2. Guide students to prepare the script for their scene, including dialogue, sound effects, and props. You may wish to videotape the scene so performers can watch themselves afterward.

FICTION

Waiting
Budge Wilson

PERSONAL CONNECTION Activating Prior Knowledge

Think about people you like to do things with, such as your friends and classmates, a brother, a sister, or a cousin. Which of these people are a lot like you? Which are not? In your opinion, do best friends usually have similar or contrasting—that is, very different—personalities? Share your views with a group of classmates or with the entire class.

SCIENCE CONNECTION

The story "Waiting," which is set in Nova Scotia, a province of Canada, is about twin sisters with contrasting appearances and personalities. Twins are born about once in every 89 births, and are either identical or fraternal. Identical twins come from a single egg and have the same genes. These twins look alike, having the same color hair and eyes and the same size and shape. Fraternal twins come from two different eggs and have different genes. Usually, they look no more alike than do any other brothers and sisters. At least two-thirds of all twins are fraternal.

Whether identical or fraternal, twins generally share a special bond.

Active Reading
Setting a Purpose
READING CONNECTION

Contrasting Characters Copy the Venn diagram below into your notebook. As you read the story, think about how the twins Juliette and Henrietta are alike and how they are different. After you finish reading, fill in details to complete the diagram.

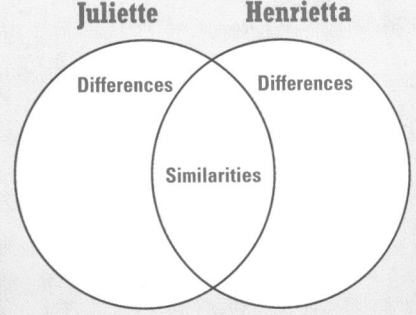

Juliette   Henrietta

Differences   Differences

Similarities

Nova Scotia

CANADA

NOVA SCOTIA
• Halifax
Atlantic
Ocean
Miles
0 100 200
N W E S

 LASERLINKS
• *GEOGRAPHICAL CONNECTION* **37**

OVERVIEW

Objectives

- To understand and appreciate a short story about contrasting characters
- To enrich reading by using active reading skills
- To identify and understand characters, particularly main characters
- To examine a writer's use of comparisons
- To express understanding of the story through a choice of writing forms, including character sketches, a journal entry, and a letter
- To extend understanding of the story through a variety of multimodal and cross-curricular activities

Skills

**READING SKILLS/
STRATEGIES**
- Connecting

LITERARY CONCEPTS
- Characters
- Plot

GENRE STUDY
- Fiction: short story

THE WRITER'S STYLE
- Elaboration with sensory details

GRAMMAR
- Verb tenses

SPELLING
- Words ending in -ance/-ant

STUDY SKILLS
- SQ3R

LISTENING
- Oral history

SPEAKING, LISTENING, AND VIEWING
- Drama performance

Cross-Curricular Connections

SOCIAL STUDIES
- Creating a multimedia presentation
- National symbols
- Native Americans

HISTORY
- World War II
- Rationing
- Gramophone

MATH
- Proportions

 GEOGRAPHICAL CONNECTION
Nova Scotia "Waiting" is set in the Canadian province of Nova Scotia. These images will help students gain an understanding of the distinctive geography of the province.

Side A, Frame 49217

PRINT AND MEDIA RESOURCES

UNIT ONE RESOURCE BOOK
Strategic Reading: Literature, p. 19
Vocabulary SkillBuilder, p. 22
Reading SkillBuilder, p. 20
Spelling SkillBuilder, p. 21

GRAMMAR MINI-LESSONS
Transparencies, p. 21
Copymasters, p. 29

WRITING MINI-LESSONS
Transparencies, pp. 34 and 38

ACCESS FOR STUDENTS ACQUIRING ENGLISH
Selection Summaries
Reading and Writing Support

FORMAL ASSESSMENT
Selection Test, pp. 9–10
 Test Generator

 AUDIO LIBRARY
See Reference Card

 LASERLINKS
Geographical Connection
Social Studies Connection

 INTERNET RESOURCES
McDougal Littell Literature
Center at http://www.hmco.com
/mcdougal/lit

SUMMARY

Juliette considers herself talented, smart, lively, and outgoing—the exact opposite of Henrietta, her pale, reserved twin. Juliette sometimes bullies and mocks Henrietta, who never complains about her sister's treatment of her. When the two girls are almost 13 years old, they and their friends put on a summer play, with Juliette in the leading role. During the final scene, as Juliette raises her arms to join in a dance, she realizes to her horror that she has ripped her dress along the back. Henrietta rescues her sister from public humiliation by gliding onstage and gracefully draping a bedspread over her, concealing the rip in the dress while making her own entrance look like part of the play. As the performers take their final bows, Juliette suddenly realizes that Henrietta has emerged as a beautiful, confident young woman who has lost her waiting look and become very appealing to boys. Juliette acknowledges that she will never have Henrietta's power.

Thematic Link: *Opening Doors*
Henrietta's serene, confident personality will open doors for her that will remain closed to Juliette.

Illustration by Meg Kelleher Aubrey.

WORDS TO KNOW

apathy (ăp′ə-thē) *n.* lack of strong feeling or interest (p. 40)
arresting (ə-rĕs′tĭng) *adj.* striking (p. 47)
dominant (dŏm′ə-nənt) *adj.* ruling or controlling (p. 40)
flamboyant (flăm-boi′ənt) *adj.* given to showy display; flashy (p. 40)
infuriatingly (ĭn-fyo͝or′ē-ā′tĭng-lē) *adv.* in a way that makes one very angry **infuriate** *v.* (p. 49)
quarantine (kwôr′ən-tēn) *n.* a place where a diseased animal is kept away from others (p. 42)
saunter (sôn′tər) *v.* to walk about slowly (p. 47)
stupefying (sto͞o′pə-fī′ĭng) *adj.* stunning **stupefy v.** (p. 46)
submissive (səb-mĭs′ĭv) *adj.* willing to give in to or obey another (p. 40)
vigor (vĭg′ər) *n.* physical or mental strength, energy, or force (p. 47)

Waiting

by Budge Wilson

"You must realize, of course, that Juliette is a very complex child." My mother was talking on the telephone. Shouting, to be more exact. She always spoke on the phone as though the wires had been disconnected, as though she were trying to be heard across the street through an open window. "She's so many-*sided*," she continued. "Being cute, of course, is not enough, although heaven knows she could charm the legs off a table. But you have to have something more than personality."

I was not embarrassed by any of this. Lying on the living room floor on my stomach, I was pretending to read *The Bobbsey Twins at the Seashore*. But after a while I closed the book. Letting her words drop around me, I lay there like a plant enjoying the benefit of a drenching and beneficial rain. My sister sat nearby in the huge wingback chair, legs tucked up under her, reading the funnies.

"I hope you don't regard this as *boasting*, but she really is so very, *very* talented. Bright as a button in school—three prizes, can you believe it, at the last school closing—and an outstanding athlete, even at eight years old."

Resting my head on my folded arms, I smiled quietly. I could see myself eight years from now, receiving my gold medal, while our country's flag rose in front of the Olympic flame. The applause thundered as the flag reached its peak, standing straight out from the pole, firm and strong. As the band broke into a moving rendition of "O Canada," I wept softly. I stood wet and waterlogged from my last race, my tears melding with the chlorine and coursing slowly down my face. People were murmuring, "So young, so small, and so attractive."

"And such a leader!" My mother's voice hammered on. "Even at her age, she seems forever to be president of this and director of that. I feel very blessed indeed to be the mother of such a child." My sister stirred in her chair and coughed slightly, carefully turning a page.

WAITING **39**

Mini-Lesson **Literary Concepts**

REVIEWING PLOT Remind students that plot is the sequence of related events that make up a story. Some of the events in a plot are actions performed by the characters in the story. Explain to students that for the plot to be convincing, the characters' motivations—or the reasons for their actions—must be plausible.

Application Have students work in small groups to create a chart, like the one shown, listing some of the actions of the characters in this story and briefly describing the motivation behind each action. Then have students discuss whether they find the motivations plausible and the plot convincing.

Action	Motivation
Juliette's mother brags about her pride in her daughter's accomplishments	

CUSTOMIZING FOR
Students Acquiring English

- Use **ACCESS FOR STUDENTS ACQUIRING ENGLISH**, *Reading and Writing Support.*
- This story may prove difficult because all the events are told from the point of view of Juliette, who is sometimes an unreliable narrator. Ask students to look, as they read, for instances in which Juliette is not being completely honest.

I Point out that *The Bobbsey Twins* was a popular series of books for young people about the adventures of a large, happy family.

STRATEGIC READING FOR
Less-Proficient Readers

Set a Purpose Invite a volunteer to role-play the mother's conversation in the opening paragraph. Then direct students to read the story to find out why Juliette's mother feels this way about her daughter.

Use **UNIT RESOURCE BOOK**, p. 19, for guidance in reading the selection.

Literary Concept: CHARACTERS

A Have students consider why the story opens with Juliette's mother's comments about her. Guide them to explain what this opening suggests about Juliette's importance in the story. *(Possible response: Opening with these comments about Juliette suggests she is the most important—or main— character.)*

Critical Thinking: SPECULATING

B Have students infer the setting of the story from the details in this passage. *(The story is set in Canada.)*

Challenge students to consider, as they read, the effect the girls' mother has on the girls' relationship. (*Possible response: The mother's obvious favoritism toward Juliette has inflamed the girls' sibling rivalry and made Juliette very self-centered. As a result, Juliette has overlooked her sister's quiet strength and its potential appeal to others.*)

CUSTOMIZING FOR
Multiple Learning Styles

C **Spatial or Graphic Learners** Invite students to draw the newspaper photo of Juliette. Then have students analyze what Juliette's extended arms and open mouth in the picture suggest about her personality. (*Possible response: She is confident, outgoing, and even brash.*)

Critical Thinking:
HYPOTHESIZING

D In this passage, Henrietta is described as looking as if she were "waiting for something." Have students connect this comment with the title of the story and speculate about what Henrietta might be waiting for. (*Possible response: maturity and a chance to assert her own personality*)

Active Reading: CLARIFY

E Guide students to consider the twins' personalities and appearances as they analyze how the girls are different. (*Possible response: Juliette is untidy and flamboyant, with a "mop of wild black curls." Henrietta is quiet and subdued, with "dim beige color" hair.*)

STRATEGIC READING FOR
Less-Proficient Readers

F Have students return to their purpose for reading and discuss Juliette's achievements: class president, drama club manager, actress, singer, and dancer.

Set a Purpose Have students pay special attention, as they read the next section, to the way Juliette treats Henrietta.

It was true. I was president of grade 4 and manager of the Lower Slocum Elementary School Drama Club. I had already starred in two productions, one of them a musical. In an ornate crêpe paper costume composed of giant overlapping yellow petals, I had played Lead Buttercup to a full house. Even Miss Prescott's aggressive piano playing had failed to drown me out, had not prevented me from stealing the show from the Flower Queen. My mother kept the clipping from *The Shelburne Coast Guard* up on the kitchen notice board. It included a blurred newspaper picture of me with extended arms and open mouth. Below it, the caption read, "Juliette Westhaver was the surprise star of the production, with three solos and a most sprightly little dance, performed skillfully and with gusto. Broadway, look out!"

Mama was still talking. "Mm? Oh. Henrietta. Yes, well, she's fine, I guess, just fine. Such a serious, responsible little girl, and so fond of her sister." I looked up at Henrietta, who was surveying me over the top of her comics. There was no expression on her face at all.

But then Henrietta was not often given to expression of any kind. She was my twin, but apart from the accident of our birth, or the coincidence, we had almost nothing in common. It was incredible to me that we had been born to the same parents at almost the same moment, and that we had been reared in the same house.

But Henrietta was my friend and I hers. We were, in fact, best friends, as is so often the case with twins. And as with most close childhood friendships, there was one <u>dominant</u> member, one <u>submissive</u>. There was no doubt in this case as to who played the leading role.

Henrietta even looked submissive. She was thin and pale. She had enormous sky-blue eyes surrounded by a long fringe of totally colorless eyelashes. Her hair was a dim beige color without gradations of light or dark, and it hung straight and lifeless from two barrettes. Her fingers were long and bony, and she kept them folded in her lap, motionless, like a tired old lady. She had a straight little nose and a mouth that seldom smiled—it was serious and still and oddly serene. She often looked as though she were waiting for something.

Untidy and <u>flamboyant</u>, my personality and my person flamed hotly beside her cool <u>apathy</u>. My temper flared, my joys exploded. With fiery red cheeks and a broad snub nose, I grinned and hooted my way through childhood, dragging and pushing Henrietta along as I raced from one adventure to the next. I had a mop of wild black curls that no comb could tame. I was small, compact, sturdy, well-coordinated and extremely healthy. Henrietta had a lot of colds.

CLARIFY

In what ways are Juliette and Henrietta different?

Using a Reading Log

When I start talking about Henrietta and me, I always feel like I'm right back there, a kid again. Sometimes, you know, I got fed up with her. If you have a lot of energy, for instance, it's no fun to go skiing with someone who's got lead in her boots. And for heaven's sake, she kept falling all the time. Scared to death to try the hills, and likely as not going down them on the seat of her pants. "Fraidy-cat! Fraidy-cat!" I'd yell at her from the bottom of the hill where I had landed right-side up, and she would start down the first part of the slope with straight and trembling knees, landing in a snow bank before the hill even got started. There were lots

WORDS TO KNOW	**dominant** (dŏm′ə-nənt) *adj.* ruling or controlling **submissive** (səb-mĭs′ĭv) *adj.* willing to give in to or obey another **flamboyant** (flăm-boi′ənt) *adj.* given to showy display; flashy **apathy** (ăp′ə-thē) *n.* lack of strong feeling or interest

40

Mini-Lesson  **Reading Skills/Strategies**

CONNECTING Remind students that active readers use several strategies to help them understand what they read. One strategy is to find ways to connect what they read with some of their own experiences.

Application Have students think about the relationship between Juliette and Henrietta. Encourage students to compare this relationship with the relationships they have with their own siblings or with sibling relationships they have observed.

Reteaching/Reinforcement
• *Unit One Resource Book,* p. 20

of fields and woods around our town, and good high hills if you were looking for thrills. You could see the sea from the top of some of them, and the wild wind up there made me feel like an explorer, a brave Micmac[1] hunter, the queen of the Maritime Provinces. Sometimes I would let out a yell just for the joy of it all—and there, panting and gasping and falling up the hill would be old Henrietta, complaining, forever complaining, about how tired she was, how cold.

But I guess I really loved Henrietta anyway, slowpoke though she was. I had lots and lots of other friends who were more interesting than she was. But it's a funny thing—she was nearly always my first choice for someone to play with.

There was a small woodlot to the east of the village, on land owned by my father. We called it The Grove. It had little natural paths in it, and there were open spaces under the trees like rooms or houses or castles, or whatever you wanted them to be that day. The grove of trees was on the edge of a cliff overhanging some big rocks, and at high tide the sea down there was never still, even when it was flat oil calm. So it could be a spooky kind of place to play in, too. I loved to go there when it was foggy and play spy. It was 1940 and wartime, and by then we were ten, going on eleven. From The Grove we could sometimes see destroyers, and once even a big aircraft carrier. In the fog, it wasn't hard to believe that the Nazis were coming, and that we were going to be blown to bits any minute.

We never told Mama or Papa about going to the cliff when the mist was thick. Henrietta hardly ever wanted to go on those foggy days. She was afraid of falling off the cliff onto the rocks, sure she would drown in the churned-up water, nervous about the ghostly shapes in the thick gray-white air. But she always went. I used to blackmail her. "If you don't go, I'll tell Mama about the time you pretended to be sick and stayed home from school because you didn't

have your homework done and were scared of Miss Garrison." Or I would just plain order her around. "I'm *going*, Henrietta, so get a move on and *hurry!*" She'd come padding out of the house in her stupid yellow raincoat, so that she wouldn't get a cold in the wet wind, and off we'd go—me fast and complaining about her slowness, and her slow and complaining about my speed. But she'd be there and we'd be together and we'd have fun. I'd be the spy, and she'd be the poor agonized prisoner of war, tied up to a tree by a bunch of Nazis. Sometimes I'd leave her tethered good and long, so she'd look *really* scared instead of pretend scared, while I prowled around and killed Nazis and searched for hidden weapons. Or we'd play Ghost, and I'd be the ghost—floating along on the edge of the cliff and shrieking in my special death shriek that I saved for ghost games. It started out low like a groan and then rose to a wail, ending in a scream so thin and high that it almost scared *me.* Sometimes, if she was especially wet and tired, Henrietta would start to cry, and that *really* made me mad. Even now, I can't stand crybabies. But you had to have a victim, and this was something she was extra good at. No point in wasting my death shriek on a person who wasn't afraid of ghosts. No fun to have the Nazis tying up someone who was big and strong and brave, particularly when the Nazis weren't actually there and you had to think them up and pretend the whole thing.

One time when we went there with a bunch of kids instead of just us two, I forgot all about her being tied to the tree and got nearly home before I raced back the whole half mile to untie her. She never said a word. It was snowing, and there were big fat snowflakes on those long white lashes of hers, and her eyes looked like they were going to pop right out of her head.

---

1. **Micmac:** a Native American people inhabiting Nova Scotia and other provinces of Canada.

Mini-Lesson   **Grammar**

VERB TENSES: CHOOSING THE RIGHT VERB Certain pairs of verbs can cause confusion. These pairs include *let* and *leave*, *lie* and *lay*, and *sit* and *set*. Explain the following rules:

let means "to allow" or "to permit"
leave means "to depart" or "to allow to stay or be"

lie means "to recline"
lay means "to put or place something"

sit means "to rest"
set means "to put something"

Application Have students write four sentences about the story using *let* or *leave*, four using *lie* or

lay, and four using *sit* or *set*. They may use the present or past form of the verb or the past participle.

	lie, lay, lain
present	Juliette *lies* on the living room floor.
past	Henrietta *lay* in bed.
past participle	Their cat has *lain* there all day.

	lay, laid, laid
present	Henrietta *lays* the book down.
past	She *laid* it near the big rock.
past participle	The stage manager *has laid* a towel over the branches.

Reteaching/Reinforcement
• *Grammar Mini-Lessons* copymasters p. 29, transparencies p. 21

 The Writer's Craft

Choosing the Right Verb, pp. 482–484

Linking to Math

K Explain to students that in 1942, when the story takes place, a 64-page comic book cost 10 cents. In 1995 a 64-page comic book cost $3.50. Invite students to calculate the percentage of the price increase, using the following proportion:

$$\frac{\text{Increase in price}}{\text{Original price}} \times 100\% = \frac{\%\ \text{of price}}{\text{increase}}$$

(3400%)

Active Reading: QUESTION

L Students might say that Henrietta wanted to seem brave and strong or that she knew it would do no good to tell on Juliette, her mother's favorite. Have the class explore what Henrietta's silence reveals about her character. *(Possible response: Henrietta is stronger and smarter than Juliette realizes.)*

Literary Concept: PLOT

M Henrietta has created a beautiful, workable set. This event prompts Juliette to disparage her sister in public. Ask students why Juliette minimizes Henrietta's artistic talent. *(Possible responses: Juliette is jealous of her sister's achievements; she wants to reassert her own superiority and make Henrietta feel unsure of herself.)*

CUSTOMIZING FOR
Students Acquiring English

2 You may want to point out to students how these two sentences are an example of Juliette's unreliability as a narrator.

STRATEGIC READING FOR
Less-Proficient Readers

N Have students return to their purpose for reading and discuss Juliette's treatment of her sister.

• Who is in charge of the summer plays? *(Juliette)* **Noting Relevant Details**

• What is Henrietta's role in these plays? *(She is in charge of costumes and set design.)* **Summarizing**

Set a Purpose Have students read on to discover how Henrietta treats Juliette in the next part of the story.

K I said I was real sorry, and next week I even bought her a couple of comic books out of my own allowance money, when she was home sick with bronchitis. Mama said she should have had the sense to wear a scarf and a warm hat, being as she was so prone to colds, and that's certainly true. She never told on me, and I don't know why. She sat up against the pillows and colored in her coloring book or read her funnies, or more often she just lay there on the bed, her hands lying limp on the quilt, with that patient, quiet, waiting look of hers.

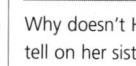

L Why doesn't Henrietta tell on her sister?
Using a Reading Log

When the spring came, a gang of us would always start going out to The Grove on weekends to start practicing for our summer play. Year after year we did this, and it had nothing to do with those school plays in which I made such a hit. We'd all talk about what stories we liked, and then we'd pick one of them and make a play out of it. I would usually select the play because I was always the one who directed it, so it was only fair that I'd get to do the choosing. If there was a king or a queen, I'd usually be the queen. If you're the director, you can't be something like a page or a minor fairy, because then you don't seem important enough to be giving out instructions and bossing people around, and the kids maybe won't pay attention to all the orders. Besides, as my mother pointed out, I was smart and could learn my lines fast, and you couldn't expect some slow dummy to memorize all that stuff.

Henrietta's voice was so soft and quiet that no one could ever hear her unless they were almost sitting on her lap; so of course it would have been stupid to give her a part. She couldn't even be the king's horse or the queen's milk-white mule because she was so darn scrawny. You can't have the lead animal looking as though it should be picked up by the Humane Society and put in quarantine. But she was really useful to the production, and it must have been very satisfying for her. She got to find all the costume parts and rigged up the stage in the biggest cleared space among the trees, making it look like a ballroom or a throne room or whatever else we needed. She did a truly good job, and if it weren't for the fact that I can't stand conceited people, I probably would even have told her so. I liked Henrietta the way she was. I didn't want her strutting around looking proud of herself and putting on airs. One time one of the kids said, "Hey, Henrietta, that's a really great royal bedroom you made," and right away she started standing and moving around in a way that showed she thought she was a pretty smart stage manager.

I hate that kind of thing, and I knew the others wouldn't like it either. So I said, "Oh, sure! And the king must have just lost his kingdom in the wars. Who ever heard of a king sleeping on a pile of branches or having an old torn dishtowel at the window? Some king!" And everyone laughed. I always think that laughter is very important. It makes everyone happy right away and is a good way to ease tensions.

We had a lot of fun practicing for those plays. No one went away for the summer. No one needed to. The sea was right there alongside the village, with a big sandy beach only a quarter mile away. Some of the fishermen let us use their smaller flats for jigging,[2] and we could always swim or dig for clams or collect mussels. Besides, the war was on; people weren't spending money on cottages or trips. Seems to me that everyone just stuck around home and saved paper and counted their ration stamps and

---

2. **jigging:** boating.

WORDS TO KNOW   **quarantine** (kwôr′ən-tēn′) *n.* a place where a diseased animal is kept away from others

42

Mini-Lesson   **The Writer's Style**

ELABORATION Discuss with students how writers use sensory details to help their readers imagine or visualize characters, scenes, or events in a plot. Remind students that sensory details show how something looks, sounds, smells, tastes, or feels. Point out specific passages in which Wilson uses sensory details, such as the following, which are highlighted on this page:
• "Henrietta's voice was so soft and quiet" (sound)
• "the queen's milk-white mule" (sight)
• "sleeping on a pile of branches" (touch)

Application Encourage students to make a chart with the following headings: Sight, Sound, Smell, Taste, and Touch. Under each heading, students should list some sensory details from the story. Then invite students to write a paragraph that uses sensory details to retell an event in the plot.

Reteaching/Reinforcement
• Writing Handbook, anthology p. 819
• *Writing Mini-Lessons* transparencies, pp. 34 and 38

The Writer's Craft

Sensory Details, p. 255

Staithes, Yorkshire (about 1900), Dame Laura Knight. Copyright © Dame Laura Knight, reproduced by permission of Curtis Brown Group Ltd., London.

listened to the news on the radio. There was a navy base nearby, and sometimes sailors came to dinner. They'd tell us about life on the base and all the dangers they were expecting and hoping to experience when they started sailing to Europe. I envied them like anything and couldn't for the life of me see why you had to be eighteen before you joined the navy, or why they wouldn't let girls run the ships or use the guns. Henrietta said she didn't want to be a sailor anyway, because she'd be too scared, which of course is only what you'd expect. Apart from that, there wasn't much excitement. So the play practices were our main entertainment during those years. In the summer, we practiced on most fine days, and in August we put on the play in front of all our mothers and fathers and uncles and aunts, and for the sisters and brothers too young to take part.

The play we put on in 1942 was about a rich nobleman called Alphonse who falls in love with an exquisitely beautiful but humble country girl called Genevieve. I played the part of Genevieve, and it was the nicest part I had ever played. In the last scene, Genevieve and the nobleman become engaged, and she gets to dress up in a very gorgeous gown for a big court ball. I had a real dress for this scene, instead of the usual pieced-together scraps of material dug out of old trunks from our attics. My mother let me use one of her long dance dresses from when she was young. It was covered with sequins and even had some sort of fluffy feather stuff around the hem; and it was pale sapphire blue and very romantic looking. I had trouble getting into it because I was almost thirteen now and sort of big through the middle. But my mother put in a new zipper instead of the buttons, and I was able to wear it after all. I had to move a little carefully and not take very deep breaths, but I was as tall as Mama now, and I felt like a real woman, a true beauty. The neck was kind of low, but I was pretty flat, so I didn't need to worry about being indecent in front of Harold Boutilier, who played the part of Alphonse. Mama put a whole lot of makeup on me, covering up the pimples I was starting to get, and I thought I looked like a movie star, a genuine leading lady. The zipper wasn't put into the dress in time for the dress rehearsal, but Harold wore a big bow at his neck and his mother's velvet shorty coat, with a galvanized chain around his waist that shone like real silver. He had on his sister's black stockings and a pair of high rubber boots, and he looked very handsome. Up until this year he had just seemed like an okay boy to me, as boys go, but this summer I'd spent a lot of time watching him and thinking about him when I went to bed at night. I guess I had a big crush

WAITING **43**

Art Note

Staithes, Yorkshire by Dame Laura Knight *Staithes, Yorkshire* is a painting of an English fishing village by Laura Knight (1877–1970), one of the leading artists of the 20th century. The towering cliff and wide ocean contrast with the sheltered little village.

Reading the Art *What details in this picture suggest that the village is safe and comfortable? Do you think Juliette pictures her village this way? Why or why not?*

Linking to History

O Explain that for civilians during World War II, items that were needed for the war effort, such as butter, eggs, meat, sugar, leather, aluminum, and gasoline, were in short supply. These items were allocated to civilians through a system of rationing. Using money and ration stamps, civilians were allowed to purchase only limited quantities of these items.

Literary Concept:
MAIN CHARACTER

P Guide students to explain what Juliette's comments about the war in this passage reveal about her character. *(Possible responses: She is adventurous and brave; she has a romantic view of war.)*

Active Reading: EVALUATE

Q Have students evaluate Juliette's image of herself as "a movie star." How does her real appearance contrast with the way she imagines herself? *(Possible response: Despite a flat chest, a wide middle, and pimples, Juliette imagines herself to be a glamorous movie star.)*

M i n i - L e s s o n **S t u d y   S k i l l s**

SQ3R Explain to students that they can use a method called SQ3R—Survey, Question, Read, Review, and Recite—to help them understand and retain information such as that found in reference books. Trace these steps in the process:

Survey Skim the title, first and last paragraphs, graphics, and subheadings. Make predictions about the reading.

Question Turn the title and subheadings into questions.

Read Read, revising your predictions as you go along.

Review Summarize at key points in the reading; focus on the main ideas.

Recite Highlight the title, headings, and key passages. Outline the material or tell someone else about it.

Application Have students use the SQ3R process as they do research for the social studies project on growing up during World War II (p. 51). Later, invite students to explain what they found most helpful about the process. Encourage students to use this study method when doing other research projects.

R If necessary, have students review Juliette's comments on page 43 about wearing the dress. Students should see that the dress makes Juliette feel glamorous, like a movie star or a genuine leading lady.

Critical Thinking:
HYPOTHESIZING

S Point out the sentences "If any of us needed anything, she [Henrietta] could get it for us" and "He [the nobleman] is of course looking for a wife, but no one even thinks of her as a possible candidate." Invite students to hypothesize about what these lines might foreshadow in the story. *(Possible response: Someone will need something and Henrietta will get it; a boy will fall in love with Henrietta, whom no one thinks is attractive.)*

CUSTOMIZING FOR
Multiple Learning Styles

T **Musical Learners** Students adept at rhythm and sound may enjoy creating music and sound effects for Juliette's play. Invite students to share these effects with the class as a volunteer reads this part of the story aloud.

Literary Concept:
MAIN CHARACTER

U Guide students to reread this passage and then to explain what it reveals about Juliette. *(Possible response: With the exception of her sister—whom she judges harshly—Juliette looks at things romantically rather than realistically.)*

---

on him. And I was pretty sure that when he saw me in that blue dress, he'd have a crush on me right away, too.

CLARIFY

R How does Juliette feel about wearing one of her mother's dresses?
Using a Reading Log

On the day of the play, all our families started arriving at The Grove theater a full hour before we got started. It didn't rain, and there wasn't even one of those noisy Nova Scotian winds that shake the trees and keep you from hearing the lines. My mother was hustling around backstage helping with clothes and makeup. Mostly she was fussing with my face and my first costume and telling me how pretty I looked. We had rigged up eight bedspreads, some torn and holey, some beautiful, depending on the fear or the pride of the mothers who lent them; and behind this strung-out curtain, we prepared ourselves for the two o'clock production. Henrietta was moving quietly about on the stage, straightening furniture, moving props, standing back to look at the effect. Later on, just before the curtain went up, or rather was drawn aside, she went off and sat down against a tree, where she'd have a good view of the performance, but where she'd be out of

S sight. If any of us needed anything, she could get it for us without the audience seeing what she was doing.

*I*n the first part of the play, the nobleman ignores the beautiful peasant girl, who comes on dressed in rags but heavily made up and therefore beautiful. He is of course looking for a wife, but no one even thinks of her as a possible candidate. She does a lot of sighing and weeping, and Alphonse rides around on his horse (George Cruikshank) looking handsome and tragic. Harold did this very well. Still, I could hardly wait for the last scene, in which I could get out of those rags and emerge as the

radiant court butterfly. But I put all I had into this first scene, because when Alphonse turns down all the eligible and less beautiful women of the land and retires to a corner of the stage to brood (with George Cruikshank standing nearby, munching grass), Genevieve arrives on the scene to a roll of drums (our wooden spoon on Mrs. Eisner's pickling kettle). As Alphonse turns to look at her dazzling beauty, he recognizes her for what she is—not just a poor commoner, but a young woman of great charm and loveliness, worthy of his hand. At this point, she places her hand on her breast and does a deep and graceful curtsy. He stands up, bends to help her rise, and in a tender and significant gesture kisses her outstretched hand.

And that's exactly how we did it, right there on the foxberry patch, which looked like a rich green carpet with a red pattern, if you happened to have the kind of imagination to see it that way. I thought I would faint with the beauty of it all. Then the string of bedspreads was drawn across the scene, curtain hoops squeaking, and the applauding audience awaited the final scene.

I didn't waste any time getting into my other costume. Dressed in my blue gown, I peeked through the hole in Mrs. Powell's bedspread to assess the audience. I had not had time to look until now, but Mama had dressed me first, and she had six other girls to get ready for the ball scene. The crowd outside was large. There must have been forty-five or fifty people of various sizes and ages sitting on the cushions placed on top of the pine needles. The little kids were crawling and squirming around like they always do, and mothers were passing out pacifiers and bags of chips and jelly beans and suckers to keep them quiet during intermission. One little boy—Janet Morash's brother—was crying his head off, and I sure as fire hoped he'd stop all that racket before the curtain went up. While I watched all this, I

44 UNIT ONE   PART 1: OPENING DOORS

Mini-Lesson   Genre Study

FICTION Draw on the chalkboard the chart shown on the right, and use it to show the class that a **short story** is a kind of fiction with the following attributes:

- It usually can be read in a single sitting.
- It focuses on one or two main characters.
- The characters deal with a problem or conflict.

Application Have students copy the chart in their notebooks and fill it in with relevant details from "Waiting" and other short stories they have read.

Short Story	"Waiting"
read in one sitting	
one or two characters	
single problem or single conflict	

Illustration by Meg Kelleher Aubrey.

Mini-Lesson   Interviewing

ORAL HISTORY Tell students that one way to learn about life in another time or place—such as Nova Scotia during World War II—is to interview someone who has a story to tell about his or her past and then to write the interview as an oral history. Direct students to plan questions that will elicit more than yes or no answers. Possible questions include these:

• What were the greatest challenges you faced?
• What experiences stand out most in your memory?

Tell students to tape-record the interview, transcribe it, and then write it as an oral history, using the subject's own words as much as possible.

Application Have students interview someone who grew up during World War II. Tell students to write the interview as an oral history and to use it as part of their research for the social studies project on page 51.

Literary Concept:
MAIN CHARACTER

V Ask students to consider what they can infer about Juliette from her reaction to the presence of the sailors and 12th-grade boys at the play. *(Possible response: Juliette seems thrilled that she will have an opportunity to perform before a larger audience than usual. She seems exuberant, confident, and self-centered, especially when she uses the phrase "my big scene.")*

Literary Concept: IRONY

W Remind students that irony is a contrast between what is expected and what actually exists or happens. Point out that Juliette is convinced that her sister is going to make a fool of herself if she wears makeup with casual clothing. Have students explain the irony here. *(It is Juliette, not Henrietta, who might be making a fool of herself with her tight gown and unrealistic expectations.)*

Linking to History

X Explain that a gramophone is a phonograph, or record player. In 1877 Thomas Alva Edison invented the phonograph, which reproduced sound on paraffin-soaked strips of paper, using a steel stylus. In 1888 Emile Berliner introduced the first phonograph record; four years later, he developed the master disc. Before that, musicians had had to repeat a performance for each copy of a recording. In 1948 the first plastic long-playing record was sold. Videodiscs, combining pictures and sound, were first sold in 1981; the first compact disc (CD) was sold in 1983.

CUSTOMIZING FOR
Students Acquiring English

3 Make sure that students understand the difference between these two uses of the verb *burst* (the first metaphorical, the second literal).

Active Reading: PREDICT

Y Urge students to think about what they have learned about Juliette and the other characters in the story and to use this information to make their predictions. Students could predict that Juliette's mother will come to her rescue or that Juliette will dash off the stage crying.

V looked over to the left and saw three sailors coming through the woods. I knew them. They'd been to our house for supper a couple of times, but I never dreamt we'd be lucky enough to have the navy at our play. My big scene was going to be witnessed by more than just a bunch of parents and kids. There was even a little group of grade 12 boys in the back row.

We were almost ready to begin. Backstage, most of the makeup was done, and Mrs. Elliot was standing by the tree, making up Henrietta just for the heck of it. Henrietta had set up the stage and handed out the costumes, and she was putting in time like some of the rest of us. She just had on that old blue sweatshirt of hers and her dungarees, and it seemed to me that all **W** that makeup was going to look pretty silly on someone who didn't have a costume on; but I didn't really care. If Henrietta wanted to make a fool of herself, it wasn't going to bother *me*.

In the last scene, all the courtiers and aristocrats are milling around in the ballroom, waiting for the nobleman to arrive with his betrothed. The orchestra is playing Strauss waltzes (on Mrs. Corkum's portable wind-up **X** gramophone), and you can see that everyone is itchy footed and dying to dance, but they have to wait around until Alphonse arrives with Genevieve. It is a moment full of suspense, and I had to do a lot of smart and fierce directing to get that bunch of kids to look happy and excited and impatient all at the same time. But they did a really good job that afternoon. You could see that they thought they actually *were* lords and ladies and that it was a real live ball they had come to.

Suddenly there is a sound of trumpets (little Horace Miller's Halloween horn), and Alphonse comes in, very slowly and stately, with Genevieve on his arm. She is shy and enters

with downcast eyes; but he turns around, bows to her, and she raises her head with new pride and confidence, lifting her arms to join him in the dance. We did all this beautifully, if I do say so myself, and as I started to raise my arms, I thought I would burst with the joy and splendor of that moment.

As it turned out, burst is just about exactly what I did. The waltz record was turned off during this intense scene, and there was total silence on the stage and in the audience. As my arms reached shoulder level, a sudden sound of ripping taffeta reached clear to the back of the audience. (Joannie Sherman was sitting in the last row, and she told me about it later.) I knew in one awful, <u>stupefying</u> moment that my dress had ripped up the back, the full length of that long zipper. I can remember standing there on the stage with my arms half raised, unable to think or feel anything beyond a paralyzed horror. After that day, whenever I heard that someone was in a state of shock, I never had to ask the meaning of that term. I knew. Joannie told me later that the whole stageful of people looked like they had been turned to stone and that it really had been a scream to see.

PREDICT

What will happen to Juliette now that her dress has ripped?
Using a Reading Log

Suddenly, as quiet and quick as a cat, Henrietta glided onstage. She was draped in one of the classier bedspreads from the curtain, and no one would have known that she wasn't supposed to be there. I don't know how anyone as slow-moving as Henrietta could have done so much fast thinking. But she did. She was carrying the very best bedspread—a lovely blue woven one that exactly matched my dress. She stopped in

| WORDS TO KNOW | **stupefying** (stoo'pə-fī'ĭng) *adj.* stunning **stupefy** *v.* |

46

Mini-Lesson: Speaking,  Listening, and Viewing

DRAMA PERFORMANCE Discuss with students Juliette's preparation for her performance as Genevieve in the play. Provide students with these guidelines for preparing for a dramatic performance:
1. Study the script so you understand the plot, the theme of the play, and any emotional messages.
2. Select the gestures, mannerisms, and actions that reveal the character.
3. Use a voice that reflects the character.
4. Stay in character. Once the play begins, all your actions must suit the character, not your own personality.

Application Arrange students in small groups to perform the last scene of Juliette's play, following the guidelines provided for the first of the Alternative Activities on page 51. Students should first create a script—imagining the dialogue between the different characters, based on details provided in the story—and then should select a director and cast the roles. Allow students time to memorize their lines and rehearse. Have the groups perform their plays for the rest of the class.

front of me, and lifting the spread with what I have to admit was a lot of ceremony and grace, she placed it gravely over my shoulders. Fastening it carefully with one of the large safety pins that she always kept attached to her sweatshirt during performances, she then moved backward two paces and bowed first to me and then to Harold before moving slowly and with great dignity toward the exit.

Emerging from my shock with the kind of presence of mind for which I was noted, I raised my arms and prepared to start the dance with Alphonse. But Harold, eyes full of amazement, was staring at Henrietta as she floated off the stage. From the back of the audience, I could hear two long, low whistles, followed by a deep male voice exclaiming, "Hubba, *hubba!*" to which I turned and bowed in graceful acknowledgement of what I felt to be a vulgar but nonetheless sincere tribute. The low voice, not familiar to me, spoke again. "Not *you*, pie-face!" he called, and then I saw three or four of the big boys from grade 12 leave the audience and run into the woods.

Somehow or other I got through that scene. Harold pulled his enchanted eyes back onstage, and the gramophone started the first few bars of "The Blue Danube" as we began to dance. Mercifully, the scene was short, and before long we were taking our curtain calls. "Stage manager! Stage manager!" shouted one of the sailors, and after a brief pause, old Henrietta came shyly forward, bedspread gone, dressed once more in her familiar blue sweatshirt and dungarees. The applause from the audience went on and on, and as we all bowed and curtsied, I stole a look at Henrietta. Slender, I thought, throat tight. Slender, not skinny anymore. All in an instant I saw everything, right in the midst of all that clapping and

bowing. It was like one of those long complicated dreams that start and finish within the space of five minutes, just before you wake up in the morning. Henrietta was standing serenely, quietly. As the clapping continued, while the actors and actresses feverishly bobbed up and down to acknowledge the applause, she just once, ever so slightly, inclined her head, gazing at the audience out of her astonishing eyes— enormous, <u>arresting</u>, fringed now with long dark lashes. Mrs. Elliot's makeup job had made us all see what must have been there all the time—a strikingly beautiful face. But there was something else there now that was new. As I continued to bow and smile, the word came to me to describe that strange new thing. *Power.* Henrietta had power. And what's more, she had it without having to *do* a single thing. All she needs to do, I thought, is *be.* The terrible injustice of it all stabbed me. There I was, the lead role, the director, the brains and <u>vigor</u> of our twinship, and suddenly, after all my years in first place, it was she who had the power. Afterwards I looked at them—the boys, the sailors, *Harold*—as they gazed at her. All she was doing was <u>sauntering</u> around the stage picking up props. But they were watching, and I knew, with a stunning accuracy, that there would always be watchers now, wherever she might be, whatever she wore, regardless of what she would be doing. And I also knew in that moment, with the same sureness, that I would never have that kind of power, not ever.

The next day, Mama stationed herself at the telephone, receiving all the tributes that came pouring in. A few moments per call were given over to a brief recognition of my acting talents and to an uneasy amusement over the split dress. The rest of the time was spent in shouted

WORDS	**arresting** (ə-rĕs′tĭng) *adj.* striking
TO	**vigor** (vĭg′ər) *n.* physical or mental strength, energy, or force
KNOW	**saunter** (sôn′tər) *v.* to walk about slowly

47

↓ **BB**

Multicultural Perspectives

EARLY USES OF MAKEUP Students may be interested to know that makeup has been traced back to 3500 B.C., when women in Egypt and Mesopotamia used henna dyes to color their feet and hands. Women also used an eye shadow called kohl—made from lead and charcoal—because it was believed to ward off danger. Around 50 B.C., Cleopatra, queen of Egypt, painted her upper eye-lids with kohl and rouged her cheeks with red ocher.

The use of makeup created a need for makeup remover. In A.D. 200, Galen, a Greek physician, recommended a makeup remover that consisted of water, beeswax, and olive oil. Today, cold cream, which is one type of makeup remover, is made from virtually the same ingredients.

Two Girls on a Cliff by Dame Laura Knight Painted in 1917, this picture captures the quiet peace of the seashore and the serene pleasure of contemplation. This work stands in sharp contrast to the artist's later pictures, which are vigorous renderings of the life of the theater, ballet, and circus.

Reading the Art *Do you think the title "Waiting" would fit this picture? Explain your reasons.*

Critical Thinking: ANALYZING

 Invite students to explain the irony in this passage. If necessary, have students reread the opening page of the story. *(Possible response: When the story opened, Juliette was listening to her mother brag about her. Now she unhappily listens to her mother brag about her sister. This is a reversal of Juliette's expectations.)*

Active Reading: EVALUATE

Invite students to evaluate whether Juliette's mother is being honest when she states that she recognized Henrietta's potential all along. *(Possible response: There is no indication that Juliette's mother had this degree of perception. In fact, she seemed so taken with Juliette's accomplishments that she practically ignored Henrietta.)*

Two Girls on a Cliff (about 1917), Dame Laura Knight. Oil on canvas, 23½″ × 28½″, courtesy of Sotheby's. Copyright © Dame Laura Knight, reproduced by permission of Curtis Brown Group Ltd., London.

discussion of Henrietta's startling and surprising beauty. I lay face downward on my bed and let the words hail down upon me. "Yes, indeed. *Yes.* I quite agree. Simply beautiful. And a real bolt from the blue. She quite astonished all of us. Although of course I recognized this quality in her all along. I've often sat and contemplated her lovely eyes, her milky skin, her delicate hands, and thought, 'Your time will come, my dear! Your time will come!' "

"Delicate hands!" I whispered fiercely into the mattress. "Bony! Bony!"

I suppose, in a way, that nothing changed too drastically for me after that play. I continued to lead groups, direct shows, spark activities with my ideas, my zeal. In school I did well in all my subjects and was good at sports, too. Henrietta's grades were mediocre, and she never even tried out for teams or anything, while I was on the swim team, the

---

Assessment **Option**

INFORMAL ASSESSMENT   You can informally assess how well students understood the story by having them write a letter from one of the main characters to the other. Writing as Juliette, students can explain how they feel about Henrietta's new-found "power" and the change in their relationship; writing as Henrietta, they can describe how they feel about the past and the new relationship.

Rubric

3 Full Accomplishment   Students accurately describe and analyze the characters and their

relationship. They maintain a consistent point of view and use events from the plot to back up their conclusions.

2 Substantial Accomplishment   Students understand the characters' previous and current relationship but do not provide enough details to back up their assertions.

1 Little or Partial Accomplishment   Students are unable to describe the characters' relationship. The point of view is inconsistent, and there are few details.

baseball team, the basketball team. She still moved slowly, languidly, as though her energy was in short supply, but there was a subtle difference in her that was hard to put your finger on. It wasn't as though she went around covered with all that highly flattering greasepaint that Mrs. Elliot had supplied. In fact, she didn't really start wearing makeup until she was fifteen or sixteen. Apparently she didn't need to. That one dramatic walk-on part with the blanket and the safety pin had done it all, although I'm sure I harbored a hope that we might return to the old Henrietta as soon as she washed her face. Even the sailors started coming to the house more often. They couldn't take her out, of course, or *do* anything with her. But they seemed to enjoy just looking at her, contemplating her. They would sit there on our big brown plush chesterfield under the stern picture of Great-great-grandmother Logan in the big gold frame, smoking cigarette after cigarette and watching Henrietta as she moved about with her <u>infuriatingly</u> slow, lazy grace, her grave confidence. Her serenity soothed and excited them, all at the same time. Boys from grades 9 and 10 hung around our backyard, our verandah, the nearest street corner. They weren't mean to me. They simply didn't know I was there, not really.

I didn't spend much time with Henrietta anymore, or boss her, or make her go to The Grove in the fog or try to scare her. I just wasn't all that crazy about having her around the entire time, with those eyes looking out at me from under those long lashes, quiet, mysterious, full of power. And of course you had to trip over boys if you so much as wanted to ask her what time it was. Every once in a while I'd try to figure out what the

thing was that made her so different now; and then, one day, all of a sudden, I understood. We were down at the beach, and she was just sitting on a rock or something, arms slack and resting on her knees, in a position I had often seen over the years. And in that moment I knew. Everything else was the same—the drab white skin; the bony, yes, bony hands; the limp hair. But she had lost her waiting look. Henrietta didn't look as though she were waiting for anything at all anymore. ❖

LITERARY INSIGHT

from *Song of Myself*
by Walt Whitman

I exist as I am, that is enough,
If no other in the world be aware
   I sit content,
And if each and all be aware I sit
   content.

One world is aware and by far the
   largest to me, and that is myself,
And whether I come to my own to-day
   or in ten thousand or ten million
   years,
I can cheerfully take it now, or with
   equal cheerfulness I can wait.

WORDS TO KNOW
infuriatingly (ĭn-fyŏŏr′ē-ā′tĭng-lē) *adv.* in a way that makes one very angry **infuriate** *v.*

49

Literary Concept: PLOT

FF Remind students that the plot of a story may suggest a theme, or a message about life or human nature. Encourage them to explain the message about life suggested by the change in Henrietta. *(Possible response: Power comes from a sense of self-assurance.)*

COMPREHENSION CHECK

1. What is the relationship between Juliette and Henrietta? *(They are twin sisters.)*
2. Before the summer play, which girl bosses the other around? *(Juliette)*
3. What happens to Juliette's costume during the play? *(It rips up the back.)*
4. What does Juliette realize about Henrietta? *(She realizes Henrietta is beautiful and has power over boys. She also realizes she won't be able to boss Henrietta around anymore.)*

INSIGHT

1. How would you explain what the speaker of the poem is waiting for? *(Possible response: The speaker is waiting to come into his own.)*
2. What words would you use to describe the speaker? *(Possible response: cheerful, poised, serene, and confident)*
3. How would you compare the speaker in the poem with Henrietta? *(Possible response: Both are content with themselves. Henrietta has stopped waiting; the speaker still waits and does so cheerfully.)*

WALT WHITMAN

Walt Whitman (1819–1892) is considered America's first modern poet. "Song of Myself," a poem of 52 groups of long lines, was the outstanding section of his masterpiece, *Leaves of Grass*, a work that Whitman first published in 1855 and revised throughout his lifetime.

Mini-Lesson   Spelling

WORDS ENDING IN *-ANCE/-ANT* Explain to students that an adjective that derives from a noun ending in *-ance* or *-ancy* ends in *-ant* rather than *-ent*. Provide these examples:

noun	adjective
dominance	**dominant**
flamboyance	**flamboyant**

Application Have students complete the chart by writing the correct spelling of the adjective that is formed from each noun.

noun	adjective
1. abundance	
2. defiance	
3. fragrance	
4. hesitance	
5. ignorance	

Urge students to look for more nouns and adjectives that fit this pattern and to add them to their personal word lists.

Reteaching/Reinforcement
• *Unit One Resource Book*, p. 21

1. Accept all reasonable responses.
2. Possible response: Henrietta becomes the dominant twin; Juliette becomes aware of her sister's beauty, self-assurance, and appeal to boys. Henrietta seems to have come into her own.
3. Possible responses: Some students may say that Henrietta loves her sister and wants to save her from embarrassment. Others may say that Henrietta wants to show her sister that now she is the superior one.
4. Some students may favor Juliette as a friend because she is imaginative and energetic; others may favor Henrietta because she is quiet, serene, and self-assured.
5. Guide students to support their views with specific examples from the story and from their own experiences with their friends.
6. Possible responses: Parental attention is limited, so some children think they have to compete with their brothers and sisters to win their share; parents sometimes foster competition by favoring one child over another or by comparing their children in an attempt to spur them to greater achievement.

Another Pathway

Encourage students to work with partners to make sure they have captured Henrietta's voice and her view of events. Partners should take turns reading their retellings aloud to help clarify the meaning and strengthen the diction.

Rubric

3 Full Accomplishment Students retell an event from Henrietta's point of view in a clear and consistent manner.

2 Substantial Accomplishment Students adequately retell an event from Henrietta's point of view and do so in a somewhat consistent manner.

1 Little or Partial Accomplishment Students have difficulty retelling an event and do not reflect Henrietta's perspective consistently.

RESPONDING OPTIONS

FROM PERSONAL RESPONSE TO CRITICAL ANALYSIS

REFLECT
1. What are your impressions of Henrietta and Juliette at the end of the story?

RETHINK
2. How would you explain the changes in the relationship between Henrietta and Juliette after the play?
Consider

Close Textual Reading
- what happens during the play
- Juliette's perceptions of herself and Henrietta
- Juliette's recognition of her sister's power
- Juliette's statement that Henrietta has "lost her waiting look"

3. Why do you think Henrietta comes to Juliette's rescue after Juliette rips her dress?

4. Which of the twins would you prefer as a friend, and why?
Consider
- the contrasts between Juliette and Henrietta listed on your diagram
- the qualities that you value in a friend

5. In a close childhood friendship, according to Juliette, one person leads and the other follows. Do you agree or disagree with her view of friendship? Use examples from your discussion on the Previewing page and from your own experiences to support your opinion.

RELATE
6. *Sibling rivalry* is a term that describes strong feelings of competition among children in the same family. Why do you think some brothers and sisters need to compete against one another?

Multimodal Learning
ANOTHER PATHWAY

Think about how Henrietta might have viewed herself, her sister, and the events in the story. Choose one event from the story, such as the play at The Grove, and retell it from Henrietta's point of view. Share your version with the class and compare it with Juliette's version.

QUICKWRITES

1. How would you turn this story into a pilot show for a new television series? Write **character sketches** for Juliette and Henrietta. Refer to the diagram you created for the Reading Connection on page 37.

2. Write a **journal entry** that Henrietta might create to express what the Insight poem on page 49 means to her.

3. Budge Wilson has written about her reasons for writing "Waiting": "I have often been interested in bullies—adult bullies as well as ones who are children. Why do they behave the way they do?" Write a **letter** to Budge Wilson, stating your ideas on this matter.

PORTFOLIO Save your writing. You may want to use it later as a springboard to a piece for your portfolio.

QuickWrites

1. Remind students to include information about each character based on the character's appearance and behavior and on what other characters say about her. You can also remind students what they learned from the mini-lesson on the writer's style (p. 42).
2. Guide students to select a specific point in the story to use as a basis for Henrietta's

interpretation of the poem. Remind students that Henrietta's sense of self changes as she matures and as the story reaches its climax.
3. Encourage students to include in their letters specific examples from the story and from their own experiences.

The Writer's Craft

Character Sketch, pp. 54–61
Letter Forms, p. 669

LITERARY CONCEPTS

Characters are the people, animals, or imaginary creatures that take part in the action of a story. Usually, a short story centers on events in the life of one person, animal, or creature, known as the **main character.** A writer develops a character by presenting the character's thoughts, words, and actions. A writer may also provide physical descriptions of characters. How does Budge Wilson develop Juliette in this story?

ART CONNECTION

Look at the reproduction of a water color illustration by Meg Kelleher Aubrey on page 38. How would you compare your impressions of the girl in this illustration with your impressions of Henrietta?

Detail of illustration by Meg Kelleher Aubrey.

THE WRITER'S STYLE

Early in the story, Juliette compares her mother's words of praise for her to rain watering a plant: "Letting her words drop around me, I lay there like a plant enjoying the benefit of a drenching rain." Find another comparison that Juliette uses in the story. What does each comparison reveal about Juliette?

ALTERNATIVE ACTIVITIES

1. Perform the last scene of the **play,** showing Henrietta's rescue of Juliette. The costumes, props, and music used in the scene should reflect the details presented in the story.

2. Draw or paint **portraits** of Juliette and Henrietta. Try to capture their contrasting appearances and personalities. Display your pictures in class.

ACROSS THE CURRICULUM

 **Social Studies** With a small group, research what it was like for people growing up in the United States or in Canada during World War II. You may want to consult reference books, listen to music of the era, or interview grandparents or other adults who recall the early 1940s. Using pictures, maps, mementos, and tape recordings, create a **multimedia presentation** for the class.

Art Connection

Guide students to compare specific colors, shapes, and lines in the art with specific descriptions of Henrietta in the text.

Across the Curriculum

Social Studies *Cooperative Learning* Group members can divide up the reference materials, with each student checking one source. In addition, you may wish to have students assume specific roles, such as facilitator and fact checker, to help them practice the social skills they need for effective group work.

ADDITIONAL SUGGESTION

Social Studies Juliette imagines that she is "a brave Micmac hunter, the queen of the Maritime Provinces." Native Americans, among them the Micmacs, represent a rich and diverse cultural heritage. They include more than 350 individual tribes, such as the Inuit of the far north and the native Hawaiians. Have students find out about the original native people who lived in their state or area. Students should find out what kinds of homes they had, how they governed themselves, and what some of their beliefs were.

SOCIAL STUDIES CONNECTION The Home Front—World War II During World War II, many American mothers, children, and grandparents kept the home fires burning while the soldiers were away. These historical images give students a glimpse into this time in our history and will help them research what life was like for those who remained stateside during the war.

Side A, Frame 49222

The Writer's Style

Invite students to show their comparisons in the form of a chart. On the left, students should write the first comparison and what it reveals about Juliette. On the right, students should jot down another comparison (e.g., "I . . . let the words hail down upon me") and what it says about Juliette. Also encourage students to identify the figure of speech in each comparison. See The Writer's Craft pages 314–315.

Alternative Activities

1. Help students draw on their specific learning styles: spatial learners, for example, might want to create the costumes; interpersonal learners can be the directors; and intrapersonal learners can draft the script. See also the directions for a drama performance in the mini-lesson on page 46.

2. Encourage students to comb the text for details about each girl's appearance and personality. Students should use these details as they plan their portraits.

Literary Concepts

Possible responses: Wilson develops Juliette by presenting her own thoughts, words, and actions and the reactions of others to her. Students should cite specific examples of each technique, such as the boy's shout "Not *you,* pie-face!" which reveals that the boy views Juliette as unattractive.

Sample responses:

1. Elton John is flamboyant because he wears flashy costumes.
2. The person could be found on an athletic field, engaged in a strenuous activity such as running.
3. No, because submissive people are too willing to give in to be good leaders.
4. Elizabeth Taylor has arresting eyes because they are a striking violet color.
5. Someone might saunter because it is too hot to walk quickly.
6. The animal might have a disease that could be passed on to other animals.
7. A terrible dance recital could have a stupefying effect, with the audience stunned by how bad the performance was.
8. No, because he or she would be uninterested in football events.
9. The coach might yell rude remarks at his players, at the other coach or team, or at the fans.
10. The dominant member would be the leader, the person taking charge.

Reteaching/Reinforcement

• *Unit One Resource Book*, Vocabulary SkillBuilder, p. 22

BUDGE WILSON

Born in Halifax, Nova Scotia, in 1927, Budge Wilson began her college education at the University of King's College (1945–1946) and earned her bachelor's degree in 1949 from Dalhousie University. She then studied at the University of Toronto for two years. Immediately after completing her graduate work, Wilson taught English and art for a year before moving on to jobs as a staff artist, librarian, freelance editor, journalist, photographer, and fitness instructor.

SOCIAL STUDIES CONNECTION
The Home Front—World War II
During World War II, many American mothers, children, and grandparents kept the home fires burning while the soldiers were away. These historical images give students a glimpse into this time in our history and will help them research what life was like for those who remained stateside during the war.

Side A, Frame 49222

WORDS TO KNOW

Write an answer for each question.

1. Name an entertainer whom you would describe as **flamboyant** and explain your choice.
2. Where might someone who is full of **vigor** be found?
3. Would a **submissive** person make a good leader? Why or why not?
4. Name a television or movie star with **arresting** eyes. What makes them so?
5. Why might someone choose to **saunter** through a park?
6. Why might an animal have to be put into **quarantine?**
7. Give an example of an event that might have a **stupefying** effect on an audience.
8. Would someone who shows **apathy** toward football make a good cheerleader? Why or why not?
9. Describe a coach who acts **infuriatingly** during a championship game?
10. How might you recognize the **dominant** member of a group of friends?

BUDGE (MARJORIE) WILSON

1927–

Although Budge Wilson wanted to be a writer ever since she was a child, she did not actually begin writing for publication until the age of fifty. "It may seem odd for someone my age to be writing for and about children," she said. "But I remember my own youth very vividly, and I've watched my own children and their friends grow up. . . . I don't find it very hard to enter the head and heart of a fictional person who is much younger than I am."

Wilson, who makes her home in Nova Scotia, Canada, where she grew up, sets many of her stories in that province. These stories reflect her deep curiosity about people and her observations of them. For example, in the short story "Waiting," she explores her curiosity about sisters and brothers:

why some are good friends and others almost seem to hate one another; why some are aggressive and others are passive. Her fiction for young adults has won several awards. For example, *The Leaving*, a collection of short stories that includes "Waiting," won the Canadian Library Association's Young Adult Book Award for 1991.

Budge Wilson has found that she loves writing more than any other thing that she has tried. As she puts it, "A person who loves to write is never lonely; within his or her own head, a writer always has a safe and very interesting place to go."

OTHER WORKS "My Cousin Clarette," "The Metaphor," "Mr. Manuel Jenkins," *Breakdown*

Extended Reading

LASERLINKS
• *SOCIAL STUDIES CONNECTION*

52 UNIT ONE   PART 1: OPENING DOORS

WHAT DO YOU THINK?

Reflecting on Theme

Have students recall the survey they created before they began reading the selections in Part 1 (page 12). Ask students to compare their thoughts now about having a brother or a sister with their thoughts then. If their thoughts are different now, invite them to create a new graph to reflect the change.

FOCUS ON NONFICTION

Whereas some readers enjoy getting lost in the imaginary world of fiction, others prefer the authenticity of stories from real life. **Nonfiction** is writing about real people, places, and events.

There are two broad categories of nonfiction. One category, called **informative nonfiction,** mainly provides factual information. Nonfiction of this type includes science and history books, encyclopedias, pamphlets, and most of the articles in magazines and newspapers.

The other category of nonfiction is called **literary nonfiction** because it is written to be read and experienced in much the same way as fiction. However, literary nonfiction differs from fiction in that real people take the place of fictional characters, and the settings and plots are not imagined but are actual places and true events.

The types of literary nonfiction you will read in this book are **autobiographies, biographies,** and **essays.**

AUTOBIOGRAPHY An **autobiography** is the true story of a person's life, told by that person. It is almost always written from the first-person point of view. In this book, you will read excerpts from several autobiographies. In each, the author focuses on a significant event in his or her life.

An autobiography is usually book length because it covers a long period of the writer's life. However, there are shorter types of autobiographical writing, such as **journals, diaries,** and **memoirs.**

BIOGRAPHY A **biography** is the true story of a person's life, told by someone else. The writer, or **biographer,** interviews the subject if possible and also researches the person's life by reading letters, books, diaries, and other sources of information. A short biography of Eleanor Roosevelt is included in this book.

As you will see, biographies and autobiographies may seem like fiction because they contain some of the same elements, such as character, setting, and plot.

Teaching Strategies:
CATEGORIES OF NONFICTION

Autobiography Read the description of autobiography to the class. Then explain that *auto* means "self," *bio* means "life," and *graphy* means "writing." Ask volunteers to explain how they can use these word parts to explain the term and remember its meaning. You may wish to have students list several other words that contain one of these word parts.

Biography Have a volunteer read this paragraph to the class. Then on the chalkboard make a web showing the characteristics of biography, as in the example below.

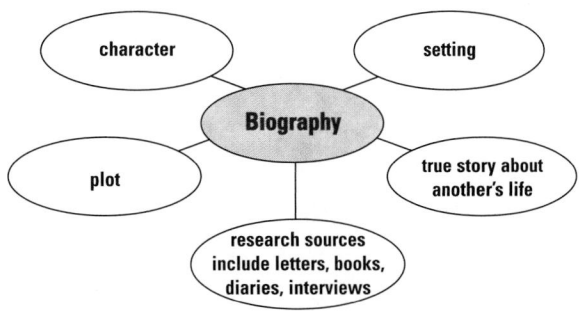

Students can copy this web into their notebooks and refer to it when reading biographies, such as the one about Eleanor Roosevelt.

Reading Strategies: MODELING

Invite volunteers to read aloud the Strategies for Reading Nonfiction. Tell students to use these strategies as they read the excerpt from *Immigrant Kids* on page 55 and other nonfiction selections in this book. Then model how to apply the strategies. You may wish to use the model provided or create your own.

- **Preview** *"I can tell from the photographs and opening sentences that this is a true story."*

- **Figure out the organization** *"The organization seems to be chronological. The events are presented in the order in which they occur."*

- **Separate facts and opinions** *"This essay presents a lot of facts, especially names, dates, statistics. The writer does express the opinion that the ordeal the immigrants went through was worth it."*

- **Predict** *"I predict that the essay will end with information about immigration today."*

- **Build** *"My father came to America from Germany, but I didn't know about Ellis Island and the rigorous examinations that the immigrants were subjected to."*

- **Evaluate** *"The immigrants had a very difficult time coming to America. I have great respect for their determination."*

ESSAY An **essay** is a short piece of nonfiction that deals with one subject. Essays often appear in newspapers and magazines. The writer of an essay might share an opinion, try to entertain or persuade the reader, or simply describe an incident that has special significance. Essays that explain how the author feels about a subject are called **informal**, or **personal**, **essays**. In this book, the selection "Homeless" is an example of an informal essay. **Formal essays** are serious and scholarly and are rarely found in literature textbooks.

STRATEGIES FOR READING NONFICTION

Nonfiction can be read as literature or as a source of information. The nonfiction you will read in this book has been included because of its literary merit.

Use the following strategies when you read nonfiction:

- **Preview** a selection before you read. Look at the title, the pictures or diagrams, and any subtitles or terms in boldface or italic type. All of these will give you an idea of what the selection is about.

- **Figure out the organization** If the work is a biography or an autobiography, the organization is probably chronological—that is, events are presented in the order in which they happened. Other selections may be organized around ideas the author wants to discuss. Understanding the organization can help you predict what will come next.

- **Separate facts and opinions** **Facts** are statements that can be proved, such as "This book contains several excerpts from autobiographies." **Opinions** are statements that cannot be proved. They simply express a person's beliefs, such as "*Boy* is the best autobiography in this book." Writers of nonfiction sometimes present opinions as if they were facts. Be sure you recognize the difference.

- **Question** as you read. Why did things happen the way they did? How did people feel? What is the writer's opinion? Do you share the writer's opinion, or do you have different views on the subject?

- During your reading, stop now and then and try to **predict** what will come next. Sometimes you will be surprised by what happens or by what an author has to say about an issue.

- As you read, **build** on your understanding. Add new information to what you have already learned, and see if your ideas and opinions change.

- Continually **evaluate** what you read. Evaluation should be an ongoing process, not just something that you do after reading a selection. Remember, too, that evaluation involves more than saying that a selection is good or bad. Form opinions about the people, events, and ideas that are presented. Decide whether or not you like the way the piece was written.

Finally, it is important to recognize that your understanding of a selection does not end when you stop reading. As you think more about what you have read and discuss it with others, you will find that your understanding continues to grow.

PREVIEWING

NONFICTION

from Immigrant Kids
Russell Freedman

PERSONAL CONNECTION Activating Prior Knowledge

What do you know about the experience of immigrating to the United States? Have you, members of your family, friends or acquaintances been through this experience? What was it like? In small groups, discuss what you know about immigration.

Building Background

HISTORICAL CONNECTION

The United States is called a nation of immigrants because most Americans' ancestors came here from other countries. Of course, Native Americans were here long before everyone else, and not everyone who came to these shores came willingly, particularly the millions of Africans who were shipped to America as slaves. The immigrants who came here voluntarily from Europe began to arrive in increasing numbers during the 1800s, and their numbers rose sharply around the turn of the century. In 1892, Ellis Island in New York Harbor became the reception center for arriving immigrants and remained so until it closed in 1943.

Poster at Ellis Island.
Photo by Karen Yamauchi for Chermayeff & Geismar Inc./MetaForm Inc.

Active Reading

READING CONNECTION

Setting Purpose for Reading With your classmates, record what you already know about immigration in the left-hand column of a chart like the one below. Then, in the middle column, list any questions whose answers you would like to find in the selection. After you read the selection, use the third column to record what you learned. Setting a Purpose

Immigration		
What We Know	**What We Want to Learn**	**What We Learned**

LASERLINKS
• HISTORICAL CONNECTION 55

OVERVIEW

Objectives

- To understand and appreciate informative nonfiction that describes the arrival of immigrants to the United States
- To understand how to set a purpose for reading
- To identify a writer's use of primary and secondary sources
- To express understanding of the selection through a choice of writing forms, including journal entries and a pro or con statement
- To extend understanding of the selection through a variety of multimodal and cross-curricular activities

Skills

READING SKILLS/ STRATEGIES
- Setting a purpose for reading

GRAMMAR
- Plural and possessive nouns

LITERARY CONCEPTS
- Informative nonfiction
- Conflict

GENRE STUDY
- Nonfiction: informative nonfiction

SPELLING
- Prefixes and base words

SPEAKING, LISTENING, AND VIEWING
- Oral report

Cross-Curricular Connections

HISTORY
- Statue of Liberty

MATH
- Percents
- Making a bar graph or pie chart

SOCIAL STUDIES
- Mapping immigration

HISTORICAL CONNECTION
European Immigrants In these vintage Ellis Island images, students will be able to see European immigrants arriving in the United States. The images may lead to a discussion about the differences between the voluntary migration of Europeans to this country during the late 1800s and the forced relocations, at various times, of Native American and African peoples.

Side A, Frame 49231

PRINT AND MEDIA RESOURCES

UNIT ONE RESOURCE BOOK
Strategic Reading: Literature, p. 25
Vocabulary SkillBuilder, p. 28
Reading SkillBuilder, p. 26
Spelling SkillBuilder, p. 27

GRAMMAR MINI–LESSONS
Transparencies, pp. 8–9
Copymasters, pp. 10–11

ACCESS FOR STUDENTS ACQUIRING ENGLISH
Selection Summaries
Reading and Writing Support

FORMAL ASSESSMENT
Selection Test, pp. 11–12
 Test Generator

 AUDIO LIBRARY
See Reference Card

LASERLINKS
Historical Connection

INTERNET RESOURCES
McDougal Littell Literature Center at http://www.hmco.com /mcdougal/lit

SUMMARY

Russell Freedman describes the hardships that European immigrants faced while sailing to the United States between 1880 and 1920. He includes an excerpt from an autobiography by Edward Corsi, who immigrated to the United States in 1907, at age ten, and later became U.S. Commissioner of Immigration. Freedman explains how officials at Ellis Island interviewed and examined immigrants and how, because of physical or mental illnesses, some immigrants were not allowed into the country. Angelo Pellegrini, who also immigrated to the United States as a child, recounts his family's experience at Ellis Island. Freedman points out that today, as in earlier times, immigrants must endure hardships as they seek to better their lives.

Thematic Link: *Opening Doors* Coming to the United States at the turn of the century opened doors to many educational, social, and economic opportunities for immigrants.

CUSTOMIZING FOR

Students Acquiring English

- Use **ACCESS FOR STUDENTS ACQUIRING ENGLISH,** *Reading and Writing Support.*

- Many students acquiring English will be able to relate to the immigrants' experiences described in this selection. If applicable, ask them to compare and contrast their own experiences with those of the immigrants.

- As you guide students through the selection, you may want to use the suggestions under Strategic Reading for Less-Proficient Readers as well as the suggestions in these boxes.

STRATEGIC READING FOR

Less-Proficient Readers

Set a Purpose Introduce students to the selection by having them describe how they would feel if they were immigrating, or moving, to another country. Then invite students to read the selection to find out if their feelings match those of the people described therein.

Use **UNIT ONE RESOURCE BOOK,** p. 25, for guidance in reading the selection.

from
IMMIGRANT KIDS

by Russell Freedman

A

In the years around the turn of the century, immigration to America reached an all-time high. Between 1880 and 1920, 23 million immigrants arrived in the United States. They came mainly from the countries of Europe, especially from

Italian girl at Ellis Island, 1926. Lewis W. Hine. Lewis W. Hine collection; United States History, Local History, and Genealogy Division; The New York Public Library; Astor, Lenox, and Tilden Foundations.

The luggage of Irish immigrants sits on the dock at Ellis Island. Brown Brothers.

56   UNIT ONE   PART 1:OPENING DOORS

WORDS TO KNOW

din (dĭn) *n.* a loud, confused mixture of noises (p. 57)

fervent (fûr′vənt) *adj.* having or expressing great warmth or depth of feeling (p. 57)

impoverished (ĭm-pŏv′ər-ĭsht) *adj.* poor (p. 57)

indomitable (ĭn-dŏm′ĭ-tə-bəl) *adj.* unconquerable (p. 60)

teeming (tē′mĭng) *adj.* full of people or things (p. 60)

impoverished towns and villages in southern and eastern Europe. The one thing they had in common was a <u>fervent</u> belief that in America, life would be better.

Most of these immigrants were poor. Somehow they managed to scrape together enough money to pay for their passage to America. Many immigrant families arrived penniless. Others had to make the journey in stages. Often the father came first, found work, and sent for his family later.

Immigrants usually crossed the Atlantic as steerage passengers. Reached by steep, slippery stairways, the steerage lay deep down in the hold of the ship. It was occupied by passengers paying the lowest fare.

Men, women, and children were packed into dark, foul-smelling compartments. They slept in narrow bunks stacked three high. They had no showers, no lounges, and no dining rooms. Food served from huge kettles was dished into dinner pails provided by the steamship company. Because steerage conditions were crowded and uncomfortable, passengers spent as much time as possible up on deck.

The voyage was an ordeal, but it was worth it. They were on their way to America.

The great majority of immigrants landed in New York City, at America's busiest port. They never forgot their first glimpse of the Statue of Liberty.

Edward Corsi, who later became United States Commissioner of Immigration, was a ten-year-old Italian immigrant when he sailed into New York harbor in 1907:

My first impressions of the New World will always remain etched in my memory, particularly that hazy October morning when I first saw Ellis Island. The steamer *Florida,* fourteen days out of Naples, filled to capacity with 1,600 natives of Italy, had weathered one of the worst storms in our captain's memory; and glad we were, both children and grown-ups, to leave the open sea and come at last through the Narrows into the Bay.

───◆◆◆───

Giuseppe and I held tightly to Stepfather's hands, while Liberta and Helvetia clung to Mother.

───◆◆◆───

My mother, my stepfather, my brother Giuseppe, and my two sisters, Liberta and Helvetia, all of us together, happy that we had come through the storm safely, clustered on the foredeck for fear of separation and looked with wonder on this miraculous land of our dreams.

Giuseppe and I held tightly to Stepfather's hands, while Liberta and Helvetia clung to Mother. Passengers all about us were crowding against the rail. Jabbered conversation, sharp cries, laughs and cheers—a steadily rising <u>din</u> filled the air. Mothers and fathers lifted up babies so that they too could see, off to the left, the Statue of Liberty. . . . **D**

Finally the *Florida* veered to the left, turning northward into the Hudson River, and now the incredible buildings of lower Manhattan came very close to us.

The officers of the ship . . . went striding up and down the decks shouting orders and directions and driving the immigrants before them. Scowling and gesturing, they pushed

WORDS TO KNOW	**impoverished** (ĭm-pŏv′ər-ĭsht) *adj.* poor
	fervent (fûr′vənt) *adj.* having or expressing great warmth or depth of feeling
	din (dĭn) *n.* a loud, confused mixture of noises

57

Multiple Learning Styles

E **Interpersonal Learners** Invite students to work in groups of four or five to conduct mock interviews with immigrants to the United States. One student should pose as the examiner, and the others should be the immigrants. Guide students to draw on their organizational and communication skills in role-playing these interviews.

Active Reading: CLARIFY

F Explore with students why the government examined people at Ellis Island. Ask why Ellis Island was known by immigrants as "Heartbreak Island." *(Immigrants who did not pass the exams at Ellis Island were not allowed to enter the country. This caused great heartbreak and anguish.)*

STRATEGIC READING FOR

Less-Proficient Readers

G Explore with students how their feelings about immigrating compare with the feelings of the immigrants described here.

• What is Ellis Island? *(the nation's chief immigrant processing center)* **Noting Relevant Details**

• What happened at Ellis Island? *(The immigrants were questioned and examined; only those who passed the exams were admitted to the United States.)* **Summarizing**

Set a Purpose Have students read on to find out how immigrants felt about the examinations at Ellis Island.

Literary Concept:
INFORMATIVE NONFICTION

H Point out the pictures on these pages. Then have students explain where they think the pictures might have come from. *(Possible response: They were taken by immigrants or their families, by immigration officials, or by newspaper or magazine photographers.)*

---

and pulled the passengers, herding us into separate groups as though we were animals. A few moments later we came to our dock, and the long journey was over.

But the journey was not yet over. Before they could be admitted to the United States, immigrants had to pass **E** through Ellis Island, which became the nation's chief immigrant processing center in 1892. There they would be questioned and examined. Those who could not pass all the exams would be detained; some would be sent back to Europe. And so their arrival in America was filled with great anxiety. Among the immigrants, Ellis Island was known as "Heartbreak Island."

When their ship docked at a Hudson River pier, the immigrants had numbered identity tags pinned to their clothing. Then they were herded onto special ferryboats that carried them to Ellis Island. Officials hurried them along, shouting "Quick! Run! Hurry!" in half a dozen languages.

Filing into an enormous inspection hall, the immigrants formed long lines separated by

A mother and her children arrive at Ellis Island. Brown Brothers.

58 UNIT ONE   PART 1: OPENING DOORS

Mini-Lesson  Literary Concepts

REVIEWING CONFLICT Remind students that conflict is a struggle between two opposing forces. In an external conflict, a character struggles against some outside person or force. Internal conflict occurs when the struggle is within a character's own mind. Discuss examples of internal and external conflicts in the selections that students have already read.

Application Have students decide whether Mrs. Pellegrini's trying to convince the immigration officials that her daughter should be allowed to enter the country is an internal or an external conflict (page 60). *(external)*

Jewish war orphans arriving from eastern Europe, 1921. American Jewish Joint Distribution Committee, Inc., New York.

I Be sure students understand that immigrants were examined and labeled in order to screen out the ones officials believed would be unable to make a living. Have students debate who should be allowed to immigrate to the United States today, and why. (*Some students will argue that since everyone deserves a chance at a better life, everyone should be allowed to immigrate; others will say that only those who have a sound mind and body and who can support themselves should be allowed to immigrate.*)

Linking to Math

J Point out to students that one immigrant out of every five or six was detained for additional examinations. Remind students that between 1880 and 1920, 23 million immigrants came to the United States. Then have students calculate how many immigrants were detained at Ellis Island. (*1 out of 5 is 20%, or 4,600,000 people; 1 out of 6 is 16.67%, or 3,834,100 people. Thus, between 3,834,100 and 4,600,000 people were detained.*)

Literary Concept: CONFLICT

K Review what students learned about conflict in the mini-lesson on page 58. Then have them tell whether they think the conflict in this passage is internal or external. (*Some students may say the conflict is external because the clerks were getting the immigrants flustered with their questions; others may say the conflict is internal because the immigrants were getting flustered in their own minds.*)

STRATEGIC READING FOR
Less-Proficient Readers

L Discuss the terror that the immigrants felt during the examinations. Explore how some people got so flustered, or upset, that they could not speak.

- What did the first doctor look for? (*physical and mental abnormalities*) **Noting Relevant Details**

- What did the second doctor watch for? (*contagious and infectious diseases*) **Noting Relevant Details**

Set a Purpose Direct students to read on to discover where today's immigrants come from.

---

iron railings that made the hall look like a great maze.

Now the examinations began. First the immigrants were examined by two doctors of the United States Health Service. One doctor looked for physical and mental abnormalities. When a case aroused suspicion, the immigrant received a chalk mark on the right shoulder for further inspection: L for lameness, H for heart, X for mental defects, and so on.

The second doctor watched for contagious and infectious diseases. He looked especially for infections of the scalp and at the eyelids for symptoms of trachoma, a blinding disease. Since trachoma caused more than half of all medical detentions, this doctor was greatly feared. He stood directly in the immigrant's path. With a swift movement, he would grab the immigrant's eyelid, pull it up, and peer beneath it. If all was well, the immigrant was passed on.

Those who failed to get past both doctors had to undergo a more thorough medical exam. The others moved on to the registration clerk, who questioned them with the aid of an interpreter: What is your name? Your nationality? Your occupation? Can you read and write? Have you ever been in prison? How much money do you have with you? Where are you going?

⟫◆⟪

About one immigrant out of every five or six was detained for additional examinations or questioning.

⟫◆⟪

Some immigrants were so flustered that they could not answer. They were allowed to sit and rest and try again.

About one immigrant out of every five or six was detained for additional examinations or questioning.

The writer Angelo Pellegrini has recalled his own family's detention at Ellis Island:

We lived there for three days—Mother

 Mini-Lesson / **Grammar**

PLURAL AND POSSESSIVE NOUNS

Remind students that plural nouns (*girls, islands, cats*) name more than one person, place, thing, or idea and that possessive nouns (*girl's, island's, cat's*) show who or what owns something. Then review the rules for forming plural nouns and possessive nouns.

Application Have students find at least five plural nouns and five possessive nouns in the excerpt from *Immigrant Kids*. Students can record the nouns on a chart like the one shown.

Reteaching/Reinforcement
- Grammar Handbook, anthology pp. 858–859
- *Grammar Mini-Lessons* copymasters pp. 10–11, transparencies pp. 8–9

 **The Writer's Craft**

Possessive Nouns, p. 420

Plural Nouns	Possessive Nouns
years	America's
immigrants	captain's
villages	Stepfather's
States	nation's

M Ask students what this incident reveals about Angelo Pellegrini's mother and many other immigrants. You can use this think-aloud to model the thinking process:

Think-Aloud Model The Pellegrinis would have had to turn back if their child wasn't allowed in. Mrs. Pellegrini must have been really resourceful and brave to make the officials understand that her daughter wasn't ill. This story helps me realize that many immigrants had to be very strong and determined to settle in our country.

STRATEGIC READING FOR
Less-Proficient Readers

N Point out that today many immigrants come to the United States from Asia and Africa. Summarizing

Reading Skills/Strategies:
SETTING A PURPOSE

O Have students follow up on the purpose they set before reading by returning to the chart they began in the Reading Connection (page 55). Invite them to review the last column, which by now should contain answers that the selection provided to their questions about immigration.

INSIGHT

1. How has immigration changed since the Native American migration? (*Possible responses: Methods of travel vary; numbers of people are regulated; origins of immigrants vary; laws affecting immigration have been established.*)

2. Why do you think the early immigrants developed into different groups with different ways of life? (*because the groups were spread so far apart*)

COMPREHENSION CHECK

1. When was immigration at an all-time high? (*at around the turn of the century*)

2. Where did most immigrants enter the country? (*Ellis Island, New York*)

3. Why did people immigrate to the United States? (*They were seeking a better life for themselves and their children.*)

---

and we five children, the youngest of whom was three years old. Because of the rigorous physical examination that we had to submit to, particularly of the eyes, there was this terrible anxiety that one of us might be rejected. And if one of us was, what would the rest of the family do? My sister was indeed momentarily rejected; she had been so ill and had cried so much that her eyes were absolutely bloodshot, and Mother was told, "Well, we can't let her in." But fortunately, Mother was an <u>indomitable</u> spirit and finally made them understand that if her child had a few hours' rest and a little bite to eat she would be all right. In the end we did get through.

Most immigrants passed through Ellis Island in about one day. Carrying all their worldly possessions, they left the examination hall and waited on the dock for the ferry that would take them to Manhattan, a mile away. Some of them still faced long journeys overland before they reached their final destination. Others would head directly for the <u>teeming</u> immigrant neighborhoods of New York City. . . .

Immigrants still come to America. Since World War II, more than 8 million immigrants have entered the country. While this is a small number compared to the mass migrations at the turn of the century, the United States continues to admit more immigrants than any other nation.

Many of today's immigrants come from countries within the Western Hemisphere, and from Asia and Africa as well as Europe. When they reach the United States, they face many of the same problems and hardships that have always confronted newcomers. And they come here for the same reason that immigrants have always come: to seek a better life for themselves and their children. ❖

M (margin marker)

HISTORICAL INSIGHT

NATIVE AMERICAN MIGRATION

People have been coming to North America from other countries for thousands of years, but do you know who the very first people were? America's first inhabitants, the Native Americans, were actually descendants of Asian migrants who traveled from Siberia to Alaska across the Bering land bridge. Though the bridge is now under water, it was exposed from around 33,000 B.C. to 10,000 B.C. During that time, glaciers covered much of the Northern Hemisphere. So much water turned into ice that the level of the ocean dropped, exposing 50 miles of land between Asia and North America.

Animals wandered across the land bridge in search of food, and hunters often followed them. Over the next several thousand years, both people and animals continued to migrate south to the warmer forests and grasslands of North and Central America. By 9000 B.C., some tribes had migrated all the way to the southern tip of South America. Over time they developed into different groups with distinctive ways of life. By the time Columbus arrived in the New World, more than 700 tribes lived in North America alone—each with its own language, customs, and system of government.

WORDS TO KNOW

indomitable (ĭn-dŏm′ĭ-tə-bəl) *adj.* unconquerable
teeming (tē′mĭng) *adj.* full of people or things **teem** *v.*

60

Mini-Lesson **Spelling**

PREFIXES AND BASE WORDS Explain that the prefixes -im and -in both mean "not." You can use the following chart to help students form new words with prefixes and base words. Point out that sometimes the form of a word changes when a prefix is added, as shown in the second example.

Base	Prefix	New Word
mature *(adj.)*	-im	immature *(adj.)*
dominate *(v.)*	-in	indomitable *(adj.)*

Application Have students write the new word that is formed when the prefix -in or -im is added to each of the following base words:

1. in + flexible
2. in + decent
3. in + conceivable
4. in + complete
5. im + modest
6. im + moderate
7. im + mobile
8. im + possibility

Remind students to look for other words that fit this pattern and to add them to their personal word lists.

Reteaching/Reinforcement
• *Unit One Resource Book*, p. 27

RESPONDING
O P T I O N S

FROM PERSONAL RESPONSE TO CRITICAL ANALYSIS

REFLECT

1. What are your reactions to the immigrants' experiences? Record your thoughts in your notebook.

RETHINK

2. Which of the hardships that immigrants face seem most difficult to you?
   Consider   Close Textual Reading
   • the voyage across the sea
   • the procedures at Ellis Island
   • the challenges after immigration

3. Do you think the immigration procedures at Ellis Island were justified? Why or why not?

4. Compare the immigrants in this selection with the "immigrants" described in the Historical Insight on page 60.

RELATE

5. Review the chart you created for the Reading Connection on page 55. Do you have any questions that the selection didn't answer? Discuss them with your classmates.

6. Many immigrants to the United States today come from Mexico, Central America, Asia, and the Caribbean. How do you think their experiences compare with earlier immigrants' experiences?

Multimodal Learning
ANOTHER PATHWAY

Working with a partner, write a letter that an immigrant might send to his or her relatives in the "old country." Describe the voyage, the passage through Ellis Island, and new challenges in America. Share the letter with the entire class.

QUICKWRITES

1. Do you think immigrant parents and children had similar or different thoughts on their voyage across the Atlantic? Write two **journal entries,** one from an immigrant child's perspective and another from his or her parents'.

2. Should anyone who wants to immigrate to the United States be allowed to do so? Write a **pro or con statement** on this question. Include your reasons.

   📁 **PORTFOLIO** Save your writing. You may want to use it later as a springboard to a piece for your portfolio.

LITERARY CONCEPTS

Informative nonfiction is written mainly to provide factual information about real people, places, and events. Writers of nonfiction often use both primary and secondary sources. **Primary sources** are original, firsthand accounts or information. **Secondary sources** are descriptions based on primary sources.

In this selection, Freedman includes primary sources in the form of letters or diary entries written by immigrants. Why do you think he included these primary sources? What do you learn that you couldn't learn any other way?

IMMIGRANT KIDS   **61**

Students should support responses to these open-ended questions with information from the selection.

1. Accept all reasonable responses.

2. Some students may say that the procedures at Ellis Island were most difficult because families had risked everything to come to the United States and might have had to turn back if even one member was sick. Other students might argue that the challenges the immigrants faced after they left Ellis Island were most difficult because they were living in a country where they did not speak the language or know the customs.

3. Students who think the procedures were justified could argue that immigrants should be able to support themselves. Students who don't agree could argue that Americans have a moral responsibility to help those less fortunate than themselves and that immigrants add immeasurably to American life.

4. Possible responses: They were different, because the Native Americans traveled by land, whereas the other immigrants traveled by sea; they were the same, because they all came seeking a better life.

5. Accept all reasonable responses.

6. Possible response: Today's immigrants have an easier time because they know a lot more about the United States before they come here, thanks to TV, radio, and newspapers.

Another Pathway

Cooperative Learning Before partners write their letters, have them brainstorm. Guide partners to cooperate in recording their ideas on a web, a chart, or some other prewriting graphic. They also should cooperate in writing and revising: one student should do the actual drafting, the other the revising. Partners should edit and proofread the letter together.

Literary Concepts

Arrange students in pairs or small groups to respond to the questions in their books. Then have them complete a chart, like the one shown, to help them consider the advantages and disadvantages of using primary sources.

Using Primary Sources	
Advantages	**Disadvantages**
firsthand accounts	hard to read
accurate observations	hard to get
real experiences	

QuickWrites

1. Help students recall what they learned about point of view, and guide them to use the first-person point of view in their journal entries. Also help students "show, not tell" by using elaboration techniques in their writing where appropriate.

2. Encourage students to use primary and secondary sources. Primary sources can include interviews with immigrants or U.S. residents; secondary sources can include newspaper and magazine articles and editorials.

 **The Writer's Craft**

Supporting Opinions, pp. 144–151

These lines suggest a positive, welcoming attitude toward immigrants coming to the United States.

Words to Know

1. fervent   4. impoverished
2. indomitable   5. din
3. teeming

Reteaching/Reinforcement
•*Unit One Resource Book*, p. 28

Across the Curriculum

Social Studies *Cooperative Learning*
Have students work in groups of three or four to complete their research and make their maps. Students can divide the task by selecting different European countries and routes to research. For example, one student can see which routes Germans used; another student can discover how the Irish traveled. Students may be most interested in researching the routes that their ancestors used.

ADDITIONAL SUGGESTION

Math *Make a Bar Graph or Pie Chart* Along with their maps, students may want to include information about how many people came to the United States from each country. Students can present their findings in a pie chart or bar graph.

RUSSELL FREEDMAN

Russell Freedman is one of the most highly respected writers of nonfiction for children. He has published more than 30 books, including *Lincoln: A Photobiography*, which was awarded the Newbery Medal in 1988. In *Immigrant Kids*, which was published in 1980, Freedman set out to tell what life was like for the children of the immigrants. The book proved a pivotal point in Freedman's career, as he turned from writing books about nature and animals to works about people.

Multimodal Learning

ALTERNATIVE ACTIVITIES

1. Interview an immigrant to the United States. Ask questions such as the following: Why did you come to this country? Where did you come from? What were your expectations of the United States? Write a transcript of the interview and then draw a **sketch** of the person interviewed.

2. Create a **family tree** showing your ancestry, or give an oral report and display family pictures and heirlooms.

LITERARY LINKS

The following lines from Emma Lazarus's poem "The New Colossus" are inscribed on the base of the Statue of Liberty:

> Give me your tired, your poor,
> Your huddled masses yearning to breathe free,
> The wretched refuse of your teeming shore.
> Send these, the homeless, tempest-tost to me,
> I lift my lamp beside the golden door!

What do these lines suggest about the attitude of the United States toward immigrants at the time the poem was written?

WORDS TO KNOW

Review the Words to Know at the bottom of the selection pages. Write the words that best complete the following paragraph.

    Immigrants often had a ____, or burning, desire to begin a new life in America. The decision to move to a new country took ____ strength of spirit. The voyage was difficult. The crowded ships were ____ with people who were leaving ____ countries for the opportunities offered by the New World. After arriving on Ellis Island, the immigrants had to listen to officers shouting directions above the ____ of many people speaking various languages. Once the immigrants passed through Ellis Island, the doors to a new life would open.

Multimodal Learning
ACROSS THE CURRICULUM

Social Studies In this selection, Freedman writes about the wave of immigration between 1880 and 1920. This wave brought 23 million people to the United States—the largest number of all time. Research the routes these immigrants took and then sketch a **map** that shows their countries of origin and their destinations.

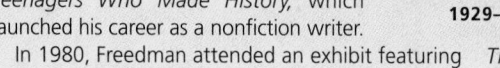

RUSSELL FREEDMAN

1929–

Even as a young boy, Russell Freedman wanted to be a writer. His first job was as a reporter. "That's where I really learned to write," he says. "I learned to organize my thoughts, respect facts, and meet deadlines." A newspaper article about a 16-year-old blind boy who invented a Braille typewriter inspired his first book, *Teenagers Who Made History*, which launched his career as a nonfiction writer.

    In 1980, Freedman attended an exhibit featuring photos of children in 19th- and early 20th-century America. He was deeply moved by the faces of the children and told the story behind the pictures in *Immigrant Kids*. "Like every writer," Freedman says, "a nonfiction writer is essentially a story-teller. Whatever my subject, I always feel that I have a story to tell that is worth telling."

OTHER WORKS *Lincoln: A Photobiography, The Wright Brothers: How They Invented the Airplane, Franklin Delano Roosevelt* Extended Reading

62   UNIT ONE   PART 1: OPENING DOORS

Alternative Activities

1. Students can tape-record or videotape their interviews to create an oral history, which can become part of a classroom exhibit. Remind students to be sure to get their subject's permission before they tape-record or videotape the interview.

2. Students uncomfortable with this activity (such as foster and adopted children) can create a family crest instead. The crest should include items that represent the student's family, such as a baseball for athletic ability.

PREVIEWING

NONFICTION

from The Autobiography of Malcolm X
Malcolm X with Alex Haley

PERSONAL CONNECTION

You are about to read an excerpt from the autobiography of the African-American leader Malcolm X. On the web shown here, Malcolm X's life has been divided into four parts. Brainstorm with your classmates to see what you and your classmates already know about each of these parts of Malcolm X's life. As you read, see if any of your ideas change. Setting a Purpose

Activating Prior Knowledge

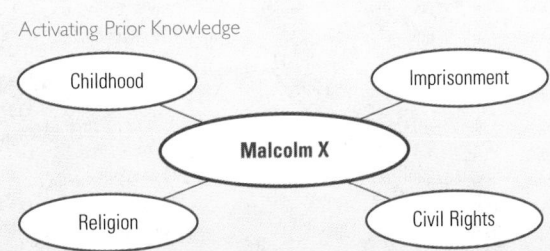

HISTORICAL CONNECTION Building Background

Malcolm Little was born in Omaha, Nebraska, in 1925. His father was murdered when Malcolm was only six. Problems that Malcolm experienced during his youth reached a climax when he was arrested in 1942 and sentenced to ten years in prison for burglary.

Prison became a turning point for Malcolm Little. In prison he joined the Black Muslims, a black religious group. He also changed his name, to represent what he was leaving behind: "Ex-smoker. Ex-drinker. Ex-Christian. Ex-Slave." Upon his release from prison, he became a Black Muslim minister. A powerful public speaker, Malcolm X preached that in order to achieve independence, African Americans should live and work completely apart from white people. Malcolm X believed that violence was acceptable in the fight for civil rights. Later, he came to believe in the possibility of brotherhood among all people. He was assassinated in 1965.

WRITING CONNECTION

In his autobiography, Malcolm X describes how a certain book opened new doors for him while he was in prison. In your notebook, write about a book that has influenced your life in some way. Identify the book and explain its importance to you.

Malcolm X addresses a rally in Harlem, 1963.
Copyright © Gordon Parks.

 LASERLINKS
• HISTORICAL CONNECTION   63

OVERVIEW

Objectives

- To understand and appreciate an autobiographical excerpt that describes a turning point in a man's life
- To enrich reading by using active reading strategies
- To identify and understand the characteristics of an autobiography
- To express understanding of the selection through a choice of writing forms, including a poem, a personal memoir, a letter, and a personal dictionary
- To extend understanding of the selection through a variety of multimodal and cross-curricular activities

Skills

GRAMMAR
- Kinds of sentences

LITERARY CONCEPTS
- Autobiography
- Point of view

GENRE STUDY
- Nonfiction: autobiography

SPELLING
- Different *a* sounds

SPEAKING, LISTENING, AND VIEWING
- Speech

Cross-Curricular Connections

HISTORY
- First dictionaries

ART
- Poster

GEOGRAPHY
- Map

SOCIAL STUDIES
- Nation of Islam

 HISTORICAL CONNECTION
Malcolm X During the civil rights movement of the 1960s, Malcolm X spoke out about issues he felt were important to African Americans. His words influenced thousands of people of all races. As they view this film, students will encounter Malcolm X and glimpse the life and times of this influential leader.

Side A, Frame 3811

PRINT AND MEDIA RESOURCES

UNIT ONE RESOURCE BOOK
Strategic Reading: Literature, p. 31
Vocabulary SkillBuilder, p. 34
Reading SkillBuilder, p. 32
Spelling SkillBuilder, p. 33

GRAMMAR MINI–LESSONS
Transparencies, p. 45

ACCESS FOR STUDENTS ACQUIRING ENGLISH
Selection Summaries
Reading and Writing Support

FORMAL ASSESSMENT
Selection Test, pp. 13–14
 Test Generator

 **AUDIO LIBRARY**
See Reference Card

 **LASERLINKS**
Historical Connection

 **INTERNET RESOURCES**
McDougal Littell Literature Center at http://www.hmco.com/mcdougal/lit

SUMMARY

In the Norfolk Prison Colony, Malcolm X found it difficult to write letters because he lacked basic language skills. As a way to educate himself, he began copying a dictionary, page by page, and then read aloud what he had written. Slowly, his vocabulary, reading skills, and writing skills improved. Once he was able to understand what he read, Malcolm X found the prison library to be a rich source of knowledge and ideas. For the first time in his life, Malcolm X felt truly free.

Thematic Link: *Opening Doors*
Knowledge—gained through the dictionary and through reading—opens the door to an entirely new life for Malcolm X.

CUSTOMIZING FOR
Students Acquiring English

- Use **ACCESS FOR STUDENTS ACQUIRING ENGLISH,** *Reading and Writing Support.*

- Students unfamiliar with U.S. history may need background information about racial tensions in this country.

- As you guide students through the selection, you may want to use the suggestions under Strategic Reading for Less-Proficient Readers as well as the suggestions in these boxes.

STRATEGIC READING FOR
Less-Proficient Readers

Set a Purpose Introduce students to the selection by telling them that Malcolm X spent ten years of his life in prison. Invite them to brainstorm a list of things he might have done to pass that time. Then invite them to read on to see if any of their predictions match what he actually did.

Use **UNIT ONE RESOURCE BOOK,** p. 31, for guidance in reading the selection.

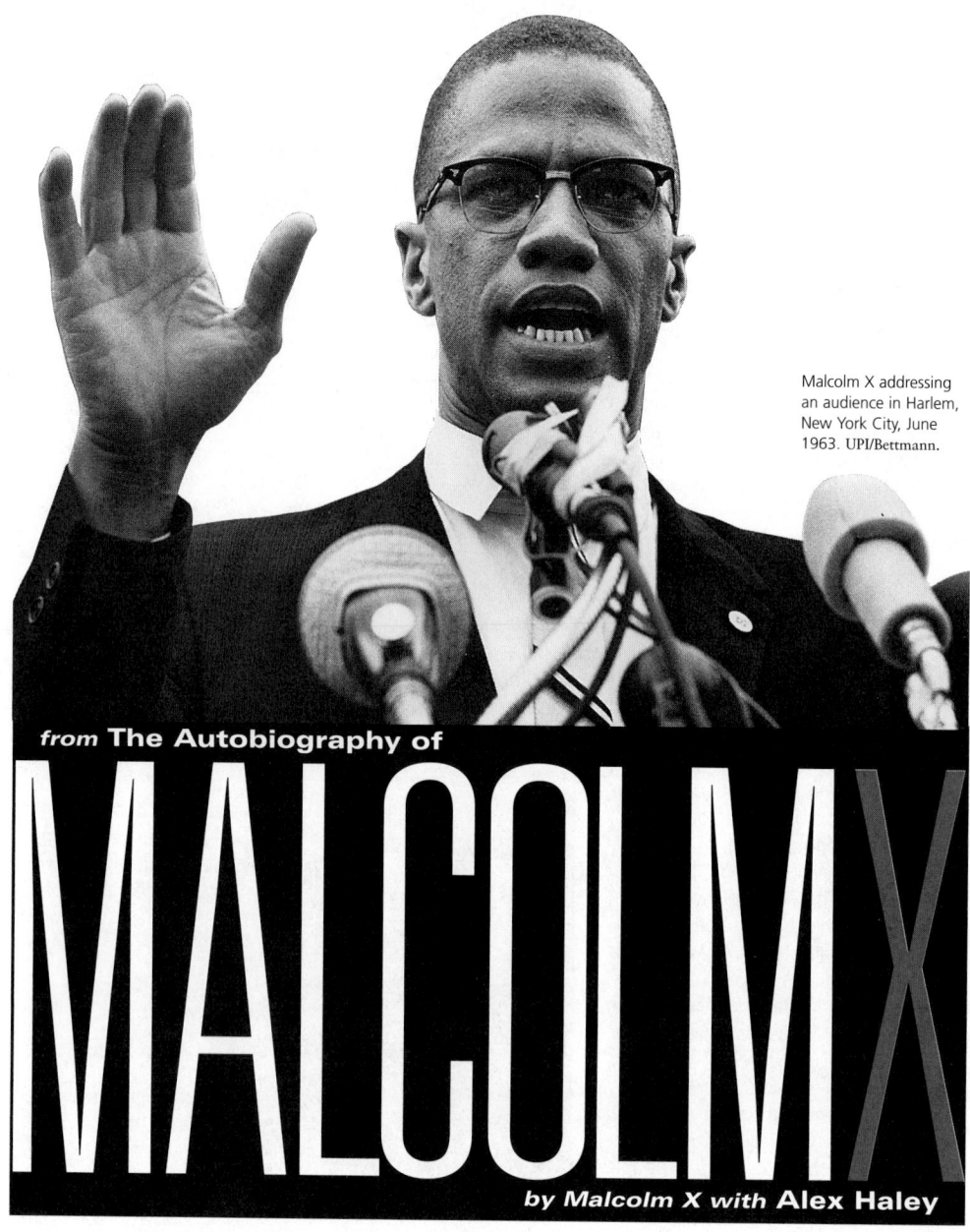

Malcolm X addressing an audience in Harlem, New York City, June 1963. UPI/Bettmann.

from **The Autobiography of**

MALCOLM X

by Malcolm X with **Alex Haley**

WORDS TO KNOW

articulate (är-tĭk′yə-lĭt) *adj.* able to express oneself clearly in words (p. 65)
emulate (ĕm′yə-lāt) *v.* to imitate or copy (p. 65)
feign (fān) *v.* to pretend (p. 67)

painstaking (pānz′tā′kĭng) *adj.* very careful (p. 65)
rehabilitation (rē′hə-bĭl′ĭ-tā′shən) *n.* the restoring of a person's ability to lead a useful life (p. 66)

t was because of my letters that I happened to stumble upon starting to acquire some kind of a homemade education. I became increasingly frustrated at not being able to express what I wanted to convey in letters that I wrote, especially those to Mr. Elijah Muhammad.[1] In the street, I had been the most <u>articulate</u> hustler out there—I had commanded attention when I said something. But now, trying to write simple English, I not only wasn't articulate, I wasn't even functional. How would I sound writing in slang, the way I would *say* it, something such as, "Look, daddy, let me pull your coat about a cat, Elijah Muhammad—"

Many who today hear me somewhere in person or on television, or those who read something I've said, will think I went to school far beyond the eighth grade. This impression is due entirely to my prison studies.

It had really begun back in the Charlestown Prison, when Bimbi[2] first made me feel envy of his stock of knowledge. Bimbi had always taken charge of any conversations he was in, and I had tried to <u>emulate</u> him. But every book I picked up had few sentences which didn't contain anywhere from one to nearly all of the words that might as well have been in Chinese. When I just skipped those words, of course, I really ended up with little idea of what the book said. So I had come to the Norfolk Prison Colony still going through only book-reading motions. Pretty soon, I would have quit even these motions, unless I had received the motivation that I did.

I saw that the best thing I could do was get hold of a dictionary—to study, to learn some words. I was lucky enough to reason also that I should try to improve my penmanship. It was sad. I couldn't even write in a straight line. It was both ideas together that moved me to request a dictionary along with some tablets and pencils from the Norfolk Prison Colony school.

I spent two days just riffling uncertainly through the dictionary's pages. I'd never realized so many words existed! I didn't know *which* words I needed to learn. Finally, just to start some kind of action, I began copying.

In my slow, <u>painstaking</u>, ragged handwriting, I copied into my tablet everything printed on that first page, down to the punctuation marks.

I'd never realized so many words existed!

I believe it took me a day. Then, aloud, I read back, to myself, everything I'd written on the tablet. Over and over, aloud, to myself, I read my own handwriting.

I woke up the next morning, thinking about those words—immensely proud to realize that not only had I written so much at one time, but I'd written words that I never knew were in the world. Moreover, with a little effort, I also could remember what many of these words meant. I reviewed the words whose meanings I didn't remember. Funny thing, from the dictionary's first page right now, that *aardvark* springs to my mind. The dictionary had a picture of it, a long-tailed, long-eared, burrowing African mammal, which lives off termites caught by sticking out its tongue as an anteater does for ants.

---

1. **Elijah Muhammad** (ē-līʹjə mōō-hämʹĭd): 1897–1975; leader of the Black Muslim movement in the United States.
2. **Bimbi:** a fellow inmate.

WORDS	**articulate** (är-tĭkʹyə-lĭt) *adj.* able to express oneself clearly in words
TO	**emulate** (ĕmʹyə-lāt') *v.* to imitate or copy
KNOW	**painstaking** (pānzʹtā'kĭng) *adj.* very careful

65

CUSTOMIZING FOR

Students Acquiring English

2 Ask students to guess the meaning of the idiom *worked up*. ("excited" or "enthusiastic")

3 Draw students' attention to the word *understand* in italic type. Explain that authors sometimes place words in italics in order to emphasize them and show their importance.

STRATEGIC READING FOR

Less-Proficient Readers

E Invite students to discuss how Malcolm X spent his time in prison.

• What benefits did Malcolm get from reading? (*Possible response: He discovered a new world, filled his time, and gained a sense of freedom.*) **Drawing Conclusions**

Set a Purpose Have students read on to find out if Malcolm continued his studies.

D I was so fascinated that I went on—I copied the dictionary's next page. And the same experience came when I studied that. With every succeeding page, I also learned of people and places and events from history. Actually the dictionary is like a miniature encyclopedia.

E Finally the dictionary's A section had filled a whole tablet—and I went on into the B's. That was the way I started copying what eventually became the entire dictionary. It went a lot faster after so much practice helped me to pick up handwriting speed. Between what I wrote in my tablet, and writing letters, during the rest of my time in prison I would guess I wrote a million words.

I never had been so truly free in my life.

I suppose it was inevitable that as my word base broadened, I could for the first time pick up a book and read and now begin to understand what the book was saying. Anyone who has read a great deal can imagine the new world that opened. Let me tell you something: from then until I left that prison, in every free moment I had, if I was not reading in the library, I was reading on my bunk. You couldn't have gotten me out of books with a wedge.[3] Between Mr. Muhammad's teachings, my correspondence, my visitors—usually Ella and Reginald[4]—and my reading of books,

F months passed without my even thinking about being imprisoned. In fact, up to then, I never had been so truly free in my life.

The Norfolk Prison Colony's library was in the school building. A variety of classes was taught there by instructors who came from such places as Harvard and Boston universities. The weekly debates between

inmate teams were also held in the school building. You would be astonished to know how worked up convict debaters and audiences would get over subjects like "Should Babies Be Fed Milk?"

Available on the prison library's shelves were books on just about every general subject. Much of the big private collection that Parkhurst[5] had willed to the prison was still in crates and boxes in the back of the library—thousands of old books. Some of them looked ancient: covers faded, old-time parchment-looking binding. Parkhurst, I've mentioned, seemed to have been principally interested in history and religion. He had the money and the special interest to have a lot of books that you wouldn't have in general circulation. Any college library would have been lucky to get that collection.

As you can imagine, especially in a prison where there was heavy emphasis on <u>rehabilitation</u>, an inmate was smiled upon if he demonstrated an unusually intense interest in books. There was a sizable number of well-read inmates, especially the popular debaters. Some were said by many to be practically walking encyclopedias. They were almost celebrities. No university would ask any student to devour literature as I did when this new world opened to me, of being able to read and *understand*.

I read more in my room than in the library itself. An inmate who was known to read a lot

---

3. **wedge:** a tapered piece of wood or metal used for splitting wood or rock.
4. **Ella and Reginald:** Malcolm's sister and brother.
5. **Parkhurst:** a millionaire interested in the education and training of prisoners.

WORDS TO KNOW **rehabilitation** (rē′hə-bĭl′ĭ-tā′shən) *n.* the restoring of a person's ability to lead a useful life

66

 Mini-Lesson Grammar

KINDS OF SENTENCES Explore with students how we use language for different purposes, and point out that there is a different kind of sentence for each purpose: *declarative, interrogative, imperative,* and *exclamatory.*

Application Have students identify the kind of sentence that each of the following represents:
1. The Norfolk Prison Colony's library was in the school building. (*declarative*)
2. Should babies be fed milk? (*interrogative*)
3. Turn your lights out at 10:00 P.M. (*imperative*)

4. Malcolm X learned so much by reading! (*exclamatory*)
5. Actually, the dictionary is like a miniature encyclopedia. (*declarative*)
6. Should I read in my room or in the library? (*interrogative*)

Reteaching/Reinforcement
• *Grammar Mini-Lessons* transparencies, p. 45

 **The Writer's Craft**

Kinds of Sentences, pp. 386–387

Sentence Type	Purpose	End Punctuation
declarative	makes a statement	period
interrogative	asks a question	question mark
imperative	tells or requests	period
exclamatory	expresses strong feeling	exclamation point

could check out more than the permitted maximum number of books. I preferred reading in the total isolation of my own room.

When I had progressed to really serious reading, every night at about ten P.M. I would be outraged with the "lights out." It always seemed to catch me right in the middle of something engrossing.

Fortunately, right outside my door was a corridor light that cast a glow into my room. The glow was enough to read by, once my eyes adjusted to it. So when "lights out" came, I would sit on the floor where I could continue reading in that glow.

At one-hour intervals the night guards paced past every room. Each time I heard the approaching footsteps, I jumped into bed and <u>feigned</u> sleep. And as soon as the guard passed, I got back out of bed onto the floor area of that light-glow, where I would read for another fifty-eight minutes—until the guard approached again. That went on until three or four every morning. Three or four hours of sleep a night was enough for me. Often in the years in the streets, I had slept less than that. ❖

 G

WORDS TO KNOW **feign** (fān) *v.* to pretend

67

LITERARY INSIGHT

AARDVARK
by Julia Fields

Since
   Malcolm died
   That old aardvark
   has got a sort of fame
   for himself—
   I mean, of late, when I read
   The dictionary the first
   Thing I see
   Is that animal staring at me.
And then
   I think of Malcolm—
   How he read
   in the prisons
   And on the planes
   And everywhere
   And how he wrote
   About old Aardvark.
Looks like Malcolm X helped
Bring attention to a lot of things
We never thought about before.

CUSTOMIZING FOR

Gifted and Talented Students

F Malcolm X says that until he learned to read in prison, he "never had been so truly free in [his] life." Ask students to interpret what he means by that statement. Ask them, What kind of freedom does reading give people that they cannot get in any other way?

STRATEGIC READING FOR

Less-Proficient Readers

G Discuss how Malcolm X studied even more as he learned to read more fluently.

• How did Malcolm X take advantage of the prison's educational facilities? *(He borrowed books from the library and attended classes.)* **Summarizing**

INSIGHT

1. How is Malcolm X like the aardvark? *(Possible response: Both are unusual and fascinating.)*
2. What does the aardvark symbolize in the poem? *(Possible responses: education; a beginning, since aardvark is one of the first words in most dictionaries)*
3. How do you think the speaker of the poem regards Malcolm X? *(Possible responses: as a hero and a leader; with fondness and respect)*

About the Author Born in 1938, Julia Fields is known for her eloquent short stories and poems about the African-American experience.

COMPREHENSION CHECK

1. Where does this portion of Malcolm X's autobiography take place? *(in the Norfolk Prison Colony)*
2. What allowed Malcolm X to feel "truly free" in prison? *(learning to read and write)*
3. In what place did he like to read? *(in his own room)*
4. Why did he continue to read when the lights were turned out? *(He hated to stop, especially if he was in the middle of something.)*

Mini-Lesson ⟨TM⟩ Spelling

DIFFERENT *A* SOUNDS Explain to students that one way they can improve their spelling is to recognize the different sounds that specific letters can have. Tell students that in this lesson you will concentrate on the letter *a.* Share with them the following information:

Spelling	Sound	Examples
a	ə	reh<u>a</u>bilitate
a, ai	ā	<u>ai</u>d, p<u>ai</u>nst<u>a</u>king
ei	ā	f<u>ei</u>gn, r<u>ei</u>gn
a	ä	<u>a</u>rticulate, <u>a</u>rt, <u>a</u>lms

Application Have students create a series of flashcards with an *a* sound on one side and an example of a word containing the sound on the other side. Encourage students to draw from the selection examples of words with each kind of *a* sound and to add them to their personal word lists.

Reteaching/Reinforcement
• *Unit One Resource Book,* p. 33

1. Accept all reasonable responses.
2. Possible responses: He was a highly motivated, intelligent, and disciplined person who loved learning and self-improvement; he was a criminal who did his best to turn his life around.
3. Possible responses: Reading gave Malcolm X a sense of power and independence that had no link to his physical captivity. Not being able to read had severely limited him; reading made him free by expanding his mind and imagination.
4. Possible responses: determination, patience, intelligence, strength.
5. Possible response: Malcolm X educated many people about matters they might not have thought deeply about before, especially racial injustice.
6. Possible response: They cannot fill out job applications, read street signs or labels on food and medicine, or learn about current events in newspapers and magazines. Malcolm X might have suggested that communities run free reading classes and offer in-home teaching to homebound people.

Another Pathway

Cooperative Learning Remind students that they are writing a persuasive speech. Explain that such a speech should appeal to reason, emotion, or ethics (a sense of right and wrong). Guide students to use the appeal or appeals that would be most effective for their audience and topic. When they have finished speaking, have them listen to feedback from their classmates.

RESPONDING OPTIONS

FROM PERSONAL RESPONSE TO CRITICAL ANALYSIS

REFLECT

1. What are your thoughts about Malcolm X's accomplishments? Write your ideas in your notebook. Close Textual Reading

RETHINK

2. Based on this excerpt, how would you describe Malcolm X?

3. Malcolm X said that when he learned to read he "had never been so truly free" in his life. What do you think he meant by this?

   Consider

   • his frustrations at being unable to communicate effectively
   • the new doors that learning to read opened for him

4. Malcolm X had many followers during his lifetime. What leadership qualities does his autobiography reveal?

5. Read or reread "Aardvark" on page 67. What do you think the last three lines might mean?

RELATE

6. While in prison, Malcolm X realized that he didn't have the reading and writing skills he needed. Today, between 21 million and 25 million people in the United States are illiterate, or unable to read or write. What are some problems illiterate people face? What do you think Malcolm X would suggest that communities do to help illiterate people acquire reading skills?

LITERARY CONCEPTS

An **autobiography** is the story of a person's life, written by that person. An autobiography usually focuses on events that shape or change a person's life. How did Malcolm X's study of the dictionary in prison change his life?

Multimodal Learning
ANOTHER PATHWAY

Imagine that Malcolm X has been asked to speak to your class about the importance of reading. Write the speech that he might give and then deliver it to a group of your classmates.

QUICKWRITES

1. Write a **poem** about Malcolm X or a quality of his that you admire.

2. Expand your Writing Connection notes into a **personal memoir** about a book that shaped or changed your life.

3. Recall your response to question 3 in column 1. Then compose a **letter** that Malcolm X might have written, explaining how he became "truly free" in jail.

4. Using a computer or index cards, set up a **personal dictionary** in which you alphabetically record new words and definitions that you want to remember throughout the school year. Start with at least ten entries.

PORTFOLIO Save your writing. You may want to use it later as a springboard to a piece for your portfolio.

Literary Concepts

Students can work together in groups of three or four to explore ways in which studying the dictionary in prison changed Malcolm X's life. Encourage students to create a web to help them brainstorm ideas. Their web might look like this:

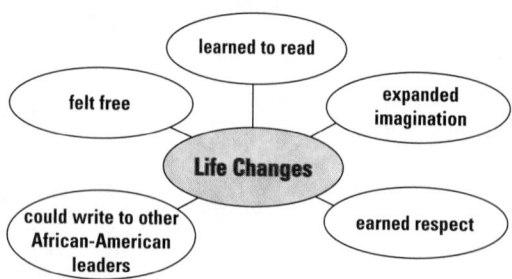

QuickWrites

1. Encourage students to use "Aardvark" (p. 67) or any other poem as a model for their own poem.
2. Guide students to narrow their focus to one important book and one episode from their lives.
3. Before students begin writing, have them review the format for writing friendly letters.
4. Students should be sure to check the spelling, pronunciation, and definitions of each word in a standard dictionary.

The Writer's Craft

Letter Forms, p. 669

ALTERNATIVE ACTIVITIES

1. Create a **mural** of Malcolm X in his years after prison.

2. Let a dictionary fall open to any page. Carefully read the page, then jot down how many entries were on it, how many were new to you, and which one (or ones) you found most interesting. Share your **dictionary study** with your classmates.

ACROSS THE CURRICULUM

Art Create a **poster** that encourages people to read. Display it in your classroom or school library.

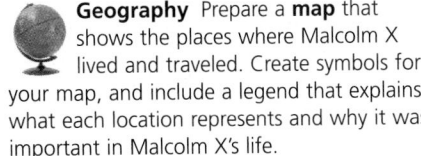 **Geography** Prepare a **map** that shows the places where Malcolm X lived and traveled. Create symbols for your map, and include a legend that explains what each location represents and why it was important in Malcolm X's life.

LITERARY LINKS

Think about the title of the O. Henry story "A Retrieved Reformation" on page 28. Could that title apply to Malcolm X? Compare and contrast Malcolm X and Jimmy Valentine.

WORDS TO KNOW

An analogy contains two pairs of words that are related in the same way, as in the example TALL : SHORT :: pretty : ugly. The analogy is read, "Tall is to short as pretty is to ugly." Review the *Words to Know* in the boxes at the bottom of the selection pages. In each item below, decide which word best completes the second pair.

1. FOLLOW : LEADER :: _____ : hero
2. GRACEFUL : DANCER :: _____ : speaker
3. LOUD : QUIET :: _____ : careless
4. RECOVERY : HOSPITAL :: _____ : prison
5. WISH : HOPE :: _____ : pretend

MALCOLM X

While Malcolm X was in prison, he began to follow the teachings of Elijah Muhammad and the Nation of Islam, also known as the Black Muslims. After his release from prison, he became a minister for this group and soon was more famous than Elijah Muhammad. Malcolm X preached in favor of black power and black nationalism, opposing white oppression and integration. However, because of a dispute within the faith, Malcolm was expelled from the group. He then traveled to Africa and Saudi Arabia, where he became a follower of traditional Islam. In 1964, Malcolm X founded the Organization of Afro-American Unity to publicize the plight of African Americans. During this same period, he and Alex Haley, who later wrote *Roots,* worked together on Malcolm X's autobiography. On February 21, 1965, while preparing to speak in Harlem, Malcolm X was assassinated. Three men, two of whom were Black Muslims, were convicted of his murder and sentenced to life in prison. His autobiography was published after his death.

1925–1965

THE AUTOBIOGRAPHY OF MALCOLM X **69**

Alternative Activities

1. Suggest that students work in small groups to create their mural. They should sketch the design in pencil and fill it in with paints or markers.

2. Students might enjoy working on this activity in pairs. One student could read the information aloud, and the other could record it. Students can then share their studies by posting them on a bulletin board.

Art Suggest that students, in creating their posters, use different media, such as photographs, paints, and markers. Urge students to create a slogan to make the message on their poster more persuasive.

Geography *Cooperative Learning* Students can work with partners to research the locations and to create legends that explain the importance of each location.

ADDITIONAL SUGGESTION

Social Studies *Nation of Islam* Students can research the history of the Nation of Islam (Black Muslims). Have them find out how the organization began, what it stands for, and how it has changed over the years. Invite students to share their findings in an oral presentation.

Literary Links

Possible response: The title could apply to both the fictional Jimmy Valentine and the real Malcolm X because both got a second chance at life, or a "retrieved reformation." Jimmy put his talents to honest use and changed his life; Malcolm X taught himself to read and changed his life.

Words to Know

1. emulate
2. articulate
3. painstaking
4. rehabilitation
5. feign

Reteaching/Reinforcement
• *Unit Resource Book,* p. 34

MALCOLM X

In late 1963, Malcolm X traveled to Mecca, in Saudi Arabia, where he experienced a religious conversion and adopted the orthodox Muslim belief in the equality of the races. He returned to the United States, established the Organization of Afro-American Unity, and preached against racism for the rest of his life.

The Scholarship Jacket

by Marta Salinas

OBJECTIVES

- To promote independent active reading
- To apply and practice skills learned in previous lessons
- To provide an opportunity to assess students' performance through an alternative assessment instrument

SUMMARY

Martha, who is being raised by her grandparents, has the best record of any eighth grader and is entitled to receive her school's highest academic honor—a scholarship jacket. Shortly before graduation, however, Martha overhears an argument between two of her teachers, Mr. Schmidt and Mr. Boone. She learns that her classmate Joann's wealthy and influential father is pressuring the teachers to award the jacket to his daughter. Mr. Schmidt, the history teacher, refuses to lie or to falsify the grades. The next day, the principal informs Martha that she must pay $15 if she wants to receive the scholarship jacket at the graduation ceremony. Martha approaches her grandfather, hoping he will give her the money. Though he can afford to pay for the award, he refuses to do so on principle. The next day, Martha informs the principal of her grandfather's decision and blurts out that he'll have to give the jacket to Joann. The principal suddenly changes his mind and decides to award Martha the jacket. Martha finds her grandfather weeding his bean field and tells him the good news.

Thematic Link: *Opening Doors* Martha opens doors for equal treatment by refusing to accept prejudice.

Reading Pathways

- Have students choose partners and do a paired reading.

- Have students read the selection on their own and write in dialogue journals.

- Invite groups of students to do a group reading, selecting parts for each student to read.

- Evaluate how well students can read, interpret, discuss, and write about the selection on their own by using the Integrated Assessment for Unit One, located in the Alternative Assessment booklet. Administer the assessment at the end of the unit after students have read all the selections and completed all the writing that was assigned. Set aside two class periods, or about two hours, for the assessment.

The small Texas school that I went to had a tradition carried out every year during the eighth-grade graduation: a beautiful gold and green jacket (the school colors) was awarded to the class valedictorian, the student who had maintained the highest grades for eight years. The scholarship jacket had a big gold S on the left front side and your name written in gold letters on the pocket.

My oldest sister, Rosie, had won the jacket a few years back, and I fully expected to also. I was fourteen and in the eighth grade. I had been a straight A student since the first grade and this last year had looked forward very much to owning that jacket. My father was a farm laborer who couldn't earn enough money to feed eight children, so when I was six I was given to my grandparents to raise. We couldn't participate in sports at school because there were registration fees, uniform costs, and trips out of town; so, even though our family was quite agile and athletic there would never be a school sports jacket for us. This one, the scholarship jacket, was our only chance.

In May, close to graduation, spring fever had struck as usual with a vengeance. No one paid any attention in class; instead we stared out the windows and at each other, wanting to speed up the last few weeks of school. I despaired every time I looked in the mirror. Pencil thin, not a curve anywhere. I was called "beanpole" and "string bean," and I knew that's what I looked like. A flat chest, no hips, and a brain; that's what I had. That really wasn't much for a fourteen-year-old to work with, I thought, as I absent-mindedly wandered from my history class to the gym. Another hour of sweating in basketball and displaying my toothpick legs was coming up. Then I remembered my P.E. shorts were still in a bag under my desk where I'd forgotten them. I had to walk all the way back and get them. Coach Thompson was a real bear if someone wasn't dressed for P.E. She had said I was a good forward and even tried to talk Grandma into letting me join the team once. Of course Grandma said no.

I was almost back at my classroom door when I heard voices raised in anger as if in some sort of argument. I stopped. I didn't mean to eavesdrop, I just hesitated, not knowing what to do. I needed those shorts and I was going to be late, but I didn't want to interrupt an argument between my teachers. I recognized the voices: Mr. Schmidt, my history teacher, and Mr. Boone, my math teacher. They seemed to be arguing about me. I couldn't believe it. I still remember the feeling of shock that rooted me flat against the wall as if I were trying to blend in with the graffiti written there.

PRINT AND MEDIA RESOURCES

UNIT ONE RESOURCE BOOK
Strategic Reading: Literature, p. 37

FORMAL ASSESSMENT
Selection Test, pp. 15–16
Part Test, pp. 17–18
 Test Generator

ALTERNATIVE ASSESSMENT
Unit One Integrated Assessment,
pp. 1–6

ACCESS FOR STUDENTS ACQUIRING ENGLISH
Selection Summaries

AUDIO LIBRARY
See Reference Card

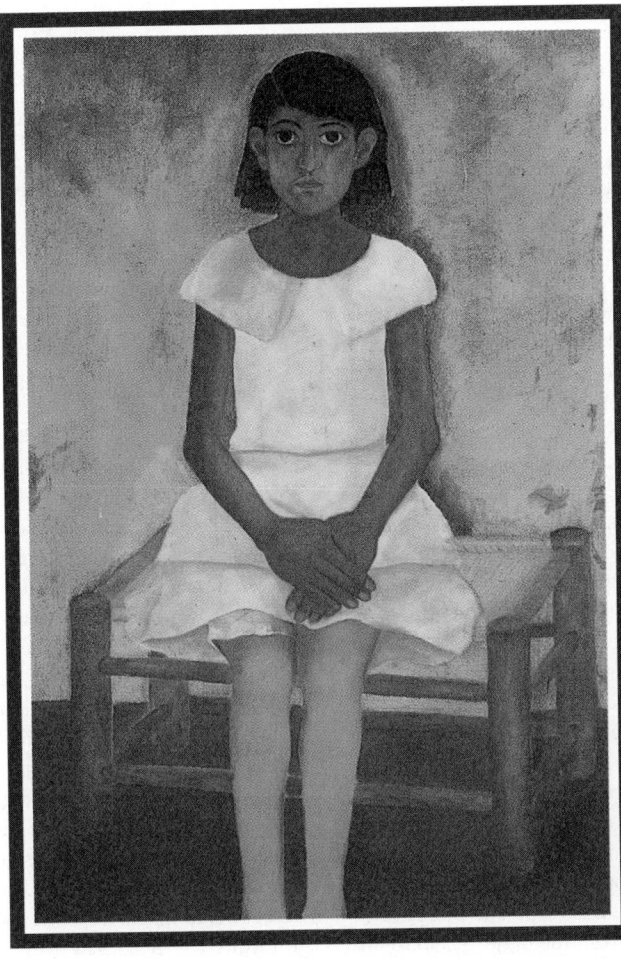

Retrato de muchacha [Portrait of a girl] (1929), Frida Kahlo. Oil on canvas, 46½″ × 31½″, collection of the Dolores Olmedo Patiño Foundation, Museo Frida Kahlo, Mexico City.

"I refuse to do it! I don't care who her father is, her grades don't even begin to compare to Martha's. I won't lie or falsify records. Martha has a straight A-plus average and you know it." That was Mr. Schmidt and he sounded very angry. Mr. Boone's voice sounded calm and quiet.

"Look. Joann's father is not only on the Board, he owns the only store in town: we could say it was a close tie and—"

The pounding in my ears drowned out the rest of the words, only a word here and there filtered through. ". . . Martha is Mexican . . . resign . . . won't do it. . . ." Mr. Schmidt came rushing out and luckily for me went down the opposite way toward the auditorium, so he didn't see me. Shaking, I waited a few minutes and then went in and grabbed my bag and fled from the room. Mr. Boone looked up when I came in but didn't say anything. To this day I

THE SCHOLARSHIP JACKET **71**

Multicultural Perspectives

In "The Scholarship Jacket," Martha explains that she was sent to live with her grandparents because her father, a farm laborer, couldn't afford to raise eight children. Large numbers of Mexican Americans work as laborers on farms. Many of them are migrant workers who move from one area to another throughout the Southwest, depending on the availability of farm work. These workers generally receive low wages and live in poverty. Since the 1960s, efforts have been made to improve the working conditions of migrant laborers. In 1962 Cesar Chavez, a labor union organizer and advocate for the poor, created the National Farm Workers Association in order to improve conditions for California grape pickers. After organizing a number of boycotts, Chavez succeeded in getting grape growers to accept the workers' union.

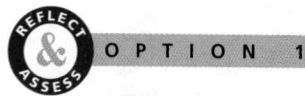

Individual Activity
GIVING A SPEECH

During the annual graduation ceremony at Martha's school, the valedictorian gives a thank-you speech for the scholarship jacket. Have students prepare and present Martha's speech, in which she explains what the jacket means to her and how she feels about her "eight years of hard work and expectation."

Teacher's Role Explain that the speech should last from two to three minutes and should reflect Martha's ideas and point of view. Have students first write an outline that lists the main ideas and shows how the speech is organized. Students can use the outline as a basis for writing the full text of the speech or the note cards that contain the main points. Tell students to practice the speech in front of as many listeners as they can. Explain the importance of a speaker's diction, tone, pacing, volume, gestures, and body language when presenting a speech.

Rubric

3 Full Accomplishment The speech explains in detail how Martha feels about winning the scholarship jacket. The speech is well organized, with a clear beginning, middle, and end. The student speaks distinctly, using appropriate diction and body language.

2 Substantial Accomplishment The speech provides some details about how Martha feels about the jacket, but the organization is somewhat unclear.

1 Little or Partial Accomplishment The speech does not explain Martha's feelings about the jacket, the organization is unclear, and the diction is weak.

---

don't remember if I got in trouble in P.E. for being late or how I made it through the rest of the afternoon. I went home very sad and cried into my pillow that night so Grandmother wouldn't hear me. It seemed a cruel coincidence that I had overheard that conversation.

The next day when the principal called me into his office I knew what it would be about. He looked uncomfortable and unhappy. I decided I wasn't going to make it any easier for him, so I looked him straight in the eyes. He looked away and fidgeted with the papers on his desk.

"Martha," he said, "there's been a change in policy this year regarding the scholarship jacket. As you know, it has always been free." He cleared his throat and continued. "This year the Board has decided to charge fifteen dollars, which still won't cover the complete cost of the jacket."

I stared at him in shock, and a small sound of dismay escaped my throat. I hadn't expected this. He still avoided looking in my eyes.

"So if you are unable to pay the fifteen dollars for the jacket it will be given to the next one in line." I didn't need to ask who that was.

Standing with all the dignity I could muster, I said, "I'll speak to my grandfather about it, sir, and let you know tomorrow." I cried on the walk home from the bus stop. The dirt road was a quarter mile from the highway, so by the time I got home, my eyes were red and puffy.

"Where's Grandpa?" I asked Grandma, looking down at the floor so she wouldn't ask me why I'd been crying. She was sewing on a quilt as usual and didn't look up.

"I think he's out back working in the bean field."

I went outside and looked out at the fields. There he was. I could see him walking between the rows, his body bent over the little plants, hoe in hand. I walked slowly out to him, trying to think how I could best ask him for the money.

There was a cool breeze blowing and a sweet smell of mesquite fruit in the air, but I didn't appreciate it. I kicked at a dirt clod. I wanted that jacket so much. It was more than just being a valedictorian and giving a little thank you speech for the jacket on graduation night. It represented eight years of hard work and expectation. I knew I had to be honest with Grandpa; it was my only chance. He saw my shadow and looked up.

He waited for me to speak. I cleared my throat nervously and clasped my hands behind my back so he wouldn't see them shaking. "Grandpa, I have a big favor to ask you," I said in Spanish, the only language he knew. He still waited silently. I tried again. "Grandpa, this year the principal said the scholarship jacket is not going to be free. It's going to cost fifteen dollars, and I have to take the money in tomorrow, otherwise it'll be given to someone else." The last words came out in an eager rush. Grandpa straightened up tiredly and leaned his chin on the hoe handle. He looked out over the field that was filled with the tiny green bean plants. I waited, desperately hoping he'd say I could have the money.

He turned to me and asked quietly, "What does a scholarship jacket mean?"

I answered quickly; maybe there was a chance. "It means you've earned it by having the highest grades for eight years and that's why they're giving it to you." Too late I realized the significance of my words. Grandpa knew that I understood it was not a matter of money. It wasn't that. He went back to hoeing the weeds that sprang up between the delicate little bean plants. It was a time-consuming job; sometimes the small shoots were right next to each other. Finally he spoke again as I turned to leave, crying.

"Then if you pay for it, Marta, it's not a scholarship jacket, is it? Tell your principal I will not pay the fifteen dollars."

I walked back to the house and locked myself in the bathroom for a long time. I was angry with Grandfather even though I knew he was right, and I was angry with the Board, whoever they were. Why did they have to change the rules just when it was my turn to win the jacket? Those were the days of belief and innocence.

It was a very sad and withdrawn girl who dragged into the principal's office the next day. This time he did look me in the eyes.

"What did your grandfather say?"

I sat very straight in my chair.

"He said to tell you he won't pay the fifteen dollars."

The principal muttered something I couldn't understand under his breath and walked over to the window. He stood looking out at something outside. He looked bigger than usual when he stood up; he was a tall, gaunt man with gray hair, and I watched the back of his head while I waited for him to speak.

"Why?" he finally asked. "Your grandfather has the money. He owns a two-hundred acre ranch."

I looked at him, forcing my eyes to stay dry. "I know, sir, but he said if I had to pay for it, then it wouldn't be a scholarship jacket." I stood up to leave. "I guess you'll just have to give it to Joann." I hadn't meant to say that, it had just slipped out. I was almost to the door when he stopped me.

"Martha—wait."

I turned and looked at him, waiting. What did he want now? I could feel my heart pounding loudly in my chest and see my blouse fluttering where my breasts should have been. Something bitter and vile tasting was coming up in my mouth; I was afraid I was going to be sick. I didn't need any sympathy speeches. He sighed loudly and went back to his big desk. He watched me, biting his lip.

"Okay, damn it. We'll make an exception in your case. I'll tell the Board, you'll get your jacket."

I could hardly believe my ears. I spoke in a trembling rush. "Oh, thank you, sir!" Suddenly I felt great. I didn't know about adrenalin in those days, but I knew something was pumping through me, making me feel as tall as the sky. I wanted to yell, jump, run the mile, do something. I ran out so I could cry in the hall where there was no one to see me.

At the end of the day, Mr. Schmidt winked at me and said, "I hear you're getting the scholarship jacket this year."

His face looked as happy and innocent as a baby's, but I knew better. Without answering I gave him a quick hug and ran to the bus. I cried on the walk home again, but this time because I was so happy. I couldn't wait to tell Grandpa and ran straight to the field. I joined him in the row where he was working, and without saying anything I crouched down and started pulling up the weeds with my hands. Grandpa worked alongside me for a few minutes, and he didn't ask what had happened. After I had a little pile of weeds between the rows, I stood up and faced him.

"The principal said he's making an exception for me, Grandpa, and I'm getting the jacket after all. That's after I told him what you said."

Grandpa didn't say anything; he just gave me a pat on the shoulder and a smile. He pulled out the crumpled red handkerchief that he always carried in his back pocket and wiped the sweat off his forehead.

"Better go see if your grandmother needs any help with supper."

I gave him a big grin. He didn't fool me. I skipped and ran back to the house whistling some silly tune. ❖

THE SCHOLARSHIP JACKET **73**

Class Discussion

SHARING IDEAS

1. What are your thoughts about the ending of the story? *(Accept all reasonable responses.)*

2. Do you think the principal would have given the jacket to Martha if she hadn't blurted out that she knew about the plan to award the jacket to Joann? *(Possible responses: No, because the slip-up made the principal feel ashamed about trying to cheat Martha; yes, because the principal knew that Martha had earned the jacket and his conscience would have prevented him from accepting the Board's decision.)*

3. Do you agree or disagree with Martha's grandfather's decision not to pay for the jacket? Why or why not? *(Some students will agree with the grandfather's view that an award is not an award if the recipient has to pay for it. Other students may say that he risked breaking Martha's heart by refusing to go along with the Board's policy.)*

4. If Joann had received the scholarship jacket, do you think Martha would have spoken out about what she had overheard? Why or why not? *(Possible responses: Some students may say that Martha would have remained silent. These students may point out that Martha never intended to blurt out that she was aware of the plan to award the jacket to Joann. Other students may say that Martha would have spoken out because nothing in her life had meant as much to her as receiving the jacket. She viewed the jacket as her family's only chance for recognition.)*

Teacher's Role The issue of unfairness is sensitive. Guide students to express their ideas about Martha's situation while also guiding them to appreciate each student's individuality and personal heritage.

OVERVIEW

In the Guided Assignment for this section, students will write a personal response essay. By writing such an essay, students will learn how to support their personal response by including their thoughts and feelings. As preparation for this assignment, The Writer's Style will help students understand how elaboration can assist in supporting the ideas and emotions in their personal essays. In Reading the World, students will consider other people's personal responses as well as their own.

Objectives

- To recognize how authors use elaboration
- To use correctly punctuated quotations to support ideas
- To write a personal response to a piece of literature
- To consider other people's responses to a photograph

Skills

LITERATURE
- Identifying and analyzing techniques of elaboration

WRITING AND LANGUAGE
- Organizing a personal response essay
- Using sensory language

GRAMMAR AND USAGE
- Punctuating quotations
- Prepositional phrases
- Placing prepositional phrases

MEDIA LITERACY
- Responding to a photograph

SPEAKING, LISTENING, AND VIEWING
- Creating descriptions with a partner
- Peer discussion

CRITICAL THINKING
- Synthesizing responses
- Classifying
- Analyzing
- Speculating

Teaching Strategy: MODELING

In the following models, the authors use incidents, details, and quotations to elaborate on their main responses to people and places.

A **Wilson** Possible responses: blackmailing or directly ordering the sister. The narrator is trying to force the sister to accompany her to The Grove.

B **Rylant** Possible responses: The details of the dark, small rooms illuminated by the television and the objects lying around on the furniture and the floor support the idea that the two people are careless.

WRITING ABOUT LITERATURE

A PERSONAL LOOK

We all have strong reactions to what we read and see. Perhaps you admired Juliette in "Waiting" and liked Ernie by the end of "A Crush." How do you share your responses with others? In the following pages you will

- study techniques writers use to support ideas
- write a personal response to a selection from Unit One, "On The Threshold"
- explore responses to real-world situations

The Writer's Style: Elaboration You can use elaboration—examples, incidents, details, and quotations—to make your writing more interesting and to support your ideas.

Read the Literature

How many ways can you develop an idea? Notice some of the techniques these writers use.

Literature Models

A **Elaboration with Incidents**
What incidents, or situations, does the narrator describe? What's her main idea?

> I used to blackmail her. "If you don't go, I'll tell Mama about the time you pretended to be sick and stayed home from school because you didn't have your homework done and were scared of Miss Garrison." Or I would just plain order her around. "I'm *going*, Henrietta, so get a move on and *hurry!*" She'd come padding out of the house in her stupid yellow raincoat, so that she wouldn't get a cold in the wet wind, and off we'd go—me fast and complaining about her slowness, and her slow and complaining about my speed.
>
> Budge Wilson, from "Waiting"

B **Elaboration with Details**
What details help you imagine this scene? What idea do you think the details support?

> They lived, the two of them, in tiny dark rooms always illuminated by the glow of a television set, Ernie's bags of Oreos and Nutter Butters littering the floor, his baseball cards scattered across the sofa, his heavy winter coat thrown over the arm of a chair so he could wear it whenever he wanted, and his box of Burpee seed packages sitting in the middle of the kitchen table.
>
> Cynthia Rylant, from "A Crush"

PRINT AND MEDIA RESOURCES

UNIT ONE RESOURCE BOOK
Writer's Style, p. 41
Prewriting, p. 42
Elaboration, p. 43
Peer Response Guide, pp. 44–45
Revising and Proofreading, p. 46
Student Model, p. 47
Rubric, p. 48

GRAMMAR MINI-LESSONS
Transparencies, pp. 33 and 44
Copymasters, p. 43

WRITING MINI-LESSONS
Transparencies, p. 34

ACCESS FOR STUDENTS ACQUIRING ENGLISH
Reading and Writing Support

FORMAL ASSESSMENT
Guidelines for Writing Assessment

WRITING COACH

Connect to Life

Elaboration appears in newspapers, magazines, and other media. The writer of the essay below uses elaboration to help explain one of astronaut Frederick Gregory's ideas.

Biographical Essay

Space exploration, Gregory has said, might be likened to a child's progress in school. Not much should be expected from a kindergartner, but by the time the student finishes graduate school, the investment is ready to pay off. As he puts it, "I think we're just in the first grade right now. The more we do it, the smarter we get."

Editors of Time-Life Books
from *Voices of Triumph: Leadership*

Elaboration with Quotations
What idea does the quotation support? How does it make the idea easier to understand?

Try Your Hand: Using Elaboration

1. **Revise a QuickWrite** Choose one of your QuickWrites and try to improve it using elaboration.

2. **Use Sensory Language** With a partner, choose a subject, such as a picnic, that can be described using your five senses: sight, sound, taste, touch, smell. Describe the subject out loud. Take turns saying one sentence for each sense. If you like, you can write your sentences or turn them into a story.

3. **Give Details or Examples** Providing a good example is a strong way to elaborate on a statement. Write a statement you have made or heard recently, such as "We did a good job on our project." Elaborate by giving examples that support or expand the basic statement.

SkillBuilder

 GRAMMAR FROM WRITING

Punctuating Quotations
Use quotation marks to show where the exact words of a speaker or writer begin and end.

I felt it when the narrator said, "Henrietta's look hit me like a dodge ball in the gut."

Place quotation marks outside commas and periods following direct quotations.

"She's such a leader," Mom said.

"In fact," she said, "I'm sure she'll be a great success."

Henrietta said, "I guess you ought to know, Mom."

APPLYING WHAT YOU'VE LEARNED
Write the following sentences using correct punctuation.

1. Lubin said to Medy I'm supposed to meet Roman at the beach.
2. Will you be home for dinner Medy asked.
3. No, he said, I don't think so.

 GRAMMAR HANDBOOK

For more information on quotation marks, see page 886 of the Grammar Handbook. For more information on elaboration, see page 819 in the Writing Handbook.

PUNCTUATING QUOTATIONS Point out to students that the quotation marks go around only the speaker's exact words. Remind them that the speaker should be indicated and that there are a variety of methods for doing this. Have students review the selections in this unit and note the position of quotation marks in relation to other punctuation.

Application Answers:
1. Lubin said to Medy, "I'm supposed to meet Roman at the beach."
2. "Will you be home for dinner?" Medy asked.
3. "No," he said, "I don't think so."

Reteaching/Reinforcement *Grammar Mini-Lessons* copymasters p. 43, transparencies p. 33 and 44

 The Writer's Craft

Punctuating Quotations, pp. 637 and 648–650

Teaching Strategy: MODELING

C Possible responses: The quotation supports the idea that space exploration is still in its early stages of development. The quotation makes this idea easier to understand because it compares the progress of space exploration with that of a small child.

Try Your Hand

1. Responses will vary. Revisions should be improved by the use of incidents, details, or quotations to elaborate.
2. Pairs should employ all five senses when describing their ideas and feelings about the scene. Invite them to make their descriptions as vivid as possible.
3. Encourage students to use a variety of methods for adding details and examples. Remind them of the techniques of writing incidents, visual descriptions, and direct speech.

Responses may be as follows: We did a good job on our project. We had enough time to really organize ourselves and to assign roles to all the group members. For instance, I was in charge of all visual aids. I found the pictures we wanted to use and made arrangements for a video monitor so we could show clips from videos. We met often enough so that we could work everything out and rehearse our presentation. I think we all feel good about the work we did.

WRITING ABOUT LITERATURE

Personal Response

Everyone responds to songs, movies, and literature differently. Your response is as valuable as anyone else's, but it's important to be able to explain why you feel the way you do.

GUIDED ASSIGNMENT

Write a Personal Response Essay In a personal response essay, tell your own thoughts and feelings about a work of literature.

① Prewrite and Explore

How did you feel about the selections in Unit One? Were there any that moved you? Any you disliked?

DISCOVERING YOUR RESPONSE

Reread some of the selections, jotting down reactions, comments, questions, predictions, and feelings in your notebook. Then reflect on what you have read and written.

- Which parts are important, interesting, or hard to follow?
- Which character or event most affected me?
- Did any of the selections remind me of my own life?
- What is my overall reaction to each piece I reread?

Response Form

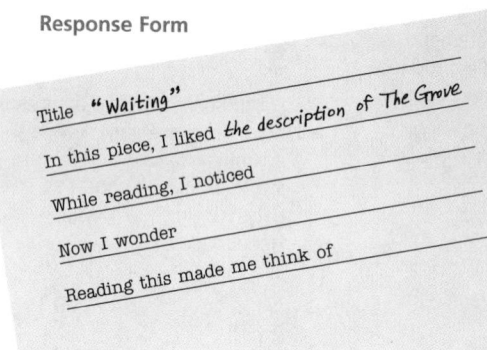

Title "Waiting"

In this piece, I liked the description of The Grove

While reading, I noticed

Now I wonder

Reading this made me think of

EXPLORING YOUR REACTIONS

Your answers to the questions at the left and any of the suggestions below can help you choose a focus for your personal response.

- Choose a selection. Copy and fill in the form at the left, supporting statements with examples from the literature or from your experience.
- Sketch the character or scene you were most impressed by.
- Discuss your selection with a partner. How do his or her responses influence you?

Decision Point You can respond to the entire selection or zero in on one part of it—a character, a description, even a word. What about the selection intrigues you?

76

 Assessment Option

SELF-ASSESSMENT

After students have completed the Exploring Your Reactions suggestions, they should assess their personal responses. Students can use the following questions to focus and clarify their responses:

- *Did I fill in the form using examples of incidents, precise details, sensory language, or quotations?*
- *Does my sketch correspond to the details in the selection?*
- *Did I alter my response as I listened to my partner and defined my feelings?*

② Freewrite to Make Connections

Spend about five minutes freewriting your thoughts and feelings about the idea you chose. The yellow notes show how one student analyzed her freewriting to see where her ideas were taking her.

Student's Freewriting Model

Will telling more of the story here make my connection clearer?

The grove where Juliette and Henrietta played reminds me of a place behind my house where I used to play with an old friend. When I read the story, I felt as if I were at my own grove again.

I remembered all the times that Tanya told me what to do, and it sounded like Juliette's voice bossing Henrietta. When Juliette finally realizes that Henrietta is powerful, she knows that she won't be able to pick on her sister any more. The same is true for Tanya and me.

I need details about my friendship and the sisters' relationship to support my comparison.

③ Draft and Share

When you write a personal response, your freewriting might become your draft. Use the questions below to help you analyze your freewriting. The SkillBuilder on organization can help you focus your draft.

- How complete is my response? Did I say what I really think or feel about this work?
- Have I included enough information about the story to help readers understand my response to it?
- What details, incidents, quotations, and examples from the literature or my life could I add to support my response?

Have a peer read your draft and answer these questions.

 PEER RESPONSE

- What would make my essay more interesting to you?
- Why do you think I responded as I did?
- What feelings came through strongly in my writing?

Writing Skill: ELABORATION

G The Discovery Draft provides an opportunity for students to think through ideas and information they've gathered. Review various methods of elaboration they have encountered in this lesson. Encourage students to find places they could elaborate their freewriting by looking for statements that may be meaningful and familiar to them but would be unfamiliar to a reader who has not shared their experiences.

Teaching Strategy: USING THE SKILLBUILDER

H You can help students analyze and organize their freewriting by teaching the SkillBuilder on Organizing a Personal Response Essay at this time. This will help them to develop an organized draft based on their freewriting.

SkillBuilder **WRITER'S CRAFT**

ORGANIZING A PERSONAL RESPONSE ESSAY Explain that all essays have three basic elements: an introduction, a body, and a conclusion. Point out that the body is the main substance of the essay and will be longer and more detailed than the introduction and conclusion. Encourage students to think about ordering their reasons for their response and to ensure that the support for each reason is in the correct place in the body.

Application Encourage students to sort through each item in their freewriting and put it where it should go in the introduction, body, or conclusion. For example, support for ideas should go with each idea in the body.

Reteaching/Reinforcement *Writing Mini-Lessons* transparencies p. 34

 The Writer's Craft

Writing from Personal Experience, pp. 32–39

78

Critical Thinking: ANALYZING

I Explain to students that the best way to edit is to respond to each question and peer comment.

CUSTOMIZING FOR
Students Acquiring English

J Some students may be unfamiliar with expressing their reactions in public or in writing. Encourage these students to trust their ideas and elaborate on the textual sources for their responses.

Teaching Strategy: MODELING

K Ask students to judge whether the writer makes a clear connection between the story and her life and whether she uses sufficient elaboration. In the first paragraph, the writer includes details about three elements—the people, place, and action—both in the story and in her own experience. Make sure students notice the quotation in the second paragraph. Also discuss with students how the student's final draft meets the Standards of Evaluation. She includes the author and title of the essay and tells enough about the selection in the first sentence. Then she states a response and provides reasons for it. The second paragraph provides another response and comparison.

Standards for Evaluation

Ideas and Content
- identifies the work by title and author
- gives a brief summary of the work
- uses details and quotations from the work as well as the writer's personal experience to support the writer's response
- ends with a summary of the response and a conclusion

Structure and Form
- demonstrates proper paragraphing
- includes transitional words to show relationships among ideas
- uses a variety of sentence structures

Grammar, Usage, and Mechanics
- contains no more than two or three minor errors in grammar and usage
- contains no more than two or three minor errors in spelling, capitalization, and punctuation

---

WRITING ABOUT LITERATURE

❹ Revise and Edit

I Your peer reviewer's comments can help you put yourself in the reader's place. Consider those comments and the Standards for Evaluation below as you edit. Reflecting on the questions below can help you learn more about writing your own final draft.

J

Student's Final Draft

What important information about the selection is included in the first paragraph?

> **Personal Response: Playing in The Grove**
>
> After reading "Waiting" by Budge Wilson a few times, I had a strange feeling about the two sisters in the story and their woodlot called The Grove. It took me a while to realize that it reminded me of Tanya, my old best friend, and the clearing in the woods behind my house where we used to play. The narrator of the story, Juliette, remembers The Grove as a favorite place where she and her twin sister played together. It's also the place where the quiet twin, Henrietta, finally escapes Juliette's shadow.

Does this writer make the connection between the story and her life clear?

K

How does the writer use elaboration to support her comparison?

> Reading about Juliette and Henrietta reminded me of how my friend Tanya used to boss me. That changed after I moved away. Now Tanya says I'm a big-city girl, that I'm more independent. It's kind of like Juliette noticing Henrietta's beauty and power. "I didn't spend much time with Henrietta anymore," Juliette says, "or boss her, or make her go to The Grove in the fog or try to scare her."

Standards for Evaluation

A personal response essay
- identifies the author and title of the literary work
- tells enough about the literature so that readers can understand the response
- states a response and gives reasons for it
- draws an overall conclusion

78 UNIT ONE: ON THE THRESHOLD

Assessment **Option**

SELF-ASSESSMENT

To help students assess their own writing, have them ask themselves the following questions:
- *Have I identified the literary work I am discussing?*
- *Have I familiarized my reader with the writing?*
- *Have I made connections between the important detail or details in the writing and my own response?*

- *Did I elaborate on my reasons? Is there anything I can add to make my elaborations clearer or more engaging?*
- *Did I punctuate quotations correctly?*

Grammar in Context

Prepositional Phrases A prepositional phrase is a group of words that begins with a preposition and ends with an object. Prepositional phrases help a writer elaborate an idea by adding precision, clarity, and details. They are often used in descriptions and to clarify when or how things happen.

In a clearing,
~~T~~here stood a tall tree stump that we used as a stage.

Tanya chose songs for us to sing. She sang the lead

After a week,
vocals, and I practiced backup. ~~Then~~ we invited our

families to a short concert.

Look at the example above.

- The first sentence has two prepositional phrases: "In a clearing" (the preposition is *In*; its object is *clearing*) and "as a stage" (the preposition is *as*; its object is *stage*).
- The last sentence has two prepositional phrases, "After a week" and "to a short concert." Identify each preposition and its object.

For more information about prepositions, see page 890 of the Grammar Handbook.

Try Your Hand:
Using Prepositional Phrases

On a separate sheet of paper, enrich the following sentences by adding one or more prepositional phrases to each.

1. The bedspread has blue trim.
2. Trees fill the grove.
3. A surprisingly large crowd came.
4. My sister is the pretty one.

SkillBuilder

G → GRAMMAR FROM WRITING

Placing Prepositional Phrases

Sometimes you can move a prepositional phrase without changing a sentence's meaning.

Tanya couldn't bully me anymore after the move.

After the move, Tanya couldn't bully me anymore.

Sometimes the placement of a prepositional phrase can make the sentence unclear.

Unclear *In the tall reeds, I watched the little birds.*

Clear *I watched the little birds in the tall reeds.*

In the first example above, note how the phrase *In the tall reeds* seems to modify *I*. The phrase should be placed closer to *birds*, the word it modifies.

APPLYING WHAT YOU'VE LEARNED
Write each sentence so that its meaning is clearer.

1. I heard Mom on the phone.
2. With a little makeup, I admired how lovely she looked.
3. In the dark, I was the one who left Henrietta alone.

Less-Proficient Writers

L Make sure students understand what a preposition and an object are before they begin this page. Explain that prepositions usually come before nouns or pronouns. Common prepositions include: *in, as, with, to,* and *by.* An object is a noun or a pronoun that receives the action of a verb or a preposition.

Teaching Strategy:
USING THE SKILLBUILDER

M You can help students identify prepositional phrases by teaching the SkillBuilder on Placing Prepositional Phrases at this time. It explains that these phrases can appear either before or after the subject of the sentence but that the placement can be important for making the meaning clear.

Try Your Hand

Answers will vary but should not make the meaning of the sentence ambiguous. The following sentences are suggestions. Note that prepositional phrases can come before or after the main part of the sentence.
1. The bedspread has blue trim with long, orange tassels.
2. Over the hill, trees fill the grove with their dark leaves.
3. After the explosion, a surprisingly large crowd came.
4. On some days, my sister is the pretty one with her short, smart haircut.

SkillBuilder GRAMMAR FROM WRITING

PLACING PREPOSITIONAL PHRASES Present this information by writing the sentences on the chalkboard. Point out how, in the second example, placing the phrase next to the correct noun makes the meaning clearer. Draw students' attention to the ambiguity in the unclear sentence.

Application Answers:
1. On the phone, I heard Mom.
2. I admired how lovely she looked with a little makeup.
3. I was the one who left Henrietta alone in the dark.

Additional Suggestions Have students rewrite the following sentences so that their meanings are made clearer.
1. With a snap, I heard the twig break.
2. I am progressing in my geometry by drawing different shapes.
3. They will be returning to the concert hall for a duet after a long break.

Reteaching/Reinforcement *Grammar Mini-Lessons* transparencies, p. 44

 The Writer's Craft

Prepositional Phrases, pp. 539 and 543

READING THE WORLD

On pages 74–78, students learned how to write a personal response to a work of literature. They should also be aware that they can use the skills they developed to structure their responses to the real world.

In this lesson, students learn to respond to a photo and to compare their response with their classmates' responses.

Critical Thinking: SPECULATING

N Students might mention that at a quick glance they noticed a kind of barricade or unusual wall. After a closer look at the photo, students might mention that they detect an upended car, a toppling stack of cardboard boxes, a stack of rubber tires, and two stacks of fenders. This unusual wall raises questions as to why someone would choose these particular objects and arrange them in this particular way.

Media Literacy:
INTERPRETING A PHOTO

O Students may say that at first the scene captured in the photo looks confusing—a heap of objects thrown together randomly. As students continue to examine the scene, they may detect a pattern in the arrangement of the objects. For example, the upended cars at each end seem to frame the objects collected within. The boxes are stacked together, as are the fenders, rather than strewn about. Students can infer that the objects are arranged according to a plan to stimulate a response in the viewer. The collection of junk makes a point about some of the things people use and then throw out.

Speaking and Listening:
GROUP DISCUSSION

P Have students work in groups to share their responses to the scene pictured in the photo. Students may cite several reasons as to why this unusual wall was made. For example, some may say that the wall was made to show viewers the vast amount of junk that piles up in a community. Students should express any connections they see between their response to this photo and experiences they have had. Students may conclude that people respond differently to scenes such as the one pictured and that people's perceptions and responses are related to their own experiences. People bring much of themselves to what they experience.

MANY RESPONSES

Every day you respond to things you see in the world around you, just as you responded to stories and poems in this unit. But do you ever wonder whether others respond the way you do?

View Take a quick glance at the scene on this page. What do you see? Now look again, more closely this time. What additional details do you notice? Do they raise questions in your mind? **N**

Interpret What was your first reaction to this scene? Did you like what you saw, or were you put off or confused? Why might these objects have been arranged the way they are? **O**

Discuss Share your responses and reactions with a few classmates. How were your first reactions the same or different? What conclusions did each of you come to about the reasons behind this unusual wall? Now talk about what your responses tell you about different ways people react to the world. **P**

SkillBuilder

 CRITICAL THINKING

Considering Other Opinions

As you saw in your group discussion, people can have very different responses to the same thing. Therefore, in order to make good judgments about what you see, hear, or read, it is a good idea to consider other people's responses first. You might even discover some surprising information along the way. For example, the "junk" wall in this picture was constructed outside an art museum to show the value of recycling. Does this change your opinion of it once again? The more information you gather, the more informed your opinions will be.

APPLYING WHAT YOU'VE LEARNED

- Review your notes. Think about your first reactions to the photo. What in your experience led to your response? Was your impression accurate or not? How can you use your personal experiences to evaluate what you see?

- With one or two classmates, examine some of the images that appear throughout the book. Which do you like? Which do they like? When there is a disagreement, take turns trying to help the others "see" the picture as you do.

Wrecked cars and other garbage are displayed outside the Taipei Fine Arts Museum in Taiwan as part of the museum's efforts to stress the importance of recycling.

READING THE WORLD **81**

SkillBuilder CRITICAL THINKING

Synthesizing Responses Encourage students to consider carefully their classmates' responses. Point out that their own responses may change as they share them with others. Remind students that being open to different views can enrich their own thinking.

Application
- Students may have thought of responding either through pictures or by writing.

- Reactions may have stemmed from a particular detail or the work as a whole. Students should mention that personal experience can support a response by providing details and adding perspective.
- Encourage students to recognize that they are repeatedly influenced by people and images around them. Point out that particularly striking details and effective use of language often influence people to reconsider their opinions.

Part 2 Lesson Planner

TIME ALLOTMENTS SHOWN ARE APPROXIMATE. DEPENDING ON YOUR GOALS AND THE NEEDS OF YOUR STUDENTS, YOU MAY WISH TO ALLOW MORE OR LESS TIME FOR CERTAIN PORTIONS OF THE LESSON.

Table of Contents	Discussion	Previewing the Selection	Reading the Selection
PART OPENER **LETTING OTHERS IN** **What Do You Think?** page 82	**20 MINUTES** • Reflect on the part theme		
SELECTION **The War of the Wall** page 84 AVERAGE		**20 MINUTES** • PERSONAL CONNECTION • COMMUNITY CONNECTION • READING CONNECTION: Dialect	**25 MINUTES** • Introduce vocabulary • Read pp. 84–91 (8 pp.)
SELECTION **Last Cover** page 96 EASY		**20 MINUTES** • PERSONAL CONNECTION • SCIENCE CONNECTION • READING CONNECTION: Context clues	**40 MINUTES** • Introduce vocabulary • Read pp. 96–105 (10 pp.)
GENRE LESSON **Focus on Poetry** page 108	**20 MINUTES** • Discuss characteristics of poetry • Discuss strategies for reading poetry		
SELECTIONS **The Pasture** **A Time to Talk** page 111 AVERAGE		**20 MINUTES** • PERSONAL CONNECTION • BIOGRAPHICAL CONNECTION • READING CONNECTION: Oral reading	**5 MINUTES** • Read pp. 1–2 (2 pp.)
SELECTIONS **There Is No Word for Goodbye** **Graduation Morning** page 116 CHALLENGING		**15 MINUTES** • PERSONAL CONNECTION • CULTURAL CONNECTION • READING CONNECTION: Understanding cultural contexts	**10 MINUTES** • Read pp. 116–118 (3 pp.)
SELECTION **Homeless** page 122 CHALLENGING		**20 MINUTES** • PERSONAL CONNECTION • COMMUNITY CONNECTION • READING CONNECTION: Author's purpose	**15 MINUTES** • Introduce vocabulary • Read pp. 122–125 (4 pp.)

Writing	Exploring Topics	Prewriting	Drafting and Revising
WRITING FROM EXPERIENCE **Firsthand and Expressive Writing**	**20 MINUTES**	**25 MINUTES**	**80 MINUTES**

Time estimates assume in-class work. You may wish to assign some of these stages as homework.

Responding to the Selection

FROM PERSONAL RESPONSE TO CRITICAL ANALYSIS	OR	ANOTHER PATHWAY	LITERARY CONCEPTS	QUICKWRITES

Extension Activities: ALTERNATIVE ACTIVITIES • LITERARY LINKS • CRITIC'S CORNER • THE WRITER'S STYLE • ACROSS THE CURRICULUM • ART CONNECTION • WORDS TO KNOW • BIOGRAPHY

50 MINUTES
• Discussion questions	OR • Letter	• Conflict • Point of view	• Speech • Newspaper article • Personal narrative	

50 MINUTES — ✔ ✔ SOCIAL STUDIES ✔ ✔ ✔

40 MINUTES
• Discussion questions	OR • Readers Theater presentation	• Setting • Conflict	• Advertising flyer • Dialogue	

40 MINUTES — ✔ ✔ SCIENCE ✔ ✔

20 MINUTES
• Discussion questions	OR • Illustrated book	• Rhyme	• Poem • Recipe	

20 MINUTES — ✔ GEO-GRAPHY ✔

30 MINUTES
• Discussion questions	OR • Comparison diagram	• Imagery	• Thesaurus entry • Graduation card • Poem or character sketch	

20 MINUTES — ✔ SOCIAL STUDIES ✔

40 MINUTES
• Discussion questions	OR • Letter	• Essay	• Editorial • Definition	

40 MINUTES — ✔ SOCIAL STUDIES ✔ ✔

30 MINUTES

Part 2 Cooperative Project

Video Pen Pals

Overview

Students create entertaining videos that capture their unique personalities and the special flavor of life at their school.

PROJECT AT A GLANCE

The selections in Unit One, Part 2 are about how people get to know one another. For this project, students will get to know one another by creating videos that introduce others to their unique personalities. Students will work together in small groups to create a videotape, or videotapes, to portray themselves and their school. They will exchange videos with a classroom in a partner school chosen by the teacher or a school administrator. If desired, the project may culminate in a field trip to the partner school.

OBJECTIVES

- To learn interesting and unique things about your fellow students and your school
- To plan and produce a videotape that accurately portrays the students in your class and life at your school
- To exchange videotapes with students in another school

SUGGESTED GROUP SIZE

4–5 students per group

MATERIALS

- one or more video cameras
- one or more videocassettes
- a VCR (videocassette recorder)

 **Getting Started**

Arranging the Project

Before students begin, find out what channels you will need to work through in order to arrange this project. You will probably need the approval of your school administration and the administration of the cooperating school. Allow plenty of time to make the preliminary arrangements.

Try to choose a school that is different from yours in some interesting ways. For example, if your school is in an urban area, you might team up with a suburban or rural school. You also might team up with a school in a different geographic region or one with a different ethnic or socioeconomic mix of students.

Once you have found a classroom willing to participate, make sure the other teacher fully understands this project. Check with one another and trade ideas at various stages.

Arranging for Videotaping

You may want to contact someone who can help you with the videotaping procedures for the project, especially if you are not very familiar with the process. Your school may have a media resource person, a librarian, or a teacher's assistant who can lend a hand. A parent with a flexible work schedule might also be willing to donate time to the project.

If your school does not have video equipment, you may be able to borrow it from a parent or a local merchant. The project can be adapted to the availability of equipment. Each group might have its own video camera or camcorder and produce a separate video. Alternately, a single camera may be passed from group to group, with the groups taping their segments on the same videocassette.

 **Creating the Videos**

Introducing the Project

Explain that students will be working in small groups to plan and produce a videotape about themselves and their school. Give them some information about their partner school and tell them that the purpose of the videos is to establish links with students at the partner school.

To spark interest, you can ask students to watch television programs intended for young people that follow a video magazine format. Often these shows consist of interviews with young people who are doing interesting things and short features on high schools or middle schools that are involved in unique projects. Use these programs to discuss the possibilities for filming and producing your own videos.

In discussion, ask students how they could present themselves in a way that will interest strangers. How could they create entertaining videos that capture their unique personalities and the special flavor of life at their school?

As a way to personalize the project, you might draft a group letter of introduction to the other class. You could solicit suggestions from your students and compose the letter on the board or on oversized paper. When the letter is complete, it can be copied onto stationery and mailed.

Group Investigations

Divide students into groups of four or five, making an effort to achieve maximum diversity in each group. For the next several days, the groups will work as teams of investigative reporters, gathering information about group members and the school. Encourage students to conduct informal interviews with group members, other students, and teachers; to take note of any newsworthy events or projects and to look for creative ways of capturing their subjects on video. As students are gathering information, hold class meetings to check on their progress and to offer help and advice. Each group should be encouraged to find its own distinctive way of gathering and presenting information.

Creating a Project Description

After students have done some preliminary planning, have each group prepare a one-page description of its project. In this way you can steer groups away from duplication and can help them keep their projects manageable. Confer with each group about what they plan to do. Here are some possible formats:

OPTION 1: VIDEO MONTAGE

Groups can create a montage (a rapid succession of visual images) with an accompanying sound track. The montage could portray aspects of everyday life at school, perhaps featuring shots of group members involved in various school activities.

OPTION 2: SCHOOL NEWS

Groups can create a newscast that focuses on interesting events or people, student opinion, or other topics of interest at their school.

OPTION 3: MUSIC NARRATIVE

Students can create their own music video that tells a story about themselves and their school. Students may create original music or use a popular recording. You may wish to approve the choice of music ahead of time to ensure its suitability.

OPTION 4: HOT TOPICS

Students can interview one another or present a panel discussion about some controversial topic, such as music censorship, prejudice, or the rights of teenagers. These topics might also be discussed in the format of a talk show in which a host interviews both guests and audience members.

Production

While each group tapes, keep the rest of the students on track to minimize disruptions. You'll probably want to set time limits, both for the finished tape and for the actual filming. For the production of a single tape, groups may need your help in developing continuity between the segments. You may wish to set aside class time to help students develop some form of credits for their tapes.

---

③ Sharing the Videos

This project could culminate in a screening party that features a single tape or multiple tapes, depending on how you shaped the project. You might invite administrators, the other class, or any other interested people from the community for a viewing of the tape. Serve popcorn and refreshments if you wish. Then make arrangements to exchange videos with the partner school. If possible, schedule a time when participating students can meet and reflect on the project.

 Assessing the Project

The following rubric can be used for group or individual assessment.

3 Full Accomplishment Students followed directions and produced a video that creatively and accurately portrays their lives and life at their school.

2 Substantial Accomplishment Students' video is complete, but the images and/or music they have chosen does not accurately portray their lives and life at their school.

1 Little or Partial Accomplishment Students' video is incomplete or does not fulfill the requirements of the assignment.

For the Portfolio

Keep master copies of all the videos in your classroom or school library for future reference. Include a copy of your written assessment in each student's portfolio. At the end of the year, you might share the videos with teachers from the next grade level.

Note: For other assessment options, see the *Teacher's Guide to Assessment and Portfolio Use.*

Cross-Curricular Options

SOCIAL STUDIES

Have students study the progress of information technology in the 20th century, including radio, movie newsreels, television, rapid satellite transmissions, computer networking, and other advances. Have them give a summary of how such technology has affected people's daily lives.

LANGUAGE ARTS

Individual students might be invited to participate in a "pen pal" adjunct to this project. Students could be given extra credit for corresponding with a partner at the other school. The letters periodically could be sent in a packet or through a computer networking system.

MUSIC

Encourage students to create an audiotape featuring segments of the songs that are most popular among students in your school. Alternatively, they could create an audiotape of a school choir or other performance group and send the tape along with the video to the partner school.

Resources

Video Power: A Complete Guide to Writing, Planning, and Shooting Videos by Tom Shachtman and Harriet Shelare gives clear instructions and tips.

Dancing in the Dark: Youth, Popular Culture, and the Electronic Media by Quentin J. Schultze investigates how television and radio affect young people and pop culture.

Film by Richard Platt and *The TV Book* by Judy Fireman are large, heavily illustrated books tracing the history of the movies and television.

WHAT DO YOU THINK?

——— Objectives ———

The activities on this page can be used to
- introduce the Part 2 theme, "Letting Others In," since each activity is connected to one or more of the selections in Part 2
- create materials for students' personal portfolios that they can later reconsider or revise
- build an understanding of theme that students can review and revise as they progress through the unit

How do you feel about change?

After students have chosen an important change in their life, encourage them to list aspects of that change that were exciting and those that were unpleasant. Students can then weigh the alternatives in order to decide how they felt overall about the change. (See "The War of the Wall," p. 83.)

What would you suggest?

Instruct partners to plan the overall format for their outline before they begin writing. To help partners explore ways in which children and their parents can learn to see eye-to-eye, encourage them to think about situations in which they and their parents were able to reach an agreement after a conflict. (See "Last Cover," p. 95.)

How do you say goodbye?

Before groups begin their role-playing, they might want to write a brief dialogue that they can refer to during role-playing. In addition, this activity may present an opportunity for you to address issues of grief and loss. (See "There Is No Word for Goodbye" and "Graduation Morning," p. 115.)

LETTING OTHERS IN

WHAT DO You THINK?

REFLECTING ON THEME

When we let others into our lives, we open ourselves up to new experiences, ideas, and emotions. What might influence your decision to let someone into your life? What might you risk or gain by letting this person get to know you? Use the activities on this page to help you think about these questions.

What would you suggest?

Suppose your parents' attitudes and beliefs are different from yours. How might you and your parent learn to see eye-to-eye?

How do you feel about change?

Do you view change as challenging and exciting, or do you view it as scary or unpleasant? Think of an important change that has occurred in your life. Write about the situation or sketch it in comic-book or storyboard form.

Looking back

At the beginning of this unit, you thought about how experiences can open doors to discoveries. After you finished reading the selections in the first part of this unit, what new discoveries had you made? Create one or more paper doors that open up to reveal something you've learned about yourself or others. Hang your doors and the messages inside them on a bulletin board for others to open.

How do you say goodbye?

People say goodbye in different ways. With some of your classmates, role-play how you would say goodbye to a parent who is going on a business trip or to a brother or sister who is going away to college.

Looking Back

Encourage students to be creative in designing their paper doors. Tell them that the doors can reveal a written description, an illustration, or a collage of images that represent what they have learned. You may wish to extend the activity by having students discuss the following questions:
- Why is this new discovery important to you?
- In what ways do you think this discovery will affect your life?

COMMUNITY OUTREACH

To broaden students' perspectives, invite members from local big brother or big sister organizations or from foster grandparent groups to speak about the importance of letting others into one's life. You may also wish to invite students to volunteer some time as "foster" grandchildren at local nursing homes. Students who do so can keep a journal that details their experience—and that of their "foster" grandparents—of letting new people into their lives.

FICTION

The War of the Wall

Toni Cade Bambara

Activating Prior Knowledge/Setting a Purpose

PERSONAL CONNECTION

Is there a place in your neighborhood that seems to belong to young people? Perhaps it is a park or a schoolyard or a mall. In your notebook, draw or describe that place and tell how people feel about it. As you read "The War of the Wall," think about how the narrator and Lou feel about a special place in their neighborhood.

Building Background

COMMUNITY CONNECTION

In the 1960s, some African-American artists began a "wall of respect" movement. The artists worked to create special places by painting murals on walls in their communities as symbols of their respect for the neighborhoods.

Walls have also been regarded as symbols for even larger ideas. For example, the Berlin Wall was a negative symbol of the split between the Communist world and the free world. The Vietnam Veterans Memorial, on the other hand, includes a positive symbol. Part of the memorial is a wall of honor, engraved with the name of every American killed or missing in action in the Vietnam conflict.

Visitors at Vietnam Veterans Memorial in Washington, D.C.
Copyright © Catherine Ursillo/Photo Researchers Inc.

Active Reading

READING CONNECTION

Dialect The neighborhood people in "The War of the Wall" use dialect as they speak with each other. A dialect is a type of language spoken in a particular place by a group of people. It may include special pronunciations of words as well as colorful expressions. Some examples of the dialect used in this story are listed in the chart below. As you read, use context clues to try to figure out what the dialect means. Then when you finish reading, copy the chart and record the meanings of each expression. If you find other examples of dialect, add them and their meanings to the chart also.

Dialect	Meaning
pot likker (p. 85)	liquid in which meat and/or vegetables have been cooked
full of sky (p. 86)	
fix her wagon (p. 86)	
heating up (p. 86)	
slapped five (p. 88)	
laying down a heavy rap (p. 89)	
sounded very tall (p. 89)	

LASERLINKS
• PERSONAL CONNECTION   83

SUMMARY

When the narrator and Lou discover a stranger preparing to paint a mural on their neighborhood wall, they try a variety of tactics to stop her. The wall is special to the children and to the neighborhood—the children have even honored Jimmy Lyons who died in Vietnam by carving his name in the wall. Unable to discourage the artist, the children later plot to deface the mural by spraying it with epoxy paint. As they approach the finished mural, they find the whole neighborhood admiring its depictions of African-American leaders and local adults and children—including Lou and the narrator. Jimmy Lyons's carved name appears in a painted rainbow, and the artist's inscription reveals that she is his cousin.

Thematic Link: *Letting Others In* Lou and the narrator think that an outsider like the painter lady could not understand how precious their wall is to them. They are surprised when they discover that she, too, thinks the wall is special.

CUSTOMIZING FOR
Students Acquiring English

- Use **ACCESS FOR STUDENTS ACQUIRING ENGLISH**, *Reading and Writing Support*.

- Encourage students acquiring English to complete the Reading Connection activity with native-speaking partners.

Ⓘ Point out that *Me and Lou* is technically ungrammatical. Standard English would be *Lou and I*. Ask students what this usage suggests about the narrator.

STRATEGIC READING FOR
Less-Proficient Readers

Set a Purpose Have students read to discover how the people in the neighborhood react to the painter lady.

Use **UNIT ONE RESOURCE BOOK,** p. 51, for guidance in reading the selection.

by Toni Cade Bambara

The War of the Wall

Me and Lou had no time for courtesies. We were late for school. So we just flat out told the painter lady to quit messing with the wall. It was our wall, and she had no right coming into our neighborhood painting on it. Stirring in the paint bucket and not even looking at us, she mumbled something about Mr. Eubanks, the barber, giving her permission. That had nothing to do with it as far as we were concerned. We've been pitching pennies against that wall since we were little kids. Old folks have been dragging their chairs out to sit in the shade of the wall for years. Big kids have been playing handball against the wall since so-called integration[1] when the crazies 'cross town poured cement in our pool so we couldn't use it. I'd sprained my neck one time boosting my cousin Lou up to chisel Jimmy Lyons's name into the wall when we found out he was never coming home from the war in Vietnam to take us fishing.

"If you lean close," Lou said, leaning

---

1. **since so-called integration:** from the time in the 1960s when segregation, the separation of the races in public places, was outlawed. The narrator is being sarcastic, suggesting that integration has not been successful.

84 UNIT ONE PART 2: LETTING OTHERS IN

WORDS TO KNOW

beckon (bĕk'ən) *v.* to summon or call, usually by a gesture or nod (p. 89)
drawl (drôl) *v.* to speak slowly, stretching the vowel sound (p. 88)
inscription (ĭn-skrĭp'shən) *n.* something written, carved, or engraved on a surface (p. 90)

liberation (lĭb'ə-rā'shən) *n.* a state of freedom reached after a struggle (p. 89)
scheme (skēm) *v.* to plot or plan in a secretive way (p. 88)

hipshot against her beat-up car, "you'll get a whiff of bubble gum and kids' sweat. And that'll tell you something—that this wall belongs to the kids of Taliaferro Street." I thought Lou sounded very convincing. But the painter lady paid us no mind. She just snapped the brim of her straw hat down and hauled her bucket up the ladder.

"You're not even from around here," I hollered up after her. The license plates on her old piece of car said "New York." Lou dragged me away because I was about to grab hold of that ladder and shake it. And then we'd really be late for school.

When we came from school, the wall was slick with white. The painter lady was running string across the wall and taping it here and there. Me and Lou leaned against the gumball machine outside the pool hall and watched. She had strings up and down and back and forth. Then she began chalking them with a hunk of blue chalk.

The Morris twins crossed the street, hanging back at the curb next to the beat-up car. The twin with the red ribbons was hugging a jug of cloudy lemonade. The one with yellow ribbons was holding a plate of dinner away from her dress. The painter lady began snapping the strings. The blue chalk dust measured off halves and quarters up and down and sideways too. Lou was about to say how hip it all was, but I dropped my book satchel on his toes to remind him we were at war.

Some good aromas were drifting our way from the plate leaking pot likker onto the Morris girl's white socks. I could tell from where I stood that under the tinfoil was baked ham, collard greens, and candied yams. And knowing Mrs. Morris, who sometimes bakes for my mama's restaurant, a slab of buttered

cornbread was probably up under there too, sopping up some of the pot likker. Me and Lou rolled our eyes, wishing somebody would send us some dinner. But the painter lady didn't even turn around. She was pulling the strings down and prying bits of tape loose.

Side Pocket came strolling out of the pool hall to see what Lou and me were studying so hard. He gave the painter lady the once-over, checking out her paint-spattered jeans, her chalky T-shirt, her floppy-brimmed straw hat. He hitched up his pants and glided over toward the painter lady, who kept right on with what she was doing.

"Whatcha got there, sweetheart?" he asked the twin with the plate.

"Suppah," she said all soft and countrylike.

"For her," the one with the jug added, jerking her chin toward the painter lady's back.

Still she didn't turn around. She was rearing back on her heels, her hands jammed into her back pockets, her face squinched up like the masterpiece she had in mind was taking shape

> **She was rearing back on her heels, her hands jammed into her back pockets, her face squinched up like the masterpiece she had in mind was taking shape on the wall by magic.**

on the wall by magic. We could have been gophers crawled up into a rotten hollow for all she cared. She didn't even say hello to anybody. Lou was muttering something about how great her concentration was. I butt him with my hip, and his elbow slid off the gum machine.

"Good evening," Side Pocket said in his best ain't-I-fine voice. But the painter lady was moving from the milk crate to the step stool to the ladder, moving up and down fast,

THE WAR OF THE WALL **85**

Mini-Lesson   Literary Concepts

REVIEWING POINT OF VIEW Remind students that point of view is the perspective from which a story is told. In first-person point of view, the narrator is one of the characters in the story and uses first-person pronouns such as *I, me,* and *we.* The reader sees the events of the story and other characters only through the eyes of the narrator.

Application Have students work in pairs to identify one sentence on each page of the story that suggests the first-person point of view. They should take turns listing each sentence and then underlining the first-person pronouns contained in the sentence. Have them discuss how the story might change if another point of view were used instead.

D When the painter lady asks Mama questions about how her food is cooked, Mama tells her, "I don't care who your spiritual leader is. . . . If you eat in the community, sistuh, you gonna eat pig by-and-by, one way or t'other." Mama is alluding to the fact that some people have dietary restrictions based on their cultural or religious traditions. For example, some people of the Jewish and Muslim cultures do not eat pork. People of the Hindu tradition do not eat any beef.

CUSTOMIZING FOR

Students Acquiring English

2 Point out that *sistuh* is an example of dialect. It is the word *sister* pronounced with a regional accent.

Literary Concept:
POINT OF VIEW

E Remind students that the story is told in first person. This means that the reader sees the action through the eyes of the narrator. Sometimes, however, the writer suggests what other people are thinking. How does she do that? *(by including other people's words and describing their actions)* Invite students to look for the places where the narrator and other characters like Lou, Mama, or Pop Johnson seem to see things differently from the narrator.

---

scribbling all over the wall like a crazy person. We looked at Side Pocket. He looked at the twins. The twins looked at us. The painter lady was giving a show. It was like those old-timey music movies where the dancer taps on the tabletop and then starts jumping all over the furniture, kicking chairs over and not skipping a beat. She didn't even look where she was stepping. And for a minute there, hanging on the ladder to reach a far spot, she looked like she was going to tip right over.

"Ahh," Side Pocket cleared his throat and moved fast to catch the ladder. "These young ladies here have brought you some supper."

"Ma'am?" The twins stepped forward. Finally the painter turned around, her eyes "full of sky," as my grandmama would say. Then she stepped down like she was in a trance. She wiped her hands on her jeans as the Morris twins offered up the plate and the jug. She rolled back the tinfoil, then wagged her head as though something terrible was on the plate.

"Thank your mother very much," she said, sounding like her mouth was full of sky too. "I've brought my own dinner along." And then, without even excusing herself, she went back up the ladder, drawing on the wall in a wild way. Side Pocket whistled one of those oh-brother breathy whistles and went back into the pool hall. The Morris twins shifted their weight from one foot to the other, then crossed the street and went home. Lou had to drag me away, I was so mad. We couldn't wait to get to the firehouse to tell my daddy all about this rude woman who'd stolen our wall.

All the way back to the block to help my mama out at the restaurant, me and Lou kept asking my daddy for ways to run the painter lady out of town. But my daddy was busy talking about the trip to the country and telling Lou he could come too because

Grandmama can always use an extra pair of hands on the farm.

Later that night, while me and Lou were in the back doing our chores, we found out that the painter lady was a liar. She came into the restaurant and leaned against the glass of the steam table, talking about how starved she was. I was scrubbing pots and Lou was chopping onions, but we could hear her through the service window. She was asking Mama was that a ham hock in the greens, and was that a neck bone in the pole beans, and were there any vegetables cooked without meat, especially pork.

"I don't care who your spiritual leader is," Mama said in that way of hers. "If you eat in the community, sistuh, you gonna eat pig by-and-by, one way or t'other."

All the way back to the block to help my mama out at the restaurant, me and Lou kept asking my daddy for ways to run the painter lady out of town.

Me and Lou were cracking up in the kitchen, and several customers at the counter were clearing their throats, waiting for Mama to really fix her wagon for not speaking to the elders when she came in. The painter lady took a stool at the counter and went right on with her questions. Was there cheese in the baked macaroni, she wanted to know? Were there eggs in the salad? Was it honey or sugar in the iced tea? Mama was fixing Pop Johnson's plate. And every time the painter lady asked a fool question, Mama would dump another spoonful of rice on the pile. She was tapping her foot and heating up in a dangerous way. But Pop Johnson was happy as he could be. Me and Lou peeked through the

86 UNIT ONE PART 2: LETTING OTHERS IN

Mini-Lesson | Reading Skills/Strategies

ACTIVE READING: QUESTIONING Explain to students that active readers ask questions and try to "get into" the selection as they read. One way to do this is to ask yourself how the characters feel about a situation or subject.

Application Copy the chart onto the board. Ask students to determine how the narrator feels about the subjects listed in the left-hand column. Then ask them what clues told them how the narrator feels.

Reteaching/Reinforcement
Unit One Resource Book, p. 52

Subject	How Narrator Feels	Evidence
school	likes it/respects it	narrator doesn't want to be late
the wall before it was painted		
the painter lady		
Mama's cooking		
New York City subway graffiti		
the wall after it was painted		

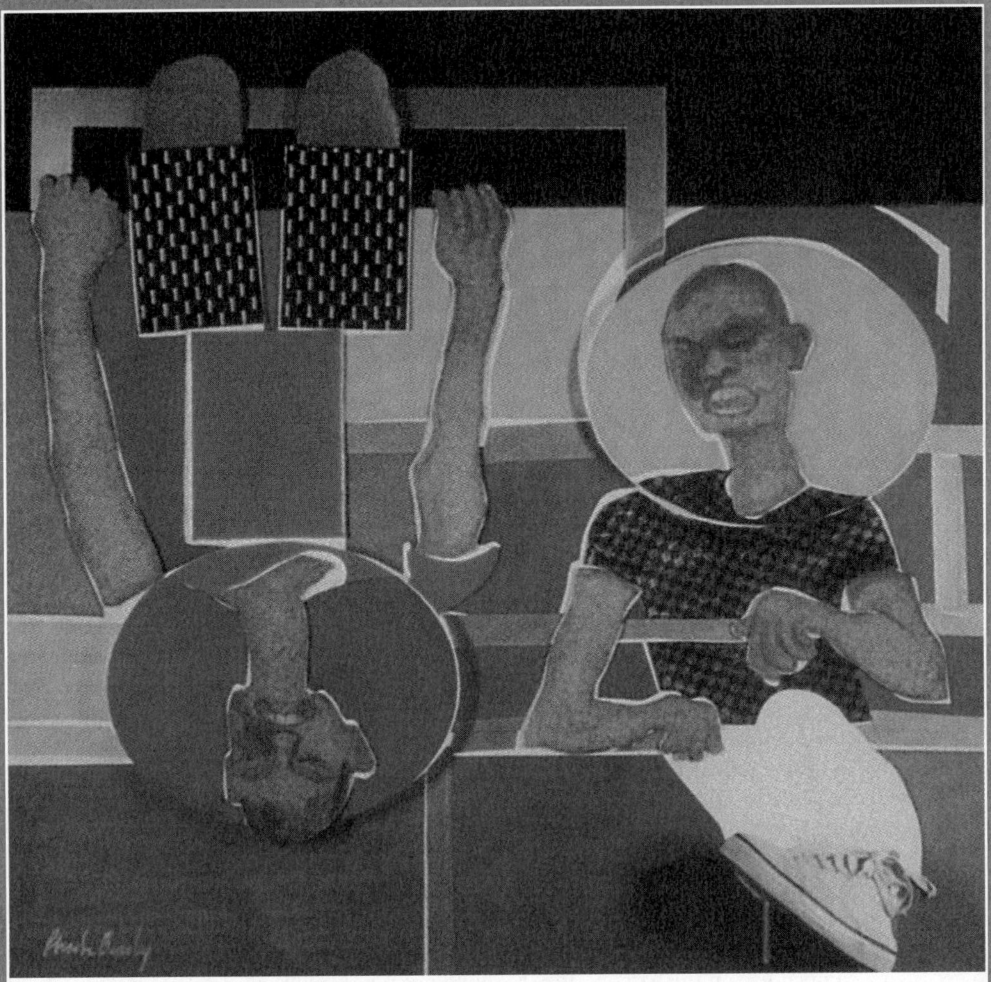

***Sibling Rivals* by Phoebe Beasley**
Phoebe Beasley is a contemporary
artist who creates paintings, lithographs,
and posters. In this collage, she has created two siblings who are at odds with
each other. Each sibling seems to have
a different view of the world.

Reading the Art *What view does each
sibling seem to have? Does either sibling
appear to be stronger than the other? If
you think so, what details tell you so?
From their expressions, which sibling do
you think feels more confident?*

Sibling Rivals (1989), Phoebe Beasley. Collage, 32″ × 40″, courtesy of the artist.

Mini-Lesson **The Writer's Style**

FORMAL AND INFORMAL LANGUAGE
Formal and informal language are types of standard
English. Both involve correct grammar, usage, and
mechanics. Formal English is suitable for book
reports and term papers. It has a serious tone and
an advanced vocabulary. Informal English is used in
everyday conversations or class discussions; it's also
used in newspapers and magazines. Informal English
has a casual tone, with simpler words, short sentences, and contractions. Informal English includes
slang expressions that appear in dictionaries. Slang
that does not appear in the dictionary is considered
to be nonstandard English.

Application Ask pairs of students to write a dialogue between two people, using informal language—the way the students themselves naturally
speak. Then have them suggest specific changes they
would make if they were using formal language.

Reteaching/Reinforcement
• *Writing Mini-Lessons* transparencies, p. 36

The Writer's Craft

Formal and Informal English, p. 311

service window, wondering what planet the painter lady came from. Who ever heard of baked macaroni without cheese, or potato salad without eggs?

"Do you have any bread made with unbleached flour?" the painter lady asked Mama. There was a long pause, as though everybody in the restaurant was holding their breath, wondering if Mama would dump the next spoonful on the painter lady's head. She didn't. But when she set Pop Johnson's plate down, it came down with a bang.

When Mama finally took her order, the starving lady all of a sudden couldn't make up her mind whether she wanted a vegetable plate or fish and a salad. She finally settled on the broiled trout and a tossed salad. But just when Mama reached for a plate to serve her, the painter lady leaned over the counter with her finger all up in the air.

"Excuse me," she said. "One more thing." Mama was holding the plate like a Frisbee, tapping that foot, one hand on her hip. "Can I get raw beets in that tossed salad?"

"You will get," Mama said, leaning her face close to the painter lady's, "whatever Lou back there tossed. Now sit down." And the painter lady sat back down on her stool and shut right up.

All the way to the country, me and Lou tried to get Mama to open fire on the painter lady. But Mama said that seeing as how she was from the North, you couldn't expect her to have any manners. Then Mama said she was sorry she'd been so impatient with the woman because she seemed like a decent person and was simply trying to stick to a very strict diet. Me and Lou didn't want to hear that. Who did that lady think she was, coming into our

neighborhood and taking over our wall?

"Welllllll," Mama drawled, pulling into the filling station so Daddy could take the wheel, "it's hard on an artist, ya know. They can't always get people to look at their work. So she's just doing her work in the open, that's all."

All weekend long me and Lou tried to scheme up ways to recapture our wall.

Me and Lou definitely did not want to hear that. Why couldn't she set up an easel downtown or draw on the sidewalk in her own neighborhood? Mama told us to quit fussing so much; she was tired and wanted to rest. She climbed into the back seat and dropped down into the warm hollow Daddy had made in the pillow.

All weekend long, me and Lou tried to scheme up ways to recapture our wall. Daddy and Mama said they were sick of hearing about it. Grandmama turned up the TV to drown us out. On the late news was a story about the New York subways. When a train came roaring into the station all covered from top to bottom, windows too, with writings and drawings done with spray paint, me and Lou slapped five. Mama said it was too bad kids in New York had nothing better to do than spray paint all over the trains. Daddy said that in the cities, even grown-ups wrote all over the trains and buildings too. Daddy called it "graffiti." Grandmama called it a shame.

We couldn't wait to get out of school on Monday. We couldn't find any black spray paint anywhere. But in a junky hardware store downtown we found a can of white epoxy[2] paint, the kind you touch up old refrigerators

---

2. **epoxy** (ĭ-pŏk′sē): a plastic used in glues and paints.

WORDS TO KNOW	**drawl** (drôl) *v.* to speak slowly, stretching the vowel sound **scheme** (skēm) *v.* to plot or plan in a secretive way

88

M i n i - L e s s o n   G r a m m a r

PRONOUN CASE: COMPOUND STRUCTURES A compound subject is made up of more than one part, such as a noun and a pronoun, as in *Lou and I*. The pronoun *we* can be substituted for *Lou and I*. A compound object is made up of more than one part, such as a noun and a pronoun. In the sentence *She gave it to Patty and me,* the compound object *Patty and me* could be replaced by the pronoun *us.*

Application Invite students to listen to the following sentences and substitute the correct pronouns.

1. [Lou and I](We/Us) went to the mall to check out the new arcade. *(We)*

2. Grandma said she was really glad to see [Freida and me](we/us) after so long. *(us)*

3. Someday, maybe [my family and I] (we/us) will get to travel to Africa. *(we)*

Reteaching/Reinforcement
• Grammar Handbook, anthology pp. 860–861
• *Grammar Mini-Lessons* copymasters, pp. 12–13, transparencies, p. 10

The Writer's Craft

Subject Pronouns, p. 435
Object Pronouns, p. 437

with when they get splotchy and peely. We spent our whole allowance on it. And because it was too late to use our bus passes, we had to walk all the way home lugging our book satchels and gym shoes, and the bag with the epoxy.

When we reached the corner of Taliaferro and Fifth, it looked like a block party or something. Half the neighborhood was gathered on the sidewalk in front of the wall. I looked at Lou, he looked at me. We both looked at the bag with the epoxy and wondered how we were going to work our scheme. The painter lady's car was nowhere in sight. But there were too many people standing around to do anything. Side Pocket and his buddies were leaning on their cue sticks, hunching each other. Daddy was there with a lineman[3] he catches a ride with on Mondays. Mrs. Morris had her arms flung around the shoulders of the twins on either side of her. Mama was talking with some of her customers, many of them with napkins still at the throat. Mr. Eubanks came out of the barbershop, followed by a man in a striped poncho, half his face shaved, the other half full of foam.

 "She really did it, didn't she?" Mr. Eubanks huffed out his chest. Lots of folks answered right quick that she surely did when they saw the straight razor in his hand.

Mama beckoned us over. And then we saw it. The wall. Reds, greens, figures outlined in black. Swirls of purple and orange. Storms of blues and yellows. It was something. I recognized some of the faces right off. There was Martin Luther King, Jr. And there was a man with glasses on and his mouth open like he was laying down a heavy rap. Daddy came up alongside and reminded us that that was

Minister Malcolm X. The serious woman with a rifle I knew was Harriet Tubman because my grandmama has pictures of her all over the house. And I knew Mrs. Fannie Lou Hamer 'cause a signed photograph of her hangs in the restaurant next to the calendar.

Then I let my eyes follow what looked like a vine. It trailed past a man with a horn, a woman with a big white flower in her hair, a handsome dude in a tuxedo seated at a piano, and a man with a goatee holding a book. When I looked more closely, I realized that what had looked like flowers were really faces. One face with yellow petals looked just like Frieda Morris. One with red petals looked just like Hattie Morris. I could hardly believe my eyes.

"Notice," Side Pocket said, stepping close to

> **I recognized some of the faces right off. There was Martin Luther King, Jr. And there was a man with glasses on and his mouth open like he was laying down a heavy rap.**

the wall with his cue stick like a classroom pointer. "These are the flags of liberation," he said in a voice I'd never heard him use before. We all stepped closer while he pointed and spoke. "Red, black and green," he said, his pointer falling on the leaflike flags of the vine. "Our liberation flag. And here Ghana, there Tanzania. Guinea-Bissau, Angola, Mozambique." Side Pocket sounded very tall, as though he'd been waiting all his life to give this lesson.

Mama tapped us on the shoulder and pointed

---

3. **lineman:** a person who sets up and maintains telephone or electric-power lines.

WORDS TO KNOW
beckon (bĕk'ən) *v.* to summon or call, usually by a gesture or nod
liberation (lĭb'ə-rā'shən) *n.* a state of freedom reached after a struggle

89

Critical Thinking: HYPOTHESIZING

J What do you think Mr. Eubanks means when he says, "she really did it, didn't she?" (*Possible responses: She really did what she said she was going to do, paint the wall; she really created something special.*)

Linking To History

 **K** Students may want to try to guess who some of the people are in the painter lady's mural. For example, the "man with a horn" could be trumpet player Louis Armstrong; the "woman with a big white flower in her hair" is probably singer Billie Holiday; the "handsome dude in a tuxedo seated at a piano" might be Duke Ellington; and the "man with a goatee holding a book" is probably writer W.E.B. Du Bois. You may want to bring photographs of these people to share with the class.

CUSTOMIZING FOR
Students Acquiring English

3 Students acquiring English may have trouble with this phrase. You may want to lead a discussion about how someone could sound tall. If necessary, point out that people who feel very proud often stand up straight and look taller.

Multicultural ● **Perspectives**

THE WALL OF RESPECT The narrator recognizes four African-American heroes on the wall, one of whom is Fannie Lou Hamer. Hamer, a poor, uneducated farmer, gained prominence in the early 1960s as a civil rights activist in Mississippi. She helped lead the voting rights movement.

Also on the wall is the African-American flag, the red, black, and green flag that Side Pocket calls "our liberation flag." This flag was introduced by Marcus Garvey in the 1920s and represents the blood (red), race (black), and hopes (green) of African Americans.

Ask students to think about the subjects of the mural and what African-American heroes, flags of various African countries, and people in the neighborhood have in common. Then have students discuss why they think the painter lady chose to connect these subjects in her work.

Art Note

Another Times Voice Remembers My Passion's Humanity by Calvin B. Jones and Mitchell Caton This street mural was created in 1979 and restored in 1993. It was painted on the Elliott Donnelley Youth Center in Chicago.

Reading the Art *What do you think the title of this mural means? What subjects can you identify on the mural? How might these subjects be connected?*

L Ask students to tell what the painter lady does to the neighborhood wall. *(She creates a mural on the wall that depicts African-American heroes, the African-American flag and the flags of various African countries, and people who live in the neighborhood.)* **Noting Relevant Details**

Ask students to discuss how they think the members of the neighborhood feel about the finished mural. *(They are awestruck and very pleased with the painter lady's work. They feel proud of this addition to their neighborhood.)* **Making Inferences**

COMPREHENSION CHECK

1. How do Lou and the narrator feel about Jimmy Lyons? *(They respect him highly; Jimmy Lyons grew up in the neighborhood and was planning to take Lou and the narrator fishing. After his death in Vietnam, Lou and the narrator chisel his name into the wall.)*

2. Why do the narrator and Lou resent the painter lady? *(She is not from their city or town; she doesn't speak to them; she is going to "deface" a place that they hold dear.)*

3. How do the children intend to make their feelings about the painter lady's work known? *(They plan to use spray paint to deface the mural with graffiti.)*

4. Why did the painter lady paint the mural? *(to honor her cousin's memory with a gift to his neighborhood)*

Another Times Voice Remembers My Passion's Humanity (1979), Calvin B. Jones and Mitchell Caton. Outdoor mural, 22′ × 48′, Elliott Donnelley Youth Center, Chicago. Restored in 1993 by Bernard Williams and Paige Hinson, Chicago Mural Project.

to a high section of the wall. There was a fierce-looking man with his arms crossed against his chest guarding a bunch of children. His muscles bulged, and he looked a lot like my daddy. One kid was looking at a row of books. Lou hunched me 'cause the kid looked like me. The one that looked like Lou was spinning a globe on the tip of his finger like a basketball. There were other kids there with microscopes and compasses. And the more I looked, the more it looked like the fierce man was not so much guarding the kids as defending their right to do what they were doing.

Then Lou gasped and dropped the paint bag and ran forward, running his hands over a rainbow. He had to tiptoe and stretch to do it, it was so high. I couldn't breathe either. The painter lady had found the chisel marks and had painted Jimmy Lyons's name in a rainbow.

"Read the inscription, honey," Mrs. Morris said, urging little Frieda forward. She didn't have to urge much. Frieda marched right up, bent down, and in a loud voice that made everybody quit oohing and ahhing and listen, she read,

> *To the People of Taliaferro Street*
> *I Dedicate This Wall of Respect*
> *Painted in Memory of My Cousin*
> *Jimmy Lyons*

WORDS
TO
KNOW

inscription (ĭn-skrĭp′shən) *n.* something written, carved, or engraved on a surface

90

Mini-Lesson **Literary Concepts**

MUSIC Throughout history, music has been used as a means of expressing emotions and relating experiences. Some of the heroes portrayed by the painter lady have used music to tell their own personal stories and express themselves. These people include the singer Billie Holiday and the musicians Louis Armstrong and Duke Ellington.

Application Play several of the recordings of the artists mentioned. Ask students to write their impressions as they listen to the music. Tell them to be sure to note any emotion or message they think the music conveys. Then have students share their impressions with the rest of the class.

CAVE PAINTINGS

Prehistoric rock painting from Tassili n'Ajjer, Algeria, depicting women, children and cattle. Musée de l'Homme, Paris. Erich Lessing/Art Resource, New York.

Although the wall-of-respect movement began in the 1960s, painting on walls is hardly a new idea. The oldest known human paintings were made during the Upper Paleolithic period about 10,000–40,000 years ago. Some of the most famous of these paintings are found on the walls of the caves of Lascaux, in France, and Altamira, in Spain.

Although the cave artists did occasionally paint people, most of their paintings are of animals, such as bison, bulls, mammoths, deer, and horses. The motives of the cave artists are unknown. They might have believed that the paintings gave them power in communicating with their gods, magical control over animals, or special strength and success in hunting.

Many of the paintings are artistically superb. The artists used the colors black, white, brown, red, and yellow, which they obtained from such natural sources as charcoal, clay, and ocher (a kind of iron ore). Each pigment was sprayed on in powder form through a bone blowpipe, mixed with grease to form a kind of crayon, or made into a paint and applied with fingers or brushes. Some of the animals painted in Lascaux span 18 feet and were painted over swellings on the walls, which give them a realistic, three-dimensional effect.

CAVE PAINTINGS **91**

Mini-Lesson Spelling

DIFFERENT K SOUNDS Explain to students that the k sound has several different spellings. Usually, the letters c, ck, and k, as in the words *inscription, lock,* and *kid* are used to spell the k sound. Sometimes, the letters ch, as in the word *scheme,* represent this sound.

Application Write the following words on the chalkboard and ask students to identify the letters that spell the k sound:
1. attack (atta**ck**)
2. describe (des**c**ribe)
3. forecast (fore**c**ast)
4. bicker (bi**ck**er)
5. character (**ch**ara**c**ter)
6. school (s**ch**ool)

Ask students to look for more words that fit this pattern, in their own writing and in things that they read, and to add these words to their personal word lists.

Reteaching/Reinforcement
• *Unit One Resource Book,* p. 53

1. Accept all reasonable responses. Some students may say that they were surprised by the ending because they thought the painter lady had no connection with the neighborhood. Others may say that they were not surprised by the ending because they had guessed who the painter lady was.

2. Possible response: She manages to connect the living neighborhood to heroes of the past, to a personal hero (Jimmy Lyons), and to the wider world that includes nations of Africa.

3. Possible responses: Yes, because when people go by the wall, they will think of Jimmy Lyons and connect themselves with the other African-American heroes on the wall. No, the people don't need a wall like that to have self-respect.

4. Possible responses: Other people in the neighborhood knew who she was; the others may have wanted to wait and see what she would do.

5. Possible responses: Yes, because the wall belonged to their neighborhood, not to some outsider. No, because the painter lady is obviously trying to create a work of art for the people of the neighborhood.

6. Possible response: They would want to include heroes who are part of their common heritage, so that neighborhood people will be inspired by them.

Another Pathway

Students should work together to select the issues they want to address in their letter and the tone and formality of the writing style. You may wish to have one student write the letter and his or her partner edit it.

Rubric

3 Full Accomplishment Students' letters are organized, grammatically correct, and consistent with the natures of the characters.

2 Substantial Accomplishment Students' letters are organized and somewhat true to character.

1 Little or Partial Accomplishment Students' letters are poorly organized and do not consistently reflect the natures of Lou and the narrator.

RESPONDING
OPTIONS

FROM PERSONAL RESPONSE TO CRITICAL ANALYSIS

REFLECT
1. What thoughts came to mind as you finished reading this story? Record them in your notebook.

RETHINK
2. What do you think the painter lady accomplishes by creating the mural?
   Consider Close Textual Reading
   - the inscription on the mural
   - the people and images depicted in the mural
   - what the "wall of respect" means to the neighborhood

3. Do you think the mural will make a difference in the lives of the neighborhood kids? Explain your answer.

4. An army of only two tries to wage war against the painter lady. Why do you think others in the neighborhood don't join the battle?

5. Do you think the narrator has a right to be upset when the painter lady first appears? Why or why not?

RELATE
6. If an artist painted a mural in your neighborhood, what heroes do you think your neighbors would want represented? Why?

Multimodal Learning
ANOTHER PATHWAY

Put yourself in the shoes of the narrator or Lou. With a partner, compose a letter that the narrator and Lou might send to the painter lady after seeing her mural. When you and your partner are finished, share your letter with the rest of the class.

THE WRITER'S STYLE

Bambara uses hyphenated expressions as adjectives to help readers better understand and imagine what she describes. For example, what kind of voice did you imagine when you read that Side Pocket used "his best ain't-I-fine voice" (page 85)? Look back through the story to find other examples of hyphenated adjectives. Then make up some of your own and use them in a description of someone or something.

QUICKWRITES

1. Write a **speech** that the painter lady might deliver to the community if she were to return for the dedication of the mural.

2. Write a **newspaper article** that a local reporter might write about the mural, explaining its creation, theme, and effect on the community.

3. Think about the place in your neighborhood that seems to belong to young people—the one you wrote about for the Personal Connection on page 83. Then write a **personal narrative** that tells why that place is special.

PORTFOLIO Save your writing. You may want to use it later as a springboard to a piece for your portfolio.

The Writer's Style

Examples in the selection include "paint-spattered" and "floppy-brimmed" on page 85. You may want to brainstorm with the students to create a list of other hyphenated expressions on the chalkboard. Students could then write a few sentences that use the examples they made up themselves.

QuickWrites

1. Speeches should acknowledge the painter lady's relationship to the community through her cousin, Jimmy Lyons.

2. Tell students that a newspaper article is made up of facts, not opinions, that answer the questions *who, what, why, where, when,* and *how.* Students should try to stay objective.

3. Remind students to use details that tell why the place is special. They should also use the first-person point of view.

The Writer's Craft

Feature Article, pp. 208–210

Multimodal Learning
ALTERNATIVE ACTIVITIES

1. The "flags of liberation" that the painter lady includes in her mural are depictions of the African-American flag. Its colors represent the blood (red), the race (black), and the hopes (green) of African Americans. Design a **flag** for your community, school, or classroom. Exhibit your flag and tell what each color or symbol on it represents.

2. Many of the words and expressions in this story are dialect or slang. Working with a partner, use three or more of these expressions in role-playing a **dialogue** between the narrator and Jimmy Lyons before he leaves for Vietnam.

LITERARY CONCEPTS

A **conflict** is a struggle between opposing forces. The struggle can be between a character and an outside force—such as another character, society, or nature—or it can be within a character's mind as he or she grapples with a problem or decision. How would you describe the main conflict in this story?

CONCEPT REVIEW: Point of View A story told from the **first-person point of view** is narrated by a character within the story. One told from the **third-person point of view** is narrated by someone outside the story. Which point of view is used in "The War of the Wall"? Why do you think Bambara chose that point of view?

Multimodal Learning
ACROSS THE CURRICULUM

History Research the wall-of-respect movement or one of the four African-American heroes that the narrator recognizes in the painter lady's mural. Prepare and deliver an **oral report** about the subject you researched.

Mural (1980), Judy Jamerson. Church St. Mission High School, San Francisco.

History *Cooperative Learning* Divide the class into five groups. Assign one group the wall-of-respect movement and each of the other groups one of the four heroes. Encourage all group members to help present the oral report.

ADDITIONAL SUGGESTION

Geography *Cooperative Learning* Invite students to look at a map of Africa and identify the places whose flags are depicted in the mural. Then divide the class into several groups to investigate more about each of the countries listed. Within the groups, students should assign one person to research history, another to research customs and culture, and another to research physical features of the country. When they have finished their research, ask each group to present its findings to the rest of the class.

HISTORICAL CONNECTION
Heroes These portraits of Martin Luther King, Jr., Mary Bethune, W.E.B. Du Bois, and Harriet Tubman can be used as an introduction to students' research on these important leaders.

Side A, Frame 49243

Alternative Activities

1. Students should think about what makes their community, school, or classroom special. They may want to brainstorm several preliminary designs before making their flags.
2. Before they begin role-playing, students will want to create brief character sketches of Jimmy Lyons and the narrator. They should also think of an appropriate scenario for the dialogue and decide on its tone.

Literary Concepts

Have students work with partners. Have each pair work to identify the conflicts in the story. Ask the students to decide whether the conflicts they identify are external or internal conflicts. Lead a discussion about which is the story's main conflict.

Concept Review Point of View Possible response: The story uses a first-person point of view so that the reader may identify with the narrator and experience the conflict with great immediacy.

ART CONNECTION

Study the illustration on page 87. Do you think it does a good job of capturing the mood of the narrator and Lou in this story? Why or why not?

Sibling Rivals (1989), Phoebe Beasley. Collage, 32″ × 40″, courtesy of the artist.

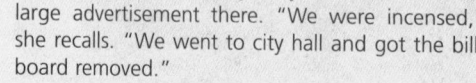

WORDS TO KNOW

EXERCISE A Review the Words to Know in the boxes at the bottom of the selection pages. Then read each book title below and choose a vocabulary word that you would expect to find in that book. Write the word on your paper and explain why you would expect to find it in the book.

1. *The Speech Patterns of Slow Talkers*
2. *The True Story of a Million-Dollar Bank Robbery*
3. *Nonverbal Communication: A Study of Gestures and Their Meanings*
4. *Memoirs of a Former Slave*
5. *History Recorded on Tombstones*

EXERCISE B Using as many of the vocabulary words as you can, retell the plot of this story to a partner.

TONI CADE BAMBARA

Toni Cade Bambara wrote numerous short stories. She was also a screenwriter and novelist and won an American Book Award. Bambara believed that writers "are everyday people who write stories that come out of their neighborhoods." "The War of the Wall" was inspired by her own memories. As a child, she and her companions created a park in a vacant city lot. One day they found a large advertisement there. "We were incensed," she recalls. "We went to city hall and got the billboard removed."

1939–1995

Bambara also worked in a welfare department, planned recreation for mentally ill patients, held community-action workshops, and taught at a college. In her later years she produced documentaries and videos for organizations that help needy people. One of her works, *The Bombing of Osage Avenue*, won several awards. Bambara was born in New York City, and also lived in Atlanta and Philadelphia.

OTHER WORKS "Raymond's Run"; "My Delicate Heart Condition"; *Gorilla, My Love; The Sea Birds Are Still Alive; The Salt Eaters*

Extended Reading

LASERLINKS
• *HISTORICAL CONNECTION*
• *ART GALLERY*

WHAT DO YOU THINK?

Reflecting on Theme

Have students recall their ideas about change that they wrote about or sketched before reading the selections in Part 2. Ask them to compare their thoughts then with their thoughts now after reading about the narrator's and Lou's response to change. If their thoughts are different now, invite them to revise their paragraphs, comic books, or storyboards to reflect those new ideas.

FICTION

Last Cover
Paul Annixter

PERSONAL CONNECTION Activating Prior Knowledge / Setting a Purpose

Do you know people who feel strong attachments to their pets? Why do you think some people develop such close ties with animals? What can a pet offer that a person cannot? Which animals do you think make especially good pets? Discuss these questions with a small group of classmates. As you read this story, think about the bond between the two boys and the red fox they raise as a pet.

Fox Hunting, the Find, Currier & Ives.
Scala/Art Resource, New York.

Building Background
SCIENCE CONNECTION

The red fox is the most common fox in the northern United States. Clever, quick, and gifted with keen hearing and a sharp sense of smell, a red fox makes an excellent hunter but a poor pet. A fox and its mate may roam many miles to stake out a territory in which to hunt and raise their young. This territory may be as large as 70 city blocks.

Foxes are often hunted for their fur, for sport, or because their raids on chicken coops are a nuisance to farmers. In some fox hunts, like the one in this story, hunters on horseback use dogs to follow the scent of a fox. The dogs' barking reveals the fox's hiding place.

Active Reading
READING CONNECTION

Context Clues In "Last Cover" you may encounter some unfamiliar words. Often you can figure out the meaning of an unfamiliar word by means of **context clues**—words or sentences around it that suggest its meaning. As you read this story for the first time, use context clues to guess at the meaning of any unfamiliar words. Then, during a second reading, use a chart like the one shown to jot down words and phrases, the context clues, and the probable meanings.

Word or Phrase	Context Clues	Probable Meaning
kit	"tiny," "pet fox Colin and I had raised"	a baby fox
pine	"set a lot of store by"	
pranking		

LASERLINKS
• SCIENCE CONNECTION   95

SCIENCE CONNECTION
The Red Fox The red fox is one of the most widespread species of animals in North America. The information in these images will help students better understand the world of the red fox.

Side A, Frame 49258

SUMMARY

Stan narrates this story of his younger brother, Colin, and their pet fox, Bandit. The boys' father, a hunter and woodsman, scorns Colin's sensitive, artistic nature. He doesn't know that when Bandit returns to the wild, Colin skillfully tracks and observes his former pet. When neighbors' chickens start disappearing, local hunters plot to kill Bandit. After Bandit is killed, Colin creates a masterful drawing that shows the fox camouflaged in the last hiding place where Colin saw him. Even the best woodsmen had never found this place. The father, seeing that Colin shares his deep affinity for nature, gains new respect for Colin and his art.

Thematic Link: *Letting Others In* A shared love of nature helps a boy and his father let each other into their lives and hearts as they strive to protect a red fox named Bandit.

CUSTOMIZING FOR
Students Acquiring English

• Use **ACCESS FOR STUDENTS ACQUIRING ENGLISH**, *Reading and Writing Support*.

• The Reading Connection activity on using context clues to guess unfamiliar vocabulary will be very helpful to many students acquiring English. You may want to pair these students with their native-speaking classmates for this activity.

STRATEGIC READING FOR
Less-Proficient Readers

Set a Purpose To help students become familiar with the story, have them read to learn the personality traits of the two boys. Ask students to watch for each boy's response to the loss of the fox.

Use **UNIT ONE RESOURCE BOOK**, p. 57, for guidance in reading the selection.

LAST COVER

by Paul Annixter

I'm not sure I can tell you what you want to know about my brother; but everything about the pet fox is important, so I'll tell all that from the beginning.

It goes back to a winter afternoon after I'd hunted the woods all day for a sign of our lost pet. I remember the way (A) my mother looked up as I came into the kitchen. Without my speaking, she knew what had happened. For six hours I had walked, reading signs, looking for a delicate print in the damp soil or even a hair that might have told of a red fox passing that way—but I had found nothing.

"Did you go up in the foothills?" Mom asked.

I nodded. My face was stiff from held-back tears. My brother, Colin, who was going on twelve, got it all from one look at me and went into a heartbroken, almost silent, crying.

Three weeks before, Bandit, the pet fox Colin and I had raised from a tiny kit, had disappeared, and not even a rumor had been heard of him since.

WORDS TO KNOW

bleak (blēk) *adj.* harsh and dreary (p. 98)
confound (kən-found′) *v.* to bewilder; confuse (p. 102)
essence (ĕs′əns) *n.* basic nature or spirit (p. 103)
harried (hăr′ēd) *adj.* worried; distressed (p. 103)
intricate (ĭn′trĭ-kĭt) *adj.* elaborately detailed (p. 105)
invalid (ĭn′və-lĭd) *n.* a sickly or disabled person (p. 99)

passive (păs′ĭv) *adj.* inactive, lacking in energy or willpower (p. 99)
sanction (săngk′shən) *v.* to give approval for (p. 102)
sanctuary (săngk′chōō-ĕr′ē) *n.* shelter; protection (p. 105)
wily (wī′lē) *adj.* crafty; sly (p. 103)

Detail of illustration by Wendell Minor reprinted from *Red Fox Running* by Eve Bunting. Copyright ©1993 by Wendell Minor, published by Clarion Books.

LAST COVER **97**

Have students look, as they read the selection, for clues that reflect Sumter's (the father's) feelings about the fox and about Colin. Invite them to look for signs of change in his feelings as the story unfolds. What makes his feelings change?

Possible responses:

- *Page 99:* "'Ever since you started talking up Colin's art, I've had an invalid for help around the place.'" (Colin and his art are useless.)

- *Page 99:* "'Watch out with all your soft ways,' Father had warned. . . . "You'll make too much of him.'" (Colin is soft-hearted and spoiled.)

- *Page 102:* "Father, who took pride in all the ritual of the hunt, had refused to be a party to such an affair, though in justice he could do nothing but sanction any sort of hunt. . . ." (Father can't bear to hunt the fox.)

- *Page 102:* "He didn't like what was on any more than I did. . . ." (Father doesn't want the fox to be killed.)

- *Page 105:* "He sat holding the picture with a sort of tenderness for a long time. . . ." (Colin's art is something to be admired.)

- *Page 105:* "When the time came for Colin to go to art school, it was Father who was his solid backer." (Father supports Colin's artistic ability.)

Literary Concept: SETTING

A Explain to students that the setting is the time and place of the action of a story, a poem, or a play. Sometimes the setting is clear and well defined, as it is in "Last Cover." At other times, the setting is left up to the reader's imagination. The setting may include geographic location, the historical period (past, present, or future), season, time of day, and customs and manners of the society. Invite students to look for clues that describe the setting of "Last Cover." (p. 96: kitchen, woods in winter)

Mini-Lesson  Literary Concepts

REVIEWING CONFLICT Remind students that a conflict is a struggle between opposing forces. An external conflict occurs when a character struggles against an outside force or person. An internal conflict occurs when the struggle is within a character's own mind.

Application Divide the class into three groups. Have each group pick a main character from the selection—Stan, Colin, or Father—and list the conflicts the character faces in the story. Have students separate external and internal conflicts. Invite each group to present its list to the class.

B What does Mom mean when she says about Bandit, "he's got to live his life same as us"? *(Possible response: She is comparing the fox's need to be free and to find a mate with that of children growing up and creating lives of their own, away from their parents.)*

Literary Concept: CONFLICT

C Remind students that conflict is a struggle between two opposing forces. Point out the conflict between Colin and his father over the fox. Ask students what the two opposing opinions are in this conflict. *(Father is sure that Bandit is a chicken and egg stealer; Colin loves the fox and thinks his bad habits are due to his being a young fox.)*

Linking to Science

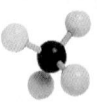

D Father recites a rhyme that tells of the seven sleepers—animals that hibernate, or lie dormant, through the winter. During hibernation, animals don't merely go to sleep, as many people think. Actually, several of their bodily functions, including temperature, breathing rate, and heart rate are dramatically reduced. Do students know why animals hibernate? *(to protect themselves from winter cold and to cut down on the amount of food they need)*

STRATEGIC READING FOR
Less-Proficient Readers

E Ask students how Colin reacts to the loss of the fox. Is the narrator's reaction the same? *(Colin cries, then decides to make a picture. The narrator wants to cry but feels he is too old for that.)* Comparing and Contrasting

Set a Purpose As students read, have them pay attention to the importance of the fox to the boys.

"He'd have had to go off soon anyway," Mom comforted. "A big, lolloping fellow like **B** him, he's got to live his life same as us. But he may come back. That fox set a lot of store by you boys in spite of his wild ways."

C "He set a lot of store by our food, anyway," Father said. He sat in a chair by the kitchen window mending a piece of harness. "We'll be seeing a lot more of that fellow, never fear. That fox learned to pine for table scraps and young chickens. He was getting to be an egg thief, too, and he's not likely to forget that."

"That was only pranking when he was little," Colin said desperately.

From the first, the tame fox had made tension in the family. It was Father who said we'd better name him Bandit, after he'd made away with his first young chicken.

"Maybe you know," Father said shortly. "But when an animal turns to egg sucking, he's usually incurable. He'd better not come pranking around my chicken run again."

It was late February, and I remember the <u>bleak</u>, dead cold that had set in, cold that was a rare thing for our Carolina hills. Flocks of sparrows and snowbirds had appeared, to peck hungrily at all that the pigs and chickens didn't eat.

"This one's a killer," Father would say of a morning, looking out at the whitened barn roof. "This one will make the shoats[1] squeal."

A fire snapped all day in our cookstove and another in the stone fireplace in the living room, but still the farmhouse was never warm. The leafless woods were bleak and empty, and I spoke of that to Father when I came back from my search.

"It's always a sad time in the woods when the seven sleepers are under cover," he said.

"What sleepers are they?" I asked. Father was full of woods lore.

"Why, all the animals that have got sense enough to hole up and stay hid in weather like this. Let's see, how was it the old rhyme named them?

> *Surly bear and sooty bat,*
> *Brown chuck and masked coon,*
> *Chippy-munk and sly skunk,*
> *And all the mouses*
> *'Cept in men's houses.*

"And man would have joined them and made it eight, Granther Yeary always said, if he'd had a little more sense."

"I was wondering if the red fox mightn't make it eight," Mom said.

Father shook his head. "Late winter's a high time for foxes. Time when they're out deviling, not sleeping."

y chest felt hollow. I wanted to cry like Colin over our lost fox, but at fourteen a boy doesn't cry. Colin had squatted down on the floor and got out his small hammer and nails to start another new frame for a new picture. Maybe then he'd make a drawing for the frame and be able to forget his misery. It had been that way with **E** him since he was five.

I thought of the new dress Mom had brought home a few days before in a heavy cardboard box. That box cover would be fine for Colin to draw on. I spoke of it, and Mom's glance thanked me as she went to get it. She and I worried a lot about Colin. He was small for his age, delicate and blond, his hair much lighter and softer than mine, his eyes deep and wide and blue. He was often sick, and I knew the fear Mom had that he

---

1. **shoats** (shōts): young pigs.

| WORDS TO KNOW | **bleak** (blēk) *adj.* harsh and dreary |

98

Mini-Lesson **Reading Skills/Strategies**

USING CONTEXT CLUES Using context clues helps readers understand new words or phrases. Context clues are the words or phrases before or after unfamiliar words. Context clues may define a word, give synonyms, give examples, provide comparisons or contrasts, or enable readers to infer meaning.

Application Have the students copy the chart on page 95. Have them extend the chart by jotting down any unfamiliar phrases and searching out

context clues to infer their meanings. Students might begin with the following examples:

"white-livered" interpretation (p. 99)

soft ways (p. 99)

held his ground (p. 100)

time-honored rules (p.102)

Reteaching/Reinforcement
• *Unit One Resource Book*, p. 58

might be predestined.[2] I'm just ordinary, like Father. I'm the sort of stuff that can take it—tough and strong—but Colin was always sort of special.

Mom lighted the lamp. Colin began cutting his white cardboard carefully, fitting it into his frame. Father's sharp glance turned on him now and again.

"There goes the boy making another frame before there's a picture for it," he said. "It's too much like cutting out a man's suit for a fellow that's, say, twelve years old. Who knows whether he'll grow into it?"

Mom was into him then, quick. "Not a single frame of Colin's has ever gone to waste. The boy has real talent, Sumter, and it's time you realized it."

"Of course he has," Father said. "All kids have 'em. But they get over 'em."

"It isn't the pox[3] we're talking of," Mom sniffed.

"In a way it is. Ever since you started talking up Colin's art, I've had an <u>invalid</u> for help around the place."

Father wasn't as hard as he made out, I knew, but he had to hold a balance against all Mom's frothing.[4] For him the thing was the land and all that pertained to it. I was following in Father's footsteps, true to form, but Colin threatened to break the family tradition with his leaning toward art, with Mom "aiding and abetting[5] him," as Father liked to put it. For the past two years she had had dreams of my brother becoming a real artist and going away to the city to study.

It wasn't that Father had no understanding of such things. I could remember, through the years, Colin lying on his stomach in the front room making pencil sketches, and how a good drawing would catch Father's eye halfway across the room, and how he would sometimes

gather up two or three of them to study, frowning and muttering, one hand in his beard, while a great pride rose in Colin, and in me too. Most of Colin's drawings were of the woods and wild things, and there Father was a master critic. He made out to scorn what seemed to him a <u>passive</u>, "white-livered" interpretation of nature through brush and pencil instead of rod and rifle.

At supper that night Colin could scarcely eat. Ever since he'd been able to walk, my brother had had a growing love of wild things, but Bandit had been like his very own, a gift of the woods. One afternoon a year and a half before, Father and Laban Small had been running a vixen through the hills with their dogs. With the last of her strength the she-fox had made for her den, not far from our house. The dogs had overtaken her and killed her just before she reached it. When Father and Laban came up, they'd found Colin crouched nearby, holding her cub in his arms.

Father had been for killing the cub, which was still too young to shift for itself, but Colin's grief had brought Mom into it. We'd taken the young fox into the kitchen, all of us, except Father, gone a bit silly over the little thing. Colin had held it in his arms and fed it warm milk from a spoon.

"Watch out with all your soft ways," Father had warned, standing in the doorway. "You'll make too much of him. Remember, you can't make a dog out of a fox. Half of that little critter has to love, but the other half is a wild

---

2. **predestined** (prē-dĕs′tĭnd): having one's fate decided beforehand; in this case, chosen by God for an early death.

3. **pox**: chickenpox, a contagious disease causing skin eruptions.

4. **frothing** (frôth′ĭng): light, meaningless talking.

5. **aiding and abetting**: helping and encouraging.

| WORDS TO KNOW | **invalid** (ĭn′və-lĭd) *n.* a sickly or disabled person |
| | **passive** (păs′ĭv) *adj.* inactive; lacking in energy or willpower |

99

F What does the statement "Father wasn't as hard as he made out, I knew, but he had to hold a balance against all Mom's frothing" indicate about Father's and Stan's relationships with Mom? *(Possible responses: They both see her as the more frivolous member of the family; they "humor" her "frothing" but leave the serious talk to themselves.)*

Literary Concept: CHARACTERIZATION

G Remind students that characterization refers to the techniques a writer uses to create and develop a character. Characterization tells the reader what the character is like. Stan, the narrator, suggests that he is like his father, whereas Colin is not. What different character traits do the two brothers have? *(Stan is interested in hunting, is confident, and refuses to cry when Bandit is lost. Colin is interested in art, is sensitive, and cries when Bandit is lost.)*

CUSTOMIZING FOR
Students Acquiring English

I Explain that the idiom *had been for* means "had been in favor of" and that *shift for itself* means "take care of itself."

Active Reading: CLARIFY

H Discuss the events in the story so far. Some of them take place in the present, and some take place in the past. The following model may help students review the action so far.

Think-Aloud Model *This story is a bit confusing. It seems to begin as if Stan is telling it in the present, but then it flashes back to the time when Bandit was lost. Then it goes even farther back to the time when Bandit first became Stan and Colin's pet. I will need to stop every once in a while to review events so I can keep track of what happened in the past and what is happening in the present.*

| Mini-Lesson | Grammar |

VERB TENSES A verb has different forms called tenses.

- The present tense places an action or existing condition in the present: Colin <u>attends</u> art school.
- The past tense places an action or condition in the past: Colin and Stan <u>loved</u> Bandit.
- The future tense places an action or condition in the future: Colin <u>will draw</u> hundreds of pictures of Bandit.

Application Have students read the following sentences and tell what tense each verb is in.
1. We <u>fed</u> the fox cub bits of meat. *(past)*

2. Colin <u>makes</u> frames for his pictures. *(present)*
3. Bandit <u>steals</u> chickens during the night. *(present)*
4. The farmers <u>will</u> <u>search</u> for him together. *(future)*
5. The fox <u>hid</u> quietly in the pool. *(past)*
6. Father <u>finds</u> the hidden fox in Colin's drawing. *(present)*

Reteaching/Reinforcement
- Grammar Handbook, anthology pp. 871–872
- *Grammar Mini-Lessons* copymasters pp. 24–26, transparencies pp. 16 and 18–19

The Writer's Craft

Tenses of Verbs, pp. 474–475

STRATEGIC READING FOR
Less-Proficient Readers

J How do the boys feel about their pet fox? (*They both love the fox and are dedicated to him.*) **Using Context Clues**

• What other traits do the boys have in common? (*They both have a deep appreciation for the woods and for each other.*) **Comparing and Contrasting**

Set a Purpose Invite students to read on to find out how Bandit behaves in the spring and early summer.

CUSTOMIZING FOR
Students Acquiring English

2 Students may need help understanding the reference to an Indian, in this case meaning a Native American. Explain that many Native American tribes, due to living in the wilderness, had developed an understanding and knowledge of wildlife and their environments.

CUSTOMIZING FOR
Multiple Learning Styles

K **Intrapersonal Learners** Invite students to imagine what it would be like to be Colin writing a journal about his experiences with Bandit. How would Colin tell the story? Ask students to create a journal entry that describes the day that he rediscovered Bandit in the woods. Then ask students to form small groups and share their entries.

Critical Thinking:
HYPOTHESIZING

L What does the author mean by "He really loved us back, with a fierce, secret love no tame thing ever gave"? (*He may mean that Bandit didn't show his affection in the way tame animals do. Instead he showed it by letting the boys see him and letting them know he trusted them.*)

---

hunter. You boys will mean a whole lot to him while he's a kit, but there'll come a day when you won't mean a thing to him and he'll leave you shorn."[6]

For two weeks after that Colin had nursed the cub, weaning it from milk to bits of meat. For a year they were always together. The cub grew fast. It was soon following Colin and me about the barnyard. It turned out to be a patch fox, with a saddle of darker fur across its shoulders.

I haven't the words to tell you what the fox meant to us. It was far more wonderful owning him than owning any dog. There was something rare and secret like the spirit of the woods about him, and back of his calm, straw-gold eyes was the sense of a brain the equal of a man's. The fox became Colin's whole life.

Each day, going and coming from school, Colin and I took long side trips through the woods, looking for Bandit. Wild things' memories were short, we knew; we'd have to find him soon, or the old bond would be broken.

Ever since I was ten, I'd been allowed to hunt with Father, so I was good at reading signs. But, in a way, Colin knew more about the woods and wild things than Father or me. What came to me from long observation Colin seemed to know by instinct.

It was Colin who felt out, like an Indian, the stretch of woods where Bandit had his den, who found the first slim, small fox-print in the damp earth. And then, on an afternoon in March, we saw him. I remember the day well, the racing clouds, the wind rattling the tops of the pine trees and swaying the Spanish moss. Bandit had just come out of a clump of laurel; in the maze of leaves behind him we caught a glimpse of a slim red vixen, so we knew he had found a mate. She melted from sight like a shadow, but Bandit turned to watch us, his mouth open, his tongue lolling as he smiled his

old foxy smile. On his thin chops, I saw a telltale chicken feather.

Colin moved silently forward, his movements so quiet and casual he seemed to be standing still. He called Bandit's name, and the fox held his ground, drawn to us with all his senses. For a few moments he let Colin actually put an arm about him. It was then I knew that he loved us still, for all of Father's warnings. He really loved us back, with a fierce, secret love no tame thing ever gave. But the urge of his life just then was toward his new mate. Suddenly, he whirled about and disappeared in the laurels.

Colin looked at me with glowing eyes. "We haven't really lost him, Stan. When he gets through with his spring sparking,[7] he may come back. But we've got to show ourselves to him a lot, so he won't forget."

"It's a go," I said.

"Promise not to say a word to Father," Colin said, and I agreed. For I knew by the chicken feather that Bandit had been up to no good.

A week later the woods were budding, and the thickets were rustling with all manner of wild things scurrying on the love scent. Colin managed to get a glimpse of Bandit every few days. He couldn't get close though, for the spring running was a lot more important to a fox than any human beings were.

Every now and then Colin got out his framed box cover and looked at it, but he never drew anything on it; he never even picked up his pencil. I remember wondering if what Father had said about framing a picture before you had one had spoiled something for him.

I was helping Father with the planting now, but Colin managed to be in the woods every

---

6. **shorn:** cut off, like hair; forsaken.
7. **spring sparking:** the springtime mating period.

Mini-Lesson **Study Skills**

REFERENCE BOOKS Reference books such as an almanac or encyclopedia can provide students with in-depth information on almost any topic they choose. Show students an almanac, an encyclopedia, and an atlas and have them flip through the books to see how they are organized.

Application Invite students to pick a topic from the story, such as foxes, or hibernation, and look it up in the encyclopedia. Have them jot down any information they find pertinent to the story. Then have them share their findings with the class.

Albert's Son (1959), Andrew Wyeth. Tempera on board, 74 cm × 61.5 cm, The National Museum of Contemporary Art, Oslo, Norway. Photo by Jacques Lathion, Nasjonalgalleriet.

Albert's Son by **Andrew Wyeth**
Andrew Wyeth is one of the most popular painters of realistic subjects in the United States. He created this painting with tempera paints in 1959. In it, he tries to show the personality and character traits of his subject.

Reading the Art *What does Wyeth want you to think about Albert's son? What details give you clues about the boy's character? Does Albert's son look like your image of one of the characters in "Last Cover"?*

Active Reading: PREDICT

 Ask students to predict what Colin might be thinking about drawing on his framed box top. *(Possible responses: the woods, Stan, Bandit)*

Assessment ✓ Option

SELF-ASSESSMENT
Retelling Students can assess their understanding of the story so far by retelling what has happened from a different point of view. Suggest that they choose to be Mom, Father, or one of the angry farmers, and have them give their side of the story to a small group of classmates.

Rubric
3 Full Accomplishment Students accurately, concisely, and specifically describe the events in the selection so far. The point of view and personality traits of the character they have chosen are easily identifiable.

2 Substantial Accomplishment Students describe most events in the selection accurately. The point of view and traits of the character they have chosen are not as easily identifiable and may need a little focusing.

I Little or Partial Accomplishment Students have difficulty describing the events in the selection, missing some, or placing some in incorrect sequence. They also have trouble telling the story from a single point of view.

N Ask students to summarize what Bandit does in early summer. *(He and his mate raid barns and poultry houses, killing farm animals.)* Summarizing

Set a Purpose Invite students to read on to discover where Bandit hides from the angry hunters.

Critical Thinking: ANALYZING

O Why doesn't Father want to participate in the hunt for Bandit? *(Possible responses: He realizes how important the fox is to his sons; he is intrigued by the fox's ability to outwit the hunters; he feels that Bandit is only doing what comes naturally; he does not approve of the hunters' breaking the time-honored rules of hunting in their search for Bandit.)*

day. By degrees, he learned Bandit's range, where he drank and rested and where he was likely to be according to the time of day. One day he told me how he had petted Bandit again and how they had walked together a long way in the woods. All this time we had kept his secret from Father.

As summer came on, Bandit began to live up to the prediction Father had made. Accustomed to human beings, he moved without fear about the scattered farms of the region, raiding barns and hen runs that other foxes wouldn't have dared go near. And he taught his wild mate to do the same. Almost every night they got into some poultry house, and by late June Bandit was not only killing chickens and ducks but feeding on eggs and young chicks whenever he got the chance.

Stories of his doings came to us from many sources, for he was still easily recognized by the dark patch on his shoulders. Many a farmer took a shot at him as he fled, and some of them set out on his trail with dogs, but they always returned home without even sighting him. Bandit was familiar with all the dogs in the region, and he knew a hundred tricks to confound them. He got a reputation that year beyond that of any fox our hills had known. His confidence grew, and he gave up wild hunting altogether and lived entirely off the poultry farmers. By September, the hill farmers banded together to hunt him down.

It was Father who brought home that news one night. All time-honored rules of the fox chase were to be broken in this hunt; if the dogs

couldn't bring Bandit down, he was to be shot on sight. I was stricken and furious. I remember the misery of Colin's face in the lamplight. Father, who took pride in all the ritual of the hunt, had refused to be a party to such an affair, though in justice he could do nothing but sanction any sort of hunt, for Bandit, as old Sam Wetherwax put it, had been "purely getting in the Lord's hair."

The hunt began next morning, and it was the biggest turnout our hills had known. There were at least twenty mounted men in the party and as many dogs.

Father and I were working in the lower field as they passed along the river road. Most of the hunters carried rifles, and they looked ugly.

Twice during the morning I went up to the house to find Colin, but he was nowhere around. As we worked, Father and I could follow the progress of the hunt by the distant hound music on the breeze. We could tell just where the hunters first caught sight of the fox and where Bandit was leading the dogs during the first hour. We knew as well as if we'd seen it how Bandit roused another fox along Turkey Branch and forced it to run for him and how the dogs swept after it for twenty minutes before they sensed their mistake.

Noon came, and Colin had not come in to eat. After dinner Father didn't go back to the field. He moped about, listening to the hound talk. He didn't like what was on any more than I did, and now and again I caught his smile of satisfaction when we heard the broken, angry notes of the hunting horn, telling that the dogs had lost the trail or had run another fox.

WORDS TO KNOW

confound (kən-found′) *v.* to bewilder; confuse
sanction (săngk′shən) *v.* to give approval for

102

Mini-Lesson: Speaking, Listening, and Viewing

STORYTELLING Explain to students that storytelling is a very old tradition. Storytellers often gathered plot ideas from rumors and legends of a particular region, so sometimes story characters included wise or crafty animals like Bandit.

Application Divide the class into groups of three or four. Invite them to imagine they are some of the

hunters who tried to capture Bandit. Have each group come up with its own "Bandit story," in which it describes its hunt for the elusive fox. (Remind students that humor is often a part of storytelling.) When the groups have prepared their stories, have them all gather to tell the collected stories of Bandit.

I was restless, and I went up into the hills in midafternoon. I ranged the woods for miles, thinking all the time of Colin. Time lost all meaning for me, and the short day was nearing an end when I heard the horn talking again, telling that the fox had put over another trick. All day he had deviled the dogs and mocked the hunters. This new trick and the coming night would work to save him. I was wildly glad as I moved down toward Turkey Branch and stood listening for a time by the deep, shaded pool where for years we boys had gone swimming, sailed boats, and dreamed summer dreams.

Suddenly, out of the corner of my eye, I saw the sharp ears and thin, pointed mask of a fox—in the water almost beneath me. It was Bandit, craftily submerged there, all but his head resting in the cool water of the pool and the shadow of the two big beeches that spread above it. He must have run forty miles or more since morning. And he must have hidden in this place before. His knowing, crafty mask blended perfectly with the shadows and a mass of drift and branches that had collected by the bank of the pool. He was so still that a pair of thrushes flew up from the spot as I came up, not knowing he was there.

Bandit's bright, <u>harried</u> eyes were looking right at me. But I did not look at him direct. Some woods instinct, swifter than thought, kept me from it. So he and I met as in another world, indirectly, with feeling but without sign or greeting.

The fox had put over another trick.

Suddenly I saw that Colin was standing almost beside me. Silently as a water snake, he had come out of the bushes and stood there. Our eyes met, and a quick and secret smile passed between us. It was a rare moment in which I really "met" my brother, when something of his <u>essence</u> flowed into me and I knew all of him. I've never lost it since.

My eyes still turned from the fox, my heart pounding. I moved quietly away, and Colin moved with me. We whistled softly as we went, pretending to busy ourselves along the bank of the stream. There was magic in it, as if by will we wove a web of protection about the fox, a ring-pass-not that none might penetrate. It was so, too, we felt, in the brain of Bandit, and that doubled the charm. To us he was still our little pet that we had carried about in our arms on countless summer afternoons.

Two hundred yards upstream, we stopped beside slim, fresh tracks in the mud where Bandit had entered the branch. The tracks angled upstream. But in the water the <u>wily</u> creature had turned down.

We climbed the far bank to wait, and Colin told me how Bandit's secret had been his secret ever since an afternoon three months before, when he'd watched the fox swim downstream to hide in the deep pool. Today he'd waited on the bank, feeling that Bandit, hard pressed by the dogs, might again seek the pool for <u>sanctuary</u>.

WORDS TO KNOW	**harried** (hăr′ēd) *adj.* worried; distressed **harry** *v.*
	essence (ĕs′əns) *n.* basic nature or spirit
	wily (wī′lē) *adj.* crafty; sly
	sanctuary (săngk′chōō-ĕr′ē) *n.* shelter; protection

103

Mini-Lesson · **Genre Study**

FICTION Most fiction is created from the writer's imagination. Fiction contains various literary elements, including setting, plot, character, theme, and tone. "Last Cover" is a **short story** written as fiction. Short stories contain most or all of the literary elements found in longer pieces of fiction.

Application Have students copy the chart and describe the setting, plot, characters, theme, and tone of "Last Cover."

Literary Element	How It Applies to "Last Cover"
setting	
plot	
characters	
theme	
tone	

***Beech Trees* by Gustav Klimt** Austrian painter Gustav Klimt is known for his jewellike paintings that resemble mosaics. He is particularly well known for his colorful portraits of women.

Reading the Art *What feeling do you get when you look at* Beech Trees? *Do these woods look safe or unprotected to you? How does the artist create the effect of light in this painting?*

CUSTOMIZING FOR

Gifted and Talented Students

Throughout the story, the writer refers to magic, secrets, and instinct to describe the relationship between Colin and Bandit. What thoughts and emotions do these words evoke in you as a reader? *(Possible response: They evoke a sense of the unknown and of love beyond human teachings or understanding.)*

Beech Trees (1903), Gustav Klimt. Österreichische Galerie, Vienna, Austria. Erich Lessing/Art Resource, New York.

Mini-Lesson The Writer's Style

AUDIENCE Help students understand that when writers choose words or a way of writing, they usually keep a particular audience in mind. The audience is who the writer hopes or expects will read his or her work.

Application Have students reread the first paragraphs of the selection. Then ask them to write one or two paragraphs explaining who they think Paul

Annixter's intended audience is. Tell them to be sure to cite specific passages from the selection as evidence in support of their opinions.

Reteaching/Reinforcement
- Writing Handbook, anthology p. 809
- *Writing Mini-Lessons* transparencies, p. 26

 The Writer's Craft

Audience, pp. 233–234

We looked back once as we turned homeward. He still had not moved. We didn't know until later that he was killed that same night by a chance hunter, as he crept out from his hiding place.

That evening Colin worked a long time on his framed box cover that had lain about the house untouched all summer. He kept at it all the next day too. I had never seen him work so hard. I seemed to sense in the air the feeling he was putting into it, how he was believing his picture into being. It was evening before he finished it. Without a word he handed it to Father. Mom and I went and looked over his shoulder.

It was a delicate and <u>intricate</u> pencil drawing of the deep branch pool, and there was Bandit's head and watching, fear-filled eyes hiding there amid the leaves and shadows, woven craftily into the maze of twigs and branches, as if by nature's art itself. Hardly a fox there at all, but the place where he was—or should have been. I recognized it instantly, but Mom gave a sort of incredulous sniff.

"I'll declare," she said, "it's mazy as a puzzle. It just looks like a lot of sticks and leaves to me."

Long minutes of study passed before Father's eye picked out the picture's secret, as few men's could have done. I laid that to Father's being a born hunter. That was a picture that might have been done especially for him. In fact, I guess it was.

Finally he turned to Colin with his deep, slow smile. "So that's how Bandit fooled them all," he said. He sat holding the picture with a sort of tenderness for a long time, while we glowed in the warmth of the shared secret. That was Colin's moment. Colin's art stopped being a pox to Father right there. And later, when the time came for Colin to go to art school, it was Father who was his solid backer. ❖

(4)

WORDS
TO
KNOW

intricate (ĭn′trĭ-kĭt) *adj.* elaborately detailed

105

S Why do you think the writer chooses to underplay Bandit's death? *(Possible response: The understanding and trust between Colin and the fox is the focus of the story; Bandit's death is not.)*

CUSTOMIZING FOR

Multiple Learning Styles

T Spatial or Graphic Learners Invite students to re-create Colin's drawing from the description on page 105. Have students interpret, as they draw, the way Bandit camouflages himself among the branches.

STRATEGIC READING FOR

Less-Proficient Readers

U Where does Bandit hide from the hunters? *(in the deep branch pool)* Noting Relevant Details

• Is Bandit ultimately successful in his attempt to elude the hunters? *(No, he is eventually found and killed, although the hunter is not part of the posse.)* Noting Relevant Details

CUSTOMIZING FOR

Students Acquiring English

(4) Call students' attention to the adjective *mazy*. Point out that the root word *maze* is a noun and that the suffix *-y* can be added to many nouns to form adjectives: *Mazy* means "complicated and mysterious; mazelike."

COMPREHENSION CHECK

1. Why are the two boys upset at the beginning of the story? *(Their pet fox has disappeared.)*
2. Why does Father disapprove of the boys' keeping Bandit as a pet? *(He thinks the fox will steal or kill the local livestock; he thinks that Colin is too emotional in his attachment to the animal.)*
3. What secret do the boys keep from their father? *(They know where Bandit is.)*
4. How does Bandit let Colin know that he trusts him? *(He lets Colin put an arm around him and see where he has been hiding.)*
5. What picture does Colin draw at the end of the story? *(Bandit in his hiding place)*
6. How does Father's opinion of Colin's art change after he sees Colin's picture of Bandit? *(He comes to appreciate Colin's art and begins supporting his work.)*

Mini-Lesson Spelling

DIFFERENT SPELLINGS OF ē Explain to students that the ē sound can be spelled in a variety of ways. Have them read aloud the following examples from the selection:

bl<u>ea</u>k   wil<u>y</u>

harr<u>ie</u>d   sl<u>ee</u>ping

Application Copy the following words onto the board and invite volunteers to underline the letters that are pronounced ē.

1. n<u>ea</u>r
2. starr<u>y</u>
3. bl<u>ea</u>ry
4. ferr<u>ie</u>d
5. d<u>ee</u>p
6. str<u>ea</u>m
7. worr<u>ie</u>d
8. prett<u>y</u>
9. l<u>ea</u>d
10. bl<u>ee</u>d

Ask students to look for more words that fit this pattern, in their own writing and in the things that they read, and add these words to their personal word list.

Reteaching/Reinforcement
• *Unit One Resource Book,* p. 59

1. Responses should reflect students' understanding of each of the characters and his or her feelings.
2. Possible response: Father may not really have disapproved of Colin's art but just did not understand it. Later he realizes that he and Colin share the same views and understanding of nature, but they have a different way of expressing it.
3. Possible response: His art tells a story and he knows that the story of Bandit is unfinished until the end, when the fox is killed.
4. Possible response: Colin might feel that he and Bandit have some things in common: they are both outcasts in a way; they both experience things in an instinctual rather than a direct way.
5. Possible response: The last cover refers to Bandit's hiding place in the water and/or Colin's last box cover.
6. Accept all reasonable responses that are adequately supported.

Another Pathway

Cooperative Learning Within each group, members should work collaboratively to decide which scene they want to portray. Then students can brainstorm for particular details they want to include in their reading. One person can write down the scene and the details, another person can research appropriate music to use, and a third person can perform the scene.

Rubric

3 Full Accomplishment Students' readings are organized and accurately reflect the selection and its characters.

2 Substantial Accomplishment Students' readings, for the most part, accurately reflect the selection and its characters but could use some reorganizing.

1 Little or Partial Accomplishment Students' readings are poorly organized and do not consistently and accurately reflect the selection and its characters.

RESPONDING
OPTIONS

FROM PERSONAL RESPONSE TO CRITICAL ANALYSIS

REFLECT 1. What are your thoughts about the relationships in this story? Share your reactions with a partner.

RETHINK 2. How would you explain Father's suddenly changing his mind about Colin's art at the end of the story?

Consider Close Textual Reading
- Father's previous disapproval of Colin's art
- Father's response to Colin's drawing
- what the drawing reveals about Colin

3. Why do you think Colin leaves the framed box cover blank for the entire summer?

4. How would you account for Colin's strong attachment to Bandit?

Consider Close Textual Reading
- Colin's first experiences with Bandit
- what Bandit offers that a dog cannot
- your prereading discussion about people and their pets

5. What do you think the title of this story means?

RELATE 6. Do you think people should raise wild animals as pets? Do you think wild animals should be raised in zoos? Give reasons for your answers.

LITERARY CONCEPTS

The **setting** of a story is the time and place in which the events of the story occur. In this story, Paul Annixter provides several details to help you picture the woods in your imagination. Which details helped you most, and why?

CONCEPT REVIEW: Conflict A **conflict** is a struggle between opposing forces. What conflicts can you identify in this story?

Multimodal Learning
ANOTHER PATHWAY

Working with a small group, rehearse a Readers Theater presentation of key episodes from this story. Select background music that is appropriate to the mood of each episode—for example, the suspense of the fox hunt or the mysteriousness of Bandit's pool. Present your reading to the class.

QUICKWRITES

1. Imagine that Colin is exhibiting his drawings and paintings for the first time. Write an **advertising flyer** about Colin and his art, inviting the public to attend the exhibition.

2. Imagine that Stan in this story and Juliette in "Waiting" are guests on a talk show. The topic for discussion is relationships with brothers or sisters. Write a brief **dialogue** between Stan and Juliette.

PORTFOLIO Save your writing. You may want to use it later as a springboard to a piece for your portfolio.

106   UNIT ONE   PART 2: LETTING OTHERS IN

Literary Concepts

Have students form four groups. Assign a section of the story to each group and ask groups to explain the setting, including the place, the time, and details that further describe where and when the story takes place.

Concept Review Conflict Be sure students give examples of external conflicts (between fox and farmers, between Father and Colin) and internal conflicts (within Colin and within Father).

CRITIC'S CORNER

According to Tai Ling Bloomfield, a seventh-grade member of the student board, "It didn't seem fair that Bandit had to die." Would you have liked the story better if Bandit had escaped the hunters? Why or why not?

LITERARY LINKS

How would you compare Colin and the painter lady in "The War of the Wall"?

Multimodal Learning

ACROSS THE CURRICULUM

Science *Cooperative Learning*
Working with a small group of classmates, create a **poster** that displays pictures of red foxes and includes interesting facts about them. One member of the group might do library research. Another might visit a zoo or interview a wildlife conservationist. A third member might design the poster.

WORDS TO KNOW

Review the Words to Know at the bottom of the selection pages. Then on your paper, write the word that is most closely related in meaning to the italicized word or phrase in each sentence below.

1. Bandit found *safety* in his hiding place.
2. The boys' father did not *support* the idea of raising a fox as a pet.
3. Bandit proved himself to be a *clever* trickster.
4. The winter was *cheerless* and bitterly cold.
5. Colin's *avoidance* of chores led his father to compare him to an *ailing, bedridden person*.
6. The fox was able to *confuse* the dogs during the hunt.
7. A person who was *lacking in spirit and force* would not have pleased Colin's father.
8. To understand Colin's *true character*, his father needed to understand his art.
9. The farmers were *irritated* by Bandit's constant attacks on their livestock.
10. Colin's picture was *complex* in its use of details.

PAUL ANNIXTER

1894–1985

"Paul Annixter" was the pen name of Howard A. Sturtzel, author of more than 500 short stories. Most of these stories are about wildlife.

When he was 9, Sturtzel and his mother were left alone, having to provide for themselves and his paralyzed grandmother. Sturtzel sold newspapers and candy and later worked as a hotel bellhop. When he was 16, he traveled across the United States and Canada, living the life of a hobo.

Eventually, Sturtzel settled on a timber claim in northern Minnesota, where he lived alone for a year and a half and began to write. About his life in Minnesota he said, "I think there is no better forcing ground for a writer than a timber claim, particularly one that is a long way from anywhere at all. By the time you get to talking to yourself in short pithy sentences, you'll be writing, if there's any of it in you."

After attending college, he married the daughter of his favorite writer and tutor, Will Levington Comfort. He and his wife, Jane, worked together to produce more than 20 novels for young people. "Where one may have a weakness," he said of himself and his wife, "the other is apt to have a strength."

OTHER WORKS *Buffalo Chief, Brought to Cover, Pride of Lions and Other Stories*

Extended Reading

Literary Links

Possible responses: Both artists are quiet and introverted; both use their art to express a personal feeling.

Across the Curriculum

Science *Cooperative Learning*
Another option is to have each group research different kinds of foxes and their habits and habitats. In this case, each group can divide up as suggested and present an overall report on their research.

ADDITIONAL SUGGESTION

Social Studies *Fox Hunting*
Invite students to research information about the two sides of the fox-hunting issue. Divide the class into two groups. Ask students to assign within the groups the roles of researcher, note taker, and presenter. After both sides have researched their side of the controversy, have them engage in a debate about whether fox hunting should be outlawed.

Words to Know

1. sanctuary	6. confound
2. sanction	7. passive
3. wily	8. essence
4. bleak	9. harried
5. invalid	10. intricate

Reteaching/Reinforcement
• *Unit One Resource Book*, p. 60

HOWARD A. STURTZEL

As early as the age of eight, Howard A. Sturtzel wrote pieces on the life and death of a cattail and the story of an acorn.

QuickWrites

1. Students may want to include in their flyer some biographical information about Colin. They can also include the kinds of subjects he draws and where he gets his inspiration.
2. Students may want to choose specific topics as questions, such as sibling rivalry, physical similarities and differences, relationship to mother or father, hobbies, or talents.

 The Writer's Craft

Advertisements, pp. 154–156
Creating Dialogue, pp. 320–322

FOCUS ON POETRY

Poetry is the most compact form of literature. In a poem all kinds of ideas, feelings, and sounds are packed into a few carefully chosen words. The words, the sounds, and even the shape of a poem all work together to create a total effect.

FORM The way a poem looks—its arrangement on the page—is its form. Poetry is written in **lines,** which may or may not be sentences. Sometimes the lines are divided into groups called **stanzas.** Remember that poets choose arrangements of words and lines deliberately. The form of a poem can add to its meaning.

SOUND Most poems are meant to be read aloud. Therefore, poets choose and arrange words to create the sounds they want the listener to hear. There are many techniques that poets can use to control the sounds of their poems. Three of these are described here.

- **Rhyme** Words that end with the same sounds are said to rhyme. In many Western cultures, poems traditionally contain rhyming words at the ends of the lines, as in this passage from "The Charge of the Light Brigade" on page 298:

  > Theirs not to reason *why,*
  > Theirs but to do and *die.*

- **Rhythm** A poem's rhythm is sometimes called its beat. The rhythm is the pattern of stressed (´) and unstressed (˘) syllables—the word parts that are read with more and less emphasis—in the poem's lines. In these lines from "The Charge of the Light Brigade," listen for a beat that sounds like the pounding of horses' hooves:

  > Cánnŏn tŏ right ŏf thĕm,
  > Cánnŏn tŏ left ŏf thĕm,

Poems that do not have a regular rhythm, sounding more like conversation, are called free verse. "Graduation Morning" on page 115 is an example of **free verse.**

- **Repetition** A poet may choose to repeat sounds, words, phrases, or whole lines in a poem. Repetition helps the poet emphasize an idea or create a particular feeling.

IMAGERY Imagery involves words and phrases that appeal to the five senses. A poet may use imagery to create a picture in the reader's mind or to remind the reader of a familiar sensation. Notice how the following lines from "The Women's 400 Meters" on page 442 create a "sound picture" as well as a visual picture. They help bring the poem inside you.

> Bang! they're off
> careening down the lanes,
> each chased by her own bright tiger.

FIGURATIVE LANGUAGE Poets use figurative language when they choose words and phrases that help readers picture ordinary things in new ways. Such words and phrases are called **figures of speech.** Three figures of speech are explained below.

• **Simile** A comparison in which the word *like* or *as* is used is called a simile. This simile from "Hockey" on page 441 compares hockey players' sticks to wolves' teeth:

> The play is fast, fierce, tense.
> Sticks click and snap like teeth
> Of wolves on the scent of a prey.

• **Metaphor** A comparison that does not contain the word *like* or *as* is called a metaphor. To what is the road compared in the following line from "The Highwayman" on page 497?

> The road was a ribbon of moonlight
> over the purple moor,

• **Personification** When a poet describes an animal or object as if it were human or had human qualities, the poet is using personification. In these lines from "Formula" on page 469, the poet gives the human characteristic of dreaming to the night and the fish:

> Perhaps the night dreams
> that it is no longer night;
> the fish, that they are boats;

THEME All the poetic elements you have read about help poets establish their poems' themes. Just as in fiction, a poem's theme is the message about life that it conveys.

STRATEGIES FOR READING POETRY

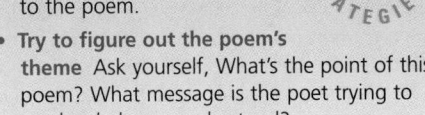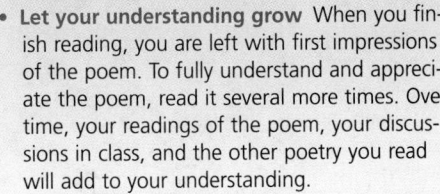

• **Preview the poem** Notice the poem's form: what shape it has on the page, how long it is, how long its lines are, and whether or not it has stanzas.

• **Read the poem aloud** Pause at the end of each complete thought, not necessarily at the ends of lines. Look for end punctuation to help you find where each thought ends. As you read, listen for rhymes and rhythm and for the overall sound of the words in the poem.

• **Visualize the images** In your mind's eye, picture the images and comparisons you find in the poem. Do the images remind you of feelings or experiences you have had?

• **Think about the words and phrases** Allow yourself to wonder about any phrases or words that seem to stand out. Think about what the

choice of those words adds to the poem.

• **Try to figure out the poem's theme** Ask yourself, What's the point of this poem? What message is the poet trying to send or help me understand?

• **Let your understanding grow** When you finish reading, you are left with first impressions of the poem. To fully understand and appreciate the poem, read it several more times. Over time, your readings of the poem, your discussions in class, and the other poetry you read will add to your understanding.

• **Allow yourself to enjoy the poem** Remember that poetry is about feelings. You may connect with a particular poem because it expresses feelings that you have felt yourself.

Figurative Language Ask students to create examples of similes, metaphors, and personification to describe aspects of the classroom or school. Provide them with some examples to spark ideas:

• **Simile** Students swarmed like bees around the guest speaker.
• **Metaphor** A good book is a passport to a world of adventure.
• **Personification** The TV screen mumbled to itself in the dark.

Theme Invite students to brainstorm a list of messages that their favorite poems or songs might convey.

Reading Strategies: MODELING

Invite volunteers to read aloud the Strategies for Reading Poetry. Tell students to use these strategies as they read "The Pasture" on page 110 and other poems in this book. Then apply the strategies to "A Time to Talk." You may wish to use the models provided or create your own.

• **Preview the poem** *"This poem is very short, only eight lines. Its title suggests it will be about farming."*

• **Read the poem aloud** Read the poem to the class. Demonstrate how end punctuation cues the reader when to pause or stop. For instance, the reader should pause after the word *spring* in line 1 but continue reading after the word *calf* in line 5 and not stop until after the word *mother* in line 6.

• **Visualize the images** *"I see a thin, trembling calf with big eyes."*

• **Think about the words and phrases** *"The word* fetch *makes me feel like I'm in the pasture too."*

• **Try to figure out the poem's theme** *"I think this poem is about the beauty of nature."*

• **Let your understanding grow** Read the poem a second time and re-address the poem's theme. *"Maybe it's about friendship or taking pleasure in the simple things outdoors."*

• **Allow yourself to enjoy the poem** *"I liked this poem because it gave me a beautiful picture of country life."*

OVERVIEW

Objectives

- To understand and appreciate two lyric poems about sharing time with others
- To practice reading poems aloud
- To examine rhyme, end rhyme, and rhyme scheme
- To express understanding of the poems through a choice of writing forms, including writing a poem and creating a recipe
- To extend understanding of the poems through a variety of multimodal and cross-curricular activities

Skills

LITERARY CONCEPTS
- Rhyme, end rhyme, and rhyme scheme
- Imagery

SPEAKING, LISTENING, AND VIEWING
- Role-playing

Cross-Curricular Connections

GEOGRAPHY
- New Hampshire

HISTORY
- Stone walls

 **GEOGRAPHICAL CONNECTION**
Views of New England Views of the New England countryside will enhance students' understanding of the settings presented in Robert Frost's poetry.

Side A, Frame 49264

POETRY

The Pasture
A Time to Talk

Robert Frost

Activating Prior Knowledge / Setting a Purpose
PERSONAL CONNECTION

During a typical week, you probably have a lot to do after school and on weekends. You probably also set aside some time to spend with people who are important to you—classmates, parents or other relatives, or friends. Use a diagram like the one shown to jot down some examples of things that you like to do with these people. Then as you read, consider how the speakers feel about sharing time with others.

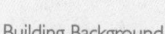

Time with Others

Building Background
BIOGRAPHICAL CONNECTION

Robert Frost's poetry has itself been described as a friendly and meaningful act of sharing. Frost draws readers into his poems by using everyday language to write about ordinary experiences.

Many of Frost's poems are set on farms in New England, where he spent much of his life. The farmers, their work, and images of nature—including streams, trees, farm animals, stone fences, and the ever-changing seasons—make up the setting of many of his poems.

An Abandoned Farm (about 1908), Ernest Lawson. National Museum of American Art, Smithsonian Institution, Washington D.C./Art Resource, New York.

Active Reading
READING CONNECTION

Oral Reading To get the most enjoyment out of these poems, read them aloud. Before you read aloud, however, practice reading each poem to yourself a few times to get a feel for its general flow and meaning. Follow the punctuation, pausing at commas and periods rather than at the end of each line. Picture the images the poet creates. Then practice reading the poem aloud, experimenting with your voice by slowing down and speeding up and by reading softer and louder. Try to imagine how the **speaker**—the voice that speaks to the reader—might sound.

 **LASERLINKS**
- *GEOGRAPHICAL CONNECTION*

110 UNIT ONE PART 2: LETTING OTHERS IN

PRINT AND MEDIA RESOURCES

UNIT ONE RESOURCE BOOK
Strategic Reading: Literature, p. 63

ACCESS FOR STUDENTS ACQUIRING ENGLISH
Reading and Writing Support

FORMAL ASSESSMENT
Selection Test, pp. 23–24
Test Generator

 **AUDIO LIBRARY**
See Reference Card

 **LASERLINKS**
Geographical Connection
Author Background
Art Gallery

INTERNET RESOURCES
McDougal Littell Literature Center at http://www.hmco.com /mcdougal/lit

---

The Pasture

by Robert Frost

Silverstrim's Farm (1989), David Bareford. Quester Gallery, Stonington, Connecticut.

I'm going out to clean the pasture spring;
I'll only stop to rake the leaves away
(And wait to watch the water clear, I may):
I shan't be gone long.—You come too.

5 I'm going out to fetch the little calf
That's standing by the mother. It's so young
It totters when she licks it with her tongue.
I shan't be gone long.—You come too.

FROM PERSONAL RESPONSE *TO* CRITICAL ANALYSIS

REFLECT   1. Would you like to share the speaker's experiences? Why or why not?

RETHINK   2. Why might the speaker want a companion?

     Consider   Close Textuial Reading
     • what a companion might add to the experience
     • the tasks the speaker describes

    3. How would you describe the speaker's attitude toward nature?

THE PASTURE   **111**

M i n i - L e s s o n   L i t e r a r y   C o n c e p t s

IMAGERY   Point out or remind students that imagery refers to the descriptive words and phrases that re-create sensory experiences for a reader. Images can appeal to any of the five senses: sight, hearing, smell, taste, and touch. The majority of images are visual, serving to stimulate pictures in the reader's mind.

Application   Have students take turns reading the poems aloud. Then have individual students identify descriptive words and phrases and the sense or senses that the words or phrases appeal to. For example, in "The Pasture," students might mention the image of the calf that totters when its mother licks it. This image appeals to the senses of sight and touch.

Sidebar

Thematic Link: *Letting Others In*
Robert Frost celebrates the simple but meaningful moments of his day by sharing them with a friend or neighbor.

CUSTOMIZING FOR
Students Acquiring English

• Use **ACCESS FOR STUDENTS ACQUIRING ENGLISH**, *Reading and Writing Support.*

 (I)   Point out the inverted word order in this line and ask students what purpose it serves. *(It makes the line end in a rhyme.)*

Art Note

Silverstrim's Farm **by David Bareford**
Although this painting of a peaceful farm landscape was created in 1989, it evokes the sense of the continuity of farm life past and present.

Reading the Art   *What mood does Silverstrim's Farm create in you? Does this painting make you feel hectic or peaceful? What about it makes you feel that way?*

Critical Thinking: ANALYZING

(A)   Ask students why in "The Pasture" the speaker mentions that he or she "shan't be gone long." *(Possible response: to emphasize that enjoying the simple beauty of nature takes only a moment of time out of the usual routine)*

From Personal Response to Critical Analysis

1. Accept all reasonable responses.
2. Possible responses: to share in the simple beauty of the surroundings; to have someone to talk to about the day.
3. Possible response: Since the speaker seems to enjoy and wants to share outdoor tasks—such as cleaning a spring and fetching a calf—he or she probably has an abiding love for nature.

B Ask students to relate the speaker's experience to something in their own lives. For example, students might mention a time when they were doing homework and were interrupted by a telephone call from a friend.

Literary Concept: IMAGERY

C Ask students to listen as you read "A Time to Talk" aloud. Have them identify the words and phrases that appeal to the sense of hearing. *(Possible responses: "a friend calls," "slows his horse to a meaning walk," "shout from where I am," "I thrust my hoe")*

CUSTOMIZING FOR
Students Acquiring English

(2) Invite students to speculate about what the speaker might mean by "a meaning walk."

Literary Concept: RHYME

D Remind students that words that rhyme end in the same or similar sounds. Ask students to find examples of rhyming words. *(road, hoed; walk, talk; around, ground; tall, wall; is it, visit)*

Art Note

Galena by Robert L. Barnum
Regarding his artistic approach, the watercolorist Robert Barnum comments, "One of my goals when I design an image is to attempt to create something that describes a substantial amount of emotional energy—a two-dimensional image that seems more spiritual, motivational, or exhilarating than the original physical act."

Reading the Art *What mood does this painting create in you? How does the painter convey a sense of distance and vastness?*

A Time to Talk

by Robert Frost

Galena (1988), Robert L. Barnum. Watercolor, private collection.

When a friend calls to me from the road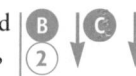
And slows his horse to a meaning walk,
I don't stand still and look around
On all the hills I haven't hoed,
5 And shout from where I am, "What is it?"
No, not as there is a time to talk.
I thrust my hoe in the mellow ground,
Blade-end up and five feet tall,
And plod: I go up to the stone wall
10 For a friendly visit.

COMPREHENSION CHECK
1. Where do both poems take place? *(outside, in the countryside)*
2. What tasks does the speaker do or intend to do in the poems? *(In "The Pasture," the speaker intends to clean the spring and fetch the little calf. In "A Time to Talk" the speaker hoes the ground.)*
3. Whom does the speaker invite to come along in "The Pasture"? *(you, or the reader)*
4. In "A Time to Talk," why does the speaker stop work to talk? *(Taking time to talk to a friend is at least as important as finishing a task.)*

Mini-Lesson: Speaking, **Listening, and Viewing**

ROLE-PLAYING Explain to students that taking on the role of a character in a story or poem helps them see things from a different perspective. It also helps them to clarify their own points of view in a situation that is similar to the character's.

Application Have students role-play a conversation between the farmer and the friend who happens along in "A Time to Talk." Have them speculate about some background information such as the ages of the characters, the closeness of their relationship, and the destination of the friend. Then have students role-play the conversation. Encourage them to have fun with this, but also to realize that their everyday conversation is worthwhile, just as Frost suggests in the poem.

RESPONDING
O P T I O N S

FROM PERSONAL RESPONSE TO CRITICAL ANALYSIS

REFLECT 1. What do you think about the speaker of "A Time to Talk"? Draw a picture to show your impression of the speaker.

RETHINK 2. Do you think the speaker is wise to stop and talk?

             Consider Close Textual Reading
- the importance of completing farm chores on time
- the importance of sharing a friendly visit

RELATE 3. Which poem did you enjoy more—"The Pasture" or "A Time to Talk"? Why?

        4. How are the speakers of "The Pasture" and "A Time to Talk" alike, and how are they different? How does each speaker "let others in"? Thematic Link

        5. Frost wrote that a poem should "begin in delight and end in wisdom." Explain whether, in your opinion, either of these poems fulfills Frost's goal.

Multimodal Learning
ANOTHER PATHWAY

Both of these poems contain vivid rural images. With a partner, create an illustrated children's book, using one of the poems as the text. Share the book with your class or with a group of younger children.

QUICKWRITES

1. Think of one or more activities that you would like to share with someone. Then write a **poem** that imitates Frost's style. Begin with "I'm going out to …" and end with "I shan't be gone long.—You come too."

2. Think about a person with whom you have really great talks. What makes it easy or interesting to talk to that person? Create a **recipe** that includes all the ingredients of a good conversation.

📁 *PORTFOLIO Save your writing. You may want to use it later as a springboard to a piece for your portfolio.*

LITERARY CONCEPTS

Rhyme is a repetition of identical or similar sounds. The most common form of rhyme is **end rhyme,** where the rhymes in a poem occur at the ends of the lines.

What examples of end rhyme can you identify in "A Time to Talk"? Chart the rhyme scheme of this poem. A **rhyme scheme** is the pattern of end rhyme in a poem. You can chart the pattern by assigning a letter of the alphabet, beginning with the letter *a,* to each line. Lines that rhyme are given the same letter. For example, you can chart the rhyme scheme of the first four lines of "The Pasture" as follows:

spring	*a*
away	*b*
may	*b*
too	*c*

Geography *Cooperative Learning*
Have students work in groups to investigate more about New England, specifically New Hampshire. One group can research general information about New England, another can research specific places in New Hampshire, a third group can provide the copy for the brochure based on the others' findings, and a fourth group can draw the illustrations for the brochure. Finally, when the brochure is complete, have each group designate a spokesperson to describe to the rest of the class the process his or her group followed in carrying out its task.

ADDITIONAL SUGGESTIONS

History *Walls of Stone* Stone walls date back to the earliest times in the United States. Although they are common in New England, they are not unique to that region. Invite students to discover how New England settlers built stone walls and what tools or machines (if any) were used.

ROBERT FROST

In 1961, President John F. Kennedy, in the spirit of encouraging the arts in the United States, invited Robert Frost to read from his work at the presidential inauguration. Frost read two of his poems: "Dedication" and "The Gift Outright." Both the President and the poet died in 1963.

AUTHOR BACKGROUND
Robert Frost In this vintage film, Robert Frost speaks candidly about his view of nature, providing students with important insights into a man whose poems were greatly influenced by his environment.

Side A, Frame 8775

ART GALLERY
Landscape Art Through these examples of representational art, students can see the influence of nature on artists. The images may lead to a discussion about the different styles and media artists have used in their presentations of nature.

Side A, Frame 49270

Multimodal Learning

ALTERNATIVE ACTIVITIES

1. Choose several of Frost's poems and, with a small group of classmates, practice and present a **choral reading** of them to your class.

2. Create a **photo or picture essay** based on the theme of this part of Unit One, "Letting Others In."

Thematic Link

Multimodal Learning

ACROSS THE CURRICULUM

 Geography Frost is often called a regional writer because his poems focus on the landscape and people of New England, especially New Hampshire. Research the region—you may want to talk to a travel agent—and then create a **travel brochure** that describes some of the places people can visit to experience "Robert Frost's New England." Be sure your brochure includes a map.

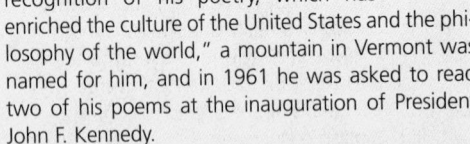

ROBERT FROST

The man who became one of America's most popular poets did not publish any poems until he was 39 years old—and he had to go to another country to do it. Robert Frost made "a late start to market," as he states in one of his poems, but he more than made up for it. He won the Pulitzer Prize for poetry four times, Congress voted him a gold medal "in recognition of his poetry, which has enriched the culture of the United States and the philosophy of the world," a mountain in Vermont was named for him, and in 1961 he was asked to read two of his poems at the inauguration of President John F. Kennedy.

Frost spent his early years in San Francisco. At the age of 11, he moved east with his widowed mother. Over the next 25 years, he attended Dartmouth and Harvard, married and raised a family, and worked as a farmer, an editor, and a schoolteacher. He and his family settled on a New Hampshire farm that his

1874–1963

grandfather had bought for him. There Frost began to write some of his best poems, but he could find no publisher for them.

In 1912 he sold the farm and moved his family to England, where he devoted most of his time to writing. His work soon interested a London publisher, and his first two books of poems came out in 1913 and 1914. Frost's poetry was so well received in England that American publishers began sending him offers. After the outbreak of World War I, Frost moved his family back to the United States. From a farm in New Hampshire, he produced a steady stream of work that received great acclaim. He also taught and lectured at several universities.

Frost's poems are often concerned with personal relationships and questions of integrity. They depict life as a rewarding struggle requiring courage, hard work, and enthusiasm.

OTHER WORKS *Complete Poems of Robert Frost*

Extended Reading

 LASERLINKS
• AUTHOR BACKGROUND
• ART GALLERY

114 UNIT ONE PART 2: LETTING OTHERS IN

Alternative Activities

1. Encourage group members to take turns reading different poems aloud and then to select the ones they want to present in their choral reading. They may want to assign an options generator to suggest various ways to interpret the lines and a direction giver to conduct the group and help the members read together. Have them practice a few times and suggest that they use a tape recorder so that they can hear their progress before presenting the final reading.

2. Students may want to think back to the other selections in this unit to see how different the interpretations of "Letting Others In" can be. Provide students with supplies, such as scissors, tape, paper, and magazines to cut up.

PREVIEWING

POETRY

There Is No Word for Goodbye
Mary TallMountain

Graduation Morning
Pat Mora

Activating Prior Knowledge
PERSONAL CONNECTION

Think about crossroads in your life—times when a part of your life ended and a new part began. For example, the transition from elementary school to middle school would be a crossroads, as would saying goodbye to a best friend who is moving far away. What feelings and thoughts do such situations produce? Why is it sometimes hard to say goodbye to the old and hello to the new? In your notebook, describe your thoughts at such times.

Building Background
CULTURAL CONNECTION

These poems present people who are moving on to new chapters in their lives. In the first poem, two relatives are about to take leave of each other. They are Athabaskans, members of a group of Native American tribes—including the Sarcee, the Beavers, and the Chipewyan of Canada—who speak Athabaskan languages. Though their numbers are now small, the Athabaskans have a long, proud history.

In the second poem, a boy called Lucero is graduating. He lives near the Rio Grande, the river that separates Texas and Mexico. In this border region, people from the United States and Mexico mix freely. On each side of the river, many residents speak both English and Spanish. A number of Mexican citizens, like the woman attending the graduation, cross the Rio Grande to work in Texas by day and return to Mexico at night.

Active Reading
READING CONNECTION

Understanding Cultural Contexts For the people in these poems, one part of life is about to end, and a new part is about to begin. As you read, think about the thoughts and feelings being described and also about the cultures reflected in the poems. After you have read both poems, think about ways in which the poems are similar, despite the differences in the cultures.

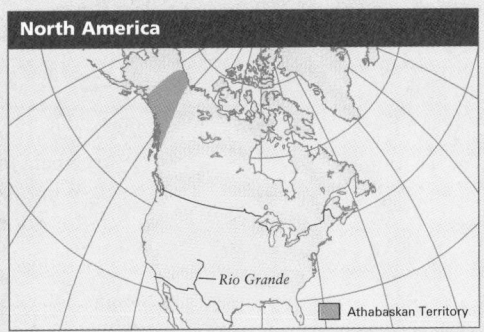

North America

Rio Grande

Athabaskan Territory

GOODBYE / GRADUATION MORNING **115**

OVERVIEW

Objectives

- To understand and appreciate two poems about crossroads in life
- To identify and understand imagery
- To express understanding of the poems through a choice of writing forms, including a thesaurus entry, a graduation card, and a poem or character sketch
- To extend understanding of the poems through a variety of multimodal and cross-curricular activities

Skills

LITERARY CONCEPTS
- Imagery
- Figurative language

GENRE STUDY
- Lyric poem

SPEAKING, LISTENING, AND VIEWING
- Interviews

Cross-Curricular Connections

SOCIAL STUDIES
- Athabaskan peoples

GEOGRAPHY
- Athabaskan regions

PRINT AND MEDIA RESOURCES

UNIT ONE RESOURCE BOOK
Strategic Reading: Literature, p. 67

ACCESS FOR STUDENTS ACQUIRING ENGLISH
Reading and Writing Support

FORMAL ASSESSMENT
Selection Test, p. 25
 Test Generator

 AUDIO LIBRARY
See Reference Card

 LASERLINKS
Art Gallery

CUSTOMIZING FOR

Students Acquiring English

- Use **ACCESS FOR STUDENTS ACQUIRING ENGLISH**, *Reading and Writing Support*.

- Help students to appreciate the qualities of poems written in free verse just as you helped them to appreciate Frost's poems that use traditional rhythm and rhyme. Encourage students to read these poems aloud and to enjoy their sounds.

STRATEGIC READING FOR

Less-Proficient Readers

Set a Purpose Ask students to read to find out how the aunt feels about saying goodbye to someone she loves.

Use **UNIT ONE RESOURCE BOOK**, p. 67, for guidance in reading the selection.

CUSTOMIZING FOR

Gifted and Talented Students

Ask the students to think about how "There Is No Word for Goodbye" would have been different if the aunt were the speaker. Have students discuss what the aunt might have noticed about her niece or nephew and whether the tone of the poem would have been different.

Active Reading: CONNECT

Ⓐ Ask students to describe a relationship they have with an older relative or friend. How is that relationship similar to the one between the niece or nephew and the aunt in the poem? How would they feel if they had to say goodbye to that person?

There Is No Word for Goodbye

by Mary TallMountain

Eskimo woman in northwestern Alaska. Werner Forman/Art Resource, New York.

Sokoya,[1] I said, looking through
the net of wrinkles into
wise black pools
of her eyes.

5   What do you say in Athabaskan
when you leave each other?
What is the word
for goodbye?

---

1. **sokoya** (sô-koi′yä): an aunt on the mother's side.

Mini-Lesson   Genre Study

POETRY On the chalkboard, draw the web shown, and use it to point out some of the qualities of a **lyric poem**:
- has short verses
- expresses personal thoughts and feelings
- uses intensely emotional language

Application Have volunteers take turns reading the two poems aloud to the class. Then have students identify words and phrases that appeal to their emotions. For example, students may mention the lines "When does your mouth / say goodbye to your heart?" from "There Is No Word for Goodbye."

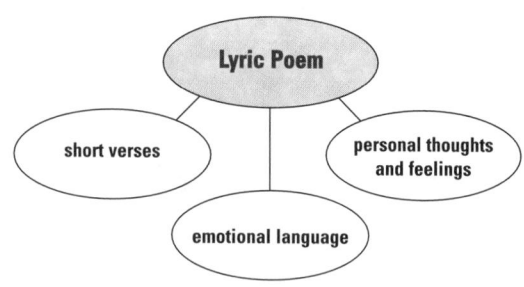

B A shade of feeling rippled
      the wind-tanned skin.
      Ah, nothing, she said,
      watching the river flash.

      She looked at me close.
      We just say, Tlaa.[2] That means,
15   See you.
      We never leave each other.
      When does your mouth
      say goodbye to your heart?

      She touched me light **C**
20   as a bluebell.
      You forget when you leave us,
      You're so small then.
      We don't use that word.

      We always think you're coming back,
25   but if you don't,
      we'll see you some place else.
      You understand.
      There is no word for goodbye. **D**

---

2. **tlaa** (tlä).

FROM PERSONAL RESPONSE TO CRITICAL ANALYSIS

REFLECT 1. What are your thoughts about the aunt's response to the speaker's question? Jot down your ideas in your notebook.

RETHINK 2. How would you explain why the Athabaskans have "no word for goodbye"?
    Consider Close Textual Reading
    • what you can infer about the aunt's feelings for the speaker
    • what the statement "we'll see you some place else" might mean

    3. What do you think the aunt means when she asks, "When does your mouth say goodbye to your heart?"

THERE IS NO WORD FOR GOODBYE **117**

Active Reading: EVALUATE

B The speaker says that the aunt displays a "shade of feeling." Ask students to discuss what this feeling might be. *(Possible responses: The aunt is surprised that her niece doesn't understand the language as well as she does; she is sad that the niece is leaving; she is pained by memories of other people leaving.)*

Literary Concept:
FIGURATIVE LANGUAGE

C Ask students to identify an example of figurative language in these lines and to discuss the comparison. *(The phrase "light / as a bluebell" is an example of a simile: it compares the lightness of the aunt's touch to the gentle touch of a flower petal.)*

STRATEGIC READING FOR
Less-Proficient Readers

D Ask students why the aunt says there is no word for goodbye. *(She believes people never really leave each other.)* Making Inferences

Set a Purpose Ask students to read the next poem and decide if the boy and the housekeeper will ever say goodbye.

From Personal Response to Critical Analysis

1. Accept all reasonable responses.
2. Possible response: Students may point out that the Athabaskans must believe that people never really leave each other emotionally, or that they will be reunited in death.
3. Possible responses: The aunt means that two people who love each other are somehow united as one, as the mouth and the heart belong to one body. She means that words can never fully express emotions.

Mini-Lesson: Speaking,   Listening, and Viewing

INTERVIEWS Use the following lists to explain to students the characteristics of an interviewer and an interviewee.

An interviewer
• prepares questions ahead of time
• sets a goal about what he or she wants to accomplish or learn
• researches the subject of the interview
• prepares open-ended questions

An interviewee
• answers each question thoughtfully

• avoids answers such as "yes," "no," or "I don't know"
• stays focused on the subject

Application Have pairs of students work together. Ask each pair to pick one character from the two poems—the aunt, the niece or nephew, the boy, or the housekeeper. One student will play this character, the interviewee. Ask the other student to act as interviewer to discover more about the character. Encourage students to keep their questions and answers consistent with information provided in the poem.

Sunrise by Edvard Munch Norwegian painter Edvard Munch (mōōngk) used a style called Expressionism in much of his work. Munch's work tends to challenge the viewer's emotions.

Reading the Art What impressions does the painting give you? How do you feel when you look at this painting?

Critical Thinking: ANALYZING

E Ask students to discuss what the poet means when she writes "snared him with sweet coffee, pennies, / Mexican milk candy, brown bony hugs." *(Possible response: The housekeeper uses treats and affection to win the boy over.)*

Literary Concept: IMAGERY

F Ask students to look at the phrase "stubborn cactus thorns" and to identify the senses that this image appeals to. *(sight and touch)*

CUSTOMIZING FOR

Multiple Learning Styles

G Bodily-Kinesthetic Learners Have students work in pairs to act out one of the poems in pantomime. After each pair acts out the poem, invite the rest of the class to comment on which gestures were most effective.

STRATEGIC READING FOR

Less-Proficient Readers

H Ask students whether they think the boy and the housekeeper will ever say goodbye. *(Possible response: Although they may not see each other after the boy grows up, they will always remember each other.)* Drawing Conclusions

COMPREHENSION CHECK
1. Why doesn't the aunt in the first poem reveal the word for goodbye in her language? *(because there is no word for goodbye)*
2. What job does the woman in "Graduation Morning" do for the boy's family? *(She cleans his family's house.)*
3. How does the woman feel about the boy? *(She loves him.)*
4. How is the woman dressed differently from the other guests at the graduation ceremony? *(She wears a black sweater and scarf instead of sparkling clothes.)*

The Sun, Edvard Munch. University Collections, Oslo, Norway. Scala/Art Resource, New York.

Graduation Morning
by Pat Mora

for Anthony

She called him *Lucero*,[1] morning star,
E snared him with sweet coffee, pennies,
Mexican milk candy, brown bony hugs.

Through the years she'd cross the Rio
5 Grande to clean his mother's home. *"Lucero,
mi*[2] *lucero,"* she'd cry, when she'd see him
running toward her in the morning,
F when she pulled stubborn cactus thorns
from his small hands, when she found him
10 hiding in the creosote.[3]

Though she's small and thin,
black sweater, black scarf,
the boy in the white graduation robe
easily finds her at the back of the cathedral,
15 finds her amid the swirl of sparkling clothes,
finds her eyes.

Tears slide down her wrinkled cheeks.
Her eyes, *luceros,* stroke his face. **G** **H**

1. **lucero** (lōō-sĕ'rô) *Spanish:* bright star.
2. **mi** (mē) *Spanish:* my.
3. **creosote** (krē'ə-sōt'): creosote bushes, shrubs found in Mexico and the southwestern United States.

Mini-Lesson **Literary Concepts**

REVIEWING FIGURATIVE LANGUAGE
Remind students that figurative language helps to create fresh and original descriptions. In a figurative expression, the words are not literally true, and one thing may be described in terms of another. Two common examples of figurative language are simile, a comparison using *like* or *as,* and metaphor, a comparison of two things without using *like* or *as.*

Application Have students reread both poems and identify examples of figurative language. Next, have them rewrite the poems using everyday prose instead of figurative language. When they are finished, ask them to discuss how the figurative language enhances the meaning of the poems.

RESPONDING
OPTIONS

FROM **PERSONAL RESPONSE** *TO* **CRITICAL ANALYSIS**

REFLECT 1. In your notebook, sketch your impressions of the woman and the boy in "Graduation Morning." Share your sketch with a partner.

RETHINK 2. Why do you think the housekeeper weeps at the end of the poem?

3. What words would you use to describe the relationship between the housekeeper and the boy?

4. The Spanish word *lucero* occurs four times in this poem. Why do you think the poet repeats this word? Why do you think the word is used in a new way in the last line?

RELATE 5. Which of the two poems comes closer to expressing your own views about the crossroads in life? Recall the ideas that you described for the Personal Connection on page 115.

6. In both poems, a young person and an adult share a strong and tender relationship. What do you think an adult might have to offer a young person? What might a young person have to offer an adult?

Multimodal Learning
ANOTHER PATHWAY

Get together with a partner and identify similarities and differences between the aunt in "There Is No Word for Goodbye" and the housekeeper in "Graduation Morning." Then create a Venn diagram to show these likenesses and differences. Share your diagram with the class.

QUICKWRITES

1. A thesaurus entry contains words or phrases that can serve as synonyms for a given word. Create a **thesaurus entry** for the word *goodbye*. In your entry, include expressions that suggest future meetings, such as "See you later."

2. Imagine that you are the housekeeper in "Graduation Morning." Write a **graduation card** that expresses the thoughts, feelings, or advice you want to share with Lucero.

3. Write a **poem** or a **character sketch** that describes an older person who has influenced your life.

📁 *PORTFOLIO Save your writing. You may want to use it later as a springboard to a piece for your portfolio.*

LITERARY CONCEPTS

Words and phrases that appeal to the reader's senses are known as **imagery.** Poets carefully choose words to help the reader imagine how things look, feel, smell, sound, and taste. For example, in "Graduation Morning," Pat Mora uses the line "black sweater, black scarf" to help you picture the housekeeper's appearance. Her dark clothes contrast with the "sparkling clothes" worn by the other guests at the graduation ceremony.

What other words in "Graduation Morning" paint vivid pictures in your imagination? What words in "There Is No Word for Goodbye" help you visualize the aunt's appearance?

---

1. Sketches should reflect information provided in the poem and draw on students' imaginations.

2. Possible responses: She realizes that the boy's graduation means that their relationship will change; she is moved by the graduation ceremony and her love for the boy.

3. Possible responses: *tender, eternal, loving, protective*

4. Possible response: By repeating the word, the poet emphasizes the boy's importance to the housekeeper. The word's new use in the last line emphasizes the housekeeper's importance to the boy.

5. Accept all reasonable answers.

6. Possible response: An adult can offer wisdom and experience, and a young person can offer energy and affection.

Another Pathway

Have each partner choose one of the women and list her characteristics. Then have one partner be the differentiator, who compares the lists and divides the characteristics into similarities and differences. The other partner can be the recorder, who creates the diagram and writes down any class responses.

Rubric

3 Full Accomplishment Students accurately recognize the similar and different characteristics of each woman and show them in the diagram.

2 Substantial Accomplishment Students have difficulty deciding which characteristics are similar and which are different and create a chart that is not entirely accurate.

1 Little or Partial Accomplishment Students have difficulty recognizing the characteristics of each woman and creating the Venn diagram.

Literary Concepts

Divide the class into two groups and assign one poem to each group. Have the students within each group designate a recorder to write down their findings about imagery. Encourage them to create a chart that includes the following heads:

Sight   Touch   Smell   Sound   Taste

Have the members of the group look for words and phrases that appeal to each of the five senses. When they have finished, have them share their charts with the class.

QuickWrites

1. Encourage students to record both words and phrases, including slang terms and expressions from foreign languages.

2. Remind students to review the poem to find references to specific shared events that might personalize the card.

3. Students may want to prepare a list of characteristics as a springboard. Have them ask themselves questions such as: What do I want to tell about this person? What is the most important feature of our relationship?

 **The Writer's Craft**

Character Sketch, pp.54–61

Social Studies *Cooperative Learning* Have each group choose a particular aspect of the Athabaskan peoples, such as art, culture, customs, housing, or food. Have each group assign a recorder and a researcher, as well as a direction giver to ensure all tasks are accomplished. Finally, have each group assign a summarizer to present the group's oral report to the class.

ADDITIONAL SUGGESTION

Geography *What's There Now?* Invite the class to look at the map on page 115 that shows where the Athabaskan people lived. Have students research the area to discover facts about its physical features, resources, and climate. If possible, have them find out what trade and/or business is generated from that area today. What is the area known for?

MARY TALLMOUNTAIN

Mary TallMountain didn't become a poet until she was in her fifties, when she met Native American scholar Paula Gunn Allen. Under her tutelage, TallMountain sometimes wrote for sixteen hours a day to create many powerful, lyrical poems.

PAT MORA

Pat Mora writes because she wants to tell the stories from her Hispanic heritage. She says she also writes because "I am fascinated by the pleasure and power of words."

ART GALLERY

Eskimo and Mexican Art Art can result from the crafting of items for everyday use or from intentional attempts to express emotion or show an appreciation of beauty. These images, which show how two very different cultures perceive art, may lead to a discussion about why different cultures create different kinds of art.

Side A, Frame 49280

Multimodal Learning

ALTERNATIVE ACTIVITIES

1. Present an **oral reading** of one or both of these poems in class.
2. Tape-record musical selections that express the sadness of saying goodbye. Play the **recording** in class.

Multimodal Learning

ACROSS THE CURRICULUM

Social Studies Work in small groups to discover more about the history and culture of the Athabaskan peoples of Canada and Alaska. Present your findings to the class in an **oral report.**

MARY TALLMOUNTAIN

1918–

Mary TallMountain was three years old when her mother, a member of the Koykon-Athabascan people of Nulato, Alaska, was fatally stricken with tuberculosis. The Nulato village council approved Mary's adoption by a white couple. In 1945, after her adoptive parents died, TallMountain moved to San Francisco, where she ran her own business. A bout with illness left her almost penniless, and she nearly became homeless. TallMountain decided to become a voice for the homeless. She moved to one of the poorest parts of the city and wrote about the people there. She still lives in California and writes about her heritage.

PAT MORA

1942–

While growing up in El Paso, Texas, Pat Mora experienced one culture at home and a different culture at school: "I spoke Spanish at home to my grandmother and aunt, but I didn't always want my friends at school to know that I spoke Spanish." As an adult, Mora takes pride in expressing her Hispanic heritage.

Much of her writing depicts the beauty and cultural diversity of the American Southwest and the harmony that exists in nature and among Mexican and Anglo peoples. The author of three poetry collections, two of which have received Southwest Book Awards, she currently resides in Ohio. She continues to write and gives readings of her poetry, essays, and children's books. For Pat Mora, writing has always been a voyage of discovery: "I write because I am curious. I am curious about me. Writing is a way of finding out how I feel about anything and everything."

OTHER WORKS *Chants, Borders* Extended Reading

120 UNIT ONE PART 2: LETTING OTHERS IN

LASERLINKS
• *ART GALLERY*

Alternative Activities

1. Encourage students to be creative in preparing their oral readings. For example, they can vary the volume, tone, accent, and speed as they say the lines. Suggest they use appropriate gestures to accompany the readings.
2. In addition to playing prerecorded music, allow students who sing or play instruments to perform selections that express the sadness of parting.

PREVIEWING

NONFICTION

Homeless
Anna Quindlen

PERSONAL CONNECTION *Activating Prior Knowledge*

At the end of the movie *The Wizard of Oz,* Dorothy keeps saying that there's no place like home. Do you agree with her? Do you think people who have no homes would agree with her? If you had no home, what would you miss most? Think of both small and large things. Then use a diagram like the one shown to rank ten things that you would miss, in order of their importance to you.

1	5	10
Least Important		**Most Important**

COMMUNITY CONNECTION *Building Background*

Every night in cities across the country, thousands of homeless people sleep on sidewalks, in bus stations, in cardboard boxes, or in other temporary shelters. In the last ten years, the number of homeless people has increased dramatically. Estimates of our nation's homeless population range from 250,000 to 3 million.

People are homeless for a number of reasons. Many cannot find low-cost housing. Others have lost their jobs, are mentally ill, are drug addicts, or are victims of abuse. Families with children make up almost one-third of the homeless population. The woman featured in this selection lived in the Port Authority Bus Terminal in New York City, which was once a "home" for hundreds of people.

A father and child at a homeless shelter in the Haight-Ashbury district of San Francisco.
Copyright © Thomas Hoepker/Magnum.

Active Reading

Setting a Purpose

READING CONNECTION

Author's Purpose Authors write for many reasons: to entertain, to explain or inform, to express opinions, or to persuade readers to do or believe something. As you read this selection, think about Anna Quindlen's purpose for writing about the homeless. What might she have wanted to accomplish by writing this essay? Do you think she had more than one goal?

LASERLINKS
• *COMMUNITY CONNECTION*   **121**

OVERVIEW

Objectives

- To understand and appreciate an essay that emphasizes the author's feelings toward homelessness
- To understand the author's purpose
- To enrich understanding of nonfiction by examining informal and personal essays
- To express understanding of the selection through a choice of writing forms, including an editorial and a definition
- To extend understanding of the selection through a variety of multimodal and cross-curricular activities

Skills

READING SKILLS/STRATEGIES	LITERARY CONCEPTS
• Author's purpose • Evaluating	• Essay • Point of view
GRAMMAR	**GENRE STUDY**
• Subject-verb agreement	• Nonfiction: essay
	SPEAKING, LISTENING, AND VIEWING
	• Interview

Cross-Curricular Connections

SOCIAL STUDIES	HISTORY
• Port Authority Bus Terminal • Real estate	• Neighborhood history

COMMUNITY CONNECTION
Faces of Homelessness

Homelessness is a growing problem in the United States. In recent years more and more women and children have become homeless. These images may generate classroom discussion about the plight of the homeless and possible solutions to the problem.

Side A, Frame 49290

PRINT AND MEDIA RESOURCES

UNIT ONE RESOURCE BOOK
Strategic Reading: Literature, p. 71
Vocabulary SkillBuilder, p. 73
Reading SkillBuilder, p. 72

GRAMMAR MINI–LESSONS
Transparencies, pp. 3–7
Copymasters, pp. 3–9

ACCESS FOR STUDENTS ACQUIRING ENGLISH
Selection Summaries
Reading and Writing Support

FORMAL ASSESSMENT
Selection Test, pp. 27–28
Part Test, pp. 29–30
Test Generator

AUDIO LIBRARY
See Reference Card

LASERLINKS
Community Connection
Social Studies Connection

by Anna Quindlen

Homeless

SUMMARY

Anna Quindlen contemplates the meaning of home and homelessness as she interviews Ann, a woman living in New York City's Port Authority Bus Terminal. Ann says that she is not homeless and shows Quindlen treasured photos of a house she once lived in. Quindlen realizes that a home provides not only shelter but also privacy, security, and pride of ownership.

Thematic Link: *Letting Others In*
When Ann lets Anna Quindlen into her life by sharing a picture of her former home, Quindlen begins to look at homelessness and homeless people differently.

CUSTOMIZING FOR
Students Acquiring English

• Use **ACCESS FOR STUDENTS ACQUIRING ENGLISH,** *Reading and Writing Support.*

• Before reading the essay, discuss with students the many different meanings of *home.* Ask them to share what home means to them.

STRATEGIC READING FOR
Less-Proficient Readers

Set a Purpose Invite students to read to find out what the writer thinks a home is.

Use **UNIT ONE RESOURCE BOOK,** p. 71, for guidance in reading the selection.

CUSTOMIZING FOR
Gifted and Talented Students

The narrator of this selection says that Ann was "somebody" when she had a home. This implies that now she is "nobody," since she no longer has a home. Have students debate these definitions of *somebody* and *nobody,* and discuss what they indicate about how our society connects material possessions and success in life.

122   UNIT ONE   PART 2: LETTING OTHERS IN

Woman in New York City. Copyright © 1982 Christopher Morris/Black Star.

WORDS TO KNOW

compassionate (kəm-păsh′ə-nĭt) *adj.* having sympathy for the sufferings of others (p. 124)
crux (krŭks) *n.* the most important point or element (p. 124)
enfeebled (ĕn-fē′bəld) *adj.* deprived of strength; made weak (p. 123)

legacy (lĕg′ə-sē) *n.* something handed down from an ancestor or from the past (p. 123)
rummage (rŭm′ĭj) *v.* to search thoroughly by moving the contents about (p. 123)

Her name was Ann, and we met in the Port Authority Bus Terminal several Januarys ago. I was doing a story on homeless people. She said I was wasting my time talking to her; she was just passing through, although she'd been passing through for more than two weeks. To prove to me that this was true, she <u>rummaged</u> through a tote bag and a manila envelope and finally unfolded a sheet of typing paper and brought out her photographs.

They were not pictures of family, or friends, or even a dog or a cat, its eyes brown-red in the flashbulb's light. They were pictures of a house. It was like a thousand houses in a hundred towns, not suburb, not city, but somewhere in between, with aluminum siding and a chainlink fence, a narrow driveway running up to a one-car garage and a patch of backyard. The house was yellow. I looked on the back for a date or a name, but neither was there. There was no need for discussion. I knew what she was trying to tell me, for it was something I had often felt. She was not adrift, alone, anonymous, although her bags and her raincoat with the grime shadowing its creases had made me believe she was. She had a house, or at least once upon a time had had one. Inside were curtains, a couch, a stove, potholders. You are where you live. She was somebody.

I've never been very good at looking at the big picture, taking the global view, and I've always been a person with an overactive sense of place, the <u>legacy</u> of an Irish grandfather. So it is natural that the thing that seems most wrong with the world to me right now is that

She had a house, or at least once upon a time had had one.

there are so many people with no homes. I'm not simply talking about shelter from the elements, or three square meals a day or a mailing address to which the welfare people can send the check—although I know that all these are important for survival. I'm talking about a home, about precisely those kinds of feelings that have wound up in cross-stitch and French knots on samplers[1] over the years.

Home is where the heart is. There's no place like it. I love my home with a ferocity totally out of proportion to its appearance or location. I love dumb things about it: the hot-water heater, the plastic rack you drain dishes in, the roof over my head, which occasionally leaks. And yet it is precisely those dumb things that make it what it is—a place of certainty, stability, predictability, privacy, for me and for my family. It is where I live. What more can you say about a place than that? That is everything.

Yet it is something that we have been edging away from gradually during my lifetime and the lifetimes of my parents and grandparents. There was a time when where you lived often was where you worked and where you grew the food you ate and even where you were buried. When that era passed, where you lived at least was where your parents had lived and where you would live with your children when you became <u>enfeebled</u>. Then, suddenly, where you lived was where you lived for three years, until you

---

1. **in cross-stitch and French knots on samplers:** spelled out in fancy stitching on embroidered decorations.

WORDS TO KNOW	**rummage** (rŭm'ĭj) v. to search thoroughly by moving the contents about **legacy** (lĕg'ə-sē) n. something handed down from an ancestor or from the past **enfeebled** (ĕn-fē'bəld) adj. deprived of strength; made weak **enfeeble** v.

123

Linking to Social Studies

A The Port Authority Bus Terminal in New York City is one of the 26 facilities in the New York/New Jersey area owned by the corporate entity known as the Port Authority of New York and New Jersey. The Port Authority owns most of the bridges, tunnels, terminals, and airports in the New York City area. It also owns the World Trade Center, which is among the tallest buildings in the world.

CUSTOMIZING FOR
Students Acquiring English

1. Explain that the idiom *passing through* means "being in a place only because it is on the route you are traveling." Help students see the irony of Ann's "passing through for more than two weeks."

2. Point out the prefix *over-* in the word *overactive* and explain that it indicates an excessive degree of a quality and can be added to many adjectives.

Critical Thinking: ANALYZING

B Ask students to explain why they think Ann carries photographs of her house with her. *(Possible responses: It makes her feel important, like "somebody"; it reminds her of a happier time; it helps her to set a goal about where she would like to be.)*

Literary Concept:
DESCRIPTION

C Quindlen gives a fairly detailed account of what Ann's house looks like. Ask students to discuss why they think she has taken such care in providing details about the house. *(Many people view homelessness as something that could never happen to them. The description of Ann's house shows that she once had a home like many other people; it helps readers identify with Ann as a person with whom they have—or could have—something in common.)*

Mini-Lesson ⊘ **Reading Skills/Strategies**

EVALUATING Explain to students that good readers form opinions while and after they read a selection. This is one way to evaluate the information presented and get the most out of it.

Application Have students write down, as students read the essay, any opinions stated or implied.

They should include opinions held by the narrator, society, and Ann. Then have them review these opinions and write a few sentences explaining why they agree or disagree with each opinion listed.

Reteaching/Reinforcement
• *Unit One Resource Book*, p. 72

D According to Quindlen, why do some homeless people tend to stay away from shelters? *(Some are afraid of being locked in or having harm done to them; others prefer to make their own homes with their own schedules.)*

Critical Thinking: ANALYZING

E Quindlen comments that "we turn an adjective into a noun: the poor, not poor people; the homeless, not Ann. . . ." Ask students to analyze what Quindlen means by this comment. *(Looking at problems without thinking about the people who have them makes it too easy to be impersonal and not to work as hard to help those people.)*

STRATEGIC READING FOR

Less-Proficient Readers

F What words does the narrator use to mean "not having a home"? *(Possible responses: without a bureau, no mirror, no wall, no drawer that holds the spoons)*
Restating

• What does a home mean to the narrator? *(Possible responses: everything, where the heart is, a place of certainty and privacy)* Summarizing

---

COMPREHENSION CHECK

1. Who is Ann? *(the homeless woman being interviewed by Anna Quindlen)*

2. Why doesn't Ann think of herself as homeless? *(because she had a home at one time—and she has a picture to prove it)*

3. What are some characteristics that the author thinks of when she thinks of home? *(certainty, stability, predictability, and privacy)*

4. Why does Quindlen think it is important to use details, rather than broad strokes, to describe homeless people? *(The details make homeless people's problems seem real; they also make sure we don't forget that homeless people are individuals just like us.)*

---

could move on to something else and something else again.

And so we have come to something else again, to children who do not understand what it means to go to their rooms because they have never had a room, to men and women whose fantasy is a wall they can paint a color of their own choosing, to old people reduced to sitting on molded plastic chairs, their skin blue-white in the lights of a bus station, who pull pictures of houses out of their bags. Homes have stopped being homes. Now they are real estate.

D **P**eople find it curious that those without homes would rather sleep sitting up on benches or huddled in doorways than go to shelters. Certainly some prefer to do so because they are emotionally ill, because they have been locked in before and they are damned if they will be locked in again. Others are afraid of the violence and trouble they may find there. But some seem to want something that is not available in shelters, and they will not compromise, not for a cot, or oatmeal, or a shower with special soap that kills the bugs. "One room," a woman with a baby who was sleeping on her sister's floor, once told me,

They are not the homeless. They are people who have no homes.

"painted blue." That was the <u>crux</u> of it; not size or location, but pride of ownership. Painted blue.

This is a difficult problem, and some wise and <u>compassionate</u> people are working hard at it. But in the main I think we work around it, just as we walk around it when it is lying on the sidewalk or sitting in the bus terminal—the problem, that is. It has been customary to take people's pain and lessen our own participation in it by turning it into an issue, not a collection of human beings. We turn an adjective into a noun: the poor, not poor people; the homeless, not Ann or the man who lives in the box or the woman who sleeps on the subway grate.

Sometimes I think we would be better off if we forgot about the broad strokes and concentrated on the details. Here is a woman without a bureau. There is a man with no mirror, no wall to hang it on. They are not the homeless. They are people who have no homes. No drawer that holds the spoons. No window to look out upon the world. My God. That is everything. ❖ **F**

WORDS TO KNOW	**crux** (krŭks) *n.* the most important point or element
	compassionate (kəm-pặsh′ə-nĭt) *adj.* having sympathy for the sufferings of others

124

Mini-Lesson 🧩 **Literary Concepts**

REVIEWING POINT OF VIEW Remind students that in most essays the narrator is the author, and the selection is being written from his or her first-person point of view. When writing in the first-person point of view, the narrator uses first-person pronouns such as *I, me,* and *we.* "Homeless" is written in the first-person point of view, making the writer's thoughts and opinions accessible. The reader sees Ann through Quindlen's eyes and gets Quindlen's view of people who are homeless.

Application Ask students to locate six sentences in the essay that contain first-person pronouns. Ask them to consider what effect it would have if these sentences were written using third-person point of view. Then have them use the first-person point of view to write a brief paragraph about what they have learned about homelessness from reading this essay.

Bums in the Attic
from The House on Mango Street
by Sandra Cisneros

I want a house on a hill like the ones with the gardens where Papa works. We go on Sundays, Papa's day off. I used to go. I don't anymore. You don't like to go out with us, Papa says. Getting too old? Getting too stuck-up, says Nenny. I don't tell them I am ashamed—all of us staring out the window like the hungry. I am tired of looking at what we can't have. When we win the lottery . . . Mama begins, and then I stop listening.

People who live on hills sleep so close to the stars they forget those of us who live too much on earth. They don't look down at all except to be content to live on hills. They have nothing to do with last week's garbage or fear of rats. Night comes. Nothing wakes them but the wind.

One day I'll own my own house, but I won't forget who I am or where I came from. Passing bums will ask, Can I come in? I'll offer them the attic, ask them to stay, because I know how it is to be without a house.

Some days after dinner, guests and I will sit in front of a fire. Floorboards will squeak upstairs. The attic grumble.

Rats? they'll ask.

Bums, I'll say, and I'll be happy.

River Under the Roof
(1985), Friedensreich
Hundertwasser.
Japanese woodcut,
work #763A.
Copyright © 1995
Harel, Vienna, Austria.

BUMS IN THE ATTIC **125**

INSIGHT

This piece is a reflection of the ideas in the main selection and is suggested for students' independent reading. Optional discussion questions follow.

1. What is the narrator's view of his or her situation? (*Possible responses: tired of it, ashamed, embarrassed, resentful*)
2. What does the narrator believe his or her future will be like? (*He or she will own a home, help the homeless, and be happy.*)
3. How do the narrator's views on owning a home compare to Ann's? (*Possible responses: Having a nice home gives a person a sense of pride and identity; it's important for everyone to have his or her own home.*)

Art Note

River Under the Roof by Friedensreich Hundertwasser This woodcut was created in 17 different colors. The process of making a woodcut like this requires several people: an artist, who draws the piece to be reproduced; a woodcutter, who reproduces the piece by carving it into a block of wood; and a printer, who prints the piece with the wood and ink.

Reading the Art *Is this piece of art abstract or realistic? Why do you think the artist included the details that he did?*

SANDRA CISNEROS

For Sandra Cisneros, writing is a way to deal with the poverty, loneliness, and instability she faced as a child in inner-city Chicago. Today she is a prolific writer who has created a unique style, blending her mother's working-class English and her father's gentle Spanish.

Mini-Lesson Grammar

SUBJECT-VERB AGREEMENT A verb must agree with its subject in number: singular (one thing or action) or plural (more than one thing or action). A verb agrees with its subject when both the verb and the subject are singular or both are plural.

Application Copy the following sentences onto the board. Ask volunteers to choose the verb form that agrees with the subject and to tell if it is singular or plural.

1. Anna Quindlen (see/sees) how important having a home is to Ann. (*sees—singular*)
2. Sometimes people (has/have) a hard time looking at the big picture. (*have—plural*)
3. Nowadays homes (is/are) just real estate. (*are—plural*)
4. Some homeless people (choose/chooses) not to live in shelters. (*choose—plural*)
5. The woman with a baby (wish/wishes) she could have a room painted blue. (*wishes—singular*)

Reteaching/Reinforcement
- Grammar Handbook, anthology pp. 851–857
- *Grammar Mini-Lessons* copymasters pp. 3–9, transparencies pp. 3–7

 The Writer's Craft

Agreement of Subject and Verb, pp. 578–580

1. The selection may have made students think beyond what was written; encourage them to record those thoughts.
2. Students may say that they now realize that people without homes are individuals like themselves.
3. Possible response: By focusing on Ann's situation, Quindlen helped her readers understand that people who are homeless are just like anybody else; therefore, she accomplished her purpose.
4. Possible response: To Ann, a home represents the idea that she is "somebody." To the narrator, it is a place where she is able to choose how she wants to live.
5. If students don't have a sense of what is being done in support of the homeless, suggest that they contact their city or town hall and do some research.

Another Pathway

Cooperative Learning Divide students into groups. Within each group, students should first point out Quindlen's opinions and tell if they agree or disagree with them. Then they should compose a letter to Quindlen. During the composing process, one student can act as the recorder, one can explain or clarify ideas, one can write the final draft, and one can read the letter to the rest of the class.

Rubric

3 Full Accomplishment Students create a letter that clearly outlines both Quindlen's and their own opinions.

2 Substantial Accomplishment Students form their own opinions but have difficulty expressing them in a letter.

1 Little or Partial Accomplishment Students have difficulty identifying Quindlen's opinions and forming opinions of their own.

RESPONDING
OPTIONS

FROM PERSONAL RESPONSE TO CRITICAL ANALYSIS

REFLECT
1. What is the strongest impression you had when you finished reading this selection? Write your impression in your notebook and share it with a partner.

RETHINK
2. Did reading this selection change any of your thoughts or opinions about homelessness? Explain your answer.

3. In your opinion, did Quindlen accomplish her purpose for writing this essay?

   Consider Close Textual Reading
   - why she focused on only one homeless person
   - why she described her own home and her feelings about it
   - what her purpose for writing might have been

4. What does having a home represent to Ann? What does it represent to the narrator of the Insight selection on page 125? Compare the two attitudes.

RELATE
5. What is your community doing to help homeless people like Ann? What other actions do you think should be taken?

LITERARY CONCEPTS

An **essay** is a short work of nonfiction in which a writer gives her or his opinion on one subject. An **informal,** or **personal,** essay reflects a writer's feelings about a topic. Find places in Quindlen's essay where she expresses her feelings and opinions about homeless people.

Multimodal Learning
ANOTHER PATHWAY

Write a letter to Anna Quindlen, explaining why you agree or disagree with her thoughts and opinions about homelessness and homeless people. Read your letter to the class so you can share and compare opinions.

QUICKWRITES

1. Work with a partner to brainstorm ways in which students like you can help homeless people. Then explain your ideas in an **editorial** for your school newspaper.

2. One of the dictionary definitions of *home* is "a dwelling place." One of the ways Quindlen defines *home* is "where the heart is." How do you define home? Write your **definition** in your notebook. How does it compare with some of your classmates' definitions?

📁 *PORTFOLIO Save your writing. You may want to use it later as a springboard to a piece for your portfolio.*

Literary Concepts

Divide students into two groups. Have each group scan a page of "Homeless" to find Quindlen's personal opinions and then write one sentence summarizing each opinion. Invite the groups to share their sentences with the class.

Words to Know

Exercise A
1. crux
2. rummage
3. enfeebled
4. legacy
5. compassionate

Exercise B
Remind students that a good speech is well organized. It also informs an audience or persuades them to do something.

Reteaching/Reinforcement
- *Unit One Resource Book,* p. 73

Multimodal Learning

ALTERNATIVE ACTIVITIES

1. Quindlen describes some of the "dumb things" she loves about her home. What dumb things do you love about your home? Make a **drawing** or **sculpture** of one of those things and explain why it is important to you.

2. **Interview** someone who works in a homeless shelter to find out about the services available for homeless people in your area. Share your findings with your classmates.

Multimodal Learning

ACROSS THE CURRICULUM

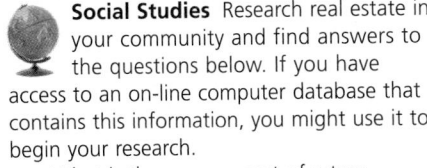

Social Studies Research real estate in your community and find answers to the questions below. If you have access to an on-line computer database that contains this information, you might use it to begin your research.

- What is the average cost of a two-bedroom home?
- What percentage of families own their own home?

WORDS TO KNOW

EXERCISE A Review the Words to Know at the bottom of the selection pages. On your paper, rewrite the sentences below, substituting a word for each italicized word or phrase.

1. Many people see providing affordable housing as the *most significant part* of the battle against homelessness.

2. Food-and-clothing drives can help homeless people, who sometimes need to *search* through garbage cans for food and supplies.

3. Homeless people can become mentally and physically *weak* when they lack adequate clothing, food, housing, and medical attention.

4. Children who grow up without homes are more likely to become parents of homeless children, thus passing the *inheritance* of homelessness to the next generation.

5. A *kind and genuinely concerned* person treats homeless people with understanding and dignity.

EXERCISE B Present a speech about homeless people that contains at least three of the vocabulary words.

ANNA QUINDLEN

After graduating from Barnard College in 1974, Anna Quindlen published her first story and started working as a newspaper reporter. In 1981 she was offered the "About New York" column in the *New York Times*. She has called writing that column her dream job, because she "got to write about anything. . . . I'd go to a cop's funeral or I'd go to Coney Island and talk to the homeless people. . . . I developed a voice of my own without using the first person and I developed the ability to come up with column ideas."

1953–

After the birth of her first child, Quindlen began writing a column about her own family, called "Life in the 30s." In her next column, "Public & Private," she tackled public and political issues on the opinion-editorial page. In 1992 she won a Pulitzer Prize for commentary.

Quindlen has published a children's book and two novels about families. According to her, families mirror society. "Real life is in the dishes," she says.

OTHER WORKS *Living Out Loud, Thinking Out Loud, The Tree That Came to Stay*

Extended Reading

LASERLINKS
- *SOCIAL STUDIES CONNECTION*

Social Studies *Cooperative Learning*
Divide the class into groups of three or four. Have each group pick a method of researching real estate: one group can use an on-line database, if available; another group can research prices in the classified section of the newspaper; and another group can make phone calls to speak to real-estate agents in the area. Have each group assign a direction giver, a researcher, and a recorder to accomplish its tasks.

ADDITIONAL SUGGESTION

History *Neighborhood History*
Invite students to interview a neighbor or someone who has lived in their neighborhood for a long time. Have them prepare questions to help them find out how the neighborhood has changed over time. For example, they might ask if the interviewee remembers a time when, as Quindlen says, "where you lived at least was where your parents had lived and where you would live with your children when you became enfeebled."

ANNA QUINDLEN

Anna Quindlen has received a great deal of attention for her columns in *The New York Times*. About her work as a journalist, she said, "I think of a column as having a conversation with a person that it just so happens I can't see. . . ."

SOCIAL STUDIES CONNECTION
Habitat for Humanity Through the organization Habitat for Humanity, volunteers have devoted thousands of hours to the building of affordable homes for people with small incomes. This film segment shows that volunteerism can be a first step in solving many of society's problems, including homelessness.

Side A, Frame 13333

Quick Writes

1. Explain that an editorial states an opinion and backs up that opinion with supporting details. Also, an editorial clearly states a recommended course of action.

2. As students write their definitions, remind them to start by saying, "Home is . . ." This will help keep them focused.

The Writer's Craft

Supporting Opinions, pp. 144–151
Informing and Defining, pp. 122–129

Alternative Activities

1. First have students discuss what Quindlen means by "dumb things." Then, after they have finished their drawings or sculptures, allow time for them to share their objects with the rest of the class.

2. Before students conduct their interviews, they should prepare their questions, remembering to ask questions that require more than just a one-word answer. Remind them to have a notebook or tape recorder handy to record the answers.

OVERVIEW

To gain a deeper appreciation of the short stories they have read in this unit, students will explore the characteristics of a narrative and then develop their own firsthand narratives in this lesson.

Objectives

- To plan a firsthand narrative by considering such elements as topic, details, and organization
- To draft a firsthand narrative and solicit a response
- To revise, edit, and publish a firsthand narrative
- To reflect on the process of writing a firsthand narrative

Skills

LITERATURE
- Chronological order
- Setting
- Imagery

WRITING AND LANGUAGE
- Showing, not telling
- Using dialogue

GRAMMAR AND USAGE
- Using verb tenses consistently

MEDIA LITERACY
- Reading cartoons
- Considering contest notices
- Exploring photographs

SPEAKING, LISTENING, AND VIEWING
- Asking questions
- Reading aloud
- Role-play
- Oral History
- Storytelling

CRITICAL THINKING
- Classifying details

Teaching Strategy:
STUMBLING BLOCK

A Students may not understand the phrase *first-person account*. Explain that in the first-person point of view, the narrator is a character in the story. The writer uses first-person pronouns such as *I*, *me*, and *we*.

Teaching Strategy: MODELING

B The letter on page 128 can be used as a springboard for topics for a firsthand narrative. Invite students to list the topics that Kat might explore in response to her friend's letter. Possible topics include working as a baby sitter, keeping children happy, facing new challenges. Ask students which of these topics they might choose to expand into a personal narrative, and why. In a response to the letter's writer, a firsthand narrative might advise the writer on how to win over Lucy or confidently handle children.

WRITING FROM EXPERIENCE

WRITING A FIRSTHAND NARRATIVE

Many of the selections in Unit One, "On the Threshold," were about experiences that both open a door to new challenges and close a door to past ways of thinking. What experiences in your life helped you grow?

GUIDED ASSIGNMENT

Write About a Personal Experience A firsthand narrative is a first-person account of a meaningful event. You can write one to help a friend with a problem you've faced yourself, to make others laugh, or to make a point.

1 Read the Sources

When might you want to share an experience you've had? The letter, the contest notice, and the cartoon on these pages might help you think of a situation that you'd like to write about and share with others.

Making Connections Try freewriting your reactions to each item on these pages. Do any incidents or memories of your own come to mind?

Choosing Possible Topics What experiences have you had that caused you to grow? Do you know anyone facing a problem who might be helped by hearing about your experience?

Letter from a Friend
How might a firsthand narrative be useful in a response to this writer?

October 15

Dear Kat,

Well, I started my first babysitting job last week It was a total disaster! What happened? You name it!

When I got there, Lucy immediately ran to her mother and started crying! Mrs. Flores tried to calm her down as Lucy wailed, "I don't want a new babysitter! I want Mimi!" After the mother finally left, Lucy backed into a corner and stared at me as if I were a monster. So I took a doll out of my bag and invited her to play with it. She threw it across the room. I thought a snack might help, so I gave her some cheese and crackers. Only then did she stop crying. But she refused to talk to me. After the snack she said, "I'm tired," got ready for bed, and fell asleep reading a book Some impression I made!

Do you have any babysitting advice? Maybe I'll try to get a paper route instead.

Love, Nan

PRINT AND MEDIA RESOURCES

UNIT ONE RESOURCE BOOK
Prewriting, p. 77
Elaboration, p. 78
Peer Response Guide, pp. 79–80
Revising and Proofreading, p. 81
Student Model, p. 82
Rubric, p. 83

GRAMMAR MINI-LESSONS
Transparencies, pp. 16 and 18–19
Copymasters, p. 24–26

WRITING MINI-LESSONS
Transparencies, p. 46

ACCESS FOR STUDENTS ACQUIRING ENGLISH
Reading and Writing Support

FORMAL ASSESSMENT
Guidelines for Writing Assessment

 **LASERLINKS**
Writing Springboard

 WRITING COACH

② QuickWrite Some Topic Ideas

On a sheet of paper, list a few experiences that were important to you. Why do you think the experiences stand out in your mind? Write a sentence that describes how each one changed you. Choose one that you remember clearly.

C
D

Contest Notice

Nan's letter reminded me of my first job. I could write about that for the contest.

KidsWorld

Magazine's Firsthand Narrative Contest

KidsWorld Magazine is sponsoring its annual national writing contest for middle school students. In 700 words or less, tell us about an important event, an unforgettable person, or a turning point in your life. Why was the event so important? What did the unforgettable person mean to you? How did the turning point change your life? Follow the rules on page 53 for writing and submitting your entry.

My turning point: I was so busy having fun at the farm that I didn't realize that I had to be responsible.

Cartoon
What personal experience does this cartoon remind you of?

E

THE FAR SIDE By GARY LARSON

Chronicle Features, 1982 Larson (6-4)

"All right! Rusty's in the club!"

💿 ▶ **LASERLINKS**
• *WRITING SPRINGBOARD*

🖥 ▶ **WRITING COACH**

CUSTOMIZING FOR
Students Acquiring English

C Generating ideas for writing may be easier for non-native speakers when they use their native languages. Reassure students that it is fine in the early stages of the writing process to think and write in the language that is most comfortable for them. Tell students that, if they wish to, they can switch back and forth between languages as they brainstorm. Guide these students to develop individual techniques that can help them achieve success.

Writing Skill:
FINDING WRITING IDEAS

D Remind students that if they write about ideas that interest them, their writing will be enthusiastic and thus likely to interest their readers.

Teaching Strategy: MODELING

E Model for students how to use the samples on this page by sharing some of your own ideas. Some possible examples include:

• My unforgettable person is my grandfather. He taught me to fish, play baseball, and ride a bike.

• The cartoon reminds me of some funny things my dog does.

• The cartoon reminds me of a time a few years ago when I joined a cooking club. We ate the strangest foods!

💿 **WRITING SPRINGBOARD**
Multicultural Communication
Patricia is a teenager who points out the different ways language is used in Korea and in the United States.

Side B, Frame 305

Writing Prompt Every culture's members have distinctive ways of communicating with one another. After listening to Patricia describe how Koreans use language, think of an incident you have seen or heard about that involved communication between two people. Write a narrative about the experience.

Less-Proficient Writers

F Inexperienced writers often have a great deal of trouble filling in the details. Help students through this part of the writing process by showing them how to use the traditional "5W's and an H" questions to generate details. Suggest that students can arrange their answers on a chart that lists:

Who?

What?

When?

Where?

Why?

How?

Speaking, Listening, and Viewing: ROLE-PLAY

G Sometimes specific objects can spark memories of vivid sensory details. Many writers have learned to build on this process by using the object in a role-playing situation. Invite small groups of students to role-play scenarios that feature selected objects. Students should select an object and re-enact a memorable situation associated with it. Encourage the rest of the group to ask questions about the situation to help the writer generate memories of sensory details.

PREWRITING

Planning Your Story

Filling In the Details You now have an experience to write about. The ideas below can help you gather the details that will make your narrative clear and lively.

① Focus on the Experience

Here are some suggestions for thinking about your experience.

- Why was the incident memorable to you?
- Describe all the emotions you felt at the time.
- **F** Run through the experience in your mind, and take notes about the order of events and the sights, smells, and sounds you associate with them.
- Who else was involved? Note any memorable words that people spoke, and write a description of each person.
- Was the setting important? Note where and when the events took place.

My first working experience

1. Alison and I were talking about boys—as usual!

2. We decided to cross the cow's pen, food in hand, to feed the sheep first.

3. The cow got mad and charged us.

4. We flung the buckets of oats and dived over the fence.

5. I decided I had better pay attention to the job.

Student's Story Line

② Fill In the Memory Gaps

If you can't remember every detail about the event, don't worry! There are ways to jog your memory.

EXPLORE DIFFERENT RESOURCES

Family Photograph Albums A picture or video of you taken at or near the time of the event may help you remember how you looked and dressed or where you lived. Consider including the photo in your narrative.

Journals or Letters Maybe you or someone else actually wrote about the experience at the time. List any details you find about the event and other people's reactions to it.

Personal Memorabilia Souvenirs such as ticket stubs, notes, or baseball cards can help you add detail to your narrative. Describe objects like these in your firsthand narrative to help you create images in the reader's mind.

Mini-Lesson: Speaking, **Listening, and Viewing**

ORAL HISTORY Discuss with students how every person has a rich store of unique memories. Explore how these memories not only tell about the person but also about his or her time and place. Invite volunteers to share some of the stories their older relatives have told them about their childhood. Explain to the class that when we tape-record or write down these memories we are creating a document called an oral history. These texts may suggest topics for personal narratives.

Application Invite students to work as partners to interview each other. Before the interview, have students prepare a list of questions, such as the following:

- What events from your life are especially important? Why?
- What do you remember about these experiences?

Have students write down their partner's answers to these questions. Their partners can use the transcription of the interview as a springboard for planning their narratives.

GET INPUT FROM OTHERS

People who experienced the event with you may remember things you've forgotten or give you another way of looking at it. Ask questions like the following:

- How do you remember the experience?
- What events or details stand out in your memory?
- What do you remember people saying or doing?

3 Tell It to Your Friends

At first, try telling your story aloud to some friends. For this version it might work best to use chronological order. This means telling the experience in the order in which the events occurred. What was your audience's reaction? Which part got the laughs? Which left them scratching their heads? Afterward, use the following tips to get feedback.

- Encourage your listeners to ask questions.
- Listen carefully to feedback and take notes about areas you need to make clearer or livelier.
- Summarize what you have learned from your peers.

Your notes will help you write your story so it is as lively as it was when you told it to your friends.

Decision Point What form should my personal narrative take? A letter? A story told aloud? A monologue?

SkillBuilder

 CRITICAL THINKING

Classifying Details

Details can fall into categories, such as sights, sounds, and smells or thoughts, feelings, and actions. A chart like the one below can help you discover and keep track of the details you want to include.

sights	?
sounds	quoting our gossip
smells	oats and molasses cow manure

APPLYING WHAT YOU'VE LEARNED
Try making a chart to help you write about your own memorable experience.

THINK & PLAN

Reflecting On Your Ideas

1. How did prewriting help you grasp the event's importance?
2. What details will have the greatest effect on readers?
3. Did listeners understand the importance of the experience? If not, how might you revise your draft so they do?

WRITING FROM EXPERIENCE **131**

Speaking, Listening, and Viewing:
COLLABORATIVE OPPORTUNITY

H Suggest that students get feedback by reading their stories aloud to the person or persons who shared the experience with them. This might be a sibling, parent, or friend. Encourage students to seek detailed comments and consider the other person's point of view carefully.

Teaching Strategy:
STUMBLING BLOCK

I Students who are having a difficult time arranging the events in chronological order will benefit from using a time line. Guide students to arrange the details of their story on a time line from the first event to last event. Encourage students to use numbers, dates, or times to help them clearly see the order in which the events occurred.

SkillBuilder CRITICAL THINKING

CLASSIFYING DETAILS Have students work in pairs to read their paper to a partner. Partners should listen closely for details and jot down words and phrases that helped them picture the experience in their imaginations. Students and partners should then work together to classify these details on the chart. Then have students repeat the process with the other paper.

Application Be sure that students have a clear method for organizing their details. By using a chart, students can classify details according to their sensory appeal and generate additional ones for their narratives.

Additional Suggestions Have students classify the details in a favorite passage from a short story in this unit.

Teaching Strategy:
STUMBLING BLOCK

J Some students may find it difficult to move from the prewriting to the drafting stage. To help dispel writer's block, share these myths and truths about writers with students:

Myth: Writers are born, not made.

Truth: Everyone can write.

Myth: Writers have to be "in the mood" to write.

Truth: If writers waited until they were in the mood, few people would write anything.

Myth: Writers have to have perfect writing skills.

Truth: Writers don't let problems with grammar, usage, and mechanics get in their way. Writers take care of these problems when they revise.

Writing Skill: DRAFTING

K Explain to students that two methods of drafting are discovery drafting and careful drafting. In discovery drafting, writers let their imaginations soar and set the direction. Discovery drafting is useful for expressing thoughts and feelings in a journal and for generating details for personal narratives and creative writing projects. Careful drafting, in contrast, is guided by a plan such as an outline. It is well suited for report writing. Encourage students to select the method of drafting that suits their topic and purpose for writing.

Starting to Write

Putting Ideas on Paper As you gather the important details about the event, start thinking about how to weave them into a story. Some people begin a firsthand narrative by listing the events in order. Others just start writing and revise later. Do whatever works best for you. The model shows how one student's thinking changed as she wrote.

1 Draft Your Narrative

Begin exploring your ideas by writing them out. Try writing as if you are telling the story aloud. At this stage, don't worry about missing information, how the ideas flow, or your spelling and grammar. The important thing is to figure out what you really think and to go wherever your draft takes you.

Student's Rough Draft

> *This is background material.*
>
> Last fall I took the job at Pain's *(spelling?)* farm to get free horseback riding lessons. ~~I had to feed the animals and clean the stalls after school.~~ Alison and I had to feed the animals and clean the stalls. Mostly, we talked about boys and school stuff. Every night I went home smelling like hay and cow manure. ~~Never heard the end of it from my brother.~~ — *Delete. Not important.*
>
> *Why is this a mistake?*
>
> One day we made the mistake of feeding the sheep before we fed Rosie the cow. Rosie was really a calf, only a coupla *(e of)* months old, but she was huge, with tiny (sharp) horns! Whhy did we do that? I only remember the conversation beforehand.
>
> *This is an example of our gossiping.*
>
> Alison claimed that Scot Rodrigeuz wanted to ask me to the carnival. All the girls I know think he's a hunk. He has dark brown hair and the greenest eyes. I had never been on anything like a date before. "No way!" I yelled back at her. We laughed. As a joke, I said tell me if Rosie started running. Half a second passed. "She's running!" Alison screamed. She freaked and jumped over the fence, with me right behind. We laughed, but we were scared to death.
>
> *Conclusion:* We weren't taking job seriously and almost got trampled because of it.

Tell why feeding the sheep first was a bad move. (I had to cross Rosie's pen with food)

Need more details! Add more information about what I learned.

Show, don't tell, what happened.

2 Analyze Your Rough Draft

Once you've written down your ideas or started drafting, look at what you've done so you can decide how to continue. Ask yourself these questions.

- What part of my narrative do I find most interesting?
- Have I told about the parts of the event I wanted to share most?
- What ideas do I really like?

GET ORGANIZED

 Narratives are usually organized chronologically. Sometimes, though, you can grab your readers' attention by beginning your story in the middle of the action. Or start out with a bit of dialogue or a description of how you felt.

3 Rework Your Draft and Share

Below are suggestions for refining and sharing your draft.

MAKE YOUR READERS CARE

If you're not careful, readers could be left asking, "So what?" To avoid this problem, try these techniques.

Show, Don't Tell Use sensory language to help your readers feel like participants in the event. See the SkillBuilder on the right.

Consider Using Dialogue Often a bit of conversation can say more than many sentences of description.

Make It Personal Let your unique personality come through. Try quoting yourself or adding details that show your quirks or sense of humor.

PEER RESPONSE

Feedback from another student can help you look at your draft objectively. Ask questions like the following.

- How did you feel after reading the piece? Why?
- What parts confused you or seemed out of place?
- Why do you think I wrote about this experience?
- How might I make the introduction more exciting?

SkillBuilder

 WRITER'S CRAFT

Showing, Not Telling
Skilled authors use examples, vivid details, and sensory language—or words that appeal to the senses—to make readers feel as if they are experiencing the story. Compare the following "tell" sentence with the "show" sentence that follows.

Tell	Alison panicked.
Show	Alison flung herself and the huge bucket over the fence, creating a snowstorm of oats.

APPLYING WHAT YOU'VE LEARNED
Turn the following "tell" sentences into "show" sentences.

1. It was nice outside.
2. Sal was ill.
3. The vacation was a failure.

 WRITING HANDBOOK

For more information about elaboration, see page 819 of the Writing Handbook.

RETHINK & EVALUATE

Preparing to Revise

1. How can you show, and not tell, your story?
2. How well do you explain the events of the experience?
3. How can your writing better reflect your personality?

Writing Skill:
USING THE COMPUTER

L Suggest that students try drafting their firsthand narratives on a computer. Point out that some writers have found that drafting on a computer helps them to write freely and take more chances because they know they can readily revise an electronic file. Guide students to use The Writing Coach, which provides detailed, specific guidelines for the drafting stage.

Writing Skill: DRAFTING

M Suggest that students set a five–minute rule at the drafting stage of the writing process. Students should give themselves five minutes to solve any problem and then move on. Explain that this will help them keep their ideas flowing.

Teaching Strategy:
STUMBLING BLOCK

N Some students may be reluctant to include dialogue because they have difficulty writing and punctuating it. Give students these guidelines to make it easier for them to incorporate dialogue:

- Use speaker's tags—such as "I shouted"—to identify the speaker.
- Put quotation marks only around the speaker's exact words.
- Capitalize the first letter of a quotation and the first letter of a new sentence within a quotation.
- Place commas and periods inside quotation marks.
- Begin a new paragraph each time the speaker changes.

SkillBuilder WRITER'S CRAFT

SHOWING, NOT TELLING Make sure that students understand the difference between providing effective sensory details and merely padding sentences with unnecessary adjectives and adverbs. Remind the class that specific nouns and verbs are often more effective than a string of adjectives and adverbs to show how a person, place, or thing is special.

Application Possible responses:
1. The soft breeze smelled like fresh clover.
2. Sal had a fever of 104°, his forehead throbbed, and his throat felt parched.
3. Torrential rain, flooded roads, and a power failure ruined the vacation.

Reteaching/Reinforcement *Writing Mini-Lessons* transparencies p. 46

 The Writer's Craft

Show Not Tell, pp. 262–265

Teaching Strategy: MODELING

O Use this model to help students understand the revision process. Invite a volunteer to read the essay aloud while students follow along silently. Then work as a class to identify vivid words and images in the first paragraph. Possibilities include *insulted calf, trampled,* and *scared us half to death.*

Readers can visualize events because of words and phrases like *holler, sweet cow with gentle brown eyes,* and *snowstorm of oats.*

Writing Skill:
CHOOSING TITLES

P Explain to students that a title serves two functions: to get the reader's interest and to suggest the contents of the writing. A direct title, such as "My First Job," tells exactly what the essay will be about. An indirect title, such as "A Wake-up Call on the Farm," gives the reader a clue as to what will follow. Be sure students understand that an indirect title should be intriguing but not obscure. The title of the student model on this page combines both the direct and indirect approaches. Encourage students to craft titles that are both interesting and informative.

REVISING AND PUBLISHING

Polishing Your Narrative

Taking a Final Look Now it's time to look carefully at your firsthand narrative to make sure it tells the whole story clearly and interestingly. You also need to correct any errors in punctuation, spelling, and grammar. Use the ideas on these pages to help you revise your draft.

Student's Revised Narrative

1 Revise and Edit

Pretend you're reading your narrative for the first time. Look for writing that is dull or events that are unclear.

- Review your peer comments. How can you make your story more interesting to readers? Is it clear why the event was important to you?
- Use the Standards for Evaluation and the Editing Checklist. Remember, you want to make your experience as clear for your readers as it is now for you.

Look at the model on the right to see how one student revised and edited her draft.

 What words or images in the first paragraph make you want to read the whole story?

How does the writer's choice of words help you see the events in your mind?

My First Job: A Wake-up Call on the Farm

Last spring Alison and I worked after school at Payne's farm. Our job was to feed the animals. But mostly, we talked about boys and school stuff. That is, until an insulted calf trampled our fun and scared us half to death.

Every afternoon we hauled big buckets of oats to three separate pens. First we fed Rosie, the giant calf. Six-month-old Rosie, who must have weighed about 200 pounds, already looked like a full-grown cow.

We climbed over the fence of Rosie's pen, laughing about some stupid thing. Half joking, I told Alison to holler if Rosie—that sweet cow with gentle brown eyes, grazing in the far corner of the pen—started running toward us. "I couldn't believe Michael said that . . ."

"She's running!" Alison wailed. She flung herself and her bucket over the fence, creating a snowstorm of oats. I spun around and saw Rosie charging us. I pictured myself being trampled to death. The next thing I remember was landing on my butt on the other side of the fence.

I looked around as if seeing the place for the first time. Alison's leg was bleeding. Rosie, our friend again, ate quietly. In the distance, Fred was struggling to fix a fence. Mrs. Payne was loading produce into the truck to sell at the market. No chatting for <u>them</u>. Suddenly, I felt foolish.

134 UNIT ONE: ON THE THRESHOLD

WRITING SPRINGBOARD

We Are Close Despite family difficulties, Eddie has stayed in school because of his older brother's encouragement and help. Eddie speaks of his brother's influence in his life.

Side B, Frame 2511

Writing Prompt Throughout life, we meet people who influence our lives in special ways. Write a narrative in which you show how a person has had an important influence on you. As an alternative, you may write about how someone you know was influenced by another person.

COW LESSONS

First day at the farm, gossiping . . . I mean working.

We decided to cross Rosie the cow's pen, oats in hand, to feed the sheep. Bad move!

Rosie expected to be fed first. "She's running!" Alison yelled. We both leapt over the fence, spilling oats everywhere.

The sheep ate the oats as we laughed and agreed to pay more attention to our jobs.

❷ Share Your Work

There are many ways you can share a firsthand narrative. Below are some possible formats. Kat decided to enter her story in the firsthand narrative contest. She also created the comic strip shown above to illustrate her story.

- Class booklet of firsthand narratives
- Monologue
- Video or dramatic skit

Standards for Evaluation

A firsthand narrative
- starts with an attention-grabbing image or idea
- gives a sense of time, place, and characters through vivid, sensory details and dialogue
- helps readers follow the order of events
- concludes by explaining the importance of the experience

Using Verb Tenses Consistently

In a firsthand narrative, the action usually takes place in one time period. To show this action consistently, be sure to use the same verb tense throughout. Consider the example below.

I spun around and saw Rosie charging us. I pictured myself being trampled to death.

 GRAMMAR HANDBOOK

For more information on verb tenses, see page 871 of the Grammar Handbook.

Editing Checklist Use the tips below as you revise your firsthand narrative.

- Are names spelled correctly?
- Is verb tense consistent?
- Are proper nouns capitalized?
- Is dialogue punctuated properly?

REFLECT & ASSESS

Evaluating the Experience

1. Did your format work well? What might have been a better way to share your story?
2. What was easiest about writing your narrative? What was hardest?

   PORTFOLIO You might ask readers to write brief reviews of your story to include in your portfolio.

Speaking, Listening, and Viewing: STORYTELLING

Q Invite students to share their writings by telling them as stories. Since storytelling is a dramatic experience, you may wish to modify your classroom environment to reinforce the listening adventure. For example, you may wish to arrange the chairs in a circle, close the shades, and dim the lights.

Teaching Strategy: MODELING

R Explore with students how this model meets the Standards for Evaluation. For example, the clear chronological order helps readers follow the sequence of events in the story. Point out the transition "the next thing I remember . . ." Also, the narrative concludes by explaining the importance of the experience: "Suddenly, I felt foolish."

PORTFOLIO

Invite students to decide whether to include their firsthand narratives in their portfolio. If they choose to include them, have students write a note to themselves, indicating what they consider the strong features of their narratives. Have students attach the note to their drafts.

Standards for Evaluation

Have students review their stories for the following:

Ideas and Content
- recounts a personal experience vividly
- draws readers in with an interesting introduction
- gives a sense of time, place, and characters through use of sensory details and dialogue
- shows why the event is important to the writer

Structure and Form
- displays a clear order of events.
- Presents a single focus in each paragraph
- uses a variety of sentence structures

Grammar, Usage, and Mechanics
- contains no more than two or three minor errors in grammar and usage
- contains no more than two or three minor errors in spelling, capitalization, and punctuation

---

SkillBuilder GRAMMAR FROM WRITING

USING VERB TENSES CONSISTENTLY

Explain to students that switching tenses confuses readers and detracts from the coherence of their writing. Also explain that a writer's choice of tense depends on the effect he or she wishes to achieve. The past tense gives a sense of authenticity, since the event is now part of history. The present tense, in contrast, gives a sense of immediacy, a "you are there" experience.

Application Have students edit this paragraph, using either the present tense or the past tense consistently.

I have a new computer game. The action was more realistic than that of any of my other computer games. It was surprisingly easy to learn. My little sister likes to play it, too.

Reteaching/Reinforcement *Grammar Mini-Lessons* copymasters pp. 24–26, transparencies pp. 16 and 18–19

 The Writer's Craft

Tenses of Verbs, pp. 474–475

This feature gives students an opportunity to reflect on what they have learned in Unit One and to assess their degree of understanding. This feature provides students with multiple opportunities for self-assessment. You may choose, however, to use some of the activities to assess specific skills, such as speaking and listening or cooperative work.

Objectives

- To allow students to reflect on and assess their understanding of theme
- To allow students to reflect on and assess their understanding of literary concepts such as character and point of view
- To provide students with the opportunity to assess and build their portfolios

Reflecting on Theme

OPTION 1

Have students consider the kinds of challenges and difficulties young people face today and how they might benefit from some of the discoveries made by characters in this unit. Have students create a chart listing contemporary challenges and characters' discoveries. Make sure students support their choices with details from the selections when writing their paragraphs.

OPTION 2

Suggest that students first review the selection in which the character they will be role-playing appears. Have students jot down notes about the character's thoughts and actions that they can refer to while role-playing.

OPTION 3

Suggest that students first restate the quotation in their own words and then review the selections to determine the character to whom the quotation best applies and the one to whom it least applies. Stress that students must support their answers with details.

 Self-Assessment Ask students to consider which selections had an impact on their ideas about experience and discovery and how the selections influenced their understanding of these issues. Students can use this information to complete their before-and-after charts.

REFLECT & ASSESS

UNIT ONE: ON THE THRESHOLD

What new insights did you develop as a result of reading the selections in this unit? Have your ideas about experience as the doorway to discovery changed? Choose one or more of the options in each of the following sections to help you reflect on what you have learned.

REFLECTING ON THEME

OPTION 1 Connecting Literature and Life The characters in this unit make many discoveries about themselves, about others, and about the world they live in. Which of these discoveries do you think are especially important for young people to apply to their own lives? Choose two or more discoveries, and explain your choice in a paragraph or two.

Consider . . .
- the discoveries that made the strongest impressions on you
- parallels between the characters' situations and those of other young people

OPTION 2 Role-Playing Select a character in Part 1 and a character in Part 2 who gain new insights from their experiences. With a partner, role-play a dialogue between the characters, in which they comment on what they have learned.

OPTION 3 Discussion Review the quotation that began this unit: "You whose day it is, / make it beautiful. / Get out your rainbow, / make it beautiful." To which of the characters in this unit do you think the quotation applies best? To which of the characters does it apply least well? Discuss these questions with a small group of classmates, citing details from the selections to support your opinions.

Self-Assessment: Make a before-and-after chart. In it, show how one or more of your ideas about experience and discovery developed after you finished reading the selections in this unit.

REVIEWING LITERARY CONCEPTS

OPTION 1 Comparing Characters A character may be classified as main or minor, depending on his or her importance to the plot, and as dynamic or static, depending on whether his or her personality changes. Make a chart in which you list and classify the characters in the selections you have read. After you complete your chart, circle the name of the dynamic character who you think changes the most.

Selection	Name of Character	Main or Minor?	Dynamic or Static?	Description of Change (If Dynamic)
"A Crush"	Ernie	Main	Dynamic	Overcomes his fear of getting involved

OPTION 2 **Examining Point of View** Most stories are told from either the first-person point of view or the third-person point of view. Work with a partner to list each story in this unit that you have read and to identify its point of view. Then discuss what would have been different in each story if the writer had used a different point of view.

Self-Assessment: Besides character and point of view, the following literary terms were introduced in Unit One, "On the Threshold." Copy this list of terms in your notebook, and then separate the ones you know well from the ones that you need to learn more about. Indicate your knowledge of the terms by giving each a ranking from 1 to 5, with 1 representing a little knowledge, 3 representing good understanding, and 5 representing total mastery.

plot	*speaker*
climax	*rhyme*
essay	*end rhyme*
autobiography	*rhyme scheme*
conflict	*imagery*
setting	*informative nonfiction*

PORTFOLIO BUILDING

- **QuickWrites** In response to the QuickWrites features in this unit, you may have written some personal narratives, letters, and journal entries. Choose from your responses one or two that show how an experience can open the door to a discovery. In a cover note, explain what you like best about these responses. Place the note with the responses in your portfolio.

- **Writing About Literature** You have now had a chance to write your own personal response to a literary work. Reread your response. Then write a letter to the author of the work, telling what you liked about the work and what you might have done differently if you had written it. Attach a copy to your response essay.

- **Writing from Experience** In your firsthand narrative, you described an event that was meaningful to you. Would you change anything if you could experience the event all over again? Explain your thoughts, and include the explanation with your narrative if you choose to keep it in your portfolio.

- **Personal Choice** Review any notes, diagrams, or records you created for the activities in this unit. Don't forget the writing and the charts you created for the Personal Connections, the Writing Connections, the Another Pathway features, and the alternative and cross-curricular activities. Consider also any writing you may have done on your own. Write a note that indicates which piece of writing or activity you enjoyed the most and why you enjoyed it. Attach the note to the piece of writing or to an evaluation of the activity, and add both to your portfolio.

Self-Assessment: At this point, you may just be beginning your portfolio. Think about the pieces that you have selected to include in your portfolio. Do you think that you will keep these pieces, or will you replace them with others as the year goes on?

SETTING GOALS

As you completed the reading and writing activities in this section, you probably recalled certain selections and types of writing that you really liked. Which authors would you like to read more works by? Which kinds of writing would you like to become more skilled at? What kinds of writing would you like to try for the first time?

Reviewing Literary Concepts

OPTION 1

Have students compare their charts with a partner's. Make sure students support their choice for the character who changes the most with details from the particular selection. Students' choices can be tallied on the chalkboard. You may wish to challenge students to create a bar graph, pie chart, or other graphic organizer to display the results. For a copy of the chart to distribute to the class, see *Unit One Resource Book*, p. 87.

OPTION 2

Tell partners to pay attention to clues in each selection that reveal its point of view. Remind students to consider how point of view affects the information that the reader receives.

 **Self-Assessment** Have students refer to the Handbook of Reading Terms and Literary Concepts (pp. 800–807) for information about terms that they wish to understand better. Then have students apply each term to a selection they have read. For instance, a student can describe the setting of a particular selection or identify the rhyme scheme of a poem in this unit.

Portfolio Building

You may wish to help students choose an option or modify the ones given to suit the needs of the class. Encourage students to include drafts as well as finished pieces in their portfolios so that they can reflect on and assess their development and progress.

Self-Assessment Students should consider the pieces that please them the most and the ones that they would like to rework. Students can create charts that list each piece in their portfolios and record their comments about it.

Setting Goals

In order to help students answer these questions and set future goals, have them identify the selections that they remember the most. Suggest that students also review their portfolio work and look at the pieces that reflect the most revision. Ask students to identify any patterns in these pieces that might suggest areas that need more work.

UNIT TWO

UNIT THEME

Unit Two

Life's Lessons In this unit, students will read selections in which the characters learn something important about life. This unit contains two parts: Part 1 "Learning the Hard Way" and Part 2 "Making Choices." Selections in both parts relate to the unit theme by focusing on characters who learn from failure or who make decisions that alter their lives.

Part 1

Learning the Hard Way Selections in Part 1 present the experiences of characters who learn valuable, though very difficult, lessons. For example, in "Thank You, M'am," a neglected boy learns a lesson in self-respect from a woman he attempts to mug.

Part 2

Making Choices The selections in Part 2 explore the choices that characters make and the lessons they learn as a result. For example, in "Say It With Flowers," a salesclerk must choose between pleasing his employer and keeping his integrity.

Links to Unit Six

The Oral Tradition Unit Six, "Across Time and Place: The Oral Tradition" contains selections that relate to the theme of this unit. You may wish to begin or conclude Unit Two by using one or more of the following selections:

- "The Wolf in Sheep's Clothing" and "The Travelers and the Purse," p. 702
- "The Old Grandfather and His Little Grandson," p. 704
- "Phaëthon," p. 706
- "Gombei and the Wild Ducks," p. 709

138

*L*IFE'S LESSONS

I THINK SUCCESS
HAS NO RULES, BUT
YOU CAN LEARN A
LOT FROM FAILURES.

Jean Kerr

*American Humorist
and dramatist*

Volley Ball III (1979), Graciela Rodo Boulanger.
Oil on canvas, 46 cm × 38 cm. Copyright ©
G. Rodo Boulanger.

139

Art Note

Volley Ball III **by Graciela Rodo
Boulanger** Graciela Rodo Boulanger's
work has evolved from her Bolivian
roots. She began formal training in
Bolivia and Argentina and continued
studying in both Vienna and Paris. Having
had her work exhibited internationally,
Rodo Boulanger is a significant force in
contemporary Latin American art.

Reading the Art *Look at the composition
of this painting. How does the painter
achieve an effect of balance and symmetry?
How would you describe the impressions
that this painting creates in you?*

To help students explore the connections between the art, the quotation,
and the unit theme, have them consider the following questions:

1. Why do you think "Life's Lessons" is
an important theme to explore?
*(Possible responses: People learn valu-
able lessons every day of their lives.
Sometimes, people are aware of having learned these lessons, but often
they aren't. Studying this theme in
detail can help raise my awareness of
the importance of the lessons I will
learn throughout my life.)*

2. How would you explain Jean Kerr's
comment about success and failure?
*(Possible responses: The comment is
ironic because it suggests that you can
learn from failure rather than success.
It's easier to learn what not to do than
what to do to become successful.)*

3. Discuss the ways in which this painting illustrates the unit theme.
*(Possible response: The game of volley-
ball involves making mistakes and
learning from them how to improve
one's game. Also, the volleyball players
are standing as a group with their
arms reaching upward. The volleyball
seems to symbolize something important; it looks like the sun, toward which
all the players are striving.)*

4. What kinds of stories do you think
you will read in this unit? *(Possible
response: The stories will involve different kinds of lessons that people learn
in their lives. Some lessons may be
painful and upsetting, while others
may be enjoyable and pleasurable.)*

5. Describe a situation in which you
learned an important lesson about
your life recently. What lesson did
you learn? What impact did this lesson have on your life? (Responses will
vary.)*

Part 1 Skills Trace

ML DENOTES MINI-LESSON IN TEACHER'S EDITION

Selections	Reading Skills and Strategies	Literary Concepts	Writing Opportunities	Speaking, Listening, and Viewing
POETRY **Casey at the Bat** Ernest Lawrence Thayer	Sound devices, PE p. 141	Rhyme and rhythm, PE p. 145 Characterization, **ML** TE p. 143	Poem, PE p. 145 Newspaper article, PE p. 145 Dialogue, PE p. 145 List of questions, PE p. 145 Sports manual, PE p. 146	Monologue, PE p. 145 Oral reading, PE p. 146 Radio sportscasts, **ML** TE p. 144
FICTION **Thank You, M'am** Langston Hughes	Cause and effect, PE p. 148 Relating cause and effect, **ML** TE p. 149	External and internal conflicts, PE p. 153 Character, PE p. 153 Dialogue, **ML** TE p. 150	Dialogue, PE p. 153 Comparison, PE p. 153	Discussion, PE p. 153 Oral report, PE p. 154
FICTION **Hollywood and the Pits** Cherylene Lee	Structure, PE p. 155 Comparing and contrasting, **ML** TE p. 158	Narrator, PE p. 165 Author's purpose, **ML** TE p. 157	Character sketch, PE p. 165 Letter, PE p. 165 Letter, **ML** TE p. 160 Adventure story, PE p. 165 Elaboration, **ML** TE p. 162	Dialogue, PE p. 165 Interviewing, PE p. 166 Role-playing, PE p. 166 Performing a routine, PE p. 166 Reading aloud, **ML** TE p. 162 Role-playing interviews, **ML** TE p. 163
NONFICTION ON YOUR OWN **from What the Dogs Have Taught Me** Merrill Markoe			List and explanations, TE p. 170	Dialogue, TE p. 169 Reading aloud, TE p. 170 Discussion, TE p. 171

Writing	Reading Skills and Strategies	Literary Concepts	Writing Opportunities	Speaking, Listening, and Viewing
WRITING ABOUT LITERATURE **Analysis**		Imagery, PE pp. 172–79 Figurative language, PE p. 175	Write word pictures, PE p. 173 Write a description, PE p. 173 Using precise verbs, PE p. 173 Analysis essay, PE pp. 174–77 Figurative language, PE p. 175	Composing descriptions, PE p. 173 Reading aloud, PE p. 174 Viewing images, PE p. 178 Interpreting images, PE p. 178 Discussion, PE p. 178 Discussing images, p. 179

Grammar, Usage, Mechanics, and Spelling	Multimodal Learning	Research and Study Skills	Vocabulary	
	Monologue, PE p. 145 Oral reading, PE p. 146 Baseball card, PE p. 146 Sports manual, PE p. 146 Radio sportscasts, (ML) TE p. 144			
Punctuating quotations, (ML) TE p. 151 Suffixes -able and -ible, (ML) TE p. 152	Discussion, PE p. 153 Theatrical sets, PE p. 154 Oral report, PE p. 154	Research Harlem history, PE p. 154	barren frail mistrust presentable suede	
Capitalizing proper nouns and adjectives, (ML) TE p. 161 Prefixes ex- and sub-, (ML) TE p. 164	Dialogue, PE p. 165 Interviewing, PE p. 166 Role-playing, PE p. 166 Performing a routine, PE p. 166 Diorama, PE p. 166 Reading aloud, (ML) TE p. 162 Role-playing interviews, (ML) TE p. 163	Research La Brea Tar Pits, PE p. 166 Outlining, (ML) TE p. 159	bewildered obsess displaced plush excavated poring glistening skewing grovel subterranean	
	Dialogue, TE p. 169 Reading aloud, TE p. 170 Discussion, TE p. 171			

Grammar, Usage, Mechanics, and Spelling	Multimodal Learning	Research and Study Skills	Media Literacy
Using precise verbs, PE p. 173 Using adverbs in comparisons, PE p. 177 Using adjectives and adverbs, PE p. 177	Composing descriptions, PE p. 173 Reading aloud, PE p. 174 Viewing images, PE p. 178 Interpreting images, PE p. 178 Discussion, PE p. 178 Discussing images, PE p. 179	Analyzing literature, PE p. 174	Analyzing advertisements, PE pp. 178–79

Part 2 Skills Trace

ML DENOTES MINI-LESSON IN TEACHER'S EDITION

Selections	Reading Skills and Strategies	Literary Concepts	Writing Opportunities	Speaking, Listening, and Viewing

FICTION
Say It with Flowers
Toshio Mori
	Question, **ML** TE p. 183	Title, PE p. 190
		Climax, PE p. 190
		Climax, **ML** TE p. 184
		Points of view, **ML** TE p. 186
			Want ad, PE p. 181
			Help-wanted ad, PE p. 190
			Profile, PE p. 190
			Sequel, PE p. 190
			Sentences, **ML** TE p. 185
			Rewriting, **ML** TE p. 186
			Critical review, **ML** TE p. 188
				Debating, PE p. 190
				Role-playing, PE p. 191
				Creating a commercial,
				  PE p. 191
				Making a speech, PE p. 191
				Oral report, PE p. 191
				Interviewing, PE p. 191
				Improvising a dialogue,
				  PE p. 192
				Analyzing writing, **ML** TE p. 186

POETRY **It Happened in Montgomery** Phil W. Petrie **Choices** Nikki Giovanni	Reading modern poetry, PE p. 193	Free verse, PE p. 196	Free-verse poem, PE p. 196 Questions, PE p. 196 Letter, PE p. 196 Written report, PE p. 197	Role-playing, PE p. 196 Oral report, PE p. 197
POETRY **Barter** Sara Teasdale **Into the Sun** Hannah Kahn		Lyric poems, PE p. 198 Imagery, PE p. 198 Figurative language, PE p. 201 Repetition, PE p. 201	Advice column, PE p. 198 Poem, PE p. 201 Letter, PE p. 201 List, PE p. 201 Lyric poem, **ML** TE p. 200	Paragraph, PE p. 201 Oral reading, PE p. 202 Music video, PE p. 202 Discussing images, **ML** TE p. 199
NONFICTION **Eleanor Roosevelt** William Jay Jacobs	Sequence, PE p. 203 Sequence of events, **ML** TE p. 205	Biography, PE p. 214 Conflict, PE p. 214 Conflict, **ML** TE p. 206	Advice column, PE p. 214 Job description, PE p. 214 Speech, PE p. 214 Written report, PE p. 215	Role-playing, PE p. 215 Poster, PE p. 215 Oral report, PE p. 215 Oral report, **ML** TE p. 212

DRAMA
A Christmas Carol
Charles Dickens, dramatized
  by Frederick Gaines
	Stage directions, PE p. 218
	Making inferences,
	  ML TE p. 220
		Theme, PE p. 243
		Imagery, **ML** TE p. 226
			Will, PE p. 243
			Plot summary, PE p. 243
			Dialogue, PE p. 243
			Rewrite dialogue, **ML** TE p. 224
				Radio play, PE p. 243
				Interviewing, PE p. 244
				Comparison, PE p. 244
				Performing, PE p. 244
				Oral report, PE p. 244
				Trivia game, PE p. 245
				Reading aloud, **ML** TE p. 223
				Discussion, **ML** TE p. 233
				Film and storyboard,
				  ML TE p. 235
				Performing, **ML** TE p. 238

Writing	**Reading Skills and Strategies**	**Literary Concepts**	**Writing Opportunities**	**Speaking, Listening, and Viewing**

WRITING FROM EXPERIENCE
Narrative and Literary Writing
		Character, PE pp. 248–49
		Plot, PE p. 248
		Conflict, PE 248
		Setting, PE p. 248
		Narrator, PE p. 250
		Show, don't tell, PE p. 251
		Dialogue, PE pp. 251, 253
			Writing a short story,
			  PE pp. 246–53
			QuickWrite, PE p. 247
			Character biography, PE p. 249
			Drafting, PE pp. 250–51
			Achieving paragraph unity,
			  PE p. 251
			Revising and publishing,
			  PE pp. 252–53
				Swapping stories, PE p. 249
				Role-playing, PE p. 249
				Performing, PE p. 253

Grammar, Usage, Mechanics, and Spelling	Multimodal Learning	Research and Study Skills	Vocabulary
Compound and complex sentences, **ML** TE p. 185 Words ending in *-ate/-ion*, **ML** TE p. 189	Debate, PE p. 190 Role-playing, PE p. 191 Create a commercial, PE p. 191 Speech, PE p. 191 Oral report, PE p. 191 Interview, PE p. 191 Improvise a dialogue, PE p. 192 Analyzing writing, **ML** TE p. 186	Research the Better Business Bureau, PE p. 191 Research flowers, PE p. 191 Taking standardized tests, **ML** TE p. 187	comeback indignantly deliberation inquisitive disarm spree ensuing temperament harmonize transaction
	Role-playing, PE p. 196 Oral report, PE p. 197	Research the Montgomery bus boycott, PE p. 197	
	Paragraph, PE p. 201 Collage, PE p. 202 Oral reading, PE p. 202 Music video, PE p. 202 Discuss images, **ML** TE p. 199		
Using adjectives, **ML** TE p. 207 Using appositives, **ML** TE p. 208 Words ending in *-ance/-ant, -ence/-ent,* **ML** TE p. 213	Role-playing, PE p. 215 Poster, PE p. 215 Oral report, PE p. 215 Oral report, **ML** TE p. 212	Research a president's wife, PE p. 215 Research the United Nations, PE p. 215 Universal Declaration of Human Rights, PE p. 215 Outlining, **ML** TE p. 209	brooding combatant migrant priority prominent
Run-on sentences, **ML** TE p. 224 Dialogue in plays and skits, **ML** TE p. 223 Words with *j, ge,* and *dge,* **ML** TE p. 242	Radio play, PE p. 243 Interview, PE p. 244 Comparison, PE p. 244 Performance, PE p. 244 Sketches, PE p. 244 Oral report, PE p. 244 Trivia game, PE p. 245 Reading aloud, **ML** TE p. 223 Discussion, **ML** TE p. 233 Film and storyboard, TE p. 235 Performance, **ML** TE p. 239	Research historic clothing, PE p. 244 Research the history of caroling, PE p. 244	abundance provision charitable reassurance currency solitude destitute summon emerge surplus finale transform mortal welfare pledge

Grammar, Usage, Mechanics, and Spelling	Multimodal Learning	Research and Study Skills	Media Literacy
Show, don't tell, PE p. 251 Achieving paragraph unity, PE p. 251 Using sentence fragments in dialogue, PE p. 253	Analyzing magazine articles, PE pp. 246–47 Interpreting newspaper statistics, PE p. 247 Story chart, PE p. 248 Swap stories, PE p. 249 Role-playing, PE p. 249 Performing, PE p. 253		Analyzing magazine articles, PE pp. 246–47 Interpreting newspaper statistics, PE p. 247

Recommended Novels

 LITERATURE CONNECTIONS WITH SOURCEBOOK FOR TEACHERS

 SPANISH VERSION AVAILABLE

Roll of Thunder, Hear My Cry
by Mildred D. Taylor

Thematic Links In this novel, set in rural Mississippi during the Great Depression, Cassie Logan discovers that life's lessons are often bitter.

About the Author Mildred D. Taylor (born 1943) draws on her experiences and heritage to write about the realities of African-American life.

Other Works by Mildred D. Taylor *Song of the Trees, Let the Circle Be Unbroken, The Friendship, The Gold Cadillac, Mississippi Bridge, The Road to Memphis*

Somewhere in the Darkness
by Walter Dean Myers

Thematic Links An escaped convict, claiming his innocence, goes on the road with his son to clear his name.

About the Author Walter Dean Myers (born 1937) is an award-winning author known for his fiction for children and young adults. Although his works often address serious topics, such as suicide, parental neglect, teen pregnancy, and adoption, his tone is usually optimistic.

Other Works by Walter Dean Myers *Fast Sam, Cool Clyde, and Stuff; The Young Landlords; Motown and Didi*

Felicia the Critic
by Ellen Conford

Thematic Links Felicia has a habit of being bluntly honest, which gets her into trouble.

About the Author Ellen Conford (born 1942) uses situations familiar to her audience to entertain and encourage through funny characters and witty dialogue.

Other Works by Ellen Conford *Lenny Kandell, Smart Aleck; If This Is Love, I'll Take Spaghetti; You Never Can Tell*

 LITERATURE CONNECTIONS WITH SOURCEBOOK FOR TEACHERS

The Giver
by Lois Lowry

Thematic Links As Jonas trains for his new role as The Giver, his perceptions of himself and his seemingly perfect community change, and he must decide how to meet the challenges brought about by his new knowledge.

About the Author Newbery Award-winning author Lois Lowry (born 1937), whose memories were the inspiration for *The Giver,* uses her writing to share with others her beliefs about the importance of communication and interdependence between people.

Other Works by Lois Lowry *A Summer to Die; Number the Stars; Find a Stranger, Say Goodbye; Anastasia Krupnik; The One Hundredth Thing About Caroline; Taking Care of Terrific*

Song of the Buffalo Boy
by Sherry Garland

Thematic Links An Amerasian teenager in Vietnam must decide whether to go to America to find her father.

About the Author Sherry Garland (born 1948) credits her high school English teacher with inspiring her to become a writer. Garland has said of her teacher, "She made us see the beauty and power of the written word. Because of her enthusiasm, . . . I wrote poetry secretly, hiding it beneath mattresses or tucked away in drawers, never showing it to anyone."

Other Works by Sherry Garland *Where the Cherry Trees Bloom, Why Ducks Sleep on One Leg, Shadow of the Dragon*

For Teacher **TEACHING LITERATURE**

Burke, Margaret. "'Now There's a Novel Idea!': Using Drama in the Secondary English Classroom." *English Quarterly* 25:4 (Summer 1993): 26–28.

Gill, Kent, et al., eds. *Ideas for the Working Classroom.* Classroom Practices, Vol. 27. Urbana, IL: National Council of Teachers of English, 1993.

O'Connor, John S. "Seeking Truth in Fiction: Teaching Unreliable Narrators." *English Journal* 83.2 (February 1994): 48–50.

 ## Recommended Readings in Cross-Curricular Areas

HISTORY

The Story of Baseball
by Lawrence S. Ritter (1983)
Ritter traces the game back to 1846 with anecdotes about some of the most historically well-known players.

Eleanor Roosevelt, With Love: A Centenary Remembrance
by Elliott Roosevelt (1984)
A personalized story told by her son with family stories and other information that only a son would know.

SOCIAL STUDIES

A Matter of Pride
by Emily Crofford (1981)
A story that focuses on the experiences of a ten-year-old girl during the Depression.

There Are No Children Here: The Story of Two Boys Growing Up in the Other America
by Alex Kotlowitz (1991)
An in-depth account of two inner-city kids and their daily struggle with life.

For Teacher CROSS-CURRICULAR INSTRUCTION

Brooks, Charlotte K. "Tapping the Potential of Our Rainbow Students (Rainbow Teachers/Rainbow Students)." *English Journal* 84.3 (March, 1995): 78–79.

Dilg, Mary A. "The Opening of the American Mind: Challenges in the Cross-Cultural Teaching of Literature." *English Journal* 84.3 (March 1995): 18–25.

Readence, John E., et al. *Content Area Literacy: An Integrated Approach.* 5th ed. Dubuque: Kendall/Hunt, 1995.

Wheat, Pam, and Brenda Whorton, eds. *Clues from the Past: A Resource Book on Archeology.* Dallas: Hendrick-Long, 1990.

 ## Recommended Media Resources

THE LANGUAGE OF LITERATURE

LASERLINKS
Videodisc, Gr.7
See *LaserLinks Teacher's Source Book,* page 16, for an overview of Unit Two.

AUDIO LIBRARY
Tapes
Unit Two: Life's Lessons
Gr. 7, Tape 3: Sides A & B
Gr. 7, Tape 4: Sides A & B
Gr. 7, Tape 5: Sides A & B
Novel in Spanish:
*Lo llamada de lo salvaje
(Call of the Wild)*

WRITING COACH
Writing Coach Software: Writing About Literature: Interpretive Essay; Short Story

OUTSIDE RESOURCES

Films/Videos/Film Strips/Audiocassettes
Where the Red Fern Grows, videocassette, Dayton Video, Inc., 1991. (108 min.)
Dickens: A Christmas Carol. Read by Patrick Horgan. Two sound cassettes. Cassette Bookshelf Listening Library.
Langston Hughes Reads. Read by Hughes. One sound cassette. (50 min.).
Casey at the Bat, videocassette, Playhouse Video, CBS/Fox Company, 1989.

Internet Resources
Literature and Language Arts Center at http://www.hmco.com/mcdougal/lit/litcent.html

For Teacher TEACHING WITH TECHNOLOGY

Sudzina, Mary R. "Technology, Teachers, Educational Reform: Implications for Teacher Preparation." Annual Meeting of the Association of Teacher Educators. Los Angeles. 13–17 Feb. 1993.

Marcus, Stephen. "The Only Technology You Really Need." *Quarterly of the National Writing Project and the Center for the Study of Writing and Literacy* 15.2 (Spring 1993): 19–21.

Means, Barbara, et al. *Using Technology to Support Education Reform.* Washington: GPO, 1993.

Professional Enrichment

Add a Dash of Dialogue!

> "You took the words right out of my mouth!" How many times have you said that? Dialogue is as crucial in literature as it is in life.

Good dialogue helps launch and propel the plot. It also helps define characters, revealing important aspects of their personalities. It helps readers hear how characters speak—and how others speak about them. Finally, it makes a story more interesting.

Before you begin discussing dialogue with your students, be sure they understand what it is. Explain that effective dialogue always sounds realistic. Point out that, like real conversation, dialogue often contains slang, informal language, and even sentence fragments. To demonstrate this, you may wish to invite volunteers to role-play a dialogue for the class. Consider using excerpts of dialogue from stories in this unit. Possibilities include "Thank You, M'am," "Hollywood and the Pits," "A Conversation with My Dogs," and "Say It With Flowers." Or you might select an excerpt from the play "A Christmas Carol." Dialogue from a play is especially suitable because it is intended to be heard rather than read.

READING DIALOGUE

After students role-play, have the rest of the class point out what made the dialogue interesting.

- Start by asking students for examples of statements that they associate with characters from famous books, television shows, plays, or movies. Then talk about how the dialogue just performed helped create equally realistic and memorable characters.
- Encourage students to talk about different ways the characters could have delivered their lines. Explore how these different deliveries might change listeners' attitudes toward the characters.
- Discuss how the short story or play would have been different if it had been written without dialogue.

WRITING DIALOGUE

- Tell students to capitalize the first word of a quotation. Also remind them to capitalize the first word of a new sentence within a quotation.
- Have students use "speaker's tags," short explanations such as *he said* and *I whispered,* to identify the speaker and tell how things are said.
- Novice writers often overuse speaker's tags. Guide them to let the speaker's words show how the speaker is feeling rather than relying on speaker's tags to tell how.
- Remind students to put quotation marks around a speaker's exact words.
- Be sure students use a comma or some other punctuation to set off quoted words from the speaker's tags. Remind students that this rule holds whether the explanatory words come before, between, or after the quoted words.

You may wish to model this rule with the the following examples:

1. **Commas and periods go inside quotation marks:**
   "I'm afraid I've forgotten your name," said James apologetically.

   Quinn smiled. "That's because it's an unusual name."

2. **Question marks and exclamation marks go inside quotation marks if they belong to the quotation itself.**
   "Did you hear that?" Charles whispered. "It's right outside the door!"

3. **Question marks and exclamation marks go outside the quotation marks if they do not belong to the quotation.**
   It's scary to hear, "The test is today"!

- Encourage students to use adverbs such as *happily, tearfully, uncertainly,* and *hopefully* to show how something is said. Model this on the board. For example, you may wish to write:
  "Thanks, but no thanks," Gina said sarcastically.
- Finally, remind students to begin a new paragraph each time the speaker changes.

Related Reading

 The Writer's Craft. Evanston, Illinois: McDougal, Littell & Company, 1995.

 Little, Jean. *Little by Little: A Writer's Education.* New York: Viking, 1988.

Family and Community Involvement

The selections in Unit Two are connected to the common theme of learning life's lessons—lessons learned through new experiences, by making mistakes, through contact with other people, and from just living life. By doing the following activities, your students, their families, and other community members can investigate the processes of learning lessons and making choices based on life's lessons.

The following Copymasters for Unit Two provide activities that students can take home and complete with a parent or other family member.

OPTION 1: INTERVIEW A WISE PERSON

- **Connection** All of the selections in Unit Two illustrate the theme of life's lessons.
- **Activity** *Copymaster, page 1* Students and family members interview someone they know to be wise about life's lessons.

OPTION 2: PERFORM AN ACT

- **Connection** In "Hollywood and the Pits," the narrator describes her days as a member of the singing and dancing Lee Sisters act.
- **Activity** *Copymaster, page 2* Students and family members create and perform a vaudeville/stage act centered around an existing or learned talent.

OPTION 3: WRITE A SHORT STORY

- **Connection** Unit Two contains several short stories in which the main character learns a powerful lesson about life.
- **Activity** *Copymaster, page 3* Students and family members write a short story about a lesson they learned and share it with others in an attempt to pass the lesson on.

OPTION 1

- **Connection** The selections in Unit Two all illustrate the theme of learning life's lessons.
- **Activity** Invite a panel of teachers to discuss with students the best methods for learning lessons inside and outside the classroom.

OPTION 2

- **Connection** Unit Two includes several poems, such as "Casey at the Bat," "It Happened in Montgomery," "Choices," and "Barter," all written by different poets using different writing methods.
- **Activity** Invite a local poet to read his or her work aloud and discuss methods of poetry writing with the class.

OPTION 3

- **Connection** The setting of "Say It with Flowers" is a flower shop where a new employee learns about the business of selling flowers.
- **Activity** Take the class on a field trip to a nursery or flower shop to learn about flower growing, selling, or arranging.

OPTION 4

- **Connection** In "Thank You, M'am," a young man learns a valuable lesson after trying to snatch Mrs. Jones's purse.
- **Activity** Organize a debate on the following topic: Should first-time thieves be given a second chance? Invite a member of a local debate team to outline rules and oversee the debate.

Part 1 Cooperative Project

A Comedy Skit

 **Getting Started**

Arranging the Project

Decide on the form the performances will take, as well as your expectations regarding them. Also decide where groups will perform. If you prefer to use an auditorium or a room other than the classroom, begin making arrangements. Decide if you would like students to memorize their lines or read from their scripts and if you expect them to create elaborate sets, collect props, or wear costumes. This project can be tailored according to groups' needs and ability levels and according to time and space constraints. Be sure groups know what is expected of them.

Some schools have a selection of scenery that can be easily erected on a stage. If this is possible, arrange with maintenance for the sets to be put into place.

Arranging for the Performances

Even if you decide to hold performances in your classroom, students might be pleased to have an audience other than just their classmates. Consider inviting school officials or other teachers. Space permitting, you might ask other seventh-grade classes to watch and to participate in a general discussion after the performances.

Overview

Students will write and act in a comedy skit in which a youth learns one of life's lessons the hard way.

PROJECT AT A GLANCE

The selections in Unit Two, Part 1 are about learning some of life's lessons the hard way. For this project, students will perform a comedy skit in which a young fictional character learns a difficult lesson. Students will work together in small groups to come up with an idea, write a script, and perform it as a skit for an audience. Culmination of the project might be a performance in front of classmates, or an evening performance for families, teachers, administrators, and other students.

OBJECTIVES

• To identify a difficult lesson of life that is relevant to students
• To write the script for a skit in which a youth learns a lesson
• To perform the skit in front of an audience

SUGGESTED GROUP SIZE

4–6 students per group

MATERIALS

• Video camera and cassette, if possible

 Creating the Skits

Introducing the Project

Explain that students will work in groups to plan and produce a comedy skit that shows a young person learning a hard lesson. Groups will brainstorm ideas for the setting, the characters, and the lesson learned; then they will develop a plot. They will write a script, assign roles, and act out the skit for an audience.

To get the ball rolling, discuss several popular television sitcoms, or ask that students watch a particular episode of a show for future discussion and reference. Many current sitcoms are youth-oriented, and most include some children. You may also opt to show a short humorous movie in class so you can discuss it on the spot. If you do, be sure the subject matter will blend with the theme of the literary selections. Students should be able to point out why the shows are humorous, as well as what lesson is being learned.

Group Investigations

Divide students into groups of four to six. Groups will work together to brainstorm ideas for the skit. They should draw on their own experiences, as well as talk to students outside class to hear about more situations that could be adapted for their use.

When groups have chosen a main idea, they should work to develop a basic plot and char-

acters. Hold class meetings to discuss the creative process in general, allowing students to share how they decided on characters and plot lines. This will also let you monitor their progress and intervene when help is needed.

Creating a Project Description

After groups have finalized the plot and characters, they should submit a brief plot summary, including a cast of characters and a brief description of each character. If cast assignments have been made, those should also be included. This will allow you to check that the projects are on schedule and on target.

OPTION 1: ADAPTING A SITCOM Groups can adapt the setting and characters from an existing or past television sitcom. They should write an entirely new plot line but have the characters keep the same personalities they have on television.

OPTION 2: ANALYSIS Groups can analyze a selected episode of an existing television sitcom. Analyses should include the lesson learned, how the lesson could have been avoided, and a description of what made the episode humorous.

OPTION 3: IN-HOUSE SKITS Ask groups to set their skits in the school. You might even go so far as to ask teachers and administrators to play themselves in the performance.

OPTION 4: HOT TOPICS Groups can select the topic of the lesson being learned from a list of serious concerns of today's youth. Ask them to interview other students about what concerns them most and to read the newspaper for more ideas.

On the day of performance, encourage the audience to laugh and enjoy themselves, but remind them to give each skit and the actors their due respect. Schedule a few extra minutes between skits for groups to trade places and prepare for the performance.

 ## 3 Sharing the Performances

If possible, videotape each skit. This allows you to review the skits for assessment, as well as to preserve the performances for reference in the future. Groups would enjoy seeing their own performances too. Try to arrange

for the taping to be done by another teacher, an older student, or a parent volunteer so you can concentrate on the performance. Tapes can later be shown in class to stimulate discussion.

 ## Assessing the Project

The following rubric can be used for group or individual assessment

3 Full Accomplishment Students follow directions and produce a comedy skit that shows a young person learning a lesson the hard way.

2 Substantial Accomplishment Students produce a skit, but it does not depict a young person learning a difficult lesson, or it is not a comedy.

1 Little or Partial Accomplishment Students' skit is incomplete or does not fulfill the requirements of the assignment.

For the Portfolio

If you made a videotape of the skits, you might keep the master copy in your classroom or in the school library for future reference. Your written assessment of the project should be inserted in each student's portfolio. Students may choose to keep a copy of the final script in their portfolio, too.

Note: For other assessment options, see the *Teacher's Guide to Assessment and Portfolio Use.*

UNIT TWO
Part 1 Lesson Planner

TIME ALLOTMENTS SHOWN ARE APPROXIMATE. DEPENDING ON YOUR GOALS AND THE NEEDS OF YOUR STUDENTS, YOU MAY WISH TO ALLOW MORE OR LESS TIME FOR CERTAIN PORTIONS OF THE LESSON.

Table of Contents	Discussion	Previewing the Selection	Reading the Selection
PART OPENER **LEARNING THE HARD WAY** **What Do You Think?** page 140	**20 MINUTES** • Reflect on the part theme		
SELECTION **Casey at the Bat** page 142 AVERAGE		**15 MINUTES** • PERSONAL CONNECTION • HISTORICAL CONNECTION • READING CONNECTION: Sound devices	**10 MINUTES** • Read pp. 142–44 (3 pp.)
SELECTION **Thank You, M'am** page 149 CHALLENGING		**20 MINUTES** • PERSONAL CONNECTION • GEOGRAPHICAL CONNECTION • READING CONNECTION: Cause and effect	**10 MINUTES** • Introduce vocabulary • Read pp. 149–52 (4 pp.)
SELECTION **Hollywood and the Pits** page 156 AVERAGE		**15 MINUTES** • PERSONAL CONNECTION • HISTORICAL CONNECTION • READING CONNECTION: Structure	**45 MINUTES** • Introduce vocabulary • Read pp. 156–64 (9 pp.)
NONFICTION ON YOUR OWN *from* **What the Dogs Have Taught Me** page 167 EASY			**10 MINUTES** • Read pp. 167–71 (5 pp.)

Writing	Writer's Style	Prewriting	Drafting and Revising
WRITING ABOUT LITERATURE **Analysis**	**30 MINUTES**	**20 MINUTES**	**80 MINUTES**

Time estimates assume in-class work. You may wish to assign some of these stages as homework.

Responding to the Selection

FROM PERSONAL RESPONSE TO CRITICAL ANALYSIS	OR	ANOTHER PATHWAY	LITERARY CONCEPTS	QUICKWRITES	ALTERNATIVE ACTIVITIES	LITERARY LINKS	CRITIC'S CORNER	THE WRITER'S STYLE	ACROSS THE CURRICULUM	ART CONNECTION	WORDS TO KNOW	BIOGRAPHY
40 MINUTES					**40 MINUTES**							
• Discussion questions	OR	• Monologue	• Rhyme and rhythm	• Poem • Newspaper article • Dialogue • List of questions	✔			✔	PHYSICAL EDUC-ATION	✔		✔
30 MINUTES					**30 MINUTES**							
• Discussion questions	OR	• Discussion	• External and internal conflict • Character	• Dialogue • Comparison	✔				SOCIAL STUDIES		✔	✔
40 MINUTES					**40 MINUTES**							
• Discussion questions	OR	• Dialogue	• Narrator	• Character sketch • Letter • Adventure story	✔	✔			SCIENCE		✔	✔ ✔

Publishing and Reflecting	Grammar in Context	Reading the World
30 MINUTES	**5 MINUTES**	**25 MINUTES**

WHAT DO YOU THINK?

Objectives

The activities on this page can be used to

- introduce the theme of "Learning the Hard Way" since each activity is connected to one or more of the selections in Part 1
- create materials for portfolios that students can return to later for reconsideration or revision
- build an understanding of theme that students can return to and develop as they progress through the unit

What would your pet say?
Encourage students to think about the possible perspectives a pet might have based on its experiences. Students first should sketch several panels from which to select for the final version of their comic strips. (See "A Conversation with My Dogs," from *What the Dogs Have Taught Me*, p. 167.)

Whom would you like to thank?
Encourage students to list some of the lessons they have learned and then select the one they consider most important. (See "Thank You, M'am," p. 147.)

How do you respond to pressure?
Have students first write a stream of consciousness description of how the situation makes them feel. Students can then use this information to select images for their collages or descriptions. (See "Casey at the Bat," p. 141; "Hollywood and the Pits," p. 155.)

How do you feel about competition?
In its discussion, each group should identify the positive and negative results of competition. You may also wish to have the groups form two teams to debate this issue. (See "Hollywood and the Pits," p. 155.)

LEARNING THE HARD WAY

WHAT DO You THINK?

REFLECTING ON THEME

According to an old saying, life is the greatest teacher. Whether you want to or not, you're always learning lessons, both inside and outside the classroom. Some lessons are easy to learn; others are learned the hard way. Use the activities on this page to help you reflect on some of life's lessons.

Whom would you like to thank?

What adult has helped you the most in growing up? Write a letter to that person, thanking him or her for teaching you a valuable lesson about life.

How do you respond to pressure?

Think of times when you have been under pressure—perhaps when giving a speech or playing in a crucial game. How do you usually respond in such situations? Create a collage that reflects your thoughts and feelings about performing under pressure, or describe them in your notebook.

What would your pet say?

If your pet could speak, what nuggets of common sense might come out of its mouth? Create a comic strip in which a pet makes comments on the way its owner feeds or trains it.

How do you feel about competition?

Should young children be encouraged to take part in competitive activities, such as gymnastic meets? With a small group of classmates, draw a scale like the one shown, and have each person mark the scale to reflect his or her views. Then discuss your ideas about competition.

1	2	3	4	5	6	7	8	9	10
harmful									beneficial

Cross-Curricular Connections

History Have students work in small groups to research a major war or battle in U.S. history. You may wish to assign a different conflict to each group. Students should research why the war or battle was fought, the casualties involved, and the outcome of the conflict. Students should also discuss what lessons they think were learned, and whether or not these lessons have had an impact on the citizens of this country. Groups can then present their findings to the class.

COMMUNITY OUTREACH

Invite students to learn more about M.A.D.D. (Mothers Against Drunk Driving) or S.A.D.D. (Students Against Drunk Driving), two organizations that attempt to raise awareness of the dangers of drunk driving. Students can write to a local chapter of M.A.D.D. for more information about the lessons to be learned from personal loss. If your school does not have a chapter of S.A.D.D., you may wish to have students write away for information about forming their own local chapter.

POETRY

Casey at the Bat

Ernest Lawrence Thayer

Activating Prior Knowledge

PERSONAL CONNECTION

Who are your favorite athletes? What do you expect of them when games are "on the line"? In your notebook, list two or three of your favorite players and tell how each one performed in a key situation. Share your list with a small group of classmates.

Favorite Athletes

Player
1.
2.
3.

Situation
1.
2.
3.

Building Background

HISTORICAL CONNECTION

Perhaps some of the favorite athletes you listed for the Personal Connection are baseball players. Baseball began in the United States in the mid-1800s. By the early 1900s, the sport was so popular that people began calling it America's national pastime. Its popularity prompted Jacques Barzun, a noted philosopher and educator, to state, "Whoever wants to know the heart and mind of America had better learn baseball." In light of the nation's continuing enthusiasm for baseball from 1888—the year "Casey at the Bat" was written—to the present, it is small wonder that "mighty Casey" has remained a popular figure for more than 100 years.

A cartoon showing baseball players and fans reacting to an umpire's call.
Culver Pictures.

Active Reading / Setting a Purpose

READING CONNECTION

Sound Devices "Casey at the Bat" is a narrative poem. Like fiction, **narrative poetry** tells a story. Unlike fiction, however, narrative poetry is written in lines and likely makes use of such sound devices as rhyme and rhythm. Read this poem silently to yourself. As you read, think about how Casey, a mighty athlete, performs in a key situation. Then read the poem aloud, listening for the rhyme and the other sound devices that help create dramatic effects.

CASEY AT THE BAT **141**

OVERVIEW

Objectives

- To understand and appreciate a narrative poem about a baseball player in a key situation
- To examine the use of sound devices in a poem
- To examine and understand rhyme and rhythm in a poem
- To appreciate and understand hyperbole
- To express understanding of the poem through a choice of writing forms, including a poem, a newspaper article, a dialogue, and a list of questions
- To extend understanding of the poem through a variety of multimodal and cross-curricular activities

Skills

LITERARY CONCEPTS
- Rhyme and rhythm
- Characterization

THE WRITER'S STYLE
- Hyperbole

GENRE STUDY
- Poetry: narrative poem

SPEAKING, LISTENING, AND VIEWING
- Radio sportscasts

Cross-Curricular Connections

PHYSICAL EDUCATION
- Sports manual

HISTORY
- Baseball biography

PRINT AND MEDIA RESOURCES

UNIT TWO RESOURCE BOOK
Strategic Reading: Literature, p. 4

ACCESS FOR STUDENTS ACQUIRING ENGLISH
Reading and Writing Support

TEACHER'S GUIDE TO ASSESSMENT AND PORTFOLIO USE

FORMAL ASSESSMENT
Selection Test, pp. 31–32
 Test Generator

 **AUDIO LIBRARY**
See Reference Card

LASERLINKS
Art Gallery

by Ernest Lawrence Thayer

Casey at the Bat

Thematic Link: Learning the Hard Way In "Casey at the Bat," Casey and his fans learn that depending on one person to win a game can lead to disappointment.

CUSTOMIZING FOR
Students Acquiring English

• Use ACCESS FOR STUDENTS ACQUIRING ENGLISH, *Reading and Writing Support.*

(1) You may want to paraphrase this line or ask students to paraphrase it: The fans' faces turned pale because they were worried that Mudville would lose the game.

(2) Point out that the prefix *a-* in *a-huggin'* is added to the verb to give it an informal, colloquial sound and to make it fit the rhythm of the poem. Have students find another verb that uses this prefix. (*a-watching*)

STRATEGIC READING FOR
Less-Proficient Readers

Set a Purpose Ask students to look, as they read, for clues that indicate the crowd's expectations of Casey. Then have students read on to find out if these expectations are met.

Use UNIT TWO RESOURCE BOOK, p. 4, for guidance in reading the selection.

Literary Concept: RHYME

(A) Read the first stanza of the poem. Ask students to identify the words that rhyme. (*day, play; same, game*) Ask what effect the rhyme has on the recitation of the poem. (*Possible response: It helps add drama to the story because there is a deliberate pause at the end of each line that rhymes.*)

It looked extremely rocky for the Mudville nine that day;
The score stood two to four, with but an inning left to play.
So, when Cooney died at second, and Burrows did the same,
A pallor wreathed the features of the patrons of the game.

5 A straggling few got up to go, leaving there the rest,
With that hope which springs eternal within the human breast.
For they thought: "If only Casey could get a whack at that,"
They'd put even money now, with Casey at the bat.

But Flynn preceded Casey, and likewise so did Blake,
10 And the former was a pudd'n, and the latter was a fake.
So on that stricken multitude a deathlike silence sat;
For there seemed but little chance of Casey's getting to the bat.

But Flynn let drive a "single," to the wonderment of all.
And the much-despised Blakey "tore the cover off the ball."
15 And when the dust had lifted, and they saw what had occurred,
There was Blakey safe at second, and Flynn a-huggin' third.

Then from the gladdened multitude went up a joyous yell—
It rumbled in the mountaintops, it rattled in the dell;
It struck upon the hillside and rebounded on the flat;
20 For Casey, mighty Casey, was advancing to the bat.

Mini-Lesson Genre Study

Beginning   Middle   End

POETRY Remind students that a **narrative poem** such as "Casey at the Bat," tells a story in a highly imaginative way. Also remind them that, like short stories, most narrative poems present a sequence of events that makes up the plot.

Application Invite students to chart the plot of "Casey at the Bat." They can create a chart with the following headings: Beginning, Middle, End. Have students decide which stanzas of the poem belong under each heading.

Then they can jot down a short summary of events under each of the headings.

Baseball Scene of Batter, Catcher, and Umpire (1915), Joseph Christian Leyendecker. Photo courtesy of the Archives of the American Illustrators Gallery, New York. Copyright © 1995 ARTShows and Products of Holderness 03245.

CASEY AT THE BAT **143**

Baseball Scene of Batter, Catcher and Umpire by Joseph Christian Leyendecker This painting by the well-known illustrator J. C. Leyendecker demonstrates the artist's talent for accurately rendering the human form. It also enables us to see of how baseball uniforms and equipment have changed since 1915.

Reading the Art *What mood does this baseball moment create for you? What clues suggest the mood? How might this illustration have been used in 1915?*

CUSTOMIZING FOR

Gifted and Talented Students

Thayer uses some long and sometimes difficult words to refer to things that have common names, such as *spheroid* for ball and *stricken multitude* for anxious crowd. Ask students to discuss what purpose these words serve throughout the poem. *(Possible responses: They show how seriously the fans and Casey take the game; the author may be poking fun at how a game can become so serious; they give the poem a humorous tone.)*

CUSTOMIZING FOR

Multiple Learning Styles

B Spatial or Graphic Learners Invite students to draw the infield of the ballpark, with the players in position as described in line 16. Remind students to include the dugout, where Casey may be waiting for his turn at bat.

Literary Concept: RHYTHM

C Have students tap out the rhythm of the fifth stanza. Ask them how the rhythm lends itself to the suspense of the poem. *(The driving, pounding rhythm reinforces the idea that the crowd's excitement is reaching fever pitch.)*

Mini-Lesson Literary Concepts

REVIEWING CHARACTERIZATION
Remind students that characterization refers to the techniques a writer uses to create and develop a character. There are four basic methods of developing a character: (1) through a physical description of the character; (2) through the thoughts, speech, or actions of the character; (3) through the thoughts or actions of other characters; and (4) through direct comments about the character's nature.

Application Copy the chart shown onto the chalkboard. Invite students to find in the poem examples of each method of characterization. Then have them fill in the chart with the lines or the numbers of the lines that show the methods of characterization.

Physical Description	Character's Thoughts/ Actions	Other Characters' Thoughts/ Actions	Direct Comments

Invite students to discuss what they can infer about Casey's character from lines 21–23. *(Casey is proud and self-assured; he is used to attention from the crowd.)*

CUSTOMIZING FOR

Students Acquiring English

(3) Ask students to guess the meaning of *doffed* from the context. Then mime the action of doffing a hat.

Critical Thinking: ANALYZING

E Ask students why they think the poet repeats Casey's name so many times in lines 21–24. *(Possible response: Emphasizing Casey's name makes him loom even larger as a hero.)*

Critical Thinking: EVALUATING

F Ask students to discuss why they think Casey has such power over the fans. *(Possible responses: Evidently, Casey has been able to come through in key situations in the past; he has rarely done anything wrong and thus seems almost godlike.)*

STRATEGIC READING FOR

Less-Proficient Readers

G Ask students to describe the crowd's expectations of Casey. *(He will hit a home run and save the game.)*
Making Inferences

COMPREHENSION CHECK

1. Who are the Mudville nine? *(a baseball team)*
2. Why is the crowd anxious for Casey to come up to bat? *(The crowd believes it can count on Casey to hit a home run and win the game.)*
3. How does Casey respond to the first two pitches? *(He refuses to swing at them, taking them for called strikes.)*
4. How does Casey respond to the third pitch? *(Casey swings and misses, striking out to end the game.)*

D
(3)
E
There was ease in Casey's manner as he stepped into his place,
There was pride in Casey's bearing and a smile on Casey's face;
And when responding to the cheers he lightly doffed his hat,
No stranger in the crowd could doubt 'twas Casey at the bat.

25 Ten thousand eyes were on him as he rubbed his hands with dirt,
Five thousand tongues applauded when he wiped them on his shirt;
Then when the writhing pitcher ground the ball into his hip,
Defiance glanced in Casey's eye, a sneer curled Casey's lip.

And now the leather-covered sphere came hurtling through the air,
30 And Casey stood a-watching it in haughty grandeur there.
Close by the sturdy batsman the ball unheeded sped;
"That ain't my style," said Casey. "Strike one," the umpire said.

From the benches, filled with people, there went up a muffled roar,
Like the beating of the storm waves on the stern and distant shore.
35 "Kill him! Kill the umpire!" shouted someone on the stand;
F And it's likely they'd have killed him had not Casey raised his hand.

With a smile of honest charity great Casey's visage shone;
He stilled the rising tumult, he made the game go on;
He signaled to the pitcher, and once more the spheroid flew;
40 But Casey still ignored it, and the umpire said, "Strike two."

"Fraud!" cried the maddened thousands, and the echo answered "Fraud!"
But one scornful look from Casey and the audience was awed;
They saw his face grow stern and cold, they saw his muscles strain,
And they knew that Casey wouldn't let the ball go by again.

45 The sneer is gone from Casey's lips, his teeth are clenched in hate,
He pounds with cruel vengeance his bat upon the plate;
And now the pitcher holds the ball, and now he lets it go,
And now the air is shattered by the force of Casey's blow.

Oh, somewhere in this favored land the sun is shining bright,
50 The band is playing somewhere, and somewhere hearts are light;
And somewhere men are laughing, and somewhere children shout,
G But there is no joy in Mudville: Mighty Casey has struck out.

Mini-Lesson: Speaking, **Listening, and Viewing**

RADIO SPORTSCASTS Explain to students that in a radio sportscast, the announcer gives a play-by-play account of what is happening in a game or an event so that listeners can visualize the action. The goal of the sportscaster is to report the action clearly and concisely so that listeners can easily follow along. At the same time, the sportscaster wants listeners to feel the excitement of the crowd, as if the listeners were actually present and watching in person.

Application Divide the class into 13 groups, if possible. Have each group select one or more stanzas of "Casey at the Bat" to "announce" as part of a radio sportscast. Have students rewrite the words so that they will sound like those of a sportscaster. For example, "Cooney died at second" in line 3 might be rewritten as "Cooney's on his way to second, and heeee's OUT! That's one away for Mudville." Groups can perform their sportscasts for the rest of the class.

RESPONDING
OPTIONS

FROM PERSONAL RESPONSE TO CRITICAL ANALYSIS

REFLECT 1. What are your impressions of Casey? Draw a sketch that reflects your impressions, and share it with a partner.

RETHINK 2. Would you have liked the poem better if Casey had hit a home run? Why or why not?

3. How would you describe Casey?
Consider Close Textural Reading
   - his attitude toward the game, the pitches, himself, and the crowd
   - his effect on the crowd

4. Why do you think this poem has remained popular for more than a hundred years?
Consider
   - what the poem suggests about fans and their expectations of athletes
   - the language of the poem

RELATE 5. Think about sports events you have watched in person or on TV. How would you compare the fans to those depicted in the poem?

Multimodal Learning
ANOTHER PATHWAY

What do you think was going through Casey's mind as he stepped up to bat? How do you think he reacted after he struck out? Pretend you are Casey and improvise a monologue that shows his perspective of the events. Perform the monologue for the class.

QUICKWRITES

1. Write a **poem** that tells what happens after Casey strikes out. Use rhythm and end rhyme.

2. Write a **newspaper article** that might appear in the *Mudville Times* the day after the game.

3. Write a **dialogue** between Casey and a teammate after the game.

4. Write a **list** of questions to ask mighty Casey during a postgame interview.

📁 *PORTFOLIO Save your writing. You may want to use it later as a springboard to a piece for your portfolio.*

LITERARY CONCEPTS

Rhyme is a repetition of identical or similar sounds. In poetry, the most common type of rhyme is **end rhyme,** where the rhymes occur at the ends of lines. Another type of rhyme is **internal rhyme,** where the rhymes occur within lines. Identify the type of rhyme in each **stanza,** or group of lines, of "Casey at the Bat."

Rhythm is a pattern of stressed and unstressed syllables. A poem may have a regular rhythm like a musical beat or an irregular rhythm that sounds more like conversation. Identify the kind of rhythm found in "Casey at the Bat." Then select a stanza that you think has a dramatic effect. How do the rhythm and rhyme create this effect?

End Rhyme	. . .rocky for the Mudville nine that **day** . . .with but an inning left to **play**
Internal Rhyme	The **score** stood two to **four**, with but . . .

CASEY AT THE BAT **145**

Physical Education *Cooperative Learning* Have students work in large groups. Within each group, four students can act as researchers to gather any information that is needed, such as rules or procedures of the sport. Two students can act as accuracy coaches to check the gathered information. A summarizer can record and edit the information, and a typist can word-process the manual.

ADDITIONAL SUGGESTION

History *Cooperative Learning* Students can work in groups of three to create a short biography of a well-known former baseball player. Each group can decide whom it would like to research, and then a researcher can gather the information from the library. Have each group assign a direction giver to help the group stay focused on the task. When students have collected all the information they need, each group can present an oral report to the class.

Art Connection

Have students review the sketch they drew of Casey in response to question 1. on page 145. Then have them compare their image of Casey with the batter in the painting by Leyendecker.

ART GALLERY
Baseball Art Over the years, a number of artists have been inspired by baseball. A few of their depictions of baseball can be seen here. You may want to use these images to generate discussion about how the artworks might enhance the reading of "Casey at the Bat."

Side A, Frames 49294

ERNEST LAWRENCE THAYER

Although actor DeWolf Hopper made "Casey at the Bat" famous through his popular recitations in the late 1880s, for years he did not know who had written the poem. When he finally met Thayer, Hopper asked him to recite the poem. Hopper later said: "I have heard many another give 'Casey.' Fond mamas have brought their sons to me to hear their childish voices lisp the poem, but Thayer's was the worst of all."

Multimodal Learning

ALTERNATIVE ACTIVITIES

1. The actor DeWolf Hopper's recitation of "Casey at the Bat" in the late 1880s made the poem a hit. Practice and perform an **oral reading** of the poem for your class.

2. Create a **baseball card** for Casey. Draw a picture of him for the front of the card, and make up the information and statistics that are typically found on baseball cards.

ACROSS THE CURRICULUM

Physical Education Write an explanation of a game or sport that you are interested in. Include descriptions of some of the fundamentals, such as the playing field or court, the equipment, the rules, and the positions. Then, with your classmates, compile the class's explanations in a manual. If you can, word-process the manual on a computer, and include pictures or diagrams to make the explanations clearer. Keep a copy of the manual on file in your school library or resource center.

ERNEST LAWRENCE THAYER

1863–1940

Although Ernest Lawrence Thayer wrote many poems for newspapers, he is remembered for just one—"Casey at the Bat." Thayer was educated at Harvard University, where he served as president of its humorous magazine, the *Lampoon*. After graduation, he joined his classmate William Randolph Hearst on the staff of the *San Francisco Examiner*, where in 1887 he began writing a poem for each Sunday issue. "Casey at the Bat" was first printed in the paper in 1888. Thayer said:

I evolved "Casey" from the situation I had seen so often in baseball—a crack batsman coming to the bat with the bases filled, and then fallen down. Every one well knows what immense excitement there is when

that situation occurs in baseball, especially when one of the best batsmen of the team comes up. The enthusiasm is at fever heat and if the batsman makes good the crowd goes wild; while, if the batsman strikes out as "Casey" did, the reverse is the case and the silence that prevails is almost appalling—and very often the army of the disappointed cannot refrain from giving vent to their feelings.

Although Thayer insisted that no particular person was the model for Casey, many ball players claimed to be the unfortunate hero of the poem. By the time of Thayer's death in 1940, "Casey" had become an American favorite. It continues to be one of the best-known sports poems ever written.

THE WRITER'S STYLE

Hyperbole is exaggeration, or bold overstatement, used for emphasis. Thayer uses hyperbole in line 18 to describe the yell of the crowd: "It rumbled in the mountaintops, it rattled in the dell." Find one other example of hyperbole in the poem and discuss why Thayer might have included it. What does the use of hyperbole add to the poem?

ART CONNECTION

Look at the reproduction of the painting *Baseball Scene of Batter, Catcher and Umpire* by Joseph Christian Leyendecker on page 143. How would you compare the batter in the painting with your image of Casey?

Detail. Photo courtesy of the Archives of the American Illustrators Gallery, New York. Copyright © 1995 ARTShows and Products of Holderness 03245.

LASERLINKS
• ART GALLERY

The Writer's Style

After students gather examples of hyperbole, invite them to replace the words or phrases they find with ordinary words or phrases. Then have them read the poem aloud, inserting the ordinary words. For example, lines 13 and 14 might read: "Flynn hit a single. Everyone was surprised. Blakey, whom everybody disliked, hit the ball really, really hard." Have students discuss how the exaggeration adds to the humor and dramatic tone of the poem.

 The Writer's Craft

Meaning and Word Choice, pp. 310–311

Alternative Activities

1. Suggest that each student select a stanza to memorize and then recite dramatically to the class. Encourage students to use different voices for individual characters in the poem.

2. Ask students who collect baseball cards to bring them in to show the class and to let others use them as models.

PREVIEWING

FICTION

Thank You, M'am
Langston Hughes

Activating Prior Knowledge
PERSONAL CONNECTION

An African proverb says, "It takes two parents to produce a child, but it takes an entire village to raise the child." Think about your own neighborhood. Is community spirit strong there? Do you know any adults who keep an eye on the young people there? Share your thoughts with some of your classmates.

Building Background
GEOGRAPHICAL CONNECTION

The action of "Thank You, M'am" takes place in the late 1950s in Harlem, a section of New York City located on Manhattan Island, as shown on the map. Earlier in this century, Harlem attracted a community of African-American musicians, artists, and writers, including Langston Hughes. The vibrant and stimulating life of Harlem had a deep influence on the work of these creative people.

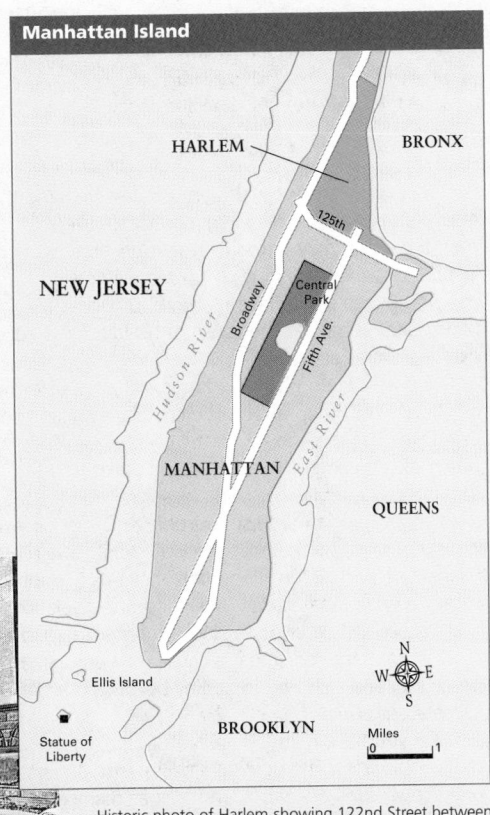

Manhattan Island

Historic photo of Harlem showing 122nd Street between 7th and 8th Avenues. Copyright © Archive Photos.

 LASERLINKS
• CULTURAL CONNECTION   **147**

OVERVIEW

Objectives

- To understand and appreciate a short story about an encounter between an adult and a young person
- To understand cause and effect
- To identify and explore conflict
- To express understanding of the story through a choice of writing forms, including a dialogue and a comparison
- To extend understanding of the story through a variety of multimodal and cross-curricular activities

Skills

READING SKILLS/ STRATEGIES
- Relating cause and effect

LITERARY CONCEPTS
- Conflict
- Dialogue

GRAMMAR
- Punctuating quotations

SPELLING
- Suffixes -able and -ible

SPEAKING, LISTENING, AND VIEWING
- Oral report

Cross-Curricular Connections

SOCIAL STUDIES
- Harlem

MUSIC
- Music of Harlem

 CULTURAL CONNECTION
Life in Harlem Harlem in the late 1950s was more than a place; it was a community that produced more art, dance, and literature than any other of its time. These images offer a glimpse into the community's vibrant lifestyle. You may wish to use them in a discussion of Harlem's daily life and culture in the 1950s.

Side A, Frames 49299

PRINT AND MEDIA RESOURCES

UNIT TWO RESOURCE BOOK
Strategic Reading: Literature, p. 7
Vocabulary SkillBuilder, p. 10
Reading SkillBuilder, p. 8
Spelling SkillBuilder, p. 9

GRAMMAR MINI–LESSONS
Transparencies, p. 34
Copymasters, p. 42

ACCESS FOR STUDENTS ACQUIRING ENGLISH
Selection Summaries
Reading and Writing Support

FORMAL ASSESSMENT
Selection Test, pp. 33–34
Test Generator

AUDIO LIBRARY
See Reference Card

LASERLINKS
Cultural Connection
Art Gallery

INTERNET RESOURCES
McDougal Littell Literature Center at http://www.hmco.com /mcdougal/lit

SUMMARY

Late one night, a boy named Roger tries to snatch the purse of Mrs. Luella Jones. She grabs him, scolds him, and drags him to her apartment. Realizing that he has not been well cared for, she tells him to wash his face and then cooks a dinner and shares it with him. He explains that his motive for snatching her purse was to get money to buy a pair of blue suede shoes. Mrs. Jones tells him that all he had to do was ask her for the money. She also tells him that when she was young, she wanted things she could not get. Mrs. Jones gives Roger ten dollars to buy the shoes and urges him to stay out of trouble. The boy thanks her as she shuts her door, and they never see each other again.

Thematic Link: *Learning the Hard Way*

Roger, who thinks he can get some easy money by snatching a woman's purse, learns a lesson about right and wrong.

READING CONNECTION Active Reading
Setting a Purpose

Cause and Effect

Events in stories are often related by **cause and effect.** In other words, one event is the reason that another event happens. The event that happens first is called the **cause.** The event produced by the cause is the **effect.** Read the excerpt on the right from "Waiting" by Budge Wilson, and then notice the chart below:

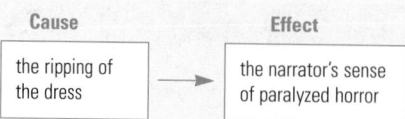

Cause		Effect
the ripping of the dress	→	the narrator's sense of paralyzed horror

Writers do not always present a cause first and then an effect. Sometimes a story begins with an effect. Later in the plot, the writer may introduce the event that is the cause. For instance, at the beginning of "A Man Who Had No Eyes," you find out that the beggar who approaches Mr. Parsons is blind. Later you learn the cause of his blindness—a chemical explosion in a factory.

Often an event in a story causes a change in a character's attitude, which then affects the character's actions. For example, near the end of "Last Cover," Colin shows his father his drawing of Bandit's hiding place. The father studies the drawing intently, discovers its secret, and for the first time is able to appreciate and support his son's artistic ambitions.

As you read, think about the way events in a plot are connected, and picture the order of events in your mind. Look for words that signal cause-and-effect relationships, such as *because, therefore, since, in order that, so that,* and *if . . . then.* Remember that a cause may produce more than one effect and that an effect may become the cause of a subsequent effect.

After you have read "Thank you M'am," think about the plot of this story. Then create a cause-and-effect chart like the one shown for "Waiting." On it, list as many examples of cause and effect as you can.

Here, the **cause** preceeds the effect.

> I knew in one awful, stupefying moment that my dress had ripped up the back, the full length of that long zipper. I can remember standing there on the stage with my arms half raised, unable to think or feel anything beyond a paralyzed horror.

Effect

WORDS TO KNOW

barren (băr′ən) *adj.* empty; deserted (p. 152)
frail (frāl) *adj.* delicate; weak and fragile (p. 150)
mistrust (mĭs-trŭst′) *v.* to have no confidence in (p. 151)

presentable (prĭ-zĕn′tə-bəl) *adj.* fit to be seen by people (p. 151)
suede (swād) *n.* leather with a soft, fuzzy surface (p. 151)

Reverie (1989), Frank Webb. Pastel, 12″ × 8″, collection of Barbara Webb.

Thank You, M'am

BY LANGSTON HUGHES

he was a large woman with a large purse that had everything in it but hammer and nails. It had a long strap, and she carried it slung across her shoulder. It was about eleven o'clock at night, and she was walking alone,

THANK YOU, M'AM **149**

Reverie by Frank Webb *Reverie* was created in pastel by contemporary artist and teacher Frank Webb. Known primarily as a watercolorist, Webb enjoys using many colors in his paintings to convey specific moods.

Reading the Art *Why do you think the artist presents a close-up side view of the person? What are your impressions of the subject of the painting?*

CUSTOMIZING FOR
Students Acquiring English

- Use **ACCESS FOR STUDENTS ACQUIRING ENGLISH,** *Reading and Writing Support.*

- Call students' attention to the word *M'am* in the title of the story. Explain that it is a contraction of the word *Madam* and is used as a form of polite address when speaking to an older woman. Invite students to share similar titles of address used in their native languages.

(①) Make sure that students understand that the word *but,* as used here, means "except."

- In addition to these suggestions, you may want to use those provided under Strategic Reading for Less-Proficient Readers.

STRATEGIC READING FOR
Less-Proficient Readers

Set a Purpose To help students become involved in the selection, have them describe Mrs. Jones. Then have them read on to find out why Roger attempts to snatch her purse.

Use **UNIT TWO RESOURCE BOOK,** p. 7, for guidance in reading the selection.

Mini-Lesson	Reading Skills/Strategies

RELATING CAUSE AND EFFECT Explain to students that writers of fiction often structure the plot of a short story around a series of events that are connected by cause and effect. If necessary, refer students to page 148 to review cause and effect. Then use the example of falling dominoes to demonstrate the relationship between a cause and an effect. Point out that the result, or effect, of one cause can itself become the cause of the next event, just as one domino knocks over the next domino and so on.

Application Have students review the cause-and-effect charts they made for this story on page 148. Then ask students to imagine a different series of events following the purse snatching—a revised story in which Mrs. Jones does not take Roger home with her. Ask students how changing some of the events in the story would change their cause-and-effect charts. Have students write a brief summary of their revised stories and create new charts.

Reteaching/Reinforcement
- *Unit Two Resource Book,* p. 8

A when a boy ran up behind her and tried to snatch her purse. The strap broke with the single tug the boy gave it from behind. But the boy's weight and the weight of the purse combined caused him to lose his balance so, instead of taking off full blast as he had hoped, the boy fell on his back on the sidewalk, and his legs flew up. The large woman simply turned around and kicked him right square in his blue-jeaned sitter. Then she reached down, picked the boy up by his shirt front, and shook him until his teeth rattled.

After that the woman said, "Pick up my pocketbook, boy, and give it here."

She still held him. But she bent down enough to permit him to stoop and pick up her purse. Then she said, "Now ain't you ashamed of yourself?"

Firmly gripped by his shirt front, the boy said, "Yes'm."

The woman said, "What did you want to do it for?"

The boy said, "I didn't aim to."

B She said, "You a lie!"

By that time two or three people passed, stopped, turned to look, and some stood watching.

C "If I turn you loose, will you run?" asked the woman.

"Yes'm," said the boy.

"Then I won't turn you loose," said the woman. She did not release him.

"I'm very sorry, lady, I'm sorry," whispered the boy.

"Um-hum! And your face is dirty. I got a great mind to wash your face for you. Ain't you got nobody home to tell you to wash your face?"

"No'm," said the boy.

"Then it will get washed this evening," said the large woman starting up the street, dragging the frightened boy behind her.

He looked as if he were fourteen or fifteen, <u>frail</u> and willow-wild, in tennis shoes and blue jeans.

The woman said, "You ought to be my son. I would teach you right from wrong. Least I can do right now is to wash your face. Are you hungry?"

"No'm," said the being-dragged boy. "I just want you to turn me loose."

"Was I bothering *you* when I turned that corner?" asked the woman.

"No'm."

"But you put yourself in contact with *me*," said the woman. "If you think that that contact is not going to last awhile, you got another thought coming. When I get through with you, sir, you are going to remember Mrs. Luella Bates Washington Jones."

Sweat popped out on the boy's face and he began to struggle. Mrs. Jones stopped, jerked him around in front of her, put a half-nelson about his neck, and continued to drag him up the street. When she got to her door, she dragged the boy inside, down a hall, and into a large kitchenette-furnished room at the rear of the house. She switched on the light and left the door open. The boy could hear other roomers laughing and talking in the large house. Some of their doors were open, too, so he knew he and the woman were not alone. The woman still had him by the neck in the middle of her room.

She said, "What is your name?"

WORDS TO KNOW
frail (frāl) *adj.* delicate; weak and fragile

150

Mini-Lesson — **Literary Concepts**

REVIEWING DIALOGUE Remind students that a conversation between two or more characters is called dialogue. In most literary forms, dialogue is set off by quotation marks. By studying the dialogue, readers can add to their knowledge about characters and plot.

Application Ask students to find in the story examples of dialogue that help them understand more about each character's background and upbringing or about the plot. Then have them write what they can infer about the characters or the plot.

"Roger," answered the boy.

"Then, Roger, you go to that sink and wash your face," said the woman, whereupon she turned him loose—at last. Roger looked at the door—looked at the woman—looked at the door—*and went to the sink.*

"Let the water run until it gets warm," she said. "Here's a clean towel."

"You gonna take me to jail?" asked the boy, bending over the sink.

"Not with that face, I would not take you nowhere," said the woman. "Here I am trying to get home to cook me a bite to eat and you snatch my pocketbook! Maybe you ain't been to your supper either, late as it be. Have you?"

"There's nobody home at my house," said the boy.

"Then we'll eat," said the woman. "I believe you're hungry—or been hungry—to try to snatch my pocketbook."

"I wanted a pair of blue <u>suede</u> shoes," said the boy.

"Well, you didn't have to snatch *my* pocketbook to get some suede shoes," said Mrs. Luella Bates Washington Jones. "You could of asked me."

"M'am?"

The water dripping from his face, the boy looked at her. There was a long pause. A very long pause. After he had dried his face and not knowing what else to do dried it again, the boy turned around, wondering what next. The door was open. He could make a dash for it down the hall. He could run, run, run, run, *run!*

The woman was sitting on the day-bed. After a while she said, "I were young once and I wanted things I could not get."

There was another long pause. The boy's mouth opened. Then he frowned, but not knowing he frowned.

The woman said, "Um-hum! You thought I was going to say *but,* didn't you? You thought I was going to say, *but I didn't snatch people's pocketbooks.* Well, I wasn't going to say that." Pause. Silence. "I have done things, too, which I would not tell you, son—neither tell God, if he didn't already know. So you set down while I fix us something to eat. You might run that comb through your hair so you will look <u>presentable</u>."

In another corner of the room behind a screen was a gas plate and an icebox. Mrs. Jones got up and went behind the screen. The woman did not watch the boy to see if he was going to run now, nor did she watch her purse which she left behind her on the day-bed. But the boy took care to sit on the far side of the room where he thought she could easily see him out of the corner of her eye, if she wanted to. He did not trust the woman *not* to trust him. And he did not want to be <u>mistrusted</u> now.

"Do you need somebody to go to the store," asked the boy, "maybe to get some milk or something?"

"Don't believe I do," said the woman, "unless you just want sweet milk yourself. I was going to make cocoa out of this canned milk I got here."

"That will be fine," said the boy.

She heated some lima beans and ham she had in the icebox, made the cocoa, and set the table. The woman did not ask the boy any-

WORDS TO KNOW	**suede** (swād) *n.* leather with a soft, fuzzy surface **presentable** (prĭ-zĕn'tə-bəl) *adj.* fit to be seen by people **mistrust** (mĭs-trŭst') *v.* to have no confidence in

151

Literary Concept: CONFLICT

D Ask students what types of conflicts Roger is experiencing. *(an external conflict with Mrs. Jones and an internal conflict that involves deciding whether to run away or to wash his face)*

CUSTOMIZING FOR

Students Acquiring English

3 Ask students why they think the words *and went to the sink* appear in italics. If necessary, explain that italics are used here to emphasize the importance of the words. The words are important because they mark a turning point in the story, when Roger makes the decision to stay rather than run away.

STRATEGIC READING FOR

Less-Proficient Readers

E Why did Roger try to snatch Mrs. Jones's purse? *(to get money to buy a pair of blue suede shoes)* **Restating**

Set a Purpose Have students read on to find out what happens to Roger and Mrs. Jones.

Critical Thinking: ANALYZING

F Ask students why they think the author repeats Mrs. Jones's full name. *(Possible responses: Repeating the name makes it more memorable; the long, weighty name reflects Mrs. Jones's powerful influence in Roger's life.)*

Active Reading: PREDICTING

G Have students predict, before they read the rest of the story, whether or not Mrs. Jones and Roger will become friends.

Mini-Lesson | **Grammar**

PUNCTUATING QUOTATIONS When writing dialogue, a writer begins a new paragraph to indicate a change in speaker and puts quotation marks around a speaker's exact words. Invite students to read the highlighted text above and to notice how the dialogue between Mrs. Jones and Roger is broken into paragraphs to indicate a change in speaker.

Reteaching/Reinforcement
• *Grammar Handbook,* anthology pp. 886–887
• *Grammar Mini-Lessons* copymasters, p. 42, transparencies, p.34

The Writer's Craft

Quotation Marks, pp. 648–650

STRATEGIC READING FOR

Less-Proficient Readers

H What happens to Roger and Mrs. Jones at the end of the story? *(After cleaning him up, feeding him, and giving him money for shoes, Mrs. Jones sends Roger on his way. They never see each other again.)* Restating

COMPREHENSION CHECK

1. What happens when Roger tries to steal Mrs. Jones's purse? *(She grabs him and drags him to her house.)*

2. What happens when Mrs. Jones gets Roger to her house? *(She feeds him and talks to him and tells him to behave himself.)*

3. Why did Roger want to steal money from Mrs. Jones? *(to buy blue suede shoes)*

4. How does Roger get the money for his shoes? *(Mrs. Jones gives it to him.)*

INSIGHT

1. What connections do you see between the poem and the short story? *(Possible responses: The speaker of the poem wishes to do what Mrs. Jones did—to help one person in a profound way; both selections address the issue of making a difference in someone else's life.)*

2. Why do you think there is no punctuation in the poem? *(Possible response: The poem is like a flash of thought or a sudden yearning. Punctuating it would have slowed down one's reading of it and made it seem less spontaneous.)*

EMILY DICKINSON

American poet Emily Dickinson (1830–1886) lived a quiet, reclusive life in Amherst, Massachusetts, and wrote nearly 1800 poems. Most of her poems are short, highly compressed lyrics that depart from conventional rhyme and meter. Few of Dickinson's poems were published or recognized during her lifetime. It was not until years after her death that she became one of America's most popular and influential poets.

---

thing about where he lived, or his folks, or anything else that would embarrass him. Instead, as they ate, she told him about her job in a hotel beauty-shop that stayed open late, what the work was like, and how all kinds of women came in and out, blondes, red-heads, and Spanish. Then she cut him a half of her ten-cent cake.

"Eat some more, son," she said.

When they were finished eating she got up and said, "Now, here, take this ten dollars and buy yourself some blue suede shoes. And next time, do not make the mistake of latching onto *my* pocketbook *nor nobody else's*—because

shoes come by devilish like that will burn your feet. I got to get my rest now. But I wish you would behave yourself, son, from here on in."

She led him down the hall to the front door and opened it. "Goodnight! Behave yourself, boy!" she said, looking out into the street.

The boy wanted to say something else other than "Thank you, m'am" to Mrs. Luella Bates Washington Jones, but he couldn't do so as he turned at the <u>barren</u> stoop and looked back at the large woman in the door. He barely managed to say "Thank you" before she shut the door. And he never saw her again. ❖

H

LITERARY INSIGHT

If I Can Stop One Heart from Breaking
by Emily Dickinson

If I can stop one Heart from breaking
I shall not live in vain
If I can ease one Life the Aching
Or cool one Pain

Or help one fainting Robin
Unto his Nest again
I shall not live in Vain.

WORDS
TO   **barren** (băr′ən) *adj.* empty; deserted
KNOW

152

Mini-Lesson  Spelling

SUFFIXES -ABLE AND -IBLE The suffixes *-able* and *-ible* are often confusing to spellers because their pronunciations are so much alike. Explain to students that an easy way to determine which suffix to use is to remember that *-able* is most often added to complete words, whereas *-ible* is most often added to roots.

present + -able = **presentable**

cred + -ible = **credible**

Application Copy the following sentences onto the chalkboard. Invite students to circle the correct suffix.

1. The test was so hard it was *imposs(-able/-ible)*.
2. The small stain was hardly *notice(-able/-ible)*.
3. Mrs. Jones believed that high goals were *attain(-able/-ible)*.
4. The decorations on the cake were *ed(-able/-ible)*.

Ask students to look for more words that fit this pattern and to add these words to their personal word lists.

Reteaching/Reinforcement
• *Unit Two Resource Book,* p. 9

RESPONDING
OPTIONS

FROM PERSONAL RESPONSE TO CRITICAL ANALYSIS

REFLECT
1. What thoughts do you have about Mrs. Jones and Roger? Jot them down and then share them with a classmate.

RETHINK
2. Why do you think Mrs. Jones treats Roger the way she does?

   Consider   Close Textural Reading
   - what she reveals about her past
   - what she seems to understand about Roger's life
   - Roger's answers to her questions

3. Is Roger likely to steal again? Why or why not?

RELATE
4. In what ways might the speaker of the Insight poem on page 152 be similar to Mrs. Jones?

5. Roger is willing to go to extreme lengths to get blue suede shoes. In what ways is he different from and similar to some of today's young people?

Multimodal Learning
ANOTHER PATHWAY

Instead of turning Roger in to the police, Mrs. Jones deals with him in her own way. With the rest of your class, discuss your thoughts about Mrs. Jones's actions. Do you think her way of dealing with Roger was effective? Why or why not? What do you think Roger might have learned from Mrs. Jones that he might not have learned from the police?

QUICKWRITES

1. Imagine that Mrs. Jones and Roger meet again ten years later. Write the **dialogue** that they might have.

2. Review the African proverb that you considered for the Personal Connection on page 147. Write a brief **comparison** between Mrs. Jones and someone who looks out for young people.

📁 *PORTFOLIO Save your writing. You may want to use it later as a springboard to a piece for your portfolio.*

LITERARY CONCEPTS

Recall that a conflict is a struggle between two opposing forces. In an **external conflict,** a character struggles against another character or an outside force. In an **internal conflict,** the struggle is within a character. What conflicts—both internal and external—does Roger face in this story?

struggle

struggle

struggle

struggle

Internal Conflict

External Conflict

CONCEPT REVIEW: Character Identify three character traits of Mrs. Jones, and explain how the author reveals them.

THANK YOU M'AM **153**

From Personal Response to Critical Analysis

1. Accept all responses that are consistent with the characters' personalities and actions.
2. Possible responses: Some students may say that Mrs. Jones has had some experiences similar to Roger's and has learned the hard way that it is important to do what is right. Others may say that Mrs. Jones realizes that Roger has no one to look after him to see that he keeps himself clean and learns the difference between right and wrong.
3. Possible responses: no, because he got Mrs. Jones's message about living an honest life; yes, because even though Mrs. Jones scared him at the time, Roger probably didn't learn his lesson.
4. Both probably feel good about making a difference in someone else's life.
5. Possible response: He is different in that he will resort to crime to get what he wants. He is similar in that he is capable of learning from his mistakes.

Another Pathway

Cooperative Learning Divide the class into two teams. Ask one team to speculate how the police might have dealt with Roger. Have the other team summarize how Mrs. Jones dealt with Roger. Have each team assign a differentiator and a recorder to help determine and record the two approaches. When the preceding steps are completed, a spokesperson from each team should discuss the team's findings.

Rubric

3 Full Accomplishment Students clearly differentiate between the two methods of handling Roger and effectively present their opinions.

2 Substantial Accomplishment Students form opinions about the different ways of handling Roger but have some difficulty presenting their opinions.

1 Little or Partial Accomplishment Students have difficulty discussing and presenting Mrs. Jones's and the police's approaches.

Literary Concepts

Invite students to form two teams. One team can look for evidence of Roger's internal conflicts, and the other can look for evidence showing how Roger's external conflict develops. Have students quote passages from the story that support their ideas about Roger's internal conflicts (*whether to run or stay; whether to stop or continue stealing*) and external conflict (*with Mrs. Jones*).

CONCEPT REVIEW: Character Mrs. Jones is powerful (*grabs Roger*), forthright (*speaks her mind*), and kind (*gives Roger food and money*).

QuickWrites

1. Suggest that students first decide on a setting for the meeting between Mrs. Jones and Roger. Where and when the conversation takes place will in part determine how the dialogue goes. The dialogue should explore the extent of Mrs. Jones's influence on Roger's life.

2. Suggest that students compare Mrs. Jones with someone they know personally, such as a family member, a teacher, or a religious leader.

 The Writer's Craft

Creating Dialogue, pp. 320–322
Comparison and Contrast, pp. 132–134

1. a person who is ill, because *frail* means "fragile or weak"
2. because it is made from the skin of animals
3. A barren neighborhood would make you depressed because there would be little to look at and it would be without beauty.
4. no, because if you mistrust someone, you have no confidence in him or her
5. Someone who doesn't look presentable would be dirty and wearing torn clothing.

Reteaching/Reinforcement
• *Unit Two Resource Book,* p. 10

Across the Curriculum

Social Studies *Cooperative Learning*
Students should work in groups of five to accomplish their research and presentation tasks. One student can make sure that everyone participates, and another can delegate the tasks that need to be accomplished. A recorder can jot down the important ideas, and a spokesperson can present the group's findings to the class.

ADDITIONAL SUGGESTION

Music from Harlem Invite students to research some of the important singers and musicians, such as Duke Ellington and Louis Armstrong, who were contemporaries of Langston Hughes and who lived or worked in Harlem.

LANGSTON HUGHES

Langston Hughes spent much of his free time talking to young, aspiring writers, encouraging them to continue their craft. He liked traveling and spent time in Mexico (where his father lived), Africa, and Europe. Widely celebrated, he became known as the poet laureate of Harlem.

ART GALLERY
African-American Art of the mid-1900s The life of Harlem's jazz clubs and streets has been depicted by many African-American artists. Students will be able to view works by several of these artists here.

Side A, Frames 49304

ALTERNATIVE ACTIVITIES

1. Draw or build models, or **sets,** for a theatrical production of "Thank You, M'am." Include both the street setting and Mrs. Jones's room.

2. Give an **oral report** comparing the music of the 1950s with the music of the 1990s. Gather examples of recorded music from both periods—including Elvis Presley's version of "Blue Suede Shoes," if possible—to support your comparison.

ACROSS THE CURRICULUM

Social Studies With a group of classmates, research the history of Harlem. Find answers to the following questions and include additional facts about this section of New York City. Present your findings in an oral report.
• Where did the name *Harlem* come from?
• Who were Harlem's first settlers?
• What was the Harlem Renaissance?

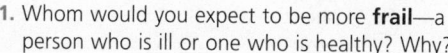
WORDS TO KNOW

On your paper, write an answer for each question below.

1. Whom would you expect to be more **frail**—a person who is ill or one who is healthy? Why?

2. Why might **suede** clothing be more expensive than cotton clothing?

3. Would a **barren** neighborhood make you happy or depressed? Why?

4. Would you give money to a person you **mistrust?** Why or why not?

5. Describe someone who definitely does not look **presentable.**

LANGSTON HUGHES

Langston Hughes has been one of the most renowned and influential of African-American poets. In fact, his poems appear in more collections than does the work of any other poet in the world. Hughes, who grew up in Lawrence, Kansas, recalls his youth thus:

"Books began to happen to me, and I began to believe in nothing but books and the wonderful world in books— where if people suffered, they suffered in beautiful language, not in monosyllables, as we did in Kansas."

Hughes was one of the first African Americans to

1902–1967

earn his living solely from writing. His first recognition came when, while working as a busboy, he left three of his poems at a table where the poet Vachel Lindsay was dining. Lindsay presented some of the young poet's works at one of his own poetry readings, and Hughes's career was launched. Hughes went on to write novels, short stories, plays, song lyrics, and radio scripts as well as poetry. To portray the African-American experience, he often focused on the ordinary people whose vitality contributed to the special atmosphere of life in Harlem.

OTHER WORKS *Not Without Laughter, The Big Sea*

Extended Reading

• ART GALLERY

Alternative Activities

1. Have students begin planning their theatrical sets by listing details from the story that describe the two settings. If students are building models, they should first list needed materials, such as cardboard, construction paper, watercolors, tape, and glue. Encourage students to have fun and to be creative.

2. If students have access to an on-line service, they may want to begin their research on the computer. Alternatively, they could interview a friend or relative familiar with the music of either or both periods.

PREVIEWING

FICTION

Hollywood and the Pits
Cherylene Lee

PERSONAL CONNECTION

Imagine that you are a child star in Hollywood. You work side by side with your favorite celebrities. Your name appears in lights. Your picture graces the cover of a magazine. The public wants to know all about you. What do you think will happen when you become an adolescent? What challenges will you face as you try to grow up and find yourself? Discuss these questions with a small group of classmates. Then as you read, think about the challenges that the main character faces.

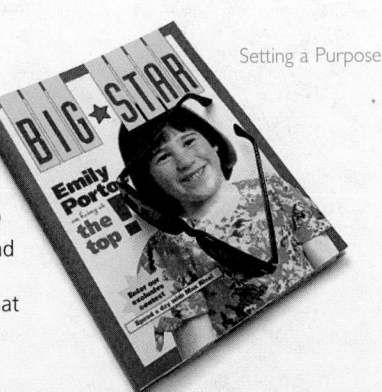

HISTORICAL CONNECTION

The main character, a former child star, lives in Los Angeles, California. Among this city's attractions are Hollywood, home of the U. S. movie industry, and the La Brea Tar Pits. Since 1906, approximately 1 million animal skeletons have been removed from the tar pits. Many of these skeletons date from the Pleistocene epoch (plĭ'stə-sēn' ĕp'ək), a period that ended about 10,000 years ago. Animals such as saber-toothed tigers, llamas, camels, giant wolves, and ground sloths stepped into shallow pools and got trapped in the tar at the bottom. Over time, the dead animals' bones became soaked with tar, which preserved them.

READING CONNECTION

Structure "Hollywood and the Pits" combines fiction and nonfiction. The main story relates the experiences of a former child star. From time to time, passages of nonfiction, printed in italic type, provide information about the tar pits. After you have read this selection, look for connections between the main story and the nonfiction passages.

LASERLINKS
• *VISUAL VOCABULARY*   **155**

California map

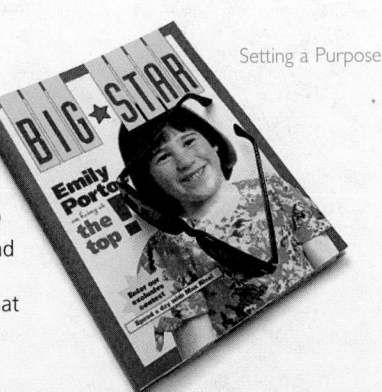

California

OREGON   IDAHO

NEVADA

CALIFORNIA

Pacific Ocean

• Los Angeles

ARIZONA

N W-E S

Miles
0   100   200

MEXICO

 VISUAL VOCABULARY
- archaeological dig (är'kē-ə-lŏj'ĭ-kəl)
- excavate (ĕk'skə-vāt')

Side A, Frames 49310

SUMMARY

As a Chinese-American child star in Hollywood, the narrator used to get many film, stage, and TV roles. Now that she has turned 15 and grown tall, however, directors no longer want to offer her parts. Hurt by their rejection and by her mother's bewilderment, she begins working as a volunteer at the La Brea Tar Pits. There she becomes fascinated with what she discovers about the animals that got trapped in tar thousands of years ago. She sees connections between her experiences in Hollywood and events that occurred eons ago. Working at the tar pits, she learns the value of observation, patience, and hard work.

Thematic Link: *Learning the Hard Way*
Facing rejection as an aging child star, the narrator discovers that growing up can cause some familiar doors to close but can open up new opportunities for self-fulfillment.

Art Note

***Grauman's Chinese Theater* by Bruce W. LaLanne** LaLanne's painting depicts the opening, on May 18, 1927, of Sid Grauman's Chinese Theater (now called Mann's Theater), one of Hollywood's first moving–picture theaters.

Reading the Art *What does the painting suggest to you about the night of the theater opening? Would you have liked to have been there? Why?*

CUSTOMIZING FOR
Students Acquiring English

- Use **ACCESS FOR STUDENTS ACQUIRING ENGLISH**, *Reading and Writing Support.*

- This story contains show business vocabulary that students may not be familiar with. You may want to discuss with students such words and expressions as *producer, director, sitcom, commercial, callback, take, role, book, eight-by-ten glossy,* and *audition.*

STRATEGIC READING FOR
Less-Proficient Readers

Set a Purpose Have students read the story to find out what challenges the narrator faces as a child star.

Use **UNIT TWO RESOURCE BOOK**, p. 13, for guidance in reading the selection.

Illustration of Grauman's Chinese Theater by Bruce W. LaLanne. From *Hollywood's Master Showman* by Charles Beardsley, Copyright © 1983 by Rosemont Publishing.

by Cherylene Lee

HOLLYWOOD
and the
PITS

156

WORDS TO KNOW

bewildered (bǐ-wǐl'dərd) *adj.* puzzled; confused **bewilder** *v.* (p. 157)
displaced (dǐs-plāst') *adj.* moved from the usual position **displace** *v.* (p. 160)
excavated (ĕk'skə-vā'tǐd) *adj.* dug-up **excavate** *v.* (p. 158)
glistening (glǐs'ə-nǐng) *adj.* shining; sparkling **glisten** *v.* (p. 157)
grovel (grŏv'əl) *v.* to lie or crawl facedown (p. 163)

obsess (əb-sĕs') *v.* to fill the mind of (p. 157)
plush (plŭsh) *adj.* luxurious (p. 157)
poring (pôr'ing) *adj.* reading or studying carefully **pore** *v.* (p. 157)
skewing (skyōō'ing) *adj.* distorting **skew** *v.* (p. 160)
subterranean (sŭb'tə-rā'nē-ən) *adj.* living beneath the earth's surface (p. 161)

In 1968 when I was fifteen, the pit opened its secret to me. I breathed, ate, slept, dreamed about the La Brea Tar Pits. I spent summer days working the archaeological dig and in dreams saw the bones glistening, the broken pelvises, the skulls, the vertebrae looped like a woman's pearls hanging on an invisible cord. I welcomed those dreams. I wanted to know where the next skeleton was, identify it, record its position, discover whether it was whole or not. I wanted to know where to dig in the coarse, black, gooey sand. I lost myself there and found something else.

My mother thought something was wrong with me. Was it good for a teenager to be fascinated by death? Especially animal death in the Pleistocene? Was it normal to be so obsessed by a sticky brown hole in the ground in the center of Los Angeles? I don't know if it was normal or not, but it seemed perfectly logical to me. After all, I grew up in Hollywood, a place where dreams and nightmares can often take the same shape. What else would a child actor do?

"Thank you very much, dear. We'll be letting you know."

I knew what that meant. It meant I would never hear from them again. I didn't get the job. I heard that phrase a lot that year.

I walked out of the plush office, leaving behind the casting director, producer, director, writer, and whoever else came to listen to my reading for a semiregular role on a family sit-com. The carpet made no sound when I opened and shut the door.

I passed the other girls waiting in the reception room, each poring over her script. The mothers were waiting in a separate room, chattering about their daughters' latest commercials, interviews, callbacks, jobs. It

sounded like every Oriental kid in Hollywood was working except me.

My mother used to have a lot to say in those waiting rooms. Ever since I was three, when I started at the Meglin Kiddie Dance Studio, I was dubbed "The Chinese Shirley Temple"— always the one to be picked at auditions and interviews, always the one to get the speaking lines, always called "the one-shot kid," because I could do my scenes in one take—even tight close-ups. My mother would only talk about me behind my back because she didn't want to hear her brag, but I knew that she was proud. In a way I was proud too, though I never dared admit it. I didn't want to be called a showoff. But I didn't exactly know what I did to be proud of either. I only knew that at fifteen I was now being passed over at all these interviews when before I would be chosen.

My mother looked at my face hopefully when I came into the room. I gave her a quick shake of the head. She looked bewildered. I felt bad for my mother then. How could I explain it to her? I didn't understand it myself. We left saying polite good-byes to all the other mothers.

I was dubbed "The Chinese Shirley Temple."

We didn't say anything until the studio parking lot, where we had to search for our old blue Chevy among rows and rows of parked cars baking in the Hollywood heat.

"How did it go? Did you read clearly? Did you tell them you're available?"

"I don't think they care if I'm available or not, Ma."

WORDS TO KNOW	**glistening** (glĭs´ə-nĭng) *adj.* shining; sparkling **glisten** *v.*
	obsess (əb-sĕs´) *v.* to fill the mind of
	plush (plŭsh) *adj.* luxurious
	poring (pôr´ĭng) *adj.* reading or studying carefully **pore** *v.*
	bewildered (bĭ-wĭl´dərd) *adj.* puzzled; confused **bewilder** *v.*

157

Have students look closely at the references to the La Brea Tar Pits as they read the selection. Ask students to consider how the information the narrator presents about the tar pits is connected with her experiences as a child star.

Possible responses:

- Page 158— The tar pits, like Hollywood, drew innocent young victims by promising something inviting.
- Page 159—The victims of the tar pits lost their future hopes, as did the narrator as a child star in Hollywood.
- Page 163—In the pits, no one fossil can tell the entire story. In Hollywood, one success story doesn't represent the experiences of most of the people who go there.

Critical Thinking: ANALYZING

A Have students read this sentence and discuss why the author included this detail in the story. *(Possible response: It symbolizes the narrator's sense of rejection and isolation. No one can hear the narrator come or go; she feels invisible.)*

I Students may not know that Shirley Temple was a famous child star of the 1930s.

Mini-Lesson 🧩 **Literary Concepts**

REVIEWING AUTHOR'S PURPOSE
Remind students that an author's purpose can be to entertain, to explain or inform, to express an opinion, or to persuade, or it can be a combination of these purposes. Lee, for instance, combines fictional incidents with facts about the La Brea Tar Pits to provide readers with a different perspective on Hollywood stardom and glamour.

Application Invite students to write a sentence that states what they think is the author's purpose in "Hollywood and the Pits." Then have them jot down several details from the story that they used as evidence to help them infer the author's purpose. Ask them if they think the author fulfilled her purpose, and have them give reasons why or why not. Use a chart, like the one shown, to help guide students in this activity.

Author's Purpose	Evidence	Purpose Fulfilled?

B Ask students why they think Lee chose to write the mother's questions as dialogue rather than having the narrator tell what her mother said—for example, "My mother asked me if I remembered to look up." (*Possible response: By having the mother pose her questions directly, Lee gives readers a better sense of the mother's urgency and enables them to empathize more with the narrator.*)

STRATEGIC READING FOR
Less-Proficient Readers

C What problem does the narrator face as a child actor in Hollywood? (*She has grown too old to be cast as a child actor.*) **Finding the Main Idea**

Set a Purpose Have students read on to find out how the narrator became a child star.

Active Reading: CONNECTING

D Ask students to relate experiences they have had that could be said to involve luck. How did being in the right place at the right time make them feel?

Think-Aloud Model *I have sometimes been lucky. Once I won a prize in a contest. I was really excited, but I also realized that it was good luck and not my abilities that won the prize. So underneath my excitement, I knew that if I were to try another time, I probably wouldn't win.*

Linking to History

E During the early part of the 20th century, vaudeville shows filled American theaters. These variety shows consisted of 10 or 15 short acts that might have included singers, dancers, jugglers, comedians, and even animals. The popularity of vaudeville declined with the advent of radio and motion pictures.

CUSTOMIZING FOR
Students Acquiring English

(2) Make sure students understand this joke. You may want to write the words *ugly* and *homely* on the board.

B "Didn't you read well? Did you remember to look up so they could see your eyes? Did they ask you if you could play the piano? Did you tell them you could learn?"

The barrage of questions stopped when we finally spotted our car. I didn't answer her. My mother asked about the piano because I lost out in an audition once to a Chinese girl who already knew how to play.

My mother took off the towel that shielded the steering wheel from the heat. "You're getting to be such a big girl," she said, starting the car in neutral. "But don't worry, there's always next time. You have what it takes. That's special." She put the car into forward, and we drove through a parking lot that had an endless number of identical cars all facing the same direction. We drove back home in silence.

C

In the La Brea Tar Pits many of the <u>excavated</u> bones belong to juvenile mammals. Thousands of years ago thirsty young animals in the area were drawn to watering holes, not knowing they were traps. Those inviting pools had false bottoms made of sticky tar, which immobilized its victims and preserved their bones when they died. Innocence trapped by ignorance. The tar pits record that well.

I suppose a lot of my getting into show business in the first place was a matter of luck—**D** being in the right place at the right time. My sister, seven years older than me, was a member of the Meglin Kiddie Dance Studio long before I started lessons. Once during the annual recital held at the Shrine Auditorium, she was spotted

WORDS
TO
KNOW   **excavated** (ĕk′skə-vā′tĭd) *adj.* dug-up **excavate** *v.*

158

---

by a Hollywood agent who handled only Oriental performers. The agent sent my sister out for a role in the CBS *Playhouse 90* television show *The Family Nobody Wanted*. The producer said she was too tall for the part. But true to my mother's training of always having a positive reply, my sister said to the producer, "But I have a younger sister . . ." which started my show-biz career at the tender age of three.

My sister and I were lucky. We enjoyed singing and dancing, we were natural hams, and our parents never discouraged us. In fact they were our biggest fans. My mother chauffeured us to all our dance lessons, lessons we begged to take. She drove us to interviews, took us to studios, went on location with us, drilled us on our lines, made sure we kept up our schoolwork and didn't sass back the tutors hired by studios to teach us for three hours a day. She never complained about being a stage mother. She said that we made her proud.

My father must have felt pride too, because he paid for a choreographer to put together our sister act: "The World Famous Lee Sisters," fifteen minutes of song and dance, real vaudeville stuff. We joked about that a lot, "Yeah, the Lee Sisters—Ug-Lee and Home-Lee," but we definitely had a good time. So did our parents. Our father especially liked our getting booked into Las Vegas at the New Frontier Hotel on the Strip. . . .

In Las Vegas our sister act was part of a show called "Oriental Holiday." The show was about a Hollywood producer going to the Far East, finding undiscovered talent, and bringing it back to the U.S. We did two shows a night in the main showroom, one at eight and one at twelve, and on weekends a third show at two in the morning. It ran the entire summer often to standing-room-only audiences—a thousand people a show.

Mini-Lesson   **Reading Skills/Strategies**

COMPARING AND CONTRASTING Explain that sometimes a literary selection may have inserts that can be compared and contrasted with the main part of the selection. The combination of fictional material and factual material in "Hollywood and the Pits" heightens readers' understanding of the meaning of the story.

Application Ask students to reread pages 158 and 159. Point out the passages in italics which con-

tain information about the La Brea Tar Pits. Ask students why Lee includes this information in the story. Invite students to select incidents from the narrator's childhood and to compare and contrast them with information in each of these passages.

Reteaching/Reinforcement
• *Unit Two Resource Book,* p. 14

Our sister act worked because of the age and height difference. My sister then was fourteen and nearly five foot two; I was seven and very small for my age—people thought we were cute. We had song-and-dance routines to old tunes like "Ma He's Making Eyes at Me," "Together," and "I'm Following You," and my father hired a writer to adapt the lyrics to "I Enjoy Being a Girl," which came out "We Enjoy Being Chinese." We also told corny jokes, but the Las Vegas audience seemed to enjoy it. Here we were, two kids, staying up late and jumping around, and getting paid besides. To me the applause sometimes sounded like static, sometimes like distant waves. It always amazed me when people applauded. The owner of the hotel liked us so much he invited us back to perform in shows for three summers in a row. That was before I grew too tall and the sister act didn't seem so cute anymore.

Many of the skeletons in the tar pits are found incomplete—particularly the skeletons of the young, which have only soft cartilage connecting the bones. In life the soft tissue allows for growth, but in death it dissolves quickly. Thus the skeletons of young animals are more apt to be scattered, especially the vertebrae protecting the spinal cord. In the tar pits, the central ends of many vertebrae are found unconnected to any skeleton. Such bone fragments are shaped like valentines, disks that are slightly lobed—heart-shaped shields that have lost their connection to what they were meant to protect.

I never felt my mother pushed me to do something I didn't want to do. But I always knew if something I did pleased her. She was generous with her praise, and I was sensitive when she withheld it. I didn't like to disappoint her.

I took to performing easily, and since I had started out so young, making movies or doing shows didn't feel like anything special. It was a part of my childhood—like going to the dentist one morning or going to school the next. I didn't wonder if I wanted a particular role or wanted to be in a show or how I would feel if I didn't get in. Until I was fifteen, it never occurred to me that one day I wouldn't get parts or that I might not "have what it takes."

When I was younger, I got a lot of roles because I was so small for my age. When I was nine years old, I could pass for five or six. I was really short. I was always teased about it when I was in elementary school, but I didn't mind because my height got me movie jobs. I could read and memorize lines that actual five-year-olds couldn't. My mother told people she made me sleep in a drawer so I wouldn't grow any bigger.

But when I turned fifteen, it was as if my body, which hadn't grown for so many years, suddenly made up for lost time. I grew five inches in seven months. My mother was amazed. Even I couldn't get used to it. I kept knocking into things, my clothes didn't fit right, I felt awkward and clumsy when I moved. Dumb things that I had gotten away with, like paying children's prices at the movies instead of junior admission, I couldn't do anymore. I wasn't a shrimp or a small fry any longer. I was suddenly normal.

Before that summer my mother had always claimed she wanted me to be normal. She didn't want me to become spoiled by the attention I received when I was working at the studios. I still had chores to do at home, went to public school when I wasn't working, was punished severely when I behaved badly. She didn't want me to feel I was different just

⊣**H**

③

HOLLYWOOD AND THE PITS **159**

Critical Thinking: ANALYZING

F Ask students to discuss why the narrator was amazed when the audience applauded her act. *(Possible response: Because it seemed as if she didn't have to work very hard to perform her act, the narrator was surprised that people would like what seemed so natural or easy for her.)*

STRATEGIC READING FOR

Less-Proficient Readers

G How did the narrator become a child star? *(Her sister was turned down for a role and she stepped in. Then the narrator and her sister formed a sister act and got many bookings.)* Summarizing

Set a Purpose Ask students to read on to find out how the narrator's mother feels about the change in her daughter's status as a star.

CUSTOMIZING FOR

Multiple Learning Styles

H Intrapersonal Learners Invite students to imagine they are the narrator and to create a journal entry that expresses her feelings about her mother's reaction to her growth. What might the mother have said to the narrator about her sudden growth? How might the narrator feel about her mother's comments?

CUSTOMIZING FOR

Students Acquiring English

③ Students should be able to infer from the context that *shrimp* and *small fry* are colloquial expressions used to describe small people.

Mini-Lesson **Study Skills**

OUTLINING Remind students that making an outline is a good way of organizing information. The purpose of outlining is to arrange main points and supporting details in logical order. In a sentence outline, main points and subpoints are stated in complete sentences. In topic outline, words or phrases are used, as in the model shown, which provides the beginning of an outline on the La Brea Tar Pits.

Application Copy the outline onto the chalkboard. Help students understand the relationship between main points and subpoints. Encourage students to create an outline as they complete the research project under Across the Curriculum on page 166.

The La Brea Tar Pits
Thesis Statement: The La Brea Tar Pits are an important source of Ice Age fossils.
I. The origin of the pits (main point)
   A. How layers of oil and tar were formed (first subpoint)
   B. How animals got trapped (second subpoint)
II. The contents of the pits
   A. Remains of giant bear excavated in 1906
   B. Skeletal remains of animals such as saber-toothed tigers, sloths, and wolves uncovered over the years

Ask students whether they think the narrator's mother is being honest when she says, "I'm not that way." *(Possible response: The mother is not being honest. That she takes her daughter to so many casting calls suggests that she does push her daughter to act.)*

STRATEGIC READING FOR
Less-Proficient Readers

 How does the narrator's mother feel about her daughter's being rejected for work? *(Possible response: She is disappointed and wonders whether there is something wrong with her daughter.)*
Noting Relevant Details

Set a Purpose Ask students to read on to find out what the narrator's grandmother thinks about the narrator's Hollywood career.

Linking to Social Studies

 A dancer, singer, choreographer, and director, Gene Kelly was a major Hollywood star, best known for his work from the 1940s through the 1960s. He performed in many movies, including *Singin' in the Rain* and *An American in Paris.*

Literary Concept:
AUTHOR'S PURPOSE

 Ask students to discuss why they think Lee includes information about the grandmother. *(Possible response: The grandmother's feelings about the narrator's Hollywood career are very different from the mother's feelings and are similar to the narrator's true feelings.)*

---

because I was in the movies. When I was eight, I was interviewed by a reporter who wanted to know if I thought I had a big head.

"Sure," I said.

"No you don't," my mother interrupted, which was really unusual, because she generally never said anything. She wanted me to speak for myself.

I didn't understand the question. My sister had always made fun of my head. She said my body was too tiny for the weight—I looked like a walking Tootsie Pop. I thought the reporter was making the same observation.

"She better not get that way," my mother said fiercely. "She's not any different from anyone else. She's just lucky and small for her age."

The reporter turned to my mother, "Some parents push their children to act. The kids feel like they're used."

"I don't do that—I'm not that way," my mother told the reporter.

But when she was sitting silently in all those waiting rooms while I was being turned down for one job after another, I could almost feel her wanting to shout, "Use her. Use her. What is wrong with her? Doesn't she have it anymore?" I didn't know what I had had that I didn't seem to have anymore. My mother had told the reporter that I was like everyone else. But when my life was like everyone else's, why was she disappointed?

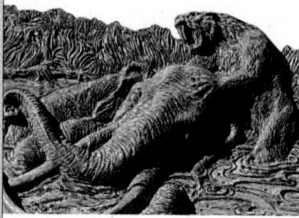

The churning action of the La Brea Tar Pits makes interpreting the record of past events extremely difficult. The usual order of deposition—the oldest on the bottom, the

youngest on the top—loses all meaning when some of the oldest fossils can be brought to the surface by the movement of natural gas. One must look for an undisturbed spot, a place untouched by the action of underground springs or natural gas or human interference. Complete skeletons become important, because they indicate areas of least disturbance. But such spots of calm are rare. Whole blocks of the tar pit can become displaced, making false sequences of the past, skewing the interpretation for what is the true order of nature.

That year before my sixteenth birthday, my mother seemed to spend a lot of time looking through my old scrapbooks, staring at all the eight-by-ten glossies of the shows that I had done. In the summer we visited with my grandmother often, since I wasn't working and had lots of free time. I would go out to the garden to read or sunbathe, but I could hear my mother and grandmother talking.

"She was so cute back then. She worked with Gene Kelly when she was five years old. She was so smart for her age. I don't know what's wrong with her."

"She's fifteen."

"She's too young to be an ingénue[1] and too old to be cute. The studios forget so quickly. By the time she's old enough to play an ingénue, they won't remember her."

"Does she have to work in the movies? Hand me the scissors."

My grandmother was making false eyelashes using the hair from her hairbrush. When she was young, she had incredible hair. I saw an old photograph of her when it flowed beyond her waist like a cascading black waterfall. At

---

1. **ingénue** (ăn'zhə-nōō'): an actress who plays inexperienced young women.

WORDS TO KNOW   **displaced** (dĭs-plâst') *adj.* moved from the usual position   **displace** *v.*
skewing (skyōō'ĭng) *adj.* distorting   **skew** *v.*

160

A s s e s s m e n t   Option

seventy, her hair was still black as night, which made her few strands of silver look like shooting stars. But her hair had thinned greatly with age. It sometimes fell out in clumps. She wore it brushed back in a bun with a hairpiece for added fullness. My grandmother had always been proud of her hair, but once she started making false eyelashes from it, she wasn't proud of the way it looked anymore. She said she was proud of it now because it made her useful.

I spent a lot of time by myself that summer, wondering what it was that I didn't have anymore.

It was painstaking work—tying knots into strands of hair, then tying them together to form feathery little crescents. Her glamorous false eyelashes were much sought after. Theatrical make-up artists waited months for her work. But my grandmother said what she liked was that she was doing something, making a contribution, and besides it didn't cost her anything. No overhead. "Till I go bald," she often joked.

She tried to teach me her art that summer, but for some reason strands of my hair wouldn't stay tied in knots.

"Too springy," my grandmother said. "Your hair is still too young." And because I was frustrated then, frustrated with everything about my life, she added, "You have to wait until your hair falls out, like mine. Something to look forward to, eh?" She had laughed and patted my hand.

My mother was going on and on about my lack of work, what might be wrong, that something she couldn't quite put her finger on. I

heard my grandmother reply, but I didn't catch it all: "Movies are just make-believe, not real life. Like what I make with my hair that falls out—false. False eyelashes. Not meant to last."

The remains in the La Brea Tar Pits are mostly of carnivorous[2] animals. Very few herbivores[3] are found—the ratio is five to one, a perversion of the natural food chain. The ratio is easy to explain.  *Thousands of years ago a thirsty animal sought a drink from the pools of water only to find itself trapped by the bottom, gooey with <u>subterranean</u> oil. A shriek of agony from the trapped victim drew flesh-eating predators, which were then trapped themselves by the very same ooze which provided the bait. The cycle repeated itself countless times. The number of victims grew, lured by the image of easy food, the deception of an easy kill. The animals piled on top of one another. For over ten thousand years the promise of the place drew animals of all sorts, mostly predators and scavengers—dire wolves, panthers, coyotes, vultures—all hungry for their chance. Most were sucked down against their will in those watering holes destined to be called the La Brea Tar Pits in a place to be named the City of Angels, home of Hollywood movie stars.* **P**

I spent a lot of time by myself that summer, wondering what it was that I didn't have anymore. Could I get it back? How could I if I didn't know what it was?

---

2. **carnivorous:** feeding on flesh.
3. **herbivores:** plant-eating animals.

WORDS TO KNOW   **subterranean** (sŭb′tə-rā′nē-ən) *adj.* lying beneath the earth's surface

161

Critical Thinking: ANALYZING

M Ask students why the narrator includes a description of how the grandmother feels about her hair— once proud of it because of its beauty but now proud because of its usefulness. (*How the grandmother feels about her hair reflects how the narrator feels about herself: she was once proud of her "cuteness" but is now proud of her hard work in the tar pits.*)

Literary Concept: NARRATOR

N Have students rewrite the passages here as if the grandmother were the narrator. Remind students to watch their use of the pronouns *I* and *she*.

STRATEGIC READING FOR
Less-Proficient Readers

O How does the grandmother feel about the narrator's career? (*Possible response: She sees it as only a brief episode in the narrator's life, not as something permanent and fulfilling; she is more interested in what would make the narrator happy.*) **Finding the Main Idea**

Set a Purpose Have students read on to discover why working at the tar pits helps the narrator feel better about herself.

Linking to Social Studies

P "City of Angels" is the English translation of the Spanish *Los Angeles*. The city was originally called *El pueblo de la Reina de Los Angeles*, which means "The Town of the Queen of the Angels." Founded in 1781, Los Angeles was part of Mexico until it was taken by the United States in 1846, during the Mexican War.

M i n i - L e s s o n   ✏   G r a m m a r

CAPITALIZING PROPER NOUNS AND ADJECTIVES Remind students that all proper nouns and proper adjectives should be capitalized. A proper noun is the name of a particular person, place, thing, or idea. A proper adjective is an adjective formed from a proper noun. Present to students the following example:

Proper noun William <u>Shakespeare</u> wrote plays.

Proper adjective Hollywood could use a <u>Shakespearean</u> screenwriter!

Application Have students rewrite the following sentences with correct capitalization.

1. Sid grauman's chinese theater was a major attraction in los angeles during the 1930s.
2. One of the places where the narrator and her sister performed was las vegas, nevada.
3. *Brea* means "tar" in spanish.

Reteaching/Reinforcement
- *Grammar Handbook,* anthology pp. 875–877
- *Grammar Mini-Lessons* copymasters, pp. 33–34, transparencies, pp. 25–26

 The Writer's Craft

Proper Nouns and Adjectives, p. 600–601

Chinese Silk **by Mark Daily** About his artwork, Mark Daily has said, "My goal is to fulfill whatever potential I have. In any profession you have to find your weak points, work on them. You must develop the discipline to do this."

Reading the Art *What effect does the artist create by having the figure look down at the viewer? What can you infer about the woman's personality?*

Active Reading: CLARIFY

Q What does the narrator like about going to the tar pits? *(She likes feeling unself-conscious and getting messy for a purpose.)*

Literary Concept: NARRATOR

R Point out to students the word *groveling.* Ask students to think about why the narrator might have used that word to describe her work in the pits. *(Possible response: The narrator literally crawls as she digs in the tar. Also she might be suggesting a connection between her work at the tar pits and her work in Hollywood. In a figurative sense, she had to grovel before powerful directors in Hollywood while she was competing for parts.)*

Chinese Silk (about 1972), Mark Daily. Oil, 24" × 20", collection of Robert Moore.

Mini-Lesson The Writer's Style

ELABORATION Authors use a variety of methods to elaborate a story's message, or theme. For example, Cherylene Lee relates several incidents to tell the story about the narrator's experiences in Hollywood and about her relationship with her mother. Each incident helps build readers' understanding of what it was like to find yourself suddenly too old at the age of 15.

Application Invite students to write about an important experience or relationship they have had. Encourage them to use several incidents in order to show readers what the experience was like or how the relationship made them feel. Before students begin writing, they should write a sentence stating the main message they want to convey and then should list examples they can use for elaboration. When students are finished, invite volunteers to read their stories aloud to the class.

Reteaching/Reinforcement
- *Writing Handbook,* anthology pp. 819–820
- *Writing Mini-Lessons* transparencies, p. 34

 The Writer's Craft

Elaboration, pp. 254–257

That's when I discovered the La Brea Tar Pits. Hidden behind the County Art Museum on trendy Wilshire Boulevard, I found a job that didn't require me to be small or cute for my age. I didn't have to audition. No one said, "Thank you very much, we'll call you." Or if they did, they meant it. I volunteered my time one afternoon, and my fascination stuck—like tar on the bones of a saber-toothed tiger.

*T*he tar pits had its lessons. I was learning I had to work slowly, become observant, to concentrate.

My mother didn't understand what had changed me. I didn't understand it myself. But I liked going to the La Brea Tar Pits. It meant I could get really messy and I was doing it with a purpose. I didn't feel awkward there. I could wear old stained pants. I could wear T-shirts with holes in them. I could wear disgustingly filthy sneakers, and it was all perfectly justified. It wasn't a costume for a role in a film or a part in a TV sit-com. My mother didn't mind my dressing like that when she knew I was off to the pits. That was okay so long as I didn't track tar back into the house. I started going to the pits every day, and my mother wondered why. She couldn't believe I would rather be <u>groveling</u> in tar than going on auditions or interviews.

While my mother wasn't proud of the La Brea Tar Pits (she didn't know or care what a fossil was), she didn't discourage me either. She drove me there, the same way she used to drive me to the studios.

"Wouldn't you rather be doing a show in Las Vegas than scrambling around in a pit?" she asked.

"I'm not in a show in Las Vegas, Ma. The Lee Sisters are retired." My older sister had married and was starting a family of her own.

"But if you could choose between . . ."

"There isn't a choice."

"You really like this tar-pit stuff, or are you just waiting until you can get real work in the movies?"

I didn't answer.

My mother sighed. "You could do it if you wanted, if you really wanted. You still have what it takes."

I didn't know about that. But then, I couldn't explain what drew me to the tar pits either. Maybe it was the bones, finding out what they were, which animal they belonged to, imagining how they got there, how they fell into the trap. I wondered about that a lot.

At the La Brea Tar Pits, everything dug out of the pit is saved— including the sticky sand that covered the bones through the ages. Each bucket of sand is washed, sieved, and examined for pollen grains, insect remains, any evidence of past life. Even the grain size is recorded—the percentage of silt to sand to gravel that reveals the history of deposition, erosion, and disturbance. No single fossil, no one observation, is significant enough to tell the entire story. All the evidence must be weighed before a semblance of truth emerges.

The tar pits had its lessons. I was learning I had to work slowly, become observant, to concentrate. I learned about time in a way that I would never experience—not in hours, days,

WORDS TO KNOW | **grovel** (grŏv′əl) *v.* to lie or crawl facedown

163

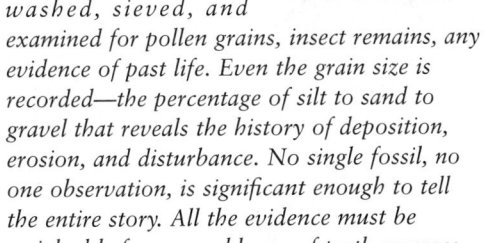

Critical Thinking: SPECULATING

S If the narrator had answered her mother and had said what she felt, what do you think she might have said? *(Possible response: She might have told her mother that she was not waiting around and that she wanted to get on with her life.)*

CUSTOMIZING FOR

Students Acquiring English

4 Explain that *You still have what it takes* means "You still have the ability to succeed (in show business)."

STRATEGIC READING FOR

Less-Proficient Readers

T Why does working at the tar pits help the narrator feel better about herself? *(Possible responses: Her experiences there allow her to reflect on the traps in her own life. Her work gives her a purpose.)* **Summarizing**

Set a Purpose Ask students to find out what personal truth the narrator discovers as a result of her work in the tar pits.

Linking to Science

U An archaeologist excavating fossils works very carefully so that no detail is overlooked. The tools of the trade range from bulldozers for deep digging to tiny dentists' picks for gently scraping away dirt from around a bone. Everything found at a fossil site is documented because each piece of information helps archaeologists tell what life was like a long time ago.

CUSTOMIZING FOR

Gifted and Talented Students

Ask students to discuss the overall message about career choices that the author conveys in this story. *(Possible response: Look for work that makes you feel useful and good about yourself.)*

Mini-Lesson: Speaking, Listening, and Viewing

INTERVIEWS Inform students that the purpose of an interview is to elicit information. Before conducting an interview, the interviewer should prepare questions that are open-ended and that invite discussion. The interviewee should answer each question thoughtfully and as fully as possible.

Application Have pairs of students write and then role-play an interview between a Hollywood reporter and the narrator as an adult. The purpose of the interview is to find out more about the narrator's life as a child star and the subsequent adjustments she has had to make. Invite students to perform their interviews in front of the class.

Literary Concept: NARRATOR

 Ask students how the narrator applies to her own life the lessons she has learned at the tar pits. (*Possible response: From her work at the tar pits, the narrator gains a deeper insight about competition and is able to put her own struggles in perspective. Even if she had continued to succeed in Hollywood, the future would have held other traps that might eventually have stifled her.*)

STRATEGIC READING FOR
Less-Proficient Readers

W What personal truth does the narrator discover as she works in the tar pits? (*She discovers that she is no longer a cute and tiny little girl. She realizes that she is growing up and can do something useful with her life.*) Finding Main Idea

COMPREHENSION CHECK

1. What was the narrator's childhood profession? (*She was an actor.*)

2. What happens after the narrator turns 15? (*She is rejected for acting jobs because she no longer is tiny and cute.*)

3. How did the narrator feel about performing in Las Vegas? (*She enjoyed it because she got to dance, jump around, and stay up late.*)

4. How does the narrator's mother react when her daughter no longer gets picked for parts? (*She is confused and upset and wonders whether there is something wrong with her daughter.*)

5. What does the narrator learn in the pits? (*that she can grow, adapt, and find work with a purpose*)

INSIGHT

1. Why do you think it is important to study fossils found in places like the La Brea Tar Pits? (*Possible response: By examining the fossils, scientists can tell more about what life was like thousands of years ago.*)

2. Why do you think some of the animals found in the tar pits became extinct? (*Possible responses: Predators killed off the population; the climate changed, and they were unable to adapt to different environmental conditions.*)

---

and months, but in thousands and thousands of years. I imagined what the past must have been like, envisioned Los Angeles as a sweeping basin, perhaps slightly colder and more humid, a time before people and studios arrived. The tar pits recorded a warming trend; the kinds of animals found there reflected the changing climate. The ones unadapted disappeared. No trace of their kind was found in the area. The ones adapted to warmer weather left a record of bones in the pit. Amid that collection of ancient skeletons, surrounded by evidence of death, I was finding a secret preserved over thousands and thousands of years. There was something cruel about natural selection and the survival of the fittest.[4] Even those successful individuals that "had what it took" for adaptation still wound up in the pits.

I never found out if I had what it took, not the way my mother meant. But I did adapt to the truth: I wasn't a Chinese Shirley Temple any longer, cute and short for my age. I had grown up. Maybe not on a Hollywood movie set, but in the La Brea Tar Pits. ❖

---

4. **natural selection . . . fittest:** a reference to the British scientist Charles Darwin's theory of evolution by natural selection, which holds that the animals best suited to their surroundings have an advantage in the competition for survival.

HISTORICAL INSIGHT

LA BREA TAR PITS

The La Brea Tar Pits in Los Angeles were formed from underground deposits of oil that seeped up through cracks in the surface of the earth. The oil evaporated and left behind pools of tar. Mammals that became trapped in these pools of tar were buried alive. As their flesh rotted away, their bones became soaked with tar and sank to the bottom of the pool. After a time, the tar hardened, forming a protective covering for the bones.

Since the first fossils were discovered in 1906, more than 100 of the tar pits have been excavated. The fossil skeletons are on display in the George C. Page Museum at the site. Many of them, including the remains of a huge bear, date back to the Ice Age, a glacial period which ended about 10,000 years ago. Although the oldest fossil discovered in the tar pits is about 38,000 years old, most of the fossils are between 14,000 and 16,000 years old.

The only human remains that have been found so far are those of a single individual. Prehistoric people may, however, have arrived in North America as early as 30,000 years ago, so the La Brea Tar Pits provide a fossil record of the kinds of animals these people probably encountered.

164 UNIT TWO PART 1: LEARNING THE HARD WAY

Mini-Lesson Ⓜ Spelling

PREFIXES *EX-* AND *SUB-* The prefix *ex-* generally means "out of." The prefix remains *ex-* before roots that begin with *c, p,* or *t,* as in *excavate* or *expire. Ex-* is changed to *ef-* before *f,* as in *efface,* and to *e-* before all other consonants, as in *ex- + vaporate = evaporate.* The prefix *sub-* means "under." Its spelling does not change when it is added to a root word, as in *sub- + terranean = subterranean.*

Application Invite students to write the correct spelling for each word that is formed by adding a prefix to a root or a base word.

1. The narrator's mother (ex + pected) her to go on with her Hollywood career.

2. When they visited agents, the narrator and her mother would ride to the top floor in an (ex + levator).

3. The narrator's mother (sub + scribed) to the belief that you should always have a positive reply.

4. Once an animal had strayed too close to the tar pits, there was no (ex + scape).

Reteaching/Reinforcement
• *Unit Two Resource Book,* p. 15

RESPONDING
OPTIONS

FROM PERSONAL RESPONSE TO CRITICAL ANALYSIS

REFLECT

1. What words describe your impressions of the main character? List three or more such words in your notebook and share them with a partner.

RETHINK

2. Why do you think the main character finds working at the tar pits so rewarding?

   Consider   Close Textual Reading
   - her experiences in Hollywood after turning 15
   - her discoveries about events in prehistoric times
   - connections that she sees between Hollywood and the tar pits

3. The main character's mother says that she wants nothing more than a normal life for her daughter. Do you think that is the case? Explain your opinion.

4. How would you compare the mother with the grandmother?

RELATE

5. For the Personal Connection on page 155, you discussed the challenges that former child stars face. What do you think the main character might say about the ideas you discussed?

6. What career do you think the main character might be most successful at? Support your choice with reasons.

Multimodal Learning
ANOTHER PATHWAY

Working with a partner improvise a dialogue between the narrator and a school counselor who helps her understand the new direction her life has taken. Perform the dialogue for your classmates.

QUICKWRITES

1. Write a **character sketch** of the narrator for an entertainment-magazine article on former child stars.

2. Write a **letter** from the narrator to her sister, presenting her new understanding of their career as "The World Famous Lee Sisters."

3. The narrator likes to imagine what the Los Angeles area was like centuries ago. Write a draft of an **adventure story** set in prehistoric times, in which the tar pits form part of the setting.

📁 **PORTFOLIO** *Save your writing. You may want to use it later as a springboard to a piece for your portfolio.*

LITERARY CONCEPTS

A **narrator** is a person who tells a story. A first-person narrator is usually a character in the story and uses the pronoun *I* or *we*. In "Hollywood and the Pits," Cherylene Lee uses a first-person narrator for the main story and the third-person point of view for the passages about the La Brea Tar Pits. Why do you think she chose to write the story this way?

From Personal Response to Critical Analysis

1. Accept all reasonable responses, such as the following: *strong, talented, hard-working, determined, resourceful.*

2. Possible responses: Some students may say that she is sympathetic to the animals that strayed into the pits because she fell into a trap as a child actor. Other students may point out that the pits offer her an opportunity to do rewarding work instead of being rewarded primarily for her looks and her size.

3. Possible responses: no, since she wants to see her daughter continue as an actor; yes, because she made sure that her daughter did not get spoiled as a child star.

4. Possible response: The mother loved her daughter's movie career, whereas the grandmother appreciates the daughter for who she is and realizes that movies falsify real life.

5. Responses should reflect the impressions students discussed earlier and their insights about the narrator's character.

6. Possible responses: archaeology, because she enjoys excavating; writing, because she can reflect on her life

Another Pathway

Invite pairs of students to brainstorm ideas about the roles they will be playing. They should review the selection for clues to the narrator's personality and style of speech. They should consider whatever experiences they may have had with a school counselor or qualities they imagine a good counselor to have. Encourage them to write down the goals that they hope to achieve in their dialogue.

Rubric

3 Full Accomplishment Students perform a dialogue that is consistent with the narrator's character.

2 Substantial Accomplishment Students perform a dialogue that is fairly consistent with the narrator's character.

1 Little or Partial Accomplishment Students are unable to perform a dialogue that is consistent with the narrator's character.

Literary Concepts

Students' responses will vary. However, most students will probably note that the first-person narration engages readers' sympathy for the narrator, while the third-person point of view provides an objective feel, which suits the factual nature of the passages.

QuickWrites

1. Provide students with a model by reading aloud a short section from an entertainment-magazine article.

2. Have students list the discoveries that the narrator makes about her career as a child star. Encourage them to include both positive and negative aspects of her career.

3. For fun, students could use and personify some of the prehistoric animals mentioned in the story.

 **The Writer's Craft**

Character Sketch, pp. 54–61
Letter Forms, p. 669

Science *Cooperative Learning* Assign two people in the group to research information about the La Brea Tar Pits. Remind them to use an outline to organize the information they find. Another member of the group can design the diorama, while a fourth member can check to be sure that the group is accurately portraying the tar pits. Invite all students to take part in creating the diorama.

SCIENCE CONNECTION

The La Brea Tar Pits Many dioramas can be seen on the grounds of the George C. Page Museum; students will have a chance to view several of them here. You may wish to use the images as a springboard to a research project about the La Brea Tar Pits.

Side A, Frames 49313

ADDITIONAL SUGGESTION

Social Studies *A Star Is Born* Invite students to research the life of Shirley Temple, now Shirley Temple Black, well-known Hollywood child star, and to compare Temple's life with the narrator's. Have students present their research to the class. Encourage them to include video clips from one of Temple's films or other visuals from their biographical resources.

Words to Know

1. b	6. b
2. a	7. c
3. c	8. d
4. d	9. c
5. c	10. a

Reteaching/Reinforcement
• *Unit Two Resource Book,* p. 16

EDITOR'S NOTE *With the permission of the author or copyright holder, potentially offensive material has been deleted from the selection.*

Multimodal Learning

ALTERNATIVE ACTIVITIES

1. **Interview** a science teacher to find out what fossils are, how they are formed, and what scientists can learn by studying them. Tape-record the interview, and play the tape in class.

2. Working with a small group of classmates, role-play a talk-show host's **conversation** with the Lee Sisters. Have one member of the group videotape the conversation, and then play the video in class.

3. With a partner, choreograph and perform a re-creation of the Lee sisters' **song-and-dance routine.** Play recordings of old tunes and tell corny jokes to enliven your performance.

CRITIC'S CORNER

According to Stephanie Hicks, a seventh-grade member of the student board, this story "would have been better if it had been only about her [the narrator's] life as an actress, or her interest in the La Brea Tar Pits. As it is, the story has too much information in too little space." Explain why you agree or disagree with this view.

WORDS TO KNOW

On your paper, write the letter of the word that is not related in meaning to the other three words in each set below.

1. (a) luxurious, (b) inexpensive, (c) stylish, (d) plush
2. (a) sturdy, (b) subterranean, (c) buried, (d) underground
3. (a) baffled, (b) bewildered, (c) determined, (d) puzzled
4. (a) shift, (b) displace, (c) move, (d) strengthen
5. (a) pore, (b) study, (c) skim, (d) examine
6. (a) cringe, (b) soar, (c) crouch, (d) grovel
7. (a) controlled, (b) obsessed, (c) relaxed, (d) haunted
8. (a) remove, (b) unearth, (c) excavate, (d) conceal
9. (a) skew, (b) twist, (c) clarify, (d) distort
10. (a) tarnish, (b) gleam, (c) shimmer, (d) glisten

Multimodal Learning

ACROSS THE CURRICULUM

SCIENCE *Cooperative Learning* With a small group of classmates, research the La Brea Tar Pits, examining photographs of the skeletons on display at the site. Then create a diorama that includes models of extinct animals from the Ice Age.

CHERYLENE LEE

Cherylene Lee, a fourth-generation Chinese American, was born and raised in Los Angeles, California. Like the narrator of her short story "Hollywood and the Pits," she was a child performer in Hollywood. She appeared in several TV sitcoms, including *Bachelor Father, Dennis the Menace,* and *My Three Sons.* Her stage credits include *A Chorus Line, The King and I,* and *Flower Drum Song,* and she

acted in the film version of *Flower Drum Song* and in the film *Donovan's Reef.*

Successful not only in Hollywood but in academic life, Lee earned degrees in paleontology and geology. In 1983, she began writing fiction, poetry, and plays. She regards writing as a path that combines the rewards of a Hollywood career with those of academic life, allowing her to be creative and to think deeply at the same time.

• SCIENCE CONNECTION

166 UNIT TWO PART 1: LEARNING THE HARD WAY

Alternative Activities

1. Remind students to prepare open-ended questions that will require thoughtful answers, but to narrow the scope of their questions so that the interviewee can be specific in his or her answers.

2. Have students prepare a character study and a dialogue for each sister. Assign a director to determine the goal of the conversation and the way he or she wants to see the conversation videotaped. Have group members discuss the characteristics of a typical talk-show conversation before they begin taping.

3. Invite students to take turns being dancers and choreographers as they develop their routines.

A Conversation with My Dogs

from *What the Dogs Have Taught Me*

BY MERRILL MARKOE

It is late afternoon. Seated at my desk, I call for my dogs to join me in my office. They do.

Me: The reason I've summoned you here today is I really think we should talk about something.

Bob: What's that?

Me: Well, please don't take this the wrong way, but I get the feeling you guys think you *have* to follow me *everywhere,* and I just want you both to know that you don't.

Stan: Where would you get a feeling like that?

Me: I get it from the fact that the both of you follow me *everywhere* all day long. Like for instance, this morning. We were all together in the bedroom? Why do you both look blank? Doesn't this ring a bell at all? I was on the bed reading the paper . . .

Bob: Where was I?

Me: On the floor sleeping.

Bob: On the floor sleepi . . . ? Oh, yes. Right. I remember that. Go on.

Me: So, there came a point where I had to get up and go into the next room to get a Kleenex. And you *both* woke up out of a deep sleep to go with me.

Stan: Yes. So? What's the problem?

Bob: We *like* to watch you get Kleenex. We happen to think it's something you do very well.

Me: The point I'm trying to make is why do you both have to get up out of a deep sleep to go *with* me. You sit there staring at me, all excited, like you think something really good is going to happen. I feel a lot of pressure to be more entertaining.

Bob: Would it help if we stood?

Stan: I think what the lady is saying is that where Kleenex retrieval is concerned, she'd just as soon we not make the trip.

Bob: Is that true?

Me: Yes. It is.

Bob (*deeply hurt*): Oh, man.

Stan: Don't let her get to you, buddy.

Bob: I know I shouldn't. But it all comes as such a shock.

Me: I think you may be taking this wrong. It's not that I don't like your company. It's just that I see no reason for you both to follow me every time I get up.

Bob: What if just one of us goes?

Stan: And I don't suppose that "one of us" would be *you?*

OBJECTIVES

- To promote independent active reading
- To practice and apply skills learned in previous selections
- To provide an opportunity to assess students' performance through an alternative assessment instrument.

Reading Pathways

- Invite students to read for enjoyment.
- Have students take turns reading dramatically.
- Encourage students to identify examples of humor.
- Evaluate how well students can read, interpret, discuss, and write about the selection on their own by using the Integrated Assessment for Unit Two, located in the Alternative Assessment booklet. Administer the assessment at the end of the unit after students have read all the selections and completed all the writing that was assigned. Set aside two class periods, or about two hours, for the assessment.

PRINT AND MEDIA RESOURCES

UNIT TWO RESOURCE BOOK
Strategic Reading: Literature, p. 19

FORMAL ASSESSMENT
Selection Test, pp. 37–38
Part Test, pp. 39–40
Test Generator

ALTERNATIVE ASSESSMENT
- *Unit Two Integrated Assessment, pp. 7–12*

ACCESS FOR STUDENTS ACQUIRING ENGLISH
Selection Summaries

AUDIO LIBRARY
See Reference Card

SUMMARY

In this humorous dialogue, the narrator tells her dogs, Bob and Stan, to stop following her around the house because she isn't going to feed them until dinnertime. The dogs then complain that she starves them. She declares firmly that the veterinarian has said they are overweight and that they will get no extra food. The narrator and the dogs then talk about instances of bad manners, such as the dogs' propensity to stick their heads into the narrator's dinner. The dogs seem to understand, but when she gets up to find her purse, both leap up and follow her.

Thematic Link: *Learning the Hard Way*
The narrator thinks she has reached a perfect understanding with her dogs but later learns they have not paid any attention to her.

Art Note

***Feather* by Beth Van Hoesen** The work of contemporary artist Beth Van Hoesen (1926–) has been praised by critics for "portray[ing] a world that is soothingly subdued, somewhat eccentric, and deceivingly simple."

Reading the Art *Do you think* Feather *is a "deceivingly simple" portrait? Why or why not? What personality traits in the dog does this painting convey?*

Feather (1985), Beth Van Hoesen. Watercolor, 14″ × 15″, collection of the artist.

Me: *Neither* of you needs to go.

Bob: Okay. Fine. No problem. Get your damn Kleenex alone from now on.

Me: Good.

Bob: I'm just curious. What's your position on pens?

Me: Pens?

Bob: Yes. How many of us can wake up out of a deep sleep to watch you look for a pen?

Me: Why would *either* of you want to wake up out of a deep sleep to follow me around while I'm looking for a pen?

Stan: Is she serious?

Bob: I can't tell. She has such a weird sense of humor.

Me: Let's just level with each other, okay? The *real* reason you both follow me every place I go is that you secretly believe there might be food involved. Isn't that true? Isn't that the real reason for the show of enthusiasm?

Stan: Very nice talk.

Bandit (1984), Beth Van Hoesen. Watercolor, 13″ × 13 ¼″, collection of the artist.

Bob: The woman has got some mouth on her.

Me: You mean you *deny* that every time you follow me out of the room it's actually because you think we're stopping for snacks?

Bob: Absolutely false. That is a bald-faced lie. We do it for the life experience. Period.

Stan: And sometimes I think it might work into a game of ball.

Bob: But we certainly don't *expect* anything.

Stan: We're *way* past expecting anything of you. We wouldn't want you to overexert yourself in any way. You have to rest and save up all your strength for all that Kleenex fetching.

Bob: Plus we know it doesn't concern you in the least that we're both *starving to death.*

Stan: We consume on the average about a third of the calories eaten daily by the typical wasted South American street dog.

Me: *One* bowl of food a day is what the *vet* said I should give you. No more.

Bob: One bowl of food is a joke. It's an hors d'oeuvre. It does nothing but whet my

A CONVERSATION WITH MY DOGS **169**

Cooperative Learning
CREATING A DIALOGUE

Have students write a dialogue between themselves and a pet they know or make up. Students can work in groups of three or four. Each group should pick a pet and discuss its personality. A group recorder can take notes as students talk. Another student can make sure group members understand one another. The recorder can read back the discussion notes, and students can then choose a writer to create the dialogue. Finally, the group can choose two readers to present the dialogue to the class. Students should aim to emulate the humor and style in "What the Dogs Have Taught Me."

Teacher's Role Monitor students, as they work, to be sure that each group member is taking part in the discussion and execution of the dialogue. After students have made their presentations, ask to discuss what part of the cooperative process was useful to them and what they might do differently next time.

Rubric

3 Full Accomplishment Students work cooperatively and present a well-written dialogue.

2 Substantial Accomplishment Students have some difficulty in reflecting a pet's personality in their completed dialogue.

1 Little or Partial Accomplishment Students have great difficulty in capturing a pet's personality in their completed dialogue.

Art Note

Reading the Art *In what way is this painting similar to* Feather *on the previous page? How is this dog's personality different from Feather's? Do either of these dogs fit the personality you imagined for Bob or for Stan? Why do you think the artist chose not to include any background details?*

THE LANGUAGE OF LITERATURE TEACHER'S EDITION **169**

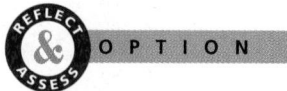

Individual Activity

MAKING A LIST

Markoe's humorous dialogue is sprinkled with irony—for example, Bob and Stan sometimes say the opposite of what they mean in an attempt to be funny. Invite students to make a list of ironic remarks made by the two dogs. Have them jot down a few notes to explain how each remark adds to the humor of the selection.

Teacher's Role One way to help students identify the ironic remarks in the selection is to have them read the dialogue aloud. You may also help students by pointing out a few examples of irony, such as Bob and Stan's remarks on page 169: "Bob: But we certainly don't expect anything. Stan: We're way past expecting anything of you."

Rubric

3 Full Accomplishment Students list several examples of irony and explain how the remarks add humor to the selection.

2 Substantial Accomplishment Students list several examples of irony but have some difficulty explaining how the examples add humor to the selection.

1 Little or Partial Accomplishment Students have difficulty listing examples of irony and explaining how they create humor.

---

appetite.

Me: Last summer, before I cut your food down, you were the size and shape of a hassock.

Bob: Who is she talking to?

Stan: You, pal. You looked like a beanbag chair, buddy.

Bob: But it was not from overeating. In summer, I retain fluids, that's all. I was in very good shape.

Stan: For a hippo. I saw you play ball back then. Nice energy. For a dead guy.

Bob: Don't talk to me about energy. Who single-handedly ate his way through the back fence. Not just once but on *four separate occasions?*

Me: So *you're* the one who did that?

Bob: One who did what?

Me: Ate through the back fence.

Bob: Is there something wrong with the back fence? I have no idea what happened. Whoever said that is a liar.

Stan: The fact remains that we are starving all day long, and you continually torture us by eating right in front of us.

Bob: Very nice manners, by the way.

Me: You have the nerve to discuss my manners? Who drinks out of the toilet and then comes up and kisses me on the face?

Bob: That would be Dave.

Me: No. That would be *you.* And while we're on the subject of manners, who keeps trying to crawl *into* the refrigerator? Who always has *mud* on their tongue?

Stan: Well, that would be Dave.

Me: Okay. That *would* be Dave. But the point I'm trying to make is that where manners are concerned, let's just say that you don't catch me trying to stick my head in *your* dinner.

Bob: Well, that may be more a function of menu than anything else.

Me: Which brings me right back to my original point. The two of you do not have to wake up and offer me fake camaraderie now that you understand that *once* a day is all you're ever going to be fed. Period. Nonnegotiable. For the rest of your natural lives. And if I want to play ball, I'll *say so.* End of sentence.

Stan: Well, I see that the nature of these talks has completely broken down.

Bob: I gotta tell you, it hurts.

Me: There's no reason to have hurt feelings.

Stan: Fine. Whatever you say.

Bob: I just don't give a damn anymore. I'm beyond that, quite frankly. Get your own Kleenex, for all I care.

Stan: I feel the same way. Let her go get all the Kleenex and pens she wants. I couldn't care less.

Me: Excellent. Well, I hope we understand each other now.

Bob: We do. Why'd you get up? Where are you going?

Me: Into the next room.

Stan: Oh. Mm hmm. I see. And why is that?

Me: To get my purse.

Stan: Hey, fatso, out of my way.

Bob: Watch out. I was first.

Stan: *I* was first.

Bob: We're getting her purse. I go first. I'm *starving.*

Stan: You don't listen at all, do you. Going for *pens* means food. She said she's getting her *purse.* That means *ball.*

 **OPTION 3**

MERRILL MARKOE

1949–

Merrill Markoe is considered one of the most talented comedy writers in show business. She was the head writer for the TV talk show *Late Night with David Letterman* from 1982 to 1983 and continued writing for the show until 1986. Markoe won four Emmy Awards for her work on Late Night and is often credited with giving the show its offbeat tone—it was she who invented one of its most popular segments, "Stupid Pet Tricks."

Although Markoe was born in New York, she and her family moved around the United States, finally settling in California. She earned a degree in painting and taught drawing at the University of Southern California. As an artist, Markoe introduced humor into her paintings and soon began to realize that comedy was her calling. In the mid-1970s, she tried standup comedy, which brought her to the attention of Letterman.

In addition to working as a situation-comedy writer and a television reporter, Markoe produced a humorous television special called *Merrill Markoe's Guide to Glamourous Living*. An admitted klutz, she says, "I can't pull off anything without tripping at the wrong spot or finding that I have a big piece of marinara sauce stuck to the corner of my face. I mean, I've never had dinner with anyone where they didn't eventually wipe my face for me or pick bread out of my eyebrows." Markoe currently writes for several national magazines and lives with her four dogs in Malibu, California.

LITERARY INSIGHT

 # DOG AROUND THE BLOCK

by E. B. White

Dog around the block, sniff,
Hydrant sniffing, corner, grating,
Sniffing, always, starting forward,
Backward, dragging, sniffing backward,
Leash at taut, leash at dangle,
Leash in people's feet entangle—
Sniffing dog, apprised of smellings,
Meeting enemies,
Loving old acquaintances, sniff,
Sniffing hydrant for reminders,
Leg against the wall, raise,

Leaving grating, corner greeting,
Chance for meeting, sniff, meeting,
Meeting, telling, news of smelling,
Nose to tail, tail to nose,
Rigid, careful, pose,
Liking, partly liking, hating,
Then another hydrant, grating,
Leash at taut, leash at dangle,
Tangle, sniff, untangle,
Dog around the block, sniff.

DOG AROUND THE BLOCK **171**

Class Discussion
SHARING IDEAS

After students have read the selection, engage them in a class discussion, using the following questions:

1. How would you explain what makes this dialogue funny? *(Possible responses: the premise—a human talking to her dogs; the dogs take on human attributes; the dogs make ironical remarks and tease their owner and each other about their antics; the narrator thinks she has come to an understanding with her dogs only to discover that they haven't understood her.)*
2. Who do you think Dave might be? *(Possible responses: another dog; another member of the household; David Letterman)*
3. How would you describe the lesson that the narrator learns? *(Even though she tries to lay down the law, the dogs are going to do exactly as they please.)*

Teacher's Role Encourage students to support their responses with specific details from the dialogue.

INSIGHT

1. How would you describe your impressions of the dog in this poem? *(Accept all reasonable responses.)*
2. How would you compare the poem with Markoe's dialogue? *(Possible response: Both are easy to read and help the reader to understand why dogs do what they do.)*
3. How would you explain why E. B. White repeats the word sniff so many times? *(Possible response: Since sniffing is what a dog does the most when out on a walk, the repetition of the word sniff calls attention to a dog's characteristic activity.)*

E. B. WHITE

Elwyn Brooks White (1899–1985) wrote for *The New Yorker* magazine and helped define English style in his book *The Elements of Style*. He is well-known for such children's classics as *Stuart Little*, *Charlotte's Web*, and *The Trumpet of the Swan*.

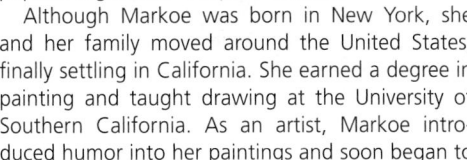

MERRILL MARKOE

Merrill Markoe worked as an art teacher and a film scriptwriter before turning to writing comedy. She says that although she was always clowning around in high school, it never occurred to her that she could make a living out of it.

EDITOR'S NOTE *With the permission of the author or copyright holder, potentially offensive material has been deleted from the selection.*

OVERVIEW

In the Guided Assignment for this section, students will write an essay analyzing imagery. By analyzing images, students will better understand how a well-chosen image can help a reader visualize a story. As preparation for this assignment, The Writer's Style will help students understand the importance of using precise verbs, similes and metaphors, and comparative adverbs to create images in their own writing. In Reading the World, students will explore the use of images in advertising.

Objectives

- To recognize how authors use description and imagery effectively
- To create effective images through the use of precise verbs
- To write an analysis of imagery in literature
- To analyze real-world images

Skills

LITERATURE
- Identifying and analyzing images

WRITING AND LANGUAGE
- Choosing precise verbs
- Using figurative language

GRAMMAR AND USAGE
- Using adverbs in comparisons

MEDIA LITERACY
- Interpreting advertisements

SPEAKING, LISTENING, AND VIEWING
- Creating a group description
- Group conferencing

CRITICAL THINKING
- Making associations
- Analyzing
- Speculating

Teaching Strategy: MODELING

In the following models, vivid imagery is used to create a picture in the reader's mind. This technique is useful in fiction, poetry, and nonfiction.

A Lee *Possible responses: images of death and destruction, created by the words* bones glistening, broken pelvises, *and* skulls.

B White *Possible responses: They appeal to our senses and create vivid images. Readers might hear the dog sniff, feel the dog straining against the leash, and see people tangled in the leash.*

EXPLORING IMAGERY

Have you noticed that you often form mental pictures, or images, of what you read? This happens because skillful writers choose words and phrases that make their descriptions vivid. What images formed in your mind as you read the poetry in Unit Two? How did you picture the La Brea Tar Pits? In the following pages you will

- study how authors use imagery effectively
- write an analysis of imagery in a selection you've read
- examine the use of images in the world around you

The Writer's Style: Imagery Writers use words and phrases to create vivid descriptions, or images, that readers can picture in their minds.

Read the Literature

The writers of each passage below chose their words and details with care. How do their choices help create strong images?

Literature Models

A **Imagery That Describes a Sight** What picture forms in your imagination when you read this passage? Which words contribute most to that picture?

> In 1968 when I was fifteen, the pit opened its secret to me. I breathed, ate, slept, dreamed about the La Brea Tar Pits. I spent summer days working the archaeological dig and in dreams saw the bones glistening, the broken pelvises, the skulls, the vertebrae looped like a woman's pearls hanging on an invisible cord.
>
> Cherylene Lee, from "Hollywood and the Pits"

B **Imagery That Shows an Event** How do these details help you picture a dog's activities? What do you see, hear, or feel?

> Dog around the block, sniff,
> Hydrant sniffing, corner, grating,
> Sniffing, always, starting forward,
> Backward, dragging, sniffing backward,
> Leash at taut, leash at dangle,
> Leash in people's feet entangle—
>
> E. B. White, from "Dog Around the Block"

172   UNIT TWO: LIFE'S LESSONS

PRINT AND MEDIA RESOURCES

UNIT TWO RESOURCE BOOK
Writer's Style, p. 23
Prewriting, p. 24
Elaboration, p. 25
Peer Response Guide, pp. 26–27
Revising and Proofreading, p. 28
Student Model, p. 29
Rubric, p. 30

GRAMMAR MINI-LESSONS
Transparencies, pp. 12–13 and 40
Copymasters, pp. 19–20

WRITING MINI-LESSONS
Transparencies, p. 39

ACCESS FOR STUDENTS ACQUIRING ENGLISH
Reading and Writing Support

FORMAL ASSESSMENT
Guidelines for Writing Assessment

 **WRITING COACH**

Connect to Nature

Vivid descriptions and imagery lend power to nonfiction writing too. In the magazine article below, instead of just writing *big, wide mouth,* the writer chose the words *cavernous, leering mouth.* Which description creates a more lifelike image? Why?

Magazine Article

The problem starts up front, with the face—the cavernous, leering mouth filled with spiky teeth; the cold, predatorial eyes; the knobby, reptilian skin. There's no sense mincing words: we're talking ugly here, nightmare dwellers, creatures from the black lagoon. Show me an alligator and I'll show you somebody truckin' hard the other way.

Donald Dale Jackson
from "Old Bigtooth Returns"
Smithsonian, January 1987

Imagery That Creates a Feeling
What images do "cold, predatorial eyes" and "knobby, reptilian skin" make you see? What do you feel?

Try Your Hand: Using Imagery

1. **Write Word Pictures** Add details to make these dull sentences shine.
   - The agent was grumpy.
   - The tar pits are interesting.
   - Her hair was mostly black with a few gray strands.

2. **Make Them Hungry** What's your favorite food? What's your idea of a mouthwatering sandwich or a delicious dessert? Describe what it looks, tastes, and smells like.

3. **Create Descriptions** In a small group, brainstorm an imaginary place. Start describing it. List items you might see, hear, or feel. Assign one item for each person to describe. Then meet as a group and read the descriptions aloud. Combine your descriptions into one composition.

SkillBuilder

 WRITER'S CRAFT

Using Precise Verbs

Skilled writers choose their words with care—avoiding the obvious and striving for the out-of-the-ordinary. Precise, colorful verbs help writers create fresh, vivid descriptions. See how poet Ernest Lawrence Thayer used precise verbs in "Casey at the Bat."

> Then from the gladdened multi-
> tude went up a joyous yell—
> It rumbled in the mountaintops,
> it rattled in the dell;
> It struck upon the hillside and
> rebounded on the flat;

APPLYING WHAT YOU'VE LEARNED
Rewrite the paragraph below, replacing the italicized words with a verb from the list.

I *said,* "Stop *swinging* at the ball." Tory *looked hurt.* I was sorry, so I *got down* beside him, *placed* my arm around him and *said,* "Don't *put* the bat on your shoulder, and don't *jump* at the ball like a ballet dancer."

shouted	flailing	crouched
rest	leap	draped
hold	whispered	winced

 **HANDBOOKS**

For information on verbs, see pages 873–874 of the Grammar Handbook. For more information on descriptive writing, see pages 820–821 in the Writing Handbook.

C Jackson *Possible responses: Readers see evil eyes awaiting a chance to attack and devour and snakelike, bumpy skin. The image of something fierce makes readers feel fear.*

Try Your Hand

1. Responses will vary. Sentences should contain vivid sensory detail, as in these examples:
   - The pot-bellied agent frowned as he replaced the heavy black phone with a thud.
   - The tar pits are an amazing treasure trove of fossils.
   - Her ebony hair was laced with silver.

2. Sample responses should appeal to sight, taste, and smell, as in this sample: "The bronzed turkey glistened on the platter. Its rich aroma was irresistible. I snatched a piece of skin as crisp as a potato chip."

3. Have students adopt a consistent point of view to unify their group descriptions. You may wish to assign students roles as voice monitor, turn-taking monitor, recorder, and direction giver.

SkillBuilder WRITER'S CRAFT

USING PRECISE VERBS Caution students that verbs must be precise but not necessarily unusual. Remind them that the primary purpose of all language is to communicate, and so they must choose their words to fit their audience and purpose. Have students review the selections in the unit and discuss the audience and some of the verbs used to communicate meaning.

Application Answer:
I *shouted,* "Stop *flailing* at the ball." Tory *winced.* I was sorry, so I *crouched* down beside him, *draped* my arm around him and whispered, "Don't *rest* the bat on your shoulder, and don't *leap* at the ball like a ballet dancer."

 **The Writer's Craft**

Verbs, pp. 464–465

WRITING ABOUT LITERATURE

Analysis

D You've seen how images create vivid pictures in a reader's mind. Images also can convey a message, emphasize an idea, or make a statement about a character. By analyzing the images in literature and in the world around you, you can better understand what you read and experience.

GUIDED ASSIGNMENT

Analyze Imagery On the next few pages, you'll explore the imagery in a piece of literature. Then you'll write an essay in which you analyze some of the imagery you found, tell why it's effective, and explain what it adds to the story or poem.

① Prewrite and Explore

The activities below can help you explore images from the literature in Unit Two.

COLLECT IMAGES

E Think about your favorite story or poem from this unit. Did it leave vivid pictures in your mind of certain people or scenes? Read the selection again, and look for strong images. You might make a chart like the one below.

TALK IT THROUGH

In a group, talk about the images in a selection from Unit Two. Read favorite lines or passages to one another. What makes the images in the passages vivid? What ideas and feelings do you get from the images?

Decision Point Now that you've explored several images, do you want to write about one image or about how a group of images work together? Or do you want to compare images from more than one selection?

Student's Image Chart

Exact words of the image	Summary of image (what it describes)	My ideas about the image
"Inviting pools had false bottoms made of sticky tar."	A water hole that had a tar bottom— a TRAP!	The images are eerie. I can see the water hole and imagine what the tar must have looked and felt like. I feel scared by the image.

Assessment ✓ **Option**

SELF-ASSESSMENT

After students have completed the "Talk It Through," discussion, they should assess their understanding of imagery. Students can consider the following questions:

• *How well did I explain to the group the images I chose?*

• *How well did I understand the images chosen by other group members?*

• *Do I feel ready to begin writing, or do I need to search through the unit for more images?*

② Write a Discovery Draft

Try freewriting about the imagery in your selection. As you explore your ideas, think about the following question: How does the author's use of imagery make the selection more effective or interesting?

Student's Discovery Draft

The description of the La Brea Tar Pits is frightening. She says, "Inviting pools had false bottoms made of sticky tar." Things aren't what they seem.

What other examples from the story can I quote?

I know! The tar pit is like Hollywood! Now, how will I support my idea?

Images like this one stick with me, "A shriek of agony from the trapped victim drew flesh-eating predators, which were then trapped themselves by the very same ooze." It's like there's no way to escape. What is the author really saying?

③ Draft and Share

You might begin your draft by introducing the story or poem and describing the image you want to explore. Then tell what you think the image means. Use details from the selection to support your ideas. Remember, your writing should be clear and easy to follow. When you finish writing, ask another student to read your draft and respond to it.

PEER RESPONSE

- Why do you think this image interests me?
- Did any of my ideas confuse you? Why?
- Where is my draft strong? Where is it weak?

WRITING ABOUT LITERATURE **175**

Writing Skill:
USING SENSORY LANGUAGE

G The Discovery Draft provides an opportunity for students to think through ideas and information they've gathered. Suggest that students focus on sensory observations as they freewrite. Guide them to think about how something looks, tastes, smells, sounds, or feels. In addition, students may find it helpful to fill in observation charts that show to which sense each image appeals.

CUSTOMIZING FOR
Less-Proficient Writers

H Remind students that an introduction should give the main idea of their essays. The body of the essay contributes details; it supports and explains the main idea. The conclusion summarizes the essay and reinforces the main idea without being repetitive. If students are having trouble organizing their drafts this way, have peer readers help suggest an organized structure.

SkillBuilder WRITER'S CRAFT

FIGURATIVE LANGUAGE Explain that metaphors and similes are figures of speech that create a comparison between two unlike things. Tell students that metaphors and similes are effective if they use fresh, vivid language to describe something familiar in a new way. Explore with students how metaphors and similes that become clichés lose their power to describe.

Application Possible responses:
1. The sun was as red as *blood.*
2. A thunderstorm is *a volcano erupting.*
3. The moon shone like *a new penny.*

Additional Suggestions Have students create similes and metaphors from these starters:
1. The cables of the bridge were intertwined like *a spider's web.*
2. The rush-hour traffic is *coursing into the city's major arteries.*

Reteaching/Reinforcement
Writing Mini-Lessons transparencies, p. 39

 The Writer's Craft

Figurative Language, pp. 314–316

WRITING ABOUT LITERATURE

4 Revise and Edit

I Don't worry if your draft isn't shaping up. Keep rethinking, getting feedback, and revising until you're satisfied. Reflect on your progress and ask yourself:

- Have I described the important images?
- Have I shown how they work in the story or poem?

J Before you revise and edit, you may want to read the Grammar in Context lesson on the next page. Also, consider the Standards for Evaluation below as you work on your final draft.

Student's Final Draft

How do the quotations support the topic of this writer's paper?

K

How does this introductory paragraph tell you what to expect from the rest of the paper?

> ### Lost in Hollywood
>
> The descriptions of the La Brea Tar Pits drew me into the story, yet they seemed to serve another purpose too. The tar pits were once pools of water that had tar bottoms. Animals that came to drink "were sucked down against their will in those watering holes destined to be called the La Brea Tar Pits in a place to be named the City of Angels, home of Hollywood movie stars." The tar pits of long ago had hidden dangers, much like the Hollywood of today.

Standards for Evaluation

An imagery analysis paper
- names the literature and states the main idea in the introduction
- identifies and discusses important imagery
- supports main ideas with examples and quotations
- is clearly written and easy to follow

Assessment ✓ **Option**

Grammar in Context

L **Adjectives and Adverbs** In this lesson you have seen how skilled writers build vivid descriptions by using precise verbs and specific nouns. Adjectives and adverbs can also help writers create descriptions, but using adjectives and adverbs that don't add new information leads to flabby writing. See how the writing in the example below improves when the student cuts unnecessary modifiers.

M The fifteen-year-old ~~teenage~~ girl in "Hollywood and the Pits" began acting when she was only three. She had been successful, but an acting career is not a ~~certain~~ sure thing. Hollywood can be inviting one moment and terrible the next, just like the La Brea Tar Pits. Ages ago, young ~~juvenile~~ animals stepped into pools of water and suddenly found themselves sinking ~~down~~ into ~~sticky~~ gooey ~~black~~ tar.

Try Your Hand: Using Adjectives and Adverbs

On a separate sheet of paper, revise each sentence. Which of the words in parentheses adds new detail? Choose the better adjective or adverb and use it in the sentence.

1. Her mother whispered (sadly, softly).
2. She (tightly, furiously) gripped the steering wheel.
3. Grandmother's eyelids fluttered (quickly, sleepily).
4. She didn't mind the (torn, colorful) jeans her granddaughter wore when she worked at the pit.

SkillBuilder

G → GRAMMAR FROM WRITING

Using Adverbs in Comparisons

Use the **comparative form** of an adverb to compare two actions. Use the **superlative form** to compare more than two actions.

*Jesse lives **close** to our school. I live **closer** to the park than he does. Lupe lives **closest** to the tar pits, which makes Abel and me jealous of her.*

In the example, *close, closer,* and *closest* are all forms of the adverb *close.* Short adverbs such as *close* often form the comparative by adding *-er,* and the superlative by adding *-est.*

*I sing **beautifully**. Many people think I used to sing **more beautifully** than I do now. However, my sister says I sing **most beautifully** when I'm sad.*

Many adverbs end in *-ly.* Most of these adverbs form the comparative with the word *more* and the superlative with the word *most.* Never use both *-er* and *more,* or both *-est* and *most.*

APPLYING WHAT YOU'VE LEARNED
Examine your draft to make sure you have used adverbs correctly in comparisons.

GRAMMAR HANDBOOK

For more information on modifiers in comparisons, see pages 867–868 in the Grammar Handbook.

WRITING ABOUT LITERATURE **177**

SkillBuilder **G** **GRAMMAR FROM WRITING**

READING THE WORLD

On pages 172–176, students analyzed images from literature. They should also be aware that images are used in the real world for a variety of reasons. In this lesson, students will examine how advertisers create images that they hope will persuade a target audience to buy a particular product.

Critical Thinking:
SPECULATING

N Students might interpret what they see literally—an ice skater with a milk mustache, for example. Students may say that they identified the product by the name milk and the milk mustache on each of the models. The ads are similar because each shows a beautiful woman with a milk mustache and emphasizes the benefits of drinking milk; they are different because each of the women shown has a different high-profile career.

Media Literacy: INTERPRETING
AN ADVERTISEMENT

O Students may infer that the models were chosen because they are beautiful, talented, and well known. Students can infer that if they drink milk, they too will be part of this accomplished group. People might be influenced to drink milk because they think it will make them beautiful, talented, and famous like the models.

Speaking and Listening:
GROUP DISCUSSION

P Have students work in groups to tell what an image is and why it is powerful. An image conveys a message, emphasizes an idea, or makes a statement about a character. Images are powerful because they appeal to the senses, often to more than one sense at a time. They help readers form vivid mental pictures.

READING THE WORLD

SELLING AN IMAGE

What do billboards, magazine ads, certain T-shirts, and even some cereal boxes have in common? They all display images. Advertisers use words and pictures to create images for products. How do images affect you?

View In your notebook describe the milk ads on this page. What do the ads have in common? What positive traits do the people pictured in the ads seem to have?

Interpret For what reasons might these people have been chosen to appear in these ads? What does seeing them in the ads lead you to believe about the product? Why might these ads influence you to drink milk?

Discuss Discuss the following questions. What messages do these ads send? How? Why are images powerful advertising tools? Use the SkillBuilder at the right to learn about the associations images can lead you to make.

6.0, 6.0, 6.0, 6.0, 6.0! If I had to rate milk as an after-sports drink, it would definitely get the gold. Besides being a better source of potassium than the leading sports drink, it has more vitamins and minerals per ounce. And how do I like it? On ice, of course.

MILK
What a surprise!™

For More Information
1-800-WHY-MILK

CRITICAL THINKING

Making Associations

Images can cause people to make **associations,** or connections, between thoughts, feelings, and ideas. People may associate figure skater Kristi Yamaguchi with athletic qualities such as grace, strength, and good health. Seeing actress Lauren Bacall makes many people think of glamour, talent, and lasting fame. Why might advertisers choose successful or famous people to represent their product? What associations do they expect their audience to make?

APPLYING WHAT YOU'VE LEARNED
Discuss one or more of the following in a small group.

- Think about an image such as a picture of a sleeping child in a cough medicine ad. What associations do the advertisers want you to make?
- How can you avoid being misled by imagery in advertising or publicity?
- Think about an appealing image such as a happy couple in a jeans ad. Use what you learned about imagery in this lesson to help you analyze the image's appeal.

SkillBuilder CRITICAL THINKING

MAKING ASSOCIATIONS Images of movie stars, sports heroes, supermodels, or other celebrities are often used to draw attention to a cause, sell a product, or elect a candidate because many people identify with these famous people. Students might bring up negative as well as positive associations that images of celebrities might convey. If these issues arise, acknowledge them openly and then move on to reasons why companies use images of celebrities for their products.

Application

- The associations might include rest, calm, and quiet, which indicate that the child's cough has been relieved.
- Students might suggest that images are created to appeal to consumers so they will purchase products. As consumers, they need to look beyond the images, searching for facts. They also should be prepared to evaluate their responses to the ads.
- Responses will vary. Students should note that the image usually presents something appealing, and the message is that the product helps consumers obtain it. For example, the image in the jeans ad appeals to people's wish for love.

UNIT TWO
Part 2 Lesson Planner

Table of Contents	Discussion	Previewing the Selection	Reading the Selection
PART OPENER **MAKING CHOICES** **What Do You Think?** page 180	**20 MINUTES** • Reflect on the part theme		
SELECTION **Say It with Flowers** page 182 CHALLENGING		**15 MINUTES** • PERSONAL CONNECTION • WRITING CONNECTION • COMMUNITY CONNECTION	**40 MINUTES** • Introduce vocabulary • Read pp. 182–89 (8 pp.)
SELECTIONS **It Happened in Montgomery/Choices** page 194 CHALLENGING		**20 MINUTES** • PERSONAL CONNECTION • HISTORICAL CONNECTION • READING CONNECTION: Reading modern poetry	**5 MINUTES** • Read pp. 194–95 (2 pp.)
SELECTIONS **Barter/Into the Sun** page 199 AVERAGE		**20 MINUTES** • PERSONAL CONNECTION • LITERARY CONNECTION • WRITING CONNECTION	**5 MINUTES** • Read pp. 199–200 (2 pp.)
SELECTION **Eleanor Roosevelt** page 204 AVERAGE		**15 MINUTES** • PERSONAL CONNECTION • HISTORICAL CONNECTION • READING CONNECTION: Sequence	**45 MINUTES** • Introduce vocabulary • Read pp. 204–13 (10 pp.)
GENRE LESSON **Focus on Drama** page 216	**20 MINUTES** • Discuss characteristics of drama • Discuss strategies for reading drama		
SELECTION **A Christmas Carol** page 219 AVERAGE		**20 MINUTES** • PERSONAL CONNECTION • BIOGRAPHICAL CONNECTION • READING CONNECTION: Stage directions	**15 MINUTES** • Introduce vocabulary • Read pp. 219–42 (24 pp.)

Writing	Exploring Topics	Prewriting	Drafting and Revising
WRITING FROM EXPERIENCE **Narrative and Literary Writing**	**25 MINUTES**	**25 MINUTES**	**80 MINUTES**

Time estimates assume in-class work. You may wish to assign some of these stages as homework.

Responding to the Selection

FROM PERSONAL RESPONSE TO CRITICAL ANALYSIS,	OR	ANOTHER PATHWAY	LITERARY CONCEPTS	QUICKWRITES	ALTERNATIVE ACTIVITIES	LITERARY LINKS	CRITIC'S CORNER	THE WRITER'S STYLE	ACROSS THE CURRICULUM	ART CONNECTION	WORDS TO KNOW	BIOGRAPHY
40 MINUTES					**40 MINUTES**							
• Discussion questions	OR	• Debate	• Title and climax	• Help-wanted ad • Profile • Sequel	✔	✔			SOCIAL STUDIES SCIENCE		✔	✔
50 MINUTES					**10 MINUTES**							
• Discussion questions	OR	• Role-playing a scene	• Free verse	• Free verse poem • Questions • Letter					SOCIAL STUDIES			✔
50 MINUTES					**40 MINUTES**							
• Discussion questions	OR	• Paragraph	• Figurative language and simile • Repetition	• Poem • Letter • List	✔					✔		✔
50 MINUTES					**40 MINUTES**							
• Discussion questions	OR	• Paragraph	• Biography and conflict	• Advice column • Job description • Speech	✔	✔			SOCIAL STUDIES		✔	✔
60 MINUTES					**60 MINUTES**							
• Discussion questions	OR	• Radio Play	• Theme	• Will • Plot summary • Dialogue	✔	✔			MUSIC		✔	✔

Publishing and Reflecting

30 MINUTES

Part 2 Cooperative Project

Issues Theater

 **1 Getting Started**

Overview

Groups of students will share their views on issues of interest through dramatic presentations.

PROJECT AT A GLANCE

The selections in Unit Two, Part 2 concern people making difficult choices in their lives. For this project, students will collaborate in small groups to plan and perform a dramatic selection with a message. Each group will choose an issue of interest to its members. Then the group will research various aspects of that issue to determine what message they would like to get across to their audience. Performances may be in any form (dance, pantomime, skit, puppet show, and so on) that best conveys the message. Students will write their own scripts, plan any costumes, and create any special scenery, props, or effects they need. The culmination of the project will be a school-wide presentation of all the performances.

OBJECTIVES

• To identify an issue of interest to students
• To choose a focus for the issue
• To determine the message they want to convey about the issue
• To work cooperatively to present the message in a dramatic form

SUGGESTED GROUP SIZE

4–6 students per group

MATERIALS

• Current newspapers and newsmagazines
• Video camera and tape (if possible)

Getting Started

Arranging the Project

Schedule a time for the final performances in a large room, such as the cafeteria, gym, or auditorium. You might coordinate this effort with any other teachers whose students are doing the same project. The entire school should be invited to watch the performances, as should school officials. Enlist students to be ushers, issue and collect tickets (if appropriate), and run the curtain or lights.

If possible, arrange for the entire presentation to be videotaped. The media person at school might be willing to do this, or you can ask for parental help. Collect a fairly wide selection of newspapers and newsmagazines for students to examine.

If an episode of a TV newsmagazine will be dealing with a youth-oriented issue, you might want to tape it and replay it in class or assign its viewing as "homework."

Arranging the Performances

Once the date, place, and time have been set, much of your work involved in arranging the performances will come later. Try to structure the performances by mixing or alternating various forms. In order to do this, you will need to know how each message will be presented (dance, mime, skit). If some groups need special props, they may turn to you for help. Offer suggestions for where they can obtain the items, contact those in charge of any school props yourself, or make suggestions about alternative items.

2 Creating the Issues Theater

Introducing the Project

Explain that students will be working together in small groups to select an issue, determine a point of view, and present that point of view to an audience through a performance of an appropriate form. Be sure to set a minimum and maximum time limit for the performances. Ask students to look through the newspapers and magazines if they need help finding an issue. If you taped a television newsmagazine episode, you might want to ask the class to watch it at this time.

Discuss a few of the issues that students have discovered. If there are opposing views, encourage students to debate them while maintaining an orderly discussion. Explain that each group will select only one point of view to present and that not all members must agree with the message. (If some students argue vehemently, you may want to assign them to different groups for this project.)

Also discuss the various forms of theater, such as mime, puppetry, dance, drama, and music. Students can talk about when each form might be appropriate to convey a particular message.

Group Investigations

Divide students into groups of four to six. The groups will work cooperatively to discuss important issues. They should also discuss these issues with other students to get a broader picture of what issues students find most important. Groups will meet and decide on a final topic of interest, the point of view that message should take, and the form of presentation. Hold class meetings to monitor groups' progress, anticipate problems, and encourage students to experiment with various forms of presentations. Obstacles that groups are experiencing can also be discussed and solved with the help of the class.

Creating a Project Description

After students have completed the preliminary planning, they should write a one-page description of their project, including the issue being addressed, the point of view being taken, and what form the performance will take and why. If issues are duplicated within the class, you might encourage groups to take opposing viewpoints or present the issue in different forms. Meet with groups periodically to discuss their progress.

OPTION 1: TELEVISION NEWSMAGAZINE
Groups can stage their own version of *60 Minutes* by having the performance take the form of a television newsmagazine. Students can act as anchorpersons and reporters, as well as the "victims," "experts," or "officials" being interviewed.

OPTION 2: FORMAL DEBATE Two groups can be assigned the same issue but take opposing points of view. They should fully research the topic and then hold a debate expressing their viewpoints.

OPTION 3: PROPAGANDA Groups can research the term *propaganda* and find examples of it to share with the class. They might also develop their own brochure of propaganda on an issue and viewpoint they select.

OPTION 4: SCHOOL ISSUES Groups can brainstorm issues that deal directly with daily school life. They should present a written argument about why a particular issue is a problem and suggestions for how it might be solved. If appropriate, groups can be encouraged to present their arguments to the school administration.

This project is a large undertaking. You might want to set aside a few minutes at the end of class every day so that groups can meet under your supervision. You also might have to make arrangements with school officials for rehearsal time and space.

3 Sharing the Performances

The idea of issues theater is to reach as large an audience as possible with your message. Therefore, the perfect culmination of this project is performances in front of the entire student body, teachers, and administration. If such arrangements cannot be made, at least try to invite another class to watch. Videotaping the performances will allow you to let other teachers use the tapes for their classes.

After the performances, meet again as a class to review and discuss the project and its successes and failures. Students should be able to explain what they might do differently if they had to do this assignment over.

 Assessing the Project

The following rubric can be used for group or individual assessment.

3 Full Accomplishment Students follow directions and produce a theatrical presentation depicting a clear point of view on an issue important to them.

2 Substantial Accomplishment Students produce a presentation on an important issue, but it lacks a clear message or is not presented in the most effective medium.

1 Little or Partial Accomplishment Students' presentation is incomplete or does not fulfill the requirements of the assignment.

For the Portfolio
If you made a video of the performances, keep the tape in your classroom or the school library for future reference. Include copies of the project descriptions and your own written assessment in each student's portfolio. You also might want to include any reviews published in the school newspaper.

Note: For other assessment options, see the *Teacher's Guide to Assessment and Portfolio Use.*

Cross-Curricular Options

LANGUAGE ARTS
Ask students to take a modern issue and turn it into an Aesop-like fable concluding with a moral. Issues can be disguised within the context of the fable, but should be spelled out clearly in the moral.

SCIENCE
 You might ask groups that have selected an environmental issue to prepare posters that explain pollution, smog, acid rain, or another topic. Encourage them to ask for help from the science teacher.

SOCIAL STUDIES
 Groups can find out if the issue they selected has been relevant to any other society or civilization. They should note what happened, if a solution was found, and what effect the solution had.

LANGUAGE ARTS
Individuals or groups can compose letters to city officials inviting them to attend the performances. Letters should explain the project and its purpose and give a list of issues to be covered. You might also alert a local television station of the event in the same way.

Resources

Who's Running Your Life? A Look at Young People's Rights by Jules Archer discusses the rights and responsibilities of young people.

Taking a Stand Against Environmental Pollution by David E. Newton stresses what every person can do to help the environment.

Mime: Basics for Beginners by Cindie Straub and Matthew Straub explains the fundamentals of mime.

UNIT TWO **PART 2**

WHAT DO YOU THINK?

───── Objectives ─────

The activities on this page can be used to

- introduce the theme of "Making Choices" since each activity is connected to one or more of the selections in Part 2
- create materials for students' personal portfolios that they can return to later for reconsideration or revision
- build an understanding of theme that students can develop as they work through the unit

How would you handle this situation?
In each small group, have students form two teams to argue for or against intervention. Each team should present an argument and reasons to support it. Then have students switch sides and argue for the opposite side. (See "Say It With Flowers," p. 181; "Choices," p. 193.)

What would you choose?
Students should also consider the results of each unpopular choice to evaluate whether the decision turned out to be good or bad. (See "Say It With Flowers," p. 181; "It Happened in Montgomery" and "Choices," p. 193; *A Christmas Carol*, p. 218.)

What's your recipe for perfection?
If students are unfamiliar with the format of a recipe, you may wish to bring in some examples to which they can refer. Suggest that students think of real-life role models to help them create their "perfect" ones. (See "Eleanor Roosevelt," p. 203.)

MAKING CHOICES

WHAT DO YOU THINK?

REFLECTING ON THEME

Some choices in life are easy and of little consequence. Others are more difficult and involve some risk. Still others can even alter the course of history. Use the activities on this page to help you consider what choices you might make, how you might make them, and what they might say about you.

What would you choose?

With a group of classmates, brainstorm a list of situations in which people have made unpopular choices. Include situations from history and from personal experience. Then share your list with other groups.

How would you handle this situation?

Suppose two of your friends are trading baseball cards. Patrick wants to trade Kenneth a worthless card for one that he knows is very valuable. Kenneth doesn't know the card's real worth. Would you choose to do nothing, or would you try to keep Kenneth from getting ripped off? Debate your ideas with a group of classmates.

Chris Clark
left field

What's your recipe for perfection?

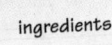
ingredients
1.
2.
3.

If you could create a role model for the world, what "ingredients" would you use? In your notebook, write your recipe for Mr. or Ms. R. Model. First, list the ingredients and quantities; then tell how to combine them, and explain why that particular mix is essential.

Looking Back

At the beginning of this unit, you thought about some of life's lessons and the choices you might make in challenging situations. Now that you have read the selections in the first part of Unit Two, have your ideas changed? In your notebook, write a paragraph about a lesson you learned from the selections, describing the effect that the lesson has had on you.

Looking Back
Self-Assessment Encourage students to review the selections in Part 1 and to identify the one that had the most impact on their thinking. Tell students to jot down their ideas about its lesson and about how that lesson has influenced them. Encourage students to think about situations to which the lesson might apply.

PARENTAL INVOLVEMENT
Invite students to write a poem about a difficult choice that a parent or a relative made. Have students first discuss with the parent or relative the situation in which the choice was made, how he or she reached a decision, and what was learned as a result. Students should then convey in a poem the ideas and feelings that the parent or relative has expressed. Invite volunteers to present their poems to the class.

PREVIEWING

FICTION

Say It with Flowers

Toshio Mori (tō'shē-ō mō'rē)

Activating Prior Knowledge
PERSONAL CONNECTION

Think of experiences that you have had with salesclerks in stores. What qualities do you value most in a salesclerk? Create a chart, like the one shown, in which you list several qualities and then rank them in order of importance. Share your chart with a small group of classmates.

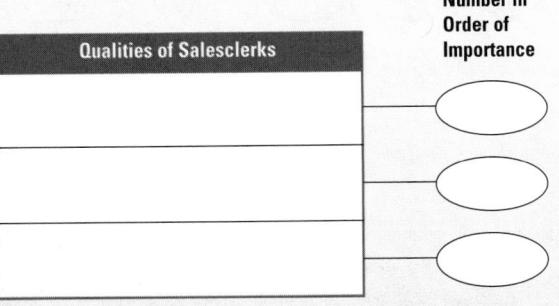

Qualities of Salesclerks	Number in Order of Importance
	◯
	◯
	◯

Setting a Purpose
WRITING CONNECTION

Imagine you are the owner of a new business opening in a shopping mall. In your notebook, create a want ad that describes the qualities you are looking for in a salesclerk who will work for you. Refer to the chart you created for the Personal Connection. Then as you read, think about the qualities of the salesclerks in this story.

Help Wanted

Building Background
COMMUNITY CONNECTION

"Say It with Flowers" is about a salesclerk who works in a flower shop in Yokohama, California, a fictional community based on the Japanese-American community where writer Toshio Mori lived in the late 1930s and early 1940s. Mori worked in a plant nursery, where he acquired firsthand experience in the flower business.

Like other business people, flower shop owners try both to please their customers and to make a profit. Selling flowers, however, can be a risky business. If cut flowers are not sold within a certain time, they wither and die, and the flower shop loses money. If the shop continues to lose money, the owner may go out of business, and the employees would then lose their jobs. Thus, shop owners must sell as much of their stock as they can—older flowers as well as fresh ones.

SAY IT WITH FLOWERS **181**

SAY IT WITH FLOWERS

by Toshio Mori

SUMMARY

The narrator and Tommy are working in Mr. Sasaki's flower shop when Teruo comes in and asks for a job. Mr. Sasaki and Tommy teach Teruo about the business. Teruo does well until he learns that he must lie to customers about the freshness of the flowers. If he doesn't lie, the older flowers won't be sold, and profits will drop. Teruo tries lying and hates it. When he answers customers' questions truthfully, Mr. Sasaki threatens to fire him. Teruo then begins selling only the freshest flowers and giving customers much more than they pay for. Mr. Sasaki fires Teruo, and Teruo cheerfully leaves.

Thematic Link: *Making Choices* Teruo must decide which is more important—pleasing his boss or maintaining his integrity.

CUSTOMIZING FOR
Students Acquiring English

- Use **ACCESS FOR STUDENTS ACQUIRING ENGLISH,** Reading and Writing Support.

- If possible, invite Japanese-American students to model the correct pronunciation of the names Toshio Mori, Sasaki, and Teruo.

Art Note

***The Flowers I Sent Myself (I'm So Very Thoughtful)* by P. S. Gordon** Unlike many contemporary artists who strive to eliminate details in an attempt to capture the essence of a subject, Gordon attempts to include as many details as possible in his paintings. This watercolor is typical of his work in its combination of precise rendering and airbrushed background.

Reading the Art *The artist has said, "For me, more is better." How does this painting express his statement?*

P. S. Gordon is an artist living in Oklahoma. He is represented by Peter Tatistcheff Gallery in New York. *The Flowers I Sent Myself (I'm So Very Thoughtful),* 1990, is a watercolor on paper, 40" × 60".

182 UNIT TWO   PART 2: MAKING CHOICES

WORDS TO KNOW

comeback (kŭm′băk′) *n.* a response, usually a witty one (p. 185)

deliberation (dĭ-lĭb′ə-rā′shən) *n.* careful thought (p. 186)

disarm (dĭs-ärm′) *v.* to overcome by using charm (p. 184)

ensuing (ĕn-sōō′ĭng) *adj.* coming afterward; following **ensue** *v.* (p. 185)

harmonize (här′mə-nīz′) *v.* to bring into agreement (p. 183)

indignantly (ĭn-dĭg′nənt-lē) *adv.* in an angry way, especially as a result of unjust treatment (p. 189)

inquisitive (ĭn-kwĭz′ĭ-tĭv) *adj.* curious; eager to learn (p. 184)

spree (sprē) *n.* a period in which someone acts very freely (p. 188)

temperament (tĕm′prə-mənt) *n.* a person's characteristic nature (p. 183)

transaction (trăn-săk′shən) *n.* an exchange of money for a product (p. 186)

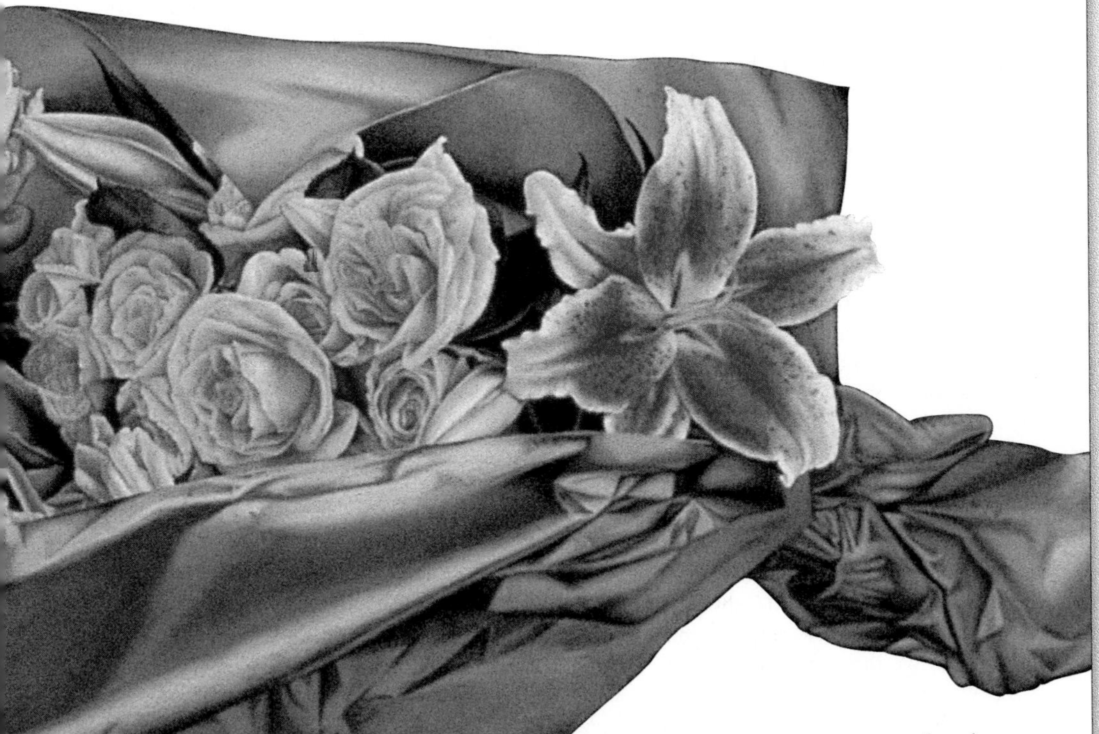

Set a Purpose Have students discuss some of the responsibilities of clerks in a flower store, such as identifying different kinds of flowers and learning how to make bouquets and ring up purchases. Then ask students to read to find out what the other employees teach the new clerk about selling flowers.

Use **UNIT TWO RESOURCE BOOK**, p. 33, for guidance in reading the selection.

CUSTOMIZING FOR
Gifted and Talented Students

As students read, have them discuss their impressions of the employees' views about selling old flowers and how the employees rationalize this practice. Ask students which, if any, opinions they agree with. Make sure that students support their responses with details from the selection and examples from their own experiences.

CUSTOMIZING FOR
Multiple Learning Styles

A **Bodily-Kinesthetic Learners** Invite students to role-play the interview between Teruo and Mr. Sasaki, with the narrator looking on. Guide students to use gestures as well as dialogue to show the interaction between these characters.

Critical Thinking: CLASSIFYING

B Ask students how they would describe the narrator's character, based on his decision to say nothing and watch Mr. Sasaki and the young man. *(Possible response: He is cautious, shrewd, and perceptive.)*

He was a queer one to come to the shop and ask Mr. Sasaki for a job, but at the time I kept my mouth shut. There was something about this young man's appearance which I could not altogether harmonize with a job as a clerk in a flower shop. I was a delivery boy for Mr. Sasaki then. I had seen clerks come and go, and although they were of various sorts of temperaments and conducts, all of them had the technique of waiting on the customers or acquired one eventually. You could never tell about a new one, however, and to be on the safe side, I said nothing and watched

A

B

WORDS
TO
KNOW

harmonize (här′mə-nīz′) *v.* to bring into agreement
temperament (tĕm′prə-mənt) *n.* a person's characteristic nature

183

Mini-Lesson Reading Skills/Strategies

ACTIVE READING: QUESTION Explain to students that active readers ask questions about what is happening as they read. Tell students that another important element in questioning is making mental notes about words or statements that confuse them. Be sure students understand that it is important not to get sidetracked by this process. Things may get clearer as they read more of the story.

Application Point out the narrator's statement that he "could not altogether harmonize [Teruo's appearance] with a job as a clerk in a flower

shop." Model how students might phrase the question, "I don't understand what the narrator means by this." Have students read on to find an answer and to jot down clues on a chart like the one shown.

Have students use their charts to answer the question. *(Possible response: The narrator means that Teruo looks and seems different from the other clerks.)* Students may find it helpful to create similar charts as they read other selections.

Reteaching/Reinforcement
• *Unit Two Resource Book,* p. 34

Teruo's "Normal" Traits	Teruo's "Odd" Traits
curious	won't lie
works hard	gives away flowers
learns fast	undercharges customers

our boss readily take on this young man. Anyhow, we were glad to have an extra hand.

Mr. Sasaki undoubtedly remembered last year's rush when Tommy, Mr. Sasaki and I had to do everything and had our hands tied behind our backs for having so many things to do at one time. He wanted to be ready this time. "Another clerk and we'll be all set for any kind of business," he used to tell us. When Teruo came around looking for a job, he got it, and Morning Glory Flower Shop was all set for the year as far as our boss was concerned.

When Teruo reported for work the following morning, Mr. Sasaki left him in Tommy's hands. Tommy was our number one clerk for a long time.

"Tommy, teach him all you can," Mr. Sasaki said. "Teruo's going to be with us from now on."

"Sure," Tommy said.

"Tommy's a good florist. You watch and listen to him," the boss told the young man.

"All right, Mr. Sasaki," the young man said. He turned to us and said, "My name is Teruo." We shook hands.

We got to know one another pretty well after that. He was a quiet fellow with very little words for anybody, but his smile <u>disarmed</u> a person. We soon learned that he knew nothing about the florist business. He could identify a rose when he saw one, and gardenias and carnations too; but other flowers and materials were new to him.

"You fellows teach me something about this business, and I'll be grateful. I want to start from the bottom," Teruo said.

Tommy and I nodded. We were pretty sure by then he was all right. Tommy eagerly went about showing Teruo the florist game. Every morning for several days Tommy repeated the prices of the flowers for him. He told Teruo

what to do on telephone orders; how to keep the greens fresh; how to make bouquets, corsages, and sprays.[1] "You need a little more time to learn how to make big funeral pieces," Tommy said. "That'll come later."

In a couple of weeks Teruo was just as good a clerk as we had had in a long time. He was curious almost to a fault and was a glutton for work. It was about this time our boss decided to move ahead his yearly business trip to Seattle. Undoubtedly he was satisfied with Teruo, and he knew we could get along without him for a while. He went off and left Tommy in full charge.

uring Mr. Sasaki's absence I was often in the shop helping Tommy and Teruo with the customers and the orders. One day when Teruo learned that I once worked in the nursery and had experience in flower growing, he became <u>inquisitive</u>.

"How do you tell when a flower is fresh or old?" he asked me. "I can't tell one from the other. All I do is follow your instructions and sell the ones you tell me to sell first, but I can't tell one from the other."

I laughed. "You don't need to know that, Teruo," I told him. "When the customers ask you whether the flowers are fresh, say yes firmly. 'Our flowers are always fresh, madam.'"

Teruo picked up a vase of carnations. "These flowers came in four or five days ago, didn't they?"

"You're right. Five days ago," I said.

"How long will they keep if a customer bought them today?" Teruo asked.

"I guess in this weather they'll hold a day or two," I said.

"Then they're old," Teruo almost gasped.

1. **sprays:** decorative flat arrangements of flowers, often used for funerals.

WORDS TO KNOW
disarm (dĭs--ärm') *v.* to overcome by using charm
inquisitive (ĭn-kwĭz'ĭ-tĭv) *adj.* curious; eager to learn

184

Mini-Lesson 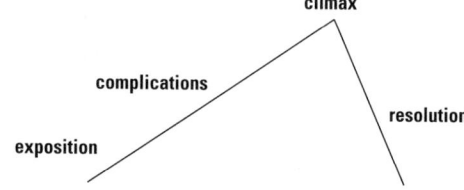 **Literary Concepts**

REVIEWING CLIMAX Remind students that the climax of a story is its turning point, the high point of interest in the plot. To help students identify the climax, review plot and its components. Explain that plot is the sequence of related events that make up a story; it is the blueprint of the action, or what happens in the story. The exposition introduces the characters and the conflict they face. Complications set in as the characters try to resolve the conflict. Eventually, the plot reaches the climax, the highest point of suspense. The final stage is the

resolution, in which loose ends are tied up and the story is brought to a close.

Application As students read "Say It with Flowers," have them complete the following plot diagram.

"Why, we have fresh ones that last a week or so in the shop."

"Sure, Teruo. And why should you worry about that?" Tommy said. "You talk right to the customers, and they'll believe you. 'Our flowers are always fresh? You bet they are! Just came in a little while ago from the market.'"

Teruo looked at us calmly. "That's a hard thing to say when you know it isn't true."

"You've got to get it over with sooner or later," I told him. "Everybody has to do it. You too, unless you want to lose your job."

"I don't think I can say it convincingly again," Teruo said. "I must've said yes forty times already when I didn't know any better. It'll be harder next time."

"You've said it forty times already, so why can't you say yes forty million times more? What's the difference? Remember, Teruo, it's your business to live," Tommy said.

"I don't like it," Teruo said.

"Do we like it? Do you think we're any different from you?" Tommy asked Teruo. "You're just a green kid. You don't know any better, so I don't get sore, but you got to play the game when you're in it. You understand, don't you?"

Teruo nodded. For a moment he stood and looked curiously at us for the first time and then went away to water the potted plants.

QUESTION

Why does Teruo look curiously at Tommy and the narrator?

a Reading Log

In the ensuing weeks we watched Teruo develop into a slick sales clerk, but for one thing. If a customer forgot to ask about the condition of the flowers, Teruo did splendidly. But if someone should mention about the freshness of the flowers, he wilted right in front of the customer's eyes. Sometimes he would sputter. On other occasions he would stand gaping speechless, without a <u>comeback</u>. Sometimes, looking embarrassedly at us, he would take the customer to the fresh flowers in the rear and complete the sale.

"Don't do that anymore, Teruo," Tommy warned him one afternoon after watching him repeatedly sell the fresh ones. "You know we got plenty of the old stuff in the front. We can't throw all that stuff away. First thing you know the boss'll start losing money, and we'll all be thrown out."

"I wish I could sell like you," Teruo said. "Whenever they ask me, 'Is this fresh? How long will it keep?' I lose all sense about selling the stuff and begin to think of the difference between the fresh and the old stuff. Then the trouble begins."

"Remember, the boss has to run the shop so he can keep it going," Tommy told him. "When he returns next week, you better not let him see you touch the fresh flowers in the rear."

On the day Mr. Sasaki came back to the shop, we saw something unusual. For the first time I watched Teruo sell old stuff to a customer. I heard the man plainly ask him if the flowers would keep good, and very clearly I heard Teruo reply, "Yes, sir. These flowers'll keep good." I looked at Tommy, and he winked back. When Teruo came back to make it into a bouquet, he looked as if he had just discovered a snail in his mouth. Mr. Sasaki came back to the rear and watched him make the bouquet. When Teruo went up front to complete the sale, Mr. Sasaki looked at Tommy and nodded approvingly.

When I went out to the truck to make my last delivery for the day, Teruo followed me. "Gee, I feel rotten," he said to me. "Those flowers I sold won't last longer than tomorrow. I feel lousy. I'm lousy. The people'll get to know my word pretty soon."

WORDS TO KNOW	**ensuing** (ĕn-sōō′ĭng) *adj.* coming afterward; following **ensue** *v.* **comeback** (kŭm′băk′) *n.* a response, usually a witty one

185

Mini-Lesson ✏ **Grammar**

COMPOUND AND COMPLEX SENTENCES
Remind students that compound sentences consist of two or more simple sentences that are joined together. The writer's choice of coordinating conjunctions *(and, but, or, for, so)* shows the relationship between ideas that are equal in importance. Then explain that complex sentences contain one main clause and one or more subordinate clauses.

Application Have students identify each of the following sentences from the story as compound or complex. Then have them write two more examples of each kind of sentence.

1. "You talk right to the customers, and they'll believe you." *(compound)*
2. If a customer forgot to ask about the condition of the flowers, Teruo did splendidly. *(complex)*
3. "When he returns next week, you better not let him see you touch the fresh flowers." *(complex)*

Reteaching/Reinforcement
- *Grammar Handbook,* anthology p. 850
- *Grammar Mini-Lessons* copymasters, p. 37, transparencies, pp. 46–47

📖 **The Writer's Craft**

Complex Sentences, pp. 565–566

K Ask students to discuss how Teruo's feelings here might foreshadow the story's climax. *(Possible responses: He feels bad because he is lying. The climax may have something to do with his feelings about lying to customers.)*

Critical Thinking: ANALYZING

L Ask students to analyze Mr. Sasaki's comments and question their validity. *(Possible responses: Mr. Sasaki is trying to rationalize his lying to his customers. By denying that the flowers are old, Mr. Sasaki can ignore any guilt he may feel because of his deceit.)*

STRATEGIC READING FOR
Less-Proficient Readers

M Ask students what reason Teruo gives for not selling the old flowers. *(Lying makes him feel rotten.)*
Summarizing

Set a Purpose Have students read to discover if Teruo heeds Mr. Sasaki's warning.

CUSTOMIZING FOR
Students Acquiring English

I Students should be able to infer from the context that *get* in these sentences means "understand."

Active Reading: CLARIFY

N Explore with students the different reasons why Mr. Sasaki feels annoyed at Teruo. Use this model to show how students might make inferences and draw conclusions.

Think-Aloud Model *First, Mr. Sasaki tells Tommy that Teruo's reason for his actions is no good for a businessman. That shows he's angry about losing money. But when he tells Teruo that he's a good boy, I think he's also annoyed because he feels he made a mistake in hiring Teruo.*

"Forget it," I said. "Quit worrying. What's the matter with you?"

K "I'm lousy," he said, and went back to the store.

Then one early morning the inevitable happened. While Teruo was selling the fresh flowers in the back to a customer, Mr. Sasaki came in quietly and watched the <u>transaction</u>. The boss didn't say anything at the time. All day Teruo looked sick. He didn't know whether to explain to the boss or shut up.

While Teruo was out to lunch, Mr. Sasaki called us aside. "How long has this been going on?" he asked us. He was pretty sore.

"He's been doing it off and on. We told him to quit it," Tommy said. "He says he feels rotten selling the old flowers."

L "Old flowers!" snorted Mr. Sasaki. "I'll tell him plenty when he comes back. Old flowers! Maybe you can call them old at the wholesale market, but they're not old in a flower shop."

"He feels guilty fooling the customers," Tommy explained.

The boss laughed impatiently. "That's no reason for a businessman."

When Teruo came back, he knew what was up. He looked at us for a moment and then went about cleaning the stems of the old flowers.

"Teruo," Mr. Sasaki called.

Teruo approached us as if steeled for an attack.

"You've been selling fresh flowers and leaving the old ones to go to waste. I can't afford that, Teruo," Mr. Sasaki said. "Why don't you do as you're told? We all sell the flowers in the front. I tell you they're not old in a flower shop. Why can't you sell them?"

"I don't like it, Mr. Sasaki," Teruo said. "When the people ask me if they're fresh, I hate to answer. I feel rotten after selling the

old ones."

"Look here, Teruo," Mr. Sasaki said. "I don't want to fire you. You're a good boy, and I know you need a job, but you've got to be a good clerk here or you're going out. Do you get me?"

"I get you," Teruo said.

CLARIFY

N Why is Mr. Sasaki annoyed?

In the morning we were all at the shop early. I had an eight o'clock delivery, and the others had to rush with a big funeral order. Teruo was there early. "Hello," he greeted us cheerfully as we came in. He was unusually high-spirited, and I couldn't account for it. He was there before us and had already filled out the eight o'clock package for me.

He was almost through with the funeral frame, padding it with wet moss and covering it all over with brake fern, when Tommy came in. When Mr. Sasaki arrived, Teruo waved his hand and cheerfully went about gathering the flowers for the funeral piece. As he flitted here and there, he seemed as if he had forgotten our presence, even the boss. He looked at each vase, sized up the flowers, and then cocked his head at the next one. He did this with great <u>deliberation</u>, as if he were the boss and the last word in the shop. That was all right, but when a customer soon after came in, he swiftly attended him as if he owned all the flowers in the world. When the man asked Teruo if he was getting fresh flowers, without batting an eye he escorted the customer into the rear and eventually showed and sold the fresh ones. He did it with so much grace, dignity and swiftness that we stood around like his stooges.[2] However, Mr. Sasaki went on with his work as if nothing had happened.

---

2. **stooges:** assistants to comedians who act as victims to pranks.

WORDS TO KNOW	**transaction** (trăn-săk'shən) *n.* an exchange of money for a product
	deliberation (dĭ-lĭb'ə-rā'shən) *n.* careful thought

Mini-Lesson **The Writer's Style**

DIFFERENT POINTS OF VIEW Remind students that point of view is the vantage point, or angle, from which a story is told. Explain that the two most common points of view are first person and third person. In the first-person point of view, the narrator is one of the characters in the story and uses first-person pronouns such as *I, me,* and *we*. The reader sees the events of the story and other characters only through the eyes of the narrator. In the third-person point of view, the narrator is not in the story and relates the story using the third-person pronouns, such as *he, she,* or *it*.

Application Have students select one portion of the story and rewrite it from Teruo's point of view. Students can exchange papers and analyze each other's writing to explore how a story can change when told from a different point of view.

Reteaching/Reinforcement
• *Writing Mini-Lessons* transparencies p. 47

 **The Writer's Craft**

Point of View, pp. 318–319

Cyclamen and White Amaryllis (1990), Eric Isenburger, Private Collection, SuperStock.

187

***Cyclamen and White Amaryllis* by Eric Isenburger** Eric Isenburger (1902–1994) spent most of his career in New York City. For many years he served as a mentor to young artists there. This painting, done when the artist was in his late 80s, is typical of his decorative style. Influenced by Henri Matisse, Isenburger liked to work with bright colors and long brush strokes.

Reading the Art *The two plants depicted in the painting are placed close together. Why do you think the artist positioned the plants in this way? How does the use of a bright blue background affect the mood of the painting?*

Mini-Lesson ⚾ Study Skills

TAKING STANDARDIZED TESTS Explain to students that no matter what type of standardized test they may take, they can use specific strategies to do well. Explain the following techniques:

1. Carefully read and listen to all directions.
2. Budget your time.
3. Complete the questions you know. Skip any items you are not sure of and return to them if you have time.
4. When using computerized answer sheets, completely fill in the circle for the correct answer. Don't make stray marks in other answer circles.

Application Have students follow these guidelines when they next take a standardized test. After the test, discuss with students how these techniques helped them improve their scores. You may wish to adapt the Comprehension Check on page 189 to follow the multiple-choice format used in many standardized tests. For example, the first question could be rewritten as:

1. Which of the following best describes Teruo's reaction after being told to sell old flowers?
   a) delighted   b) scared   c) shocked
   d) envious   e) complacent

<table><tr><td>

CUSTOMIZING FOR

2 Explain that *fairly* in this sentence means "almost."

3 Make sure that students understand that *not only . . . but* is not a negative construction. Teruo went back to the rear for fresh ones, *and* added three or four extras.

Critical Thinking:
HYPOTHESIZING

O Have students hypothesize about why Teruo disobeys the boss by selling the fresh flowers—even adding extra flowers. Students can debate which hypothesis is most likely to be correct. *(Possible responses: Teruo is deliberately spiting the boss; Teruo is hoping to get fired; Teruo is a good-hearted person who wants to make people happy with the flowers they buy.)*

Linking to Science

P Orchids are one of the largest groups of flowering plants, with more than 30,000 species. Apart from their popularity as display flowers, one species of orchid, *Vanilla planifolia,* is the source of vanilla flavoring used in cookies, cakes, candies, and ice cream.

Active Reading: PREDICT

Q Students might predict that Teruo will admit what he has done or even quit his job. Guide students to see how the plot is building to the climax, Teruo's confrontation with Mr. Sasaki.

STRATEGIC READING FOR
Less-Proficient Readers

R Ask students to summarize Teruo's actions that suggest he did not heed Mr. Sasaki's warning. *(He continues to sell the fresh flowers and even gives some away.)* **Summarizing**
Set a Purpose Students can read to see what finally happens to Teruo.

</td><td>

2

3 **O**

A long towards noon Teruo attended his second customer. He fairly ran to greet an old lady who wanted a cheap bouquet around fifty cents for a dinner table. This time he not only went back to the rear for the fresh ones but added three or four extras. To make it more irritating for the boss, who was watching every move, Teruo used an extra lot of maidenhair[3] because the old lady was appreciative of his art of making bouquets. Tommy and I watched the boss fuming inside of his office.

When the old lady went out of the shop, Mr. Sasaki was furious. "You're a blockhead. You have no business sense. What are you doing here?" he said to Teruo. "Are you crazy?"

Teruo looked cheerful enough. "I'm not crazy, Mr. Sasaki," he said. "And I'm not dumb. I just like to do it that way, that's all."

The boss turned to Tommy and me. "That boy's a sap,"[4] he said. "He's got no head."

Teruo laughed and walked off to the front with a broom. Mr. Sasaki shook his head. "What's the matter with him? I can't understand him," he said.

While the boss was out to lunch, Teruo went on a mad <u>spree</u>. He waited on three customers at one time, ignoring our presence. It was amazing how he did it. He hurriedly took one customer's order and had him write a birthday greeting for it, jumped to the second customer's side and persuaded her to buy roses because they were the freshest of the lot. She wanted them delivered, so he jotted the address down on the sales book and leaped to the third customer.

"I want to buy that orchid in the window," she stated without deliberation.

"Do you have to have orchid, madam?"

"No," she said. "But I want something nice for tonight's ball, and I think the orchid will

</td><td>

match my dress. Why do you ask?"

"If I were you, I wouldn't buy that orchid," he told her. "It won't keep. I could sell it to you and make a profit, but I don't want to do that and spoil your evening. Come to the back, madam, and I'll show you some of the nicest gardenias in the market today. We call them Belmont, and they're fresh today."

He came to the rear with the lady. We watched him pick out three of the biggest gardenias and make them into a corsage. When the lady went out with her package, a little boy about eleven years old came in and wanted a twenty-five-cent bouquet for his mother's birthday. Teruo waited on the boy. He was out in the front, and we saw him pick out a dozen of the two-dollar-a-dozen roses and give them to the kid.

Tommy nudged me. "If he was the boss, he couldn't do those things," he said.

"In the first place," I said, "I don't think he could be a boss."

"What do you think?" Tommy said. "Is he crazy? Is he trying to get himself fired?"

"I don't know," I said.

When Mr. Sasaki returned, Teruo was waiting on another customer, a young lady.

PREDICT

What will Teruo do now that his boss has returned?
Using a Reading Log

"Did Teruo eat yet?" Mr. Sasaki asked Tommy.

"No, he won't go. He says he's not hungry today," Tommy said.

We watched Teruo talking to the young lady. The boss shook his head. Then it came. Teruo came back to the rear and picked out a

---

3. **maidenhair:** a fern with delicate fronds, used to provide fullness in bouquets.
4. **sap:** slang for stupid person.

WORDS
TO **spree** (sprē) *n.* a period in which someone acts very freely
KNOW

188

</td></tr></table>

Assessment ✓ Option

INFORMAL ASSESSMENT You may wish to assess students' understanding of "Say It with Flowers" by having them write a critical review of the story. The review should evaluate the author's success in handling such elements as plot, characters, setting, conflict, and suspense. Direct students to use details from the story to make their point, but caution them against merely summarizing the plot. Students should include at least three literary elements in their analyses.

Rubric

3 Full Accomplishment Students evaluate the story by considering at least three story elements. Each point is supported with specific examples drawn from the story.

2 Substantial Accomplishment Students evaluate the story but are unable to provide detailed support for their opinions. Fewer than three literary elements are included.

I Little or Partial Accomplishment Students summarize rather than evaluate the story; they have difficulty using literary terms.

dozen of the very fresh white roses and took them out to the lady.

"Aren't they lovely!" we heard her exclaim.

We watched him come back, take down a box, place several maidenhairs and asparagus,[5] place the roses neatly inside, sprinkle a few drops, and then give it to her. We watched him thank her, and we noticed her smile and thanks. The girl walked out.

Mr. Sasaki ran excitedly to the front. "Teruo! She forgot to pay!"

Teruo stopped the boss on the way out. "Wait, Mr. Sasaki," he said. "I gave it to her."

"What!" the boss cried <u>indignantly</u>.

"She came in just to look around and see the flowers. She likes pretty roses. Don't you think she's wonderful?"

"What's the matter with you?" the boss said. "Are you crazy? What did she buy?"

"Nothing, I tell you," Teruo said. "I gave it to her because she admired it, and she's pretty enough to deserve beautiful things, and I liked her."

"You're fired! Get out!" Mr. Sasaki spluttered. "Don't come back to the store again."

"And I gave her fresh ones too," Teruo said.

Mr. Sasaki rolled out several bills from his pocketbook. "Here's your wages for this week. Now get out," he said.

"I don't want it," Teruo said. "You keep it and buy some more flowers."

"Here, take it. Get out," Mr. Sasaki said.

Teruo took the bills and rang up the cash register. "All right, I'll go now. I feel fine. I'm happy. Thanks to you." He waved his hand to Mr. Sasaki. "No hard feelings."

On the way out Teruo remembered our presence. He looked back. "Good-bye. Good luck," he said cheerfully to Tommy and me.

He walked out of the shop with his shoulders straight, head high, and whistling. He did not come back to see us again. ❖

5. **asparagus:** a plant with fine, fernlike leaves.

LITERARY INSIGHT

old age sticks
by E. E. Cummings

old age sticks
up Keep
Off
signs)&

youth yanks them
down(old
age
cries No

Tres)&(pas)
youth laughs
(sing
old age

scolds Forbid
den Stop
Must
n't Don't

&)youth goes
right on
gr
owing old

WORDS TO KNOW

indignantly (ĭn-dĭg'nənt-lē) *adv.* in an angry way, especially as a result of unjust treatment

189

Literary Concept: TITLE

S Have students discuss what flowers mean to Teruo and Mr. Sasaki. *(Possible response: To Teruo, flowers are a way to express tender concern for another person's feelings; to Mr. Sasaki, flowers have only monetary value as a source of profits.)*

COMPREHENSION CHECK

1. How does Teruo react when he is first told to sell old flowers? *(He is shocked.)*
2. Why do Teruo's co-workers ask him to lie to customers? *(to sell the old flowers before they must be thrown out, thereby keeping the business profitable)*
3. What does Mr. Sasaki do when Teruo gives flowers away? *(He fires Teruo.)*

INSIGHT

1. What do you consider unusual about this poem? *(no formal sentences; unusual capitalization and punctuation)*
2. How would you explain what the last stanza means? *(Possible response: Youth rebels against old age but can't prevent itself from getting old too.)*
3. What connections do you see between this poem and "Say It with Flowers"? *(Possible response: This poem is about the inevitable conflict between the old and the young because of their different perspectives; Mori's short story is about the conflict between Mr. Sasaki and a young sales clerk because of their different views about how to run a business.)*

E. E. CUMMINGS

Cummings (1894–1962) wrote poems that were strikingly original in form and style—with intentional spelling, punctuation, and grammatical irregularities. Harvard-educated and wealthy, he drove an ambulance during World War I, painted extensively, and continued his experiments with "typographical poetry" throughout his life. His efforts on behalf of free, individual expression reflected his belief in the importance of the self.

Mini-Lesson Spelling

WORDS ENDING IN -ATE/-ION Often when a suffix is added to a word, it changes the part of speech of the word. For example, the adjective *deliberate* becomes the noun *deliberation* when the suffix *-ion* is added; the verb *transact* becomes the noun *transaction*. Students should note that a final silent e is dropped before adding *-ion*.

Application Have students add the suffix *-ate* or *-ion* to each of the following words: *alien, regulate, passion, recess,* and *dissect.*

Ask students to look for more words that fit this pattern, in their own writing and in things that they read, and to add those words to their personal word lists.

Reteaching/Reinforcement
• *Unit Two Resource Book,* p. 35

From Personal Response to Critical Analysis

1. Accept all reasonable responses.
2. Some students may say that Teruo acted irrationally or spitefully in giving away flowers. Other students may say that Teruo showed great kindness to his customers.
3. Possible responses: Some students may predict that the shop would have gone out of business or had much lower profits. Others may say that Teruo's honesty and generosity would have attracted more customers and increased profits.
4. Possible response: Teruo is too honest to lie about the freshness of the flowers. He does not want to compromise his own integrity and deceive people who trust him.
5. He might agree that youth rebels against the old, or he might not see his actions as a rebellion at all.
6. Possible responses: Teruo was an excellent clerk because he helped the customers; he was a very poor clerk because he gave customers more than they paid for and made the shop less profitable, thereby putting the business in jeopardy. Mr. Sasaki would agree with the latter assessment.

Another Pathway

Cooperative Learning Arrange students in groups of six. Within each group, have one pair of students argue that Teruo could be a boss and another pair of students argue that he couldn't. Have each pair present its position and supporting arguments to the other. Assign a group differentiator to help the whole group discuss the issue and critically evaluate the opposing positions. Finally, have a group recorder write a report that includes both positions and their supporting evidence.

Rubric

3 Full Accomplishment Students prepare well-supported arguments and a thorough, well-written report.

2 Substantial Accomplishment Students prepare partially supported arguments and a partially completed report.

1 Little or Partial Accomplishment Students are unable to argue both positions, and they provide an incomplete and poorly written report.

RESPONDING OPTIONS

FROM PERSONAL RESPONSE TO CRITICAL ANALYSIS

REFLECT
1. Did you expect the story to end the way it did? Share your response with a partner.

RETHINK
2. How would you evaluate Teruo's conduct on his last day at work?
   Consider Close Textual Reading
   • his treatment of the customers
   • his motives for acting as he does
   • other ways he might have handled his conflict with Mr. Sasaki

Thematic Link
3. What if Mr. Sasaki had chosen not to fire Teruo? What do you think would have happened to the Morning Glory Flower Shop?

4. Why do you think Teruo finds it so difficult to follow Mr. Sasaki's orders for selling flowers?

RELATE
5. How do you imagine Teruo would respond to the views expressed by the speaker of the Insight poem on page 189?

6. Look back at the chart you created for the Personal Connection on page 181. How would you evaluate Teruo as a salesclerk? How would you compare your evaluation with Mr. Sasaki's?

Multimodal Learning
ANOTHER PATHWAY

The narrator says that he does not think Teruo could be a boss. Do you agree or disagree with this opinion? Debate this issue with other students in a small group. Then present a summary of the group's arguments to the rest of the class.

QUICKWRITES

1. What qualities might Mr. Sasaki think a good salesclerk should have? Describe these qualities in a **help-wanted ad** that Mr. Sasaki might place in a local newspaper.

2. In what occupations do you think Teruo would be successful? List two or more careers and explain your recommendations in a **profile** that a job counselor might write after having interviewed Teruo.

3. Write a **sequel** to this story, telling what happens to Teruo on his next job.

📁 *PORTFOLIO Save your writing. You may want to use it later as a springboard to a piece for your portfolio.*

LITERARY CONCEPTS

The **title** of a work of literature often says something significant about the work as a whole. The title of this story, "Say It with Flowers," is an advertising slogan. What statement do you think Teruo makes with flowers at the end of the story?

CONCEPT REVIEW: Climax The **climax** of a story is the point at which the conflict is resolved. At what point does Teruo act as if he has made his decision? Is that the climax of the story? Support your opinion with evidence from the story.

Literary Concepts

Have students work in pairs to analyze the title. Students might see the title as an ironic comment on flowers as symbols of love, affection, and sympathy. When Teruo tries to use flowers as they are intended, he is fired. Other students might say that Teruo uses the flowers to tell his boss that he does not respect him.

CONCEPT REVIEW Some students may argue that the climax occurs when Teruo goes on his mad spree; others will say it occurs when Mr. Sasaki fires Teruo.

QuickWrites

1. Guide students to analyze Mr. Sasaki's words and actions to discover what he particularly values in his salesclerks.
2. Students should first create Teruo's character profile to discover what jobs best suit him.
3. Remind students that Teruo's character should be consistent with the way Mori presented him in the story.

 The Writer's Craft

Advertisement, pp.154–156
Character Sketch, pp. 54–61
Short Story, pp. 78–85

Multimodal Learning

ALTERNATIVE ACTIVITIES

1. Imagine that a customer returns to the flower shop either to complain about flowers that did not last or to praise Teruo for his salesmanship. Role-play a **conversation** between the customer and Mr. Sasaki.

2. Create a **television commercial** advertising the Morning Glory Flower Shop. Videotape the commercial and play it for your classmates.

3. Imagine that Teruo now runs his own business, perhaps even a flower shop. Present the **speech** Teruo might give to motivate new employees.

LITERARY LINKS

If you have read "A Crush" on page 15, compare the importance of flowers to Ernie with their importance to Mr. Sasaki.

ACROSS THE CURRICULUM

 Social Studies Working in a small group, research the Better Business Bureau, a corporation organized by businesses to protect consumers against unfair business practices. Find out about the procedures that consumers should follow if they wish to file a complaint against a particular business. Present your group's findings to the class in an **oral report.**

Science Research and report on what happens to flowers after they are cut. Consult reference books and, if possible, interview a science teacher or a local florist. Find answers to the following questions:
- What causes cut flowers to wilt?
- How can you prolong their freshness?
- Why do some cut flowers last longer than others?
- Which cut flowers last longest?

What flowers mean to Ernie

What flowers mean to Mr. Sasaki

What flowers mean to both Ernie and Mr. Sasaki

Social Studies *Cooperative Learning*
Encourage groups to divide the task and form cooperative note-taking pairs. Partners should take notes from their sources independently and then compare what they have found. Tell partners to take something from each other's notes to improve their own. The group should come together to write and present their oral report.

Science Remind students to consider varied aspects of their topic, such as the climate and when the flowers are cut. To help students generate a list of these variables, you may wish to have them begin the project by making a word web around the phrase "cut flowers."

ADDITIONAL SUGGESTIONS

Math *Average Costs* The story mentions specific prices for flowers, such as a twenty-five-cent bouquet and two-dollar-a-dozen roses. Have students call or visit several florists to find out what each shop charges for a bouquet, a dozen roses, and a corsage. Then direct students to calculate the average price for a bouquet, a dozen roses, and a corsage today.

Literary Link

Possible response: To Ernie, flowers represent beauty and a way of showing love. To Mr. Sasaki, flowers represent money in his pocket.

Alternative Activities

1. Before students plan their role-playing, remind them that complaints are treated more seriously when the dissatisfied customer is courteous. Outline the steps in making a complaint: provide brief background, state the problem, and request specific compensation.

2. Suggest that students block out the commercials by preparing storyboards that show what will happen in each brief scene. You may wish to set a time limit for each commercial, such as one to two minutes.

3. Remind students that speeches can be persuasive, informative, or entertaining. Guide them to create a speech that suits the occasion.

EXERCISE A

1. harmonize	6. indignantly
2. temperament	7. deliberation
3. disarm	8. spree
4. inquisitive	9. transaction
5. comeback	10. ensuing

EXERCISE B

Sample dialogue:

"I know I'm being *inquisitive*," I said, "but I'd really like to know if Teruo's selling *spree* was the last straw."

"I doubt it," Tommy replied. "Teruo just didn't have the right *temperament* for this job."

"What about that *transaction* when he gave the boy a dozen two-dollar-a-dozen roses for twenty-five cents!" I said. "No wonder Mr. Sasaki reacted so *indignantly*."

Reteaching/Reinforcement
• *Unit Two Resource Book*, p. 36

TOSHIO MORI

Mori published his first story in 1938, six years after he started working at his family's nursery. Within three years, his stories were being printed in national literary journals. Unfortunately, World War II interrupted Mori's career. It was not until the late 1970s that his writing once more gained attention.

WORDS TO KNOW

EXERCISE A Review the Words to Know in the boxes at the bottom of the selection pages. On your paper, write the word that best completes each sentence below.

1. Will Teruo learn to _____ his ideas with those of his boss?
2. Teruo's quiet yet friendly behavior hinted at his mild ____.
3. With his cheerful smile, Teruo could ____ even an angry customer.
4. Teruo's ____ nature caused him to ask many questions about the flower business.
5. The other clerks told Teruo to respond with a persuasive ____ when a customer asked about the freshness of the flowers.
6. Mr. Sasaki watched ____ as Teruo gave the customers extra flowers.
7. Teruo acted with ___ when he carefully selected and arranged flowers on his last day of work.
8. When Teruo began his selling ____, he moved like a whirlwind through the shop.
9. In one ___, Teruo discouraged a woman from buying orchids and sold her fresh gardenias instead.
10. In the ___ weeks after his firing, how do you think Teruo will feel?

EXERCISE B Using five or more of the Words to Know, improvise a dialogue between the narrator and Tommy about the firing of Teruo.

TOSHIO MORI

Toshio Mori was born and raised in California. His first language was Japanese, which his mother and father spoke at home. In his youth he read between 500 and 1,000 library books each year. For a time, Mori wanted to be a professional baseball player. Later, he considered becoming a monk. Then he decided to become a writer at the age of 22. He was inspired by the stories his mother had related. "She told me of the past and the present, all subjects, human nature, faith, greed, how to live, with frank examples from her own or someone else's life, good or bad." To achieve his goal of becoming a writer, he wrote for 4 hours each night, after working a 12-hour day in his family's nursery and flower shop.

During World War II, Mori was sent to live at the

1910–1980

Topaz, Utah, Relocation Center, one of ten camps in which Japanese Americans were detained after Japan's attack on Pearl Harbor in 1941. During his time there, Mori kept writing. He worked as a historian for the camp and helped to create a camp magazine called *Trek*.

When the war ended, he returned home, only to find that bookworms had destroyed the manuscripts for more than 200 of his stories, which had been hurriedly stored in a barn when his family was forced to leave California. Despite this setback, Mori eventually became the first Japanese American to have a collection of short stories published in the United States.

Mori wrote hundreds of short stories and five novels. Many of his stories show the strength of the human spirit in dealing with the struggles of life.

WHAT DO YOU THINK?

Reflecting on Theme

Have students recall the debate they held before reading the selections in this part of Unit Two. Ask them to recall some of their reasons for or against getting involved if one of their friends were trying to deceive another about the value of a baseball card. Have students consider any new ideas they now wish to add to the debate.

PREVIEWING

POETRY

It Happened in Montgomery
Phil W. Petrie

Choices
Nikki Giovanni

Activating Prior Knowledge
PERSONAL CONNECTION

The two poems that follow are about making choices. What do you think is the most important choice you have had to make in your life so far? On a chart like the one shown, describe that choice.

Building Background
HISTORICAL CONNECTION

A simple choice made by an individual can change the course of history. On December 1, 1955, a tired Rosa Parks, an African American, boarded a city bus in Montgomery, Alabama, and sat down in the middle section. According to city law, African Americans had to vacate middle rows when white passengers could find no seats in front and wished to sit in the middle. When a white passenger wished to sit in Parks's row, the driver ordered her to give up her seat. Parks refused and was arrested at the next bus stop. Her choice inspired Dr. Martin Luther King, Jr., to organize a bus boycott, which became the beginning of the civil rights movement. A little more than a year after the boycott began, the U.S. Supreme Court ruled that segregation on public transportation was unconstitutional. Thereafter, Rosa Parks became known as the mother of the civil rights movement.

Portrait of Dr. Martin Luther King, Jr. Brown Brothers.

I chose to _____

The people who helped me make my choice were
_____
_____
_____

The options I had were
_____
_____
_____

I made my choice because
_____
_____
_____

READING CONNECTION   Active Reading

Reading Modern Poetry Two of the choices modern poets must make when composing a poem are whether or not to use rhyme and whether or not to follow the standard rules for punctuation and capitalization. In addition, modern poets must decide on the length of lines and stanzas. As you read the following poems aloud, think about the choices the speakers describe. Then read the poems again and think about the choices the poets made.

LASERLINKS
• HISTORICAL CONNECTION   **193**

PRINT AND MEDIA RESOURCES

UNIT TWO RESOURCE BOOK
Strategic Reading: Literature, p. 39

FORMAL ASSESSMENT
Selection Test, pp. 43–44
 Test Generator

ACCESS FOR STUDENTS ACQUIRING ENGLISH
Reading and Writing Support

 AUDIO LIBRARY
See Reference Card

 LASERLINKS
Historical Connection

 INTERNET RESOURCES
McDougal Littell Literature Center at http://www.hmco.com /mcdougal/lit

---

OVERVIEW

— **Objectives** —

• To understand and appreciate two modern poems about making choices
• To explore ways to read modern poetry
• To understand free verse
• To express understanding of the poems through a choice of writing forms, including a free-verse poem, a list of questions, and a letter
• To extend understanding of the poems through a variety of multimodal and cross-curricular activities

— **Skills** —

LITERARY CONCEPTS	**SPEAKING, LISTENING, AND VIEWING**
• Free verse	• Role-playing • Oral report

— **Cross-Curricular Connections** —

SOCIAL STUDIES	**MATH**
• Montgomery bus boycott	• Making a pie chart of major ethnic groups

ALTERNATIVE

Previewing

Pairs of students can use the following prompts to preview these poems orally.

Personal Connection

Discussion Prompts *It's good to have the chance to make choices—or is it? How do you feel about making choices? Describe your feelings to your partner. Then listen as your partner describes his or her feelings. You can use these questions to start the discussion:*

• *What choices are easy to make?*

• *Which choices are hard?*

• *What is good about being able to choose?*

• *Why do some people avoid making choices?*

HISTORICAL CONNECTION
I Have a Dream Throughout the 1950s and 1960s, many African Americans made great contributions to the civil rights movement. Among them was the great Martin Luther King, Jr. Here, his entire "I Have a Dream" speech is presented as a backdrop to historical images of the civil rights movement.

Side A, Frame 16092

It Happened in

Montgomery

Rosa Park's arrest on December 1, 1955, for refusing to give up her seat to a whte passenger, touched off a boycott of Montgomery's bus lines by black residents. UPI/Bettmann.

by Phil W. Petrie B

for Rosa Parks

A Then he slammed on the brakes—
Turned around and grumbled.

But she was tired that day.
Weariness was in her bones.
5 And so the thing she's done yesterday,
And yesteryear,
On her workdays,
Churchdays,
Nothing-to-do-guess-I'll-go-and-visit Sister Annie
10 Days—

She felt she'd never do again

And he growled once more

So she said:
No sir . . . I'm stayin' right here.

15 And he gruffly grabbed her,
Pulled and pushed her
Then sharply shoved her through the doors

The news slushed through the littered streets
Slipped into the crowded churches,
20 Slimmered onto the unmagnolied side of town
While the men talked and talked and talked.

She—
Who was tired that day,
Cried and sobbed that she was glad she'd done it.
25 That her soul was satisfied.

That Lord knows,
A little walkin' never hurt anybody;

That in one of those unplanned, unexpected
Unadorned moments—
30 A weary woman turned the page of History.

FROM PERSONAL RESPONSE TO CRITICAL ANALYSIS

REFLECT 1. What words or phrases would you use to describe Rosa Parks? Jot them down in your notebook.

RETHINK 2. Why do you think Rosa Parks chose not to give up her seat?

Choices

by Nikki Giovanni

if i can't do
what i want to do
then my job is to not
do what i don't want
5 to do

it's not the same thing
but it's the best i can
do

if i can't have
10 what i want   then
my job is to want
what i've got
and be satisfied
that at least there
15 is something more
to want

since i can't go
where i need
to go   then i must   go
20 where the signs point
though always understanding
parallel movement
isn't lateral

when i can't express
25 what i really feel
i practice feeling
what i can express
and none of it is equal
i know
30 but that's why mankind
alone among the mammals
learns to cry

Gemini I (1969), Lev T. Mills. Etching, The Evans-Tibbs Collection, Washington, D.C.

CHOICES   **195**

1. Responses will vary.
2. Possible responses: confused, defeated, frustrated, bitter, angry, sad
3. Possible responses: Some students may say that these lines show the speaker's sorrow or anger at not having true freedom of choice and that without these lines the poem would be less sad and less memorable. Other students may say that these lines suggest that everyone shares the speaker's predicament.
4. Possible response: The poem flows more smoothly without punctuation and reflects the uninterrupted flow of thought through the speaker's mind.
5. Possible responses: Rosa Parks might not agree with the speaker's views because she kept her seat and refused to make concessions. The speaker in "Choices" might applaud Parks's bravery.

Literary Link

Have students compare and contrast Rosa Parks to Malcolm X. (*Possible responses: Both people made significant choices and were leaders in the African-American struggle for civil rights. Although both made important contributions, today Malcolm X is the better known of the two.*)

Another Pathway

Groups should have at least ten students, three to take the principal roles and the rest to be passengers. Before they begin, have students discuss the speaker of "Choices" and decide whether he or she would get involved in the incident, and, if so, how.

Rubric

3 Full Accomplishment Students create a skit that accurately reflects the speaker's character in this situation.

2 Substantial Accomplishment Students create a less complete skit.

1 Little or Partial Accomplishment Students misinterpret the speaker's personality and actions.

RESPONDING
OPTIONS

FROM PERSONAL RESPONSE TO CRITICAL ANALYSIS

REFLECT 1. What is your impression of the speaker of "Choices"? Is the speaker male or female, young or old, quiet or outgoing? Discuss your impressions with a partner.

RETHINK 2. How do you think the speaker feels about the choices that he or she must make?

Close Textual Reading 3. How would "Choices" be different without the last three lines?

4. What effect do you think Giovanni creates by omitting capitalization and punctuation? Cite lines from the poem as you explain your opinion.

RELATE 5. How do you think Rosa Parks might respond to the speaker's views in "Choices"? What do you think the speaker in "Choices" might say about Parks's decision in "It Happened in Montgomery"?

LITERARY CONCEPTS

Poetry without regular rhyme, rhythm, or line length is called **free verse.** When you read "It Happened in Montgomery" and "Choices" aloud, you will notice the absence of regular rhyme and rhythm. What other differences do you notice between these two poems and poems with regular rhyme and rhythm, such as "Casey at the Bat" on page 141?

Multimodal Learning
ANOTHER PATHWAY

Imagine that the speaker of "Choices" was on the bus when Rosa Parks decided not to give up her seat. Might the speaker have said or done anything in response to Parks's actions? With a group of classmates, take the parts of Rosa Parks, the bus driver, the speaker of "Choices," and the passengers on the bus and role-play the scene for the rest of the class.

QUICKWRITES

1. Recall the choice you wrote about in Personal Connection on page 193 and write a **free-verse poem** about it. Try to use some of the techniques that Petrie and Giovanni used in their poems.

2. If you could talk to Rosa Parks, what would you ask her? Write a list of five **questions** that you would ask her in an interview about her life.

3. How might Teruo in "Say It with Flowers" respond to the speaker of "Choices"? Write a **letter** that Teruo might write, expressing his reaction.

📁 *PORTFOLIO Save your writing. You may want to use it later as a springboard to a piece for your portfolio.*

Literary Concepts

Cooperative Learning Divide the class into two groups, one to analyze "It Happened in Montgomery" and the other to analyze "Choices." Have each group select a recorder and facilitator. Students can arrange their findings in a chart.

"Casey at the Bat"	*"Choices"*
rhyme scheme	no rhyme
regular beat	uneven rhythm
regular line length	irregular lines

QuickWrites

1. Encourage students to whisper the words of their poem aloud as they write to help them achieve a conversational rhythm.
2. Suggest that students use reporters' 5W's and H—who, what, when, where, why, and how—to spark ideas.
3. Encourage students to reread the story to look at the choices Teruo made. Have students list Teruo's qualities to help them accurately reflect his character.

The Writer's Craft

Interviewing Skills, p. 357

ADDITIONAL SUGGESTIONS

Math *Making a Pie Chart* The United States is a multicultural country. Invite students to look in an almanac to identify the major ethnic groups in the United States and each one's percentage of the total population. Students can create a pie chart to show the results of their research.

PHIL W. PETRIE

In an essay entitled "What Shall I Tell My Sons Who Are Black?" Petrie explains that he tries not to burden his sons' future with the bitterness of the past. "I do not want them to become class conscious and racially myopic," he says. He guides them to provide for and protect their families by getting a good education.

NIKKI GIOVANNI

Giovanni was the subject of the 1987 PBS documentary *Spirit to Spirit: Nikki Giovanni*, directed by Mirra Bank. Giovanni says, "I don't know if I'm a fighter as much as a basic rebel.... The '60s were a successful revolution.... The next battle then is the battle for an individual. Can an individual be who *she* is?"

ACROSS THE CURRICULUM

Social Studies Find out more about the Montgomery bus boycott. Look for answers to the following questions: Who organized it, and why? How long did it last? What were the results? Why was it a success? If you have access to a computer, you might want to begin your research by conducting an on-line search. Present your findings to the class in the form of an oral or written report.

The Bus (1941), Jacob Lawrence. George & Joyce Wein Collection. Photo by Jim Strong, Inc.

PHIL W. PETRIE

Phil Petrie (1921–) has worked as a senior editor at a New York publishing company and as a freelance magazine writer. A graduate of Tennessee State University, Petrie's interests at school were poetry writing, political science, and English.

Petrie tries to reveal people's rights, not only in poems such as "It Happened in Montgomery," but in real life as well. "Regardless of the roles we play, or expect others to play," he said, "it is important that we respond to other humans as persons with desires and needs. We should respect those needs and when we can, support them."

NIKKI GIOVANNI

1943–

Nikki Giovanni, born Yolande Cornelia Giovanni, Jr., has received many awards for her poetry, nonfiction, and recordings. Born in Knoxville, Tennessee, Giovanni graduated with honors from Fisk University and also attended the University of Pennsylvania and Columbia University. A teacher and lecturer as well as a writer, Giovanni founded her own publishing company at the age of twenty-seven. Giovanni's poems often reflect her childhood in Tennessee and her experiences as an African American. She says, "I write out of my own experiences—which also happen to be the experiences of my people. Human beings fascinate me. I just keep trying to dissect them poetically to see what's there."

OTHER WORKS *Ego Tripping and Other Poems for Young People; Black Feeling, Black Talk; Black Judgement;* "Truth Is on Its Way" Extended Reading

IT HAPPENED IN MONTGOMERY/CHOICES **197**

Alternative Activities

1. Have students research another key event from the civil rights movement. Then have them create a poster or collage that shows what the event was and why it was important to the movement.
2. Ask students to think of examples of choices made that changed someone's life or changed history. Have them write a short story about one of these events.

OVERVIEW

Objectives

- To understand and appreciate two lyric poems that give advice about getting the most out of life
- To examine figurative language
- To express understanding of the poems through a choice of writing forms, including a poem, a letter, and a list
- To extend understanding of the story through a variety of multimodal and cross-curricular activities

Skills

LITERARY CONCEPTS
- Figurative language
- Repetition

GENRE STUDY
- Lyric poetry

SPEAKING, LISTENING, AND VIEWING
- Collage
- Oral reading
- Music video

Cross-Curricular Connections

SCIENCE
- Wild horses

ALTERNATIVE

Previewing

Pairs of students can use the following prompts to preview these poems orally.

Writing Connection

Discussion Prompts *Advice takes many forms. It can be casual suggestions to friends or more serious directions on how to live a meaningful life. What advice would you give a friend about life? Talk with a classmate about goals. Start this way:*

- *Here are five important life goals: money, family, career, charity, and having fun. Arrange these from most to least important. Explain to your partner the reasons for your choices.*

POETRY

Barter
Sara Teasdale

Into the Sun
Hannah Kahn

Activating Prior Knowledge

PERSONAL CONNECTION

One of the most popular features in a daily newspaper is the advice column, which contains questions from readers and answers from the columnist. Millions of people read advice columns, looking for little nuggets of good sense or a chuckle. Suppose that you are the writer of such a column and that you are asked to give advice about how to get the most out of middle school or an activity that you enjoy. Get together in a small group to brainstorm ideas.

Building Background

LITERARY CONNECTION

The speakers of "Barter" and "Into the Sun" also give advice—about how to get the most out of life. Both of these poems are examples of lyric poems. **Lyric poems** are personal expressions of ideas and emotions. The language in lyric poems is usually concise and rich in **imagery,** or words and phrases that appeal to the senses—sight, hearing, taste, touch, and smell.

Writing the words

SOARING FIRE

is more appealing | than simply writing

fire

Ask Norm
Advice that Works

Dear Norm,
Help! I've got a problem with my little sister. She always wants to

Setting a Purpose

WRITING CONNECTION

Recall the ideas you discussed for the Personal Connection. Using some of these ideas, write a brief column of advice. Then read the poems several times—silently and aloud. As you read, compare the advice you wrote down with the advice provided by each of the speakers.

198   UNIT TWO   PART 2: MAKING CHOICES

PRINT AND MEDIA RESOURCES

UNIT TWO RESOURCE BOOK
Strategic Reading: Literature, p. 43

ACCESS FOR STUDENTS ACQUIRING ENGLISH
Reading and Writing Support

FORMAL ASSESSMENT
Selection Test, pp. 45–46
Test Generator

AUDIO LIBRARY
See Reference Card

Barter

by Sara Teasdale

Life has loveliness to sell,
   All beautiful and splendid things,
Blue waves whitened on a cliff,
   Soaring fire that sways and sings,
5 And children's faces looking up
Holding wonder like a cup.

Life has loveliness to sell,
   Music like a curve of gold,
Scent of pine trees in the rain,
10   Eyes that love you, arms that hold,
And for your spirit's still delight,
Holy thoughts that star the night.

Spend all you have for loveliness,
   Buy it and never count the cost;
15 For one white singing hour of peace
   Count many a year of strife well lost,
And for a breath of ecstasy
   Give all you have been, or could be.

BARTER   **199**

FROM **PERSONAL RESPONSE** *TO* **CRITICAL ANALYSIS**

REFLECT   1. Which image from this poem appeals to you the most? Share your response with a partner.

RETHINK   2. The word *barter* means "to trade or exchange." Why do you think the poet selected this word as the title of the poem?

          3. How would you explain what the speaker means by the line "Spend all you have for loveliness"?

RELATE   4. How do you think the speaker of this poem would respond to the old saying "The best things in life are free"? Explain your answer.

Mini-Lesson   Genre Study

POETRY Remind students that **lyric poetry** is a type of poetry that expresses ideas and feelings in compact, imaginative, and musical language, using rich imagery. Then draw on the chalkboard the chart shown and use it to explore the effect of an image.

Application Have students copy the chart into their notebooks. Then have students work in pairs to find at least three other images from the two poems, identify the senses to which they appeal, and discuss their effect on the reader.

Image	Sense(s)	Effect
"Life has loveliness to sell"	sight, hearing	

Thematic Link: *Making Choices*

Both speakers offer advice about the choices that lead to self-fulfillment.

CUSTOMIZING FOR
Students Acquiring English

- Use **ACCESS FOR STUDENTS ACQUIRING ENGLISH**, Reading and Writing Support.

(I) Make sure students understand the meanings of the tenses used in the last line of this poem. "Have been" implies the past; "could be" implies the future.

STRATEGIC READING FOR
Less-Proficient Readers

Set a Purpose Have students discuss what makes a beautiful sunset or a delicious meal so pleasurable. Explore how the five senses help us enjoy life's beauty. Then have students read to discover what the speakers enjoy most.

Use **UNIT TWO RESOURCE BOOK**, p. 43, for guidance in reading the poems.

Literary Concept:
FIGURATIVE LANGUAGE

(A) Explain that personification is a figure of speech in which human qualities are attributed to an animal, object, or idea. Then have students identify examples of personification in lines 1 and 4 and explain the effect of this technique. *(Possible response: By personifying life and fire, the speaker creates sensory images that give the reader a fresh look at familiar things.)*

From Personal Response to Critical Analysis

1. Responses will vary.
2. Possible response: The poem urges trading all you have for beauty.
3. Possible responses: Use all your energy to enjoy life; don't let the beauty of life pass you by.
4. Possible response: Some students may say that the speaker would agree because life's beauty costs nothing in dollars and cents. Other students may say that the speaker would disagree because moments of ecstasy may require supreme sacrifices, costing "all you have been, or could be."

Have students imagine and then role-play a dialogue between the speakers of the two poems about how to lead a fulfilling life.

CUSTOMIZING FOR

Multiple Learning Styles

B **Spatial or Graphic Learners** Invite students to draw a picture or create a sculpture of the wild horse.

Literary Concept:
RHYME AND RHYTHM

C Have students identify the rhyme scheme and hypothesize why the poet used rhyme here. *(Possible responses: head/red; sky/die, undone/sun. The rhyme helps create a rhythm which captures the horse's gallop.)*

Art Note

Design for the cover of *Der Blaue Reiter* by Wassily Kandinsky Kandinsky (1866–1944) was co-founder of *Der Blaue Reiter* (The Blue Rider), a journal written by artists. This painting, exhibited in 1911, is considered to be an important starting point of the abstract movement in painting.

Reading the Art *What are your impressions of the figure in this painting? What do you think the other forms represent?*

COMPREHENSION CHECK
1. What does life have to sell? *(loveliness)*
2. What does the poet suggest you do in "Barter"? *(spend everything you have for beauty)*
3. What should you do before you die, according to the second poem? *(ride a wild horse into the sun)*

Into the Sun

Design for the cover of *Der Blaue Reiter* [The Blue Rider] (1911), Wassily Kandinsky. Glue-based paint, Indian ink, 27.9 cm × 21 cm, Karl Flinker Collection, Paris.

by Hannah Kahn

Ride a wild horse
   with purple wings
   striped yellow and black
   except his head
5   which must be red.

Ride a wild horse
   against the sky
   hold tight to his wings . . .
   Before you die
10   whatever else you leave
      undone,
   once, ride a wild horse
   into the sun.

200   UNIT TWO   PART 2: MAKING CHOICES

Assessment   Option

INFORMAL ASSESSMENT To assess students' understanding of both poems' lyric qualities and *carpe diem* (seize the day) theme, have them create a new image that captures their ideas about living life to the fullest. Guide students to develop their image into a lyric poem of four to eight lines. Encourage them to use figurative language in their poems.

Rubric
3 Full Accomplishment Student creates a lyric poem that expresses the importance of living life to the fullest. The poem has a central image and uses poetic techniques.
2 Substantial Accomplishment Student creates a poem, but the imagery lacks sufficient vividness and clarity.
1 Little or Partial Accomplishment Student writes unclear statements that create no images.

RESPONDING OPTIONS

FROM PERSONAL RESPONSE *TO* CRITICAL ANALYSIS

REFLECT
1. In your notebook, draw the picture that the words in "Into the Sun" create in your imagination.

RETHINK
2. The speaker does not really intend that the reader should ride a multicolored wild horse into the sun. Explain in your own words what the speaker is encouraging the reader to do.

3. Do you consider the speaker's advice worthwhile or not? Explain.

RELATE
4. Which poem do you think offers better advice? Give reasons to support your opinion.

Multimodal Learning
ANOTHER PATHWAY

Sara Teasdale once wrote, "Oh how I should love to make one really fine poem before there is no more *me*." Do you think she achieved her goal by writing "Barter"? Is "Into the Sun" a fine poem too? Write a paragraph that states and explains your opinion. Share the paragraph with the class.

LITERARY CONCEPTS

Figurative language is language that is used creatively to extend ideas beyond their literal or dictionary meanings. One example of figurative language is a **simile,** a comparison that uses words such as *like* or *as*. "Neat as a pin" and "strong as an ox" are examples of familiar similes. Lines 5 and 6 of "Barter" contain a simile: "And children's faces looking up/ Holding wonder like a cup." This simile compares children's faces that fill with wonder to a cup that fills with a liquid. Find another simile in this poem, and explain the comparison that it makes.

Strong as an **ox**

CONCEPT REVIEW: Repetition Poets often repeat sounds, words, phrases, or whole lines to emphasize an idea or stir a feeling. What effect does Hannah Kahn create in "Into the Sun" by repeating the words "ride a wild horse"?

QUICKWRITES

1. Write a **poem** of advice for middle schoolers, using the ideas you developed for the Writing Connection on page 198.

2. Think of a character from a selection you have read who could benefit from the advice given in one of these poems. Write a **letter** to that character explaining the importance of the speaker's advice.

3. What "beautiful and splendid things" would you add to those that the speaker of "Barter" mentions? Make a **list** of at least six things, and use figurative language to describe each of them.

 PORTFOLIO *Save your writing. You may want to use it later as a springboard to a piece for your portfolio.*

From Personal Response to Critical Analysis

1. Drawings will vary.
2. Possible responses: The speaker advocates placing feeling above reason, taking risks, or doing something you always dreamed of doing.
3. Possible responses: No, because people have responsibilities to others. Yes, because we must strive to fulfill our dreams and destiny.
4. Possible responses: The first poem, because it describes specific examples of things we should seek, like "loveliness"; the second poem, because it inspires us to follow our dreams.

Literary Link

Have students compare the advice in these poems to the choice Teruo made in "Say It with Flowers" (page 182). Would these poets support Teruo's choice? Why or why not? (*Possible responses: Yes, because he embraced beauty and followed his heart; no, because his dream was too narrow.*)

Another Pathway

Encourage students to make specific references to each poem as they explain their opinions.

Rubric
3 Full Accomplishment Student thoroughly evaluates the poems.
2 Substantial Accomplishment Student creates a less-detailed critical evaluation.
1 Little or Partial Accomplishment Student summarizes rather than evaluates.

Literary Concepts

Arrange the class in small groups to reread "Barter" to find the other simile, "music like a curve of gold." Each group should then select a recorder to write the group's suggestions and a direction giver to direct the conversation. Groups can then write three similes that apply to the poem's theme.

CONCEPT REVIEW Students can work in pairs to analyze the effect of the repetition in "Into the Sun." (*Possible responses: It reinforces the importance of taking risks or following your dream; it helps create the poem's rhythm.*)

QuickWrites

1. Encourage students to include examples of figurative language and of repetition.
2. Have students skim the table of contents to list characters from the selections they have read and then identify the one who most needs to experience beauty or to take a risk.
3. Encourage students to draw on all five senses as they list their "beautiful and splendid things."

The Writer's Craft

Using Language Imaginatively, pp 314–317

Science *Cooperative Learning Wild Horses* Have students work in groups of four or five to make a map showing where horses originated. Using encyclopedias or biology books, students can research their topic individually, then pool their results in a group discussion. The group should elect a moderator and a recorder. A map maker can draw the final product.

ART CONNECTION

Encourage students to consider, as they frame their responses, the difference between the written images in poetic language and the visual images in a painting. Students may respond that Kandinsky's soaring horse captures the spirit of Kahn's image of a horse with wings.

SARA TEASDALE

"The planning of the pattern of a poem is largely subconscious with me," Teasdale wrote in 1920. "Naturally the idea needs more or less space according to whether it is simply a statement of an emotion, or whether added to the statement, a deduction is made. The patterns of most of my lyrics are a matter of balance and speed rather than a matter of design which can be perceived by the eye."

HANNAH KAHN

Praising Kahn's work, one reviewer noted, "A willingness to probe the blackness, to find the sweetness where others might not, gives [Hannah Kahn] the poet's edge over the rest of us. Using herself as a catalyst, she both lives her feelings and steps away to describe them."

Multimodal Learning

ALTERNATIVE ACTIVITIES

1. Create a **collage** based on the message that one of the poems conveys.

2. Present an **oral reading** of one of the poems. Tape-record appropriate background music to accompany your reading.

3. Create a **music video** based on one of the poems. Turn the poem into a song, and videotape brief scenes that reflect its images.

ART CONNECTION

Look at the reproduction of a painting by Wassily Kandinsky on page 200. How would you compare your experience of viewing this picture with your experience of reading "Into the Sun"?

Design for the cover of *Der Blaue Reiter* [The Blue Rider] (1911), Wassily Kandinsky. Glue-based paint, Indian ink, 27.9 cm × 21 cm, Karl Flinker Collection, Paris.

SARA TEASDALE

1884–1933

Sara Teasdale was born and educated in St. Louis, Missouri. She remembered spinning funny little stories to herself long before she knew how to read. Her first volume of poetry, published in 1907, was praised for the delicate simplicity of the verse. Teasdale, who sometimes composed entire poems in her mind before writing them down, once said, "For me one of the greatest joys of poetry is to know it by heart—perhaps that is why the simple song-like poems appeal to me most—they are the easiest to learn."

In 1918, her book *Love Songs* won the Columbia University Poetry Society prize, which was the forerunner of the Pulitzer Prize in poetry. Although her works were widely read, her personal life was unhappy. Shy and withdrawn, she avoided public appearances and remained in semi-seclusion after an unhappy marriage. She died at 48 following a bout with pneumonia.

OTHER WORKS *Rivers to the Sea* Extended Reading

HANNAH KAHN

A winner of more than 25 awards for her verse, Hannah Kahn (1911–) loved poetry as a child but never thought she would grow up to be a poet. She was born in New York City in 1911 but lived in a small town from the age of 12 until the age of 15. During those years, illness prevented her from attending high school. At age 15, Kahn went to work. She later married, had children, and began to write poetry. Although she had little formal education, some of her poems appeared in such literary magazines as *American Scholar*. At the age of 50, Kahn started taking classes one night a week, and at 62, she earned a college degree. In addition to writing poetry, Kahn has worked as a teacher and lecturer and as poetry review editor for the *Miami Herald*.

OTHER WORKS *Eve's Daughter; Wind Song; Time, Wait* Extended Reading

202 UNIT TWO PART 2: MAKING CHOICES

Alternative Activities

1. Encourage students to gather materials from a wide variety of sources, including magazines, newspapers, and found objects.
2. Invite students to include appropriate sound effects as well as music, such as the roar of the ocean's surf or the gentle swish of trees in the wind.
3. Guide students to select images and music that reflect the theme and mood of the poem they selected to film.

PREVIEWING

NONFICTION

Eleanor Roosevelt
William Jay Jacobs

Activating Prior Knowledge
PERSONAL CONNECTION

You may know that Eleanor Roosevelt was the wife of Franklin Delano Roosevelt, the 32nd president of the United States. She was also one of the most famous and influential women of the 20th century. What else do you know about Eleanor Roosevelt? Share your knowledge in a class discussion.

Building Background
HISTORICAL CONNECTION

As you will learn, Eleanor Roosevelt was much more than a president's wife. Her life spanned a period of dramatic changes in the United States and the world. The time line below shows some events that occurred during Eleanor's lifetime.

Active Reading/Setting A Purpose
READING CONNECTION

Sequence The order in which events occur is called time order, or **chronological order.** The author of this selection presents events in Eleanor Roosevelt's life in chronological order. As you read, look for dates and for signal words such as *before, during, after, first, next, while,* and *later* in order to follow the sequence of events. After you've finished reading, copy the time line shown below and add to it important events in Eleanor's life.

Chronological Order	
Event	**First,** Eleanor Roosevelt is born in 1884.
Event	**Next,** women win the right to vote in the United States.
Event	**Later,** the Supreme Court ends segregation in schools.

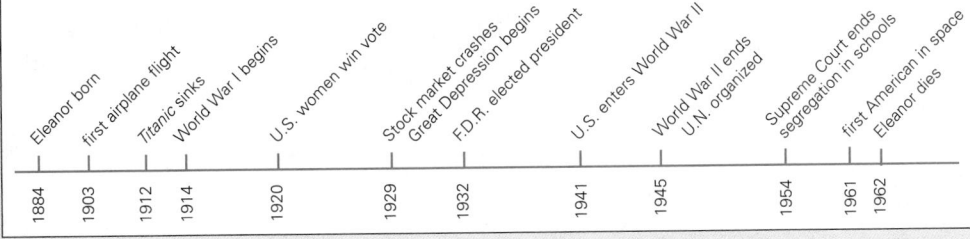

LASERLINKS
• HISTORICAL CONNECTION   **203**

PRINT AND MEDIA RESOURCES

UNIT TWO RESOURCE BOOK
Strategic Reading: Literature, p. 47
Vocabulary SkillBuilder, p. 50
Reading SkillBuilder, p. 48
Spelling SkillBuilder, p. 49

GRAMMAR MINI–LESSONS
Transparencies, pp. 12 and 39
Copymasters, p. 19

WRITING MINI–LESSONS
Transparencies, p. 41

ACCESS FOR STUDENTS ACQUIRING ENGLISH
Selection Summaries
Reading and Writing Support

FORMAL ASSESSMENT
Selection Test, pp. 47–48
 Test Generator

 **AUDIO LIBRARY**
See Reference Card

LASERLINKS
Historical Connection

OVERVIEW
Objectives

• To understand and appreciate a biography of one of the most famous women in U.S. history
• To understand the importance of the sequence of events
• To analyze biography as a literary genre
• To express understanding of the selection through a choice of writing forms, including an advice column, a job description, and a speech
• To extend understanding of the selection through a variety of multimodal and cross-curricular activities

Skills

READING SKILLS/STRATEGIES
• Noting sequence of events

THE WRITER'S STYLE
• Using appositives

GRAMMAR
• Using adjectives

LITERARY CONCEPTS
• Biography
• Conflict

GENRE STUDY
• Nonfiction: Biography

SPELLING
• Words ending in -ance/-ant, -ence/-ent

STUDY SKILLS
• Outlining

SPEAKING, LISTENING, AND VIEWING
• Role-playing

Cross-Curricular Connections

SOCIAL STUDIES
• Settlement houses
• League of Women Voters

• The United Nations Universal Declaration of Human Rights

SCIENCE
• Polio

HISTORICAL CONNECTION
Eleanor Roosevelt This film examines Eleanor Roosevelt's influence on government during the 1930s. Students will see her addressing the United Nations and engaging in humanitarian activities. You may wish to use the film to generate a discussion comparing women's roles in politics at that time with their roles in politics today.

Side A, Frame 22423

SUMMARY

Eleanor Roosevelt, daughter of Theodore Roosevelt's brother Elliott and Elliott's wife Anna, survived a difficult childhood to become a force for reform throughout the world. She married her distant cousin, Franklin Delano Roosevelt, helping him recover from polio and supporting his political career. Gradually, she lost her shyness and insecurity and began to speak up for her own beliefs. When her husband was elected president, she persuaded him to work for social reforms, and she led relief efforts during the Depression and World War II. After FDR died, Eleanor helped to found the United Nations. Until her death, she remained a tireless worker for human rights.

Thematic Link: *Making Choices* Eleanor Roosevelt chose to use her talents and energies to fight for human rights throughout the world.

Eleanor Roosevelt
by William Jay Jacobs

President Franklin Delano Roosevelt and First Lady Eleanor Roosevelt. UPI/Bettmann.

WORDS TO KNOW

brooding (broō'dĭng) *adj.* full of worry; troubled
brood *v.* (p. 209)
combatant (kəm-băt'nt) *n.* fighter (p. 209)
migrant (mī'grənt) *adj.* moving from place to place (p. 210)

priority (prī-ôr'ĭ-tē) *n.* something that must receive attention first (p. 210)
prominent (prŏm'ə-nənt) *adj.* well-known; widely recognized (p. 209)

E leanor Roosevelt was the wife of President Franklin Delano Roosevelt. But Eleanor was much more than just a president's wife, an echo of her husband's career.

Sad and lonely as a child, Eleanor was called "Granny" by her mother because of her seriousness. People teased her about her looks and called her the "ugly duckling." . . .

Yet despite all of the disappointments, the bitterness, the misery she experienced, Eleanor Roosevelt refused to give up. Instead she turned her unhappiness and pain to strength. She devoted her life to helping others. Today she is remembered as one of America's greatest women.

Eleanor was born in a fine townhouse in Manhattan. Her family also owned an elegant mansion along the Hudson River, where they spent weekends and summers. As a child Eleanor went to fashionable parties. A servant took care of her and taught her to speak French. Her mother, the beautiful Anna Hall Roosevelt, wore magnificent jewels and fine clothing. Her father, Elliott Roosevelt, had his own hunting lodge and liked to sail and to play tennis and polo. Elliott, who loved Eleanor dearly, was the younger brother of Theodore Roosevelt, who in 1901 became president of the United States. The Roosevelt family, one of America's oldest, wealthiest families, was respected and admired.

To the outside world it might have seemed that Eleanor had everything that any child could want—everything that could make her happy. But she was not happy. Instead her childhood was very sad.

Almost from the day of her birth, October 11, 1884, people noticed that she was an unattractive child. As she grew older, she could not help but notice her mother's extraordinary beauty, as well as the beauty of her aunts and cousins. Eleanor was plain looking, ordinary, even, as some called her, homely. For a time she had to wear a bulky brace on her back to straighten her crooked spine. **A**

When Eleanor was born, her parents had wanted a boy. They were scarcely able to hide their disappointment. Later, with the arrival of two boys, Elliott and Hall, Eleanor watched her mother hold the boys on her lap and lovingly stroke their hair, while for Eleanor there seemed only coolness, distance.

Feeling unwanted, Eleanor became shy and withdrawn. She also developed many fears. She was afraid of the dark, afraid of animals, afraid of other children, afraid of being scolded, afraid of strangers, afraid that people would not like her. She was a frightened, lonely little girl.

ELEANOR ROOSEVELT **205**

CUSTOMIZING FOR

Students Acquiring English

- Use ACCESS FOR STUDENTS ACQUIRING ENGLISH, Reading and Writing Support.

- In addition to these boxes, you may want to use the suggestions under Strategic Reading for Less-Proficient Readers.

(1) You may want to point out that "ugly duckling" refers to an unattractive child and comes from a Hans Christian Andersen tale about an ugly duckling that grows up to be a beautiful swan. Encourage interested students to find and read the story.

STRATEGIC READING FOR

Less-Proficient Readers

Set a Purpose Ask students to find out, as they read, what Eleanor's childhood was like.

Use UNIT RESOURCE BOOK, p. 47, for guidance in reading the selection.

CUSTOMIZING FOR

Gifted and Talented Students

Challenge students to brainstorm a list of other women whose accomplishments and character they think rank with Eleanor's. Have students support their choices. (Possible responses: Mother Teresa, Mother Hale, Amelia Earhart, Indira Gandhi)

Literary Concept: BIOGRAPHY

A Ask students what circumstances made Eleanor Roosevelt's childhood an unhappy one. (She was ridiculed because of her unattractive appearance; she had to wear a back brace; her parents were disappointed because they had wanted a boy.)

Mini-Lesson   **Reading Skills/Strategies**

NOTING SEQUENCE OF EVENTS Students may expect the events in a biographical work to be presented in chronological order. Although this usually is true, authors sometimes include facts out of sequence. Have students read the first three paragraphs on this page and note that they are not written in chronological order. Discuss how this technique suggests the contrast between the great lady Eleanor Roosevelt became and the frightened child she once was.

Application Have students read the five paragraphs on pages 208 and 209 beginning "In May 1906 . . ." Ask students what happened to Eleanor during the nine years that followed 1906. (She had five children and later worked tirelessly in support of the war effort.) Then ask what happened to Franklin during those nine years. (He was elected to the New York State Senate, then appointed assistant secretary of the navy.)

Reteaching/Reinforcement
- Unit Two Resource Book, p. 48

B Ask students to explain why Jacobs included this detail in the biography. *(Possible response: It shows that some of Eleanor's strengths were apparent even at an early age—she was kind, compassionate, and capable of forgiving others.)*

CUSTOMIZING FOR
Multiple Learning Styles

C **Spatial or Graphic Learners** Invite students to add the tragic events described so far in the biography to the time line that they began for the Reading Connection.

Critical Thinking: ANALYZING

D Have students analyze the influence Eleanor's parents had on her life. Which parent do they think had the greater influence? Why? *(Possible response: Mr. Roosevelt had the greater influence. Because of his love, Eleanor decided to live the selfless life he had described in his letters.)*

Active Reading: EVALUATE

E Ask students to share their opinions of Theodore Roosevelt, based on what they read in this passage and anything they already know about his life. *(Possible responses: He was playful, fun, outgoing, daring, and risk-taking.)*

The one joy in the early years of her life was her father, who always seemed to care for her, love her. He used to dance with her, to pick her up and throw her into the air while she laughed and laughed. He called her "little golden hair" or "darling little Nell."

Then, when she was six, her father left. An alcoholic, he went to live in a sanitarium[1] in Virginia in an attempt to deal with his drinking problem. Eleanor missed him greatly.

B Next her mother became ill with painful headaches. Sometimes for hours at a time Eleanor would sit holding her mother's head in her lap and stroking her forehead. Nothing else seemed to relieve the pain. At those times Eleanor often remembered how her mother had teased her about her looks and called her "Granny." But even at the age of seven Eleanor was glad to be helping someone, glad to be needed —and noticed.

C The next year, when Eleanor was eight, her mother, the beautiful Anna, died. Afterward her brother Elliott suddenly caught diphtheria[2] and he, too, died. Eleanor and her baby brother, Hall, were taken to live with their grandmother in Manhattan.

A few months later another tragedy struck. Elliott Roosevelt, Eleanor's father, also died. Within eighteen months Eleanor had lost her mother, a brother, and her dear father.

For the rest of her life Eleanor carried with her the letters that her father had written to her from the sanitarium. In them he had told her to be brave, to become well educated, and to grow up into a woman he could be proud of, a woman who helped people who were suffering.

The one joy in the early years of her life was her father, who always seemed to care for her, love her.

Only ten years old when her father died, Eleanor decided even then to live the kind of life he had described—a life that would have made him proud of her.

Few things in life came easily for Eleanor, but the first few years after her father's death proved exceptionally hard. Grandmother Hall's dark and gloomy townhouse had no place for children to play. The family ate meals in silence. Every morning Eleanor and Hall were expected to take cold baths for their health. Eleanor had to work at better posture by walking with her arms behind her back, clamped over a walking stick.

Instead of making new friends, Eleanor often sat alone in her room and read. For many months after her father's death she pretended that he was still alive. She made him the hero of stories she wrote for school. Sometimes, alone and unhappy, she just cried.

Some of her few moments of happiness came from visiting her uncle, Theodore Roosevelt, in Oyster Bay, Long Island. A visit with Uncle Ted meant playing games and romping outdoors with the many Roosevelt children.

Once Uncle Ted threw her into the water to teach her how to swim, but when she started to sink, he had to rescue her. Often he would read to the children old Norse tales and poetry. It was at Sagamore Hill, Uncle Ted's home, that Eleanor first learned how much fun it could be to read books aloud.

---

1. **sanitarium** (săn´ĭ-târ´ē-əm): an institution for the care of people with a specific disease or other health problem.
2. **diphtheria** (dĭf-thîr´ē-ə): a serious infectious disease.

Mini-Lesson  **Literary Concepts**

REVIEWING CONFLICT Remind students that conflict is a struggle between two opposing forces. In an external conflict, a character struggles against some outside person or force, as in the struggle between Eleanor and her mother-in-law. An internal conflict occurs when the struggle is within a character. Eleanor's internal conflicts include her struggles with her many fears—of the dark, animals, and other children.

Application Arrange students in small groups. Have each group select one external and one internal conflict that Eleanor faces, and brainstorm ways that she might have resolved the conflict. Invite each group to share its suggestions with the class. Then have the class debate which conflicts were the most difficult to resolve and why.

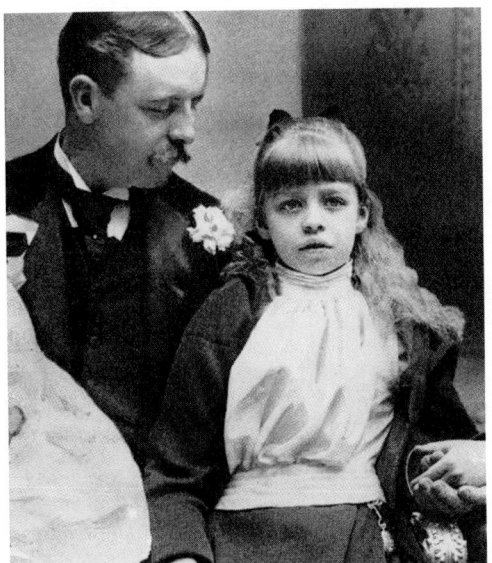

For most of the time Eleanor's life was grim. Although her parents had left plenty of money for her upbringing, she had only two dresses to wear to school. Once she spilled ink on one of them, and since the other was in the wash, she had to wear the dress with large ink stains on it to school the next day. It was not that Grandmother Hall was stingy. Rather, she was old and often confused. Nor did she show much warmth or love for Eleanor and her brother. Usually she just neglected them.

Just before Eleanor turned fifteen, Grandmother Hall decided to send her to boarding school in England. The school she chose was Allenswood, a private academy for girls located on the outskirts of London.

It was at Allenswood that Eleanor, still thinking of herself as an "ugly duckling," first dared to believe that one day she might be able to become a swan.

At Allenswood she worked to toughen herself physically. Every day she did exercises in the morning and took a cold shower. Although she did not like competitive team sports, as a matter of self-discipline she tried out for field hockey. Not only did she make the team but, because she played so hard, also won the respect of her teammates.

They called her by her family nickname, "Totty," and showed their affection for her by putting books and flowers in her room, as was

Elliott Roosevelt and his daughter, Eleanor, aged six. Eleanor adored her father, who called her "little golden hair" or "darling little Nell." UPI/Bettmann.

the custom at Allenswood. Never before had she experienced the pleasure of having schoolmates actually admire her rather than tease her.

At Allenswood, too, she began to look after her health. She finally broke the habit of chewing her fingernails. She learned to eat nutritious foods, to get plenty of sleep, and to take a brisk walk every morning, no matter how miserable the weather.

Under the guidance of the school's headmistress, Mademoiselle Souvestre, (or "Sou"), she learned to ask searching questions and think for herself instead of just giving back on tests what teachers had said.

She also learned to speak French fluently, a skill she polished by traveling in France, living for a time with a French family. Mademoiselle Souvestre arranged for her to have a new red dress. Wearing it, after all of the old, worn dresses Grandmother Hall had given her, made her feel very proud.

Eleanor was growing up, and the joy of young womanhood had begun to transform her personality.

In 1902, nearly eighteen years old, she left Allenswood, not returning for her fourth year there. Grandmother Hall insisted that, instead, she must be introduced to society as a debutante—to go to dances and parties and begin to take her place in the social world with other wealthy young women.

ELEANOR ROOSEVELT **207**

STRATEGIC READING FOR
Less-Proficient Readers

F Ask students what Eleanor was like as a child. (*shy, withdrawn, fearful*) **Making Inferences**

• What tragic events occurred in her childhood? (*Her mother, brother Elliott, and father all died within 18 months.*) **Summarizing**

Set a Purpose Have students read to find out what event becomes a turning point in Eleanor's life.

Linking to Literature

G Jacobs is alluding to the fairy tale "The Ugly Duckling" by the Danish writer Hans Christian Andersen (1805–1875). As a child, Andersen was tall and awkward. Like the young swan in his famous story, Andersen was teased by his classmates and treated harshly by his teachers. Although Andersen did not grow up to be beautiful like the swan, he did become a successful writer of novels, poems, plays, and fairy tales.

Critical Thinking:
SYNTHESIZING

H Have students speculate why Eleanor was accepted by her schoolmates at Allenswood when she had never been accepted before. (*Possible responses: In the past she was withdrawn, whereas at Allenswood she became a team player; her schoolmates respected her effort and determination.*)

CUSTOMIZING FOR
Students Acquiring English

② Point out that *Mademoiselle* is a French title of address for an unmarried woman and that the comparable English title is *Miss* or *Ms.*

Mini-Lesson 🖊 Grammar

USING ADJECTIVES Explain that adjectives are words that modify or describe nouns or pronouns. Tell students that they can usually identify an adjective by finding a word that answers the questions *what kind*, *which one*, or *how many*. Define each type of adjective shown, using the chalkboard. Using details from the selection, guide students to see how adjectives help the reader visualize what is being described.

Application Have students read the two highlighted paragraphs and look for adjectives and the nouns they modify. Then ask students to list

alternative adjectives and describe any effect their substitutions have on the meaning of the two paragraphs.

Reteaching/Reinforcement
• *Grammar Handbook*, anthology p. 866
• *Grammar Mini-Lessons* copymasters, p. 19, transparencies, pp. 12 and 39

 **The Writer's Craft**

Adjectives, pp. 496–497

Some Types of Adjectives

Common	Proper	Articles
fearless women, warm sun, that book, another test	Italian food, April showers	a, an, the

Active Reading: EVALUATE

J Ask students why Eleanor is so concerned about the extent of Franklin's love. Use the following think-aloud model.

Think-Aloud Model *Marrying for love seems very important to Eleanor. I remember that she always felt unattractive and insecure. I think she's afraid that Franklin couldn't really love her because she's not pretty. Maybe she's also insecure because her mother made fun of her.*

CUSTOMIZING FOR
Students Acquiring English

3 Make sure students are familiar with this wedding custom. You may want to invite students to share wedding customs from their native cultures.

STRATEGIC READING FOR
Less-Proficient Readers

K Discuss how Eleanor experienced a turning point in her life when she fell in love with Franklin.

- How did Eleanor feel at her wedding? *(serious and very much in love)* Noting Relevant Details

Set a Purpose Have students read to find out about Eleanor's role and accomplishments as First Lady.

Literary Concept: CONFLICT

L Is the conflict described here internal or external? *(The conflict between Eleanor and her mother-in-law is external, but it results in some internal conflict for Eleanor.)*

Away from Allenswood, Eleanor's old uncertainty about her looks came back again. She saw herself as too tall, too thin, too plain. She worried about her buckteeth, which she thought made her look horselike. The old teasing began again, especially on the part of Uncle Ted's daughter, "Princess" Alice Roosevelt, who seemed to take pleasure in making Eleanor feel uncomfortable.

I Eleanor, as always, did as she was told. She went to all of the parties and dances. But she also began working with poor children at the Rivington Street Settlement House on New York's Lower East Side. She taught the girls gymnastic exercises. She took children to museums and to musical performances. She tried to get the parents interested in politics in order to get better schools and cleaner, safer streets.

Meanwhile Eleanor's life reached a turning point. She fell in love! The young man was her fifth cousin, Franklin Delano Roosevelt.

Eleanor and Franklin had known each other since childhood. Franklin recalled how once he had carried her piggyback in the nursery. When she was fourteen, he had danced with her at a party. Then, shortly after her return from Allenswood, they had met by chance on a train. They talked and almost at once realized how much they liked each other.

For a time they met secretly. Then they attended parties together. Franklin—tall, strong, handsome—saw her as a person he could trust. He knew that she would not try to dominate him.

But did he really love her? Would he always? She wrote to him, quoting a poem she knew: " 'Unless you can swear, "For life, for death!" . . . Oh, never call it loving!' "

J Franklin promised that his love was indeed "for life," and Eleanor agreed to marry him. It was the autumn of 1903. He was twenty-one.

She was nineteen.

On March 17, 1905, Eleanor and Franklin were married. "Uncle Ted," by then president of the United States, was there to "give the bride away." It was sometimes said that the dynamic, energetic Theodore Roosevelt had to be "the bride at every wedding and the corpse at every funeral." And it was certainly true that day. Wherever the president went, the guests followed at his heels.

Before long Eleanor and Franklin found themselves standing all alone, deserted. Franklin seemed annoyed, but Eleanor didn't mind. She had found the ceremony deeply moving. And she stood next to her husband in a glow of idealism—very serious, very grave, very much in love.

In May 1906 the couple's first child was born. During the next nine years Eleanor gave birth to five more babies, one of whom died in infancy. Still timid, shy, afraid of making mistakes, she found herself so busy that there was little time to think of her own drawbacks.

Still, looking back later on the early years of her marriage, Eleanor knew that she should have been a stronger person, especially in the handling of Franklin's mother, or, as they both called her, "Mammá." Too often Mammá made the decisions about such things as where they would live, how their home would be furnished, how the children would be disciplined. Eleanor and Franklin let her pay for things they could not afford—extra servants, vacations, doctor bills, clothing. She offered, and they accepted.

Before long, trouble developed in the relationship between Eleanor and Franklin. Serious, shy, easily embarrassed, Eleanor could not share Franklin's interests in golf and tennis. He enjoyed light talk and flirting with women. She could not be lighthearted. So she stayed on the sidelines. Instead of losing her temper, she bottled up her anger and did not talk to him at all. As he used to say, she "clammed up." Her

---

Mini-Lesson | **The Writer's Style**

USING APPOSITIVES Explain that an appositive is a noun or phrase that identifies or explains the person or thing preceding it. An appositive that adds extra information is set off from the rest of the sentence with commas.

no appositive: "Uncle Ted" was there to give the bride away. He was the President.

with appositive: "Uncle Ted," the President, was there to give the bride away.

Application Have students combine each of the following sentences by using appositives.

1. Her father left the family. He was an alcoholic.

2. Eleanor and her baby brother lived with their grandmother. Her baby brother's name was Hall.

3. Elliott Roosevelt died. Elliott Roosevelt was Eleanor's father.

4. At Sagamore Hill Eleanor learned how much fun it could be to read books aloud. Sagamore Hill was Uncle Ted's home.

Reteaching/Reinforcement
- *Writing Mini-Lessons* transparencies, p. 41

The Writer's Craft

Using Appositives, p. 307

silence only made things worse, because it puzzled him. Faced with her coldness, her <u>brooding</u> silence, he only grew angrier and more distant.

Meanwhile Franklin's career in politics advanced rapidly. In 1910 he was elected to the New York State Senate. In 1913 President Wilson appointed him Assistant Secretary of the Navy—a powerful position in the national government, which required the Roosevelts to move to Washington, D.C.

In 1917 the United States entered World War I as an active <u>combatant</u>. Like many socially <u>prominent</u> women, Eleanor threw herself into the war effort. Sometimes she worked fifteen and sixteen hours a day. She made sandwiches for soldiers passing through the nation's capital. She knitted sweaters. She used Franklin's influence to get the Red Cross to build a recreation room for soldiers who had been shell-shocked in combat. . . .

In 1920 the Democratic Party chose Franklin as its candidate for vice-president of the United States. Even though the Republicans won the election, Roosevelt became a well-known figure in national politics. All the time, Eleanor stood by his side, smiling, doing what was expected of her as a candidate's wife.

She did what was expected—and much more—in the summer of 1921 when disaster struck the Roosevelt family. While on vacation Franklin suddenly fell ill with infantile paralysis—polio—the horrible disease that each year used to kill or cripple thousands of children, and many adults as well. When Franklin became a victim of polio, nobody knew what caused the disease or how to cure it.

Franklin lived, but the lower part of his body remained paralyzed. For the rest of his life he never again had the use of his legs. He had to be lifted and carried from place to place. He had to wear heavy steel braces from his waist to the heels of his shoes.

His mother, as well as many of his advisers, urged him to give up politics, to live the life of a country gentleman on the Roosevelt estate at Hyde Park, New York. This time, Eleanor, calm and strong, stood up for her ideas. She argued that he should not be treated like a sick person, tucked away in the country, inactive, just waiting for death to come.

Franklin agreed. Slowly he recovered his health. His energy returned. In 1928 he was elected governor of New York. Then, just four years later, he was elected president of the United States.

Meanwhile Eleanor had changed. To keep Franklin in the public eye while he was recovering, she had gotten involved in politics herself. It was, she thought, her "duty." From childhood she had been taught "to do the thing that has to be done, the way it has to be done, when it has to be done."

With the help of Franklin's adviser Louis Howe, she made fund-raising speeches for the Democratic Party all around New York State. She helped in the work of the League of Women Voters, the Consumer's League, and the Foreign

> Eleanor threw herself into the war effort. Sometimes she worked fifteen and sixteen hours a day.

WORDS TO KNOW	**brooding** (brōō′dǐng) *adj.* full of worry; troubled **brood** *v.*
	combatant (kəm-bắt′nt) *n.* fighter
	prominent (prŏm′ə-nənt) *adj.* well-known; widely recognized

209

M Explore what purpose this incident serves in the biography. Guide students to explain what this conflict might foreshadow about Eleanor and Franklin's life together. (*Possible response: Their different styles makes communication between them difficult. As a result, they may grow apart.*)

Literary Concept: **BIOGRAPHY**

CUSTOMIZING FOR

Multiple Learning Styles

N **Musical Learners** Students might enjoy researching and sharing some of the songs from World War I and II that inspired patriotism and participation in the war efforts.

Linking to Science

O Polio, or poliomyelitis, is an infectious viral disease that affects the central nervous system and sometimes results in paralysis. First described in 1840, the disease cannot be cured, only prevented through vaccination. Dr. Jonas Salk developed the first polio vaccine in 1954; Dr. Albert Sabin created an oral version in 1963. As a result of immunizations, the number of polio cases declined from a high of 57,879 in 1952 to only a few each year.

Active Reading: QUESTION

P Have students stop and record any questions they have at this point. (*Possible response: Why did Eleanor become stronger at this point in her life?*)

Mini-Lesson **Study Skills**

OUTLINING Explain that many students find outlining a useful strategy for organizing information. In an outline, ideas are shown by roman numerals, subheads by capital letters, and details by Arabic numbers. Copy on the chalkboard the outline shown and explain each division.

Application Have students work in pairs to outline "Eleanor Roosevelt" as a study aid. Invite volunteers to write their outlines on the board. As a class, combine each sample to produce an outline that students can use as they answer the Responding Options.

I. Main Idea
   A. Subhead
   B. Subhead
     1. Detail
     2. Detail
II. Main Idea
   A. Subhead
     1. Detail

     2. Detail
   B. Subhead
     1. Detail
     2. Detail
   C. Subhead

Policy Association. After becoming interested in the problems of working women, she gave time to the Women's Trade Union League (WTUL).

It was through the WTUL that she met a group of remarkable women—women doing exciting work that made a difference in the world. They taught Eleanor about life in the slums. They awakened her hopes that something could be done to improve the condition of the poor. She dropped out of the "fashionable" society of her wealthy friends and joined the world of reform—social change.

For hours at a time Eleanor and her reformer friends talked with Franklin. They showed him the need for new laws: laws to get children out of the factories and into schools; laws to cut down the long hours that women worked; laws to get fair wages for all workers.

By the time that Franklin was sworn in as president, the nation was facing its deepest depression. One out of every four Americans was out of work, out of hope. At mealtimes people stood in lines in front of soup kitchens for something to eat. Mrs. Roosevelt herself knew of once-prosperous families who found themselves reduced to eating stale bread from thrift shops or traveling to parts of town where they were not known to beg for money from house to house.

Eleanor worked in the charity kitchens, ladling out soup. She visited slums. She crisscrossed the country learning about the suffering of coal miners, shipyard workers, migrant farm workers, students, housewives—Americans caught up in the paralysis of the Great Depression. Since Franklin himself remained crippled, she became his eyes and ears, informing him of what the American people were really thinking and feeling.

Eleanor also was the president's conscience, personally urging on him some of the most compassionate, forward-looking laws of his presidency, including, for example, the National Youth Administration (NYA), which provided money to allow impoverished young people to stay in school.

She lectured widely, wrote a regularly syndicated[3] newspaper column, "My Day," and spoke frequently on the radio. She fought for equal pay for women in industry. Like no other First Lady up to that time, she became a link between the president and the American public.

Above all she fought against racial and religious prejudice. When Eleanor learned that the DAR (Daughters of the American Revolution) would not allow the great black singer Marian Anderson to perform in their auditorium in Washington, D.C., she resigned from the organization. Then she arranged to have Miss Anderson sing in front of the Lincoln Memorial.

Similarly, when she entered a hall where, as often happened in those days, blacks and whites were seated in separate sections, she made it a point to sit with the blacks. Her example marked an important step in making the rights of blacks a matter of national priority.

On December 7, 1941, Japanese forces launched a surprise attack on the American naval base at Pearl Harbor, Hawaii, as well as on other American installations in the Pacific. The United States entered World War II, fighting not only against Japan but against the brutal dictators who then controlled Germany and Italy.

Eleanor helped the Red Cross raise money. She gave blood, sold war bonds. But she also did the unexpected. In 1943, for example, she visited barracks and hospitals on islands throughout the South Pacific. When she visited a hospital, she stopped at every bed. To each soldier she said

---

3. **syndicated:** sold to many newspapers for publication.

WORDS
TO
KNOW

migrant (mī'grənt) *adj.* moving from place to place
priority (prī-ôr'ĭ-tē) *n.* something that must receive attention first

210

Multicultural Perspectives

MARIAN ANDERSON Marian Anderson, born in Philadelphia in 1902, received her early musical training while singing in church choirs. When she was 23 years old, she won a singing competition, an honor that brought with it the opportunity for her to appear with the New York Philharmonic in 1925. During the 1930s, she toured both Europe and the United States, sometimes performing in as many as 100 concerts in a season. When Anderson performed on the steps of the Lincoln Memorial in 1939, after being barred from singing in Constitution Hall, a crowd of 75,000 people were in attendance. In 1955 she became the first African American to sing with the Metropolitan Opera, as Ulrica in Verdi's *Un ballo in maschera*. An outstanding humanitarian as well as a great singer, Anderson was appointed in 1958 as an alternate American delegate to the United Nations. She died April 8, 1993.

(T) Ask students what this anecdote reveals about Eleanor Roosevelt's character. Use students' answers as a springboard for an analysis of how this passage is characteristic of the biographer's attitude toward his subject. *(Possible response: The anecdote reveals Eleanor's sensitivity, kindness, and humanitarianism. It suggests that the biographer admires his subject greatly.)*

CUSTOMIZING FOR

Multiple Learning Styles

(U) **Bodily-Kinesthetic Learners** The death of Franklin Roosevelt was a watershed event in the lives of the World War II generation, just as the assassination of President John F. Kennedy would prove to be a pivotal event in the lives of many people in the 1960s. Invite students who process knowledge through body language to create a skit showing how they imagine the nation reacted to the news of Roosevelt's death.

Critical Thinking:
SYNTHESIZING

(V) Have students compare the period after Franklin Roosevelt's death with the period Eleanor spent at Allenswood. *(Possible responses: At both times Eleanor found new strengths, new interests, and a new way of life.)*

Nobody else had done so much to help raise the spirits of the men.

Eleanor Roosevelt talks animatedly as she has lunch with American soldiers in their mess hall, September 26, 1943.
AP/Wide World Photos.

something special, something that a mother might say. Often, after she left, even battle-hardened men had tears in their eyes. Admiral Nimitz, who originally thought such visits would be a nuisance, became one of her strongest admirers. Nobody else, he said, had done so much to help raise the spirits of the men.

By spring 1945 the end of the war in Europe seemed near. Then, on April 12, a phone call brought Eleanor the news that Franklin Roosevelt, who had gone to Warm Springs, Georgia, for a rest, was dead.

As Eleanor later declared, "I think that sometimes I acted as his conscience. I urged him to take the harder path when he would have preferred the easier way. In that sense, I acted on occasion as a spur, even though the spurring was not always wanted or welcome.

"Of course," said Eleanor, "I loved him, and I miss him."

After Franklin's funeral, every day that Eleanor was home at Hyde Park, without fail, she placed flowers on his grave. Then she would stand very still beside him there.

With Franklin dead, Eleanor Roosevelt might have dropped out of the public eye, might have been remembered in the history books only as a footnote to the president's program of social reforms. Instead she found new strengths within herself, new ways to live a useful, interesting life—and to help others. Now, moreover, her successes were her own, not the result of being the president's wife.

In December 1945 President Harry S Truman

ELEANOR ROOSEVELT **211**

Mini-Lesson **Genre Study**

NONFICTION Explain to students that the word **biography** comes from the Greek words *bios* ("life") and *graphia* ("writing"). From this, have students deduce that biographies are a type of nonfiction, or writings about real life events. Tell the class that good biographies paint a complete picture of the subject, revealing flaws as well as admirable traits. Explain that descriptions of conflicts make biographies more suspenseful and dramatic because readers want to find out how they are resolved.

Application Have students make a web like the one shown, indicating the different aspects of a biography. Then invite students to add details from "Eleanor Roosevelt" to their webs.

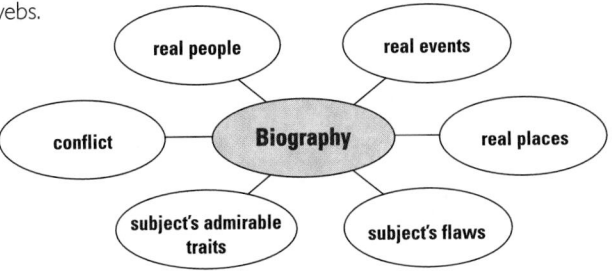

invited her to be one of the American delegates going to London to begin the work of the United Nations. Eleanor hesitated, but the president insisted. He said that the nation needed her; it was her duty. After that, Eleanor agreed.

W In the beginning some of her fellow delegates from the United States considered her unqualified for the position, but after seeing her in action, they changed their minds.

X It was Eleanor Roosevelt who, almost single-handedly, pushed through the United Nations General Assembly a resolution giving refugees from World War II the right *not* to return to their native lands if they did not wish to. The Russians angrily objected, but Eleanor's reasoning convinced wavering delegates. In a passionate speech defending the rights of the refugees she declared, "We [must] consider first the rights of man and what makes men more free—not governments, but man!"

Next Mrs. Roosevelt helped draft the United Nations Declaration of Human Rights. The Soviets wanted the declaration to list the duties people owed to their countries. Again Eleanor insisted that the United Nations should stand for individual freedom—the rights of people to free speech, freedom of religion, and such human needs as health care and education. In December 1948, with the Soviet Union and its allies refusing to vote, the Declaration of Human Rights won approval of the UN General Assembly by a vote of forty-eight to zero.

Even after retiring from her post at the UN, Mrs. Roosevelt continued to travel. In places around the world she dined with presidents and kings. But she also visited tenement slums[4] in Bombay, India; factories in Yugoslavia; farms in Lebanon and Israel.

> "She would rather light a candle than curse the darkness."

Everywhere she met people who were eager to greet her. Although as a child she had been brought up to be formal and distant, she had grown to feel at ease with people. They wanted to touch her, to hug her, to kiss her.

Eleanor's doctor had been telling her to slow down, but that was hard for her. She continued to write her newspaper column, "My Day," and to appear on television. She still began working at seven-thirty in the morning and often continued until well past midnight. Not only did she write and speak, she taught retarded children and raised money for health care of the poor.

As author Clare Boothe Luce put it, "Mrs. Roosevelt has done more good deeds on a bigger scale for a longer time than any woman who ever appeared on our public scene. No woman has ever so comforted the distressed or so distressed the comfortable."

Gradually, however, she was forced to withdraw from some of her activities, to spend more time at home.

On November 7, 1962, at the age of seventy-eight, Eleanor died in her sleep. She was buried in the rose garden at Hyde Park, alongside her husband.

Adlai Stevenson, the American ambassador to the United Nations, remembered her as "the First Lady of the World," as the person—male or female—most effective in working for the cause of human rights. As Stevenson declared, "She would rather light a candle than curse the darkness."

And perhaps, in sum, that is what the struggle for human rights is all about. ❖

---

4. **tenement slums:** parts of a city where poor people live in crowded, shabby buildings.

Assessment ✓ Option

INFORMAL ASSESSMENT To help students assess their own work, have them prepare an oral report that answers the question, "Why is Eleanor Roosevelt a fitting subject for a biography?" They should use several details from the selection to back up their opinions. Have them present the report to the class.

Rubric

3 Full Accomplishment Students write and present a concise, informative report supported by many details.

2 Substantial Accomplishment Students write and present a report that is not concise or well supported with selection details.

I Little or Partial Accomplishment Students have difficulty completing or presenting a finished report.

from The Autobiography of Eleanor Roosevelt

by Eleanor Roosevelt

In the beginning, because I felt, as only a young girl can feel it, all the pain of being an ugly duckling, I was not only timid, I was afraid. Afraid of almost everything, I think: of mice, of the dark, of imaginary dangers, of my own inadequacy. My chief objective, as a girl, was to do my duty. This had been drilled into me as far back as I could remember. Not my duty as I saw it, but my duty as laid down for me by other people. It never occurred to me to revolt. Anyhow, my one overwhelming need in those days was to be approved, to be loved, and I did whatever was required of me, hoping it would bring me nearer to the approval and love I so much wanted.

As a young woman, my sense of duty remained as strict and rigid as it had been when I was a girl, but it had changed its focus. My husband and my children became the center of my life, and their needs were my new duty. I am afraid now that I approached this new obligation much as I had my childhood duties. I was still timid, still afraid of doing something wrong, of making mistakes, of not living up to the standards required by my mother-in-law, of failing to do what was expected of me.

As a result, I was so hidebound by duty that I became too critical, too much of a disciplinarian. I was so concerned with bringing up my children properly that I was not wise enough just to love them. Now, looking back, I think I would rather spoil a child a little and have more fun out of it.

from No Ordinary Time

by Doris Kearns Goodwin

It was said jokingly in Washington during the war years that Roosevelt had a nightly prayer: "Dear God, please make Eleanor a little tired." But in the end, he often came around to her way of thinking. Labor adviser Anna Rosenberg had been one of those who criticized Eleanor's unceasing pressure on the president, but years later she changed her mind. "I remember him saying, 'We're not going to do that now. Tell Eleanor to keep away; I don't want to hear about that anymore.'

And then 2-3 weeks later he would say, 'Do you remember that thing Eleanor brought up? Better look into it, maybe there's something to it—I heard something to indicate that maybe she's right.' I'm not sure she would have had the opportunity to bring things to his attention unless she pressured him—I mean he was so involved and in retrospect it was never anything for herself. . . . He would never have become the kind of President he was without her."

THE AUTOBIOGRAPHY OF ELEANOR ROOSEVELT / NO ORDINARY TIME **213**

COMPREHENSION CHECK
1. Who raised Eleanor after her parents died? *(her grandmother)*
2. How did Eleanor feel about Allenswood, the boarding school she attended in England? *(She liked it.)*
3. Why was Eleanor called Franklin's "eyes and ears" during his presidency? *(His polio kept him in Washington, so she traveled and reported what she saw.)*
4. For what organization did Eleanor work after Franklin Roosevelt died? *(the United Nations)*

INSIGHT

1. After reading a passage from Eleanor's autobiography, what advice would you give Eleanor if you could? *(Possible response: Don't look back with regret, just focus on the present.)*
2. Which would you prefer to read more of, Eleanor's autobiography or Jacobs's biography? Why? *(Possible responses: Eleanor's because it is more personal; Jacobs's because it is more objective)*
3. In the passage from *No Ordinary Time,* what does Roosevelt's joking prayer mean? *(Possible response: If Eleanor is tired, she won't keep Franklin awake, discussing a new reform she has in mind.)*
4. Why do you think Franklin eventually came around to Eleanor's way of thinking on so many issues? *(Possible response: Franklin knew that Eleanor was right, but he needed to be prodded to act.)*

DORIS KEARNS GOODWIN

Doris Kearns Goodwin, born in 1943, was a professor of government at Harvard University and served as a special consultant to the President from 1969–1973. Goodwin won a 1995 Pulitzer prize for *No Ordinary Time.*

Mini-Lesson TM **Spelling**

WORDS ENDING IN -ANCE/-ANT, -ENCE/-ENT Explain to students that they should spell an adjective with *-ant* if they can trace it to a noun ending in *-ance.* Similarly, they should spell an adjective with *-ent* if they can trace it to a noun ending in *-ence.* Provide these examples:

Noun	Adjective
prominence	prominent
dominance	dominant
existence	existent

Application Have students complete this chart. Then have them look for more words with these endings to add to their personal word lists.

Reteaching/Reinforcement
• *Unit Two Resource Book,* p. 49

Noun	Adjective
	eminent
instance	
elegance	
permanence	
	fragrant

1. Possible responses: *compassionate, strong, determined*

2. Possible responses: her work for human rights and the UN, her bravery and outspokenness in the fight for racial equality, her work for women and the poor, her role as First Lady and political activist

3. Possible response: She had been trained to do her duty as a child, so she chose to act dutifully later in life.

4. Possible responses: It helped by giving her energy and focus when life was difficult; it hurt by causing her to repress her own ideas.

5. Possible responses: Some students may say that Franklin Roosevelt might not have fought so strongly for human rights. Other students may add that, without his wife's influence, he never would have been so aware of the sufferings of many Americans. His wife could make insistent, deeply personal appeals.

6. Possible responses: She would probably continue to work for human rights and oppose persecution, racism, hunger, and poverty throughout the world. She probably would help people who have AIDS, the homeless, and victims of drug abuse.

Another Pathway

Before students write, invite them to look through the selection and pick out details and examples that support their interpretation.

Rubric

3 Full Accomplishment Students complete a well-thought-out and well-written paragraph that includes appropriate details.

2 Substantial Accomplishment Students complete the paragraph, but they do not include appropriate details.

1 Little or Partial Accomplishment Students are unable to complete the paragraph, or they include inappropriate details.

RESPONDING
OPTIONS

FROM **PERSONAL RESPONSE** *TO* **CRITICAL ANALYSIS**

REFLECT
1. What words and phrases would you use to describe Eleanor Roosevelt? Record them in your notebook.

RETHINK
2. Which of Eleanor's accomplishments do you find most impressive? Why?

Thematic Link
3. How do you think Eleanor's childhood experiences might have affected the kinds of choices she made later in life?

   Consider
   • how she felt about herself
   • her goals and values

Close Textual Reading
   • what she says in her autobiography (first Insight on page 213)

4. Do you think Eleanor's sense of duty helped or hurt her? Support your response with information from the biography and the Insights.

5. How might Franklin Roosevelt's presidency have been different if he had not had Eleanor's help and support? Explain.

RELATE
6. If Eleanor Roosevelt were alive today, which national and world issues do you think would concern her? Explain your answer.

Multimodal Learning
ANOTHER PATHWAY

Adlai Stevenson said of Eleanor Roosevelt, "She would rather light a candle than curse the darkness." Using details from this selection, write a paragraph explaining what you think Stevenson meant by this statement. Share your paragraph with the class.

QUICKWRITES

1. Write an **advice column** that Eleanor would have written in response to a teenager's question about how to build self-confidence. Use examples from Eleanor's own life in your column.

2. Write a **job description** of Eleanor's role as First Lady.

3. Russell Freedman, the author of another biography of Eleanor Roosevelt, writes: "Her critics . . . called her a meddlesome busybody, a do-gooder, a woman who did not know her place." Write a draft of a **speech** that Eleanor Roosevelt might have given to defend her actions.

PORTFOLIO *Save your writing. You may want to use it later as a springboard to a piece for your portfolio.*

LITERARY CONCEPTS

A **biography** is the story of a person's life, written by another person. Some biographies show both the strengths and the weaknesses of the subject. Other biographies are more one-sided, either praising the subject or finding fault. How would you describe the style of Jacobs's biography? What details from the selection support your opinion?

CONCEPT REVIEW Conflict Name the most important conflicts Eleanor faced—both internal and external.

ELEANOR ROOSEVELT
First Discovery
RUSSELL FREEDMAN

Literary Concepts

Students may find the biography balanced in describing Eleanor as a child but biased in its description of her as an adult. Have students work in small groups to find details that support their view. Appoint a direction giver in each team to make sure that the discussion stays on track.

CONCEPT REVIEW Possible responses: *internal:* her feelings of being unloved; *external:* her struggles against those who would deny human rights

QuickWrites

1. To help students use the right tone, bring in some advice columns from newspapers for students to use as writing models.

2. Discuss how expectations of the First Lady have changed since 1945. Guide students to set their descriptions in either Eleanor Roosevelt's time or the present.

3. Remind students that the purpose of their speech is to persuade. As such, it should support opinions with facts.

The Writer's Craft

Personal Voice, pp 312–313
Supporting Opinions, pp. 144–151

ALTERNATIVE ACTIVITIES

1. Eleanor called herself "the President's conscience." Think about a world or national problem that she would care about if she were First Lady today. Recall the ideas you discussed for question 6 on page 214. Then, with a partner, **role-play** the conversation she might have with her husband about solving the problem.

2. Research the wife of any president who served after Franklin D. Roosevelt. Compare and contrast that First Lady with Eleanor Roosevelt. Make a **poster** that shows the women's similarities and differences, and share it with your class.

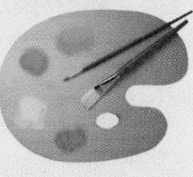

LITERARY LINKS

Which poem do you think would mean more to Eleanor Roosevelt, "Choices" on page 193 or "Into the Sun" on page 198? Why?

ACROSS THE CURRICULUM

Social Studies Find out more about the United Nations Universal Declaration of Human Rights. Consider using an encyclopedia program on a computer as a reference tool. Present your findings in an oral or written report.

WORDS TO KNOW

On your paper, answer each of the following questions.

1. Since working for social justice was a **priority** in Eleanor's life, how much of her time might she have devoted to it?

2. How might being **prominent,** as Eleanor was, help a person promote a worthy cause?

3. Can a person like Eleanor Roosevelt, who fought for human rights, be considered a **combatant** for social justice? Why or why not?

4. Would wounded soldiers have enjoyed talking to Mrs. Roosevelt if she had been a **brooding** visitor? Why or why not?

5. What special hardships might **migrant** farm workers face?

WILLIAM JAY JACOBS

William Jay Jacobs admires Eleanor Roosevelt for her strength of character: "The more I learned about Eleanor Roosevelt, the more I saw her as a woman of courage. She turned her pain to strength." Jacobs believes that young people need role models like Eleanor Roosevelt—historical figures who faced tests and persisted. He says that by writing biographies he is "able to reach a very special audience: young people searching for models, trying to understand themselves." Jacobs

1933–

has written many biographies for young people, including biographies of Hernando Cortés, Edgar Allan Poe, Abraham Lincoln, and Winston Churchill. Jacobs says that perhaps his primary task in writing biographies for young people "is to introduce them to that great reservoir of recorded history from which our civilization has drawn inspiration."

OTHER WORKS *Mother, Aunt Susan and Me: The First Fight for Women's Rights* Extended Reading

ELEANOR ROOSEVELT **215**

Across the Curriculum

Social Studies **Cooperative Learning** Arrange students in groups of four or five to complete their research. Members can divide the reference material, each student checking one source. Invite students who used on-line reference sources to share their experiences with the rest of the class.

ADDITIONAL SUGGESTION

Science *Thanks, Technology!* In small groups, students can report on the technology that developed during Eleanor Roosevelt's lifetime. Have students vote on which change most affected her ability to achieve her goals.

Words to Know

Possible responses:
1. She might have devoted most of her time to it.
2. She would have influential, wealthy friends who could give time and money to her causes.
3. Yes, because Eleanor Roosevelt fought for justice.
4. No, because she would have been sullen and grim.
5. They might have difficulty finding a place to live and getting consistent medical care and education because they move frequently.

Reteaching/Reinforcement
• *Unit Two Resource Book*, p. 50

Literary Links

Possible response: "Into the Sun," because Eleanor's sad childhood experiences gave her the strength to take great risks as a champion of the rights of the oppressed

WILLIAM JAY JACOBS

In addition to being a writer, Jacobs has taught history and social studies since 1975 in public schools in Darien, Connecticut. Before that, he taught at several colleges and universities.

Alternative Activities

1. Suggest that students create a brief script or note cards for their role-playing. Allow students time to rehearse their skit.
2. Helpful sources of information include books about the White House and first ladies, biographies, and back issues of magazines and newspapers.

Teaching Strategies:
ELEMENTS OF DRAMA

Cast of Characters Have students read the Cast of Characters for *A Christmas Carol* on page 219. Then have students imagine they are adapting "Say it with Flowers" on page 181 as a drama. Ask them to create a cast of characters.

Dialogue Arrange students in pairs. Have partners create and write down a brief dialogue about a special holiday. Invite volunteers to share their dialogue by acting it out for the class.

Stage Directions Read the explanation of stage directions to the class. Then have students write stage directions for their dialogues.

A **drama,** or **play,** is a form of literature that is performed for an audience, either on stage or before a camera. We can see drama on television, in movies, in videos, and on stage.

The elements of drama are similar to the elements of fiction. Like fiction, drama usually tells a story with characters, plot, and setting. Unlike fiction, drama is written to be performed for an audience. For this reason, drama is written in a special form called a **script,** in which lines are written out for the characters to speak. The script has various parts, which are described below.

CAST OF CHARACTERS A script usually begins with a list of the characters in the play. Often a short description appears next to a character's name.

DIALOGUE A play consists almost entirely of dialogue—conversation between the characters. Both the plot of the play and the characters' personalities are revealed through dialogue. The dialogue appears in lines next to the characters' names, as in this example from *The Monsters Are Due on Maple Street* (page 358):

Steve. What was that? A meteor?
Don. That's what it looked like. I didn't hear any crash though, did you?

STAGE DIRECTIONS A play includes instructions for the director, the performers, and the stage crew. These are called stage direc-

tions, and they are printed in italic type in this book. Often they are also enclosed in parentheses. Many stage directions tell actors how to speak or move. Stage directions also describe the **scenery**—all the decorations on stage that help create the setting. Some stage directions describe **props**—the objects that actors need and use during the play. Many scripts also include suggestions for lighting and sound. Notice how the following stage directions from *A Christmas Carol,* on page 226, tell the actor what to do and what props to use.

Scrooge. Yes, here's the key. (*He turns with the key toward the door, and Marley's face swims out of the darkness. Scrooge watches, unable to speak. He fumbles for a match, lights the lantern, and swings it toward the figure, which melts away.*)

The stage directions in dramas that are meant to be filmed must also include camera directions. Through the medium of the camera, the audience might see a close-up of a character, a look between characters while someone else is speaking, or a quick shot of the outside of a building. These types of camera shots are carefully planned by the playwright and are an important element in the play.

ACTS AND SCENES The action of a play is divided into scenes. A scene changes whenever the setting—time, place, or both time and place—changes. Sometimes scenes are grouped into acts. In *The Monsters Are Due on Maple Street,* for example, four scenes are grouped into two acts.

STRATEGIES FOR READING DRAMA

- **Read the play silently** Before you try to read the play aloud with others, read it to yourself. You need to know the entire plot and understand the characters before you perform the play.

- **Figure out what is happening** When you watch a movie, it takes you a while to understand exactly what the movie is about. The same is true when you read a play. Be patient —you will need to read several pages to understand what is happening.

- **Read the stage directions carefully** If you were watching a drama on stage or on television, you would see the action and the scenery. When you read a drama, you have to imagine both. The stage directions tell exactly where and when each scene is happening, and they help you visualize the action. If you skip over the stage directions, you will miss important information.

- **Get to know the characters** In drama, you get to know the characters through dialogue— through the characters' own words and through what others say to and about them.

Analyze the characters' words carefully and try to discover the feelings behind them, just as if you were reading fiction.

- **Keep track of the plot** As in fiction, the plot of a drama centers on a main conflict that the characters try to resolve. Look for the conflict and let yourself become involved in the story. Watch for the action to build to a climax, and then evaluate how the conflict is resolved.

- **Read the play aloud with others** When drama is performed, it takes on a whole new aspect: it becomes almost like real life. When you read the part of a character, you become an actor. You will play the part differently than anyone else because you bring your own interpretation to the role. Let yourself become that character for a while. React to what other characters say and do to you. Be ready with your character's lines and read only the words your character says. Do not read the stage directions aloud. You may find that you really enjoy playing the part of someone who is totally different from you.

FOCUS ON DRAMA **217**

OVERVIEW

Objectives

- To understand and appreciate a dramatization of Charles Dickens's classic story about a character who changes for the better
- To understand how to follow stage directions to enrich reading
- To identify and understand theme
- To express understanding of the drama through a choice of writing forms, including a will, a plot summary, and a dialogue
- To extend understanding of the drama through a variety of multimodal and cross-curricular activities

Skills

READING SKILLS/STRATEGIES
- Making inferences

THE WRITER'S STYLE
- Dialogue in plays and skits

GRAMMAR
- Run-on sentences

LITERARY CONCEPTS
- Theme
- Imagery

GENRE STUDY
- Drama

SPELLING
- Words with *j*, *ge* and *dge*

SPEAKING, LISTENING, AND VIEWING
- Fllm/Drama
- Drama performance

Cross-Curricular Connections

HISTORY
- Christmas in England
- Victorian sleepwear
- Boarding schools
- Accents

SOCIAL STUDIES
- Victorian England
- Family holidays

SCIENCE
- Electric lights

MATH
- Computing cost

MUSIC
- Carols and caroling

HISTORICAL CONNECTION
The Industrial Revolution During the 1800s, Britain was undergoing great industrial and social change. In his novels and stories, Dickens depicted some of the unfortunate results of such change. Here, students will get a glimpse of the living conditions that Dickens and many others endured.

Side A, Frames 49318

PREVIEWING

DRAMA

A Christmas Carol

Charles Dickens
Dramatized by Frederick Gaines

Activating Prior Knowledge
PERSONAL CONNECTION

How people lead their lives depends partly on the choices they make. In a small group, discuss the people and characters you've read about so far in this part of the unit. How did their choices affect them and the people around them? Did any of their choices change their attitudes and behavior? Why or why not? As you read this dramatization of *A Christmas Carol,* consider the choices the characters make and the effects of those choices.

Character	Choices/Effects
_____	_____
_____	_____
_____	_____
_____	_____
_____	_____
_____	_____
_____	_____

Building Background
BIOGRAPHICAL CONNECTION

Charles Dickens chose to write novels that criticized the attitudes of the greedy and exposed the abuses of the poor. When Dickens published *A Christmas Carol* in 1843, about one-third of the people in London, England, lived in poverty. Factories had changed the face of London, with people flooding the city, abandoning rural areas for a new way of life. The city quickly became dirty and overcrowded; wages were low, the crime rate was high, and children were hungry. Jobs and housing were in short supply. The Poor Law of 1834 forced the homeless into workhouses, where they worked for room and board. By exposing the suffering of the poor in a vivid and sympathetic manner, Dickens convinced many readers that conditions had to be corrected. His novels helped bring about reforms.

READING CONNECTION Active Reading

Stage Directions In adapting Dickens's novel into a play, Frederick Gaines chose to depict some of the poor people and conditions of London in his stage directions. **Stage directions** are italicized notes in the scripts of plays. They guide actors and readers by explaining the settings of scenes, the movements of actors, the tones of voice of the **dialogue,** and the sound effects. When you read a play, don't skip the stage directions. They give you information that you won't get any other way.

A London street in the 19th century. Culver Pictures.

LASERLINKS
- *HISTORICAL CONNECTION*

218   UNIT TWO   PART 2: MAKING CHOICES

PRINT AND MEDIA RESOURCES

UNIT TWO RESOURCE BOOK
Strategic Reading: Literature, p. 53
Vocabulary SkillBuilder, p. 56
Reading SkillBuilder, p. 54
Spelling SkillBuilder, p. 55

GRAMMAR MINI–LESSONS
Transparencies, p. 2
Copymasters, p. 2

WRITING MINI–LESSONS
Transparencies, p. 48

ACCESS FOR STUDENTS ACQUIRING ENGLISH
Selection Summaries
Reading and Writing Support

FORMAL ASSESSMENT
Selection Test, pp. 49–50
Part Test, pp. 51–52
Test Generator

AUDIO LIBRARY
See Reference Card

LASERLINKS
Historical Connection
Author Background

INTERNET RESOURCES
McDougal Littell Literature
Center at http://www.hmco.com
/mcdougal/lit

218 THE LANGUAGE OF LITERATURE TEACHER'S EDITION

A Christmas Carol

by Charles Dickens

Dramatized by Frederick Gaines

Illustrations Copyright © 1990 Roberto Innocenti, reprinted by permission of The Creative Company, Mankato, Minnesota.

SUMMARY

Christmas is coming, but Bob Cratchit, an underpaid clerk, knows better than to expect any kindness from his employer, the mean and stingy Ebenezer Scrooge. On Christmas Eve, Scrooge is visited by four spirits: the ghost of Jacob Marley, his dead business partner; the Spirit of Christmas Past; the Spirit of Christmas Present; and the Spirit of Christmas Yet to Come. They show him the value of charity. They also show him that Bob Cratchit's frail young son, Tiny Tim, will not live long without help. They also show Scrooge that if he does not change his ways, people will not be sorry when he dies. Scrooge changes his ways and provides a merry Christmas for the Cratchits and everyone else, including himself.

Thematic Link: *Making Choices* When he chooses to embrace the Christmas spirit, Ebenezer Scrooge regains his humanity and realizes that real joy comes from doing good things for others.

WORDS TO KNOW

abundance (ə-bŭn′dəns) *n.* wealth (p. 224)

charitable (chăr′ĭ-tə-bəl) *adj.* generous in giving (p. 234)

currency (kûr′ən-sē) *n.* money (p. 231)

destitute (dĕs′tĭ-tōōt′) *n.* people lacking the necessities of life (p. 224)

emerge (ĭ-mûrj′) *v.* to come into sight (p. 225)

finale (fə-năl′ē) *n.* the concluding part (p. 242)

mortal (môr′tl) *adj.* of the earth; not a spirit (p. 228)

pledge (plĕj) *n.* something given to guarantee fulfillment of a promise (p. 231)

provision (prə-vĭzh′ən) *n.* a supplying of needs (p. 224)

reassurance (rē′ə-shŏŏr′əns) *n.* a restoring of confidence (p. 227)

solitude (sŏl′ĭ-tōōd) *n.* the state of being alone (p. 222)

summon (sŭm′ən) *v.* to call for or send for with authority or urgency; to order to come or appear (p. 227)

surplus (sûr′pləs) *adj.* extra; more than is needed (p. 224)

transform (trăns-fôrm′) *v.* to change the form or appearance of (p. 221)

welfare (wĕl′fâr′) *n.* well-being (p. 228)

CUSTOMIZING FOR
Students Acquiring English

- Use **ACCESS FOR STUDENTS ACQUIRING ENGLISH**, *Reading and Writing Support.*

- Because this play is set in Victorian England, students may have difficulty with some of the vocabulary. Encourage them to read as far as they can before looking up words in a dictionary.

STRATEGIC READING FOR
Less-Proficient Readers

Set a Purpose Review the Biographical Connection with students and ask if they think that more fortunate people have a responsibility to share with the less fortunate. Invite students to read to see how Scrooge feels about the poor and his duty toward them.

Use **UNIT TWO RESOURCE BOOK**, p. 53, for guidance in reading the selection.

CUSTOMIZING FOR
Gifted and Talented Students

This drama blends elements of comedy and tragedy. Challenge students, as they read, to list which characterizations and events are comic and which are serious. Ask them why Dickens's story mixes both. *(Possible responses: Scrooge can be seen as a comic character because of his exaggerated reactions to everything and everyone. The play's plot of a rich man getting his "comeuppance" has some very comedic moments. However, the drama's four spirits and the visions Scrooge sees of Tiny Tim's death, poverty, and Scrooge's own loneliness and death are tinged with tragedy. Dickens mixes both dark and light elements in imitation of real life; Dickens mixes both because audiences need comic relief after sad scenes.)*

Critical Thinking:
HYPOTHESIZING

A Ask students to speculate about why the characters are listed in this order. *(It is the order of their appearance in the play.)*

Characters

Carolers, Families, Dancers	Jacob Marley	Second Spirit *(the Spirit of Christmas Present)*
First Boy	Priest	Poorhouse Children
Second Boy	Leper	Mrs. Cratchit
Third Boy	First Spirit *(the Spirit of Christmas Past)*	Several Cratchit Children
Girl with a doll		Tiny Tim
Ebenezer Scrooge	Jack Walton	Beggar Children, Hunger and Ignorance
Bob Cratchit, Scrooge's clerk	Ben Benjamin	
Fred, Scrooge's nephew	Child Scrooge	Third Spirit *(the Spirit of Christmas Yet to Come)*
Gentleman Visitor	Fan, Scrooge's sister	
Warder and Residents of the Poorhouse	Fezziwig	Peter, a Cratchit child
	Young Ebenezer	Boy
Sparsit, Scrooge's servant	Dick Wilkins	Butcher
Cook	Sweetheart of Young Ebenezer	Coachman
Charwoman		

Prologue

The play begins amid a swirl of street life in Victorian London. Happy groups pass; brightly costumed carolers *and* families *call out to one another and sing "Joy to the World." Three* boys *and a* girl *are grouped about a glowing mound of coal. As the* carolers *leave the stage, the lights dim and the focus shifts to the mound of coals, bright against the dark. Slowly, the children begin to respond to the warmth. A piano plays softly as the children talk.*

Mini-Lesson	Reading Skills/Strategies

MAKING INFERENCES In fiction, characters don't always state exactly how they feel. The reader must infer what each character is feeling. Characters' gestures and other actions offer hints about ideas and feelings not spoken. In a drama, these hints appear in the form of stage directions. Although directors and actors add their own interpretation, stage directions indicate much of the characters' behavior. Have students read the highlighted directions on page 221. The stage directions hint at Scrooge's unpleasant manner as the children scatter and retreat from him.

Application Ask students to read the stage directions on page 225 and note Cratchit's interaction with the children. What can students infer about Cratchit's personality?

Reteaching/Reinforcement
- *Unit Two Resource Book*, p. 54

First Boy. I saw a horse in a window. (*pause*) A dapple . . . gray and white. And a saddle, too . . . red. And a strawberry mane down to here. All new. Golden stirrups. (*People pass by the children, muttering greetings to one another.*)

Second Boy. Christmas Eve.

Third Boy. Wish we could go.

First Boy. So do I.

Third Boy. I think I'd like it.

First Boy. Oh, wouldn't I . . . wouldn't I!

Second Boy. We're going up onto the roof. (*The boys look at him quizzically.*) My father has a glass. Telescope. A brass one. It opens up and it has twists on it and an eyepiece that you put up to look through. We can see all the way to the park with it.

Third Boy. Could I look through it?

Second Boy. Maybe . . . where would you look?

(*The* Third Boy *points straight up.*) Why there?

Third Boy. I'd like to see the moon. (*The boys stand and look upward as the* girl *sings to her doll. One of the boys makes a snow angel on the ground.*)

Girl (*singing*)

Christ the King came down one day,
Into this world of ours,
And crying from a manger bed,
Began the Christmas hour.

(*speaking*)

Christ the King, my pretty one,
Sleep softly on my breast,
Christ the King, my gentle one,
Show us the way to rest.

(*She begins to sing the first verse again. As snow starts to fall on the boy making the snow angel, he stands up and reaches out to catch a single flake.*)

Scene 1

SCROOGE IN HIS SHOP

The percussion thunders. Scrooge *hurls himself through the descending snowflakes and sends the children scattering. They retreat, watching.* Cratchit *comes in. He takes some coal from the mound and puts it into a small bucket; as he carries it to a corner of the stage, the stage area is* transformed *from street to office.* Scrooge's *nephew* Fred *enters, talks with the children, gives them coins, and sends them away with a "Merry Christmas."*

Fred. A Merry Christmas, Uncle! God save you!

Scrooge. Bah! Humbug!

Fred. Christmas a humbug, Uncle? I hope that's meant as a joke.

Scrooge. Well, it's not. Come, come, what is it you want? Don't waste all the day, Nephew.

Fred. I only want to wish you a Merry Christmas, Uncle. Don't be cross.

Scrooge. What else can I be when I live in such a world of fools as this? Merry Christmas! Out with Merry Christmas! What's Christmas to you but a time for paying bills without money, a time for finding yourself a year

WORDS TO KNOW	**transform** (trăns-fôrm′) *v.* To change the form or appearance of

221

Linking to History

B Dickens wrote *A Christmas Carol* in 1843, when the traditional Christmas celebrations had fallen out of favor. Employers, for example, were actively discouraged from giving workers time off to celebrate. *A Christmas Carol* was so influential in sparking a renewal of the Christmas spirit that Dickens has been credited with almost single-handedly reviving the holiday customs.

CUSTOMIZING FOR

Multiple Learning Styles

C Bodily-Kinesthetic Learners Invite volunteers to demonstrate how they would make a snow angel.

Literary Concept: IMAGERY

D Have students name the senses to which the images in these stage directions appeal. Then ask students to make predictions about the scene based on these images. (*Possible responses: The images appeal to hearing, touch, and sight. Their violence— "percussion thunders" and "hurls"—suggests that the scene might present a confrontation.*)

CUSTOMIZING FOR

Students Acquiring English

I Many students acquiring English come from non-Christian backgrounds, so you may want to provide background information on Christmas and the customs associated with it in the English-speaking world.

E Have students analyze Scrooge's personality based on what Dickens reveals here. *(Possible responses: Scrooge's actions and comments reveal that he is rude, mean-spirited, and stingy.)*

Literary Concept: CHARACTER

F Ask students what Fred's comments in this passage reveal about his character. *(Possible responses: Fred is generous, warm, gracious, more interested in being friendly than in being right, and slow to take offense.)*

Active Reading: CLARIFY

G Have students compare and contrast Fred's actions here with his earlier discussion with Scrooge to clarify why Fred hesitates. If necessary, use the following model:

Think-Aloud Model *I remember that earlier Fred wished Scrooge a Merry Christmas and invited him to dinner. Scrooge rudely turned Fred down. From the stage directions I can see that Scrooge has turned his back on Fred. I guess Fred hesitates because he wants to say more. But he can see that Scrooge is not interested, and he can predict that Scrooge's response will be negative.*

CUSTOMIZING FOR

Students Acquiring English

2 Explain that *liberality* means "generosity" and that the word is used ironically here, since it is already obvious to the audience that Scrooge is anything but generous.

E older and not an hour richer. If I could work my will, every idiot who goes about with "Merry Christmas" on his lips should be boiled with his own pudding and buried with a stake of holly through his heart.

Fred. Uncle!

Scrooge. Nephew, keep Christmas in your own way and let me keep it in mine.

Fred. But you don't keep it.

Scrooge. Let me leave it alone then. Much good may it do you. Much good it has ever done you.

F **Fred.** There are many things from which I might have derived good by which I have not profited, I daresay, Christmas among the rest. And though it has never put a scrap of gold in my pocket, I believe it has done me good and will do me good, and I say, God bless it!

Scrooge. Bah!

Fred. Don't be angry, Uncle. Come! Dine with us tomorrow.

Scrooge. I'll dine alone, thank you.

Fred. But why?

Scrooge. Why? Why did you get married?

Fred. Why, because I fell in love with a wonderful girl.

Scrooge. And I with <u>solitude</u>. Good afternoon.

Fred. Nay, Uncle, but you never came to see me before I was married. Why give it as a reason for not coming now?

Scrooge. Good afternoon.

Fred. I am sorry with all my heart to find you so determined; but I have made the attempt in homage to Christmas, and I'll keep that good spirit to the last. So, a Merry Christmas, Uncle.

Scrooge. Good afternoon!

Fred. And a Happy New Year!

Scrooge. Good afternoon! (*Fred hesitates as if to say something more. He sees that Scrooge has gone to get a volume down from the shelf, and so he starts to leave. As he leaves, the doorbell rings.*) Bells. Is it necessary to always have bells? (*The gentleman visitor enters, causing the doorbell to ring again.*) Cratchit!

Cratchit. Yes, sir?

Scrooge. The bell, fool! See to it!

Cratchit. Yes, sir. (*He goes to the entrance.*)

Scrooge (*muttering*). Merry Christmas . . . Wolves howling and a Merry Christmas . . .

Cratchit. It's for you, sir.

Scrooge. Of course it's for me. You're not receiving callers, are you? Show them in.

Cratchit. Right this way, sir. (*The gentleman visitor approaches Scrooge.*)

Scrooge. Yes, yes?

Gentleman Visitor. Scrooge and Marley's, I believe. Have I the pleasure of addressing Mr. Scrooge or Mr. Marley?

Scrooge. Marley's dead. Seven years tonight. What is it you want?

Gentleman Visitor. I have no doubt that his liberality is well represented by his surviving partner. Here, sir, my card. (*He hands Scrooge his business card.*)

Scrooge. Liberality? No doubt of it? All right, all right, I can read. What is it you want? (*He returns to his work.*)

Gentleman Visitor. At this festive season of the year . . .

Scrooge. It's winter and cold. (*He continues his work and ignores the gentleman visitor.*)

Gentleman Visitor. Yes . . . yes, it is, and the more reason for my visit. At this time of the year it

WORDS TO KNOW	**solitude** (sŏl′ĭ-to͞od) *n.* the state of being alone

222

Multicultural Perspectives

NEW YEAR CELEBRATIONS New Year's Day is celebrated on January 1—but it wasn't always so. During the Middle Ages, most European countries followed the Julian calendar. As a result, New Year's Day was celebrated on March 25. Called Annunciation Day, it was honored as the day on which, according to Christian belief, it was revealed to Mary that she would give birth to the Son of God. When the Gregorian calendar was introduced in the late 1500s, New Year's Day shifted to January 1 in most of Western Europe. Great Britain and the American colonies did not begin using that date until 1752.

The Jewish New Year falls on the first and second days of the month of Tishri, usually around the end of September or the beginning of October. The Jewish New Year is called Rosh Hashanah, and along with Yom Kippur (the Day of Atonement), is the most important holiday of the year. Traditionally, Chinese people celebrate the New Year somewhere between January 21 and February 19. The Vietnamese New Year, called Tet, lasts for three days. It falls at the same time as the Chinese New Year.

Active Reading: PREDICT

H Have students predict why the Gentleman Visitor has come to see Scrooge. Guide students to use the setting—time and place—as they make their predictions. *(Possible responses: Since it is Christmas, the Gentleman Visitor will probably ask for a charitable donation or invite Scrooge to a party.)*

(I) *A Christmas Carol* was written during the Victorian Era (1837–1901), representing the reign of Queen Victoria. During this time, Britain was a great world power both on sea and land. After Great Britain's victory in the Napoleonic Wars at the beginning of the century, the country became the world's greatest naval power, with control over most of the world's commerce. Furthermore, England was the world's leader in manufacturing. Scrooge represents most industrialists' attitude at the time. He voices the Social Darwinist theory of "survival of the fittest." According to that doctrine, the poor are poor because of some fault on their part. This belief allows Scrooge to ignore the problems of the downtrodden.

Literary Concept: IMAGERY

(J) Have students notice the contrasting images of Cratchit and Scrooge. Then guide them to infer what the images suggest about Cratchit's character. *(Possible response: The images contrast Cratchit, who is dancing, and Scrooge, who is working. Unlike Scrooge, Cratchit is still able to enjoy life's simple pleasures.)*

is more than usually desirable to make some slight provision for the poor and destitute who suffer greatly from the cold. Many thousands are in want of common necessaries; hundreds of thousands are in want of common comforts, sir.

Scrooge. Are there no prisons?

Gentleman Visitor. Many, sir.

Scrooge. And the workhouse? Is it still in operation?

Gentleman Visitor. It is; still, I wish I could say it was not.

Scrooge. The poor law is still in full vigor then?

Gentleman Visitor. Yes, sir.

Scrooge. I'm glad to hear it. From what you said, I was afraid someone had stopped its operation.

Gentleman Visitor. Under the impression that they scarcely furnish Christian cheer of mind or body to the multitude, a few of us are endeavoring to raise a fund to buy the poor some meat and drink and means of warmth. We choose this time because it is the time, of all others, when want is keenly felt and abundance rejoices. May I put you down for something, sir?

Scrooge (*retreating into the darkness temporarily*). Nothing.

Gentleman Visitor. You wish to be anonymous?

Scrooge. I wish to be left alone. Since you ask me what I wish, sir, that is my answer. I don't make merry myself at Christmas, and I can't afford to make idle people merry. I help support the establishments I have mentioned . . . they cost enough . . . and those who are poorly off must go there.

Gentleman Visitor. Many can't go there, and many would rather die.

Scrooge. If they would rather die, they had better do it and decrease the surplus population. That is not my affair. My business is. It occupies me constantly. (*He talks both to the gentleman visitor and to himself while he thumbs through his books.*) Ask a man to give up life and means . . . fine thing. What is it, I want to know? Charity? . . . (*His nose deep in his books, he vaguely hears the dinner bell being rung in the workhouse; he looks up as if he has heard it but never focuses on the actual scene. The warder of the poorhouse stands in a pool of light at the far left, slowly ringing a bell.*)

Warder. Dinner. All right. Line up. (*The poorly clad, dirty residents of the poorhouse line up and file by to get their evening dish of gruel,[1] wordlessly accepting it and going back to eat listlessly in the gloom. Scrooge returns to the business of his office. The procession continues for a moment, then the image of the poorhouse is obscured by darkness. The dejected gentleman visitor exits.*)

Scrooge. Latch the door, Cratchit. Firmly, firmly. Draft as cold as Christmas blowing in here. Charity! (*Cratchit goes to the door, starts to close it, then sees the little girl with the doll. She seems to beckon to him; he moves slowly toward her, and they dance together for a moment. Scrooge continues to work. Suddenly carolers appear on the platform, and a few phrases of their carol, "Angels We Have Heard on High," are heard. Scrooge looks up.*) Cratchit! (*As soon as Scrooge shouts, the*

---

1. **gruel** (grōō'əl): a thin, watery food made by boiling ground grain in water or milk.

WORDS TO KNOW	**provision** (prə-vĭzh'ən) *n.* a supplying of needs
	destitute (dĕs'tĭ-tōōt') *n.* people lacking the necessities of life
	abundance (ə-bŭn'dəns) *n.* wealth
	surplus (sûr'pləs) *adj.* extra; more than is needed

224

Mini-Lesson **Grammar**

RUN-ON SENTENCES A run-on sentence occurs when two or more sentences are written as one. A run-on sentence combines ideas that should be separate. Normally, run-on sentences should not be used. However, writers sometimes use them in dialogue. In the highlighted run-on sentence on page 224, Scrooge is rambling as he speaks about poorhouses. If a new sentence began with "They cost enough," the passage would be grammatically correct.

Application Have students look at Scrooge's highlighted dialogue on page 228. Ask them to rewrite the dialogue in complete sentences.

Reteaching/Reinforcement
- *Grammar Handbook,* anthology p. 849–850
- *Grammar Mini-Lessons* copymasters p. 2, transparencies p. 2

 **The Writer's Craft**

Run-on Sentences, pp. 395–396

girl *and the* carolers *vanish and* Cratchit *begins to close up the shop.*) Cratchit!

Cratchit. Yes, sir.

Scrooge. Well, to work then!

Cratchit. It's evening, sir.

Scrooge. Is it?

Cratchit. Christmas evening, sir.

Scrooge. Oh, you'll want all day tomorrow off, I suppose.

Cratchit. If it's quite convenient, sir.

Scrooge. It's not convenient, and it's not fair. If I was to deduct half a crown[2] from your salary for it, you'd think yourself ill-used, wouldn't you? Still you expect me to pay a day's wage for a day of no work.

Cratchit. It's only once a year, sir.

Scrooge. Be here all the earlier the next morning.

Cratchit. I will, sir.

Scrooge. Then off, off.

Cratchit. Yes, sir! Merry Christmas, sir!

Scrooge. Bah! (*As soon as* Cratchit *opens the door, the sounds of the street begin, very bright and loud.* Cratchit *is caught up in a swell of people hurrying through the street. Children pull him along to the top of an ice slide, and he runs and slides down it, disappearing in darkness as the stage suddenly is left almost empty.* Scrooge *goes around the room blowing out the candles, talking to himself.*) Christmas Eve. Carolers! Bah! There. Another day. (*He opens his door and peers out.*) Black, very black. Now where are they? (*The children are heard singing carols for a moment.*) Begging pennies for their songs, are they? Oh, boy! Here, boy! (*The little* girl *emerges from the shadows.* Scrooge *hands her a dark lantern, and she holds it while he lights it with an ember from the pile of coals.*)

---

2. **half a crown:** an amount of British money, equal to 2½ shillings or one-eighth of a pound.

FROM **PERSONAL RESPONSE** TO **CRITICAL ANALYSIS**

REFLECT   1. What was your response to the meeting between Ebenezer Scrooge and his nephew, Fred? Describe your reaction in your notebook.

RETHINK   2. What is your opinion of Ebenezer Scrooge?
   Consider
   • how he chooses to live his life
   • how he treats others, such as Bob Cratchit
   • his response to the Gentleman Visitor's request

   3. Skim the stage directions. How is the **mood**—the feeling the writer wants the reader to get—outside Scrooge's office different from the mood within the office?

WORDS
TO   **emerge** (ĭ-mûrj′) *v.* to come into sight
KNOW

225

Literary Concept: CHARACTER

N Explain to students that it is customary to give servants a gift of extra money at holidays. Ask students what Scrooge's actions toward Cook and Sparsit reveal about his character. *(his extreme stinginess, his inability to enjoy the Christmas spirit)*

Active Reading: EVALUATE

O Remind students that active readers develop their own ideas about characters and events. Invite students to evaluate how well the author builds suspense in this scene. *(Possible response: The author is very successful at building suspense in this scene. The darkness, Marley's unintelligible mumbling, Scrooge's confusion over what he hears, and Marley's echoing voice—all contribute to create suspense.)*

Scene 2
Scrooge Goes Home

M

Scrooge (*talking to the little* Girl). Hold it quiet! There. Off now. That's it. High. Black as pitch. Light the street, that's it. You're a bright lad! Good to see that. Earn your supper, boy. You'll not go hungry this night. Home. You know the way, do you? Yes, that's the way. The house of Ebenezer Scrooge. (*As the two find their way to* Scrooge's *house, the audience sees and hears a brief image of a cathedral interior with a living crèche and a large choir singing "Amen!"; the image ends in a blackout. The lights come up immediately, and* Scrooge *is at his door.*) Hold the light up, boy, up. (*The girl with the lantern disappears.*) Where did he go? Boy? No matter. There's a penny saved. Lantern's gone out. No matter. A candle saved. Yes, here's the key. (*He turns with the key toward the door, and Marley's face swims out of the darkness.* Scrooge *watches, unable to speak. He fumbles for a match, lights the lantern, and swings it toward the figure, which melts away. Pause.* Scrooge *fits the key in the lock and turns it as the door suddenly is opened from the inside by the porter,* Sparsit. Scrooge *is startled, then recovers.*) Sparsit?

Sparsit. Yes, sir?

Scrooge. Hurry, hurry. The door . . . close it.

Sparsit. Did you knock, sir?

Scrooge. Knock? What matter? Here, light me up the stairs.

Sparsit. Yes, sir. (*He leads* Scrooge *up the stairs. They pass the* cook *on the way.* Scrooge *brushes by her, stops, looks back, and she leans toward him.*)

Cook. Something to warm you, sir? Porridge?

Scrooge. Wha . . . ? No. No, nothing.

Cook (*waiting for her Christmas coin*). Merry Christmas, sir. (Scrooge *ignores the request and the* cook *disappears. Mumbling,* Scrooge *follows* Sparsit.)

Scrooge (*looking back after the* cook *is gone*). Fright a man nearly out of his life . . . Merry Christmas . . . bah!

Sparsit. Your room, sir.

Scrooge. Hmmm? Oh, yes, yes. And good night.

Sparsit (*extending his hand for his coin*). Merry Christmas, sir.

Scrooge. Yes, yes . . . (*He sees the outstretched hand; he knows what* Sparsit *wants and is infuriated.*) Out! Out! (*He closes the door after* Sparsit, *turns toward his chamber, and discovers the* charwoman *directly behind him.*)

Charwoman. Warm your bed for you, sir?

Scrooge. What? Out! Out!

Charwoman. Aye, sir. (*She starts for the door.* Marley's *voice is heard mumbling something unintelligible.*)

Scrooge. What's that?

Charwoman. Me, sir? Not a thing, sir.

Scrooge. Then, good night.

Charwoman. Good night. (*She exits, and* Scrooge *pantomimes shutting the door behind her. The voice of* Marley *over an offstage microphone whispers and reverberates: "Merry Christmas, Scrooge!" Silence.* Scrooge *hears the voice but cannot account for it. He climbs up to open a window and looks down. A cathedral choir singing "O Come, All Ye Faithful" is heard in the distance.* Scrooge *listens a moment, shuts the window, and prepares for bed. As soon as he has shut the sound out of his room, figures appear; they seem to be coming down the main aisle of a church, bearing gifts to the living*

REVIEWING IMAGERY Remind students that words and phrases that appeal to the reader's senses are known as imagery. Explain that writers use details to help readers imagine how things look, feel, smell, sound, and taste. Point out the images of sight and touch in the highlighted passage on page 227.

Application Have students skim the stage directions and the dialogue to identify other examples of words and phrases that appeal to the senses.

crèche. The orchestra plays "O Come, All Ye Faithful" as the procession files out. Scrooge, ready for bed, warms himself before the heap of coals. As he pulls his nightcap from a chair, a small hand-bell tumbles off onto the floor. Startled, he picks it up and rings it for reassurance; *an echo answers it. He turns and sees the little girl on the street; she is swinging her doll, which produces the echo of his bell. Scrooge escapes to his bed; the girl is swallowed up in the darkness. The bell sounds grow to a din, incoherent as in a dream, then suddenly fall silent. Scrooge sits up in bed, listens, and hears the chains of Marley coming up the stairs. Scrooge reaches for the bell pull to* summon *Sparsit. The bell responds with a gong, and Marley appears. He and Scrooge face one another.)*

Scrooge. What do you want with me?

Marley (*in a ghostly, unreal voice*). Much.

Scrooge. Who are you?

Marley. Ask who I was.

Scrooge. Who were you?

Marley. In life, I was your partner, Jacob Marley.

Scrooge. He's dead.

Marley. Seven years this night, Ebenezer Scrooge.

Scrooge. Why do you come here?

Marley. I must. It is commanded me. I must wander the world and see what I can no longer share, what I would not share when I walked where you do.

Scrooge. And must go thus?

Marley. The chain? Look at it, Ebenezer, study it. Locks and vaults and golden coins. I forged it, each link, each day when I sat in these chairs, commanded these rooms. Greed, Ebenezer Scrooge, wealth. Feel them, know them. Yours was as heavy as this I wear seven years ago, and you have labored to build it since.

Scrooge. If you're here to lecture, I have no time for it. It is late; the night is cold. I want comfort now.

Marley. I have none to give. I know not how you see me this night. I did not ask it. I have sat invisible beside you many and many a day. I am commanded to bring you a chance, Ebenezer. Heed it!

Scrooge. Quickly then, quickly.

Marley. You will be haunted by three spirits.

Scrooge (*scoffing*). Is that the chance?

Marley. Mark it.

Scrooge. I do not choose to.

Marley (*ominously*). Then you will walk where I do, burdened by your riches, your greed.

Scrooge. Spirits mean nothing to me.

Marley (*slowly leaving*). Expect the first tomorrow, when the bell tolls one, the second on the next night at the same hour, the third upon the next night when the last stroke of twelve has ended. Look to see me no more. I must wander. Look that, for your own sake, you remember what has passed between us.

Scrooge. Jacob . . . Don't leave me! . . . Jacob! Jacob!

Marley. Adieu, Ebenezer. (*At* Marley's *last words a funeral procession begins to move across the stage. A boy walks in front; a priest follows, swinging a censer; sounds of mourning and the suggestion of church music are heard. Scrooge calls out, "Jacob, don't leave me!" as if talking in the midst of a bad dream. At the end of the procession is the little girl, swinging her doll and singing softly.*)

Girl.
Hushabye, don't you cry,
Go to sleep, little baby.
When you wake, you shall have

WORDS TO KNOW
reassurance (rē′ə-shŏŏr′əns) *n.* a restoring of confidence
summon (sŭm′ən) *v.* To call for or send for with authority or urgency; to order to come or appear

227

Linking To Social Studies

P Explain that in the 19th century both men and women wore soft cotton or woolen caps to bed at night to protect them from the cold. Many people also warmed their beds by passing long-handled brass pans filled with hot coals over the sheets.

Critical Thinking:
HYPOTHESIZING

Q Have students identify Marley and infer why his spirit has appeared to Scrooge. Guide students to recall Scrooge's actions to help them guess why Marley has appeared. (*Possible responses: Marley was Scrooge's business partner; this Christmas Eve is the seventh anniversary of his death. He may be haunting Scrooge because of some unfinished business; perhaps he wants to warn Scrooge about the consequences of his greed.*)

CUSTOMIZING FOR
Multiple Learning Styles

R **Musical Learners** Invite students to select background music for this scene. Remind students to refer to the stage directions as well as to the dialogue to determine the scene's mood. Their music choices should reflect this mood.

CUSTOMIZING FOR
Students Acquiring English

3 Point out that *adieu* is a French word for "goodbye." Marley's use of it gives his leaving of Scrooge a very formal final feeling.

Literary Concept: SYMBOL

S Challenge students to explain what the funeral procession symbolizes. (*Possible responses: Marley's death, Scrooge's death, the death of the Christmas spirit*)

T Have students think about what the little girl and the leper might represent. *(Possible responses: The little girl might represent hope; the leper, disease and death.)*

Active Reading: PREDICT

U Ask students to predict how Scrooge will react to Marley's warning. *(Possible responses: He will ignore it; he will try to mend his ways.)*

STRATEGIC READING FOR

Less-Proficient Readers

V Discuss Marley's appearance and possible reasons for it.

• What is Marley's chain and why does he wear it? *(Marley's chain represents the wealth he hoarded during his life; it is punishment for his greed.)* **Making Inferences**

• Why has Marley appeared? *(to warn Scrooge he is destined for the same sad fate)* **Finding the Main Idea**

Set a Purpose Have students find out what the Spirit of Christmas Past reveals.

Active Reading: PREDICT

W Guide students to combine the information from the stage directions and opening dialogue to predict what this spirit will reveal. *(Possible response: Scrooge's childhood and early years)*

All the pretty little horses,
Blacks and bays, dapples and grays,
All the pretty little horses.

T (*She stops singing and looks up at* Scrooge; *their eyes meet, and she solemnly rings the doll in greeting.* Scrooge *pulls shut the bed curtains, and the* girl *exits. The bell sounds are picked up by the bells of a* leper *who enters, dragging himself along.*)

Leper (*calling out*). Leper! Leper! Stay the way! Leper! Leper! Keep away! (*He exits and the clock begins to chime, ringing the hours.* Scrooge *sits up in bed and begins to count the chimes.*)

Scrooge. Eight . . . nine . . . ten . . . eleven . . . it can't be . . . twelve. Midnight? No. Not twelve. It can't be. I haven't slept the whole day through. Twelve? Yes, yes, twelve noon. (*He hurries to the window and looks out.*) Black. Twelve midnight. (*pause*) I must get up. A day wasted. I must get down to the office. (*Two small chimes are heard.*) Quarter past. But it just rang twelve. Fifteen minutes haven't gone past, not so quickly. (*Again two small chimes are heard.*) A quarter to one. The spirit . . . It's to come at one. (*He hurries to his bed as the chimes ring again.*) One.

Scene 3

THE SPIRIT OF CHRISTMAS PAST

The hour is struck again by a large street clock, and the first spirit *appears. It is a figure dressed to look like the little girl's doll.*

W **Scrooge.** Are you the spirit whose coming was foretold to me?

First Spirit. I am.

Scrooge. Who and what are you?

First Spirit. I am the Ghost of Christmas Past.

Scrooge. Long past?

First Spirit. Your past.

Scrooge. Why are you here?

First Spirit. Your <u>welfare</u>. Rise. Walk with me.

Scrooge. I am <u>mortal</u> still. I cannot pass through air.

First Spirit. My hand. (Scrooge *grasps the* spirit's *hand tightly, and the doll's bell rings softly.* Scrooge *remembers a scene from his past in which two boys greet each other in the street.*)

First Voice. Halloo, Jack!

Second Voice. Ben! Merry Christmas, Ben!

Scrooge. Jack Walton. Young Jack Walton. Spirits . . . ?

First Voice. Have a good holiday, Jack.

Scrooge. Yes, yes, I remember him. Both of them. Little Ben Benjamin. He used to . . .

First Voice. See you next term, Jack. Next . . . term . . .

Scrooge. They . . . they're off for the holidays and going home from school. It's Christmas time . . . all of the children off home now . . . No . . . no, not all . . . there was one . . . (*The* spirit *motions for* Scrooge *to turn, and he sees a young* boy *playing with a teddy bear and talking to it.*) Yes . . . reading . . . poor boy.

First Spirit. What, I wonder?

WORDS TO KNOW	**welfare** (wĕl′fâr′) *n.* well-being
	mortal (môr′tl) *adj.* of the earth; not a spirit

228

Mini-Lesson  **The Writer's Style**

DIALOGUE IN PLAYS AND SKITS Explain to students that writers use dialogue, or a conversation between two or more characters, in stories, poems, and plays. Mention that plays and skits are made up almost entirely of dialogue. Tell the class that dialogue moves the action along, makes it more interesting, and helps readers understand the characters by providing clues about their thoughts and feelings. Look at some examples of dialogue from the play to show students that Scrooge's attitudes are suggested by what he says.

Application Have students reread the dialogue on pages 228–232 to find examples of how Scrooge becomes childlike when he recalls his early experiences. Then have students select passages of dialogue to read aloud, telling what each passage suggests about the thoughts and feelings of Scrooge or the other characters in the scene.

Reteaching/Reinforcement
• *Writer's Handbook,* anthology p. 815
• *Writing Mini-Lessons* transparencies, p. 48

 **The Writer's Craft**

Creating Dialogue, pp. 320–322

Critical Thinking:
HYPOTHESIZING

X Have students analyze why Scrooge's dialogue changes and becomes childlike. *(Possible response: By speaking like a child and imitating the parrot, Scrooge is reliving his past, losing himself in the delight in reading that he once knew as a child.)*

Literary Concept:
FLASHBACK

Y Guide students to identify the portion of the plot that is out of chronological order and explain its purpose. *(Possible responses: The events from Scrooge's childhood are out of order. Reliving the past allows Scrooge to learn from both pleasures and miseries, and the audience can compare Scrooge as a child with Scrooge as an old man.)*

Linking To History

Z In the 19th century, many boys from middle-class and upper-class British families attended boarding schools rather than day schools. Most boys returned to their families during holidays and vacations, but some others, like Scrooge, remained at school year-round.

Active Reading: EVALUATE

AA Ask students what they think the Spirit is trying to teach Scrooge and what—if anything—he has learned. *(Possible responses: The Spirit wants Scrooge to learn charity, sympathy, generosity, and enjoyment of life's offerings. It appears that Scrooge has not learned this lesson.)*

Scrooge. Reading? Oh, it was nothing. Fancy,[3] all fancy and make-believe and take-me-away. All of it. Yes, nonsense.

Child Scrooge. Ali Baba.[4]

Scrooge. Yes . . . that was it. . . .

Child Scrooge. Yes, and remember . . . and remember . . . remember Robinson Crusoe?[5]

Scrooge. And the parrot!

Child Scrooge. Yes, the parrot! I love him best.

X **Scrooge** (*imitating the parrot*). With his stripy green body and yellow tail drooping along and couldn't sing—awk—but could talk, and a thing like a lettuce growing out the top of his head . . . and he used to sit on the very top of the tree—up there.

Child Scrooge. And Robinson Crusoe sailed around the island, and he thought he had escaped the island, and the parrot said, the parrot said . . .

Scrooge (*imitating the parrot*). Robinson Crusoe, where you been? Awk! Robinson Crusoe, where you been?

Child Scrooge. And Robinson Crusoe looked up in the tree and saw the parrot and knew he hadn't escaped and he was still there, still all alone there.

Scrooge. Poor Robinson Crusoe.

Child Scrooge (*sadly replacing the teddy bear*). Poor Robinson Crusoe.

Scrooge. Poor child. Poor child.

First Spirit. Why poor?

Y **Scrooge.** Fancy . . . fancy . . . (*He tries to mask his feelings by being brusque.*) It's his way, a child's way to . . . to lose being alone in . . . in dreams, dreams . . . Never matter if they are all nonsense, yes, nonsense. But he'll be all right, grow out of it. Yes. Yes, he did outgrow it, the nonsense. Became a man and left there, and he became, yes, he became a man and . . . yes, successful . . . rich! (*The sadness returns.*) Never matter . . . never matter. ((*Fan runs in and goes to* Child Scrooge.) Fan!

Fan. Brother, dear brother! (*She kisses* Child Scrooge.)

Child Scrooge. Dear, dear Fan.

Fan. I've come to bring you home, home for good and ever. Come with me, come now. (*She takes his hand, and they start to run off, but the* spirit *stops them and signals for the light on them to fade. They look at the* spirit, *aware of their role in the* spirit's *"education" of* Scrooge.)

Scrooge. Let me watch them go? Let them be happy for a moment! (*The* spirit *says nothing.* Scrooge *turns away from them, and the light goes out.*) A delicate, delicate child. A breath might have withered her.

First Spirit. She died a woman and had, as I remember, children.

Scrooge. One child.

First Spirit. Your nephew.

Scrooge. Yes, yes, Fred, my nephew. (Scrooge *pauses, then tries to bluster through.*) Well? Well, all of us have that, haven't we? Childhoods? Sadnesses? But we grow and we become men, masters of ourselves. (*The* spirit *gestures for music to begin. It is heard first as from a great distance, then* Scrooge *becomes aware of it.*) I've no time for it, Spirit. Music and all of your Christmas folderol. Yes, yes, I've learnt what you have to show me. (Fezziwig, Young Ebenezer, *and* Dick *appear, busily preparing for a party.*)

Fezziwig. Yo ho, there! Ebenezer! Dick!

---

3. **fancy:** illusion.

4. **Ali Baba** (ä′lē bä′bə): in the *Arabian Nights*, a poor woodcutter who discovers the treasure-filled cave of 40 thieves.

5. **Robinson Crusoe:** in the novel *Robinson Crusoe* by Daniel Defoe, a shipwrecked sailor who survives for years on a small island.

Scrooge. Fezziwig! It's old Fezziwig that I 'prenticed[6] under.

First Spirit. Your master?

Scrooge. Oh, aye, and the best that any boy could have. There's Dick Wilkins! Bless me. He was very much attached to me was Dick. Poor Dick. Dear, dear.

Fezziwig. Yo ho, my boys! No more work tonight. Christmas Eve, Dick! Christmas, Ebenezer! Let's have the shutters up before a man can say Jack Robinson! (*The music continues. Chandeliers are pulled into position, and mistletoe, holly, and ivy are draped over everything by bustling servants. Dancers fill the stage for Fezziwig's wonderful Christmas party. In the midst of the dancing and the gaiety servants pass back and forth through the crowd with huge platters of food. At a pause in the music,* Young Ebenezer, *who is dancing, calls out.*)

Young Ebenezer. Mr. Fezziwig, sir, you're a wonderful master!

Scrooge and Young Ebenezer. A wonderful master!

Scrooge (*echoing the phrase*). A wonderful master! (*The music changes suddenly, and the dancers jerk into distorted postures and then begin to move in slow motion. The celebrants slowly exit, performing a macabre dance to discordant sounds.*)

First Spirit. Just because he gave a party? It was very small.

Scrooge. Small!

First Spirit. He spent a few pounds[7] of your "mortal" money, three, four at the most. Is that so much that he deserves this praise?

Scrooge. But it wasn't the money. He had the power to make us happy, to make our service light or burdensome. The happiness he gives is quite as great as if it cost a fortune. That's what . . . a good master is.

First Spirit. Yes?

Scrooge. No, no, nothing.

First Spirit. Something, I think.

Scrooge. I should like to be able to say a word or two to my clerk just now, that's all.

First Spirit. But this is all past. Your clerk, Cratchit, couldn't be here.

Scrooge. No, no, of course not, an idle thought. Are we done?

First Spirit (*motioning for the waltz music to begin*). Nearly.

Scrooge (*hearing the waltz and remembering it*). Surely it's enough. Haven't you tormented me enough? (Young Ebenezer *is seen waltzing with his* Sweetheart.)

First Spirit. I only show the past, what it promised you. Look. Another promise.

Scrooge. Oh. Oh, yes. I had forgotten . . . her. Don't they dance beautifully? So young, so young. I would have married her if only . . .

Sweetheart. Can you love me, Ebenezer? I bring no dowry[8] to my marriage, only me, only love. It is no currency that you can buy and sell with, but we can live with it. Can you? (*She pauses, then returns the ring* Scrooge *gave her as his pledge.*) I release you, Ebenezer, for the love of the man you once were. Will that man win me again, now that he is free?

Scrooge (*trying to speak to her*). If only you had held me to it. You should not have let me go. I was young; I did love you.

Sweetheart (*speaking to* Young Ebenezer). We

---

6. **'prenticed:** short for apprenticed, here meaning "learned a trade while working."

7. **pounds:** basic British units of money, each equal to 20 shillings.

8. **dowry:** the property a bride brings to her husband when they marry.

| WORDS TO KNOW | **currency** (kûr′ən-sē) *n.* money |
| | **pledge** (plĕj) *n.* something given to guarantee fulfillment of a promise |

231

Literary Concept: CHARACTER

BB Ask students to compare and contrast the way Fezziwig and Scrooge treat their employees and to explore what their behavior reveals about each character. (*Possible responses: Fezziwig is a kind, generous, jovial master; Scrooge is a nasty, stingy, and disagreeable master.*)

Active Reading: CLARIFY

CC Ask students to explain why the First Spirit shows Scrooge the Christmas scene with his first master. (*Possible response: The Spirit wants Scrooge to learn from his former master how to treat people. The Spirit hopes Scrooge will become a better master— and person.*)

Critical Thinking: SPECULATING

DD Ask students what they think Scrooge would like to say to Cratchit. (*Possible response: Scrooge would like to apologize to Cratchit for the unkind way he has treated him or to wish Cratchit a "Merry Christmas."*)

CUSTOMIZING FOR

Multiple Learning Styles

EE Interpersonal Learners Invite students to create a dialogue or skit that shows Scrooge and his sweetheart resolving their differences.

Multicultural Perspectives

Christmas in Latin America is deeply swathed in rich tradition. In Santa Domingo, Puerto Rico, Venezuela, and some other Latin American countries, groups serenade outside other friends' houses, a custom called *trulla* or *asalto*. The host rewards his friends with food and drink and joins the party. A Mexican tradition calls for children and sometimes adults to form a procession. Holding a decorated tree branch, the people go from house to house singing and asking for their *aguindaldo*, which are Christmas presents in the form of candy and coins. Epiphany is a special part of the Christmas celebration. In Puerto Rico, for instance, friends and family gather to sing and pray to the three kings at a celebration called *Vigilia de los Reyes*. At dawn, the vigil ends and the families have a feast, which often includes roasted pig, rice and pigeon peas, sausages, and banana croquettes. To prepare for the kings, children put shoeboxes lined with grass under their beds. The kings come during the night and leave toys for the children; their camels eat the grass!

FF Ask students why Scrooge didn't marry his sweetheart. *(Possible response: because she didn't have a dowry, and he wanted money more than love.)*

GG Explore what the Spirit of Christmas Past reveals about Scrooge's childhood and early manhood.

• What was Scrooge like as a child? *(lonely; he loved books and his sister.)* **Drawing Conclusions**

• According to Scrooge, why was Fezziwig a good master? *(He made his workers happy and their service light.)* **Noting Relevant Details**

• What does the Ghost show Scrooge? *(the good times and mistakes of his youth)* **Summarizing**

Set a Purpose Have students find out what lessons Scrooge learns from the Spirit of Christmas Present.

From Personal Response to Critical Analysis

1. Possible response: child Scrooge, because he seems so vulnerable
2. Possible responses: Both Scrooge and Marley have wasted their lives pursuing money. Scrooge is cruel, whereas Fezziwig is kind, especially to his employees.
3. Possible responses: He let love slip through his fingers because of greed; he never told his sister how much she meant to him.
4. Possible response: They make him recall his childhood and rethink his opinions about the poor.

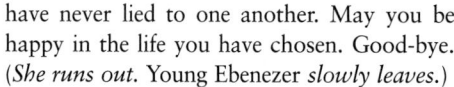

have never lied to one another. May you be happy in the life you have chosen. Good-bye. (*She runs out.* Young Ebenezer *slowly leaves.*)

FF **Scrooge.** No, no, it was not meant that way . . . !

First Spirit. You cannot change now what you would not change then. I am your mistakes, Ebenezer Scrooge, all of the things you could have done and did not.

Scrooge. Then leave me! I have done them. I shall live with them. As I have, as I do; as I will.

First Spirit. There is another Christmas, seven years ago, when Marley died.

Scrooge. No! I will not see it. I will not! He died. I could not prevent it. I did not choose for him to die on Christmas Day.

First Spirit. And when his day was chosen, what did you do then?

Scrooge. I looked after his affairs.

First Spirit. His business.

Scrooge. Yes! His business! Mine! It was all that I had, all that I could do in this world. I have nothing to do with the world to come after.

First Spirit. Then I will leave you.

Scrooge. Not yet! Don't leave me here! Tell me what I must do! What of the other spirits?

First Spirit. They will come.

Scrooge. And you? What of you?

First Spirit. I am always with you. (*The little girl appears with her doll; she takes* Scrooge's *hand and gently leads him to bed. Numbed, he follows her. She leans against the foot of the bed, ringing the doll and singing. The* first spirit *exits as she sings.*)

Girl.

When you wake, you shall have
All the pretty little horses,
Blacks and bays, dapples and grays,
All the pretty little horses.

(*She rings the doll, and the ringing becomes the chiming of* Scrooge's *bell. The* girl *exits.* Scrooge *sits upright in bed as he hears the chimes.*)

Scrooge. A minute until one. No one here. No one's coming. (*A larger clock strikes one o'clock.*)

FROM PERSONAL RESPONSE TO CRITICAL ANALYSIS

REFLECT 1. Which character in Scenes 2 and 3 made the strongest impression on you, and why? In your notebook, jot down words and phrases to describe that character.

RETHINK 2. Compare and contrast Scrooge with his late partner, Jacob Marley, and with his old master, Fezziwig.

3. The Spirit of Christmas Past reveals memories of Scrooge's youth. What are the most serious mistakes Scrooge has made?
   Consider
   • his childhood
   • his sister, Fan, and her son
   • his old master, Fezziwig
   • his sweetheart

4. In Scenes 2 and 3, Scrooge encounters a number of different children, such as the girl with the doll and even himself as a child. What effect do you think these children have on Scrooge?

232 UNIT TWO PART 2: MAKING CHOICES

Scene 4

THE SPIRIT OF CHRISTMAS PRESENT

A light comes on. Scrooge *becomes aware of it and goes slowly to it. He sees the* second spirit, *the Spirit of Christmas Present, who looks like* Fezziwig.

Scrooge. Fezziwig!

Second Spirit. Hello, Scrooge.

Scrooge. But you can't be . . . not Fezziwig.

Second Spirit. Do you see me as him?

Scrooge. I do.

Second Spirit. And hear me as him?

Scrooge. I do.

Second Spirit. I wish I were the gentleman, so as not to disappoint you.

Scrooge. But you're not . . . ?

Second Spirit. No, Mr. Scrooge. You have never seen the like of me before. I am the Ghost of Christmas Present.

Scrooge. But . . .

Second Spirit. You see what you will see, Scrooge, no more. Will you walk out with me this Christmas Eve?

Scrooge. But I am not yet dressed.

Second Spirit. Take my tails, dear boy, we're leaving.

Scrooge. Wait!

Second Spirit. What is it now?

Scrooge. Christmas Present, did you say?

Second Spirit. I did.

Scrooge. Then we are traveling here? In this town? London? Just down there?

Second Spirit. Yes, yes, of course.

Scrooge. Then we could walk? Your flying is . . . well, too sudden for an old man. Well?

Second Spirit. It's your Christmas, Scrooge; I am only the guide.

Scrooge (*puzzled*). Then we can walk? (*The* spirit *nods.*) Where are you guiding me to?

Second Spirit. Bob Cratchit's.

Scrooge. My clerk?

Second Spirit. You did want to talk to him? (Scrooge *pauses, uncertain how to answer.*) Don't worry, Scrooge, you won't have to.

Scrooge (*trying to change the subject, to cover his error*). Shouldn't be much of a trip. With fifteen bob[9] a week, how far off can it be?

Second Spirit. A world away, Scrooge, at least that far. (Scrooge *and the* spirit *start to step off a curb when a funeral procession enters with a child's coffin, followed by the* poor-house children, *who are singing. Seated on top of the coffin is the little* girl. *She and* Scrooge *look at one another.*) That is the way to it, Scrooge. (*The procession follows the coffin offstage;* Scrooge *and the* spirit *exit after the procession. As they leave, the lights focus on* Mrs. Cratchit *and her* children. Mrs. Cratchit *sings as she puts* Tiny Tim *and the other children to bed, all in one bed. She pulls a dark blanket over them.*)

Mrs. Cratchit (*singing*).
When you wake, you shall have
All the pretty little horses,
Blacks and bays, dapples and grays,
All the pretty little horses.

---

9. **bob:** a British slang term for shilling.

A CHRISTMAS CAROL **233**

Active Reading: PREDICT

HH Invite students to predict who the Third Spirit will be, based on the identity of the First and Second Spirits. (*Possible response: Since the First Spirit is the Spirit of Christmas Past, and the Second Spirit is the Spirit of Christmas Present, the Third Spirit probably will be the Spirit of Christmas Yet to Come.*)

Literary Concept: HUMOR

II Explain that playwrights sometimes create humor through the use of situational irony, as when the reader expects one thing to happen, but something surprising happens instead. Then have students explain what they find ironic about Scrooge's remark. (*Possible response: It is ironic that Scrooge is afraid to fly on the Spirit's coattails when he has calmly accepted ghosts and visions of his past.*)

Critical Thinking: MAKING JUDGMENTS

JJ Ask students if "a world away" is an appropriate way to describe Cratchit's home. Have students explain their answers. (*Possible response: Yes, physically, Cratchit's home is very close by. However, symbolically, it is very far away, because it represents a very different social class and is a happy place, in contrast to Scrooge's unhappy home.*)

Mini-Lesson / **Genre Study**

DRAMA On the board or chart paper, draw the web shown. Use the web as a springboard to explain that **drama** is a kind of writing with the following qualities:
- It is meant to be performed.
- The story is told through dialogue and the characters' actions.
- Stage directions suggest how the actors should move and speak.
- The action may be divided into acts and scenes.

Application Have students copy the web into their notebooks. Ask them to add details to the web based on their reading of *A Christmas Carol*. For instance, they might jot down ideas about how the play could be performed, list characters' actions that are particularly vivid, or record lines of dialogue that they find appealing. After they are finished, divide students into groups of four or five to share their webs and discuss their notations.

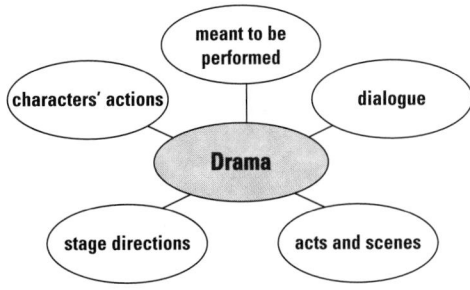

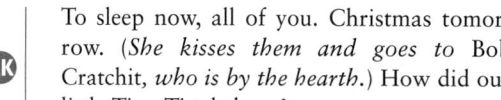

KK To sleep now, all of you. Christmas tomorrow. (*She kisses them and goes to* Bob Cratchit, *who is by the hearth.*) How did our little Tiny Tim behave?

Bob Cratchit. As good as gold and better. He told me, coming home, that he hoped the people saw him in church because he was a cripple and it might be pleasant to them to remember upon Christmas Day who made the lame to walk and the blind to see.

Mrs. Cratchit. He's a good boy. (*The second spirit and* Scrooge *enter.* Mrs. Cratchit *feels a sudden draft.*) Oh, the wind. (*She gets up to shut the door.*)

Second Spirit. Hurry. (*He nudges* Scrooge *in before* Mrs. Cratchit *shuts the door.*)

Scrooge. Hardly hospitable is what I'd say.

LL **Second Spirit.** Oh, they'd say a great deal more, Scrooge, if they could see you.

Scrooge. Oh, they should, should they?

Second Spirit. Oh yes, I'd think they might.

Scrooge. Well, I might have a word for them . . .

Second Spirit. You're here to listen.

Scrooge. Oh. Oh yes, all right. By the fire?

Second Spirit. But not a word.

Bob Cratchit (*raising his glass*). My dear, to Mr. Scrooge. I give you Mr. Scrooge, the founder of the feast.

Mrs. Cratchit. The founder of the feast indeed! I wish I had him here! I'd give him a piece of my mind to feast upon, and I hope he'd have a good appetite for it.

Bob Cratchit. My dear, Christmas Eve.

Mrs. Cratchit. It should be Christmas Eve, I'm sure, when one drinks the health of such an odious, stingy, hard, unfeeling man as Mr. Scrooge. You know he is, Robert! Nobody knows it better than you do, poor dear.

Bob Cratchit. I only know one thing on Christmas: that one must be <u>charitable</u>.

Mrs. Cratchit. I'll drink to his health for your sake and the day's, not for his. Long life to him! A Merry Christmas and a Happy New Year. He'll be very merry and very happy, I have no doubt.

Bob Cratchit. If he cannot be, we must be happy for him. A song is what is needed. Tim!

Mrs. Cratchit. Shush! I've just gotten him down, and he needs all the sleep he can get.

Bob Cratchit. If he's asleep on Christmas Eve, I'll be much mistaken. Tim! He must sing, dear; there is nothing else that might make him well.

Tiny Tim. Yes, Father?

Bob Cratchit. Are you awake?

Tiny Tim. Just a little.

Bob Cratchit. A song then! (*The* children *awaken and, led by* Tiny Tim, *sit up to sing "What Child Is This?" As they sing,* Scrooge *speaks.*)

Scrooge. Spirit. (*He holds up his hand; all stop singing and look at him.*) I . . . I have seen enough. (*When the* spirit *signals to the children, they leave the stage, singing the carol quietly.* Tiny Tim *remains, covered completely by the dark blanket, disappearing against the black.*) Tiny Tim . . . will he live?

Second Spirit. He is very ill. Even song cannot keep him whole through a cold winter.

Scrooge. But you haven't told me!

Second Spirit (*imitating* Scrooge). If he be like to die, he had better do it and decrease the surplus population. (Scrooge *turns away.*) Erase, Scrooge, those words from your thoughts. You are not the judge. Do not judge, then. It may be that in the sight of heaven you are more worthless and less fit to live than millions like this poor man's child. Oh God! To hear an insect on a leaf pronouncing that

WORDS
TO
KNOW

charitable (chăr′ĭ-tə-bəl) *adj.* generous in giving

234

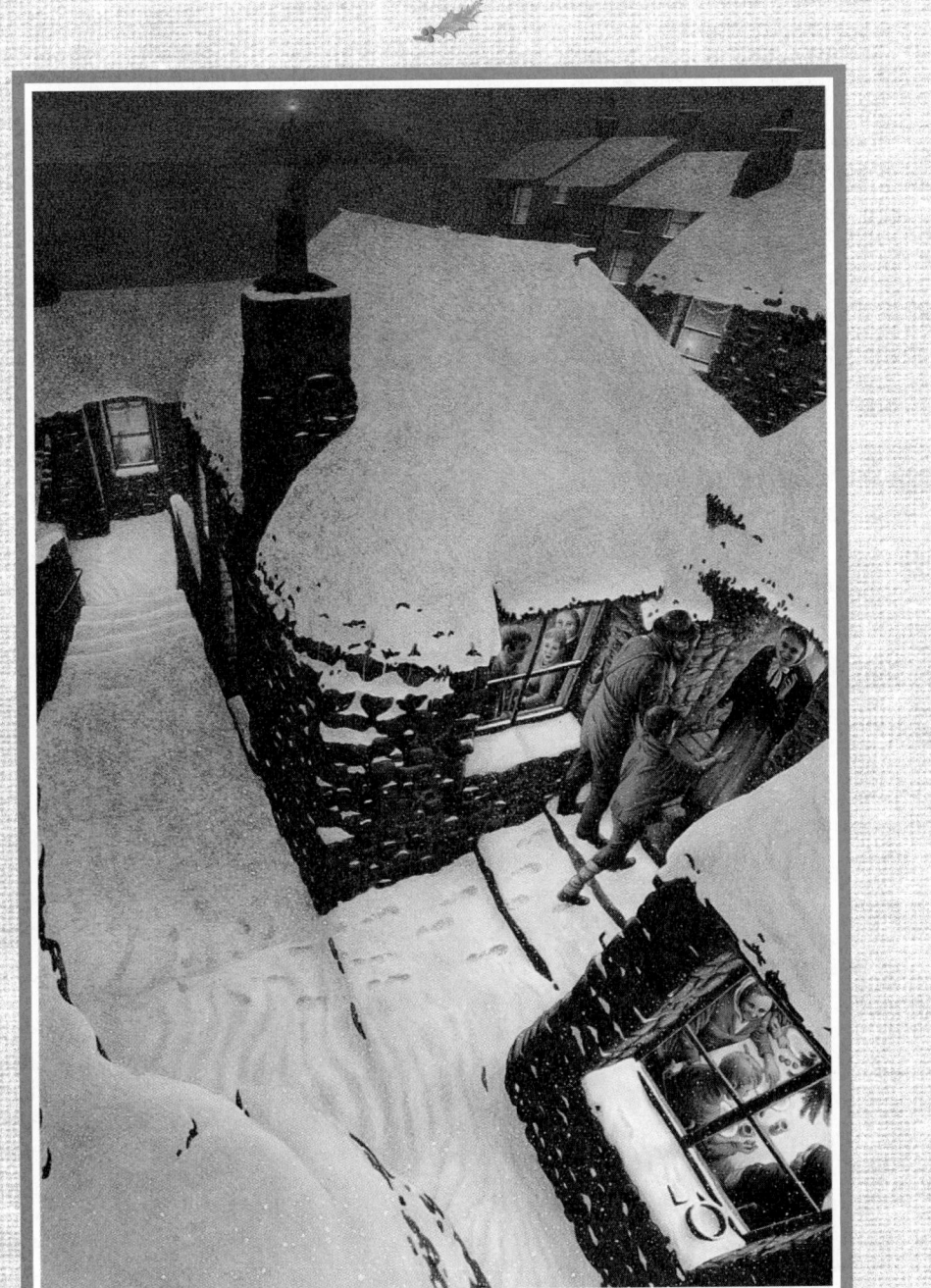

A CHRISTMAS CAROL **235**

| Mini-Lesson Speaking, | Listening, and Viewing |

FILM/DRAMA The first filmed version of *A Christmas Carol* appeared in 1908; since then, many versions have been produced and are available on video. You may wish to show a video of *A Christmas Carol* so that students can compare their images of the play with a filmed version. The Michael Redgrave production, part of The Christmas Collection, runs 30 minutes, so it can be shown during a class period. The 1951 British version by Brian Desmond-Hurst, starring Alastair Sim as Scrooge, is also widely available and runs 86 minutes.

Application After students have seen the video, ask them to explain whether it captured the play the way they envision it. Explain that filmmakers plan each scene with storyboards, or rough sketches depicting the plot, action, and characters. Arrange students in small groups to create storyboards for different scenes of the play, based on their interpretation and the video. As each group displays its storyboards, have them explain what elements they took from the filmed version and what elements from the written one.

PP Ask students why they think Scrooge refuses to go to his nephew Fred's house. Guide students to find details about Scrooge's character that can help them infer his reasons. *(Possible responses: Scrooge is too proud to go to Fred's house because he was so surly in refusing Fred's earlier gracious invitation. Scrooge is afraid of seeing more that will hurt him.)*

Literary Concept: SYMBOL

QQ Have students explain the significance of the children who represent Hunger and Ignorance. Ask why they are shown as children, and what the Spirit means by the last line here. *(Possible response: Just as children grow, the problems of hunger and ignorance only get greater. If Scrooge ignores hunger and ignorance, they will get worse.)*

STRATEGIC READING FOR
Less-Proficient Readers

RR Discuss what Scrooge learns from the second Spirit.

• What do the Cratchits have that Scrooge doesn't? *(Possible responses: a loving family; a happy home; kind, charitable natures)* Comparing and Contrasting

• What does the Second Spirit tell Scrooge about the needs of the poor? *(that the hunger and ignorance of the poor are real; that if he continues to ignore the needs of the poor, their needs will only increase)* Summarizing

Set a Purpose As students read the rest of the play, have them see if Scrooge changes as a result of his experiences with the spirits.

---

there is too much life among his hungry brothers in the dust. Good-bye, Scrooge.

Scrooge. But is there no happiness in Christmas Present?

Second Spirit. There is.

Scrooge. Take me there.

Second Spirit. It is at the home of your nephew . . .

Scrooge. No!

Second Spirit (*disgusted with* Scrooge). Then there is none.

Scrooge. But that isn't enough . . . You must teach me!

Second Spirit. Would you have a teacher, Scrooge? Look at your own words.

Scrooge. But the first spirit gave me more . . . !

Second Spirit. He was Christmas Past. There was a lifetime he could choose from. I have only this day, one day, and you, Scrooge. I have nearly lived my fill of both. Christmas Present must be gone at midnight. That is near now. (*He speaks to two* beggar children *who pause shyly at the far side of the stage. The* children *are thin and wan; they are barefoot and wear filthy rags.*) Come. (*They go to him.*)

Scrooge. Is this the last spirit who is to come to me?

Second Spirit. They are no spirits. They are real. Hunger, Ignorance. Not spirits, Scrooge, passing dreams. They are real. They walk your streets, look to you for comfort. And you deny them. Deny them not too long, Scrooge. They will grow and multiply, and they will not remain children.

Scrooge. Have they no refuge, no resource?

Second Spirit (*again imitating* Scrooge). Are there no prisons? Are there no workhouses? (*tenderly to the* children) Come. It's Christmas Eve. (*He leads them offstage.*)

Scene 5

THE SPIRIT OF CHRISTMAS YET TO COME

Scrooge *is entirely alone for a long moment. He is frightened by the darkness and feels it approaching him. Suddenly he stops, senses the presence of the* third spirit, *turns toward him, and sees him. The* spirit *is bent and cloaked. No physical features are distinguishable.*

Scrooge. You are the third. (*The* spirit *says nothing.*) The Ghost of Christmas Yet to Come. (*The* spirit *says nothing.*) Speak to me. Tell me what is to happen—to me, to all of us. (*The* spirit *says nothing.*) Then show me what I must see. (*The* spirit *points. Light illumines the shadowy recesses of* Scrooge's *house.*) I know it. I know it too well, cold and cheerless. It is mine. (*The* cook *and the* char-woman *are dimly visible in* Scrooge's *house.*) What is . . . ? There are . . . thieves! There are thieves in my rooms! (*He starts forward to accost them, but the* spirit *beckons for him to stop.*) I cannot. You cannot tell me that I must watch them and do nothing. I will not. It is mine still. (*He rushes into the house to claim his belongings and to protect them. The* two women *do not notice his presence.*)

Cook. He ain't about, is he? (*The* charwoman *laughs.*) Poor ol' Scrooge 'as met 'is end.[10] (*She laughs with the* charwoman.)

Charwoman. An' time for it, too; ain't been alive in deed for half his life.

Cook. But the Sparsit's nowhere, is he . . . ?

Sparsit (*emerging from the blackness*). Lookin' for someone, ladies? (*The* cook *shrieks, but the* charwoman *treats the matter more practically, anticipating competition from* Sparsit.)

Charwoman. There ain't enough but for the two of us!

Sparsit. More 'an enough . . . if you know where to look.

Cook. Hardly decent is what I'd say, hardly decent, the poor old fella hardly cold and you're thievin' his wardrobe.

Sparsit. You're here out of love, are ya?

Charwoman. There's no time for that. (Sparsit *acknowledges* Scrooge *for the first time, gesturing toward him as if the living* Scrooge *were the corpse.* Scrooge *stands as if rooted to the spot, held there by the power of the spirit.*)

Sparsit. He ain't about to bother us, is he?

Charwoman. Ain't he a picture?

Cook. If he is, it ain't a happy one. (*They laugh.*)

Sparsit. Ladies, shall we start? (*The three of them grin and advance on* Scrooge.) Cook?

Cook (*snatching the cuff links from the shirt* Scrooge *wears*). They're gold, ain't they?

Sparsit. The purest, madam.

Charwoman. I always had a fancy for that nightcap of his. My old man could use it. (*She takes the nightcap from* Scrooge's *head.* Sparsit *playfully removes* Scrooge's *outer garment, the coat or cloak that he has worn in the previous scenes.*)

Sparsit. Bein' a man of more practical tastes, I'll go for the worsted[11] and hope the smell ain't permanent. (*The three laugh.*) Cook, we go round again.

Cook. Do you think that little bell he's always ringing at me is silver enough to sell? (*The three of them move toward the nightstand, and* Scrooge *cries out.*)

Scrooge. No more! No more! (*As the spirit directs* Scrooge's *attention to the tableau[12] of the three thieves standing poised over the silver bell,* Scrooge *bursts out of the house, clad only in his nightshirt.*) I cannot. I cannot. The room is . . . too like a cheerless place that is familiar. I won't see it. Let us go from here. Anywhere. (*The spirit directs his attention to the* Cratchit *house; the children are sitting together near* Mrs. Cratchit, *who is sewing a coat.* Peter *reads by the light of the coals.*)

Peter. "And he took a child and set him in the midst of them."

Mrs. Cratchit (*putting her hand to her face*). The light tires my eyes so. (*pause*) They're better now. It makes them tired to try to see by firelight, and I wouldn't show reddened eyes to your father when he comes home for the world. It must be near his time now.

Peter. Past it, I think, but he walks slower than he used to, these last few days, Mother.

Mrs. Cratchit. I have known him to walk with . . . I have known him to walk with Tiny Tim upon his shoulder very fast indeed. (*She catches herself, then hurries on.*) But he was very light to carry and his father loved him, so that it was no trouble, no trouble. (*She hears* Bob Cratchit *approaching.*) Smiles, everyone, smiles.

10. **'as met 'is end:** Cockney dialect for "has met his end." Cockneys (residents of the East End of London) drop the letter h when pronouncing words.

11. **worsted:** a smooth woolen fabric.

12. **tableau** (tăb′lō′): a portion of a play in which the actors momentarily freeze in their positions for dramatic effect.

A CHRISTMAS CAROL **237**

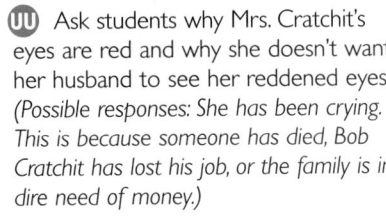

Multicultural **Perspectives**

Christmas, like many holidays, is associated with traditional foods. In England, turkey or goose and plum pudding are often served. In America, people of Italian heritage often enjoy fish dinners on Christmas Eve and pasta as a first course on Christmas Day. On the Caribbean island of Barbados, people have a tangy red fruit drink called *sorrel* on Christmas morning.

VV Have students infer from the details in this passage what is going to happen on Sunday and where Bob Cratchit just came from. *(Possible responses: Sunday will be Tiny Tim's funeral; Bob just came from arranging the funeral.)*

Active Reading: PREDICT

WW Ask students to predict how Scrooge will react to Tiny Tim's death. Guide students to consider the message about human behavior that the playwright is building with these events. *(Possible responses: He will be heartbroken. Scrooge has observed the depth of love in the Cratchit family and how much the loss of Tiny Tim will mean to them. Moreover, Scrooge realizes that he did nothing to help the boy stay alive.)*

From Personal Response to Critical Analysis

1. Possible response: I was pleasantly surprised that Scrooge cared.
2. Possible responses: Scrooge feels guilty because he thinks he could have done something to help Tiny Tim live; Scrooge associates his own death with that of Tiny Tim and feels sorry for them both.
3. Possible responses: Scrooge wants to see Fezziwig again because he was so fond of his old master; Scrooge is very confused by everything that has happened to him and isn't thinking straight.
4. Students may express pity, sorrow, or pain.

Bob Cratchit (*entering*). My dear, Peter . . . (*He greets the other* children *by their real names.*) How is it coming?

VV **Mrs. Cratchit** (*handing him the coat*). Nearly done.

Bob Cratchit. Yes, good, I'm sure that it will be done long before Sunday.

Mrs. Cratchit. Sunday! You went today then, Robert?

Bob Cratchit. Yes. It's . . . it's all ready. Two o'clock. And a nice place. It would have done you good to see how green it is. But you'll see it often. I promised him that, that I would walk there on Sunday . . . often.

Mrs. Cratchit. We mustn't hurt ourselves for it, Robert.

Bob Cratchit. No. No, he wouldn't have wanted that. Come now. You won't guess who I've seen. Scrooge's nephew, Fred. And he asked after us and said he was heartily sorry and to give his respect to my good wife. How he ever knew that, I don't know.

Mrs. Cratchit. Knew what, my dear?

Bob Cratchit. Why, that you were a good wife.

Peter. Everybody knows that.

Bob Cratchit. I hope that they do. "Heartily sorry," he said, "for your good wife, and if I can be of service to you in any way—" and he gave me his card—"that's where I live"—and Peter, I shouldn't be at all surprised if he got you a position.

Mrs. Cratchit. Only hear that, Peter!

Bob Cratchit. And then you'll be keeping company with some young girl and setting up for yourself.

Peter. Oh, go on.

Bob Cratchit. Well, it will happen, one day, but remember, when that day does come—as it must—we must none of us forget poor Tiny Tim and this first parting in our family.

Scrooge. He died! No, no! (*He steps back and the scene disappears; he moves away from the spirit.*)

FROM **PERSONAL RESPONSE** TO **CRITICAL ANALYSIS**

REFLECT 1. What thoughts came to mind when you read Scrooge's reaction to Tiny Tim's death? Describe your thoughts in your notebook.

RETHINK 2. Why do you think Tiny Tim's death affects Scrooge so deeply?

3. Why do you think Scrooge sees the Ghost of Chistmas Present as his old master Fezziwig?

4. Cratchit tells his wife that Tiny Tim thought it might be pleasant for people to see him in church and "remember upon Christmas Day who made the lame to walk and the blind to see." If you had seen Tiny Tim, is that what you would have thought? If not, what might you have thought instead?

Mini-Lesson: Speaking, **Listening, and Viewing**

DRAMA PERFORMANCE Because of its form and content, *A Christmas Carol* is an ideal play for students to perform for families and for other classes. If you have not already done so, you may wish to show students a filmed version of the play to get a visual understanding of some of the elements of stagecraft. Then make a web that is like the one shown and that lists each of the tasks involved in staging a play.

Application Assign each student a role in the production, according to his or her interests and learning style. Bodily-kinesthetic learners will enjoy performing the play, whereas interpersonal learners can be directors. Spatial learners can prepare scenery, lighting, costumes, and playbills; musical learners can create or find background music and sound effects. Assign logical-mathematical learners the task of designing the set and stage area; request that intrapersonal learners videotape rehearsals and the production. Then stage the play!

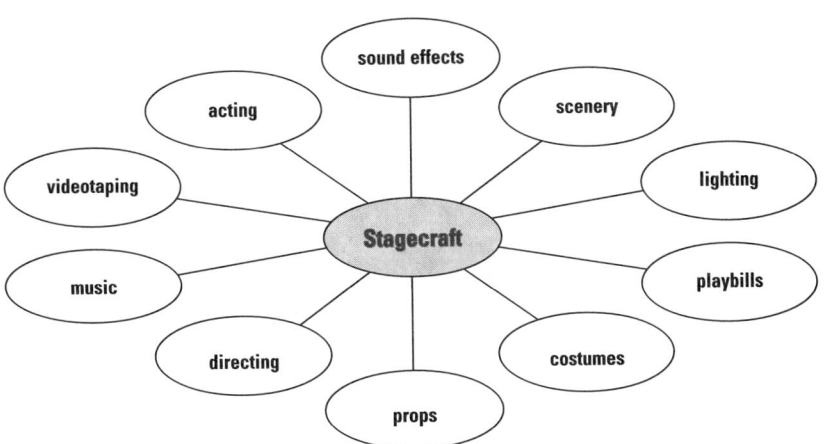

sound effects

acting

scenery

videotaping

lighting

Stagecraft

music

playbills

directing

costumes

props

Scene 6

The Spirit of Christmas Present

Scrooge. Because he would not . . . no! You cannot tell me that he has died, for that Christmas has not come! I will not let it come! I will be there . . . It was me. Yes, yes, and I knew it and couldn't look. I won't be able to help. I won't. (*pause*) Spirit, hear me. I am not the man I was. I will not be that man that I have been for so many years. Why show me all of this if I am past all hope? Assure me that I yet may change these shadows you have shown me. Let the boy live! I will honor Christmas in my heart and try to keep it all the year. I will live in the Past, the Present, and the Future. The spirits of all three shall strive within me. I will not shut out the lessons that they teach. Oh, tell me that I am not too late! (*A single light focuses on the little* girl, *dressed in a blue cloak like that of the Virgin Mary. She looks up, and from above a dove is slowly lowered in silence to her; she takes it and encloses it within her cloak, covering it. As soon as she does this, a large choir is heard singing "Gloria!" and the bells begin to ring. Blackout. When the lights come up again,* Scrooge *is in bed. The* third spirit *and the figures in the church have disappeared.* Scrooge *awakens and looks around his room.*) The curtains! They are mine and they are real. They are not sold. They are here. I am here; the shadows to come may be dispelled. They will be. I know they will be. (*He dresses himself hurriedly.*) I don't know what to do. I'm as light as a feather, merry as a boy again. Merry Christmas! Merry Christmas! A Happy New Year to all the world! Hello there! Whoop! Hallo! What day of the month is it? How long did the spirits keep me? Never mind. I don't care. (*He opens the window and calls to a boy in the street below.*) What's today?

Boy. Eh?

Scrooge. What's the day, my fine fellow?

Boy. Today? Why, Christmas Day!

Scrooge. It's Christmas Day! I haven't missed it! The spirits have done it all in one night. They can do anything they like. Of course they can. Of course they can save Tim. Hallo, my fine fellow!

Boy. Hallo!

Scrooge. Do you know the poulterers[13] in the next street at the corner?

Boy. I should hope I do.

Scrooge. An intelligent boy. A remarkable boy. Do you know whether they've sold the prize turkey that was hanging up there? Not the little prize; the big one.

Boy. What, the one as big as me?

Scrooge. What a delightful boy! Yes, my bucko!

Boy. It's hanging there now.

Scrooge. It is? Go and buy it.

Boy. G'wan!

Scrooge. I'm in earnest! Go and buy it and tell 'em to bring it here that I may give them the direction where to take it. Come back with the butcher and I'll give you a shilling.[14] Come back in less than two minutes and I'll give you half a crown!

Boy. Right, guv! (*He exits.*)

Scrooge. I'll send it to Bob Cratchit's. He shan't

---

13. **poulterers** (pōl′tər-ərz): people who sell poultry.
14. **shilling:** a British coin. Five shillings equal a crown.

Assessment ✓ Option

INFORMAL ASSESSMENT You can informally assess how well your class understood the play by inviting them to create a before-and-after chart showing Scrooge's life, personality, and actions before and after the Spirits' visits. Have students look through the play for specific examples, details, and quotations to include in their diagram.

Rubric

3 Full Accomplishment Students use specific details from the play to show Scrooge's successful transformation from wretched miser to blissful benefactor.

2 Substantial Accomplishment Students accurately describe the effect of the Spirits' visit on Scrooge's personality, but include insufficient or inappropriate details from the play.

1 Little or Partial Accomplishment Students are unable to accurately show the change in Scrooge's personality as a result of his encounter with the three Spirits.

Literary Concept: THEME

A Ask students to identify the Gentleman Visitor and explain why Scrooge gives him the money. Have students explain how Scrooge's actions here relate to the play's main message. *(Possible response: In Scene 1, Scrooge refused to give this same caller money for the poor. Now Scrooge donates a great sum of money willingly. He now cares deeply about the suffering of others.)*

STRATEGIC READING FOR
Less-Proficient Readers

B Explore with students how Scrooge changes as a result of his experiences with the spirits. *(Scrooge becomes generous and kind.)* **Relating Cause and Effect**

COMPREHENSION CHECK

1. Who tells Scrooge that he will be haunted by three spirits? *(Marley's ghost)*
2. Who is the Second Spirit? *(the Spirit of Christmas Present)*
3. What does the Second Spirit show Scrooge? *(the Cratchit household)*
4. Who is the Third Spirit? *(the Spirit of Christmas Yet to Come)*
5. What does Scrooge send to the Cratchits in Scene 6? *(a turkey)*
6. With whom does Scrooge spend Christmas? *(with his nephew Fred and the Cratchits)*

EDITOR'S NOTE *With the permission of the copyright holder, some material was deleted to shorten and focus this selection.*

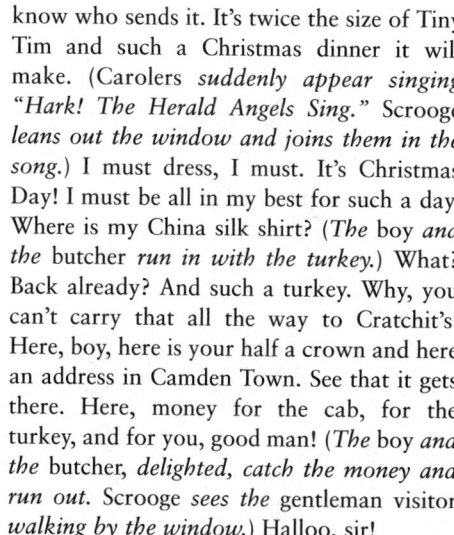

know who sends it. It's twice the size of Tiny Tim and such a Christmas dinner it will make. (*Carolers suddenly appear singing "Hark! The Herald Angels Sing." Scrooge leans out the window and joins them in the song.*) I must dress, I must. It's Christmas Day! I must be all in my best for such a day. Where is my China silk shirt? (*The boy and the butcher run in with the turkey.*) What? Back already? And such a turkey. Why, you can't carry that all the way to Cratchit's. Here, boy, here is your half a crown and here an address in Camden Town. See that it gets there. Here, money for the cab, for the turkey, and for you, good man! (*The boy and the butcher, delighted, catch the money and run out. Scrooge sees the gentleman visitor walking by the window.*) Halloo, sir!

Gentleman Visitor (*looking up sadly, less than festive*). Hello, sir.

Scrooge. My dear sir, how do you do? I hope you succeeded yesterday. It was very kind of you to stop by to see me.

Gentleman Visitor (*in disbelief*). Mr. Scrooge?

Scrooge. Yes, that is my name, and I fear it may not be pleasant to you. Allow me to ask your pardon, and will you have the goodness to add this (*throwing him a purse*) to your good work!

Gentleman Visitor. Lord bless me! My dear Mr. Scrooge, are you serious?

Scrooge. If you please, not a penny less. A great many back payments are included in it, I assure you. Will you do me that favor?

Gentleman Visitor. My dear sir, I don't know what I can say to such generosity . . .

Scrooge. Say nothing! Accept it. Come and see me. Will you come and see me?

Gentleman Visitor. I will.

Scrooge. Thank 'ee. I am much obliged to you. I thank you fifty times. God bless you and Merry Christmas!

Gentleman Visitor. Merry Christmas to you, sir!

Scrooge (*running downstairs, out of his house, and onto the street*). Now which is the way to that nephew's house. Girl! Girl!

Girl (*appearing immediately*). Yes, sir?

Scrooge. Can you find me a taxi, miss?

Girl. I can, sir. (*She rings her doll, and a coachman appears.*)

Scrooge (*handing the coachman a card*). Can you show me the way to this home?

Coachman. I can, sir.

Scrooge. Good man. Come up, girl. (*They mount to the top of the taxi. This action may be stylistically suggested.*) Would you be an old man's guide to a Christmas dinner?

Girl. I would, sir, and God bless you!

Scrooge. Yes, God bless us every one! (*raising his voice almost in song*) Driver, to Christmas! (*They exit, all three singing "Joy to the World." Blackout. The lights come up for the finale at Fred's house. The Cratchits are there with Tiny Tim. All stop moving and talking when they see Scrooge standing in the center, embarrassed and humble.*) Well, I'm very glad to be here at my nephew's house! (*He starts to cry.*) Merry Christmas! Merry Christmas!

All (*softly*). Merry Christmas. (*They sing "Deck the Halls," greeting one another and exchanging gifts. Scrooge puts Tiny Tim on his shoulders.*)

Tiny Tim (*shouting as the carol ends*). God bless us every one!

Scrooge (*to the audience*). Oh, yes! God bless us every one!

WORDS TO KNOW	**finale** (fə-năl′ē) *n.* the concluding part

242

Mini-Lesson   T M   Spelling

WORDS WITH J, GE, and DGE Tell students that the sound *j* can be spelled *j*, *ge*, or *dge*. *Ge* and *dge* usually appear at the ends of words; *j* appears at the beginning or in the middle.

Examples: justice, emerge, pledge

Application Say the following words and ask students to spell them.

1. damage
2. dodge
3. pajamas
4. badge
5. juice
6. judge
7. injury
8. challenge
9. journal
10. mileage
11. jumbo
12. marriage

Ask students to find other words that fit this pattern, in their own writing and in things that they read, and to add them to their personal word lists.

Reteaching/Reinforcement
• *Unit Two Resource Book*, p. 55

RESPONDING OPTIONS

FROM PERSONAL RESPONSE TO CRITICAL ANALYSIS

REFLECT
1. If you had just seen this play on stage, what is the first thing you would say to a friend about it? Write your response in your notebook.

RETHINK
2. What words or phrases would you use to describe Scrooge's character in the last scene?

3. Which spirit do you think had the greatest influence in motivating Scrooge to change his life? Explain.

4. Which character's life is likely to be changed the most in the future? Explain your answer.

RELATE
5. Charles Dickens wrote about many serious problems of his time. How would you compare the problems of the poor today with the problems of the poor in Dickens's time? Explain.

LITERARY CONCEPTS

In a work of literature, the **theme** is the message about life or human nature that the writer presents to the reader. Sometimes a theme is stated directly. Often, however, a theme is merely suggested, and the reader must figure it out. What do you think is the theme of *A Christmas Carol*?

An artist's rendering of poor people in 19th-century London. Culver Pictures.

Multimodal Learning
ANOTHER PATHWAY

Cooperative Learning
With some classmates, present A *Christmas Carol* as a radio play. Ask some students to read parts and others to provide sound effects. If possible, record your drama on audiocassette or videocassette so you can play it for another class later.

QUICKWRITES

1. Write a new **will** for Scrooge, explaining how he will share his wealth since his change of heart.

2. Has Scrooge been permanently changed by his experience? What will happen to the Cratchits? Write the **plot summary** for a sequel to this play, based on what you know about Scrooge and human nature.

3. Compose an imaginary **dialogue** in which two people or characters in this part of Unit Two discuss the choices they have made and the lessons they have learned from those choices.

Thematic Link

📁 *PORTFOLIO Save your writing. You may want to use it later as a springboard to a piece for your portfolio.*

A CHRISTMAS CAROL **243**

From Personal Response to Critical Analysis

1. Possible response: This play tells an interesting story about human nature's ability to change.
2. Possible responses: *kind, decent, loving, warm, generous, joyful, compassionate, filled with faith*
3. Possible responses: Some students may mention the First Spirit because it shows Scrooge important experiences from his past. Other students may mention the Second Spirit because it shows Scrooge what he was missing in life. Still others may choose the Third Spirit because it is the most frightening and helps Scrooge see the kind of future he is creating.
4. Possible responses: Scrooge, because he will enjoy the pleasure of being with people and giving generously; Tiny Tim, because he will get stronger instead of dying.
5. Possible responses: The problems are different today because poor people are not as desperate as they were in Dickens's time because of social welfare programs; the problems are the same because poor people are still struggling to get adequate food, clothing, shelter, education, and health care.

Another Pathway

Cooperative Learning Assign a specific time frame for completion. Also tell students that their goal is to make sure that every member of the group learns the material as well as delivers a high-quality performance. Remind students that radio plays depend on effective communication of plot and characters through sound alone. Be sure to allow time for group processing.

Rubric
3 Full Accomplishment Students present a well-acted play in which characters are accurately portrayed.
2 Substantial Accomplishment Students complete the play but portray some characters inaccurately.
1 Little or Partial Accomplishment Students have much difficulty working cooperatively and fail to portray most characters accurately.

Literary Concepts

Possible responses: It is better to give than to receive; real joy comes from doing good for others; we can have the Christmas spirit all year long; people can change for the better. You may choose to have students work in pairs to identify the theme. Encourage them to make graphic organizers to relate prior knowledge and textual details.

QuickWrites

1. Encourage students to use some legal words and phrases in drafting the will. Guide them to study the play's level of diction for guidelines in choosing other suitable words.
2. Remind students to arrange the events in chronological order. You may also wish to have the sequel include conflict, climax, and resolution.
3. Have students write their dialogue in the correct form, putting quotation marks around the characters' exact words and beginning a new paragraph each time the speaker changes.

 The Writer's Craft

Creating Dialogue, pp. 320–322

Literary Links

Possible responses: After his change of heart, Scrooge is loving, warm, generous, and compassionate. Mr. Sasaki remains the same throughout the story: hard-nosed, businesslike, and deceitful. Scrooge could teach Mr. Sasaki the importance of generosity; Mr. Sasaki could teach Scrooge (before his change of heart) patience.

Across the Curriculum

Music *Cooperative Learning* Students can work in groups of four to discover more about carols and caroling. Have group members work on their own to locate material and then come together to compare their findings. In addition, you may wish to appoint a direction-giver in each group to help everyone stay on track.

ADDITIONAL SUGGESTIONS

Social Studies *Family Holidays* Invite students to explore a holiday that their family celebrates. Students can interview family members and consult reference sources to learn more about the music, foods, customs, dances, and ceremonies associated with the holiday. To share their findings, students might present a multicultural festival.

Math *Computing Cost* Scrooge buys a huge turkey for the Cratchits' Christmas dinner. Have students compute how much a 25-pound turkey would cost based on the current price per pound of turkey in a local food store. Then have students plan a complete Christmas dinner, listing the cost of each item and then computing the total cost.

Multimodal Activities

ALTERNATIVE ACTIVITIES

1. Scrooge buys a huge turkey for the Cratchits' Christmas dinner. What do organizations in your community do to help bring cheer to others over the holidays? **Interview** members of some community organizations to find out what they do. Post the names and phone numbers of these organizations so others can get involved.

2. With your classmates, watch a video of *A Christmas Carol*. Then get together in small groups and compare the video and play versions. When you have finished, share your group's **comparison** with the other groups.

3. How might you produce a modern-day version of *A Christmas Carol*? Working in groups, decide how you might change such elements as the setting, the plot, and the characters while maintaining the same theme. Then write dialogue and stage directions for one scene and stage a **performance** of the scene for the class.

4. Research the clothing that the upper and lower classes wore during Charles Dickens's time. Using your research as a guide, draw **sketches** of some original costumes for a stage production of this play.

Women's fashions of the mid-19th century. Copyright © Archive Photos.

LITERARY LINKS

Compare Scrooge before or after his change of heart and Mr. Sasaki in "Say It With Flowers" on page 181? What do you think each character might learn from the other?

Scrooge	Mr. Sasaki

What they might learn from one another:

Multimodal Learning

ACROSS THE CURRICULUM

Music Research the history of carols and caroling. Present your findings to the class in an oral report or speech. Try to include recordings or your own renditions of some of the carols mentioned in this play.

Alternative Activities

1. Students can contact their local Chamber of Commerce or public library for a community calendar that lists the names and telephone numbers of all the civic, religious, and social organizations in town.

2. Suggest that students arrange their findings on a comparison/contrast chart or Venn diagram to make it easier for them to organize and remember key points.

3. Remind students that the dialogue reflects Dickens's time period and the different dialects of London. Before students begin writing, have them discuss how their dialogue will reflect the time and region of their present-day setting. Students may be familiar with the 1988 Richard Donner film, *Scrooged*, starring comedian Bill Murray as a modern-day Scrooge employed as a TV executive.

4. Students can consult fashion books, history texts, and encyclopedias for ideas.

WORDS TO KNOW

EXERCISE A For each item below, write *S* if the words are synonyms. Write *A* if they are antonyms.

1. finale—ending
2. pledge—promise
3. surplus—lack
4. destitute—wealthy
5. transform—change
6. solitude—isolation
7. summon—dismiss
8. provision—supplies
9. mortal—human
10. charitable—stingy
11. welfare—well-being
12. reassurance—discouragement
13. abundance—lack
14. currency—money
15. emerge—disappear

EXERCISE B Use five or more vocabulary words to make up questions for a trivia game on *A Christmas Carol*. Play the game with a group of classmates.

CHARLES DICKENS

Charles Dickens was the most popular British writer of his time. One evening, after finishing a speech about the conditions of the poor, Dickens was touched by the audience's enthusiastic applause. Upon returning home, he conceived the story of *A Christmas Carol*. Although he had intended to write a pamphlet called "An Appeal to the People of England, on Behalf of the Poor Man's Child," he instead used the form of a story to get across his idea. When *A Christmas Carol* came out in December 1843, about 6,000 copies were sold on Christmas Day alone. Since then, *A Christmas Carol* has become a holiday tradition and has helped define the spirit of the Christmas season in England.

1812–1870

Dickens's own unhappy childhood provided material for a number of his works. When Dickens was 12, his father was sent to a debtors' prison, and Dickens had to leave school and go to work in a rat-infested factory. The hopelessness and shame he experienced there affected him deeply. One of his novels, *David Copperfield*, was based partly on his experiences in that factory. In such other novels as *Oliver Twist* and *Little Dorrit*, Dickens draws on childhood memories to depict the plight of the poor in a materialistic society.

OTHER WORKS *A Tale of Two Cities, Great Expectations, Bleak House*

Extended Reading

LASERLINKS
• *AUTHOR BACKGROUND*

Words To Know

EXERCISE A

1. S	8. S
2. S	9. S
3. A	10. A
4. A	11. S
5. S	12. A
6. S	13. A
7. A	14. S
	15. A

EXERCISE B

Possible responses: With what *currency* did Scrooge tip the boy who went to find the butcher? *(half a crown)* What *mortal* was Scrooge's first master? *(Fezziwig)*

Reteaching/Reinforcement
• *Unit Two Resource Book*, p. 56

CHARLES DICKENS

After the publication of *A Christmas Carol* in 1843, Dickens became so closely identified with the holiday that upon his death a child was said to have cried, "Dickens dead? Then will Father Christmas die too?"

AUTHOR BACKGROUND
Charles Dickens This film dealing with the life and times of Charles Dickens will introduce students to illustrations from some of his works and will give them a better understanding of the settings that inspired the author.

Side A, Frames 26038

WHAT DO YOU THINK?

Reflecting on Theme

Ask students to refer to the "perfect person" recipes they created before reading the selections in Part 2 of this unit. Ask students if, after reading *A Christmas Carol* and seeing Scrooge's change of heart, their ideas of what makes a perfect person have changed. Invite students to revise their recipes, adding any new ingredients that come to mind now that they have read this play.

OVERVIEW

To gain a deeper appreciation of the short stories they have read in this unit, students will explore the characteristics of a short story and create a story themselves in this lesson.

Objectives

- To plan the story by considering elements such as character, plot, conflict, and setting
- To draft the story and solicit response
- To revise and publish the story
- To reflect on the process of writing a short story

Skills

LITERATURE
- Identifying story elements
- Exploring point of view

WRITING AND LANGUAGE
- Show don't tell
- Using paragraphs

GRAMMAR AND USAGE
- Using sentence fragments in dialogue

MEDIA LITERACY
- Reading a pie chart

SPEAKING, LISTENING, AND VIEWING
- Group composing
- Role-playing
- Performing the story

CRITICAL THINKING
- Generating information

Teaching Strategy: MODELING

A Have students look at the badge displayed on page 246. Ask what they can determine about the person whose badge is shown. Some possibilities are:
- Her name is Sumi.
- She is a volunteer at the Community Nursing Home.
- She wants people to call her by her first name.

Then students would need to invent details to write a narrative about Sumi. Questions like these can help:
- Why is she working at the nursing home?
- What does she like about her work?
- Who are her favorite patients and why?

CUSTOMIZING FOR

Students Acquiring English

B Point out the phrase *bald eagles* in the "Kindest Cut" and tell students that the eagle is often used as a symbol for the United States. Explain that it represents independence and courage. Then invite students to explain how the young men in this article embody similar qualities to those that the bald eagle represents.

WRITING A NARRATIVE

Should you betray a friend's secret in order to help him? Have you ever been tempted to cheat on a test? The selections in Unit Two, "Life's Lessons," deal with people making difficult choices. Where did the writers get their story ideas? Sometimes a real-life event can form the basis of a story. Other times, writers create imaginary situations in order to explore an idea or share a lesson.

GUIDED ASSIGNMENT

Write a Short Story A short story is a narrative with a plot, a setting, a conflict, and characters. In this lesson, you'll write a short story based on a real or an imaginary event. In the process, you'll explore how an event or an idea becomes good fiction.

① Look for Inspiration

The articles on these pages are similar to those you read in newspapers and magazines. They describe real-life examples of young people making tough choices and learning life's lessons. Can you discover a story in each one?

A **Making Connections** As you read each article, try to imagine some characters, a conflict, a plot, and a setting. Perhaps you could add some imaginative details or invent a conversation between characters. These are some ways in which writers turn facts into fiction.

Getting Personal Now think of situations from your own life. How would you change the details to create a fictional story?

Decision Point Choose an idea, either from the articles or from your own life, that you would like to expand into a story.

KINDEST CUT

B IF COMPASSION WERE A subject, the Bald Eagles, of San Marco, Calif., would clearly get A's. They took notice in early February that their friend Ian O'Gorman, 11, was starting to lose weight. Then on Feb. 18, doctors removed a tumor the size of an orange from Ian's small intestine. The diagnosis was non-Hodgkins lymphoma, which has a 68 percent survival rate after five years for children under the age of 15. Two days later, Ian's best friend, Taylor Herber, came to the hospital. He learned that the chemotherapy to treat Ian's disease would make his hair fall out. "At first I said I would shave my head as a joke, but then I decided to really do it," says Taylor. "I thought it would be less traumatizing for Ian." At school he told the other boys what he was planning, and they jumped on the bandwagon. Soon, says another friend, "just about everyone wanted to shave their heads."

from "Kindest Cut"
People Magazine, April 11, 1994

PRINT AND MEDIA RESOURCES

Remind these students to concentrate on getting their ideas down on paper. Reassure them that spelling, grammar, and mechanical skills, such as punctuation, are not crucial at this stage.

C Helpful Hint Students might find that their thoughts flow more easily if they do their freewriting on a computer since it's easier to quickly adjust or reverse a thought as they input.

② QuickWrite

③ What are the first things that come to your mind when you think about your idea? Choose one aspect of the story that interests you the most—a scene, a person, the character's thoughts, causes of the problem, even the ending—and write about it for five or ten minutes. Follow your thoughts wherever they lead you.

Newspaper Statistics

Magazine Article

The Worst Day I Ever Had

In 1994, Adonal Foyle, number 31, was third in the nation in blocked shots. That year, he led Colgate University to the NCAA tournament. Below Adonal describes how his first basketball game changed his life.

D

The next time I got a rebound, I ran downcourt to shoot a layup. The only problem was, I ran the length of the court without dribbling! I didn't know that I had to.

All the players stopped in their tracks and stared at me, then laughed hysterically. I was totally embarrassed.

Now I *really* wanted to learn how to play basketball. I joined a local team that practiced at

night. About four months later, I went back to the court. Not only did I dribble, but I also blocked every shot in sight.

I've come a long way in my basketball career since making a fool of myself in that first game. Basketball even helped me get to college. Learning something new can be frustrating—but it pays off to keep trying. Just think what I would have missed out on if I had never picked up that basketball!

Adonal Foyle
from "The Worst Day I Ever Had"
Sports Illustrated for Kids, July 1995

D The basketball jargon in "The Worst Day I Ever Had" might be difficult for students unfamiliar with the sport. Explain the following terms:
rebound: to get the ball after someone else has thrown it to the basket
downcourt: the other end of the basketball court
lay-up: a jumping one-hand shot made off the backboard from close under the basket
dribbling: to bounce the ball repeatedly while moving down the court

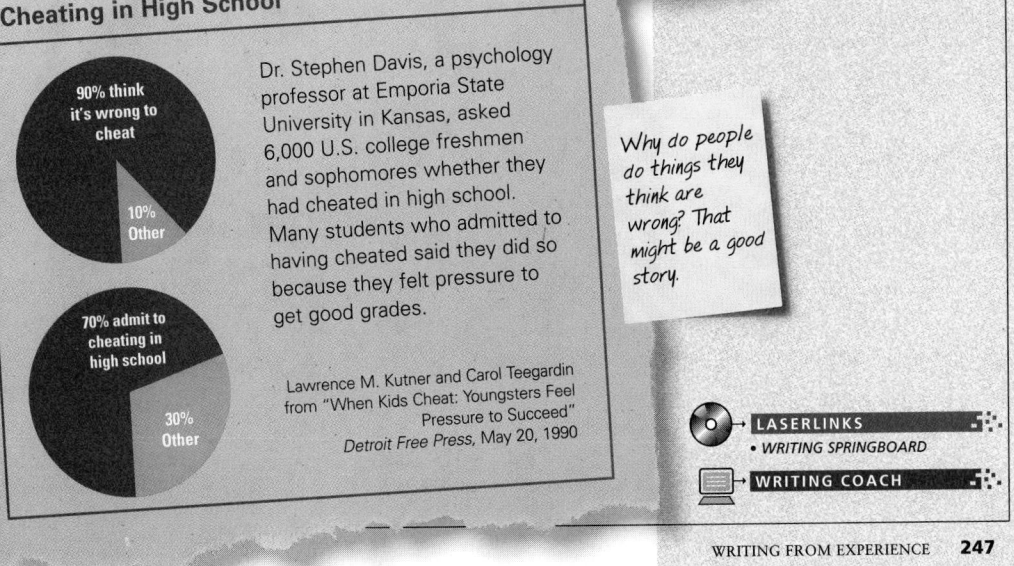

I cheated on a test once. I felt so horrible afterward! I'm surprised so many kids cheat.

Cheating in High School

90% think it's wrong to cheat

10% Other

70% admit to cheating in high school

30% Other

Dr. Stephen Davis, a psychology professor at Emporia State University in Kansas, asked 6,000 U.S. college freshmen and sophomores whether they had cheated in high school. Many students who admitted to having cheated said they did so because they felt pressure to get good grades.

Lawrence M. Kutner and Carol Teegardin
from "When Kids Cheat: Youngsters Feel
Pressure to Succeed"
Detroit Free Press, May 20, 1990

Why do people do things they think are wrong? That might be a good story.

LASERLINKS
• *WRITING SPRINGBOARD*

WRITING COACH

Media Literacy:
READING A PIE CHART

E Have students look at the pie charts. Point out that the whole circle represents 100% of the population being surveyed, which, in this case, is 6,000 U.S. college freshmen and sophomores. You may want to explain to students that *other* means students who do not think it is wrong to cheat (in the first circle) and students who do not admit to cheating in high school (in the second circle). Then ask students to find each of the following:
1. 10% of 6,000 (600)
2. 90% of 6,000 (5,400)
3. 70% of 6,000 (4,200)
4. 30% of 6,000 (1,800)

WRITING SPRINGBOARD
Making Choices Jordan, an African-American teenager, tells how an unpleasant experience led him to make a difficult decision about his future.

Side B, Frame 07940

Writing Prompt Sometimes our misbehavior or misjudgments get us in trouble. Often such mistakes lead us to make difficult decisions about our lives. Have you ever known someone whose life was changed by something that happened to him or her? Write a short story in which that person narrates the life-changing experience.

F If the chart does not help students imagine where the idea might lead, suggest they write a simplified outline of a familiar story. Students can then substitute different characters, alter the plot slightly, and change the setting. Guide students to study the outline to help them develop a plot line.

CUSTOMIZING FOR

Less-Proficient Writers

G If students are overwhelmed by the idea of developing all the story elements together, guide them with the following method:
1. Select a character.
2. Get the character involved in a conflict.
3. Increase the conflict.
4. Resolve the conflict.

After students have developed the plot, guide them to consider each of the other story elements in turn.

PREWRITING

Planning Your Story

Letting the Story Unfold Just by having an idea to explore, you're on your way to writing a short story. The next two pages will help you tap your imagination and begin a journey of discovery. Where do you think your idea will lead?

❶ Examine Your Idea

How do you feel as you read your Quick-Write? Your reaction can help you decide whether the idea you picked is a good basis for a story. If your idea seems boring or if you're having trouble imagining where the idea might lead, try creating a story chart like the one below. Ask yourself "what if?" questions to turn the real-life facts into a story. You can always choose another idea if your first one doesn't work.

❷ Consider the Story Elements

All short stories, no matter what they are about, have four elements in common. Writers vary the elements to make each story unique. Fill in your story chart with details about each element.

Character Who is at the center of the action? How does he or she talk, move, look, and dress? What is he or she thinking?

Plot What happens in your story? You may not know everything at this point. That's okay. You'll fill in the blanks as you write.

Conflict What problem or decision does the main character face?

Setting When and where does the action take place?

❸ Identify the Conflict

As you explore your story, it's important to know the problem or decision that is at its center. For example, a character might be trying to decide whether or not to cheat on a test. Think about some concrete details you can include in your story to help the reader understand the problem.

Student's Story Chart

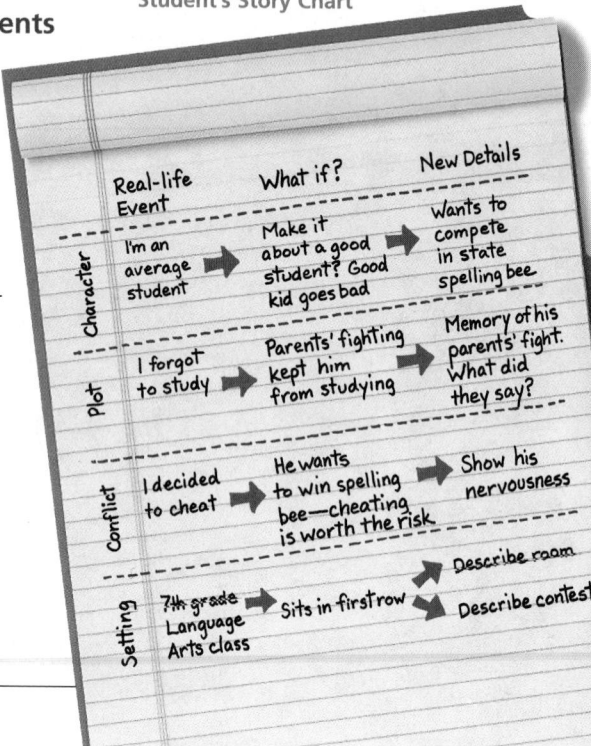

Mini-Lesson: Speaking, **Listening, and Viewing**

GROUP COMPOSING Group composing is an excellent way to help less-proficient writers plan a story and all writers to expand on their story ideas. Professional writers often join workshops where they can share and compare ideas. Brainstorming a story with others helps writers create believable characters, logical plots, dramatic conflicts, and realistic settings. Have students follow these guidelines:
• Only one person at a time should speak. Each person should speak for a specific, brief amount of time.
• One person should serve as a recorder, writing down the story. Or, the recorder can tape record

the story and later transcribe it or play it back for the group.

Application Arrange students in groups of three to create and tell a group story. One person should start the story, the next person continue it, and the last person end it. Invite the recorder for each group to share the story with the class. Then have volunteers describe the composing process, focusing on ways they planned their story and developed their ideas.

4 Follow the Characters' Lead

Once you understand the conflict, begin thinking about how the characters will react to it. This might become the plot of your story. The tips below might help.

Be the Characters Imagine yourself as each character and think about the problem as he or she sees it. The key is to put yourself in the story to see how the character feels.

Model Characters After Real People Think about how you and other people might react to the conflict. A character can be based on several real people.

5 Share Ideas with Other Writers

One of the best ways to develop your ideas is to share them with other writers. Get together with other students and ask for their ideas and suggestions about what you've done so far. Consider the following ideas.

Swap Stories Meet with a friend or group of friends to discuss and respond to each other's story ideas. Ask for the specific help you need—for example, help deciding what a character would look like or how the story might end.

Role-play Try role-playing your story-in-progress with your friends. Tell them what you know about the characters and the conflict. One idea is to assign roles to your friends. Encourage them to use their imaginations to act out their roles. Write down any interesting dialogue or plot twists your friends come up with.

SkillBuilder

 CRITICAL THINKING

Generating Information
How can you keep your characters from sounding like cardboard cutouts? A biography sheet like the one below can help you invent a detailed history for your main characters. It can help you understand them better and imagine details that help readers see them clearly.

Main Character's Name: Ray

Personality: Shy, studious, imaginative, dresses plainly

Background: Parents fighting, he wants to qualify for spelling bee

APPLYING WHAT YOU'VE LEARNED
Adapt your character biography sheet to fit your story. How can you add some details to make your characters seem real? If you can't come up with ideas, try role-playing the story or sharing your ideas with others.

THINK & PLAN

Reflecting on Your Ideas

1. How can you make your characters seem real?
2. How can you make readers care about the conflict?
3. Why do you think your idea will interest readers?

WRITING FROM EXPERIENCE **249**

H Students may also wish to work in groups to present their drafts as a Reader's Theater for the class. The audience can present feedback in the form of a brief critical review, including both praise and suggestions for revision.

 SkillBuilder **CRITICAL THINKING**

GENERATING INFORMATION Encourage students to include as much detail as they can in their biography sheets. If students are having difficulty generating ideas, partner students to "interview" each other. Each student should pretend to be a character in the partner's short story. Students can then ask each other questions to get more biographical information.

Application Possible response: Use dialogue to add the information from your extended character biography sheet.

Additional Suggestions To extend the activity, students can create book jacket biographies for their characters. The biographies can include facts about character's appearance, such as height, weight, hair color, eye color, and distinguishing marks. The biographies can also have a brief description of the character's past, including birthplace, education, marriage status, and career as appropriate. Finally, students can include a sketch of the character.

I Students may find it easier to write their stories on a computer. If students are using computers, remind them to save all drafts separately on a disk. Before students start writing, show them how to title each draft to make sure that nothing is lost or overwritten in successive drafts. For example, students can select a key word and number drafts consecutively—basketball.1, basketball.2, etc.

CUSTOMIZING FOR
Students Acquiring English

J If students are having difficulty drafting their stories, encourage them to talk about the central point they want their readers to understand. Arrange students in groups. Help members elicit a peer response with this question: "What part of the story do you think is most important for my readers?" Then help students make changes that will clarify their point.

Teaching Strategy:
MANAGING THE PAPER LOAD

K Students often desire detailed feedback at this stage of the composing process. Instead, as you read the drafts, concentrate on only the one element that each student finds most troublesome, such as conflict or plot. Students can work out less serious story problems in a peer review setting.

DRAFTING

Putting It All Together

Making the Pieces Fit Now that you've gathered some ideas about your characters, setting, conflict, and plot, it's time to organize them. Sometimes you will have a detailed story plan. At other times, you may have only a beginning or a key scene in mind. As you write, let your characters come to life in your mind and begin to "tell" you where to take the story.

1 Write a Rough Draft

To start, write the part of the story that you know most about at this stage—the ending, the setting, or a description of a character. Below is a model of one student's rough draft. The notes show suggestions from peer reviewers.

Student's Rough Draft

2 Choose a Narrator

The narrator is the person who tells your story. Here are two types of narrator. Which works best for you?

First-Person Narrator This type of narrator is part of the story and describes the action from his or her point of view. A first-person narrator describes his or her thoughts and feelings and uses such pronouns as *I, me, we,* and *our.*

Third-Person Narrator This type of narrator is not a story character but an observer who tells what happens. The narrator may also describe how the characters feel or what they think. This type of narrator uses such pronouns as *he, she,* and *they.*

> *Why don't you add some dialogue? Have Miss T. say the words?*
> *Jessica*

> *Standing right in front of Ray,*
> Miss Thompson gave the first word of the spelling test. Occasion. He closed his eyes. Then he thought about the note in his sleeve. Ray looked around the room. He saw Miss Thompson at the far end of the classroom. He slid the note under his *test* paper, *and copied the answer. O-c-c-a-s-i-o-n.*
>
> "Number Two. Disappoint," announced Miss Thompson. *for an answer* Ray looked at the note. He wrote the answer down next to number 4. Then he looked up. Miss Thompson was standing behind him. She looked as if someone had kicked her dog. Ray wanted to crawl under the desk.

> *You're just kind of telling things. Can you add details to make it more interesting*
> *Alex*

> *He couldn't see Miss Thompson. Where was she? Ray turned around and there she was,*

WRITING SPRINGBOARD

Amin's Experience An Armenian teenager recounts her journey from Armenia to the United States. She remembers her parents' decision not to reveal their true destination, the anticipation she felt when she found out they were going to the United States, and her feelings about not knowing the truth.

Writing Prompt Think about Amin's story and the events that happened to her. What events in your life or in the life of someone you know could you shape into a short story?

Side B, Frame 05525

3 See the Action as You Write

As you write, picture each event. Be careful not to leave out details that help readers understand what is happening. To find out about ways to organize a story, see pages 824–825 of the Writing Handbook.

4 Make Your Characters Seem Real

Show, Don't Tell Use vivid words and imagery to breathe life into your characters. Don't just describe what they're like, let their actions speak for them. For example, instead of saying that a character is nervous, show him sweating!

Let Them Talk to Each Other A good way to show what characters are thinking is having them talk to one another. Try rewriting some scenes as dialogue to find out where this method works best.

Draw a Picture Sketch a picture of your characters. Maybe you'll like the picture so much you'll use it to illustrate your story. See page 253 for other ideas for presenting your story.

Make the Dialogue Realistic Believe it or not, using sentence fragments might help! To find out how, check out the SkillBuilder on page 253.

5 Share Your Draft

Before you revise your story, invite a friend to read and comment on it. Try asking the following questions.

 **PEER RESPONSE**

- How did my story make you feel? What words or images made you feel that way?
- What do you want to know more about?
- Where can I add details to help you imagine the people or events better?

SkillBuilder

 WRITER'S CRAFT

Achieving Paragraph Unity

Paragraphs develop from the ideas you're trying to express. Use the guidelines below to make your paragraphs unified.

- Group related details together as a paragraph.
- Start a new paragraph when there's a change in action.
- Start a new paragraph when the speaker or setting changes.

APPLYING WHAT YOU'VE LEARNED
Consider the following dialogue.

Sally sat down. "Are you going to my party?" "Can't. It's my dad's birthday." "Too bad. Yuck. Tuna fish." "Have my turkey."

How would you revise the passage to identify the speakers?

 WRITING HANDBOOK

For more information about paragraphing, see pages 815–816 of the Writing Handbook.

RETHINK & EVALUATE

Preparing to Revise

1. What part of the story is most important to you?
2. What details can you add about the setting?
3. How can you make the action flow more smoothly?

WRITING FROM EXPERIENCE **251**

Teaching Strategy:
STUMBLING BLOCK

L Encourage students who are having difficulty with plot to arrange events on a flow chart or time line. Students can then move the events around to see which variation is most effective.

Speaking and Listening:
ROLE PLAY

M To help students create realistic-sounding dialogue, suggest they read the dialogue aloud to themselves to hear how it sounds. Guide students to redraft any dialogue that sounds stilted or unnatural. Writers of effective dialogue are often said to have a "good ear" for the way people speak. Have students spend a lunch hour listening to conversations around them and jotting down possible dialogue they could use in their writing

Critical Thinking: ANALYZING

N Guide students to consider how the dialogue would change if the point of view shifts. Remind students to pay special attention to word choice. For example, would the character use formal or informal English?

Teaching Strategy:
COLLABORATIVE OPPORTUNITY

O Have peer readers read the entire story all the way through before they make any comments. During a second reading, they should jot down any comments and suggestions. Remind students to include specific suggestions for revision such as recommending simile or details to make a paragraph interesting.

SkillBuilder WRITER'S CRAFT

USING PARAGRAPHS As students revise their stories, remind them to follow these tips:
- Look for paragraphs that have too many ideas. Guide students to break these paragraphs into shorter, more cohesive paragraphs.
- Make sure paragraphs focus on one main idea. Remind students that these paragraphs may need to include a specific topic sentence.
- Check for unity and coherence. Add transitions to link ideas.

Application Possible Responses:
"Sally sat down and said, "Are you going to my party?"
"Can't," said Tom. "It's my dad's birthday."
"Too bad," she replied. Then Sally made a face and said, "Yuck. Tuna fish."
Tom handed her a sandwich and said, "Have my turkey."

Reteaching/Reinforcement
Writing Mini-Lessons transparencies pp. 29–31

 The Writer's Craft
Using Paragraphs, pp. 251–252

Writing Skill: REVISING

P As students revise and edit their stories, they will work to improve their drafts by:

1. Adding needed words, sentences, and paragraphs.
2. Cutting unnecessary material. Direct students to look for information that is not closely related to the topic or restates what has already been said.
3. Replacing parts by substituting new words, sentences, and paragraphs for what has been cut.
4. Rearranging words, sentences, and paragraphs to create better logic, coherence, and suspense.

Many students think that revisers are not good writers. Good writers, they think, get it right the first time. Explain to students that all writers revise and that extensive revision is the mark of a thoughtful writer. Also, students are often unwilling to make major changes in a draft because it makes the paper messy. To overcome this problem, you may wish to encourage students to write on a computer or revise successive drafts in different colored ink.

Research Skill:
USING THE COMPUTER

Q Some students might wish to publish their writing on an on-line bulletin board. Encourage students to ask for reader's reactions via E-mail. Or, they can set up an on-line conversation with others in a "chat room" about the story. Students can download and print the comments about their stories.

REVISING AND PUBLISHING

Fine-Tuning Your Story

Making It Final A story is like a puzzle—all of the pieces work together to create a whole. Take a step back from your story to see whether everything fits together. Cut out any information that will distract readers, and revise anything that seems confusing or choppy.

① Revise and Edit

P These tips can help you fine-tune your story.

- Read the Standards for Evaluation and the Editing Checklist on the next page.
- Look at your story from a reader's point of view. How can you show, and not tell, what's happening?
- Review peer comments, notes to yourself, and your story map. Make changes that will help make your story work. Create new characters, add more events, or even change the ending.
- Make sure your narrator speaks from a consistent point of view, whether it's first person or third person.
- Read the model to see how revisions improved one writer's story.

Student's Final Story

What details does the writer use to show you how Ray is feeling?

Which paragraph shows the turning point of the story? Why?

Cheating Spells T-r-o-u-b-l-e
by Marie Ho

Cheating Spells T-r-o-u-b-l-e
by Marie Ho

Standing right in front of Ray, Miss Thompson gave the first word. "Occasion." His mind went blank except for the memory of his parents' fight the night before. I can't flunk this test! he thought.

Ray remembered the note. He looked around the room. Miss Thompson was walking away from him. His heart pumping fast, Ray shook the note from his sleeve and hid it under his test paper. She turned around and smiled at Ray, her best student.

"Number four. 'Disappoint,'" announced Miss Thompson, walking to the other end of the classroom.

Ray froze. He looked at the note for the answer and wrote it down next to number 4. Then he wiped his sweaty hands on his jeans. Let this be over soon, he thought.

When Ray looked up again, he couldn't find the teacher anywhere. Where was she? Ray turned all the way around and almost bumped his nose into the gold buttons of her dress. His whole head burned as he looked up.

One student presented her story in the form of a play. Her script includes dialogue, a description of the setting, and a description of the characters' actions.

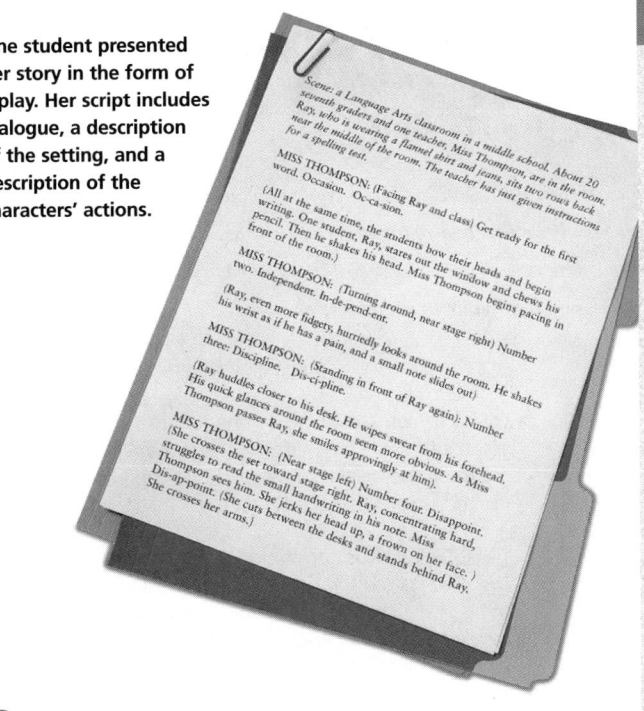

Scene: a Language Arts classroom in a middle school. About 20 seventh graders and one teacher, Miss Thompson, are in the room. Ray, who is wearing a flannel shirt and jeans, sits two rows back near the middle of the room. The teacher has just given instructions for a spelling test.

MISS THOMPSON: (Facing Ray and class) Get ready for the first word. Occasion. Oc-ca-sion.

(All at the same time, the students bow their heads and begin writing. One student, Ray, stares out the window and chews his pencil. Then he shakes his head. Miss Thompson begins pacing in front of the room.)

MISS THOMPSON: (Turning around, near stage right) Number two. Independent. In-de-pend-ent.

(Ray, even more fidgety, hurriedly looks around the room. He shakes his wrist as if he has a pain, and a small note slides out.)

MISS THOMPSON: (Standing in front of Ray again) Number three. Discipline. Dis-ci-pline.

(Ray huddles closer to his desk. He wipes sweat from his forehead. His quick glances around the room seem more obvious. As Miss Thompson passes Ray, she smiles approvingly at him).

MISS THOMPSON: (Near stage left) Number four. Disappoint. (She crosses the set toward stage right. Ray, concentrating hard, struggles to read the small handwriting in his note. Miss Thompson sees him. She jerks her head up, a frown on her face.) Dis-ap-point. (She cuts between the desks and stands behind Ray. She crosses her arms.)

② Consider Other Publishing Formats

There are many ways you can share your finished story with other people. You might write a script based on your story and invite some peers to act in it. Or, you might come up with a format on your own. Following are some other ideas you might try.

- Create a classroom anthology.
- Perform your story out loud.
- Publish your story in the school or local newspaper.

Standards for Evaluation

A short story
- grabs and holds the reader's interest
- uses natural-sounding dialogue
- maintains a consistent point of view
- presents events in an order readers can understand

SkillBuilder

 GRAMMAR FROM WRITING

Using Sentence Fragments in Dialogue

A sentence fragment is a phrase that doesn't express a complete idea. It omits the subject, verb, or both. Sentence fragments can be used in dialogue to show how people really talk, as in the example below.

"Number four. 'Disappoint,'" announced Miss Thompson.

Spend some time listening to how people really talk and write down exactly what you hear.

GRAMMAR HANDBOOK

Page 848 of the Grammar Handbook has more information about sentence fragments.

Editing Checklist Ask yourself the questions below.

- Is the paragraphing correct?
- Is the point of view consistent?
- Do details support the plot?

REFLECT & ASSESS

Evaluating the Experience

1. How did you find your story idea?
2. How would you make your characters more real next time?

PORTFOLIO Create a cover to include with your story.

R Students can work in groups and submit their story to an organization sponsoring writing contests. The magazines *Market Guide for Young Writer's* and *Writer's Market* list organizations that sponsor writing contests for middle-school writers. The National Council of Teachers of English (1111 Kenyon Road, Urbana, IL) also sponsors several young writer's contests.

Teaching Strategy: MANAGING THE PAPER LOAD

S While shorthand codes for mechanical or usage errors (such as sp for "spelling error") can save a great deal of time, many issues of substance in fiction writing are difficult to identify by code. Therefore, whenever possible, phrase your comments as questions that encourage students to reflect and assess. For example, instead of writing "Unclear," try "What does this reveal about the character?" A good question helps elicit positive, rather than defensive, comments.

Standards for Evaluation

Have students review their stories for the following:

Ideas and Content
- creates believable characters who use natural-sounding dialogue
- introduces, develops, and resolves conflict through a realistic plot
- uses sensory details and description to create a setting readers can picture in their minds
- maintains a consistent point of view: first or third person

Structure and Form
- demonstrates proper and effective paragraphing
- includes transitional words and phrases to show relationships among ideas
- uses variety of sentence structures

Grammar, Usage, and Mechanics
- contains no more than two or three minor errors in grammar and usage
- contains no more than two or three minor errors in spelling, capitalization, and punctuation

---

SkillBuilder GRAMMAR FROM WRITING

USING SENTENCE FRAGMENTS IN DIALOGUE You may wish to remind students that quotation marks are used to enclose a speaker's exact words. Be sure they understand that when a quotation is interrupted by explanatory words, each part of the quote is enclosed in quotation marks. Remind students to place commas and end marks inside the quotation marks. Tell students to use tags, such as *she yelled,* to identify the speaker and describe more vividly how things are said.

Application Students can work in pairs to label each line of dialogue in their stories as "fragment"

or "sentence." Then have partners discuss whether the fragments or complete sentences are more effective in portraying each character's personality or the story situation.

Reteaching/Reinforcement
Writing Mini-Lessons copymasters, p. 1, transparencies, p. 1

 The Writer's Craft

Dialogue, p. 322
Sentence Fragments, p. 394

UNIT REVIEW

This feature allows students to reflect on what they have learned in Unit Two and to assess how their thinking has developed as a result. This feature provides students with several options for self-assessment. However, you may choose to use some of the activities to assess specific skills, such as speaking and listening or cooperative work.

Objectives

- To allow students to reflect on and assess their understanding of theme
- To allow students to reflect on and assess their understanding of literary concepts, such as conflict and climax
- To provide students with the opportunity to assess and build their portfolios

Reflecting on Theme

OPTION 1

Have students work together to select characters for their skits. Suggest that each student refer back to the selection in which his or her character appears to jot down notes to use in creating the dialogue. Make sure students write dialogue that is consistent with the characters' actions and thoughts.

OPTION 2

Have students skim the selections to determine which lessons they might apply to their own lives. Suggest that students consider how the age difference between their two characters might have an influence on the lessons they learn.

OPTION 3

Explain to students that characters who change a great deal are called dynamic characters and those who change very little are static characters. Groups can create before-and-after character sketches to determine whether a character changes and to what extent.

 Self-Assessment In order to help students choose a selection, have them create a chart that lists the ways that each selection shows how life can be a teacher. Suggest that students consider some situations in which they might apply the insights that they derived from their chosen selection.

UNIT TWO: LIFE'S LESSONS

Before reading the selections in this unit, you explored some of your ideas about life's lessons. Now that you have finished reading the selections, some of your ideas may have developed. Use one or more of the options in each of the following sections to assess how your thinking has changed.

REFLECTING ON THEME

OPTION 1 Portraying Characters Many of the characters in Unit Two learn from their experiences. With a group of classmates, choose three or more of those characters and prepare and perform a skit in which they discuss the expression "Live and learn."

Consider . . .
- which characters learn lessons
- how you would describe the lesson each character learns
- why the characters might consider the lessons important
- how learning the lessons might change the characters

OPTION 2 Comparing Lessons In this unit, both young people and adults have learning experiences. From the selections that you have read, choose a young person and an adult who learn lessons that you might apply to your own life. Write a paragraph or two, explaining your choices and comparing the lessons that the characters learn.

OPTION 3 Discussion Which of the characters in Unit Two do you think develops the most as a result of his or her choices? Which of the characters develop little or not at all? Discuss these questions with a small group of classmates, supporting your views with examples from the selections and insights from your own experience.

Self-Assessment: Which of the selections in this unit made you think most deeply about how life can be a teacher? Write a short paragraph in which you explain how the selection has influenced your thinking.

REVIEWING LITERARY CONCEPTS

OPTION 1 Exploring Conflict The characters in Unit Two are involved in a variety of conflicts. Some are external, others are internal, and still others may be a combination of the two. Think back over the characters in the selections you have read. Then make a chart like the one shown, listing each character who experiences a conflict, briefly describing the conflict, and classifying it as external, internal, or both. Then, identify the conflict that you consider most difficult to resolve.

CONFLICT

Character	Description	Type
Casey	Casey struggles against the pitcher, trying to get a hit with the game on the line.	External

OPTION 2 **Identifying Climax** As you may recall, a climax is the point of greatest interest or suspense in the plot of a story or play. Work with two or three classmates to identify the climax of each story or play that you have read in this unit. Then choose the selection that you think has the most interesting climax, and think of a way to change its plot so that the climax would occur at a different point. Jot down an outline of your revised plot, and share the outline with other groups.

Self-Assessment: *In your notebook, copy this list of the other literary terms that were presented in this unit. Then sort the terms into three groups. In group A, list terms that you can* easily use in discussing literary works; in group B, list terms than you understand fairly well; and in group C, list the terms about which you need basic information. Jot down a strategy for getting the information you need in order to understand the terms in group C.

rhyme	free verse
end rhyme	figurative language
internal rhyme	simile
stanza	biography
rhythm	mood
narrator	theme
title	

PORTFOLIO BUILDING

- **QuickWrites** In some of your responses for the QuickWrites features in this unit, you wrote from the perspective of characters who gain new insights from experience. Select one response that you think reflects a character's thoughts and feelings especially well. In a cover note, explain what you did to make this response so true to character. Then add the response and the cover note to your portfolio.

- **Writing About Literature** Earlier in this unit, you studied how writers use imagery to help create vivid pictures for readers. Try drawing a picture that represents the imagery you analyzed. Attach the picture to your imagery-analysis essay.

- **Writing from Experience** You now have experience in writing a short story of your own. What if someone wanted to turn your story into a movie? Would you keep the same ending? Would you put in new characters? Write down any changes you might make in turning your piece of creative writing into a movie script.

- **Personal Choice** Review all the writing, charts, drawings, and evaluations that you created for the activities in this unit. Don't forget to look back on any writing that you did on your own.

Which work do you think reflects your best ideas about life as the greatest teacher? Write a note explaining your choice, and attach the note to the piece of writing or to an evaluation of the activity. Add both to your portfolio.

Self-Assessment: *Review all the writing samples in your portfolio. Which ones reflect your particular strengths as a writer? What skills would you like to keep improving as the year goes on? Write a brief note to answer these questions, and file it in your portfolio.*

SETTING GOALS

In this unit, you have read short stories, poems, nonfiction works, and even a full-length play. Which of these types of literature appeals most to you, and why? What other works of this type do you plan to read during the coming year? Explore these questions in a paragraph or two.

REFLECT AND ASSESS **255**

Setting Goals

In order to help students answer these questions and set future goals, have students consider which selections had the greatest impact on them and why they were affected by them. Ask students if they think the genre of the work might have had something to do with their reaction.

Reviewing Literary Concepts

OPTION 1

Remind students that a character may have more than one conflict. Encourage them to list and describe all conflicts. You may wish to have students work in small groups to compare their charts. In addition, make sure students support their choice of the most difficult conflict with details from the particular selection. For a copymaster of the chart, please see *Unit Two Resource Book*, p. 69.

OPTION 2

Students should compare outlines and discuss how their revised plots differ from the original ones.

 Self-Assessment You may choose to have students refer to the Handbook of Reading Terms and Literary Concepts (pp. 800–807) for information about each term that they list in group C. Then have students apply each term to a selection they have read. For instance, a student can identify an example of figurative language in a selection or discuss the theme of a particular work.

Portfolio Building

You may wish to help students choose options or modify the ones provided. Encourage students to incorporate in their portfolios several samples of their best work, including drafts in addition to final products.

 **Self-Assessment** Students should identify the pieces that they regard as their best work and the ones that they would like to revise further.

UNIT THREE

UNIT THEME

Unit Three

Stepping Forward In this unit, students will read about situations that test the characters' inner strength. This unit contains two parts: Part 1, "Showing Courage," and Part 2, "A Change of Heart." The selections in each part relate to the unit theme by presenting characters who show courage or who experience inner change.

Part 1

Showing Courage In Part 1 the characters find themselves in situations that demand great courage. For example, in "The Chief's Daughter," a young girl must decide whether to risk her life to follow her conscience.

Part 2

A Change of Heart The selections in Part 2 emphasize the new perspectives that characters can gain in challenging situations. For example, in "Koden," a family tragedy opens the doors to understanding for an adolescent girl.

Links to Unit Six
The Oral Tradition Unit Six, "Across Time and Place: The Oral Tradition," contains three selections that relate to the theme of "Stepping Forward":
• "How Odin Lost His Eye," p. 718
• "Where the Girl Saved Her Brother," p. 721
• "Waters of Gold," p. 725
You may wish to use one or more of these selections to introduce or conclude Unit Three.

STEPPING FORWARD

YOU GAIN COURAGE, STRENGTH,

AND CONFIDENCE BY EVERY

EXPERIENCE IN WHICH YOU

REALLY STOP TO LOOK FEAR

IN THE FACE. . . . YOU MUST

DO THE THINGS YOU THINK

YOU CANNOT DO.

—ELEANOR ROOSEVELT

AMERICAN DIPLOMAT, WRITER, AND FORMER

FIRST LADY OF THE UNITED STATES

256

Confrontation at the Bridge (1975), Jacob Lawrence. Courtesy of the artist and Francine Seders Gallery, Seattle, Washington.

257

To help students explore the connections between the art, the quotation, and the unit theme, have them discuss the following questions:

1. What does the phrase "stepping forward" mean to you? *(Possible responses: It refers to the need people have to stand up and be counted, to face challenges, and to take risks to achieve goals. Most people want to move forward and to learn, develop, and grow.)*

2. How do you think the quotation by Eleanor Roosevelt relates to the theme of "stepping forward"? *(Possible response: The quotation conveys the idea that in order to make positive changes you have to overcome fear, take risks, and believe in yourself.)*

3. What connection do you see between this painting and the ideas of stepping forward and facing fear? *(Possible response: In order to cross the bridge, these people will have to show courage and face the threatening animal. The bridge is symbolic of the path of life, and the animal is symbolic of the great challenges, difficulties, and conflicts that sometimes stand in the way.)*

4. What kinds of stories do you think you will read in this unit? *(Possible response: The stories will deal with the challenges that characters face and the ways they respond to them.)*

5. Think of a challenge or confrontation that you faced successfully. How did you respond to this situation? What did you learn about yourself? Do you feel your experience helped you grow in any way? How? *(Responses will vary.)*

Art Note

Confrontation at the Bridge by Jacob Lawrence Jacob Lawrence (1917–) portrays the lives and struggles of African Americans. His paintings often focus on the day-to-day realities of the poor. In 1941, at the age of 24, he became the first African-American artist to be represented by a New York gallery when the Downtown Gallery featured his *Migration of the Negro* series.
Reading the Art *Consider the artist's use of color and line to depict the figures and the animal on the bridge. How would you describe the mood that the painting gives you? What other elements of the painting contribute to this mood?*

Part 1 Skills Trace

ML DENOTES MINI-LESSON IN TEACHER'S EDITION

Selections	Reading Skills and Strategies	Literary Concepts	Writing Opportunities	Speaking, Listening, and Viewing
FICTION **The Chief's Daughter** Rosemary Sutcliff	Inference, PE p. 260 Making inferences, **ML** TE p. 262	Description, PE p. 271 Simile, PE p. 271 Character, **ML** TE p. 264 Point of view, **ML** TE p. 265	Sequel, PE p. 271 Speech, PE p. 271 Review, PE p. 271 Rewriting, **ML** TE p. 267 Letter, **ML** TE p. 269	Role-playing, PE p. 271 Bulletin board, PE p. 272 Oral report, **ML** TE p. 266 Storytelling, **ML** TE p. 267
NONFICTION **The Noble Experiment** *from* **I Never Had It Made** Jackie Robinson, as told to Alfred Duckett	Distinguishing fact and opinion, **ML** TE p. 276	Motivation, PE p. 283 Autobiography, PE p. 283 Sources, **ML** TE p. 277	Write about prejudice, PE p. 273 Letter, PE p. 283 Speech, PE p. 283 Definition, PE p. 283 Paragraph, **ML** TE p. 282	Stage an interview, PE p. 283 Oral report and time line, PE p. 284 Sportscast, **ML** TE p. 275 Film/drama, **ML** TE p. 282
FICTION **The Medicine Bag** Virginia Driving Hawk Sneve	Connecting, **ML** TE p. 287	Exposition, PE p. 295 Setting, **ML** TE p. 288	Write about heritage, PE p. 285 Poem or paragraph, PE p. 285 Essay, PE p. 295 Dialogue, PE p. 295 Song lyrics, PE p. 295 Tale, PE p. 295 Editorial, PE p. 295 Paragraph, TE p. 288 Story summary, **ML** TE p. 293	Essay, PE p. 295 Oral or written report, PE p. 296 Medicine bag, PE p. 296 Oral history, **ML** TE p. 290 Paraphrase, **ML** TE p. 294
POETRY **The Charge of the Light Brigade** Alfred, Lord Tennyson	Noticing rhythm, PE p. 298	Rhythm, PE p. 301	Write about the military, PE p. 298 Letter, PE p. 301 News report, PE p. 301 Dialogue, PE p. 301	Reading aloud, PE p. 298 Letter, PE p. 301 Choral reading, PE p. 302 Oral history and interviews, PE p. 302
NONFICTION ON YOUR OWN *from* **Susan Butcher and the Iditarod Trail** Ellen M. Dolan				Press conference, TE p. 310 Discussion, TE p. 311

Writing	Reading Skills and Strategies	Literary Concepts	Writing Opportunities	Speaking, Listening, and Viewing
WRITING ABOUT LITERATURE **Interpretation**	Analyzing main idea and details, PE pp. 312–13 Responding to literature, PE pp. 314–17 Making inferences, PE p. 319	Analyzing main idea and details, PE pp. 312–13	Topic sentences, PE p. 313 Supporting sentences, PE p. 313 Revising, PE p. 313 Interpretive essay, PE pp. 314–17 Writing a conclusion, PE p. 315	Viewing a scene, PE p. 318 Interpreting a scene, PE p. 318 Discussion, PE p. 318 Discussing inferences, PE p. 319

Grammar, Usage, Mechanics, and Spelling	Multimodal Learning	Research and Study Skills	Vocabulary	
Adjectives and adverbs, ML TE p. 263 Unstressed vowels, ML TE p. 270	Role-playing, PE p. 271 Bulletin board, PE p. 272 Oral report, ML TE p. 266 Story telling, ML TE p. 267	Research springs, PE p. 272 Reference books, ML TE p. 266 Research prehistoric Wales, ML TE p. 266	anxious clambering headland hover kindred	scouring scuffle sullen thatch waver
Capitalizing titles, ML TE p. 278 Correcting empty sentences, ML TE p. 279 Spelling with suffixes, ML TE p. 280	Stage an interview, PE p. 283 Oral report and time line, PE p. 284 Sportscast, ML TE p. 275 Film/drama, ML TE p. 282	Research Jackie Robinson, PE p. 284 Research segregation policies, PE p. 284	cynical eloquence incredulous insinuation integrated	retaliate shrewdly speculating taunt ultimate
Subject-verb agreement, ML TE p. 289 Unity, ML TE p. 291 Prefixes and roots, ML TE p. 292	Essay, PE p. 295 Oral or written report, PE p. 296 Medicine bag, PE p. 296 Picture book, PE p. 296 Visual representation, PE p. 297 Oral history, ML TE p. 290 Paraphrase, ML TE p. 294	Research Sioux crafts, PE p. 296 Paraphrasing, ML TE p. 294	confines descendant fatigue reluctantly unseemly	
Sound devices, ML TE p. 299	Reading aloud, PE p. 298 Letter, PE p. 301 Choral reading, PE p. 302 Poster, PE p. 302 Video game, PE p. 302 Oral history and interviews, PE p. 302	Research weapons, PE p. 302 Research the Crimean War, PE p. 302		
	Design an award, TE p. 309 Press conference, TE p. 310 Discussion, TE p. 311			

Grammar, Usage, Mechanics, and Spelling	Multimodal Learning	Research and Study Skills	Media Literacy
Using topic sentences, PE p. 313 Using subordinating conjunctions, PE p. 317 Subordinate clauses, PE p. 317	Viewing a scene, PE p. 318 Interpreting a scene, PE p. 318 Discussion, PE p. 318 Discussing inferences, PE p. 319		Interpreting scientific articles, PE p. 313 Interpreting a scene, PE pp. 318–19

Selections	Reading Skills and Strategies	Literary Concepts	Writing Opportunities	Speaking, Listening, and Viewing
FICTION **What I Want to Be When I Grow Up** Martha Brooks	Making inferences, **ML** TE p. 323	Humor and exaggeration, PE p. 329 Simile, **ML** TE p. 325	Write about an experience, PE p. 321 Prediction, PE p. 329 Sequel, PE p. 329 Editorial, PE p. 329 Rewriting, **ML** TE pp. 322, 327	Paragraph, PE p. 329 Dialogue, PE p. 330 Interview, PE p. 330 Oral report, PE p. 330
FICTION **Koden** Judith Nihei	Reading dialogue, PE p. 331 Questioning, **ML** TE p. 333	Characterization, PE p. 340 Point of view, **ML** TE p. 334	Adage, PE p. 340 Character sketch, PE p. 340 Letter, PE p. 340 Rewriting, **ML** TE p. 334 Paragraph, **ML** TE p. 336	List characters, PE p. 340 Dialogue, PE p. 341 Description, PE p. 341 Questionnaire, PE p. 341 Oral report, PE p. 341 Storyboard, **ML** TE p. 337 Oral report, **ML** TE p. 338
NONFICTION **I Am a Native of North America** Chief Dan George, as told to Helmut Hirnschall	Making judgments, **ML** TE p. 347	Persuasion, PE p. 348 Repetition, **ML** TE p. 345	Summary, PE p. 342 Definition, PE p. 348 Speech, PE p. 348 Poem, PE p. 348 Rewriting, **ML** TE p. 343	Diagram, PE p. 348 Dance, PE p. 349 Scale model, PE p. 349
POETRY **Direction** Alonzo Lopez **Your World** Georgia Douglas Johnson		Metaphor, PE p. 353	Write about the future, PE p. 350 Personal response, PE p. 353 Poem, PE p. 353 Essay, PE p. 353	Dialogue, PE p. 353 Oral interpretation or dance, PE p. 354 Oral report, PE p. 354 Dramatic reading, **ML** TE p. 351
DRAMA **The Monsters Are Due on Maple Street** Rod Serling	Reading a teleplay, PE p. 355 Distinguishing fact and opinion, **ML** TE p. 358	Dialogue, PE p. 369 Theme, PE p. 369 Theme, **ML** TE p. 361	Summary, PE p. 369 Stage directions, PE p. 369 Proposal, PE p. 369 Description, PE p. 371 Summary, **ML** TE p. 361	Role-playing, PE p. 369 Interview, PE p. 370 Oral report, PE p. 370 Music, PE p. 370 Reading aloud, **ML** TE p. 357 Readers theater, **ML** TE pp. 363, 365

Writing	Reading Skills and Strategies	Literary Concepts	Writing Opportunities	Speaking, Listening, and Viewing
WRITING FROM EXPERIENCE **Informative Exposition**		Details, PE p. 375 Main idea, PE p. 377 Audience and purpose, PE p. 377	Writing a definition, PE pp. 372–79 Drafting, PE pp. 376–77 Elaborating with specific examples, PE p. 377 Revising and publishing, PE pp. 378–79	Discussion group, PE p. 374 Interviews, PE p. 374 Poster, PE p. 379

Grammar, Usage, Mechanics, and Spelling	Multimodal Learning	Research and Study Skills	Vocabulary
Direct quotations, (ML) TE p. 326 Informal language, (ML) TE p. 327 Compound words and contractions, (ML) TE p. 328	Paragraph, PE p. 329 Dialogue, PE p. 330 Interview, PE p. 330 Oral report, PE p. 330	Research Alcoholics Anonymous, PE p. 330 Paraphrasing, (ML) TE p. 324	
Antecedent agreement, (ML) TE p. 335 Author's purpose and goal, (ML) TE p. 336 Hard and soft c and g (ML) TE p. 339	List characters, PE p. 340 Dialogue, PE p. 341 Description, PE p. 341 Questionnaire, PE p. 341 Oral report, PE p. 341 Storyboard, (ML) TE p. 337 Oral report, (ML) TE p. 338	Research a Japanese custom, PE p. 341	
Silent gh, (ML) TE p. 344 Subject-verb agreement, (ML) TE p. 346	Diagram, PE p. 348 Dance, PE p. 349 Poster or billboard, PE p. 349 Scale model, PE p. 349	Research a Salishan smoke house, PE p. 349	
	Dialogue, PE p. 353 Oral interpretation or dance, PE p. 354 Collage, PE p. 354 Poster, PE p. 354 Oral report, PE p. 354 Dramatic reading, (ML) TE p. 351	Research animals connected to Native American traditions, PE p. 354	
Dialogue in plays, (ML) TE p. 357 Interjections, (ML) TE p. 359 Suffixes -ance/-ant and -ence/-ent, (ML) TE p. 360	Role-playing, PE p. 369 Set design, PE p. 370 Interview, PE p. 370 Oral report, PE p. 370 Comic book, PE p. 370 Music, PE p. 370 Reading aloud, (ML) TE p. 357 Readers theater, (ML) TE pp. 363, 365 Story log, (ML) TE p. 366	Research UFOs, PE p. 370 Research prejudice, PE p. 370 Taking essay tests, (ML) TE p. 367	antagonism incriminate contorted intense defiant legitimate flustered optimistic idiosyncrasy persistent

Grammar, Usage, Mechanics, and Spelling	Multimodal Learning	Research and Study Skills	Media Literacy
Elaborating with specific examples, PE p. 377 Punctuating appositives, PE p. 379	Analyzing movie dialogue, PE p. 372 Interpreting journals, newspapers, magazine articles, business charts, and advertisements, PE pp. 372–73 Discussion group, PE p. 374 Interviews, PE p. 374 Poster, PE p. 379	Dictionaries and thesauri, PE p. 374 On-line E-mail sources, PE p. 374 Books of quotations, PE p. 374 Newspaper, television, and radio sources, PE p. 375 Using a dictionary, PE p. 375	Analyzing movie dialogue, PE p. 372 Interpreting journals, newspapers, magazine articles, business charts, and advertisements, PE pp. 372–73 Using reference, on-line, television, and radio sources, PE p. 374

Recommended Resources

Recommended Novels

**LITERATURE CONNECTIONS WITH
SOURCEBOOK FOR TEACHERS**

Across Five Aprils
by Irene Hunt

Thematic Links During the Civil War, a young farm boy must step forward and take responsibility when the rest of his family members are split over the war and choose to face varying enemies. **About the Author** Irene Hunt (born 1907) grew up in southern Illinois and listened to her grandfather's stories of the Civil War, which she turned into award-winning historical novels for young people. **Other Works by Irene Hunt** *The Lottery Rose, No Promises in the Wind, Up a Road Slowly*

**LITERATURE CONNECTIONS WITH
SOURCEBOOK FOR TEACHERS**

The Glory Field
by Walter Dean Myers

Thematic Links In this multi-generational novel, the descendants of a slave discover strength and identity in their vital connection to family and land. Each descendant steps forward in his or her own way.
About the Author Walter Dean Myers (born 1937) has been a prolific writer of both fiction and nonfiction works for young adults.
Other Works by Walter Dean Myers *Somewhere in the Darkness, Scorpions, Fallen Angels, Motown and Didi*

Midnight Is a Place
by Joan Aiken

Thematic Links A young boy steps forward to fight for his rightful inheritance in England during the industrial age. **About the Author** Joan Aiken (born 1924) has been applauded for her lively imagination, humorous characters, and intricate plots. **Other Works by Joan Aiken** *The Whispering Mountain; Night Fall; A Bundle of Nerves*

**LITERATURE CONNECTIONS WITH
SOURCEBOOK FOR TEACHERS**

SPANISH VERSION AVAILABLE

The Call of the Wild
by Jack London

Thematic Links When the dog Buck is forced into battle for control of his destiny, he responds by following the call of the wild.
About the Author Jack London (1876–1916) drew upon his experiences in the Klondike during the Gold Rush to write this classic dog story.
Other Works by Jack London *The Sea-Wolf, The Son of the Wolf: Tales of the Far North, White Fang, Lost Face, Tales of the Fish Patrol*

The Last Monster
by Jane Annixter and Paul Annixter

Thematic Links A young boy is determined to kill the grizzly bear that crippled his father.
About the Authors Jane Annixter (born 1903) and Paul Annixter (1894–1985) began writing together in 1954. They said that working together was steadier, for if one slowed down, the other urged him or her on.
Other Works by Jane Annixter and Paul Annixter *Buffalo Chief, The Phantom Stallion, The Great White, Windigo, The Runner*

The Clown
by Barbara Corcoran

Thematic Links An American girl smuggles a clown from Russia, who is in danger for political reasons, using her uncle's passport and clothes.
About the Author Barbara Corcoran (born 1911) usually writes fiction that looks into the physical and emotional problems of young adults.
Other Works by Barbara Corcoran *Sam; A Row of Tigers; Don't Slam the Door When You Go; The Winds of Time; Make No Sound; Hey, That's My Soul You're Stomping On*

For Teacher TEACHING LITERATURE

Gebhard, Ann O. "The Emerging Self: Young Adult and Classic Novels of the Black Experience." *English Journal* 82.5 (September 1993): 50–54.

Kaywell, Joan. "Using Young Adult Problem Fiction and Nonfiction to Produce Critical Readers." *ALAN Review* 21.2 (Winter 1994): 29–32.

Smith, Pamela. "Interpreters Theatre: A Tool for Teaching Literature." *English Journal* 82.7 (November 1993): 71–72.

Recommended Readings in Cross-Curricular Areas

HISTORY

Celtic Warrior Chiefs
by John Matthews and
Bob Stewart (1994)
Describes fantastic and real
exploits. Links to Rosemary
Sutcliff's "The Chief's
Daughter."

One More River to Cross
by Jim Haskins (1992)
Features inspirational stories
of men and women who fol-
lowed their dreams. Links to
Jackie Robinson's *I Never Had
it Made.*

SOCIAL STUDIES

Dakota Dream
by James Bennett (1994)
A young man wants to be-
come Sioux. Links to Virginia
Driving Hawk Sneve's "The
Medicine Bag" and Chief Dan
George's "I Am a Native of
North America."

Arctic Expedition
by Mike Salisbury (1989)
A young person prepares to
explore the Arctic. Includes
descriptions of physical features and equipment necessary for survival. Links to
*Susan Butcher and the
Iditarod Trail.*

For Teacher   CROSS-CURRICULAR INSTRUCTION

Christensen, Joel. "Capture Your Entire
Audience." *Legacy* 5.4 (July-August 1994):
17–19.

Gibbs, Linda J., and Edward J. Earley.
*Using Children's Literature to Develop Core
Values.* Bloomington, IN: Phi Delta Kappa
Educational Foundation, 1994.

Heathcote, Dorothy. "Excellence in Teaching:
What It Takes to Do It Well." *Teaching
Theatre* 4.1 (Fall 1992): 3–6.

Recommended Media Resources

THE LANGUAGE OF LITERATURE

LASERLINKS
Videodisc, Gr. 7
See *LaserLinks
Teacher's Source
Book,* pages 23–24,
for an overview of
Unit Three.

AUDIO LIBRARY
Tapes
Unit Three: Stepping
Forward
Gr. 7, Tape 6: Sides A & B
Gr. 7, Tape 7: Sides A & B
Gr. 7, Tape 8: Sides A & B

WRITING COACH
Writing Coach
Software: Writing
About Literature:
Interpretive Essay;
Explanation of an Idea

OUTSIDE RESOURCES

Films/Videos/Film Strips/Audiocassettes
Past Eight O'Clock. Read by Jane Asher.
Chivers Children's Audio Books.
The Shining Company. Read by Ron
Keith. Seven sound cassettes. (9.5 hrs.)
A History of Native Americans, video-
cassette, Indians of Native America
Video Collection II, 1994. (30 min.)

Internet Resources
Literature and Language Arts Center at
http://www.hmco.com/mcdougal/lit/
litcent.html

For Teacher   TEACHING WITH TECHNOLOGY

Courtney, Tim, et al. "The Impact of Com-
puter Technology on the Teaching of English
(The Round Table)." *English Journal* 82.8
(December 1993): 68–70.

Bruder, Isabelle, et al. "School Reform: Why
You Need Technology to Get There." *Electronic Learning* 11.8 (May-June 1992): 22–28.

Cannings, Terence R., and LeRoy Finkel, eds.
The Technology Age Classroom. Wilsonville,
OR: Franklin, Beedle & Associates, Inc., 1993.

Professional Enrichment

Developing Educated Viewers

Here's a statistic guaranteed to shock you: During winter, the average seventh grader watches television 7 hours and 17 minutes a day.

Things are a bit better in the summer, when that same seventh grader watches TV 6 hours and 47 minutes a day. We all know that excessive television viewing cuts down on the time that teenagers can spend reading, writing, and improving verbal skills. Even a TV insider once called the media "chewing gum for the eyes." So how can a language arts teacher combat this "vast wasteland"? Here's how—by teaching your students to be educated viewers.

A VIEWER'S "GLOSSARY"
The basic language of television is the picture, or visual image. People who write teleplays consider visual images the principal means of communication. Words function to complement and clarify the images on the screen, not the other way around. In this unit, your students will read the teleplay *The Monsters Are Due on Maple Street.* You can help them get the most from reading and viewing teleplays by explaining how a teleplay is constructed. As your students prepare to read *The Monsters Are Due on Maple Street,* share the following terms and explanations:
- **Shot list** A shot list is a roster of the major scenes that are going to be "shot," or filmed. Quick and simple to prepare, a shot list records all the scenes the director wants to include in the teleplay.
- **Storyboards** A storyboard is a visual way of planning a scene. Compare it to the graphic organizers that students use to brainstorm writing ideas. Explore with the class how storyboards enable teleplay writers to think in more detail about what they will include in each scene. Students may be interested in knowing that Walt Disney (1901–1966) was the first television illustrator to use storyboards to plan cartoons.
- **Scripts** A script is a written plan for a teleplay. Unlike essays, scripts can be written in many different ways. For example, some scripts are arranged in columns, with the directions for the crew on the left and the narrative on the right.

VIEWING FOR INFORMATION
Discuss with students how we view some teleplays for enjoyment and others for information. Then share the following guidelines for viewing teleplays.
- Show students how to look for the organizational structure of the teleplay. If the structure is chronological, for example, students should be able to recognize the sequence of events.
- Remind students to be active viewers. They should ask themselves questions as they watch. Elicit from the class how asking questions will help them identify the most important parts of the teleplay and isolate aspects they did not understand and therefore might not remember as clearly. Questions also help viewers be more interested in the show's topic.
- Guide students to paraphrase key points in the show into their own words. Be sure students understand that paraphrasing is the process of putting a person's dialogue into your own words. Explain that paraphrasing allows viewers to sort out the main points and make sure they are clear.

VIEWING CRITICALLY
Explain to students that viewing critically is different from viewing for information. Here, viewers judge to what extent they agree with the show's message.
- To view critically, students should first establish their standards for evaluating the message. Next they should collect information about the topic. Finally, students should apply their standards to the information.
- Students must be alert and informed as they view critically. They can ask themselves if the show is suppressing or distorting facts and being consistent with previous shows on the same subject.

Invite students to prepare a checklist to help them evaluate a teleplay and their reasons for watching it. Here are some questions that students can ask themselves:
- Do I think this teleplay will be worth watching?
- Have I enjoyed other shows like this? Have I learned something from them?
- The last time I watched a show like this, what was my reaction?
- Is there anything else I would like to do or should be doing instead of watching this show?

Related Reading

 Alexander, Allison, ed. *Taking Sides: Clashing Views on Controversial Issues in Mass Media and Society.* Dushkin, 1993.

 Bennett, Steven. *Kick the TV Habit: A Simple Program for Changing Your Family's Viewing and Videogame Habits.* New York: Penguin, 1994.

 Polk, Lee, and LeShan, Eda. *The Incredible Television Machine.* New York: Macmillan, 1977.

Family and Community Involvement

From risking one's life for a friend to facing racial prejudice, all of the selections in Unit Three are connected to the theme of stepping forward. By completing some of the following activities, your students, their families, and other community members can make important connections outside the classroom as they explore real-life examples of stepping forward.

The following Copymasters for Unit Three provide activities that students can take home and complete with a parent or other family member.

OPTION 1: WRITE A POEM
- **Connection** All of the selections in Unit Three illustrate the theme of stepping forward.
- **Activity** *Copymaster, page 1* Students and family members use poetry to tell the story of a brave act of stepping forward.

OPTION 2: DESIGN A GAME
- **Connection** In "The Noble Experiment," Jackie Robinson braves racial prejudice to play major-league baseball.
- **Activity** *Copymaster, page 2* Students and family members design and make a trivia game about baseball or another topic related to the selection.

OPTION 3: BUILD A REPLICA
- **Connection** The fictional story "The Chief's Daughter" is set in prehistoric Wales, sometime between 3000 and 50 B.C.
- **Activity** *Copymaster, page 3* Students and family members build a three-dimensional replica of a prehistoric structure.

OPTION 1
- **Connection** All of the selections in Unit Three illustrate the theme of stepping forward.
- **Activity** Invite a community activist involved in a local social cause to tell students about his or her cause and discuss what's involved in stepping forward to promote change in your community.

OPTION 2
- **Connection** The author of "I Am a Native of North America" and the grandfather in "The Medicine Bag" both demonstrate pride in their Native American heritage.
- **Activity** Take the class on a field trip to a museum that houses Native American artifacts and crafts.

OPTION 3
- **Connection** In "What I Want to Be When I Grow Up," the main character considers a career as a journalist.
- **Activity** Organize a career fair by inviting parents and community members to discuss their professions with students. Ask a career counselor to talk about the process of choosing a career.

Part 1 Cooperative Project

A Newsmagazine

 **Getting Started**

Arranging the Project

Make arrangements with the school so students can photocopy important pictures to accompany their written articles. You might want to set a limit on the number of pictures allowed so things don't get out of hand. Gather a fairly large selection of newsmagazines such as *Time, Newsweek,* and even *People* for students to examine. These magazines need not be current—any issues are fine. If possible, try to find other magazines with a historical slant, along the lines of *American Heritage.* There are several dozen historically focused magazines that are too esoteric to be found in school libraries, but you may be able to borrow some from another teacher or a friend who has a special interest in a particular historical era.

Arranging for Printing

If students have access to computers, they may want to type up their final articles in a typical two- or three-column magazine format. If not, a parent might volunteer to do this. Stress to students that their articles should be neatly and legibly written, whether or not they are to be typed later. If the typing is to be done by someone other than themselves, students should also indicate where in each article any pictures should appear.

 **Creating the Newsmagazine**

Introducing the Project

Explain that students will be working cooperatively to write an article in the style of a newsmagazine about a historical figure whose courage they admire. The article should tell the background of the person, the events and circumstances leading up to the event, the specific act of courage, and the results of the act on that person and others.

Have students look over the newsmagazines. They should note the general layout of the magazines, as well as the general tone and style of the reporting. Help students note that opinions are clearly labeled as such, and most good reporting is done on a factual, unemotional level. If you can find an article similar to the project assignment, ask all students to read it and discuss it as a class.

Group Investigation

Divide students into groups of two to four. The groups will work as teams of investigative reporters and will select a historical figure to write about. This person should have performed a courageous act above and beyond that of the average person. Encourage students to do general research on several figures before selecting one on which to focus. When groups have selected an appropriate person to write about, members can divide responsibilities for portions of the article. One student can find background information on the historical era, one can research the background of the person, one can describe in detail the events leading up to and the act of courage itself, while another can describe the aftermath of the event. The group can meet to assemble the article, decide on which pictures to include, and put finishing touches on the writing.

Creating a Project Description

After groups have narrowed the field and selected a courageous figure, they should also have some knowledge of the basic event. Ask each group to submit a brief description of the person and the act of courage, telling why they chose that particular person. This will allow you to encourage diversity in the subject matter and give you an idea of how the groups are progressing on their project. Meet individually with each group to discuss the project from time to time.

OPTION 1: SAY IT FOR THE CAMERA If your school has access to a video camera, the article and a reading of it might be videotaped for presentation. Students can model the "program" on any of several documentaries that use a narrator and a montage of still photos and pictures instead of actors.

OPTION 2: TODAY'S HEROES Students can complete a newsmagazine about people in today's news rather than a figure from the past.

OPTION 3: THE SUPERHERO DEBATE Groups can select well-known cartoon superheros and debate the amount of courage each demonstrates. Opinions should be backed up with facts, such as specific examples of heroism, what superpowers they possess, and in what ways they are vulnerable.

OPTION 4: A SPECIFIC ERA Assign students a specific historical era in which to find their courageous person, such as the Wild West, the Renaissance, the Civil War, or the Birth of America. This effort might be coordinated with the history or social studies teacher.

If fancy printing or typesetting is not available to students, they can write the articles in a two-column format, inserting pictures in appropriate places. The class can think up a title, make a table of contents, and bind the pages into one magazine.

3 Sharing the Magazine

If you have the resources, you might photocopy the entire magazine for each student to take home. The original can be placed in the school library for interested students to read. (This way it will also be available for next year's students as an example of the project.)

& Assessing the Project

The following rubric can be used for group or individual assessment.

3 Full Accomplishment Students follow directions and produce an article that describes a historical figure who performed a significant act of courage.

2 Substantial Accomplishment Students produce an article about a historical figure, but the description of the act of courage or its significance is unfocused.

1 Little or Partial Accomplishment Students' article is incomplete or does not fulfill the requirements of the assignment.

For the Portfolio
If you place the original magazine in the school library, you might want to keep a photocopy in your classroom. Individual students' portfolios should include a copy of your final written assessment, as well as a copy of the brief description they wrote earlier in the project.

Note: For other assessment options, see the *Teacher's Guide to Assessment and Portfolio Use.*

Cross-Curricular Options

ART/LANGUAGE ARTS
Ask students to write a children's story about the person they selected. This can be accompanied by illustrations showing the person and the events of the story.

MUSIC
Ask students to find and record songs that tell about a person doing something courageous. The audiotape can be played in class for review and discussion.

MATH

Students can design and take a survey about the most admired courageous person. The results of the survey can be shown in a bar graph or pie chart.

Resources

The Story of Folk Music by Melvin Berger provides information about the origins and characteristics of folk music.

Part 1 Lesson Planner

TIME ALLOTMENTS SHOWN ARE APPROXIMATE. DEPENDING ON YOUR GOALS AND THE NEEDS OF YOUR STUDENTS, YOU MAY WISH TO ALLOW MORE OR LESS TIME FOR CERTAIN PORTIONS OF THE LESSON.

Table of Contents	Discussion	Previewing the Selection	Reading the Selection
PART OPENER **SHOWING COURAGE** **What Do You Think?** page 258	**20 MINUTES** • Reflect on the part theme		
SELECTION **The Chief's Daughter** page 261 CHALLENGING		**20 MINUTES** • PERSONAL CONNECTION • HISTORICAL CONNECTION • READING CONNECTION: Inference	**45 MINUTES** • Introduce vocabulary • Read pp. 261–70 (10 pp.)
SELECTION **The Noble Experiment** *from* **I Never Had It Made** page 274 AVERAGE		**20 MINUTES** • PERSONAL CONNECTION • HISTORICAL CONNECTION • WRITING CONNECTION	**35 MINUTES** • Introduce vocabulary • Read pp. 274–82 (9 pp.)
SELECTION **The Medicine Bag** page 286 EASY		**20 MINUTES** • PERSONAL CONNECTION • HISTORICAL CONNECTION • WRITING CONNECTION	**35 MINUTES** • Introduce vocabulary • Read pp. 286–94 (9 pp.)
SELECTION **The Charge of the Light Brigade** page 299 CHALLENGING		**15 MINUTES** • PERSONAL CONNECTION • HISTORICAL CONNECTION • READING CONNECTION: Noticing rhythm	**5 MINUTES** • Read pp. 299–300 (2 pp.)
NONFICTION ON YOUR OWN *from* **Susan Butcher and the Iditarod Trail** page 303 AVERAGE			**35 MINUTES** • Read pp. 303–11 (9 pp.)

Writing	Writer's Style	Prewriting	Drafting and Revising
WRITING ABOUT LITERATURE **Interpretation**	**25 MINUTES**	**25 MINUTES**	**75 MINUTES**

Time estimates assume in-class work. You may wish to assign some of these stages as homework.

Responding to the Selection

FROM PERSONAL RESPONSE TO CRITICAL ANALYSIS	OR	ANOTHER PATHWAY	LITERARY CONCEPTS	QUICKWRITES
50 MINUTES				
• Discussion questions	OR	• Role-playing	• Description and simile	• Sequel • Speech • Review
40 MINUTES				
• Discussion questions	OR	• Stage an interview	• Motivation • Autobiography	• Letter • Speech • Definition
50 MINUTES				
• Discussion questions	OR	• Essay	• Exposition	• Dialogue • Song lyrics • Tale • Editorial
40 MINUTES				
• Discussion questions	OR	• Letter	• Rhythm	• News report • Dialogue

Extension Activities

ALTERNATIVE ACTIVITIES	LITERARY LINKS	CRITIC'S CORNER	THE WRITER'S STYLE	ACROSS THE CURRICULUM	ART CONNECTION	WORDS TO KNOW	BIOGRAPHY
40 MINUTES							
			✔	SCIENCE	✔	✔	
30 MINUTES							
✔				SOCIAL STUDIES	✔	✔	
50 MINUTES							
✔	✔			✔	✔	✔	
50 MINUTES							
✔	✔			SOCIAL STUDIES		✔	
						✔	

Publishing and Reflecting

30 MINUTES

Grammar in Context

15 MINUTES

Reading the World

30 MINUTES

WHAT DO YOU THINK?

Objectives

The activities on this page can be used to

• introduce the theme of "Showing Courage," since each activity is connected to one or more of the selections in Part 1

• create materials for personal portfolios that students can return to later for reconsideration or revision

• build an understanding of theme that students can return to and develop as they progress through the unit

What brave people are part of your family history?

Invite students to write a series of thought-provoking questions before they interview their relatives. Encourage students to bring photos or draw illustrations to accompany their class presentations. (See "The Medicine Bag," p. 285.)

What people in history impress you?

Encourage students to plan their designs for each card. Students should select pictures or illustrations that reflect the courageous qualities of each person chosen. (See "The Noble Experiment," p. 273.)

Who is your personal hero?

After the class has compiled a master list, you may wish to have volunteers role-play each person on the list. Each volunteer can present a campaign speech that details his or her courageous accomplishments. (See the excerpt from *Susan Butcher and the Iditarod Trail,* p. 303.)

Who's the bravest of them all?

Make sure that students do not choose characters too obscure for partners to guess. You may wish to have students present the reasons for their choice of character to the entire class. (See "The Chief's Daughter," p. 259 and "The Charge of the Light Brigade," p. 298.)

SHOWING COURAGE

WHAT DO YOU THINK?

REFLECTING ON THEME

Throughout your life, you will be called upon to show courage again and again. You'll need to accept responsibilities, defend your beliefs, and admit mistakes. You may face a deep fear or fight to overcome great odds. Use the activities on this page to examine your views about courage.

What brave people are part of your family history?

Interview an older relative, asking him or her to tell you about an ancestor who acted with courage. Tape-record the interview, transcribe it, and write an oral history based on it. Read your oral history to your classmates.

What people in history impress you?

Brainstorm a list of people who have done something remarkable—such as discover a cure for polio or walk on the moon. For each person, create a trading card that presents a key fact.

Who is your personal hero?

master list

1.
2.
3.
4.
5.

Whom do you consider the most courageous person in your school or community? With a small group, create a list of three names. Then share your list with other groups, compile a master list, and hold an election to determine the class's choice.

Who's the bravest of them all?

Think of the bravest character you have ever read about or seen in a movie. Then have a partner try to guess the character's identity after asking you no more than ten yes-or-no questions. Share your reasons for choosing the character you did.

Cross-Curricular Connections

Art Have students work in small groups to create collages based on the theme of showing courage. Students should work together to generate a list of words and images that come to mind when they think about the quality of courage. Students can draw from this list when designing their collages. Encourage groups to use a variety of materials, including drawings, photos, and clippings from magazines and newspapers. Groups can display their finished collages in the classroom for all to see.

COMMUNITY OUTREACH

Instruct students to write a short biography of someone they consider courageous in their school or community. Students may choose to write about one of the people they nominated for the personal hero activity on this page. Students should interview the individual chosen and then outline the information they gather. The biographies can be collected and bound into a class book for students to read.

FICTION

The Chief's Daughter
Rosemary Sutcliff

Activating Prior Knowledge
PERSONAL CONNECTION

When you think about courage, what individuals come to mind? In your notebook, create a chart like the one shown, listing three or more people and their brave deeds. Then, as you read "The Chief's Daughter," think about the main characters in the story and how they show their courage.

Courage	
People	Brave Deeds
1.	1.
2.	2.
3.	3.

Building Background
HISTORICAL CONNECTION

"The Chief's Daughter" is a story about two courageous young people that is set in prehistoric Wales, sometime between 3000 and 50 B.C. This age was full of danger and mystery. Families banded together in clans to increase their chances of survival and chose a courageous warrior to be their chief, or protector. They built their *bothies,* or huts, on high ground so that they could detect enemy warriors at a distance. When threatened, the entire clan took refuge within a *stockade*—a stronghold protected by a barrier of stakes driven into the ground. Above all, a clan needed to protect its source of water. Some clans prayed to a mother-goddess that they associated with water. In her honor, clans sometimes erected a tall stone, called a *menhir.* They even resorted to human sacrifice to appease the mother-goddess.

Great Britain and Ireland

Atlantic Ocean
SCOTLAND
North Sea
NORTHERN IRELAND
IRELAND
Irish Sea
ENGLAND
WALES
English Channel
FRANCE
Miles
0 100 200

THE CHIEF'S DAUGHTER **259**

SUMMARY

Nessan, the daughter of a Celtic chieftain in ancient Wales, has befriended the boy Dara, a 12-year-old Irish prisoner. Nessan's clan plans to sacrifice Dara to the Earth Goddess to restore the clan's spring, which has mysteriously dried up. Nessan helps Dara escape. Then, to save an innocent guard's life, she confesses to the crime, knowing that she will be sacrificed in Dara's place. As Dara runs through the hills behind the village, he finds a shallow pond that contains a shrine to the Goddess. He steals one of the offerings there, a spear. He is unaware that removing the spear helps to unclog an outlet to an underground stream. Water flows into the spring, which feeds the clan's spring. The spring flows again, and Nessan is spared.

Thematic Link: *Showing Courage* Nessan shows extraordinary courage when she frees Dara and offers to be sacrificed in his place.

CUSTOMIZING FOR
Students Acquiring English

- Use **ACCESS FOR STUDENTS ACQUIRING ENGLISH,** *Reading and Writing Support.*

- This story combines difficult vocabulary with an unfamiliar context, so it may prove difficult for many students. Encourage students acquiring English to read through once for a basic understanding of the plot, without interrupting their reading to look up unfamiliar words. Have them follow this first reading with a brief comprehension check, then do a second reading for in-depth understanding.

- In addition to these boxes, you may want to use the suggestions under Strategic Reading for Less-Proficient Readers.

Inference

An inference is a logical guess or conclusion based on evidence. As you read a story, you pick up details that help you understand what is going on. Using these details and what you know from your own experience, you figure out more than what the words say. For example, look at the following paragraphs from Anna Quindlen's "Homeless":

> Her name was Ann, and we met in the Port Authority Bus Terminal several Januarys ago. <u>I was doing a story on homeless people.</u> She said I was wasting my time talking to her; she was just passing through, although she'd been passing through for more than two weeks. To prove to me that this was true, she rummaged through a tote bag and a manila envelope and finally unfolded a sheet of typing paper and brought out her photographs.
>
> They were not pictures of family, or friends, or even a dog or cat, its eyes brown-red in the flashbulb's light. <u>They were pictures of a house.</u>

From the **detail** that the narrator "was doing a story on homeless people," you can **infer** that she is a newspaper or magazine writer.

From the **detail** that Ann produces a photograph of a house, you can **infer** that the house is important to her for some reason.

Making inferences is a natural part of the reading process, and you make many inferences while reading a story. Often you change your mind and make new inferences after you have gathered more details. Your inferences may differ from those made by other readers because you are using your own knowledge and experience to make connections as you read. While reading "The Chief's Daughter," you might record some of your inferences about the courage of the characters and about other aspects of the story.

Story Detail

Mr. Parsons gives the beggar two half dollars.

Knowledge

Experience

Reader

Inference

Mr. Parsons is sensitive to the needs of others.

WORDS TO KNOW

anxious (ăngk′shəs) *adj.* worried; uneasy in mind (p. 263)

clambering (klăm′bər-ĭng) *n.* the act of climbing with effort, using the hands and feet **clamber** *v.* (p. 267)

headland (hĕd′lənd) *n.* a point of land, usually high and with a sheer drop, extending out into a body of water (p. 262)

hover (hŭv′ər) *v.* to stay or wait near a place (p. 265)

kindred (kĭn′drĭd) *n.* one's relatives (p. 262)

scouring (skour′ĭng) *adj.* going about in a quick but thorough way, especially in a search or pursuit **scour** *v.* (p. 262)

scuffle (skŭf′əl) *n.* the act or sound of feet shuffling (p. 267)

sullen (sŭl′ən) *adj.* depressing; dismal (p. 263)

thatch (thăch) *v.* to make a roof out of plant stems (p. 262)

waver (wā′vər) *v.* to move unsteadily back and forth or to become unsure (p. 270)

The Chief's Daughter

by Rosemary Sutcliff

Illustration by Marco Ventura. From *Anna dei Porci* by Piero and Marco Ventura. Copyright © 1987 Mondadori.

CUSTOMIZING FOR

Gifted and Talented Students

Challenge students to compare and contrast the values of the Clan with the values of modern American society as they read. *(Possible response: The Clan values unquestioning allegiance and obedience to its leader, physical courage, and personal sacrifice. While American society values these qualities, it also places value on personal fulfillment, emotional growth, and independence.)*

Literary Concept:
DESCRIPTION

A Ask students to share their impressions of prehistoric Wales, based on the opening description. Invite students to explain the mood created by this description. *(Possible response: Prehistoric Wales is exciting, dangerous, and mysterious. The mood created is thrilling, tense, and frightening.)*

CUSTOMIZING FOR
Multiple Learning Styles

B **Spatial or Graphic Learners** Invite students to use this scene as a starting point for a drawing that reveals more about Dara and Nessan and their relationship.

A The Dun, the Strong-Place, stood far out on the <u>headland</u>, seeming almost to overhang the Western Sea. Three deep turf banks ringed it round, and where the hawthorn stakes of the stockade had taken root here and there, their small stunted branches with salt-burned leaves grew bent all one way by the sea wind.

The Chief's big round Hall, where the Fire of the Clan never died on the hearth, stood at the highest part of the enclosure, with his byres and barns and stables, and the women's huts clumped about it. But in quiet times only the Chief himself and his <u>kindred</u> and household warriors lived there, while the rest of the Clan lived in the stone and turf bothies scattered over the landward side of the headland. Only when the raiders came out of the West in their skin-covered war boats would the whole Clan drive their cattle into the spaces between the sheltering turf banks and take refuge in the Chief's stronghold.

It was such a time now, the whole enclosure crowded with men and women and children and dogs and lean pigs, while the cattle lowed and fidgeted uneasily in their cramped space. For three days ago, the war boats had come again, and the Irish raiders were loose along the coast of Wales, <u>scouring</u> the hills for cattle and slaves.

On the sloping roof of the hut where the black herd bull lived, a boy and a girl were sprawling side by side. The boy would rather have climbed to the roof of the Hall, because from there you could get a further view to the west, but the turf of the Hall roof, tawny as a hound's coat, was growing slippery with the dryness of late summer, while the bull-house

was <u>thatched</u> with heather that gave you something to dig your toes and heels into, so that you did not keep sliding off all the time.

The girl was ten years old, dark and slight, like most of the folk in the headland Strong-Place below her. She had found a grey and white seagull's feather caught in the rough thatch, and was trying to twist it into her long dark hair. The boy, who lay propped on one elbow staring out to sea, was older, with hair and eyes almost the same color as the string of amber[1] round his neck. He did not belong to the girl's People, but was a prisoner in their hands, left behind wounded, the last time the Irish war boats came.

The girl gave up trying to make the feather stay in her hair, and sat chewing the end of it instead. "Dara, why will you always be staring out toward the sunset?"

The boy went on staring. "I look toward my home."

"If you loved it so much, why did you leave it and come raiding in ours?"

He shrugged. "I am a man. When the other men go raiding, should I sit at home spinning with the women?"

"A *man!* You're only twelve, even now! Only two years older than I am!"

That time the boy did not answer at all. The sea creamed on the rocks under the headland, and from beneath the heather thatch came the soft heavy puffing of the herd bull. After a while the girl threw the feather away, and said crossly, "All right, go on staring into the sunset. *I* am not wanting to talk to you."

---

1. **amber:** a hard yellow, orange, or brownish yellow fossil resin used for making jewelry.

WORDS
TO
KNOW

headland (hĕd′lənd) *n.* a point of land, usually high and with a sheer drop, extending out into a body of water
kindred (kĭn′drĭd) *n.* one's relatives
scouring (skour′ĭng) *adj.* going about in a quick but thorough way, especially in a search or pursuit **scour** *v.*
thatch (thăch) *v.* to make a roof out of plant stems

262

Mini-Lesson Reading Skills/Strategies

MAKING INFERENCES Tell students that when they read between the lines to find information that is not directly stated, they are making inferences. For example, Dara never says that he misses his home. However, students can infer this because he stares toward the west, where his home is.

Application Have students read the dialogue between Dara and Nessan on pages 262 and 263.

Have students discuss what inferences they can make about the relationship between these characters. Ask students to indicate what clues from the story they used to make their inferences. You may wish to have students complete a two-column chart indicating inferences made and clues used.

Reteaching/Reinforcement
• *Unit Three Resource Book* p. 5

"Why should you want to talk to a prisoner?" Dara snapped, looking round at last. "You did not have to come climbing up here after me."

"You would not have been even a prisoner, if I had not pleaded for you. They meant to sacrifice you to the Black Mother; you know that, don't you?"

"I know that. You've reminded me often enough," Dara said between his teeth. "It is a great honor that Nessan the Chief's daughter should plead for me. I must remember and be grateful."

The girl seemed to have got over her sudden crossness, and looked at him consideringly. "Yes, I think you should," she said after a moment, "for besides pleading for you with Father *and* with Laethrig the Priest, ¿I gave my best blue glass arm-ring to the Mother, that she might not be angry with us for keeping you alive!"

And then someone came past the bull-house with a clanking pail, and looked up and called to Dara that it was time he came down and took his share of the work, for the cattle needed watering.

Just below the Chief's Hall, where the land began to drop, a spring burst out from under a grey boulder. It filled a small deep pool almost like a well, then spilled over and away down the narrow gulley it had worn for itself, through the gap left for it in the encircling banks, and dropped over the cliff edge making a thread of white water among the rocks, until it reached the sea. That evening it seemed to the men watering the cattle that it was running unusually low, and when the pails were

"Dara, why will you always be staring out toward the sunset?"

brought up out of the well-pool, it took longer than usual to refill. Some of them looked at each other a little anxiously. But the spring had never been known to dry up, no matter how many men and cattle drank from it. They were imagining things . . . It would be its usual self in the morning. . . .

But in the morning, when it was time to water the cattle again, and the women came to draw the day's pitcher-full for their households, there was scarcely any water spilling over into the little gully at all.

"It has been a dry summer, I am thinking," one woman said.

Another shook her head. "We have had dry summers before."

"It is in my mind," said a man standing by with a pail for his cattle, "that this thing must be told quickly to the Chief."

The Chief came, and looked into the <u>sullen</u> stillness of the well, and then up into the heat-milky sky, pulling the dark front-locks of hair on either side of his face as he always did when troubled. "It must surely rain soon," he said after a while. "Maybe rain is all we need. But meanwhile the cattle must be doing with half measure, and see that the women take their pitchers away only half full."

What he did not say, and no one else said either, for even to speak of such a thing would be unlucky, was, "If the water fails, the stronghold fails also."

All that day the people went about with <u>anxious</u> eyes, returning again and again to look at the spring. By evening, the pool had

WORDS TO KNOW | **sullen** (sŭl'ən) *adj.* depressing; dismal
anxious (ăngk'shəs) *adj.* worried; uneasy in mind

263

I Invite students to guess what tone of voice Dara used when he *snapped.* Then model appropriate intonation of these words.

Critical Thinking: SYNTHESIZING

C Have students analyze what Nessan means here. Guide them to combine story clues with what they learned from the Historical Connection on page 259 in their analysis. *(Possible response: Dara would be dead if Nessan hadn't stepped in. They were going to make Dara a human sacrifice to appease the Black Mother.)*

Active Reading: EVALUATE

D Explore with students Nessan's efforts on Dara's behalf. Then have students evaluate what Nessan's actions suggest about her feelings for Dara. Ask them to consider what her prior offering of the "blue glass arm-ring" might suggest about her future actions on Dara's behalf. *(Possible responses: Nessan might feel pity, affection, or sympathy for Dara. Her offering of the arm-ring suggests she might sacrifice more for him in the future.)*

Linking to Social Studies

E The use of fresh spring water for drinking continues to this day. In fact, an entire commercial industry has developed that bottles water obtained from natural springs and transports it all over the world for sale. The International Bottled Water Association was established in 1982 to promote the use of bottled drinking water worldwide.

Mini-Lesson  Grammar

ADJECTIVES AND ADVERBS Tell students that adjectives and adverbs are descriptive words that are often misused. Explain that writers can avoid making mistakes with such descriptive words by checking to see what word they want to modify. An adjective modifies a noun or pronoun; it tells *which one, what kind,* or *how many.* An adverb modifies a verb, adjective, or adverb; it tells *when, where, how,* or *to what extent.*

Application Have students identify the adjectives and adverbs in the highlighted paragraph above.

Then have them rewrite the paragraph with alternative adjectives and adverbs.

Reteaching/Reinforcement
• Grammar Handbook, anthology p. 866
• *Grammar Mini-Lessons* copymasters, p. 19, transparencies p. 12

The Writer's Craft

Adjective or Adverb?, pp. 522–523

View of Donner Lake, California by **Albert Bierstadt** Bierstadt (1830–1902) was known for his majestic panoramic landscapes of the American West. The lavish detail and monumental scale of these landscapes capture the grand poetry of the wilderness.

Reading the Art *How does the artist suggest the wonder and grandeur of this scene? Do you think Nessan's prehistoric Wales looked much the same? Why or why not?*

View of Donner Lake, California (1871 or 1872), Albert Bierstadt. Oil on paper mounted on canvas, 29 ¼″ × 21 ¼″, The Fine Arts Museum of San Francisco, gift of Anna Bennett and Jessie Jonas in memory of August F. Jonas, Jr.

Mini-Lesson Literary Concepts

REVIEWING CHARACTER Remind students that characters are the people, animals, or imaginary creatures that take part in the action of a literary work. There are four basic methods a writer can use to develop a character: (1) presenting a character's words and actions, (2) showing a character's thoughts, (3) describing a character's appearance, (4) telling what others think about a character.

Application As students read the story, have them describe the main characters, Nessan and Dara, by completing a character analysis chart like the one shown.

Character	Trait	How Revealed

barely filled up again, and not one drop was spilling over into the stony runnel.[2]

Then the Chieftain sent for Laethrig the Priest. And Laethrig came, very old and brittle, like a withered leaf, in his mantle of beaver skins with his necklaces of dried seed pods and slender seabird bones rustling and rattling about his neck. And he sat down beside the spring and went away small inside himself so that looking into his eyes was like looking through the doorway of an empty hut. And it seemed a long time, to the men and women waiting about him, before he came back and looked out of his eyes again.

"What is it?" they asked, softly like a little wind through the headland grasses. "What is it, Old Wise One?"

The old man said, "It is as I feared. The Black Mother is angry with us because we did not slay in her honor the Irish captive."

The Chieftain had grown fond of the red-haired boy, and a shadow crossed his face, but he only said, "The Will of the Goddess is the Will of the Goddess. What must we do, Old Wise One?"

Laethrig the Priest got slowly to his feet, and drew his beaver-skin mantle about him. "At first dark, we must begin to cry to the Goddess, on the sacred drums, and at moonset we must make the sacrifice. Then the Black Mother will no longer be angry with us, and she will give us back the living water, so that our spring will run full again."

Nessan, on the outskirts of the crowd, had the sudden dreadful feeling of being tangled in a bad dream. In the dream she saw Dara standing quite still in the grip of the huge

Nessan . . . had the sudden dreadful feeling of being tangled in a bad dream.

warrior who had caught hold of him. He looked more bewildered than afraid, and she thought that he had not really understood what Laethrig said. He and she could manage well enough when they talked together, but the tongue of the Irish raiders was different in many ways from the tongue that her own people spoke, and he might not have understood.

Despite the hot evening, her feet seemed to have frozen to the ground, and she could not move or make a sound; and still in the bad dream she saw them take Dara away. She knew that he had begun to be afraid now; he looked back once as though with a desperate hope that someone would help him. And then he was gone.

Nessan unfroze, and her head began to work again. It whirled with thoughts and half-ideas chasing each other round and round, while she still <u>hovered</u> on the edge of the murmuring crowd. And then quite suddenly, out of the chase and whirl, a plan began to come, detail after detail, until she knew exactly what she must do.

The three Drummers of the Clan stepped into the open space beside the spring and began to make a soft eery whispering and throbbing with their fingertips on the sacred wolfskin drums, and all the Clan who were not already there came gathering as though at a call. The sun was down and the shadows crowding in, made sharp-edged and thin by the moon, as she slipped away unnoticed by the crowd. The rest of the Dun was almost

___
2. **runnel:** a narrow channel for water.

WORDS TO KNOW
hover (hŭv'ér) *v.* to stay or wait near a place

265

②

②

↓ H

F Have students analyze the figurative language and imagery used in this passage to describe Laethrig's character. *(Possible responses: The simile* like a withered leaf *suggests that he is wrinkled and frail. The images of the skins and necklaces suggest he is special, magical, and set apart from the others.)*

STRATEGIC READING FOR

Less-Proficient Readers

G Discuss what the Clan decides to do when the spring runs dry.

• What does Laethrig want to do to get the spring to run full again? *(sacrifice Dara)* **Summarizing**

• What is the Clan's attitude toward the Black Mother? *(Possible responses: fear, awe, faith)* **Making Inferences**

Set a Purpose As students read, they should note how Nessan disobeys the Priest's decree.

CUSTOMIZING FOR

Students Acquiring English

② Explain that *tongue* here means "language." Students who speak French will recognize that the word for tongue and language is the same.

Active Reading: PREDICT

H Ask students to predict what they think Nessan will do. *(Possible responses: She will pray for Dara; she will offer herself in Dara's place; she will contact Dara's people.)*

Mini-Lesson   The Writer's Style

POINT OF VIEW Point of view is the perspective from which a story is told. Remind students that in the first-person point of view, the narrator is one of the characters in the story and uses the pronouns *I, me, my, we,* and *our.* When the story is told from the third-person point of view, the narrator does not participate in the story and relates the story using the pronouns *he, she, him, her, it, they,* and *them.* Any story can change dramatically when told from a different point of view.

Application Have students determine the story's third-person point of view. Then divide students into groups of three or four and have them analyze the differences between what the characters know and what the reader finds out. For instance, ask students which character knows why the spring comes back to life. Have the groups explain how these differences add to the story's tension.

Reteaching/Reinforcement
• Writing Handbook, anthology pp. 824–825
• *Writing Mini-Lessons* transparencies, p. 47

The Writer's Craft
Point of View, pp. 318–319

Critical Thinking:
HYPOTHESIZING

I Have students make inferences about Nessan's plans, based on her actions here. *(Possible responses: She plans to warn Dara about the Clan's intentions; she is going to set Dara free.)*

Literary Concept: CHARACTER

J Ask students how the author reveals Nessan's character here. *(through her actions)* Then have them explain why the author selected this method of revealing her character. *(Possible response: Her actions are dramatic and provide the best way of showing her courageous and heroic traits.)*

CUSTOMIZING FOR
Multiple Learning Styles

K **Interpersonal Learners** Invite students to rewrite this scene from Dara's first-person point of view. Then have students analyze the difference a change in point of view makes in characterization and plot.

CUSTOMIZING FOR
Students Acquiring English

3 Point out that Nessan uses *shan't*, which is a contraction of "shall not."

I deserted now; no one to notice her as she slipped by like another shadow. She ran to the place where the stream gully zigzagged out through its gap at the cliff's edge—everything depended on that—then to the out-shed where tomorrow's bread was stored; then to a certain dark bothie among the sleeping-places. It was easy to find the right one, for the huge warrior who had taken Dara away stood on guard before its door-hole, leaning on his spear. Her heart was beating right up in her throat as she started to work her way round to the back of the bothie, so that she was sure only the throbbing of the drums kept the spear man from hearing it, and was terrified that they might stop.

But she reached the back of the bothie, and checked there, carefully thinking out her next move.

Many of the living huts had a loose strip of turf in the roof, which could be turned back to let in more air in hot summer weather, and by good fortune, this was one of **J** them. She reached up (the rough stone walls were so low that the edge of the roof came down to only just above her head) and felt for the rope of twisted heather that held the loose end of the summer-strip in place, and found it. She pulled it free, but standing on the ground, she could not reach up far enough to raise the turf flap more than a few fingers' lengths. Well, that did not matter, so long as she could get a hand inside. She got a good hold on the top of the hut wall; it was easy enough to find a toehold in a chink between two stones, and she was as light as a cat. Next instant she was crouching belly-flat along the edge of the roof, listening for any sound from the man on the far side of the hut.

No sound came. She found the edge of the summer-strip again, and lifted it a little and then a little more, until she could let it fold back on itself, with no more sound than a mouse might have made in the thatch.

In the pitch darkness below the square hole, she thought she heard quick breathing and then a tiny startled movement. She ducked her head and shoulders inside. "Dara! It's me—Nessan."

And Dara's voice whispered back, "Nessan!"

"Don't make a sound! There's a man with a spear outside. Have they tied you up?"

"Yes—to the house-post."

"I am coming down." Nessan felt for the right hold, and swung her legs into the hole, and dropped. Any sound that she made was covered by the wolfskin drums which woke at that moment into a coughing roar. Then she had found Dara and pulled her little food knife from her belt and was feeling for the rawhide ropes that lashed his hands behind him to the tall center pole of the bothie.

"What does it all mean?" he whispered. "What have I done?"

"They say the Black Mother is angry, and that is why the spring is failing. They say that they must kill you at moon-set tonight, and then she will not be angry any more."

Dara gave a gasp, and jerked in his bonds.

"Hold still, or I shall cut you! But they shan't do it! I will not let them!"

"How can you stop them?" Dara's voice shook a little in the dark. "Go away, Nessan—go away before they find you!"

Nessan didn't bother to answer that. She

> *"They say the Black Mother is angry, and that is why the spring is failing."*

Mini-Lesson   Study Skills

REFERENCE BOOKS On the board, draw a web like the one shown and invite students to brainstorm some reference sources that Sutcliff may have consulted when researching background information: history books, encyclopedias, and atlases. Demonstrate how to use an atlas by looking up *Ireland* in the index and then finding its location on a map.

Application Invite students to work cooperatively in small groups to find out more about prehistoric Wales. Direct students to use history books, encyclopedias, and atlases, among other sources. Point out to students that many print resources are now available on CD-ROM. Assign students roles as voice monitor and recorder to help ensure that everyone contributes. Then have students present their findings to the class as brief oral reports.

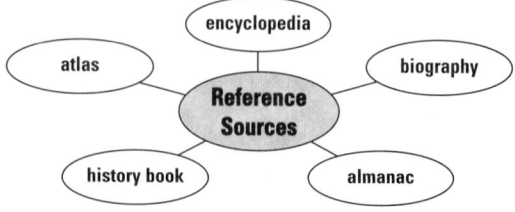

went on sawing at the rawhide ropes, until suddenly the last strand parted. She gave a little sound like a whimper, under her breath. "There. Now come!"

She could feel him rubbing his wrists to get the feeling back. "You first; you're lighter than me."

She did not argue. There was no time. She reached up for the rough wall top, and felt Dara heave from below. She came up through the glimmering sky-square, and went right over in a kind of swooping scramble, to land on the earth outside. There was a faint grunt and a <u>scuffle</u>, the dark shape of Dara's head and shoulders appeared through the hole, and next instant he had dropped onto his feet beside her.

She caught his hand and began to run, out toward the seaward side of the Dun, away from those terrible drums. When she pulled up, panting, they were at the gap in the turf walls where the stream gully passed through.

"Look! This is the way you must go—they don't guard this side. And when you're away, you'll be able to find a war band of your own people."

They had scrambled down the dry runnel-bed, right to the far edge of the gap, and the cliff plunged almost from their feet to the sea creaming among the rocks far below. Dara looked down—and down—and down—and swallowed as though he felt sick.

"You've got to go that way!" she whispered fiercely. "It's easy."

"If it's so easy, why don't they guard it?"

"Because the water from the spring makes it slippery, and no one could keep his footing on the wet rocks. But now it's dry. Don't you see? It's dry!" She fished hurriedly down the front of her tunic and held something out to him. "Here's a barley cake. Now go quick!"

But the boy Dara hesitated an instant longer.

"Nessan, why are you doing this?"

"I—don't want you to be killed."

"I don't want to be killed either. But Nessan, what will they do to you?"

"They will not do anything. No one will know that I had anything to do with it, if only you go quickly."

Dara tried to say something more, then flung an arm round her neck in a small fierce hug and next instant was creeping forward alone.

She was half crying, as he crouched and slithered away, feeling for every hand- and foothold along the grass-tufted cliff edge, and disappeared in the black moon-shadow of the turf wall. She waited, shivering, ears on the stretch for any sound. Once she heard the rattle of a falling pebble, but nothing more. At last she turned back toward the Chief's Hall, and the quickening throb of the wolfskin drums.

To Dara, that time of clinging and <u>clambering</u> along the shelving ledges of bare rocks and summer-burned grass, with the turf wall rising steeply on his right side, and on his left the empty air and the drop to the fanged rocks and the sea, was the longest that he had ever known. And at every racing heartbeat he was terrified of a false step that would send him whirling down into that dreadful emptiness with the rocks at the bottom of it, or betray him to the terrible little dark men within the Dun. But at last the space between the turf wall and cliff edge grew wider, and then wider still, and soon he was clear of the Dun, and the deserted turf huts scattered inland of it, and he gathered himself together and ran.

After a while he slowed down. No sense in

WORDS TO KNOW

scuffle (skŭf'əl) *n.* the act or sound of feet shuffling
clambering (klăm'bər-ĭng) *n.* the act of climbing with effort, using the hands and feet
clamber *v.*

267

Active Reading: EVALUATE

L Have students decide if they would like to have Nessan as a friend. Why or why not? (*Possible responses: yes, because she is courageous and intelligent; no, because she is foolhardy*)

Active Reading: QUESTION

M Ask students what they would like to know about the spring and the Black Mother at this point in the story. If necessary, guide students with the following model.

Think-Aloud Model *I really don't know much about these issues, and both are central to the plot. I would like to know why the spring isn't flowing. Is the heat the cause, as some people think? Or could there be a curse on the spring? And who or what is the Black Mother?*

STRATEGIC READING FOR
Less-Proficient Readers

N Explore with students how Nessan disobeys the Priest's decree.

• Why does Nessan free Dara? (*She cares about him and doesn't want him to die.*) **Making Inferences**

• How does Nessan get into the hut where Dara is being held prisoner? (*She climbs in through the top.*) **Summarizing**

Set a Purpose Have students read to find out who the Black Mother is and what Dara takes from her.

Literary Concept:
DESCRIPTION

O Ask students which details in this passage help them best imagine the scene. (*Possible responses: "bare rocks," "empty air," or "fanged rocks"*)

Mini-Lesson: Speaking, Listening, and Viewing

STORYTELLING Explain that many stories about prehistoric people come from poems, songs, legends, and myths that have been passed down by word of mouth through the oral tradition. To make these stories easier to remember, storytellers included refrains, or lines repeated at the end of stanzas. They also included the repetition of a sound, word, phrase, line, or grammatical structure. Describe to students how repetition links related ideas and emphasizes key points.

Application Invite students to recast "The Chief's Daughter" as a story suitable for younger children

and then, if possible, share the story with them. Encourage students to develop an animated delivery. Suggest the storytellers try using refrains, repetition, and different voices and postures for the different characters. Also urge students to allow the children to talk about the story after they have finished telling it. If an actual performance for a younger audience isn't possible, have the class perform in front of a group of peers as if for a younger audience. Post-performance discussion might then address speculations regarding its effectiveness for younger children.

simply running like a hare across country, and he had no idea in what direction he would find the war bands of his own people. And at that moment he realized that he had no weapon. Nessan had slipped her knife back into her belt after she had cut his bonds, and neither of them had thought of it again. He was alone and unarmed in an enemy country. Well, there was nothing to do but keep going and hope that he would not need to kill for food or run into any kind of trouble before he found his own people.

P Presently, well into the hills, he came upon a moorland pool, where two streamlets met. It was so small and shallow that he could have waded through it in several places, and scarcely get wet to the knee. And the moon, still high in the glimmering sky, showed him an upright black stone that stood taller than a man, exactly between the two streamlets where they emptied themselves into the pool. A black stone, in a countryside where other stones were grey; and twisted about the narrowest part near the top, a withered garland of tough moorland flowers: ling and rag-wort and white-plumed bog-grasses.

Q Dara stood staring at it with a feeling of awe. And as he did so, a little wind stirred the dry garland, and from something fastened among the brittle flowerheads, the moonlight struck out a tiny blaze of brilliant blue fire! Nessan's blue glass arm-ring! He caught his breath, realizing that this must be the Goddess herself, the Black Mother. But at the same instant, he noticed the spear which stood upright in the tail of the

pool. A fine spear, its butt ending in a ball of enamelled bronze; an Irish spear!

His own people must have passed this way and come across the Goddess whose People they had been raiding, and left an offering to turn aside her anger. He noticed also that the spear, set up in what seemed to be the place where the two streams joined before the feet of the Black Mother, had caught a dead furze branch on its way down and twigs and birch leaves and clumps of dry grass, even the carcass of some small animal, had drifted into the furze branch and clung there, building up into something like a small beaver's dam, and blocking the stream so that it had spread out into a pool. And as the pool grew high enough, it had begun to spill over into a new runnel that it was cutting for itself down the hillside.

Dara was not interested in the changed course of a stream, but he needed that spear; needed it so badly that his need was greater even than his fear of taking it.

He caught a deep breath and turned to the tall garlanded stone that seemed to him now to stand like a queen in the moonlight. "Black Mother, do not be angry. I must have the spear. See, I will leave you a barley cake and my amber necklace instead. That is two gifts for one!"

And his heart racing, he stepped into the water and pulled up the spear. For a moment he expected the sky to fall on him or the hillside to open and close again over his head. But nothing

A European sword that was made in about 1300. Copyright © The British Museum.

268 UNIT THREE PART 1: SHOWING COURAGE

Mini-Lesson **Genre Study**

FICTION Draw a web like the one shown and use it to explain that **historical fiction** is a type of fiction with the following characteristics:
- It is prose.
- It may be based on or include real events from the past.
- The setting is a real historical place.
- The story describes real or realistic historical figures.
- There are a plot, conflict, and theme.

Application Have students copy the web into their notebooks. Direct them to refer to it as they

review "The Chief's Daughter." Then have students note which genre characteristics the story contains using examples from the story.

happened, and he went on his way, following the faint track of the war band that he could pick up here and there by trampled grass or a thread of dark wool caught on a bramble spray, and the droppings left by driven cattle.

And behind him, now that the spear that had held it was gone, little by little the dam washed away, and the pool sank, as the water returned to its old stream bed and sang its way downhill, to disappear under a bramble bush in the place where it had always gone underground before the raider left his spear for the Black Mother.

And where it went from there, under the turf and the rocks and the hawthorn bushes on its way to the sea, was a secret that neither Dara nor the Irish raiders nor Nessan's People knew. Only the stream singing to itself in the dark, knew that secret.

At moon-set, when the drumming grew still, and the pine knot torches all round the space below the Chief's Hall began to flare more brightly in the dark time before the dawn, several warriors of the Chief's kin went to fetch Dara from his prison. They came running back shouting that the boy was gone!

The word ran like a squall of wind through the crowd, and the Chief sprang up from his seat of piled oxhides. "Gone?"

"There's not a sign of him —not a shadow."

"And his cut bonds lying beside the center post, and the summer-strip turned back from the roof edge!"

The Chief turned upon the warrior who had guarded the door hole. "Istoreth, what do you say as to this?"

The warrior looked his Chief steadily in the

"I helped him to escape, my Father, through the gap where the spring water goes."

eye, but in the light of the torches his face was ashy, for he knew what to expect. "I kept my watch. I saw nothing, I heard nothing," he said.

"Ill have you kept your watch! And the Black Mother waits for her sacrifice. If the boy is not found, then you must take his place. Is it fair and just?"

"It is fair and just," the man said.

The Chief turned from him to the warriors standing close around. "Go you and search all within the stockade—every corner, every hut."

But before they could move to obey him, Nessan, on the dark fringe of the crowd, heard her own voice, high and silvery and very clear, as though it were not hers at all but somebody else's, "You will not find him! He is not here!"

There was a sudden hush, everyone looked toward her, and in the hollow heart of the hush, the Chief her father demanded in a terrible voice, "Nessan, what thing have you done?"

Nessan walked forward into the torchlight, the people parting to let her through. "I helped him to escape, my Father, through the gap where the spring water goes. It is dry, not slippery, now that the water —does not run."

The Chief groaned and covered his face with his hands, and Laethrig the Priest, who had been standing by all this while, spoke for the first time. "And you are daring to come forth here and tell us of it?"

"Yes, Old Holy One." Nessan tried desperately to steady her voice.

"You are very brave, my child, or very foolish!"

Nessan drew a long shivering breath. "You

T Discuss with students Dara's removal of the spear.

• What is the Black Mother? *(a tall stone and goddess)* Noting Relevant Details

• Why does Dara remove the spear from the stream? *(He needs a weapon.)* Relating Cause and Effect

• What does Dara leave in place of the spear? *(His barley cake and amber necklace.)* Noting Relevant Details

Set a Purpose As students complete the story, ask them to discover what happens to Nessan.

Active Reading: PREDICT

U Invite students to predict what will happen now that the Clan has discovered Dara's absence. *(Possible responses: The guard will be punished; Nessan will confess.)*

CUSTOMIZING FOR
Students Acquiring English

④ Students may have trouble understanding what the Chief means when he says, "Ill have you kept your watch!" Ask what it means for a guard to have "kept watch." *(stood guard)* Then ask for a word that means the opposite of *ill. (well)* Help students put these ideas together to conclude that the Chief means that the guard hasn't done his job very well.

Literary Concept:
CHARACTER

V Have students explain what the guard's reaction reveals about his character. *(Possible responses: He is courageous; he follows the rules of his society.)*

Assessment **Option**

INFORMAL ASSESSMENT To assess how well students understood the story, have them write a letter from Nessan to Dara. The letter should explain why Nessan defied the decree of her people to free the Irish slave. Students should also explore why Nessan came forward and took the blame for her actions. Guide students to make inferences and include details from the story.

Rubric

3 Full Accomplishment Letters are written from Nessan's point of view and thoroughly explain her actions.

2 Substantial Accomplishment Letters describe most of Nessan's reasons, but also include extraneous information.

1 Little or Partial Accomplishment Letters are not written from Nessan's point of view and do not accurately explain her actions.

Literary Concept:
CHARACTER

W Have students analyze what Nessan's actions in this scene tell about her character. *(Possible response: Her hesitation shows that she is human; its brevity shows that she is extremely courageous.)*

Active Reading: CLARIFY

X Have students explain what the priest means by "the willingness is enough." *(Possible response: The Black Mother was satisfied with Nessan's offer of personal sacrifice.)*

Y Ask students what happens to Nessan. *(She offers to be sacrificed but is spared, because the spring starts to flow again.)* **Summarizing**

COMPREHENSION CHECK

1. Who is Dara and why is he with the Clan? *(He is a 12-year-old Irish prisoner they captured.)*
2. Why didn't the Clan kill Dara? *(Nessan, the Chief's daughter, successfully pleaded for his life.)*
3. What did the Clan decide to to do to get the spring flowing again? *(sacrifice Dara)*
4. What happened as a result of Dara's removing the spear? *(The spring flowed again.)*
5. Why does Nessan confess that she helped Dara escape? *(to prevent the Clan from killing Istoreth, the innocent guard)*

---

cannot kill Istoreth. It was not his fault. I—I knew when I helped Dara away, that if the well did not fill again, I must come here instead of him."

"It is of your own choosing," said the old priest, very gently. "So be it, then; come here to me."

"No!" cried the Chief.

"Yes!" said the old priest, as gently as ever. He was holding the black pottery bowl that was used for only one thing, to hold the drink that brought the Long Sleep at the time of sacrifice.

Nessan took a step toward him, and <u>wavered</u> for a moment, then walked steadily forward.

Everything was very quiet, nobody moved or whispered in all the crowd; the only sound was the restless stirring of the thirsty cattle. And then into the quiet, there fell a tiny sound; a soft "plop" and then a faint trickling from the well that had been sullenly silent all night long.

"No, wait!" one of the women cried. "Listen!"

"What to, then?"

"There it is again!"

"It is the well! The spring is coming back to life!"

That time all those near enough to the spring heard it, and a great gasp went up from them. They crowded round the well-pool; then they were parting and pushing back to make a path for the Chief and Laethrig to pass through.

Nessan did not move. She stood where she was, and shut her eyes tight; she heard another plop and a wet green trickling, and the murmur of the crowd; and then her father crying out in a great triumphant voice, "The water is rising! You see, Old Holy One? You hear?"

"I see and I hear," said the old priest. "It is in my heart that the Black Mother is no longer angry with us . . ."

And she knew from his voice that he had gone away small inside himself, so that if you looked into his eyes it would be like looking through the doorway of an empty hut.

Everyone waited, hearing the plop and ripple of the refilling well. And then at last Nessan heard the old man sigh, and the dry rustle of his necklaces, as he stirred and came back to himself. "The Black Mother has spoken to me. She calls for no more sacrifice in this matter; she says the willingness is enough—the willingness is enough." ❖

| WORDS |
| TO |
| KNOW |

270

waver (wā'vər) *v.* to move unsteadily back and forth or to become unsure

---

Mini-Lesson ⓣⓜ **Spelling**

UNSTRESSED VOWELS Explain to students that words with unstressed vowels cause spelling problems, because you cannot hear what the vowel is when the word is pronounced. Write the word *relative* on the chalkboard and ask why the middle syllable is most likely to cause spelling problems. Lead students to see that an unstressed vowel is difficult to identify. Write the word *related* and ask why the *a* in *related* is easier to hear than the *a* in *relative*. Mark the stressed *a* in *related*.

Application Read aloud the following words and ask students to write them, paying careful attention to unstressed vowels.

1. kindred	5. waver
2. headland	6. waited
3. sullen	7. necklaces
4. scuffle	8. sacrifice

Ask students to look for more words that fit this pattern, in their own writing and in things that they read, and to add these words to their personal word lists.

Reteaching/Reinforcement
• *Unit Three Resource Book* p. 6

RESPONDING
OPTIONS

FROM PERSONAL RESPONSE TO CRITICAL ANALYSIS

REFLECT 1. Draw a sketch of Nessan that conveys your impressions of her. Share your sketch with a partner.

RETHINK 2. How would you have responded to this story if Nessan had been sacrificed at the end?

3. Laethrig the Priest tells Nessan that she is either very brave or very foolish. Which do you think she is, and why?

Consider Close Textual Reading
- the way she helps Dara to escape
- why she takes Istoreth's place at the sacrifice

RELATE 4. Look back at the chart you created for the Personal Connection on page 259. How would you compare the courage of the people you listed with the courage shown by either Nessan or Dara?

Thematic link

5. Dara is regarded as a *scapegoat,* or a person who is held responsible for a bad thing. Why do you think groups sometimes single out an individual as the cause of a misfortune?

Multimodal Learning
ANOTHER PATHWAY

Get together with a partner and role-play a conversation between Nessan and her father after her release at the end of the story. Improvise a dialogue in which they discuss her reasons for rescuing Dara and her views about friendship.

QUICKWRITES

1. Write a **sequel** to this story, telling what happens to Dara after his return to his people.

2. Do you think Nessan is qualified to lead the clan someday? Write a **speech** that the Chief might give to the leaders of the clan, explaining whether or not his daughter has the courage that a chief needs.

3. Is Sutcliff's story realistic, or does it contain too many coincidences to be believable? State and support your opinion in a **review** of the story for your school paper.

📂 **PORTFOLIO** *Save your writing. You may want to use it later as a springboard to a piece for your portfolio.*

LITERARY CONCEPTS

Writers use **description** to help readers imagine a scene, an event, or a character. For example, in the opening paragraph of this story, Sutcliff provides phrases such as "small stunted branches" and "salt-burned leaves" to help you imagine the windblown stockade. Skim the story to identify other examples of vivid description.

CONCEPT REVIEW: Simile A **simile** is a comparison that uses the word *like* or *as.* For example, Sutcliff uses the simile "like a withered leaf" to suggest Laethrig's age and brittleness. What does Sutcliff suggest by stating that looking into Laethrig's eyes "was like looking through the doorway of an empty hut"?

THE CHIEF'S DAUGHTER **271**

From Personal Response to Critical Analysis

1. Drawings will vary.
2. Students may say that they would have been horrified, shocked, or saddened.
3. Possible responses: She is brave because she courageously followed her heart, took action, and fully accepted responsibility for her actions. She is foolish because she stepped forward and risked death.
4. Students might say that the people they listed are more or less courageous than Nessan or Dara.
5. Possible responses: Some students may say that groups want to avoid having to take responsibility themselves. Others may say that groups want to find an easy answer instead of coming to grips with a problem.

Literary Links

In "A Retrieved Reformation," Jimmy Valentine rescues a child locked in a bank vault. Ask students to compare his motives for doing this with those of Nessan when she rescues Dara. *(Possible response: In both cases, the motive was love.)*

Another Pathway

Although dialogue should be improvised, students should agree in advance on some points to be included.

Rubric

3 Full Accomplishment Students fully explore Nessan's reasons for saving Dara.

2 Substantial Accomplishment Students describe some reasons Nessan had for rescuing Dara.

1 Little or Partial Accomplishment Students do not cover the primary issues or remain in roles.

Literary Concepts

Student responses will vary. Invite students to work together in small groups to skim the story for vivid images and descriptions, such as the details about the Black Mother. Students can arrange their findings according to the senses to which the descriptions appeal: sight, sound, taste, touch, and smell. Invite each group to presents its findings to the class.

CONCEPT REVIEW Possible response: His eyes didn't show any feeling, and he had an eerie, other-worldly quality.

QuickWrites

1. Have students first prepare a story map or time line to help them arrange the information in chronological order.
2. Remind students that persuasive speeches can appeal to reason, emotion, or ethics. Guide them to structure their speeches with a clear beginning, middle, and end.
3. Have students first outline their review to make sure that they have included at least two specific supporting statements for each assertion.

The Writer's Craft

Short Story, pp. 78–85
Supporting Opinions, pp. 144–151

Science Arrange students in small groups. To ensure that students work together productively, you may wish to assign a voice monitor, a turn-taking monitor, and a direction giver. You may also wish to use role cards to help students practice the social skills they need for effective group work.

ADDITIONAL SUGGESTION

Science *Save Our Water* Remind students that, just like the Clan, people today still depend on a supply of fresh water. Have students work in teams to come up with a list of rules for conserving water. Have students explore ways to implement these rules in school and at home.

Words to Know

1. scouring	6. kindred
2. headland	7. scuffle
3. clamber	8. thatch
4. anxious	9. hover
5. sullen	10. waver

Reteaching/Reinforcement

• *Unit Three Resource Book* p. 7

ROSEMARY SUTCLIFF

Sutcliff's first book on Celtic and Saxon legends was submitted by a friend to a respected publisher. The publisher decided to publish the book but asked Sutcliff to write a children's book on Robin Hood. The book was a success, and her writing career was launched.

CRITIC'S CORNER

According to Scott Terrill, a seventh-grade member of our student board, the writer of "The Chief's Daughter" describes actions very well, but not the setting. Explain whether or not you agree with Scott's opinion, citing evidence from the story.

Multimodal Learning

ACROSS THE CURRICULUM

Science Work with a small group of classmates to create a bulletin board display about springs. Do research to answer the following questions as well as questions of your own: How does the water in an underground spring rise to the surface? Where does the water in a spring originate? Where are springs usually found? If you have access to an encyclopedia CD-ROM on your computer, use it to begin your research.

WORDS TO KNOW

Review the Words to Know at the bottom of the selection pages. On your paper, write the word that best completes each sentence.

1. In prehistoric times, bands of warriors sometimes were on the prowl, _____ the coast in search of settlements to raid.
2. Clans built stockades on a _____ so that they could spot these warriors.
3. In times of danger, an entire clan would _____ up the cliffs to seek shelter within the stockade.
4. Many of the clan were _____, afraid of what the future might hold.
5. The chief looked _____ and gloomy.
6. The chief's hall was well guarded and large enough to accommodate his _____ .
7. Sometimes, only the _____ of villagers' feet broke the silence.
8. Most of all, the clan feared that raiders would set the _____ roof of the stockade on fire.
9. Therefore, guards would _____ near the outskirts to prevent surprise attacks.
10. Most raiders, however, would _____, uncertain whether to attack such a well-protected place.

ROSEMARY SUTCLIFF

British author Rosemary Sutcliff wrote fiction that enables her readers to imagine the lives of people of long ago. Her novel *Warrior Scarlet,* for example, tells about a boy growing up in England during the Bronze Age, sometime between 2500 and 650 B.C. Sutcliff liked to immerse herself in the historical period she depicted in a story: "To me half the fun of writing a book is the research entailed," she said. "I love trying to piece together historical background and to catch the right smell of the period."

In her autobiography, Sutcliff describes her sense

1920–1992

of isolation as a child. She suffered from a form of rheumatoid arthritis, and until the age of 10, was educated at home by her mother, who read to her extensively. For the next four years, she attended school, but she was often ill and hospitalized.

Reflecting on her career as a writer, Sutcliff said that her mother's reading aloud to her gave her a feeling for good writing that helped her later when she created her own stories.

OTHER WORKS *The Lantern Bearers, The Witch's Brat, Tristan and Iseult* Extended Reading

Alternative Activities

1. Have students create a three-dimensional model of the Strong-Place on the headland. They should include the stockade, the dwellings inside of it, and the turf banks that ring the cliff.
2. Ask students what kind of music they imagine as they read about the throbbing of the wolfskin drums. Invite students to select and record background music that suits the mood of this story. Students can play the music in class as they give an oral reading of part of the story.

PREVIEWING

NONFICTION

The Noble Experiment

from *I Never Had It Made*
Jackie Robinson *as told to* Alfred Duckett

PERSONAL CONNECTION Activating Prior Knowledge

What is prejudice? What causes people to feel prejudice or to commit acts of prejudice? Recall instances of prejudice that you have read or heard about—or experienced yourself. Then, with your classmates, fill out a web like the one below.

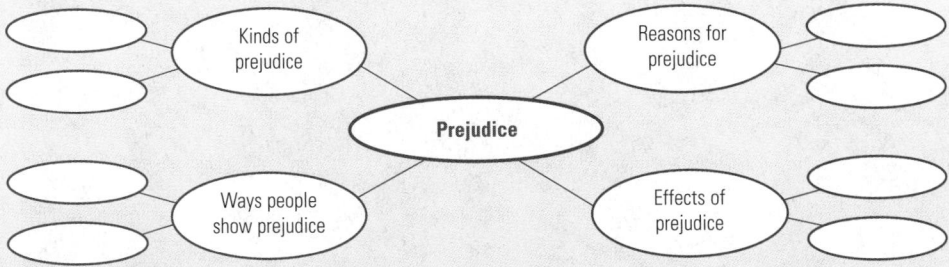

Kinds of prejudice

Reasons for prejudice

Prejudice

Ways people show prejudice

Effects of prejudice

HISTORICAL CONNECTION Building Background

In the 1940s, African Americans faced many barriers created by prejudice. In the South, "Jim Crow" laws kept blacks from mixing with whites in schools, restaurants, hospitals, and parks. African Americans were forced to use separate restrooms and water fountains.

Athletic competition did not escape this segregation. In baseball, blacks played in separate "Negro leagues"; they were barred from the majors. In 1947, Jackie Robinson became the first African American to break the major-league "color barrier." A superb athlete, he helped the Brooklyn Dodgers win six league championships and was named the league's most valuable player in 1949. He was inducted into the Baseball Hall of Fame in 1962.

Setting a Purpose
WRITING CONNECTION

What are your views on prejudice? Can you think of any ways that prejudice can be eliminated? In your notebook, explain your thoughts. Use the web and your discussion from Personal Connection to get started.

THE NOBLE EXPERIMENT **273**

The Noble

SUMMARY

Jackie Robinson recalls the events that led to his becoming the first African-American baseball player in the Major Leagues in the 20th century. Branch Rickey, president of the Brooklyn Dodgers, had always opposed segregation. In 1945, he convinced the team's board of directors to let him hire an African-American player. Working in secrecy, he chose Jackie Robinson not only for his skill, but for his character. The player would have to be able to endure other people's hatred and threats without fighting back. If the player fought back, race riots might erupt and it might be a long time before any other African Americans were allowed to play in the big leagues. Yet he also had to retain his dignity. At twenty-six, telling only his mother and his girlfriend Rachel of his decision, Robinson accepted the challenge.

Thematic Link: _Showing Courage_ Jackie Robinson showed courage when he agreed to become the first African American to break the color barrier in baseball.

CUSTOMIZING FOR

Students Acquiring English

- Use **ACCESS FOR STUDENTS ACQUIRING ENGLISH,** _Reading and Writing Support._

- Because students from many cultures may be avid baseball fans, invite volunteers to explain the baseball terms used in this selection, such as _coach, scout, farm club, box score,_ and _shortstop._

STRATEGIC READING FOR

Less-Proficient Readers

Set a Purpose Ask students if they would enjoy being the first person ever to do something difficult. Have them explain why or why not. Then invite students to read to find out what the "noble experiment" was. Use **UNIT THREE RESOURCE BOOK,** p. 11, for guidance in reading the selection.

Jackie Robinson steals home during a Braves-Dodgers game at Ebbets Field in Brooklyn, August 22, 1948. UPI/Bettmann.

WORDS TO KNOW

cynical (sĭn′ĭ-kəl) _adj._ mistrustful of other's sincerity (p. 277)

eloquence (ĕl′ə-kwəns) _n._ forceful, convincing speech (p. 276)

incredulous (ĭn-krĕj′ə-ləs) _adj._ unable or unwilling to believe something (p. 278)

insinuation (ĭn-sĭn′yōō-ā′shən) _n._ a suggestion or hint intended to insult (p. 278)

integrated (ĭn′tĭ-grâ′tĭd) _adj._ open to people of all races or ethnic groups without restriction; desegregated (p. 277)

retaliate (rĭ-tăl′ē-āt′) _v._ to get revenge; get even (p. 276)

shrewdly (shrōōd′lē) _adv._ wisely; in a clever way (p. 276)

speculating (spĕk′yə-lâ′tĭng) _adj._ thinking about different possibilities; guessing what might happen **speculate** _v._ (p. 278)

taunt (tônt) _v._ to make fun of; jeer (p. 280)

ultimate (ŭl′tə-mĭt) _adj._ final; most important (p. 280)

from *I Never Had It Made*

Experiment

by Jackie Robinson as told to Alfred Duckett

In 1910 Branch Rickey was a coach for Ohio Wesleyan. The team went to South Bend, Indiana, for a game. The hotel management registered the coach and team but refused to assign a room to a black player named Charley Thomas. In those days college ball had a few black players. Mr. Rickey took the manager aside and said he would move the entire team to another hotel unless the black athlete was accepted. The threat was a bluff because he knew the other hotels also would have refused accommodations to a black man. While the hotel manager was thinking about the threat, Mr. Rickey came up with a compromise. He suggested a cot be put in his own room, which he would share with the unwanted guest. The hotel manager wasn't happy about the idea, but he gave in.

Years later Branch Rickey told the story of the misery of that black player to whom he had given a place to sleep. He remembered that Thomas couldn't sleep.

"He sat on that cot," Mr. Rickey said, "and was silent for a long time. Then he began to cry, tears he couldn't hold back. His whole body shook with emotion. I sat and watched him, not knowing what to do until he began tearing at one hand with the other—just as if he were trying to scratch the skin off his hands with his fingernails. I was alarmed. I asked him what he was trying to do to himself.

"'It's my hands,' he sobbed. 'They're black. If only they were white, I'd be as good as anybody then, wouldn't I, Mr. Rickey? If only they were white.'"

"Charley," Mr. Rickey said, "the day will come when they won't have to be white."

Thirty-five years later, while I was lying awake nights, frustrated, unable to see a future, Mr. Rickey, by now the president of the Dodgers, was also lying awake at night, trying to make up his mind about a new experiment.

He had never forgotten the agony of that black athlete. When he became a front-office executive in St. Louis, he had fought, behind the scenes, against the custom that consigned black spectators to the Jim Crow section of the Sportsman's Park, later to become Busch Memorial Stadium. His pleas to change the rules were in vain. Those in power argued that if blacks were allowed a free choice of seating, white business would suffer.

Branch Rickey lost that fight, but when he became the boss of the Brooklyn Dodgers in 1943, he felt the time for equality in baseball had come. He knew that achieving it would be

A

Mini-Lesson: Speaking, **Listening, and Viewing**

SPORTSCAST (Play-by-play) Invite students to name sportscasters—for example, Marv Albert, Pat Summerall, and Al Michaels. Discuss what makes their play-by-play so exciting: thorough preparation, an alert attitude, and colorful words. Go over these sportscast guidelines with students:
- Be informed about the players and coaches. Find out the players' statistics, backgrounds, and controversies.
- Know the specialized sports vocabulary.
- Be enthusiastic.

Application Invite students to work in pairs or groups of three to write and present a play-by-play broadcast of Jackie Robinson's first day playing major-league baseball with the Brooklyn Dodgers. Guide students to return to the story to infer how the players and audience reacted to Robinson's debut. Students should study Jackie Robinson's remarks and personality to predict how he might react under stress. Encourage students to use baseball vocabulary in their sportscast.

B Have readers evaluate Rickey's skill as a negotiator. Then ask what his plans show about his personality. *(Possible responses: His careful planning—and success—reveals that he is a master negotiator, intelligent, and shrewd.)*

STRATEGIC READING FOR
Less-Proficient Readers

C To see if students understand the story so far, ask them what "the noble experiment" was. *(Rickey's plan to end segregation in major-league baseball by bringing in a black player.)* **Restating**

Set a Purpose Have students read to find out why Branch Rickey selected Jackie Robinson to be the player to break the color barrier.

Literary Concept:
AUTOBIOGRAPHY

D Have students explain at least two ways they can tell that this selection is an autobiography. *(Possible responses: It is the story of the author's life; it is told using a first-person point of view; it is nonfiction.)*

---

terribly difficult. There would be deep resentment, determined opposition, and perhaps even racial violence. He was convinced he was morally right, and he <u>shrewdly</u> sensed that **B** making the game a truly national one would have healthy financial results. He took his case before the startled directors of the club, and using persuasive <u>eloquence</u>, he won the first battle in what would be a long and bitter campaign. He was voted permission to make the Brooklyn club the pioneer in bringing blacks into baseball.

Winning his directors' approval was almost insignificant in contrast to the task which now lay ahead of the Dodger president. He made certain that word of his plans did not leak out, particularly to the press. Next, he had to find the ideal player for his project, which came to be called "Rickey's noble experiment." This player had to be one who could take abuse, name-calling, rejection by fans and sportswriters and by fellow players not only on opposing teams but on his own. He had to be able to stand up in the face of merciless persecution and not <u>retaliate</u>. On the other hand, he had to be a contradiction in human terms; he still had to have spirit. He could not be an "Uncle Tom."[1]

Jackie Robinson after he signed a contract with the Brooklyn Dodgers, April 10, 1947. AP/Wide World Photos.

His ability to turn the other cheek had to be predicated[2] on his determination to gain acceptance. Once having proven his ability as player, teammate, and man, he had to be able to cast off humbleness and stand up as a full-fledged participant whose triumph did not carry the poison of bitterness.

nknown to most people and certainly to me, after launching a major scouting program, Branch Rickey had picked me as that player. The Rickey talent hunt went beyond national borders. Cuba, Mexico, Puerto Rico, Venezuela, and other countries where dark-skinned people lived had been checked out. Mr. Rickey had learned that there were a number of black players, war veterans mainly, who had gone to these countries, despairing of finding an opportunity in their own country. The manhunt had to be camouflaged. If it became known he was looking for a black recruit for the Dodgers, all hell would have broken loose. The gimmick he used as a coverup was to make the world believe that he was about to establish a new Negro league. In the spring of 1945 he called a press conference and announced that the Dodgers were organizing the United States League, composed of all black teams. This, of course, made blacks and prointegration whites indignant. He was accused of trying to uphold the existing segregation and, at the same time, capitalize on black players. Cleverly, Mr. Rickey replied that his league would be better organized than the current ones. He said its main purpose, eventually, was to be absorbed

---

1. **Uncle Tom:** an offensive term for a black person who is regarded as trying overly hard to please white people; originally from the novel *Uncle Tom's Cabin*, written by Harriet Beecher Stowe in 1852.

2. **predicated** (prĕd′ĭ-kā′tĭd): based

WORDS
TO
KNOW

shrewdly (shrōōd′lē) *adv.* wisely; in a clever way
eloquence (ĕl′ə-kwəns) *n.* forceful, convincing speech
retaliate (rĭ-tăl′ē-āt′) *v.* to get revenge; get even

276

DISTINGUISHING FACT AND OPINION
Explain that a fact is a statement that can be proved, such as "Jackie Robinson was the first African American to play major-league baseball." In contrast, an opinion cannot be proved, such as "Jackie Robinson was the best baseball player ever." Opinions usually reflect personal beliefs and are often debatable.

Application Have students complete the following chart by placing a check in the appropriate column.

Reteaching/Reinforcement
• *Unit Three Resource Book*, p. 12

Statement	Fact	Opinion
1. Branch Rickey was the president of the Brooklyn Dodgers.	✔	
2. Rickey sent his scouts to find dark-skinned players.	✔	
3. Jackie Robinson was the best player for the "experiment."		✔
4. Sukeforth looked like a sincere person.		✔

---

into the majors. It is ironic that by coming very close to telling the truth, he was able to conceal that truth from the enemies of integrated baseball. Most people assumed that when he spoke of some distant goal of integration, Mr. Rickey was being a hypocrite on this issue as so many of baseball's leaders had been.

Black players were familiar with this kind of hypocrisy. When I was with the Monarchs, shortly before I met Mr. Rickey, Wendell Smith, then sports editor of the black weekly Pittsburgh *Courier,* had arranged for me and two other players from the Negro league to go to a tryout with the Boston Red Sox. The tryout had been brought about because a Boston city councilman had frightened the Red Sox management. Councilman Isadore Muchneck threatened to push a bill through banning Sunday baseball unless the Red Sox hired black players. Sam Jethroe of the Cleveland Buckeyes, Marvin Williams of the Philadelphia Stars, and I had been grateful to Wendell for getting us a chance in the Red Sox tryout, and we put our best efforts into it. However, not for one minute did we believe the tryout was sincere. The Boston club officials praised our performance, let us fill out application cards, and said, "So long." We were fairly certain they wouldn't call us, and we had no intention of calling them.

Incidents like this made Wendell Smith as <u>cynical</u> as we were. He didn't accept Branch Rickey's new league as a genuine project, and he frankly told him so. During this conversation, the Dodger boss asked Wendell whether any of the three of us who had gone to Boston was really good major league material. Wendell said I was. I will be forever indebted to Wendell because, without his even knowing it,

his recommendation was in the end partly responsible for my career. At the time, it started a thorough investigation of my background.

In August 1945, at Comiskey Park in Chicago, I was approached by Clyde Sukeforth, the Dodger scout. Blacks have had to learn to protect themselves by being cynical but not cynical enough to slam the door on potential

---

> Unknown to most people and certainly to me, after launching a major scouting program, Branch Rickey had picked me as that player.

---

opportunities. We go through life walking a tightrope to prevent too much disillusionment. I was out on the field when Sukeforth called my name and beckoned. He told me the Brown Dodgers were looking for top ballplayers, that Branch Rickey had heard about me and sent him to watch me throw from the hole.[3] He had come at an unfortunate time. I had hurt my shoulder a couple of days before that, and I wouldn't be doing any throwing for at least a week.

Sukeforth said he'd like to talk with me anyhow. He asked me to come to see him after the game at the Stevens Hotel.

Here we go again, I thought. Another time-wasting experience. But Sukeforth looked like a sincere person, and I thought I might as well listen. I agreed to meet him that night. When we met, Sukeforth got right to the point. Mr. Rickey wanted to talk to me about the possi-

---

3. **throw from the hole:** to throw from deep in the infield to first base.

277

CUSTOMIZING FOR
Students Acquiring English

(1) Point out that "It is ironic that ..." introduces an idea opposite to what the reader expects. Here, readers expect that Rickey would give away his secret by telling so much of the truth, but actually he fools his enemies.

(2) Students may need to be reminded that *to push a bill through* means to have the local legislature pass a law.

Linking to Social Studies

(E) Before Robinson broke the color barrier, African Americans played baseball in the so-called Negro leagues. The Negro National League (1920–1948) and Negro America League (1937–1950) produced such sports legends as Willie Mays, Hank Aaron, Roy Campanella, Satchel Paige, Josh Gibson, and James "Cool Papa" Bell—all of whom earned a place in the Baseball Hall of Fame.

Critical Thinking: ANALYZING

(F) Ask students what Robinson means by his reference to "walking a tightrope." *(Possible response: If African Americans become too distrustful, they might miss real opportunities. If they become too trusting, they might get cheated.)*

CUSTOMIZING FOR
Multiple Learning Styles

(G) **Interpersonal Learners** Invite students to role-play the encounter between Robinson and Sukeforth, creating dialogue that captures each man's personality, aims, and feelings.

Mini-Lesson   Literary Concepts

REVIEWING SOURCES Guide students to recall that writers use primary and secondary sources to get the details they need when they write nonfiction. Copy the information on the chalkboard to use as you explain the difference between primary and secondary sources. Invite students to add sources to the list.

Application Have students complete the chart by speculating about the most likely sources that Robinson and his co-author used to write "The Noble Experiment." Students should then classify each source as primary or secondary.

Information	Possible Source	Type
1. 1945 press conference		
2. Boston Red Sox tryout		
3. Sukeforth meeting		
4. contract signing		

Sources
Primary   *Secondary*
interviews   *encyclopedias*
diaries   *almanacs*
letters   *periodicals*
photographs   *on-line sources*

H Ask students why Robinson was reluctant to go to Brooklyn for a try-out. You may wish to guide students by using this model.

Think-Aloud Model *I read on page 275 that Robinson felt frustrated because he couldn't see a future for himself. So why wouldn't he jump at this chance? I remember that he had already been deceived by the Red Sox. Perhaps he may have been afraid of being tricked and of losing his position with the Kansas City Monarchs.*

Critical Thinking:
HYPOTHESIZING

I Invite students to hypothesize about the function of farm teams, making inferences from the information in this passage. *(They train and develop players for their parent teams in the major leagues.)*

CUSTOMIZING FOR
Students Acquiring English

3 Because different cultures describe emotions in different ways, you may want to ask students acquiring English what Jackie Robinson was feeling when he *felt the heat* come up into his cheeks. *(anger)*

bility of becoming a Brown Dodger. If I could get a few days off and go to Brooklyn, my fare and expenses would be paid. At first I said that I couldn't leave my team and go to Brooklyn just like that. Sukeforth wouldn't take no for an answer. He pointed out that I couldn't play for a few days anyhow because of my bum arm. Why should my team object?

H I continued to hold out and demanded to know what would happen if the Monarchs fired me. The Dodger scout replied quietly that he didn't believe that would happen.

I shrugged and said I'd make the trip. I figured I had nothing to lose.

Branch Rickey was an impressive-looking man. He had a classic face, an air of command, a deep, booming voice, and a way of cutting through red tape and getting down to basics. He shook my hand vigorously and, after a brief conversation, sprang the first question.

"You got a girl?" he demanded.

It was a hell of a question. I had two reactions: why should he be concerned about my relationship with a girl; and, second, while I thought, hoped, and prayed I had a girl, the way things had been going, I was afraid she might have begun to consider me a hopeless case. I explained this to Mr. Rickey and Clyde.

Mr. Rickey wanted to know all about Rachel. I told him of our hopes and plans.

"You know, you *have* a girl," he said heartily. "When we get through today, you may want to call her up because there are times when a man needs a woman by his side."

My heart began racing a little faster again as I sat there speculating. First he asked me if I really understood why he had sent for me. I told him what Clyde Sukeforth had told me.

"That's what he was supposed to tell you," Mr. Rickey said. "The truth is you are not a

candidate for the Brooklyn Brown Dodgers. I've sent for you because I'm interested in you as a candidate for the Brooklyn National League Club. I think you can play in the major leagues. How do you feel about it?"

My reactions seemed like some kind of weird mixture churning in a blender. I was thrilled, scared, and excited. I was incredulous. Most of all, I was speechless.

"You think you can play for Montreal?" he demanded.

> Here was a guy questioning my courage. That virtually amounted to him asking me if I was a coward.

I got my tongue back. "Yes," I answered. Montreal was the Brooklyn Dodgers' top farm club. The players who went there and made it had an excellent chance at the big time.

I was busy reorganizing my thoughts while Mr. Rickey and Clyde Sukeforth discussed me briefly, almost as if I weren't there. Mr. Rickey was questioning Clyde. Could I make the grade?

Abruptly, Mr. Rickey swung his swivel chair in my direction. He was a man who conducted himself with great drama. He pointed a finger at me.

"I know you're a good ballplayer," he barked. "What I don't know is whether you have the guts."

I knew it was all too good to be true. Here was a guy questioning my courage. That virtually amounted to him asking me if I was a coward. Mr. Rickey or no Mr. Rickey, that was an insinuation hard to take. I felt the heat coming up into my cheeks.

WORDS TO KNOW

speculating (spĕk'yə-lā'-tĭng) *adj.* thinking about different possibilities; guessing what might happen **speculate** *v.*
incredulous (ĭn-krĕj'ə-ləs) *adj.* unable or unwilling to believe something
insinuation (ĭn-sĭn'yōō-ā'shən) *n.* a suggestion or hint intended to insult

---

Mini-Lesson **Grammar**

CAPITALIZING TITLES Explain the following rules of capitalization to students.

1. Capitalize titles used with names of persons and abbreviations standing for those titles. *Example:* **Mr.** Jackie Robinson

2. Do not capitalize titles used as common nouns. *Example: Rickey was the* **coach.**

3. Capitalize the following titles when they refer to the current holders of positions: royalty, The Pope, President and Vice-President of the United States. *Example: The new* **President** is a fan.

Application Have students correctly capitalize the titles in each of the following sentences:

1. One of the (coaches/Coaches) called on Robinson. *(coaches)*
2. My friend (professor/Professor) Harris once saw (mr./Mr.) Robinson play at Ebbets Field in Brooklyn. *(Professor, Mr.)*
3. It is a tradition that the (president/President) throws out the first baseball each year. *(president)*

Reteaching/Reinforcement
• Grammar Handbook, anthology p. 875
• *Grammar Mini-Lessons* copymasters, p. 33 transparencies, p. 25

Before I could react to what he had said, he leaned forward in his chair and explained.

I wasn't just another athlete being hired by a ball club. We were playing for big stakes. This was the reason Branch Rickey's search had been so exhaustive. The search had spanned the globe and narrowed down to a few candidates, then finally to me. When it looked as though I might be the number-one choice, the investigation of my life, my habits, my reputation, and my character had become an intensified study.

"I've investigated you thoroughly, Robinson," Mr. Rickey said.

One of the results of this thorough screening were reports from California athletic circles that I had been a "racial agitator"[4] at UCLA. Mr. Rickey had not accepted these criticisms on face value. He had demanded and received more information and came to the conclusion that if I had been white, people would have said, "Here's a guy who's a contender, a competitor."

(From left) Gil Hodges, Gene Hermanski, Branch Rickey, and Jackie Robinson at Yankee Stadium during the World Series, October 4, 1949. The Bettmann Archive.

 fter that he had some grim words of warning. "We can't fight our way through this, Robinson. We've got no army. There's virtually nobody on our side. No owners, no umpires, very few newspapermen. And I'm afraid that many fans will be hostile. We'll be in a tough position. We can win only if we can convince the world that I'm doing this because you're a great ballplayer and a fine gentleman."

He had me transfixed as he spoke. I could feel his sincerity, and I began to get a sense of how much this major step meant to him.

Because of his nature and his passion for justice, he had to do what he was doing. He continued. The rumbling voice, the theatrical gestures were gone. He was speaking from a deep, quiet strength.

"So there's more than just playing," he said. "I wish it meant only hits, runs, and errors—only the things they put in the box score. Because you know—yes, you would know, Robinson, that a baseball box score is a democratic thing. It doesn't tell how big

4. **racial agitator** (ăj´ĭ-tā´tər): a negative term used for someone who tried to stir up trouble between the races.

THE NOBLE EXPERIMENT   **279**

Active Reading: EVALUATE

J Ask students to summarize why Rickey had to conduct an extensive investigation into Robinson's background. Then have students evaluate whether such an investigation was really necessary. *(Rickey was trying to make sure that Robinson was the right person for his "experiment." Students might argue that Rickey was justified in making sure that Robinson had the necessary courage. Or they might say that Rickey was out of line to investigate such personal things without Robinson's knowledge.)*

STRATEGIC READING FOR
Less-Proficient Readers

K Ask students what qualities Robinson had that made him the best choice for Rickey's "noble experiment." *(Possible responses: He was a superb ballplayer, courageous, a contender, and a competitor.)* Classifying

• Why does Rickey want to know if Robinson has a girlfriend? *(Rickey feels that Robinson is going to need someone to stand by his side.)* Restating

Set a Purpose Ask students to find out why Robinson accepts Rickey's offer to join the Brooklyn Dodgers.

Literary Concept:
AUTOBIOGRAPHY

L Ask students what kind of sources the authors most likely used to re-create Rickey's actions and words. *(primary sources such as interviews and diaries; Robinson is telling this story to Duckett based on his own memories.)*

Mini-Lesson      The Writer's Style

CORRECTING EMPTY SENTENCES
Explain to students that empty sentences don't provide enough details. There are two kinds of empty sentences. The first type simply repeats an idea. The other type makes a claim that is not supported with a fact, reason, or example. Refer students to the highlighted paragraph above. Point out the use of detail and description. Then write on the chalkboard the examples shown in the box to the right.

Application Have students revise each of these empty sentences.
1. Branch Rickey was great.
2. Today, baseball tickets are expensive, and they cost a lot, too.
3. Prejudice is bad.

Reteaching/Reinforcement
• *Writing Mini-Lessons* transparencies, p. 44

The Writer's Craft

Empty Sentences, p. 297

Weak: Skillful ballplayers are speedy and fast runners.

Repetition eliminated: Skillful ballplayers are fast runners.

Weak: I admire Jackie Robinson, because he is the best.

Details added: I admire Jackie Robinson, because he had the courage to withstand prejudice.

Literary Concept: MOTIVATION

M Ask students why Rickey keeps testing Robinson's courage like this. *(Possible responses: He knows how difficult Robinson's task will be; he wants to make sure Robinson knows what he's getting into.)*

CUSTOMIZING FOR
Students Acquiring English

4 Make sure that students understand that the racial epithet *nigger* is highly offensive and should never be used.

Active Reading: EVALUATE

N Ask students if they agree with Robinson's statement about dignity. Explore the reasons why Robinson might place such importance on his personal dignity. *(Possible responses: His own dignity had likely been attacked often because of his race; he was a fighter who didn't give in to others.)*

Literary Concept: MOTIVATION

O Ask students why Rickey acts out the part of a white player this way. *(Possible responses: He wants to see how Robinson will react in such a situation; he wants to show Robinson how difficult things will get.)*

CUSTOMIZING FOR
Multiple Learning Styles

P **Logical-Mathematical Learners**
Invite students to find out the capacity of their school's gymnasium or outdoor stadium and calculate how many spectators must attend to reach 10 percent, 25 percent, 50 percent, and 80 percent of capacity. Students can show their results on bar graphs.

---

you are, what church you attend, what color you are, or how your father voted in the last election. It just tells what kind of baseball player you were on that particular day."

I interrupted. "But it's the box score that really counts—that and that alone, isn't it?"

"It's all that *ought* to count," he replied. "But it isn't. Maybe one of these days it *will* be all that counts. That is one of the reasons I've got you here, Robinson. If you're a good enough man, we can make this a start in the right direction. But let me tell you, it's going to take an awful lot of courage."

He was back to the crossroads question that made me start to get angry minutes earlier. He asked it slowly and with great care.

"Have you got the guts to play the game no matter what happens?"

"I think I can play the game, Mr. Rickey," I said.

The next few minutes were tough. Branch Rickey had to make absolutely sure that I knew what I would face. Beanballs[5] would be thrown at me. I would be called the kind of names which would hurt and infuriate any man. I would be physically attacked. Could I take all of this and control my temper, remain steadfastly loyal to our ultimate aim?

He knew I would have terrible problems and wanted me to know the extent of them before I agreed to the plan. I was twenty-six years old, and all my life—back to the age of eight when a little neighbor girl called me a nigger—I had believed in payback, retaliation. The most luxurious possession, the richest treasure anybody has, is his personal dignity. I looked at Mr. Rickey guardedly, and in that second I was looking at him not as a partner in a great experiment, but as the enemy—a white man. I had a question, and it was the

> Beanballs would be thrown at me. I would be called the kind of names which would hurt and infuriate any man. I would be physically attacked.

age-old one about whether or not you sell your birthright.

"Mr. Rickey," I asked, "are you looking for a Negro who is afraid to fight back?"

I never will forget the way he exploded.

"Robinson," he said, "I'm looking for a ballplayer with guts enough not to fight back."

After that, Mr. Rickey continued his lecture on the kind of thing I'd be facing.

He not only told me about it, but he acted out the part of a white player charging into me, blaming me for the "accident" and calling me all kinds of foul racial names. He talked about my race, my parents, in language that was almost unendurable.

"They'll taunt and goad you," Mr. Rickey said. "They'll do anything to make you react. They'll try to provoke a race riot in the ballpark. This is the way to prove to the public that a Negro should not be allowed in the major league. This is the way to frighten the fans and make them afraid to attend the games."

If hundreds of black people wanted to come to the ballpark to watch me play and Mr. Rickey tried to discourage them, would I understand that he was doing it because the emotional enthusiasm of my people could harm the experiment? That kind of enthusiasm

---

5. **beanballs:** pitches thrown purposely at a batter's head.

WORDS TO KNOW	**ultimate** (ŭl′tə-mĭt) *adj.* final; most important
	taunt (tônt) *v.* to make fun of; jeer

280

Mini-Lesson  Spelling

SPELLING WITH SUFFIXES Explain to students that when a suffix beginning with a vowel is added to a word ending in a silent e, the e is usually dropped. Present the following examples from "A Noble Experiment."

base word	suffix	new word
speculate	-ing	speculating
integrate	-ed	integrated
insinuate	-ion	insinuation

Application Have students write each word using the suffix shown.

1. use + age
2. continue + ous
3. mature + ity
4. confuse + ion
5. refuse + al
6. create + ive
7. survive + al
8. believe + able

Encourage students to find five words ending with a silent e in the highlighted passage and add suffixes to them. *(courage, care, game, make, face, infuriate, take, ultimate, age)* Students can add these words to their personal word lists.

Reteaching/Reinforcement
• *Unit Three Resource Book* p. 13

---

would be as bad as the emotional opposition of prejudiced white fans.

Suppose I was at shortstop. Another player comes down from first, stealing, flying in with spikes high, and cuts me on the leg. As I feel the blood running down my leg, the white player laughs in my face.

"How do you like that, nigger boy?" he sneers.

Could I turn the other cheek? I didn't know how I would do it. Yet I knew that I must. I had to do it for so many reasons. For black youth, for my mother, for Rae, for myself. I had already begun to feel I had to do it for Branch Rickey.

I was offered, and agreed to sign later, a contract with a $3,500 bonus and $600-a-month salary. I was officially a Montreal Royal. I must not tell anyone except Rae and my mother. ❖

The pennant-winning 1949 Brooklyn Dodgers team. Jackie Robinson is second from the right in the third row.
UPI/Bettmann.

THE NOBLE EXPERIMENT **281**

Active Reading: CLARIFY

Q Ask students why other players would treat Robinson so cruelly. If students are having difficulty judging motivation, you may wish to use this think-aloud model.

Think-Aloud Model *I remember from the Historical Connection on page 273 that blacks faced many barriers created by prejudice. The white players might envy Robinson's talent and fear that black players will displace whites.*

Linking to History

R Robinson went on to play baseball with skill and determination that has rarely been matched in sports history. Upon retirement from baseball at the end of the 1956 season, Robinson had compiled a career batting average of .311 and had played for six pennant winners and one world-championship team.

STRATEGIC READING FOR
Less-Proficient Readers

S Explore with students Robinson's reasons for agreeing to become Rickey's "noble experiment." *(He accepted for the benefit of black youth, his mother, his girlfriend Rae, Rickey, and himself.)* **Drawing Conclusions**

• What does Rickey say may happen if Robinson accepts his offer? *(He could be hit with beanballs, called terrible names, and physically attacked.)* **Summarizing**

CUSTOMIZING FOR
Gifted and Talented Students

Have students speculate about what effect Robinson's career and autobiography could have on fans and readers. *(Possible responses: They could inspire readers of any race to take courageous risks, help fight prejudice, shatter stereotypes, and knock down barriers to promotion.)*

Assessment ✓ Option

SELF-ASSESSMENT To help students assess their understanding of the selection, you may wish to have them ask themselves and then answer the following questions.
• What was "noble" about Branch Rickey's "experiment"?
• Which of Robinson's qualities do I find especially admirable?

• Why do I think other people admire Jackie Robinson?
• What advice would I have given to Jackie Robinson when he was considering Branch Rickey's offer?
• Would I have liked to have been in Jackie Robinson's place? Why or why not?

INSIGHT

1. Do you think baseball star Mickey Mantle was a good choice for writing a tribute about Robinson? Why or why not? *(Possible response: Yes. As a ballplayer, Mantle was qualified to judge Robinson's skills. Also, because Mantle wasn't a close friend of Robinson's, he could be objective.)*
2. What do you think Mantle admires most about Jackie Robinson? *(Possible responses: his courage, control, and independence)*
3. Do you think Robinson would like Mantle's tribute to him? Why or why not? *(Possible response: yes, because it shows great respect for Robinson)*

MICKEY MANTLE

Mickey Mantle (1931–1995) was one of the greatest switch hitters in baseball. Elected unanimously to the Baseball Hall of Fame, Mantle, like Robinson, became a legend to baseball fans and players alike.

COMPREHENSION CHECK

1. What does Rickey show about his beliefs when he shares a room with an African American? *(He rejects racism; he believes in equality.)*
2. What are Rickey's plans for Robinson? *(to make him the first African-American player to break the color barrier in the major leagues)*
3. What does Rickey warn Robinson about? *(that Robinson must be prepared for insults and attacks)*
4. How does the interview between Robinson and Rickey end? *(Robinson accepts Rickey's offer and signs a contract.)*

LITERARY INSIGHT

from The Quality of Courage
by Mickey Mantle

Sometimes courage is very quiet. People who saw Jackie Robinson play baseball remember him as a hard, aggressive, noisy ball player who was always in the middle of every argument—when he wasn't winning a game by stealing home or driving in the go-ahead run or making a game-saving play in the field. I thought he was one of the best ball players I ever saw, and when he played against teams that I was on—in the World Series of 1952 and 1953 and 1955 and 1956—he always showed a lot of guts.

But he had even more courage his first year in the majors, 1947, when I was still a young high school kid in Oklahoma. That year Robinson hardly ever opened his mouth, he never argued, he didn't get into any fights, he was the quietest, politest player anyone ever saw. When you think of Jackie's natural personality—he liked action, arguments, rough games, give and take, and he liked to be in the center of the stage, talking, yelling, taking charge—you wonder how he ever was able to control

himself that first year. Especially in the face of the riding he took, the things he was called. . . .

There's an odd thing about Jackie Robinson. I myself was never very friendly with him, and I have found that a lot of people who knew him in and out of baseball really dislike him. He's a hard man for some people to like because he isn't soft and smooth-talking and syrupy. He's tough and independent, and he says what he thinks, and he rubs people the wrong way. But I have never heard of anyone who knew Jackie Robinson, whether they liked him or disliked him, who didn't respect him and admire him. That might be more important than being liked.

282   UNIT THREE   PART 1: SHOWING COURAGE

Mini-Lesson: Speaking, Listening, and Viewing

FILM/DRAMA Explain to students that comparing a film and text version of the same work offers them an opportunity to practice the skill of evaluation in a different way. Discuss how this also gives them the chance to compare characterization in two- and three-dimensional media. Then invite students to view *The Jackie Robinson Story* (black and white, 76 minutes), the 1950 film version of Robinson's autobiography in which Robinson plays himself.

Application To help students compare the film with what they have read in "The Noble Experiment," have them write a paragraph that answers these questions:
- What did the film version add to your impression of Jackie Robinson and Branch Rickey? What new insights about their characters did you gain?
- Compare and contrast how you visualized the characters with the way they appeared in the film.
- How would you rate this film? Excellent? Good? Fair? Explain the reasons for your evaluation.

RESPONDING
OPTIONS

1. Possible response: He was talented and brave.
2. Possible responses: It was courageous, because Rickey faced great opposition. It was ingenious, because it tricked the opposition. It was long overdue, because ethnic groups should not be segregated.
3. Possible responses: Robinson, because he faced others' cruelty; Rickey, because he took a stand against injustice when he had nothing to gain personally.
4. Possible responses: Yes, because without pride a person cannot have self-respect. No, because everyone wants to be liked.
5. Possible responses: Some students may say that athletes should be role models, because young people do look up to them. Other students may say that athletes should be judged only for what they are being paid for, their athletic performance.

FROM PERSONAL RESPONSE TO CRITICAL ANALYSIS

REFLECT
1. What are your impressions of Jackie Robinson? Write your thoughts about him in your notebook.

RETHINK
2. What is your opinion of Branch Rickey's plan to integrate baseball?
   Consider
   • his reasons for wanting to carry out the plan
   • how and why he kept it secret
   • the final results of the plan

Thematic Link
3. Think about the difficulties both Rickey and Robinson faced. Who showed the greater courage? Give reasons for your answer.

RELATE
4. In the Insight on page 282, Mickey Mantle says that whether people liked or disliked Jackie Robinson, they respected and admired him. Do you think that being respected and admired might be more important than being liked? Why or why not?
5. Many saw Jackie Robinson as a role model for young people. Should we expect professional athletes to be role models, or should we judge them only on their athletic performance?

Close Textual Reading

Multimodal Learning
ANOTHER PATHWAY

If you had had an opportunity to interview Jackie Robinson and Branch Rickey, what questions would you have asked them? Working with two other students, practice and then stage an interview with Robinson and Rickey for your class.

QUICKWRITES

1. What do you think Jackie Robinson would have said to Charley Thomas, the player whose suffering affected Branch Rickey? Write a **letter** that Robinson might have sent to Thomas after signing with the Dodgers.

2. Using information from the selection, write a **speech** that Jackie Robinson might have given to a group of baseball officials about the effects of prejudice on baseball.

3. Branch Rickey said that he was "looking for a ballplayer with guts enough not to fight back." Write a **definition** of courage that you think Rickey would have agreed with.

📁 *PORTFOLIO Save your writing. You may want to use it later as a springboard to a piece for your portfolio.*

LITERARY CONCEPTS

The reasons for a person's actions are known as **motivation.** What motivated Branch Rickey and Jackie Robinson? How were their motivations alike, and how were they different?

CONCEPT REVIEW: Autobiography An autobiography usually focuses on events that shape or change a person's life. How did the meeting with Branch Rickey change Jackie Robinson's life?

Another Pathway

To help students work collaboratively, assign a voice monitor to ensure that all group members speak clearly; a recorder to transcribe the interview; and a direction giver to keep the group on task. Remind interviewers to prepare questions that require more than a yes or no response and that relate to issues important to Robinson and Rickey. Students role-playing Robinson and Rickey should review the selection to note their characters' actions, reactions, and motivations.

Rubric
3 Full Accomplishment Students ask questions that tap both men's motivations and evaluate their actions and accomplishments.
2 Substantial Accomplishment Students ask questions that reveal what Robinson and Rickey were able to accomplish.
1 Little or Partial Accomplishment Students have difficulty preparing and/or staging an interview.

THE NOBLE EXPERIMENT **283**

Literary Concepts

Possible response: Both men were motivated to end segregation. Robinson was motivated to set an example for African-American youth, whereas Rickey was not. Invite students to work in pairs to explore each man's perception of justice and competitiveness.

CONCEPT REVIEW Rickey changed Robinson's life by helping him become a world-famous leader and role model.

QuickWrites

1. Suggest that students imagine how Jackie Robinson might have felt about the injustice that Charley Thomas endured.
2. Guide students to structure their informative speech with a clear introduction, body, and conclusion. Remind students to include sufficient details and examples to make their point clearly.
3. Encourage students to think about Rickey's point that sometimes not fighting back is the sign of real courage.

 The Writer's Craft

Letter Forms, p. 669
Informing and Defining, pp. 122–129

Social Studies Arrange students in groups of four to complete their research. You may want to have group members divide the reference material, with each student checking a different source. The PBS documentary series "Eyes on the Prize" provides an excellent visual history of the civil rights movement. It may be available in libraries or for rent in local video stores.

ADDITIONAL SUGGESTION

Math *Batter Up !* Students can research and prepare a report on Robinson's statistical average during his career. Invite students to calculate yearly averages for Robinson's achievements in batting, home runs, triples, doubles, bases on balls, games played, errors, and stolen bases. Have students provide a clear explanation of how they determined the player's batting average.

Words to Know

1. shrewdly	6. retaliate
2. incredulous	7. integrated
3. speculating	8. insinuation
4. cynical	9. eloquence
5. taunt	10. ultimate

Reteaching/Reinforcement
• *Unit Three Resource Book*, p. 14

ALFRED DUCKETT

Duckett's most famous speech, "I Have a Dream," was written with Dr. Martin Luther King, Jr., and delivered by King in front of the Lincoln Memorial in Washington, D.C., on August 28, 1963.

Multimodal Learning

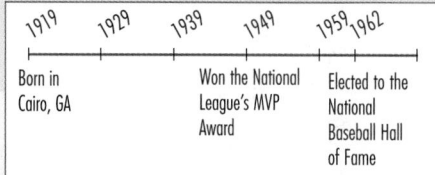

ALTERNATIVE ACTIVITIES

Read the rest of Jackie Robinson's autobiography, *I Never Had It Made*. Create a **time line** of his accomplishments and give a report on his experiences in baseball and his other achievements.

1919	1929	1939	1949	1959	1962
Born in Cairo, GA			Won the National League's MVP Award		Elected to the National Baseball Hall of Fame

ACROSS THE CURRICULUM

Social Studies Jackie Robinson experienced prejudice and discrimination in breaking the "color barrier" in major-league baseball. Find out more about segregation policies, such as "Jim Crow" laws, that existed during Robinson's lifetime. How did these policies affect African Americans? When and how were the laws changed?

Review the Words to Know at the bottom of the selection pages. On your paper, write the vocabulary word that is the best substitute for each boldfaced word or phrase below.

1. Branch Rickey **cleverly** devised a cover story for the press.
2. Some **unbelieving** fans gasped when Jackie Robinson walked onto the field for his first major-league game.
3. The majority of fans who were sitting home, **guessing,** were wrong about Rickey's plans.
4. Many blacks felt very **mistrustful** about promises made by whites.
5. Some ballplayers on other teams would **mock** Robinson and try to anger him.
6. Robinson was not allowed to **fight back.**
7. The goal of the experiment was to have **desegregated** major leagues.
8. Sometimes a sportswriter would put in his column a **sly negative comment** about Robinson's character.
9. Several ministers spoke with **great verbal skill** about the evils of prejudice.
10. The **final** result of Rickey's "noble experiment" was highly successful.

ALFRED DUCKETT

It seems natural that Alfred Duckett would want to tell Jackie Robinson's story, since Duckett was born in Brooklyn and was a baseball fan as well as a journalist. Robinson and Duckett worked together to produce *I Never Had It Made: The Autobiography of Jackie Robinson*. Besides writing books, Duckett also wrote poetry, magazine articles, and speeches.

1917–1984

Duckett also co-founded *Equal Opportunities* magazine and was the director of Associated Negro Press International, Inc. He appeared on national television programs and lectured in many schools, churches, and universities. Duckett ran a public relations firm in Chicago until his death in 1984.

Alternative Activities

Remind students that time lines highlight key events in history, not every single event. Suggest that students jot down notes as they read to help them track key events in Robinson's life. Encourage students to include in their reports their own reactions to the events of Robinson's life. To extend the activity, you may wish to have students mark key events in the civil rights movement on their time lines in order to place Robinson's ground-breaking achievements in a broader historical context.

PREVIEWING

FICTION

The Medicine Bag
Virginia Driving Hawk Sneve

Objectives

- To understand and appreciate a short story about the importance of tradition and culture
- To identify and analyze exposition
- To express understanding of the story through a choice of writing forms, including a dialogue, a song lyric, a tale, and an editorial
- To extend understanding of the story through a variety of multimodal and cross-curricular activities

---

Skills

READING SKILLS/ STRATEGIES
- Connecting

THE WRITER'S STYLE
- Unity

GRAMMAR
- Subject-verb agreement

LITERARY CONCEPTS
- Exposition
- Setting

SPELLING
- Prefixes and roots

STUDY SKILLS
- Paraphrasing

SPEAKING, LISTENING, AND VIEWING
- Oral history

Cross-Curricular Connections

GEOGRAPHY
- Native American reservations

HISTORY
- American Indian Movement (AIM)

SCIENCE
- Adolescence

SOCIAL STUDIES
- Vision quests
- Belief systems

Activating Prior Knowledge
PERSONAL CONNECTION

Most people in the United States can trace their roots to one or more ethnic groups. Their ethnic heritage can be traced to a country in Africa, Asia, Europe, or Latin America, or perhaps to a Native American people. What is your ethnic heritage? How much does it mean to you? What customs or traditions are important in your ethnic culture? Which people in your family are especially important in preserving these customs and traditions? Jot down your thoughts in your literature notebook.

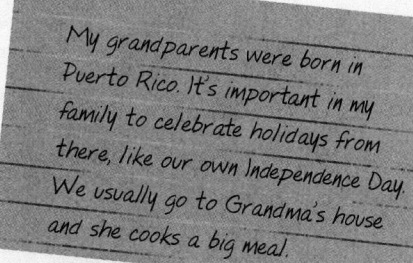

My grandparents were born in Puerto Rico. It's important in my family to celebrate holidays from there, like our own Independence Day. We usually go to Grandma's house and she cooks a big meal.

Building Background
HISTORICAL CONNECTION

The narrator of this story traces part of his heritage to the Sioux, a Native American people. The Sioux are North American Plains Indians who became well-known for their skills in hunting and battle. Their chiefs included Sitting Bull and Crazy Horse.

During the 1800s, the Sioux gradually lost their land and their independence to white settlers. After being defeated by the U.S. Army, the Sioux were moved onto reservations where they were forced to change their ways of living. Many of their customs gradually died out. Today most Sioux still live on reservations, in North Dakota, South Dakota, Montana, and Nebraska. Their lives are far different from those of their ancestors, and many Sioux live in poverty. The great-grandfather in this story comes from the Rosebud Reservation in South Dakota, where 18,000 Sioux currently live.

Sioux dancer at Cheyenne River Reservation, South Dakota.
Copyright © 1987 Allen Russell/ Profiles West.

Setting a Purpose
WRITING CONNECTION

Which of your relatives—either living or deceased—stands out most in your mind? Perhaps it is a grandparent who taught you about your heritage or an aunt who tells funny stories. In your notebook, write a poem or a paragraph describing your relative and telling what makes him or her special. Then, as you read "The Medicine Bag," compare your experiences with your relative with the narrator's experiences with his great-grandfather.

LASERLINKS
- *HISTORICAL CONNECTION*

285

HISTORICAL CONNECTION
The Sioux Nation European contact permanently changed the culture of the Sioux. Students will see paintings showing the methods used by the Sioux to hunt buffalo prior to European contact, as well as postcontact pictures of a tribal delegation and a tribal policeman. These images may be used to generate discussion about how European contact changed the Sioux culture.

Side A, Frame 49325

PRINT AND MEDIA RESOURCES

UNIT THREE RESOURCE BOOK
Strategic Reading: Literature, p. 17
Vocabulary SkillBuilder, p. 20
Reading SkillBuilder, p. 18
Spelling SkillBuilder, p. 19

GRAMMAR MINI-LESSONS
Transparencies, p. 3
Copymasters, p. 3

WRITING MINI-LESSONS
Transparencies, p. 31

ACCESS FOR STUDENTS ACQUIRING ENGLISH
Selection Summaries
Reading and Writing Support

FORMAL ASSESSMENT
Selection Test, pp. 57–58
 Test Generator

 **AUDIO LIBRARY**
See Reference Card

LASERLINKS
Historical Connection
Art Gallery

SUMMARY

Martin and Cheryl's great-grandfather, a Sioux named Joe Iron Shell, comes to visit them. "Grandpa" knows that he is dying. He wants to pass on to Martin his sacred medicine bag, an old leather pouch worn around the neck. Martin is secretly ashamed of the shabby, frail old man and does not want to wear the medicine bag. However, Grandpa's quiet dignity and colorful stories earn the respect of Martin's friends and of Martin himself. When Grandpa finally tells Martin the story of the medicine bag and presents the bag to him, Martin gains a sense of responsibility and a pride in his heritage.

Thematic Link: *Showing Courage*
Grandpa's courage enables Martin to embrace his Sioux heritage.

CUSTOMIZING FOR
Students Acquiring English

- Use **ACCESS FOR STUDENTS ACQUIRING ENGLISH**, *Reading and Writing Support*.

- Students acquiring English may be able to relate to the narrator's embarrassment at his great-grandfather's traditional dress, language, and customs. If it seems appropriate, you may want to invite them to share similar experiences they have had. They may find it more comfortable to do so in writing than in speaking aloud.

STRATEGIC READING FOR
Less-Proficient Readers

Set a Purpose Ask students how different people show they value their ethnic heritage. Discuss holidays, foods, and language. Then have students read to find out what happens to Grandpa upon reaching the house.

Use **UNIT THREE RESOURCE BOOK**, p. 17, for guidance in reading the selection.

The Medicine Bag

by Virginia Driving Hawk Sneve

My kid sister Cheryl and I always bragged about our Sioux grandpa, Joe Iron Shell. Our friends, who had always lived in the city and only knew about Indians from movies and TV, were impressed by our stories. Maybe we exaggerated and made Grandpa and the reservation sound glamorous, but when we'd return home to Iowa after our yearly summer visit to Grandpa, we always had some exciting tale to tell.

WORDS TO KNOW

confines (kŏn'fīnz') *n.* limits; boundaries (p. 292)
descendant (dĭ-sĕn'dənt) *n.* an immediate or remote offspring of a person (p. 289)
fatigue (fə-têg') *n.* extreme weariness or exhaustion (p. 288)

reluctantly (rĭ-lŭk'tənt-lē) *adv.* unwillingly (p. 288)
unseemly (ŭn-sēm'lē) *adj.* not decent or proper (p. 288)

Challenge students, as they read the story, to explain what the medicine bag symbolizes. *(Possible responses: The importance of heritage; the continuation of culture and traditions.)*

CUSTOMIZING FOR

Students Acquiring English

(1) Explain that *man* here is an exclamation that shows the speaker's strong emotions. Be sure that students understand that this exclamation is different from the literal meaning of the word *man*.

(2) You may want to use the word *mutts* to show that a speaker's choice of words can reveal his or her attitudes and feelings. Although *mutts* means "dogs," it is usually used when the speaker has a negative feeling toward the animals in question.

Active Reading: CONNECT

(A) Ask students if this description differs from their image of Native Americans. Invite volunteers to share their images of Native Americans. As a class, explore the sources of these images. *(Possible response: Students might say that they envision Native Americans as tall and stately, as shown in movies such as* Dances with Wolves.*)*

Literary Concept: EXPOSITION

(B) Invite students to compare the description of the narrator's neighborhood with the description of Grandpa's home. Ask students to speculate why the author includes this information at the beginning of the story. *(Possible response: It shows the different backgrounds of the two characters and introduces the conflicted feelings the narrator has about his grandfather.)*

We always had some authentic Sioux article to show our listeners. One year Cheryl had new moccasins that Grandpa had made. On another visit he gave me a small, round, flat, rawhide drum which was decorated with a painting of a warrior riding a horse. He taught me a real Sioux chant to sing while I beat the drum with a leather-covered stick that had a feather on the end. Man, that really made an impression.

We never showed our friends Grandpa's picture. Not that we were ashamed of him, but because we knew that the glamorous tales we told didn't go with the real thing. Our friends would have laughed at the picture, because Grandpa wasn't tall and stately like TV Indians. His hair wasn't in braids but hung in stringy gray strands on his neck, and he was old. He was our great-grandfather, and he didn't live in a tipi but all by himself in a part log, part tar-paper shack on the Rosebud Reservation in South Dakota. So when Grandpa came to visit us, I was so ashamed and embarrassed I could've died.

There are a lot of yippy poodles and other fancy little dogs in our neighborhood, but they usually barked singly at the mailman from the safety of their own yards. Now it sounded as if a whole pack of mutts were barking together in one place.

I got up and walked to the curb to see what the commotion was. About a block away I saw a crowd of little kids yelling, with the dogs yipping and growling around someone who was walking down the middle of the street.

I watched the group as it slowly came closer and saw that in the center of the strange procession was a man wearing a tall black hat. He'd pause now and then to peer at something in his hand and then at the houses on either side of the street. I felt cold and hot at the same time as I recognized the man. "Oh, no!" I whispered. "It's Grandpa!"

I stood on the curb, unable to move, even though I wanted to run and hide. Then I got mad when I saw how the yippy dogs were growling and nipping at the old man's baggy pant legs and how wearily he poked them away with his cane. "Stupid mutts," I said as I ran to rescue Grandpa.

When I kicked and hollered at the dogs to get away, they put their tails between their legs and scattered. The kids ran to the curb where they watched me and the old man.

Mesquakie Pouch. Courtesy of Morning Star Gallery, Santa Fe, New Mexico. Photo by Addison Doty.

THE MEDICINE BAG **287**

Mini-Lesson 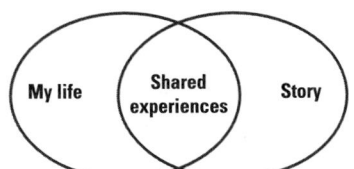 Reading Skills/Strategies

ACTIVE READING: CONNECT Explain to students that when they use the reading strategy of connecting, they look for similarities between what is described in the selection and what they have experienced directly, heard about, or read about elsewhere.

Application Ask students to review the selection and to create Venn diagrams that show connections between the story and their own experiences. If students have difficulty making connections, ask them to list the story's key events and the feelings of each character. Ask students if they can remember having similar things happen to them or experiencing similar emotions.

Reteaching/Reinforcement
• *Unit Three Resource Book* p. 18

My life / Shared experiences / Story

C Explain that Martin's voice cracks probably because he is going through adolescence. As boys mature, increasing amounts of the hormone testosterone bring about the deepening of their voices, mainly through the enlargement of the larynx and doubling in length of the vocal cords. As a result, the pitch of the voice changes, often abruptly.

CUSTOMIZING FOR
Students Acquiring English

3 Use the word *getup* as another example of word choice that reveals the narrator's feelings. *Getup* literally means "clothing," but it has a negative connotation that reflects the narrator's embarrassment about his great-grandfather.

Active Reading: PREDICT

D Invite students to explain the conflict in this story as revealed here and earlier. Then have students predict how the conflict will develop and be resolved. *(Possible responses: The conflict is the narrator's clashing feelings of shame and love for his great-grandfather. The boy might overcome his embarrassment, or his great-grandfather might change.)*

Literary Concept:
FORESHADOWING

E Ask students what grandfather's collapse leads them to expect in the story. *(Possible response: Grandpa's illness or death.)*

Critical Thinking: ANALYZING

F Have students analyze Martin's actions to explain what they reveal about his character. *(Possible response: Martin's good sense in an emergency and willingness to help show that he is mature and responsible.)*

C "Grandpa," I said and felt pretty dumb when my voice cracked. I reached for his beat-up old tin suitcase, which was tied shut with a rope. But he set it down right in the street and shook my hand.

"*Hau, Takoza,* Grandchild," he greeted me formally in Sioux.

All I could do was stand there with the whole neighborhood watching and shake the hand of the leather-brown old man. I saw how his gray hair straggled from under his big black hat, which had a drooping feather in its crown. His rumpled black suit hung like a sack over his stooped frame. As he shook my hand, his coat fell open to expose a bright red, satin shirt with a beaded bolo tie under **3** the collar. His getup wasn't out of place on the reservation, but it sure was here, and I wanted to sink right through the pavement.

"Hi," I muttered with my head down. I tried to pull my hand away when I felt his bony hand trembling and looked up to see **D** fatigue in his face. I felt like crying. I couldn't think of anything to say, so I picked up Grandpa's suitcase, took his arm, and guided him up the driveway to our house.

Mom was standing on the steps. I don't know how long she'd been watching, but her hand was over her mouth, and she looked as if she couldn't believe what she saw. Then she ran to us.

"Grandpa," she gasped. "How in the world did you get here?"

She checked her move to embrace Grandpa, and I remembered that such a display of

I knew that everybody felt as guilty as I did— especially Mom. Mom was all Grandpa had left.

affection is unseemly to the Sioux and would embarrass him.

"*Hau,* Marie," he said as he shook Mom's hand. She smiled and took his other arm.

As we supported him up the steps, the door banged open and Cheryl came bursting out of the house. She was all smiles and was so obviously glad to see Grandpa that I was ashamed of how I felt.

"Grandpa!" she yelled happily. "You came to see us!"

Grandpa smiled, and Mom and I let go of him as he stretched out his arms to my ten-year-old sister, who was still young enough to be hugged.

"*Wicincala,* little girl," he greeted her and then collapsed.

He had fainted. Mom and I carried him into her sewing room, where we had a spare bed.

After we had Grandpa on the bed, Mom stood there helplessly patting his shoulder.

"Shouldn't we call the doctor, Mom?" I suggested, since she didn't seem to know what to do.

"Yes," she agreed with a sigh. "You make Grandpa comfortable, Martin."

I reluctantly moved to the bed. I knew Grandpa wouldn't want to have Mom undress him, but I didn't want to, either. He was so skinny and frail that his coat slipped off easily. When I loosened his tie and opened his shirt collar, I felt a small leather pouch that hung from a thong around his neck. I left it alone and

WORDS TO KNOW	**fatigue** (fə-tēg′) *n.* extreme weariness or exhaustion
	unseemly (ŭn-sēm′lē) *adj.* not decent or proper
	reluctantly (rĭ-lŭk′tənt-lē) *adv.* unwillingly

288

Mini-Lesson 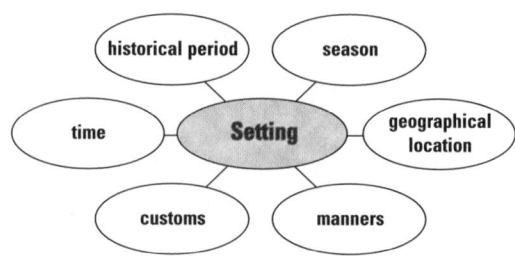 Literary Concepts

REVIEWING SETTING Remind students that setting is the time and place of the action of a story, poem, or play. Sometimes the setting is clear and well defined; other times it is left to the reader's imagination. Setting may include geographic location, the historical period (past, present, or future), season, time of day, and customs and manners of the society. Use the word web on the chalkboard to reinforce these characteristics of setting.

Application Have students list any descriptions in the text that provide clues about the setting. Then, in a short paragraph, ask them to describe the setting of "The Medicine Bag" and to analyze its effect on the characters and events in the story.

moved to remove his boots. The scuffed old cowboy boots were tight, and he moaned as I put pressure on his legs to jerk them off.

I put the boots on the floor and saw why they fit so tight. Each one was stuffed with money. I looked at the bills that lined the boots and started to ask about them, but Grandpa's eyes were closed again.

Mom came back with a basin of water. "The doctor thinks Grandpa is suffering from heat exhaustion," she explained as she bathed Grandpa's face. Mom gave a big sigh, "Oh hinh, Martin. How do you suppose he got here?"

We found out after the doctor's visit. Grandpa was angrily sitting up in bed while Mom tried to feed him some soup.

"Tonight you let Marie feed you, Grandpa," spoke my dad, who had gotten home from work just as the doctor was leaving. "You're not really sick," he said as he gently pushed Grandpa back against the pillows. "The doctor said you just got too tired and hot after your long trip."

Grandpa relaxed, and between sips of soup, he told us of his journey. Soon after our visit to him, Grandpa decided that he would like to see where his only living <u>descendants</u> lived and what our home was like. Besides, he admitted sheepishly, he was lonesome after we left.

I knew that everybody felt as guilty as I did—especially Mom. Mom was all Grandpa had left. So even after she married my dad, who's a white man and teaches in the college in our city, and after Cheryl and I were born, Mom made sure that every summer we spent a week with Grandpa.

I never thought that Grandpa would be lonely after our visits, and none of us noticed how old and weak he had become. But Grandpa knew, and so he came to us. He had ridden on buses for two and a half days. When

he arrived in the city, tired and stiff from sitting for so long, he set out, walking, to find us.

He had stopped to rest on the steps of some building downtown, and a policeman found him. The cop, according to Grandpa, was a good man who took him to the bus stop and waited until the bus came and told the driver to let Grandpa out at Bell View Drive. After Grandpa got off the bus, he started walking again. But he couldn't see the house numbers on the other side when he walked on the sidewalk, so he walked in the middle of the street. That's when all the little kids and dogs followed him.

I knew everybody felt as bad as I did. Yet I was proud of this 86-year-old man who had never been away from the reservation, having the courage to travel so far alone.

"You found the money in my boots?" he asked Mom.

"Martin did," she answered, and roused herself to scold. "Grandpa, you shouldn't have carried so much money. What if someone had stolen it from you?"

Grandpa laughed. "I would've known if anyone had tried to take the boots off my feet. The money is what I've saved for a long time—a hundred dollars—for my funeral. But you take it now to buy groceries so that I won't be a burden to you while I am here."

"That won't be necessary, Grandpa," Dad said. "We are honored to have you with us, and you will never be a burden. I am only sorry that we never thought to bring you home with us this summer and spare you the discomfort of a long trip."

Grandpa was pleased. "Thank you," he answered. "But do not feel bad that you didn't bring me with you, for I would not have come

WORDS
TO
KNOW

descendant (dĭ-sĕn′dənt) *n.* an immediate or remote offspring of a person

289

↓ I

J

K

Active Reading: CONNECT

G Point out how Mom uses a Sioux term here. Invite students to recall an instance when they or their parents used a term from the language of their heritage. Then have students explain what this reveals about Martin's mother and the situation. If applicable, guide students by using a think-aloud model like the following.

Think-Aloud Model *My father was born in Puerto Rico. He speaks in Spanish when he is very upset, for example, when I was hurt or came home very late. This makes me think the mother is very worried. This tells me that she cares deeply for her grandfather.*

CUSTOMIZING FOR

Multiple Learning Styles

H **Musical Learners** Invite students to write or find a song that expresses the need to stay connected with one's ethnic heritage.

Literary Concept: SETTING

I Have students analyze this passage to discover what it reveals about the story's setting. *(Possible responses: The society includes kind, helpful people and many children and pets. The residential neighborhood has sidewalks and wide streets.)*

STRATEGIC READING FOR

Less-Proficient Readers

J Ask students what happened to Grandpa after he reached the house and family. *(He fainted.)* **Noting Sequence of Events**

Set a Purpose Invite students to read to find out why Grandpa has come for a visit.

Active Reading: CONNECT

K Ask students if they have ever known anyone with this kind of courage and determination. Invite students to explain how the person showed these traits.

Mini-Lesson Grammar

SUBJECT-VERB AGREEMENT Explain that a verb must agree with its subject in number. That is, if the subject is plural, the verb must be plural, and if the subject is singular, the verb must be singular. Share the examples on the chalkboard.

Application Have students correct the errors in agreement in these sentences.
1. Mom have a basin of water. *(has)*
2. The boot are stuffed with money. *(is)*
3. Grandpa show the effects of his long walk. *(shows)*

4. Grandpa sit on the patio. *(sits)*
5. Cheryl and her friends comes to meet Grandpa. *(come)*
6. "You looks fine, Grandpa," he said. *(look)*

Reteaching/Reinforcement
• Grammar Handbook, anthology p. 851–852
• *Grammar Mini-Lessons* copymasters, p. 3, transparencies p. 3

📖 **The Writer's Craft**

Agreement of Subject and Verb, pp. 578–580

A Native American (singular subject) *is* (singular verb) *a member of a specific tribe.*

Native Americans (plural subject) *were* (plural verb) *the first inhabitants of North America.*

Art Note

The Tribesman by Hubert Shuptrine
Hubert Shuptrine refers to his approach to art as *realization*—an attempt to communicate to viewers his love for the subject he is painting. The subject of this painting is James Chiltoskey, nicknamed "Going Back" by the medicine men of his tribe, who visited him repeatedly when he was a sick child.

Reading the Art *What impression do you have of the subject of this painting? What do the positioning of the man, his appearance, and his facial expression tell you about his character? Are your impressions similar to or different from your impression of Grandpa? Why?*

Active Reading: CONNECT

M Ask students to explain what Martin means by "hot and cold feeling." Then invite volunteers to share instances when they felt the same way Martin does here. *(Possible responses: He feels both proud and embarrassed. Students might say that they have felt this way about their parents, siblings, or other relatives.)*

The Tribesman (1982), Hubert Shuptrine. Montgomery (Alabama) Museum of Art, Blount Collection. Copyright © 1982 Hubert Shuptrine, all rights reserved.

then. It was not time." He said this in such a way that no one could argue with him. To Grandpa and the Sioux, he once told me, a thing would be done when it was the right time to do it, and that's the way it was.

"Also," Grandpa went on, looking at me, "I have come because it is soon time for Martin to have the medicine bag."

We all knew what that meant. Grandpa thought he was going to die, and he had to follow the tradition of his family to pass the medicine bag, along with its history, to the oldest male child.

"Even though the boy," he said, still looking at me, "bears a white man's name, the medicine bag will be his."

I didn't know what to say. I had the same hot and cold feeling that I had when I first saw Grandpa in the street. The medicine bag was the dirty leather pouch I had found around his neck. "I could never wear such a thing," I almost said aloud. I thought of having my friends see it in gym class, at the swimming pool, and could imagine the smart things they would say. But I

Mini-Lesson: Speaking, Listening, and Viewing

ORAL HISTORY When he gives the medicine bag to Martin, Grandpa also passes along the history of his family. Explain to students that in addition to passing on physical objects from the past, people transmit their traditions by sharing stories of their lives, as Grandpa does on the next few pages. This history may never be written down, but it can be preserved by being passed down from generation to generation.

Application Have students invite an older relative, neighbor, or friend to share the story of his or her life as an oral history, as Grandpa does for Martin. If possible, have students tape-record the stories. Have students list some questions to start the conversation and keep it going. Here are some questions students can use:
• What customs and traditions did you follow in your family? Which ones did you like the best? Why?
• What was your favorite childhood meal?
• What did your family do for recreation?

just swallowed hard and took a step toward the bed. I knew I would have to take it.

But Grandpa was tired. "Not now, Martin," he said, waving his hand in dismissal. "It is not time. Now I will sleep."

So that's how Grandpa came to be with us for two months. My friends kept asking to come see the old man, but I put them off. I told myself that I didn't want them laughing at Grandpa. But even as I made excuses, I knew it wasn't Grandpa that I was afraid they'd laugh at.

Nothing bothered Cheryl about bringing her friends to see Grandpa. Every day after school started there'd be a crew of giggling little girls or round-eyed little boys crowded around the old man on the patio, where he'd gotten in the habit of sitting every afternoon.

Grandpa would smile in his gentle way and patiently answer their questions, or he'd tell them stories of brave warriors, ghosts, and animals, and the kids listened in awed silence. Those little guys thought Grandpa was great.

Finally, one day after school, my friends came home with me because nothing I said stopped them. "We're going to see the great Indian of Bell View Drive," said Hank, who was supposed to be my best friend. "My brother has seen him three times, so he oughta be well enough to see us."

When we got to my house, Grandpa was sitting on the patio. He had on his red shirt, but today he also wore a fringed leather vest that was decorated with beads. Instead of his usual cowboy boots, he had solidly beaded moccasins on his feet that stuck out of his black trousers. Of course, he had his old black hat on—he was seldom without it. But it had been brushed, and the feather in the beaded headband was proudly erect, its tip a brighter white. His hair lay in silver strands over the red shirt collar.

I stared just as my friends did, and I heard one of them murmur, "Wow!"

Grandpa looked up, and when his eyes met mine, they twinkled as if he were laughing inside. He nodded to me, and my face got all hot. I could tell that he had known all along I was afraid he'd embarrass me in front of my friends.

"*Hau, hoksilas,* boys," he greeted and held out his hand.

My buddies passed in a single file and shook his hand as I introduced them. They were so polite I almost laughed. "How, there, Grandpa," and even a "How-do-you-do, sir."

"You look fine, Grandpa," I said as the guys sat on the lawn chairs or on the patio floor.

"*Hanh,* yes," he agreed. "When I woke up this morning, it seemed the right time to dress in the good clothes. I knew that my grandson would be bringing his friends."

"You guys want some lemonade or something?" I offered. No one answered. They were listening to Grandpa as he started telling how he'd killed the deer from which his vest was made.

Grandpa did most of the talking while my friends were there. I was so proud of him and amazed at how respectfully quiet my buddies were. Mom had to chase them home at supper time. As they left, they shook Grandpa's hand again and said to me:

"Martin, he's really great!"

"Yeah, man! Don't blame you for keeping him to yourself."

"Can we come back?"

But after they left, Mom said, "No more visitors for a while, Martin. Grandpa won't admit it, but his strength hasn't returned. He likes having company, but it tires him."

That evening Grandpa called me to his room before he went to sleep. "Tomorrow," he said, "when you come home, it will be time to give you the medicine bag."

I felt a hard squeeze from where my heart is supposed to be and was scared, but I answered,

THE MEDICINE BAG **291**

Critical Thinking:
HYPOTHESIZING

N Have students speculate about what Martin is afraid his friends will laugh at. (*Possible response: Martin fears his friends will laugh at him because he has a great-grandfather who is from a different culture.*)

Active Reading: EVALUATE

O Ask students if they believe that Martin is right to feel worried that his friends will laugh at his great-grandfather or at himself. (*Possible responses: Yes, because Hank's remark could mean that Martin's friends see Grandpa as some sort of curiosity and will judge him harshly; no, because the way Cheryl's friends reacted suggests that Martin's friends will be impressed with Grandpa.*)

Literary Concept:
CHARACTER

P Invite students to explain what this passage reveals about Martin and Grandpa. (*Possible responses: Martin shows his feelings easily; Grandpa knows a great deal about human nature; Grandpa is observant and perceptive.*)

STRATEGIC READING FOR
Less-Proficient Readers

Q Discuss with students how much Martin's friends liked Grandpa and how impressive they found him.

- How did Martin's friends behave during the visit? (*They were polite and respectful.*) **Summarizing**

- Why did Grandpa change his clothing when Martin's friends came to visit? (*Grandpa didn't want to embarrass Martin.*) **Making Inferences**

Set a Purpose Have students read on to find out the history of the medicine bag and its contents.

Mini-Lesson **The Writer's Style**

UNITY Ask students what they think of when they hear the word *unity*. Discuss how unity helps teams, students, and nations work together to achieve common goals. Relate this discussion to the purpose of unity in writing: to focus all ideas on a single purpose. Explain that if all the sentences in a paragraph are not focused on the main idea, the writing is likely to confuse readers.

Application Have students work in pairs to analyze the highlighted passage, noticing how the writer achieves unity by presenting related events in chronological order.

Reteaching/Reinforcement
- *Writing Handbook,* anthology p. 816
- *Writing Mini-Lessons* transparencies, p. 31

The Writer's Craft

Unity, pp. 266–268

Linking to Social Studies

Vision quests were a vital rite of passage for the Plains Indians. Both male and female teenagers sought supernatural visions by traveling to a remote location where they fasted and reflected to find a spiritual being. The spiritual being taught the person prayers and songs and told the person what objects to gather and carry in a medicine bag as talismans. The youth could then call on this spiritual guardian throughout life.

Cultural Note

The religious beliefs of nearly all Native American tribes connect humans to every other living thing. Some Native American tribes believe that the spirits of all people join to form a single spiritual force. This force has the power to direct and influence them. The Sioux call this force *Wakantanka;* the Iroquois, *Orenda;* the Algonquians, *Manitou.*

Active Reading: CONNECT

Ask students what role dreams play in their lives. Invite volunteers to relate experiences they have had in which a dream affected their lives in some way.

 "OK, Grandpa."

All night I had weird dreams about thunder and lightning on a high hill. From a distance I heard the slow beat of a drum. When I woke up in the morning, I felt as if I hadn't slept at all. At school it seemed as if the day would never end, and when it finally did, I ran home.

Grandpa was in his room, sitting on the bed. The shades were down, and the place was dim and cool. I sat on the floor in front of Grandpa, but he didn't even look at me. After what seemed a long time, he spoke.

"I sent your mother and sister away. What you will hear today is only for a man's ears. What you will receive is only for a man's hands." He fell silent, and I felt shivers down my back.

"My father in his early manhood," Grandpa began, "made a vision quest to find a spirit guide for his life. You cannot understand how it was in that time, when the great Teton Sioux were first made to stay on the reservation. There was a strong need for guidance from *Wakantanka,* the Great Spirit. But too many of the young men were filled with despair and hatred. They thought it was hopeless to search for a vision when the glorious life was gone and only the hated <u>confines</u> of a reservation lay ahead. But my father held to the old ways.

"He carefully prepared for his quest with a purifying sweat bath, and then he went alone

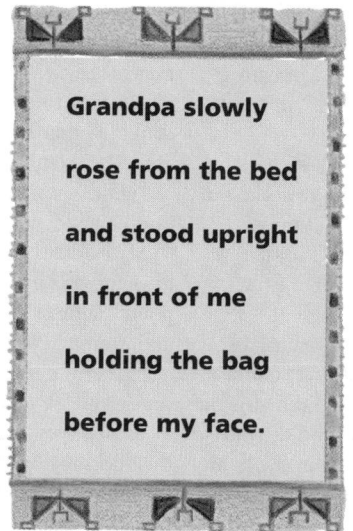

Grandpa slowly rose from the bed and stood upright in front of me holding the bag before my face.

to a high butte[1] top to fast and pray. After three days he received his sacred dream—in which he found, after long searching, the white man's iron. He did not understand his vision of finding something belonging to the white people, for in that time, they were the enemy. When he came down from the butte to cleanse himself at the stream below, he found the remains of a campfire and the broken shell of an iron kettle. This was a sign which reinforced his dream. He took a piece of the iron for his medicine bag, which he had made of elk skin years before, to prepare for his quest.

"He returned to his village, where he told his dream to the wise old men of the tribe. They gave him the name Iron Shell, but neither did they understand the meaning of the dream. This first Iron Shell kept the piece of iron with him at all times and believed it gave him protection from the evils of those unhappy days.

"Then a terrible thing happened to Iron Shell. He and several other young men were taken from their homes by the soldiers and sent far away to a white man's boarding school. He was angry and lonesome for his parents and the young girl he had wed before he was taken away. At first Iron Shell resisted the teachers' attempts to change him, and he did not try to learn. One day it was his turn to work in the school's blacksmith shop. As he walked

---

1. **butte** (byo͞ot): a flat-topped hill.

WORDS TO KNOW   **confines** (kŏn'fīnz') *n.* limits; boundaries

292

Mini-Lesson **Spelling**

PREFIXES AND ROOTS Explain to students that different words can be formed from the same roots by adding different prefixes. On the board, write the prefixes and roots shown below. Ask volunteers for examples of words made from these prefixes and roots.

Prefixes
pre, in, de, ex, con

Roots
scribe, clude, flict vent, cision

Application Divide students in teams and challenge them to make as many words as they can by combining the prefixes with the roots. *(conflict, inflict, describe, inscribe, prescribe, invent, prevent, decision, precision, incision, include, exclude, conclude)* Then have students build their personal word lists by changing the prefixes on these words from page 292:

resisted (in, per)   received (de, con, per)

Reteaching/Reinforcement
• *Unit Three Resource Book* p. 19

into the place, he knew that his medicine had brought him there to learn and work with the white man's iron.

"Iron Shell became a blacksmith and worked at the trade when he returned to the reservation. All of his life he treasured the medicine bag. When he was old, and I was a man, he gave it to me, for no one made the vision quest any more."

Grandpa quit talking, and I stared in disbelief as he covered his face with his hands. His shoulders were shaking with quiet sobs, and I looked away until he began to speak again.

"I kept the bag until my son, your mother's father, was a man and had to leave us to fight in the war across the ocean. I gave him the bag, for I believed it would protect him in battle, but he did not take it with him. He was afraid that he would lose it. He died in a faraway place."

Again Grandpa was still, and I felt his grief around me.

"My son," he went on after clearing his throat, "had only a daughter, and it is not proper for her to know of these things."

He unbuttoned his shirt, pulled out the leather pouch, and lifted it over his head. He held it in his hand, turning it over and over as if memorizing how it looked.

"In the bag," he said as he opened it and removed two objects, "is the broken shell of the iron kettle, a pebble from the butte, and a piece of the sacred sage." He held the

pouch upside down and dust drifted down.

"After the bag is yours, you must put a piece of prairie sage within and never open it again until you pass it on to your son." He replaced the pebble and the piece of iron and tied the bag. I stood up, somehow knowing I should. Grandpa slowly rose from the bed and stood upright in front of me holding the bag before my face. I closed my eyes and waited for him to slip it over my head. But he spoke. "No, you need not wear it." He placed the soft leather bag in my right hand and closed my other hand over it. "It would not be right to wear it in this time and place where no one will understand. Put it safely away until you are again on the reservation. Wear it then, when you replace the sacred sage."

Grandpa turned and sat again on the bed. Wearily he leaned his head against the pillow. "Go," he said. "I will sleep now."

"Thank you, Grandpa," I said softly, and left with the bag in my hands.

That night Mom and Dad took Grandpa to the hospital. Two weeks later I stood alone on the lonely prairie of the reservation and put the sacred sage in my medicine bag. ❖

THE MEDICINE BAG **293**

Ask students to explain what they think the objects in the medicine bag symbolize. *(Possible responses: The iron shell may symbolize work, the coming of modern times, or the family name; the pebble may represent a tie to the land; the sage may symbolize spirituality or nature.)*

COMPREHENSION CHECK

1. Whom does Grandpa come to visit at the beginning of the story? *(the narrator and his family)*
2. Where does Grandpa live? *(on a Sioux reservation in South Dakota)*
3. What mixed feelings does Martin have about his great-grandfather? *(pride and shame)*
4. How do Martin's friends react to Grandpa when they finally meet him? *(They are impressed.)*
5. What gift does Grandpa give Martin? *(his medicine bag)*

INSIGHT

1. Why do you think the vision quest was so important in the Sioux culture? *(Possible responses: It put people in touch with their spiritual side, which was a focus for these people; it signaled maturity and adult responsibilities.)*
2. Would you have liked to have been a member of the Sioux? Why or why not? *(Possible responses: Yes, because they were brave and spiritual; no, because they led a harsh, difficult life.)*
3. How do the living conditions described here compare with Martin and Grandpa's living situation. *(Possible responses: The Sioux were a free-roaming people; Martin and Grandpa seem to live in one place most of the time. The Sioux lived in teepees, Martin lives in a comfortable house, and Grandpa lives in a shack on a reservation. Grandpa has less money than Martin's parents have.)*

HISTORICAL INSIGHT

The Sioux

The Sioux Indians descend from immigrants who, in prehistoric times, crossed the Bering Strait between Siberia and Alaska. Over time, different bands of these Stone Age hunters eventually spread across the North American continent. Before Columbus came to America, the Sioux lived and traveled in the eastern half of the continent. During the 1700s, they crossed the Missouri River into the Great Plains and settled near the Black Hills of South Dakota.

French explorers gave the name *Sioux* to the people who called themselves the Lakotas. There were seven large Sioux tribes, called the Seven Council Fires. Over the centuries, these tribes developed different dialects and spread across large areas of the country. In the mid-1700s, the Sioux acquired horses that Europeans had brought to the New World. The horses enabled the Sioux to hunt buffalo and transport their tepees and other belongings on *travois*, platforms supported by harnesses made of two poles. Buffalo were as important to the

Frame of Sioux steam lodge, Standing Rock Agency, 1905. State Historical Society of North Dakota. Photo by Francis Densmore.

Sioux as horses because they supplied the Sioux with almost everything they needed.

One of the most important rites, or ceremonies, among the Sioux was the vision quest undertaken by a young boy entering manhood. A boy began a vision quest by purifying his body, soul, and mind in the hot steam of a sweat lodge. Then he was taken to a special place to sit alone for up to four days, waiting for a vision that might help him decide his future. This ordeal of fasting and enduring the elements took great courage and strong faith.

During the 1800s, the Sioux battled white settlers and buffalo hunters, as well as the U.S. Army and government, to save the land, the buffalo, and the Sioux way of life. By 1885, the 50 million buffalo that had roamed the plains in 1850 and had been the Sioux's main source of food had all but disappeared. By the late 1800s, the free-roaming Sioux were forced to give up their way of life and live on reservations, where many have remained to this day.

Mini-Lesson Study Skills

PARAPHRASING Tell students that when they paraphrase, they rewrite something in their own words. Explain that a paraphrase usually is about as long as the original passage.

Students should follow these steps when they paraphrase:
1. Find the main idea.
2. List supporting details.
3. Simplify the language.
4. Revise the paraphrase.

Application Invite students to paraphrase a paragraph or two from the Historical Insight feature, "The Sioux." Then have students work with partners to revise their paraphrases. Invite volunteers to share their work with the class, showing how they restated the main ideas in different words.

RESPONDING
OPTIONS

FROM PERSONAL RESPONSE TO CRITICAL ANALYSIS

REFLECT 1. What thoughts do you have at the end of this story? Describe them in your notebook and then share them with a partner.

RETHINK 2. Do you think Martin's life will be different because of his experiences with his great-grandfather? Explain your answer.

3. Do you admire Grandpa? Explain why or why not.

Thematic Link 4. Do Martin and his great-grandfather show courage? Give reasons for your answer.

RELATE 5. Think about the relative you described for the Writing Connection on page 285. What connections can you make between your experiences with your relative and Martin's experiences with Grandpa?

6. What difficulties do you think Native Americans face in the effort to pass down their traditions? Give examples drawn from "The Medicine Bag," the Historical Insight, and your own knowledge.

Multimodal Learning
ANOTHER PATHWAY

Imagine that Martin must write an essay about a person he admires, and he chooses to write about Grandpa. With a partner or a small group, draft the essay that Martin might write, using details from the story to help you. When you have finished your essay, share it with your classmates.

QUICKWRITES

1. Imagine that Martin has grown up and has a son of his own. Write the **dialogue** that they might have as Martin passes the medicine bag on to his son.

2. Write a **song lyric** that tells the story of Grandpa and his gift.

3. Write a **tale** that Grandpa might have told to Martin's friends.

4. Sneve's purpose for writing was to correct people's misconceptions of Native Americans. What misconceptions do you think she tries to correct in "The Medicine Bag"? Explain those misconceptions in a draft of an **editorial** for your school newspaper.

📁 *PORTFOLIO Save your writing. You may want to use it later as a springboard to a piece for your portfolio.*

LITERARY CONCEPTS

Exposition usually occurs at the beginning of a story or play. In the exposition, the writer introduces the main characters, describes the setting, and often establishes the conflict. What do you learn from the exposition in "The Medicine Bag" about the narrator, about the differences between his neighborhood and Grandpa's neighborhood, and about the narrator's internal conflict? If any of this information had been omitted, how might your understanding of the story have been affected?

THE MEDICINE BAG **295**

From Personal Response to Critical Analysis

1. Responses will vary.
2. Possible response: Yes, because Martin learned to be proud of his Sioux heritage. This might make him more secure and more appreciative of the cultures of others.
3. Possible responses: Yes, because Grandpa is brave and determined to pass on Sioux traditions. No, because Grandpa clings too much to the past.
4. Possible responses: Yes, Grandpa shows courage when he travels to visit his granddaughter's family; Martin shows courage when he accepts his heritage in the face of possible prejudice.
5. Responses will vary.
6. Possible responses: They face poverty and exclusion; many leave the reservation and integrate themselves into mainstream society, losing their ties to their heritage.

Another Pathway

Students should plan collaboratively to ensure their essays have unity, coherence, and a consistent voice. Appoint an integrator to combine group members' ideas and reasoning into a single position that everyone can support. You may also wish to appoint a seeker of justification to assess story details.

Rubric

3 Full Accomplishment Students fully explain Martin's reasons for admiring Grandpa.

2 Substantial Accomplishment Students partly explain why Martin selected Grandpa as a role model.

I Little or Partial Accomplishment Students are unable to explain why Martin considers Grandpa praiseworthy.

Literary Concepts

Possible responses: Martin feels love and tenderness for Grandpa but is also ashamed of him. Martin lives in comfortable circumstances in a suburban neighborhood; his great-grandfather, in reduced circumstances on a reservation in South Dakota. If this information had been omitted, you might not understand the importance Grandpa places on passing down the family traditions to Martin.

QuickWrites

1. Before students write, they should reread the dialogue in which Grandpa passes on the medicine bag to Martin. Tell students to think about how Martin's life will be different from Grandpa's and how that would affect the dialogue.

2. Encourage students to use rhythm and rhyme to make their lyrics melodic.

3. To help students capture Grandpa's "voice" in their tale, guide them to choose words that Grandpa might have used. Suggest that students reread dialogue in which Grandpa takes part and study his diction.

4. Remind students that an editorial is a persuasive essay. While it should appeal to reason, emotion, or ethics, it also should be free from errors in logic and reasoning.

The Writer's Craft

Creating Dialogue, pp. 320–322
Short Story, pp. 78–85
Supporting Opinions, pp. 144–151

Literary Links

Possible response: Both selections are about the relationship between an elderly Native American and a much younger person. The poem is much shorter than the story and concerns only a single conversation. Sokoya and Grandpa are both spiritual people. Grandpa has come to say goodbye to his family; Sokoya believes that Athabaskans do not need to say goodbye.

Across the Curriculum

Geography *Cooperative Learning* Have students find out more about the locations of reservations in the United States today. Divide students into small groups of three or four. Each group can select either a region or a tribe for the focus of their research. Students can create historical maps that show where Native Americans formerly lived and where they were forced to go to live on a particular reservation. Groups can use their maps to create classroom displays.

ADDITIONAL SUGGESTIONS

Social Studies *Belief Systems* Have students find out more about the belief systems of the Sioux or other Native American groups. If possible, have students contact local Native American organizations or local Native Americans to interview or invite to class as guest speakers.

History *AIM* Have students research the American Indian Movement (AIM). Ask students to find out how this organization developed and what its goals are. Have students conduct research on the group's activities in the 1970s and its clashes with the Federal Bureau of Investigation (FBI), especially in South Dakota (Wounded Knee and Ogala). Helpful sources include history books, autobiographies by AIM members, and documentary videos.

LITERARY LINKS

What similarities and differences are there between this story and the poem "There Is No Word for Goodbye" on page 115? Compare Sokoya with Martin's great-grandfather. What are their feelings and attitudes?

Sokoya's feelings and attitudes

Martin's Grandpa's feelings and attitudes

How Sokoya and Grandpa's feelings and attitudes are alike

ALTERNATIVE ACTIVITIES

1. Present an oral or written **report** on Native American reservations. Include information on the schools, laws, government, housing, population, and social conditions of reservations today.

2. Choose three or four small objects that you think represent your life or your destiny. Make a **medicine bag** for them, complete with a string or rope. Explain the significance of the objects to a group of your classmates.

3. Put together a **picture book** of Sioux crafts or objects. On each page, explain the meaning and purpose of each object.

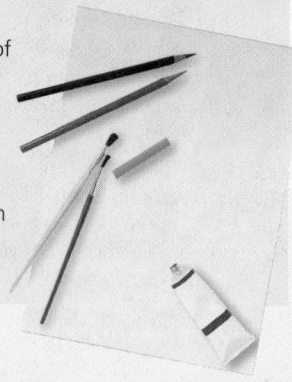

ART CONNECTION

Look at the reproduction of Hubert Shuptrine's *The Tribesman* on page 290. What are your impressions of its subject? How would you compare these impressions with your impressions of Martin's great-grandfather?

Detail of *The Tribesman* (1982), Hubert Shuptrine. Montgomery (Alabama) Museum of Art, Blount Collection. Copyright © 1982 Hubert Shuptrine, all rights reserved.

Alternative Activities

1. Suggest that students look to computer or print encyclopedias, on-line sources, and almanacs for information. Guide students to arrange their information in a logical manner.

2. Encourage students to select objects that are important to their lives, but respect students' privacy. Remind students that they do not have to reveal anything that would make them feel uncomfortable.

3. Students should do careful research to make sure that their illustrations are accurate.

WORDS TO KNOW

EXERCISE A Using your understanding of the boldfaced words below, write the letter of the word or phrase that best completes each sentence.

1. Martin's **descendant** would be born (a) the same year as Martin, (b) before Martin, (c) after Martin.

2. If Martin greeted Grandpa **reluctantly,** his manner would show (a) excitement, (b) a lack of enthusiasm, (c) bitter anger.

3. The **confines** of a reservation might be shown by (a) lines on a map, (b) photographs of daily life, (c) the tired faces of residents.

4. If Grandpa did not want to appear **unseemly** for an important occasion, he might put on (a) work clothes, (b) old worn clothes, (c) good clothes.

5. Grandpa's **fatigue** is most obvious when (a) he decides to take a bus trip, (b) he collapses, (c) he tells stories of his past glory.

EXERCISE B Draw a visual representation of one or more of the Words to Know. For example, you might portray something you find *unseemly* or draw a family tree that shows the *descendants* of your ancestors.

VIRGINIA DRIVING HAWK SNEVE

1933–

Virginia Driving Hawk Sneve grew up on the Sioux Rosebud Reservation in South Dakota in a family she describes as "secure, warm, and loving." "I never realized that I was an Indian," she reports, "until I went to college at South Dakota State University. It was a shock to realize I was different. People expected me not to speak English well and to wear feathers and beads."

Sneve began to write as a way of correcting people's misconceptions of Native Americans. Her first book, *Jimmy Yellow Hawk,* was awarded the Interracial Council for Minority Books for Children Award. The award gave her the confidence to continue writing. Since then, she has gone on to write 11 more books as well as book reviews and magazines articles. "The Medicine Bag" is based on the experience of a friend whose grandmother left her reservation for the first time to visit her family in Minneapolis.

Sneve writes in the summer and works as a counselor at Rapid City Central High School in South Dakota during the school year. She also has worked to promote coverage of Native American issues by the Corporation for Public Broadcasting.

Exercise A
1. c
2. b
3. a
4. c
5. b

Exercise B
Accept all visual representations that reflect one or more Words to Know.

Reteaching/Reinforcement
• *Unit Three Resource Book* p. 20

VIRGINIA DRIVING HAWK SNEVE

The author's other books include *When Thunders Spoke* (1974) and *Dancing Teepees: Poems of American Indian Youth* (1989).

ART GALLERY
Sioux Indian Art Some of the Sioux artifacts on display in museums were made to be used in rituals; others were not. All, however, express aspects of traditional Sioux belief and culture. Both ritual and utilitarian objects are shown in these images.

Side A, Frame 49338

LASERLINKS
• *ART GALLERY*

THE MEDICINE BAG **297**

WHAT DO YOU THINK?

Reflecting on Theme

Refer students to the oral histories they transcribed before reading the selections in Part One. Have them compare and contrast their oral histories to Grandpa's history. Ask students to describe how both Grandpa and the person they interviewed showed courage. Invite volunteers to reread to the class the oral histories they wrote and then, as a class, discuss what courage means and the different ways it can be shown by different people.

OVERVIEW

Objectives

- To understand and appreciate a classic narrative poem about a heroic, tragic battle
- To examine and appreciate rhythm in a poem
- To express understanding of the selection through a choice of writing forms, including a news report and a dialogue
- To extend understanding of the story through a variety of multimodal and cross-curricular activities

Skills

THE WRITER'S STYLE
- Sound devices

LITERARY CONCEPTS
- Rhythm

SPEAKING, LISTENING, AND VIEWING
- Oral history
- Oral report
- Choral reading

Cross-Curricular Connections

HISTORY
- Crimean War

SOCIAL STUDIES
- Oral history

MATH
- Cost of war

ALTERNATIVE

Previewing

Students can choose partners and use the following prompts to preview "The Charge of the Light Brigade" orally.

Personal Connection

Discussion Prompts Discuss with your partner what you know about the giving and taking of orders in the military. As you read "The Charge of the Light Brigade," notice the poet's attitude toward obeying military orders.

 HISTORICAL CONNECTION
The Crimean War 1853–1856
The poem describes a brave but doomed attack by British cavalry during the Crimean War in 1854. Six hundred soldiers advance. Many fewer ride back. However, the soldiers' brave attack has not been forgotten, and their glory lives on in the memory of the British nation.

Side A, Frame 49344

POETRY

The Charge of the Light Brigade
Alfred, Lord Tennyson

PERSONAL CONNECTION Activating Prior Knowledge

What do you know about the giving and taking of orders in the military? Must all orders be obeyed? Can you think of any circumstances in which obeying military orders might have tragic results? Jot down your ideas in your notebook and then share them with a small group of classmates.

HISTORICAL CONNECTION Building Background

"The Charge of the Light Brigade" is a narrative poem inspired by a tragic event that occurred during the Crimean (krī-mē'ən) War, 1853–1856. This war was fought between Russia and a group of nations that included Great Britain. Russia eventually lost the war. On October 25, 1854, at Balaklava in southern Ukraine, the Light Brigade, a British cavalry unit, was ordered to charge Russian gunners at the end of a valley. The Light Brigade was armed only with swords. As the poem begins, Tennyson depicts the Light Brigade riding toward the Russian artillery.

READING CONNECTION Active Re

Noticing Rhythm In this poem, Tennyson recreates what it might have been like for British soldiers to charge the Russian gunners. He uses short lines and phrases to create a fast-paced beat, or rhythm, as he describes the sounds and sights of battle. As you read the poem for the first time, think about the soldiers and how they respond to a tragic situation. Then read the poem aloud several times, listening to its rhythm as you read.

Engraving of artillery emplacement from the Crimean War. Copyright © Archive Photos.

 **LASERLINKS**
- HISTORICAL CONNECTION

298 UNIT THREE PART 1: SHOWING COURAGE

PRINT AND MEDIA RESOURCES

UNIT THREE RESOURCE BOOK
Strategic Reading: Literature, p. 23

ACCESS FOR STUDENTS ACQUIRING ENGLISH
Reading and Writing Support

FORMAL ASSESSMENT
Selection Test, p 59
Test Generator

 **AUDIO LIBRARY**
See Reference Card

LASERLINKS
Historical Connection

The Charge of the Light Brigade

by Alfred, Lord Tennyson

Thematic Link: *Showing Courage* The soldiers show great courage when they ride into battle, realizing that the order to charge is a mistake that likely will cost them their lives.

Half a league,[1] half a league,
Half a league onward,  **A**
All in the valley of Death
    Rode the six hundred.
5 "Forward, the Light Brigade!
Charge for the guns!" he said:
Into the valley of Death
    Rode the six hundred.

    "Forward, the Light Brigade!" **I**
10 Was there a man dismay'd?
Not tho' the soldier knew
    Some one had blunder'd:
Theirs not to make reply,
Theirs not to reason why,
15 Theirs but to do and die:
Into the valley of Death
    Rode the six hundred.

Cannon to right of them,
Cannon to left of them,
20 Cannon in front of them
    Volley'd and thunder'd;
Storm'd at with shot and shell,
Boldly they rode and well,
Into the jaws of Death,
25 Into the mouth of Hell **B**
    Rode the six hundred.

---

1. **league:** a distance of about three miles.

THE CHARGE OF THE LIGHT BRIGADE **299**

Small sword and scabbard (about 1790).
The Hermitage, St. Petersburg, Russia.

Art Note

Small sword This sword, which is on display at the British Museum in London, dates from approximately 1790.

Reading the Art *Why do you think the person who made this sword engraved it in such detail? How would you explain why this weapon is etched with roses?*

CUSTOMIZING FOR
Students Acquiring English

• Use **ACCESS FOR STUDENTS ACQUIRING ENGLISH**, *Reading and Writing Support.*

I Explain that 19th-century poets often deleted the letter e in past participles such as *dismayed.* Let students know that this does not change the pronunciation.

STRATEGIC READING FOR
Less-Proficient Readers

Set a Purpose Have students read to find out what happened to the soldiers and how the poet wants them to be remembered.

Use **UNIT THREE RESOURCE BOOK**, p. 23, for guidance in reading the selection.

Literary Concept: RHYTHM

A Have volunteers read these lines aloud while other students tap out the beat that the recurrence of stressed syllables creates.

Literary Concept: IMAGERY

B Ask students to locate images in these lines and explain how they help readers visualize events. *(Possible responses: "Jaws of Death" and "mouth of Hell" appeal to the senses of sight, sound, and touch, creating a picture of destruction personified as a gnashing mouth.)*

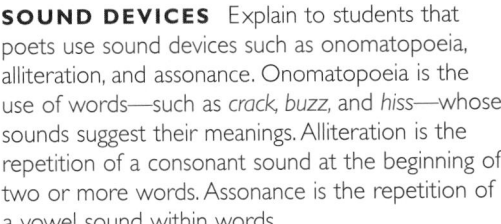

Mini-Lesson | **The Writer's Style**

SOUND DEVICES Explain to students that poets use sound devices such as onomatopoeia, alliteration, and assonance. Onomatopoeia is the use of words—such as *crack, buzz,* and *hiss*—whose sounds suggest their meanings. Alliteration is the repetition of a consonant sound at the beginning of two or more words. Assonance is the repetition of a vowel sound within words.

Application Have students identify each of the following sound devices from "The Charge of the Light Brigade."
1. Theirs but to do and die *(alliteration)*
2. thunder'd *(onomatopoeia)*

3. Not tho' the soldier knew *(assonance)*
4. Storm'd at with shot and shell *(alliteration)*
5. While horse and hero fell *(alliteration)*

The Writer's Craft

Sound Devices, pp. 316–317

Challenge students to debate the issue of a soldier's responsibilities to follow orders without question. Ask them if there are situations where a soldier has a responsibility to disobey orders. You may wish to discuss with students the Nuremberg Trials that followed World War II, which rejected the argument that soldiers following orders from their superiors cannot be held responsible for the war crimes they commit.

Art Note

The Charge of the Light Brigade by **Christopher Clark** The British painter Christopher Clark (1875–1942) focused on the confusion of the battle. Only the colorful rider in the center is shown clearly. In the rest of the scene, the figures are blurred by the smoke.

Reading the Art *How does the painter suggest that the charge of the Light Brigade is doomed? What details help create an impression of action and movement?*

Active Reading: EVALUATE

C Ask students to evaluate the effect of verbs such as *volley'd, thunder'd,* and *storm'd.* Guide students by using this model.

Think-Aloud Model *These verbs are very powerful and specific. They help me visualize the action clearly and recreate the sounds of battle in my imagination.*

D Have students explain the result of the battle. *(The British fought well, but many died.)* **Summarizing**

How does the poet want the Light Brigade remembered? *(as heroes)*
Finding the Main Idea

COMPREHENSION CHECK
1. About how many soldiers were in the Light Brigade? *(600)*
2. What weapons did they carry? *(sabers)*
3. What weapons did they face? *(cannons)*
4. Why did the men charge? *(They were following orders.)*

Detail of *The Charge of the Light Brigade* (early 1900s), Christopher Clark. Historical Pictures/Stock Montage.

Flash'd all their sabers bare,
Flash'd as they turn'd in air
Sabring the gunners there,
30 Charging an army, while
    All the world wonder'd:
Plunged in the battery-smoke,
Right thro' the line they broke;
Cossack and Russian
35 Reel'd from the saber-stroke,
    Shatter'd and sunder'd.[2]
Then they rode back, but not,
    Not the six hundred.

    Cannon to right of them,
40 Cannon to left of them,
    Cannon behind them
        Volley'd and thunder'd;
    Storm'd at with shot and shell,   C
    While horse and hero fell,
45 They that had fought so well
    Came thro' the jaws of Death,
    Back from the mouth of Hell,
    All that was left of them,
        Left of six hundred.

50 When can their glory fade?
    O the wild charge they made!
        All the world wonder'd.   D
    Honor the charge they made!
    Honor the Light Brigade,
55   Noble six hundred!

2. **sunder'd:** split; broken apart.

300 UNIT THREE PART 1: SHOWING COURAGE

Assessment **Option**

SELF-ASSESSMENT To help students assess their own work, have them ask themselves and then answer the following questions about the poem:
• How did the rhythm affect my understanding and enjoyment of the poem?
• The poet repeats phrases such as "Cannon to right of them, / Cannon to left of them, / Cannon behind them." What purposes do I think the repetition achieves?

• In what ways do the members of the Light Brigade suffer?
• Which images are particularly effective? Why?
• What would it have been like to have been a soldier in the Light Brigade?
• What did I like most about this poem?

RESPONDING
OPTIONS

FROM PERSONAL RESPONSE TO CRITICAL ANALYSIS

REFLECT
1. What images go through your mind as you read this poem? Discuss them with a partner.

RETHINK
2. Do you consider the soldiers of the Light Brigade to be heroes? Why or why not?

Close Textual Reading

Consider
- lines 11–12 of the poem
- how the soldiers fought
- the outcome of the tragic charge

3. How do you think the speaker of the poem feels about the Light Brigade? Why do you think so?

4. What if a number of the soldiers had refused to obey the order to charge? What do you think might have happened?

5. How might the Russian gunners have perceived the charge? Describe the attack from their point of view.

RELATE
6. Do you think a tragedy like this suicidal charge could happen today? Why or why not?

Multimodal Learning
ANOTHER PATHWAY

What do you think a soldier in the Light Brigade might have written his wife after the tragic charge? Write a letter in which a soldier describes the battle and expresses his views of a soldier's duty. Read your letter to the class.

QUICKWRITES

1. Imagine that you are a war correspondent at the Battle of Balaklava. Write a **news report** for the *Times* of London describing what you observe.

2. Imagine that you are a soldier who has survived the charge and that you happen to meet the poet Tennyson. Write the **dialogue** that you would have with Tennyson, presenting your response to the ideas and emotions that "The Charge of the Light Brigade" conveys.

📁 *PORTFOLIO Save your writing. You may want to use it later as a springboard to a piece for your portfolio.*

LITERARY CONCEPTS

Rhythm is the pattern of stressed and unstressed syllables in a line of poetry. You can understand the rhythm of a poem more clearly if you mark the stressed and unstressed syllables. The syllables you read with more emphasis (stress) are marked with ´. The weaker-sounding syllables (unstressed) are marked with ˘.

"Fórward, thĕ Líght Brĭgáde!

Chárge fŏr thĕ gúns!" hĕ sáid:

Working in pairs, copy the first stanza of this poem into your notebook. Then mark the rhythmic pattern of each line, as shown in the example.

From Personal Response to Critical Analysis

1. Possible response: A blur of action and loud noises.

2. Possible responses: Some students may say that they are heroes because they nobly followed orders and endangered their lives in battle. Other students may say that they are not heroes because they foolishly followed orders that they knew were a mistake.

3. Possible responses: He feels that they deserve to be honored or admired for their bravery, as shown in the final lines of the poem.

4. Possible responses: The other soldiers might have followed their lead and many lives could have been saved. The mutineers might have been shot by their officers and even more lives would have been lost.

5. Possible responses: The Russians might have admired the soldiers' patriotism and bravery. The Russians might have judged them suicidal fools.

6. Responses will vary. Some students may point out that in any age military disasters occur, claiming many lives.

Another Pathway

Direct students to page 669 in *The Writer's Craft* for the correct letter format. Remind students to use first-person point of view.

Rubric

3 Full Accomplishment Students provide an accurate description of the battle and clearly state the British soldier's views about duty.

2 Substantial Accomplishment Students explain the battle but may not fully explain the soldier's sense of responsibility.

1 Little or Partial Accomplishment Students cannot describe the battle or express the soldier's point of view.

Literary Concepts

The first stanza might be scanned as follows:

Hálf ă leágue, hálf ă leágue,

Hálf ă leágue ónwărd,

Áll ĭn tħe válleў ŏf Déath

Róde tħe síx húndrĕd.

"Fórwărd, tħe Líght Brĭgăde!

Chárge fŏr tħe gúns!" hĕ sáid:

Ínto tħe válleў of Déath

Róde tħe síx húndrĕd.

QuickWrites

1. Tell students to begin by writing a lead paragraph that states *who, what, when, where, why,* and *how.* The details should then be arranged from most to least important.

2. Make sure students use the correct punctuation with the dialogue. Students may either support or challenge the views that Tennyson presents in the poem.

 The Writer's Craft

Informing and Defining, pp. 122-129
Creating Dialogue, pp. 320–322

Possible responses: Both Nessan and the soldiers risked their lives. Nessan did so from a belief in justice, whereas the soldiers did so from devotion to duty. Students may argue that Nessan's courage was greater, because she was so young, or that the soldiers' courage was greater, because they knew their fight was futile.

Across the Curriculum

History Students can consult an on-line or print encyclopedia for information. Suggest that students include pictures and other visuals to make their oral reports more dramatic and effective.

Social Studies *Cooperative Learning* Encourage groups to contact their local veterans organizations. Tell students that they should explain the goals of the project to the people they wish to interview and obtain permission from them before conducting and tape-recording the interviews. You may wish to direct students to collected oral histories of soldiers available in print or in documentary videos.

ADDITIONAL SUGGESTIONS

 Math *Cost of War* Have students select any five wars, such as the Crimean War, the Civil War, World War I, World War II, and the Vietnam War, and use an encyclopedia or almanac to find out which one was the most devastating in terms of loss of life. Students can show their results in a bar graph. Caution students to make sure that the numbers given in their sources represent the same categories (i.e., all numbers are total casualties or all numbers are just United States casualties).

ALFRED, LORD TENNYSON

Tennyson wrote "The Charge of the Light Brigade" after reading a newspaper account of the battle. Historians believe the tragedy was caused by rivalry between two stubborn British commanding officers. His words, "Theirs but to do and die" have become synonymous with the idea of following orders unquestioningly.

Multimodal Learning

ALTERNATIVE ACTIVITIES

1. Present a **choral reading** of the poem. Tape-record sound effects, such as the booming of cannon or the neighing of horses, to accompany the reading.

2. Research the weapons used at the Battle of Balaklava. Then create a **poster** that presents drawings of these weapons and captions describing their use.

3. Design a **video game** that if played skillfully, allows a player to move a soldier of the Light Brigade safely through the charge. Write a summary of the game, indicating several right and wrong moves that a player might make.

LITERARY LINKS

How would you compare the courage shown by the Light Brigade with the courage shown by Nessan in "The Chief's Daughter" on page 259?

ACROSS THE CURRICULUM

 History Research the Crimean War, and then present an oral report that answers the following questions: What were the causes of the war? Which countries fought against the Russians? Who was Lord Cardigan? Who was known as "the Lady with the Lamp," and why was she famous? What happened to the surviving members of the Light Brigade?

Social Studies: *Cooperative Learning* Working with a group of classmates, compile an oral history in which former soldiers express their views about a soldier's responsibilities and the consequences of following or disobeying orders. Try to interview at least three former soldiers. One member of the group might prepare questions for the interviews, another member might conduct the interviews, a third member might tape-record them, and a fourth member might provide a commentary on the taped interviews.

ALFRED, LORD TENNYSON

Even today, Alfred Tennyson is one of the most well-known poets in English literature. The fourth son in a family of 12 children, Tennyson grew up in Somersby, England. In 1827, he and his brother Charles published a collection of poems titled *Poems by Two Brothers*. When this collection drew favorable notice, Alfred felt encouraged to continue writing.

In 1833, Tennyson's best friend, Arthur Henry Hallam, died suddenly. Overwhelmed with grief, Tennyson did not publish anything for the next ten years. In 1836, he fell in love with Emily Sellwood, but poverty forced the couple to postpone marriage. In 1850, Tennyson's luck changed. *In Memoriam*, a collection of 133 poems in memory of Hallam,

1809–1892

became hugely popular, as did his poems about King Arthur and the Round Table. Financially secure at last, he was finally able to marry Emily Sellwood. Queen Victoria named him poet laureate, or court poet—a lifetime honor. As poet laureate, Tennyson wrote poems about national events. One of the poems he wrote was "The Charge of the Light Brigade."

Tennyson's mastery of rhythm and rhyme and his gift for using sound to support meaning helped make him one of the most popular poets of his time. He is buried in the Poets' Corner of Westminster Abbey.

OTHER WORKS "Break, Break, Break"; "Tears, Idle Tears"; *Idylls of the King* Extended Reading

---

Alternative Activities

1. Allow students time to rehearse and prepare thoroughly before they present their choral reading.
2. Students can consult history books and reference texts such as encyclopedias for information.
3. You may also wish to encourage students familiar with a simple program such as Q-Basic to program their video game on a computer so others can play it.

from **Susan Butcher and**

THE IDITAROD TRAIL

by Ellen M. Dolan

Illustrations by John Sandford.

OVERVIEW

Objectives

- To promote independent active reading
- To apply and practice skills learned in previous selections
- To provide an opportunity to assess students' performance through an alternative assessment instrument

Reading Pathways

- Invite students to read the selection independently and take notes in their reading logs.

- Have students choose partners and do a paired reading.

- Encourage small groups of students to do a choral reading, choosing parts for each student to read.

- Evaluate how well students can read, interpret, discuss, and write about the selection on their own by using the Integrated Assessment for Unit Three, located in the Alternative Assessment booklet. Administer the assessment at the end of the unit after students have read all the selections and completed all the writing that was assigned. Set aside two class periods, or about two hours, for the assessment.

In January, in the year 1925, the "Black Death" struck two children in Nome, a gold-rush town on the northwest coast of Alaska. "Black Death" was the northern name for diphtheria, a deadly disease. Its name alone terrified parents, for it was often young children who were infected. Symptoms of the disease were a sore throat and fever. These could quickly lead to rapid heartbeat, difficult breathing, choking, and soon . . . death.

THE IDITAROD TRAIL **303**

PRINT AND MEDIA RESOURCES

UNIT THREE RESOURCE BOOK
Strategic Reading: Literature, p. 27

FORMAL ASSESSMENT
Selection Test, p. 61
Part Test, pp. 63–64
■ Test Generator

ALTERNATIVE ASSESSMENT
• Unit Three Integrated Assessment, pp. 13–18

ACCESS FOR STUDENTS ACQUIRING ENGLISH
Selection Summaries

■ **AUDIO LIBRARY**
See Reference Card

■ **INTERNET RESOURCES**
McDougal Littell Literature Center at http://www.hmco.com/mcdougal/lit

SUMMARY

During the harsh winter of 1925, a doctor in Nome, Alaska, fears that there may be an outbreak of diphtheria. His supply of vaccine is limited. The safest way to get more vaccine to Nome is by dog sled from Nenana, more than 600 miles away. The area's best mushers are recruited to help transport the serum in dog-sled relays along the treacherous Iditarod trail in frigid weather. The efforts of Leonhard Seppala, with his lead dog Togo, and Gunnar Kaasen, with his lead dog Balto, are especially heroic. Thanks to the extraordinary work of the drivers and dogs, the vaccine reaches Nome in only five days. Many children's lives are saved.

Thematic Link: *Showing Courage* The men and sled dogs show great courage in braving the Arctic winter to transport a vaccine to Nome, Alaska.

Curtis Welch was the only doctor in Nome, but fortunately he was a good one. Dr. Welch had seen no signs of the "Black Death" for many years. Now he recognized its telltale white spots in the children's throats and knew it was back. Diphtheria spread quickly. More than fifteen hundred people, many of them children, were at risk.

In addition to the children, Dr. Welch was especially worried about the Indians in the town and nearby villages. They had not yet built up immunity to white people's diseases and would likely be the first ones to succumb to the infection. Except for trappers and fishermen, the natives had few disturbances in the North until 1898. Then their entire world changed.

In the late 1800s adventurers searching for oil accidentally found gold near Resurrection Creek in southern Alaska. Prospectors continued the search north and west and made several more strikes. Then in 1898 they discovered a bonanza of a field on the beach at Cape Nome.

Gold! Much gold! The word spread quickly, and thousands of hopeful adventurers raced to get a share of the prize. Almost thirty thousand prospectors arrived in Nome, set up a jumble of tents on the beach, and eventually mined $2 million in gold.

By 1925 the rush was over. Many of the successful miners had become worthy citizens, most of the disappointed prospectors had left, and the

Two Eskimo boys with handcrafted Eskimo baskets in Teller, Alaska, 1904. The Bettmann Archive.

population of Nome was reduced to fifteen hundred. Nome became an orderly frontier town in place of a wild dangerous settlement filled with thieves and murderers. There were stout timber family houses on the side streets. And several main streets were lined with offices and shops offering supplies and services of all kinds: hardware, groceries, laundry, banking, lodging, barbers, lawyers, a post office, Town Council and Health Board offices, and a hospital.

The hospital was a large, two-story building, but Dr. Welch decided not to admit the diphtheria patients. He kept them isolated in their homes and treated them there one at a time. This would help contain the disease. But the only really effective way to stop an epidemic from spreading through the entire town was to vaccinate people against it. The doctor had a small amount of vaccine, or serum, but it was five years old—possibly useless—and would not go far. He must find more.

He went to the mayor, George Maynard, and the Town Council to ask for help. They recognized the emergency and immediately sent a wireless message to the territorial governor, Scott Bond, in Juneau. He in turn telegraphed requests for serum to hospitals and clinics in the Alaska Territory and the states.

At last doctors from a hospital in Anchorage, Alaska, almost one thousand miles southeast, answered. They found 300,000 units of the serum among their supplies. It was, however, the middle of winter in the frigid North. How should they ship the serum?

This was a difficult problem. There were three ways to get from Anchorage to Nome: by sea, by air, or by combined train/dogsled on land. Winter in Nome was so cold that the Bering Sea froze in rippling waves of ice. So no ship could get up the coast from Anchorage to Nome until the spring thaw. The second choice, by air, was risky. There were only two small single-engine biplanes near Fairbanks, Alaska, but they had been dismantled and stored for the winter. The third choice was a three-hundred-mile journey by train from Anchorage to Nenana, a town near Fairbanks, and then a six- or seven-hundred-mile sled-dog drive along a U.S. mail and supply route through the desolate, forbidding country in the Alaskan interior.

Many of the officials thought that one of the planes, reassembled, was the best answer. But it had an open cockpit, and its pilot had never flown at night or in January's subzero temperatures. If the plane iced up or crashed, both the pilot and the serum could be lost. On the other hand, it normally took almost a month to complete a dogsled journey from Nenana to Nome. It was a difficult choice.

Then the two sick children died in Nome and more were ill. The governor made his decision; it would be sled-dog teams on the land route.

> It normally took almost a month to complete a dogsled journey from Nenana to Nome. It was a difficult choice.

This trail through the mountains and tundra of the interior had once been used by Athapascan and Inuit peoples. Then the U.S. government marked, excavated, and maintained it as a route for mail and supplies to serve a network of gold-rush towns. The trail took its name from one of these towns, Iditarod. Along the route was a series of roadhouses and cabins, each spaced about a day's journey from the next.

Governor Bond sent out an appeal for volunteers. He needed sturdy drivers and fast dogs. Members of the Northern Commission Company, which managed the trail, knew where to find them. Within two days, the plans were complete and the teams were in place. Some of the drivers and the dogs waited in the cabins and shelters along the trail. Many of these men were regular drivers on the mail route. The rest were all experienced mushers who either owned or borrowed strong dogs. They would relay the serum from musher to musher until it reached Nome.

The word "musher" is a corruption of the French-Canadian verb "marcher," meaning "to march" or "to go." In the early days, sled-dog drivers' word for their animals to move forward was "mush." "Musher" became part of the frontier vocabulary as the term for a person who drove sled dogs.

At the hospital in Anchorage on January 27, doctors carefully packed the vials of serum. They wrapped them in several layers of quilting and

Diphtheria is a bacterial infection caused by the Klebs-Löffler bacillus, named after Edwin Klebs, the German doctor who discovered it in 1883, and Friedrich Löffler, the German scientist who isolated it in 1884.

The bacteria attack the mucous membranes in the mouth, nose, and throat. Within a week, the bacteria can create a false membrane that can block the air passages. In some cases, doctors have to operate to prevent the patient from suffocating.

The serum used to vaccinate children against diphtheria was synthesized by Pierre Roux and Emil von Behring in 1894. Before their discovery, nearly a third of the people who contracted the disease died; in some epidemics, nearly all the victims succumbed.

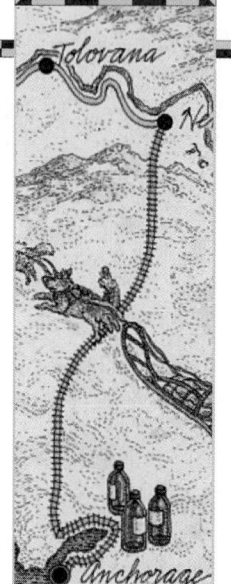

then canvas to protect them against breakage and cold. They included written instructions on how to warm the serum along the route. This compact, twenty-pound package could make the difference between life and death for children one thousand miles away. They rushed it to the train station, put it in the hands of conductor Frank Knight, and watched as Engine No. 66 pulled out.

As the serum traveled north from Anchorage, "Wild Bill" Shannon, an experienced musher, waited in Nenana with nine dogs. It was dark and very cold when the train arrived. "Wild Bill" took the package of serum, tied it to his sled, and called up his dogs. With a "hike" to the team and a swish of the sled runners, the serum was on its way across the Alaskan interior.

Leonhard Seppala and his dog team, October 12, 1928.
AP/Wide World Photos.

The next day Leonhard Seppala left Nome with twenty dogs and started south to meet the relay at a halfway point. His goal was the town of Nulato, 250 miles down the trail from Nome on the frozen Yukon River. Because of his fine reputation as a sled-dog racer, Seppala had been the first to be pressed into service by members of Nome's Health Board. At this time, he was the most famous man in Alaska. Driving his fastest lead dog, Togo, Seppala had won every important sled-dog race in the North. Twelve-year-old Togo, a small Siberian husky, was to be his leader again on this—the most important race of all.

Meanwhile "Wild Bill" faced a number of problems. The temperature had dropped to fifty degrees below zero. Speed was important, but he could not push his team too hard. The dogs' lungs might frost from breathing heavily in the

Multicultural   Perspectives

SLED DOGS The first settlers in Alaska, the Eskimo, found that sled dogs were the most useful means of transportation in the frigid climate. Part wolf, part domesticated dog, these sturdy animals have a furry, thick outer coat and a dense, waterproof inner coat that enables them to survive the freezing air and water. Their flat feet, also cushioned in fur, are suited for traveling over snow drifts and crusts of ice. To the Eskimo and some non-native settlers, the dogs were not only pets but a vital part of the household.

Arctic air. To protect his own lungs, Bill breathed only through his nose. The bitter wind howled and hurled snow in his face. The trail was a blur.

Bill stopped once to rest the dogs and then quickly moved on. Fifty-two miles out of Nenana, he reached the first relay cabin. He was exhausted, but the serum was still safely tucked in his sled. He gave it to the driver waiting at Tolovana and then went inside to rest.

Musher after musher took the precious package. They went over icy patches, up mountain slopes, down into valleys. Most of the cabins were about thirty miles apart. At many of them, the musher brought the serum in to warm it before continuing. The relay went on through the night into the day and the next night.

On January 29, Edgar Nollner waited in a dark cabin at Whiskey Creek, close to the halfway point. Suddenly he sat up. Bells! Was he hearing things? He ran to the window and found that it was Bill McCarty, who had tied sleigh bells to his dogs, coming in from the Ruby relay cabin. Mushers, either by choice or in some towns by law, often tied bells on their lead dogs to warn people they were coming up behind them. Edgar had not expected to hear Bill's bells for several days, but he wasted no time. He took the serum and started north along the frozen Yukon River.

The temperature was forty degrees below zero with a wind chill of sixty below. Edgar drove straight into the wind as the trail wound through desolate country. He brought the serum to his brother, George, at Galena, and George went on to Bishop Mountain.

THE IDITAROD TRAIL **307**

Alaska, the 49th state, takes its name from an Aleut word meaning "great land" or "that which the sea breaks against." Alaska's area constitutes nearly 20 percent of the area of the continental United States. In 1867, Secretary of State William Seward purchased the land from Russia for $7.2 million. Although the cost broke down to about two cents an acre, Seward was ridiculed, and the transaction was called Seward's Folly. In 1880, when the United States took the first census, there were 33,426 Alaskans, nearly all native people. The Gold Rush of 1898 more than doubled the population.

In 1968, scientists discovered huge deposits of gas and oil—10 billion barrels of oil, 27 trillion cubic feet of gas—near Prudhoe Bay on the Arctic Coast. Nine years later, the Trans-Alaskan pipeline was completed. Other Alaskan landmarks include Denali National Park, Mendenhall Glacier, and the Katmai National Park.

After Bishop Mountain, the Yukon curves and turns south. The temperature continued to drop. It was sixty degrees below zero when Charlie Evans started his stretch of the relay. Before long, he noticed that two of his dogs were actually starting to freeze. He put them in the sled, covered them, and ran in front of the team himself to encourage the other dogs.

Charlie pulled into Nulato early in the morning of January 30. In less than three days, the relay teams had reached the halfway point. This was much faster than anyone had expected. Seppala was still traveling south from Nome. Instead of waiting for him to arrive and lose precious time, Tommy Patsy took the serum and went on north to the next stop.

That day the relay runners passed through three more villages. On the following day, January 31, Harry Invanoff left Shaktoolik and started north into a blizzard. For five miles he struggled through the wind.

Suddenly a team appeared out of the swirling snow. It was Seppala. He was very surprised to see Harry—long before he expected to reach the relay. Seppala, Togo, and the team had already traveled 170 miles from Nome. But he knew, better than anyone, how urgent this relay was. His own young daughter had died earlier from diphtheria. Seppala turned the team around and immediately started back to Nome.

> Seppala prepared to start again, but could find no trace of a land trail. The wind continued to blow almost at hurricane force.

Seppala had been leaving several dogs at stops along the way south so there would be a fresh team for the return trip. He would need them soon. Just north of Shaktoolik, the coast curves in around frozen Norton Bay. If he went along the shoreline, he would lose several hours, perhaps even a day. But if he cut across the pack ice on the frozen bay, it could break loose and carry them out to open water. There would be no way back. Seppala had great faith in his leader and was willing to stake his life on Togo's instincts. He decided to risk the bay.

The wind was fierce, often blowing the sled over and keeping the dogs at a slow trot. Togo went steadily on. The storm had swept much of the snow off the trail and exposed the glare ice below. The dogs frequently slipped and skidded sideways, endangering Seppala's grasp on the sled. The light began to fade. As night approached, it was only Togo's remarkable sense of direction and Seppala's determination that brought them across the bay and back onto the original trail.

Once safely on land, Seppala fed his dogs and rested for the night. It had been an exceptionally long run—over one hundred miles on the trail. As they slept, yesterday's trail broke off and floated out to sea.

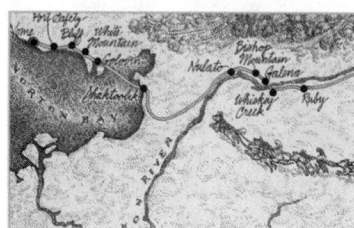

The next morning Seppala prepared to start again, but could find no trace of a land trail. The wind continued to blow almost at hurricane force. Seppala could not even see the front of his team through this total "whiteout." It was Togo who felt beneath the snow, found the trail, and started for the next relay point.

Downtown Ruby.
The Anchorage (Alaska) Museum of History and Art. (B74.5.146)

In Nome more children were ill. Although Seppala did not know it, the Town Council had decided to send extra teams to help bring in the serum on its final run to Nome. Three more teams driven by Charlie Olson, Ed Rohn, and Gunnar Kaasen left Nome. They were to space themselves in cabins along the last eighty miles of coastline.

Seppala and his team were battered and exhausted when they reached Olson, who was waiting at Golovin. Togo had led the teams all the way—250 miles. Olson transferred the serum, went out into fifty-mile-per-hour winds, and battled his way through treacherous weather for another twenty-five miles. At Bluff he passed the serum to Kaasen, who was to bring it on to Ed Rohn.

At the head of Kaasen's team was a handsome black dog, Balto. He was not as fast as Togo, but he was strong and steady. Although Seppala used Balto to haul freight, he did not choose him for his relay team. Kaasen had always thought Balto was a brave dog. He

would be proved right.

The wind was still roaring when Kaasen and the team started out. Snow piled in drifts around the dogs and covered them up to their stomachs in places. Balto pulled with all his strength and the rest of the team followed. The sled moved forward haltingly. Balto had found the trail again, and the relay continued.

Then, abruptly, Balto stopped. Kaasen shouted at him to go on, but the dog would not move. Kaasen ran forward to see what was wrong. Balto was standing in several inches of icy water. They were on the bank of the Topkop River, and the ice below was beginning to give way. Had they continued, the team and sled would have pitched forward into the river. Balto knew what he was doing. As soon as Kaasen dried the dog's feet, Balto made a turn and led the team around the river and back to the trail.

Once during the trip the sled overturned and the serum flew through the air. Blinded by the whirling snow, Kaasen could not find it. He grew frantic as he searched. Had it come all this way, just to be lost on the final fifty miles?

Desperately he felt around. It had to be somewhere in the snow. The dogs watched curiously as Kaasen yanked off his gloves, got down on his knees, and dug in the snow. He

Individual Activity
CREATE AN AWARD

The brave men and dogs described in this selection risked their lives to help save the lives of scores of children. For their heroism, these mushers and their sled dogs were honored in a number of ways, including the establishment of a Hall of Fame, the presentation of cash awards, and the erection of a bronze statue. Invite students to design another award to honor these courageous men and their dogs.

Teacher's Role Explain that the award should recognize the courage and accomplishment of these men and their dogs. Guide students to tap into their different learning styles as they plan and create the award. For example, musical learners could write a ballad; spatial or graphic learners could design a medal or a plaque; logical-mathematical learners could plan a medical-research fund; linguistic learners could write a formal speech.

Rubric

3 Full Accomplishment Students create awards that fully recognize the courage shown by the mushers and their dogs. They describe the award thoroughly or actually produce it.

2 Substantial Accomplishment Students create awards that somewhat recognize the mushers' courage but do not describe the award in detail or fully complete it.

1 Little or Partial Accomplishment Students create awards that do not satisfactorily recognize the achievement of the mushers and their dogs.

Cooperative Learning
HOLD A PRESS CONFERENCE

The dramatic Alaskan rescue operation captivated the entire country. People clamored for news of the mushers, their dogs, the trail, weather conditions, and the fate of the ill children. Invite students to imagine that they lived in 1925 and were in charge of informing the world of the success of the rescue mission. Have students work in groups to hold a press conference to announce the news of the successful mission.

Teacher's Role Guide students to gather details by referring to the selection and outside reference sources, such as almanacs, encyclopedias, and magazine articles about Alaska. Assign group roles to ensure that every student contributes fully to the group effort. A turn-taking monitor can make sure that group members share responsibilities, a recorder can write the script, and an accuracy coach can reread the selection and correct errors in any member's explanation. You may wish to videotape the press conferences so participants can view their performances later.

Rubric

3 Full Accomplishment Groups summarize the dramatic rescue mission completely, capturing the drama and excitement of the mission.

2 Substantial Accomplishment Groups summarize the rescue, but some details are missing or are out of chronological order.

1 Little or Partial Accomplishment Groups do not arrange events in chronological order, the presentation is somewhat flat, and important details are missing.

---

was afraid to move too far from the sled and lose his sense of direction. At last his hand closed on the package. This time he tied it very tightly to his sled. Balto moved on.

When they reached Port Safety, where Rohn was waiting, Kaasen did not see the light that usually signaled that a musher was inside. The storm had destroyed all of Nome's telegraph communications, so Kaasen did not know that the Town Council had called a temporary halt to the relay. Kaasen was not sure what to do—to stop or go on. At last he decided that even if Rohn was inside, he must be asleep. It would take him precious time to dress and harness his dogs. Balto and the team were going well, the weather was improving, and Nome was now twenty-five miles away. Kaasen decided to keep going.

Just after dawn on February 2, Balto led the final relay team into Nome. The dogs and Kaasen were half-frozen and bone tired. At 5:30 A.M. Kaasen knocked on Dr. Welch's door. When

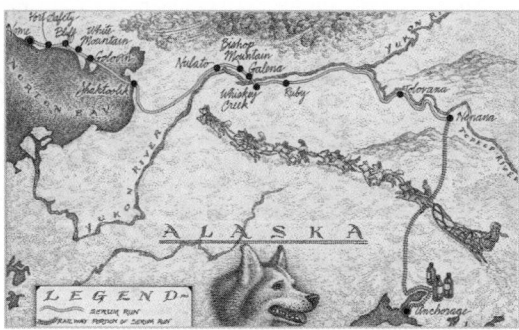

the doctor, thinking someone else was ill, answered it, he was astonished. It had taken just five days, seven and a half hours to complete a journey that usually took at least twenty-five days.

The doctor got busy. With a good supply of fresh serum, he was able to continue vaccinations. From then on, there were no new cases of diphtheria. Within three weeks, the quarantine was lifted and the people of Nome were safe again.

This dramatic rescue caught the attention of the entire country, and mushers and their dogs

became instant heroes. Medals, citations, and other rewards were heaped on the courageous men. Seppala, who was the best-known of the mushers, later moved to New England and continued to race his sled dogs for many years. Togo, somewhat lamed by the long relay, remained his favorite leader until he was retired at sixteen years of age. Seppala, who raced for over forty-five years and traveled an estimated

A statue of Balto stands in New York City's Central Park. It was erected in 1925, the year of the serum run. Sara Cedar Miller/Central Park Conservancy.

310   UNIT THREE   PART 1: SHOWING COURAGE

Multicultural Perspectives

WHAT'S IN A NAME? The town and trail name *Iditarod* comes from the Eskimo word *Haiditarod*, which means "distant, far place." For the first Eskimo settlers, this area deep in the Alaskan interior was very remote from the usual fishing places. Later, the gold miners dropped the h and a from the name, and the town became known as Iditarod.

250,000 miles by dog team, was the first to introduce the Siberian husky breed to the "lower forty-eight" states. In 1966 when the Dog Mushers' Hall of Fame was built near Knik, Alaska, Seppala and Togo were among the first chosen as members.

Kaasen and Balto, who made the final run into Nome, received $1,000 from the company that produced the serum plus movie offers and newspaper coverage around the world. Later that same year a bronze statue of Balto was placed in Central Park in New York City. It is still there. Children can sit astride his bronze back, pat his sides, and imagine a snow-covered trail in the distance.

A plaque under the statue says, "Dedicated to the indomitable spirit of the sled dogs that relayed antitoxin six hundred miles . . ." At the base of the statue is a salute to all brave sled dogs: "Endurance-fidelity-intelligence." ❖

ELLEN DOLAN

When Ellen Dolan (1929–) first read about the Iditarod race in 1986, she became eager to know more about it. Being an avid winter-sports fan ("I once had the opportunity to ski cross-country with a headlamp late at night to a ghost town near Aspen, Colorado. Spooky!"), Dolan dove into her new project, and the book *Susan Butcher and the Iditarod Trail* resulted.

Dolan grew up with her parents and three brothers in a suburb of St. Louis, Missouri. She spent many Sundays at family gatherings in her grandparents' home nearby. During those gatherings, she says, "My Irish uncles told me impossible stories and taught me to swing a baseball bat and shoot a basketball. My aunts played and sang beautiful music. I have loved stories, music, and sports ever since."

Although Dolan began her professional career as a concert pianist and also taught elementary school, her first love was writing. In an eighth-grade essay, she wrote that her goal was to become a writer; however, it was not until her children were in grade school that she fulfilled her goal. Dolan enjoys writing for young people and has often found inspiration in her students.

OTHER WORKS *The Republic of Ireland, Europe (World Myths and Legends II)* Extended Reading

Class Discussion

SHARING IDEAS

Teacher's Role Act as discussion facilitator by reading questions aloud for the class. Assign one student the role of turn-taking monitor to ensure that all students have a chance to express their opinions.

1. How did you feel about the mushers and their sled dogs? Explain. *(Students probably will be impressed by their perseverance.)*

2. Do you think that reassembling one of the airplanes would have been a better method for transporting the vaccine? Why or why not? *(Possible response: No. It might have been faster, but it could have been more dangerous and posed a greater risk of failure because of the weather and the open cabin.)*

3. Why do you think the men and dogs were able to transport the vaccine so quickly? *(Possible responses: They pushed themselves to the limit, because many lives were at stake; everyone cooperated and worked together as a team.)*

4. Do you think the children would have survived without the vaccine? Why or why not? *(Possible response: Even with a quarantine and the best of care, it seems unlikely that so many unvaccinated children would have survived, given diphtheria's high death rate and extreme contagion.)*

5. Would you have liked to have been a part of this rescue mission? If so, explain why and what part you would have liked to have played. If not, explain why not. *(Possible responses: No, because there was too much danger—from the cold and diphtheria. Yes, because it would have been exciting and fulfilling to have helped save so many lives.)*

ELLEN M. DOLAN

Ellen Dolan's first publication was a short story about two brothers who water-ski. She then wrote a humor column each month for a local newspaper. When that ended three years later, Dolan began writing a weekly social column, describing the parties, teas, and charity events in her community.

Dolan continued to write while raising four children. Her other publications include a series of retellings of children's classics, such as *The Ugly Duckling, Peter Rabbit, Henny Penny,* and *Little Red Riding Hood.* She has also retold a number of Native American legends and has written numerous magazine articles for children and young adults.

OVERVIEW

In the Guided Assignment for this section, students will write a paper that answers a big question about a story or a poem. By learning to interpret a selection, students will better understand the choices a writer makes in creating a piece of literature. As preparation for this assignment, The Writer's Style will help students understand how all the sentences in a paragraph work together to create unity. In Reading the World, students will apply what they have learned about interpreting a piece of writing to interpret a scene in the real world.

Objectives

- To understand how writers achieve unity in a paragraph
- To write unified paragraphs
- To write an interpretation of a work of literature
- To interpret a real-world situation

Skills

LITERATURE
- Analyzing character

WRITING AND LANGUAGE
- Using topic sentences
- Writing a conclusion

GRAMMAR AND USAGE
- Using subordinating conjunctions

MEDIA LITERACY
- Interpreting a scene from everyday life

SPEAKING, LISTENING, AND VIEWING
- Group discussion
- Peer response
- Group conferencing

CRITICAL THINKING
- Making inferences

ANSWER A BIG QUESTION

Characters and events in stories can be confusing. For example, why was Martin ashamed of his grandpa? Why did the Chief's daughter help Dara? The skills you use to find meaning in literature can help you make sense of the world around you as well. In the following pages you will

- study how writers express unified ideas
- find meaning in a selection you've read
- answer a big question about a real-world situation

The Writer's Style: Unity in Paragraphs How do writers present their ideas clearly? One way is by making sure that every paragraph has unity. A paragraph has unity when every sentence supports the same main idea.

Read the Literature

Notice how the sentences in each paragraph work together.

Literature Models

A **Topic Sentences**
A topic sentence states the main idea of a paragraph. What is the topic sentence of this paragraph? What details support it?

W e always had some authentic Sioux article to show our listeners. One year Cheryl had new moccasins that Grandpa had made. On another visit he gave me a small, round, flat, rawhide drum which was decorated with a painting of a warrior riding a horse. He taught me a real Sioux chant to sing while I beat the drum with a leather-covered stick that had a feather on the end. Man, that really made an impression.

Virginia Driving Hawk Sneve
from "The Medicine Bag"

B **Flow of Details**
In narrative paragraphs a clear flow of events gives a paragraph unity. How does each sentence in this paragraph connect to what follows?

B ill stopped once to rest the dogs and then quickly moved on. Fifty-two miles out of Nenana, he reached the first relay cabin. He was exhausted, but the serum was still safely tucked in his sled. He gave it to the driver waiting at Tolovana and then went inside to rest.

Ellen M. Dolan
from *Susan Butcher and the Iditarod Trail*

312 UNIT THREE: STEPPING FORWARD

Teaching Strategy: MODELING

The following models use carefully structured paragraphs. By learning to write topic sentences and to support them with details, students can create unified paragraphs.

A **Sneve** *Possible responses: The topic sentence is the first sentence of the paragraph. The rest of the sentences in the paragraph support this sentence by showing the various "authentic Sioux" articles or the narrator's reactions.*

B **Dolan** *Possible response: Each sentence shows another stage in Bill's journey. The sentences reflect the sequence in which the events occurred.*

PRINT AND MEDIA RESOURCES

UNIT THREE RESOURCE BOOK
Writer's Style, p. 31
Prewriting, p. 32
Elaboration, p. 33
Peer Response Guide, pp. 34–35
Revising and Proofreading, p. 36
Student Modeling, p. 37
Rubric, p. 38

GRAMMAR MINI-LESSONS
Transparencies, pp. 42 and 47

WRITING MINI-LESSONS
Transparencies, pp. 29–31

ACCESS FOR STUDENTS ACQUIRING ENGLISH
Reading and Writing Support

FORMAL ASSESSMENT
Guidelines for Writing Assessment

WRITING COACH

Connect to Science

Writers of newspapers, magazines, textbooks, instruction manuals, and similar works are trying to convey a great deal of information to readers. Why is unity particularly important in such writing?

Scientific Article

Sugar can drain energy, too. Sweet foods, such as candy bars and regular sodas, give quick energy because they provide a rapid supply of simple sugar, but the body burns this sugar very quickly. This often results in a lower energy level than before the food was eaten.

Terry Lykins
(Knight-Ridder Tribune Syndicate)
from "'Fuel Up' Your Body to
Cruise Through Stress"
Phoenix Gazette, June 8, 1994

Supporting Details in Paragraphs
What is the main idea? How do you know? How is this main idea supported by details?

Try Your Hand: Writing Unified Paragraphs

1. **Write a Topic Sentence** For each topic below, write an interesting topic sentence that could begin a paragraph.

   - a big event (getting glasses, performing, moving)
   - meeting somebody for the first time

2. **Add Events** To each of the topic sentences from the first activity, add three or four sentences that develop the main idea.

3. **Check Your Details** Revise the following paragraph so that all the sentences support the topic sentence. You may have to remove some sentences.

   Martin worries about his friends' opinions. My brother is the same way! Martin was afraid they wouldn't like his grandpa. But when a bunch of his friends met the old man, they liked him. Then Martin felt proud. I'm proud of my grandpa.

WRITER'S CRAFT

Using Topic Sentences

Main ideas are sometimes implied rather than stated. However, a good way to begin a unified paragraph is to state the main idea in a topic sentence. When you're writing a paragraph, a topic sentence can help you focus on the most important idea. A topic sentence also helps the reader understand what the paragraph is about.

APPLYING WHAT YOU'VE LEARNED
Write an interesting topic sentence for each main idea below.

1. a paragraph explaining why your new bike is fun to ride
2. a paragraph describing the best scene in a movie
3. a paragraph about a favorite place to hang out

Now review some of your earlier writing assignments. Choose a few paragraphs that need improvement. For each one, identify the main idea and write a topic sentence that states the main idea clearly. Then revise the paragraph to eliminate any unrelated ideas.

WRITING HANDBOOK

For more information on paragraphs, see pages 815–816 in the Writing Handbook.

Teaching Strategy: MODELING

C **Lykins** Encourage students to recognize that the first sentence expresses the main idea of the paragraph: Sugar can drain energy. They can infer this from the paragraph because the other sentences show how this occurs, thus supporting the main idea.

Try Your Hand

1. Sentences will vary. Here is a sample for each topic:
   - We always seem to be moving to a new home.
   - When Akiko and I first met, everything was just fine.

2. Guide students to make sure that all the sentences they add to each topic sentence are related to that sentence. Students should not add details that are unrelated to the topic sentence. Here is a sample for the first sentence: *We always seem to be moving to a new home. Actually, I like it. Every time, you get a new room and a new neighborhood. However, it can get kind of lonely at times.*

3. Guide students to identify the topic sentence (the first sentence). Here is a sample: *Martin worries about his friends' opinions. He was afraid they wouldn't like his grandpa. But when a bunch of his friends met the old man, they liked him. Then Martin felt proud.*

USING TOPIC SENTENCES Remind students that writing sentences that support a central idea produces a unified paragraph. The topic sentence states the central idea of a paragraph. Guide students to note that a topic sentence usually is found at the beginning of a paragraph, so that the reader immediately knows what the paragraph is about.

Applications Possible responses:
1. For looks and speed, my new bike is second to none.
2. At the climax, the monster turns out to be still breathing.
3. The skating rink is the place to be on Saturday afternoons.

Help students identify the topic sentences in their paragraphs.

Reteaching/Reinforcement
Writing Mini-Lessons transparencies, pp. 29–31

 The Writer's Craft

Topic Sentences, pp. 247–248 and 267

WRITING ABOUT LITERATURE

Interpretation

Sometimes after reading a story or poem you may be left with a question twirling in your mind. Learning how to answer your questions about what you read can help you make sense of the things that puzzle you in everyday life.

GUIDED ASSIGNMENT

D **Answer a Big Question** On the next few pages, you will look closely at a story or poem you have read. Then you will write a paper in which you focus on why something happened, what something means, or why the writer included something.

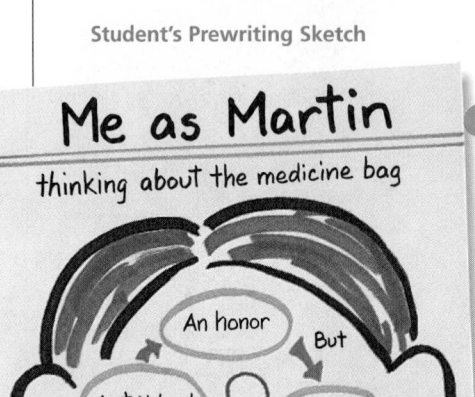

Student's Prewriting Sketch

❶ Prewrite and Explore

Choose a story or poem and review it. Which people or events puzzled or surprised you? Why? Record your questions and responses in your reading log. The following questions may help you begin to explore.

E
- Which parts did I have to read more than once?
- Do any characters do things that don't make sense?
- Does something happen that surprised me?
- Is the ending what I expected?

Decision Point Based on your notes, which of your **F** questions do you think would be the most interesting to explore further?

❷ Looking for Answers

How can you find an answer to your question? Completing one or more of the activities below can help.

- Reread passages that you have questions about. Look for clues that might provide answers.
- If you wish, discuss your question with a few classmates. They may have some helpful ideas.
- If a character has puzzled you, try asking yourself, If I were this character, what would I think and feel? You might want to arrange your ideas in a sketch like the one at the left.

Assessment ✓ **Option**

SELF-ASSESSMENT After students have completed the Looking for Answers discussion, they can assess their understanding by asking themselves the following questions:
- *What in the passage is interesting or puzzling?*
- *Why do I find the passage interesting?*

- *If I wanted to express to a friend why the passage is interesting or confusing, what would I say?*
- *Could I write a sentence that expresses what is interesting or confusing and why?*

③ Write and Analyze a Discovery Draft

In your discovery draft, be honest about what you do and do not understand. Try to work out what puzzles you. When you read your discovery draft, circle or underline the parts that seem most important or come closest to answering your questions about the story or poem.

Student's Discovery Draft

Martin doesn't want the medicine bag. So I don't get it when he says, "I knew I would have to take it." Why doesn't he just say no thanks? Why is he willing to take it?

I should tell that I thought the author left out information.

This reminds me. Something just like this happened to me, when my aunt gave me that ugly sweater. I nearly told her, "I'll never wear that." But before I could, she said, "Your grammy always wanted you to have it." That's when I knew I had to keep it—and wear it.

Now I understand Martin!

④ Draft and Share

Begin your next draft by expanding your discovery draft. You can use what you've learned about paragraphs to help you organize your ideas and unify your paragraphs. When you finish, feel free to invite another student to read your writing. Ask him or her to answer the questions below.

 PEER RESPONSE

- Can you tell me the main idea of my writing?
- Will you point out phrases, sentences, and ideas that you like and tell me why you like them?

SkillBuilder

 WRITER'S CRAFT

Writing a Conclusion
There are many ways to conclude, or end, a piece of writing. One way is to repeat the main idea and the most important points of your essay. When you write this type of conclusion, you help your reader remember the point of your essay. In the conclusion below, the first sentence states the main idea, and the following sentences sum up important points in the essay.

Since the author left open a very big question about Martin, I was interested in the story. To answer the question, I had to think hard about Martin. And eventually I found an answer. That turned out to be pretty exciting, because I figured out Martin's feelings about his grandpa and learned something about myself too.

APPLYING WHAT YOU'VE LEARNED
Decide whether the type of conclusion shown above could make a strong ending for your essay. Remember, if one sentence restates your main idea, the other sentences should use details to support the idea.

 WRITING HANDBOOK

For more information on writing conclusions, see pages 822–823 of the Writing Handbook.

WRITING ABOUT LITERATURE **315**

Writing Skill: ELABORATION

G The Discovery Draft provides an opportunity for students to think about their questions and sort through their answers. Students should be specific about which aspects they do and do not understand or that they find interesting. Encourage them to reread the difficult or interesting passages. Students can write about one part of their chosen selection at a time, providing details about their reactions.

Teaching Strategy: MANAGING THE PAPER LOAD

H Guide students to analyze their own Discovery Drafts. Have them read through their drafts and underline topic sentences. Tell them to write these sentences on a new sheet of paper. Then students can group the appropriate details under each topic sentence before they write the next draft.

 SkillBuilder **WRITER'S CRAFT**

WRITING A CONCLUSION Remind students that the main parts of an essay are the introduction, body, and conclusion. The introduction contains a thesis, the body contains the main points of the essay, and the conclusion sums up the essay.

Application Possible response: A conclusion like this could make a strong ending to my essay. I had the same experience. I was interested because of a problem in the story, too. I didn't know what to think at first. Then I figured out what I thought it meant.

Additional Suggestions Have students work in pairs to write conclusions. Students should exchange essays and see if they can discover each other's main idea. If they want, students can write conclusions for each other's essays.

Reteaching/Reinforcement

 The Writer's Craft

Writing Conclusions, pp. 278–280

I To evaluate and revise their inter-pretation of a poem or story, students should make sure that their papers have a beginning, middle, and an end and that the sentences in the middle paragraph support the idea stated in the topic sentence.

Teaching Strategy: MODELING

J Help students analyze the student's final draft, and show how it meets the Standards for Evaluation below. Point out that in the first sentence, the writer gives the title and author. The second paragraph shows why the student was interested in and puzzled by the story. It includes details and quotations from the story to show exactly what the student found puzzling. The final para-graph is a conclusion that shows the importance of the passage and the stu-dent's process in reaching a decision.

Standards for Evaluation

Have students review their stories for the following:

Ideas and Content
- gives the author, title, and brief summary of the literature
- explains what the writer thinks a passage means
- is supported with quotes, reasons, and other evidence
- shows why the writer thinks the passage is important

Structure and Form
- uses well-organized paragraphs and a clear organization
- includes transitional words and phrases to show relationships among ideas
- uses a variety of sentence structures

Grammar, Usage, and Mechanics
- contains no more than two or three minor errors in grammar and usage
- contains no more than two or three minor errors in spelling, capitalization, and punctuation

---

WRITING ABOUT LITERATURE

⑤ Revise and Edit

Readers need to understand how you arrived at your interpreta-tion. As you revise, explain your thinking by quoting the litera-ture and by referring to your own experience. When you are done, make a final copy. Reread it and reflect on what you learned by writing this paper.

What important infor-mation does the first sentence contain?

Student's Final Draft

The first time I read "The Medicine Bag" by Virginia Driving Hawk Sneve, I thought that the author didn't tell enough about Martin. After reading it again and giving it careful thought, I real-ized that I understood Martin very well.

When Martin's Sioux grandpa comes to stay at his house, Martin is very embarrassed by the way the old man looks and acts. After he learns that he will inherit his grandpa's medicine bag, he gets worried since his friends might tease him. I could feel that Martin didn't really want the bag, so I was shocked when he said, "I knew I would have to take it." Why didn't he just say no thanks?

What is the purpose of the second paragraph? How do the rest of the sentences support the purpose?

What does the con-cluding paragraph tell?

Since the author left open a very big question about Martin, I was interested in the story. To answer the question, I had to think hard about Martin. And eventually I found an answer. That turned out to be pretty exciting, because I figured out Martin's feelings about his grandpa and learned something about myself too.

Standards for Evaluation

An interpretive essay
- gives the author, the title, and a brief summary of the literature
- explains what the writer thinks a passage means
- supports ideas with quotations, reasons, and other evidence
- shows why the writer thinks the passage is important

Assessment Option

SELF-ASSESSMENT To help students assess their own writing, have them ask themselves the fol-lowing questions:
- *Is it clear which passage I am interpreting?*
- *Have I included a topic sentence for each middle paragraph?*

- *Do the other sentences in each middle paragraph relate to its topic sentence?*
- *Does my conclusion remind the reader of the main point of my essay?*

Grammar in Context

Subordinate Clauses In an interpretive essay, you'll need to show relationships between ideas or events. Subordinate clauses can help you do that. A subordinate clause, such as *when the rain stopped*, adds information but cannot stand by itself as a sentence. Notice how the student added subordinate clauses to connect events in this draft.

When
Martin's Sioux grandpa comes to stay at his house,

Martin is very embarrassed by the way the old man

After
looks and acts. he learns that he will inherit his grandpa's

medicine bag. He gets worried.

since his friends might tease him.

Try Your Hand: Using Subordinate Clauses Correctly

On a separate sheet of paper, revise the paragraph below so that it reads more smoothly. You might first want to look at the SkillBuilder about subordinating conjunctions at the right.

Grandpa's eyes were closed. He looked almost sad. So I turned my attention back to my book. I tried to read. I saw his sad face in my mind. I didn't want to look again. I knew I might cry. A minute passed. I couldn't concentrate. I looked up. I didn't think he'd be awake. I was wrong. He was looking straight at me.

SkillBuilder

 **GRAMMAR FROM WRITING**

Using Subordinating Conjunctions

 The first word in many subordinate clause is a **subordinating conjunction.** The conjunction links the clauses it introduces to the main clause to form a complete sentence. Here is a list of some commonly used subordinating conjunctions.

after	although	as
as if	as long as	because
before	if	so that
since	though	unless
until	when	where
while	wherever	

APPLYING WHAT YOU'VE LEARNED
Connect each pair of sentences with a subordinating conjunction.

1. The dog barked. He was scared of Grandpa.
2. He looked exhausted. He'd been walking for days.
3. I wanted to run into the street. I saw him.

 Check your draft to make sure you have used subordinating conjunctions effectively.

 GRAMMAR HANDBOOK

For more information on subordinate clauses, see pages 848 and 888 of the Grammar Handbook.

Teaching Strategy:
USING THE SKILLBUILDER

K To help students write subordinate clauses, teach the SkillBuilder on Subordinating Conjunctions at this time. It provides a list of words students can use to introduce their subordinate clauses.

CUSTOMIZING FOR
Less-Proficient Writers

L Tell students that subordinate clauses can never be punctuated as sentences because they do not express a complete thought. Encourage students to make sure that they attach each subordinate clause to a main clause to form a complete sentence.

Try Your Hand

Remind students that a comma comes at the end of a subordinate clause when the clause begins a sentence. Revisions of the paragraph will vary. Here is a sample:
When Grandpa's eyes were closed, he looked almost sad. So I turned my attention back to my book. I tried to read, although I saw his sad face in my mind. I didn't want to look again, as I knew I might cry. A minute passed. Since I couldn't concentrate, I looked up. Although I didn't think he'd be awake, I was wrong. He was looking straight at me.

PORTFOLIO

Invite students to review the conclusions they wrote and to write a note explaining the challenges they faced in writing an effective ending. Have students attach the note to their interpretive essays.

SkillBuilder **G** GRAMMAR FROM WRITING

USING SUBORDINATING CONJUNCTIONS Encourage students to refer back to this list of subordinating conjunctions to help them with their writing. Show them that a subordinate clause that begins a sentence is followed by a comma to set it off from the rest of the sentence. Advise students to note sentences that begin with a subordinating conjunction and to punctuate them with a comma.

Application Possible responses:
1. The dog barked because he was scared of Grandpa.

2. He looked exhausted since he'd been walking for days.
3. I wanted to run into the street when I saw him.

Additional Suggestions Have students continue with the following sentences. Make sure they use commas where necessary.
1. I waited. I was dying to go meet him.
2. Grandpa was going to move. I was going to wait.
3. The dog kept barking. It recognized Grandpa.

Reteaching/Reinforcement
Grammar Mini-Lessons transparencies, pp. 42 and 47

The Writer's Craft
Subordinate Clauses, pp. 565–566

READING THE WORLD

On pages 314–317, students interpreted a passage from a poem or story. They should also be aware that they interpret scenes from everyday life all the time. In this lesson, they can interpret a situation by applying the techniques they used to interpret a work of literature.

Critical Thinking: ANALYZING

M Students should note that the place is a farm stand in a rural area that is probably run by people who live in the house behind it. They will note the house is on fire and a crane from a fire engine is over it. They may be puzzled about what the firefighter is doing.

Media Literacy: GATHERING FACTS

N Students may infer that a fire started and that a truck came to put it out. There may be few people around because the house is empty or because the firefighters have warned people to leave. The firefighter may be investigating the farm stand to make sure no one is there and that it is not burning.

Speaking and Listening: GROUP DISCUSSION

O Have student groups notice as many details about the scene as possible. If they take notes, encourage them to group related notes about ideas and details together under headings such as "People," "Fire Service," "House," "Surroundings," and so on.

R E A D I N G THE WORLD

WHAT'S GOING ON?

Just as you may not understand a story or poem right away, often you can't interpret a situation at first glance.

View Suppose that you have just come upon this scene. In your notebook, describe the place, the people, and the actions. Make a note of anything puzzling or meaningful to you.

Interpret How might this scene have come about? Try to imagine why it is the way it is. Why are so few people around? Why is the firefighter not fighting the fire?

Discuss In a group, share ideas about the situation. Take notes if you wish. Use the SkillBuilder at the right to learn more about making inferences.

 CRITICAL THINKING

Making Inferences

When you're faced with a situation you don't understand, you can gather details about it and think about how they might fit together. Then you can make an inference about what is going on. When you make an inference, you fill in information based on your knowledge of the world. Making inferences can help you understand situations even when some information and details are missing.

APPLYING WHAT YOU'VE LEARNED

In a small group, discuss one or more of the following:

1. One day, a friend hobbles into class on crutches. By simply observing, what inference might you make? Why?
2. Gari plays in the orchestra and the marching band. He plays the drums, the xylophone, and the piano. On the basis of these facts, what can you infer about Gari?
3. What inferences did you make about the scene shown at the left? Why did you make them? Which of your questions about the scene did making inferences help you answer?

SkillBuilder CRITICAL THINKING

MAKING INFERENCES Encourage discussion about whether gathering details can follow a certain order. For instance, it may be interesting to ask students whether they first noticed a particular detail in the picture and then moved on to another one. Then ask students how they used these details to make inferences about the situation.

Applications Possible responses:

1. Groups will probably infer that the friend had some sort of accident.
2. Students may infer that Gari likes music and may have some talent as a musician. They may also speculate that Gari enjoys more than one instrument.
3. Students may have inferred that the firefighter is checking on the stand to make sure it is safe. They may have brought together a variety of evidence to infer this. A question that may have prompted this response is why the firefighter is down by the farm stand.

UNIT THREE
Part 2 Lesson Planner

TIME ALLOTMENTS SHOWN ARE APPROXIMATE. DEPENDING ON YOUR GOALS AND THE NEEDS OF YOUR STUDENTS, YOU MAY WISH TO ALLOW MORE OR LESS TIME FOR CERTAIN PORTIONS OF THE LESSON.

Table of Contents	Discussion	Previewing the Selection	Reading the Selection
PART OPENER **A CHANGE OF HEART** **What Do You Think?** page 320	**20 MINUTES** • Reflect on the part theme		
SELECTION **What I Want to Be When I Grow Up** page 322 EASY		**20 MINUTES** • PERSONAL CONNECTION • COMMUNITY CONNECTION • WRITING CONNECTION	**25 MINUTES** • Read pp. 322–28 (7 pp.)
SELECTION **Koden** page 332 EASY		**20 MINUTES** • PERSONAL CONNECTION • CULTURAL CONNECTION • READING CONNECTION: Reading dialogue	**30 MINUTES** • Read pp. 332–39 (8 pp.)
SELECTION **I Am a Native of North America** page 343 AVERAGE		**20 MINUTES** • PERSONAL CONNECTION • CULTURAL CONNECTION • WRITING CONNECTION	**20 MINUTES** • Read pp. 343–47 (5 pp.)
SELECTIONS **Direction** page 351 AVERAGE **Your World** page 352 AVERAGE		**20 MINUTES** • PERSONAL CONNECTION • LITERARY CONNECTION • WRITING CONNECTION	**5 MINUTES** • Read pp. 351–52 (2 pp.)
SELECTION **The Monsters Are Due on Maple Street** page 356 AVERAGE		**20 MINUTES** • PERSONAL CONNECTION • HISTORICAL CONNECTION • READING CONNECTION: Reading a teleplay	**50 MINUTES** • Introduce vocabulary • Read pp. 356–68 (13 pp.)

Writing	Exploring Topics	Prewriting	Drafting and Revising
WRITING FROM EXPERIENCE **Informative Exposition**	**25 MINUTES**	**30 MINUTES**	**80 MINUTES**

Time estimates assume in-class work. You may wish to assign some of these stages as homework.

Responding to the Selection

FROM PERSONAL RESPONSE TO CRITICAL ANALYSIS	OR	ANOTHER PATHWAY	LITERARY CONCEPTS	QUICKWRITES	ALTERNATIVE ACTIVITIES	LITERARY LINKS	CRITIC'S CORNER	THE WRITER'S STYLE	ACROSS THE CURRICULUM	ART CONNECTION	WORDS TO KNOW	BIOGRAPHY
50 MINUTES					**50 MINUTES**							
• Discussion questions	OR	• Paragraph	• Humor and exaggeration	• Prediction • Sequel • Editorial	✔	✔	✔		HEALTH	✔		✔
40 MINUTES					**50 MINUTES**							
• Discussion questions	OR	• List characters	• Characterization	• Adage • Character sketch • Letter	✔	✔	✔		SOCIAL STUDIES			✔
40 MINUTES					**60 MINUTES**							
• Discussion questions	OR	• Venn diagram	• Persuasion	• Definition • Speech • Poem	✔				SOCIAL STUDIES		✔	✔
40 MINUTES					**40 MINUTES**							
• Discussion questions	OR	• Role-playing a dialogue	• Metaphor	• Personal response • Poem • Essay	✔	✔						✔
50 MINUTES					**60 MINUTES**							
• Discussion questions	OR	• Role-playing a trial	• Dialogue and theme	• Summary • Stage directions • Proposal	✔	✔			SOCIAL STUDIES MUSIC		✔	✔

Publishing and Reflecting

30 MINUTES

A Mock Town Council Meeting

Overview

Students will investigate community problems, recommend solutions, and draft and present resolutions at a mock Town Council meeting.

PROJECT AT A GLANCE

The selections in Unit Three, Part 2 all concern change. Some are the result of long-fought public battles, while others concern more intimate changes of heart. For this project, students will learn about working for change as they investigate how lower-level government functions. They will examine their neighborhood or community to identify existing problems and possible solutions. They will draft a solution into a resolution and present it in a speech to a mock Town Council. Groups will debate the pros and cons of each resolution. Resolutions passed by the council may be put to all students for a "town" vote. If possible, the class will choose the best resolution to present to the actual legislative body of the community.

OBJECTIVES

- To identify community problems that are of interest to students
- To research different perspectives on and possible solutions to the problems
- To work together to prepare resolutions that address the problems
- To prepare and deliver speeches that support the resolutions
- To respond critically to resolutions presented by other groups

SUGGESTED GROUP SIZE

4–5 students per group

MATERIALS

- Community or neighborhood newspapers that call attention to local problems
- Videotape of legislative body discussing an issue (optional)

1 Getting Started

Arranging the Project

Decide how you will assemble the council officers for the mock meeting. You may want to ask three to five adults to act as the officers, or you can hold class elections or appoint the officers yourself. For their convenience, schedule any adults well ahead of time.

Gather back copies of local newspapers that deal with issues from your community. Also look for a "local" section of a metropolitan newspaper if you live in or around a large city. Often these inserts are distributed only in the area they cover. If a videotape of a local council session is not available, tape or ask someone else to tape a legislative session from a cable television channel. While this might not accurately reflect the outstanding issues in your community, students can get a flavor of the legislative process from the taped proceedings.

You might want to draft a resolution of your own, so students have a model to follow.

Arranging for a Mock Town Council Meeting

A large room is best for this meeting. The room should have tables at the front for council members, chairs for the audience, and a lectern from which students can address the council. Check the schedule for the room in school that would best suit your purpose and make reservations now.

2 Creating the Resolutions

Introducing the Project

Explain that students will be working in small groups to identify a problem in the community that interests them and to investigate possible solutions to the problem. They will then draft resolutions to be presented in front of a mock Town Council meeting.

Discuss some of the things students might be interested in helping to change in the community. Allow them to scan the newspapers to find issues, but encourage them to stay within realistic expectations. A resolution supporting world peace is commendable but somewhat out of reach. Help them focus on issues more along the lines of unsafe parks, unsightly public places, a lack of recreational facilities for teens, or a need for supervised day care in the area.

Have students view the videotape of a legislative session and note how the proceedings are organized. You might introduce them to *Robert's Rules of Order,* if they are not already familiar with the document.

This is the time to show students the model resolution you drafted, so they can follow the same general form and language.

Group Investigations

Divide students into groups of four or five. Groups should select a problem and investigate it thoroughly. Their investigation should include input from people directly involved with the problem, other adults in the community, and several of the students' peers. The investigation also should include research about how other communities have handled a similar problem. Groups can meet to discuss what point of view to take and to draft a resolution along those lines.

Creating a Project Description

At this point, ask students to hand in a copy of their resolution, along with some brief supporting information or reasons. You can make suggestions about amending the resolution, or discuss the reasoning and logic behind the supporting statements. Group members should each prepare a one-to-three minute statement of support that can be read aloud at the mock town meeting. Remind students to practice their speeches beforehand and to speak loudly and clearly when their turn comes.

OPTION 1: A MOCK TRIAL Invent a "lawsuit" in which a landowner has failed to keep his or her property clean, thus affecting the entire neighborhood's property values. Appoint a judge, jury, lawyers, and a defendant and hold a mock trial.

OPTION 2: A REAL TOWN MEETING Arrange for students to attend a real town meeting. Obtain a copy of the agenda for the meeting and ask groups to prepare statements about issues that interest them. You might let students actually read some statements if opportunities present themselves.

OPTION 3: STUDENT COUNCIL Arrange for the entire class to attend a meeting of your school's student council. By special arrangement, students might be allowed to address the council and offer opinions on the current subjects under discussion while watching and learning correct legislative procedure.

Don't allow students to become overwhelmed with this project. Urge them to keep the issues simple and the resolutions down-to-earth. At the same time, urge those fascinated with the process of change to continue their involvement beyond completion of the project.

3 Sharing the Resolutions

Even if you cannot act out an entire Town Council meeting, have groups present resolutions and arguments in class. The class can discuss the merits and drawbacks of each resolution or offer suggestions as to how they could be made stronger or more realistic. If any of the resolutions demonstrate special merit, you might forward them to the Town Council with an explanation of the project.

Assessing the Project

The following rubric can be used for group or individual assessment.

3 Full Accomplishment Students follow directions and present a clear resolution and supporting arguments for change in the community.

2 Substantial Accomplishment Students present a resolution and supporting arguments, but the reasoning is illogical, weak, or not sufficiently based in reality.

1 Little or Partial Accomplishment Students' resolution or argument is incomplete or does not fulfill the requirements of the assignment.

For the Portfolio
A copy of each group's resolution should be placed in individual students' portfolios, along with a draft of the supporting argument and your written assessment of the project.

Note: For other assessment options, see the *Teacher's Guide to Assessment and Portfolio Use.*

Cross-Curricular Options

SOCIAL STUDIES

Have students research and analyze how local, state, and federal legislative bodies pass laws. The methods can be compared and contrasted. Students can also compare such methods from other countries.

MATH

Ask students to find the ratio of the number of U.S. representatives to the population of the state they represent. Then have them decide whether or not this ratio demonstrates equal representation.

ART

Students can make a photo display illustrating their chosen problem.

SCIENCE

Have students research how animals such as wolves establish a social order.

Resources

Our Federal Government: How It Works by Patricia C. Acheson provides a general introduction to the government.

Pack, Band, and Colony: The World of Social Animals by Judith and Herbert Kohl investigates the social communities formed by wolves.

TOWN COUNCIL MEETING

5th period

Auditorium A

WHAT DO YOU THINK?

Objectives

The activities on this page can be used to
- introduce the theme of "A Change of Heart," since each activity is connected to one or more of the selections in Part 2
- create materials for personal portfolios that students can return to later for reconsideration or revision
- build an understanding of theme that can be returned to and revised as students progress through the unit

What made you change your mind?
You may wish to have students also consider how their impressions of people change as they come to know them better. (See "What I Want to be When I Grow Up," p. 321; "Koden," p. 331; and "The Monsters Are Due on Maple Street," p. 355.)

What's your direction in life?
Encourage students to think of ways in which they can make their public service announcements persuasive to other students. Students may want to watch or listen to examples of successful PSAs to get ideas for their own. You may wish to have students tape-record or videotape their public service announcements. (See "Direction" and "Your World," p. 350.)

How can you influence people's attitudes?
Students should first decide on a current issue that they think readers should know more about. Once they have chosen that issue, students can brainstorm possible images or photos that convey a message and grab readers' attention. (See "I Am a Native of North America," p. 342.)

A CHANGE OF HEART

WHAT DO  YOU THINK?

REFLECTING ON THEME

Did you ever learn something about a person that made you see him or her in a different light? Perhaps, then, you—like Ebenezer Scrooge in *A Christmas Carol*—have experienced a change of heart. Use the activities on this page to think about what causes a change of heart and what happens as a result.

What made you change your mind?

Did you ever form a first impression of someone only to find out later that you had misjudged the person? In your notebook, write about or sketch both your first impression and your later impression of such a person. What caused your impression to change?

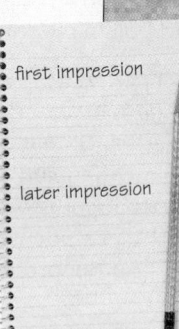

What's your direction in life?

Write a public-service announcement that encourages students to make positive changes, such as learning a new skill; getting involved in sports, the school band, or other activities; or doing volunteer work.

How can you influence people's attitudes?

Imagine that you are on the staff of a newsmagazine. You are planning an article on an important issue—such as the problems of the elderly or of homeless people. With a group, design a magazine cover to interest readers in the article.

Looking Back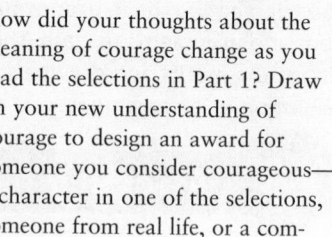

How did your thoughts about the meaning of courage change as you read the selections in Part 1? Draw on your new understanding of courage to design an award for someone you consider courageous—a character in one of the selections, someone from real life, or a composite of a number of character traits. Then write and deliver a brief speech, explaining the reasons for your choice.

Looking Back
Have students create charts that list their ideas about courage before and after reading the selections in Part 1. Students can use this information when designing their awards and writing their speeches.

PARENTAL INVOLVEMENT
Invite students to work with a parent or a relative to write lyrics for a song about courage. Students can choose to write about an imaginary person or a real-life individual. Encourage students to set their lyrics to a familiar melody. Students can then perform their songs for the class.

FICTION

What I Want to Be When I Grow Up
Martha Brooks

Activating Prior Knowledge
PERSONAL CONNECTION

Think about a time when you were in a crowd of strangers. Maybe you were strolling through a shopping mall during the holiday season, standing in line for a popular ride at an amusement park, or cheering for your favorite team in a packed arena. What might have led you to form a good impression of one of the strangers? What might have led you to form a bad impression? In your notebook, create a web like the one shown here, listing some of your reasons. Compare your reasons with those of your classmates.

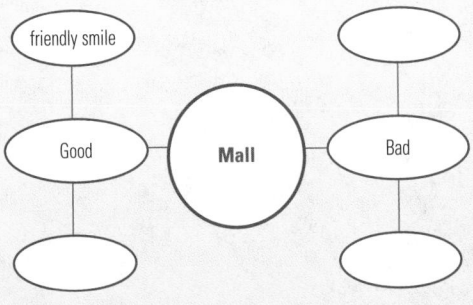

Building Background
COMMUNITY CONNECTION

In this story, the narrator is a junior-high-school student who forms impressions of strangers he observes while riding a city bus. In large cities such as New York City, Los Angeles, Boston, and Chicago—and in many smaller ones—taking a bus can be the most convenient, efficient, and economical way of getting from one place to another. Thousands of people from all walks of life are regular riders. For these people, traveling with strangers is part of the daily routine.

Passengers boarding a city bus. Copyright © Don Smetzer/Tony Stone Images.

Setting a Purpose
WRITING CONNECTION

In this story, the narrator's mother says that "taking the bus is an education." Think about times when you have ridden on a bus or used another kind of public transportation. In your notebook, briefly describe an experience on one of the rides that caused you to form impressions of strangers and learn something about people. Then, as you read, consider how the narrator forms impressions of strangers and what he learns about people.

PRINT AND MEDIA RESOURCES

UNIT THREE RESOURCE BOOK
Strategic Reading: Literature, p. 41
Reading SkillBuilder, p. 42
Spelling SkillBuilder, p. 43

GRAMMAR MINI–LESSONS
Transparencies, p. 33
Copymasters, p. 43

WRITING MINI–LESSONS
Transparencies, p. 36

ACCESS FOR STUDENTS ACQUIRING ENGLISH
Selection Summaries
Reading and Writing Support

FORMAL ASSESSMENT
Selection Test, pp. 65–66
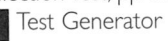 Test Generator

AUDIO LIBRARY
See Reference Card

OVERVIEW
Objectives

- To understand and appreciate a short story about a junior-high-school student's experiences and impressions
- To identify and appreciate humor and exaggeration in a short story
- To express understanding of the story through a choice of writing forms, including writing a prediction, a sequel, and an editorial
- To extend understanding of the story through a variety of multimodal and cross-curricular activities

Skills

READING SKILLS/ STRATEGIES
- Making inferences

THE WRITER'S STYLE
- Informal language

GRAMMAR
- Direct quotations

LITERARY CONCEPTS
- Humor
- Simile

SPELLING
- Compound words and contractions

STUDY SKILLS
- Paraphrasing

SPEAKING, LISTENING, AND VIEWING
- Dialogue
- Interview
- Oral report

Cross-Curricular Connections

GEOGRAPHY
- Guatemala

SOCIAL STUDIES
- Buses

HEALTH
- Alcoholics Anonymous

MATH
- Calculating duration

ALTERNATIVE
Previewing

Instead of creating a word web, students can choose partners and discuss their impressions.

Personal Connection

Discussion Prompts: *Think back to a specific time when you remember being in the midst of strangers and noticing one or more of them. Describe the time to your partner. If you need help getting started, try thinking about the following questions:*

- *Where were you?*
- *Were you alone or with a friend?*
- *What made you notice a stranger nearby?*
- *What were your impressions? Why do you think you formed them?*
- *Did you have any interaction with the stranger?*
- *If so, did your impressions change after the interaction?*

As you read, notice Andrew's impressions of the strangers he observes.

SUMMARY

Fourteen-year-old Andrew is having a hard time deciding what he wants to be when he grows up. He considers journalism, and he shows a journalist's skill at observation, as he describes his visits to the orthodontist and his encounters with a large, loud bus passenger named Earl. At first, Andrew thinks Earl is rude and obnoxious. However, when Andrew becomes ill on the bus, Earl helps him, and Andrew discovers that Earl is really a kind person who believes in helping others.

Thematic Link: *A Change of Heart*
Andrew experiences a deeper understanding of those around him—and of himself—as he looks beyond his first impressions.

Art Note

The Subway from ***Ruckus Manhattan,* 1975, by Red Grooms** The set designer Red Grooms (1937–) is noted for depicting vivid environments, where the viewer must step into the artwork to appreciate it. His caricatures reflect both careful observation and wild fantasy.

Reading the Art *What do you think the personalities of the characters shown are like? How would you describe the mood the artwork creates in you?*

CUSTOMIZING FOR
Students Acquiring English

- Use **ACCESS FOR STUDENTS ACQUIRING ENGLISH,** *Reading and Writing Support.*

- You may want to call students' attention to U.S. slang words and expressions, such as "gunk," "grossed out," "jerk," and "he wasn't dealing with a full deck."

Detail of *The Subway* (1976), Red Grooms. From *Ruckus Manhattan.* Mixed media, 9′ × 18′ 7″ × 37′ 2″, courtesy of Marlborough Gallery, New York. Copyright © 1995 Red Grooms/Artists Rights Society.

Assessment Option

INFORMAL ASSESSMENT Assess students' understanding of the story by asking them to rewrite a part of it as if it were told by one of the following characters: Andrew's mother, Earl, or a third-person narrator. Tell students to be sure to include details that suggest the new point of view.

Rubric

3 Full Accomplishment Students accurately rewrite a section of the story from the new point of view, keeping the plot development clear and the characterizations consistent.

2 Substantial Accomplishment Students are able to trace the plot events but have some difficulty retelling them from a new point of view.

1 Little or Partial Accomplishment Students have difficulty rewriting the story from a new point of view and fail to include some important events of the plot..

When I Grow Up

by Martha Brooks On the third Thursday afternoon of every month, I take my mother's hastily written note to the office where the school secretary, Mrs. Audrey Plumas, a nervous lady with red blotchy skin, looks at it and tells me I can go. Then I leave George J. Sherwood Junior High, walk down to the corner, and wait for the 2:47 bus which will get me downtown just in time for my four o'clock orthodontic appointment.

I hate taking the bus. It's always too hot even in thirty-below-zero weather. The fumes and the lurching make me sick. The people are weird.

Mom says with the amount of money she's forking out to give me a perfect smile I shouldn't complain. "Andrew," she says cheerfully, "taking the bus is an education. It's a rare opportunity for people of all types and from all walks of life to be in an enforced environment that allows them to really get a close look at one another." She then adds, meaningfully, "Think of it as research for your life's work." She goes on like that even though she can't possibly know what she's talking about because she's a business executive who drives a brand-new air-conditioned Volvo to work every day.

I made the mistake, a while ago, of telling her I want to be a journalist when I grow up. Out of all the things I've ever wanted to be—an undersea photographer, a vet for the London Zoo, a missionary in Guatemala— she feels this latest choice is the most practical and has **B**

CUSTOMIZING FOR
Gifted and Talented Students

Remind students that the author creates vivid characters by using only a few carefully chosen words. Have students look for and list the character traits of Andrew's mother, Dr. Fineman, Mrs. Blahuta, and "the suit" on the bus. Then, based on their impressions of these characters, have students extend these "portraits" by writing brief descriptions of each character.

STRATEGIC READING FOR
Less-Proficient Readers

Set a Purpose Invite students to share some of their ideas about careers and their impressions of adults in those careers. Then have students read to see how Andrew describes some of the adults around him.

Use **UNIT THREE RESOURCE BOOK**, p. 41, for guidance in reading the selection.

Critical Thinking: ANALYZING

A Ask students why they think the writer includes so many details in the first paragraph. (*Possible responses: The details help get the reader right into the story; the writer hopes to suggest that the narrator is especially observant.*)

Linking to Geography

B Guatemala is located in Central America, bordered by Mexico to the northwest, Belize to the east, and El Salvador and Honduras to the southeast. A Spanish-speaking country, Guatemala has an area of about 42,000 square miles (109,000 square kilometers) and a population of more than 9 million.

Mini-Lesson Reading Skills/Strategies

MAKING INFERENCES Explain to students that when they make inferences, they use information from their reading as well as prior knowledge to judge, reason, or draw a conclusion about something that is not stated directly.

Application Have students list the inferences they made about Andrew's feelings about various topics. They should base their inferences on their reading and their own experiences and record them in a chart like the one shown. If students are having difficulty, provide them with the first entry in the chart as an example.

Evidence	Inference
Andrew's mother says that riding the bus is an education, but she herself drives to work	Her statement may be insincere.

Reteaching/Reinforcement
• *Unit Three Resource Book*, p. 42

C Ask students to identify an example of humor in this passage. *(Possible response: the thought of Andrew choosing a career when he has barely outgrown sucking his thumb)*

Literary Concept: SIMILE

D Remind students that a simile is a comparison using *like* or *as*. Ask them to discuss how the simile "like floppy little doughnuts" heightens their visual image of the woman and her stockings. *(Possible response: By describing an image everyone can relate to, the simile helps to transport readers to the bus as if they themselves are seeing the woman.)*

CUSTOMIZING FOR

Students Acquiring English

I Make sure that students understand Andrew is exaggerating his discomfort when he says he wished he could die. Invite them to infer what this tells about his personality and to find another example of exaggeration later on this page. *(He is prone to dramatics: "The backs of girls' necks make me crazy.")*

STRATEGIC READING FOR

Less-Proficient Readers

E Discuss with students how Andrew's frequent changes in career plans and his attitude toward adults highlight his immaturity. Ask students how Andrew reacts to the women he deals with. *(They annoy him or cause him trouble. His mother nags him about career choices, a woman on the bus crowds him, and the receptionist scolds him.)* **Summarizing**

Set a Purpose Have students read on to find out what Andrew's first impression of the "pork chop man" is.

---

latched on to it like it's the last boat leaving the harbor.

She feels that, at fourteen, I have to start making "important career choices." This, in spite of the fact that my teeth stick out from having stopped sucking my thumb only six years ago.

On the bus last month, I happened to sit across the aisle from a girl with pasty white skin and pale eyes lined in some kind of indigo gunk. We were right at the front, near the driver. The bus was so full there was no escape. She kept smiling like she had an imaginary friend. Every so often she'd lean forward and go, "Phe-ew," breathing right on me. The woman beside me wanted the whole bench to herself and edged me over with her enormous thighs until I was flattened against the metal railing. (I can't stand older women who wear stockings rolled, like floppy little doughnuts, down to their ankles.) She then took the shopping bag from her lap and mashed it between her ankles and mine as a further precaution that I wouldn't take up any more room than I had coming to me. Hot, numb with misery, and totally grossed out, I closed my eyes and lost track of time. I went six extra stops and was fifteen minutes late for my appointment.

I was left staring at the pork chop man's thick, freckled neck.

The old lady who runs the orthodontist's office also seems to run Dr. Fineman, who only appears, molelike, to run his fingers along your gums and then scurries off to other patients in other rooms. This old lady doesn't like kids unless they are with a parent. The first few months I went with my mother. Mrs. G. Blahuta, Receptionist (that's the sign on this dinosaur's desk), smiled and told me what a brave boy I was. She even exchanged recipes with my mother. That was four years ago. This past time, when I arrived late and gasping because I'm slightly asthmatic, Mrs. Blahuta (the orthodontist calls her Gladys; she has purple hair) scowled and asked me to come to the desk, where I stood, wishing I could die, while she shrilled at me about inconsiderate teenagers who think of no one but themselves and show so little responsibility and motivation it's a wonder they can dress themselves in the morning.

Shaking with humiliation, I sat down to wait my turn beside a blond girl with gold hairs on her beautiful tanned legs. She had been pretending to read a glamour magazine. Her eyebrows shot up as I sat down. She primly inched away and gave me her back like she was a cat and I was some kind of bug she couldn't even be bothered to tease.

On the trip home another gorgeous pristine-type girl swayed onto the bus two stops after mine. She sat down in the empty seat in front of me and opened the window I'd been too weak from my previous ordeals to tackle. This life-saving breeze hit my face, along with the sweet, stirring scent of her musky perfume. Gratefully I watched the back of her neck. (She wore her hair up. The backs of girls' necks make me crazy.)

After about five more stops a sandy-haired man, whose stomach rolled like a pumpkin over the belt of his green work pants, got on the bus and sat down beside this breath-stopping girl. She didn't even seem to know he was there, and with great interest stretched her long neck to get a close look at a passing trailer truck loaded with pigs. Their moist snouts poked at whatever

324 UNIT THREE PART 2: A CHANGE OF HEART

Mini-Lesson | **Study Skills**

PARAPHRASING Explain to students that when doing research for a report they should paraphrase, or rewrite a passage in their own words. The paraphrase should be about as long as the original passage. Students should follow these steps when paraphrasing a passage: 1. find the main idea; 2. list supporting details; 3. simplify the language; 4. revise the paraphrase.

Application Tell students to use this skill to gather information about Alcoholics Anonymous for their oral reports under Across the Curriculum on page 330. Students might bring to class a reference source, paraphrase a passage from it, and then read the paraphrase to the rest of the class.

air they could get at and you could tell they were on their way to the slaughterhouse. (Why else would pigs be spending a day in the city?)

The sandy-haired man readjusted his cap that was almost too small for his very large head. "Look at all them sausages!" he exclaimed, laughing really loudly at his dumb joke. The girl kept right on looking at the pigs. I could have died for her, but except for her nostrils that flared delicately and her slightly stiffened neck and shoulders, she didn't appear to be bothered at all.

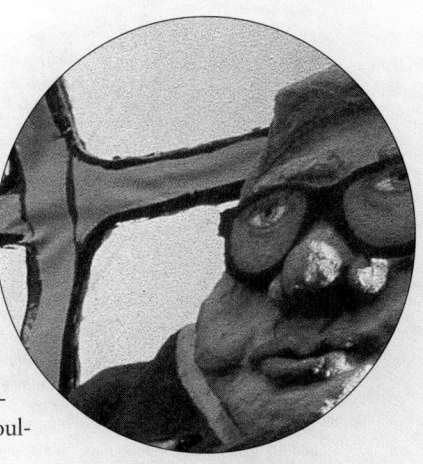

The man playfully nudged her. "Hey!" he chortled, in a voice that could be heard all over the bus. "You like pork chops?"

She turned from the pigs (I noticed her incredibly long eyelashes that were light at the tips) and stared straight at him. His face went into a silly fixed smile. "Excuse me," she said coolly, and got up to leave.

"Oh, your stop comin' up, little lady?" he bellowed as he got up quickly. Pulling at his cap brim, he let her past.

She walked about four steps down the aisle and moved in beside an expensively dressed Chinese lady with bifocals who looked suspiciously back at us, then frowned. I frowned at the fat man so she'd know it had been him, and not me, causing all the commotion.

I couldn't believe it when the man, calling more attention to himself, leaned forward and poked a business-type suit person! He said, in what possibly for him was a whisper, "Guess she don't like pigs." The suit person gave him a pained over-the-shoulder smile.

The man finally settled back. "I used to live on a farm. Yup. I did. I really did," he continued to nobody in particular because everybody near was pretending to look out of windows, or read, or be very concerned with what time their watches gave.

"Whew! It's hot!" He all of a sudden got up and reached over the suit person, ruffling his hair. "Oh sorry," he said. "Mind if I open this?" He tugged open the suit's window. The suit shot him a look that suggested he wasn't dealing with a full deck. Which he probably wasn't.

I prayed he would leave, but ten minutes later the girl of my dreams got off the bus. I was left staring at the pork chop man's thick, freckled neck.

His stop wasn't until one before mine. As we pulled away I watched him walk over and strike up a conversation with another complete stranger who was too polite to ignore him.

Like I said, you have to put up with some very weird people when you take the bus.

Today, I pleaded with my mother to drive me downtown. She lay on the couch popping painkillers because yesterday she fell and twisted an ankle and suffered a very small fracture as well. She isn't in a cast or anything and it's her left foot so she doesn't need it to drive with. When I asked her nicely for the second time, explaining that she wouldn't even have to get out of the car, she glared at me a moment and burst into tears. I don't understand why she's so selfish. I hope she gets a migraine from watching soap operas all day.

WHAT I WANT TO BE WHEN I GROW UP **325**

CUSTOMIZING FOR
Students Acquiring English

(2) Point out that while the sentence "Look at all them sausages!" is grammatically incorrect, it gives the reader a sense of the character's lively way of speaking. Invite students to identify another example of this character's incorrect use of language on this page. (*"Guess she don't like pigs."*)

Active Reading: EVALUATE

F Ask students why they think Andrew "couldn't believe" what the man did and why Andrew cares at all what the man does. (*Possible response: Andrew is surprised that anyone would violate the unstated rules about crowding or taking up too much space. He was probably afraid that the man would speak to him and he would be forced to respond.*)

Literary Concept: HUMOR

G Ask students if they think that the girl on the bus was really the girl of Andrew's dreams. Why does he call her this? (*No, it adds humor to the situation. By exaggerating his attachment to her, he suggests that the pork chop man's presence has been a huge obstacle in his path.*)

STRATEGIC READING FOR
Less-Proficient Readers

H Discuss how calling the passenger "the pork chop man" reflects Andrew's impression of the character.

• What is Andrew's first impression of the pork chop man? (*Possible responses: He is large, loud, weird, and silly, and he crashes in on people's personal space.*) **Summarizing**

Set a Purpose Ask students to read to find out whether Andrew's impression of this man changes in the story.

Mini-Lesson **Literary Concepts**

REVIEWING SIMILE Remind students that a simile is a comparison of two unlike things that have some quality in common. Similes make a direct comparison using words such as *like, as,* or *resembles.*

Application Have students identify examples of simile, listing each comparison and explaining how it adds humor to the story. For example, Andrew uses the simile "like a cat" to describe the way the girl shows him her back and suggests his insignificance.

❶ Ask students to notice the detail that Andrew uses to describe the receptionist. Invite students to rewrite this sentence, replacing the metaphor with a simile. (*Possible response: I tried to explain to the purple-haired receptionist, who seemed as ancient as a dinosaur, that I missed my bus on account of being kept late in science class.*)

CUSTOMIZING FOR

Students Acquiring English

③ Explain that *youse* is a colloquial (and grammatically incorrect) way of saying *you* (plural).

④ Ask students what word is missing from "Name's Earl." If necessary, explain that leaving off the first words of sentences is part of this character's informal, clipped, friendly way of speaking. Ask them to identify similar instances on the same page.

---

❶ Can you believe it? I was late again for my appointment. I tried to explain to the purple-haired dinosaur that I'd missed my bus on account of being kept late in science class. (I had to rewrite a test I'd messed up the first time because I was away sick the day the teacher told us to study for it and my friend Gordon, the jerk, was supposed to tell me and forgot to.)

Mrs. Blahuta said snidely that she was surprised I was only twenty minutes late and did I intend to put in an appearance at my next monthly appointment or would they all be kept in suspense until the final moment of the working day, which was five o'clock. Sharp!

She kept me until every last person, except myself, had been checked over. At five to five she ushered me in to the orthodontist as his last appointment for the day. He processed me as if I were some dog in a laboratory and then Gladys dismissed me by holding out my next month's appointment slip like it was a bone I'd probably bury.

I got out onto the street, saw my bus departing, and made a silent vow that for at least a month I wasn't going to speak to any person over the age of eighteen.

At five twenty-two I boarded my bus and all the seats were taken. As we got under way, I suddenly felt sick. I clung to the nearest pole while the bus lurched, braked, accelerated, and picked up three or four passengers at every stop. Heated bodies armed with parcels, babies, books, and briefcases pressed past me. Into his

microphone, the driver ordered everyone to the back. I didn't budge. When his voice began to sound as if it were coming from inside a vacuum cleaner, another wave of nausea overcame me and my hands, hot and wet, slipped down the pole.

I hate getting motion sickness. I'm sometimes so sensitive that just looking at, say, a movie of people going fast in a roller coaster can almost make me lose my last meal. Whenever I'm sick in the car, Mom says, "Fix your eyes on objects that are the furthest away. Don't look at anything that'll pass you by."

Remembering that, I turned to face the front of the bus. The furthest thing in my view was the pork chop man. As he was coming straight toward me, I shifted my gaze past his shoulder to a spot of blue that was, I guess, the sky. The bus took another shift and the sudden lurch swung me quickly around to where I'd been. I very nearly lost my battle with nausea to the skirts of a person wearing purple paisley.

Somebody gripped my arm, and said, "One of youse has to get up. This boy's going to be sick."

Immediately two people vacated their seats. Next thing I knew I was sitting beside a window with the pork chop man. He reached around behind me and tugged until wind hit my face.

"Hang your head out, now," he roared. "If you have to puke your guts out just go ahead and don't be shy." He patted my back in a fatherly way with one enormous hand while the other hung like a grizzly paw along the back end of my seat.

I did as I was told, breathed deeply for several seconds, and brought my head back in to have a look at him. I don't think I've ever seen such an enormous man. Up close, I realized he wasn't

326 UNIT THREE PART 2: A CHANGE OF HEART

Mini-Lesson Grammar

DIRECT QUOTATIONS Explain that a direct quotation is a restatement of someone's exact words. Instruct students to use quotation marks to show where the exact words of a speaker or writer begin and end. Quotation marks are not used with indirect quotations, which summarize or paraphrase what someone has said.

Application Have students label any indirect quotations and punctuate any direct quotes they identify in the following sentences.
1. Andrew said he wanted his mother to drive him to his appointment.

2. Please drive me to my appointment! Andrew pleaded to his mother.
3. Mrs. Blahuta told Andrew he would have to wait until the last appointment of the day.
4. Thanks, Andrew said to Earl. I'm not sure what would have happened if you hadn't helped me.

Reteaching/Reinforcement
• Grammar Handbook, anthology pp. 886–887
• *Grammar Mini-Lessons* copymasters p. 43, transparencies p. 33

really so much fat as there was just an awful lot of him. "Name's Earl," he said, solemnly.

"Thanks, Earl," I said. "I'm Andrew."

"Don't have to thank me, Andrew. I joined A.A. two years ago. Haven't touched a drop since. I remember how it felt to be real sick."

I wanted to explain that I wasn't a drinker, but was overcome by another terrible feeling that I might lose control. Earl said, "Hold on, kid," and shoved my head out the window again.

We didn't talk much after that. It wasn't until my stop was coming up that I realized he'd just missed his.

I pulled the buzzer cord and said, "You missed your stop."

"How'd you know that?"

"I noticed you when you were on the bus one other time," I mumbled, embarrassed.

Earl sat back and looked straight ahead. He looked like a man who'd been struck by a thought that was almost too big to handle.

The bus arrived at my stop and Earl hurriedly got to his feet to let me past. I stepped off the bus with him right behind. On the street he said, still amazed, "You noticed me?"

The bus fumed noisily on past us.

"Yeah. Well—there was this girl, first. You came and sat beside her . . ." I trailed off.

"You know," said Earl, "just between you and me, city people aren't friendly. They don't notice nothing. See that old lady, there?"

At the light, an old girl tottered off the curb and started to cross the street. She carried two plastic Safeway bags full of groceries.

Out of the corner of his mouth, in a lisping whisper, Earl informed me, "If she was to fall and hurt herself just enough so she could

still walk, not one person would stop and offer to help her home with those bags."

"That's true," I said, thinking that if they did, they'd probably turn around and help themselves to her purse.

We started across the street. I felt better, now that we were off the bus. I actually started to feel a little hungry. I wondered how I was going to say goodbye to Earl. I was afraid he might want to talk to me for a long time. He walked slowly and I felt obliged to keep pace with him.

We reached the other side and stopped on the sidewalk. All the while he kept going on about the time he'd taken some guy to emergency at the General Hospital. The guy had almost bled to death before they could get anybody's attention.

Without hardly pausing to breathe, Earl cornered me with his desperately lonely eyes and launched into another story. I made out like I was really interested, but to tell the truth I was thinking about my favorite TV program, which would be on that very moment, and about how Mom sits with me on the sofa, sometimes, while we eat our dinner and watch it together.

"Well," said Earl, too heartily, "I can see that you're going to be okay and I shouldn't keep you. Probably missed your supper, eh?"

He stuck out his hand, that massive freckled paw. Surprised, I took it and it surrounded mine in an amazingly gentle way.

"Thanks," I said again.

"Told you not to mention it," said Earl. "We've all got to help each other out, don't we, buddy? But I can see I don't have to tell you that. You're different. You notice things." ❖

Next thing I knew I was sitting beside a window with the pork chop man.

Mini-Lesson ✒ The Writer's Style

INFORMAL LANGUAGE Informal language differs from formal language in that it has a more casual tone and does not reflect strict rules of usage. Informal language is often used in casual writing, such as may be found in letters, magazines, and newspapers. It uses simpler words, short sentences, and contractions such as *you'll* and *she's*.

Application The dialogue in "What I Want to Be When I Grow Up" contains examples of informal

language. Have students rewrite the highlighted dialogue using formal language. Then ask students to discuss their impressions of the difference between informal and formal language.

Reteaching/Reinforcement
• *Writing Mini-Lessons* transparencies, p. 36

The Writer's Craft
Formal and Informal English, p. 311

Active Reading: EVALUATE

J Ask students what effect the use of Earl's name, rather than "pork chop man," has on their impression of him. *(Possible response: Now that the narrator calls him by name, Earl appears to be more human and less of a caricature, as he was previously portrayed.)*

Critical Thinking: ANALYZING

K Ask students what they think the writer means by stating that Earl looked "like a man who'd been struck by a thought that was almost too big to handle." *(Possible response: Earl was surprised and touched that anyone had noticed him.)*

Linking to Social Studies

L The word *bus* is short for *omnibus*, a Latin word that means "for all." The first bus developed was the steam-driven stagecoach, which was first operated in England in 1830. By 1915, buses were a form of transportation used in many countries.

Active Reading: CONNECT

M Andrew expresses fear that Earl might want to talk to him for a long time. Ask students who have had a similar experience to describe the situation to the class. You may wish to share the following thought process with students:

Think-Aloud Model *I remember a time when I was with someone who made me uncomfortable. I wasn't sure what to do. She wasn't a bad person, just someone I didn't feel like spending a lot of time with. Also, I was afraid that if I started talking to her, she would keep talking and not want to stop. Still, I felt kind of sorry for this person, so I didn't want to bolt right away.*

STRATEGIC READING FOR
Less-Proficient Readers

N Ask students to describe how Andrew's impressions of Earl have changed. *(Andrew now thinks that Earl is a kind, if lonely, person who is much more sensitive than he once thought.)* Drawing Conclusions

Ask students to discuss the merits and drawbacks of noticing details the way Andrew does throughout the selection.

COMPREHENSION CHECK

1. Why does Andrew ride the bus? *(to get to and from his orthodontist's appointment)*
2. How does Andrew feel about riding the bus? *(It makes him feel sick, and he thinks a lot of weird people ride the bus.)*
3. What seemingly obnoxious person does Andrew observe on his ride home on the bus? *(The pork chop man, Earl)*
4. How does this person help Andrew? *(by coming to Andrew's rescue when he gets motion sickness on the bus)*

INSIGHT

1. What do you think Andrew would think of the poet's ideas? *(Possible responses: After his encounter with Earl, Andrew might be inclined to agree with the poet's sentiments about caring for others.)*
2. What do you think is the main message of the poem? *(Possible response: If you assume you understand how something really is, you lose its mystery or the possibility of discovering something new. If you act as if you were born today, you will see things in a new way and relate to others differently.)*

AMADO NERVO

Amado Nervo (1870–1919) was one of Mexico's most highly regarded poets. His work, which includes poems, short stories, novels, and essays, often deals with the quest for spiritual truth and the meaning of existence. Nervo emerged as an independent and profound writer in his few years of work.

LITERARY INSIGHT

I Was Born Today
by Amado Nervo

Every day that dawns, you must say to
  yourself,
"I was born today!
The world is new to me.
This light that I behold
Strikes my unclouded eyes for the
  first time;
The rain that scatters its crystal drops
Is my baptism!

"Then let us live a pure life,
A shining life!
Already, yesterday is lost. Was it bad?
  Was it beautiful?
. . . Let it be forgotten.
And of that yesterday let there remain
  only the essence,
The precious gold of what I loved
  and suffered
As I walked along the road . . .

"Today, every moment shall bring
  feelings of well being and cheer.

And the reason for my existence.
My most urgent resolve
Will be to spread happiness all over the
  world,
To pour the wine of goodness into the
  eager mouths around me . . .

"My only peace will be the peace of others;
Their dreams, my dreams;
Their joy, my joy;
My crystal tear,
The tear that trembles on the eyelash of
  another;
My heartbeat,
The beat of every heart that throbs
Throughout worlds without end!"

Every day that dawns, you must say to
  yourself,
"I was born today!"

328   UNIT THREE   PART 2: A CHANGE OF HEART

Mini-Lesson   (T M)   Spelling

Compound word
down + town = downtown

Contraction
do + not = don't

COMPOUND WORDS AND CONTRACTIONS Words may be combined to form other words in several different ways. When two words are simply connected with no change in either word, the word formed is called a compound word. When an apostrophe is used to show that one or more letters have been omitted after two words are joined, the resulting word is called a contraction. Copy the examples shown on the chalkboard to share with students.

Application Ask students to create compound words or contractions from the boldfaced words in the following sentences.

1. Earl said **he would** be glad to talk to Andrew again.
2. Andrew waited in the **arm chair** as the clock ticked.
3. "**She is** the most beautiful girl **I have** ever seen," Andrew thought to **him self**.
4. "**I am** Andrew," he told Earl. "Thanks for all **you have** done."

Reteaching/Reinforcement
• *Unit Three Resource Book*, p. 43

RESPONDING OPTIONS

FROM PERSONAL RESPONSE TO CRITICAL ANALYSIS

REFLECT 1. Draw a sketch that conveys your impressions of Earl. Share your sketch with a partner.

RETHINK 2. At the end of the story, Earl says to Andrew, "You notice things." Do you think Andrew is more observant than most people his age? Support your opinion with evidence from the story.

3. Why, in your opinion, does Earl help Andrew when Andrew is suffering from motion sickness?

Close Textual **Consider**
Reading
  • what Earl reveals about his background
  • Earl's attitude toward strangers
  • your impressions of Earl's character

4. What do you think Andrew will do the next time he sees Earl on the bus? Give reasons for your answer.

RELATE 5. Review what you wrote for the Writing Connection on page 321. How does what Andrew learns about people compare with what you learned while taking public transportation?

6. Reread the Insight poem on page 328. What do you think Earl might say about the speaker's message?

LITERARY CONCEPTS

The quality that makes a piece of writing funny or amusing is called **humor.** Writers can create humor in many ways. One way is through the use of **exaggeration**—an extreme overstating of an idea, as when Andrew insists that he isn't going to speak to any person over the age of 18 for at least a month. Find other examples of exaggeration in this story. What makes each exaggeration humorous?

Multimodal Learning
ANOTHER PATHWAY

Working with a partner, discuss Andrew's attitude toward Earl at the end of the story. Then write a brief paragraph explaining whether Andrew's impressions of Earl change during the course of the story. Read your paragraph to the
Thematic Link entire class.

QUICKWRITES

1. Predict the career that Andrew will choose for his life's work. Support your **prediction** with evidence from the story.

2. Write a **sequel** to this story, in which Andrew and the "breath-stopping girl" meet and share their experiences as bus riders.

3. Mrs. Blahuta claims that teenagers are inconsiderate and selfish. Write an **editorial** that supports or refutes her opinion.

📁 **PORTFOLIO** *Save your writing. You may want to use it later as a springboard to a piece for your portfolio.*

From Personal Response to Critical Analysis

1. Students' sketches should reflect the narrator's description of Earl.

2. Possible response: Yes, his descriptions include tiny details, like the appearance of someone's stockings or neck. No, many people his age observe others carefully and notice things.

3. Possible response: Earl helps Andrew because he knows what it is like to feel sick and because he is not afraid to get involved with others.

4. Possible response: Because Andrew finds Earl embarrassing to be around, Andrew will probably acknowledge him but will be reluctant to strike up a conversation.

5. Possible response: We both learned that first impressions are sometimes wrong.

6. Possible response: Earl might think that the language was too flowery and formal, but he would agree that people should act lovingly toward one another.

Another Pathway

Encourage pairs to reread the final paragraphs of the story to look for any clues that suggest whether or not Andrew's impressions of Earl have changed. Each partner should read part of his or her paragraph aloud.

Rubric

3 Full Accomplishment Students write a concise paragraph, thoroughly explaining whether or not Andrew's impressions have changed.

2 Substantial Accomplishment Students have some difficulty explaining their opinion in a clear, concise paragraph.

1 Little or Partial Accomplishment Students' paragraphs do not clearly state and explain an opinion about Andrew's impressions of Earl.

Literary Concepts

Students may cite any of Andrew's descriptions of the people he sees on the bus or his experience at the orthodontist's office as examples of exaggeration. Students should understand that exaggeration often enlarges or overstates an idea to such an extent that it becomes amusing.

QuickWrites

1. Besides the career choices that Andrew mentions in the selection, have students consider other occupations that might suit someone so observant.

2. Students should reread the passage about the girl to make inferences about her personality. Remind them to try to capture Andrew's personality in their sequels.

3. Remind students that an editorial begins with a statement of opinion that is later supported with details and facts.

📁 **The Writer's Craft**

Short Story, pp. 78–85
Supporting Opinions, pp. 144–151

Literary Links

Possible response: Both relationships are between adults who have something to teach and younger people who have something to learn from them.

Across the Curriculum

Health *Cooperative Learning* Have students work in groups of three to research topics such as slogans associated with AA and similar organizations based on the principles of AA. One student should oversee and facilitate the group's research. Another student should record the group's research results, and the remaining student should present the group's findings to the class. Remind students to use their skills in paraphrasing as they gather information for their reports.

ADDITIONAL SUGGESTIONS

Math *How much longer?* Have students reread the first paragraph to determine how long Andrew has to ride the bus to get to the orthodontist. Tell students to assume he has a five-minute walk from the bus stop to the office. *(68 minutes, or 1 hour and 8 minutes)*

Art Connection

Possible response: Both are humorous exaggerations of other people.

MARTHA BROOKS

About her work Martha Brooks writes, "I try to be true to the characters I invent—listening to them, letting them tell their stories, and respecting the lives they live.... I always keep in mind, though, the aspects of healing and hope because life is full of possibilities."

ALTERNATIVE ACTIVITIES

1. What do you think Andrew might tell his mom about being helped by Earl on the bus? With a partner, improvise a **dialogue** for the class.

2. Conduct an **interview** with a journalist to find out about the rewards and challenges of a career in journalism and about the skills good journalists need. If possible, have someone videotape the interview, then show the video to your classmates.

ACROSS THE CURRICULUM

Health Earl tells Andrew that he has stopped drinking since joining AA, or Alcoholics Anonymous. Research this organization to learn about its origin and the support it provides recovering alcoholics. Share your research in an oral report.

LITERARY LINKS

Compare the relationship between Andrew and Earl with the relationship between Roger and Mrs. Jones in "Thank You, M'am" (page 147).

CRITIC'S CORNER

According to Gabriel Bonilla, a seventh-grade member of our student board, the title of this story "went perfectly with the last words." Explain why you agree or disagree with Gabriel's opinion.

ART CONNECTION

Look at the photograph of Red Grooms's set design for *Ruckus Manhattan* on page 322. How would you compare the artist's caricatures of people with Andrew's impressions of strangers?

MARTHA BROOKS

A playwright, novelist, and writer of short stories, Martha Brooks often writes from the teenage point of view: "I write fiction which is about that particular time in life when the senses are sharp and life is bewildering and pain and love have very blurry borders."

Born in Manitoba, Canada, Brooks began writing in 1972 but had to wait ten years for a publisher to accept her work. She says she persisted because she had learned how to cope with disappointment. Not only did she suffer from recurring bouts of childhood pneumonia, but she grew up on the premises of a tuberculosis sanatorium. "Tuberculosis in the 1950s was still a disease as serious as cancer or Acquired Immune Deficiency Syndrome (AIDS) is today," she says. "Children who grow up to be artists very often have unusual beginnings, so these were mine—surrounded by people who were fighting to cure, or be cured of, a life-threatening disease." Brooks believes that these experiences made her a sharp observer of the human condition: "I learned very early that failure, adversity, and unfairness are all part of living."

330 UNIT THREE PART 2: A CHANGE OF HEART

Alternative Activities

1. Remind each partner to use the following listening strategies as they enact their dialogue:
   - Show interest in what the speaker has to say.
   - Maintain eye contact with the speaker.
   - Respond to what the speaker has said; repeat a word or phrase if necessary to clarify understanding.

2. When students are preparing for their interviews, remind them to use questions that are open-ended and prompt discussion rather than questions that can be answered with a yes or no. Have students prepare questions ahead of time but suggest they also listen for answers during the interview that might lead them to other questions they have not prepared.

FICTION

Koden
Judith Nihei

OVERVIEW

Objectives

OVERVIEW

Objectives

- To understand and appreciate a short story about a character who expresses her individuality within a tradition
- To enrich reading by using active reading strategies
- To understand and appreciate characterization
- To express understanding of the story through a choice of writing forms, including an adage, a character sketch, and a letter
- To extend understanding of the story through a variety of multimodal and cross-curricular activities

---

Activating Prior Knowledge   *Setting a Purpose*

PERSONAL CONNECTION

What kinds of things do you do to show others the real you? In your notebook, create a web similar to the one shown here to record some of the ways in which you like to express your individuality. Then, as you read "Koden," think about the main character and the ways in which she expresses her individuality.

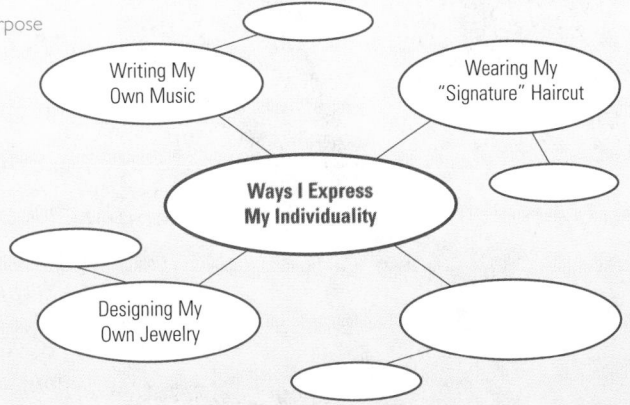

Writing My Own Music

Wearing My "Signature" Haircut

Ways I Express My Individuality

Designing My Own Jewelry

Skills

READING SKILLS/ STRATEGIES	GENRE STUDY
• Questioning	• Fiction: short story
THE WRITER'S STYLE	**SPELLING**
• Author's purpose and goals	• Hard and soft c and g
GRAMMAR	**SPEAKING, LISTENING, AND VIEWING**
• Antecedent agreement	• Storyboards
LITERARY CONCEPTS	• Oral report
• Characterization	• Oral history
• Point of view	

Cross-Curricular Connections

GEOGRAPHY	SOCIAL STUDIES
• San Francisco area place names	• Japanese funeral rites
	HISTORY
	• The life of Buddha

CULTURAL CONNECTION   *Building Background*

People from different cultures express their individuality through unique customs. The story you are about to read describes a Japanese funeral custom called *koden*. In the Japanese culture, most wakes and funerals are conducted according to Buddhist rites. During a wake, a Buddhist priest recites sutras (passages from Buddhist scriptures), and mourners burn incense. After the wake, the family of the deceased usually serves food, and mourners give *koden* ("incense money") as an expression of respect. Traditionally, the money is given in white envelopes tied with black and white or silver and white strings.

Mourners at a funeral in Japan. Copyright © 1983 Bernard Pierre Wolff/ Photo Researchers.

READING CONNECTION   *Active Reading*

Reading Dialogue As you read "Koden," you will notice that the author sometimes does not include phrases, such as "he said" and "she said," that identify the speakers of dialogue. In such cases, you must infer, or figure out, which character is speaking by paying close attention to the dialogue itself. The indentions in the text will help you infer who is speaking. Each indented line of dialogue represents a new speaker.

KODEN   **331**

PRINT AND MEDIA RESOURCES

UNIT THREE RESOURCE BOOK
Strategic Reading: Literature, p. 47
Reading SkillBuilder, p. 48
Spelling SkillBuilder, p. 49

GRAMMAR MINI-LESSONS
Transparencies, p. 10
Copymasters, pp. 15–16

WRITING MINI-LESSONS
Transparencies, p. 26

ACCESS FOR STUDENTS ACQUIRING ENGLISH
Selection Summaries
Reading and Writing Support

FORMAL ASSESSMENT
Selection Test, pp. 67–68
 Test Generator

AUDIO LIBRARY
See Reference Card

LASERLINKS
Author Background

INTERNET RESOURCES
McDougal Littell Literature Center at http://www.hmco.com /mcdougal/lit

SUMMARY

The narrator's 12-year-old cousin Kenny dies in an accident. After the funeral, the narrator helps her family keep a written record of the *koden,* the traditional Japanese gifts of money to the family of someone who has died. That evening, Kenny's mother, Auntie Harumi, mentions that the narrator's father was once quietly rebellious, just as the narrator is. The narrator discovers a new closeness with her father, from whom she had been growing apart, and she realizes the depth of their love for each other.

Thematic Link: *A Change of Heart* The tragic death of a family member makes the narrator and her father realize how much they care about each other.

CUSTOMIZING FOR
Students Acquiring English

- Use **ACCESS FOR STUDENTS ACQUIRING ENGLISH,** *Reading and Writing Support.*

- If possible, invite students with a Japanese background to explain the custom of *koden* and other traditions of Buddhism.

- In addition to these boxes, you may want to use the suggestions under Strategic Reading for Less-Proficient Readers.

STRATEGIC READING FOR
Less-Proficient Readers

Set a Purpose Ask students to discuss their knowledge of funeral customs in different cultures. Then have students read to discover what *koden* is. Use **UNIT THREE RESOURCE BOOK,** p. 47, for guidance in reading the selection.

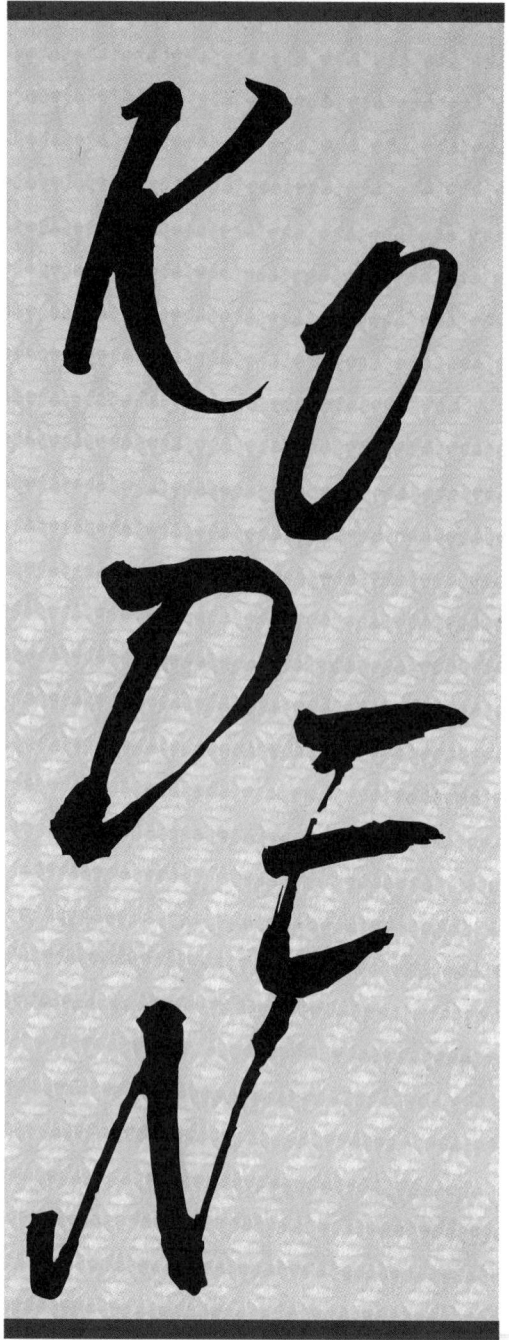

KODEN
by Judith Nihei

I guess you could say I was having a bad year. If you asked me to tell you why, I probably couldn't. Or maybe I could say a lot of things but they wouldn't mean anything to anyone but me. A lot of people say they want to know, but I'm not sure if they really do or not.

I was supposed to be doing a lot of things. I was supposed to get my driver's license and I was supposed to start thinking about college and I was supposed to be, I don't know, moody and difficult. I was moody, I guess, but I think the only difficult thing about me was that I wasn't being difficult. I didn't want anything. I didn't refuse what I was given, and I spoke when I was spoken to, and I kept my grades up. I quit softball and piano lessons, but everyone was expecting me to do that anyway.

Multicultural   Perspectives

FUNERAL RITES The majority of funerals in Japan are conducted according to Buddhist traditions. While specific details differ among sects, there are many common rites and customs. Traditionally, the period of mourning *(kichú)* lasts from 7 to 49 days. A written notice is placed on the front door of the house or the outside gate. The wake *(tsuya)* is held the night before the funeral service. Mourners customarily bring *koden* and send flowers. Funeral rites begin with a Buddhist priest reciting sutras and conclude with family and other mourners burning pinches of incense. Cremation is widely practiced, and some of the remains of the deceased are placed in a small jar *(kotsutsubo)* to be kept at home on a special altar. Every seventh day throughout the 49 days, family and friends gather around the altar. After this period, the *kotsutsubo* is buried at the gravesite.

Have students hypothesize about why the characters do not openly acknowledge or express their emotions about Kenny's death throughout most of the selection. Only some of their actions betray what is going on. Ask students to find examples of this behavior in the selection.

Possible responses:

• *Holding back emotions may be characteristic family behavior; it's too painful for them to show what they really feel.*

• *Page 334—"Russell played with the knob of the gearshift, jiggling it from side to side in neutral. The quiet bothered me."*

• *Page 335—"Uncle Ed thanked everybody . . . sometimes cracking jokes like he does, which seemed kind of weird although I guess it really wasn't."*

• *Page 335—"The funeral was sad, and I'm still not sure what I think about that."*

A I did get a second hole pierced in my left ear, which no one can even see if my hair is down, and two holes in one ear is nothing compared with what some people at my school are doing. But my dad never wanted me to get my ears pierced in the first place, so I guess it really burned him that I hadn't even asked before I got the second hole done. I might have discussed it with him if I hadn't felt like I had to have an army of lawyers to prove my case every time I disagreed with him. Not that he yells. He just slowly and quietly convinces you how wrong you are.

"You don't think," he'd say, which really hurt because it felt like I was thinking all the time—like I could be who they wanted me to be if only I could *stop* thinking. And if I got mad, he'd get even more annoyed.

"Don't get so upset," he would say. "No big deal."

CONNECT

Have you ever had thoughts or experiences similar to the narrators?

Using a Reading Log

Anyway, the day Kenny died, my mom was still at work and I'd just gotten home from school when Dad called.

"Hello?"

"Yeah," he said. "This is Dad."

"Hi," I said. "Mom's not home yet."

He cleared his throat. "You know, in life there is both happiness and sorrow."

I could almost see him holding the phone, standing with his head up, shoulders back, throwing out his chest like he did when he'd show us how he delivered his big speech for the Japanese School program when he was twelve. I couldn't believe it. He was performing for me.

Who died? I wanted to ask. Somebody's dead. Grandma had a bad heart and Grandpa was always wandering around by himself with his cane. At my brother's graduation the summer before, when I'd had my picture taken with them, I got a funny feeling that if I went away to college in a couple of years, I might not be home when they died, that I might not be home for a lot of things.

"Yeah," I said, "so—?"

"Kenny's dead," he said.

I was so surprised that I actually shouted into the phone, which is something you never did to my dad.

"WHAT?"

KODEN **333**

Literary Concept:
POINT OF VIEW

A Ask students to identify from whose point of view the story is being told. *(The narrator tells the story in the first person.)*

Active Reading: CONNECT

B If students have difficulty relating similar thoughts or experiences, ask them to explain how they think they would feel or act if someone were to say, "You don't think."

Mini-Lesson **Reading Skills/Strategies**

ACTIVE READING: QUESTIONING
Remind students that active readers ask questions as they read, exploring reasons for what is going on and looking for motivations for the characters' actions. Active readers also ask questions about things they do not understand but hope to have clarified later in the selection.

Application Ask students to list questions they have as they read the selection. On a chart like the one shown, students should list their questions as well as the answers they discover. If students find that they have unanswered questions, encourage them to work with partners to discuss these questions and possible answers to them.

Reteaching/Reinforcement
• *Unit Three Resource Book,* p. 48

Questions   Answers

Students Acquiring English

① If possible, have students who speak Japanese model correct pronunciation of Umetsu and other Japanese names in the story, and the author's name.

② Point out that the narrator and her brother communicate using as few words as possible. You may need to paraphrase "Figures" and "Grow up. This isn't about you" in order to help them understand this exchange.

Active Reading: QUESTION

Ⓒ Ask students to write their questions about what the accident might have been. To help them answer their questions, use the following model:

Think-Aloud Model *When I read that the boy had died, the first thing I thought of was that he might have been in a car accident. Or maybe he was playing and had a biking or swimming accident.*

Linking to Geography

Ⓓ The story takes place in and around San Francisco in western California. The narrator mentions "Berkeley," meaning the University of California at Berkeley, and "the Bay," meaning the San Francisco Bay. The cities of Berkeley and San Francisco are joined by the San Francisco Bay Bridge.

Critical Thinking: ANALYZING

Ⓔ Ask students what the narrator means when she says, "The scratch marks had become scars." *(Possible response: In the past, the narrator and her brother hurt each other's feelings, and, though they now mostly avoid rather than confront each other, the memory of that emotional pain stays with them both.)*

---

① My cousin Kenny had been the next Umetsu to be born after me. Russ and I were the oldest cousins and our dad was the oldest brother. Then came Uncle Ben, Uncle Jack, Uncle Ed and Uncle Bill. The first wedding I remember going to was when Uncle Ben, Kenny's father, married Auntie Harumi. The reason I remember it so well is because the whole time my mom was getting mad at me for scratching and fussing my way through the wedding ceremony, and the thing was she had left some pins in my dress when she made it. Kenny was their first-born son. He had just turned twelve.

"It was an accident," my dad said.

The day of the funeral I ended up waiting for my brother on the bench outside the main doors of my school. My parents had taken the day off to go over to the East Bay early, but I wasn't supposed to have my education disrupted. Anyway, they were making Russ come back for me. He was in his first year at Berkeley, and I knew he wasn't going to be happy about having to drive across the Bay to get me and then drive all the way back, but that was his tough luck for being born first.

> **PREDICT**
>
> What do you think the accident was?
>
> Using a Reading Log

Ⓒ

Ⓓ

I stood up just in time to see the paleyellow Volkswagen Bug maneuver toward the curb. The car pulled up, and Russ leaned over and opened the passenger door from the inside. I threw my bag into the backseat, got inside and slammed the door shut. All the windows were closed, and the pressure thudded in my ear.

Auntie Harumi used to say that Russell and I were like two cats forced to share a territory, glaring and avoiding, showing our claws from a distance, occasionally hissing and spitting and mixing it up. This last year it had mostly been avoiding. The scratch marks had become scars. We didn't talk much.

When we got through Golden Gate Park, he downshifted and we exited into the busy traffic on Fell Street, stopping at the light by the DMV. It was suddenly quiet enough for me to feel my ears tingling from the noise. Russell played with the knob of the gearshift, jiggling it from side to side in neutral. The quiet bothered me.

"How is everybody?" I asked.

"I haven't really talked to Auntie and Uncle yet," he said, staring at the light. "I think everybody's pretty upset. Do you know how it happened?"

"No," I said, "do you?"

"Yeah."

"Who told you?"

"Dad."

"Figures."

"Grow up. This isn't about you."

"So tell me, then."

"Kenny was playing in their backyard. The kids had this rope and they were up in that big tree and Kenny slipped."

"And hit his head?"

"And hanged himself," Russell said, pounding into first gear as the light changed to green.

I guess no one told me because they thought I would cry or something, which is something you never do in front of my parents. I think Russell thought I was going to cry, too, but I never cry in front of anyone anymore.

"Where are we going?" I said instead.

"Grandma and Grandpa's. So you'd better keep your hair over those ears."

I didn't know what was going to happen. I

Mini-Lesson  **Literary Concepts**

REVIEWING POINT OF VIEW Remind students that the point of view is the perspective from which a story is told. In the first-person point of view, the narrator is one of the characters in the story and uses first-person pronouns such as *I, me,* and *we*. The reader sees the events of the story and other characters only through the eyes of the narrator. In the third-person point of view, the narrator is not in the story and relates the story using third-person pronouns such as *he, she,* or *it*.

Application Have students rewrite the highlighted passage in the third person. Ask them to describe how the change in point of view changes the mood of the story.

The Reader (1980), Will Barnet. Copyright © Will Barnet/VAGA, New York.

had only been to one funeral before, when my mom's father died, and I was really little then so all I remembered was the smell of the Buddhist incense and the sleepy drone of the priest chanting. My father's family were Presbyterians, so I knew there wouldn't be any chanting or anything, but I thought that might make it worse because then you could understand everything. When we got to the funeral parlor on the night of the service and I saw the table, I did remember the *koden*.

It was a small oak table in the middle of the lobby. I saw my Uncle Ed, representing our family, sitting behind it next to one of Auntie Harumi's brothers, who represented theirs. As people came in, they'd stop and put a white envelope in front of Uncle Ed. Sometimes it was the size of a greeting card, and sometimes it was long and narrow and covered with Japanese characters. Uncle Ed thanked everybody, nodding or sharing hands, sometimes cracking jokes like he does, which seemed kind of weird although I guess it really wasn't. Then he'd hand the envelope to Auntie's brother, who put it in

a covered, lacquered box, like the kind Grandma used for sushi on New Year's Day.

I knew this was the *koden,* the money. In each envelope was anywhere from five to fifty dollars. I had seen my parents get their envelopes ready for other funerals—my mom writing their name and address on the envelope because her handwriting was better, my dad making sure that the five-, ten- or twenty-dollar bill was crisp and new.

"What's the money for?" I asked my mom once.

"It's a custom," she said.

I wanted to know what they did with the money and she said sometimes they used it to pay for the funeral and sometimes they gave it away to people who really needed it, like the cancer society. When I asked my dad why they gave *koden,* he said it was out of respect.

The funeral was sad, and I'm still not sure what I think about that. They buried Kenny the next day. The people who came to the burial were invited to my uncle and aunt's house, and all of a sudden everyone was busy—making food and unfolding chairs and shaking hands. Being the oldest, my dad took

KODEN   **335**

J Ask students what they can infer about the father's character from the fact that he always took charge and acted as if this were any other family party. *(Possible response: He liked to be in control of his emotions and everything around him.)*

Active Reading: CLARIFY

K Ask students why they think the aunts washed the dishes twice. *(Possible responses: They were distracted and not really thinking about what they were doing; they were trying to keep busy to keep from thinking about the great sadness they felt.)*

Critical Thinking: ANALYZING

L Ask students what they think the narrator means by everyone having someone to be except her. *(Possible response: Everybody had a role to play to make him or her appear busy except the narrator.)*

J charge, like he always does, greeting people and thanking people, like this was no different from any other big family party. Russ played with the cousins, and the uncles made drinks and took care of our grandparents, and the aunts cooked and **K** served and washed all the dishes twice. It seemed like everyone had something to do **L** and someone to be except me.

It was the most time I had spent with the family in a long time, and I don't know, it was different. I felt like I'd lost my place in a favorite book I'd been rereading, that each page was familiar but I couldn't quite find the exact place where I needed to be. I stood as long as I could in one spot and then sat in one chair or another until I felt like standing up again.

inally, just the family was left and it was time to clear the dining-room table. Uncle Jack went out to his car and brought back two brand-new notebooks and some pens and pencils. He gave them to me to put on the table, where someone had already replaced the punch bowls and salami and sushi with an adding machine, a shoe box and the lacquer box from the night before. There were six chairs, two on each side and one on either end. My dad sat at one end, with Teri, Uncle Jack's wife, on his left and my mom on his right. Uncle Bill's wife, Sue, sat next to her, and Uncle Bill sat at the other end, with the adding machine in front of him. Someone turned down the volume of the TV in the next room, and then it was time to count the *koden.*

Auntie Teri had the lacquer box open in front of her. She took out an envelope, wrote a number on it and handed it to Dad.

He opened it.

"Mrs. Yoneko Omi. Ten dollars."

Mom wrote the name and amount in her notebook each time Dad spoke. He handed the card to her and she recorded its number, then gave the envelope to Auntie Sue, Bill's wife, who was sitting at her right. In a book like Mom's, Auntie Sue recorded the address if there was one. She then stored the card or envelope in a shoe box and handed the money or check to Uncle Bill, who kept a running tally on the adding machine.

"Motomo and Edna Ishigashi. Twenty dollars."

I wandered into the kitchen. Auntie Harumi was swinging a large pan of chow mein out of the oven. I watched her pour the noodles onto a platter and spread the vegetables over the top with her chopsticks, standing at a distance to keep the sauce from splattering her neat black dress.

"Hey, how's it going out there?" she asked.

"Okay, I guess. Um, how are you doing?"

Auntie Harumi wiped her hands on a dishtowel.

"Oh, okay. It'll be different when everybody goes home, but for now . . ."

She dropped her voice and took my arm, looking over my shoulder to make sure no one else would hear.

". . . you know, while you're here, I want to tell you something."

"What?"

"I told your uncle—"

"Which one?"

"My husband, smart aleck. I told your Uncle Ben, I said, 'Your family is the best.' Gee, your dad-folks are just taking care of everything. Auntie's family is here, huh? But they're not lifting a finger."

Mini-Lesson ✒ **The Writer's Style**

AUTHOR'S PURPOSE AND GOALS The author's purpose is the general reason for writing. Goals are the specific aims the writer hopes to achieve for himself or herself and for the readers. The four main purposes for writing are to express an opinion, to entertain, to inform, and to persuade.

Application Ask students to write a paragraph describing what they think the author's purpose is in writing "Koden." Remind them that an author may combine two or more of the four purposes listed above. Students should include at least three examples from the selection to support their opinions.

Reteaching/Reinforcement
• Writing Handbook, anthology p. 808
• *Writing Mini-Lessons* transparencies, p. 26

📖 **The Writer's Craft**

General Purpose, pp. 231–232

"That's because Dad won't let them," I said.

Auntie laughed. She reached over and pushed my hair behind my ears.

"Oh, you got a second hole. Neat!"

I let the hair fall back onto my face.

"Dad had a cow,"I said.

"Not happy," she said, smiling.

"I waited until last year to even ask if I could have my ears pierced. I think Mom was on my side, but . . . you know. So I figured, they're my ears—"

Auntie laughed again.

"You and your dad," she said. "You know, he was always the different one."

"My dad?"

"He grew this beard once, and your grandmother had a fit! She thought it was the most horrible thing she had ever seen, couldn't stand to have any of her friends see him like that."

"Dad had a beard?"

"Oh, long time ago—before Ben and I were even dating. I remember her coming over to our house and almost apologizing to my mother, because no matter what she said, he wouldn't shave it off."

"Well it's gone now."

"Yeah, but not because anyone told him to get rid of it. Your dad has his own mind. Just like you."

Japanese portable cabinet [Sage-dansu] (late 16th century), The Seattle (Washington) Art Museum, Eugene Fuller Memorial Collection (72.16). Photo by Paul Macapia.

I walked back into the dining room and stood behind my dad's chair. Work at the table went on slowly, methodically. I watched and waited for a break in the rhythm. Finally they stopped so that Mom could turn the page of her notebook.

"Can I get anybody anything?" I asked. They all shifted in their seats and stretched. Auntie Teri sipped her coffee and made a face.

"Cold," she said.

She picked up her cup and headed for the kitchen, where we could hear Uncle Ben and Uncle Jack arguing over someone's golf handicap. Auntie Sue walked around the table and took Auntie Teri's place. Uncle Ed wandered in with a glass in his hand and sat in Sue's empty seat. Mom took off her glasses and massaged her eyes.

"Yeah," my dad said. "Why don't you give Mom a break, there."

Mom stood up, pressed her hands to the small of her back and walked toward the kitchen. I looked down at her place, and Uncle Ed shifted to his right. I sat down and pulled the chair closer to the table. I picked up the ballpoint pen Mom had been using. It was warm. I looked at the notebook to see where she was, the number where she'd stopped. I wiped my hand on my thigh and moved her coffee cup way beyond where it could do any harm.

Mini-Lesson: Speaking,   Listening, and Viewing

STORYBOARDS Explain that storyboards are like comic-strip illustrations and are used in the film industry to plan how a scene will be filmed. Storyboards act as a kind of map for everyone who is involved in a production: the actors, the sound crew, the lighting crew, and the director.

Application Invite students to create a storyboard for any scene in "Koden" as if they were preparing to videotape the story. They should choose the scenes they want to portray and then determine the angles from which they want the camera to shoot. The storyboards should also detail who and what will appear in the scene.

"Ready?" Dad asked.

I nodded and the rhythm began again.

"Tominaga. Harry and Alice. Twenty-five dollars."

I wrote. He glanced at my writing. He repeated:

"Tominaga. Harry and Alice. Twenty-five dollars."

He handed me the envelope. I checked the number and I handed it to my uncle.

"The Mas Ninomiya Family. Twenty-five dollars. . . ."

We worked from twilight to darkness. My grandparents were taken upstairs to rest. I blended into the rhythm and pattern of the table, until at last it was finished.

P It was almost nine o'clock. My dad never did take a break. He gave the box of money to Auntie Harumi's brother-in-law, who was an accountant, and asked him to please count it again to be sure that the total was correct. While everyone else was stretching and gathering up their things, I handed my notebook to my dad so that he could double-check it. I knew if any money was lost or anything, he would question my work first, but he just took it and placed it on the table with the rest.

"How about a cup of coffee?" he asked.

I turned to go to the kitchen, but he placed his hand gently on my arm.

"Ayako," he called to my mom, "how about bringing us some coffee?"

He opened the French doors that led to the backyard, and we stepped outside. The fog was coming in from the Bay, rolling through the top of the tree where Kenny had been playing. Its coolness made me realize how warm I had been. My dad reached into his shirt pocket and pulled out a new pack of cigarettes. He tore off the cellophane wrapper and tore into the foil. He tapped the pack against his left hand so that two cigarettes poked out, and then he offered one to me.

I shook my head.

"I don't smoke, Dad."

"Well, that's something."

He pulled one out for himself and lit it with his heavy square lighter, cupping his hand around the flame against the wind.

"Maybe we ought to cut this tree down," he said, squinting through the smoke at the big tree.

"Why?"

"I don't know. I guess it's not the tree's fault."

"Maybe it would make Auntie and Uncle feel better, though."

"I don't know what could help them feel better. Your kids aren't supposed to die before you do."

 hen I was little and we spent every Sunday at our grandparents' house, playing with our uncles before they married and had their own families, I thought my father and his brothers were an unbeatable force. But as the day of the funeral had approached, they had been different, shaky, like they had to fight to stay in charge, like it was their fault, somehow, that they couldn't protect Kenny, prevent it from happening.

I didn't know what to say, so I shoved my hair behind my ears and then covered them up as soon as I realized what I'd done. I looked away.

"Do you want your coffee out here, Dad? I'll go get it."

Mini-Lesson   **Genre Study**

FICTION Explain to students that a **short story** is a work of fiction that usually has the following features:
- focuses on one or two main characters
- can be read in one sitting
- is built around a single problem or conflict faced by the main characters

Application Invite students to prepare an oral report that lists the ways "Koden" fits the profile of a short story. Students should discuss who the one or two main characters are and what the single conflict is that the characters face.

Instead of answering, he put his hand on my head and turned it toward him. I looked up at him, and he pushed my hair back behind my ears.

"I like to see your face," he said.

I couldn't help it. I started to cry then, which really made me mad because I knew it would upset him. But instead of telling me to stop, Dad put his arm around me, which made me cry even more. After a while I kind of stopped and he gave me his handkerchief.

"I'm sorry, Daddy," I said.

"No big deal," he said, lighting another cigarette. "Go inside now. It's getting cold."

Dad turned away from me then, walking deeper into the yard toward my brother and my cousins, and I watched the tip of his cigarette glow in the darkness, floating like a small torch in the dark night. ❖

CUSTOMIZING FOR

Gifted and Talented Students

Ask students what purpose they think rituals like the koden serve. Have them describe rituals that are part of their own lives and discuss what functions these rituals serve for them.

HISTORICAL INSIGHT

Buddhism

The narrator of this story attended a Buddhist funeral when she was young and remembers the smell of incense and the tradition of *koden*. Many of the traditions and art forms practiced in the Japanese culture today—such as the tea ceremony, rock gardens, flower arranging, incense blending, and ink painting—have been influenced by Buddhism.

Buddhism is a religion that began in India and was introduced into Japan in the sixth century A.D. Its founder was Siddhartha Gautama. Not much is known about his early life, but according to tradition, when Gautama was about 29 years old, he had four visions. The fourth vision made him decide to leave his wife and newborn child in search of religious enlightenment. After six years of extreme self-denial and self-torture (he lived in extreme poverty and filth, often ate only one grain of rice a day,

and pulled out his beard one hair at a time) he stopped to meditate under a tree. Several hours later, he experienced enlightenment.

After others learned of Gautama's enlightenment, they began to call him Buddha, "Enlightened One." Buddha began preaching the message of the dharma, or "saving truth," urging his followers to pursue a "Noble Eightfold Path" to peace and happiness. The main elements of this path are knowing the truth, knowing and controlling one's own thoughts and feelings, resisting evil, and holding a job that does not harm others.

Today, Buddhism is one of the major religions of the world. It has about 300 million followers, most of whom live in Southeast Asia and Japan.

Head of Buddha (late 8th/early 9th century), unknown Korean artist. Detroit Institute of Arts, Founders Society Purchase with funds from an anonymous bequest, the Joseph H. Boyer Memorial Fund, Macauley Fund, K. T. Keller Fund, and G. Albert Lyon Foundation.

BUDDHISM **339**

INSIGHT

1. Explain how you think self-denial might lead someone to enlightenment. *(Possible response: When you are not distracted by choices of what to do, what to eat, and what to wear, you can focus on one goal—enlightenment.)*
2. Which elements of the path to peace and happiness do you consider most important? Explain. *(Responses will vary.)*

COMPREHENSION CHECK
1. What tragedy happens to the narrator's family? *(Her cousin Kenny accidentally hangs himself.)*
2. What ritual does the family practice after the funeral of a loved one? *(counting koden, the money given by mourners)*
3. How does everyone in the family react to the tragedy? *(They keep busy and repress emotion.)*
4. How does the father treat his daughter at the end of the story? *(When she begins to cry, he comforts her and shows her sympathetic understanding.)*

Art Note

Head of Buddha Sculptures and busts like this one of Buddha are common sights in countries and cultures where Buddhism is practiced.

Reading the Art *Many say looking into the face of Buddha makes them feel calm. What feelings does it evoke in you?*

Mini-Lesson **(M)** Spelling

HARD AND SOFT C AND G Explain that when the letters *c* and *g* have a hard sound, they will be followed by the letters *a, o,* or *u*. When they have a soft sound (pronounced like *s* and *j*), they will be followed by the letters *i, e,* or *y*. Suffixes that follow a soft *c* or *g* will always begin with an *i* or an *e*, such as *-ian, -ion, -ious,* or *-ence*. Copy the examples shown on the board to share with students.

Application In the following words, invite students to indicate if the *c* or *g* is soft or hard and fill in the missing letters.

1. The narrator c_ncealed her feelings of sadness over Kenny's death. *(hard; o)*
2. Kenny's death was a horrible trag_dy for the family. *(soft; e)*
3. Kenny's death was the end of innoc_nce for the narrator. *(soft; e)*
4. The narrator and her father often arg_ed. *(hard; u)*

Reteaching/Reinforcement
• *Unit Three Resource Book,* p. 49

From Personal Response to Critical Analysis

1. Responses will vary. Possible response: Parents and their children are often more alike than they realize.

2. Possible response: She has been holding back tears for Kenny all day and can do so no longer.

3. Possible response: The narrator realizes how deeply Kenny's death has upset her father, and the narrator's father realizes how much he loves his daughter, who is becoming an adult. The father and the narrator begin to see each other as individuals, rather than as a parent and a child.

4. Possible response: We are both willing to take extreme steps (like piercing our ears) to express our individuality.

5. Invite students to share their own funeral customs and experiences, such as holding wakes, conducting burial rites, and singing traditional songs. Purposes might include showing respect, honoring the dead, and comforting the living.

Another Pathway

Cooperative Learning Divide the class into five groups. Have each group pick a character to discuss: the narrator, her father, Russell, Aunt Harumi, or Uncle Ed. Within each group, assign the roles of facilitator (to make sure all students in the group are participating), elaborator (to develop the group's ideas), and recorder (to record the group's ideas). Then have the other students in the group create a chart that describes how their character felt and why that character reacted as he or she did.

Rubric

3 Full Accomplishment Students discern the character's feelings and thoroughly explain his or her reactions.

2 Substantial Accomplishment Students identify the character's feelings but have difficulty explaining his or her reactions.

1 Little or Partial Accomplishment Students are unable to identify the character's feelings and explain his or her reactions.

RESPONDING
O P T I O N S

FROM **PERSONAL RESPONSE** *TO* **CRITICAL ANALYSIS**

REFLECT
1. What thoughts were going through your mind as you finished this story? Record them in your notebook.

RETHINK
2. Why do you think the narrator starts to cry at the end of the story?

3. How would you explain the change in the narrator's relationship with her father?

Close Textual Reading
Consider
• what her aunt tells her about her father's beard
• her participation in the recording of the *koden*
• how her father feels when he says "Your kids aren't supposed to die before you do"

RELATE
4. How would you compare the ways the narrator expresses her individuality with the ways you express yours?

5. This story involves the Japanese funeral custom of *koden*. What funeral customs or traditions are you familiar with? How would you compare the purposes of those customs with the purpose of *koden*?

LITERARY CONCEPTS

Characterization is the way that writers make their characters seem real. A writer may use any of the following methods to make a character come alive:
• showing the character in action or conversation
• explaining the character's thoughts
• describing the character's physical appearance
• telling how other people respond to the character
Look back through "Koden" to find an example of each method. Share your examples with your classmates.

Multimodal Learning
ANOTHER PATHWAY

With a small group of classmates, list the characters in this story and describe how each reacts to Kenny's death. Then discuss the following questions: Why does each character react as he or she does? Why don't all the characters react in the same manner? Share your group's ideas with the rest of the class.

QUICKWRITES

1. An adage is an old saying that expresses an accepted truth, like "In life, there is both happiness and sorrow." Make up an **adage** that fits this story and explain what it means.

2. Write a **character sketch** that would help an actor playing the role of the narrator or her father in a movie version of "Koden."

3. Imagine that the narrator has gone away to college. Write a **letter** that she might write to her father, expressing her views about his expectations of her and her need to express her individuality

📁 **PORTFOLIO** *Save your writing. You may want to use it later as a springboard to a piece for your portfolio.*

Literary Concepts

You may wish to have students choose one character and focus on the ways that character comes to life in the selection. Students can create charts that list the four methods and examples from the selection for each of these methods.

QuickWrites

1. Remind students that an adage reflects a universal or general truth, so theirs should express a truth about human life that they discovered in "Koden."

2. Encourage students to include details about the character's appearance, age, and personality, as well as any information that helps to explain his or her actions.

3. Students' letters should comment on events in this story and the new understanding that the narrator and her father reach at the conclusion.

 The Writer's Craft

Character Sketch, pp. 54–61
Letter Forms, p. 669

Multimodal Learning

ALTERNATIVE ACTIVITIES

1. To help readers "hear" how a character's words are spoken, a writer may use an adverb, as in the phrase "he said *angrily.*" Rewrite some of the **dialogue** in this story by adding adverbs to the phrases that introduce it. Then have classmates read the speeches aloud, following the direction of each adverb. Discuss how using different adverbs might affect the way the dialogue would be spoken.

2. Every culture has unique customs. Write a **description** of a custom that your family practices, and explain its significance to the class.

3. Comforting people who have lost a loved one can be difficult. Create a **questionnaire** and survey people of different ages and cultural backgrounds to find out what they think are the best ways to comfort the bereaved. Present your findings to the class.

LITERARY LINKS

In this story the narrator changes as a result of her experiences. Compare the narrator with another character who changes, such as Juliette in the story "Waiting" (page 37). Which character do you think develops a stronger sense of individuality because of her experiences?

CRITIC'S CORNER

When members of the student board were asked to give their impressions of "Koden," Michael Regula responded that the story "needs an ending," and Chrissy Kennedy said that "the situation was realistic and something I could relate to." Do you agree with either student—or both? Discuss your opinions with a partner.

ACROSS THE CURRICULUM

Social Studies Research a Japanese custom, such as the tea ceremony, bowing, or the removal of shoes before entering a house. In an oral report, present the history of the custom and explain its importance.

JUDITH NIHEI

An author, director, and actor, Judith Nihei was born in San Francisco, California. She received a bachelor's degree in English and creative writing from the University of Washington in Seattle, where she was also on the staff of the Asian Multi-Media Center.

Besides writing plays and short stories, Nihei is on the writing staff of *The Puzzle Place,* a PBS series about diversity and ethics, and she has written scripts for the Emmy-winning KRON-TV children's program *Buster and Me.* She is also the artistic director of the Northwest Asian American Theatre and has been active in companies such as the Asian American Theater Company of San Francisco and the Committee, San Francisco's original improvisational comedy troupe.

LASERLINKS
• AUTHOR BACKGROUND

Literary Links

Possible response: The narrator in "Koden" develops a stronger sense of individuality, indicated by the fact that she remains independent, whereas Juliette's happiness remains linked to what others think of her.

Across the Curriculum

Social Studies If possible, have students interview someone familiar with Japanese customs. In addition, students should look in the library for research materials dealing with the cultural history of Japan. Encourage students to draw illustrations to show during their presentations.

ADDITIONAL SUGGESTIONS

History *The Life of Buddha* Invite students to research (in religious and history books) and summarize Buddha's life story. Then ask students to act as storytellers and present Buddha's story as an oral history.

AUTHOR BACKGROUND

Judith Nihei In this interview, the author speaks about her two cultures and her life as a writer.

Side A, Frame 28571

Alternative Activities

1. Tell students to select an important passage of dialogue, such as the exchange between the narrator and her father at the end of this story. Students should try to imagine what each character is feeling and choose an adverb to capture that feeling.

2. Remind students that, as they describe the custom, they should also explain the purpose that it serves.

3. Students may want to choose family members, neighbors, and friends to interview. Have students compile the results and present them in chart or poster form to the class.

OVERVIEW

Objectives

- To understand and appreciate an essay in which a Native American expresses his culture's attitude toward living things
- To understand and appreciate persuasion
- To express understanding of the selection through a choice of writing forms, including a definition, a speech, and a poem
- To extend understanding of the selection through a variety of multimodal and cross-curricular activities

Skills

**READING SKILLS/
STRATEGIES**
- Making judgments

GRAMMAR
- Subject-verb agreement

LITERARY CONCEPTS
- Persuasion
- Repetition

SPELLING
- Silent *gh*

SPEAKING, LISTENING, AND VIEWING
- Oral report

Cross-Curricular Connections

SOCIAL STUDIES
- Chinese communes
- Salishan smoke house

- Salishan art

CULTURAL CONNECTION
Salishan Culture The Salishan people of the Pacific Northwest participate in an annual ritual called a potlatch. These historical images show potlatches and other aspects of the Salishan culture. You may wish to use them to illustrate the importance of the ritual in this culture.

Side A, Frame 49354

NONFICTION

I Am a Native of North America
Chief Dan George, *as told to* Helmut Hirnschall

Activating Prior Knowledge
PERSONAL CONNECTION

What is your attitude toward human beings and other living things? Fill out a chart like the one shown, then compare your views with those of your classmates.

Attitude Scale					
	Strongly disagree				Strongly agree
	1	2	3	4	5
I respect all living things.					
I feel a strong link to other people.					
It is important to respect others' opinions and ways of life.					
It is important to take care of the environment.					

Building Background
CULTURAL CONNECTION

In the essay you are about to read, Chief Dan George discusses his attitudes toward human beings and other living things. His attitudes were greatly influenced by the Salishan culture into which he was born. Salishan peoples once lived throughout the Puget Sound region of Washington and in southern British Columbia, Canada. One of their greatest annual ceremonies was called the potlatch ("giving" or "gift"). This ceremony included several days of feasting, singing, and dancing. During the festivities people gave away their possessions as a way of gaining prestige and respect. Sometimes they gave away nearly everything except their house.

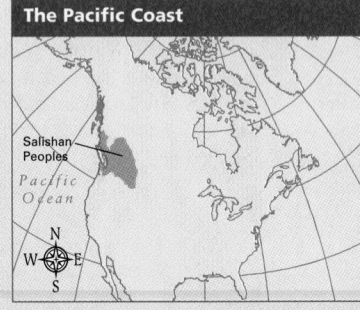

The Pacific Coast

Salishan Peoples

Pacific Ocean

N W E S

Setting a Purpose
WRITING CONNECTION

Review the attitude scale you made for the Personal Connection, then write a brief summary of your attitude toward human beings and other living things. Wherever possible, support or illustrate your statements with examples. As you read this essay, compare your attitude with Chief Dan George's.

LASERLINKS
- *CULTURAL CONNECTION*

342 UNIT THREE PART 2: A CHANGE OF HEART

PRINT AND MEDIA RESOURCES

UNIT THREE RESOURCE BOOK
Strategic Reading: Literature, p. 53
Reading SkillBuilder, p. 54
Spelling SkillBuilder, p. 55

GRAMMAR MINI-LESSONS
Transparencies, p. 7
Copymasters, p. 7

ACCESS FOR STUDENTS ACQUIRING ENGLISH
Selection Summaries
Reading and Writing Support

FORMAL ASSESSMENT
Selection Test, pp. 69–70
 Test Generator

 **AUDIO LIBRARY**
See Reference Card

 **LASERLINKS**
Cultural Connection
Art Gallery

INTERNET RESOURCES
McDougal Littell Literature Center at http://www.hmco.com/mcdougal/lit

I AM A NATIVE OF NORTH AMERICA

by Chief Dan George as told to Helmut Hirnschall

The Birth of Ikce Wicasa (1990), Colleen Cutschall. Courtesy of Art Gallery of Southwestern Manitoba, Canada.

I AM A NATIVE OF NORTH AMERICA **343**

SUMMARY

Chief Dan George discusses what he learned during his early days in a community of Salish people in the Pacific Northwest: acceptance of others, respect for nature, generosity, and trust. He contrasts his Native American upbringing with the ways of the white culture and questions whether those raised in the white culture know the true meaning of love. He believes that love and forgiveness are essential if civilization is to continue. He urges people to learn from his culture before it vanishes.

Thematic Link: *A Change of Heart* Chief Dan George urges people to experience a change of heart by seeking a deeper understanding of each other and all living things.

Art Note

The Birth of the Ikce Wicasa by Colleen Cutschall (Lakota/Sioux) *Ikce Wicasa* means the "common people." This piece of art shows man (on the right) and woman (on the left) making their way across the dark underworld toward the surface light where *Tokahe* is already standing—the first man to emerge into the light.

Reading the Art *What do you think the images shown in this painting might represent?*

CUSTOMIZING FOR
Students Acquiring English

- Use **ACCESS FOR STUDENTS ACQUIRING ENGLISH**, *Reading and Writing Support.*
- Students acquiring English will probably be able to relate to the Native American's experience of living in two different cultures. Encourage them to write their impressions of U.S. culture.

STRATEGIC READING FOR
Less-Proficient Readers

Set a Purpose Have students identify, as they read the selection, the two cultures Chief Dan George describes.

Use **UNIT THREE RESOURCE BOOK**, p. 53, for guidance in reading the selection.

Assessment Option

INFORMAL ASSESSMENT Have students rewrite the essay as if it were a letter from Chief Dan George to the President of the United States. Remind students to try to imitate some of Chief Dan George's techniques of persuasion in their letters.

Rubric

3 Full Accomplishment Students write an effective and persuasive letter reflecting the issues that Chief Dan George addresses in his essay.

2 Substantial Accomplishment Students address the issues in their letters but have difficulty writing convincing arguments.

1 Little or Partial Accomplishment Students have difficulty translating the issues raised in the essay into letter form or are unable to complete the letter.

In the course of my lifetime I have lived in two distinct cultures. I was born into a culture that lived in communal houses. My grandfather's house was eighty feet long. It was called a smoke house, and it stood down by the beach along the inlet. All my grandfather's sons and their families lived in this large dwelling. Their sleeping apartments were separated by blankets made of bull rush reeds, but one open fire in the middle served the cooking needs of all. In houses like these, throughout the tribe, people learned to live with one another; learned to serve one another; learned to respect the rights of one another. And children shared the thoughts of the adult world and found themselves surrounded by aunts and uncles and cousins who loved them and did not threaten them. My father was born in such a house and learned from infancy how to love people and be at home with them. **A**

And beyond this acceptance of one another there was a deep respect for everything in nature that surrounded them. My father loved the earth and all its creatures. The earth was his second mother. The earth and everything it contained was a gift from See-see-am . . . and the way to thank this great spirit was to use his gifts with respect.

I remember, as a little boy, fishing with him up Indian River, and I can still see him as the sun rose above the mountaintop in the early morning . . . I can see him standing by the water's edge with his arms raised above his head while he softly moaned . . . "Thank you, thank you." It left a deep impression on my young mind. **I**

And I shall never forget his disappointment when once he caught me gaffing for fish "just for the fun of it." "My son," he said, "the Great Spirit gave you those fish to be your brothers, to feed you when you are hungry. You must respect them. You must not kill them just for the fun of it."

344   UNIT THREE   PART 2: A CHANGE OF HEART

Mini-Lesson ⟨M⟩ Spelling

SILENT *gh* Remind students that the letters *gh* are often silent, as in *ought, tight,* and *weight.* Explain to students that words containing a silent *gh* are often misspelled. By familiarizing themselves with this silent letter combination, students can improve their spelling skills.

Application Ask students to find four words containing *gh* in the highlighted paragraph above. Then read the following words aloud to the class and have students spell them.

1. might	5. caught
2. flight	6. though
3. night	7. sight
4. sought	8. dough

Ask students to look for more words that fit this pattern, in their own writing and in things that they read, and to add these words to their personal word lists.

Reteaching/Reinforcement
• *Unit Three Resource Book,* p. 55

This then was the culture I was born into and for some years the only one I really knew or tasted. This is why I find it hard to accept many of the things I see around me.

I see people living in smoke houses hundreds of times bigger than the one I knew. But the people in one apartment do not even know the people in the next and care less about them.

It is also difficult for me to understand the deep hate that exists among people. It is hard to understand a culture that justifies the killing of millions in past wars and is at this very moment preparing bombs to kill even greater numbers. It is hard for me to understand a culture that spends more on wars and weapons to kill than it does on education and welfare to help and develop.

It is hard for me to understand a culture that not only hates and fights his brothers but even attacks nature and abuses her. I see my white brother going about blotting out nature from his cities. I see him strip the hills bare, leaving ugly wounds on the face of mountains. I see him tearing things from the bosom of mother earth as though she were a monster who refused to share her treasures with him. I see him throw poison in the waters, indifferent to the life he kills there; and he chokes the air with deadly fumes.

My white brother does many things well, for he is more clever than my people, but I wonder if he knows how to love well. I wonder if he has ever really learned to love at all. Perhaps he only loves the things that are his own but never learned to love the things that are outside and beyond him. And this is, of course, not love at all, for man must love all creation or he will love none of it. Man must love fully or he will become the lowest of the animals. It is the power to love that makes him the greatest of them all . . . for he alone of all animals is capable of love.

I AM A NATIVE OF NORTH AMERICA **345**

CUSTOMIZING FOR

Students Acquiring English

② Point out that the expression "for some years" indicates an indefinite but significant number of years. Similar expressions are used with other periods of time ("for some months," "for some weeks").

Active Reading: EVALUATE

Ⓑ The narrator describes the "white man's" culture as one that justifies the killing of millions. Ask students whether they agree with his assessment. *(Possible responses: The "white man's" culture doesn't believe in killing millions but does believe in a defense against other nations that do. The "white man's" culture does think that killing is acceptable because innocent people are often killed in the name of defense.)*

Literary Concept: REPETITION

Ⓒ Ask students why Chief Dan George repeats the word *love* in this paragraph. *(Possible response: to emphasize how very important he feels love is)*

STRATEGIC READING FOR

Less-Proficient Readers

Ⓓ Ask students what the two cultures are that Chief Dan George has experienced. *(Growing up, he experienced the Native American culture of his family, and later he experienced the "white man's" culture.)* Summarizing

Set a Purpose Have students read to find out how Chief Dan George thinks his people can be best helped by others.

Mini-Lesson Literary Concepts

REVIEWING REPETITION Repetition is the repeated use of any element of language—a sound, a word, a phrase, a line, or a grammatical structure. Writers use repetition to stress important ideas and to create memorable sound effects.

Application Invite students to read the highlighted passage aloud and then to point out examples of repetition in it. Have students assess the effect of this technique on their thinking and emotions.

E Invite students to explain what they think Chief Dan George means when he states that when we know we are loved "we are able to sacrifice for others." Ask students to suggest examples of the kinds of sacrifices he might mean. *(Possible response: He means that love is a powerful force that can inspire people to make great sacrifices; sacrifices might include giving up some material things or sharing food with others.)*

CUSTOMIZING FOR
Multiple Learning Styles

F **Bodily-Kinesthetic Learners**
Invite students to create an interpretive dance that suggests Chief Dan George's loneliness.

Linking to Social Studies

G The Salishan culture is not the only one that values communal living. In China, many people in rural areas live in agricultural communes. Within the communes, 80 to 160 people are responsible for farming up to 95 acres (38 hectares) of land. Because the Chinese communes were created by government decree, however, the communal spirit is somewhat different than that of the Salishan culture.

Literary Concept: PERSUASION

H Ask students to explain how Chief Dan George appeals to both reason and emotion in this passage. *(Possible responses: The author uses logic to persuade, as suggested by the evidence that everyone likes to give as well as receive; he uses stirring language, as in the words beautiful and good things, to appeal to emotions.)*

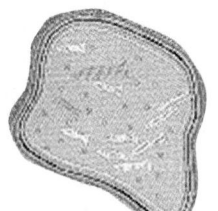

Love is something you and I must have. We must have it because our spirit feeds upon it. We must have it because without it we become weak and faint. Without love our self-esteem weakens. Without it our courage fails. Without love we can no longer look out confidently at the world. Instead we turn inwardly and begin to feed upon our own personalities, and little by little we destroy ourselves.

You and I need the strength and joy that comes from knowing that we are loved. With it we are creative. With it we march tirelessly. With it, and with it alone, we are able to sacrifice for others. **E**

There have been times when we all wanted so desperately to feel a reassuring hand upon us . . . there have been lonely times when we so wanted a strong arm around us . . . I cannot tell you how deeply I miss my wife's presence when I return from a trip. Her love was my greatest joy, my strength, my greatest blessing. **F**

I am afraid my culture has little to offer yours. But my culture did prize friendship and companionship. It did not look on privacy as a thing to be clung to, for privacy builds up walls, and walls promote distrust. My culture lived in big family communities, and from infancy people learned to live with others. **G**

My culture did not prize the hoarding of private possessions; in fact, to hoard was a shameful thing to do among my people. The Indian looked on all things in nature as belonging to him, and he expected to share them with others and to take only what he needed.

Everyone likes to give as well as receive. No one wishes only to receive all the time. We have taken much from your culture . . . I wish you had taken something from our culture . . . for there were some beautiful and good things in it. **H**

Mini-Lesson **Grammar**

SUBJECT-VERB AGREEMENT Explain that a verb must agree with its subject in number. A singular subject needs a singular verb, and a plural subject needs a plural verb. Even in an inverted sequence, where the subject comes after (rather than before) the verb, the verb must still agree with the subject in number.

Application Have students choose the correct form of the verb and its subject in the following sentences.
1. At the heart of Chief Dan George's pleas (is/are) his desire to share love. *(is; desire)*
2. From his past (comes/come) the chief's strong cultural ties. *(come; ties)*

3. Rooted in his relationships with his father (is/are) Chief Dan George's feelings about respecting the earth. *(are; feelings)*
4. (Do/Does) most readers agree with Chief Dan George? *(Do; readers)*

Reteaching/Reinforcement
- Grammar Handbook, anthology pp. 855–857
- *Grammar Mini-Lessons* copymasters, p. 7, transparencies, p. 7

 **The Writer's Craft**

Agreement in Inverted Sentences, p. 584

Soon it will be too late to know my culture, for integration is upon us and soon we will have no values but yours. Already many of our young people have forgotten the old ways. And many have been shamed of their Indian ways by scorn and ridicule. My culture is like a wounded deer that has crawled away into the forest to bleed and die alone.

The only thing that can truly help us is genuine love. You must truly love us, be patient with us and share with us. And we must love you—with a genuine love that forgives and forgets . . . a love that forgives the terrible sufferings your culture brought ours when it swept over us like a wave crashing along a beach . . . with a love that forgets and lifts up its head and sees in your eyes an answering love of trust and acceptance.

This is brotherhood . . . anything less is not worthy of the name.

I have spoken.

LITERARY INSIGHT

The Time We Climbed Snake Mountain
by Leslie Marmon Silko

Seeing good places
      for my hands
I grab the warm parts of the cliff
                  and I feel the mountain as I climb.
Somewhere   around here
            yellow spotted snake is sleeping   on his rock
                  in the sun.
So
    please, I tell them
          watch out,
don't step on the spotted yellow snake
                  he lives here.
The mountain is his.

THE TIME WE CLIMBED SNAKE MOUNTAIN   **347**

From Personal Response to Critical Analysis

1. Possible response: the ideas of respecting the earth and accepting other cultures
2. Possible responses: a love of and respect for nature and for the earth; the concept of sharing with others
3. Possible responses: Advantages include the sharing of material possessions and the support of an extended family; disadvantages include the lack of privacy and having to share everything.
4. Possible response: Yes, he shows love and acceptance by saying he forgives the "white man" for what he did to his people. No, he does not mention positive achievements and values of the culture of white Americans.
5. Possible response: Both involve respect for living things.

Another Pathway

Cooperative Learning Divide the class into groups of five. Have each group select a recorder to create the diagram and a summarizer to help keep their tasks focused. Invite each group to present its diagrams to the class.

Rubric

3 Full Accomplishment Students identify the differing values and common characteristics and record them in the diagram.

2 Substantial Accomplishment Students find the differing values but are unable to identify some of the common characteristics.

1 Little or Partial Accomplishment Students have difficulty identifying similarities and differences between the two groups.

RESPONDING
OPTIONS

FROM PERSONAL RESPONSE TO CRITICAL ANALYSIS

REFLECT
1. What images or ideas from this essay stand out most in your mind? Sketch or describe them in your notebook. Then share them with a partner.

RETHINK
2. Chief Dan George says that his culture has taken much from the white man's culture. What do you think are some "beautiful and good things" in George's culture that his "white brother" might have taken in exchange?

3. What do you think are some advantages and disadvantages of communal living?
   Consider
   • the experiences George describes
   • your own experiences of living with other people

4. Throughout the essay, George urges people to love and accept one another. Do you think he shows love and acceptance in this essay? Support your opinion with evidence.

RELATE
5. Reread the Insight poem on page 347. How does the speaker's attitude toward the snake compare with the Salishan attitude toward living things?

LITERARY CONCEPTS

Persuasion is a type of writing that is meant to influence a reader's feelings, beliefs, or actions. In a persuasive essay, such as "I Am a Native of North America," a writer tries to convince readers to accept a point of view or to take certain actions. To argue for his or her point of view convincingly, a writer may use logic and evidence to appeal to readers' thinking and use stirring language and images to appeal to readers' emotions. Working with a partner, find examples of how George appeals to both reason and emotion in this essay.

Multimodal Learning
ANOTHER PATHWAY

Chief Dan George compares the Salishan culture with the culture of white Americans. With a small group of classmates use a Venn diagram to show George's perceptions of the similarities and differences between the two cultures. When you have finished, share your diagram with the rest of the class.

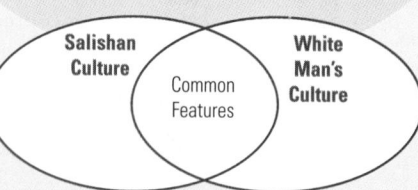

Salishan Culture — Common Features — White Man's Culture

QUICKWRITES

1. Write a **definition** of love from Chief Dan George's point of view.

2. Write a **speech** to persuade students to get involved in environmental activities. Review the examples that you identified for the Literary Concepts activity.

3. Create a **poem** in response to this essay. To get started, review the summary you wrote for the Writing Connection on page 342.

📁 **PORTFOLIO** Save your writing. You may want to use it later as a springboard to a piece for your portfolio.

Literary Concepts

Have each pair of students make a chart, using the heads Reason and Emotion and listing examples in the appropriate columns. (*Possible responses: The stirring language about the power of love, on page 345, appeals to emotion; the argument about killing only when hungry, on page 344, appeals to logic.*)

QuickWrites

1. Students should provide examples from the essay to illustrate their definition of love.
2. Students' speeches should appeal to readers' reason and emotions. Remind students to support the logical parts of their arguments with facts.
3. Have students review the Insight poem and other poems in this book as models. Students should also consider using figurative language, as Chief Dan George did in the simile "my culture is like a wounded deer."

 **The Writer's Craft**

Informing and Defining, pp. 122–129
Supporting Opinions, pp. 144–151

ALTERNATIVE ACTIVITIES

1. Select music and choreograph and perform a **dance** that expresses the spirit or theme of "I Am a Native of North America" or of the Insight poem.

2. Since pictures can say more than words, create a **poster** or **billboard** based on one of the images you sketched or wrote about for the Reflect question on page 348.

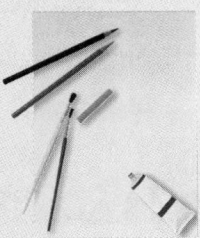

WORDS TO KNOW

WORDPLAY Copy this diagram in your notebook. Then fill in the copy of the diagram with information about the word *communal*.

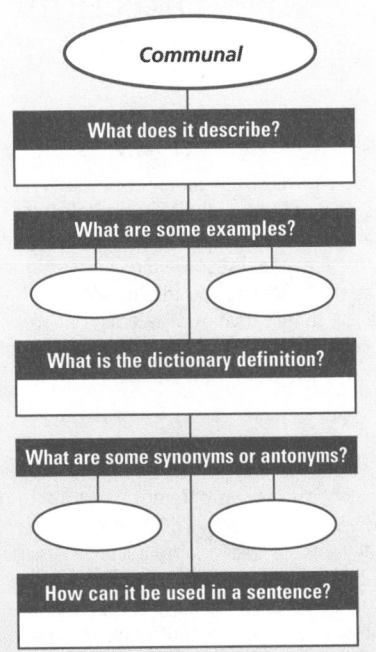

Communal

What does it describe?

What are some examples?

What is the dictionary definition?

What are some synonyms or antonyms?

How can it be used in a sentence?

ACROSS THE CURRICULUM

Social Studies Using George's descriptions and your own research, work with a partner to construct a three-dimensional scale model of a Salishan smoke house. Leave a side of the model open to show the sleeping apartments inside the house. Write explanatory information to accompany your model, and display the model for your class or school.

CHIEF DAN GEORGE

Best known as an actor, Chief Dan George (1899–1981) was the leader of the Tell-lall-watt tribe of the Coast Salish Nation from 1951 to 1963. George, whose tribal name was Geswanouth Slaholt, was born and raised on the Burrard Reserve in British Columbia, Canada. For many years he worked as a longshoreman, loading and unloading ships on Vancouver's waterfront.

George began his 20-year career as an actor at the age of 62, when his son, a television performer, suggested that he replace an ailing white actor playing an Indian character in a Canadian television series. Later, George received international acclaim for his role as an aging Cheyenne warrior in the 1970 film *Little Big Man*. George once told a reporter that his Academy Award nomination for best supporting actor helped him realize a goal he had set for himself —"to do something that would give a name to the Indian people." George appeared in a number of other U.S. and Canadian feature films and served as a spokesperson for Native American rights and environmental protection.

LASERLINKS
• *ART GALLERY*

I AM A NATIVE OF NORTH AMERICA   **349**

Students may find information about this concept in dictionaries, encyclopedias, thesauruses, and on-line services.

Across the Curriculum

Social Studies Suggest that students do library research using encyclopedias and history books. Provide them with a variety of building materials such as glue, paper, cardboard, and paint to use in constructing their models.

ADDITIONAL SUGGESTIONS

Social Studies Invite students to present an oral report on the art and artifacts of the Salishan and other cultures of Puget Sound and British Columbia. Ask them to point out, in their report, connections between the art and the values of these cultures.

CHIEF DAN GEORGE

During his acting career, Chief Dan George appeared in several made-for-television movies and more than 15 motion pictures. He won awards for best supporting actor from both the National Society of Film Critics and the New York Film Critics. In 1971, he won a human relations award from the Canadian Council of Christians and Jews.

ART GALLERY
Harmony with Nature Salishan people have had a very close relationship with nature. These images show some of the ways in which Salishan and European artists have represented that relationship. They may be used to generate discussion about other cultures' relationships with nature.

Side A, Frame 49361

Alternative Activities

1. Encourage students to use music that expresses their own feelings about the essay or poem. Alternatively, they may want to research some Native American music to use as accompaniment.

2. Students may want to use a variety of media to complete their poster or billboard. Encourage them to be creative in their choice of tools and materials.

OVERVIEW

Objectives

- To understand and appreciate two lyric poems about human possibilities
- To identify and understand metaphor and extended metaphor
- To express understanding of the poems through a choice of writing forms, including a personal response, a poem, and an essay
- To extend understanding of the poems through a variety of multimodal and cross-curricular activities

Skills

GENRE STUDY
- Lyric poetry

SPEAKING, LISTENING, AND VIEWING
- Dramatic reading
- Oral interpretation
- Oral report

Cross-Curricular Connections

SOCIAL STUDIES
- Medicine wheels

ALTERNATIVE

Previewing

Instead of creating a chart or jotting down notes about the directions their life might take, students can work in discussion groups to preview "Direction" and "Your World" orally.

Personal Connection

Discussion Prompts: *As a group, consider and discuss the different directions you think your lives might take. Use the following questions to get started:*

- *What are your greatest interests?*

- *How do you pursue these interests?*

- *What are your educational and career goals?*

- *What qualities would it take to realize your goals?*

As you read the two poems, look for the views expressed by each speaker about life's possibilities.

POETRY

Direction
Alonzo Lopez

Your World
Georgia Douglas Johnson

PERSONAL CONNECTION Activating Prior Knowledge

Picture yourself five or ten years from now. What directions do you think your life might take? In your notebook, create a chart like the one shown here. On the left side, list some directions your life might take or challenges you might face. On the right side, list some qualities or talents that you might develop to meet new challenges. Share your chart with a small group of classmates.

Possibilities	
Direction or Challenge	**Quality or Talent**
1. getting a good education	1. persistence
2.	2.
3.	3.

LITERARY CONNECTION Building Background

These two poems express different views about directions that people's lives can take. The poem "Direction" reflects the traditional values of the Papago, a Native American people who inhabit the desert region of southern Arizona and northwest Mexico. In the poem, the speaker recalls advice for living handed down by a grandfather. The grandfather associates different directions with qualities he wants the speaker to acquire. The poem "Your World" was written by Georgia Douglas Johnson, an African-American poet. It describes a change of direction that opens up a whole new world of possibilities for the speaker.

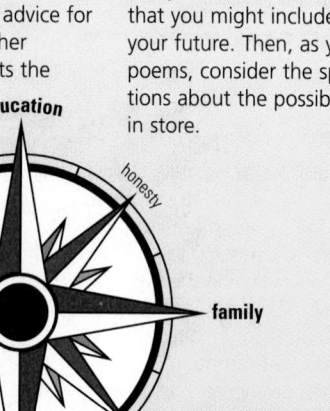

WRITING CONNECTION Setting

Review the chart that you created for the Personal Connection. Select one of the directions or challenges you listed, and jot down a few words or phrases that you might include in a poem about your future. Then, as you read the two poems, consider the speakers' suggestions about the possibilities that life has in store.

350 UNIT THREE PART 2: A CHANGE OF HEART

PRINT AND MEDIA RESOURCES

UNIT THREE RESOURCE BOOK
Strategic Reading: Literature, p. 59

ACCESS FOR STUDENTS ACQUIRING ENGLISH
Reading and Writing Support

FORMAL ASSESSMENT
Selection Test, pp. 71–72
 Test Generator

AUDIO LIBRARY
See Reference Card

Direction

by Alonzo Lopez

I was directed by my grandfather
To the East,
   so I might have the power of the bear;
To the South,
5   so I might have the courage of the eagle;
To the West,
   so I might have the wisdom of the owl;
To the North,
   so I might have the craftiness of the fox;
10 To the Earth,
   so I might receive her fruit;
To the Sky,
   so I might lead a life of innocence. **A**

FROM PERSONAL RESPONSE TO CRITICAL ANALYSIS

REFLECT 1. What are your impressions of the grandfather's advice? Share them with a partner.

RETHINK 2. If the speaker could acquire only one of the qualities mentioned in the poem, which quality would you recommend? Why?

       3. If the speaker were to acquire all the qualities mentioned in the poem, what words would you use to describe him or her?

       4. Put yourself in the grandfather's place and imagine that you have directed the speaker to the sun and the moon. What qualities might the grandfather want the speaker to acquire from these celestial bodies?

RELATE 5. How do the possibilities that you listed for the Personal Connection on page 350 compare with the possibilities that the speaker describes?

DIRECTION **351**

Mini-Lesson: Speaking, Listening, and Viewing

DRAMATIC READING Explain that when a person gives a dramatic reading, he or she is acting out a role. The focus is on shedding one's own personality and expressing the qualities of the character being portrayed.

Application Have each student develop a character from one of the poems—such as the speaker, the grandfather, or one of the animals mentioned—by writing a short paragraph in which that character gives advice to someone looking for direction in life. Then have students assume the role of the character and give a dramatic reading of their paragraph.

Your World

by Georgia Douglas Johnson

Your world is as big as you make it.
I know, for I used to abide
In the narrowest nest in a corner,
My wings pressing close to my side. **C**

5   But I sighted the distant horizon
Where the sky line encircled the sea
And I throbbed with a burning desire
To travel this immensity.

I battered the cordons around me
10   And cradled my wings on the breeze
Then soared to the uttermost reaches
With rapture, with power, with ease!

Mini-Lesson   **Genre Study**

POETRY Copy onto the chalkboard the web that shows the characteristics of a **lyric poem**. Explain to students that a lyric poem expresses intense, personal feelings and may also
• convey ideas by suggestion rather than directly
• contain rhythm and/or rhyme
• use repetition
• use imagery and/or figurative language

Application Ask students to reread the two poems. Have them list evidence that suggests these are lyric poems. Invite them to present their findings to the rest of the class.

RESPONDING
OPTIONS

FROM PERSONAL RESPONSE TO CRITICAL ANALYSIS

REFLECT

1. Sketch "before and after" pictures that reflect your impressions of the speaker of "Your World." When you are finished, share your sketches with a partner.

RETHINK

2. Why do you think the speaker compares himself or herself to a bird?

3. Do you agree with the view of human possibilities that the speaker conveys? Why or why not?

   Consider Close Textual Reading

   • the line "Your world is as big as you make it"

   • the change that the speaker experiences

4. In "Your World," the speaker suggests that people must break down certain barriers in order to change their life. Describe an important change that you have made or have heard about. What barriers were overcome?

RELATE

5. How would you compare the speaker of "Direction" with the speaker of "Your World"?

Multimodal Learning
ANOTHER PATHWAY

Imagine that the speaker of "Your World" and the grandfather in "Direction" meet to discuss their views about human possibilities. Working with a partner, role-play a dialogue between them for the entire class.

QUICKWRITES

1. What does the line "Your world is as big as you make it" mean to you? Write a **personal response,** using examples from your reading and experiences to explain your understanding.

2. Write a draft of a **poem** about your own possibilities. Include some of the words and phrases you jotted down for the Writing Connection on page 350.

3. How does the grandfather in "Direction" compare with an older relative whom you admire? Write a draft of a comparison-and-contrast **essay** to explore this question.

   📁 **PORTFOLIO** *Save your writing. You may want to use it later as a springboard to a piece for your portfolio.*

LITERARY CONCEPTS

Like a simile, a **metaphor** is a figure of speech that compares two things. Unlike a simile, though, a metaphor does not express the comparison by means of the word *like* or *as.* Instead, a metaphor states that something is something else. For example, "The eye is like a window to the soul" is a simile, but "The eye is a window to the soul" is a metaphor. Sometimes, a poet develops an **extended metaphor**—a series of comparisons between two things. What words in "Your World" develop a series of comparisons between the speaker and a bird?

DIRECTION / YOUR WORLD **353**

Possible response: Andrew in "What I Want to Be When I Grow Up" would benefit the most. He tends to think negatively and avoids taking risks.

Across the Curriculum

Social Studies *Cooperative Learning* Explain to students that a shaman's medicine wheel, like the poem "Direction," associates values such as courage and humility with a specific direction of the compass. Invite groups of five to research Native American medicine wheels and share their findings in an oral report to the class. Ask each group to assign a support giver to encourage participation. Suggest students include visuals, either those gathered from research or ones they create, in their presentations.

Social Studies *Take My Advice* Have students research the education and training that professional counselors receive. Students can interview school guidance counselors or contact community organizations that employ career counselors, substance abuse counselors, or psychologists and psychiatrists. Remind students to explain the project to the person they wish to interview and prepare a list a questions in advance.

Multimodal Learning

ALTERNATIVE ACTIVITIES

1. Perform for your classmates an **oral interpretation** of, or an **interpretive dance** based on, one of these poems.

2. Create a **collage** to illustrate the theme of "Your World."

3. Survey several adults to find out their views on teenagers' future possibilities. Then share the results of the survey in an **oral report.**

4. Research one of the animals mentioned in "Direction" to learn about its traditional importance to Native Americans. You might begin your research by consulting an on-line computer encyclopedia. Create a **poster** to show your findings.

LITERARY LINKS

Which character in this unit do you think would benefit the most from following the example of the speaker of "Your World"? Why?

THE SPIRIT BEAR

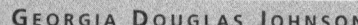

ALONZO LOPEZ

Alonzo Lopez (1949–) was born in Pima County, Arizona. At the Institute of American Indian Arts, he studied creative writing, participated in drama and dance, and practiced the traditional crafts of his people—the Papago. He later attended Yale University, then transferred to Wesleyan University in Connecticut, where he studied the Navajo language and majored in anthropology. After graduation, he returned to work among the Papago. His poems deal with the Papago, their traditional values, and their love of the land.

GEORGIA DOUGLAS JOHNSON

1886–1966

A Georgia native, Georgia Douglas Johnson studied music and literature at Atlanta University and Oberlin College. Eventually, she settled in Washington, D.C., where she worked as a writer, teacher, and government employee. One of the first African-American women to gain wide recognition as a poet, she helped pave the way for later African-American poets, such as Langston Hughes and Mari Evans. She inspired many young black people, encouraging them to have pride in their heritage and confidence in their writing ability.

A year before her death, Johnson received an honorary doctorate in literature from Atlanta University. She died leaving behind three uncompleted manuscripts, including a book about her husband, a lawyer and politician who died in 1925. **OTHER WORKS** *The Heart of a Woman and Other Poems, An Autumn Love Cycle* Extended Reading

354 UNIT THREE PART 2: A CHANGE OF HEART

Alternative Activities

1. Suggest that students prepare for their oral interpretations by deciding on the volume, speed, and emphasis they will use while reading. Encourage dancers to be creative and dramatic in their choice of music and choreography. For instance, ask them how they might use body movement and music to suggest the flight of a bird in "Your World."

2. Provide students with a variety of papers and found materials to use in their collages. Suggest that they scan art books for inspiration.

3. Have students prepare survey questions and a tally chart for recording answers before they begin surveying. Encourage students to create a pie chart or a bar graph to display their results and to use it as a visual aid in their presentations.

4. Suggest that students find animal photos in reference books to use as models for their drawings or that they cut out animal photos from old newspapers and magazines. Many on-line computer encyclopedias include images as well as text.

DRAMA

The Monsters Are Due on Maple Street
Rod Serling

PERSONAL CONNECTION Activating Prior Knowledge Setting a Purpose

How do you react to fear of the unknown? What happens to you when you think that danger may be lurking around the corner? How does your body react? What goes through your mind? With your classmates, use a chart like the one below to brainstorm some of the ways in which you and other people react to fear. Then, as you read this selection, think about the characters and how they react to their fear of the unknown.

Individuals	Groups
dry mouth	cling together

HISTORICAL CONNECTION Building Background

Rod Serling. Culver Pictures.

The Twilight Zone was a television series created by Rod Serling. Eerie and very suspenseful, the series became one of the most popular shows in television history during its 1959–1965 run. Its stories often involved ordinary people in suburban settings typical of the late 1950s. The events in the stories were far from ordinary, however; they were a window into an imaginary world beyond ours—the twilight zone. As the characters faced the unknown, they reacted in both typical and unexpected ways.

READING CONNECTION Active Reading

Reading a Teleplay The script of a television show is called a **teleplay**. Like all drama scripts, a teleplay includes stage directions. Printed in italic type in this selection, the stage directions provide suggestions for the actors and the director, explain the setting, and describe props and lighting and sound effects. The stage directions in a teleplay, however, also include camera directions. These help readers imagine what a television performance of the drama might look like. They also help the producer of the television program know what details the author wants to emphasize or focus on.

THE MONSTERS ARE DUE ON MAPLE STREET **355**

OVERVIEW

Objectives

- To understand and appreciate a teleplay about how ordinary people react to fear of the unknown
- To learn more about the reading of a teleplay
- To identify and understand dialogue
- To express understanding of a selection through a choice of writing forms, including a summary, stage directions, and a proposal
- To extend understanding of the selection through a variety of multimodal and cross-curricular activities

Skills

READING SKILLS/STRATEGIES
- Distinguishing between fact and opinion

THE WRITER'S STYLE
- Dialogue in plays

GRAMMAR
- Interjections

LITERARY CONCEPTS
- Dialogue
- Theme

GENRE STUDY
- Drama: teleplay

SPELLING
- Suffixes -ance/-ant, -ence/ -ent

STUDY SKILLS
- Taking essay tests

SPEAKING, LISTENING, AND VIEWING
- Drama performance
- Film/drama

Cross-Curricular Connections

SCIENCE
- Meteoroids, meteors, and meteorites
- Sunspots

HISTORY
- Dark Ages

SOCIAL STUDIES
- Prejudices throughout history

MUSIC
- Background music

PRINT AND MEDIA RESOURCES

UNIT THREE RESOURCE BOOK
Strategic Reading: Literature, p. 63
Vocabulary SkillBuilder, p. 66
Reading SkillBuilder, p. 64
Spelling SkillBuilder, p. 65

GRAMMAR MINI–LESSONS
Transparencies, pp. 29 and 43
Copymasters, p. 39

WRITING MINI–LESSONS
Transparencies, p. 48

ACCESS FOR STUDENTS ACQUIRING ENGLISH
Selection Summaries
Reading and Writing Support

FORMAL ASSESSMENT
Selection Test, pp. 73–74
 Test Generator

AUDIO LIBRARY
See Reference Card

SUMMARY

A bright object roars over peaceful Maple Street, and suddenly the power goes off, the phones stop working, and cars will not start. Steve Brand and a neighbor, Charlie, plan to walk downtown for help, but young Tommy insists that aliens have landed and they don't want anyone to leave the block. When Les Goodman's car starts by itself, people suspect that Les is an agent of the aliens. A panic ensues as the residents look for someone to blame for all the strange events. One man, Pete Van Horn, is accidentally shot to death by Charlie. The group of neighbors turns into an angry mob. From a distance, aliens watch with satisfaction, commenting that human beings are their own worst enemies.

Thematic Link: *A Change of Heart* Fear of the unknown turns once-friendly neighbors against one another as they try to account for a bizarre series of events.

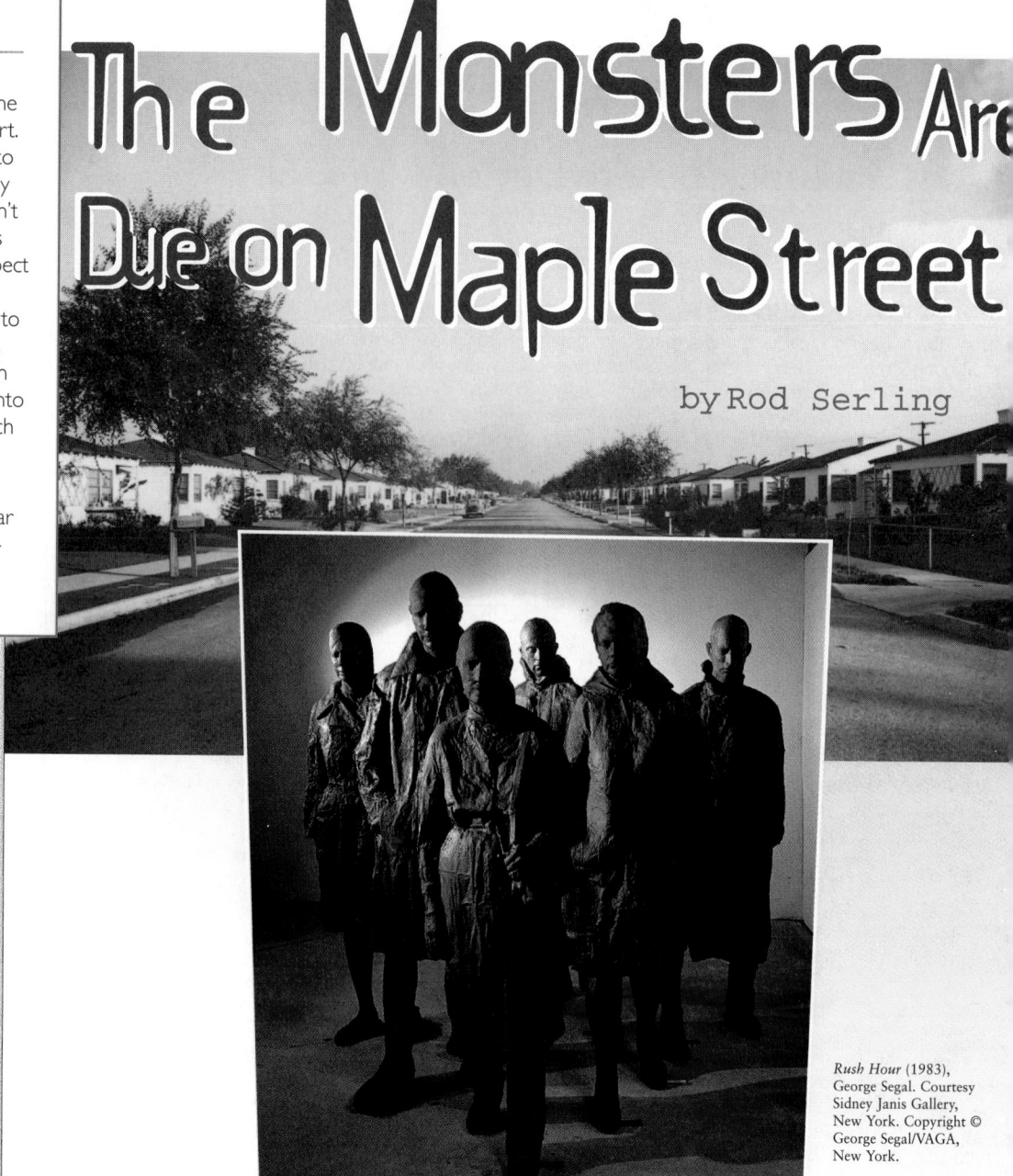

The Monsters Are Due on Maple Street

by Rod Serling

Rush Hour (1983), George Segal. Courtesy Sidney Janis Gallery, New York. Copyright © George Segal/VAGA, New York.

356   UNIT THREE   PART 2: A CHANGE OF HEART

Art Note

Rush Hour by George Segal George Segal (1924–) is best known for his life-size sculptures of real people in real situations. Many of his works are in public areas, and at first glance his figures are often mistaken for living people.

Reading the Art *What feelings do these sculptures stir in you, and why?*

CUSTOMIZING FOR
Students Acquiring English

- Use **ACCESS FOR STUDENTS ACQUIRING ENGLISH**, *Reading and Writing Support.*

- Encourage all students to read aloud passages from this play. Some students may prefer to read the roles of Voices Four or Five, or Man Two, which have only one line each.

STRATEGIC READING FOR
Less-Proficient Readers

Set a Purpose To help students become involved in the selection, have them discuss what they think a typical suburban street is like. Then ask them to read to find out what strange events have occurred on Maple Street.

Use **UNIT THREE RESOURCE BOOK**, p. 63, for guidance in reading the selection.

WORDS TO KNOW

antagonism (ăn-tăg′ə-nĭz′əm) *n.* hostility; unfriendliness (p. 361)

contorted (kən-tôr′tĭd) *adj.* twisted or pulled out of shape **contort** *v.* (p. 366)

defiant (dĭ-fī′ənt) *adj.* willing to stand up to opposition; bold (p. 361)

flustered (flŭs′tərd) *adj.* nervous or confused **fluster** *v.* (p. 359)

idiosyncrasy (ĭd′ē-ō-sĭng′krə-sē) *n.* a personal way of acting; an odd mannerism (p. 365)

incriminate (ĭn-krĭm′ə-nāt′) *v.* to cause to appear guilty (p. 363)

intense (ĭn-tĕns′) *adj.* showing great concentration or determination (p. 360)

legitimate (lə-jĭt′ə-mĭt) *adj.* in accordance with accepted practices; reasonable (p. 364)

optimistic (ŏp′tə-mĭs′tĭk) *adj.* hopeful about the future; confident (p. 360)

persistent (pər-sĭs′tənt) *adj.* refusing to give up; continuing stubbornly (p. 360)

CUSTOMIZING FOR

Gifted and Talented Students

Ask students to identify the various points in the story where the neighbors turn on one another and to explain why they do so in each case.

Possible responses:

- *Pages 361–362—Because Les's car starts by itself and his neighbors' cars do not, Les is set apart from the rest, and his neighbors become suspicious.*

- *Page 363—Because Les looks at the sky late at night, neighbors assume he has alien friends.*

- *Page 365—Since no one has seen Steve's ham radio, neighbors assume he uses it to contact aliens.*

- *Page 366—Because Charlie can't see what is approaching, he assumes the figure is an alien and shoots.*

- *Page 366—Because Charlie's lights go on, the neighbors assume he is different and dangerous.*

- *Page 367—Because Tommy gave an explanation for what was happening, the neighbors assume he is the monster.*

CUSTOMIZING FOR

Multiple Learning Styles

A **Bodily-Kinesthetic Learners** Invite students to pantomime the actions of the characters in the opening scene.

CUSTOMIZING FOR

Students Acquiring English

I Point out that the narrator describes an idyllic small town in the 1950s or 1960s. You may need to explain front-porch gliders, hopscotch, and the bell of an ice-cream vendor.

CAST OF CHARACTERS

Narrator	**Voice One**	**Man One**
Tommy	**Voice Two**	**Les Goodman**
Steve Brand	**Voice Three**	**Ethel Goodman**, *Les's wife*
Don Martin	**Voice Four**	**Man Two**
Myra Brand, *Steve's wife*	**Voice Five**	**Figure One**
Woman	**Pete Van Horn**	**Figure Two**
	Charlie	
	Sally, *Tommy's mother*	

A ct One

A (*Fade in on a shot of the night sky. The various heavenly bodies stand out in sharp, sparkling relief. The camera moves slowly across the heavens until it passes the horizon and stops on a sign that reads "Maple Street." It is daytime. Then we see the street below. It is a quiet, tree-lined, small-town American street. The houses have front porches on which people sit and swing on gliders, talking across from house to house. Steve Brand is polishing his car, which is parked in front of his house. His neighbor, Don Martin, leans against the fender watching him. An ice-cream vendor riding a bicycle is just in the process of stopping to sell some ice cream to a couple of kids. Two women gossip on the front lawn. Another man is watering his lawn with a garden hose. As we see these various activities, we hear the* Narrator's *voice.*)

Narrator. Maple Street, U.S.A., late summer. A tree-lined little world of front-porch gliders, **I** hopscotch, the laughter of children, and the bell of an ice-cream vendor.

(*There is a pause, and the camera moves over to a shot of the ice-cream vendor and two small boys who are standing alongside just buying ice cream.*)

Mini-Lesson   The Writer's Style

DIALOGUE IN PLAYS Explain that plays consist mostly of dialogue. The dialogue must sound natural, show what is happening offstage, and reveal what the characters are thinking and feeling. The speeches of characters appear—without quotation marks—after their names. Stage directions, shown in parentheses and italics, give information about the setting and tell how the characters move or look.

Application Ask students to reread aloud the scene on pages 366 and 367 where Charlie is accused by the crowd. Then have students work in small groups to write several lines of dialogue to extend the scene. Have the groups read aloud the dialogue that they create.

Reteaching/Reinforcement
- *Writing Mini-Lessons* transparencies, p. 48

 The Writer's Craft

Creating Dialogue, pp. 320–322

B Meteoroids are rock fragments traveling through space. Meteoroids that are drawn into Earth's atmosphere by its gravitational field are called meteors. As they enter the atmosphere, they are traveling at speeds of up to 5,200 miles (8,400 kilometers) per hour. Friction caused by traveling through atmospheric gases results in most meteors vaporizing before they reach the ground. Those rare meteors that reach the Earth's surface are called meteorites.

Literary Concept: DIALOGUE

C The dialogue of Voices One, Two, Three, Four, and Five consists of brief, clipped sentences that suggest the urgency triggered by fear of the unknown.

Active Reading: PREDICT

D Ask students to predict what will be revealed as the cause of the flash and subsequent power outage. (*Possible responses: aliens, a meteor, a bomb*)

Narrator. At the sound of the roar and the flash of the light, it will be precisely six-forty-three p.m. on Maple Street.

(*At this moment* Tommy, *one of the two boys buying ice cream from the vendor, looks up to listen to a tremendous screeching roar from overhead. A flash of light plays on the faces of both boys and then moves down the street and disappears. Various people leave their porches or stop what they are doing to stare up at the sky.* Steve Brand, *the man who has been polishing his car, stands there transfixed, staring upwards. He looks at* Don Martin, *his neighbor from across the street.*)

B **Steve.** What was that? A meteor?

Don. That's what it looked like. I didn't hear any crash though, did you?

Steve. Nope. I didn't hear anything except a roar.

Myra (*from her porch*). What was that?

Steve (*raising his voice and looking toward the porch*). Guess it was a meteor, honey. Came awful close, didn't it?

Myra. Too close for my money! Much too close.

(*The camera moves slowly across the various porches to* people *who stand there watching and talking in low conversing tones.*)

Narrator. Maple Street. Six-forty-four p.m. on a late September evening. (*He pauses.*) Maple Street in the last calm and reflective moment (*pause*) before the monsters came!

(*The camera takes us across the porches again. A man is replacing a light bulb on a front porch. He gets off his stool to flick the switch and finds that nothing happens. Another man is working on an electric power mower. He plugs in the plug, flicks the switch of the mower off and on, but nothing happens. Through a window we see a woman pushing her finger up and down on the dial hook of a telephone. Her voice sounds far away.*)

Woman. Operator, operator, something's wrong on the phone, operator! (Myra Brand *comes out on the porch and calls to* Steve.)

Myra (*calling*). Steve, the power's off. I had the soup on the stove, and the stove just stopped working.

Woman. Same thing over here. I can't get anybody on the phone either. The phone seems to be dead.

(*We look down again on the street. Small, mildly disturbed voices are heard coming from below.*)

Voice One. Electricity's off.

Voice Two. Phone won't work.

Voice Three. Can't get a thing on the radio.

Voice Four. My power mower won't move, won't work at all.

Voice Five. Radio's gone dead!

(Pete Van Horn, *a tall, thin man, is seen standing in front of his house.*)

Pete. I'll cut through the back yard to see if the power's still on, on Floral Street. I'll be right back!

(*He walks past the side of his house and disappears into the back yard. The camera pans down slowly until we are looking at ten or eleven people standing around the street and overflowing to the curb and sidewalk. In the background is* Steve Brand's *car.*)

Steve. Doesn't make sense. Why should the power go off all of a sudden and the phone line?

Don. Maybe some kind of an electrical storm or something.

Charlie. That don't seem likely. Sky's just as blue as anything. Not a cloud. No lightning. No thunder. No nothing. How could it be a storm?

Woman. I can't get a thing on the radio. Not even the portable.

Mini-Lesson **Reading Skills/Strategies**

DISTINGUISHING BETWEEN FACT AND OPINION Tell students that it is important to distinguish fact from opinion as they read works of literature. A fact is a statement that can be proved, such as "Rod Serling is the author of *The Monsters Are Due on Maple Street.*" An opinion is a statement that cannot be proved, such as "*The Monsters Are Due on Maple Street* is the best drama that Rod Serling ever wrote."

Application Have students classify each of the following statements as fact or opinion and explain the reason why.

1. Charlie kills Pete Van Horn in *The Monsters Are Due on Maple Street.* (*fact*)
2. Charlie is the most evil character in the play. (*opinion*)
3. Pete Van Horn probably was a spy for the alien invaders. (*opinion*)
4. Reading a teleplay is more enjoyable than watching one. (*opinion*)

Reteaching/Reinforcement
• *Unit Three Resource Book,* p. 64

(*The people again begin to murmur softly in wonderment.*)

Charlie. Well, why don't you go downtown and check with the police, though they'll probably think we're crazy or something. A little power failure and right away we get all <u>flustered</u> and everything—

Steve. It isn't just the power failure, Charlie. If it was, we'd still be able to get a broadcast on the portable.

(*There is a murmur of reaction to this. Steve looks from face to face and then at his car.*)

Steve. I'll run downtown. We'll get this all straightened out.

(*He gets in the car and turns the key. Looking through the open car door, we see the crowd watching* Steve *from the other side. He starts the engine. It turns over sluggishly and then stops dead. He tries it again, and this time he can't get it to turn over. Then very slowly he turns the key back to "off" and gets out of the car. The people stare at* Steve. *He stands for a moment by the car and then walks toward them.*)

Steve. I don't understand it. It was working fine before—

Don. Out of gas?

Steve (*shakes his head*). I just had it filled.

Woman. What's it mean?

Charlie. It's just as if (*pause*) as if everything had stopped. (*Then he turns toward* Steve.) We'd better walk downtown.

(*Another murmur of assent to this.*)

Steve. The two of us can go, Charlie. (*He turns to look back at the car.*) It couldn't be the meteor. A meteor couldn't do this.

(*He and* Charlie *exchange a look. Then they start to walk away from the group.* Tommy *comes into view. He is a serious-faced young*

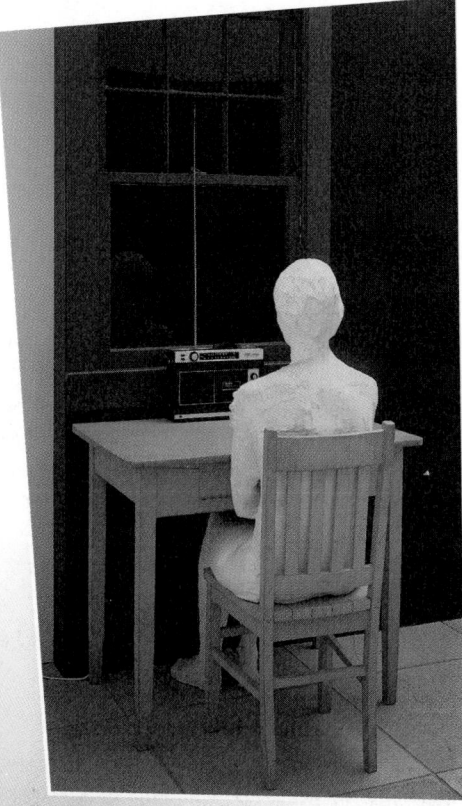

Alice Listening to Her Poetry and Music (1970), George Segal. Bayer Staatsgemäldesammlungen–Staatsgalerie Moderner Kunst, Munich, Germany. Copyright © George Segal/VAGA, New York.

boy in spectacles. He stands halfway between the group and the two men, who start to walk down the sidewalk.*)

Tommy. Mr. Brand—you'd better not!

Steve. Why not?

Tommy. They don't want you to.

(*Steve *and* Charlie *exchange a grin, and* Steve *looks back toward the boy.*)

Steve. Who doesn't want us to?

Tommy (*jerks his head in the general direction of*

WORDS TO KNOW

flustered (flŭs′tərd) *adj.* nervous or confused **fluster** *v.*

359

Active Reading: EVALUATE

G Ask students why they think the adults are willing to listen to Tommy's explanation about what is happening on Maple Street. Use the following model.

Think-Aloud Model *Adults don't usually pay attention to children during a crisis. Maybe because they have no explanation of their own and they are frightened of the unknown, the adults are willing to listen to any explanation. Perhaps they know Tommy to be a particularly bright child and worth listening to.*

Critical Thinking: ANALYZING

H Ask students why they think Tommy's mother wants him to stop talking. *(Possible responses: Tommy is voicing everyone's hidden fears; Tommy's mother is afraid that the neighbors might turn against her son.)*

Linking to Science

I Scientist George Hale discovered sunspots in 1750. They occur on the photosphere, or surface, of the sun and are caused by changes in the sun's magnetic field. Depending on its size, a sunspot can last for only a few hours or for as long as several months. Some scientists think that the solar storms associated with sunspots interfere with radio and television reception on earth.

---

the distant horizon). Them!

Steve. Them?

Charlie. Who are them?

Tommy *(intently).* Whoever was in that thing that came by overhead.

(Steve knits his brows for a moment, cocking his head questioningly. His voice is intense.*)*

Steve. What?

Tommy. Whoever was in that thing that came over. I don't think they want us to leave here.

(Steve leaves Charlie, walks over to the boy, and puts his hand on the boy's shoulder. He forces his voice to remain gentle.)

G

Steve. What do you mean? What are you talking about?

Tommy. They don't want us to leave. That's why they shut everything off.

Steve. What makes you say that? Whatever gave you that idea?

Woman *(from the crowd).* Now isn't that the

Detail of *Rush Hour* (1983), George Segal.

---

craziest thing you ever heard?

Tommy *(persistent but a little frightened).* It's always that way, in every story I ever read about a ship landing from outer space.

Woman *(to the boy's mother, Sally, who stands on the fringe of the crowd).* From outer space yet! Sally, you better get that boy of yours up to bed. He's been reading too many comic books or seeing too many movies or something!

Sally. Tommy, come over here and stop that kind of talk.

Steve. Go ahead, Tommy. We'll be right back. And you'll see. That wasn't any ship or anything like it. That was just a . . . a meteor or something. Likely as not— *(He turns to the group,* now trying very hard to sound more optimistic than he feels.*)* No doubt it did have something to do with all this power failure and the rest of it. Meteors can do some crazy things. Like sunspots.

Don *(picking up the cue).* Sure. That's the kind of thing—like sunspots. They raise Cain[1] with radio reception all over the world. And this thing being so close—why, there's no telling the sort of stuff it can do. *(He wets his lips and smiles nervously.)* Go ahead, Charlie. You and Steve go into town and see if that isn't what's causing it all.

(Steve and Charlie walk away from the group down the sidewalk as the people watch silently. Tommy stares at them, biting his lips, and finally calls out again.)

---

1. **raise Cain:** cause trouble; create a disturbance. (In the Bible, Adam and Eve's son Cain becomes the first murderer when he kills his brother Abel.)

WORDS TO KNOW
intense (ĭn-tĕns′) *adj.* showing great concentration or determination
persistent (pər-sĭs′tənt) *adj.* refusing to give up; continuing stubbornly
optimistic (ŏp′tə-mĭs′tĭk) *adj.* hopeful about the future; confident

360

Mini-Lesson Spelling

SUFFIXES *-ance/-ant -ence/-ent* The suffixes *-ance* and *-ant* are commonly added to complete words. The suffixes *-ence* and *-ent* are commonly added to roots after the letters *ci, qu,* and *sc.* Tell students that many words that begin with *a* use the suffixes that begin with *a.*

Application Invite the students to choose the correct suffix to complete the words in the following sentences.

1. Charlie's consci(<u>ence</u>/ance) didn't bother him one bit after shooting Pete.
2. All of the inhabit(ents/<u>ants</u>) of Maple Street were

afraid of the unseen danger.

3. All of the appli(ences/<u>ances</u>) stopped working after the blinding flash.
4. Steve offered little guid(ence/<u>ance</u>) to the mob, already wild with fright.

Ask students to look for more words that fit this pattern, in their own writing and in things that they read, and to add these words to their personal word lists.

Reteaching/Reinforcement
• *Unit Three Resource Book,* p. 65

Tommy. Mr. Brand!

(*The two men stop.* Tommy *takes a step toward them.*)

Tommy. Mr. Brand . . . please don't leave here.

(Steve *and* Charlie *stop once again and turn toward the* boy. *In the crowd there is a murmur of irritation and concern, as if the boy's words— even though they didn't make sense—were bringing up fears that shouldn't be brought up.* Tommy *is both frightened and* defiant.)

Tommy. You might not even be able to get to town. It was that way in the story. Nobody could leave. Nobody except—

Steve. Except who?

Tommy. Except the people they sent down ahead of them. They looked just like humans. And it wasn't until the ship landed that— (*The boy suddenly stops, conscious of the people staring at him and his mother and of the sudden hush of the crowd.*)

Sally. (*in a whisper, sensing the* antagonism *of the crowd*). Tommy, please son . . . honey, don't talk that way—

Man One. That kid shouldn't talk that way . . . and we shouldn't stand here listening to him. Why this is the craziest thing I ever heard of. The kid tells us a comic book plot, and here we stand listening—

(Steve *walks toward the camera and stops beside the boy.*)

Steve. Go ahead, Tommy. What kind of story was this? What about the people they sent out ahead?

Tommy. That was the way they prepared things for the landing. They sent four people. A mother and a father and two kids who looked just like humans . . . but they weren't.

(*There is another silence as* Steve *looks toward the crowd and then toward* Tommy. *He wears a tight grin.*)

Steve. Well, I guess what we'd better do then is to run a check on the neighborhood and see which ones of us are really human.

(*There is laughter at this, but it's a laughter that comes from a desperate attempt to lighten the atmosphere. The people look at one another in the middle of their laughter.*)

Charlie (*rubs his jaw nervously*). I wonder if Floral Street's got the same deal we got. (*He looks past the houses.*) Where is Pete Van Horn anyway? Isn't he back yet?

(*Suddenly there is the sound of a car's engine starting to turn over. We look across the street toward the driveway of* Les Goodman's *house. He is at the wheel trying to start the car.*)

Sally. Can you get started, Les?

(Les Goodman *gets out of the car, shaking his head.*)

Les. No dice.

(*He walks toward the group. He stops suddenly as, behind him, the car engine starts up all by itself.* Les *whirls around to stare at the car. The car idles roughly, smoke coming from the exhaust, the frame shaking gently.* Les's *eyes go wide, and he runs over to his car. The people stare at the car.*)

Man One. He got the car started somehow. He got *his* car started!

(*The people continue to stare, caught up by this revelation and wildly frightened.*)

Woman. How come his car just up and started like that?

Sally. All by itself. He wasn't anywheres near it.

WORDS
TO
KNOW

defiant (dǐ-fī′ənt) *adj.* willing to stand up to opposition; bold
antagonism (ăn-tăg′ə-nǐz′əm) *n.* hostility; unfriendliness

361

Literary Note

J One of Rod Serling's models for the plot of this teleplay was *The Crucible* by Arthur Miller. In this 1953 play, a community virtually destroys itself trying to find the source of evil during the Salem witch trials.

Literary Concept: THEME

K Explain to students that the theme of a literary work is the message about life or human nature that it conveys. Ask them what Tommy's comment about what the aliens looked like suggests about the theme. (*It supports the idea that the monsters or enemies may be "normal" human beings like the neighbors on Maple Street.*)

Active Reading: CONNECT

L Ask students what they think Steve's "tight grin" suggests about how he feels. Invite them to describe times when they have felt the same way Steve does. (*Possible response: Steve is trying to look calm and amused, but he is actually frightened.*)

STRATEGIC READING FOR
Less-Proficient Readers

M Ask students who Tommy seems to think is responsible for the flash of light and other strange events. (*aliens*)
Noting Relevant Details

Set a Purpose Have students find out what causes the neighbors to be suspicious of Les.

Mini-Lesson Literary Concepts

REVIEWING THEME Tell students that the theme is the message about life or human nature communicated by a work of literature. Explain that, in most cases, the reader must infer the theme. One way of figuring out a theme is to identify the lessons that the main characters learn and then to consider how these lessons might apply to all people.

Application Ask students to write a one-sentence summary of the theme of *The Monsters Are Due on Maple Street.* Have them discuss how this theme might apply to all people.

Man Leaning on a Car Door by George Segal By including the door of a flashy 1956 Mercury sedan in this sculpture, Segal paid tribute to his own love of cars and driving.

Reading the Art *What do you think the sculpture represents? What does the posture of the figure suggest?*

Critical Thinking:
MAKING JUDGMENTS

 Ask students if they think that "real oddball" is an accurate description of Les. Ask them what this description suggests about Charlie's expectations of his neighbors. *(Possible response: This isn't a good description, since Les probably does only one or two minor things differently from his neighbors. This description suggests that Charlie wants everyone else to live the way he does, without any variation.)*

CUSTOMIZING FOR
Students Acquiring English

(3) Point out that the word *mob* means "a crowd," but that the word conveys a negative meaning, suggesting a crowd that has gone wild and is bent on carrying out destructive actions that an individual would hesitate to do.

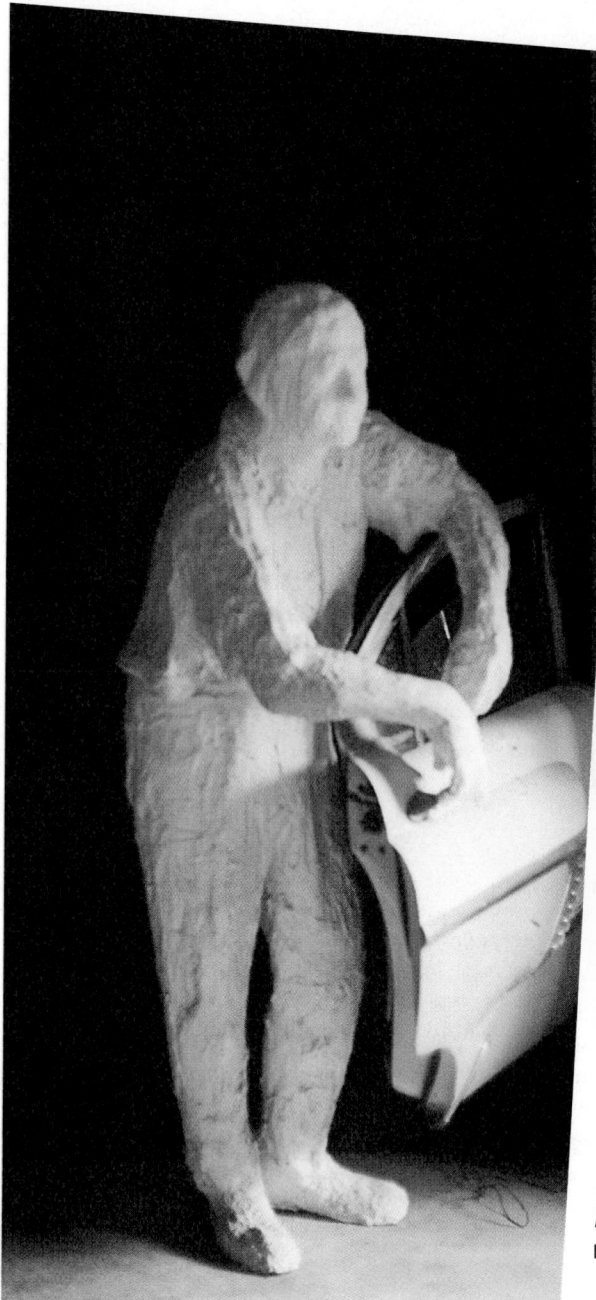

Man Leaning on a Car Door (1963), George Segal. Courtesy Sidney Janis Gallery, New York. Copyright © George Segal/VAGA, New York.

362 UNIT THREE PART 2: A CHANGE OF HEART

It started all by itself.

(Don Martin *approaches the group and stops a few feet away to look toward Les's car.*)

Don. And he never did come out to look at that thing that flew overhead. He wasn't even interested. (*He turns to the group, his face taut and serious.*) Why? Why didn't he come out with the rest of us to look?

Charlie. He always was an oddball. Him and his whole family. Real oddball.

Don. What do you say we ask him?

(*The group starts toward the house. In this brief fraction of a moment, it takes the first step toward changing from a group into a mob. The group members begin to head purposefully across the street toward the house. Steve stands in front of them. For a moment their fear almost turns their walk into a wild stampede, but Steve's voice, loud, incisive, and commanding, makes them stop.*)

Steve. Wait a minute . . . wait a minute! Let's not be a mob!

(*The people stop, pause for a moment, and then, much more quietly and slowly, start to walk across the street. Les stands alone facing the people.*)

Les. I just don't understand it. I tried to start it, and it wouldn't start. You saw me. All of you saw me.

(*And now, just as suddenly as the engine started, it stops, and there is a long silence that is gradually intruded upon by the frightened murmuring of the people.*)

Les. I don't understand. I swear . . . I don't understand. What's happening?

Don. Maybe you better tell us. Nothing's

| **Mini-Lesson** **Genre Study** |

DRAMA Explain to students that in a drama the story is related through the characters' dialogue and actions. The plot of a drama usually has the following parts:
- Introduction: Setting and characters are introduced.
- Conflict or problem: Some difficulty arises.
- Complications: Characters try to figure out how to solve the conflict or problem.
- Crisis/climax: Characters do something that changes the course of action.
- Resolution: Problems are solved through action or explanation.

Application Have students create a chart that includes all of the parts of the plot of a drama and then list details from *The Monsters Are Due on Maple Street* to illustrate each part.

working on this street. Nothing. No lights, no power, no radio, (*then meaningfully*) nothing except one car—yours!

The people's murmuring becomes a loud chant filling the air with accusations and demands for action. Two of the men pass Don *and head toward* Les, *who backs away from them against his car. He is cornered.*)

Les. Wait a minute now. You keep your distance—all of you. So I've got a car that starts by itself—well, that's a freak thing—I admit it. But does that make me a criminal or something? I don't know why the car works—it just does!

(*This stops the crowd momentarily, and* Les, *still backing away, goes toward his front porch. He goes up the steps and then stops, facing the mob.*)

Les. What's it all about, Steve?

Steve (*quietly*). We're all on a monster kick, Les. Seems that the general impression holds that maybe one family isn't what we think they are. Monsters from outer space or something. Different from us. Aliens from the vast beyond. (*He chuckles.*) You know anybody that might fit that description around here on Maple Street?

Les. What is this, a gag? (*He looks around the group again.*) This a practical joke or something?

(*Suddenly the car engine starts all by itself, runs for a moment, and stops. One woman begins to cry. The eyes of the crowd are cold and accusing.*)

Les. Now that's supposed to <u>incriminate</u> me, huh? The car engine goes on and off, and that really does it, doesn't it? (*He looks around at the faces of the people.*) I just don't understand it . . . any more than any of you do! (*He wets his lips, looking from face to face.*)

Look, you all know me. We've lived here five years. Right in this house. We're no different from any of the rest of you! We're no different at all. . . . Really . . . this whole thing is just . . . just weird—

Woman. Well, if that's the case, Les Goodman, explain why— (*She stops suddenly, clamping her mouth shut.*)

Les (*softly*). Explain what?

Steve (*interjecting*). Look, let's forget this—

Charlie (*overlapping him*). Go ahead, let her talk. What about it? Explain what?

Woman (*a little reluctantly*). Well . . . sometimes I go to bed late at night. A couple of times . . . a couple of times I'd come out here on the porch, and I'd see Mr. Goodman here in the wee hours of the morning standing out in front of his house . . . looking up at the sky. (*She looks around the circle of faces.*) That's right, looking up at the sky as if . . . as if he were waiting for something, (*pauses*) as if he were looking for something.

(*There's a murmur of reaction from the crowd again as* Les *backs away.*)

Les. She's crazy. Look, I can explain that. Please . . . I can really explain that . . . . She's making it up anyway. (*Then he shouts.*) I tell you she's making it up!

(*He takes a step toward the crowd, and they back away from him. He walks down the steps after them, and they continue to back away. Suddenly he is left completely alone, and he looks like a man caught in the middle of a menacing circle as the scene slowly fades to black.*)

P

Q

WORDS TO KNOW

incriminate (ĭn-krĭm′ə-nāt′) v. to cause to appear guilty

363

Mini-Lesson: Speaking,   Listening, and Viewing

DRAMA PERFORMANCE Tell students that they can increase their understanding and enjoyment of a teleplay by reading the script aloud. Explain to students that when performing a part in a Readers Theater performance, they should think of themselves as reading scripts in a recording studio. They must rely solely on their voices to make a character come alive for their audience.

Application Invite students to present a Readers Theater performance of an act of *The Monsters Are Due on Maple Street*. Remind students to speak clearly and expressively so that the audience will understand every word.

Act Two

Scene One

(Fade in on Maple Street at night. On the sidewalk, little knots of people stand around talking in low voices. At the end of each conversation they look toward Les Goodman's house. From the various houses, we can see candlelight but no electricity. The quiet that blankets the whole area is disturbed only by the almost whispered voices of the people standing around. In one group Charlie stands staring across at the Goodmans' house. Two men stand across the street from it in almost sentrylike poses.)

Sally *(in a small, hesitant voice).* It just doesn't seem right, though, keeping watch on them. Why . . . he was right when he said he was one of our neighbors. Why, I've known Ethel Goodman ever since they moved in. We've been good friends—

Charlie. That don't prove a thing. Any guy who'd spend his time lookin' up at the sky early in the morning—well, there's something wrong with that kind of person. There's something that ain't <u>legitimate</u>. Maybe under normal circumstances we could let it go by, but these aren't normal circumstances. Why, look at this street! Nothin' but candles. Why,

it's like goin' back into the Dark Ages or somethin'!

(Steve walks down the steps of his porch, down the street to the Goodmans' house, and then stops at the foot of the steps. Les is standing there; Ethel Goodman behind him is very frightened.)

Les. Just stay right where you are, Steve. We don't want any trouble, but this time if anybody sets foot on my porch—that's what they're going to get—trouble!

Steve. Look, Les—

Les. I've already explained to you people. I don't sleep very well at night sometimes. I get up and I take a walk and I look up at the sky. I look at the stars!

Ethel. That's exactly what he does. Why, this whole thing, it's . . . it's some kind of madness or something.

Steve *(nods grimly).* That's exactly what it is—some kind of madness.

Charlie's Voice *(shrill, from across the street).* You best watch who you're seen with, Steve! Until we get this all straightened out, you ain't exactly above suspicion yourself.

Steve *(whirling around toward him).* Or you, Charlie. Or any of us, it seems. From age eight on up!

Woman. What I'd like to know is—what are we gonna do? Just stand around here all night?

Charlie. There's nothin' else we *can* do! *(He turns back, looking toward Steve and Les again.)* One of 'em'll tip their hand. They got to.

Steve *(raising his voice).* There's something you can do, Charlie. You can go home and keep your mouth shut. You can quit strutting around like a self-appointed judge and climb into bed and forget it.

WORDS TO KNOW **legitimate** (lə-jĭt′ə-mĭt) *adj.* in accordance with accepted practices; reasonable

364

Charlie. You sound real anxious to have that happen, Steve. I think we better keep our eye on you, too!

Don (*as if he were taking the bit in his teeth, takes a hesitant step to the front*). I think everything might as well come out now. (*He turns toward Steve.*) Your wife's done plenty of talking, Steve, about how odd you are!

Charlie (*picking this up, his eyes widening*). Go ahead, tell us what she's said.

(Steve *walks toward them from across the street.*)

Steve. Go ahead, what's my wife said? Let's get it all out. Let's pick out every <u>idiosyncrasy</u> of every single man, woman, and child on the street. And then we might as well set up some kind of citizens' court. How about a firing squad at dawn, Charlie, so we can get rid of all the suspects. Narrow them down. Make it easier for you.

Don. There's no need gettin' so upset, Steve. It's just that . . . well . . . Myra's talked about how there's been plenty of nights you spent hours down in your basement workin' on some kind of radio or something. Well, none of us have ever seen that radio—

(*By this time* Steve *has reached the group. He stands there defiantly.*)

Charlie. Go ahead, Steve. What kind of "radio set" you workin' on? I never seen it. Neither has anyone else. Who do you talk to on that radio set? And who talks to you?

Steve. I'm surprised at you, Charlie. How come you're so dense all of a sudden? (*He pauses.*) Who do I talk to? I talk to monsters from outer space. I talk to three-headed green men who fly over here in what look like meteors.

(Myra Brand *steps down from the porch, bites her lip, calls out.*)

Myra. Steve! Steve, please. (*Then looking around, frightened, she walks toward the group.*) It's just a ham radio set, that's all. I bought him a book on it myself. It's just a ham radio set. A lot of people have them. I can show it to you. It's right down in the basement.

Steve (*whirls around toward her*). Show them nothing! If they want to look inside our house—let them go and get a search warrant.

Charlie. Look, buddy, you can't afford to—

Steve (*interrupting him*). Charlie, don't start telling me who's dangerous and who isn't and who's safe and who's a menace. (*He turns to the group and shouts.*) And you're with him, too—all of you! You're standing here all set to crucify—all set to find a scapegoat—all desperate to point some kind of a finger at a neighbor! Well now, look, friends, the only thing that's gonna happen is that we'll eat each other up alive—

(He stops abruptly as Charlie *suddenly grabs his arm.*)

Charlie (*in a hushed voice*). That's not the only thing that can happen to us.

(*Down the street, a figure has suddenly materialized in the gloom. In the silence we hear the clickety-clack of slow, measured footsteps on concrete as the figure walks slowly toward them. One of the women lets out a stifled cry. Sally grabs her boy, as do a couple of other mothers.*)

Tommy (*shouting, frightened*). It's the monster! It's the monster!

(*Another woman lets out a wail, and the people fall back in a group staring toward the darkness and the approaching figure. The people stand in the shadows watching. Don Martin joins them, carrying a shotgun. He holds it up.*)

idiosyncrasy (ĭd'ē-ō-sĭng'krə-sē) *n.* a personal way of acting; odd mannerism

365

Active Reading: CLARIFY

U Ask students what they think Steve means when he asks Charlie, "How come you're so dense all of a sudden?" (*Possible response: Steve is being sarcastic and is really asking why Charlie doesn't just come right out and accuse him of talking to aliens.*)

Critical Thinking: ANALYZING

V Ask students why they think that Steve's wife tries to stop him from talking anymore. (*Possible response: She may be afraid that people will believe his sarcastic remarks or that his protestations will be interpreted as symptoms of his guilt.*)

STRATEGIC READING FOR
Less-Proficient Readers

W Discuss with students how the neighbors begin to suspect another person each time they learn something new about someone else. Then have students explain why Steve becomes a suspect. (*because he works on a radio in the basement and no one has ever seen this radio*) **Noting Relevant Details**

Set a Purpose Have students read to find out what happens when the neighbors on Maple Street think they see and hear a monster coming.

CUSTOMIZING FOR
Multiple Learning Styles

X Logical-Mathematical Learners Ask students to use logical reasoning to list several possibilities for who or what might be walking toward the crowd. (*Possible responses: someone from a different part of town who wants to offer or ask for an explanation of what is going on; someone who has been hurt and needs assistance; the neighbor who went to check on the other street*)

Mini-Lesson: Speaking, Listening, and Viewing

FILM/DRAMA When viewing a film or dramatic performance, the viewer needs to work hard to interpret all that is going on. For example, a good viewer must infer the characters' qualities from the clues that the dialogue provides. Viewers also should observe how the characters interact, in order to infer how the characters feel about one another.

Application After students have viewed the Readers Theater performance described in the Mini-Lesson on page 363, ask them to explain how they used the dialogue to form interpretations of Charlie and Steve.

Critical Thinking: SPECULATING

Y Ask students to speculate about what Steve wanted to say by finishing his sentence, "What good would a shotgun do against—" (*Possible responses: something more powerful than we are; an alien; a monster; the unknown*)

Active Reading: EVALUATE

Z Ask students why they think that Charlie is now willing to believe that what is happening is a "gag." (*Possible answer: because now it is his reputation that is at risk, whereas before it was easier to suspect others*)

Don. We may need this.

Steve. A shotgun? (*He pulls it out of Don's hand.*) No! Will anybody think a thought around here! Will you people wise up. What good would a shotgun do against—

(*The dark figure continues to walk toward them as the people stand there, fearful, mothers clutching children, men standing in front of their wives.*)

Charlie (*pulling the gun from Steve's hands*). No more talk, Steve. You're going to talk us into a grave! You'd let whatever's out there walk right over us, wouldn't yuh? Well, some of us won't!

(*Charlie swings around, raises the gun, and suddenly pulls the trigger. The sound of the shot explodes in the stillness. The figure suddenly lets out a small cry, stumbles forward onto his knees, and then falls forward on his face. Don, Charlie, and Steve race forward to him. Steve is there first and turns the man over. The crowd gathers around them.*)

Steve (*slowly looks up*). It's Pete Van Horn.

Don (*in a hushed voice*). Pete Van Horn! He was just gonna go over to the next block to see if the power was on—

Woman. You killed him, Charlie. You shot him dead!

Charlie (*looks around at the circle of faces, his eyes frightened, his face contorted*). But . . . but I didn't know who he was. I certainly didn't know who he was. He comes walkin' out of the darkness—how am I supposed to know who he was? (*He grabs Steve.*) Steve—you know why I shot! How was I supposed to know he wasn't a monster or something? (*He grabs Don.*) We're all scared of the same thing. I was just tryin' to . . . tryin' to protect my home, that's all! Look, all of you, that's all I was tryin' to do. (*He looks down wildly at the*

body.) I didn't know it was somebody we knew! I didn't know—

(*There's a sudden hush and then an intake of breath in the group. Across the street all the lights go on in one of the houses.*)

Woman (*in a hushed voice*). Charlie . . . Charlie . . . the lights just went on in your house. Why did the lights just go on?

Don. What about it, Charlie? How come you're the only one with lights now?

Les. That's what I'd like to know.

(*Pausing, they all stare toward Charlie.*)

Les. You were so quick to kill, Charlie, and you were so quick to tell us who we had to be careful of. Well, maybe you had to kill. Maybe Pete there was trying to tell us something. Maybe he'd found out something and came back to tell us who there was amongst us we should watch out for—

(*Charlie backs away from the group, his eyes wide with fright.*)

Charlie. No . . . no . . . it's nothing of the sort! I don't know why the lights are on. I swear I don't. Somebody's pulling a gag or something.

(*He bumps against Steve, who grabs him and whirls him around.*)

Steve. A gag? A gag? Charlie, there's a dead man on the sidewalk, and you killed him! Does this thing look like a gag to you?

(*Charlie breaks away and screams as he runs toward his house.*)

Charlie. No! No! Please!

(*A man breaks away from the crowd to chase Charlie. As the man tackles him and lands on top of him, the other people start to run toward them. Charlie gets up, breaks away from the other man's grasp, and lands a couple of des-*

WORDS TO KNOW   **contorted** (kən-tôr′tĭd) *adj.* twisted or pulled out of shape   **contort** *v.*

366

Assessment ✓ Option

SELF-ASSESSMENT Help students evaluate their understanding by showing them how to create a story log of this selection. Point out that they can record time and place in their logs. For example, they can start by recording that the story begins on Maple Street at 6:43 p.m. Then have them write the events that took place. Similarly, have students create time/place entries for each act or scene and

then log in the events that took place. To help students assess their own work, have them ask themselves and then respond to the following questions:
• What did I most enjoy about creating the story log?
• What was the most difficult part?
• If I were creating a new log, what would I do differently?

erate punches that push the man aside. Then
e forces his way, fighting, through the crowd
nd jumps up on his front porch. Charlie *is on*
is porch as a rock thrown from the group
mashes a window beside him, the broken glass
lying past him. A couple of pieces cut him. He
tands there perspiring, rumpled, blood running
down from a cut on the cheek. His wife breaks
away from the group to throw herself into his
arms. He buries his face against her. We can see
he crowd converging on the porch.)

Voice One. It must have been him.

Voice Two. He's the one.

Voice Three. We got to get Charlie.

(*Another rock lands on the porch.* Charlie *push-*
es his wife behind him, facing the group.)

Charlie. Look, look I swear to you. . . . it isn't me
. . . but I do know who it is . . . I swear to
you, I do know who it is. I know who the
monster is here. I know who it is that doesn't
belong. I swear to you I know.

Don (*pushing his way to the front of the crowd*).
All right, Charlie, let's hear it!

(Charlie*'s eyes dart around wildly.*)

Charlie. It's . . . it's . . .

Man Two (*screaming*). Go ahead, Charlie.

Detail of *Man Leaning on a Car Door* (1963), George Segal.

Charlie. It's . . . it's the kid. It's Tommy. He's the **AA**
one!

(*There's a gasp from the crowd as we see* Sally
holding the boy. Tommy *at first doesn't under-*
stand and then, realizing the eyes are all on him,
buries his face against his mother.)

Sally (*backs away*). That's crazy! He's only a boy.

Woman. But he knew! He was the only one! He
told us all about it. Well, how did he know?
How could he have known?

(*Various people take this up and repeat the*
question.)

Voice One. How could he know?

Voice Two. Who told him?

Voice Three. Make the kid answer.

(*The crowd starts to converge around the moth-*
er, who grabs Tommy *and starts to run with him.*
The crowd starts to follow, at first walking fast,
and then running after him. Suddenly Charlie's
lights go off and the lights in other houses go on,
then off.)

Man One (*shouting*). It isn't the kid . . . it's Bob
Weaver's house.

Woman. It isn't Bob Weaver's house, it's Don
Martin's place.

Charlie. I tell you it's the kid.

Don. It's Charlie. He's the one.

(*People shout, accuse, and scream as the lights*
go on and off. Then, slowly, in the middle of
this nightmarish confusion of sight and sound,
the camera starts to pull away until, once again, **BB**
we have reached the opening shot looking at the
Maple Street sign from high above.) **CC**

Scene Two

(*The camera continues to move away while grad-*
ually bringing into focus a field. We see the metal
side of a spacecraft that sits shrouded in darkness.
An open door throws out a beam of light from

THE MONSTERS ARE DUE ON MAPLE STREET **367**

Active Reading: EVALUATE

AA Ask students if they think that
Charlie really believes that Tommy is
the monster. Have them explain their
answers. (*Possible response: He probably*
doesn't think it's Tommy, but he says so
because he wants to take the attention
off himself.)

Literary Concept: THEME

BB Ask students how the view of
Maple Street from high above is con-
nected to the theme of the story.
(*Possible response: Anyone looking at*
Maple Street from this angle would
think—as the reader does at the begin-
ning—that it is a typical, normal
American suburb. As the theme suggests,
things are not always as they appear,
Maple Street included.)

STRATEGIC READING FOR
Less-Proficient Readers

CC Ask students the following
questions:

• What happens when a dark figure is
seen walking toward the crowd?
(*Charlie shoots at it and kills Pete*
Van Horn.) **Restating**

• Why does Charlie shoot? (*He is terri-*
fied that the figure is a monster that
will do harm.) **Making Inferences**

• Whom does Charlie accuse of being
the monster? (*Tommy, an eight-year-*
old neighbor) **Noting Relevant Details**

Set a Purpose Have students read to
the end of the selection to find out
who the "monster" really is.

Mini-Lesson | **Study Skills**

TAKING ESSAY TESTS Explain to students
that when they take an essay test, they must
write in-depth answers to any question posed.
Also they should support their answers with evidence or examples. Tell students it is helpful to
plan or outline their answers before beginning
to write.

Application Tell students to act as if they are
taking an essay test and plan the answer to this
essay-type question:

Which man do you think would make a better
leader, Charlie or Steve? Support your answer with
evidence from the selection.

Suggest that students organize their notes in a
chart like the one shown.

Answer: Steve

Evidence: Charlie: is quick to react;
shoots Pete without looking first.
Steve: tries to remain calm; doesn't
back down

the illuminated interior. Two figures appear, silhouetted against the bright lights. We get only a vague feeling of form.)

Figure One. Understand the procedure now? Just stop a few of their machines and radios and telephones and lawn mowers. . . . Throw them into darkness for a few hours, and then just sit back and watch the pattern.

Figure Two. And this pattern is always the same?

Figure One. With few variations. They pick the most dangerous enemy they can find . . . and it's themselves. And all we need do is sit back . . . and watch.

Figure Two. Then I take it this place . . . this Maple Street . . . is not unique.

Figure One *(shaking his head)*. By no means. Their world is full of Maple Streets. And we'll go from one to the other and let them destroy themselves. One to the other . . . one to the other . . . one to the other—

Detail of *Rush Hour* (1983), George Segal.

Scene Three

(The camera slowly moves up for a shot of the starry sky, and over this we hear the Narrator's *voice.)*

Narrator. The tools of conquest do not necessarily come with bombs and explosions and fallout.[2] There are weapons that are simply thoughts, attitudes, prejudices—to be found only in the minds of men. For the record, prejudices can kill and suspicion can destroy. A thoughtless, frightened search for a scapegoat has a fallout all its own for the children . . . and the children yet unborn, *(a pause)* and the pity of it is . . . that these things cannot be confined to . . . The Twilight Zone!

(Fade to black.)

---

2. **fallout:** radioactive particles that fall to earth after a nuclear explosion.

RESPONDING OPTIONS

FROM PERSONAL RESPONSE TO CRITICAL ANALYSIS

REFLECT   1. In your notebook, jot down words and phrases that describe your reaction to the ending of the teleplay. Then share your reactions with a partner.

RETHINK   2. Do you think the aliens are correct in their judgment of human behavior? Why or why not?

3. In your opinion, are the monsters on Maple Street the aliens or the residents? Give reasons for your answer.

4. Why do you think the author chose Maple Street as the setting of this teleplay?

RELATE   5. This teleplay shows what can happen when a crowd becomes a mob. How does being in a crowd change the way people act? What other examples of "mob mentality" do you know about?

LITERARY CONCEPTS

In drama, stories are told mostly through **dialogue,** or conversations between characters. The characters' dialogue also reveals their beliefs and values. According to the dialogue in this teleplay, which characters react most strongly to fear of the unknown?

CONCEPT REVIEW: Theme A literary work's theme is a message about life or human nature that the work conveys to readers. A work's theme may not be stated directly, and a work might have more than one theme. What do you think is the main theme of *The Monsters Are Due on Maple Street*?

Multimodal Learning
ANOTHER PATHWAY

Cooperative Learning
Put Charlie on trial for the death of Pete Van Horn. Some class members should role-play the parts of the judge, the trial lawyers, and witnesses from the neighborhood. The rest of the class should act as the jury and decide whether Charlie killed Pete in self-defense or is guilty of manslaughter.

QUICKWRITES

1. Write a short **summary** of this teleplay, like one that might appear in a videotape catalog. Remember to entice readers to make them want to rent or buy the video.

2. Write **stage directions** to describe what a visitor would find on Maple Street the day after the events of this teleplay.

3. Revise *The Monsters Are Due on Maple Street* to present a more positive perspective on human behavior. Write a **proposal** for changing the script, describing the reason for each change and the way it would affect the theme of the teleplay.

📁 *PORTFOLIO Save your writing. You may want to use it later as a springboard to a piece for your portfolio.*

THE MONSTERS ARE DUE ON MAPLE STREET   **369**

---

1. Possible response: I was surprised that aliens were involved at all.
2. Possible responses: Yes, because people tend to suspect others whom they regard as different. No, since people sometimes show true heroism and concern for others in an emergency.
3. Possible responses: The monsters are the aliens because they started the trouble. The monsters are the neighbors because they turned on each other.
4. Possible response: By using a typical suburban street like Maple Street, the author suggests that this pattern of behavior could happen anywhere.
5. Possible responses: People seem to take less personal responsibility for their actions when they are in a crowd. An example of "mob mentality" might be a crowd "stampede" at a sports event.

Another Pathway

Cooperative Learning Have students begin by looking up *self-defense* and *manslaughter* in a dictionary. Students can form teams of three or more to act as the defense and the prosecution. Allow them time to search for evidence in the selection and to prepare their arguments. Select a direction giver to keep students on track.

Rubric

3 Full Accomplishment Students prepare arguments, back up their statements with evidence, stay on track, and reach a verdict.

2 Substantial Accomplishment Students prepare arguments but have difficulty supporting their positions with evidence and staying on track.

1 Little or Partial Accomplishment Students have difficulty presenting the two arguments and are unable to translate information from the selection into a mock trial.

Literary Concepts

Have students trace the dialogues of characters to compare and contrast the ways they deal with their fear of the "monster." *(Possible responses: Tommy, because he looks to fantasy for an explanation; Charlie, because his fear leads to murder)*

Concept Review Have each student create a sentence that expresses the theme and read it aloud. *(Possible response: When we let prejudice and suspicion control us, we become our own worst enemy.)*

QuickWrites

1. Remind students to aim for enticing the reader without giving away the ending.
2. Tell students to create new stage directions by adapting the existing ones, taking into account the events suggested at the end of the play.
3. Help students get started by asking them to consider how the effect of this play would have been different if Pete Van Horn had not been killed.

 The Writer's Craft

Summarizing, pp. 342–343
Stage Directions, p. 321

Possible responses: Nessan's clan wants to sacrifice Dara, thinking that his death will make water flow again from their spring. Similarities: Neither scapegoat has anything to do with his group's problems; blaming someone as the cause of misfortune just makes the accusers feel better because they now have a known person whom they can attack as a way of solving a problem. Differences: The killing of scapegoats is common in Dara's culture, whereas on Maple Street it is unheard of and criminal.

Across the Curriculum

Social Studies *Cooperative Learning* Students may want to discuss the Holocaust, the reign of the Khmer Rouge in Cambodia, the issues surrounding the civil rights movement, women's rights, or any current events involving prejudice. Suggest they check encyclopedias, history books, and on-line reference sources. Divide students into groups of three or four. Each group can focus on one issue and present its findings to the class. As a class, students can create a social history time line showing when, where, and what kind of prejudice occurred. If feasible, students can display their time line in a place for the whole school to view.

Music *Monster Mash* Students who cannot play an instrument may wish to experiment with using drums or triangles to create their own simple compositions. Another suggestion might be to have students act as "disc jockeys" to select current songs that reflect the theme of *The Monsters Are Due on Maple Street.*

Multimodal Learning

ALTERNATIVE ACTIVITIES

1. Using details from the teleplay, create a **set design** showing what you think Maple Street looks like. Include houses, cars, and other objects mentioned in the script.

2. Rod Serling wanted to write meaningful plays about important social issues. Conduct a mock television **interview** with Serling, in which you discuss the social issue that he explores in this teleplay.

3. Research the controversy about the existence of UFOs (unidentified flying objects). Find out what the U.S. Air Force and others have to say about the possibility that aliens have visited the earth. If you have access to an on-line computer service, you might use it to begin your research. Present your findings to the class in an **oral report.**

4. Create a **comic book** based on the teleplay. Draw key scenes and write the accompanying dialogue.

Claude Akins as Steve Brand and Jack Weston as Charlie in the teleplay, *The Monsters Are Due on Maple Street.* Photofest.

Multimodal Learning

LITERARY LINKS

How does Dara become a scapegoat in "The Chief's Daughter" (page 259)? In what ways is the situation in that story similar to and different from the situation in this teleplay? Think about the settings as well as the beliefs, fears of the unknown, and motivations of the characters in both selections.

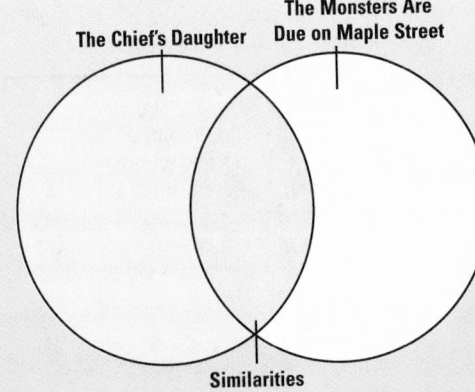

The Chief's Daughter | The Monsters Are Due on Maple Street

Similarities

ACROSS THE CURRICULUM

Social Studies How have prejudices and suspicions served to hurt and destroy people throughout history? Find out by looking through books about American and world history. Write a short summary of a tragic situation that was caused by irrational fear and prejudice, such as the Salem witch trials or the "Red scare." Then explain how you think people could avoid repeating such mistakes in the future.

Music Choose or compose appropriate background music for different scenes in *The Monsters Are Due on Maple Street.* Play the music for the class, explaining why you chose each piece.

Alternative Activities

1. Encourage students to present their set design as a sketch, painting, or scale model.
2. Have the students prepare questions that they would want to ask Serling. Then have them role-play the interview, basing Serling's responses on what they think the selection suggests about his attitudes.
3. Remind students that the existence of UFOs is controversial, so they must discuss each side of the issue in their oral reports. Prompt them to offer and support their own opinions as well.
4. Students can work in pairs for this activity. Each member can choose whether to write or draw, but they must work collaboratively.

WORDS TO KNOW

EXERCISE Use your understanding of the vocabulary words to help you complete the following sentences. Write the letter of each correct answer on your paper.

1. A student who is flustered is probably (a) confused, (b) happy, (c) asleep, (d) mean.
2. Intense fans might (a) clap softly, (b) show boredom, (c) scream, (d) leave early.
3. Optimistic students expect (a) punishment, (b) failure, (c) homework, (d) success.
4. A legitimate answer to a question is (a) silly, (b) sensible, (c) false, (d) dishonest.
5. If one's face is contorted, it is (a) clean, (b) red, (c) pale, (d) twisted.
6. A child who is defiant answers (a) boldly, (b) promptly, (c) cautiously, (d) timidly.
7. A persistent talker is (a) shy, (b) seldom quiet, (c) dishonest, (d) bragging.

8. If the police found evidence to incriminate you, you would be (a) relieved, (b) in trouble, (c) thankful, (d) released.
9. A nurse may feel antagonism toward a patient who (a) is insulting, (b) is considerate, (c) arrives on time, (d) feels feverish.
10. An idiosyncrasy is (a) a persistent drip, (b) a repeated sound, (c) a personal habit, (d) a stupid person.

WORDPLAY Use a dictionary to find the origin of the word *scapegoat.* Then, in your notebook, describe an example of a scapegoat that you have recently read or heard about.

ROD SERLING

Though the public knew Rod Serling as a creator of exciting television shows, those in the entertainment business knew him as "the angry young man of television." Serling began his career by writing for radio and television in Cincinnati. In 1955, he scored his first big hit with his television drama *Patterns,* which won an Emmy Award. Although Serling wanted to write meaningful plays about important social issues, television sponsors and executives often found his topics too controversial. Thus began his long battle with those who con-

1924–1975

trolled the networks.

Serling turned to writing science fiction and fantasy in series such as *The Twilight Zone* and *Night Gallery.* Because these shows were not realistic, he had more freedom to deal with issues such as prejudice and intolerance. Serling eventually won six Emmy Awards and many other honors for the extraordinary quality of his work.

OTHER WORKS *Stories from the Twilight Zone, Requiem for a Heavyweight, Planet of the Apes* (screenplay) Extended Reading

THE MONSTERS ARE DUE ON MAPLE STREET   **371**

WHAT DO YOU THINK?
Reflecting on Theme

Have students recall the writing or sketches showing first and later impressions that they created before reading the selections in Part 2. Having read Serling's teleplay, students may have additional thoughts about

why first impressions can change. Have students write about these ideas, or draw sketches showing their first and later impressions of the people on Maple Street.

OVERVIEW

To gain a deeper appreciation of the selections they have read in this unit, students will explore the qualities of informative writing and then write an essay that defines an idea.

Objectives

- To plan an essay by considering such elements as audience, purpose, specific examples, and organization
- To draft an essay that defines an idea and to solicit a response
- To revise, edit, and publish an essay
- To reflect on the process of writing a definition essay

Skills

LITERATURE
- Determining purpose

WRITING AND LANGUAGE
- Exploring definition
- Elaborating with specific examples
- Considering audience and purpose

GRAMMAR AND USAGE
- Punctuating appositives

MEDIA LITERACY
- Interpreting movie dialogue

- Studying business charts
- Reading magazine articles
- Finding examples in the media
- Gathering information on video

RESEARCH SKILLS
- Using KWL charts
- Using a dictionary

SPEAKING, LISTENING, AND VIEWING
- Conducting a group discussion
- Staging a game show
- Reading aloud

Critical Thinking: ANALYZING

A Explain to students that the choice of topic is especially important. Encourage students to select a term such as courage or patriotism that lends itself to in-depth analysis. Suggest that students begin with a basic dictionary definition to see if the term is suitable for an essay. Then, have students expand the dictionary definition with supporting details from their own personal experience and research.

Teaching Strategy: MODELING

B Discuss with students the way the Lion and the Wizard of Oz view courage. The definitions of courage in the movie dialogue are similar in that they both are connected to fear and bravery. They are different because the first involves not being afraid whereas the second involves facing danger even when you are afraid.

WRITING FROM EXPERIENCE

WRITING TO EXPLAIN

What is success? Who is truly beautiful? What is a hero? Each of us probably answers these questions differently. In Unit Three, "Stepping Forward," you saw how different authors portrayed the idea of courage. Did any of the examples surprise you?

GUIDED ASSIGNMENT

Define an Idea Writing about a difficult idea like courage can often help you and others understand it better. On the following pages you will have a chance to choose a quality and explore just what it means to you.

❶ Analyze Examples

The items on these two pages give examples of courage. How does each add to your understanding of courage? Which example do you think is most effective? Why? On the basis of these examples, write a definition of courage.

❷ Find an Idea to Explore

A Now think about other complex ideas, such as justice, success, and friendship. You may want to brainstorm additional ideas with some classmates.

Choose one idea that you'd like to explore. Talk to your friends about what the idea means to them, or look in your journal or at newspapers, magazines, or advertisements to find as many examples of your idea as possible.

❸ QuickWrite a Definition

Try jotting down a quick definition of the idea you've chosen.

372 UNIT THREE: STEPPING FORWARD

Movie Dialogue
The dialogue shows two different interpretations of courage. How are they similar? different? **B**

The Wizard of Oz
by L. Frank Baum

In this story, the Cowardly Lion thinks he lacks courage because he is afraid of wicked witches and other scary things. In the first of two excerpts below, he tells Dorothy why this is so. But in the second excerpt, the Wizard explains what true courage is and tells the Lion why he really has it.

* * *

"What makes you a coward?" asked Dorothy, looking at the great beast in wonder, for he was as big as a small horse.

"It's a mystery," replied the Lion. "I suppose I was born that way. All the other animals in the forest naturally expect me to be brave, for the Lion is everywhere thought to be the King of Beasts."

* * *

"But how about my courage?" asked the Lion anxiously.

"You have plenty of courage, I am sure," answered Oz. "All you need is confidence in yourself. There is no living thing that is not afraid when it faces danger. True courage is in facing danger when you are afraid, and that kind of courage you have in plenty."

PRINT AND MEDIA RESOURCES

UNIT THREE RESOURCE BOOK
Prewriting, p. 69
Elaboration, p. 70
Peer Response Guide, pp. 71–72
Revising and Proofreading, p. 73
Student Model, pp. 74–75
Rubric, p. 76

GRAMMAR MINI-LESSONS
Transparencies, p. 30
Copymasters, p. 39

WRITING MINI-LESSONS
Transparencies, pp. 4–5, 26 and 34

ACCESS FOR STUDENTS ACQUIRING ENGLISH
Reading and Writing Support

FORMAL ASSESSMENT
Guidelines for Writing Assessment

 **LASERLINKS**
Writing Springboard

 WRITING COACH

Business Chart

Which jobs seem most risky? Why do you think people choose dangerous jobs?

Risky Businesses

The danger of various jobs can be measured by the amount of money businesses spend for workers' compensation, insurance that covers job-related injuries and deaths.

Source: National Council on Compensation Insurance, Inc.

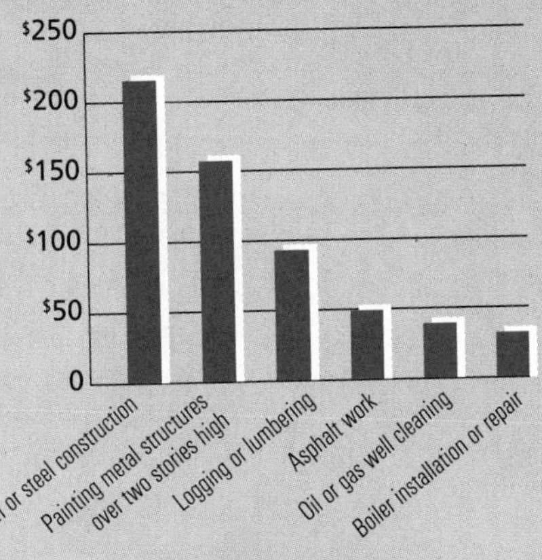

Monthly Workers'-Compensation Costs

$250
$200
$150
$100
$50
0

Iron or steel construction
Painting metal structures over two stories high
Logging or lumbering
Asphalt work
Oil or gas well cleaning
Boiler installation or repair

Magazine Article

Ryan White was 13 when he learned he had been infected with HIV. He became a spokesperson for people with AIDS during the long legal battle over his right to attend school. He died in 1990 at the age of 18.

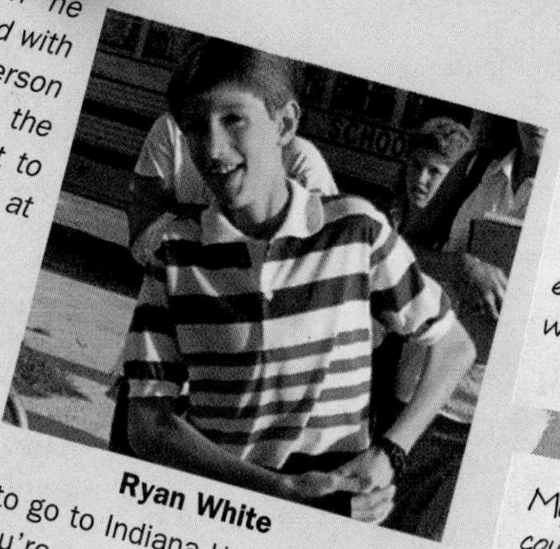

"Are you afraid of dying?" asks a student at Boys Town.

"No," Ryan says. "If I were worried about dying, I'd die. I'm not afraid, I'm just not ready yet. I want to go to Indiana University."

"How does it feel knowing you're going to die?" another boy wonders.

"Someday you'll die too," says Ryan. The boy, about Ryan's age, looks shocked. "Things could always be worse," Ryan adds, not wanting to cause discomfort. "It's how you live your life that counts."

from "The Quiet Victories of Ryan White"
People Weekly, May 30, 1988

Ryan White

Ryan White was certainly brave. I guess courage can be emotional as well as physical.

My mother's courageous in that sense. She's raising two kids alone and going to night school.

Jack Friedman

→ **LASERLINKS**
• *WRITING SPRINGBOARD*

→ **WRITING COACH**

WRITING FROM EXPERIENCE **373**

WRITING SPRINGBOARD

A Teen Volunteer Regina Hall, a teen volunteer, discusses her feelings about being a peer tutor.

Side B, Frame 10945

Writing Prompt Showing compassion or understanding for someone else's situation can sometimes be difficult. Using Regina's experience and other people's experiences that you know about, define *compassion*.

Writing Skill: DEFINITION

E Explain to students that to write a definition of a term, they should classify it and then list the characteristics that distinguish it from all other members of that class. Tell students that if at first they do not identify the qualities that distinguish a term from others in the same class, they must continue exploring the term until they do so.

CUSTOMIZING FOR
Less-Proficient Writers

F For inexperienced writers, use the following prompts to help them focus their thinking as they do their research:
- What are the qualities of the thing you are defining?
- How does it work?
- How is it different from others like it?
- Why do readers need to know about it?

Media Literacy: VIDEO

G Suggest that students look for video as well as print sources to gather information on their topic. Tell students that many public libraries have video collections that include documentaries on science, social studies, and the arts.

PREWRITING

Thinking on Paper

A Definition in Progress Before you can define your idea, you need to find out as much about it as possible. The suggestions below can help you start gathering information and asking questions that will help you shape your definition.

1 Think About Ways to Define

E What kind of information should you gather in order to define your idea? Below are ways you can define an idea. What types of details would you use in each one?

Dictionary Definition You might start with the basic meaning of the word. A dictionary definition might suggest different ways the word can be used.

Examples Give specific examples of the idea to help readers understand it.

Contrast Show what your idea is by describing what it isn't.

Anecdote Tell a story from your life that illustrates the idea.

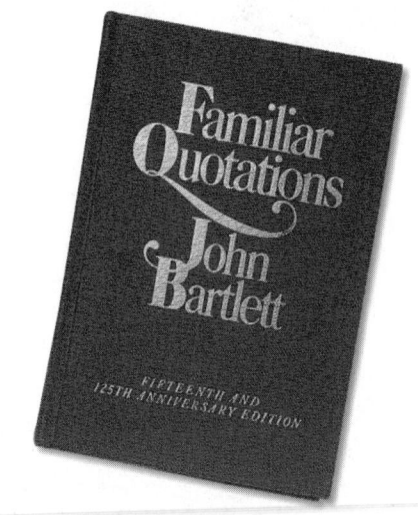

2 Research Every Angle

You've seen many methods you can use to create a definition. Now, how do you gather the actual details? Try any of the ideas below.

Gather Other Definitions Dictionaries and thesauri are good starting points. Gather some definitions, synonyms, and antonyms to get your ideas flowing. The SkillBuilder on the right will give you tips for using a dictionary to start exploring.

Brainstorm Form a discussion group in class or on e-mail to brainstorm definitions. Other people might have ideas you've never considered!

Check Out a Book of Quotations Books like Bartlett's *Familiar Quotations* list thoughtful and funny definitions of ideas, given by famous people.

Collect Anecdotes Ask people to describe the best example of your idea they've ever seen.

Find Examples in the Media Newspaper, television, and radio stories can provide real-life examples of your idea.

Mini-Lesson **Research Skills**

USING KWL CHARTS Explain to students that they can use the KWL method as they research their definition. Explain that KWL works equally well with brainstorming, researching, and interviewing. On the board, list the three steps in the KWL process:

  K: What do I already *know* about it?
  W: What do I *want* to know?
  L: What did I *learn*?

Describe each step. Then complete a sample KWL chart for a concept such as courage.

Application Invite students to make a KWL chart for the idea they wish to define. Suggest that students be as detailed as possible as they gather definitions, brainstorm, and collect anecdotes. Encourage students to refer to the chart as they draft their essays.

Focus Your Definition

By now you have probably collected several pages of notes about your idea. it's time to see how the pieces fit together. Try making a cluster diagram similar to the one below.

Write your idea in the middle of a piece of paper. Around it, write all the details that you've gathered and any others that come to mind. Each time you write a detail, draw a circle around it. Then draw lines to connect related ideas. Look for ways to group the details into categories.

Student's Cluster Diagram

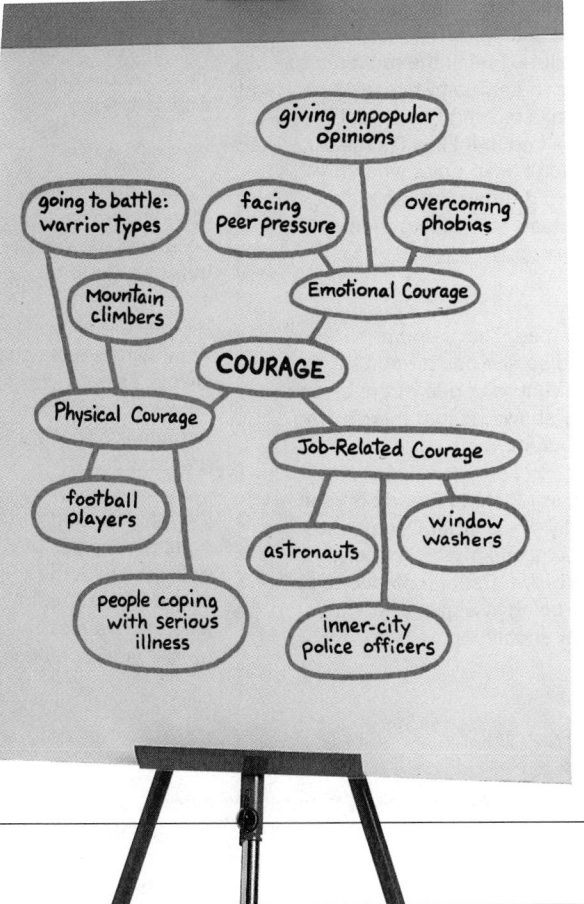

Using a Dictionary

A dictionary is a good resource for defining ideas, but it is just a starting point. For example, read the entry below.

cour•age n. 1 *the attitude of facing and dealing with anything recognized as dangerous, difficult, or painful, instead of withdrawing from it.*

This definition suggests that courage has many sides. It involves both the body and the mind, and actually facing the challenge, deciding not to hide from it. An essay about courage might give examples of some, or all, of these sides.

APPLYING WHAT YOU'VE LEARNED
Look up your idea in a dictionary. How many different sides does the idea have?

THINK & PLAN

Reflecting on Your Ideas

1. What examples best convey the idea you're trying to define?
2. What examples from your own life illustrate your idea?
3. What do other people think about the idea?
4. How might you organize the examples you've gathered?

Teaching Strategy:
STUMBLING BLOCK

H Students may think that cluster diagrams and other graphic organizers must be grammatically correct and logically organized. Explain to students that the purpose of a cluster diagram is to focus ideas. As a result, grammar, punctuation, and spelling are not important at this stage in the writing process. Also reassure students that it's all right to have a few redundancies in their chart. In fact, they may get a better grip on a slippery idea the second time they write it.

CUSTOMIZING FOR
Students Acquiring English

I Students from other cultures may define courage differently. If possible, use these cultural differences as a springboard to greater exploration of the topic.

SkillBuilder   **RESEARCH SKILLS**

USING A DICTIONARY Remind students that good dictionaries show how words have been used and are currently being used. Model how to find each part of a dictionary entry:

• spelling and syllabication
• pronunciation
• part of speech
• grammatical forms
• etymology
• definitions
• related words and synonyms

Application Explain that sometimes different dictionaries provide different information about specific words. To identify differences (and contradictions), invite students to use several dictionaries.

Additional Suggestions Have students use several dictionaries to look up the following words: *gumbo, cab, broadcast, rhetoric,* or *nachos.*

J Some students may find it helpful to keep a writing log. At the top of each piece of writing, have them note when, where, and how they are working. Explain that the more detailed the notations, the more the log will help them draw conclusions about their writing. After students make a number of such notations, have them write a brief paragraph evaluating the approaches they have used and assessing the effectiveness of each. Guide students to apply what they learn as they write their essays.

Writing Skill:
USING THE COMPUTER

K Ask students how they can tell that the draft shown on this page was written on a computer. *(Possible responses: by the computer screen, icons, arrows, computer typeface)* Discuss some of the advantages of drafting on a computer, such as speed, ease of revision, less worry about spelling corrections. Encourage students to draft their papers on the computer and use the Writing Coach, which provides detailed, specific guidelines for the drafting stage.

DRAFTING

Shaping Your Ideas

The Next Stage Now it's time to start drafting. As you write, it might help you to think about who your audience will be, how you might organize your ideas, and how you might present your definition. You can begin with your prewriting notes and continue expanding your definition.

1 Write and Analyze a Discovery Draft

Are you ready to put your thoughts into words? The Writing Coach may help you draft your definition. Just relax and start writing. Then take a break and reread what you wrote. Look at the quick definition you jotted down. How has it changed?

Student's Discovery Draft

Courage	
My Discovery Draft	**My Comments** My Discovery Draft
Most of the kids who answered my survey said courage is fighting an enemy. They gave examples like warrior-type movie characters and fighter pilots. I think the most courageous thing a person can do is to be true to himself and his beliefs. I mean, if I say I think smoking is stupid, I shouldn't let my friends talk me into it. If I say it's mean to pick on people, then I shouldn't keep quiet when my friends do it. But it takes guts to do that. Courage is also facing problems in your life instead of avoiding them. It's definitely not taking the easy way out.	I really don't agree with this definition. I should show another way of looking at it.
	Standing up for your beliefs takes courage, but it needs to be explained better.
My mom's raising two kids alone. That's courage. She started night school a year ago so she could get a better job. That took courage. Ryan White was one of the bravest people I can think of. His story shows us that there's emotional courage and physical courage.	What is that thing she always says? "The only way out of it is through it." That's a great quote.
Some kids defined courage as "Kicking Freddy Spinner's butt." Freddy is the school bully. My brother Danny once asked him, "How can hurting kids make you feel good about yourself?" That's pretty brave. Beating someone up is not. Being brave is also not being in a gang, hurting people on purpose, tagging, or shoplifting.	It might be good to compare the popular definition with my own. Maybe I could also make a poster for the youth center.

WRITING SPRINGBOARD
Ryan White Speaks Out Ryan White was a young AIDS patient who contracted the disease from a blood transfusion. He fought to stay in school against the protest of many members of his Indiana community. In this film, Ryan speaks to the presidential commission on AIDS.

Side B, Frame 13229

Writing Prompt Before he died of AIDS in 1990, Ryan White showed a great deal of courage in his fight against ignorance and intolerance. Define *courage*.

② Think About Audience and Purpose

As you get ready to start a new draft, think about whose attention you're trying to get and why. Will you present your writing to other students? your parents? the community? Now think about your purpose. How do you want people to react to your ideas? Your definition can

- change the way people think about the idea
- show many sides of it
- focus on one side of the idea
- show how you disagree with other definitions

③ Play with Format

Now think about ways to present your definition, such as in an essay, a poem, a mural, or posters. Speeches, articles, and posters can inform, persuade, or inspire. Ads persuade people to do something. An anthology or a bulletin-board display can show how several people define one idea. Try one of those formats or brainstorm with some friends.

④ Rework and Reflect

It's time to decide how to organize your ideas into an effective definition. If you used a cluster to brainstorm, each grouping there might be a paragraph. If your idea is complex, try starting with a dictionary definition or a quotation. If you have personal reasons for exploring the idea, include an anecdote from your own life. Don't worry if the first method of organization you try doesn't work. Just try another.

 PEER RESPONSE

After you have drafted a definition, you may want to get reactions from your peers. Try using the questions below.

- How would you restate my definition of the idea in your own words?
- Is my writing clearly organized? If not, what other type of organization might I use?
- How well do the examples support my definition?

N Remind students that narrative writing often uses informal language, especially in dialogue. In contrast, writing that explains, such as extended definitions, often uses formal diction. Tell students that they should think about the words they plan to use. Explain that some word-processing programs have special "Grammar Checkers" that check not only grammar and usage but also informal language and slang.

Writing Skill: REVISING

O Remind students that it is easier to spot weak organization and poor examples if they let a few hours elapse between writing and revising. If possible, encourage students to wait a little while before revising their writing. Be sure that students refer to the Standards for Evaluation as they revise their papers.

Teaching Strategy: MODELING

P Invite a volunteer to read the revised student essay aloud. Then discuss the questions in the side column. Possible responses include:
- The survey grabs the reader's attention. It is an effective opening.
- Comparing and contrasting allows the writer to add specific details and examples, which make the definition more specific.

REVISING AND PUBLISHING

Taking a Final Look

One Last Look Even the best writers revise their work again and again. When they do, they add new ideas and interesting details and improve its form. The following suggestions will help you refine your definition and get it ready for presentation.

① Revise and Edit

N Take a careful look at your definition. Is it clear and to the point? Have you included helpful examples? You might want to use the following ideas as you revise and edit your definition:

O
- Review your peer comments, the Standards for Evaluation, and your own reactions to your writing. How do the organization and the examples support your definition?

- Be sure your ideas flow smoothly. Find any gaps in thought and add details to fill in missing links. Use transitions to link ideas.
- Grab readers' attention. If a certain detail jumps out at you, try using it in your introduction. You might also start your definition with a statistic, a vivid description, a question, an anecdote, or a quotation.

Student's Revised Essay

Courage

When I asked the kids in 7B what courage is, 15 out of 28 said that courage is about physically fighting an enemy. Some of them mentioned warriors and fighter pilots. I agree that courage is about fighting enemies. But in my mind, the toughest enemies include sickness, pressure from other kids, family problems, and bad luck.

I asked kids to write about the most courageous act they could imagine. Many said "beating up the class bully." But would that show courage? In my opinion, that would be acting as badly as the bully. I think that talking to him would be the bravest thing to do. Is the bully brave? Some people might think so. But I think he's a coward. He's really scared but hides this by picking on kids smaller and weaker than he is.

Courage is in your muscle _and_ in your mind. My mom, a single mother and college student, says, "The only way out of it is through it," and she should know. She's always tired.

P Why do you think the writer begins with the survey results? Do you think this approach works?

How does comparing and contrasting help the writer define courage?

378

② Present Your Definition

The following illustration shows how one student turned his definition of courage into a pair of posters that he hung in the youth center. The posters compared some teens' misconceptions about courage with his own definition.

Student's Poster Series

SkillBuilder

GRAMMAR FROM WRITING

Punctuating Appositives
An **appositive** is a noun or phrase that explains the noun it follows. Use commas to set off an appositive that adds information unnecessary to understanding the sentence. Do not use commas when the appositive completes the sentence's meaning. Explain why commas are or are not used in these sentences.

My mom, a single mother and college student, says, . . .

The cat Ginger is my favorite.

GRAMMAR HANDBOOK

For more information, see pages 880–882 of the Grammar Handbook.

Editing Checklist The questions below can help you revise.

- Are the facts correct?
- Did you use transitions?
- Are your sentences varied?

REFLECT & ASSESS

Evaluating the Experience

1. What makes your definition a good one? How could you improve your next definition?
2. What ways of defining ideas can you use in other subjects?

📁 **PORTFOLIO** Your definition of the idea might change as you get older. Save it in your portfolio to reread later.

Speaking, Listening, and Viewing: GAME SHOW

Ⓠ Invite students to create a question-and-answer game show based on their written definitions. Invite each student to submit five questions and answers about his or her topic. Then have the class decide on the format for their game show, perhaps modeled on a TV game show. Assign a group to select the best questions and one student to act as the show host. Allow students time to read each other's essays in preparation for being contestants on the show.

PORTFOLIO
Invite students to rank their papers for possible inclusion in their portfolios. Encourage students to devise their own ranking systems to help them sort their work.

Standards for Evaluation

Have students review their essays for the following:

Ideas and Content
- defines an idea and uses specific details to explain it
- uses comparisons or other ways to clarify the explanation
- supports explanations with descriptions and examples
- has a strong introduction and satisfying ending

Structure and Form
- uses well-organized paragraphs and a clear organization
- includes transitional words and phrases to show relationships among ideas
- uses a variety of sentence structures

Grammar, Usage, and Mechanics
- contains no more than two or three minor errors in grammar and usage
- contains no more than two or three minor errors in spelling, capitalization, and punctuation

---

SkillBuilder Ⓖ GRAMMAR FROM WRITING

PUNCTUATING APPOSITIVES You may wish to show students how to combine sentences by reducing one of them to an appositive and inserting it in the other. Write two sentences on the chalkboard, circle the noun or phrase that will become an appositive, and draw an arrow to show where it will be inserted in the first sentence. Then read the combined sentence. Here is a model:

Separate: People value courage above other characteristics. It is a mysterious quality.

Combined: People value courage, a mysterious quality, above other characteristics.

Application Have students add punctuation to these sentences, where necessary:

1. The story "The Last Cover" is about a fox.
2. My sister a straight-A student always has her nose in a book.
3. I wanted to go to the mall my favorite place on Saturday afternoon.

Reteaching/Reinforcement
Grammar Mini-Lessons copymasters p. 39, transparencies p. 30

 The Writer's Craft

Commas with Appositives, p. 634

This feature allows students to reflect on the selections they have read and the activities they have done in Unit Three and to assess how well they understand what they have learned. Although this feature provides students with several opportunities for self-assessment, you may wish to use some of the activities to assess specific skills—such as speaking and listening or cooperative work—informally.

──────── **Objectives** ────────

- To allow students to reflect on and assess their understanding of theme
- To allow students to reflect on and assess their understanding of literary concepts such as characterization and dialogue
- To provide students with the opportunity to assess and build their portfolios

REFLECTING ON THEME

OPTION 1

Encourage students to review the selections they have read and the notes they have taken before writing down the messages about stepping forward. Remind students to focus on the ways in which each message might be relevant to young people.

OPTION 2

Students may want to review their two chosen selections and take notes about the characters and their situations. Encourage students to make sure that their dialogues reflect the traits of their chosen characters.

OPTION 3

Have each group review the selections in this unit and jot down ideas about the ways in which particular characters are good role models. Students can refer to this information in their panel discussions. Make sure students are able to support their opinions with details from the selections and from their own experiences.

Self-Assessment In order to help students answer these questions, have them consider which selections had the greatest impact on them and why they were affected so strongly. Suggest that students discuss in their paragraphs some situations to which they might apply what they learned from reading a particular selection.

REFLECT & ASSESS

UNIT THREE: STEPPING FORWARD

As you read the selections in this unit, you probably thought deeply about what it means to step forward. Now is a good time for you to reflect on what you have learned in this unit. Choose one of the options in each of the following sections to assess how your thinking has evolved.

REFLECTING ON THEME

OPTION 1 **Making Connections** Jot down the messages about stepping forward that you got from the selections you read in this unit. Then choose two or more messages that you think young people might take to heart as words to live by. Write a paragraph or two, explaining your choices.

Consider . . .

- the challenges that the characters in the selections face
- the challenges that young people face today
- the messages that might inspire young people the most

OPTION 2 **Writing a Dialogue** Choose a character from a selection in Part 2, and imagine that character in the situation of one of the characters in Part 1. How do you think the character from Part 2 would respond to the situation? What do you think he or she might learn about showing courage? Write a dialogue between the two characters to explore your ideas.

OPTION 3 **Holding a Panel Discussion** Work with a small group of classmates to select three or more characters whom you consider good role models for young people today. Then hold a panel discussion to explore reasons why you chose those characters over all the others. Cite examples from the selections and from your own experience to support your ideas.

Self-Assessment: Which selection influenced your thinking the most? Which influenced your thinking the least? Write a paragraph or two to explore these questions.

REVIEWING LITERARY CONCEPTS

OPTION 1 **Examining Characterization** Characterization includes all the techniques that writers use to create and develop characters. In your notebook, make a chart like the one shown, listing at the top each main character in the stories you have read. Then assign a number to each technique to indicate its importance in making the character come alive for you. Use a scale from 1 to 5, with 1 for least important and 5 for most important. Identify the characters that made the strongest impressions on you, and compare your ratings of the authors' techniques.

	Nessan				
Presenting character's words and actions	5				
Showing character's thoughts	4				
Describing character's appearance	2				
Telling what others think about character	3				

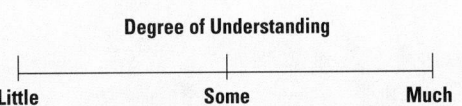 **Evaluating Dialogue** Writers of plays and stories use dialogue—conversation between two or more characters—to advance plot and to reveal the traits of characters. With a partner, choose three stories from this unit and identify an important passage of dialogue in each. If these passages were deleted from the stories, how would your understanding of the plots and characters change? Which story would be affected the most?

 Self-Assessment: Besides characterization *and* dialogue, *other key terms presented in this unit include* description, motivation, exposition, persuasion, metaphor, *and* simile. *In your notebook, create a scale like the one shown to rate your understanding of these terms, writing each where you think it belongs. Use the Handbook of Reading Terms and Literary Concepts to look up any terms on the left end of the scale.*

Degree of Understanding

Little   Some   Much

PORTFOLIO BUILDING

- **QuickWrites** For some of the QuickWrites features in this unit, you wrote speeches, both from your own perspective and from the perspectives of characters in the selections. Choose the response in which you think you best developed your main points. Write a note identifying the details that work especially well, attach the note to the response, and place both in your portfolio.

- **Writing About Literature** You have learned how writing an interpretive essay about a passage in a story can help you understand the story as a whole. How would you describe what you learned by writing the interpretive essay? What effect do you think writing the essay had on your understanding of the story? Write a note to answer these questions, and attach the note to your interpretive essay.

- **Writing from Experience** Earlier in this unit, you wrote an essay about a concept. Reread your essay. Who is the first person that comes to mind when you think of this concept? Write a note to that person, explaining why he or she reminds you of the concept. Include the note with your essay if you choose to keep it in your portfolio.

- **Personal Choice** Review everything you created in your work for this unit—charts, drawings, evaluations, and writing, including any pieces you did on your own. Select one piece of writing or one activity that you consider your best work. Write a note explaining how the writing or activity influenced your ideas about stepping forward. Attach the note to the piece of writing or to your record of the activity, and add both to your portfolio.

 Self-Assessment: At this point, your portfolio probably contains both old and recent pieces of writing. Write a note comparing a recent piece with an earlier one. In it, identify one or more strengths that only the recent piece reflects.

SETTING GOALS

As you completed the reading and writing activities in this unit, you probably noticed that you are strong in certain skills but not in others. In your notebook, list one or two skills that you intend to develop as you work through the selections in the next unit.

REFLECT AND ASSESS **381**

OPTION 1

Students may wish to skim the selections and jot down their ideas and thoughts about the techniques of characterization used. Remind students that a selection may not reflect every technique listed in the chart. You may wish to have students compare their charts with a partner's after completing the activity. For a copy of the chart to distribute to the class, see *Unit Three Resource Book,* p. 79.

OPTION 2

Have partners consider the information that is presented in the dialogue and how their understanding of each story would be affected without this information. You may wish to have students share their thoughts and ideas with other partners.

Self-Assessment Have students write a definition of each term that they include on the left end of the scale. Then have students apply each term to a selection they have read. For instance, a student can identify an example of metaphor in a selection or discuss a particular character's motivation in a story.

PORTFOLIO BUILDING

You may wish to help students choose options or modify the ones given to suit the portfolio system you have established for the class. Encourage students to incorporate in their portfolios drafts in addition to final products so that they can reflect on and assess their development and progress.

Self-Assessment Students should identify a recent piece that they are proud of and an older piece that they would like to improve. Ask students to look for patterns to their revising processes that might indicate areas in which they have strengthened their writing.

SETTING GOALS

You may wish to have students create charts that list what they consider their strengths and weaknesses as readers and writers. Remind students to set reasonable goals for developing their skills and to list practical suggestions to which they can refer in the future.

UNIT THEME

Unit Four

Meeting Challenges In this unit, students will read selections in which characters meet challenges head on in a variety of ways. This unit contains two parts: Part 1 "The Will to Win" and Part 2 "High Stakes." Selections in each part relate to the unit theme by focusing on characters who show an indomitable spirit or who risk themselves in pursuit of a goal.

Part 1

The Will to Win Selections in Part 1 detail the experiences of characters who refuse to give up in the face of great odds, such as the brave mongoose who fights a pair of cobras to the death in "Rikki-tikki-tavi."

Part 2

High Stakes The selections in Part 2 feature characters who take great risks to achieve personal goals, such as the boy in "The Christmas Hunt" who goes out hunting alone to prove himself to his father.

Links to Unit Six

The Oral Tradition Unit Six, "Across Time and Place: The Oral Tradition" contains three selections that relate to the theme of "Meeting Challenges":
- "The Arrow and the Lamp: The Story of Psyche," p. 744
- "Pumpkin Seed and the Snake," p. 750
- "Kelfala's Secret Something," p. 754

You may choose to introduce or conclude Unit Four by using one or more of these selections.

UNIT FOUR

MEETING CHALLENGES

THE CHALLENGE
IS IN THE MOMENT,
THE TIME IS
ALWAYS NOW.

James Baldwin
African-American writer

Copyright © Reggie Holladay/SIS.

382

383

To help students explore the connections between the art, the quotation, and the unit theme, have them discuss the following questions:

1. What do you already know about the theme of meeting challenges that might prepare you for this unit? *(Possible responses: Facing a challenge involves strength, determination, and courage. Meeting challenges prepares you for the future by teaching you about yourself and the qualities you need in order to succeed.)*

2. Paraphrase the quotation by James Baldwin. *(Possible response: The quotation reflects the idea that one must seize the moment to face challenges. There is no time like the present to tackle obstacles and pursue goals.)*

3. What connection do you see between the artwork on this page and the idea of meeting challenges? *(Possible response: The artwork combines two very challenging sports—skateboarding and surfboarding. By putting the skateboarders in the setting of a large wave, the artist emphasizes the challenges facing them. This would not have been as apparent if the skateboarders were depicted in a realistic setting.)*

4. What do you predict the selections in this unit will be about? *(Possible response: The selections will focus on the challenges that characters face and what they learn from their experiences. Some characters will probably be successful, while others may not be able to rise to the occasion.)*

5. With a small group of classmates, take turns describing challenges that you have faced. What did meeting this challenge entail? What did you learn about yourself from the experience? *(Responses will vary.)*

Art Note

Reading the Art *How would you describe the feelings this artwork creates in you? How does the artist suggest the rapid movements of the wave and the skateboarders in this still image?*

Part 1 Skills Trace
ML DENOTES MINI-LESSON IN TEACHER'S EDITION

Selections	Reading Skills and Strategies	Literary Concepts	Writing Opportunities	Speaking, Listening, and Viewing
FICTION **Rikki-tikki-tavi** Rudyard Kipling	Noticing personification, PE p. 385 Predicting, **ML** TE p. 388	Minor characters, PE p. 400 Setting, PE p. 400 Point of view, **ML** TE p. 389 Plot, **ML** TE p. 394	Lyrics, PE p. 400 Summary, PE p. 400 Battle scene, PE p. 400 Rewriting point of view, **ML** TE p. 389	List and ranking, PE p. 400 Radio reading, PE p. 401 Visual display, oral report, or booklet, PE p. 401 Dramatic reading, **ML** TE p. 392 Debate, **ML** TE p. 395
FICTION **Amigo Brothers** Piri Thomas	Comparing and contrasting, **ML** TE p. 404	Surprise ending, PE p. 413 Motivation, **ML** TE p. 405 Point of view, **ML** TE p. 411	Paragraph, PE p. 402 Definition, PE p. 413 Editorial, PE p. 413 Profile, PE p. 413 Rewriting point of view, **ML** TE p. 411	Role-playing, PE p. 413 Interview and oral report, PE p. 414 Film, **ML** TE p. 409
FICTION **The Serial Garden** Joan Aiken	Making predictions, PE p. 415 Drawing conclusions, **ML** TE p. 417	Irony, PE p. 433 Humor, PE p. 433 Setting, **ML** TE p. 421 Figurative language, **ML** TE p. 427	Predicting, PE p. 415 Fantasy story, PE p. 432 Escape plan, PE p. 432 Recipe, PE p. 432 Conversation, PE p. 432 Matching test, **ML** TE p. 429	List, PE p. 432 Monologue, PE p. 433 Readers Theater, **ML** TE p. 425 Assessing a performance, **ML** TE p. 426 Evaluating art, **ML** TE p. 428
NONFICTION **The Eternal Frontier** Louis L'Amour	Making inferences, **ML** TE p. 437	Title, PE p. 439	Writing about space exploration, PE p. 435 Personal response, PE p. 439 Letter, PE p. 439 Profile, PE p. 439 Draft, PE p. 439 Summary, **ML** TE p. 438	Class vote, PE p. 439 Multimedia presentation, PE p. 440 Panel discussion, PE p. 440
POETRY ON YOUR OWN **Hockey** Scott Blaine **The Women's 400 Meters** Lillian Morrison **74th Street** Myra Cohn Livingston **I'll Walk the Tightrope** Margaret Danner **To Satch** Samuel Allen			Newspaper article, TE p. 443	Performance, TE p. 444 Discussion, TE p. 445

Writing	Reading Skills and Strategies	Literary Concepts	Writing Opportunities	Speaking, Listening, and Viewing
WRITING ABOUT LITERATURE **Creative Response**	Analyzing dialogue, PE pp. 446–47 Responding to literature, PE pp. 448–51	Analyzing dialogue, PE pp. 446–47 Characters, PE pp. 448–49	Rewriting, PE p. 447 Dialogue, PE p. 447 Speaker's tags, PE p. 447 Creative response, PE pp. 448–51 Creating paragraphs, PE p. 449	Role-playing, PE pp. 447, 448 Viewing a scene, PE p. 452 Interpreting a scene, PE p. 452 Discussion, PE p. 452 Discussing a situation, PE p. 453

Grammar, Usage, Mechanics, and Spelling	Multimodal Learning	Research and Study Skills	Vocabulary	
Quotations, (ML) TE p. 387 Point of view, (ML) TE p. 389 The letters *j*, *ge*, and *dge*, (ML) TE p. 390	List and ranking, PE p. 400 Comic book, PE p. 401 Radio reading, PE p. 401 Visual display, oral report, or booklet, PE p. 401 Dramatic reading, (ML) TE p. 392 Debate, (ML) TE p. 395	Research the mongoose or cobra, PE p. 401 Assignment logs, (ML) TE p. 397 Summarizing, (ML) TE p. 399	consolation cower cunningly revive scuttle	
Commas with interrupters, (ML) TE p. 406 Words from French, (ML) TE p. 407 Point of view, (ML) TE p. 411	Role-playing, PE p. 413 Interview and oral report, PE p. 414 Film, (ML) TE p. 409 Yearbook page, (ML) TE p. 412	Research conditioning of boxers, PE p. 414 Note-taking, (ML) TE p. 410	barrage bedlam dispel evading feint	game improvise pensively perpetual unbridled
Semicolons separating a series, (ML) TE p. 422 Suffixes, *-able* and *-ible*, (ML) TE p. 424 Using figurative language, (ML) TE p. 427	List, PE p. 432 Cereal box, PE p. 433 Model garden, PE p. 433 Tune, PE p. 433 Video or board game, PE p. 433 Monologue, PE p. 433 Illustrations, (ML) TE p. 419 Readers theater, (ML) TE p. 425 Assessing a performance, (ML) TE p. 426 Evaluating art, (ML) TE p. 428	K-W-L approach, (ML) TE p. 418 Taking essay tests: planning your answers, (ML) TE p. 423 Taking objective tests: matching questions, (ML) TE p. 429	aggrievedly chaos convalesce forage gaudy	incalculable susceptible tantalizing vigil wan
	Class vote, PE p. 439 Multimedia presentation, PE p. 440 Time line, PE p. 440 Panel discussion, PE p. 440	Research "famous firsts," PE p. 440 Research scientists' predictions, PE p. 440	antidote devastating impetus incorporate multitude	

Grammar, Usage, Mechanics, and Spelling	Multimodal Learning	Research and Study Skills	Media Literacy
Using speakers' tags, PE p. 447 Capitalizing dialogue, PE p. 451 Punctuating dialogue, PE p. 451	Role-playing, PE pp. 447, 448 Sketch, PE p. 448		Interpreting a scene, PE pp. 452–53

Selections	Reading Skills and Strategies	Literary Concepts	Writing Opportunities	Speaking, Listening, and Viewing
FICTION **The Christmas Hunt** Borden Deal	Making predictions, PE p. 456 Predicting, ML TE p. 464	Foreshadowing, PE p. 471 Description, ML TE p. 458 Simile, ML TE p. 467	Explanation, PE p. 470 Analysis, PE p. 470 Persuasive essay, PE p. 470 Paragraph, ML TE p. 461 Letter, ML TE p. 465	Role-playing, PE p. 470 Oral presentation, PE p. 471 Artwork, PE p. 471 Music and reading aloud, PE p. 471 Acting out, PE p. 472 Role-playing, ML TE p. 459 Directions, ML TE p. 469
NONFICTION *from* **Boy: Tales of Childhood** Roald Dahl	Noting sequence of events, ML TE p. 476 Distinguishing fact and opinion, ML TE p. 482	Dialect, PE p. 486 Imagery, ML TE p. 477 Irony, ML TE p. 481	Letter, PE p. 486 Story, PE p. 486 Conversation, PE p. 486 Writing about a prank, PE p 473 Description, ML TE p. 477 Paragraph, ML TE p. 481 Letter, ML TE p. 483	Dialogue, PE p. 486 Oral interpretation, PE p. 487 Portrait, PE p. 487 Pantomime, ML TE p. 480 Understanding dialect, ML TE p. 484
FICTION **All Summer in a Day** Ray Bradbury	Identifying contrasts, PE p. 488 Comparing and contrasting, ML TE p. 491	Simile and metaphor, PE p. 495 Figurative language, ML TE p. 490 Dialogue, ML TE p. 493	Plan, PE p. 495 Dialogue, PE p. 495 Profile, PE p. 495 Letter, ML TE p. 490	Paragraph, PE p. 495 Oral reading, PE p. 496 Weather forecast, PE p. 496 Role-playing, ML TE p. 493
POETRY **The Highwayman** Alfred Noyes	Identifying narrative elements in poetry, PE p. 497	Onomatopoeia, PE p. 503 Rhythm, PE p. 503 Metaphor, ML TE p. 499 Rhythm, ML TE p. 501	Essay, PE p. 503 Epitaph, PE p. 503 Article, PE p. 503 Short story, ML TE p. 502	Dialogue, PE p. 503 Interview, PE p. 504 Choral reading, PE p. 504 Background music, PE p. 504 Dramatic reading, ML TE p. 498 Reading aloud, ML TE pp. 499, 501
NONFICTION *from* **Commodore Perry in the Land of the Shogun** Rhoda Blumberg	Visualizing, PE p. 505 Visualizing, ML TE p. 509	Imagery, PE p. 516 Conflict, ML TE p. 511	Account, PE p. 516 Profile, PE p. 516 Letter, PE p. 516 Provocative introductions, ML TE p. 507	Journal entry, PE p. 516 Noh play, PE p. 517 Rewriting, ML TE p. 510 Skit, ML TE p. 511 Discussion and debate, ML TE p. 512 Oral history, ML TE p. 513

Writing	Reading Skills and Strategies	Literary Concepts	Writing Opportunities	Speaking, Listening, and Viewing
WRITING FROM EXPERIENCE **Report**	Drawing conclusions, PE p. 523	Main idea, PE p. 521	Writing a report, PE pp. 518–25 Drafting, PE pp. 522–23 Using facts and statistics, PE p. 523 Revising and publishing, PE pp. 524–25	Brainstorming, PE p. 518

Grammar, Usage, Mechanics, and Spelling	Multimodal Learning	Research and Study Skills	Vocabulary	
Time transitions, (ML) TE p. 461 Compound sentences, (ML) TE p. 463 1+1+1 words, (ML) TE p. 468	Role-playing, PE p. 470 Oral presentation, PE p. 471 Artwork, PE p. 471 Music and reading aloud, PE p. 471 Acting out, PE p. 472 Role-playing, (ML) TE p. 459 Directions, (ML) TE p. 469	Research trained dogs, PE p. 471 Research sporting dogs, PE p. 471 Reference books, (ML) TE p. 460	brashness cavorting clamor contempt indifference	irate lithe mimicry refuge tactic
Sensory details, (ML) TE p. 478 Subordinate clauses, (ML) TE p. 479 Compound words, (ML) TE p. 485	Dialogue, PE p. 486 Ballad, PE p. 487 Oral interpretation, PE p. 487 Ad, PE p. 487 Portrait, PE p. 487 Pantomime, (ML) TE p. 480 Understanding dialect, (ML) TE p. 484	Research British preparatory schools, PE p. 487 Glossaries, (ML) TE p. 475	elaborate flourishing jaunty loathsome malignant	
Figurative language, (ML) TE p. 490 Reflexive pronouns, (ML) TE p. 492 Spelling with the suffix -ly, (ML) TE p. 494	Paragraph, PE p. 495 Oral reading, PE p. 496 Weather forecast, PE p.496 Poster, PE p. 496 Role-playing, (ML) TE p. 493	Research Venus, PE p. 496	apparatus concussion resilient savor tumultuously	
	Dialogue, PE p. 503 Interview, PE p. 504 Choral reading, PE p. 504 Background music, PE p. 504 Dramatic reading, (ML) TE p. 498 Reading aloud, (ML) TE pp. 499, 501			
Provocative introductions, (ML) TE p. 507 Subject-verb agreement in inverted sentences, (ML) TE p. 514	Journal entry, PE p. 516 Sketch, PE p. 517 Diagram, PE p. 517 Noh play, PE p. 517 Painting or mural, (ML) TE p. 509 Rewriting, (ML) TE p. 510 Skit, (ML) TE p. 511 Discussion and debate, (ML) TE p. 512 Oral history, (ML) TE p. 513	Research Noh plays, PE p. 517 Indexes, (ML) TE p. 508	appall furor incessant inept mystifying omen replenish resolve seclude turmoil	

Grammar, Usage, Mechanics, and Spelling	Multimodal Learning	Research and Study Skills	Media Literacy
Using facts and statistics, PE p. 523 Formatting quotations, PE p. 525	Analyzing newspaper articles, pictures, and maps, PE pp. 518–19 Brainstorming, PE p. 518	Library sources, PE p. 520 Using a research plan and source cards, PE p. 520 Creating an outline, PE p. 521	Analyzing newspaper articles, pictures, and maps, PE pp. 518–19 Library sources, PE p. 520

Recommended Resources

Recommended Novels and Drama

 LITERATURE CONNECTIONS WITH SOURCEBOOK FOR TEACHERS

The Clay Marble
by Minfong Ho

Thematic Links Dara and her family learn to cope with their losses as they meet the challenge of crossing war-torn Cambodia to get to a refugee camp. Dara's need to belong is met in unexpected ways as she gains self-confidence.

About the Author Minfong Ho (born 1951) writes to make people aware of the suffering endured by others and as a tribute to their perseverance. This novel was inspired by Ho's experience with a young Cambodian refugee in the 1980s.

Other Works by Minfong Ho *Sing to the Dawn, Rice without Rain*

 LITERATURE CONNECTIONS WITH SOURCEBOOK FOR TEACHERS

The Diary of Anne Frank
by Frances Goodrich and Albert Hackett

Thematic Links In this dramatic adaptation of Anne Frank's diary, eight people meet many challenges as they hide in a secret annex in Amsterdam during the Nazi occupation of the Netherlands.

About the Author Frances Goodrich (1891–1984) and Albert Hackett (1900–1995) were a highly successful husband-and-wife team who wrote plays. Many of their works were made into popular Hollywood movies and stage plays.

Other Works by Frances Goodrich and Albert Hackett *Up Pops the Devil, Bridal Wise, The Great Big Doorstep*

LITERATURE CONNECTIONS WITH SOURCEBOOK FOR TEACHERS

Where the Red Fern Grows
by Wilson Rawls

Thematic Links A young boy saves money to buy two dogs and is heartbroken when they die.

About the Author Although Wilson Rawls (born 1913) never made it through the eighth grade, he loved to read and, at an early age, fell in love with Jack London's *The Call of the Wild*. The book inspired in him a dream of writing a book like London's.

Other Works by Wilson Rawls *Summer of the Monkeys*

The Dark Secret of Weatherend
by John Bellairs

Thematic Links A young man and his friend, a librarian, find themselves at the mercy of a sinister man until they unravel his challenging mystery.

About the Author John Bellairs (1938–1991) created mysteries featuring enterprising young detectives, drawing upon his childhood and vivid imagination for inspiration.

Other Works by John Bellairs *The Letter, the Witch, and the Ring; The House with a Clock in Its Walls; A Figure in the Shadows; The Face in the Frost*

The Chief
by Robert Lipsyte

Thematic Links Showing a strong will to win, the Tomahawk Kid dreams of becoming a boxing champion.

About the Author Works by Robert Lipsyte (born 1938) feature characters who go through a transformation due to hard work and adherence to ethics.

Other Works by Robert Lipsyte *The Contender, Free to Be Muhammad Ali, One Fat Summer, The Brave, Jock and Jill, Summer Rules*

For Teacher   TEACHING LITERATURE

Barbieri, Maureen and Linda Rief, eds. *Workshop 6 by and for Teachers: The Teacher as Writer.* Portsmouth, NH: Heinemann, 1994.

Felter, Douglas P. "Skeleton Keys: Teaching the Fiction of Narrative Truth." *English Journal* 83.2 (February 1994): 43–47.

Kobrin, Beverly. "Don't Neglect Nonfiction." *American Educator: The Professional Journal of the American Federation of Teachers* 15.3 (Winter 1991): 36+.

 ## Recommended Readings in Cross-Curricular Areas

HISTORY

A Pictorial History of Boxing
by Nat Fleischer and Sam Andre (1989)
Gives a historical look at boxing through vivid pictures. Links to Piri Thomas's "Amigo Brothers."

SOCIAL STUDIES

Japan
by Carol Greene (1983)
Describes the history and geography of Japan. Links to Rhoda Blumberg's *Commodore Perry in the Land of the Shogun.*

SCIENCE

Snakes
by Ruth Belov Gross (1990)
This book starts with a step-by-step analysis of snake life-cycles and closes with a pictorial essay on 23 types of snakes. Links to Kipling's "Rikki-tikki-tavi."

Space Colony: Frontier of the 21st Century
by Franklyn M. Branley (1982)
Looks at life in a space colony through letters from colonists. Links to "The Eternal Frontier" and "All Summer in a Day."

For Teacher CROSS-CURRICULAR INSTRUCTION

Crawford, Leslie W. *Language and Literacy Learning in Multicultural Classrooms.* Needham Heights, MA: Simon & Schuster, 1993.

Culp, Mary Beth and Jamee Osborn Sosa. "The Influence of Nonfiction on Attitudes, Values, and Behavior." *English Journal* 82.8 (December 1993): 60–64.

Everson, Barbara J. "Considering the Possibilities with Improvisation." *English Journal* 82.7 (November 1993): 64–66.

Vogt, Gregory L. and Cheryl A. Manning, eds. *Suited for Spacewalking: Teacher's Guide with Activities.* Washington, DC: National Aeronautics and Space Administration, 1992.

 ## Recommended Media Resources

THE LANGUAGE OF LITERATURE

LASERLINKS
Videodisc, Gr. 7
See *LaserLinks Teacher's Source Book,* pages 30–31, for an overview of Unit Four.

AUDIO LIBRARY
Tapes
Unit Four: Meeting Challenges
Gr. 7, Tape 9: Sides A & B
Gr. 7, Tape 10: Sides A & B
Gr. 7, Tape 11: Sides A & B

WRITING COACH
Writing Coach Software: Writing About Literature: Direct Response; Explanation of an Idea

OUTSIDE RESOURCES

Films/Videos/Film Strips/Audiocassettes
Kim. Read by Margaret Hilton. Ten sound cassettes. (13.5 hrs.)
Anne Frank: The Diary of a Young Girl. Read by Susan Adams. Six sound cassettes. (9 hrs.)
Rikki-tikki-tavi, videocassette. Orson Welles narrates. (30 min.)
Ray Bradbury—Tales of Fantasy. Read by Ray Bradbury. Two sound cassettes. Listening Library, Inc.

Internet Resources
Literature and Language Arts Center at http://www.hmco.com/mcdougal/lit/litcent.html

For Teacher TEACHING WITH TECHNOLOGY

Finkel, LeRoy. *Technology Tools in the Information Age Classroom.* Using Technology in the Classroom Series. Wilsonville, OR: Franklin, Beedle & Associates, Inc., 1991.

Henry, M .J. "Profile of a Technology-Using Teacher." Annual Convention of the Eastern Educational Research Association. Clearwater, FL. 17–23 Feb. 1993.

New York City Board of Education. *Computer Literacy: Intermediate and Secondary Grades.* 2nd ed. Brooklyn: New York City Board of Education, 1983.

To Boldly Go Where No One Has Gone Before

> Margie even wrote about it that night in her diary. On the page headed May 17, 2155, she wrote, "Today Tommy found a real book!"

As the opening of Isaac Asimov's science fiction story "The Fun They Had" shows, science fiction takes readers on a wild ride to visit otherworldly people and places. Before your students read the science fiction selections in this unit, help them understand the definition and characteristics of the genre.

What exactly *is* science fiction? Open the discussion by asking students which science fiction novels and short stories they have read and which science fiction movies and televisions shows they have seen. Jot down their responses on the board. Then invite students to briefly describe some of the plots in their favorite science fiction books and shows. Lastly, elicit the following characteristics of the genre.

Science fiction . . .

- is usually set in another world or in the future
- probes the impact of sudden or cataclysmic change on people
- may be populated by exotic creatures and unfamiliar life-forms
- is often rooted in scientific fact or probability, such as nuclear power, space travel, and advanced weaponry
- deals with time and space travel, life on other planets, ideal worlds, and crises created by technology or alien creatures and environments

Explain to students that it was not until about 1950 that science fiction became an accepted genre. Today, about ten percent of the books published annually are shelved as science fiction. Nearly all major colleges and universities teach science fiction today, as do many secondary schools. There are many well-respected critical journals covering science fiction, as well as on-line computer chat rooms and bulletin boards devoted to the topic.

THE HISTORY OF SCIENCE FICTION WRITING

Although science fiction seems like the most modern of genres, it's is actually one of the most ancient. The roots of "sci-fi" stretch all the way back to ancient times. For example, the Babylonian *Gilgamesh Epic* revolved around a search for immortality and ultimate knowledge, the Greek myth of Daedalus and Icarus with the technology of flight, and Lucian of Samosata's *True History* with a voyage to the moon. The Greeks and Romans wrote many stories about imaginary voyages to alien lands. In the 1600s, French writer Cyrano de Bergerac and German astronomer Johannes Kepler both wrote stories about voyages to the moon.

- The first great science fiction writer was Jules Verne. His most famous books include *Journey to the Center of the Earth* (1864), *A Trip to the Moon* (1865), and *20,000 Leagues Under the Sea* (1870).
- The title of "father of science fiction" was reserved for the first major writer of science fiction in English—H.G. Wells. His science fiction books include *The Time Machine* (1895), *The Island of Dr. Moreau* (1896), *The Invisible Man* (1897), *The War of the Worlds* (1899), and *The First Men on the Moon* (1901).
- Famous modern science fiction writers include Robert Heinlein (*Stranger in a Strange Land*), Isaac Asimov (*I, Robot*) Ray Bradbury (*Fahrenheit 451*), Frank Herbert (*Dune*), and Ursula K. LeGuin (*The Left Hand of Darkness*).

SCIENCE FICTION MOVIES AND TV SHOWS

Traditionally, science fiction was the domain of teenage boys, especially those in the sixth to eighth grades. Today, however, teenage girls are equally likely to be sci-fi fans. Many experts credit the media with this broadening of audience. See how many of these famous science fiction movies students have seen:

- 1970s: *Star Wars, 2001: A Space Odyssey, The Andromeda Strain, Alien*
- 1980s: *Close Encounters of the Third Kind, Starman, The Empire Strikes Back*
- 1990s: *Demolition Man, Total Recall,* the *Star Trek* series, *Johnny Mnemonic, Congo*

Then invite students to list their favorite science fiction TV shows. Here are some especially beloved ones: *The Twilight Zone, The Outer Limits, Lost in Space, Star Trek, My Favorite Martian.*

To help students appreciate the rich history of science fiction, invite them to work in small research groups and to present their findings on a time line. The can correlate each science fiction work with key inventions and discoveries of the age.

Related Reading

 Asimov, Isaac, and Conklin, Groff, eds. *50 Short Science Fiction Tales.* New York: Macmillan, 1963.

 Jakubowski, Maxim. *The SF Book of Lists.* New York: Berkeley Books, 1983.

 Yep, Laurence. *Sweetwater.* New York: Harper, 1975.

Family and Community Involvement

 ## Family

By completing some of the following activities, your students, their families, and other community members can make important connections outside the classroom as they explore real-life examples of meeting challenges.

The following Copymasters for Unit Four provide activities that students can take home and complete with a parent or other family member.

OPTION 1: CREATE A CHALLENGE CALENDAR
- **Connection** All of the selections in Unit Four illustrate the theme of meeting challenges.
- **Activity** *Copymaster, page 1* Students and family members create a calendar that encourages them to meet new challenges.

OPTION 2: ROLE-PLAY A DIALOGUE
- **Connection** In "All Summer in a Day," futuristic colonists live and work on the planet Venus, meeting the challenges that such a home presents.
- **Activity** *Copymaster, page 2* Students and family members think about and discuss the planet Venus through role-playing.

OPTION 3: WATCH A VIDEO ABOUT A PET
- **Connection** In "Rikki-tikki-tavi" and "The Christmas Hunt," humans and animals form a special bond and face challenges together.
- **Activity** *Copymaster, page 3* Students and family members watch a movie about a boy and his dog. After watching, they discuss the relationship between pets and their owners and the challenges of pet ownership.

 ## Community

OPTION 1
- **Connection** All of the selections in Unit Four illustrate the theme of meeting challenges.
- **Activity** Have the class survey community athletes about the challenges that must be met in various sports.

OPTION 2
- **Connection** The poem "The Highwayman" tells of the tragic love of a robber and an innkeeper's daughter.
- **Activity** Invite a local actor to give a dramatic reading of "The Highwayman" to the class.

OPTION 3
- **Connection** In "All Summer in a Day," Margot lives on Venus and waits for the one day of the year when the sun will shine.
- **Activity** Arrange a field trip to a planetarium to find out about the sun and Venus and how to spot Venus in the night sky.

OPTION 4
- **Connection** Young Roald Dahl has a love of candy in the excerpt from *Boy: Tales of Childhood.*
- **Activity** Take a trip to a candy factory or invite a confectioner to explain candy-making to the class.

Part 1 Cooperative Project

A Sports Banquet

Overview

Students plan a sports banquet to honor a team or individual that has shown exceptional fortitude while playing the game.

PROJECT AT A GLANCE

The selections in Unit Four, Part 1 are about people who have persevered and overcome obstacles and setbacks to achieve success. For this project, students will work in cooperative groups to select a sports figure or team that has overcome obstacles to achieve success to some degree. They will plan a full banquet honoring that person or team and write several speeches that point out the obstacles and how they were overcome, as well as the level of success achieved. The plan should include a full written description of who would be invited; the food served; the featured speakers; and the speeches, which can be read aloud for the class.

OBJECTIVES

- To select a sports figure or team that has overcome obstacles to achieve success
- To plan a full banquet honoring that person or team
- To write a speech reviewing the obstacles and achievements of the person or team

SUGGESTED GROUP SIZE

3–4 students

MATERIALS

Several issues of sports magazines

1 Getting Started

Arranging the Project

Gather as many sports magazines as possible. If the school library doesn't have a wide selection, ask your school's physical education teachers to lend you magazines, with the promise to return them. Since events need not be current, don't overlook older issues.

If you are not already familiar with today's sports heroes, you might want to leaf through these magazines to give yourself some basic knowledge of which sports and sports figures students are raving about.

Arranging the Banquet

If your school has an annual sports banquet, you may wish to invite the coordinator to speak to the class about the steps necessary in organizing such an event.

If possible, arrange for your class to have a reserved table in the cafeteria at lunchtime, where the banquet could be acted out to the best of their ability. Coordinate this with the cafeteria staff as well as the school administration. Otherwise, the banquet can be described and held in class.

2 Creating the Banquets

Introducing the Project

Explain that students will be working in groups to select a sports figure or team that has overcome difficulties or obstacles to achieve some degree of success. Point out that these successes need not be making it to the World Series or the Olympics. The football team that loses its star quarterback, running back, and linebacker in one season and still makes it to the first playoff round before elimination has certainly overcome difficulties.

Groups will then plan a banquet for the selected person or team. Plans should include where the banquet would be held, how many people would be invited, the menu, and a list of people asked to speak at the banquet. Groups should also write a speech that reviews the difficulties encountered, how these difficulties were overcome, and the resulting success achieved. These speeches will be read in class.

Some students will know immediately who they would like to select as a subject, while others will be at a loss. Ask that groups meet, go through the magazines, and select a person or team they can all admire. Stress that the person or team must have overcome an obstacle or difficulty. Natural talent, however enviable, does not qualify for this award.

Group Investigations

Divide students into teams of three or four. Be sure that non-sports-minded students are

grouped with sports fans. As groups meet to select a figure or team, encourage them to consider sports not usually in the public eye, as well as the Special Olympics, as they make their selection. Ask groups to report their final selection to you so you can avoid duplication and make alternative suggestions. Since price is irrelevant, groups can dream! If their banquet will fill the Convention Center, that's fine.

Creating a Project Description

After students have gathered some preliminary information, they should write a brief description of the banquet as they envision it. You can meet with each group to review the early stages of the plans, make suggestions, and help them make revisions, if necessary. The speeches should be written after everything else is planned. Students may work independently to write their own personal speech honoring the chosen person or team.

OPTION I: SPORTS CONVENTION Students can design and plan a sports convention. Each group should be responsible for a booth at the convention, which will include persons who are well-known and respected in that sport, as well as some of the equipment used in the sport. Some equipment will have to be shown in pictures, but encourage students to bring in what they can.

OPTION 2: ANIMAL OF THE YEAR Groups can honor fictional animals from literature, television, or the movies that overcame obstacles—for example, the dogs and the cat in *The Incredible Journey*, the tortoise who outran the hare, and the pig Babe who didn't become bacon. Students should be sure to invite the hero or heroine's animal pals to the banquet and serve appropriate chow.

OPTION 3: THE ROAST Groups can plan a "roast"-type banquet honoring a person or team. If necessary, explain that the speeches at a roast are generally humorous and tease the honoree, but they finish on a note of honest admiration.

Again, encourage groups to select figures that are perhaps not as well known as some others. Suggest that they look to a sport that they have seen only in the Olympics or have just heard about and launch an investigation in that direction.

3 Sharing the Banquet Speeches

All speeches should be read in front of the whole class. You may wish to alternate the subjects by rotating groups or to complete all speeches about one particular person or team so they may be contrasted immediately. All speeches should be given from behind a lectern, if possible, or at least from behind a desk at the front of the room. Encourage students to speak with clarity, to enunciate carefully, and to speak slowly enough so that they can be understood.

Assessing the Project

The following rubric may be used for group or individual assessment.

3 Full Accomplishment Students follow directions and produce a plan for a banquet and a speech honoring a person or team for overcoming hardship to achieve success.

2 Substantial Accomplishment Students produce a plan for a banquet and a speech honoring a person or team, but the focus of the speech is unclear or the subject poorly chosen.

1 Little or Partial Accomplishment Students' plan and speech are incomplete or do not fulfill the requirements of the assignment.

For the Portfolio

Keep a copy of each student's speech in his or her portfolio, along with a copy of your written assessment. You may also wish to include a copy of the group's plans for the banquet.

Note: For other assessment options, see the *Teacher's Guide to Assessment and Portfolio Use.*

Cross-Curricular Options

MATH

Students can plan the banquet, then contact caterers, hotels, or simply visit the local grocery store to calculate the total cost of such a banquet. They can also calculate how much they would have to charge for tickets to cover their cost.

MUSIC

Have students plan a banquet for a musical group. Students could put together a collection of some of the group's songs, especially any that mention overcoming hardships.

ART

Students can make a drawing of the room in which the banquet would be held and show how they would like to have it decorated. The drawing should also show how the room would be arranged.

Resources

The Giant Book of More Strange but True Sports Stories by Howard Liss retells 150 unusual happenings in a variety of sports.

The World's Best Street & Yard Games by Glen Vecchione describes the rules and requirements of approximately 100 games.

Winners Under 21 edited by Phyllis Hollander and Zander Hollander profiles athletes who won sports fame before they reached age 21.

UNIT FOUR

Part 1 Lesson Planner

TIME ALLOTMENTS SHOWN ARE APPROXIMATE. DEPENDING ON YOUR GOALS AND THE NEEDS OF YOUR STUDENTS, YOU MAY WISH TO ALLOW MORE OR LESS TIME FOR CERTAIN PORTIONS OF THE LESSON.

Table of Contents	Discussion	Previewing the Selection	Reading the Selection
PART OPENER **THE WILL TO WIN** **What Do You Think?** page 384	**20 MINUTES** • Reflect on the part theme		
SELECTION **Rikki-tikki-tavi** page 386 EASY		**15 MINUTES** • PERSONAL CONNECTION • HISTORICAL CONNECTION • READING CONNECTION: Noticing personification	**45 MINUTES** • Introduce vocabulary • Read pp. 386–99 (14 pp.)
SELECTION **Amigo Brothers** page 403 AVERAGE		**20 MINUTES** • PERSONAL CONNECTION • HISTORICAL CONNECTION • WRITING CONNECTION	**35 MINUTES** • Introduce vocabulary • Read pp. 403–12 (10 pp.)
SELECTION **The Serial Garden** page 416 AVERAGE		**20 MINUTES** • PERSONAL CONNECTION • LITERARY CONNECTION • READING CONNECTION: Making predictions	**50 MINUTES** • Introduce vocabulary • Read pp. 416–31 (16 pp.)
SELECTION **The Eternal Frontier** page 436 CHALLENGING		**20 MINUTES** • PERSONAL CONNECTION • SCIENCE CONNECTION • WRITING CONNECTION	**10 MINUTES** • Introduce vocabulary • Read pp. 436–38 (3 pp.)
POETRY ON YOUR OWN **Hockey** page 441 AVERAGE **The Women's 400 Meters** page 442 AVERAGE **74th Street** page 443 AVERAGE **I'll Walk the Tightrope** page 444 AVERAGE **To Satch** page 445 AVERAGE			**10 MINUTES** • Read pp. 441–45 (5 pp.)

Writing	Writer's Style	Prewriting	Drafting and Revising
WRITING ABOUT LITERATURE **Creative Response**	**30 MINUTES**	**30 MINUTES**	**80 MINUTES**

Time estimates assume in-class work. You may wish to assign some of these stages as homework.

Responding to the Selection

FROM PERSONAL RESPONSE TO CRITICAL ANALYSIS	OR	ANOTHER PATHWAY	LITERARY CONCEPTS	QUICKWRITES
40 MINUTES				
• Discussion questions	OR	• List	• Minor characters and setting	• Lyrics • Summary • Battle scene
50 MINUTES				
• Discussion questions	OR	• Role-playing	• Surprise ending	• Definition • Editorial • Profile
40 MINUTES				
• Discussion questions	OR	• List	• Irony and humor	• Fantasy story • Escape plan • Recipe • Conversation
40 MINUTES				
• Discussion questions	OR	• Class vote	• Title	• Personal response • Letter • Profile • Draft

Extension Activities

ALTERNATIVE ACTIVITIES	LITERARY LINKS	CRITIC'S CORNER	THE WRITER'S STYLE	ACROSS THE CURRICULUM	ART CONNECTION	WORDS TO KNOW	BIOGRAPHY
40 MINUTES							
✔				SCIENCE		✔	✔
30 MINUTES							
		✔	✔	PHYSICAL EDUCATION		✔	✔
40 MINUTES							
✔	✔					✔	✔
30 MINUTES							
✔				SCIENCE		✔	✔
							✔

Publishing and Reflecting   **Grammar in Context**   **Reading the World**

30 MINUTES   **10 MINUTES**   **30 MINUTES**

WHAT DO YOU THINK?

Objectives

The activities on this page can be used to
- introduce the theme of "The Will to Win" since each activity is connected to one or more of the selections in Part 1
- create materials for students' personal portfolios that they can return to later for reconsideration or revision
- build an understanding of theme that can be returned to and revised as students progress through the unit

Whom would you honor?

Have students plan the kind of image that best suits their chosen individual. You may wish to have students examine examples of commemorative stamps to get ideas. (This activity connects to all the selections in this part.)

What does it take to win?

Encourage students to jot down examples of "underdogs" who have achieved stunning upsets. Tell students to make sure the tone of their speeches is inspirational and persuasive. (See "Amigo Brothers," p. 402.)

What advice would you give?

Have groups first think of the actions and attitudes of individuals who seem to have the will to win. Encourage the class to select or design appropriate photos and illustrations to accompany the manual. (This activity connects to all the selections in this part.)

What is "the right stuff"?

Have students first brainstorm a list of the challenges that someone living in outer space might face and the qualities needed in order to surmount them. (See "The Eternal Frontier," p. 435.)

THE WILL TO WIN

WHAT DO **You** THINK?

REFLECTING ON THEME

An Olympic runner with a badly twisted ankle hobbles toward the finish line. A scientist spends countless hours searching for a cure for a deadly disease. Some people never give up. Use the activities on this page to explore your own views about what it means to have the will to win.

Whom would you honor?

Suppose that you have been asked to plan a series of postage stamps commemorating individuals who had the will to win. Design the stamp for one of the individuals you would honor.

What does it take to win?

Imagine that you are the coach of a team that is the underdog in a championship game. Compose a pregame motivational speech—a pep talk—to fire up your players. In the speech, tell about individuals or teams who have done the seemingly impossible. Deliver your speech to the class, having a classmate videotape your presentation if possible.

What advice would you give?

How can you tell if someone has the will to win? With a small group, brainstorm a list of actions and attitudes that are indications of this quality. Share your list with the rest of your classmates, and work with them to compile a "Will to Win" manual that provides advice on setting goals, overcoming obstacles, and learning from failure.

What is "the right stuff"?

Imagine that you are the director of a training program at NASA. Your staff is conducting interviews to select people for the first colony in outer space. Draft a memo (or tape-record a message) to your staff, describing the qualities you are looking for in the ideal candidate.

384   UNIT FOUR   PART 1: THE WILL TO WIN

COMMUNITY OUTREACH

Encourage students to volunteer at a local Special Olympics. You may wish to contact an organizer ahead of time to learn more about the ways in which students might participate. Remind students that the Special Olympics encourages all participants to believe that they are winners. Afterward, have students work in small groups to write brief reports on their experiences as volunteers.

PARENTAL INVOLVEMENT

Have students tape-record or videotape an interview with a parent or relative about the importance of having the will to win. Students should ask their parents or relatives to tell about their own experiences and to offer advice about the importance of refusing to give up. Students can present their interviews to the class.

FICTION

Rikki-tikki-tavi
Rudyard Kipling

Activating Prior Knowledge
PERSONAL CONNECTION

Natural enemies fight or fear each other by instinct. What natural enemies in the animal kingdom can you name? Think about common enemies, such as cats and birds, as well as exotic animals you may have heard or read about. With a partner, brainstorm a list of natural enemies. Share your list with your classmates.

Building Background
HISTORICAL CONNECTION

If you lived in India, you almost certainly would mention the mongoose and the cobra as a pair of natural enemies—a pair that will fight to the death. The mongoose, growing only to a length of 16 inches, seems hardly a match for the poisonous cobra, a snake that averages 6 feet in length and 6 inches in diameter.

You will learn more about these animals in the story you are about to read, which is set in India during the late 1800s. At that time the British ruled India. British families lived in open, airy houses called bungalows—one-story homes with big windows and large shaded porches to protect the inhabitants from the hot sun. Because of the heavy seasonal rains, vines and creepers covered every outside wall, and bushes could grow to be as big as an average-sized American garage. The jungle often grew so close to the bungalows that it was not uncommon to find snakes, insects, and other animals around and in these homes.

Mongoose and cobra.
Copyright © Norman
Myers/Bruce Coleman, Inc.

Active Reading
READING CONNECTION

Noticing Personification Kipling uses a technique called **personification** in "Rikki-tikki-tavi," giving the animals human characteristics. Personification allows readers to imagine what the animals think, feel, and say about each other. As you read, think about the human qualities that each animal has, especially Rikki-tikki-tavi and his cobra enemies.

Setting a Purpose

LASERLINKS
• CULTURAL CONNECTION   385

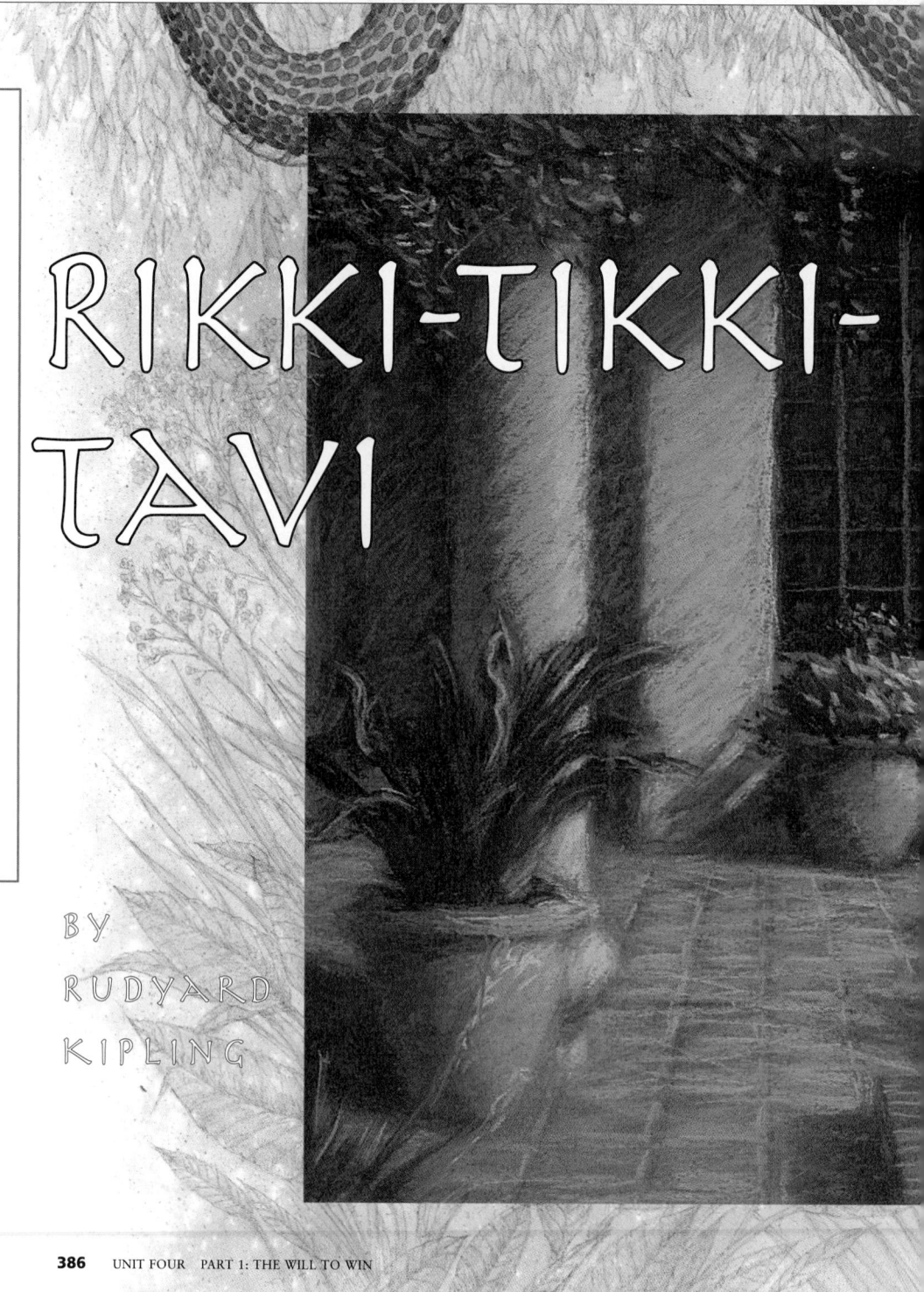

RIKKI-TIKKI-
TAVI

BY
RUDYARD
KIPLING

SUMMARY

A young mongoose, Rikki-tikki-tavi, becomes the house pet of an English family living in colonial India. While exploring the garden, Rikki meets the cobra Nag and narrowly escapes the bite of his wife, Nagaina. Rikki-tikki becomes the family hero when he kills a small poisonous snake and saves the boy Teddy. That night the mongoose overhears Nag and Nagaina plotting to kill the entire family. After Nag sneaks into the bathroom, Rikki-tikki attacks the snake. Teddy's father shoots the snake to death. The next morning, as the wife of Darzee the Tailorbird distracts Nagaina, Rikki-tikki begins destroying the cobra's eggs. Learning that the vengeful Nagaina has gone to the house, Rikki finds her on the veranda poised to strike Teddy. Rikki-tikki distracts Nagaina with her last egg, giving Teddy's father the chance to rescue Teddy. The cobra grabs her egg and carries it into her hole, where Rikki-tikki bravely follows and kills her. Pampered and praised by Teddy's family, Rikki continues to guard the garden.

Thematic Link: *The Will to Win* Rikki-tikki-tavi shows his will to win when he defends his "family" against the cobras.

CUSTOMIZING FOR
Students Acquiring English

• Use **ACCESS FOR STUDENTS ACQUIRING ENGLISH**, *Reading and Writing Support.*

• There is a reference in the story to Brahm (Brahma). Invite volunteers who know about Hinduism to give background information about the religion to their classmates.

• As you guide students through the selection, you may want to use the suggestions in these boxes, as well as the questions under Strategic Reading for Less-Proficient Readers.

386   UNIT FOUR   PART 1: THE WILL TO WIN

WORDS TO KNOW

consolation (kŏn′sə-lā′shən) *n.* something that comforts (p. 396)

cower (kou′ər) *v.* to crouch or shrink down in fear (p. 389)

cunningly (kŭn′ĭng-lē) *adv.* in a clever way that is meant to trick or deceive (p. 396)

revive (rĭ-vīv′) *v.* to become conscious; wake up (p. 387)

scuttle (skŭt′l) *v.* to run quickly, with hurried movements (p. 396)

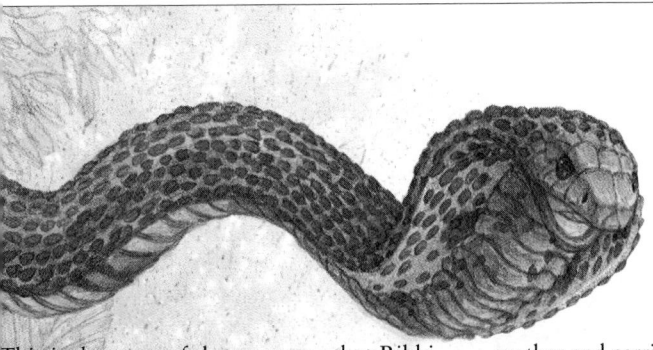

STRATEGIC READING FOR

Less-Proficient Readers

Set a Purpose To help spark interest in the reading, invite students to preview the story. Guide them to look at the illustrations, read the captions, and skim the interlinear questions. Discuss some of students' impressions and predictions. Then ask students to read to discover how Rikki-tikki-tavi comes to live in Teddy's house.

Use **UNIT FOUR RESOURCE BOOK**, p. 4, for guidance in reading the selection.

This is the story of the great war that Rikki-tikki-tavi fought single-handed, through the bathrooms of the big bungalow in Segowlee cantonment.[1] Darzee, the tailorbird, helped him, and Chuchundra, the muskrat, who never comes out into the middle of the floor but always creeps round by the wall, gave him advice; but Rikki-tikki did the real fighting.

He was a mongoose, rather like a little cat in his fur and his tail but quite like a weasel in his head and his habits. His eyes and the end of his restless nose were pink; he could scratch himself anywhere he pleased with any leg, front or back, that he chose to use; he could fluff up his tail till it looked like a bottle-brush, and his war cry as he scuttled through the long grass was: *Rikk-tikk-tikki-tikki-tchk!*

One day, a high summer flood washed him out of the burrow where he lived with his father and mother and carried him, kicking and clucking, down a roadside ditch. He found a little wisp of grass floating there and clung to it till he lost his senses. When he <u>revived</u>, he was lying in the hot sun on the middle of a garden path, very draggled indeed, and a small boy was saying, "Here's a dead mongoose. Let's have a funeral."

"No," said his mother, "let's take him in and dry him. Perhaps he isn't really dead."

They took him into the house, and a big man picked him up between his finger and thumb and said he was not dead but half choked; so they wrapped him in cotton wool and warmed him over a little fire, and he opened his eyes and sneezed.

CUSTOMIZING FOR

Gifted and Talented Students

Have students imagine the story being told from the cobra's perspective. Challenge students to explain how their view of the action and the characters differs.

Literary Concept: PERSONIFICATION

A Ask students to explain how Kipling makes Rikki seem human in this passage. Explore with students why Kipling would personify the mongoose in this story. *(Possible responses: Kipling describes Rikki as he might a human soldier, as a fighter in a "great war." The personification helps readers identify with the wild creature and become interested in his exploits.)*

Cultural Note

B India's annual rainy season lasts from mid-June through September. Rivers often flood the land, destroying crops and houses.

1. **cantonment** (kăn-tōn′mənt): a military base.

WORDS
TO
KNOW   **revive** (rĭ-vīv′) *v.* to become conscious; wake up

387

Mini-Lesson   ✎   Grammar

CAPITALIZATION IN QUOTATIONS
Direct students to the highlighted quotation above. Point out that the first word of a direct quotation is capitalized. Explain that in a divided quotation, students should capitalize the first word of the second part only when it begins a new sentence or is a proper noun or proper adjective.

Application Have students correct the capitalization errors in the following sentences.
1. "don't be frightened, Teddy," said his father.
2. "good gracious," said Teddy's mother, "And that's a wild creature!"
3. "all mongooses are like that," said her husband.

4. "there are more things to find out about in this house," he said to himself, "than all my family could find out in all their lives."
5. "bother my white teeth! have you ever heard where she keeps her eggs?"

Reteaching/Reinforcement
• Grammar Handbook, anthology pp. 886–887
• *Grammar Mini-Lessons* copymasters, p. 35, transparencies, p. 27

 The Writer's Craft

Quotations, p. 611

C Ask students why they think a mongoose's curiosity would make it difficult to frighten him. *(Possible response: If a mongoose is very inquisitive and tries to investigate everything around him, it might not be easy to catch him off guard and scare him.)*

CUSTOMIZING FOR

Students Acquiring English

1 Explain that *Ouch!* is an exclamation used by someone in pain.

2 Students should infer from the context that *Good gracious* is an exclamation that shows surprise.

Active Reading: PREDICT

D Point out that Teddy's mother fears that the mongoose will cause trouble, whereas his father thinks that Rikki will prevent trouble. Invite students to make predictions about what might happen as a result of Rikki's moving inside the bungalow. *(Possible responses: He will bite Teddy; he will protect Teddy.)*

STRATEGIC READING FOR

Less-Proficient Readers

E Make sure students understand how Rikki-tikki comes to stay with Teddy.

• How does Rikki-tikki end up in Teddy's house? *(He is found lying in the middle of a garden path after a summer flood and is brought inside by Teddy and his mother.)* **Noting Relevant Details**

• Why is he allowed to stay? *(He is fun and a good "watchdog.")* **Relating Cause and Effect**

Set a Purpose Have students read to find out how Rikki becomes a hero.

"Now," said the big man (he was an Englishman who had just moved into the bungalow), "don't frighten him, and we'll see what he'll do."

C It is the hardest thing in the world to frighten a mongoose, because he is eaten up from nose to tail with curiosity. The motto of all the mongoose family is "Run and Find Out;" and Rikki-tikki was a true mongoose. He looked at the cotton wool, decided that it was not good to eat, ran all round the table, sat up and put his fur in order, scratched himself, and jumped on the small boy's shoulder.

"Don't be frightened, Teddy," said his father. "That's his way of making friends."

1 "Ouch! He's tickling under my chin," said Teddy.

Rikki-tikki looked down between the boy's collar and neck, snuffed at his ear, and climbed down to the floor, where he sat rubbing his nose.

2 "Good gracious," said Teddy's mother, "and that's a wild creature! I suppose he's so tame because we've been kind to him."

"All mongooses are like that," said her husband. "If Teddy doesn't pick him up by the tail or try to put him in a cage, he'll run in and out of the house all day long. Let's give him something to eat."

They gave him a little piece of raw meat. Rikki-tikki liked it immensely; and when it was finished, he went out into the veranda[2] and sat in the sunshine and fluffed up his fur to make it dry to the roots. Then he felt better.

"There are more things to find out about in this house," he said to himself, "than all my family could find out in all their lives. I shall certainly stay and find out."

He spent all that day roaming over the house. He nearly drowned himself in the bathtubs, put his nose into the ink on a writing table, and burnt it on the end of the big man's cigar, for he climbed up in the big man's lap to see how writing was done. At nightfall he ran into Teddy's nursery to watch how kerosene lamps were lighted, and when Teddy went to bed, Rikki-tikki climbed up too; but he was a restless companion, because he had to get up and attend to every noise all through the night and find out what made it. Teddy's mother and father came in, the last thing, to look at their boy, and Rikki-tikki was awake on the pillow.

"I don't like that," said Teddy's mother; "he may bite the child."

"He'll do no such thing," said the father. "Teddy is safer with that little beast than if he had a bloodhound to watch him. If a snake came into the nursery now—"

But Teddy's mother wouldn't think of anything so awful.

Early in the morning Rikki-tikki came to early breakfast in the veranda, riding on Teddy's shoulder, and they gave him banana and some boiled egg; and he sat on all their laps one after the other, because every well-brought-up mongoose always hopes to be a house mongoose some day and have rooms to run about in; and Rikki-tikki's mother (she used to live in the general's house at Segowlee) had carefully told Rikki what to do if ever he came across white men.

Then Rikki-tikki went out into the garden to see what was to be seen. It was a large garden, only half-cultivated,[3] with bushes, as big as

---

2. **veranda** (və-răn′də): a long open porch.
3. **cultivated:** cleared for the growing of garden plants.

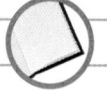

Mini-Lesson **Reading Skills/Strategies**

| Prediction | Information Used to Make Prediction |

ACTIVE READING: PREDICTING Tell students that when readers predict, they try to figure out what will happen next in a story. Discuss with students how readers combine information they already know with information they gather from the story in order to make predictions. Discuss with students the importance of revising predictions as they continue reading so that they can take into account new information from the story.

Application Have students create a chart like the one shown. Ask them to recall some of the predictions they made while reading the story and to jot them down in the first column. In the second column, students should list details from the story and events from their own experiences that they used to make the prediction.

Reteaching/Reinforcement
• *Unit Four Resource Book*, p. 5

summerhouses, of Marshal Niel roses, lime and orange trees, clumps of bamboos, and thickets of high grass. Rikki-tikki licked his lips. "This is a splendid hunting ground," he said, and his tail grew bottlebrushy at the thought of it; and he scuttled up and down the garden, snuffing here and there till he heard very sorrowful voices in a thorn bush. It was Darzee, the tailorbird, and his wife. They had made a beautiful nest by pulling two big leaves together and stitching them up the edges with fibers and had filled the hollow with cotton and downy fluff. The nest swayed to and fro, as they sat on the rim and cried.

"What is the matter?" asked Rikki-tikki.

"We are very miserable," said Darzee. "One of our babies fell out of the nest yesterday, and Nag ate him."

"H'm!" said Rikki-tikki, "that is very sad—but I am a stranger here. Who is Nag?"

Darzee and his wife only <u>cowered</u> down in the nest without answering, for from the thick grass at the foot of the bush there came a low hiss—a horrid, cold sound that made Rikki-tikki jump back two clear feet. Then inch by inch out of the grass rose up the head and spread hood of Nag, the big black cobra, and he was five feet long from tongue to tail. When he had lifted one-third of himself clear of the ground, he stayed, balancing to and fro exactly as a dandelion tuft balances in the wind; and he looked at Rikki-tikki with the wicked snake's eyes that never change their expression,

THEN INCH BY INCH OUT OF THE GRASS ROSE UP THE HEAD AND SPREAD HOOD OF NAG, THE BIG BLACK COBRA . . .

whatever the snake may be thinking of.

"Who is Nag?" said he. "*I* am Nag. The great god Brahm[4] put his mark upon all our people when the first cobra spread his hood to keep the sun off Brahm as he slept. Look, and be afraid!"

 **H**

I

He spread out his hood more than ever, and Rikki-tikki saw the spectacle mark on the back of it that looks exactly like the eye part of a hook-and-eye fastening. He was afraid for the minute, but it is impossible for a mongoose to stay frightened for any length of time; and though Rikki-tikki had never met a live cobra before, his mother had fed him on dead ones, and he knew that all a grown mongoose's business in life was to fight and eat snakes. Nag knew that too, and at the bottom of his cold heart, he was afraid.

"Well," said Rikki-tikki, and his tail began to fluff up again, "marks or no marks, do you think it is right for you to eat fledglings out of a nest?"

Nag was thinking to himself and watching the least little movement in the grass behind Rikki-tikki. He knew that mongooses in the garden meant death sooner or later for him and his family; but he wanted to get Rikki-tikki off his guard. So he dropped his head a little, and put it on one side.

"Let us talk," he said. "You eat eggs. Why should not I eat birds?"

"Behind you! Look behind you!" sang Darzee.

---

4. **Brahm:** another name for Brahma, creator of the universe in the Hindu religion.

WORDS TO KNOW **cower** (kou'ər) *v.* to crouch or shrink down in fear

389

Multiple Learning Styles

F Spatial or Graphic Learners
Students might enjoy creating a picture that shows how they visualize the garden setting.

Linking to Science

G A mongoose kills snakes, rats, and mice for food. It also eats young birds and birds' eggs. It is a fierce animal but can be tamed. A cobra uses its poison either by injecting or by spitting it. When the poison is spit into a person's eyes, it can blind him or her if it is not washed out immediately. Cobras eat frogs, birds, fish, and small mammals.

Critical Thinking: ANALYZING

H Have students analyze Nag's speech in this passage and explain what it reveals about his character. *(Possible response: The stately diction and reference to Brahm make Nag seem mythical, terrifying, and unbeatable.)*

Literary Concept: PLOT

I Remind students that the plot of a story develops because of a conflict, or struggle between opposing forces. Remind them that an external conflict is a struggle between a character and outside forces and that an internal conflict involves a character's inner struggles. Have students identify the conflicts in this passage. *(Possible responses: Rikki faces an external conflict with Nag; both Nag and Rikki face internal struggles to overcome their fear as they prepare for battle.)*

Mini-Lesson  **The Writer's Style**

POINT OF VIEW Explain that when the narrator is not a character in the story, the writer is using the third-person point of view. Point out to students how Kipling uses third-person pronouns such as *he, she, him, her, they,* and *them.* Instruct students that third-person narration can be either from a limited point of view, in which the narrator brings the reader into the mind of only one character, or from an omniscient (all-knowing) point of view, in which the narrator knows everything about the characters and can see into all of their minds. Tell students that this story is told from the third-person omniscient point of view.

Application Ask students to rewrite and extend the highlighted passage above using the third-person limited point of view. Students can choose to write from the point of view of either Rikki or Nag.

Reteaching/Reinforcement
• Writing Handbook, anthology pp. 824–825
• *Writing Mini-Lessons* transparencies, p. 47

The Writer's Craft

Point of View, pp. 318–319

J Discuss Rikki's inexperience as a fighter. Point out that he did not recognize the right time to break Nagaina's back, nor did he bite her long enough. Invite students to predict what will happen in the story as a result of Rikki's mistakes here. (*Possible responses: Nagaina or Nag will kill or badly injure him; he will learn from his mistakes and kill the cobras.*)

CUSTOMIZING FOR

Multiple Learning Styles

K **Logical-Mathematical Learners**
Invite students to plan different ways that Rikki could defeat Nag and Nagaina with the least possible danger to himself. Have students present their plans to the class for a vote on the best plan.

Active Reading: QUESTION

L Call on volunteers to add to a list of problems that Rikki faces. (*Possible responses: He faces two enemies working together against him, Nag and Nagaina; he is a young and inexperienced fighter; he is fighting in unfamiliar territory.*)

Rikki-tikki knew better than to waste time in staring. He jumped up in the air as high as he could go, and just under him whizzed by the head of Nagaina, Nag's wicked wife. She had crept up behind him as he was talking, to make an end of him; and he heard her savage hiss as the stroke missed. He came down almost across her back, and if he had been an old mongoose, he would have known that then was the time to break her back with one bite; but he was afraid of the terrible lashing return stroke of the cobra. He bit, indeed, but did not bite long enough; and he jumped clear of the whisking tail, leaving Nagaina torn and angry.

"Wicked, wicked Darzee!" said Nag, lashing up as high as he could reach toward the nest in the thorn bush; but Darzee had built it out of reach of snakes, and it only swayed to and fro.

Rikki-tikki felt his eyes growing red and hot (when a mongoose's eyes grow red, he is angry), and he sat back on his tail and hind legs like a little kangaroo and looked all around him and chattered with rage. But Nag and Nagaina had disappeared into the grass. When a snake misses its stroke, it never says anything or gives any sign of what it means to do next. Rikki-tikki did not care to follow them, for he did not feel sure that he could manage two snakes at once. So he trotted off to the gravel path near the house and sat down to think. It was a serious matter for him.

If you read the old books of natural history, you will find they say that when the mongoose fights the snake and happens to get bitten, he runs off and eats some herb that cures him. That is not true. The victory is only a matter of quickness of eye and quickness of foot—snake's blow against mongoose's jump—and as no eye can follow the

QUESTION

L What problems does Rikki face?

Using a Reading Log

390 UNIT FOUR PART 1: THE WILL TO WIN

Illustration by Michael Foreman. Copyright © 1987 Michael Foreman.

Mini-Lesson **⟨TM⟩** Spelling

THE LETTERS *j, ge,* **AND** *dge* Explain to students that the sound *j* can be spelled *j, ge,* or *dge*. Tell them that familiarity with the following rules will help them improve their spelling.
- The letter *j* spells the *j* sound only at the beginning or in the middle of words—*just, enjoy.*
- The letters *ge* spell the *j* sound at the end of words—*cage.*
- The letters *dge* appear at the end of one-syllable words with a short vowel—*edge.*

Application Have students write the following words as you read them aloud.

1. stranger	6. justice	11. fledglings
2. jealous	7. advantage	12. rejoice
3. bridge	8. pajamas	13. danger
4. plunged	9. badge	14. pledge
5. marriage	10. dodge	15. injury

Ask students to look for more words that fit this pattern, in their own writing and in things that they read, and to add them to their personal word lists.

Reteaching/Reinforcement
- *Unit Four Resource Book,* p. 6

motion of a snake's head when it strikes, this makes things much more wonderful than any magic herb. Rikki-tikki knew he was a young mongoose, and it made him all the more pleased to think that he had managed to escape a blow from behind.

It gave him confidence in himself, and when Teddy came running down the path, Rikki-tikki was ready to be petted. But just as Teddy was stooping, something wriggled a little in the dust, and a tiny voice said, "Be careful. I am Death!" It was Karait, the dusty brown snakeling that lies for choice on the dusty earth; and his bite is as dangerous as the cobra's. But he is so small that nobody thinks of him, and so he does the more harm to people.

Rikki-tikki's eyes grew red again, and he danced up to Karait with the peculiar rocking, swaying motion that he had inherited from his family. It looks very funny, but it is so perfectly balanced a gait that you can fly off from it at any angle you please; and in dealing with snakes this is an advantage.

If Rikki-tikki had only known, he was doing a much more dangerous thing than fighting Nag; for Karait is so small and can turn so quickly, that unless Rikki bit him close to the back of the head, he would get the return stroke in his eye or his lip. But Rikki did not know: his eyes were all red, and he rocked back and forth, looking for a good place to hold. Karait struck out. Rikki jumped sideways and tried to run in, but the wicked little dusty gray head lashed within a fraction of his shoulder, and he had to jump over the body, and the head followed his heels close.

Teddy shouted to the house, "Oh, look here! Our mongoose is killing a snake"; and Rikki-tikki heard a scream from Teddy's mother. His father ran out with a stick, but by the time he came up, Karait had lunged out once too far, and Rikki-tikki had sprung, jumped on the snake's back, dropped his head far between his forelegs, bitten as high up the back as he could get hold, and rolled away. That bite paralyzed Karait, and Rikki-tikki was just going to eat him up from the tail, after the custom of his family at dinner, when he remembered that a full meal makes a slow mongoose; and if he wanted all his strength and quickness ready, he must keep himself thin. He went away for a dust bath under the castor-oil bushes, while Teddy's father beat the dead Karait.

"What is the use of that?" thought Rikki-tikki; "I have settled it all."

And then Teddy's mother picked him up from the dust and hugged him, crying that he had saved Teddy from death; and Teddy's father said that he was a providence,[5] and Teddy looked on with big scared eyes. Rikki-tikki was rather amused at all the fuss, which, of course, he did not understand. Teddy's mother might just as well have petted Teddy for playing in the dust. Rikki was thoroughly enjoying himself.

That night at dinner, walking to and fro

> **CLARIFY**
>
> Why is Rikki amused by the fuss?
>
> *Using a Reading Log*

 O

 P

---

5. **providence:** blessing; something good given by God.

THE LANGUAGE OF LITERATURE TEACHER'S EDITION **391**

Critical Thinking: CLASSIFY

M Have students classify Rikki's fighting abilities by judging how well prepared they think he is for a showdown with the cobras. (*Possible responses: Rikki is well prepared, as shown by Nag's fear of him and his escape from Nagaina's attack; Rikki is poorly prepared, because he is young and inexperienced.*)

Literary Concept: SUSPENSE

N Remind students that suspense is a feeling of growing tension and excitement. Have students identify the details that build suspense here. (*Possible responses: The narrator says that fighting Karait is more dangerous than fighting Nag. Rikki does not know the technique for biting Karait, so this passage helps to create tension and excitement.*)

Active Reading: CLARIFY

O Ask students to explain Rikki's amused reaction. (*Possible response: Rikki doesn't understand why the humans praise him so much for doing what comes naturally.*)

STRATEGIC READING FOR
Less-Proficient Readers

P Review with students the story so far.

- Why does Rikki attack Karait? (*They are natural enemies; Rikki wants to protect Teddy.*) **Making Inferences**

- Why is the family so delighted with Rikki? (*He saved Teddy from being bitten by Karait the snake.*) **Summarizing**

Set a Purpose Have students read to find out what plans Rikki has for Nag.

Assessment ✓ **Option**

SELF-ASSESSMENT To help students assess their own understanding of the story, you may wish to have them respond to the following questions in writing or in brief oral reports.

- Would a snake or a mongoose make a good pet? Would wild animals act the way they do in this story?

- If I were filming this story, how would I have it narrated? What are the advantages and disadvantages of different methods of narrating a movie version of this story?

- Would I recommend this story to a friend? Why or why not?

- What aspects of the story interested me the most? Why?

The Rose Arch, Wendy Jelbert. From *Gardens in Watercolor*, by Wendy Jelbert, published by B. T. Batsford Ltd.

392   UNIT FOUR   PART 1: THE WILL TO WIN

among the wineglasses on the table, he might have stuffed himself three times over with nice things; but he remembered Nag and Nagaina, and though it was very pleasant to be patted and petted by Teddy's mother and to sit on Teddy's shoulder, his eyes would get red from time to time, and he would go off into his long war cry of *"Rikk-tikk-tikki-tikki-tchk!"*

Teddy carried him off to bed and insisted on Rikki-tikki sleeping under his chin. Rikki-tikki was too well-bred to bite or scratch, but as soon as Teddy was asleep, he went off for his nightly walk around the house; and in the dark he ran up against Chuchundra, the muskrat, creeping around by the wall. Chuchundra is a brokenhearted little beast. He whimpers and cheeps all the night, trying to make up his mind to run into the middle of the room; but he never gets there.

"Don't kill me," said Chuchundra, almost weeping. "Rikki-tikki, don't kill me!"

"Do you think a snake killer kills muskrats?" said Rikki-tikki scornfully.

"Those who kill snakes get killed by snakes," said Chuchundra, more sorrowfully than ever. "And how am I to be sure that Nag won't mistake me for you some dark night?"

"There's not the least danger," said Rikki-tikki; "but Nag is in the garden, and I know you don't go there."

"My cousin Chua, the rat, told me—" said Chuchundra, and then he stopped.

"Told you what?"

"H'sh! Nag is everywhere, Rikki-tikki. You should have talked to Chua in the garden."

"I didn't—so you must tell me. Quick, Chuchundra, or I'll bite you!"

Chuchundra sat down and cried till the tears rolled off his whiskers. "I am a very poor man," he sobbed. "I never had spirit enough to run out into the middle of the room. H'sh! I

---

mustn't tell you anything. Can't you *hear*, Rikki-tikki?"

Rikki-tikki listened. The house was as still as still, but he thought he could just catch the faintest *scratch-scratch* in the world—a noise as faint as that of a wasp walking on a windowpane— the dry scratch of a snake's scales on brickwork.

"That's Nag or Nagaina," he said to himself, "and he is crawling into the bathroom sluice.[6] You're right, Chuchundra; I should have talked to Chua."

He stole off to Teddy's bathroom, but there was nothing there, and then to Teddy's mother's bathroom. At the bottom of the smooth plaster wall, there was a brick pulled out to make a sluice for the bath water, and as Rikki-tikki stole in by the masonry curb where the bath is put, he heard Nag and Nagaina whispering together outside in the moonlight.

"When the house is emptied of people," said Nagaina to her husband, "*he* will have to go away, and then the garden will be our own again. Go in quietly, and remember that the big man who killed Karait is the first one to bite. Then come out and tell me, and we will hunt for Rikki-tikki together."

"But are you sure that there is anything to be gained by killing the people?" said Nag.

"Everything. When there were no people in the bungalow, did we have any mongoose in the garden? So long as the bungalow is empty, we are king and queen of the garden; and remember that as soon as our eggs in the melon bed hatch (as they may tomorrow), our children will need room and quiet."

"I had not thought of that," said Nag. "I will go, but there is no need that we should hunt for Rikki-tikki afterward. I will kill the big man and his wife, and the child if I can, and come away quietly. Then the bungalow will be empty, and Rikki-tikki will go."

Rikki-tikki tingled all over with rage and hatred at this, and then Nag's head came through the sluice, and his five feet of cold body followed it. Angry as he was, Rikki-tikki was very frightened as he saw the size of the big cobra. Nag coiled himself up, raised his head, and looked into the bathroom in the dark, and Rikki could see his eyes glitter.

"Now, if I kill him here, Nagaina will know; and if I fight him on the open floor, the odds are in his favor. What am I to do?" said Rikki-tikki-tavi.

Nag waved to and fro, and then Rikki-tikki heard him drinking from the biggest water jar that was used to fill the bath. "That is good," said the snake. "Now, when Karait was killed, the big man had a stick. He may have that stick still, but when he comes in to bathe in the morning, he will not have a stick. I shall wait here till he comes. Nagaina—do you hear me?—I shall wait here in the cool till daytime."

There was no answer from outside, so Rikki-tikki knew Nagaina had gone away. Nag coiled himself down, coil by coil, around the bulge at the bottom of the water jar, and Rikki-tikki stayed still as death. After an hour he began to move, muscle by muscle, toward the jar. Nag

---

6. **bathroom sluice** (slo͞os): a channel and opening in a wall through which the water in a bathtub can be drained outdoors.

T Ask students to classify Chuchundra as a main or minor character and explain their classification. Then have students explain what function Chuchundra has in this part of the story. (*Possible responses: He is a minor character, because he plays a small role in the story's plot. His function is to warn Rikki about Nag.*)

Linking to History

U In the late 1800s, when this story takes place, homes in India did not have indoor plumbing with water faucets and drains for bathtubs. As a result, a tub had to be filled with water from a jar. The dirty water was drained through a sluice, or passageway, in the wall.

Critical Thinking: ANALYZE

V Ask students what this passage reveals about Nag and how it affects their appreciation of the story. (*Possible responses: It reveals how formidable an enemy Nag really is, which makes Rikki's actions seem even more heroic. It makes the story more exciting and suspenseful.*)

Active Reading: PREDICT

W Have students predict whether Rikki will attack Nag now or later. Encourage them to base their predictions on what they already know about Rikki from the story. (*Possible responses: He will attack now because he is inexperienced; he will attack later because he is cautious and intelligent.*)

X Have students analyze this passage to discover how Kipling creates suspense and builds the plot toward its climax. *(Possible response: Repeated words and phrases such as "muscle by muscle" help slow the action and build suspense.)*

Active Reading: CLARIFY

Y Possible response: Rikki attacked Nag, who began flinging Rikki back and forth. Teddy's father entered and shot and killed Nag.

STRATEGIC READING FOR

Less-Proficient Readers

Z Make sure students are following the story to this point.

• What plan did Rikki have for attacking Nag in the bathroom? Did it work? *(Rikki planned to jump on Nag while the snake was asleep, biting his head and breaking his back. Rikki jumped on Nag. The noise of the attack awakened the man, who shot Nag.)*
Summarizing

• Why do you think Rikki was concerned about Nagaina's eggs? *(If they hatched, there would be new cobras to battle in the garden.)* Making Inferences

Set a Purpose Have students read on to find out what happens to Nagaina's eggs.

X was asleep, and Rikki-tikki looked at his big back, wondering which would be the best place for a good hold. "If I don't break his back at the first jump," said Rikki, "he can still fight; and if he fights—O Rikki!" He looked at the thickness of the neck below the hood, but that was too much for him; and a bite near the tail would only make Nag savage.

"It must be the head," he said at last; "the head above the hood. And, when I am once there, I must not let go."

Then he jumped. The head was lying a little clear of the water jar, under the curve of it; and, as his teeth met, Rikki braced his back against the bulge of the red earthenware to hold down the head. This gave him just one second's purchase,[7] and he made the most of it. Then he was battered to and fro as a rat is shaken by a dog—to and fro on the floor, up and down, and round in great circles; but his eyes were red, and he held on as the body cart-whipped over the floor, upsetting the tin dipper and the soap dish and the flesh brush, and banged against the tin side of the bath.

As he held, he closed his jaws tighter and tighter, for he made sure he would be banged to death; and, for the honor of his family, he preferred to be found with his teeth locked. He was dizzy, aching, and felt shaken to pieces when something went off like a thunderclap just behind him; a hot wind knocked him senseless, and red fire singed his fur. The big man had been awakened by the noise and had fired both barrels of a shotgun into Nag just behind the hood.

CLARIFY

Y What happened in the fight?

Using a Reading Log

Rikki-tikki held on with his eyes shut, for now he was quite sure he was dead; but the head did not move, and the big man picked him up and said, "It's the mongoose again, Alice; the little chap has saved *our* lives now."

Then Teddy's mother came in with a very white face and saw what was left of Nag, and Rikki-tikki dragged himself to Teddy's bedroom and spent half the rest of the night shaking himself tenderly to find out whether he really was broken into forty pieces, as he fancied.

When morning came, he was very stiff but well pleased with his doings. "Now I have Nagaina to settle with, and she will be worse than five Nags, and there's no knowing when the eggs she spoke of will hatch. Goodness! I must go and see Darzee," he said. **Z**

Without waiting for breakfast, Rikki-tikki ran to the thorn bush where Darzee was singing a song of triumph at the top of his voice. The news of Nag's death was all over the garden, for the sweeper had thrown the body on the rubbish heap.

"Oh, you stupid tuft of feathers!" said Rikki-tikki angrily. "Is this the time to sing?"

"Nag is dead—is dead—is dead!" sang Darzee. "The valiant Rikki-tikki caught him by the head and held fast. The big man brought the bang stick, and Nag fell in two pieces! He will never eat my babies again."

"All that's true enough; but where's Nagaina?" said Rikki-tikki, looking carefully round him.

"Nagaina came to the bathroom sluice and

---

7. **purchase:** secure grasp or hold.

Mini-Lesson 🧩 Literary Concepts

Climax
Complications Resolution
Exposition

REVIEWING PLOT Remind students that the plot is the sequence of related events that make up a story; it is the blueprint of the action, or what happens in the story. Point out that most plots follow a pattern. Copy the diagram shown, and use it as you explain the following stages in the plot. The exposition introduces the characters and the conflicts they face.

Complications set in as the characters try to resolve the conflict. Eventually, the plot reaches a climax, the highest point of interest. The final stage is the resolution, in which the loose ends are tied up and the story is brought to a close.

Application Have students draw the diagram in their notebooks and add details from the story to explain the different parts of the plot.

r Birds and Fruit-Bearing Convolvulus, William Hooker. From *tal Memoirs*, 1813.

THE NEWS OF NAG'S DEATH WAS ALL OVER THE GARDEN, FOR THE SWEEPER HAD THROWN THE BODY ON THE RUBBISH HEAP.

called for Nag," Darzee went on; "and Nag came out on the end of a stick—the sweeper picked him up on the end of a stick and threw him upon the rubbish heap. Let us sing about the great, the red-eyed Rikki-tikki!" And Darzee filled his throat and sang.

"If I could get up to your nest, I'd roll your babies out!" said Rikki-tikki. "You don't know when to do the right thing at the right time. You're safe enough in your nest there, but it's war for me down here. Stop singing a minute, Darzee." **AA**

> ### QUESTION
> What danger does Rikki still face?
>
> *Using a Reading Log*

"For the great, the beautiful Rikki-tikki's sake I will stop," said Darzee. "What is it, O Killer of the terrible Nag?" **BB**

"Where is Nagaina, for the third time?"

"On the rubbish heap by the stables, mourning for Nag. Great is Rikki-tikki with the white teeth."

"Bother my white teeth! Have you ever heard where she keeps her eggs?" **③**

"In the melon bed, on the end nearest the wall, where the sun strikes nearly all day. She hid them there weeks ago."

"And you never thought it worthwhile to tell me? The end nearest the wall, you said?"

"Rikki-tikki, you are not going to eat her eggs?"

"Not eat exactly, no. Darzee, if you have a grain of sense, you will fly off to the stables and pretend that your wing is broken and let Nagaina chase you away to this bush. I must get to the melon bed, and if I went there now, she'd see me."

Darzee was a featherbrained little fellow who could never hold more than one idea at a time in his head; and just because he knew that Nagaina's children were born in eggs like his own, he didn't think at first that it was fair to

RIKKI-TIKKI-TAVI **395**

Art Note

Taylor Birds by William Hooker after James Forbes Civil servant James Forbes was one of the earliest and best amateur artists painting Indian scenes. His drawings were published in 1813. Professional artist William Hooker colored the pictures for the plates.

Reading the Art *How would you describe the way this picture is drawn? How would you compare your impressions of these birds with your impressions of Darzee and his wife?*

Active Reading: CLARIFY

AA Ask students why Rikki is so annoyed at Darzee, who is supposed to be a friend. Use the following model if students are having difficulty making connections.

Think-Aloud Model *Rikki knows that only half his job is done, but Darzee is cheerfully singing away. I would be angry if someone were chattering when he should be helping me! I think Rikki is angry that Darzee is not helping him find Nagaina. Or it could be that Rikki is sore and stiff and is not in the mood for Darzee's cheerfulness. That would annoy me too!*

Active Reading: QUESTION

BB Point out Rikki's repeated query about Nagaina's location and ask students what danger Rikki still faces. *(Possible responses: He still faces Nagaina's anger, which will be even greater now that her husband is dead. He must get to Nagaina's eggs before they hatch.)*

CUSTOMIZING FOR
Students Acquiring English

③ Remind students that the family in this story originally came from Great Britain and that the expression *bother* is British slang. It corresponds to the American English phrase *never mind*.

Mini-Lesson: Speaking, Listening, and Viewing

DEBATE Explain that a debate is a formal contest in which two teams argue opposing sides of a question in an organized fashion. Invite the class to conduct a debate using the following rules:

1. Team members should work together cooperatively to decide which major arguments each person will present and in which order people will speak.
2. To prepare the rebuttal, team members should listen closely and critically to the debaters for the other side.
3. Each team has 15 minutes to present its arguments and then 5 minutes to present its rebuttals.

Application Have students debate whether "wild" animals, like Rikki, should be kept as pets. Divide the class into several small groups and allow them sufficient time to research the issues in magazine and newspaper articles and prepare outlines and other notes.

CC Invite students to describe the difference between Darzee and his wife. *(Possible response: Darzee is scatterbrained and weak; his wife is sensible and strong.)*

Active Reading: PREDICT

DD Discuss Nagaina's character with students. Guide students to draw on what they already know about the cobra from the story. Then have students predict how Nagaina will react to the trick Darzee's wife uses. *(Possible responses: Nagaina is clever, so she will turn the tables and use her own trick on Rikki; Nagaina is blinded by pride and arrogance, so she will fall for the trick and then get mad.)*

Literary Concept: PLOT

EE Ask students to explain why Rikki must crush the eggs immediately. Encourage students to explain why Kipling may have chosen to include this race against time in the story. *(Possible responses: Rikki must crush the eggs now because they are about to hatch; Nagaina may return at any minute. This race against time builds suspense and creates interest in what will happen next.)*

---

kill them. But his wife was a sensible bird, and she knew that cobra's eggs meant young cobras later on; so she flew off from the nest and left Darzee to keep the babies warm and continue his song about the death of Nag. Darzee was very like a man in some ways.

She fluttered in front of Nagaina by the rubbish heap and cried out, "Oh, my wing is broken! The boy in the house threw a stone at me and broke it." Then she fluttered more desperately than ever.

Nagaina lifted up her head and hissed, "You warned Rikki-tikki when I would have killed him. Indeed and truly, you've chosen a bad place to be lame in." And she moved toward Darzee's wife, slipping along over the dust.

"The boy broke it with a stone!" shrieked Darzee's wife.

"Well! It may be some <u>consolation</u> to you when you're dead to know that I shall settle accounts with the boy. My husband lies on the rubbish heap this morning, but before night the boy in the house will lie very still. What is the use of running away? I am sure to catch you. Little fool, look at me!"

Darzee's wife knew better than to do *that,* for a bird who looks at a snake's eyes gets so frightened that she cannot move. Darzee's wife fluttered on, piping sorrowfully, and never leaving the ground, and Nagaina quickened her pace.

Rikki-tikki heard them going up the path from the stables, and he raced for the end of the melon patch near the wall. There, in the warm litter above the melons, very <u>cunningly</u> hidden, he found twenty-five eggs, about the size of a bantam's eggs[8] but with whitish skins instead of shells.

"I was not a day too soon," he said, for he could see the baby cobras curled up inside the skin, and he knew that the minute they were hatched they could each kill a man or a mongoose. He bit off the tops of the eggs as fast as he could, taking care to crush the young cobras, and turned over the litter from time to time to see whether he had missed any. At last there were only three eggs left, and Rikki-tikki began to chuckle to himself when he heard Darzee's wife screaming.

"Rikki-tikki, I led Nagaina toward the house, and she has gone into the veranda and—oh, come quickly—she means killing!"

Rikki-tikki smashed two eggs and tumbled backward down the melon bed with the third egg in his mouth and <u>scuttled</u> to the veranda as hard as he could put foot to the ground. Teddy and his mother and father were there at early breakfast; but Rikki-tikki saw that they were not eating anything. They sat stone still, and their faces were white. Nagaina was coiled up on the matting by Teddy's chair, within easy striking distance of Teddy's bare leg; and she was swaying to and fro, singing a song of triumph.

LOOK AT YOUR FRIENDS, RIKKI-TIKKI. THEY ARE STILL AND WHITE. THEY ARE AFRAID. THEY DARE NOT MOVE.

---

8. **bantam's eggs:** the eggs of a small hen.

WORDS
TO
KNOW

consolation (kŏn′sə-lā′shən) *n.* something that comforts
cunningly (kŭn′ĭng-lē) *adv.* in a clever way that is meant to trick or deceive
scuttle (skŭt′l) *v.* to run quickly, with hurried movements

396

Mini-Lesson **Genre Study**

FICTION Draw the web shown and use it to explain that a **short story** is a kind of fiction with the following characteristics:
• It can generally be read in one sitting.
• It usually focuses on one or two main characters.
• The characters usually face a single problem or conflict.

Application Have students copy the web into their notebooks. Direct them to refer to it as they jot down notes applying the definition of a short story to "Rikki-tikki-tavi."

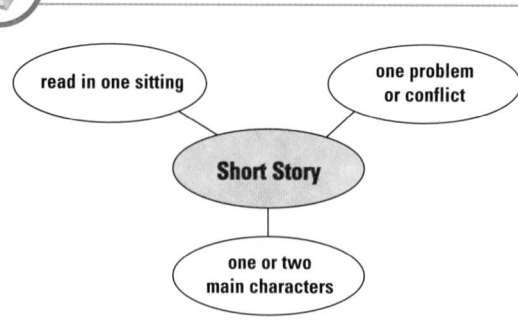

read in one sitting • one problem or conflict • **Short Story** • one or two main characters

"Son of the big man that killed Nag," she hissed, "stay still. I am not ready yet. Wait a little. Keep very still, all you three! If you move, I strike, and if you do not move, I strike. Oh, foolish people who killed my Nag!"

Teddy's eyes were fixed on his father, and all his father could do was to whisper, "Sit still, Teddy. You mustn't move. Teddy, keep still."

Then Rikki-tikki came up and cried, "Turn round, Nagaina; turn and fight!"

"All in good time," said she, without moving her eyes. "I will settle my account with you presently. Look at your friends, Rikki-tikki. They are still and white. They are afraid. They dare not move, and if you come a step nearer, I strike."

"Look at your eggs," said Rikki-tikki, "in the melon bed near the wall. Go and look, Nagaina!"

The big snake turned half round and saw the egg on the veranda. "Ah-h! Give it to me," she said.

Rikki-tikki put his paws one on each side of the egg, and his eyes were blood-red. "What price for a snake's egg? For a young cobra? For a young king cobra? For the last—the very last of the brood? The ants are eating all the others down by the melon bed."

Nagaina spun clear round, forgetting everything for the sake of the one egg; and Rikki-tikki saw Teddy's father shoot out a big hand, catch Teddy by the shoulder, and drag him across the little table with the teacups, safe and out of reach of Nagaina.

"Tricked! Tricked! Tricked! *Rikk-tck-tck!*" chuckled Rikki-tikki. "The boy is safe, and it was I—I—I that caught Nag by the hood last night in the bathroom." Then he began to jump up and down, all four feet together, his head close to the floor. "He threw me to and fro, but he could not shake me off. He was dead before the big man blew him in two. I did it! *Rikki-tikki-tck-tck!* Come then, Nagaina. Come and fight with me. You shall not be a widow long."

Nagaina saw that she had lost her chance of killing Teddy, and the egg lay between Rikki-tikki's paws. "Give me the egg, Rikki-tikki. Give me the last of my eggs, and I will go away and never come back," she said, lowering her hood.

"Yes, you will go away, and you will never come back, for you will go to the rubbish heap with Nag. Fight, widow! The big man has gone for his gun! Fight!"

Rikki-tikki was bounding all round Nagaina, keeping just out of reach of her stroke, his little eyes like hot coals. Nagaina gathered herself together and flung out at him. Rikki-tikki jumped up and backwards. Again and again and again she struck, and each time her head came with a whack on the matting of the veranda, and she gathered herself together like a watch spring. Then Rikki-tikki danced in a circle to get behind her, and Nagaina spun round to keep her head to his head, so that the rustle of her tail on the matting sounded like dry leaves blown along by the wind.

He had forgotten the egg. It still lay on the veranda, and Nagaina came nearer and nearer to it, till at last, while Rikki-tikki was drawing

STRATEGIC READING FOR

Less-Proficient Readers

FF Ask students to summarize what has become of Nagaina's eggs. *(Rikki found them, bit off their tops, and crushed the young cobras inside. He carried one last remaining egg to the verandah.)* Summarizing

Set a Purpose Have students read to find out what happens to Nagaina.

Critical Thinking: SYNTHESIZE

GG Invite students to explain why Rikki is bragging to Nagaina now. Guide students to apply what they have already learned about Nagaina and Rikki. *(Possible response: He is drawing her attention away from the family and is trying to provoke her into a fight.)*

CUSTOMIZING FOR

Students Acquiring English

④ Explain that a widow is a woman whose husband has died. You may want to give students the corresponding word for a man, *widower.*

Active Reading: EVALUATE

HH Ask students what they think of Rikki's insistence on destroying Nagaina's children and of Nagaina's devotion to her eggs. Ask students if they feel any sympathy for Nagaina and her unborn children. *(Possible responses: I feel sympathy for Nagaina, because she is a living creature and protective of her children; I do not feel sympathy for Nagaina, because she wants to kill the family.)*

Mini-Lesson **Study Skills**

ASSIGNMENT LOGS Tell students that when they finish reading "Rikki-tikki-tavi," they will have a choice of assignments. Suggest that students keep track of their assignments in an assignment log. In this special notebook or folder, they should

- write all assignments and record any important information about them, such as instructions and due dates
- keep a weekly schedule of assignments, in which they budget the time needed for completion
- break long assignments into parts. For example, when writing a report, they should break the assignment into tasks that can be done each day

Application Have students create an assignment log to use for their Alternate Activities, QuickWrites, and Across the Curriculum assignments. Students should be sure to list what materials they will need, record when each assignment is due, and budget their time. Encourage students to see page 335 of The Writer's Craft for additional information.

II Invite volunteers to identify the similes in this passage and analyze if they succeed in making the passage more vivid. *(Possible responses: The similes are "flew like an arrow" and "goes like a whiplash." They are much more effective in creating vivid descriptions than the simple statement that Nagaina sped away.)*

Critical Thinking:
MAKING JUDGMENTS

JJ Ask students if they think Rikki's decision to follow Nagaina into the rat hole is wise. Guide students to support their judgments. *(Possible responses: It is unwise, because it traps Rikki in the dark and because the cobra can maneuver underground better than the mongoose; it is wise, because it is the only way to trap the cobra.)*

Linking to Social Studies

KK The garden and snakes are potent symbols. In the Bible, for example, the garden represents paradise; the snake or serpent, pure evil. Adam and Eve are expelled from Eden, the garden paradise, when Eve falls prey to the serpent's treachery. The garden paradise in this story is restored to harmony when the serpent is eliminated.

II breath, she caught it in her mouth, turned to the veranda steps, and flew like an arrow down the path, with Rikki-tikki behind her. When the cobra runs for her life, she goes like a whiplash flicked across a horse's neck. Rikki-tikki knew that he must catch her, or all the trouble would begin again.

She headed straight for the long grass by the thorn bush, and as he was running, Rikki-tikki heard Darzee still singing his foolish little song of triumph. But Darzee's wife was wiser. She flew off her nest as Nagaina came along and flapped her wings about Nagaina's head. If Darzee had helped, they might have turned her; but Nagaina only lowered her hood and went on. Still, the instant's delay brought Rikki-tikki up to her, and as she plunged into the rat hole where she and Nag used to live, his little white teeth were clenched on her tail, and he went down with her—and very few mongooses, however wise and old they may be, care to follow a cobra into its hole.

It was dark in the hole; and Rikki-tikki never knew when it might open out and give Nagaina room to turn and strike at him. He held on savagely and stuck out his feet to act as brakes on the dark slope of the hot, moist earth.

Then the grass by the mouth of the hole stopped waving, and Darzee said, "It is all over with Rikki-tikki! We must sing his death song. Valiant Rikki-tikki is dead! For Nagaina will surely kill him underground."

So he sang a very mournful song that he made up on the spur of the minute; and just as he got to the most touching part, the grass

quivered again, and Rikki-tikki, covered with dirt, dragged himself out of the hole leg by leg, licking his whiskers. Darzee stopped with a little shout. Rikki-tikki shook some of the dust out of his fur and sneezed. "It is all over," he said. "The widow will never come out again." And the red ants that live between the grass stems heard him and began to troop down one after another to see if he had spoken the truth.

Rikki-tikki curled himself up in the grass and slept where he was—slept and slept till it was late in the afternoon, for he had done a hard day's work.

"Now," he said, when he awoke, "I will go back to the house. Tell the coppersmith, Darzee, and he will tell the garden that Nagaina is dead."

The coppersmith is a bird who makes a noise exactly like the beating of a little hammer on a copper pot; and the reason he is always making it is because he is the town crier to every Indian garden and tells all the news to everybody who cares to listen. As Rikki-tikki went up the path, he heard his "attention" notes like a tiny dinner gong, and then the steady *"Ding-dong-tock!* Nag is dead—*dong!* Nagaina is dead! *Ding-dong-tock!"* That set all the birds in the garden singing and the frogs croaking, for Nag and Nagaina used to eat frogs as well as little birds.

When Rikki got to the house, Teddy and Teddy's mother (she looked very white still, for she had been fainting) and Teddy's father came out and almost cried over him; and that night he ate all that was given him till he could eat no more and went to bed on Teddy's shoulder,

---

Multicultural Perspectives

SNAKES To many people, snakes are loathsome creatures best left undisturbed. Indeed, snakes can be deadly—especially mambas, cobras, coral snakes, rattlesnakes, bushmasters, fer-de-lances, and vipers. In some cultures, snakes are worshiped and handled as part of important rituals.

For example, the Hopi, or Moqui, people of northeastern Arizona hold a snake dance every two years in the latter part of August. Many Hopi believe that

snakes have special powers and are their brothers, the children of the ancestors of the Snake Maid and the Snake Hero, who were transformed into snakes. The Snake Dance is intended to petition the nature gods to bring rain.

The first part of the ritual consists of eight days of secret ceremonies. After that, the Snake Dance is held in public.

where Teddy's mother saw him when she came to look late at night.

"He saved our lives and Teddy's life," she said to her husband. "Just think, he saved all our lives."

Rikki-tikki woke up with a jump, for the mongooses are light sleepers.

"Oh, it's you," said he. "What are you bothering for? All the cobras are dead; and if they weren't, I'm here."

Rikki-tikki had a right to be proud of himself; but he did not grow too proud, and he kept that garden as a mongoose should keep it, with tooth and jump and spring and bite, till never a cobra dared show its head inside the walls. ❖

For centuries, European nations struggled to gain control of India, the so-called "Jewel of the East." In the 1500s, the Portuguese discovered the first sea routes to India and eastern Asia. They established bases in India and the Spice Islands so that they could transport spices from these lands to Europe, where they were in great demand. The British recognized the profitability of this spice trade and challenged Portugal's monopoly of the trade routes. In 1599, eighty London merchants joined together to finance the East India Company. The next year, the company received a charter, or official document, that granted it exclusive trading rights in the East Indies and the power to maintain an army and a navy, declare war, and govern new territories.

By the mid-1700s, the British East India Company had become the leading power in India. For about the next hundred years, it continued to wage wars with surrounding countries, each time gaining more territory. After an Indian rebellion against the East India Company in 1857, however, the British government decided it was time to step in and take direct control of India. This marked the beginning of a golden age for the British in India. By the time Kipling was writing in the late 1800s, British-born government officials and their families, such as Teddy's family in this story, were enjoying a high standard of living in colonial India. India remained a British colony until 1947, when it finally gained its independence after a century-long struggle with the British government.

THE COLONIZATION OF INDIA **399**

CUSTOMIZING FOR

Gifted and Talented Students

Explain that some critics have charged that Kipling's writing affirms his nationalistic views. Have students discuss whether they think Rikki's role as the family's bodyguard suggests the relationship between Britain and her colonies. You may wish to have students read Kipling's poem "Gunga Din" and have them compare Rikki and Gunga Din.

STRATEGIC READING FOR

Less-Proficient Readers

LL Ask students to infer what happens to Nagaina. (*Rikki kills her in the rat hole.*) **Making Inferences**

COMPREHENSION CHECK
1. How does Rikki end up at Teddy's house? (*A summer flood carries him from his burrow to a garden path near Teddy's house.*)
2. How does Nagaina want to get rid of Rikki? (*by killing Teddy's family*)
3. Who shoots Nag? (*Teddy's father*)
4. Who kills Nagaina? (*Rikki*)
5. Where does Nagaina die? (*in the rat hole, her home*)

INSIGHT
1. Why do you think India was called the "Jewel of the East"? (*Possible response: because of its beauty and its strategic location in the spice trade*)
2. How do you think life for the Indian people changed when British rule ended? (*Possible response: They became more independent, because they were no longer expected to serve the British.*)

Mini-Lesson — Study Skills

SUMMARIZING Describe how writers summarize by expressing the main ideas of a passage in their own words, leaving out details. Point out that a summary is much shorter than the original text. Copy the steps shown onto the board and discuss them with students.

Application Invite students to summarize the Historical Insight on page 399. Then have students choose partners to revise each other's summary. Invite volunteers to share their work with the class, showing how they isolated the key ideas and checked their work for accuracy. Students have another opportunity to practice summarizing in QuickWrites, on page 400.

Steps in Summarizing
Step 1: Reread the passage.
Step 2: Rewrite key ideas in simple words.
Step 3: Check for accuracy.

From Personal Response to Critical Analysis

1. Responses will vary.
2. Possible responses: Students might say that they would feel sad, angry, betrayed, or depressed.
3. Possible responses: He fights to protect the family, since he is fond of them; he acts only from instinct, since it is a mongoose's nature to battle snakes.
4. Possible responses: Some students may say the fight with Karait takes the greatest courage, because the snake is both elusive and lethal. Other students may choose the battle with Nag, because Rikki is inexperienced and vastly overpowered. Still others may mention the battle with Nagaina, because Rikki is at a disadvantage in the dark rat hole.
5. Possible responses: The main character is heroic and admirable; the story is suspenseful and fast moving; the writing is brisk and colorful.

Literary Links

Have students compare how heroism and courage are portrayed in "Rikki-tikki-tavi" and "The Charge of the Light Brigade." *(Possible response: In this selection, the heroic and courageous character is a mongoose battling cobras. In "The Charge of the Light Brigade," soldiers are heroic and courageous as they charge into the valley of death against unbeatable enemy troops.)*

Another Pathway

Cooperative Learning To help students work together, each group can select an explainer of ideas to share everyone's ideas and opinions, a support giver to give verbal and nonverbal acceptance, and a recorder to write the list and rankings.

Rubric

3 Full Accomplishment Students list all the animals in the story and their qualities. The ranking is thoughtful and balanced.

2 Substantial Accomplishment Students list most of the animals and their qualities. Students cannot explain some of the reasons for their rankings.

1 Little or Partial Accomplishment Students list only some of the animals and their qualities. Students cannot justify their rankings.

RESPONDING
OPTIONS

FROM **PERSONAL RESPONSE** TO **CRITICAL ANALYSIS**

REFLECT   1. What did you think of Rikki-tikki by the end of the story? Jot down your thoughts in your notebook. Then share them with your classmates.

RETHINK   2. How might you react to this story if Rikki-tikki or Teddy were killed by one of the cobras?

3. In your opinion, does Rikki-tikki fight Nag and Nagaina mainly to protect Teddy and his parents, or does he act only from instinct? Explain your answer.

Thematic Link   4. Which of Rikki-tikki's battles do you think takes the greatest courage? Explain your choice.

RELATE   5. "Rikki-tikki-tavi" is considered by many to be a classic story—one that has been read and enjoyed by many generations. How would you explain what gives this story its classic appeal?

Multimodal Learning
ANOTHER PATHWAY

With a small group of classmates, make a list of the animals in this story and brainstorm the qualities that each shows. Rank the qualities on a scale from 1 to 10, with 10 being most admirable. Then share your list with the rest of the class, giving reasons for your rankings.

QUICKWRITES

1. In the story, Darzee sings a song about Rikki-tikki's killing of Nag. Write **lyrics** for that song, beginning with the words quoted in the story.

2. Most, but not all, of the characters in the story consider Rikki-tikki to be a hero. Write a **summary** of the story from Nagaina's point of view.

3. Choose a pair of natural enemies from the list you created for the Personal Connection on page 385, and write a **battle scene** between the two animals. Use details, as Kipling does, to make the battle exciting and easy to follow.

📁 *PORTFOLIO Save your writing. You may want to use it later as a springboard to a piece for your portfolio.*

LITERARY CONCEPTS

Characters that play a small role in a work's plot are called **minor characters.** An author often uses minor characters to keep the plot moving or to provide a contrast to a main character. For example, Chuchundra advances the plot (when he tells Rikki-tikki where Nag is) and contrasts with Rikki-tikki (Chuchundra is a coward). Who are some other minor characters? How do they function in the story?

CONCEPT REVIEW: Setting What if the bungalow in this story didn't have a garden? How might the story be different?

400   UNIT FOUR   PART 1: THE WILL TO WIN

Literary Concepts

Students might say that Darzee warns Rikki about Nagaina and by his stupidity makes Rikki seem clever. Darzee's wife distracts Nagaina. Karait is used to show how tough Rikki is. Teddy's father helps Rikki during his battle with Nag. Teddy's vulnerability makes Rikki seem heroic.

Concept Review Students might say that without the garden the story would not have had the cobras that generate the basic conflict of the plot.

QuickWrites

1. Encourage students to set the words to a popular, familiar tune. Encourage students to use a tune with a melody and rhythm that suit the mood of the words.
2. Remind students to use what they learned about summarizing from the mini-lesson on page 399.
3. Have students use dialogue to make their battle scene more dramatic.

 **The Writer's Craft**

Summarizing, pp. 342–343
Creating Dialogue, pp. 320–322
Sensory Details, p. 255

Multimodal Learning

ALTERNATIVE ACTIVITIES

1. Make a **comic-book** version of part of this story. Reread the story to determine the important scenes you want to portray and the dialogue you want to include in the talk balloons. Illustrate your scenes and then share your book with younger audiences.

2. Stage a **radio reading** of the story. Assign students to perform the parts of the characters and the narrator and to provide sound effects. Rehearse your performance, then tape-record it for other classes.

ACROSS THE CURRICULUM

Science Prepare a report on either the mongoose or the cobra. Skim the story for details about mongooses or cobras, then check an encyclopedia, other books, or a computer database for additional information. Present your findings in the form of a visual display, an oral report, or a booklet. Be sure to include information about the animal's habitat, prey, and enemies, as well as common myths about the animal.

WORDS TO KNOW

For each boldfaced word, write the letter of the phrase that best illustrates its meaning.

1. **revive**
   a. a package sent to a faraway country
   b. a man opening his eyes after an operation
   c. a teacher telling a student to correct mistakes in a paper

2. **cower**
   a. a scared child reacting to a bully
   b. a bird hopping from branch to branch
   c. a snake moving silently through the grass

3. **consolation**
   a. a girl whose friends go to the park without her
   b. a meeting of people who work together on a problem
   c. a boy who gets a puppy after his best friend moves away

4. **cunningly**
   a. a fox that fools its enemy
   b. a lion that rules the jungle
   c. a mouse that is frightened by every noise

5. **scuttle**
   a. kittens playing with yarn
   b. cows grazing in a meadow
   c. chicks that see a hawk approaching

JOSEPH RUDYARD KIPLING

1865–1936

Though educated in England, Rudyard Kipling was born and raised in India, where his father was a school principal. Kipling loved to read as a child, and his first job was as a journalist on a British newspaper in India. His stories about his Indian travels made him extremely popular, and when he returned to London in 1889, he was already famous.

When he had children of his own, Kipling turned to writing children's stories. His first collections, *The Jungle Book* and *The Second Jungle Book,* included stories about an Indian boy raised by wolves and animal stories set in India. "Rikki-tikki-tavi" is one of these.

Kipling received numerous honors and awards. In 1907 he won the Nobel Prize in literature. He is buried in London in the Poets' Corner of Westminster Abbey.

OTHER WORKS *Just So Stories, The Light That Failed,* "Gunga Din"   Extended Reading

LASERLINKS
• *SCIENCE CONNECTION*

Across the Curriculum

Science Encourage students to use recycled materials and found objects to create their visual displays. Suggest that oral reports include visual aids, such as photographs from books and magazines.

ADDITIONAL SUGGESTION

Social Studies *Freedom!* Have students research and prepare a report on India's long struggle for independence from Great Britain. Have students include a time line listing key people, dates, and events.

SCIENCE CONNECTION
The Mongoose and the Cobra
Seeing the cobra and the mongoose in their natural habitat will help students better understand how these two animals interact.

Side A, Frames 49378

Words to Know

1. b
2. a
3. c
4. a
5. c

Reteaching/Reinforcement
• *Unit Four Resource Book,* p. 7

JOSEPH RUDYARD KIPLING

Kipling believed it was the duty of the British Empire to spread its culture around the world, and much of his writing glorifies the British Empire. Although his popularity as a writer has faded somewhat over the years, he is generally regarded as a master of the short adventure story.

Alternative Activities

1. Encourage students to decide how many panels they will include in their comic and what each panel will show. You may want to make comic books available so students can familiarize themselves with this type of art and its storytelling techniques.

2. First play for students a radio version or a recording of another, similar story. Then have them discuss what was effective about the recording and apply what they learn to their own radio reading.

OVERVIEW

Objectives

- To understand and appreciate a short story about two good friends who must compete against each other
- To analyze a surprise ending
- To appreciate the use of images and figures of speech
- To express understanding of the story through a choice of writing forms, including a definition, an editorial, and a profile
- To extend understanding of the story through a variety of multimodal and cross-curricular activities

Skills

READING SKILLS/ STRATEGIES
- Comparing and contrasting

THE WRITER'S STYLE
- Point of view

GRAMMAR
- Commas with interrupters

LITERARY CONCEPTS
- Surprise ending
- Motivation

SPELLING
- Words from French

STUDY SKILLS
- Note taking

SPEAKING, LISTENING, AND VIEWING
- Film

Cross-Curricular Connections

PHYSICAL EDUCATION
- Conditioning programs
- Planning exercise

HISTORY
- Jack Broughton

SOCIAL STUDIES
- Amateur boxing

ALTERNATIVE

Previewing

Instead of writing answers in their notebooks, students can discuss their responses with a partner.

Personal Connection

Discussion Prompts Think about an incident in which you and a friend were both competing for the same thing. Describe this incident to your partner and then listen carefully to your partner's description. Next, discuss what happens when friends compete. Use the following questions to help you get started.

- *What was it that you and your friend were competing for?*
- *Were you upset to find you were competing against someone you liked?*
- *What was the result of the competition, and how did it affect your friendship?*
- *Do you think friends should compete? Why or why not?*

As you read, look at how competition affects Antonio and Felix's friendship.

FICTION

Amigo Brothers
Piri Thomas

Activating Prior Knowledge
PERSONAL CONNECTION

Think about a time when you had to compete against a good friend in order to win something you really wanted. Maybe you and your friend were competing on opposing teams for a championship trophy or were running against each other in a class election. What was it like to be your good friend's rival? Did your friendship affect the way you competed? Did the competition affect your friendship? In your notebook, jot down answers to these questions.

Building Background
HISTORICAL CONNECTION

In "Amigo Brothers," two good friends compete against each other in a boxing tournament. Boxing is one of the oldest forms of athletic competition. More than 5,000 years ago, boxing was popular in Sumeria, and boxing later was an event in the Olympic games of ancient Greece. For most of the history of the sport, boxers fought without gloves. Then, in the mid-1860s, the marquis of Queensberry, an English nobleman, helped to establish rules in an effort to protect boxers from serious injury. The Queensberry rules called for the use of padded gloves, three-minute rounds separated by one-minute rest periods, and a ten-second count for a knockout. Today, boxers fight in different divisions according to their weights. Amateur boxers are not paid for their bouts and compete in tournaments sponsored by local and national organizations. Of all the amateur tournaments, none is more famous than the annual Golden Gloves tournament.

Herbert Slade of Australia (left) and James Mace of England, two famous bare-knuckle boxers of the late 1800s. Culver Pictures.

Setting a Purpose
WRITING CONNECTION

Review the answers you wrote for the Personal Connection. In your notebook, write a paragraph explaining which force you consider stronger—friendship or competition. Then, as you read this selection, think about the main characters and the ways in which they respond to a competition that tests their friendship.

PRINT AND MEDIA RESOURCES

UNIT FOUR RESOURCE BOOK
Strategic Reading: Literature, p. 11
Vocabulary SkillBuilder, p. 14
Reading SkillBuilder, p. 12
Spelling SkillBuilder, p. 13

GRAMMAR MINI-LESSONS
Transparencies, p. 29
Copymasters, p. 39

WRITING MINI-LESSONS
Transparencies, p. 47

ACCESS FOR STUDENTS ACQUIRING ENGLISH
Selection Summaries
Reading and Writing Support

FORMAL ASSESSMENT
Selection Test, pp. 79–80
 Test Generator

 **AUDIO LIBRARY**
See Reference Card

INTERNET RESOURCES
McDougal Littell Literature Center at http://www.hmco.com /mcdougal/lit

AMIGO BROTHERS

by Piri Thomas

SUMMARY

Seventeen-year-olds Antonio Cruz and Felix Varga are best friends who both dream of being lightweight boxing champions. When they are paired against each other in the Boys Club division finals, the *amigo* brothers decide to train separately and fight as if they were strangers. On the day of the match, they square off in the ring, each not knowing quite what to expect. But when the bell sounds, they give their all. Antonio dances gracefully around the ring and jabs. Felix delivers his powerhouse punches. After two rounds, the fight is even. In the third and final round, the boys pound wildly at each other, delivering blows even after the final bell has rung. Once the referee and trainers pry them apart, the friends rush toward each other and hug. Then, before the announcer can name the winner, Antonio and Felix leave the ring arm in arm.

Thematic Link: *The Will to Win* Antonio Cruz and Felix Varga have the will to win, both in the ring and as friends.

403

WORDS TO KNOW

barrage (bə-räzh′) *n.* a rapid, heavy attack (p. 405)

bedlam (bĕd′ləm) *n.* a noisy confusion (p. 411)

dispel (dĭ-spĕl′) *v.* to scatter; get rid of (p. 409)

evading (ĭ-vā′dĭng) *adj.* avoiding; escaping **evade** *v.* (p. 411)

feint (fānt) *v.* to make a pretended attack in order to draw attention away from one's real purpose or target (p. 411)

game (gām) *adj.* ready and willing to proceed (p. 411)

improvise (ĭm′prə-vīz′) *v.* to speak or perform without preparation (p. 408)

pensively (pĕn′sĭv-lē) *adv.* in a way that suggests deep thought (p. 406)

perpetual (pər-pĕch′ōō-əl) *adj.* continual; unending (p. 408)

unbridled (ŭn-brīd′ld) *adj.* lacking in restraint or control (p. 408)

Antonio Cruz and Felix Vargas were both seventeen years old. They were so together in friendship that they felt themselves to be brothers. They had known each other since childhood, growing up on the lower east side of Manhattan in the same tenement building on Fifth Street between Avenue A and Avenue B.

Flight (1988), Douglas Safranek. Egg tempera on panel, 40″ × 32″, courtesy of Schmidt Bingham Gallery, New York.

Antonio was fair, lean, and lanky, while Felix was dark, short, and husky. Antonio's hair was always falling over his eyes, while Felix wore his black hair in a natural Afro style.

Each youngster had a dream of someday becoming lightweight champion of the world. Every chance they had the boys worked out, sometimes at the Boy's Club on 10th Street and Avenue A and sometimes at the pro's gym on 14th Street. Early morning sunrises would find them running along the East River Drive, wrapped in sweatshirts, short towels around their necks, and handkerchiefs Apache style around their foreheads.

While some youngsters were into street negatives, Antonio and Felix slept, ate, rapped, and dreamt positive. Between them, they had a collection of *Fight* magazines second to none, plus a scrapbook filled with torn tickets to every boxing match they had ever attended and some clippings of their own. If asked a question about any given fighter, they would immediately zip out from their memory banks divisions,[1] weights, records of fights, knockouts, technical knockouts, and draws or losses.

Each had fought many bouts representing

---

1. **divisions:** weight groups into which boxers are separated.

| Mini-Lesson | Reading Skills/Strategies |

COMPARE AND CONTRAST Explain to students that when they use the reading strategy of comparing and contrasting, they identify similarities and differences between two items, people, or settings, for example. Tell students that comparing is showing how two items are the same, and contrasting is showing how they are different.

Application Have students create and fill in a chart like the one shown that compares and contrasts Antonio and Felix.

Reteaching/Reinforcement
- *Unit Four Resource Book,* p. 12

Attributes	Antonio	Felix

their community and had won two gold-plated medals plus a silver and bronze medallion. The difference was in their style. Antonio's lean form and long reach made him the better boxer, while Felix's short and muscular frame made him the better slugger. Whenever they had met in the ring for sparring sessions, it had always been hot and heavy.

Now, after a series of elimination bouts,[2] they had been informed that they were to meet each other in the division finals that were scheduled for the seventh of August, two weeks away—the winner to represent the Boys Club in the Golden Gloves Championship Tournament.

The two boys continued to run together along the East River Drive. But even when joking with each other, they both sensed a wall rising between them.

One morning less than a week before their bout, they met as usual for their daily workout. They fooled around with a few jabs at the air, slapped skin, and then took off, running lightly along the dirty East River's edge.

Antonio glanced at Felix, who kept his eyes purposely straight ahead, pausing from time to time to do some fancy leg work while throwing one-twos followed by upper cuts to an imaginary jaw. Antonio then beat the air with a <u>barrage</u> of body blows and short devastating lefts with an overhand, jawbreaking right.

After a mile or so, Felix puffed and said, "Let's stop for awhile, bro. I think we both got something to say to each other."

Antonio nodded. It was not natural to be acting as though nothing unusual was happening when two ace boon buddies were going to be blasting . . . each other within a few short days.

They rested their elbows on the railing separating them from the river. Antonio wiped his face with his short towel. The sunrise was now creating day.

Felix leaned heavily on the river's railing and stared across to the shores of Brooklyn. Finally, he broke the silence.

". . . , man. I don't know how to come out with it."

Antonio helped. "It's about our fight, right?"

"Yeah, right." Felix's eyes squinted at the rising orange sun.

"I've been thinking about it too, *panin*.[3] In fact, since we found out it was going to be me and you, I've been awake at night, pulling punches[4] on you, trying not to hurt you."

"Same here. It ain't natural not to think about the fight. I mean, we both are *cheverote*[5] fighters, and we both want to win. But only one of us can win. There ain't no draws in the eliminations."

Felix tapped Antonio gently on the shoulder. "I don't mean to sound like I'm bragging, bro. But I wanna win, fair and square."

Antonio nodded quietly. "Yeah. We both know that in the ring the better man wins. Friend or no friend, brother or no . . ."

Felix finished it for him. "Brother. Tony, let's promise something right here. Okay?"

"If it's fair, *hermano*,[6] I'm for it." Antonio admired the courage of a tugboat pulling a barge five times its welterweight[7] size.

"It's fair, Tony. When we get into the ring, it's gotta be like we never met. We gotta be like two heavy strangers that want the same thing, and only one can have it. You understand, don'tcha?" (I)

---

2. **elimination bouts:** matches to determine which boxers advance in a competition.

3. *panin* (pä′nēn) *American Spanish:* pal; buddy.

4. **pulling punches:** holding back in delivering blows.

5. *cheverote* (chĕ-vĕ-rô′tĕ) *American Spanish:* really cool.

6. *hermano* (ĕr-mä′nô) *Spanish:* brother.

7. **welterweight:** one of boxing's weight divisions, with a maximum weight of 147 pounds.

WORDS TO KNOW   **barrage** (bə-räzh′) *n.* a rapid, heavy attack

405

Active Reading: PREDICT

A Have students predict what might happen to the boys' friendship as a result of their fight. *(Possible responses: Their friendship might be shattered; they could emerge as even better friends.)*

Critical Thinking: HYPOTHESIZE

B Have students infer what Felix wants to say to Antonio. Guide students to use context clues as they formulate their hypotheses. *(Possible responses: Felix wants to talk about how the fight will affect their friendship; he wants to talk about how they can get out of the fight; he wants to talk about boxing strategies.)*

Literary Concept: MOTIVATION

C Invite students to explain what motivates the boys to discuss their upcoming fight. Challenge students to explain what the boys' language reveals about their relationship. *(Possible response: They are motivated by a strong desire to keep the friendship intact. Their forms of address reveal mutual respect, admiration, and affection. Using words from their native language shows how relaxed the boys are with each other.)*

CUSTOMIZING FOR
Students Acquiring English

(I) Point out that the spelling of *don'tcha* reflects the way that "don't you" is often pronounced in informal spoken English.

Mini-Lesson   **Literary Concepts**

REVIEWING MOTIVATION Remind students that motivation explains why a character acts, feels, or thinks a certain way. Create a word web like the one shown to help students brainstorm concepts that motivate people's actions. Encourage students to volunteer other common motivations in their lives.

Application Have students create and fill in a chart that traces the two main characters' actions and the motivations of these actions.

El Abrazo [The hug] by Fletcher
Martin Fletcher Martin (1904–) hails
from pioneer stock: his ancestors were
English, Irish, and French settlers who
landed in America in the 1600s. He
grew up in the West, where his father
was a newspaper publisher and ranch-
er. Largely self-taught, Martin attained
prominence in the art world.

Reading the Art *What kind of relationship do you think exists between the two
subjects? Do you think Antonio and Felix
would express their friendship in this
manner? Why or why not?*

CUSTOMIZING FOR

Students Acquiring English

② Guide students to understand that
the word *heads* in the phrase *it would
be better for our heads* is not used literally. Rather, *heads* refers to the feelings
and attitudes of the two characters.

STRATEGIC READING FOR

Less-Proficient Readers

Ⓓ Ask students the following questions.

• How are the boys the same? How
are they different? *(The boys grew up
in the same neighborhood and are both
successful prizefighters. They have different fighting styles: Antonio is the better boxer; Felix is the better slugger.)*
Comparing and Contrasting

• How do the boys resolve their conflict and deal with the upcoming
competition? *(They decide to fight their
best and act as if they are strangers in
the ring.)* **Summarizing**

Set a Purpose Have students read to
find out how each boy spends the
night before the fight and how Antonio
decides to deal with Felix once inside
the ring.

"Let's stop for a while, bro."
"It's about our fight, right?"
"If it's fair, hermano, I'm for it."

"*Sí*, I know." Tony smiled. "No pulling
punches. We go all the way."

"Yeah, that's right. Listen, Tony. Don't you
think it's a good idea if we don't see each
other until the day of the fight? I'm going to
stay with my Aunt Lucy in the Bronx. I can
use Gleason's Gym for working out. My
manager says he got some sparring partners
with more or less your style."

Tony scratched his nose <u>pensively</u>. "Yeah, it

would be better for our heads." He held out
his hand, palm upward. "Deal?"

"Deal." Felix lightly slapped open skin.

"Ready for some more running?" Tony
asked lamely.

"Naw, bro. Let's cut it here. You go on. I
kinda like to get things together in my head."

"You ain't worried, are you?" Tony asked.

"No way, man." Felix laughed out loud. "I
got too much smarts for that. I just think it's

El Abrazo [The Hug] (1966), Fletcher Martin. Acrylic on paper, 22″ × 17″, private collection.

WORDS
TO   **pensively** (pĕn′sĭv-lē) *adv.* in a way that suggests deep thought
KNOW

406

Mini-Lesson **Grammar**

COMMAS WITH INTERRUPTERS Explain
that interrupters are words or phrases that break
the flow of thought in a sentence. Commas are
used to mark pauses before and after the interruption. If the interrupter appears at the end of
the sentence, end punctuation takes the place of
a second comma. The examples illustrate how
commas are used with interrupters (underlined).

Application Have students punctuate following
sentences.
1. "*Sí* I know." Tony smiled.
2. "Yeah that's right."

3. Antonio groggy bobbed and weaved.
4. August 7 the day of the fight was sunny.
5. "No way man" Felix laughed.
6. "You watch yourself too *sabe?*"
7. Antonio danced a joy to behold.

Reteaching/Reinforcement
• Grammar Handbook, anthology pp. 880–882
• *Grammar Mini-Lessons* copymasters p. 39,
 transparencies, p. 29

 The Writer's Craft

Interrupting Words and Phrases, p. 580

cooler if we split right here. After the fight, we can get it together again like nothing ever happened."

The amigo brothers were not ashamed to hug each other tightly.

"Guess you're right. Watch yourself, Felix. I hear there's some pretty heavy dudes up in the Bronx. *Suavecito,*[8] okay?"

"Okay. You watch yourself too, *sabe*[9]?"

Tony jogged away. Felix watched his friend disappear from view, throwing rights and lefts. Both fighters had a lot of psyching up to do before the big fight.

The days in training passed much too slowly. Although they kept out of each other's way, they were aware of each other's progress via the ghetto grapevine.

The evening before the big fight, Tony made his way to the roof of his tenement. In the quiet early dark, he peered over the ledge. Six stories below, the lights of the city blinked, and the sounds of cars mingled with the curses and the laughter of children in the street. He tried not to think of Felix, feeling he had succeeded in psyching his mind. But only in the ring would he really know. To spare Felix hurt, he would have to knock him out, early and quick.

Up in the South Bronx, Felix decided to take in a movie in an effort to keep Antonio's face away from his fists. The flick was *The Champion* with Kirk Douglas, the third time Felix was seeing it.

The champion was getting . . . beat . . . , his face being pounded into raw, wet hamburger. His eyes were cut, jagged, bleeding, one eye swollen, the other almost shut. He was saved only by the sound of the bell.

Felix became the champ and Tony the challenger.

The movie audience was going out of its head, roaring in blood lust at the butchery going on. The champ hunched his shoulders,

grunting and sniffing red blood back into his broken nose. The challenger, confident that he had the championship in the bag, threw a left. The champ countered with a dynamite right that exploded into the challenger's brains.

Felix's right arm felt the shock. Antonio's face, superimposed on the screen, was shattered and split apart by the awesome force of the killer blow. Felix saw himself in the ring, blasting Antonio against the ropes. The champ had to be forcibly restrained. The challenger was allowed to crumble slowly to the canvas, a broken, bloody mess.

When Felix finally left the theatre, he had figured out how to psyche himself for tomorrow's fight. It was Felix the Champion vs. Antonio the Challenger.

He walked up some dark streets, deserted except for small pockets of wary-looking kids wearing gang colors. Despite the fact that he was Puerto Rican like them, they eyed him as a stranger to their turf. Felix did a last shuffle, bobbing and weaving, while letting loose a torrent of blows that would demolish whatever got in its way. It seemed to impress the brothers, who went about their own business.

Finding no takers, Felix decided to split to his aunt's. Walking the streets had not relaxed him, neither had the fight flick. All it had done was to stir him up. He let himself quietly into his Aunt Lucy's apartment and went straight to bed, falling into a fitful sleep with sounds of the gong for Round One.

Antonio was passing some heavy time on his rooftop. How would the fight tomorrow affect his relationship with Felix? After all, fighting was like any other profession. Friendship had nothing to do with it. A gnawing doubt crept in. He cut negative thinking real quick by

---

8. *Suavecito* (swä-vĕ-sē′tô) *American Spanish:* Take it easy.
9. *sabe?* (sä′bĕ) *Spanish:* you know?

E Ask students what the preparations for the fight made by Antonio and Felix reveal about their personalities and friendship. If necessary, guide students by using the following model:

Think-Aloud Model *Tony spends the night before the fight all alone, thinking about the fight and his friend. Felix spends the night at a movie. It seems like he's with others, but he's really alone, just like Tony. This tells me that both boys need time alone to think. They are both thoughtful, concerned people.*

Literary Concept: ALLITERATION

F Invite students to identify examples of alliteration in this passage and discuss how the author uses the sounds of words to help readers visualize the scene. *(Possible response: "superimposed, screen, shattered, split," "crumble, canvas," "broken, bloody"; the alliteration helps readers get a mental picture of the speed and force of the fight.)*

CUSTOMIZING FOR
Students Acquiring English

3 Point out that *split* is a slang word meaning "to leave."

CUSTOMIZING FOR
Multiple Learning Styles

G **Intrapersonal Learners** Invite students to explain what they think Antonio is thinking, based on their own experiences.

M i n i - L e s s o n   Spelling

WORDS FROM FRENCH Explain to students that English has incorporated words from many languages, including French. To make it easier to remember how to spell these words, point out the following letter combinations.

- **age** (pronounced /äzh/)
- **et** (pronounced /ā/)
- **eur** (pronounced /œr/)

Application Ask students to spell the following words as you read them aloud.

1. barrage	6. beret
2. ballet	7. mirage
3. corsage	8. espionage
4. amateur	9. chauffeur
5. buffet	10. grandeur

Have students look for more words that fit this pattern, in their own writing and in things that they read, and then add these words to their personal word lists.

Reteaching/Reinforcement
- *Unit Four Resource Book*, p. 13

Critical Thinking: SYNTHESIZE

H Ask students why they think the fight has generated so much interest in the community. *(Possible responses: because the boys are liked and well respected and each has his own loyal following; because boxing is an important sport in their neighborhood)*

Literary Concept: SUSPENSE

I Invite students to explain how the author builds suspense. Suggest analyzing this passage as a jumping-off point. *(Possible responses: The "beehive" of activity, the move to a larger space, and the boys' internal conflicts all create a sense of anticipation before the fight.)*

CUSTOMIZING FOR

Multiple Learning Styles

J **Interpersonal Learners** Invite students to imagine that they are one of the community leaders or dignitaries at the fight. Have students write and deliver a brief speech suitable to the occasion and their status in the community.

STRATEGIC READING FOR

Less-Proficient Readers

K Make sure students are following the story to this point.

• Where does each boy spend the evening before the fight? *(Felix goes to see The Champion; Antonio spends time thinking on his rooftop.)*
Summarizing

• How does Antonio decide to think of Felix in the ring? *(as another opponent, not as his friend Felix)* **Noting Relevant Details**

Set a Purpose Have students read to find out how the fight goes and why boxing is so important to the boys.

doing some speedy fancy dance steps, bobbing and weaving like mercury. The night air was blurred with <u>perpetual</u> motions of left hooks and right crosses. Felix, his *amigo* brother, was not going to be Felix at all in the ring. Just an opponent with another face. Antonio went to sleep, hearing the opening bell for the first round. Like his friend in the South Bronx, he prayed for victory via a quick, clean knockout in the first round.

Large posters plastered all over the walls of local shops announced the fight between Antonio Cruz and Felix Vargas as the main bout.

The fight had created great interest in the neighborhood. Antonio and Felix were well liked and respected. Each had his own loyal following. Betting fever was high and ranged from a bottle of Coke to cold, hard cash on the line.

Antonio's fans bet with <u>unbridled</u> faith in his boxing skills. On the other side, Felix's admirers bet on his dynamite-packed fists.

Felix had returned to his apartment early in the morning of August 7th and stayed there, hoping to avoid seeing Antonio. He turned the radio on to *salsa* music sounds and then tried to read while waiting for word from his manager.

The fight was scheduled to take place in Tompkins Square Park. It had been decided that the gymnasium of the Boys Club was not large enough to hold all the people who were sure to attend. In Tompkins Square Park, everyone who wanted could view the fight, whether from ringside or window fire escapes or tenement rooftops.

The morning of the fight, Tompkins Square was a beehive of activity with numerous workers setting up the ring, the seats, and the guest speakers' stand. The scheduled bouts began shortly after noon, and the park had begun filling up even earlier.

The local junior high school across from Tompkins Square Park served as the dressing room for all the fighters. Each was given a separate classroom, with desktops, covered with mats, serving as resting tables. Antonio thought he caught a glimpse of Felix waving to him from a room at the far end of the corridor. He waved back just in case it had been him.

The fighters changed from their street clothes into fighting gear. Antonio wore white trunks, black socks, and black shoes. Felix wore sky blue trunks, red socks, and white boxing shoes. Each had dressing gowns to match their fighting trunks with their names neatly stitched on the back.

The loudspeakers blared into the open window of the school. There were speeches by dignitaries, community leaders, and great boxers of yesteryear. Some were well prepared, some <u>improvised</u> on the spot. They all carried the same message of great pleasure and honor at being part of such a historic event. This great day was in the tradition of champions emerging from the streets of the lower east side.

Interwoven with the speeches were the sounds of the other boxing events. After the sixth bout, Felix was much relieved when his trainer, Charlie, said, "Time change. Quick knockout. This is it. We're on."

Waiting time was over. Felix was escorted from the classroom by a dozen fans in white T-shirts with the word FELIX across their fronts.

Antonio was escorted down a different stairwell and guided through a roped-off path.

As the two climbed into the ring, the crowd exploded with a roar. Antonio and Felix both bowed gracefully and then raised their arms in acknowledgment.

Antonio tried to be cool, but even as the roar was in its first birth, he turned slowly to

WORDS	**perpetual** (pər-pěch′ōō-əl) *adj.* continual; unending
TO	**unbridled** (ŭn-brīd′ld) *adj.* lacking in restraint or control
KNOW	**improvise** (ĭm′prə-vīz′) *v.* to speak or perform without preparation

408

Multicultural **Perspectives**

BOXING Ancient boxing, dating back at least 5,000 years, was a ruthless sport. Each match usually ended with the death of the loser. There were no rules governing the sport until 1743, when boxing champion Jack Broughton devised a set of rules that standardized some practices and eliminated others. In 1838, based upon Broughton's set, the Original London Prize Ring rules were devised. These were updated in 1853 and renamed the Revised London Prize Ring rules. By the end of the 19th century, the rules had undergone the last major revision and had become the Queensberry rules.

The Queensberry rules emphasized boxing skill and agility. They prohibited wrestling, hugging, barefisted fighting, hitting an opponent when he is helpless, and fighting to the death. This set of rules, which remains the basis of today's rules, made the sport more civil.

meet Felix's eyes looking directly into his. Felix nodded his head and Antonio responded. And both as one, just as quickly, turned away to face his own corner.

Bong, bong, bong. The roar turned to stillness.

"Ladies and Gentlemen, *Señores y Señoras.*"

The announcer spoke slowly, pleased at his bilingual efforts.

"Now the moment we have all been waiting for—the main event between two fine young Puerto Rican fighters, products of our lower east side."

"Loisaida,"[10] called out a member of the audience.

"In this corner, weighing 131 pounds, Felix Vargas. And in this corner, weighing 133 pounds, Antonio Cruz. The winner will represent the Boys Club in the tournament of champions, the Golden Gloves. There will be no draw. May the best man win."

The cheering of the crowd shook the windowpanes of the old buildings surrounding Tompkins Square Park. At the center of the ring, the referee was giving instructions to the youngsters.

"Keep your punches up. No low blows. No punching on the back of the head. Keep your heads up. Understand. Let's have a clean fight. Now shake hands and come out fighting."

Both youngsters touched gloves and nodded. They turned and danced quickly to their corners.

Their head towels and dressing gowns were lifted neatly from their shoulders by their trainers' nimble fingers. Antonio crossed himself. Felix did the same.

BONG! BONG! ROUND ONE. Felix and Antonio turned and faced each other squarely in a fighting pose. Felix wasted no time. He came in fast, head low, half hunched toward his right shoulder, and lashed out with a straight left. He missed a right cross as Antonio slipped the punch and countered with one-two-three lefts that snapped Felix's head back, sending a mild shock coursing through him. If Felix had any small doubt about their friendship affecting their fight, it was being neatly dispelled.

Antonio danced, a joy to behold. His left hand was like a piston pumping jabs one right after another with seeming ease.

Felix bobbed and weaved and never stopped boring in. He knew that at long range he was at a disadvantage. Antonio had too much reach on him. Only by coming in close could Felix hope to achieve the dreamed-of knockout.

Antonio knew the dynamite that was stored in his *amigo* brother's fist. He ducked a short right and missed a left hook. Felix trapped him

---

10. **Loisaida** (lô′-ē-sī′dä): a Hispanic slang pronunciation of *Lower East Side.*

WORDS TO KNOW	**dispel** (dĭ-spĕl′) *v.* to scatter; get rid of

409

[Poster in body:]

Antonio Cruz y Felix Vargas

THE MAIN EVENT

AUGUST 7

Tompkins Square Park

Active Reading: PREDICT

L Have students predict who they think will win the fight and why. You may wish to use this model:

Think-Aloud Model *I remember from page 405 that Felix is a better slugger and Antonio is a better boxer. Since I know from this passage that the fight can't end in a draw, I think Antonio will win, because he is a better boxer.*

Linking to History

M Jack Broughton, the so-called father of English boxing, drew up the first set of rules for the game in 1743. Broughton was also credited with inventing boxing gloves, but originally these "mufflers" were used only in training sessions to teach "the manly art of self-defense."

Literary Concept: MOTIVATION

N Ask students what motivates Felix to try to land the first punch. (*Possible responses: He really wants to win, and he believes that the boxer who lands the first punch will have the advantage; he wants to appear aggressive to his supporters and the crowd of people gathered to watch.*)

Mini-Lesson: Speaking, **Listening, and Viewing**

FILM Explain to students that many people feel that boxing is an especially dramatic sport because the winner must prevail in a one-on-one fight. Tell students this might be one reason why so many films have been made about boxing. Invite students to brainstorm a list of famous boxing movies, such as the *Rocky* series and *The Champion.*

Application Show portions of one of the boxing movies brainstormed by the class. After you play the video, have the class compare and contrast viewing a boxing match on film and reading about it in a short story. To promote discussion, ask students the following questions:

- Were you able to visualize the boxing match better by reading it in "Amigo Brothers" or watching it in the video?
- What did you learn about boxing from the video that you did not learn from the story?
- What did you learn about boxing from the story that you did not learn from the video?

Right to the Jaw by Mahonri Mackintosh Young Although well-known for his paintings, prints, and drawings, American painter Mahonri Mackintosh Young (1877–1957) received the greatest accolades for his sculptures. Showing common people, especially laborers and prizefighters, his work established new directions in American sculpture.

Reading the Art *How is movement suggested by the figures of the two boxers?*

Critical Thinking:
MAKING JUDGMENTS

O Point out how the writer uses the word *amigos* in the middle of the fight to remind readers that the boys are very close friends. Ask students if they think that it is easier or harder for the boys to fight each other because they know each other so well. *(Possible responses: It is easier, because they know where to hit to inflict the maximum damage; it is harder, because they do not want to hurt each other, which adds to their internal conflicts.)*

Active Reading: CLARIFY

P Have students describe the tactics the boys use as they fight. *(Possible responses: They try to trick each other with feints, rush each other, send a barrage of blows, and bob and weave.)*

CUSTOMIZING FOR
Multiple Learning Styles

Q Musical Learners Have students select background music for this scene that reflects its excitement and suspense.

Right to the Jaw (about 1926), Mahonri Mackintosh Young. Bronze, courtesy of Wood River Gallery, Mill Valley, California.

against the ropes just long enough to pour some punishing rights and lefts to Antonio's hard midsection. Antonio slipped away from Felix, crashing two lefts to his head, which set Felix's right ear to ringing.

O *Bong!* Both *amigos* froze a punch well on its way, sending up a roar of approval for good sportsmanship.

Felix walked briskly back to his corner. His right ear had not stopped ringing. Antonio gracefully danced his way toward his stool none the worse, except for glowing glove burns, showing angry red against the whiteness of his midribs.

"Watch that right, Tony." His trainer talked into his ear. "Remember Felix always goes to the body. He'll want you to drop your hands for his overhand left or right. Got it?"

Antonio nodded, spraying water out between his teeth. He felt better as his sore midsection was being firmly rubbed.

Felix's corner was also busy.

"You gotta get in there, fella." Felix's trainer poured water over his curly Afro locks. "Get in there or he's gonna chop you up from way back."

Bong! Bong! Round two. Felix was off his stool and rushed Antonio like a bull, sending a hard right to his head. Beads of water exploded from Antonio's long hair.

Antonio, hurt, sent back a blurring barrage of lefts and rights that only meant pain to

410 UNIT FOUR PART 1: THE WILL TO WIN

Mini-Lesson Study Skills

NOTE TAKING Explain to students that when they write reports, they need to take notes on their research. Give students the following rules for taking good research notes:

1. *Keep your notes in a single place.* Use a separate folder, notebook, or notebook section for each subject.
2. *Use a modified outline form, not complete sentences.* Jot down main ideas. Write related ideas beneath the main ones. Indent the related ideas.
3. *Look and listen for key words.*
4. *Use abbreviations and symbols.*
5. *Go back and revise your notes.*

Application Invite students to practice their note-taking skills by taking notes as they research conditioning programs for their Across the Curriculum report. You might also encourage students to practice these note-taking skills in their future research.

Felix, who returned with a short left to the head followed by a looping right to the body. Antonio countered with his own flurry, forcing Felix to give ground. But not for long.

Felix bobbed and weaved, bobbed and weaved, occasionally punching his two gloves together.

Antonio waited for the rush that was sure to come. Felix closed in and <u>feinted</u> with his left shoulder and threw his right instead. Lights suddenly exploded inside Felix's head as Antonio slipped the blow and hit him with a pistonlike left, catching him flush on the point of his chin.

<u>Bedlam</u> broke loose as Felix's legs momentarily buckled. He fought off a series of rights and lefts and came back with a strong right that taught Antonio respect.

Antonio danced in carefully. He knew Felix had the habit of playing possum when hurt, to sucker an opponent within reach of the powerful bombs he carried in each fist.

A right to the head slowed Antonio's pretty dancing. He answered with his own left at Felix's right eye that began puffing up within three seconds.

Antonio, a bit too eager, moved in too close, and Felix had him entangled into a rip-roaring, punching toe-to-toe slugfest that brought the whole Tompkins Square Park screaming to its feet.

Rights to the body. Lefts to the head. Neither fighter was giving an inch. Suddenly a short right caught Antonio squarely on the chin. His long legs turned to jelly, and his arms flailed out desperately. Felix, grunting like a bull, threw wild punches from every direction. Antonio, groggy, bobbed and weaved, <u>evading</u>

most of the blows. Suddenly his head cleared. His left flashed out hard and straight catching Felix on the bridge of his nose.

Felix lashed back with a haymaker, right off the ghetto streets. At the same instant, his eye caught another left hook from Antonio.  Felix swung out, trying to clear the pain. Only the frenzied screaming of those along ringside let him know that he had dropped Antonio. Fighting off the growing haze, Antonio struggled to his feet, got up, ducked, and threw a smashing right that dropped Felix flat on his back.

Felix got up as fast as he could in his own corner, groggy but still <u>game</u>. He didn't even hear the count. In a fog, he heard the roaring of the crowd, who seemed to have gone insane. His head cleared to hear the bell sound at the end of the round. He was damned glad. His trainer sat him down on the stool.

In his corner, Antonio was doing what all fighters do when they are hurt. They sit and smile at everyone.

The referee signaled the ring doctor to check the fighters out. He did so and then gave his okay. The cold-water sponges brought clarity to both *amigo* brothers. They were rubbed until their circulation ran free.

Bong! Round three—the final round. Up to now it had been tick-tack-toe, pretty much even. But everyone knew there could be no draw and that this round would decide the winner.

This time, to Felix's surprise, it was Antonio who came out fast, charging across the ring. Felix braced himself but couldn't ward off the barrage of punches. Antonio drove Felix hard against the ropes.

The crowd ate it up. Thus far the two had

WORDS
TO
KNOW

feint (fānt) *v.* to make a pretended attack in order to draw attention away from one's real purpose or target
bedlam (bĕd′ləm) *n.* a noisy confusion
evading (ĭ-vā′dĭng) *adj.* avoiding; escaping **evade** *v.*
game (gām) *adj.* ready and willing to proceed

411

U   Ask students why Felix and Antonio didn't wait to hear the name of the winner announced. *(Possible responses: It did not matter to them; they had already both won by fighting their hardest and keeping their friendship intact.)*

STRATEGIC READING FOR
Less-Proficient Readers

V   Ask students the following questions to make sure they understand the story.

- Who won the fight? Explain. *(Possible responses: Both boys won, because each fought his hardest and so emerged with his pride, self-respect, and friendship intact; readers don't know who actually won, because the author chose not to include this information.)* Making Judgments
- Why is boxing so important to the boys? *(Possible response: It helps them achieve recognition in their neighborhood.)* Drawing Conclusions

CUSTOMIZING FOR
Gifted and Talented Students

Have students explain what Antonio and Felix learned from this experience and debate whether it is likely that a real-life friendship would survive in a similar situation.

EDITOR'S NOTE *With the permission of the author or copyright holder, potentially offensive material has been deleted from the selection.*

COMPREHENSION CHECK
1. Where do the boys live? *(on the lower east side of Manhattan)*
2. What dream do the boys share? *(to become the world's lightweight boxing champion)*
3. Which boy is the better boxer? *(Antonio)*
4. What agreement do the boys make before the fight? *(They will fight as strangers and fight to win.)*
5. When do the boys leave the ring? *(before the winner is announced)*

---

fought with *mucho corazón*.[11] Felix tapped his gloves and commenced his attack anew. Antonio, throwing boxer's caution to the winds, jumped in to meet him.

Both pounded away. Neither gave an inch, and neither fell to the canvas. Felix's left eye was tightly closed. Claret red blood poured from Antonio's nose. They fought toe-to-toe.

The sounds of their blows were loud in contrast to the silence of a crowd gone completely mute. The referee was stunned by their savagery.

Bong! Bong! Bong! The bell sounded over and over again. Felix and Antonio were past hearing. Their blows continued to pound on each other like hailstones.

Finally the referee and the two trainers pried Felix and Antonio apart. Cold water was poured over them to bring them back to their senses.

They looked around and then rushed toward each other. A cry of alarm surged through Tompkins Square Park. Was this a fight to the death instead of a boxing match?

The fear soon gave way to wave upon wave of cheering as the two *amigos* embraced.

No matter what the decision, they knew they would always be champions to each other.

Bong! Bong! Bong! "Ladies and Gentlemen. *Señores* and *Señoras*. The winner and representative to the Golden Gloves Tournament of Champions is . . ."

The announcer turned to point to the winner and found himself alone. Arm in arm, the champions had already left the ring.

---

11. *mucho corazón* (mōō′chô kô-rä-sôn′) *Spanish:* a lot of heart; great courage

---

Assessment ✓ Option

Have students illustrate their understanding of Antonio and Felix by creating a yearbook page for each one. Students should sketch—or look through a magazine for—a picture that fits their impressions of the character; mount the picture on paper, and then add a written profile of the character. Students should include in their profiles as much of the following information as possible: nicknames, activities, sports, class awards, a quotation that tells something about the character, hobbies, favorite songs, last book read, and plans after high school.

Rubric

3 Full Accomplishment Students thoroughly analyze the characters and list many of their accomplishments.

2 Substantial Accomplishment Students explain the characters but do not include all of their likely values, activities, and accomplishments.

1 Little or Partial Accomplishment Students have difficulty analyzing the characters and what they value.

RESPONDING
OPTIONS

FROM PERSONAL RESPONSE TO CRITICAL ANALYSIS

REFLECT

1. What are your impressions of Antonio and Felix? Describe your impressions in your notebook and share them with a partner.

RETHINK

2. Why, in your opinion, do Antonio and Felix leave the ring together before the victor is announced?

3. How do you think the community will regard Antonio and Felix after the fight? Explain your ideas.

4. If either Antonio or Felix had knocked the other out, what effect do you think the knockout would have had on their friendship?

5. What is your opinion of the way Antonio and
Close Textual Felix handle their inner conflicts as two good
Reading friends competing for the same prize?

Consider
- the promise they exchange while training for the fight
- how each of them gets psyched for the fight
- why each wants to score a quick knockout
- their conduct in the ring

RELATE

6. Review the paragraph you wrote for the Writing Connection on page 402. How would you compare your ideas about friendship and competition with the views expressed in this story?

LITERARY CONCEPTS

A **surprise ending** is an unexpected twist in the plot at the end of a story. For example, at the end of "A Retrieved Reformation" (page 27), Ben Price allows Jimmy Valentine to go free instead of arresting him. Get together with a partner and brainstorm other ways in which Piri Thomas might have ended "Amigo Brothers." Why do you think he chose the ending he did?

Multimodal Learning
ANOTHER PATHWAY
Cooperative Learning

Work with two classmates to role-play a sportscaster's postfight interview with the two boxers. Have Antonio and Felix express their ideas about competition between good friends. Perform the interview for the class, having a classmate videotape it if you can.

QUICKWRITES

1. How do you think Felix and Antonio would define the word *champion*? Write a **definition** from their perspective.

2. Although many people are opposed to boxing because of its violence, some people—like the writer Joyce Carol Oates—are avid followers of the sport. According to Oates, "Boxing, like any sport, or art, or vocation in life, is about character." Write an **editorial** in favor of or against boxing. Support your opinion with details from the story, and comment on Oates's opinion.

3. Using details from the story, write a **profile** of either Antonio or Felix for a boxing magazine.

📁 **PORTFOLIO** Save your writing. You may want to use it later as a springboard to a piece for your portfolio.

AMIGO BROTHERS **413**

Physical Education Have students work in pairs to complete their research. Suggest that partners take notes from different sources. They then can combine and edit their notes to assemble the report.

ADDITIONAL SUGGESTIONS

Physical Education *No Pain, Lots of Gain* Have students plan and follow an exercise program. Suggest that they select familiar exercises such as jogging, jumping jacks, running in place, leg lifts, pushups, and arm circles. Have students chart their progress in terms of the length of time they spend on each type of exercise. Caution students that to avoid injury, they should set realistic goals based upon their current physical fitness level. You may want to ask a physical education instructor to review the plans before students begin following them.

Words to Know

Exercise A
1. fear
2. deceive
3. a trap
4. quickly
5. forgot their lines

Exercise B
1. b
2. e
3. d
4. a
5. c

Reteaching/Reinforcement
• *Unit Four Resource Book,* p. 14

PIRI THOMAS

Piri Thomas lives on the lower east side of Manhattan, where his story takes place. He draws upon his African-American and Puerto Rican heritage, along with intimate knowledge of kids like Antonio and Felix, to make his writing realistic and believable.

THE WRITER'S STYLE

Piri Thomas uses powerful images and figures of speech in the fight scenes in "Amigo Brothers." For example, on page 411, he describes Felix as carrying "powerful bombs" in each fist. What other images or figures of speech made the fight scenes come alive for you?

Multimodal Learning

ACROSS THE CURRICULUM

Physical Education Research the conditioning programs that boxers typically follow to prepare for their bouts. If possible, interview a boxer or a gym instructor as part of your research. Then present your findings in an oral report to the class.

CRITIC'S CORNER

Tommy Bartsch, a seventh-grade member of our student board, wrote that the ending of this story is not satisfying because it doesn't reveal the outcome of the fight. How would you respond to Tommy's opinion?

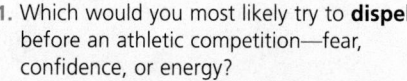

WORDS TO KNOW

EXERCISE A Answer the following questions on a sheet of paper.

1. Which would you most likely try to **dispel** before an athletic competition—fear, confidence, or energy?

2. Is a person who is **feinting** trying to deceive someone, to comfort someone, or to communicate with someone?

3. Would a fox be most likely to try to **evade** a chicken, a safe burrow, or a trap?

4. If you had to face a **barrage** of questions, would the questions be asked intelligently, politely, or quickly?

5. Would actors be most likely to **improvise** if they forgot their lines, were facing a noisy audience, or were performing an emotional scene?

EXERCISE B Match each vocabulary word on the left with the phrase on the right that suggests its meaning.

1. unbridled   a. till the end of time
2. pensively   b. full speed ahead
3. bedlam   c. standing your ground
4. perpetual   d. unable to hear yourself think
5. game   e. sadly and dreamily

PIRI THOMAS

While serving a prison sentence, Piri Thomas (1928–) decided to turn his life around. He began writing his autobiography as a step toward accomplishing this goal. For him, writing became a tool to discover his real nature and to depict his Puerto Rican and African-American heritage honestly. After his release from prison, Thomas suffered a severe setback—the manuscript he had labored over for four years was accidentally destroyed. Choosing to begin writing his autobiography anew, he spent more than five years in completing the work. When *Down These Mean Streets* was finally published in 1967, critics praised its power and honesty as well as its creative use of language and imagery.

Both *Down These Mean Streets* and Thomas's short stories are set in "El Barrio," the Puerto Rican community in New York City where Thomas grew up. His writing, which draws upon his memories of his experiences in Spanish Harlem, celebrates his people's vitality, strength, and determination.

The Writer's Style

Encourage students to select images that appeal to two or more senses at the same time. For example, "Claret red blood poured from Antonio's nose" (p. 412) appeals to sight and touch simultaneously. In addition, point out to students that the author uses similes to vividly describe the action during the fight scene. For example, Antonio's left hand is described as being "like a piston pumping jabs" (p. 409).

PREVIEWING

FICTION

The Serial Garden
Joan Aiken

Activating Prior Knowledge

PERSONAL CONNECTION

The story you are about to read is a fantasy. What other fantasies have you read or seen? Do you have any favorites? In your notebook, jot down the titles of at least three of your favorite fantasy stories. When you have finished, compare your list with your classmates' lists. Do certain fantasies appear on almost everyone's list?

LITERARY CONNECTION

Fantasy is a type of literature in which impossible, unbelievable, and often wondrous events occur. The word *fantasy* comes from the Greek word *phantasia,* meaning "a making visible." Unlike **science fiction,** which often involves a future world that is explainable in terms of scientific or technological advances, fantasy involves magic, which cannot be explained. Fantasy stories can take place in realistic settings or in make-believe ones.

Illustration by John R. Neill. From *Ozma of Oz* by L. Frank Baum, Books of Wonder/Morrow Junior Books.

Active Reading/Setting a Purpose

READING CONNECTION

Making Predictions Below are ten terms that relate to "The Serial Garden." Use these terms, the story's title, and your knowledge of fantasy to help you predict what might happen in the story. Write your prediction (or predictions) in your notebook. Then, as you read, compare your prediction with the actual events. You may wish to change your prediction as you uncover new clues.

1. **boy**
2. **corner store**
3. **cereal box**
4. **cereal**
5. **garden**
6. **princess**
7. **magic spell**
8. **teacher**
9. **shaggy dog**
10. **spring cleaning**

THE SERIAL GARDEN **415**

SUMMARY

One morning Mark Armitage buys a packet of Brekkfast Brikks cereal from a dingy shop across the street. On the back of the packet is a cutout of a garden, which he eagerly assembles in his playroom. Mark discovers that whenever he sings a special tune, the small cardboard garden changes into a real one. He rushes back to the shop and buys the last five packets of Brekkfast Brikks, each picturing a different section of the garden. When Mark assembles the next-to-last section and enters it, he meets Princess Sophia Maria Louisa. She tells him how she magically slipped inside the pages of a garden book over 50 years ago. Ever since, she has been waiting there for her beloved music teacher to play the special tune and join her. Mark questions his own music teacher, Mr. Johansen, about the tune and learns that the elderly musician is Princess Sophia's long-lost love. They go together to Mark's playroom to enter the magic garden—only to find that Mrs. Armitage has tossed the cardboard model in the furnace. Knowing that the original garden book has also been destroyed, Mark's only hope for reuniting the lovers is to advertise for Brekkfast Brikks packets in the newspaper.

Thematic Link: *The Will to Win* Mark doesn't give up as he races to assemble a magical garden and meet the challenge of the unknown.

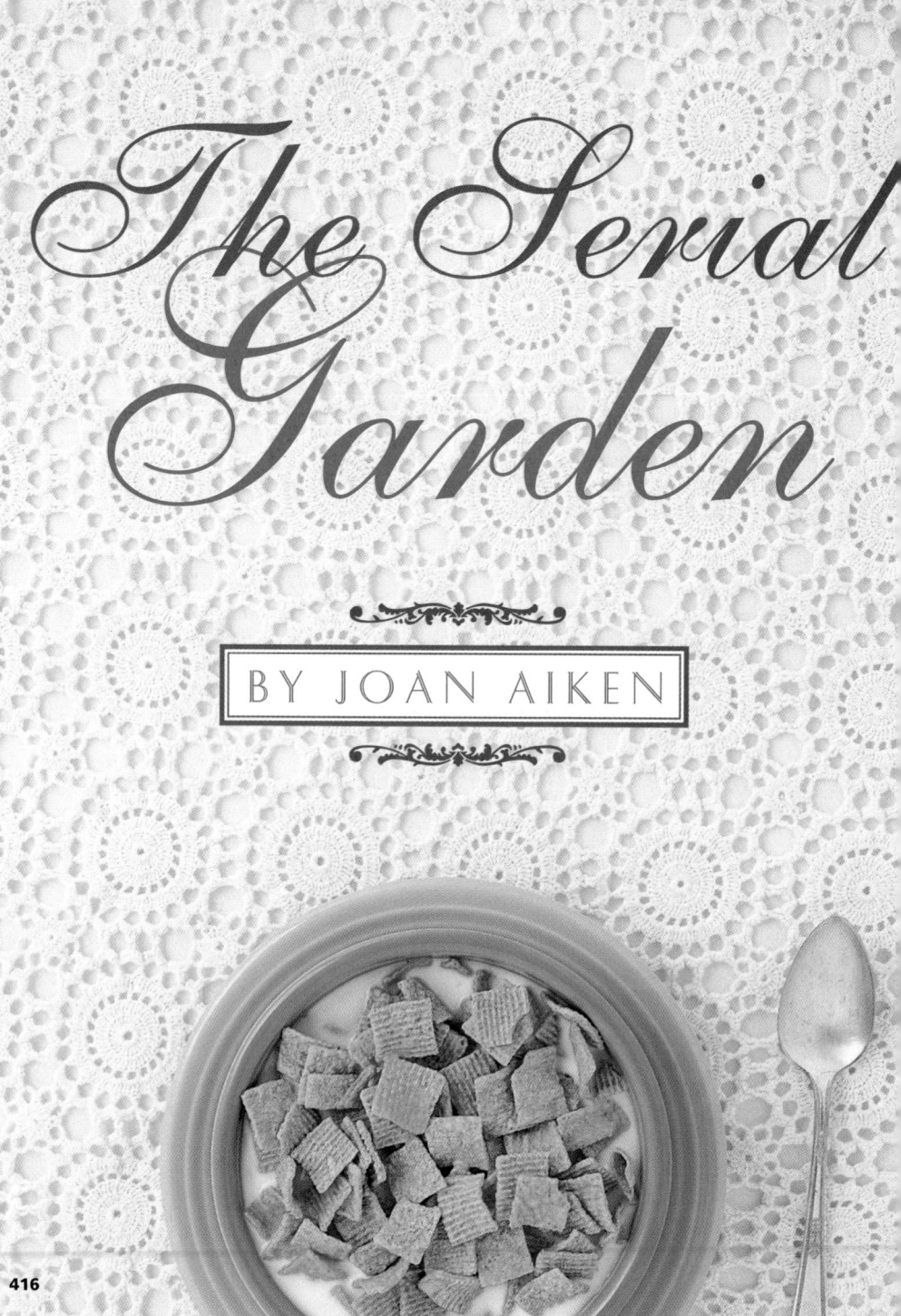

The Serial Garden

BY JOAN AIKEN

416

WORDS TO KNOW

aggrievedly (ə-grē'vĭd-lē) *adv.* in a manner suggesting that one has been badly treated (p. 421)

chaos (kā'ŏs) *n.* extreme confusion or disorder (p. 430)

convalescing (kŏn'və-lĕs'ĭng) *adj.* recovering gradually from an illness **convalesce** *v.* (p. 422)

forage (fôr'ĭj) *v.* to search for what one wants or needs, especially for food (p. 428)

gaudy (gô'dē) *adj.* excessively bright and showy (p. 420)

incalculable (ĭn-kăl'kyə-lə-bəl) *adj.* too great to be measured or counted (p. 428)

susceptible (sə-sĕp'tə-bəl) *adj.* easily affected or influenced (p. 427)

tantalizing (tăn'tə-lī'zĭng) *adj.* arousing interest without satisfying it **tantalize** *v.* (p. 423)

vigil (vĭj'əl) *n.* a time of staying awake in order to keep watch or guard something (p. 417)

wan (wŏn) *adj.* sickly; pale (p. 417)

Cold rice pudding for breakfast?" said Mark, looking at it with disfavor.

"Don't be fussy," said his mother. "You're the only one who's complaining." This was unfair, for she and Mark were the only members of the family at table, Harriet having developed measles while staying with a school friend, while Mr. Armitage had somehow managed to lock himself in the larder.[1] Mrs. Armitage never had anything but toast and marmalade for breakfast anyway.

Mark went on scowling at the chilly-looking pudding. It had come straight out of the fridge, which was not in the larder.

"If you don't like it," said Mrs. Armitage, "unless you want Daddy to pass you corn flakes through the larder ventilator, flake by flake, you'd better run down to Miss Pride and get a small packet of cereal. She opens at eight; Hickmans doesn't open till nine. It's no use waiting till the blacksmith comes to let your father out; I'm sure he won't be here for hours yet."

There came a gloomy banging from the direction of the larder, just to remind them that Mr. Armitage was alive and suffering in there.

"*You're* all right," shouted Mark heartlessly as he passed the larder door. "There's nothing to stop you having corn flakes. Oh, I forgot, the milk's in the fridge. Well, have cheese and pickles then. Or treacle tart."[2]

Even through the zinc grating on the door he could hear his father shudder at the thought of treacle tart and pickles for breakfast. Mr. Armitage's imprisonment was his own fault, though; he had sworn that he was going to find out where the mouse got into the larder if it took him all night, watching and waiting.

He had shut himself in, so that no member of the family should come bursting in and disturb his vigil. The larder door had a spring catch which sometimes jammed; it was bad luck that this turned out to be one of the times.

Mark ran across the fields to Miss Pride's shop at Sticks Corner and asked if she had any corn flakes.

"Oh, I don't think I have any left, dear," Miss Pride said woefully. "I'll have a look. . . . I think I sold the last packet a week ago Tuesday."

"What about the one in the window?"

"That's a dummy, dear."

Miss Pride's shop window was full of nasty, dingy old cardboard cartons with nothing inside them, and several empty display stands which had fallen down and never been propped up again. Inside the shop were a few small, tired-looking tins and jars, which had a worn and scratched appearance as if mice had tried them and given up. Miss Pride herself was small and wan, with yellowish gray hair; she rooted rather hopelessly in a pile of empty boxes. Mark's mother never bought any groceries from Miss Pride's if she could help it, since the day when she had found a label inside the foil wrapping of a cream cheese saying, "This cheese should be eaten before May 11, 1899."  **B**

"No corn flakes I'm afraid, dear."

"Any wheat crispies? Puffed corn? Rice nuts?"

"No, dear. Nothing left, only Brekkfast Brikks."

"Never heard of *them*," said Mark doubtfully.

"Or I've a jar of Ovo here. You spread it on bread. That's nice for breakfast," said Miss

---

1. **larder:** pantry.
2. **treacle** (trē′kəl) **tart:** a small pastry made with molasses.

<table>
<tr><td>WORDS
TO
KNOW</td><td>**vigil** (vĭj′əl) *n.* a time of staying awake in order to keep watch or guard something
wan (wŏn) *adj.* sickly; pale</td></tr>
</table>

417

CUSTOMIZING FOR

Students Acquiring English

- Use **ACCESS FOR STUDENTS ACQUIRING ENGLISH**, *Reading and Writing Support*.

- The story takes place in Great Britain, and the characters speak British English. Help students understand that British and American speakers use many of the same words. Invite students to "translate" examples of British usage.

STRATEGIC READING FOR

Less-Proficient Readers

Set a Purpose Ask students what they like to eat for breakfast. List their favorite foods on the board. Then have students read to find out what Mark does when his mother serves him something that he does not like for breakfast.

Use **UNIT FOUR RESOURCE BOOK**, p. 17, for guidance in reading the selection.

CUSTOMIZING FOR

Gifted and Talented Students

Challenge students to explain what the garden symbolizes. (*Possible responses: a perfect world that is impossible to obtain, immortality, ideal love, hope, possibility*)

Literary Concept: SETTING

A Have students determine the story's setting, citing clues that helped them identify it. (*Possible response: The story is set in England in the present. Clues include the British words* larder, treacle tart, *and* packet.)

Literary Concept: HUMOR

B Ask students to explain the humor in this passage and what creates it. (*Possible response: The humor—the cheese being wildly out of date—comes from exaggeration.*)

Mini-Lesson · **Reading Skills/Strategies**

DRAWING CONCLUSIONS Explain to students that when they draw conclusions, they combine their own knowledge with clues in the story. Then explain these steps:

1. Read the passage or story.
2. Think about a similar situation.
3. Draw a conclusion.
4. Check your conclusion by thinking about whether you had enough information.

Application On a chart like the one shown, have students list the characters in this story, a conclusion about each character, and the evidence that supports the conclusion.

Reteaching/Reinforcement
- *Unit Four Resource Book,* p. 18

Character	Conclusion	Evidence
Mr. Johansen	He is kind to animals.	He feeds the dogs before leaving to be reunited with Princess Sophia.

Pride, with a sudden burst of salesmanship. Mark thought the Ovo looked beastly, like yellow paint, so he took the packet of Brekkfast Brikks. At least it wasn't very big. . . . On the front of the box was a picture of a fat, repulsive, fair-haired boy, rather like the chubby Augustus, banging on his plate with his spoon.

"They look like tiny doormats," said Mrs. Armitage, as Mark shoveled some Brikks into the bowl.

"They taste like them too. Gosh," said Mark, "I must hurry or I'll be late for school. There's rather a nice cutout garden on the back of the packet though; don't throw it away when it's empty, Mother. Good-by, Daddy," he shouted through the larder door; "hope Mr. Ellis comes soon to let you out." And he dashed off to catch the school bus.

At breakfast next morning Mark had a huge helping of Brekkfast Brikks and persuaded his father to try them.

"They taste just like esparto grass,"[3] said Mr. Armitage fretfully.

"Yes I know, but do take some more, Daddy. I want to cut out the model garden; it's so lovely."

"Rather pleasant, I must say. It looks like an eighteenth-century German engraving," his father agreed. "It certainly was a stroke of genius putting it on the packet. No one would ever buy these things to eat for pleasure. Pass me the sugar, please. And the cream. And the strawberries."

It was the half-term holiday, so after breakfast Mark was able to take the empty packet

> "THEY LOOK LIKE TINY DOORMATS"
>
> . . .
>
> "THEY TASTE LIKE THEM TOO."

away to the playroom and get on with the job of cutting out the stone walls, the row of little trees, the fountain, the yew arch, the two green lawns, and the tiny clumps of brilliant flowers. He knew better than to "stick tabs in slots and secure with paste," as the directions suggested; he had made models from packets before and knew they always fell to pieces unless they were firmly bound together with transparent sticky tape.

It was a long, fiddling, pleasurable job.

Nobody interrupted him. Mrs. Armitage only cleaned the playroom once every six months or so, when she made a ferocious descent on it and tidied up the tape recorders, roller skates, meteorological sets, and dismantled railway engines, and threw away countless old magazines, stringless tennis rackets, abandoned paintings, and unsuccessful models. There were always bitter complaints from Mark and Harriet; then they forgot, and things piled up again till next time.

As Mark worked, his eye was caught by a verse on the outside of the packet:

> "Brekkfast Brikks to start the day
> Make you fit in every way.
> Children bang their plates with glee
> At Brekkfast Brikks for lunch and tea!
> Brekkfast Brikks for supper too
> Give peaceful sleep the whole night through."

---

3. **esparto** (ĭ-spär′tō) grass: long, coarse grass used in making rope, shoes, and paper.

Mini-Lesson   Study Skills

KWL APPROACH Explain to students that one of the most effective ways to get the most from their study time is through the KWL approach. Direct students to ask themselves these three questions as they study:

K   What do I already **know** about the subject?

W   What do I **want** to learn?

L   What did I **learn?**

Tell students that to answer the first question, they should list their prior knowledge of the subject. Next, they should list questions they would like to have answered. Finally, after they have studied, students should list the things they learned.

Application Have students work in small groups to investigate fantasy as a type of literature or film, using the KWL approach.

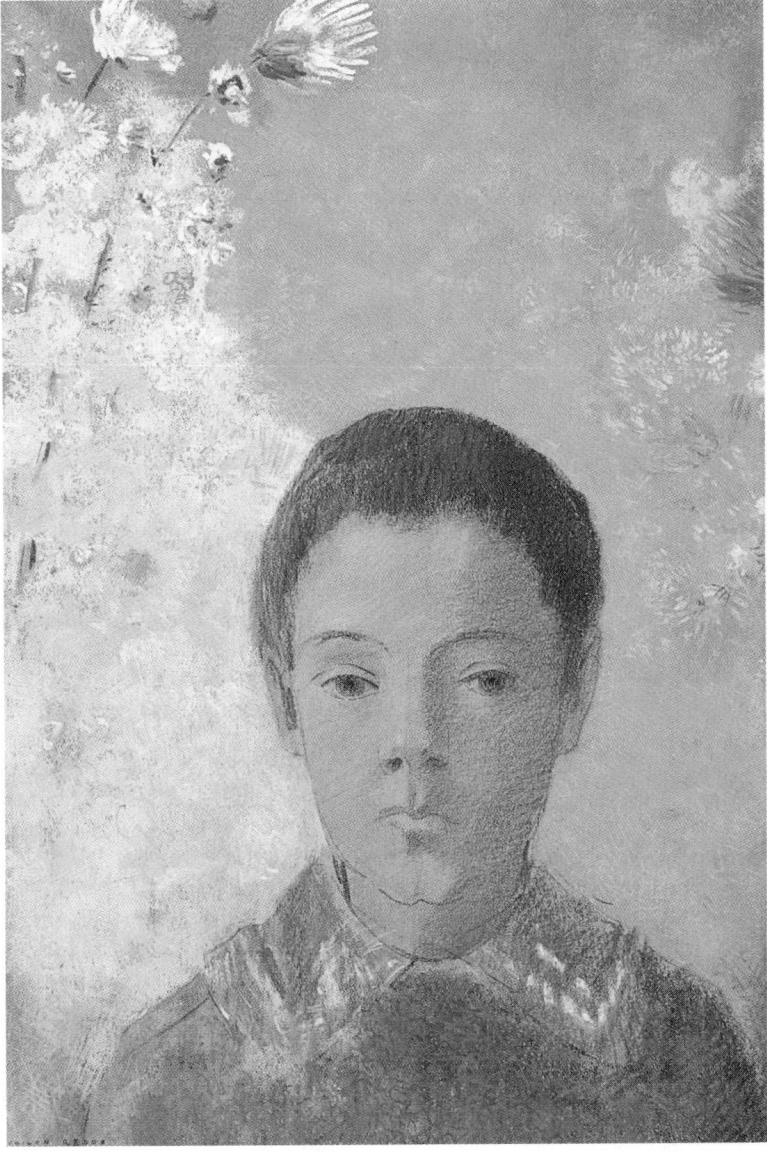

Portrait of Ari Redon (about 1898), Odilon Redon. Pastel on paper, 44.8 × 30.8 cm, The Art Institute of Chicago, gift of Kate L. Brewster (1950.130). Photo Copyright © 1994 The Art Institute of Chicago, all rights reserved.

THE SERIAL GARDEN   **419**

Ari Redon **by Odilon Redon** This portrait by French painter Odilon Redon (1840–1916) is typical of the Impressionist school of art with its soft and dreamy light and charming poetic quality. Redon departed from the Impressionists, however, in his attempt to portray the realm of mystery that other Impressionists avoided.

Reading the Art *Look at the painting's composition. Is the subject centered? Is this composition similar to or different from other portraits you've seen? Do you visualize Mark Armitage this way? Why or why not?*

Mini-Lesson **Genre Study**

FICTION Review with students the information they read about **fantasy** in the Literature Connection on page 415. Draw on the chalkboard the word web shown to remind them of the characteristic elements of fantasy.
• unbelievable or wondrous events
• an element of magic
• realistic or make-believe settings

Application Have students review "The Serial Garden" to see how the story blends realistic and make-believe elements. Have students create a two-column chart that describes which aspects of the story are realistic, like Mark's bedroom, and which are fantastic, like Princess Sophia's garden. Then have students select one item from each column and illustrate it using details from the story.

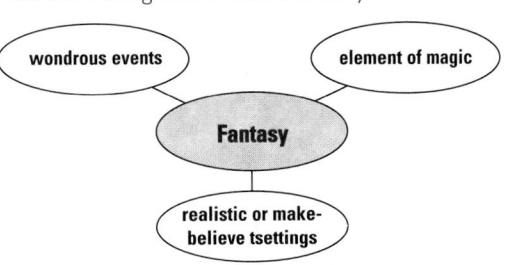

wondrous events

element of magic

Fantasy

realistic or make-believe tsettings

E **Musical Learners** Invite musical learners to write a song for their favorite breakfast food. Remind them that the tune should be catchy, lively, and brisk.

Literary Concept: SETTING

F Ask students how Mark is able to enter the garden. *(Possible response: It magically grows to life size, part of the story's fantasy.)* Ask if this setting is realistic or make-believe. *(Possible responses: It's make-believe, because cardboard gardens don't grow and become real; it's both—it's make-believe because it comes to life and realistic because it contains a gate, walls, trees, and fog like real gardens.)*

Critical Thinking:
HYPOTHESIZE

G Invite students to hypothesize why Mark has to sing the jingle rather than just say the rhyme to enter and leave the garden. *(Possible response: Music is an important part of the garden's magic.)*

STRATEGIC READING FOR
Less-Proficient Readers

H Ask volunteers to explain what surprise Mark experiences when he finishes putting together the model garden. *(The garden becomes real and life-size, and Mark can enter it.)* Summarizing

- What does Mark sing as he assembles the model? *(the rhyme on the Brekkfast Brikks box)* Noting Relevant Details

Set a Purpose Have students find out what Mark discovers in the garden and how he gets the money to buy more sections of the garden.

"Blimey," thought Mark, sticking a cedar tree into the middle of the lawn and then bending a stone wall round at dotted lines A, B, C, and D. "I wouldn't want anything for breakfast, lunch, tea, and supper, not even Christmas pudding. Certainly not Brekkfast Brikks."

He propped a clump of <u>gaudy</u> scarlet flowers against the wall and stuck them in place.

The words of the rhyme kept coming into his head as he worked, and presently he found that they went rather well to a tune that was running through his mind, and he began to hum, and then to sing; Mark often did this when he was alone and busy.

E "Brekkfast Brikks to sta-art the day,
Ma-ake you fi-it in every way—

"Blow, where did I put that little bit of sticky tape? Oh, there it is.

"Children bang their pla-ates with glee
At Brekkfast Brikks for lunch and tea

"Slit gate with razor blade, it says, but it'll have to be a penknife.

"Brekkfast Brikks for supper toohoo
Give peaceful sleep the whole night throughoo. . . .

F "Hullo. That's funny," said Mark.

It was funny. The openwork iron gate he had just stuck in position now suddenly towered above him. On either side, to right and left, ran the high stone wall, stretching away into foggy distance. Over the top of the wall he could see tall trees, yews and cypresses and others he didn't know.

"Well, that's the neatest trick I ever saw," said Mark. "I wonder if the gate will open."

He chuckled as he tried it, thinking of the larder door. The gate did open, and he went through into the garden.

One of the things that had already struck him as he cut them out was that the flowers were not at all in the right proportions. But they were all the nicer for that. There were huge velvety violets and pansies the size of saucers; the hollyhocks were as big as dinner plates, and the turf was sprinkled with enormous daisies. The roses, on the other hand, were miniature, no bigger than cuff buttons. There were real fish in the fountain, bright pink.

"I made all this," thought Mark, strolling along the mossy path to the yew arch. "Won't Harriet be surprised when she sees it. I wish she could see it now. I wonder what made it come alive like that."

He passed through the yew arch as he said this and discovered that on the other side there was nothing but gray, foggy blankness. This, of course, was where his cardboard garden had ended. He turned back through the archway and gazed with pride at a border of huge scarlet tropical flowers which were perhaps supposed to be geraniums but certainly hadn't turned out that way. "I know! Of course, it was the rhyme, the rhyme on the packet."

He recited it. Nothing happened. "Perhaps you have to sing it," he thought, and (feeling a little foolish) he sang it through to the tune that fitted so well. At once, faster than blowing out a match, the garden drew itself together and shrank into its cardboard again, leaving Mark outside.

"What a marvelous hiding place it'll make when I don't want people to come bothering,"

WORDS
TO
KNOW   **gaudy** (gô′dē) *adj.* excessively bright and showy

420

Multicultural **Perspectives**

TRANSATLANTIC TRANSLATIONS Explain that American and British English are very similar and easily understood by people on both sides of the Atlantic, yet some words and expressions are very different. The following are examples:

American English	*British English*
apartment	flat
buddy	mate
candy	sweets
elevator	lift
[car] trunk	boot
windshield	windscreen
truck	lorry
call on the telephone	ring up
diaper	nappy
TV	telly

he thought. He sang the spell once more, just to make sure that it worked, and there was the high mossy wall, the stately iron gate, and the treetops. He stepped in and looked back. No playroom to be seen, only gray blankness.

At that moment he was startled by a tremendous clanging, the sort of sound the Trump of Doom[4] would make if it was a dinner bell. "Blow," he thought, "I suppose that's lunch." He sang the spell for the fourth time; immediately he was in the playroom, and the garden was on the floor beside him, and Agnes was still ringing the dinner bell outside the door.

"All right, I heard," he shouted. "Just coming."

He glanced hurriedly over the remains of the packet to see if it bore any mention of the fact that the cutout garden had magic properties. It did not. He did, however, learn that this was Section Three of the Beautiful Brekkfast Brikk Garden Series, and that Sections One, Two, Four, Five, and Six would be found on other packets. In case of difficulty in obtaining supplies, please write to Fruhstucksgeschirrziegelsteinindustrie (Great Britain), Lily Road, Shepherds Bush.

"Elevenpence a packet," Mark murmured to himself, going to lunch with unwashed hands. "Five elevens are thirty-five. Thirty-five pennies are—no, that's wrong. Fifty-five pence are four-and-sevenpence. Father, if I mow the lawn and carry coal every day for a month, can I have four shillings and sevenpence?"

"You don't want to buy another space gun, do you?" said Mr. Armitage looking at him suspiciously. "Because one is quite enough in this family."

"No, it's not for a space gun, I swear."

"Oh, very well."

"And can I have the four-and-seven now?"

Mr. Armitage gave it reluctantly. "But that lawn has to be like velvet, mind," he said. "And if there's any falling off in the coal supply, I shall demand my money back."

"No, no, there won't be," Mark promised in reply. As soon as lunch was over, he dashed down to Miss Pride's. Was there a chance that she would have Sections One, Two, Four, Five, and Six? He felt certain that no other shop had even heard of Brekkfast Brikks, so she was his only hope, apart from the address in Shepherds Bush.

"Oh, I don't know, I'm sure," Miss Pride said, sounding very doubtful—and more than a little surprised. "There might just be a couple on the bottom shelf—yes, here we are."

They were Sections Four and Five, bent and dusty, but intact, Mark saw with relief. "Don't you suppose you have any more anywhere?" he pleaded.

"I'll look in the cellar, but I can't promise. I haven't had deliveries of any of these for a long time. Made by some foreign firm they were; people didn't seem very keen on them," Miss Pride said <u>aggrievedly</u>. She opened a door revealing a flight of damp stone stairs. Mark followed her down them like a bloodhound on the trail.

The cellar was a fearful confusion of mildewed, tattered, and toppling cartons, some full, some empty. Mark was nearly knocked cold by a shower of pilchards

---

4. **Trump of Doom:** the trumpet that, according to the Bible, will be blown to signal the end of the world.

WORDS
TO
KNOW

aggrievedly (ə-grē′vĭd-lē) *adv.* in a manner suggesting that one has been badly treated

421

I Ask students what conclusions they can draw about Mark's character based on his attitude toward the garden. You may wish to guide students by using this model:

Think-Aloud Model *Mark calmly enters the garden, looks around, and leaves only when he is called to lunch. I don't think I'd be so relaxed about a visit to a magical garden—especially if I wasn't sure I could get out! From Mark's actions, I can conclude that he is independent, self-confident, and brave. He likes a challenge.*

CUSTOMIZING FOR

Students Acquiring English

2 Use this description to help explain the story title, "The Serial Garden." Make sure students understand the difference between the homophones *serial* and *cereal*.

Literary Concept: HUMOR

J Point out that in German, many compound words are very long, and here the author is making fun of those words. Invite volunteers to try to pronounce the name.

Linking to Math

K Pounds and pence are British units of money.

Pence is the British plural of penny. Elevenpence, therefore, is eleven pennies. Have students assume that the current exchange rate between the pound and the dollar is 1.60 dollars to 1 pound. Ask them which is worth more: a dollar or a pound. *(A pound; 1 pound equals $1.60. Even though 1.6 is greater than 1, you would have to spend almost 2 dollars to get the same thing for 1 pound.)*

Critical Thinking: ANALYZE

L Ask students to analyze why Miss Pride would be "aggrieved" about the sales of Brekkfast Brikks, given what they know about her character. *(Possible response: The cereal did not sell well, and she was left with unwanted, out-of-date stock.)*

Mini-Lesson 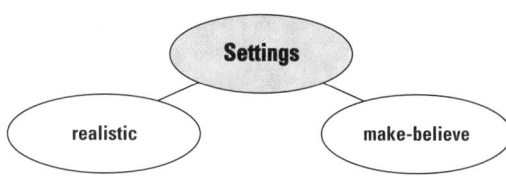 **Literary Concepts**

REVIEWING SETTING Explain to the class that the setting is the time and place of the action in a literary work. Setting may include geographic location, the historical period (past, present, or future), season, time of day, and customs and manners of the society. In some stories, the setting is well defined; in others, it is left to the reader's imagination.

Application Have students create and fill in a chart like the one shown to jot down details about the two settings in "The Serial Garden": the realistic setting that includes the Armitage residence and the make-believe setting of the magical garden.

Settings

realistic

make-believe

Literary Concept: IRONY

 Have students explain the irony in this passage. Remind students that irony occurs when something happens that is different from what is expected. *(Possible response: The reader does not expect that Miss Pride will find the rest of the cereal packets. The reversal of expectations produces irony.)*

Active Reading: CLARIFY

N Ask students why Mark is eating Brekkfast Brikks at every meal. *(Possible response: Mark has to finish each box of cereal before he can cut out and assemble the garden on the box.)*

Critical Thinking: SYNTHESIZE

O Invite students to share what they can infer about the garden and its possible owners from these and earlier details. *(Possible response: The garden is an elegant, upper-class, fantastical place, probably owned by wealthy or even royal people.)*

Literary Concept: SETTING

P Point out the imagery in this passage and have volunteers explain what senses it appeals to. Explore with the class reasons why the writer included this imagery to describe the garden. *(Possible response: The imagery appeals to the reader's senses of sight [huge, blue cabbages], touch [hugging himself], and smell [spicy perfume]. The imagery helps readers visualize the setting more clearly.)*

---

in tins,[5] which he dislodged onto himself from the top of a heap of boxes. At last Miss Pride, with a cry of triumph, unearthed a little cache of Brekkfast Brikks, three packets which turned out to be the remaining sections, Six, One, and Two.

"There, isn't that a piece of luck now!" she said, looking quite faint with all the excitement. It was indeed rare for Miss Pride to sell as many as five packets of the same thing at one time.

Mark galloped home with his booty and met his father on the porch. Mr. Armitage let out a groan of dismay.

"I'd almost rather you'd bought a space gun," he said. Mark chanted in reply:

"Brekkfast Brikks for supper too
Give peaceful sleep the whole night through."

"I don't want peaceful sleep," Mr. Armitage said. "I intend to spend tonight mouse watching again. I'm tired of finding footprints in the Stilton."[6]

During the next few days Mark's parents watched anxiously to see, Mr. Armitage said, whether Mark would start to sprout esparto grass instead of hair. For he doggedly ate Brekkfast Brikks for lunch, with soup, or sprinkled over his pudding; for tea, with jam; and for supper lightly fried in dripping, not to mention, of course, the immense helpings he had for breakfast with sugar and milk. Mr.

> "BREKKFAST BRIKKS FOR SUPPER TOO GIVE PEACEFUL SLEEP THE WHOLE NIGHT THROUGH."

Armitage for his part soon gave out; he said he wouldn't taste another Brekkfast Brikk even if it were wrapped in an inch-thick layer of *pâté de foie gras.*[7] Mark regretted that Harriet, who was a handy and uncritical eater, was still away, convalescing from her measles with an aunt.

In two days the second packet was finished (sundial, paved garden, and espaliers[8]). Mark cut it out, fastened it together, and joined it onto Section Three with trembling hands. Would the spell work for this section, too? He sang the rhyme in rather a quavering voice, but luckily the playroom door was shut and there was no one to hear him. Yes! The gate grew again above him, and when he opened it and ran across the lawn through the yew arch, he found himself in a flagged garden full of flowers like huge blue cabbages.

Mark stood hugging himself with satisfaction and then began to wander about smelling the flowers, which had a spicy perfume most unlike any flower he could think of. Suddenly he pricked up his ears. Had he caught a sound? There! It was like somebody crying

---

5. **pilchards** (pĭl′chərdz) **in tins:** cans of sardines.
6. **Stilton:** a rich, crumbly cheese.
7. *pâté de foie gras* (pä-tā′ də fwä grä′) French: a food made of chopped goose livers, often eaten spread on crackers.
8. **espaliers** (ĭ-spăl′yərz): trees or shrubs trained to grow flat against a wall.

WORDS TO KNOW	**convalescing** (kŏn′və-lĕs′ĭng) *adj.* recovering gradually from an illness **convalesce** *v.*

422

Mini-Lesson Grammar

SEMICOLONS SEPARATING A SERIES

Remind students that a semicolon indicates a longer pause and a more definite break than a comma does. A semicolon separates items in a series that are already punctuated with commas. Write on the chalkboard the example sentence.

Application Have students replace commas with semicolons correctly in these sentences.

1. He doggedly ate Brekkfast Brikks for lunch, with soup, or sprinkled over his pudding, for tea, with jam, and for supper lightly fried in dripping. (after *pudding* and after *jam,* p. 422)

Miss Pride found sections Six, One, and Two; five stale, moldy boxes of spaghetti; and some old, tattered tea bags.

2. Mark made rings round Mr. Johansen all the way to the village, the music master limped quietly along, smiling a little, from time to time he said, "Gently, my friend." (after *village* and after *little,* p. 430)

Reteaching/Reinforcement

- *Grammar Mini-Lessons* copymasters p. 40, transparencies p. 31

The Writer's Craft

The Semicolon, p. 641

and seemed to come from the other side of the hedge. He ran to the next opening and looked through. Nothing: only gray mist and emptiness. But, unless he had imagined it, just before he got there, he thought his eye had caught the flash of white-and-gold draperies swishing past the gateway.

"Do you think Mark's all right?" Mrs. Armitage said to her husband next day. "He seems to be in such a dream all the time."

"Boy's gone clean off his rocker if you ask me," grumbled Mr. Armitage. "It's all these doormats he's eating. Can't be good to stuff your insides with moldy jute.[9] Still I'm bound to say he's cut the lawn very decently and seems to be remembering the coal. I'd better take a day off from the office and drive you over to the shore for a picnic; sea air will do him good."

Mrs. Armitage suggested to Mark that he should slack off on the Brekkfast Brikks, but he was so horrified that she had to abandon the idea. But, she said, he was to run four times round the garden every morning before breakfast. Mark almost said, "Which garden?" but stopped just in time. He had cut out and completed another large lawn, with a lake and weeping willows, and on the far side of the lake had a <u>tantalizing</u> glimpse of a figure dressed in white and gold who moved away and was lost before he could get there.

After munching his way through the fourth packet, he was able to add on a broad grass walk bordered by curiously clipped trees. At the end of the walk he could see the white-and-gold person, but when he ran to the spot, no one was there—the walk ended in the usual gray mist.

When he had finished and had cut out the fifth packet (an orchard), a terrible thing happened to him. For two days he could not remember the tune that worked the spell. He tried other tunes, but they were no use. He sat in the playroom singing till he was hoarse or silent with despair. Suppose he never remembered it again?

His mother shook her head at him that evening and said he looked as if he needed a dose. "It's lucky we're going to Shinglemud Bay for the day tomorrow," she said. "That ought to do you good."

"Oh, *blow*. I'd forgotten about that," Mark said. "Need I go?"

His mother stared at him in utter astonishment.

But in the middle of the night he remembered the right tune, leaped out of bed in a tremendous hurry, and ran down to the playroom without even waiting to put on his dressing gown and slippers.

The orchard was most wonderful, for instead of mere apples its trees bore oranges, lemons, limes and all sorts of tropical fruits whose names he did not know, and there were melons and pineapples growing, and plantains and avocados. Better still, he saw the lady in her white and gold waiting at the end of an alley and was able to draw near enough to speak to her.

"Who are you?" she asked. She seemed very much astonished at the sight of him.

"My name's Mark Armitage," he said politely. "Is this your garden?"

---

9. **jute:** a strong fiber used for making mats, rope, and sacks.

| WORDS TO KNOW | **tantalizing** (tăn′tə-lī′zĭng) *adj.* arousing interest without satisfying it **tantalize** *v.* |

423

Active Reading: PREDICT

Q Invite students to predict who—or what—is behind the flash of the white-and-gold draperies. Guide students to base their predictions on story clues and their prior knowledge. You may wish to use the following model:

Think-Aloud Model *I remember that the garden is very lush and rich. It has many expensive features, such as a sundial, paving, and espaliers. This suggests to me that a royal person has swished past. It might be a king, queen, or princess, for example. Or, since this is a fantasy, there might be an evil witch or magician waiting to put a spell on Mark.*

Literary Concept: IRONY

R Ask students what is ironic about Mr. Armitage's belief that it's the bad-tasting cereal that is making Mark act so strangely. *(Possible response: It's ironic because it's not what is <u>inside</u> the box that's making Mark act that way; it's what's on the <u>outside</u> of the box—the cutout of the garden.)*

CUSTOMIZING FOR
Students Acquiring English

3 Point out that "Need I go?" is British usage. American speakers would say, "Do I have to go?"

CUSTOMIZING FOR
Multiple Learning Styles

S Spatial or Graphic Learners Invite students to create a picture or model of an imaginary or magical place they would like to visit. It might be Oz, Wonderland, or Atlantis, for example.

Mini-Lesson **Study Skills**

TAKING ESSAY TESTS: PLANNING YOUR ANSWERS Tell students that essay tests often will ask them to write a paragraph or more in answer to a question. Explain that in English class, for example, students might be asked to explain why "The Serial Garden" can be classified as a fantasy. Provide students with these guidelines for planning their answers:

• Make sure you understand what topic the question is addressing.
• Identify the approach you should take by looking for key words, such as *compare, contrast, explain, identify,* or *discuss.*

• Check to see what the form of the answer should be—for example, a paragraph or a letter.

Application Have students plan and outline their response to one of the following essay questions about "The Serial Garden":

1. Compare and contrast Princess Sophia's garden with an actual garden.
2. Describe Mark's relationship with Rudi.
3. Explain how Princess Sophia ended up in the serial garden.

Reading the Art *Describe the setting and subject of this painting. Is your own idea of what Princess Sophia and her garden look like similar to the image in the painting? Explain why or why not.*

Illustration by Ruth Sanderson.

424 UNIT FOUR PART 1: THE WILL TO WIN

Mini-Lesson  Spelling

THE SUFFIXES *-ABLE* AND *-IBLE* Write **change + able** = _____ on the chalkboard and have students create the resulting word. Repeat the procedure with **suscept + ible** = _____. Explain that the suffix *-able* usually is added to complete words to form adjectives meaning "able to [base word]"; *-ible* usually is added to roots. When either suffix is added to a word ending in silent *e*, the *e* is dropped—unless the *e* is preceded by *c* or *g*.

Application Have students add the suffix *-ible* or *-able* to the following roots and words.

1. avail
   (available)
2. aud
   (audible)
3. cred
   (credible)
4. agree
   (agreeable)
5. vis
   (visible)
6. tang
   (tangible)
7. notice
   (noticeable)
8. poss
   (possible)
9. attain
   (attainable)

Remind students that when they aren't sure how to spell a word—especially tricky ones like these—they should use the dictionary.

Reteaching/Reinforcement
• *Unit Four Resource Book*, p. 19

Close to, he saw that she was really very grand indeed. Her dress was white satin, embroidered with pearls, and swept the ground; she had a gold scarf, and her hair, dressed high and powdered, was confined in a small gold-and-pearl tiara. Her face was rather plain, pink with a long nose, but she had a kind expression and beautiful gray eyes.

"Indeed it is," she announced with hauteur. "I am Princess Sophia Maria Louisa of Saxe-Hoffenpoffen-und-Hamster. What are you doing here, pray?"

"Well," Mark explained cautiously, "it seemed to come about through singing a tune."

"Indeed. That is most interesting. Did the tune, perhaps, go like this?"

The princess hummed a few bars.

"That's it! How did you know?"

"Why, you foolish boy, it was I who put the spell on the garden, to make it come alive when the tune is played or sung."

"I say!" Mark was full of admiration. "Can you do spells as well as being a princess?"

She drew herself up. "Naturally! At the court of Saxe-Hoffenpoffen, where I was educated, all princesses were taught a little magic, not so much as to be vulgar, just enough to get out of social difficulties."

"Jolly useful," Mark said. "How did you work the spell for the garden, then?"

"Why, you see," (the princess was obviously delighted to have somebody to talk to; she sat on a stone seat and patted it, inviting Mark to do likewise) "I had the misfortune to fall in love with Herr Rudolf, the court Kapellmeister,[10] who taught me music. Oh, he was so kind and handsome! And he was most talented, but my father, of course, would not hear of my marrying him because he was only a common person."

"So what did you do?"

"I arranged to vanish, of course. Rudi had given me a beautiful book with many pictures of gardens. My father kept strict watch to see I did not run away, so I used to slip between the pages of the book when I wanted to be alone. Then, when we decided to marry, I asked my maid to take the book to Rudi. And I sent him a note telling him to play the tune when he received the book. But I believe that spiteful Gertrud must have played me false and never taken the book, for more than fifty years have now passed and I have been here all alone, waiting in the garden, and Rudi has never come. Oh, Rudi, Rudi," she exclaimed, wringing her hands and crying a little, "where can you be? It is so long—so long!"

"Fifty years," Mark said kindly, reckoning that must make her nearly seventy. "I must say you don't look it."

"Of course I do not, dumbhead. For me, I make it that time does not touch me. But tell me, how did you know the tune that works the spell? It was taught me by my dear Rudi."

"I'm not sure where I picked it up," Mark confessed. "For all I know it may be one of the Top Ten. I'll ask my music teacher; he's sure to know. Perhaps he'll have heard of your Rudolf too."

Privately Mark feared that Rudolf might very well have died by now, but he did not like to depress Princess Sophia Maria by such a suggestion, so he bade her a polite good night, promising to come back as soon as he could with another section of the garden and any news he could pick up.

---

10. **Kapellmeister** (kə-pĕl′mī′stər): the leader of a choir or orchestra.

THE SERIAL GARDEN **425**

Active Reading: PREDICT

T Have students predict who this character might be, based on what they have read and what they know about characters in fantasies. (*Possible response: This is the figure Mark caught a glimpse of earlier. She fits the traditional fairy-tale image of a princess.*)

Literary Concept: HUMOR

U Invite students to explain why the author gave the princess this name. (*Possible responses: Her name creates humor and prevents the story from being too serious; it's another funny "German" word, like the cereal company's name.*)

Critical Thinking: HYPOTHESIZE

V Ask students to guess how Mark might have learned the tune. (*Possible responses: from the radio, a friend, a relative, or his music teacher*)

STRATEGIC READING FOR Less-Proficient Readers

W Discuss with students what exciting things Mark finds in the garden. (*Possible responses: Mark finds beautiful, magical things including huge flowers, fruits, and a princess.*) **Noting Relevant Details**

- How does Mark get the money to buy the rest of the garden? (*He gets an advance from his father for promising to mow the lawn and carry coal for a month.*) **Noting Sequence of Events**

Set a Purpose Ask students to discover how Mark learned the special song.

Mini-Lesson: Speaking, Listening, and Viewing

READERS THEATER Explain to students that a Readers Theater performance provides an oral interpretation of a work of literature, such as a short story. Different readers interpret the parts of different characters, and a narrator presents the story's exposition and description. Explain that students sit on chairs or stools facing the audience, using their voices to convey their interpretation of the characters and the action.

Application Have students work in small groups to perform passages of "The Serial Garden" as a Readers Theater presentation. Guide students to go over their parts and make notes about characters, motivation, and interpretation.

X Ask students why Mark is eager to speak to his music teacher, Mr. Johansen. *(Possible responses: Mark wants to find out about the tune and the princess's beloved Rudolph; Mark is worried that he will forget the song while he is in the garden and get stuck there for eternity.)*

Linking to Social Studies

Y Cricket, generally considered the national game of England, is also popular in Canada, the West Indies, South Africa, and Australia. The game is played outdoors, with a red leather ball and a flat, paddle-shaped bat, by two teams of 11 players each. The central action of the game takes place between the batman, who stands behind a crease (a white line), and the bowler, who throws the ball from behind an opposite crease.

CUSTOMIZING FOR
Students Acquiring English

4 Explain that *straightaway* is British slang for "right away."

CUSTOMIZING FOR
Multiple Learning Styles

Z Bodily-Kinesthetic Learners Invite students to role-play this scene, suggesting through their actions and gestures the personalities of Mark and the princess.

X He planned to go and see Mr. Johansen, his music teacher, next morning, but he had forgotten the family trip to the beach. There was just time to scribble a hasty post card to the British office of Fruhstucksgeschirrziegelsteinindustrie, asking them if they could inform him from what source they had obtained the pictures used on the packets of Brekkfast Brikks. Then Mr. Armitage drove his wife and son to Shinglemud Bay, gloomily prophesying wet weather.

Y In fact, the weather turned out fine, and Mark found it quite restful to swim and play beach cricket and eat ham sandwiches and lie in the sun. For he had been struck by a horrid thought: suppose he should forget the tune again when he was inside the garden—would he be stuck there, like Father in the larder? It was a lovely place to go and wander at will, but somehow he didn't fancy spending the next fifty years there with Princess Sophia Maria. Would she oblige him by singing the spell if he forgot it, or would she be too keen on company to let him go? He was not inclined to take any chances.

It was late when they arrived home, too late, Mark thought, to disturb Mr. Johansen, who was elderly and kept early hours. Mark ate a huge helping of sardines on Brekkfast Brikks for supper—he was dying to finish Section Six—but did not visit the garden that night.

Next morning's breakfast (Brikks with hot milk, for a change) finished the last packet—and just as well, for the larder mouse, which Mr. Armitage still had not caught, was discovered to have nibbled the bottom left-hand corner of the packet, slightly damaging an ornamental grotto[11] in a grove of lime trees. Rather worried about this, Mark

decided to make up the last section straightaway, in case the magic had been affected. By now he was becoming very skillful at the tiny fiddling task of cutting out the little tabs and slipping them into the little slots; the job did not take long to finish. Mark attached Section Six to Section Five and then, drawing a deep breath, sang the incantation[12] once more. With immense relief he watched the mossy wall and rusty gate grow out of the playroom floor; all was well.

He raced across the lawn, round the lake, along the avenue, through the orchard, and into the lime grove. The scent of the lime flowers was sweeter than a cake baking.

Princess Sophia Maria came towards him from the grotto, looking slightly put out.

"Good morning!" she greeted Mark. "Do you bring me any news?"

"I haven't been to see my music teacher yet," Mark confessed. "I was a bit anxious because there was a hole—"

"Ach, yes, a hole in the grotto! I have just been looking. Some wild beast must have made its way in, and I am afraid it may come again. See, it has made tracks like those of a big bear." She showed him some enormous footprints in the soft sand of the grotto floor. Mark stopped up the hole with prickly branches and promised to bring a dog when he next came, though he felt fairly sure the mouse would not return.

"I can borrow a dog from my teacher—he has plenty. I'll be back in an hour or so—see you then," he said.

"*Auf Wiedersehen,*[13] my dear young friend." Mark ran along the village street to Mr.

---

11. **grotto:** a structure made to look like a small cave.
12. **incantation** (ĭn'kăn-tā'shən): magic spell.
13. **auf Wiedersehen** (ouf vē'dər-zā'ən) German: goodbye.

426 UNIT FOUR PART 1: THE WILL TO WIN

Mini-Lesson: Speaking,  Listening, and Viewing

ASSESSING A PERFORMANCE Explain to students that assessing a presentation, such as a Readers Theater performance, involves a three-step process.

Step 1: Think about what you already know about the work to be performed. Try not to prejudge the performance, but do establish appropriate guidelines for evaluation. For example, a humorous work probably would include comic exaggeration, whereas a serious work probably would stir deep emotional responses.

Step 2: Listen critically to the performers' reading or speaking of the lines to identify both strengths and weaknesses in the interpretation.

Step 3: Write a brief evaluation, jotting down the key ideas and describing your emotional response to the performance.

Application Invite students to assess the performances presented for the mini-lesson on page 425. Then have students work in small groups to discuss their responses. Have each group elect a recorder to summarize the group's reactions for sharing with the class.

Johansen's house, Houndshaven Cottage. He knew better than to knock at the door because Mr. Johansen would be either practicing his violin or out in the barn at the back, and in any case the sound of barking was generally loud enough to drown any noise short of gunfire.

Besides giving music lessons at Mark's school, Mr. Johansen kept a guest house for dogs whose owners were abroad or on holiday. He was extremely kind to the guests and did his best to make them feel at home in every way, finding out from their owners what were their favorite foods, and letting them sleep on his own bed, turn about. He spent all his spare time with them, talking to them and playing either his violin or long-playing records of domestic sounds likely to appeal to the canine fancy—such as knives being sharpened, cars starting up, and children playing ball games.

Mark could hear Mr. Johansen playing Brahms's lullaby in the barn, so he went out there; the music was making some of the more susceptible inmates feel homesick: howls, sympathetic moans, and long shuddering sighs came from the numerous comfortably carpeted cubicles all the way down the barn.

Mr. Johansen reached the end of the piece as Mark entered. He put down his fiddle and smiled welcomingly.

"Ach, how *gut!* It is the young Mark."

"Hullo, sir."

"You know," confided Mr. Johansen, "I play to many audiences in my life all over the world, but never anywhere do I get such a response as from zese dear doggies—it is really remarkable. But come in; come into ze house

and have some coffee cake."

Mr. Johansen was a gentle, white-haired elderly man; he walked slowly with a slight stoop and had a kindly, sad face with large dark eyes. He looked rather like some sort of dog himself, Mark always thought, perhaps a collie or a long-haired dachshund.

"Sir," Mark said, "if I whistle a tune to you, can you write it down for me?"

"Why, yes, I shall be most happy," Mr. Johansen said, pouring coffee for both of them.

So Mark whistled his tune once more; as he came to the end, he was surprised to see the music master's eyes fill with tears, which slowly began to trickle down his thin cheeks.

"It recalls my youth, zat piece," he explained, wiping the tears away and rapidly scribbling crotchets and minims on a piece of music paper. "Many times I am whistling it myself—it is wissout doubt from me you learn it—but always it is reminding me of how happy I was long ago when I wrote it."

"You *wrote* that tune?" Mark said, much excited.

"Why yes. What is so strange in zat? Many, many tunes haf I written."

"Well—" Mark said, "I won't tell you just yet in case I'm mistaken—I'll have to see somebody else first. Do you mind if I dash off right away? Oh, and might I borrow a dog—preferably a good ratter?"

"In zat case, better have my dear Lotta—alzough she is so old she is ze best of zem all," Mr. Johansen said proudly. Lotta was his own dog, an enormous shaggy lumbering animal with a tail like a palm tree and feet the size of electric polishers; she was reputed to be of incalculable age; Mr. Johansen called her his strudel-hound.

WORDS
TO
KNOW

susceptible (sə-sĕp′tə-bəl) *adj.* easily affected or influenced
incalculable (ĭn-kăl′kyə-lə-bəl) *adj.* too great to be measured or counted

427

Critical Thinking: ANALYZE

AA Explain to students that English houses sometimes have names, such as Pembroke or Foxworth Manor. Ask students to explain how the name of Mr. Johansen's house relates to his life and interests. (*Possible response: The name Houndshaven suggests that his house is a shelter [haven] for dogs [hounds]. This implies that Mr. Johansen likes dogs. Besides teaching, Mr. Johansen boards other people's dogs.*)

Literary Concept: HUMOR

BB Have students explain the humor in this scene. (*Possible response: The animals' enjoyment of the music is comic and vivid. Also, readers don't know if the animals are howling in delight or in pain.*)

CUSTOMIZING FOR
Students Acquiring English

5 Point out that the spellings *zese* and *ze* reflect Mr. Johansen's German-accented English, in which the *z* sound is substituted for *th*.

STRATEGIC READING FOR
Less-Proficient Readers

CC Ask students who taught Mark the Brekkfast Brikks melody. (*Mr. Johansen*) **Noting Relevant Details**

• What job does Mr. Johansen do in addition to teaching music? (*He boards dogs.*) **Summarizing**

Set a Purpose Ask students to continue reading to find out the relationship between the princess and Mr. Johansen.

Literary Concept: FORESHADOWING

DD Ask students why they think the author includes this detail about the dog's age. Guide them to explain what it may hint about upcoming events in the plot. (*Perceptive readers might recall that it has been 50 years since the princess has seen her beloved Rudi; these readers might make the connection between the dog's master and the princess's lost love. This detail foreshadows Rudi's identity.*)

Mini-Lesson		The Writer's Style

USING FIGURATIVE LANGUAGE Figurative language is the imaginative use of words to create pictures. Explain the following types:
Similes: Comparisons using *like* or *as.*
  His face was as round as the moon.
Metaphors: Comparisons without *like* or *as.*
  The castle was a whale adrift on a sea of grass.
Personification: Giving human qualities to nonhuman things.
  The sun crept across the sky, as if nervous.

Application Have students identify the figurative language in these sentences.

1. Miss Pride's cellar was a graveyard of tattered cartons, (*metaphor*)
2. The music was making some of the more susceptible inmates (dogs) feel homesick: howls, sympathetic moans, and long shuddering sighs . . . (*personification*)
3. He looked rather like some sort of dog himself, Mark always thought. (*simile*)

Reteaching/Reinforcement
• *Writing Mini-Lessons* transparencies, p. 39

 The Writer's Craft

Using Language Imaginatively, pp. 314–316

Le jardin potager, Yerres by Gustave Caillebotte

Reading the Art *Would you like to visit the garden pictured? Why or why not?*

Active Reading: EVALUATE

EE Have students explain what information Mark gets from the letter and why it is important. *(Possible responses: He learns that the princess's book was destroyed and its owner, the firm that made the cereal, is out of business. Therefore, unless Mark or someone else can get another complete set of Brekkfast Brikks boxes, Mark has the last remaining model of the garden.)*

Le Jardin potager, Yerres [The kitchen garden, Yerres] (1875–77), Gustave Caillebotte. Private collection.

She knew Mark well and came along with him quite biddably, though it was rather like leading a mammoth.

Luckily his mother, refreshed by her day at the sea, was heavily engaged with Agnes the maid in spring cleaning. Furniture was being shoved about, and everyone was too busy to notice Mark and Lotta slip into the playroom.

A letter addressed to Mark lay among the clutter on the table; he opened and read it while Lotta <u>foraged</u> happily among the piles of magazines and tennis nets and cricket bats and rusting electronic equipment, managing to upset several things and increase the general state of huggermugger in the room.

Dear Sir, (the letter said—it was from Messrs. Digit, Digit, & Rule, a firm of chartered accountants)—We are in receipt of your inquiry as to the source of pictures on packets of Brekkfast Brikks. We are pleased to inform you that these were reproduced from the illustrations of a little-known 18th-century German work, *Steinbergen's Gartenbuch.* Unfortunately the only known remaining copy of this book was burnt in the disastrous fire which destroyed the factory and premises of Messrs. Fruhstucksgeschirrziegelsteinindustrie two months ago. The firm has now gone into liquidation and we are winding up their effects. Yours faithfully, P. J. Zero, Gen. Sec.

WORDS
TO   **forage** (fôr′ĭj) *v.* to search for what one wants or needs, especially for food
KNOW

428

ART Explain to students that paintings and drawings are viewed and evaluated differently from other art forms, such as movies, dance, and music. Provide students with the following list of qualities to consider in evaluating the art that accompanies this selection.

- *Light and shadow* The interplay of the light and dark sections of the canvas that create the sense of depth and dimension in a flat field of view
- *Line* The thickness of the line and how it is used to create figures and objects

- *Medium* The material the artist used to create the picture, such as oil or acrylic paint, watercolors, pastels, or colored paper
- *Color* The intensity of the hues and tones
- *Composition* The arrangement of figures, objects, and white space on the canvas

Application Invite students to select one of the pieces of fine art reproduced in this story and analyze the qualities explained above. Students can share their reactions in a small group discussion or in a brief oral presentation.

"Steinbergen's Gartenbuch," Mark thought. "That must have been the book that Princess Sophia Maria used for the spell—probably the same copy. Oh, well, since it's burned, it's lucky the pictures were reproduced on the Brekkfast Brikks packets. Come on, Lotta, let's go and find a nice princess then. Good girl! Rats! Chase 'em!"

He sang the spell, and Lotta, all enthusiasm, followed him into the garden.

They did not have to go far before they saw the princess—she was sitting sunning herself on the rim of the fountain. But what happened then was unexpected. Lotta let out the most extraordinary cry—whine, bark, and howl all in one—and hurled herself towards the princess like a rocket.

"Hey! Look out! Lotta! *Heel!*" Mark shouted in alarm. But Lotta, with her great paws on the princess's shoulders, had about a yard of salmon-pink tongue out, and was washing the princess's face all over with frantic affection.

The princess was just as excited. "Lotta, Lotta! She knows me; it's dear Lotta; it must be! Where did you get her?" she cried to Mark, hugging the enormous dog, whose tail was going round faster than a turboprop.

"Why, she belongs to my music master, Mr. Johansen, and it's he who made up the tune," Mark said.

The princess turned quite white and had to sit down on the fountain's rim again.

"*Johansen?* Rudolf Johansen? My Rudi! At last! After all these years! Oh, run, run, and

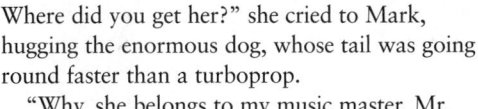

"IT'S LUCKY THE PICTURES WERE REPRODUCED ON THE BREKKFAST BRIKKS PACKETS."

fetch him immediately, please! Immediately!"

Mark hesitated a moment.

"Please make haste!" she besought him. "Why do you wait?"

"It's only—well, you won't be surprised if he's quite *old*, will you? Remember he hasn't been in a garden keeping young like you."

"All that will change," the princess said confidently. "He has only to eat the fruit of the garden. Why, look at Lotta—when she was a puppy, for a joke I gave her a fig from this tree, and you can see she is a puppy still, though she must be older than any other dog in the world! Oh, please hurry to bring Rudi here."

"Why don't you come with me to his house?"

"That would not be correct etiquette," she said with dignity. "After all, I *am* royal."

"Okay," said Mark. "I'll fetch him. Hope he doesn't think I'm crackers."

"Give him this." The princess took off a locket on a gold chain. It had a miniature of a romantically handsome young man with dark curling hair. "My Rudi," she explained fondly. Mark could just trace a faint resemblance to Mr. Johansen.

He took the locket and hurried away. At the gate something made him look back: the princess and Lotta were sitting at the edge of the fountain, side by side. The princess had an arm round Lotta's neck; with the other hand she waved to him, just a little.

THE SERIAL GARDEN **429**

Literary Concept: FORESHADOWING

FF Invite students to speculate, based on this comment, about what might happen later in the story. (*Possible responses: The yew arch might burn down; the remaining packets of Brekkfast Brikks might be destroyed by fire.*)

Active Reading: CLARIFY

GG Ask students to explain the relationship between the princess and Mr. Johansen. (*Possible response: They had fallen in love more than 50 years before. They planned to marry, but they were betrayed, and the princess has been trapped in the garden, waiting for her love.*)

CUSTOMIZING FOR
Multiple Learning Styles

HH **Spatial or Graphic Learners** Suggest that students who express themselves through visual images and pictures design the locket and miniature portrait of a youthful Mr. Johansen.

Mini-Lesson Study Skills

TAKING OBJECTIVE TESTS: MATCHING QUESTIONS Explain to the class that matching questions ask test-takers to connect items in one column with items in a second column. Provide students with the following test-taking strategies:

- Match the items you know first. This will leave fewer choices.
- Check to see if some items are used more than once and if some items are not used at all. This will help you eliminate choices.

- Check your answers carefully to make sure that you have marked every answer in the correct place on the answer sheet.

Application Have students work in pairs to make a ten-question matching test based on "The Serial Garden." Ask each pair to switch papers with another pair and to complete the test, using the test-taking strategies they learned.

Active Reading: EVALUATE

II Invite students to find the three instances when spring cleaning is mentioned in the story. Have students evaluate the author's reasons for mentioning cleaning so much. *(Possible responses: She wanted to make the story seem more real; the cleaning is a key aspect of the plot and will be very important to the story's outcome.)*

STRATEGIC READING FOR

Less-Proficient Readers

JJ Have volunteers explain how Mr. Johansen is connected to the princess. *(He is her lost love, Rudi, of more than 50 years ago.)* **Summarizing**

Set a Purpose Have students finish the story to discover if the lovers are reunited in the garden.

Literary Concept: IRONY

KK Ask students to explain what is ironic about the dogs' diets. *(Possible responses: What the dogs in the story eat is not what is normally thought of as dog food.)*

Literary Concept: PLOT

LL Invite students to explain why this is the climax of the story's plot. *(Possible response: All the details in the story lead up to this moment, the point of highest interest.)*

"Hurry!" she called again.

II Mark made his way out of the house, through the spring-cleaning <u>chaos</u>, and flew down the village to Houndshaven Cottage. Mr. Johansen was in the house this time, boiling up a noisome mass of meat and bones for the dogs' dinner. Mark said nothing at all, just handed him the locket. He took one look at it and staggered, putting his hand to his heart; anxiously, Mark led him to a chair.

"Are you all right, sir?"

"Yes, yes! It was only ze shock. Where did you get ziss, my boy?"

So Mark told him.

Surprisingly, Mr. Johansen did not find anything odd about the story; he nodded his head several times as Mark related the various points.

"Yes, yes, her letter, I have it still—" he pulled out a worn little scrap of paper, "but ze *Gartenbuch* it reached me never. Zat wicked Gertrud must haf sold it to some bookseller who sold it to Fruhstucksgeschirrziegelsteinindustrie. And so **JJ** she has been waiting all ziss time! My poor little Sophie!"

"Are you strong enough to come to her now?" Mark asked.

"*Natürlich!* But first we must give ze dogs zeir dinner; zey must not go hungry."

So they fed the dogs, which was a long job as there were at least sixty and each had a different diet, including some very odd preferences like Swiss roll spread with Marmite and yeast pills wrapped in slices of caramel. Privately, **KK** Mark thought the dogs were a bit spoiled, but Mr. Johansen was very careful to see that each visitor had just what it fancied.

"After all, zey are not mine! Must I not take good care of zem?"

At least two hours had gone by before the last willow-pattern plate was licked clean, and they were free to go. Mark made rings round Mr. Johansen all the way up the village; the music master limped quietly along, smiling a little; from time to time he said, "Gently, my friend. We do not run a race. Remember I am an old man."

That was just what Mark did remember. He longed to see Mr. Johansen young and happy once more.

The chaos in the Armitage house had changed its location: the front hall was now clean, tidy, and damp; the rumpus of vacuuming had shifted to the playroom. With a black hollow of apprehension in his middle, Mark ran through the open door and stopped, aghast. All the toys, tools, weapons, boxes, magazines, and bits of machinery had been rammed into the cupboards; the floor where his garden had been laid out was bare. Mrs. Armitage was in the playroom taking down the curtains.

"*Mother!* Where's my Brekkfast Brikks garden?"

"Oh, darling, you didn't want it, did you? It was all dusty; I thought you'd finished with it. I'm afraid I've burned it in the furnace. Really you *must* try not to let this room get into such a clutter; it's perfectly disgraceful. Why, hullo, Mr. Johansen," she added in embarrassment. "I didn't see you; I'm afraid you've called at the worst possible moment. But I'm sure you'll understand how it is at spring-cleaning time."

She rolled up her bundle of curtains, glancing worriedly at Mr. Johansen; he looked rather odd, she thought. But he gave her his tired,

WORDS TO KNOW   **chaos** (kā′ŏs′) *n.* extreme confusion or disorder

430

---

gentle smile and said, "Why, yes, Mrs. Armitage, I understand; I understand very well. Come, Mark. We have no business here, you can see."

Speechlessly, Mark followed him. What was there to say?

"Never mind," Mrs. Armitage called after Mark. "The Rice Nuts pack has a helicopter on it."

Every week in The Times newspaper you will see this advertisement:

BREKKFAST BRIKKS PACKETS. £100 offered for any in good condition, whether empty or full.

So, if you have any, you know where to send them.

But Mark is growing anxious; none have come in yet, and every day Mr. Johansen seems a little thinner and more elderly. Besides, what will the princess be thinking? ❖

 Have students figure out how much the reward would be in American dollars, using an exchange rate of 1.60 dollars to 1 pound. *($160.00.)*

STRATEGIC READING FOR

Less-Proficient Readers

Ask students to explain what happens to the lovers. *(They are not reunited because Mrs. Armitage burns the model.)* **Summarizing**

CUSTOMIZING FOR

Gifted and Talented Students

Have students discuss the appeal of fantasy. Ask them why people enjoy fantasy stories, even though they know these stories contain unlikely, and sometimes even impossible, events. *(Possible responses: These stories are entertaining because they are creative and different from everyday life; they help us enrich our own dream life.)*

COMPREHENSION CHECK
1. Where does Mark get the Brekkfast Brikks? *(at Miss Pride's shop)*
2. How does Mark get into the magic garden? *(He sings the Brekkfast Brikks rhyme.)*
3. Who does Mark meet in the garden? *(Princess Sophia)*
4. How does Mr. Johansen know the Brekkfast Brikks song? *(He wrote it.)*
5. Why aren't Mr. Johansen and the princess reunited? *(Mrs. Armitage burns the model garden while spring cleaning.)*

Assessment **Option**

INFORMAL ASSESSMENT Have students show their understanding of the story by creating a story triangle, as follows:

Line 1 (top): Name of main character

Line 2: Two words describing the main character

Line 3: Three words describing the setting

Line 4: Four words stating the main problem

Line 5: Five words describing one problem

Line 6: Six words describing another problem

Line 7: Seven words about a third problem

Line 8: Eight words describing the solution

Rubric

3 Full Accomplishment Students follow the directions fully and are creative in their choice of words and phrases.

2 Substantial Accomplishment Students describe the plot but may exceed the number of words.

1 Little or Partial Accomplishment Students cannot describe the plot within the required framework.

From Personal Response to Critical Analysis

1. Responses will vary.
2. Responses will vary.
3. Possible responses: Mark might have prevented the garden from being destroyed by hiding the model; he might have reunited the lovers by insisting that Mr. Johansen visit the garden before feeding the dogs.
4. Possible responses: Yes, because the ad will help Mark get another set of cereal boxes to reconstruct the garden; no, because Mr. Johansen will be dead before Mark can gather all the pieces he needs.
5. Possible responses: Yes, because it is exciting and fun; no, because I would be afraid that I would probably forget the melody and get trapped in the garden.
6. Possible response: They are different from Romeo and Juliet, because they survive at the end.
7. Possible response: It is a "cereal garden" because it is a cutout from a cereal box; it is a "serial garden" because the garden pieces are provided on different boxes that are purchased one after another.

Another Pathway

Cooperative Learning To help everyone work together smoothly, assign a direction giver to keep the group focused, a voice monitor to keep the volume in check, and a recorder to jot down the characters' flaws.

Rubric

3 Full Accomplishment Students list key flaws that affect the plot.

2 Substantial Accomplishment Students list some character flaws that are important to the plot.

I Little or Partial Accomplishment Students cannot isolate the key character flaws.

RESPONDING
OPTIONS

FROM PERSONAL RESPONSE TO CRITICAL ANALYSIS

REFLECT
1. What were your thoughts as you finished reading this story? Record them in your notebook before discussing them with your classmates.

RETHINK
2. How do the predictions you made for the Reading Connection on page 415 compare with the actual events of the story? If you changed any of your predictions as you were reading, what clues led you to do so?

3. What are some things Mark might have done to bring about a different ending to this story?

4. Do you think Mr. Johansen and Princess Sophia will ever be reunited? Why or why not?
Consider

Close Textual Reading
- the advertisement that appears in *The Times* every week
- Mr. Johansen's age and physical condition
- the princess's knowledge of magic
- other possible solutions to the problem

RELATE
5. If you were in Mark's place, would you go back and forth into the magic garden? Why or why not?

6. People like Mr. Johansen and Princess Sophia are often called star-crossed lovers because they seem prevented by fate from living happily ever after. How do Mr. Johansen and Princess Sophia compare with other star-crossed lovers you have read about?

7. The words *serial* and *cereal* are homophones—words with the same pronunciation for different spellings and meanings. In what sense is the garden in this story both a "serial garden" and a "cereal garden"?

Multimodal Learning
ANOTHER PATHWAY

Although the timing of Mrs. Armitage's spring cleaning contributes to the sad ending of this story, weaknesses or flaws in some of the characters also play a part. With a small group of classmates, list the flaws in Mark, Mr. Johansen, and Princess Sophia that influence the events of the story. Compare your list with other groups' lists.

QUICKWRITES

1. Use your imagination and details from the story to write a **fantasy story** about how Miss Pride first got hold of her boxes of Brekkfast Brikks cereal.

2. At one point, Mark fears that he might forget the magic tune and that Princess Sophia might keep him in the garden for company. If that happened, how could Mark get back home? Write the **escape plan** he might devise.

3. Using the descriptions of Brekkfast Brikks as a guide, write a humorous **recipe** for making the cereal.

4. Write the **conversation** Mark and Harriet (his sister) might have about the Princess and Mr. Johansen

📁 **PORTFOLIO** Save your writing. You may want to use it later as a springboard to a piece for your portfolio.

QuickWrites

1. Direct students to make a story map to help them list the new details about Miss Pride.
2. Suggest that students make a diagram to show possible escape plans. Remind students that they are in the realm of fantasy, so they can include imaginative and even impossible elements in their plan.
3. Encourage students to use cooking terms such as *blend, mix, stir,* and *pour* in their recipe. Guide them to use some of the humorous ingredients that Mr. Armitage suggests.

4. Remind students to follow the conventions of dialogue, including quotation marks and tags such as "he said" and "she replied."

 **The Writer's Craft**

Creating Dialogue, pp. 320–322

LITERARY LINKS

You listed three of your favorite fantasy stories for the Personal Connection on page 415. How would you compare "The Serial Garden" with these other stories?

Multimodal Learning

ALTERNATIVE ACTIVITIES

1. Make a **cereal box** for Brekkfast Brikks, complete with the verse and a part of the model garden on the back.

2. Create a three-dimensional **model garden** based on the description in the story.

3. Compose the **tune** to which Mark might have sung the Brekkfast Brikks rhyme. Perform the song for the class.

4. With a partner, design a **video game** or **board game** in which the object is to help Mr. Johansen find a way back to Princess Sophia. Include setbacks, detours, extra points, and other devices to make the game challenging. Study other video or board games for ideas.

5. Present a **monologue** that shows how Princess Sophia might react when she finds out that Mark and Mr. Johansen have failed to return. If possible, have a classmate videotape your presentation.

THE SERIAL GARDEN **433**

Alternative Activities

1. Have students cover an empty cereal box with white paper to use as the base for their model box.
2. Guide students first to create a scale, such as 1 inch = 1 foot, so their model will be easy to assemble. Encourage them to be creative in their use of materials.
3. Remind students to match the tune to the rhythm of the words. Provide a tape recorder so students can play back their tunes.
4. Help students design their board game with a specific audience in mind, such as students in grades 6 through 8. Also be sure that students include a rule book with their game. Have students check their work by playing the game with some classmates.
5. Encourage students to base their monologue on a close textual reading of the story.

WORDS TO KNOW

EXERCISE A On your paper, write the letter of the word that is an antonym of each boldfaced word.

1. **susceptible:** (a) pleasant, (b) insensitive, (c) friendly

2. **wan:** (a) rosy, (b) unhealthy, (c) gather

3. **tantalizing:** (a) attractive, (b) lucky, (c) disgusting

4. **aggrievedly:** (a) contentedly, (b) quietly, (c) slowly

5. **chaos:** (a) happiness, (b) warmth, (c) order

EXERCISE B Answer the following questions.

1. Is a person who is **foraging** likely to be arguing, relaxing, or moving about quickly?

2. Would a person who has been keeping a **vigil** be most likely to be sleepy, happy, or careless?

3. Are the **convalescing** people in a hospital the doctors, the visitors, or the patients?

4. Would a person be most likely to wear a **gaudy** outfit to a funeral, a costume party, or a job interview?

5. On a lonely beach, which might you find in **incalculable** numbers—seagulls, swimmers, or grains of sand?

JOAN AIKEN

Joan Aiken, daughter of the American poet Conrad Aiken, was born in Rye, England, and grew up as a British citizen. Her parents divorced when she was 4, and her mother taught her at home until Aiken turned 12.

Since there were no children her age in the neighborhood, Aiken spent much of her time reading and making up stories to amuse herself and her younger stepbrother. She says that she knew at an early age that she wanted to become a writer, having filled notebooks with her poems and stories from the time she was five.

When Aiken's own children were young, their father died, and Aiken had to work to support her family. She took a job as a story editor for a maga-

1924–

zine, supplementing her income by publishing her short stories. In 1960, she published her first novel, *The Kingdom and the Cave*. She is perhaps best known for her series of novels set in 19th-century England, beginning with *The Wolves of Willoughby Chase*.

Aiken explains her writing habits this way: "Generally, I'll start rather slowly, with a lot of revising and going back and crossing out words. As I get warmed up, it may come out faster and faster." About her story ideas she says, "Often I just get ideas from things I hear or read. I keep a little notebook."

OTHER WORKS *Go Saddle the Sea, Dido and Pa, Up the Chimney Down and Other Stories*

Extended Reading

434   UNIT FOUR   PART 1: THE WILL TO WIN

WHAT DO YOU THINK?

Reflecting on Theme

Have students look back at the "Will to Win" manual they prepared before they began reading the selections in this part of Unit Four. Ask them to consider what they learned about meeting challenges from reading "The Serial Garden." Have students add to their manuals any new tips or pieces of advice that they now have.

PREVIEWING

NONFICTION

The Eternal Frontier

Louis L'Amour (lōō′ē lə-mŏŏr′)

Setting a Purpose

Activating Prior Knowledge
PERSONAL CONNECTION

What do you know about the exploration of outer space? What achievements in this field impress you the most? What progress might occur in your own lifetime? In your notebook, list some of your ideas about space exploration. Share your list with a partner.

SCIENCE CONNECTION Building Background

In the 1920s, the American rocket scientist Dr. Robert Goddard asserted, "It is difficult to say what is impossible, for the dream of yesterday is the hope of today and the reality of tomorrow." Nowhere is this idea more evident than in the field of space exploration. For centuries, people dreamed of leaving the earth and exploring the moon. This dream became reality on July 20, 1969, when Neil Armstrong stepped from the *Apollo 11* lunar module and walked on the moon. Other achievements followed, shedding more and more light on the mysteries of the universe. For example, the Voyager space probes, launched in 1977, sent back close-up pictures of the planets Jupiter, Saturn, Uranus, and Neptune. In 1987–1988, two Soviet cosmonauts set a record by orbiting the earth for 366 days.

WRITING CONNECTION

In "The Eternal Frontier," Louis L'Amour, the author of many novels set in the Old West, shares his views about space exploration. Select one of the ideas about space exploration that you listed for the Personal Connection. Write about that idea in your notebook. Then, as you read this essay, consider the views that L'Amour presents.

Photo of Edwin E. "Buzz" Aldrin, Jr., walking on the moon, July 20, 1969. NASA.

LASERLINKS
• *SCIENCE CONNECTION*   **435**

In this essay, Louis L'Amour discusses people's need to challenge the frontier, which he describes as "the line that separates the known from the unknown." He cites past examples of people crossing frontiers. These examples include immigrants sailing to new lands, pioneers moving westward, and amazing scientific and technological advances of the 20th century. L'Amour states that today's frontier is outer space and predicts that humans will soon be exploring areas outside our solar system.

Thematic Link: *The Will to Win* Humans have the will to conquer the frontier of the future: space.

CUSTOMIZING FOR
Students Acquiring English

- Use **ACCESS FOR STUDENTS ACQUIRING ENGLISH,** *Reading and Writing Support.*

- In this selection, the author compares future space exploration with past migrations to the United States and offers possible reasons for both types of journeys. You may want to invite students acquiring English to talk or write about their families' reasons for coming to the United States.

Ⓘ Explain that the prefix *trans-* means "across." Have students infer the meaning of *transcontinental* and *transoceanic flight.*

STRATEGIC READING FOR
Less-Proficient Readers

Set a Purpose Ask students how TV programs, such as *Star Trek,* or movies, such as *The Right Stuff* and *Apollo 13,* portray space exploration. Have students read to discover L'Amour's attitude toward space exploration.

THE ETERNAL FRONTIER
by Louis L'Amour

The question I am most often asked is, "Where is the frontier now?"

The answer should be obvious. Our frontier lies in outer space.

The moon, the asteroids, the planets, these are mere stepping stones, where we will test ourselves, learn needful lessons, and grow in knowledge before we attempt those frontiers beyond our solar system. Outer space is a frontier without end, the eternal frontier, an everlasting challenge to explorers not alone of other planets and other solar systems but also of the mind of man.

All that has gone before was preliminary. We have been preparing ourselves mentally for what lies ahead. Many problems remain, but if we can avoid a <u>devastating</u> war we shall move with a rapidity scarcely to be believed. In the past seventy years we have developed the automobile, radio, television, transcontinental and transoceanic flight, and the electrification of the country, among a <u>multitude</u> of other such developments. In 1900 there were 144

Ⓘ

miles of surfaced road in the United States. Now there are over 3,000,000. Paved roads and the development of the automobile have gone hand in hand, the automobile being civilized man's <u>antidote</u> to overpopulation.

What is needed now is leaders with perspective; we need leadership on a thousand fronts, but they must be men and women who can take the long view and help to shape the outlines of our future. There will always be the nay-sayers,[1] those who cling to our lovely green planet as a baby clings to its mother, but there will be others like those who have taken us this far along the path to a limitless future.

We are a people born to the frontier. It has been a part of our thinking, waking, and sleeping since men first landed on this continent. The frontier is the line that separates the known from the unknown wherever it may be, and we have a driving need to see what lies beyond. It

---

1. **nay-sayers:** people who disagree or have negative attitudes.

WORDS
TO
KNOW

devastating (dĕv′ə-stā′tǐng) *adj.* extremely destructive **devastate** *v.*
multitude (mŭl′tǐ-tōōd′) *n.* a very great number
antidote (ăn′tǐ-dōt′) *n.* something that prevents the evil effects of something else; remedy

436

WORDS TO KNOW

antidote (ăn′tǐ-dōt′) *n.* something that prevents the evil effects of something else; remedy (p. 436)

devastating (dĕv′ə-stā′tǐng) *adj.* extremely destructive **devastate** *v.* (p. 436)

impetus (ǐm′pǐ-təs) *n.* a force that produces motion or action; impulse (p. 438)

incorporate (ǐn-kôr′pə-rāt′) *v.* to make part of another thing; merge (p. 438)

multitude (mŭl′tǐ-tōōd′) *n.* a very great number (p. 436)

 B

Challenge students to evaluate L'Amour's comparisons to space exploration. *(Possible response: Comparisons to immigration, Western pioneering, and advances in technology are valid, because they all involve enormous personal risks and challenges for the sake of exploring new frontiers.)*

(2) To clarify this sentence, lead students to understand that *this* refers to *a driving need to see what lies beyond,* from the previous sentence.

Literary Concept: ESSAY

(A) Invite volunteers to explain how they know that this selection is an essay. *(Possible responses: It is a nonfiction work that centers on a single subject.)*

Active Reading: EVALUATE

(B) Ask students if they think L'Amour admires people like pioneers and immigrants who go beyond barriers. If necessary, guide students by using this model:

Think-Aloud Model *It seems from what he says that these people had no choice, because they were born with the desire and bravery to welcome challenges. Yet phrases such as "impassable forests" suggest how difficult it is to take risks. From this I'd conclude he admires people who go beyond barriers.*

was this that brought people to America, no matter what excuses they may have given themselves or others.

Freedom of religion, some said, and the need for land, a better future for their children, the lust for gold, or the desire to escape class restrictions—all these reasons were given. The fact remains that many, suffering from the same needs and restrictions, did not come.

Why then did some cross the ocean to America and not others? Of course, all who felt that urge did not come to America; some went to India, Africa, Australia, New Zealand, or elsewhere. Those who did come to America began almost at once to push inland, challenging the unknown, daring to go beyond the thin line that divides the known and the unknown. Many had, after landing from the old country, developed good farms or successful businesses; they had become people of standing in their communities. Why then did they move on, leaving all behind?

I believe it to be something buried in their genes, some inherited trait,[2] perhaps something essential to the survival of the species.

They went to the edge of the mountains; then they crossed the mountains and found their way through impassable forests to the Mississippi. After that the Great Plains, the Rocky Mountains, and on to Oregon and California. They trapped fur, traded with Indians, hunted buffalo, ranched with cattle or sheep, built towns, and farmed. Yet the genes lay buried within them, and after a few months, a few years, they moved on.

Each science has its own frontiers, and the future of our nation and the world lies in research and development, in probing what lies beyond.

A few years ago we moved into outer space. We landed men on the moon; we sent a vehicle beyond the limits of the solar system, a vehicle still moving farther and farther into that limit-

---

2. **something buried . . . inherited trait:** a characteristic passed on from ancestors, such as eye color or height.

Mini-Lesson **Reading Skills/Strategies**

MAKING INFERENCES Explain to students that good readers often make inferences as they gather information from a selection. That is, they draw a conclusion or make a guess based on the evidence that the author presents or suggests.

Application Have students review L'Amour's essay. Ask them to jot down in their reading logs several inferences they can make about his attitude toward space exploration. For each inference, have them list the evidence that supports it. Then have students write a brief paragraph to explain the author's views.

Reteaching/Reinforcement
• *Unit Four Resource Book,* p. 24

less distance. If our world were to die tomorrow, that tiny vehicle would go on and on forever, carrying its mighty message to the stars. Out there, someone, sometime, would know that once we existed, that we had the vision and we made the effort. Mankind is not bound by its atmospheric envelope or by its gravitational field, nor is the mind of man bound by any limits at all.

One might ask—why outer space, when so much remains to be done here? If that had been the spirit of man we would still be hunters and food gatherers, growling over the bones of carrion[3] in a cave somewhere. It is our destiny to move out, to accept the challenge, to dare the unknown. It is our destiny to achieve.

Yet we must not forget that along the way to outer space whole industries are springing into being that did not exist before. The computer age has arisen in part from the space effort, which gave great impetus to the development of computing devices. Transistors, chips, integrated circuits, Teflon, new medicines, new ways of treating diseases, new ways of performing operations, all these and a multitude of other developments that enable man to live and to live better are linked to the space effort. Most of these developments have been so incorporated into our day-to-day life that they are taken for granted, their origin not considered.

If we are content to live in the past, we have no future. And today is the past. ❖ **E**

---

3. **carrion** (kăr′ē-ən): the flesh of dead animals.

| WORDS TO KNOW | **impetus** (ĭm′pĭ-təs) *n.* a force that produces motion or action; impulse |
| | **incorporate** (ĭn-kôr′pə-rāt′) *v.* to make part of another thing; merge |

438

Assessment ✓ **Option**

INFORMAL ASSESSMENT Ask students to distinguish between the main idea and the supporting details in the essay by summarizing what they read, as follows:

1. List the important points made by the author.
2. For each point listed, write down at least two supporting details.
3. Using your list of important points and supporting details, write a summary of the main idea.

Rubric

3 Full Accomplishment Students follow the directions carefully and distinguish between the main idea and supporting details.

2 Substantial Accomplishment Students summarize the essay but may include extraneous details.

1 Little or Partial Accomplishment Students cannot summarize the essay or distinguish between main ideas and supporting details.

RESPONDING OPTIONS

FROM PERSONAL RESPONSE TO CRITICAL ANALYSIS

REFLECT
1. If you could talk to Louis L'Amour, what would you say to him after reading his essay? Get together with a partner, pretend that your partner is the author, and share your response.

RETHINK
Close Textual Reading
2. At the end of the essay, L'Amour asserts, "If we are content to live in the past, we have no future. And today is the past." In your own words, explain what you think he means.

3. How would you compare your ideas about space exploration with the views that L'Amour presents in his essay? Refer to the ideas you listed for the Personal Connection on page 435.

4. L'Amour mentions several achievements of the 20th century. Which achievement do you consider the most important? Give reasons for your choice.

RELATE
Thematic Link
5. What do you think might be the greatest benefit of space exploration to human beings? Support your opinion with reasons.

LITERARY CONCEPTS

The **title** of a work may suggest its theme, or main message. Think about L'Amour's main message and the title of his essay. Why do you think he called the essay "The Eternal Frontier"?

Multimodal Learning
ANOTHER PATHWAY
Cooperative Learning

With a small group of classmates, brainstorm similarities and differences between modern space explorers and the early settlers and pioneers. Share your ideas with other groups, then hold a class vote on whether L'Amour's comparison is appropriate.

QUICKWRITES

1. If you could explore a new frontier, which one would it be? Write a **personal response,** describing the frontier and explaining your reasons for wanting to explore it.

2. Write a **letter** to a representative in Congress, supporting or opposing a proposal to raise taxes to obtain more funds for space exploration.

3. Write a **profile** of the type of person who would succeed as a pioneer in the first moon colony.

4. At the beginning of the essay, L'Amour poses the question "Where is the frontier now?" Write a **draft** of an essay that provides an answer different from L'Amour's.

📁 *PORTFOLIO Save your writing. You may want to use it later as a springboard to a piece for your portfolio.*

THE ETERNAL FRONTIER **439**

From Personal Response to Critical Analysis

1. Responses will vary.
2. Possible response: Technology is advancing so rapidly that what seems current is already out of date. We must move ahead, or we will not survive.
3. Possible response: L'Amour and I both recognize the importance of space exploration.
4. Possible response: Medical advances are the most important, because they save lives or alleviate suffering.
5. Possible responses: Finding new places for people to live, because the earth is getting overcrowded; discovering new species, because they may be able to teach us needed skills.

Another Pathway

Cooperative Learning To ensure successful group work, have each group select a turn-taking monitor to make sure everyone takes turns, an explainer of ideas to share opinions, and a summarizer to restate the group's major conclusions. Groups may wish to discuss explorers and pioneers separately before comparing and contrasting them.

Rubric

3 Full Accomplishment Students fully explore similarities and differences between modern space explorers and early pioneers.

2 Substantial Accomplishment Students identify some similarities and differences between space explorers and early pioneers.

1 Little or Partial Accomplishment Students cannot compare and contrast space explorers and early pioneers.

Literary Concepts

Suggest that students look at the topic sentence in each paragraph to find L'Amour's main idea. *(Possible response: L'Amour's message concerns the importance of space exploration. The title suggests that space, unlike our earthly frontiers, offers limitless possibilities for exploration. Space and opportunities for its exploration are eternal because they are never-ending, or infinite.)*

QuickWrites

1. Remind students to use the first-person point of view in their personal response. Guide them to include details and examples to support their reasons for wanting to explore the new frontier.
2. Remind students that their letters should be persuasive and that they should support their viewpoints with details and facts.
3. Students should include psychological and physical traits in their profile.
4. Encourage students to write their drafts on a computer to make later revisions easier.

 The Writer's Craft

Personal Voice, pp. 312–313

Literary Links

Have students compare the social and political frontiers that Eleanor Roosevelt explored with the frontiers that Louis L'Amour discusses in this essay. *(Possible response: The frontiers, although different in nature, all challenge the courage and persistence of the explorers.)*

Across the Curriculum

Science *Cooperative Learning* Have each group member independently research a specific subtopic. Then have group members work together to compile their findings and prepare their report.

ADDITIONAL SUGGESTIONS

Science *Blast Off!* Have students find out what it takes to become an astronaut. Invite them to do library research to find out about the U.S. space program. Have them present their findings in an oral report.

Words to Know

Exercise A
1. e
2. d
3. b
4. a
5. c

Exercise B
Possible response: Today's *multitude* of *devastating* diseases calls for an *antidote;* fortunately, the *impetus* already exists to *incorporate* new technology with traditional cures.

Reteaching/Reinforcement
• *Unit Four Resource Book,* p. 26

LOUIS L'AMOUR

To many critics, L'Amour's style was the key to his success. These critics praised L'Amour's ability to write fast-paced action novels rich in authentic descriptions of the setting, especially the Old West.

Multimodal Learning

ALTERNATIVE ACTIVITIES

1. Create a **multimedia presentation** about one or more "famous firsts"—either in space or on another frontier, such as medicine or communications. If possible, include pictures, slides, and recordings in your presentation. If you have access to a computer encyclopedia, you may want to use it as a starting point for gathering information.

2. Create **a time line** that shows important milestones in space exploration, such as the launching of the first Sputnik, the first lunar landing, and the launching of the first interplanetary probe.

ACROSS THE CURRICULUM

Science *Cooperative Learning* Get together with a large group of classmates to research scientists' predictions of what everyday life will be like 25 or 50 years from now. Different members of the group should focus on the following topics: information, transportation, communication, industry, health and medicine, education, leisure, and space exploration and colonization. Hold a panel discussion to share the group's findings with the rest of the class.

LOUIS L'AMOUR

When Louis L'Amour left Jamestown, North Dakota, at the age of 15, few would have predicted that he would become one of the most popular writers of the 20th century. L'Amour wandered about, working as a hay shocker, a longshoreman, a lumberjack, a fruit picker, a miner, an elephant handler, an amateur archaeologist, and a professional boxer. During his travels he got to know people who told him stories about the frontier. A descendant of pioneers, L'Amour said, "I don't have to

1908–1988

imagine what happened in the old West—I know what happened."

L'Amour drew on his experiences to make his stories of the frontier seem true to life. Over the years, he wrote 86 novels and more than 400 short stories. L'Amour received two of the country's highest honors, a Congressional National Gold Medal and the Presidential Medal of Freedom.

OTHER WORKS *How the West Was Won*

Extended Reading

WORDS TO KNOW

EXERCISE A For each phrase in the first column, write the letter of the rhyming phrase in the second column that matches its meaning.

1. add a new quality
2. a guaranteed antidote
3. a multitude of fish
4. an impetus to add salt
5. pausing before putting out a forest fire

a. a reason to season
b. masses of basses
c. devastating hesitating
d. a sure cure
e. incorporate a trait

EXERCISE B Write a sentence, using as many of the vocabulary words as possible. Describing a humorous or unlikely situation is fine, as long as the words are used accurately.

Alternative Activities

1. Suggest that students carefully plan and rehearse their presentation to make sure that all the media are smoothly integrated. Students may be able to locate historical news broadcasts or political speeches to include in their presentations.

2. Students can use almanacs and encyclopedias to find the key events in the history of space exploration. Encourage students to include drawings or other graphics to make their time line visually interesting and easy to read.

Hockey

by Scott Blaine

The ice is smooth, smooth, smooth.
The air bites to the center
Of warmth and flesh, and I whirl.
It begins in a game . . .
5 The puck swims, skims, veers,[1]
Goes leading my vision
Beyond the chasing reach of my stick.

The air is sharp, steel-sharp.
I suck needles of breathing,
10 And feel the players converge.[2]
It grows to a science . . .
We clot, break, drive,
Electrons in motion
In the magnetic pull of the puck.

15 The play is fast, fierce, tense.
Sticks click and snap like teeth
Of wolves on the scent of a prey.
It ends in the kill . . .
I am one of the pack in a mad,
20 Taut[3] leap of desperation
In the wild, slashing drive for the goal.

---

1. **veers:** changes direction.
2. **converge:** come together.
3. **taut:** strained; tense.

HOCKEY **441**

Objectives

- To promote independent active reading
- To practice and apply skills learned in previous selections
- To provide an opportunity to assess students' performance through an alternative assessment instrument

Reading Pathways

- Invite students to read the poems independently and take notes about them in their dialogue journals.
- Have students choose partners and do a paired reading..
- Encourage small groups of students to do a choral reading, choosing lines from the poems for each individual to read.
- Evaluate how well students can read, interpret, discuss, and write about the selection on their own by using the Integrated Assessment for Unit Four, located in the Alternative Assessment booklet. Administer the assessment at the end of the unit after students have read all the selections and completed all the writing that was assigned.

Art Note

Hockey Players by Calvin Nicholls

Reading the Art *How does this sculpture give you a sense of motion? Do you think it portrays hockey realistically? Why or why not?*

PRINT AND MEDIA RESOURCES

UNIT FOUR RESOURCE BOOK
Strategic Reading: Literature, p. 29

FORMAL ASSESSMENT
Selection Test, p. 85
Part Test, pp. 87–88
Test Generator

ALTERNATIVE ASSESSMENT
Unit Four Integrated
  Assessment, pp. 19–24

AUDIO LIBRARY
See Reference Card

The Women's 400 Meters

by Lillian Morrison

Skittish,[1]
they flex knees, drum heels and
shiver at the starting line

waiting the gun
5 to pour them over the stretch
like a breaking wave.

Bang! they're off
careening[2] down the lanes,
each chased by her own bright tiger.

---

1. **Skittish:** restlessly active; nervous.
2. **careening:** lurching from side to side while m[...]
rapidly.

LILLIAN MORRISON

Lillian Morrison has made a career of writing books for young people. Born in New Jersey, she graduated from Columbia University with a degree in library science. Her love of sports is so great that she wrote an entire collection of poems about sports, called *Sprints and Distances*. As Morrison says, "I am drawn to athletes, dancers, drummers, jazz musicians, who . . . symbolize for us something joyous, ordered, and possible in life."

1917–

OTHER WORKS *The Sidewalk Racer and Other Poems of Sports and Motion, Overheard in a Bubble Chamber and Other Science Poems*

Extended Reading

74th Street

by Myra Cohn Livingston

Hey, this little kid gets roller skates.
She puts them on.
She stands up and almost
flops over backwards.
5 She sticks out a foot like
she's going somewhere and
falls down and
smacks her hand. She
grabs hold of a step to get up and
10 sticks out the other foot and
slides about six inches and
falls and
skins her knee.

And then, you know what?

15 She brushes off the dirt and the
blood and puts some
spit on it and then
sticks out the other foot

again.

MYRA COHN LIVINGSTON

Myra Cohn Livingston has devoted most of her life to writing poetry and to helping young people learn to write. Livingston says she had an "ideal, happy childhood" while growing up in Omaha, Nebraska. She lived on a block with many children, with whom she would "make mud pies, put on plays, swing into the apple tree, [and] play games each night in the empty lot after supper."

1926–

Livingston has kept a journal since she was ten years old. Describing it, she says, "All of the feelings and observations I have go into that journal. Some eventually come out as poems, others are snatches of conversations or ideas that I may use someday."

OTHER WORKS *O Sliver of Liver, Whispers and Other Poems, I'm Hiding* Extended Reading

74TH STREET **443**

Individual Activity
WRITING AN ARTICLE

Invite students to read the five poems and then work independently to write a newspaper article about one or more of the characters whose feats are described in the poems. The article can be a news story describing the events in the poem, an editorial commenting on those events, or an interview with a character, for example.

Teacher's Role Explain to the class that the news stories should follow the *5W's and 1H* format by answering *who, what, when, where, why,* and *how.* The story should open with a "lead" sentence or two that contains the 5W's and 1H. Then details should be arranged from most to least important. Explain that editorials, in contrast, appeal to reason and emotion to change someone's mind about an issue. An interview presents questions and answers to explore someone's experiences. The interview should be written in dialogue form. Have students combine their articles, editorials, and interviews into a class newspaper.

Rubric

3 Full Accomplishment The newspaper article is thorough and presents an interesting slant on one or more of the poems.

2 Substantial Accomplishment The article probes the poem and the issues it raises but it may lack sufficient details and examples.

1 Little or Partial Accomplishment The article does not focus on the poem and its themes. The writing has serious weaknesses in both form and content.

Cooperative Learning
CREATIVE DRAMA

These poems describe or suggest some exciting efforts to meet challenges. Invite groups of three students to select an exciting effort described or suggested in one of the poems, flesh it out in script form, and perform it for the class. For example, after reading "Hockey," students might create a dialogue between three of the players after a goal is scored. After reading "To Satch," a group might create a scene in which Satch shares his triumph with God.

Teacher's Role Guide students to reread the poems to find details they can use as they write their scripts. Remind students to include stage directions in their scripts as well. In each group, appoint a turn-taking monitor to make sure that group members share responsibilities and a recorder to write the script. Allow sufficient rehearsal time and then have each group present its skit to the class. You may wish to videotape the skits so the actors can watch their performance later.

Rubric

3 Full Accomplishment The group writes and performs a skit that reflects the poem they select.

2 Substantial Accomplishment The group writes and performs a skit, but some details are missing or incorrect.

1 Little or Partial Accomplishment The group writes a script that does not reflect the content or tone of the poem selected.

Illustration by Sally Wern Comport. Copyright © 1990 Howard, Merrell & Partners Advertising, Raleigh, North Carolina.

I'll Walk The Tightrope
by Margaret Danner

I'll walk the tightrope that's been stretched for me,
and though a wrinkled forehead, perplexed[1] why,
will accompany me, I'll delicately
step along. For if I stop to sigh
5 at the earth-propped stride
of others, I will fall. I must balance high
without a parasol to tide
a faltering step, without a net below,
without a balance stick to guide.

---

1. **perplexed:** puzzled.

MARGARET DANNER

Margaret Danner (1915–1984) began writing poetry in junior high school, winning first prize in a poetry competition while in the eighth grade. After college she became the first African-American assistant editor of *Poetry,* a magazine that publishes the work of new poets. One of the many awards she received for her poetry enabled her to travel to Africa. She said she was particularly interested in studying African art because "man reveals a sensitivity through his creative work that is a clue to his present-day reactions to problems and pleasures."

MARGARET DANNER

Danner believes that "a writer should write what he feels, and yet I believe we should help each other. . . . Because of the predicament that the black man is in, and faces, those of us who are black should unite to extricate ourselves and each other."

To Satch

by Samuel Allen

Sometimes I feel like I will never stop
Just go on forever
Till one fine mornin'
I'm gonna reach up and grab me
5   a handfulla stars
Throw out my long lean leg
And whip three hot strikes burnin'
    down the heavens
And look over at God and say
10 *How about that!*

SAMUEL ALLEN

Samuel Allen is (1917–) both a distinguished poet and a lawyer—after graduating from Fisk University, he received a degree from Harvard Law School. Most of his poems are rooted in the African-American culture and folk heritage. Many celebrate African-American historical figures, such as Satchel Paige, and depict the painful racial discrimination they faced. Allen once said that "to enter into another culture is to risk misunderstanding. The danger is lessened, however, if we are introduced through the creative arts."

TO SATCH   **445**

SAMUEL ALLEN

Allen is also a scholar, reviewer, translator, editor, and lecturer on African-American and African literature. His statement in *The Forerunners: Black Poets in America* summarizes his literary credo: "Black poets are continuing with an increasingly sharpened sense of direction both to define and to vivify the black experience."

Class Discussion
SHARING IDEAS

Teacher's Role Use the following questions to spark a whole-class discussion of each of the poems. Then invite students to make comparisons and contrasts among the five poems.

1. How do you think the narrator in "Hockey" feels about the sport? *(Possible response: The narrator loves the sport because he or she finds it "fast, fierce, tense.")*
2. What feeling about hockey did you get from the image of "wolves on the scent of a prey"? *(Possible response: Hockey can be a brutal, killing sport.)*
3. How would you explain the "bright tiger" that chases each of the runners in "The Women's 400 Meters"? *(Possible response: The tiger could be the will to win or the fear of defeat that motivates each runner, or the runner's shadow.)*
4. Why do you think the little kid in "74th Street" gets back on her skates? *(Possible responses: She welcomes the challenge; she doesn't want to admit defeat.)*
5. Do you think the speaker in "74th Street" admires the little kid? Why or why not? *(Possible response: Yes, because of her determination and grit)*
6. What could the tightrope in "I'll Walk the Tightrope" symbolize? *(Possible responses: life itself; specific challenges with a great risk of failure)*
7. Why do you think Satch in "To Satch" feels that he "will never stop"? *(Possible responses: He enjoys playing baseball so much that he will play it for all eternity; his skill and fame earn him immortality.)*
8. Which of these poems did you like best? Explain the reasons for your reaction. *(Possible response: I liked "74th Street," because the skater has spunk.)*

OVERVIEW

In the Guided Assignment for this section, students will extend a story by writing a scene that takes place either before the story begins or after it ends. By extending a story, students learn how to present events in a logical order and add details to make writing realistic. As preparation for this assignment, The Writer's Style will help students write interesting and believable dialogue. In Reading the World, students will interpret a scene based on clues they have identified.

--- **Objectives** ---

- To understand how dialogue works and what it can reveal
- To create effective writing by adding dialogue
- To write an extension of a story
- To infer what is taking place in a real-world situation

--- **Skills** ---

LITERATURE
- Analyzing dialogue

WRITING AND LANGUAGE
- Using speaker's tags
- Creating paragraphs

GRAMMAR AND USAGE
- Capitalizing dialogue

MEDIA LITERACY
- Interpreting a scene

SPEAKING, LISTENING, AND VIEWING
- Role-playing
- Peer discussion
- Partnered analysis

CRITICAL THINKING
- Examining context

Teaching Strategy: MODELING

In the following model, dialogue is used to move the story along. Students will learn how to use this technique to help them create and develop their own stories.

Ⓐ **Thomas** Possible responses: The boys are going to fight each other in the boxing ring. The problem is that they are close friends. Each wants to win, but neither wants to hurt the other. The dialogue shows this through their agreement to pretend the other is a stranger and their admission that each of them ultimately wants to win.

WRITING ABOUT LITERATURE

EXTENDING THE STORY

You're caught up in a story—the "Amigo Brothers." Tony and Felix are pounding through the championship round. The story ends. But who won? And what about Mark? Does he ever find more Brekkfast Brikks? Stories, and real-life situations as well, can leave you wondering, "Then what happened?" Instead of just wondering, continue the story yourself. In the following pages you will

- study what dialogue adds to a story
- write a new beginning or ending to a story you've read
- explore what could be going on in a real-life situation

The Writer's Style: Writing Dialogue Writers use dialogue, the conversations of characters or actual people, to enliven their characters and to move the story along.

Read the Literature

Notice how the dialogue puts you into Felix and Tony's world. What do you learn as you read what they say?

Literature Model

Ⓐ **Dialogue That Moves the Story Along**
What's happening in the boys' lives? What is their relationship? What does each of them want? How does the dialogue reveal this information?

> Felix tapped Antonio gently on the shoulder. "I don't mean to sound like I'm bragging, bro. But I wanna win, fair and square."
>
> Antonio nodded quietly. "Yeah. We both know that in the ring the better man wins. Friend or no friend, brother or no . . ."
>
> Felix finished it for him. "Brother. Tony, let's promise something right here. Okay?"
>
> "If it's fair, *hermano*, I'm for it." Antonio admired the courage of a tugboat pulling a barge five times its welterweight size.
>
> "It's fair, Tony. When we get into the ring, it's gotta be like we never met. We gotta be like two heavy strangers that want the same thing, and only one can have it. You understand don'tcha?"
>
> Piri Thomas
> from "Amigo Brothers"

PRINT AND MEDIA RESOURCES

UNIT FOUR RESOURCE BOOK
Writer's Style, p. 33
Prewriting, p. 34
Elaboration, p. 35
Peer Response Guide, pp. 36–37
Revising and Proofreading, p. 38
Student Model, p. 39
Rubric, p.40

GRAMMAR MINI-LESSONS
Transparencies, pp. 33–34
Copymasters, pp. 35, and 42

WRITING MINI-LESSONS
Transparencies, pp. 29, and 48

ACCESS FOR STUDENTS ACQUIRING ENGLISH
Reading and Writing Support

FORMAL ASSESSMENT
Guidelines for Writing Assessment

WRITING COACH

Connect to Life

The interviews you read in magazines and newspapers actually start out as a dialogue between the writer and the subject. When you read an interview you sometimes learn something about the subject's character.

Interview

Lauren. What are you most proud of in your career?

Ellerbee. Three achievements: *NBC News Overnight; Our World* on ABC; and the news shows I do now, because I think television has an obligation to give back something useful and worthwhile to kids. I did the special with Magic Johnson on AIDS because I feel kids have a right to information about AIDS, and they have a right to it sooner rather than later.

Lauren Persons and Seth Guiñals
from "Meet . . . Linda Ellerbee"
National Geographic World

Dialogue That Reveals Character
What does the dialogue tell you about Ms. Ellerbee? What is she like?

Try Your Hand: Writing Dialogue

1. Put Words in His Mouth Rewrite the following sentence, adding dialogue to make it tell more about Ajay.

Ajay began to dance, shouting for us to join him.

2. Move the Story Along In a small group, take turns adding dialogue to the scene below. If you wish, role-play the scene first and then write the dialogue.

You and a few friends go to a concert. You're waiting outside the theater when one of the stars comes walking along the street. To your surprise, the star greets you and stops to talk. What do you talk about?

3. Recreate a Situation Have you ever wished you could go back to a situation and say something that you didn't think of at the time? Write new dialogue for yourself and the others involved in the situation.

SkillBuilder

WRITER'S CRAFT

Using Speaker's Tags
When writing dialogue, you can use **speaker's tags** such as *Tony said* or *Felix asked* to identify who is speaking. But the words *said* and *asked* are not very descriptive. You can help the reader know how dialogue sounds by using words like *whispered, shouted, pleaded,* and *mumbled* in your speaker's tags.

When it's clear who is speaking, you don't need to use speaker's tags. For example,

"Tony, try to understand what I'm saying," Felix pleaded.
"I'm tryin', Felix. But it's not easy."

APPLYING WHAT YOU'VE LEARNED
Read the dialogue below. Then rewrite it, adding speaker's tags to show who is speaking. Remember, you don't always need to use a speaker's tag when it is clear who is speaking.

"Tony, can we talk?"
"Sure, Felix. What is it?"
"You're going to hate me."
"What are you talking about? You know I'll never hate you."
"Well, about the fight. It wasn't exactly fair."
"What do you mean?"
"My coach rigged it. I knew, Tony, but I wanted to win so bad. I'm so sorry."

WRITING ABOUT LITERATURE **447**

CUSTOMIZING FOR
Less-Proficient Writers

B Some students may be unaware of exactly how an interview works and is written. Guide them to see that in the interview below, Lauren Persons is one of two interviewers who have interviewed the television personality Linda Ellerbee. Instruct students that the two interviewers met and talked with Ellerbee, probably writing down or tape-recording her answers to their questions. Later, they edited and revised what they had written to make the interview clear and direct.

Teaching Strategy: MODELING

C The dialogue tells you that Ellerbee has many television achievements and is proud of her work. She seems to enjoy doing important things for young people and giving something back to the community.

**Teaching Strategy:
USING THE SKILLBUILDER**

D To help students understand how to use dialogue correctly in their writing, introduce the SkillBuilder on Using Speaker's Tags at this time. It teaches students how to add appropriate tags to a dialogue to show who is speaking.

Try Your Hand

1. Responses will vary. Here is a sample: Ajay began to dance, shouting, "Come on, you guys. Join me. It's fun!"
2. Responses will vary. Students can imagine themselves there, waiting in line. Prompt them by asking what they might be talking about before the star comes along. Ask what the star would say and who would reply first.
3. Responses will vary. Encourage students to think of a situation in which they wished they had the right words, such as a clever response to someone they are arguing with or a correct reply to a difficult or awkward question.

SkillBuilder

WRITER'S CRAFT

USING SPEAKER'S TAGS Advise students to think about what is happening in the story and the way a speaker is likely to be talking. Students should consider adding adverbs or adverbial phrases to describe the way something is said—for instance: *Tony said quietly* or *Tony said in a quiet voice.*

Application Possible response:

"Tony, can we talk?" Felix asked nervously.

"Sure, Felix. What is it?"

"You're going to hate me."

"What are you talking about?" inquired Tony. "You know I'll never hate you."

Felix hesitated, "Well, about the fight. It wasn't exactly fair."

"What do you mean?" Tony asked in a puzzled voice.

"My coach rigged it. I knew, Tony, but I wanted to win so bad. I'm so sorry."

Reteaching/Reinforcement *Writing Mini-Lessons* transparencies, p. 48

The Writer's Craft
Dialogue in Fiction, pp. 320–321

Speaking and Listening:
ROLE-PLAY

E Guide students to imagine themselves in the characters' situation. Ask them to think how their character may be feeling at this point in the story before they continue with their dialogue.

Critical Thinking: SPECULATING

F Students can speculate about what may happen or what may have happened before the story started. Point to dialogue in the story that indicates how a particular character speaks. Students can then choose an appropriate adverb such as *nervously, slowly, intelligently,* and so on. Choosing such an adverb can help students imagine themselves as that character in a particular situation.

WRITING ABOUT LITERATURE

Creative Response

Have you ever finished reading a story and found yourself imagining all sorts of things that could happen next? When your mind races with possibilities, it's time for you to create a new adventure for the characters you just read about. In the process, you'll satisfy your curiosity and learn more about the story as well.

GUIDED ASSIGNMENT

Extend the Story On the next few pages, you'll extend one of the stories you read in Unit Four. When you extend a story, you create a set of events that take place before the original story begins or after it ends.

❶ Prewrite and Explore

Which story do you want to continue? Once you've decided, reread the story and answer the questions below. Then complete one or both of the activities at the right.

- How did the story make you feel?
- What do you know about the characters and events?
- What questions remain unanswered?

Student's Sketch

Felix and Tony are on a morning run by the East River.

I ain't gonna box no more, man.

Say what!

Serious bro, I just don't care.

You're loco, man. Crazy. You just need a little rest.

ROLE-PLAY

E With a partner, examine the questions below.

- What might the characters' lives have been like before the story began?
- What might happen after the story ends?

Explore the possibilities by role-playing a conversation that might occur between the characters. You might want to begin by choosing roles and reading dialogue from the story. When you run out of dialogue from the story, try to keep your conversation going and see what happens.

WHAT IF?

F If you let the characters talk, they might say things that move the story in an exciting new direction. Ask a specific question about the story, such as "What if Felix won?" Then plunge into that situation. Try to imagine what the characters might feel, think, say, or do. You can get your creative juices flowing by drawing a sketch like the one at the left.

 A s s e s s m e n t ✓ **O p t i o n**

SELF-ASSESSMENT After students have completed the Role-Play and What If? exercises, they can assess their own character and role. Students should consider the following questions:
- *What is my character feeling?*

- *How does my character talk?*
- *Are both the characters acting the way they act in the story?*
- *How does what they say reveal more about the story or the characters?*

2 Discovery Draft

Now that you have some idea of what's going to happen in your story extension, begin writing and see where the characters lead you. Write freely, making discoveries as you go.

Student's Discovery Draft

> Felix stops running and then he says, "Tony, we need to talk about the fight." Tony knows Felix is upset, so he tells Felix "Hey, we both fought tough, but you won. Fair and square." Then Felix tells Tony that the fight wasn't fair, and that's the problem.

Okay! I can see where I want to go with this idea. I just need to add details and dialogue.

3 Draft and Share

Whether you write in your own style or try to follow the author's way of writing, be sure to include details and dialogue that make the characters and their surroundings match the original story. Before you begin your first draft, ask yourself questions such as the following:

- What kinds of details should I include so that my series of events flows naturally from the original story?
- How can I make my characters' actions believable?

After you finish your draft, consider asking another student to read your writing and give you feedback.

 PEER RESPONSE

- Do the events follow logically?
- Do the characters' actions match their personalities?
- Does the dialogue sound the way people talk?
- What details made my writing seem real to you?
- What might I add to or remove from the story?

SkillBuilder

 WRITER'S CRAFT

Creating Paragraphs

Creating paragraphs in your story extension can help you organize your ideas. Paragraphs will also help readers follow the action and the dialogue. Remember to begin a new paragraph at these times:

- when a different character begins speaking
- when there is a change in the action
- when the scene changes

APPLYING WHAT YOU'VE LEARNED
Revise the passage below. Begin new paragraphs according to the guidelines above.

Efrain was pacing the living room and chewing on his fingernails. He turned to his sister and said nervously, "The boxing match is tomorrow." "That's nice, *niño*," Blanca mumbled. She was staring out the window, lost in her own thoughts. Meanwhile, Carlito was getting psyched up—strutting through his neighborhood as if he'd won the championship already. Getting nervous wasn't his style.

 WRITING HANDBOOK

For more information on paragraphing, see pages 815–816 of the Writing Handbook.

WRITING ABOUT LITERATURE **449**

Writing Skill:
DEVELOPING CHARACTER

G The Discovery Draft provides an opportunity for students to analyze the characters they began to develop in the Prewrite and Explore. Help them decide which character should begin talking and what he or she should say. Suggest that a problem that needs to be solved or a conflict between characters can generate a story.

Writing Skill: ELABORATION

H Encourage students to add details about the setting, the characters' actions, and the way the characters speak. Suggest that they read through the selection to see what details and words the author uses to make the story realistic and to convey information.

SkillBuilder WRITER'S CRAFT

CREATING PARAGRAPHS Remind students to indent the beginnings of all paragraphs. They may be concerned that in a story with a lot of dialogue, there will be many paragraph indents. Tell them that this is expected and necessary. Guide students to see that writers break up their dialogue with action to vary their writing.

Application Answer:

Efrain was pacing the living room and chewing on his fingernails. He turned to his sister and said nervously, "The boxing match is tomorrow."

"That's nice, *niño*," Blanca mumbled. She was staring out her window, lost in her own thoughts.

Meanwhile, Carlito was getting psyched up—strutting through his neighborhood as if he'd won the championship already. Getting nervous wasn't his style.

Additional Suggestions Have students select and revise a piece of their own writing by adding dialogue and strengthening the paragraphing.

Reteaching/Reinforcement *Writing Mini-Lessons* transparencies, p. 29

 **The Writer's Craft**

Paragraphs at Work, p. 82

Critical Thinking: ANALYZING

I As students revise their dialogue, they should use a variety of speaker's tags and make sure their characters are consistent.

Teaching Strategy: MODELING

J Discuss with students how this sample meets the Standards for Evaluation on this page. Show how it has a logical order that develops the realistic dialogue, which is similar to that used in the original story. Encourage them to refer to the Student's Discovery Draft. They will see that the author first shows Felix's hesitation and then shows Tony's confusion by having him ask a question and then insist on what he thinks Felix needs. The writer uses some Spanish and some slang to make the dialogue seem realistic. Details such as Felix's looking through the mist toward Brooklyn make the action seem realistic.

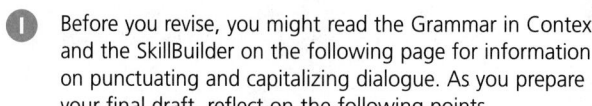

WRITING ABOUT LITERATURE

④ Revise and Edit

I Before you revise, you might read the Grammar in Context and the SkillBuilder on the following page for information on punctuating and capitalizing dialogue. As you prepare your final draft, reflect on the following points.

- Does my dialogue move the story along and reveal the characters' personalities?
- Is the dialogue correctly capitalized and punctuated?
- Have I used paragraphs correctly and effectively?
- Does my ending tie my writing together?

Student's Final Draft

J How did this writer expand on the dialogue from her prewriting?

What details make the characters and events seem real?

> The morning after the fight the two boys met as usual for a run along East River Drive. It was almost as if the fight never happened, except for Felix. He was running slower than usual. He wasn't talking at all. Finally, he just stopped.
>
> Antonio ran on a few steps before he noticed. "Hey, Felix. *Que pasa?* You feel all right?" Antonio asked.
>
> "No. I feel weird," Felix answered and looked through the mist toward Brooklyn. Then he said, "I ain't gonna box no more, man."
>
> "What! You gone crazy or something?" Antonio put his hands on Felix's shoulders and shook him gently. "You just need a rest, *hermano*. You been training too hard."
>
> "No, man, that's not it." Felix stepped away from Tony.

Standards for Evaluation

A creative response that extends a story
- presents events in logical order
- uses natural-sounding dialogue
- has characters whose actions match their personalities
- makes sense when compared with the original story

A s s e s s m e n t ✓ **O p t i o n**

SELF-ASSESSMENT To assess their own writing, students should ask themselves the following questions:
- *Are my characters and their actions realistic?*
- *Can I add details and vivid language to make my writing more interesting?*

- *Will my readers be able to follow the dialogue and understand who is speaking?*
- *Will my readers understand why the characters say what they say?*
- *Is my scene exciting or revealing?*

Grammar in Context

Punctuating Dialogue To write effective dialogue, you need to remember a few special rules of punctuation.

- Put quotation marks only around characters' exact words.
- Place commas and periods inside quotation marks.
- Place question marks or exclamation points inside quotation marks if they belong to the dialogue itself.

The model below shows how one student corrected the punctuation in a draft.

> "What! You gone crazy or something "Antonio put his hands on Felix's shoulder and shook him gently. "You just need a rest, *hermano*. You been training too hard"
>
> "No, that's not it."Felix stepped away from Tony. "An' I ain't crazy"

Try Your Hand: Punctuating Dialogue

On a separate sheet of paper, revise the following sentences to correct the punctuation errors.

1. "How was it staying at your aunt's" Tony asked?
2. "Felix answered, Kinda weird. I didn't know anyone."
3. Tony nodded. "Did any guys give you trouble"?
4. "No way, man" Felix said!
5. "No offense" Felix said "but I want to beat you."
6. "Was I too honest" Felix asked apologetically

SkillBuilder

GRAMMAR FROM WRITING

Capitalizing Dialogue

The following tips will help you correctly capitalize dialogue.

- Capitalize the first word inside quotation marks. Also capitalize the first word of a new sentence that begins within quotation marks.
- If you divide a sentence of dialogue with a speaker's tag, don't capitalize the first word that comes inside the second set of quotation marks.

Examine the capitalization in the following excerpt from Rudyard Kipling's story "Rikki-tikki-tavi."

> *"We are very miserable," said Darzee. "One of our babies fell out of the nest yesterday, and Nag ate him."*
>
> *"H'm!" said Rikki-tikki, "that is very sad—but I am a stranger here. Who is Nag?"*

APPLYING WHAT YOU'VE LEARNED
Revise the following sentences. Capitalize the dialogue correctly.

1. Hector said, "no."
2. "why not?" Perry whined.
3. "I don't want to go," Answered Hector impatiently. "besides, the gym is closed."

GRAMMAR HANDBOOK

For more information on capitalization and punctuation in dialogue, see pages 886–887 in the Grammar Handbook.

Writing Skill: PROOFREADING

K Draw students' attention to the proofreading marks to show how to transpose, or move, copy and how to insert quotation marks. Show how the transpose marks indicate the quotation marks and punctuation marks should be in reverse order. The little inverted carets point to exactly where the quotation marks go in relation to the beginning of the dialogue and after the final punctuation.

Try Your Hand

Advise students that they may have to add or change punctuation in some examples.

1. "How was it at your aunt's?" Tony asked.
2. Felix answered, "Kinda weird. I didn't know anyone."
3. Tony nodded. "Did any guys give you trouble?"
4. "No way, man!" Felix said.
5. "No offense," Felix said, "but I want to beat you."
6. "Was I too honest?" Felix asked apologetically.

PORTFOLIO

Have students write a note to themselves identifying a passage of dialogue that they are especially proud of. They can then attach the note to their final drafts.

SkillBuilder **G** GRAMMAR FROM WRITING

CAPITALIZING DIALOGUE Remind students to capitalize only the first letter of the first word in each case. Encourage them to notice that the first word inside the second set of quotation marks is capitalized only when the tag ends a sentence.

Application Answers:
1. Hector said, "No."
2. "Why not?" Perry whined.
3. "I don't want to go," answered Hector impatiently. "Besides, the gym is closed."

Additional Suggestions Have students correct the errors in capitalization in the following sentences:
1. "But," interrupted Perry, "That was the deal. You promised."
2. "that was before I knew it was closed," Replied Hector.
3. "That's not fair," Perry continued. "you always go back on your deals."

Reteaching/Reinforcement *Grammar Mini-Lessons* copymasters pp. 35 and 42, transparencies pp. 33–34

The Writer's Craft

Quotations, p. 611

READING THE WORLD

On pages 446–451, students learned how to extend a story by adding realistic dialogue. To do so, they speculated about what could have happened before the story began or after it ended. In this lesson, students will apply the skills they learned to infer what might have happened in a real-world situation.

Critical Thinking: ANALYZING

L Students should note the man's clothing and his eyes and hand. Lead them to pay attention to the boy's unusual clothing and to look at his facial expression. Invite them to think about the size of the man and the boy and about the way the man is probably crouching to talk to the boy. This may guide students to think about the boy's age.

Media Literacy: READING A SCENE

M Tell students who don't recognize the man's shirt that he is a referee. Students may speculate that the boy is a wrestler. They may decide that the man is warning the boy about something the boy has done, or he is encouraging the boy not to cry. Perhaps the boy has just done something that is not allowed or is about to fight in a match and does not want to. Encourage students to create dialogue that is suitable to their chosen interpretation.

Speaking and Listening: GROUP DISCUSSION

N Advise students that there will be several valid interpretations of the scene. All students should have sufficient time to explain their interpretation to the group. They may want to make their interpretation convincing by basing their ideas on as many details from the scene as possible. The group can help each student develop a realistic explanation.

R E A D I N G
THE WORLD

THE REST OF THE STORY

Have you ever glimpsed a situation and wanted to know more about what was going on? By observing closely, you can pick up clues that will help you interpret the event and decide how to react.

L **View** Look at the scene carefully and make note of as many details as possible about the man and the boy.

M **Interpret** Who might the man be? Who might the boy be? What could they be talking about? What might have led the man and the boy to this encounter? What do you think these people might say to each other?

N **Discuss** In a group share your ideas about this situation. What did each of you base your ideas on? Use the SkillBuilder at the right to learn about examining context.

Examining Context

You won't know what is going on in every situation you encounter. But you can gain an understanding, by examining the context and asking yourself the following questions.

- What details in this situation give me clues about who the people are and what the situation is?
- Have I had experiences that relate to this situation? Could what happened to me happen in this situation?
- When I think about possible outcomes, which one makes the most sense? Why?

APPLYING WHAT YOU'VE LEARNED
With a partner try to reach a greater understanding of the following situation.

It's not rush hour, but traffic on the highway has slowed to a crawl. Up ahead you see red lights flashing. Slowly you drive past a police car, a police officer, a fire truck, and an ambulance. On the roadside a man and a woman are holding each other. The woman has her face buried in the man's shoulder, and he stares blankly ahead. You see two cars in the ditch on one side of the road and one car in the ditch on the other side. None of the cars look damaged. What could be going on here?

SkillBuilder CRITICAL THINKING

EXAMINING CONTEXT Explain to students that context refers to the circumstances that relate to a central scene. Often the context can suggest what happens and why. For instance, in the scene on this page, the details suggest that the man is a referee and the boy is a wrestler. Students may have had similar experiences playing sports and may have had similar emotions of sadness or embarrassment.

Application Students initially may think there has been a serious accident, but they should note that none of the cars is damaged. However, they may conclude that some sort of accident has taken place. Perhaps one of the three vehicles caused all the cars to spin off the road. The ambulance and the man and woman's reaction may suggest someone has been injured even though no cars are damaged. On the other hand, students may propose that the man and woman are upset because they narrowly escaped serious injury.

UNIT FOUR

Part 2 Lesson Planner

TIME ALLOTMENTS SHOWN ARE APPROXIMATE. DEPENDING ON YOUR GOALS AND THE NEEDS OF YOUR STUDENTS, YOU MAY WISH TO ALLOW MORE OR LESS TIME FOR CERTAIN PORTIONS OF THE LESSON.

Table of Contents	Discussion	Previewing the Selection	Reading the Selection
PART OPENER **HIGH STAKES** **What Do You Think?** page 454	**20 MINUTES** • Reflect on the part theme		
SELECTION **The Christmas Hunt** page 457 AVERAGE		**15 MINUTES** • PERSONAL CONNECTION • BACKGROUND CONNECTION • READING CONNECTION: Making predictions	**45 MINUTES** • Introduce vocabulary • Read pp. 457–69 (13 pp.)
SELECTION *from* **Boy: Tales of Childhood** page 474 AVERAGE		**20 MINUTES** • PERSONAL CONNECTION • CULTURAL CONNECTION • WRITING CONNECTION	**45 MINUTES** • Introduce vocabulary • Read pp. 474–85 (12 pp.)
SELECTION **All Summer in a Day** page 489 AVERAGE		**15 MINUTES** • PERSONAL CONNECTION • LITERARY CONNECTION • READING CONNECTION: Identifying contrasts	**20 MINUTES** • Introduce vocabulary • Read pp. 489–94 (6 pp.)
SELECTION **The Highwayman** page 498 CHALLENGING		**15 MINUTES** • PERSONAL CONNECTION • HISTORICAL CONNECTION • READING CONNECTION: Identifying narrative elements in poetry	**15 MINUTES** • Read pp. 498–502 (5 pp.)
SELECTION *from* **Commodore Perry in the Land of the Shogun** page 506 CHALLENGING		**20 MINUTES** • PERSONAL CONNECTION • HISTORICAL CONNECTION • READING CONNECTION: Visualizing	**40 MINUTES** • Introduce vocabulary • Read pp. 506–15 (10 pp.)

Writing	Exploring Topics	Prewriting	Drafting and Revising
WRITING FROM EXPERIENCE **Writing a Report**	**25 MINUTES**	**25 MINUTES**	**75 MINUTES**

Time estimates assume in-class work. You may wish to assign some of these stages as homework.

Responding to the Selection

FROM PERSONAL RESPONSE TO CRITICAL ANALYSIS	OR	ANOTHER PATHWAY	LITERARY CONCEPTS	QUICKWRITES	ALTERNATIVE ACTIVITIES	LITERARY LINKS	CRITIC'S CORNER	THE WRITER'S STYLE	ACROSS THE CURRICULUM	ART CONNECTION	WORDS TO KNOW	BIOGRAPHY
40 MINUTES					**50 MINUTES**							
• Discussion questions	OR	• Role-Playing	• Foreshadowing	• Explanation • Analysis • Persuasive essay	✔	✔	✔		SCIENCE		✔	✔
50 MINUTES					**40 MINUTES**							
• Discussion questions	OR	• Dialogue	• Dialect	• Letter • Story • Conversation	✔				SOCIAL STUDIES	✔	✔	✔
40 MINUTES					**40 MINUTES**							
• Discussion questions	OR	• Paragraph	• Simile and metaphor	• Plan • Dialogue • Profile	✔	✔			SCIENCE		✔	✔
50 MINUTES					**30 MINUTES**							
• Discussion questions	OR	• Dialogue	• Onomatopoeia and rhythm	• Essay • Epitaph • Article	✔	✔				✔		✔
50 MINUTES					**60 MINUTES**							
• Discussion questions	OR	• Journal entry	• Imagery	• Account • Profile • Letter	✔				DRAMA	✔	✔	✔

Publishing and Reflecting

15 MINUTES

Part 2 Cooperative Project

A New Adventure Game

Overview

Students will create and model an adventurous new game that has high stakes for those willing to take a risk.

PROJECT AT A GLANCE

The selections in Unit Four, Part 2 are about people who risk things in hopes of larger rewards. Some are life-and-death risks; others are moral or emotional risks. For this project, students will design and model a new game with an adventure theme. This game should have built-in situations that will give players choices between taking safe and sure paths (worth a few points) and risky paths (worth a larger number of points, and with a penalty for failure). Games may be board games, card games, arcade games, video games, or in any other format students choose. Students will study each other's games and decide if they meet the criteria for the project. They will also vote for the game they would most like to play.

OBJECTIVES

• To recognize situations where taking risks can lead to higher rewards or more dramatic failures
• To create a game that involves the choice of taking a risk or playing it safe
• To review other games and evaluate them on a given set of criteria

SUGGESTED GROUP SIZE

3–4 students

MATERIALS

• Poster board
• Art supplies (markers, paint, scissors, glue, rulers)
• Spinners or number cubes
• Playing cards
• Selection of various types of games
• Box and slips of paper

1 Getting Started

Arranging the Project

Assemble a wide selection of games for students to examine. Be sure there are board games, card games (a standard deck as well as those using different cards, such as Old Maid), electronic games, and games that are made up of unique playing pieces, such as dominoes.

Also gather art supplies, or make arrangements with the art teacher so that students will have access to the supplies they need. You might even consider making this a cooperative project with the art teacher, thus giving students a place to work, freer access to supplies, and a little extra help along the way.

Arranging for Making the Games

If you cannot involve the art teacher, make arrangements for a place where students can use paint and glue and can clean up, or limit students to sketches using colored markers or crayons. Since making the games will involve a good deal of conversation and moving around, be sure you are not likely to disturb any other classes in your choice of location.

2 Creating the Games

Introducing the Project

Explain that students will be creating and modeling a new adventure game. Each game should contain, at some point, a choice between taking a safe path that leads to a minor reward and taking a high-risk path that leads either to a great reward or a major setback. They will create a model of their game and will write a set of rules that cover all possible situations. Groups will examine each other's games and decide whether each meets the criteria of the project. By secret ballot, students will vote for the game they would most like to play.

Allow students plenty of time to examine the selection of games you have brought to class. Students probably will be familiar with many of them, but they may need to refresh their memories and look over a few new ones carefully. Hold a class discussion on which games have an adventurous theme and which offer players a chance to take a risk. If possible, keep the risk-taking games in the classroom throughout the project period so groups can refer to them.

Group Investigations

Divide students into groups of three or four. Group members should brainstorm a theme and a form for their game (board game, card game, video game, and so on). Then they should begin laying out the general path or progression of the game, adding details later. It is at this point that the elements of choice and risk will first become apparent. A full set of rules should be developed to encompass any situation that might arise during play. Meet a few times with each group to keep track of their progress and help them overcome any difficulties they are encountering.

Creating a Project Description

When groups have decided on a theme and form and have done some preliminary planning on how the game will progress, ask them to prepare a brief description of their game. This description should include some indication about the risk factor of the game, although it does not need to be detailed at this point. Confer with each group about their plans to help them solidify their ideas and move on to the actual making of the game.

OPTION 1: COMPUTER GAME Students can create an interactive computer game. Instead of modeling the game, they can draw several scenes from the adventure and write a full description of the progression of the game. Creative students can also act out the game for the class.

OPTION 2: HAUNTED HOUSE Groups can design a community haunted house, similar to those set up by charitable organizations for Halloween. They can draw up a floor plan of how people would walk through the house and write a full description of each ghoul, ghost, and creepy creature that the public would encounter.

OPTION 3: PLAYGROUND FOR THE ADVENTUROUS Groups can design a new playground for students their age. Students can, at least on paper, ignore the common safety precautions usually found and design a real adventure.

OPTION 4: CARNIVAL Groups can design the rides and booths at a fund-raising carnival. Among the attractions should be several involving risk, but they need not be hazardous.

3 Sharing the Games

Set up the completed games around the classroom. Allow students to examine all the games, read the rules, and perhaps even to play a few. Then discuss the games one at a time as a class, determining which games demonstrate risk-taking features as well as what penalty there is for failure. At the end of the time, ask each student to privately write his or her favorite game on a slip of paper and put it in the "voting box." You can tabulate the results and announce the winner.

Assessing the Project

The following rubric can be used for group or individual assessment.

3 Full Accomplishment Students follow directions and create a game that includes a place for players to make a risky or safe choice.

2 Substantial Accomplishment Students create a game, but the risk factor is minimal or the rules are unclear.

1 Little or Partial Accomplishment Students' game is incomplete or does not fulfill the requirements of the assignment.

For the Portfolio
If possible, take a photograph of the final game to keep in each student's portfolio, along with a copy of your written assessment and the group's written description. Games may be donated to the school library or kept in the classroom for reference and use by future students.

Note: For other assessment options, see the *Teacher's Guide to Assessment and Portfolio Use.*

Cross-Curricular Options

ART
Students can draw several scenes from the game, or show people playing the game, for an advertising poster.

SOCIAL STUDIES

Have students research games from other countries and cultures. They can learn if the games are still being played today and can examine the games for indications of risk.

LANGUAGE ARTS
Ask students to write a short story about their game. This could be a "prequel" telling how the adventure came to the starting point of the game, or a companion story about people actually having the adventure.

Resources

More New Games! And Playful Ideas from the New Games Foundation describes 60 activity games that require no special equipment.

Play It! Over 400 Great Games for Groups by Wayne Rice and Mike Yaconelli describes a wide variety of games from thinking games to outdoor activities.

Kids' Games: Traditional Indoor and Outdoor Activities for Children of All Ages by Phil Wiswell includes board games as well.

WHAT DO YOU THINK?

─── **Objectives** ───

The activities on this page can be used to
- introduce the theme of "High Stakes," since each activity is connected to one or more of the selections in Part 2
- create materials for students' personal portfolios that they can return to later for reconsideration or revision
- build an understanding of theme that can be returned to and revised as students progress through the unit

What would you do?
Have students jot down some details about their parents' views and their own. Make sure that students support both positions logically so that they can argue their points convincingly. (See "The Christmas Hunt," p. 455.)

Was the risk worth taking?
Remind them that risks need not be physical. Make sure students express their views in a manner consistent with the character they choose. (See the excerpt from *Boy: Tales of Childhood*, p. 473, and "All Summer in a Day," p. 488.)

What approach would you take?
Remind students that their plan probably will be more convincing if it indicates the advantages that the other group will derive from acceding to it. (See the excerpt from *Commodore Perry in the Land of the Shogun*, p. 505.)

HIGH STAKES

WHAT DO YOU THINK?

REFLECTING ON THEME

When the stakes are high, the rewards can be high too. That is why some people choose to take great risks. For example, a doctor may decide to perform a dangerous operation in hopes of saving a patient's life. Use the activities on this page to examine how you might respond in some high-stakes situations.

Was the risk worth taking?

Think about a character in a movie who has taken a great risk. Write a journal entry in which that character expresses his or her views about whether the risk was worth taking. Read the journal entry to your classmates.

What approach would you take?

Imagine that your friends ask you to patch up a disagreement between them and another group of students. In your notebook, outline a plan for getting the group's leader to share your point of view.

Strategy
1. Find out why the two groups are not getting along.
2.
3.

What would you do?

Suppose you wanted to do something that your parents thought you were not quite ready for—such as taking part in an environmental-cleanup project in another city. Would you accept your parents' views or try to convince them that you were ready to take on the new responsibility? With two partners, role-play a discussion between your parents and yourself.

Looking Back

At the beginning of this unit, you thought about what is involved in meeting challenges. Review the selections you read in Part 1, your QuickWrites, and any ideas you may have jotted down. Then in your notebook write your own definition of the will to win. Use examples to illustrate your definition.

Looking Back
Students can review some of the selections in Part 1 and consider how their ideas about the will to win may have changed as a result of reading them. You may wish to have volunteers read their definitions aloud to the class to stimulate a whole class discussion.

Cross-Curricular Connections

History Have students work in small groups to research the risks and benefits of space exploration. Groups can focus their attention on particular space missions, but they should also consider the risks that the entire space program has entailed for the United States. Encourage groups not only to provide facts about space exploration but also to assess whether the benefits outweigh the risks.

FICTION

The Christmas Hunt
Borden Deal

Activating Prior Knowledge/Setting a Purpose

PERSONAL CONNECTION

Think about some of the responsibilities you now handle. Maybe you manage a paper route, baby-sit for a neighborhood family, or do several chores at home. What additional responsibility would you like to take on in the next few years? Why? Briefly answer these questions in your notebook. Then, as you read this story, think about what the main character learns about handling responsibility.

New things that I would like to try, and the responsibilities they would bring.

Building Background

BACKGROUND CONNECTION

Tom, the main character in this story, is a ten-year-old boy who believes that he is ready to handle a hunter's responsibilities. Every Christmas, his father and a group of skilled hunters use trained bird dogs to hunt quail. A bird dog instinctively stops quartering, or searching, a field when it detects the birds' scent on the ground. It then freezes, lifts a front paw, and points its nose toward the birds. On command, it flushes the quail—scares the birds into the air—and

then the hunters fire. The dog finds the fallen birds and carries them back to the hunters in its mouth. Bird dogs are sometimes entered in field trials—contests in which they are judged on their ability to obey orders, search a field, flush game birds, and retrieve the birds without damaging them.

LASERLINKS
• *BACKGROUND CONNECTION*   **455**

Previewing

Involve students in a class discussion, using the following prompts to preview "The Christmas Hunt" orally.

Personal Connection

Discussion Prompts: *Think of a responsibility you wanted very much and how you felt when you asked for and did or did not get it.*

- *What responsibility would you like to take on? Why?*

- *What can you do to show you are ready for this responsibility?*

- *What are some benefits that make you want more responsibility?*

- *Are there any disadvantages that go with increased responsibility?*

As you read, think about the responsibility Tom wants and how he tries to get it.

Art Note

Pheasant Shoot, by Ogden Pleissner
Ogden Pleissner (1905–1983) was an American artist who painted landscapes in a realistic way. In this painting, he shows a broad, spacious landscape that seems to include the viewer as part of the action.

Reading the Art *What elements in the painting help to direct your attention toward the center? What does the setting remind you of?*

Active Reading
READING CONNECTION

Making Predictions

Using what you already know to figure out what might happen in the future is called **predicting.** Reading a story can be more fun when you try to predict what will happen next in it. To make a prediction, you gather clues as you read and then use them to make a guess about what will occur later in the story.

In "The Serial Garden," for example, this paragraph appears just after Mark has set up his model garden:

> Nobody interrupted him. Mrs. Armitage only cleaned the playroom once every six months or so, when she made a ferocious descent on it and tidied up the tape recorders, roller-skates, meteorological sets, and dismantled railway engines, and threw away countless old magazines, stringless tennis rackets, abandoned paintings, and unsuccessful models. There were always bitter complaints from Mark and Harriet; then they forgot, and things piled up again till next time.

The chart below shows a clue from the paragraph and a prediction based on the clue.

Clues from the Story	Prediction
• Mark's mother throws away models when she cleans the playroom.	• Mark's mother might throw away Mark's model garden.

As you read "The Christmas Hunt," pause from time to time to think about what has happened so far. Like a good detective, look for clues about characters and events. Use the clues to predict what might happen next and how the story might end. If you wish, record the clues and predictions in a chart like the one shown here.

WORDS TO KNOW

brashness (brăsh′nĭs) *n.* foolish daring; recklessness (p. 465)

cavorting (kə-vôr′tĭng) *adj.* leaping about; prancing **cavort** *v.* (p. 461)

clamor (klăm′ər) *n.* a loud noise; uproar (p. 458)

contempt (kən-tĕmpt′) *n.* a feeling of disgust at something worthless; scorn; disrespect (p. 461)

indifference (ĭn-dĭf′ər-əns) *n.* a lack of concern or interest (p. 463)

irate (ī-rāt′) *adj.* very angry (p. 464)

lithe (līth) *adj.* bending easily; gracefully flexible (p. 459)

mimicry (mĭm′ĭ-krē) *n.* an imitation (p. 459)

refuge (rĕf′yōōj) *n.* a place of safety (p. 464)

tactic (tăk′tĭk) *n.* a method used to accomplish something; strategy (p. 458)

Pheasant Shoot, Ogden Pleissner. Courtesy of Godel & Co. Fine Art, New York.

The Christmas Hunt

BY BORDEN DEAL

457

SUMMARY

Ten-year-old Tom feels he is mature enough to go on the Christmas Day hunt. When he asks if he can go, his father says no. Tom devises a plan to prove to his father that he is a capable hunter. He takes Calypso Baby, his father's special dog, out hunting. In frustration and panic, however, Tom accidentally shoots the dog, wounding her severely. Filled with remorse, Tom tells his father that he does not deserve the bicycle that he wants for Christmas. On the morning of the Christmas Day hunt, Tom's father, who realizes that his son has faced up to the consequences of his mistake, gives him a surprise gift—a puppy—and tells him that someday both he and the puppy will be trained and may become good enough to go on the Christmas Day hunt. The gift of the puppy makes this Christmas the best ever for Tom.

Thematic Link: *High Stakes* Tom plays for high stakes when he takes his father's prize dog out hunting without permission.

CUSTOMIZING FOR

Students Acquiring English

- Use **ACCESS FOR STUDENTS ACQUIRING ENGLISH**, *Reading and Writing Support.*

- Responsibilities children take on as they grow differ from culture to culture. Discuss with students the different kinds of responsibilities a ten-year-old would be expected to have in their native cultures. You may wish to explain why hunting might be considered a rite of passage.

STRATEGIC READING FOR

Less Proficient Readers

Set a Purpose Have students read to find out how Tom gets his father's attention and if Tom's father gives him permission to go on the Christmas hunt.

Use **UNIT FOUR RESOURCE BOOK**, p. 43, for guidance in reading the selection.

It should have been the best Christmas of them all, that year at Dog Run. It started out to be, anyway. I was so excited, watching my father talking on the telephone, that I couldn't stand still. For I was ten years old, and I had never been on a quail shoot in my whole life. I wanted to go on the big Christmas Day hunt even more than I wanted that bicycle I was supposed to get. And I really needed the bicycle to cover with speed and ease the two miles I had to walk to school.

I WANTED TO GO ON THE BIG CHRISTMAS DAY HUNT EVEN MORE THAN I WANTED THAT BICYCLE I WAS SUPPOSED TO GET.

The Christmas Day hunt was always the biggest and best of the season. It was almost like a field trial; only the best hunters and the finest dogs were invited by my father. All my life I had been hearing great tales of past Christmas Day hunts. And now I knew with a great ten-year-old certainty that I was old enough to go.

My father hung up the phone and turned around, grinning. "That was Walter," he said. "There'll be ten of them this year. And Walter is bringing his new dog. If all he claims for that dog is true—"

"Papa," I said.

"Lord," my mother said. "That'll be a houseful to feed."

My father put his arm around her shoulders, hugging her. "Oh, you know you like it," he said. "They come as much for your cooking as they do for the hunting, I think."

My mother pursed her lips in the way she had and then smiled. "Wild turkey," she said. "You think you could shoot me four or five nice fat wild turkeys?"

I wanted to jump up and down to attract attention. But that was kid stuff, a <u>tactic</u> for the five-year-olds, though I had to admit it was effective. But I was ten. So I said, "Papa."

My father laughed. "I think I can," he said. "I'll put in a couple of mornings trying."

"Papa," I said desperately.

"Wild turkey stuffed with wild rice," my mother said quickly, thoughtfully, in her planning voice. "Giblet gravy, mashed potatoes, maybe a nice potato salad—"

"If I don't fail on the turkeys," my father said.

"Papa!" I said.

My father turned to me. "Come on, Tom," he said. "We've got to feed those dogs."

That's the way parents are, even when you're ten years old. They can talk right on and never hear a word you say. I ran after my father as he left the kitchen, hoping for a chance to get my words in edgewise. But my father was walking fast, and already the <u>clamor</u> of the bird dogs was rising up to cover any speech I might want to make.

The dogs were standing on the wire fence in long, dappled rows, their voices lifted in greeting. Even in my urgent need I had to stop and admire them. There's nothing prettier in the whole world than a good bird dog. There's a nobleness to its head, an intelligence in its eyes, that no other animal has. Just looking at them sent a shiver down my backbone, and the thought of shooting birds over them—well, the shiver just wasn't in my backbone now; I was shaking all over.

| WORDS TO KNOW | **tactic** (tăk′tĭk) *n.* a method used to accomplish something; strategy |
| | **clamor** (klăm′ər) *n.* a loud noise; uproar |

458

 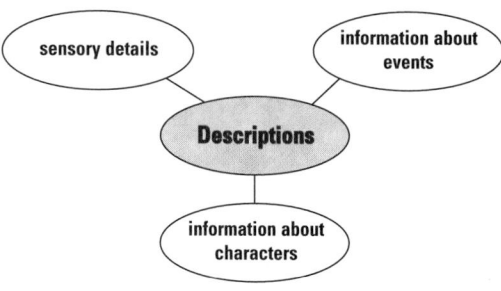

All of the dogs except one were in the same big run. But my father kept Calypso Baby in her own regal pen. I went to her and looked into her soft brown eyes. She stood up tall on the fence, her strong, <u>lithe</u> body stretched to its full height, as tall as I was.

"Hello, Baby," I whispered, and she wagged her tail. "You gonna find me some birds this Christmas, Baby? You gonna hunt for me like you do for Papa?"

She lolled her tongue, laughing at me. We were old friends. Calypso Baby was the finest bird dog in that part of the country. My father owned a number of dogs and kept and trained others for his town friends. But Calypso Baby was his personal dog, the one that he took to the field trials, the one he shot over in the big Christmas Day hunt held at Dog Run.

My father was bringing the sack of feed from the shed. I put out my hand, holding it against the wire so Calypso Baby could lick my fingers.

"This year," I whispered to her. "This year I'm going." I left Calypso Baby, went with determination toward my father. "Papa," I said, in a voice not to be denied this time.

My father was busy opening the sack of dog food.

"Papa," I said firmly. "I want to talk to you." It was the tone and the words my father used often toward me, so much of <u>mimicry</u> that my father looked down at me in surprise, at last giving me his attention.

"What is it?" he said. "What do you want?"

"Papa, I'm ten years old," I said.

My father laughed. "Well, what of it?" he said. "Next year you'll be eleven. And the next year twelve."

"I'm old enough to go on the Christmas hunt," I said.

Incredibly, my father laughed. "At ten?" he said. "I'm afraid not."

I stood, stricken. "But—" I said.

"No," my father said, in the voice that meant No, and no more talking about it. He hoisted the sack of feed and took it into the wire dog pen, the bird dogs crowding around him, rearing up on him in their eagerness.

"Well, come on and help me," my father said impatiently. "I've got a lot of things to do."

Usually I enjoyed the daily feeding of the dogs. But not today; I went through the motions dumbly, silently, not paying any attention to the fine bird dogs crowding around me. I cleaned the watering troughs with my usual care, but my heart was not in it.

After the feeding was over, I scuffed stubbornly about my other tasks and then went up to my room, not even coming down when my father came home at dusk excited with the two wild turkeys he had shot. I could hear him talking to my mother in the kitchen, and the ring of their voices had already the feel of Christmas, a hunting cheer that made them brighter, livelier, than usual. But none of the cheer and the pleasure came into me, even though Christmas was almost upon us and yesterday had been the last day of school.

That night I hunted. In my dreams I was out ahead of all the other men and dogs, Calypso Baby quartering the field in her busy way, doing it so beautifully I ached inside to watch her. All the men and dogs stopped their own hunting to watch us, as though it were a field trial. When Calypso Baby pointed, I raised the twelve-gauge shotgun,[1] moved in on her on the

---

1. **twelve-gauge** (gāj) **shotgun:** a wide-barreled gun that shoots a load of small pellets (shot) and is often used to hunt birds.

WORDS TO KNOW	**lithe** (līth) *adj.* bending easily; gracefully flexible **mimicry** (mĭm′ĭ-krē) *n.* an imitation

459

Active Reading: EVALUATE

C Have students discuss their impressions of the father's reaction to his son's request. You may wish to use the following model to give students an idea of what they might be thinking about.

Think-Aloud Model *I didn't care for the way Tom's father acted and talked to Tom. I don't think the father understood how important the hunt was for his son. Even though the father was busy, I think it would have been better if he had taken the time to explain why Tom couldn't go.*

STRATEGIC READING FOR
Less Proficient Readers

D Help students understand the significance of what happened during the conversation between Tom and his father.

- How did Tom finally get his father's attention? *(by speaking firmly)* **Noting Relevant Details**
- Why doesn't Tom's father let him go on the hunt? *(because he thinks Tom is too young)* **Making Inferences**

Set a Purpose Have students read to find out what Tom does to convince his father he's old enough to go on the Christmas hunt and the consequences of his actions.

Literary Concept:
FORESHADOWING

E Have students describe how Tom feels after his father turns down his request and how his emotions might foreshadow what is to come. *(Possible response: Tom is depressed and not looking forward to Christmas, suggesting that more sadness is to come. He will probably have a disappointing holiday.)*

CUSTOMIZING FOR
Students Acquiring English

3 Explain that *almost upon us* means "almost here."

F Ask students if they think the dream foreshadows what will happen or if it is just Tom's wishful thinking. Encourage students to defend their opinions using examples from the selection. *(Possible response: In his dream, Tom's hunting accomplishments and the level of admiration they inspire seem unrealistic. This suggest it is just a boy's wishful fantasy.)*

CUSTOMIZING FOR
Students Acquiring English

④ Point out that *Me and you are going hunting* is incorrect usage but commonly occurs in informal speech. In formal English, the correct sentence would be "You and I are going hunting."

Critical Thinking:
MAKING JUDGMENTS

G Have students evaluate the wisdom of Tom's plan to hunt solo to prove himself. Ask students if they think his plan is sensible or foolish. Make sure students support their responses. *(Possible response: His plan is foolish because it is not well thought out; he hasn't considered the dangers of hunting without experience.)*

---

ready, and Calypso Baby flushed the birds in her fine, steady way. They came up in an explosive whir, and I had the gun to my shoulder, squeezing off the shot just the way I'd been told to do. Three quail dropped like stones out of the covey,[2] and I swung the gun, following a single. I brought down the single with the second barrel, and Calypso Baby was already bringing the first bird to me in her soft, unbruising mouth. I knelt to pat her for a moment, and Baby whipped her tail to tell me how fine a shot I was, how much she liked for me to be the one shooting over her today.

F Soon there was another covey, and I did even better on this one, and then another and another; and nobody was hunting at all, not even my father, who was laughing and grinning at the other men, knowing this was his boy, Tom, and his dog, Calypso Baby, and just full of pride with it all. When it was over, the men crowded around and patted me on the shoulder, hefting the full game bag in admiration; and then there was my father's face close before me, saying, "I was wrong, son, when I said a ten-year-old boy isn't old enough to go bird hunting with the best of us."

Then I was awake, and my father, dressed in his hunting clothes, was shaking me, and it was morning. I looked up dazedly into his face, unable to shake off the dream, and I knew what it was I had to do. I had to show my father. Only then would he believe.

"Are you awake?" my father said. "You'll have to change the water for the dogs. I'm going to see if I can get some more turkeys this morning."

"All right," I said. "I'm awake now."

My father left. I got up and ate breakfast in the kitchen, close to the warm stove. I didn't say anything to my mother about my plans. I went out and watered the dogs as soon as the sun was up, but I didn't take the time, as I usually did, to play with them.

"Me and you are going hunting," I told Calypso Baby as I changed her water. She jumped and quivered all over, knowing the word as well as I did.

I went back into the house, listening for my mother. She was upstairs, making the beds. I went into the spare room where my father kept all the hunting gear. I was trembling, remembering the dream, as I went to the gun rack and touched the cold steel of the double-barreled twelve-gauge. But I knew it would be very heavy for me. I took the single-barrel instead, though I knew that pretty near ruined my chances for a second shot unless I could reload very quickly.

I picked up a full shell bag and hung it under my left arm. I found a game bag and hung it under my right arm. The strap was too long, and the bag dangled emptily to my knees, banging against me as I walked. I tied a knot in the strap so the bag would rest comfortably on my right hip. The gun was heavy in my hands as I walked into the hallway, listening for my mother. She was still upstairs.

"Mamma, I'm gone," I shouted up to her. "I'll be back in a little while." That was so she wouldn't be looking for me.

"All right," she called. "Don't wander far off. Your father will be back in an hour or two and might have something for you to do."

I hurried out of the house, straight to Calypso Baby's pen. I did not look up, afraid that my mother might be watching out of the window.

---

2. **covey** (kŭv′ē): a small flock.

Mini-Lesson   **Study Skills**

REFERENCE BOOKS Point out to students that, to write this story in a convincing way, the author either had to know or learn about hunting, bird dogs, and hunting rifles, among other subjects. A writer can use reference books to do research about unfamiliar subjects. Reference books provide succinct information about many subjects and usually list other helpful sources of information.

Application Have students use reference books as they do their research on sporting dogs for Across the Curriculum on page 471. Students can go to the library and create a list of reference books containing information on their subject. Have students share their reference lists and any helpful research strategies they learned.

That was a danger I could do nothing about, so I just ignored it. I opened the gate to Baby's pen, and she came out, circling and cavorting.

"Come on, Baby," I whispered. "Find me some birds now. Find me a whole lot of birds."

We started off, circling the barn so we would not be seen from the house and going straight away in its shadow as far as we could. Beyond the pasture we crossed a cornfield, Calypso Baby arrowing straight for the patch of sedge grass beyond. Her tail was whiplike in its thrash, her head high as she plunged toward her work, and I had to hurry to keep up. The gun was clumsy in my hands, and the two bags banged against my hips. But I remembered not to run with the gun, remembered to keep the breech[3] open until I was ready to shoot. I knew all about hunting; I just hadn't had a chance to practice what I knew. When I came home with a bag full of fine birds, my father would have to admit that I knew how to hunt, that I was old enough for the big Christmas Day hunt when all the great hunters came out from town for the biggest day of the season.

When I ducked through the barbed-wire fence, Calypso Baby was waiting for me, standing a few steps into the sedge grass, her head up watching me alertly. Her whole body quivered with her eagerness to be off. I swept my arm in the gesture I had seen my father use so many times, and Calypso Baby plunged instantly into the grass. She was a fast worker, quartering back and forth with an economical use of her energy. She could cover a field in half the time it took any other dog. The first field was empty, and we passed on to the second one. Somehow Calypso Baby knew that birds were here. She steadied down, hunting slowly, more thoroughly.

Then, startling me though I had been expecting it, she froze into a point, one foot up, her tail straight back, her head flat with the line of her backbone. I froze too. I couldn't move; I couldn't even remember to breech the gun and raise it to my shoulder. I stood as still as the dog, all of my knowledge flown out of my head; and yet far back under the panic, I knew that the birds weren't going to hold, they were going to rise in just a moment. Calypso Baby, surprised at my inaction, broke her point to look at me in inquiry. Her head turned toward me, and she asked the question as plain as my father's voice: *Well, what are you going to do about these fine birds I found for you?*

I could move then. I took a step or two, fumblingly breeched the gun, raised it to my shoulder. The birds rose of their own accord in a sudden wild drum of sound. I yanked at the trigger, unconsciously bracing myself against the blast and the recoil. Nothing happened. Nothing at all happened. I tugged at the trigger wildly, furiously, but it was too late, and the birds were gone.

I lowered the gun, looking down at it in bewilderment. I had forgotten to release the safety. I wanted to cry at my own stupidity; I could feel the tears standing in my eyes. This was not at all like my dream of last night, when I and the dog and the birds had all been so perfect.

Calypso Baby walked back to me and looked up into my face. I could read the puzzled contempt in her eyes. She lay down at my feet, putting her muzzle on her paws. I looked down at her, ashamed of myself and knowing that she was ashamed. She demanded perfection, just as my father did.

---

3. **breech:** the rear end of the gun's barrel. A shotgun cannot be fired while the breech is open.

| WORDS TO KNOW | **cavorting** (kə-vôr′tĭng) *adj.* leaping about; prancing **cavort** *v.* |
| | **contempt** (kən-tĕmpt′) *n.* a feeling of disgust at something worthless; scorn; disrespect |

461

 Mini-Lesson | **The Writer's Style**

TIME TRANSITIONS Help students understand that throughout this selection the author describes a sequence of events that happen in chronological order. The author uses specific words and phrases to indicate the sequence of events. For example, on page 461, the words *started*, *when*, and *then* indicate the sequence of events.

Application Have students brainstorm a list of words that show time transitions. Then have pairs of students write a descriptive paragraph from the point of view of the birds flushed by Calypso Baby. The paragraph should utilize time transition words and phrases to describe the sequence of events. Encourage students to share their writing with the class.

Reteaching/Reinforcement
• *Writing Handbook*, anthology p. 817
• *Writing Mini-Lessons*, transparencies, p.33

 **The Writer's Craft**

Using Transitions, pp. 271–272

Time Transition Words

start	begin	since
finish	when	continue
end	then	soon
after	eventually	suddenly
later		

Leda, an English Setter by Percival L. Rosseau Percival L. Rosseau (1859–1937) is considered one of America's greatest painters of dogs. He was born on a Louisiana plantation, and his father was killed fighting in the Civil War. Even as a child, Rosseau was an avid hunter who was intimately familiar with all aspects of hunting—especially the looks and characters of prime hunting dogs. Rosseau painted hunting dogs in their natural setting, which gave his paintings a sense of immediacy and realism. Leda, pictured here, is an English setter Rosseau painted in 1906.

Reading the Art *Compare and contrast this painting with the one on page 457. Does one painting seems more vivid and intense to you? Explain why or why not.*

Leda, an English Setter (1906), Percival Rosseau. Oil on canvas, collection of American Kennel Club.

CALYPSO BABY POINTED SUDDENLY; I JERKED THE GUN TO MY SHOULDER, REMEMBERING THE SAFETY THIS TIME, AND THEN CALYPSO BABY FLUSHED THE BIRDS.

462   UNIT FOUR   PART 2: HIGH STAKES

Multicultural **Perspectives**

CUSTOMS AND BELIEFS For many people in the world, hunting is not a part of their culture. For example, the Jains, a religious sect in India, believe all life is sacred and all living things have souls. As a result, Jains are careful never to hurt or kill any animal and are strict vegetarians. Devout Jains often walk with a small broom to sweep insects out of their path to make sure that they do not accidentally injure or kill any living thing. Many Buddhist sects also teach the sacredness of all life. Buddhists believe that showing compassion for all living things is one of the highest forms of spirituality. As a result, they proscribe hunting and the eating of flesh.

"It was my fault, Baby," I told her. I leaned over and patted her on the head. "You didn't do anything wrong. It was me."

I started off then, looking back at the bird dog. She did not follow me. "Come on," I told her. "Hunt."

She got up slowly and went out ahead of me again. But she worked in a puzzled manner, checking back to me frequently. She no longer had the joy, the confidence, with which she had started out.

"Come on, Baby," I coaxed her. "Hunt, Baby. Hunt."

We crossed into another field, low grass this time, and when we found the covey, there was very little time for setting myself. Calypso Baby pointed suddenly; I jerked the gun to my shoulder, remembering the safety this time, and then Calypso Baby flushed the birds. They rose up before me, and I pulled the trigger, hearing the blast of the gun, feeling the shock of it into my shoulder knocking me back a step.

But not even one bird dropped like a fateful stone out of the covey. The covey had gone off low and hard on an angle to the left, and I had completely missed the shot, aiming straight ahead instead of swinging with the birds. Calypso Baby did not even attempt to point singles. She dropped her head and her tail and started away from me, going back toward the house.

I ran after her, calling her, crying now but with anger rather than hurt. Baby would never like me again; she would hold me in the <u>indifference</u> she felt toward any person who was not a bird hunter. She would tolerate me as she tolerated my mother and the men who came out with shiny new hunting clothes and walked all over the land talking about how the dogs didn't hold the birds properly so you could get a decent shot.

I couldn't be one of those. I ran after the dog, calling her, until at last she suffered me to come near. I knelt, fondling her head, talking to her, begging her for another chance.

"I'll get some birds next time," I told her. "You just watch. You hear?"

At last, reluctantly, she consented to hunt again. I followed her, my hands gripping the heavy gun, determined this time. I knew it was my last chance; she would not give me another. I could not miss this time.

We hunted for an hour before we found another covey of birds. I was tired, the gun and the frustration heavier with every step. But, holding only last night's dream in my mind, I refused to quit. At last Calypso Baby froze into a beautiful point. I could feel myself sweating, my teeth gritted hard. I had to bring down a bird this time.

It seemed to be perfect. I had plenty of time, but I hurried anyway, just to be sure. Then the birds were rising in a tight cluster, and I was pulling the trigger before I had the heavy gun lined up—and in the midst of the thundering blast I heard Calypso Baby yell with pain as the random shot tore into her hip.

I threw down the gun and ran toward her, seeing the blood streaking down her leg as she staggered away from me, whimpering. I knelt, trying to coax her to me, but she was afraid. I was crying, feeling the full weight of the disaster. I had committed the worst crime of any bird hunter; I had shot my own dog.

Calypso Baby was trying to hide in a clump of bushes. She snapped at me in her fear when I reached in after her, but I did not feel the pain in my hand. I knelt over her, looking at the shredded hip. It was a terrible wound; I could see only blood and raw flesh. I snatched

463

Active Reading: PREDICT

K Have students analyze Calypso Baby's reactions to Tom's behavior (and lack of success) during this hunt. Ask them to use the dog's behavior to predict what will happen next. *(Possible response: The dog's disappointment and reluctance suggest that Tom will not shoot a bird and that they will return home empty-handed.)*

Critical Thinking: ANALYZING

L Ask students why they think Tom is determined to persist in his solo hunt after so many things have gone wrong. Ask them what events have occurred so far that suggest that Tom is not really ready for the Christmas Day hunt. *(Possible responses: Tom's forgetting to release the gun's safety, becoming exhausted carrying the gun, and shooting wildly without aiming)*

Mini-Lesson Grammar

COMPOUND SENTENCES Sometimes writers connect two complete sentences with a comma followed by a coordinating conjunction or with a semicolon. Two sentences connected in this way make a compound sentence.

Application In the highlighted passage, have students identify three compound sentences. Then have students write the following pairs of sentences as compound sentences.
1. Tom had plenty of time. He hurried anyway.
2. Calypso Baby stopped. She stared straight ahead.
3. Tom had a dream. It gave him confidence.
4. Tom pushed himself to continue the hunt. He was really exhausted.
5. The dog looked at me sadly. I had to go on.

Reteaching/Reinforcement
- Grammar Handbook anthology p. 879
- *Grammar Mini-Lessons,* copymasters, p. 37 transparencies, p. 28

 **The Writer's Craft**

Compound Sentences, p. 559

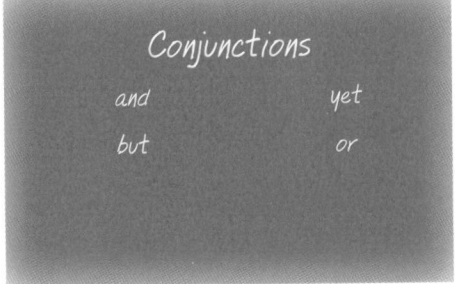
Conjunctions

and *yet*

but *or*

STRATEGIC READING FOR

Less Proficient Readers

M Make sure students understand the sequence of events that lead to the disastrous end of Tom's solo hunt.

- What accident occurs during Tom's solo hunt? *(He accidentally shoots his father's dog.)* **Restating**

- What do you think was the cause of the accident? *(Tom's inexperience with hunting and shooting)* **Relating Cause and Effect**

Set a Purpose Have students read to find out how Tom's father's reacts to what happened on the hunt.

CUSTOMIZING FOR

Students Acquiring English

6 Point out that the dashes used as punctuation in the narrator's speech indicate pauses. Tom pauses often throughout this part of the story because he is upset and does not want to tell his father what he has done.

off the empty hunting bag I had donned so optimistically, the shell bag, and took off my coat. I wrapped her in the coat and picked her **M** up in my arms. She was very heavy, hurting, whining with each jolting step as I ran toward the house.

I came into the yard doubled over with the catch in my side from the running, and my legs were trembling. My father was sitting on the back porch with three wild turkeys beside him, cleaning his gun. He jumped to his feet when he saw the wounded dog.

"What happened?" he said. "Did some fool hunter shoot her?"

I stopped, standing before my father and holding the wounded dog; I looked into his angry face. They were the most terrible words I had ever had to say. "I shot her, Papa," I said.

My father stood very still. I did not know what would happen. I had never done anything so bad in my whole life, and I could not even guess how my father would react. The only thing justified would be to wipe me off the face of the earth with one <u>irate</u> gesture of his hand.

I gulped, trying to move the pain in my throat out of the way of the words. "I took **6** her out bird hunting," I said. "I wanted to show you—if I got a full bag of birds, I thought you'd let me go on the Christmas Day hunt—"

"I'll talk to you later," my father said grimly, taking the dog from me and starting into the kitchen. "I've got to try to save this dog's life now."

I started into the kitchen behind my father. He turned. "Where's the gun you shot her with?" he said.

"I—left it."

"Don't leave it lying out there in the field," my father said in a stern voice.

I wanted very badly to go into the kitchen,

find out that the dog would live. But I turned, instead, and went back the way I had come, walking with my head down, feeling shrunken inside myself. I had overreached; I had risen up today full of pride beyond my ability, and in the stubbornness of the pride I had been blind until the terrible accident had opened my eyes so that I could see myself clearly—too clearly. I found the gun, the two bags, where I had dropped them. I picked them up without looking at the smear of blood where Calypso had lain. I went back to the house slowly, not wanting to face it, reluctant to see the damage I had wrought.

hen I came into the kitchen, my father had the dog stretched out on the kitchen table. My mother stood by his side with bandages and ointment in her hands. The wound was cleaned of the birdshot and dirt and blood. Calypso Baby whined when she saw me, and I felt my heart cringe with the rejection.

My father looked at me across the dog. The anger was gone out of him; his voice was slow and searching and not to be denied. "Now I want to know why you took my gun and my dog without permission," he said.

"David," my mother said to him.

My father ignored her, kept his eyes hard on my face. I knew it wouldn't do any good to look toward my mother. This was between me and my father, and there was no <u>refuge</u> for me anywhere in the world. I didn't want a refuge; I knew I had to face not only my father but myself.

"I—I wanted to go on the Christmas Day hunt," I said again. "I thought if I—" I stopped. It was all that I had to say; it seemed pretty flimsy to me now.

My father looked down at the dog. I was

| WORDS TO KNOW | **irate** (ī-rāt′) *adj.* very angry |
| | **refuge** (rĕf′yōōj) *n.* a place of safety |

464

Mini-Lesson   **Reading Skills/Strategies**

ACTIVE READING: PREDICT Remind students that when they make guesses about what will happen next in a story, they are predicting. Active readers predict what will happen next based on what they have read thus far. Explain that they can also predict events in a story by using prior knowledge about the subject of a story.

Application Have students refer to the predictions that they listed on their prediction charts (see page 456). Then have students analyze their predictions to see which proved true and which didn't. Remind students that readers often mispredict events or revise their predictions based on new information or clues the author reveals. Ask students if they enjoy reading literature that "keeps them guessing."

Reteaching/Reinforcement
- *Unit Four Resource Book,* p. 44

surprised at the lack of anger in him. I could read only sadness in his voice. "She may be ruined for hunting," he said. "Even if the wound heals good, if she doesn't lose the use of her leg, she may be gun-shy for the rest of her life. At best, I'll never be able to show her in field trials again. You understand what you've done?"

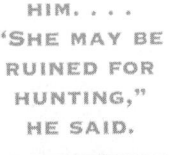

"Yes, sir," I said. I wanted to cry. But that would not help, any more than anger from my father would help.

"You see now why I said you weren't old enough?" my father said. "You've got to be trained for hunting, just like a dog is trained. Suppose other men had been out there; suppose you had shot a human being?"

"David!" my mother said.

My father turned angrily toward her. "He's got to learn!" he said. "There's too many people in this world trying to do things without learning how to do them first. I don't want my boy to be one of them."

"Papa," I said. "I'm—I'm sorry. I wouldn't have hurt Calypso Baby for anything in the world."

"I'm not going to punish you," my father said. He looked down at the dog. "This is too bad for a whipping to settle. But I want you to think about today. I don't want you to put it out of your mind. You knew that when the time came ripe for it, I intended to teach you, take you out like I'd take a puppy, and hunt with you. After a while, you could hunt by yourself. Then if you were good enough—and

only if you were good enough—you could go on the Christmas Day hunt. The Christmas Day hunt is the place you come to, not the place you start out from. Do you understand?"

"Yes, sir," I said. I would have been glad to settle for a whipping. But I knew that a mere dusting of the breeches would be inadequate for my <u>brashness</u>, my overconfidence, for the hurt I had given not only to the fine bird dog but also to my father—and to myself.

"You've got to take special care of Calypso Baby," my father said. "Maybe if you take care of her yourself while she's hurt, she'll decide to be your friend again."

I looked at the dog, and I could feel the need of her confidence and trust. "Yes, sir," I said. Then I said humbly, "I hope she will be friends with me again."

I went toward the hall, needing to be alone in my room. I stopped at the kitchen doorway, looking back at my father and mother watching me. I had to say it in a hurry if I was going to say it at all.

"Papa," I said, the words rushing softly in my throat, threatening to gag there before I could get them out. "I—I don't think I deserve that bicycle this Christmas. I don't deserve it at all."

My father nodded his head. "All right, son," he said gravely. "This is your own punishment for yourself."

"Yes," I said, forcing the word, the loss empty inside me, and yet feeling better too. I turned and ran out of the room and up the stairs.

Christmas came, but without any help from me at all. I went to bed on Christmas Eve heavy with the knowledge that tomorrow morning there would be no shiny new bicycle under the tree; there would be no Christmas Day hunt for me. I couldn't prevent myself

WORDS TO KNOW	**brashness** (brăsh'nĭs) *n.* foolish daring; recklessness

465

Critical Thinking: CLASSIFYING

N Tom's father feels it is important to learn how to hunt before you attempt to hunt. Have students brainstorm a list of activities they feel someone should not attempt before receiving the proper training. Have students determine what common characteristics these activities have that justifies their inclusion on the list. *(Possible responses: scuba diving, parachuting, diving, driving an automobile. All these activities can be life-threatening.)*

STRATEGIC READING FOR
Less Proficient Readers

O Make sure students understand Tom's father's reaction to what Tom did.

• How would you describe Tom's father's reaction after learning of the shooting of the dog? *(Possible responses: angry, sad, shocked, disappointed)* **Classifying**

Set a Purpose Have students read to find out what Tom gets for Christmas.

Literary Concept:
DESCRIPTION

P Have students point out descriptive words or phrases that reveal how upset Tom still is about the accident. *(Possible responses: "said humbly"; "rushing softly in my throat, threatening to gag there"; "forcing the word")*

Assessment ✓ Option

INFORMAL ASSESSMENT You can informally assess students' understanding of the selection by setting up the following scenario:

Pretend you are Tom on the evening after the accident. Write a letter to your father in which you explain what happened, why it happened, and how you feel about it. Be sure to express your understanding of why your father didn't punish you and of what your father was trying to teach you.

Rubric
3 Full Accomplishment Students show an understanding of the sequence of events, of how Tom

feels and has matured, and of his appreciation for his father's views.

2 Substantial Accomplishment Students describe the significant events and relate to Tom's feelings but have some difficulty expressing Tom's father's intentions.

1 Little or Partial Accomplishment Students have limited success in describing the sequence of events, Tom's motives, and his feelings after the disaster. They show little understanding of the father and his intentions.

Early Autumn by **Ken Danby** Ken Danby's (1940–) first watercolor paintings were inspired by the forest hikes he took with his father in his native Canada. He later attended the Ontario College of Art and began painting realistic scenes, such as the one included here.

Reading the Art *What do you think the boy might be feeling? What mood does this painting give you? Look at the use of light and shadows. What time of day do you think the painting captures?*

CUSTOMIZING FOR

Multiple Learners

Q **Spatial or Graphic Learners** Have students draw or describe a favorite place where they like to sit and think. Ask them to compare and contrast their settings to the one in the painting.

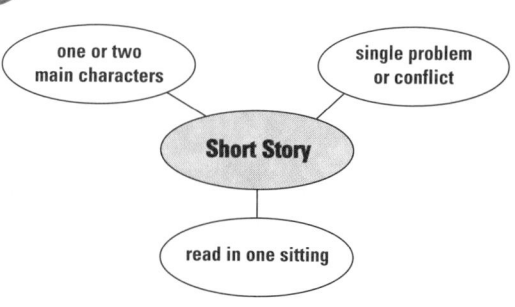

Early Autumn (1971), Ken Danby. Edition 100, a 19 color serigraph, 45.7 cm × 61 cm, by permission of the artist and Gallery Moos, Toronto, Canada.

IT WAS PERFECT QUAIL-
HUNTING WEATHER, COLD
BUT NOT TOO COLD, WITH A
SMOKY HAZE LYING OVER
THE EARTH. THE DOGS KNEW
THAT TODAY WAS FOR HUNTING.

466   UNIT FOUR   PART 2: HIGH STAKES

Mini-Lesson   Genre Study

FICTION "The Christmas Hunt" is a form of fiction known as a **short story.** Use the word web shown to remind students that a short story generally has the following characteristics:
- A short story is usually intended to be read in one sitting.
- It focuses on one or two main characters.
- It focuses on a single problem or conflict.

Application Have students fill in a word web like the one shown by jotting down details about the characters and conflict in "The Christmas Hunt."

> one or two main characters
>
> single problem or conflict
>
> **Short Story**
>
> read in one sitting

from waking up at the usual excited time, but I made myself turn over and go back to sleep. When I did, reluctantly, go downstairs, the Christmas tree did not excite me, nor the usual gifts I received every year, the heavy sweater, the gloves, the scarf, the two new pairs of blue jeans. I just wouldn't let myself think about the bicycle.

After my father had gone outside, my mother hugged me to her in a sudden rush of affection. "He would have given you the bicycle anyway," she said, "if you hadn't told him you didn't want it."

I looked up at her. "I didn't deserve it," I said. "Maybe next year I will."

She surprised me then by holding me and crying. I heard the first car arrive outside, the voices of the men excited with the promise of hunting. My mother stood up and said briskly, "Well, this is not getting that big dinner cooked," and went into the kitchen without looking back.

I went out on the front porch. It was perfect quail-hunting weather, cold but not too cold, with a smoky haze lying over the earth. The dogs knew that today was for hunting; I could hear them from around behind the house, standing on the wire fence in broad-shouldered rows, their voices yelping and calling. All except Calypso Baby. All except me.

I stood aside, watching the men arrive in their cars, my father greeting them. Their breaths hung cloudy in the air, and they moved with a sharp movement to their bodies. These were the best hunters in the whole countryside, and today would be a great comradeship and competition. Any man invited on this hunt could be proud of the invitation alone.

I felt almost remote as I watched, as I went with them around the side of the house to the dogs. They all went to examine Calypso Baby,

and I felt a freezing inside; but my father only said, "She got shot by accident," and did not tell the whole terrible story.

Then my father looked at his watch and said, "Let's wait for a few more minutes. Walter ought to be here soon. Hate to start without him."

One of the men called, "Here he comes now," and Walter drove up in his battered car.

"Come here, son," my father said, speaking to me for the first time this morning, and I went reluctantly to his side. I was afraid it was coming now, the whole story, and all the men would look at me in the same way that Calypso Baby had after I had shot her.

My father drew me to the side of Walter's car, reached in, and brought out a basket. "You wanted a bicycle," he said. "Then you decided yourself you should wait. Because you made the decision yourself, I decided you were old enough for this."

I looked at the bird-dog puppy in the basket. All of a sudden Christmas burst inside me like a skyrocket, out of the place where I had kept it suppressed all this time.

"Papa," I said. "Papa—"

"Take him," my father said.

I reached into the basket and took out the puppy. The puppy licked my chin with his harsh, warm tongue. He was long, gangly, his feet and head too big for his body—but absolutely beautiful.

My father knelt beside me, one hand on the puppy. "I told Walter to bring me the finest bird-dog puppy he could find," he said. "He's kin to Calypso Baby; he's got good blood." ⑦

"Thank you, Papa," I said in a choking voice. "I—I'd rather have him than the bicycle. I'll name him Calypso Boy, I'll—"

"When this puppy is ready for birds, we'll train him," my father said. "While we train the puppy, we'll train you too. When the time comes, you can both go on the Christmas Day hunt—if you're good enough."

CUSTOMIZING FOR

Multiple Learning Styles

Ⓡ **Intrapersonal Learners** Have students write a journal or diary entry that conveys how Tom is feeling at this point in the story. Students can choose to write using either a third-person observation of Tom or a first-person account imagining they are Tom.

CUSTOMIZING FOR

Students Acquiring English

⑦ Students should be able to guess from the context that *kin to* means "related to." Explain that *good blood* refers to the planned breeding of pure-bred dogs, also called blood lines.

Active Reading: CONNECT

Ⓢ Invite students to talk about a time they did something that they regretted but were forgiven and even given a chance to redeem themselves. Ask students if they had feelings similar to Tom's. Make sure students understand that sharing a personal story is voluntary—students who do not want to share a personal experience need not do so.

Mini-Lesson Literary Concepts

REVIEWING SIMILE Review with students that a simile is a comparison of two unlike things that have some quality in common. Similes make a direct comparison using words such as *like, as,* or *resembles.*

Application Have students locate the simile in the highlighted passage and identify the two unlike things being compared. Then have students choose a scene from this story and write a paragraph describing it, using one or more similes. The similes can describe landscape, a character's (human or nonhuman) feelings, or another aspect of the scene. Have students share their writing with the class. You may have less-proficient students rewrite the sentence cited above, using different similes to convey the same emotion.

Woodland Walk (1989), Burt Silverman. Copyright © Burt Silverman.

IT WAS THREE YEARS MORE BEFORE
I GOT TO GO ON MY FIRST CHRISTMAS HUNT.
PAPA HAD BEEN RIGHT, OF COURSE.
IN THE TIME BETWEEN I HAD LEARNED
A GREAT DEAL MYSELF WHILE TRAINING
CALYPSO BOY TO HUNT.

Mini-Lesson Spelling

I + I + I WORDS Tell students to double the final consonant of a I + I + I word (a word that has *one* syllable, *one* vowel, and *one* final consonant) before adding a suffix that begins with a vowel, such as *-ing, -ed,* or *-er.* Do not double the final consonant before a suffix that begins with a consonant. The rule does not apply to one-syllable words with two vowels that precede the final consonant.

Application Have students add the following endings to the words shown.

1. fit + ed
2. sit + ing
3. stab + ed
4. near + ing
5. mat + ed
6. kneel + ed
7. foot + ing
8. fan + ed
9. hit + ing
10. hot + er

Ask students to look for more words that fit this pattern, in their own writing and in things that they read, and to add these words to their personal word lists.

Reteaching/Reinforcement
• *Unit Four Resource Book,* p. 45

"We'll be good enough," I said. "Both of us will be good enough."

"I hope so," my father said. He stood up and looked at the men standing around us, all of them smiling down at me and Calypso Boy. "Let's go," he said. "Those birds are going to get tired of waiting on us."

They laughed and hollered, and the dogs moiled and sounded[4] in the excitement as they were let out of the pen. They fanned out across the pasture, each man or two men taking a dog. I stood watching, holding the puppy warm in my arms. I looked at Calypso Baby, standing crippled in her pen looking longingly after the hunters. I went over and spoke to her. She whined; then for the first time since the accident, she wagged her tail at me.

I looked down at the puppy in my arms. "We'll be going," I told him, as he licked at my chin. "One of these days, when you're a dog and I'm a man, we'll be right out there with the best of them."

It was three years more before I got to go on my first Christmas hunt. Papa had been right, of course. In the time between I had learned a great deal myself while training Calypso Boy to hunt. With the good blood in him he turned out to be a great bird dog—second only, I guess, to Calypso Baby, who recovered well from her wound and was Papa's dog the day Calypso Boy and I made our first Christmas hunt.

But of all the Christmases, before and since, I guess I remember best the one when Calypso Baby was hurt—and Calypso Boy first came to me. ❖

---

4. **moiled and sounded:** churned about and howled.

LITERARY INSIGHT

FORMULA
ANA MARIA IZA

To dream,
you don't have to ask permission,
nor cry out,
nor humble yourself,
nor put on lipstick;
it's enough to close your eyes halfway
and feel distant.
Perhaps the night dreams
that it is no longer night;
the fish, that they are boats;
the boats, fish;
the water, crystal.

To dream . . .
is a simple thing;
it doesn't cost a cent,
you need only to turn your back
on the hours that pass
and cover over pain,
your ears,
your eyes
and stay so,
stay . . .
until we are awakened
by a blow upon the soul.

Translated by Ron Connally

FORMULA   **469**

CUSTOMIZING FOR

Gifted and Talented Students

U Ask students to discuss what they think the memory of each dog will symbolize for Tom as he matures.

INSIGHT

1. Do you think the speaker regards dreaming as a positive or a negative act? Explain. *(Possible response: positive, because you don't need to ask permission and it's free)*

2. What do you think the speaker means by "a blow upon the soul"? *(Possible response: anything that takes us out of our dreams)*

3. How do you think this poem relates to the story? *(Possible response: Tom's "blow upon the soul" comes when his dream hunt is blown apart by the reality of shooting Calypso Baby.)*

COMPREHENSION CHECK

1. What inspired Tom to prove to his father that he was capable of going on the Christmas Day hunt? *(his dream)*

2. What goes wrong on Tom's solo hunt? *(He forgets to release the safety; he forgets to aim; he shoots his father's dog.)*

3. What punishment does Tom inflict on himself? *(not getting the Christmas bicycle he hoped for)*

4. Who is Calypso Boy? *(the bird-dog puppy related to Calypso Baby that Tom receives for Christmas)*

Mini-Lesson: Speaking, **Listening, and Viewing**

DIRECTIONS Explain to students that hunting is an activity that requires careful safety training and the mastery of specific skills. Discuss with students why it's necessary for a person who wants to do something like hunting to be willing and able to follow directions to learn the skills needed.

Application Have students list any special skills they have, such as playing the flute or doing a dance step. Have them choose one simple skill and give to the class step-by-step directions (preferably, with hands-on practice) for doing that skill.

From Personal Response to Critical Analysis

1. Encourage students to consider their reactions to the relationship between Tom and his father.
2. Possible responses: Yes, Tom was sufficiently sorry and showed he had matured; no, Tom seriously wounded Calypso Baby and should not receive something special.
3. Possible response: Tom's father is fair, treating him with respect when he acts responsibly.
4. Possible response: Tom has matured and learned to accept responsibility for his actions. He may never again take on a responsibility before he is mature enough to handle it.
5. Possible response: more open and honest communication; greater trust between parent and child; trying to see things from the other's point of view
6. Possible response: The poem relates to Tom's confidence arising from his wonderful dream of a successful hunt. Tom's dream differs from reality in that in his dream he performs like the most skilled and experienced hunter, whereas in reality he blunders terribly and wounds his own dog.
7. Possible responses: No, since consequences sometimes hurt others, as when Calypso Baby got shot, and self-punishment is rarely harsh enough. Yes, because dealing with the consequences of one's own actions and determining a suitable punishment are important steps toward maturity.

Another Pathway

Have pairs outline the dialogue, rehearse the scene, and then present it to the class. Make sure students pay attention to details in the selection that provide clues about the personalities of Tom's mother and father.

Rubric

3 Full Accomplishment Students accurately portray the emotions and points of view of each parent, and the topic of their conversation follows logically from information presented in the story.

2 Substantial Accomplishment Students accurately present the parents' points of view, but their topic of conversation does not logically follow information presented.

1 Little or Partial Accomplishment Students do not always present their character's point of view accurately and introduce tangential topics.

RESPONDING
OPTIONS

FROM PERSONAL RESPONSE TO CRITICAL ANALYSIS

REFLECT
1. What were your thoughts as you finished reading the story? Jot them down in your notebook.

RETHINK
2. Do you think Tom should have received a puppy at the end of the story? Explain your opinion.

3. How would you evaluate the way Tom's father treats him?
   Consider
   Close Textual Reading
   - the father's attitude toward Tom before the accident
   - his reaction when he learns that Tom has shot Calypso Baby
   - his response to Tom's statement that he doesn't deserve the bicycle
   - his words and actions on Christmas Day

4. How do you think Tom's experience has changed him? Base your answer on the information in the story and on your own experiences.

RELATE
5. Parents and children often disagree about whether the children are ready to participate in an activity or handle a responsibility. What are some ways parents and children can resolve their disagreements and come to an understanding?

6. In what way does the Insight poem on page 469 relate to Tom's experience? How does Tom's dream differ from reality?

7. Do you think parents should allow children to experience the consequences of their wrongdoing and dictate their own punishment? Why or why not? Use examples from the story or from your own experience to support your answer.

Multimodal Learning
ANOTHER PATHWAY

While Tom's father is scolding Tom for shooting Calypso Baby, Tom's mother twice starts to say something but never finishes her sentences. With another student, role-play for the rest of the class the conversation that Tom's mother and father might have had after Tom left the kitchen.

QUICKWRITES

1. Tom's father says, "The Christmas Day hunt is the place you come to, not the place you start out from." Write an **explanation** of what he means.

2. Imagine that you are a psychologist analyzing Tom's hunting dream. Write an **analysis** of the dream, describing what it shows about Tom and explaining why he may have dreamed it.

3. What are your thoughts and feelings about the hunting of birds? Using what you know as well as what you have learned from the story, write a **persuasive essay** arguing for or against this sport.

📁 **PORTFOLIO** Save your writing. You may want to use it later as a springboard to a piece for your portfolio.

QuickWrites

1. Encourage students to write their explanations from the father's point of view.
2. Consider discussing with students what psychoanalysts do and that some of them think that dreams are one way to express emotions and desires that cannot be expressed openly. Suggest that students relate the events in Tom's dream to his intense desire to prove himself as a hunter.
3. Before students write this essay, they should outline the arguments they will use to support their position.

 **The Writer's Craft**

Supporting Opinions, pp. 144–151

LITERARY CONCEPTS

When a writer hints at a future event in a story, the writer is using a technique called **foreshadowing.** Borden Deal uses foreshadowing in the first two sentences of this story. When Tom says, "It should have been the best Christmas of them all. . . . It started out to be, anyway," you get a clue that this Christmas will not turn out the way Tom expects. Review the story to find other clues that foreshadow what will happen. Which of those clues, if any, did you use to make predictions as you were reading the story?

Multimodal Learning
ALTERNATIVE ACTIVITIES

1. From herding sheep to hunting quail, dogs have served humans for many centuries. Today, specially trained dogs can assist people with disabilities. Research one of the many ways dogs have been trained to help people. Look in CD-ROM encyclopedias, videos, or books about dogs. Give an **oral presentation** of your findings, using pictures, slides, and other visual aids.

2. Think about the setting, sounds, and colors, as well as Tom's feelings, in the scene in which he shoots Calypso Baby. Then choose an art form and depict the scene. Share your **artwork** with your classmates.

3. Tom's feelings change a great deal during the course of this story. Find passages in the story that most clearly show those mood changes. Then select pieces of music that correspond to Tom's moods. Ask a classmate to make an **audiotape** of your performance as you read each passage aloud and then play its corresponding music.

LITERARY LINKS

Both Tom's father and Colin's father in "Last Cover" (page 95) are hunters. In what ways are the father-son relationships in these two stories similar, and in what ways are they different? If the two fathers could talk to each other, what might they say about teaching and raising children?

CRITIC'S CORNER

Eric de Armas, a seventh-grade member of the student board, felt that the boy in this story "does not get punished for what he did." Do you agree with this opinion? If so, what do you think would have been a fair punishment for what the boy did?

ACROSS THE CURRICULUM

Science *Cooperative Learning* Work with a group of classmates to research sporting dogs. Each member of the group should gather information about a particular breed, such as pointers, setters, retrievers, or spaniels. Then create a bulletin-board display that compares the characteristics of various breeds of dogs.

Hunting dogs: left to right, pointer, English setter, Brittany spaniel, Irish setter. Copyright © Walter Chandoha.

Handler training a pointer. Copyright © Dale C. Spartas.

Literary Links

Possible responses: They are similar in that the fathers come to have greater respect for their sons and different in that Tom and his father share a love of hunting whereas Colin and his father don't share a love of art. Both fathers would agree that children need their parents' attention.

Across the Curriculum

Science *Cooperative Learning* Suggest that groups consult encyclopedias, veterinary texts, and biology books or interview a local veterinarian. Have them search through old magazines to identify dog photos that they can cut out to display on their bulletin boards.

ADDITIONAL SUGGESTIONS

Math *How Much Is That Doggy?* Have students research and tally up all the costs associated with buying and keeping a dog for three years. Have them choose a specific breed and make sure they consider feeding, housing, dog toys, and veterinary costs. Encourage students to calculate and display their costs using spreadsheet software, if available.

Literary Concepts

Have students form small groups to review examples of foreshadowing in the story. *(Possible responses: Tom's resentful attitude while helping take care of the dogs suggests that he might want to prove himself later. Tom's dream foreshadows that he will act out of overconfidence.)*

Alternative Activities

1. Suggest that students use on-line encyclopedias and reference books to look up subjects such as Seeing Eye dogs and dogs used in law enforcement. Have students prepare an outline of the oral presentation.
2. Have students reread the scene. Students may work in groups to create realistic or abstract art.
3. Provide students with audio equipment as available and needed. Suggest that students try several different types of music for their performances.

BORDEN DEAL

Childhood memories of the South weave their way into much of Borden Deal's prolific work, as do themes of human growth and fallibility. In many of his stories, including "The Christmas Hunt," a mystical element is added by his references to dreams and to lessons learned in the wilderness. Deal was influenced by psychologist C. G. Jung's theories about myths and archetypes.

WORDS TO KNOW

EXERCISE A Review the Words to Know in the boxes at the bottom of the selection pages. Then write the vocabulary word that best completes each of the following sentences.

1. Although fox-hunting dogs raise quite a _____ when they are on a trail, bird dogs do their work in silence.

2. Bird dogs are _____, so they are able to move around very easily.

3. A bird dog's amazing sense of smell makes it difficult for quail to find _____.

4. When they are puppies, bird dogs must learn the _____ of hunting.

5. They learn the strategy by _____, or imitating what they see.

6. It may be difficult for a playful, _____ puppy to learn to freeze into a "point."

7. If a puppy shows _____, it probably won't be a very good hunter.

8. A good trainer looks upon a reckless or cruel dog handler with _____.

9. Tom's _____ in taking Calypso Baby hunting against his father's wishes got him into trouble.

10. No wonder he expected his father to be _____ with him for his disobedience

WORD PLAY Working with a partner, act out the meaning of *lithe, mimicry, cavorting, contempt, indifference,* or *irate* while another pair of students tries to guess the word. Then switch, with you and your partner trying to guess the word that the other pair of students is acting out. Continue until all the words have been acted out.

BORDEN DEAL

1922–1985

Borden Deal once said that his characters "live and work in real time in real places." Much of his fiction is set in the South, which Deal knew well. Born in Pontotoc, Mississippi, he worked on his father's cotton farm during the Great Depression. As a teenager, he traveled around the country and did odd jobs, including working in a circus, on a showboat, and as a forest-fire fighter. After graduating from the University of Alabama, he wrote adver- tisements before beginning his own full-time writing career.

Deal's novels and short stories have been translated into more than 20 languages and adapted for the stage, movies, radio, and television. More than 100 of his stories, poems, and reviews have been published in magazines.

OTHER WORKS *Walk Through the Valley, The Least One, The Loser, The Advocate, The Insolent Breed*

Extended Reading

WHAT DO YOU THINK?

Reflecting on Theme

Have students return to the activity on role-playing that they did before reading the selections in Part Two. Ask students how they might change their discussion after reading this selection. Have them role-play any new discussions they create.

NONFICTION

from Boy: Tales of Childhood

Roald Dahl (rōō'əl däl')

PERSONAL CONNECTION Activating Prior Knowledge/Setting a Purpose

Sometimes, it is hard to resist the urge to play a prank. Pranks can take many forms—funny or not so funny, harmless or harmful. They may also have unforeseen consequences. Get together with a small group of classmates. Describe some pranks you have played or have heard about. What were their consequences?

Building Background

CULTURAL CONNECTION

Roald Dahl, a well-known British author of books for young people, played his share of pranks when he was a schoolboy. In this excerpt from his autobiography, he describes a prank he played as a seven-year-old at Llandaff Cathedral School in Wales. This school was what the British call a preparatory school—an elementary school for students planning to attend private secondary schools. Tuition at preparatory schools can be costly, and they are known for high standards and rigorous academic training. At Dahl's school the headmaster and teachers were strict, and discipline was rigid.

WRITING CONNECTION

In your notebook, write about one of the pranks you discussed for the Personal Connection. As you write, consider the following questions: How did you or someone else feel while playing the prank and afterward? What do you think the victim of the prank might have thought about it? Then, as you read this selection, compare the prank you wrote about with the one that Roald Dahl describes.

Schoolchildren in Great Britain. Archive Photos.

OVERVIEW

Objectives

- To understand and appreciate an autobiographical excerpt about a schoolboy prank and its consequences
- To identify and understand a character's dialect
- To express understanding of the excerpt through a choice of writing forms, including a letter, a story, and conversation
- To extend understanding of the excerpt through a variety of multimodal and cross-curricular activities

Skills

READING SKILLS/ STRATEGIES
- Noting sequence of events
- Distinguishing fact and opinion

THE WRITER'S STYLE
- Sensory details

GRAMMAR
- Subordinate clauses

LITERARY CONCEPTS
- Dialect
- Imagery
- Irony

SPELLING
- Compound words

STUDY SKILLS
- Glossaries

SPEAKING, LISTENING, AND VIEWING
- Oral interpretation
- Pantomime
- Understanding dialect

Cross-Curricular Connections

SOCIAL STUDIES
- British preparatory schools

SCIENCE
- Saliva
- Making candy

PRINT AND MEDIA RESOURCES

UNIT FOUR RESOURCE BOOK
Strategic Reading: Literature, p. 49
Vocabulary SkillBuilder, p. 52
Reading SkillBuilder, p. 50
Spelling SkillBuilder, p. 51

GRAMMAR MINI-LESSONS
Transparencies, pp. 44 and 47

WRITING MINI-LESSONS
Transparencies, p. 38

ACCESS FOR STUDENTS ACQUIRING ENGLISH
Selection Summaries
Reading and Writing Support

FORMAL ASSESSMENT
Selection Test, pp. 91–92
 Test Generator

AUDIO LIBRARY
See reference Card

LASERLINKS
Author Background

SUMMARY

Roald Dahl recounts his memories of attending the Llandaff Cathedral School, including an incident at the local sweetshop, run by stingy, filthy Mrs. Pratchett. Playing a prank on Mrs. Pratchett, Dahl puts a dead mouse in a candy jar while his friends distract her. Because the sweetshop is closed the next day, the boys fear that they have caused Mrs. Pratchett to die of a heart attack. Instead, she appears at school and identifies the boys from a lineup of students. Later, each of the boys receives a caning as punishment for the prank.

Thematic Link: *High Stakes* Dahl and his friends risk punishment to play a prank on the mean owner of their favorite candy store.

CUSTOMIZING FOR
Students Acquiring English

- Use **ACCESS FOR STUDENTS ACQUIRING ENGLISH,** *Reading and Writing Support.*

- This story contains British names for a large variety of candies. Reassure students acquiring English that their English-speaking classmates are also unfamiliar with these names. As students read, they can use their reading logs to record their guesses about what kinds of candy each name describes. Ask them to note any other names they know for similar candy, such as *licorice stick* for *licorice straw.*

- In addition to these boxes, you may want to use the suggestions under Strategic Reading for Less Proficient Readers.

from

WORDS TO KNOW

elaborate (ĭ-lăb′ə-rāt′) *v.* to state at greater length or in greater detail (p. 478)
flourishing (flûr′ ĭ-shĭng) *adj.* getting along well and successfully; thriving **flourish** *v.* (p. 475)
jaunty (jôn′tē) *adj.* showing confidence and cheerfulness (p. 476)

loathsome (lōth′səm) *adj.* disgusting (p. 479)
malignant (mə-lĭg′nənt) *adj.* filled with evil; threatening (p. 481)

Y

Tales of Childhood

by Roald Dahl

The Bicycle and the Sweetshop

When I was seven, my mother decided I should leave kindergarten and go to a proper boys' school. By good fortune, there existed a well-known preparatory school for boys about a mile from our house. It was called Llandaff Cathedral School, and it stood right under the shadow of Llandaff cathedral. Like the cathedral, the school is still there and still <u>flourishing</u>.

But here again, I can remember very little about the two years I attended Llandaff Cathedral School, between the age of seven and nine. Only two moments remain clearly in my mind. The first lasted not more than five seconds, but I will never forget it.

A

WORDS TO KNOW	**flourishing** (flûr′ĭ-shĭng) *adj.* getting along well and successfully; thriving **flourish** *v.*

475

STRATEGIC READING FOR
Less Proficient Readers

Set a Purpose Have students read to determine the first memorable event the author describes and what the author's reaction to it reveals.

Use **UNIT FOUR RESOURCE BOOK**, p. 49, for guidance in reading the selection.

CUSTOMIZING FOR
Gifted and Talented Students

Have students note British slang terms as they read. Have them use context clues to determine the American English equivalents.

Possible responses:

• *Page 481*—"Hold on a tick . . ." Wait

• *Page 483*—"Sixth Form over there!" A form is a class.

• *Page 484*—"Nasty, cheeky lot . . ." Cheeky is fresh or sassy.

• *Page 484*—"They nick things . . ." They steal things.

Literary Note

A Llandaff is a Welsh name. In Welsh, many words start with *ll*. The Anglicized pronunciation of *ll* is the same as an *l* (lan daff). The correct pronunciation in Welsh, however, is "hlan daff," with a slight, soft *ch* sound.

Mini-Lesson — **Study Skills**

GLOSSARIES Explain to students that a glossary is a list of words and/or phrases and their definitions found at the end of a book. Sometimes dictionary-style books also are called glossaries. Point to the Handbook of Reading Terms and Literary Concepts, which begins on page 800, as an example of one kind of glossary.

Application Have students look up the following terms in the glossary of this book and write a definition of each term. Tell students to paraphrase each definition. Then have them write a sentence or two to relate each term to this excerpt.

1. character
2. dialect
3. imagery
4. setting

STRATEGIC READING FOR

Less Proficient Readers

B Ask students to describe the author's first vivid memory about his school days at Llandaff. *(The author remembers seeing an older boy riding full speed down the slope on a bicycle with his hands off the handlebars and recalls his wish to do the same.)* Restating

• What does young Roald's reaction to the biker reveal about the author? *(Possible response: He is immature and impressionable.)* Making Judgments

Set a Purpose Have students read to find out how the boys feel about Mrs. Pratchett and why they feel this way.

Active Reading: EVALUATE

C Have students evaluate the intensity of the boys' feelings for the sweetshop. You may wish to use the following model to demonstrate a possible thought process.

Think-Aloud Model *The sweetshop seems to bring the boys together, and stopping there is something they all look forward to. It must be very important to them, since they stop there just about every day. I think the sweetshop must play an important part in this story.*

It was my first term, and I was walking home alone across the village green after school when suddenly one of the senior twelve-year-old boys came riding full speed down the road on his bicycle about twenty yards away from me. The road was on a hill, and the boy was going down the slope, and as he flashed by he started back-pedaling very quickly so that the free-wheeling mechanism of his bike made a loud whirring sound. At the same time, he took his hands off the handlebars and folded them casually across his chest. I stopped dead and stared after him. How wonderful he was! How swift and brave and graceful in his long trousers with bicycle clips around them and his scarlet school cap at a jaunty angle on his head! One day, I told myself, one glorious day I will have a bike like that, and I will wear long trousers with bicycle clips, and my school cap will sit jaunty on my head, and I will 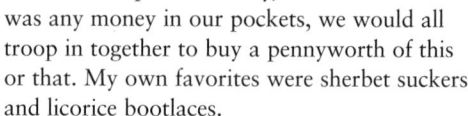 go whizzing down the hill pedaling backwards with no hands on the handlebars!

I promise you that if somebody had caught me by the shoulder at that moment and said to me, "What is your greatest wish in life, little boy? What is your absolute ambition? To be a doctor? A fine musician? A painter? A writer? Or the Lord Chancellor[1]?" I would have answered without hesitation that my only ambition, my hope, my longing was to have a bike like that and to go

Llandaf Cathedral Green (1986), Hildred Falcon. Courtesy National Library of Wales.

whizzing down the hill with no hands on the handlebars. It would be fabulous. It made me tremble just to think about it.

My second and only other memory of Llandaff Cathedral School is extremely bizarre. It happened a little over a year later, when I was just nine. By then I had made some friends, and when I walked to school in the mornings I would start out alone but would pick up four other boys of my own age along the way. After school was over, the same four boys and I would set out together across the village green and through the village itself, heading for home. On the way to school and on the way back we always passed the sweetshop. No we didn't; we never passed it. We always stopped. We lingered outside its rather small window, gazing in at the big glass jars full of bull's-eyes and old-fashioned humbugs and strawberry bonbons and glacier mints and acid drops and pear drops and lemon drops and all the rest of them. Each of us received sixpence[2] a week for pocket money, and whenever there was any money in our pockets, we would all troop in together to buy a pennyworth of this or that. My own favorites were sherbet suckers and licorice bootlaces.

---

1. **Lord Chancellor:** a high-ranking British government official who presides over the House of Lords.

2. **sixpence:** in Great Britain, six pennies.

| WORDS TO KNOW | **jaunty** (jôn′tē) *adj.* showing confidence and cheerfulness |

476

Mini-Lesson  **Reading Skills/Strategies**

NOTING SEQUENCE OF EVENTS Remind students that the sequence of events is the order in which the action occurs in a story. Point out that this sequence may not always be chronological. For example, a mystery may start with a murder or a theft and then show the events that led to it. Readers enjoy trying to figure out "whodunnit" before the author reveals the criminal's identity. In this story, the sequence in which events are related is the sequence in which Dahl experienced them, a technique often used for a first-person narrative.

Application Have students list events in the order of their occurrence, starting with the boys' discovery of the dead mouse. Discuss with students how Dahl's withholding of information about Mrs. Pratchett adds to the suspense of the story.

CUSTOMIZING FOR

Multiple Learning Styles

D **Spatial or Graphic Learners** Have students create a comic strip showing the sequence of events, as described by Thwaites's father, in making the candy called licorice bootlaces. Encourage them to use creativity and humor in their work. Have students share their comic strips with the class.

One of the other boys, whose name was Thwaites, told me I should never eat licorice bootlaces. Thwaites's father, who was a doctor, had said that they were made from rats' blood. The father had given his young son a lecture about licorice bootlaces when he had caught him eating one in bed. "Every rat catcher in the country," the father had said, "takes his rats to the Licorice Bootlace Factory, and the manager pays tuppence[3] for each rat. Many a rat catcher has become a millionaire by selling his dead rats to the factory."

"But how do they turn the rats into licorice?" the young Thwaites had asked his father.

"They wait until they've got ten thousand rats," the father had answered, "then they dump them all into a huge, shiny steel cauldron[4] and boil them up for several hours. Two men stir the bubbling cauldron with long poles, and in the end they have a thick, steaming rat stew. After that, a cruncher is lowered into the cauldron to crunch the bones, and what's left is a pulpy substance called rat mash."

"Yes, but how do they turn that into licorice bootlaces, Daddy?" the young Thwaites had asked, and this question, according to Thwaites, had caused his father to pause and think for a few moments before he answered it. At last he had said, "The two men who were doing the stirring with the long poles now put on their Wellington boots[5] and climb into the cauldron and shovel the hot rat mash out onto a concrete floor. Then they run a steamroller over it several times to flatten it out. What is left looks rather like a gigantic black pancake, and all they have to do after that is to wait for it to cool and to harden so they can cut it up into strips to make the bootlaces. Don't ever eat them," the father had said. "If you do, you'll get ratitis."

"What is ratitis, Daddy?" young Thwaites had asked.

"All the rats that the rat catchers catch are poisoned with rat poison," the father had said. "It's the rat poison that gives you ratitis."

"Yes, but what happens to you when you catch it?" young Thwaites had asked.

"Your teeth become very sharp and pointed," the father had answered. "And a short, stumpy tail grows out of your back just above your bottom. There is no cure for ratitis. I ought to know. I'm a doctor."

D

We all enjoyed Thwaites's story, and we made him tell it to us many times on our walks to and from school. But it didn't stop any of us except Thwaites from buying licorice bootlaces. At two for a penny they were the best value in the shop. A bootlace, in case you haven't had the pleasure of handling one, is not round. It's like a flat black tape about half an inch wide. You buy it rolled up in a coil, and in those days it used to be so long that when you unrolled it and held one end at arm's length above your head, the other end touched the ground.

E

Sherbet suckers were also two a penny. Each sucker consisted of a yellow cardboard tube filled with sherbet powder, and there was a hollow licorice straw sticking out of it. (Rat's blood again, young Thwaites would warn us, pointing at the licorice straw.) You sucked the sherbet up through the straw, and when it was finished you ate the licorice. They were delicious, those sherbet suckers. The sherbet fizzed in your mouth, and if you knew how

Critical Thinking: CLASSIFYING

E Ask students to classify Thwaites and then the other boys as believers or nonbelievers of Dr. Thwaites's description of how licorice bootlaces are made. Have them explain their classifications. *(Possible response: Thwaites must have been a believer, since he never ate licorice bootlaces. The boys must have been nonbelievers—since they enjoyed hearing the story over and over, but it didn't stop them from eating this candy.)*

Mini-Lesson Literary Concepts

REVIEWING IMAGERY Remind students that words and phrases that appeal to the reader's senses are known as imagery. Writers use imagery to help the reader imagine how things look, feel, smell, sound, and taste.

Application Have students analyze the author's use of imagery in Thwaites's tale about how licorice bootlaces are made. Have them list words and phrases that appeal to specific senses and describe the feeling that each image conveys. Then invite pairs of students to write their own description of how this candy is made, using imagery that makes the candy seem delicious. Invite students to share their writing with the class.

F When Thwaites says, "It's your spit that does it," he's partly correct. Although Thwaites implies that the saliva causes a chemical reaction, which is not true, he has identified the agent that causes a physical change. The gobstopper is made mostly of sugar and food coloring, which can be dissolved in water. Saliva is mostly water. As the different-colored layers of the candy are dissolved by the saliva, new layers, and new colors, are exposed.

Active Reading: CONNECT

G Ask students if there is a place they feel is very important. Ask them what characteristics make it special. Invite students to use their reading logs to draw parallels between the sweet-shop and their own special places.

CUSTOMIZING FOR

Students Acquiring English

2 Explain that tonsils are small masses of tissue located at the back of the mouth. They are part of the body's immune system.

3 Lead students to understand that the analogies used here show how important the sweetshop is to the boys.

---

to do it, you could make white froth come out of your nostrils and pretend you were throwing a fit.

Gobstoppers, costing a penny each, were enormous, hard round balls the size of small tomatoes. One gobstopper would provide about an hour's worth of nonstop sucking, and if you took it out of your mouth and inspected it every five minutes or so, you would find it had changed color. There was something fascinating about the way it went from pink to blue to green to yellow. We used to wonder how in the world the Gobstopper Factory managed to achieve this magic. "How *does* it happen?" we would ask each other. "How *can* they make it keep changing color?"

F "It's your spit that does it," young Thwaites proclaimed. As the son of a doctor, he considered himself to be an authority on all things that had to do with the body. He could tell us about scabs and when they were ready to be picked off. He knew why a black eye was blue and why blood was red. "It's your spit that makes a gobstopper change color," he kept insisting. When we asked him to elaborate on this theory, he answered, "You wouldn't understand it if I did tell you."

Pear drops were exciting because they had a dangerous taste. They smelled of nail varnish, and they froze the back of your throat. All of us were warned against eating them, and the result was that we ate them more than ever.

The sweetshop in Llandaff in the year 1923 was the very center of our lives.

Then there was a hard brown lozenge called the tonsil tickler. The tonsil tickler tasted and smelled very strongly of chloroform. We had not the slightest doubt that these things were saturated in the dreaded anesthetic which, as Thwaites had many times pointed out to us, could put you to sleep for hours at a stretch.

"If my father has to saw off somebody's leg," he said, "he pours chloroform onto a pad, and the person sniffs it and goes to sleep, and my father saws his leg off without him even feeling it."

"But why do they put it into sweets and sell them to us?" we asked him.

You might think a question like this would have baffled Thwaites. But Thwaites was never baffled. "My father says tonsil ticklers were invented for dangerous prisoners in jail," he said. "They give them one with each meal, and the chloroform makes them sleepy and stops them rioting."

"Yes," we said, "but why sell them to children?"

"It's a plot," Thwaites said. "A grown-up plot to keep us quiet."

The sweetshop in Llandaff in the year 1923 was the very center of our lives. To us, it was what a bar is to a drunk or a church is to a bishop. Without it, there would have been little to live for. But it had one terrible drawback, this sweetshop. The woman who owned it was a horror. We hated her, and we had good reason for doing so.

Her name was Mrs. Pratchett. She was a

WORDS TO KNOW **elaborate** (ĭ-lăb′ə-rāt′) *v.* to state at greater length or in greater detail

478

Mini-Lesson   The Writer's Style

Subjects Described	Details	Sensory Appeal

SENSORY DETAILS Help students understand that the author uses vivid descriptions that appeal to the reader's sense of sight, sound, smell, taste, and touch. These descriptions are called sensory details.

Application Have students reread pages 478 and 479 to identify sensory details about Mrs. Pratchett, gobstoppers, and pear drops. Then have them create a chart like the one shown on which they list the subjects described, the sensory details that describe them, and the

senses to which the details appeal. Invite students to share their information and create a cumulative class chart.

Reteaching/Reinforcement
• Writing Handbook anthology, p. 819
• *Writing Mini-Lessons*, transparencies, p. 38

 The Writer's Craft

Sensory Details, p. 255

small, skinny old hag with a moustache on her upper lip and a mouth as sour as a green gooseberry. She never smiled. She never welcomed us when we went in, and the only times she spoke were when she said things like, "I'm watchin' you, so keep yer thievin' fingers off them chocolates!" Or "I don't want you in 'ere just to look around! Either you *forks* out or you *gets* out!"

But by far the most <u>loathsome</u> thing about Mrs. Pratchett was the filth that clung around her. Her apron was grey and greasy. Her blouse had bits of breakfast all over it, toast crumbs and tea stains and splotches of dried egg yolk. It was her hands, however, that disturbed us most. They were disgusting. They were black with dirt and grime. They looked as though they had been putting lumps of coal on the fire all day long. And do not forget, please, that it was these very hands and fingers that she plunged into the sweet jars when we asked for a penny-worth of treacle toffee[6] or wine gums or nut clusters or whatever. There were precious few health laws in those days, and nobody, least of all Mrs. Pratchett, ever thought of using a little shovel for getting out the sweets as they do today. The mere sight of her grimy right hand with its black fingernails digging an ounce of chocolate fudge out of a jar would have caused a starving tramp to go running from the shop. But not us. Sweets were our life-blood. We would have put up with far worse than that to get them. So we simply stood and watched in sullen silence while this

disgusting old woman stirred around inside the jars with her foul fingers.

The other thing we hated Mrs. Pratchett for was her meanness. Unless you spent a whole sixpence all in one go, she wouldn't give you a bag. Instead you got your sweets twisted up in a small piece of newspaper which she tore off a pile of old *Daily Mirrors* lying on the counter.

So you can well understand that we had it in for Mrs. Pratchett in a big way, but we didn't quite know what to do about it. Many schemes were put forward, but none of them was any good. None of them, that is, until suddenly, one memorable afternoon, we found the dead mouse.

The Great Mouse Plot

My four friends and I had come across a loose floorboard at the back of the classroom, and when we prised it up with the blade of a pocketknife, we discovered a big hollow space underneath. This, we decided, would be our secret hiding place for sweets and other small treasures such as conkers[7] and monkey nuts and birds' eggs. Every afternoon, when the last lesson was over, the five of us would wait until the classroom had emptied; then we would lift up the floorboard and examine our secret hoard, perhaps adding to it or taking something away.

One day, when we lifted it up, we found a dead mouse lying among our treasures. It was an exciting discovery. Thwaites took it out by its tail and waved it in front of our faces.

---

6. **treacle toffee:** a hard, chewy candy made from molasses.

7. **conkers:** large brown nuts threaded on strings for use in a children's game.

WORDS TO KNOW

loathsome (lōth'səm) *adj.* disgusting

479

Literary Concept: IMAGERY

H Ask students to look at the images Dahl uses to show the boys' disgust. Ask why the author adds these details, even though he has already stated that the boys found Mrs. Pratchett's hands disgusting. (*Possible responses: These details help readers visualize the character and experience why the boys find her hands repulsive.*)

Active Reading: EVALUATE

I Have students note the author's description of Mrs. Pratchett. Then have them list other adjectives they could use to describe a character like Mrs. Pratchett. (*Possible responses: scary, mean, unpleasant, gross*) Ask students if they think the boys' perception is accurate. (*Possible responses: yes, because they include many details that seem to support their description; no, because the description seems exaggerated*)

STRATEGIC READING FOR
Less Proficient Readers

J Make sure students understand how the boys feel about the shopkeeper and why.

- How do the boys feel about Mrs. Pratchett? (*They hate her.*) **Classifying**
- Why do the boys feel this way? (*They consider her mean, ugly, and filthy.*) **Making Generalizations**

Set a Purpose Have students read to find out what the boys do to "get back at" Mrs. Pratchett.

Mini-Lesson **Grammar**

SUBORDINATE CLAUSES Explain to students that a clause is a group of words that contains a subject and a verb. A clause that cannot stand by itself as a complete sentence is a subordinate clause. In the highlighted sentence on page 478, the subordinate clause is "if I did tell you." A subordinate clause is introduced by a subordinating conjunction, in this case *if*.

Application List on the chalkboard the examples of subordinating conjunctions. Then have students use these conjunctions to introduce

subordinate clauses to add to the beginning or the end of each of the following sentences.
1. The boys were excited.
2. Mrs. Pratchett was suspicious.
3. The headmaster frowned.
4. The boys ran the rest of the way to school.

Reteaching/Reinforcement
- *Grammar Mini-Lessons* transparencies, pp. 44 and 47

The Writer's Craft

Subordinate Clauses, pp. 565–566

Subordinating Conjunctions

after	before	when
as	if	whenever
although	than	where
because	until	while

Art Note

Three Boys with a Mouse by Terry Mimnaugh As a child, Mimnaugh (1954–) was always told that she could succeed at anything she tried. She decided to be a sculptor and wasn't discouraged when she was told that women couldn't be "real" artists. She graduated from art school anyway. Today she spends six months each year planning her next year's work. She has said, "Motivation comes from within. Someone can tell you how to go over a mountain, but the only way to do it is on your own two feet."

Reading the Art *What do the expressions on the boys' faces suggest about how they feel?*

Three Boys with a Mouse (1981), Terry Mimnaugh. Bronze, 10½″ × 9″ × 7″, from the series *What Little Boys Are Made Of.*

Mini-Lesson: Speaking, Listening, and Viewing

PANTOMIME Explain to students that pantomime is the use of gestures and actions rather than spoken words to play a part. Since words are not used, the person performing a pantomime tells a story or communicates an emotion using bodily movements, gestures, and facial expressions.

Application Have students work in groups of three to five to choose a scene from the story and create a pantomime based on it. Scenes might include finding the mouse or tricking Mrs. Pratchett in the sweetshop.

After choosing a scene, groups should decide what actions and emotions they want to convey and how to pantomime them. Have each student portray one character. You may want to supply students with any props they need.

After each group presents the pantomime, encourage the rest of the class to guess what scene was presented, who the characters were, and what emotions were conveyed.

"What shall we do with it?" he cried.

"It stinks!" someone shouted. "Throw it out of the window quick!"

"Hold on a tick," I said. "Don't throw it away."

Thwaites hesitated. They all looked at me.

When writing about oneself, one must strive to be truthful. Truth is more important than modesty. I must tell you, therefore, that it was I and I alone who had the idea for the great and daring Mouse Plot. We all have our moments of brilliance and glory, and this was mine.

"Why don't we," I said, "slip it into one of Mrs. Pratchett's jars of sweets? Then when she puts her dirty hand in to grab a handful, she'll grab a stinky dead mouse instead."

The other four stared at me in wonder. Then, as the sheer genius of the plot began to sink in, they all started grinning. They slapped me on the back. They cheered me and danced around the classroom. "We'll do it today!" they cried. "We'll do it on the way home! *You* had the idea," they said to me, "so *you* can be the one to put the mouse in the jar."

Thwaites handed me the mouse. I put it into my trouser pocket. Then the five of us left the school, crossed the village green, and headed for the sweetshop. We were tremendously jazzed up. We felt like a gang of desperados setting out to rob a train or blow up the sheriff's office.

"Make sure you put it into a jar which is used often," somebody said.

"I'm putting it in gobstoppers," I said. "The gobstopper jar is never behind the counter."

"I've got a penny," Thwaites said, "so I'll ask for one sherbet sucker and one bootlace. And while she turns away to get them, you slip the mouse in quickly with the gobstoppers."

Thus everything was arranged. We were strutting a little as we entered the shop. We were the victors now, and Mrs. Pratchett was the victim. She stood behind the counter, and her small, <u>malignant</u> pig-eyes watched us suspiciously as we came forward.

"One sherbet sucker, please," Thwaites said to her, holding out his penny.

I kept to the rear of the group, and when I saw Mrs. Pratchett turn her head away for a couple of seconds to fish a sherbet sucker out of the box, I lifted the heavy glass lid of the gobstopper jar and dropped the mouse in. Then I replaced the lid as silently as possible. My heart was thumping like mad, and my hands had gone all sweaty.

"And one bootlace, please," I heard Thwaites saying. When I turned around, I saw Mrs. Pratchett holding out the bootlace in her filthy fingers.

"I don't want all the lot of you troopin' in 'ere if only one of you is buyin'," she screamed at us. "Now beat it! Go on, get out!"

As soon as we were outside, we broke into a run. "Did you do it?" they shouted at me.

"Of course I did!" I said.

"Well done, you!" they cried. "What a super show!"

I felt like a hero. I *was* a hero. It was marvelous to be so popular.

Mr. Coombes

The flush of triumph over the dead mouse was carried forward to the next morning as we all met again to walk to school.

> WORDS TO KNOW
> **malignant** (mə-lĭg′nənt) *adj.* filled with evil; threatening

481

Have students discuss the differences between the sweetshop and what they know about modern candy stores. Ask if the same prank could be played today. Have them explain why or why not. *(Possible response: probably not, because most candy today is packaged, not loose in jars)*

STRATEGIC READING FOR

Less Proficient Readers

Review with students the imagery the author uses to convey the post-prank condition in the sweetshop.

• What do the boys see at the sweetshop the morning after the prank? *(a smashed gobstopper jar on the floor; a "closed" sign on the door)* **Noting Relevant Details**

• Why do "alarm bells" ring in the boys' ears? *(They know the shop is never closed at this time.)* **Drawing Conclusions**

• What conclusion does Thwaites draw about what happened to Mrs. Pratchett? *(The discovery of the mouse gave her a terrible shock, and she had a heart attack.)* **Restating**

Set a Purpose Have students read the rest of the excerpt to discover the consequence of the boys' prank.

CUSTOMIZING FOR

Multiple Learning Styles

Bodily-Kinesthetic Learners Have students hypothesize what happened when Mrs. Pratchett reached into the gobstopper jar and found the dead mouse. Then have them enact their scene for the class.

"Let's go in and see if it's still in the jar," somebody said as we approached the sweetshop.

"Don't," Thwaites said firmly. "It's too dangerous. Walk past as though nothing has happened."

As we came level with the shop we saw a cardboard notice hanging on the door.

We stopped and stared. We had never known the sweetshop to be closed at this time in the morning, even on Sundays.

"What's happened?" we asked each other. "What's going on?"

We pressed our faces against the window and looked inside. Mrs. Pratchett was nowhere to be seen.

"Look!" I cried. "The gobstopper jar's gone! It's not on the shelf! There's a gap where it used to be!"

"It's on the floor!" someone said. "It's smashed to bits, and there's gobstoppers everywhere!"

"There's the mouse!" someone else shouted.

We could see it all, the huge glass jar smashed to smithereens with the dead mouse lying in the wreckage and hundreds of many-colored gobstoppers littering the floor.

"She got such a shock when she grabbed hold of the mouse that she dropped everything," somebody was saying.

"But why didn't she sweep it all up and open the shop?" I asked.

Nobody answered me.

We turned away and walked towards the school. All of a sudden we had begun to feel slightly uncomfortable. There was something not quite right about the shop being closed. Even Thwaites was unable to offer a reasonable explanation. We became silent. There was a faint scent of danger in the air now. Each one of us had caught a whiff of it. Alarm bells were beginning to ring faintly in our ears.

After a while, Thwaites broke the silence. "She must have got one heck of a shock," he said. He paused. We all looked at him, wondering what wisdom the great medical authority was going to come out with next.

"After all," he went on, "to catch hold of a dead mouse when you're expecting to catch hold of a gobstopper must be a pretty frightening experience. Don't you agree?"

Nobody answered him.

"Well now," Thwaites went on, "when an old person like Mrs. Pratchett suddenly gets a very big shock, I suppose you know what happens next?"

"What?" we said. "What happens?"

"You ask my father," Thwaites said. "He'll tell you."

"You tell us," we said.

"It gives her a heart attack," Thwaites announced. "Her heart stops beating, and she's dead in five seconds."

For a moment or two my own heart stopped beating. Thwaites pointed a finger at me and said darkly, "I'm afraid you've killed her."

"*Me?*" I cried. "Why just *me?*"

"It was *your* idea," he said. "And what's more, *you* put the mouse in."

All of a sudden, I was a murderer.

At exactly that point, we heard the school bell ringing in the distance, and we had to gallop the rest of the way so as not to be late for prayers.

Prayers were held in the Assembly Hall. We all perched in rows on wooden benches while the teachers sat up on the platform in armchairs, facing us. The five of us scrambled into our places just as the Headmaster marched in, followed by the rest of the staff.

| Mini-Lesson | Reading Skills/Strategies |

DISTINGUISHING FACT AND OPINION
Remind students that a fact is a statement that can be proved; an opinion is a statement that cannot be proved. Opinions generally reflect personal beliefs and are often debatable.

Application Have groups of five students determine which of the following statements are facts and which are opinions.

1. Mrs. Pratchett got a shock and had a heart attack.
2. After the prank, the gobstopper jar was not where it used to be.
3. Using chloroform in sweets is a grown-up plot to keep kids quiet.
4. Young Dahl was responsible for the prank.

Reteaching/Reinforcement
• *Unit Four Resource Book,* p. 50

The Headmaster is the only teacher at Llandaff Cathedral School that I can remember, and for a reason you will soon discover, I can remember him very clearly indeed. His name was Mr. Coombes, and I have a picture in my mind of a giant of a man with a face like a ham and a mass of rusty-colored hair that sprouted in a tangle all over the top of his head. All grown-ups appear as giants to small children. But Headmasters (and policemen) are the biggest giants of all and acquire a marvelously exaggerated stature. It is possible that Mr. Coombes was a perfectly normal being, but in my memory he was a giant, a tweed-suited giant who always wore a black gown over his tweeds and a waistcoat under his jacket.

Mr. Coombes now proceeded to mumble through the same old prayers we had every day; but this morning, when the last amen had been spoken, he did not turn and lead his group rapidly out of the hall as usual. He remained standing before us, and it was clear he had an announcement to make.

"The whole school is to go out and line up around the playground immediately," he said. "Leave your books behind. And no talking."

Mr. Coombes was looking grim. His hammy pink face had taken on that dangerous scowl which only appeared when he was extremely cross and somebody was for the high jump. I sat there small and frightened among the rows and rows of other boys; and to me at that moment the Headmaster, with his black gown draped over his shoulders, was like a judge at a murder trial.

We stopped and stared. We had never known the sweetshop to be closed at this time.

"He's after the killer," Thwaites whispered to me.

I began to shiver.

"I'll bet the police are here already," Thwaites went on. "And the Black Maria's[8] waiting outside."

As we made our way out to the playground, my whole stomach began to feel as though it was slowly filling up with swirling water. *I am only eight years old,* I told myself. *No little boy of eight has ever murdered anyone. It's not possible.*

Out in the playground on this warm, cloudy September morning, the Deputy Headmaster was shouting, "Line up in forms! Sixth Form over there! Fifth Form next to them! Spread out! Spread out! Get on with it! Stop talking all of you!"

Thwaites and I and my other three friends were in the Second Form, the lowest but one, and we lined up against the red-brick wall of the playground shoulder to shoulder. I can remember that when every boy in the school was in his place, the line stretched right around the four sides of the playground—about one hundred small boys altogether, aged between six and twelve, all of us wearing identical grey shorts and grey blazers and grey stockings and black shoes.

"Stop that *talking!*" shouted the Deputy Head. "I want absolute silence!"

But why for heaven's sake were we in the playground at all? I wondered. And why were we lined up like this? It had never happened before.

---

8. **Black Maria** (mə-rī′ə): a police patrol wagon.

BOY: TALES OF CHILDHOOD **483**

Literary Concept: FORESHADOWING

Q Ask students to describe what Mr. Coombes normally does immediately after finishing the prayers. *(leads his group out)* Ask what he does on this day. *(remains standing)* Ask students to predict what they think his actions foreshadow. *(Possible response: He will announce Mrs. Pratchett's death.)*

Literary Concept: IRONY

R Have students contrast the narrator's feelings while plotting the prank with his emotions at this point in the excerpt. *(Before, he felt daring, brilliant, and glorious; whereas now, he feels scared and ashamed of being suspected.)*

CUSTOMIZING FOR

Multiple Learning Styles

S Intrapersonal Learners Point out that the italics used here indicates Roald's thoughts. Have students write a paragraph showing what Mr. Coombes's thoughts are likely to be during this scene.

Assessment ✓ **Option**

INFORMAL ASSESSMENT You can informally assess students' understanding of the selection by having each student write a letter based on the following scenario:

Pretend that nine-year-old Roald is sent to prison for the prank. Write a letter from Roald to Thwaites or from Thwaites to his imprisoned friend. In either case, discuss the prank and its consequences.

Rubric

3 Full Accomplishment Students convey the character's voice and point of view, using accurate details to retell the prank and its consequences.

2 Substantial Accomplishment Students use the character's voice and summarize the prank but fail to include some important details.

1 Little or Partial Accomplishment Students have difficulty maintaining the character's voice and point of view. The letters include irrelevant details and leave out important ones.

T Discuss Thwaites's lack of response to finding out that Mrs. Pratchett is alive. Ask students why they think Thwaites keeps silent. *(Possible responses: Thwaites keeps silent because he can't bear being proven wrong—he swore that Mrs. Pratchett was dead. Thwaites is simply terrified that he'll get caught and be punished.)*

Literary Concept: DIALECT

U Remind students that dialect is a form of language as it is spoken in a certain place or among a certain group of people. It has its own pronunciations, spellings, and expressions. Ask students what Mrs. Pratchett's use of *'uns* and *'ands* represent. *("ones" and "hands")*

I half expected to see two policemen come bounding out of the school to grab me by the arms and put handcuffs on my wrists.

A single door led out from the school onto the playground. Suddenly it swung open, and through it, like the angel of death, strode Mr. Coombes, huge and bulky in his tweed suit and black gown; and beside him, believe it or not, right beside him trotted the tiny figure of Mrs. Pratchett herself!

Mrs. Pratchett was alive!

The relief was tremendous.

"She's alive!" I whispered to Thwaites standing next to me. "I didn't kill her!" Thwaites **T** ignored me.

"We'll start over here," Mr. Coombes was saying to Mrs. Pratchett. He grasped her by one of her skinny arms and led her over to where the Sixth Form was standing. Then, still keeping hold of her arm, he proceeded to lead her at a brisk walk down the line of boys. It was like someone inspecting the troops.

"What on earth are they doing?" I whispered.

Thwaites didn't answer me. I glanced at him. He had gone rather pale.

"Too big," I heard Mrs. Pratchett saying. "Much too big. It's none of this lot. Let's 'ave a look at some of them titchy ones."

Mr. Coombes increased his pace. "We'd better go all the way round," he said. He seemed in a hurry to get it over with now, and I could see Mrs. Pratchett's skinny goat's legs trotting to keep up with him. They had already inspected

From *Boy* by Roald Dahl. Copyright © 1984, courtesy of Farrar, Straus & Giroux, Inc.

one side of the playground where the Sixth Form and half the Fifth Form were standing. We watched them moving down the second side . . . then the third side.

"Still too big," I heard Mrs. Pratchett croaking. "Much too big! Smaller than these! Much smaller! Where's them nasty little ones?"

They were coming closer to us now . . . closer and closer.

They were starting on the fourth side . . .

Every boy in our form was watching Mr. Coombes and Mrs. Pratchett as they came walking down the line towards us.

"Nasty, cheeky lot, these little 'uns!" I heard Mrs. Pratchett muttering. "They comes into my shop, and they thinks they can do what they damn well likes!" Mr. Coombes made no reply to this.

"They nick things when I ain't lookin'," she went on. "They put their grubby 'ands all over everything, and they've got no manners. I don't mind girls. I never 'ave no trouble with girls, but boys is 'ideous and 'orrible! I don't 'ave to tell *you* that, 'Eadmaster, do I?"

"These are the smaller ones," Mr. Coombes said.

I could see Mrs. Pratchett's piggy little eyes staring hard at the face of each boy she passed.

Suddenly she let out a high-pitched yell and pointed a dirty finger straight at Thwaites. "That's 'im!" she yelled. "That's one of 'em!

Mini-Lesson: Speaking,  **Listening, and Viewing**

UNDERSTANDING DIALECT Point out to students that having "a good ear" is an important part of writing realistic dialogue. For example, Dahl needed to be familiar with the kind of dialect a British sweetshop owner might have in order to convey Mrs. Pratchett's character effectively.

Application Have students find audio or videotape recordings that provide samples of different dialects. Have students play their samples for the class. Tell students to listen carefully and note if they can detect any patterns, like dropping the *h* at the beginning of words.

I'd know 'im a mile away, the scummy little bounder!"

The entire school turned to look at Thwaites. "W-what have *I* done?" he stuttered, appealing to Mr. Coombes.

"Shut up," Mr. Coombes said.

Mrs. Pratchett's eyes flicked over and settled on my own face. I looked down and studied the black asphalt surface of the playground.

"'Ere's another of 'em!" I heard her yelling. "That one there!" She was pointing at me now.

"You're quite sure?" Mr. Coombes said.

"Of course I'm sure!" she cried. "I never forgets a face, least of all when it's as sly as that! 'Ee's one of 'em all right! There was five altogether! Now where's them other three?"

The other three, as I knew very well, were coming up next.

Mrs. Pratchett's face was glimmering with venom as her eyes traveled beyond me down the line.

"There they are!" she cried out, stabbing the air with her finger. "'Im . . . and 'im . . . and 'im! That's the five of 'em all right! We don't need to look no farther than this, 'Eadmaster! They're all 'ere, the nasty, dirty little pigs! You've got their names, 'ave you?"

"I've got their names, Mrs. Pratchett," Mr. Coombes told her. "I'm much obliged to you."

"And I'm much obliged to *you*, 'Eadmaster," she answered.

As Mr. Coombes led her away across the playground, we heard her saying, "Right in the jar of gobstoppers it was! A stinkin' dead mouse which I will never forget as long as I live!"

"You have my deepest sympathy," Mr. Coombes was muttering.

"Talk about shocks!" she went on. "When my fingers caught 'old of that nasty, soggy, stinkin' dead mouse . . . " Her voice trailed away as Mr. Coombes led her quickly through the door into the school building. ❖

Editor's Note: After being identified by Mrs. Pratchett in the schoolyard lineup, Roald and his friends were ordered into the Head-master's office. There they received a caning (beating) from Mr. Coombes, while Mrs. Pratchett watched. When Roald's mother saw her son's bruises, she promised to send him to school in England. The following year, Roald went to boarding school.

BOY: TALES OF CHILDHOOD **485**

Mini-Lesson ⟨TM⟩ **Spelling**

COMPOUND WORDS Remind students that a compound word is a word formed by combining two or more words without changing their spelling, for example, *fireproof.*

Application Write on the chalkboard the list shown and the incomplete sentences. Have students create compound words from this list and use them to complete each sentence.
1. The _____ sold candy, such as _____ and _____. *(shopkeeper, gobstoppers, humbugs)*

2. Mr. Coombes, the school's _____, wore a _____ under his jacket. *(headmaster, waistcoat)*
3. We found a loose _____ in the classroom and pried it up with the blade of a _____. *(floorboard, pocketknife)*
4. We were afraid the _____ would arrest us and put our hands in _____. *(policemen, handcuffs)*

Reteaching/Reinforcement
• *Unit Four Resource Book,* p. 51

board	floor	keeper	pocket
bugs	gob	knife	police
coat	hand	master	shop
cuffs	head	men	stopper
	hum		waist

From Personal Response to Critical Analysis

1. Encourage students to explain why they chose the part that they did.

2. Possible response: Yes, the boys' prank was unfair, and they should be punished. No, using a lineup and inflicting corporal punishment are inappropriate responses to Mrs. Pratchett's complaint.

3. Possible response: No, because the boys got in deep trouble and they might have injured Mrs. Pratchett seriously.

4. Possible response: The author's humorous writing style suggests that he viewed the prank as funny.

5. Possible response: My prank was a lot funnier and had less-severe consequences.

6. Possible response: when the severity of the consequences outweighs the humor of the prank

7. Possible responses: Dahl's love of candy; Dahl's closeness to his friends

Another Pathway

Remind students to give a dramatic reading in which they attempt to sound and act like two nine-year-old boys.

Rubric

3 Full Accomplishment The dialogue includes all the subjects specified. Each student is true to his or her character.

2 Substantial Accomplishment The dialogue covers most of the specified topics. Each student stays in character most of the time.

1 Little or Partial Accomplishment The dialogue covers few of the specified topics. Students rarely convey the point of view of the character they are portraying.

RESPONDING OPTIONS

FROM PERSONAL RESPONSE TO CRITICAL ANALYSIS

REFLECT

1. Which part of this selection did you enjoy most? Share that part with a classmate.

RETHINK
Close Textual Readings

2. Do you agree with the way Headmaster Coombes responds to Mrs. Pratchett's complaint? Why or why not?

3. Do you think the boys are right in playing their prank on Mrs. Pratchett? Give reasons to support your opinion.

   Consider
   • the consequences of the prank
   • other ways that the boys might treat Mrs. Pratchett

4. How do you think the grown-up Dahl felt about his schoolboy prank?

RELATE

5. How would you compare the boys' prank with the one you described for the Writing Connection on page 473?

6. In your opinion, when does a prank go too far to be acceptable?

7. Which of Dahl's experiences remind you the most of your own experiences when you were his age?

Multimodal Learing
ANOTHER PATHWAY

Working with a partner, write a dialogue between Roald Dahl and Thwaites. Have them discuss the prank, its consequences, and their feelings about whether it was worth doing and whether they'll go into the sweetshop again. After you have written the dialogue, rehearse and then perform it for the rest of the class.

LITERARY CONCEPTS

As you may remember, *characterization* refers to the methods that a writer uses to make characters come alive for the reader. One of these methods is to write what a character says in a way that reflects the character's **dialect**—a type of language spoken by people of a particular class or region. A dialect may differ from standard language in both vocabulary and pronunciation. One way Roald Dahl re-creates Mrs. Pratchett's British working-class dialect is by dropping *h* at the beginning of words, as in *'ere* for *here*. Find other devices he uses to depict her dialect. Then read some of her speeches aloud. What impressions do you form of her on the basis of the way she speaks?

QUICKWRITES

1. What character that you've read or heard about do you think would fit in well with Roald Dahl's gang of friends? Write a **letter** to persuade Dahl and his friends to accept the character as part of their group.

2. Using Thwaites's "rat-mash" account as a model, create a **story** about the making of your favorite candy.

3. Write the **conversation** that Mrs. Pratchett and Mr. Coombes might have had when she reported the boys' prank. Review what you learned about dialect in the Literary Concepts feature, and try to imitate the way these characters speak.

📁 *PORTFOLIO Save your writing. You may want to use it later as a springboard to a piece for your portfolio.*

486   UNIT FOUR   PART 2: HIGH STAKES

Literary Concepts

Have students form groups of three to locate one or more of Mrs. Pratchett's speeches in the text. *(Possible responses: dropping the final g in words ending in -ing; use of unusual word forms, such as "'uns" for "ones"; use of odd grammatical forms, such as "They comes into," "they thinks"; use of slang, such as "ain't" and "nick." Based on her harsh language, students may form the impression that Mrs. Pratchett is rude and nasty.)*

QuickWrites

1. Suggest that students list characteristics they think represent the author's group of friends and then match as many of these characteristics as possible with their chosen character. Have them mention the matching characteristics in their persuasive letter.

2. Have each student choose a favorite candy and list its characteristics, the creation of which should be described in the story. Encourage students to use creativity and imagination.

3. Have students first review the dialogue exchange between Mrs. Pratchett and Mr. Coombes on pages 484 and 485.

The Writer's Craft

Letter Forms, p. 669
Story Maps, p. 228
Creating Dialogue, pp. 320–322

Multimodal Learning

ALTERNATIVE ACTIVITIES

1. A ballad is a song or poem that tells a story. Using some of the events in this excerpt, write a **ballad** titled "The Ballad of the Dead Mouse." Set the words to a song you already know.

2. With a partner, read other excerpts from *Boy: Tales of Childhood.* Then present an **oral interpretation** of your favorite tale.

3. Create an illustrated **ad** for one of the candies Dahl describes in this excerpt, such as licorice bootlaces, sherbet suckers, gobstoppers, or tonsil ticklers.

4. Using the medium of your choice, create a **portrait** of Mrs. Pratchett based on Dahl's descriptions. Display your portrait in class.

ACROSS THE CURRICULUM

Social Studies What were British preparatory schools, such as Llandaff Cathedral School, like in the 1920s? Do research about the curriculum, the facilities, and the responsibilities of students at these schools. If you have access to a computer encyclopedia, use it as a research tool. Share your findings in an oral report.

ART CONNECTION

Look at the photograph of Terry Mimnaugh's sculpture *Three Boys with a Mouse* on page 480. How well do you think the sculpture captures the feelings of the boys in the selection?

WORDS TO KNOW

Review the Words to Know in the boxes at the bottom of the selection pages. Then write the word that is suggested by each phrase below.

1. turn one's stomach
2. rise in the world
3. give a blow-by-blow description
4. free and easy
5. rotten to the core

ROALD DAHL

As a schoolboy, Roald Dahl apparently showed little promise. One report about him included the comments "I have never met a boy who so persistently writes the exact opposite of what he means. He seems incapable of marshaling his thoughts on paper" and "vocabulary negligible, sentences malconstructed. He reminds me of a camel."

Dahl, however, went on to become a writer of best-selling children's books—some of which dealt with unpleasant subjects and featured obnoxious characters. For example, in *The Gremlins,*

1916–1990

his first book for children, tiny creatures cause mysterious malfunctions in airplanes. In defense of his books, Dahl remarked, "I never get any protests from children. All you get are giggles of mirth and squirms of delight. I know what children like." Dahl also credited his being a parent for his inspiration as a writer. "Had I not had children of my own," he said, "I would have never written books for children, nor would I have been capable of doing so."

OTHER WORKS *Matilda, James and the Giant Peach, Charlie and the Chocolate Factory*

Extended Reading

 LASERLINKS
• *AUTHOR BACKGROUND*

Alternative Activities

1. Explain that, ballads often are romantic or sad. Suggest that students begin by brainstorming a list of details they'd like to include in their ballads. Have students sing their ballads or recite them to music for the class.

2. Suggest that students make their oral interpretations dramatic by acting out any dialogue and including sound effects.

3. Provide students with art materials such as crayons, paint, brushes, and poster paper. Have students brainstorm creative ways of advertising the candy, emphasizing one of its main characteristics in the ad. Remind students that their ads should include writing as well as art.

4. Students may sketch their portraits in pencil, charcoal, or pastels.

ART CONNECTION

Invite students to reread the section of the story where the boys put the dead mouse in the jar. Some students may say that the general impression of intensity and excitement matches the boys' mood. Others may point out that the boys in the story "strutted" into the sweetshop while the boys in the sculpture appear to be sneaking quietly.

Across the Curriculum

Social Studies Cooperative Learning
Have students work in groups of five. Choose a direction giver to coordinate the group's activities and a recorder to organize the oral report. Individual members can present different parts of the group's research.

ADDITIONAL SUGGESTIONS

Science *Candy, Anyone?* Have students research the making of candy and its nutritional value. Suggest that they use encyclopedias and nutrition books to conduct their research. Have them present their findings in a poster.

Words to Know

1. loathsome
2. flourishing
3. elaborate
4. jaunty
5. malignant

Reteaching/Reinforcement
• *Unit Four Resource Book,* p. 52

AUTHOR BACKGROUND
Roald Dahl The author talks about his life as a writer and his approach to creating stories for children.

Side A, Frame 36854

ROALD DAHL

Dahl's memoir, *Boy: Tales of Childhood,* was selected as one of the Best Books for Young Adults by the Young Adult Library Services Association in 1985. This selection is an excerpt from this memoir.

OVERVIEW

Objectives

- To understand and appreciate a short story about a little girl who is different from her classmates
- To enrich reading by identifying contrasts
- To identify and understand metaphor and simile
- To express understanding of the story through a choice of writing forms, including a plan, a dialogue, and a profile
- To extend understanding of the story through a variety of multimodal and cross-curricular activities

Skills

READING SKILLS/ STRATEGIES
- Comparing and contrasting

THE WRITER'S STYLE
- Figurative language

GRAMMAR
- Reflexive pronouns

LITERARY CONCEPTS
- Simile and metaphor
- Dialogue

SPELLING
- The suffix *-ly*

SPEAKING, LISTENING, AND VIEWING
- Oral reading

Cross-Curricular Connections

SCIENCE
- Sunlight
- Conditions on Venus

- Models of space housing

ALTERNATIVE

Previewing

To extend class discussion, you may wish to ask students the following questions:

Personal Connection

Discussion Prompts:

- *The word* clique *is sometimes used to describe a particularly close-knit group of people that does not easily allow outsiders in. Why do you think cliques act like that?*

- *Why do you think others may want to be part of such a group or may not want to be?*

- *How do you suppose it feels to want to be part of a group, but you aren't allowed or welcomed?*

- *Do you think teenagers treat those who are different more harshly than adults do? Why or why not?*

As you read, think about how Margot's classmates treat her and how their treatment makes Margot feel.

FICTION

All Summer in a Day
Ray Bradbury

PERSONAL CONNECTION Activating Prior Knowledge

Think of some groups that you have belonged to or that you look forward to joining. In your opinion, how do groups usually treat individuals who are different from the other members of the group? Why do you think groups act that way? Discuss your views with the class.

Building Background
LITERARY CONNECTION

The main character in "All Summer in a Day" is a little girl who is different from her classmates. The action takes place in and near a classroom—a classroom on the planet Venus sometime in the future, when humans have developed the technology to set up a colony on that planet. As the story begins, the children and their teacher are eagerly awaiting an event that occurs only once every seven years.

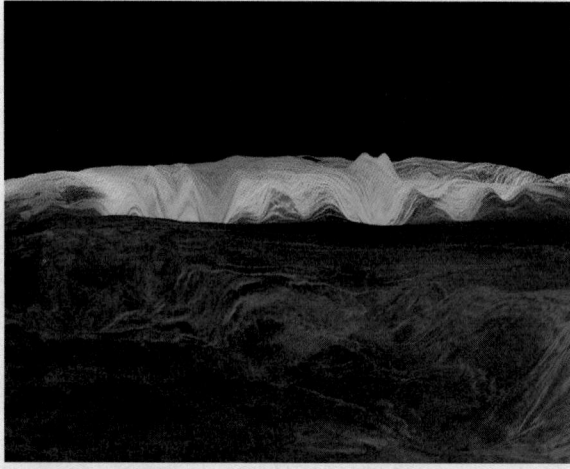

Computer-generated view of Venus from the *Magellan* spacecraft, October 6, 1994. NASA.

488 UNIT FOUR PART 2: HIGH STAKES

Active Reading / Setting a Purpose
READING CONNECTION

Identifying Contrasts Sometimes writers emphasize **contrasts**—differences—between characters, events, places, or ideas. As you read "All Summer in a Day," think about the differences between the main character and her classmates. After you finish reading, list some of the differences in a chart like the one shown.

Contrasts	
Main Character	**Her Classmates**
1.	
2.	
3.	

PRINT AND MEDIA RESOURCES

UNIT FOUR RESOURCE BOOK
Strategic Reading: Literature, p. 55
Vocabulary SkillBuilder, p. 58
Reading SkillBuilder, p. 56
Spelling SkillBuilder, p. 57

GRAMMAR MINI–LESSONS
Transparencies, p. 11
Copymasters, p. 18

WRITING MINI–LESSONS
Transparencies, p. 39

ACCESS FOR STUDENTS ACQUIRING ENGLISH
Selection Summaries
Reading and Writing Support

FORMAL ASSESSMENT
Selection Test, pp. 93–94
■ Test Generator

 **AUDIO LIBRARY**
See Reference Card

ALL SUMMER IN A DAY

BY RAY BRADBURY

Detail of *The Sower* (1888), Vincent van Gogh. Oil on canvas, Rijksmuseum Kroeller-Mueller, Otterlo, The Netherlands, Erich Lessing/Art Resource, New York. Photo Copyright © Erich Lessing.

Background photo Copyright © 1994 Thomas Wiewandt.

489

SUMMARY

Margot's classmates resent her because she remembers the sun. They can't remember it because it shines on Venus for one hour every seven years. Margot yearns to see it, but, moments before it appears, her classmates lock her in a closet. After their hour of sunlit play, her classmates suddenly think of her and let her out.

Thematic Link: *High Stakes* To Margot, the opportunity to see the sun is worth more than anything in the world.

CUSTOMIZING FOR

Students Acquiring English

- Use **ACCESS FOR STUDENTS ACQUIRING ENGLISH**, *Reading and Writing Support*.

- This story is an example of science fiction, and its imaginative elements may prove difficult for students. Have students acquiring English read it through once, without interruptions, to understand the basic plot. Then have them reread it for deeper understanding of Bradbury's rich, descriptive language.

STRATEGIC READING FOR

Less-Proficient Readers

Set a Purpose Ask students to discuss how they feel when someone shows them their dislike. Then have students read to find out how Margot's classmates treat her and why they dislike her.

Art Note

Sonoran Desert, Downpour and Hail, Tucson by Thomas Wiewandt

Reading the Art *How does the artist make you "feel" the violence of the storm?*

Art Note

Detail from *The Sower* by Vincent van Gogh Van Gogh (1853–1890) was a master of natural outdoor scenes. His images shimmer with vivid colors and deep textures that draw the viewer into his vision.

Reading the Art *How would you describe the sun in this painting?*

WORDS TO KNOW

apparatus (ăp′ə-ră′təs) *n.* a device or set of equipment used for a specific purpose (p. 492)

concussion (kən-kŭsh′ən) *n.* a strong shaking (p. 490)

resilient (rĭ-zĭl′yənt) *adj.* flexible and springy (p. 493)

savor (sā′vər) *v.* to take great pleasure in (p. 493)

tumultuously (tōō-mŭl′chōō-əs-lē) *adv.* in a wild and disorderly way (p. 493)

CUSTOMIZING FOR
Gifted and Talented Students

Have students note the author's use of dialogue and action to characterize Margot's classmates and his use of description to characterize Margot. Have students find examples of each and discuss why these different techniques are appropriate.

Possible responses:

• *Pages 490 and 491— "She was an old photograph dusted from an album, whitened away..."*

• *Page 492— "'Get away!' The boy gave her another push."*

These techniques use vivid description and action well-suited to a science fiction short story and the characters come alive in the reader's mind.

CUSTOMIZING FOR
Students Acquiring English

① Point out that the author uses vivid imagery in describing the weather. Ensure that students understand that *gold or a yellow crayon or a coin large enough to buy the world with* describes the children's memories of the sun.

② Lead students to understand that *the tatting drum, the endless shaking down of clear bead necklaces* are images that suggest rain.

Literary Concept: METAPHOR

Ⓐ Remind students that a comparison of two unlike things that have something in common is called a metaphor. Metaphors don't use direct words of comparison such as *like* and *as*. Have students identify the metaphor in Margot's poem. *("the sun is a flower")*

"Ready?"

"Ready."

"Now?"

"Soon."

"Do the scientists really know? Will it happen today, will it?"

"Look, look; see for yourself!"

The children pressed to each other like so many roses, so many weeds, intermixed, peering out for a look at the hidden sun.

It rained.

It had been raining for seven years; thousands upon thousands of days compounded and filled from one end to the other with rain, with the drum and gush of water, with the sweet crystal fall of showers and the concussion of storms so heavy they were tidal waves come over the islands. A thousand forests had been crushed under the rain and grown up a thousand times to be crushed again. And this was the way life was forever on the planet Venus, and this was the schoolroom of the children of the rocket men and women who had come to a raining world to set up civilization and live out their lives.

"It's stopping, it's stopping!"

"Yes, yes!"

Margot stood apart from them, from these children who could never remember a time when there wasn't rain and rain and rain. They were all nine years old, and if there had been a day, seven years ago, when the sun came out for an hour and showed its face to the stunned world, they could not recall. Sometimes, at night, she heard them stir, in remembrance, and she knew they were dreaming and remembering gold or a yellow crayon or a coin large enough to buy the world with. She knew that they thought they remembered a warmness, like a blushing in the face, in the body, in the arms and legs and trembling hands. But then they

always awoke to the tatting drum, the endless shaking down of clear bead necklaces upon the roof, the walk, the gardens, the forest; and their dreams were gone.

> It had been raining for seven years; thousands upon thousands of days . . .

All day yesterday they had read in class about the sun, about how like a lemon it was and how hot. And they had written small stories or essays or poems about it:

I think the sun is a flower,
That blooms for just one hour.

That was Margot's poem, read in a quiet voice in the still classroom while the rain was falling outside.

"Aw, you didn't write that!" protested one of the boys.

"I did," said Margot. "I *did*."

"William!" said the teacher.

But that was yesterday. Now, the rain was slackening, and the children were crushed to the great thick windows.

"Where's teacher?"

"She'll be back."

"She'd better hurry; we'll miss it!"

They turned on themselves, like a feverish wheel, all tumbling spokes.

Margot stood alone. She was a very frail girl who looked as if she had been lost in the rain for years, and the rain had washed out the blue from her eyes and the red from her mouth and the yellow from her hair. She was an old photo-

---

WORDS TO KNOW

concussion (kən-kŭsh′ən) *n.* a strong shaking

490

Mini-Lesson	The Writer's Style

FIGURATIVE LANGUAGE Tell students that figurative language goes beyond dictionary meanings of words to create fresh and original descriptions. In a figurative expression, the words are not literally true, and one thing may be described in terms of another. The three most common forms of figurative language are *metaphor, simile,* and *personification.*

Application Have students identify the form of figurative language in the highlighted text on this page. *(metaphor)* Then have students pretend they are colonists on either Mercury or Neptune and

write a letter to a friend back on Earth describing their planet's weather. Tell students Mercury is blazingly hot; Neptune is frigid. Instruct students to use figurative language to describe the planet's weather.

Reteaching/Reinforcement

• *Writing Mini-Lessons,* transparencies, p. 39

The Writer's Craft

Using Language Imaginatively, pp. 314–316

graph dusted from an album, whitened away; and if she spoke at all, her voice would be a ghost. Now she stood, separate, staring at the rain and the loud, wet world beyond the huge glass.

"What're *you* looking at?" said William.

Margot said nothing.

"Speak when you're spoken to." He gave her a shove. But she did not move; rather, she let herself be moved only by him and nothing else.

They edged away from her; they would not look at her. She felt them go away. And this was because she would play no games with them in the echoing tunnels of the underground city. If they tagged her and ran, she stood blinking after them and did not follow. When the class sang songs about happiness and life and games, her lips barely moved. Only when they sang about the sun and the summer did her lips move as she watched the drenched windows.

And then, of course, the biggest crime of all was that she had come here only five years ago from Earth, and she remembered the sun and the way the sun was and the sky was when she was four, in Ohio. And they, they had been on Venus all their lives, and they had been only two years old when last the sun came out and had long since forgotten the color and heat of it and the way that it really was. But Margot remembered.

Wee Maureen (1926), Robert Henri. Oil on canvas, 24" × 20", The Pennsylvania Academy of the Fine Arts, Philadelphia, gift of Mrs. Herbert Cameron Morris.

"It's like a penny," she said once, eyes closed.

"No, it's not!" the children cried.

"It's like a fire," she said, "in the stove."

"You're lying; you don't remember!" cried the children.

But she remembered and stood quietly apart from all of them and watched the patterning windows. And once, a month ago, she had refused to shower in the school shower rooms, had clutched her hands to her ears and over her head, screaming the water mustn't touch her head. So after that, dimly, dimly, she sensed it;

ALL SUMMER IN A DAY   **491**

Art Note

Wee Maureen by Robert Henri
American artist Robert Henri (1865–1929) loved to paint pictures of children. However, his pictures never idealized children or childhood but expressed the emotions children experience in their lives.

Reading the Art *What do you think the girl is feeling? What does her unadorned front-facing pose express about her personality?*

CUSTOMIZING FOR

Multiple Learning Styles

B Musical Learners Have pairs or groups of students write a song these children might sing in class about happiness, life, or the sun. Have students perform their songs for the class.

STRATEGIC READING FOR

Less-Proficient Readers

C Make sure that students understand how the other children treat Margot, giving examples of the children's meanness.

- Why do the children resent Margot so much? *(because she remembers the sun)* Finding the Main Idea

- What words would you to use to describe their treatment of Margot? *(Possible responses: cruel, mean, hurtful)* Classifying

Set a Purpose Have students read to see what happens when the rain stops.

Mini-Lesson **Reading Skills/Strategies**

COMPARING AND CONTRASTING Explain that when readers compare and contrast people or things, they look for similarities and differences. Remind students that the difference between two or more things is called contrast. Point out that the crux of this story is the contrast between Margot and her classmates.

Application Have students share the contrast charts they made to record the differences between Margot and her classmates for the Reading Connection on page 488. Then ask students to select a character from another story and make a

chart like the one shown. Remind them this time their charts should include comparisons as well as contrasts.

Reteaching/Reinforcement
- *Unit Four Resource Book,* p. 56

Margot and _____	Similarities	Differences

D Ask students who shows greater energy and emotion—Margot or her classmates. Then ask how the children's hatred of Margot might affect her personality. If needed, use the following model.

Think-Aloud Model *I think the children are more active and take more interest in life than Margot does. Maybe her depression is due not only to lack of sunlight but also to how her classmates treat her. Perhaps their strong but cruel personalities keep her isolated from them.*

Critical Thinking: ANALYZING

E Ask students what Margot's reaction was to the threat of being locked in the closet and what her reaction suggests about how much seeing the sun means to her. *(Possible responses: She protests and cries. This unusual show of emotion suggests that seeing the sun means a great deal to her.)*

CUSTOMIZING FOR
Multiple Learners

F **Linguistic Learners** Ask students to describe how *silence* can be "immense and unbelievable." *(Possible response: In contrast to all the previous noise, the sudden silence is surprising and more noticeable.)*

---

she was different, and they knew her difference and kept away.

There was talk that her father and mother were taking her back to Earth next year; it seemed vital to her that they do so, though it would mean the loss of thousands of dollars to her family. And so, the children hated her for all these reasons, of big and little consequence. They hated her pale, snow face, her waiting silence, her thinness, and her possible future.

"Get away!" The boy gave her another push. "What're you waiting for?"

Then, for the first time, she turned and looked at him. And what she was waiting for was in her eyes.

"Well, don't wait around here!" cried the boy, savagely. "You won't see nothing!"

Her lips moved.

"Nothing!" he cried. "It was all a joke, wasn't it?" He turned to the other children. "Nothing's happening today. *Is* it?"

They all blinked at him and then, understanding, laughed and shook their heads.

Then, for the first time, she turned and looked at him. And what she was waiting for was in her eyes.

"Nothing, nothing!"

"Oh, but," Margot whispered, her eyes helpless. "But, this is the day, the scientists predict, they say, they *know*, the sun . . ."

"All a joke!" said the boy and seized her roughly. "Hey, everyone, let's put her in a closet before teacher comes!"

"No," said Margot, falling back.

They surged about her, caught her up, and bore her, protesting and then pleading and then crying, back into a tunnel, a room, a closet, where they slammed and locked the door. They stood looking at the door and saw it tremble from her beating and throwing herself against it. They heard her muffled cries. Then, smiling, they turned and went out and back down the tunnel, just as the teacher arrived.

"Ready, children?" She glanced at her watch.

"Yes!" said everyone.

"Are we all here?"

"Yes!"

The rain slackened still more.

They crowded to the huge door.

The rain stopped.

It was as if, in the midst of a film concerning an avalanche, a tornado, a hurricane, a volcanic eruption, something had, first, gone wrong with the sound apparatus, thus muffling and finally cutting off all noise, all of the blasts and repercussions and thunders, and then, secondly, ripped the film from the projector and inserted in its place a peaceful tropical slide which did not move or tremor. The world ground to a standstill. The silence was so immense and unbelievable that you felt that your ears had been stuffed or you had lost your hearing altogether. The children put their hands to their ears. They stood apart. The door slid back, and the smell of the silent, waiting world came in to them.

The sun came out.

WORDS
TO **apparatus** (ăp′ə-rā′təs) *n.* a device or set of equipment used for a specific purpose
KNOW

492

Mini-Lesson ✏ **Grammar**

me	*myself*	*her/him*	*herself*
you	*yourself*		*himself*
	yourselves	*it*	*itself*
us	*ourselves*		
them	*themselves*		

REFLEXIVE PRONOUNS Point out to students that reflexive pronouns refer to an action of the subject of a sentence. Share the chart shown with students and, in the highlighted sentence, point out the use of the reflexive pronoun *herself*.

Application Have students write reflexive pronouns for the underlined pronouns in the following sentences.

1. Margot wrote the poem <u>her</u>.
2. On Venus, the Sun showed <u>it</u> for only one hour every seven years.

3. The children enjoyed <u>them</u> playing in the sunlight.
4. Margot tried to defend <u>her</u> from the other children.
5. When the story ends, do you think the children will say, "We are ashamed of <u>our</u>"?

Reteaching/Reinforcement
• Grammar Handbook anthology, pp. 860–861
• *Grammar Mini-Lessons,* copymasters, p. 18, transparencies, p. 11

The Writer's Craft

Reflexive and Intensive Pronouns, p. 443

It was the color of flaming bronze, and it was very large. And the sky around it was a blazing blue tile color. And the jungle burned with sunlight as the children, released from their spell, rushed out, yelling, into the summertime.

"Now, don't go too far," called the teacher after them. "You've only one hour, you know. You wouldn't want to get caught out!"

But they were running and turning their faces up to the sky and feeling the sun on their cheeks like a warm iron; they were taking off their jackets and letting the sun burn their arms.

"Oh, it's better than the sun lamps, isn't it?"

"Much, much better!"

They stopped running and stood in the great jungle that covered Venus, that grew and never stopped growing, <u>tumultuously</u>, even as you watched it. It was a nest of octopuses, clustering up great arms of fleshlike weed, wavering, flowering in this brief spring. It was the color of rubber and ash, this jungle, from the many years without sun. It was the color of stones and white cheeses and ink.

The children lay out, laughing, on the jungle mattress and heard it sigh and squeak under them, <u>resilient</u> and alive. They ran among the trees, they slipped and fell, they pushed each other, they played hide-and-seek and tag; but most of all they squinted at the sun until tears ran down their faces, they put their hands up at that yellowness and that amazing blueness, and they breathed of the fresh, fresh air and listened and listened to the silence which suspended them in a blessed sea of no sound and no motion. They looked at everything and <u>savored</u> everything. Then, wildly, like animals escaped from their caves, they ran and ran in shouting circles. They ran for an hour and did not stop running.

And then—

In the midst of their running, one of the girls wailed.

Everyone stopped.

The girl, standing in the open, held out her hand.

"Oh, look, look," she said, trembling.

They came slowly to look at her opened palm.

In the center of it, cupped and huge, was a single raindrop.

She began to cry, looking at it.

They glanced quickly at the sky.

"Oh. Oh."

A few cold drops fell on their noses and their cheeks and their mouths. The sun faded behind a stir of mist. A wind blew cool around them. They turned and started to walk back toward the underground house, their hands at their sides, their smiles vanishing away.

A boom of thunder startled them, and like leaves before a new hurricane, they tumbled upon each other and ran. Lightning struck ten miles away, five miles away, a mile, a half mile. The sky darkened into midnight in a flash.

They stood in the doorway of the underground for a moment until it was raining hard. Then they closed the door and heard the gigantic sound of the rain falling in tons and avalanches everywhere and forever.

"Will it be seven more years?"

"Yes. Seven."

Then one of them gave a little cry.

"Margot!"

"What?"

"She's still in the closet where we locked her."

"Margot."

They stood as if someone had driven them, like so many stakes, into the floor. They

Linking to Science

G In this selection the sun rarely shines on Venus because of the constant rain. On Earth, places near the poles get no sunlight for up to six months during the winter because the tilt of Earth and its roundish shape prevent sunlight from reaching these places.

STRATEGIC READING FOR

Less-Proficient Learners

H Help students summarize what happens when the rain stops.

- How does the environment change when the rain stops? (*The sun comes out, and it becomes warm.*) **Noting Relevant Details**

- What do the children find outside? (*a dull-colored jungle*) **Summarizing**

- Why doesn't Margot get to see this change? (*She's locked in the closet.*) **Relating Cause and Effect**

Set a Purpose Have students read on to discover how the children feel at the end of the story.

Literary Concept: DIALOGUE

I Point out to students the repeated use of *oh* in the children's dialogue as the children race and play outside. Ask students why Bradbury chose to use this word repeatedly. (*Possible response: It shows the surprise and wonderment of children who have never seen the sun.*)

WORDS TO KNOW	**tumultuously** (tŏŏ-mŭl′chōō-əs-lē) *adv.* in a wild and disorderly way
	resilient (rĭ-zĭl′yənt) *adj.* flexible and springy
	savor (sā′vər) *v.* to take great pleasure in

493

Mini-Lesson **Literary Concepts**

REVIEWING DIALOGUE Remind students that dialogue is a conversation between two or more characters. Explain that authors may use the words of a dialogue, their emphasis, and their inflection to convey the feelings or motivations of a character. As an example, point to the author's use of italics in one boy's remark, "Nothing's happening today. *Is* it?" This adds emphasis that helps to convey sarcasm.

Application Have pairs of students write and role-play a scene between Margot and a new classmate who has compassion for Margot and likes her. Encourage students to attempt to create dialogue that conveys the emotions of each character. After writing and rehearsing their scenes, have students present them to the class.

Less-Proficient Readers

J Ask students how the children feel when they remember that Margot is still locked in the closet. *(guilty)* Drawing Conclusions

CUSTOMIZING FOR
Gifted and Talented Students

K Have students write a sentence, in the author's style, about what Margot might say or do when she leaves the closet.

CUSTOMIZING FOR
Student Acquiring English

3 Students may be afraid they didn't "get" the story's ending. Assure them it is deliberately ambiguous.

COMPREHENSION CHECK

1. What special weather event is expected on Venus? *(The sun will come out.)*
2. Why is Margot the only child who remembers the sun? *(She was living on Earth until five years ago, whereas the others were born on Venus.)*
3. How do the other children show their hatred for Margot? *(They are mean to her and lock her in a closet.)*
4. How do the children feel when they remember that Margot is locked in the closet? *(guilty)*

INSIGHT

1. What might Margot's answer be to the poem's title question? *(Possible response: communicate and show acceptance)*
2. How would you explain the difference between "work for it to disappear" and "for barriers to fall down"? *(The first line doesn't tolerate difference; the second accepts and acknowledges difference and simply wants the barriers people raise against difference to disappear.)*

JAMES BERRY

James Berry was born on the island of Jamaica but moved to England when he was 23. Berry often writes about problems faced by minority children growing up in places where they are considered different.

---

looked at each other and then looked away. They glanced out at the world that was raining now and raining and raining steadily. They could not meet each other's glances. Their faces were solemn and pale. They looked at their hands and feet, their faces down.

"Margot."

One of the girls said, "Well . . . ?"

No one moved.

"Go on," whispered the girl.

They walked slowly down the hall in the sound of cold rain. They turned through the doorway to the room, in the sound of the storm and thunder, lightning on their faces, blue and terrible. They walked over to the closet door slowly and stood by it.

Behind the closet door was only silence.

They unlocked the door, even more slowly, and let Margot out. ❖

LITERARY INSIGHT

WHAT DO WE DO WITH A VARIATION?

BY JAMES BERRY

What do we do with a difference?
Do we stand and discuss its oddity
or do we ignore it?

Do we shut our eyes to it
or poke it with a stick?
Do we clobber it to death?

Do we move around it in rage
and enlist the rage of others?
Do we will it to go away?

Do we look at it in awe
or purely in wonderment?
Do we work for it to disappear?

Do we pass it stealthily[1]
or change route away from it?
Do we will it to become like ourselves?

What do we do with a difference?
Do we communicate to it,
let application[2] acknowledge it
for barriers to fall down?

---

1. **steathlily:** in a quiet, sneaky way
2. **application:** This could have either or both meanings of "close attention" or "the act of putting something to a use or purpose."

---

494   UNIT FOUR   PART 2: HIGH STAKES

Mini-Lesson  Spelling

SPELLING WITH THE SUFFIX -LY Tell students that when a word ends in a consonant, it usually retains its spelling when the suffix -ly is added. Explain that words ending in -ly are adverbs. Show students the following examples:

tumultuous + ly = **tumultuously**

creative + ly = **creatively**

Two exceptions are words that end in y—the y changes to an i before the suffix is added—and words that end in able or ible—the le becomes ly.

Application Have students write the adverbs that would correctly replace the underlined adjectives.
1. The children treated Margot <u>hateful</u>.
2. The children gathered <u>eager</u> in front of the window.
3. The children <u>guilty</u> opened the closet door.
4. It will <u>probable</u> rain on Venus tomorrow.

Ask students to look for more words that fit this pattern, and to add these words to their personal word lists.

Reteaching/Reinforcement
• *Unit Four Resource Book,* p. 57

RESPONDING
OPTIONS

FROM PERSONAL RESPONSE TO CRITICAL ANALYSIS

REFLECT
1. What are your impressions of this story? Describe them in your notebook, and then share them with a partner.

RETHINK
Close Textual Reading

2. What words would you use to describe Margot's feelings at the end of the story?

3. If you were Margot's teacher, what would you say to her classmates about their treatment of her?

4. Why do you think Margot's classmates play a prank on her?
   Consider
   • how Margot is different from them
   • the ideas you discussed for the Personal Connection on page 488

5. What do you predict Margot's future relationship with her classmates will be like?

RELATE
6. Reread the Insight poem on page 494. Which lines remind you of the way Margot's classmates treat her? Which lines, if any, reflect your own views about how a group should treat an individual who is different?

Multimodal Learning
ANOTHER PATHWAY
Cooperative Learniing

With two classmates, brainstorm ideas for an additional paragraph at the end of this story. After you select a good idea, one member of the group should dictate the paragraph, another member should transcribe and edit it, and a third member should read it to the rest of the class.

QUICKWRITES

1. Imagine that some of Margot's classmates want to do something to make up for their cruel treatment of her. Write a **plan** for what they might do.

2. Write a **dialogue** between Margot's parents and her teacher about the prank her classmates played on her.

3. What kind of people would be able to live on the Venus that Bradbury depicts in this story? How would these people be different from ordinary humans? Write a **profile** of the "rocket men and women" for a popular newsmagazine.

📁 *PORTFOLIO Save your writing. You may want to use it later as a springboard to a piece for your portfolio.*

LITERARY CONCEPTS

Writers use similes and metaphors to create pictures in readers' imaginations. A **simile** is a comparison between two things that contains the word *like* or *as;* a **metaphor** compares two things without the use of the word *like* or *as.* "The sun is like a golden coin" is an example of a simile; "The sun is a golden coin" is an example of a metaphor. Work with a partner to identify two or more examples of simile or metaphor in "All Summer in a Day." For each example, explain the comparison and describe the picture that the figure of speech creates. Then create your own similes and metaphors to complete the following sentences:
The rain was _____; Margot's classmates were _____;
The classroom was _____.

ALL SUMMER IN A DAY **495**

From Personal Response to Critical Analysis

1. Possible response: I felt sorry for Margot and found the others cruel.
2. Possible responses: shocked, sad, despairing, defiant
3. Possible response: "You children must understand how cruel your actions were and learn to accept someone you perceive as different."
4. Possible response: because they envy her experiences in the sunlight
5. Possible responses: The relationship may improve because now everyone has seen the sun and the children feel guilty for locking Margot in the closet. The relationship may get worse because Margot won't forgive or forget their cruel treatment of her.
6. Possible responses: All lines except those of the last stanza are like the way Margot's classmates treat her. The last stanza reflects my views.

Another Pathway

Cooperative Learning Help students brainstorm ideas for an additional paragraph by having them suggest and list the emotions Margot and the others might be feeling when the closet door opens and what these emotions may lead them to do or say. Then have students choose an idea from this list to translate into a paragraph.

Rubric
3 Full Accomplishment Students' paragraph is well written and consistent with the plot and characterizations.
2 Substantial Accomplishment Students' paragraph is consistent with the story's plot and most of the characterizations.
1 Little or Partial Accomplishment Students' paragraph is incomplete or inconsistent with the plot and characterizations.

Literary Concepts

Have students read aloud the figures of speech they find or create. *(Possible responses: pages 490–491, "She was an old photograph . . . ," metaphor; page 490, "a warmness, like a blushing in the face . . . ," simile; page 490, "the storms . . . were tidal waves," metaphor; The rain was an unwelcome guest; Margot's classmates were vultures; The classroom was like a prison.)*

QuickWrites

1. Divide students into small groups to brainstorm a list of things the students might do to make up with Margot.
2. Remind students to create a character profile for Margot's parents and teacher first.
3. Have students list the conditions on Venus, as described by Bradbury. Then have them brainstorm traits that someone would need to live on that planet.

The Writer's Craft

Ways of Organizing, pp. 238–242
Creating Dialogue, pp. 320–322
Character Sketch, pp. 54–61

1. savor
2. apparatus
3. concussion
4. tumultuously
5. resilient

Reteaching/Reinforcement
• *Unit Four Resource Book,* p. 58

Literary Links

Possible response: The children in the two stories learn different lessons from playing their pranks.

The Landaff boys learn that a prank may have consequences that are worse for you than for the person you played the prank on. The Venusian children learn that their cruel actions may cause another's emotional pain.

Across the Curriculum

Science *Cooperative Learning* Divide students into groups of three or four. Each member should be responsible for finding one type of reference source. Encourage groups to make their posters both informative and creative. Provide them with a variety of art supplies including scissors, magazines to cut up, paints, brushes, and markers.

ADDITIONAL SUGGESTIONS
Science *Spaceward, Ho!* Have students use the data they gathered above on the conditions on Venus to design a structure to house the first colonists on Venus. Have them present their designs as either sketches or scale models.

RAY BRADBURY

Ray Bradbury has won many awards for science fiction and fantasy writing. Unlike other science fiction writers who are dazzled by high-tech gadgets, Bradbury is concerned with how technology and science affect ordinary people.

LITERARY LINKS

How would you compare the prank played on Margot with the one played on Mrs. Pratchett in the excerpt from *Boy: Tales of Childhood* on page 473. Consider the motives of the pranksters and the consequences of each prank.

Multimodal Learning

ALTERNATIVE ACTIVITIES

1. With a group of classmates, present an **oral reading** of this story for the rest of the class.
2. Imagine that you are a TV meteorologist on Venus. Present a **weather forecast** for the day when the sun will appear. If possible, have a classmate videotape your performance.

ACROSS THE CURRICULUM

Science Working with a small group of classmates, research what scientists currently know about the climate and surface of Venus. Use reference books, periodicals, and, if possible, an on-line or CD-ROM encyclopedia as research tools. Create a poster to show your findings.

WORDS TO KNOW

Review the Words to Know in the boxes at the bottom of the selection pages. Then write the word that best completes each of the following sentences.

1. Readers who enjoy science fiction _____ the fascinating details of writers' imaginary worlds.
2. We know something about rockets, space suits, and oxygen tanks, so we can imagine the _____ a writer may describe in a story about space travel.
3. Experience with being jarred and jolted by airplane landings helps people imagine the _____ a spaceship might undergo while entering another planet's atmosphere.
4. Unless equipment and people are strapped down, they will be tossed about _____ during a rough landing.
5. What we know about the effect of rain on the soil helps us imagine how _____ the damp surface of a planet would be.

RAY BRADBURY

1920–

As a boy in Illinois, Ray Bradbury had a passion for adventure stories, secret-code rings, and comic strips. When he was unable to compete in sports, he turned to writing, creating imaginary worlds of his own. In these worlds, Bradbury says, "I could be excellent all to myself."

By the time he was in high school, Bradbury was already writing about a thousand words a day—pounding out stories on his typewriter, illustrating them by hand, and putting together his own magazines. About his early writing, Bradbury says, "I was in love with everything I did. I did not warm to a subject, I boiled over." After high school, he earned his living selling newspapers. In the early 1940s, he began selling his first stories.

Today, Bradbury ranks among the foremost U.S. writers of fantasy and science fiction. His writing often explores the impact of scientific developments on human lives. His works have appeared in more than 700 anthologies, and several of his stories have been made into movies.

Though he often writes about future technology and space travel, in some ways Bradbury is a bit old-fashioned. For example, he has never learned to drive a car and rarely flies in an airplane. His favorite way to get around is by riding a bicycle. According to one critic, Bradbury is "the grown-up child who still remembers, still believes."

OTHER WORKS *The Martian Chronicles, Dandelion Wine* Extended Reading

496 UNIT FOUR PART 2: HIGH STAKES

Alternative Activities

1. Divide the class into three groups, with each group to prepare its own oral interpretation. Allow students time for rehearsal before their oral presentations.
2. Allow students to work in groups to develop and present their Venusian weather reports. Have one student play the anchor who can ask questions; have another be the meteorologist who answers questions; have remaining group members create the weather map and write the weather report. Encourage students to have fun, caricaturing weather reports they see on TV.

POETRY

The Highwayman
Alfred Noyes

Activating Prior Knowledge

PERSONAL CONNECTION

What sacrifices would you be willing to make for someone you love? In your notebook, create a chart like the one shown, rating each kind of sacrifice on a scale from 1 to 5. Then get together with a small group of classmates to compare your ratings.

What Would You Sacrifice for Love?					
	Completely Unwilling			Very Willing	
	1	2	3	4	5
Money					
Personal Property					
Personal Goals					
Safety					
Freedom					
Life					

Building Background

HISTORICAL CONNECTION

"The Highwayman," a narrative poem set in 18th-century England, is about the sacrifices that two lovers make for each other. One of the lovers is an innkeeper's daughter; the other is a highwayman—a thief on horseback. Usually young and daring, highwaymen streaked through the night, skillfully racing their horses down dark and lonely country roads. They held up stagecoaches, stealing jewels and money from rich passengers. These raiders of the night were pursued relentlessly by redcoat troops—English soldiers like those who fought against the American colonists in the Revolutionary War.

Active Reading / Setting a Purpose

READING CONNECTION

Identifying Narrative Elements in Poetry Like a work of fiction, a narrative poem tells a story. As you read "The Highwayman" for the first time, think about the main characters and their sacrifices. Then reread the poem, and create in your notebook a sequence diagram like the one shown. On it, list the narrative elements you find in the poem, such as setting, characters, and details of events in the plot.

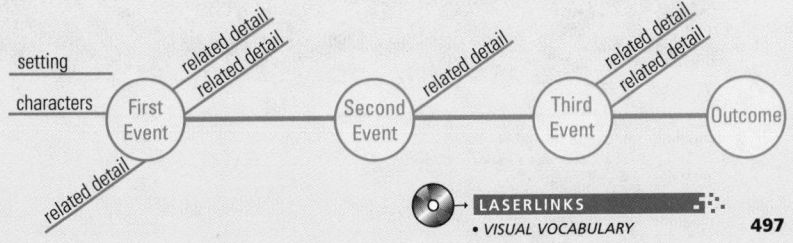

 LASERLINKS
• *VISUAL VOCABULARY*   **497**

── **Objectives** ──

• To understand and appreciate a narrative poem about two lovers and their sacrifices for each other
• To identify narrative elements in poetry
• To examine onomatopoeia in a poem
• To express understanding of the poem through a choice of writing forms, including an essay, an epitaph, and an article
• To extend understanding of the poem through a variety of multimodal and cross-curricular activities

── **Skills** ──

LITERARY CONCEPTS
• Onomatopoeia
• Metaphor
• Rhythm

GENRE STUDY
• Narrative poetry

SPEAKING , LISTENING, AND VIEWING
• Choral reading
• Dramatic reading

── **Cross-Curricular Connections** ──

SCIENCE
• Adrenaline

HISTORY
• Legendary highwaymen

 **VISUAL VOCABULARY**
The words illustrated here will help students understand the setting of the poem:
• **cobbles** (kŏb'əlz)
• **galleon** (găl'ē-ən)
• **moor** (mŏŏr)
• **rapier hilt** (rā'pē-ər hĭlt)

Side A, Frame 49399

PRINT AND MEDIA RESOURCES

UNIT FOUR RESOURCE BOOK
Strategic Reading: Literature, p. 61

ACCESS FOR STUDENTS ACQUIRING ENGLISH
Reading and Writing Support

FORMAL ASSESSMENT
Selection Test, p. 95
 Test Generator

AUDIO LIBRARY
See Reference Card

LASERLINKS
Visual Vocabulary
Art Gallery

CUSTOMIZING FOR
Students Acquiring English

- Use **ACCESS FOR STUDENTS ACQUIRING ENGLISH**, *Reading and Writing Support.*

- Help students appreciate the appealing rhythms of this narrative poem by reading several stanzas aloud with dramatic emphasis.

STRATEGIC READING FOR
Less-Proficient Readers

Set a Purpose Ask students to describe what they think a highwayman does. Then have students read to find out more about the relationship between the main characters and what the highwayman plans to do.

Use **UNIT FOUR RESOURCE BOOK**, p. 61, for guidance in reading the selection.

CUSTOMIZING FOR
Gifted and Talented Students

Encourage students to think about the complexity of the highwayman, who is both a scoundrel (thief) and a devoted lover. Have students find examples in the selection that reflect each of these sides of his personality.

Possible responses:

- *Page 499—* "His pistol butts a-twinkle... His rapier hilt a-twinkle..." (thief)

- *Page 499—* "One kiss, my bonny sweetheart..." (lover)

- *Page 499—* "I'm after a prize tonight..." (thief)

- *Page 500—* "And he kissed its waves in the moonlight," (lover)

The Highwayman

BY ALFRED NOYES

Illustrations by Charles Mikolaycak.
Copyright © 1995 Carole Kismaric Mikolaycak.

Mini-Lesson: Speaking, **Listening, and Viewing**

DRAMATIC READING Have students note that the repetition of a word within a stanza helps create rhythm in the poem. Tell them that, when a poem is read aloud, repetition can add to the dramatic impact.

Application Have partners find examples of the repetition of words within the stanzas. Tell them to read a stanza silently and then aloud to notice how the repetition helps to create a strong rhythm. Then have one partner present a dramatic reading of the stanza and explain how the repetition reinforces the rhythm and adds to the drama. To further illustrate this point, have the other partner read the stanza with synonyms substituted for the repeated words. Have the class discuss how the use of a synonym changes the rhythm and dramatic effect.

Part One

The wind was a torrent of darkness among the gusty trees.
The moon was a ghostly galleon[1] tossed upon cloudy seas.
The road was a ribbon of moonlight over the purple moor,[2]
And the highwayman came riding—
5   Riding—riding—
The highwayman came riding, up to the old inn-door.

He'd a French cocked-hat on his forehead, a bunch of lace at his chin,
A coat of the claret[3] velvet, and breeches of brown doeskin.
They fitted with never a wrinkle. His boots were up to the thigh.
10   And he rode with a jeweled twinkle,
      His pistol butts a-twinkle.
His rapier hilt[4] a-twinkle, under the jeweled sky.

Over the cobbles[5] he clattered and clashed in the dark inn-yard.
He tapped with his whip on the shutters, but all was locked and barred.
15   He whistled a tune to the window, and who should be waiting there
But the landlord's black-eyed daughter,
      Bess, the landlord's daughter,
Plaiting[6] a dark red love-knot into her long black hair.

And dark in the dark old inn-yard a stable wicket[7] creaked
20   Where Tim the ostler[8] listened. His face was white and peaked.
His eyes were hollows of madness, his hair like moldy hay,
But he loved the landlord's daughter,
      The landlord's red-lipped daughter.
Dumb as a dog he listened, and he heard the robber say—

25   "One kiss, my bonny sweetheart, I'm after a prize tonight,
But I shall be back with the yellow gold before the morning light;
Yet, if they press me sharply, and harry me through the day,

---

1. **galleon** (găl'ē-ən): a large sailing ship.
2. **moor**: an open, rolling wasteland, usually covered with low-growing shrubs.
3. **claret**: dark red, like red wine.
4. **rapier** (rā'pē-ər) **hilt**: sword handle.
5. **cobbles**: rounded stones used for paving roads.
6. **plaiting**: braiding.
7. **wicket**: a small door or gate.
8. **ostler** (ŏs'lər): a worker who takes care of horses at an inn.

THE HIGHWAYMAN   **499**

Critical Thinking: CLASSIFYING

A Ask students what adjectives they would use to describe the highwayman. *(Possible responses: handsome, dashing, dramatic)*

Literary Concept: SIMILE

B Remind students that a simile makes a comparison between two things using the words *like* or *as*. Ask students what this simile suggests about Tim's hair *(It is probably blond or light brown and messy.)*

Active Reading: PREDICT

C Ask students to predict what role Tim will play in the highwayman's future. Use the following model to prompt students.

Think-Aloud Model: *I know Tim is in love with Bess, so he must be jealous of the highwayman. I think he might betray the thief or kidnap Bess to keep the lovers apart.*

Mini-Lesson   Literary Concepts

METAPHOR Use the word web shown to remind students that a comparison of two things that have some quality in common is called a metaphor. Emphasize that a metaphor does not contain the word *like* or *as*. Explain that writers often use metaphors to describe settings and characters in a way that evokes an emotional response from the reader.

Application Have volunteers read the highlighted section aloud. Then have them identify the metaphors in this stanza. Ask them how the metaphors make them feel. Ask what mood the writer conveys about the setting. Have volunteers create additional metaphors about the wind, moon, and the road.

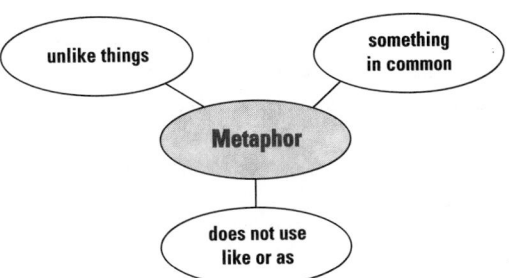

D Make sure that students understand who the main characters are and what their feelings are for each other.

- Who is Bess? (the landlord's daughter; the woman the highwayman loves)

- Why does the highwayman leave Bess? (to commit a robbery) **Drawing Conclusions**

- When does he promise to return to her? (the next night) **Making Inferences**

Set a Purpose Have students read to find out the fate of the two lovers.

Critical Thinking: ANALYZING

E Have students analyze why the redcoats tie up Bess with a musket pointing at her. (Possible response: They expect her to be so frightened of dying that she wouldn't call out to warn her lover of the ambush.)

Literary Concept: RHYTHM

F Have students analyze the rhythm and repetition in the fourth and fifth lines of each stanza on this page. Ask what effect this repetition has. (Possible response: The emphasis on moonlight, marching, and midnight increases suspense, making readers share Bess's fear for the highwayman's life.)

Then look for me by moonlight,
    Watch for me by moonlight,
30 I'll come to thee by moonlight, though hell should bar the way."

He rose upright in the stirrups. He scarce could reach her hand,
But she loosened her hair in the casement.[9] His face burnt like a brand
As the black cascade of perfume came tumbling over his breast;
And he kissed its waves in the moonlight,
D 35   (O, sweet black waves in the moonlight!)
Then he tugged at his rein in the moonlight, and galloped away to the west.

 *Part Two*

He did not come in the dawning. He did not come at noon;
And out of the tawny sunset, before the rise of the moon,
When the road was a gypsy's ribbon, looping the purple moor,
40 A redcoat troop came marching—
    Marching—marching—
King George's men came marching, up to the old inn-door.

They said no word to the landlord. They drank his ale instead.
But they gagged his daughter, and bound her, to the foot of her narrow bed.
45 Two of them knelt at her casement, with muskets at their side!
There was death at every window;
    And hell at one dark window;
For Bess could see, through her casement, the road that *he* would ride.

They had tied her up to attention, with many a sniggering jest.
E 50 They had bound a musket beside her, with the muzzle beneath her breast!
"Now, keep good watch!" and they kissed her. She heard the doomed man say—
Look for me by moonlight;
F   *Watch for me by moonlight;*
I'll come to thee by moonlight, though hell should bar the way!

55 She twisted her hands behind her; but all the knots held good!
She writhed her hands till her fingers were wet with sweat or blood!
They stretched and strained in the darkness, and the hours crawled by like years,
Till, now, on the stroke of midnight,
    Cold, on the stroke of midnight,
60 The tip of one finger touched it! The trigger at least was hers!

---

9. **casement:** a window that opens outward on side hinges.

500   UNIT FOUR   PART 2: HIGH STAKES

 **Mini-Lesson**   **Genre Study**

POETRY Tell students that poetry that tells a story is called **narrative poetry.** Like a story, a narrative poem has characters, setting, and a plot. Narrative poems also have elements of poetry. Share with students the word web that shows the elements of a narrative poem.

Application Have students create a chart listing the elements of a narrative poem. Then have them fill in the chart with examples from "The Highwayman."

Linking to Science

G When people are frightened or stressed, their bodies release adrenaline, a hormone that gives the body a burst of energy. One of adrenaline's effects is to make the heart pump more blood, thus supplying muscles with added oxygen.

The tip of one finger touched it. She strove no more for the rest.
Up, she stood up to attention, with the muzzle beneath her breast.
She would not risk their hearing; she would not strive again;
For the road lay bare in the moonlight;
65 Blank and bare in the moonlight;
And the blood of her veins, in the moonlight, throbbed to her love's refrain. **G**

Tlot-tlot; tlot-tlot! Had they heard it? The horse hoofs ringing clear; **H**
Tlot-tlot, tlot-tlot, in the distance? Were they deaf that they did not hear?
Down the ribbon of moonlight, over the brow of the hill,
70 The highwayman came riding—
 Riding—riding—
The redcoats looked to their priming![10] She stood up, straight and still.

Tlot-tlot, in the frosty silence! *Tlot-tlot,* in the echoing night!
Nearer he came and nearer. Her face was like a light.
75 Her eyes grew wide for a moment; she drew one last deep breath,
Then her finger moved in the moonlight,
 Her musket shattered the moonlight,
Shattered her breast in the moonlight and warned him—with her death.

He turned. He spurred to the west; he did not know who stood
80 Bowed, with her head o'er the musket, drenched with her own blood!

---

10. **looked to their priming:** prepared their muskets by pouring in the explosive used to fire them.

THE HIGHWAYMAN **501**

Literary Concept:
ONOMATOPOEIA

H Remind students that onomatopoeia is the use of words whose sound suggests their meaning. Have students assess what *tlot-tlot* represents. (*sound of a horse's hooves hitting the ground*) Then have students create their own onomatopoeic words based on descriptions from the poem. For example, they might try to represent the sounds of the wind on the moors, the blowing trees, the creaking garden gate, the sniggering redcoats, the musket firing. Suggest that students use their words in descriptive sentences and share them with the class.

Mini-Lesson **Literary Concepts**

REVIEWING RHYTHM Remind students that the pattern of stressed and unstressed syllables in poetry is called rhythm. Explain that when the stressed syllables—syllables that are emphasized—are arranged in a pattern, the poem has a regular beat.

Application Have students copy lines 61 and 62 in their notebooks. Have them count the syllables in each line and mark the stressed syllables. Then have them describe and compare the rhythm in the two lines. Have volunteers read the two lines aloud, conveying the rhythm through the emphasis they give the syllables.

I Have students reread these lines and formulate a hypothesis about why the highwayman rides back toward the redcoats. *(Possible responses: He wants revenge; he wants to be killed or caught.)*

CUSTOMIZING FOR
Gifted and Talented Students

J Have students discuss whether they think the highwayman can still be called both a scoundrel and a lover at the end of the poem. *(Possible response: He stops being a scoundrel when he knowingly rides toward his death.)* Have them debate whether or not they find his actions heroic. *(Possible responses: Yes, he's heroic because he is willing to sacrifice his life to avenge his love. No, his love was dead already, so his sacrifice was a waste. No, it was the fact that he was a thief that put Bess's life in danger.)*

STRATEGIC READING FOR
Less-Proficient Readers

K Make sure students understand what sacrifices the landlord's daughter and the highwayman make for each other.

- How does Bess warn the highwayman of the redcoats' trap? *(She shoots herself, and he hears the sound.)*
  Summarizing

- How does the highwayman die? *(When he turns and rides at the redcoats, they shoot him down.)* **Restating**

COMPREHENSION CHECK
1. Whom does the highwayman love? *(the landlord's daughter Bess)*
2. Who overhears the highwayman's plans to meet his love? *(Tim, the ostler)*
3. How does Bess save the highwayman? *(by shooting herself)*

Not till the dawn he heard it, his face grew grey to hear
How Bess, the landlord's daughter,
   The landlord's black-eyed daughter,
Had watched for her love in the moonlight, and died in the darkness there.

85 Back, he spurred like a madman, shouting a curse to the sky,
With the white road smoking behind him and his rapier brandished high.
Blood-red were his spurs in the golden noon; wine-red was his velvet coat;
When they shot him down on the highway,
   Down like a dog on the highway,
90 And he lay in his blood on the highway, with a bunch of lace at his throat.

And still of a winter's night, they say, when the wind is in the trees,
When the moon is a ghostly galleon tossed upon cloudy seas,
When the road is a ribbon of moonlight over the purple moor,
A highwayman comes riding—
95   *Riding—riding—*
A highwayman comes riding, up to the old inn-door.

Over the cobbles he clatters and clangs in the dark inn-yard.
He taps with his whip on the shutters, but all is locked and barred.
He whistles a tune to the window, and who should be waiting there
100 *But the landlord's black-eyed daughter,*
   Bess, the landlord's daughter,
Plaiting a dark red love-knot into her long black hair.

Assessment ✓ **Option**

INFORMAL ASSESSMENT Have pairs of students brainstorm changes in the plot that would give this poem a happy ending. Then have them rewrite the poem as a short story with a happy ending. They should stay true to the poet's characters and characterizations.

Rubric

3 Full Accomplishment Students' stories show a good understanding of the poem, adhere to its characterizations, and have creative endings.

2 Substantial Accomplishment Students' stories show an understanding of the poem, but their characterizations are sometimes inconsistent with those in the original poem.

1 Little or Partial Accomplishment Students' stories show little understanding of the poem and its characters.

RESPONDING OPTIONS

FROM PERSONAL RESPONSE TO CRITICAL ANALYSIS

REFLECT

1. What images stay in your mind after your reading of this poem? Sketch one or more images in your notebook.

RETHINK

2. Would you like the poem better if the last two stanzas were not included? Why or why not?

3. Both Bess and the highwayman make great sacrifices for love. In your opinion, whose sacrifice shows greater courage? Explain your choice.

4. What words would you use to express your evaluation of the conduct of the redcoats?

Close Textual Reading

Consider
- their duty to uphold the law
- their treatment of Bess
- other actions they might have taken to apprehend the highwayman

5. How do you think Tim the ostler might feel about the deaths of Bess and the highwayman? Give reasons for your opinion.

RELATE

6. Think about the sacrifices of other lovers whom you have read about or seen in movies. How would you compare their sacrifices with the ones made by Bess and the highwayman?

Literary Link

Multimodal Learning
ANOTHER PATHWAY

The last two stanzas of this poem suggest that the two lovers are reunited after death. What do you think each might say to the other? Work with a small group of classmates to write a dialogue between Bess and the highwayman. Have two members of the group read the dialogue to the rest of the class.

QUICKWRITES

1. Do you think people who make great sacrifices for love are noble or foolish? Write a draft of an **essay** that states and supports your opinion. Review the ratings you recorded for the Personal Connection on page 497, and use the sacrifices of Bess and the highwayman as examples.

2. Write an **epitaph**—a brief statement in memory of a dead person—for either Bess or the highwayman.

3. Write an **article** about Bess and the highwayman for a tabloid newspaper, complete with a shocking headline and gripping details.

📁 *PORTFOLIO Save your writing. You may want to use it later as a springboard to a piece for your portfolio.*

LITERARY CONCEPTS

Onomatopoeia (ŏn'ə-măt'ə-pē'ə) is the use of words whose sound suggests their meaning—words such as *whiz, buzz, boom, pop, screech,* and *sizzle.* What examples of onomatopoeia can you identify in this poem? What does Noyes achieve by creating these echoing effects?

BOOM!

CONCEPT REVIEW: Rhythm Read aloud the last two stanzas, listening to the beat of the lines. Then make a copy of the stanzas, marking the syllables that are emphasized by the rhythm. Discuss the effects that the rhythm creates.

---

1. Responses will vary
2. Possible response: no, since these stanzas suggest that the lovers are still together in an afterlife
3. Possible response: Bess's sacrifice, because she knows she has no chance to live
4. Possible responses: immoral, cruel, excessive, unfair
5. Possible responses: guilty, because he loved Bess; triumphant, because he was jealous of the highwayman
6. Possible response: The sacrifices made by Bess and the highwayman are as heroic as those of Romeo and Juliet.

Another Pathway

Cooperative Learning Have students work in groups of three or four. Suggest that the group first decide what the subject of the dialogue should be; for example, Bess and the highwayman might talk about their relationship or the events that led to their deaths. Assign a recorder to write the dialogue and a direction giver to keep the group on track.

Rubric

3 Full Accomplishment Students write and perform a dialogue that is true to the poet's characterizations.

2 Substantial Accomplishment Students write a dialogue that for the most part reflects the poet's characterizations.

1 Little or Partial Accomplishment Students write an incomplete dialogue that is not true to the poet's characterizations.

Literary Concepts:

Possible responses: *Tlot-tlot;* Noyes makes the action seem vivid and creates an experience for the reader. The sound suggests the highwayman's return without directly stating it—this adds suspense.

Concept Review Encourage students to read the stanzas aloud to help them identify the rhythm. *(Possible responses: The regular rhythm creates suspense and mystery; the rhythm is similar to the pounding hooves of the highwayman's horse.)*

QuickWrites

1. Suggest that students begin by listing reasons why they think these sacrifices are foolish or noble.
2. Ask students to consider what Bess and the highwayman would want written on their tombstones, based on their lives and characters.
3. Remind students to provide vivid details that will create a powerful experience for their readers.

 The Writer's Craft

Personal Voice, pp. 312–313
Character Sketch, pp. 54–61
Creating Interest, p. 248

History *Cooperative Learning*
Highway Robbery Explain to students that highwaymen have often been the subjects of romantic legends and ballads. Divide students into groups and have them select one of the following figures to research: Robin Hood, Pancho Villa, Zorro, Jesse James, Sam Bass. Have group members look for both fact-based and fictional accounts of these figures and compare them. Groups can present their comparisons in a chart for a bulletin-board display. Students may wish to provide illustrations with their charts.

Literary Links

Possible responses: The poems differ in rhythm, but are similar in that both deal with violence. Also, in both poems, people willingly sacrifice their lives for what they believe is important.

ART CONNECTION
Have students use examples from the poem to support their responses. They can quote lines to show similarities or differences between how they imagined the scene and how it was illustrated.

ART GALLERY
Rural England The setting of the poem—rural England in the 1800s—is illustrated in these artworks. You may wish to generate discussion about English life at the time.

‖‖‖‖‖‖‖‖‖‖‖‖‖‖‖‖

Side A, Frame 49404

ALFRED NOYES

Alfred Noyes took popular themes and elevated them through his mastery of rhythm. Though critics of his time sometimes denigrated his poetry as excessively romantic and not "intellectual" enough, his use of vivid metaphor and compelling rhythm has appealed to generations of readers.

Multimodal Learning

ALTERNATIVE ACTIVITIES

1. Work with a group of classmates to role-play an investigative news reporter's **interviews** with the innkeeper, Tim the ostler, guests at the inn, and one or more redcoats about the deaths of Bess and the highwayman. If possible, have someone videotape the interviews, and show the tape to the class.

2. Present a **choral reading** of the poem, with different groups of students reading different stanzas. Make sure to vary the pitch and volume of your voice and the pace of your reading to reflect changes in mood.

3. Select **background music** that you think is appropriate for one or more stanzas of the poem. Play or perform this music for your classmates, and explain why you chose it.

ART CONNECTION
Review Charles Mikolaycak's illustrations that accompany the poem. Do the illustrations match the pictures that you imagined while reading the poem? Explain your answer.

LITERARY LINKS
Alfred Noyes greatly admired the poems of Alfred, Lord Tennyson. Read or reread "The Charge of the Light Brigade" on page 298. What similarities and differences between that poem and "The Highwayman" do you see?

ALFRED NOYES

1880–1958

Alfred Noyes was born in Wolverhampton, England, and spent much of his childhood on the Welsh coast, where he loved to read and daydream in a "mountain nook" overlooking the sea. Educated at Oxford University, he had written eight books of poetry by the time he was 30. He became one of the most popular poets in England in the early 1900s—popular enough to support himself solely from his writing. He wrote most of his poetry before 1942, when glaucoma cost him his eyesight. He continued to dictate prose works, however, including an autobiography and two children's books.

Noyes's best-known work is "The Highwayman," with its driving rhythm and haunting refrain. Generations of students have read this poem. Noyes said he wrote it in only two days when he was 24 years old.

OTHER WORKS "A Song of Sherwood," "The Admiral's Ghost"

Extended Reading

LASERLINKS
• ART GALLERY

Alternative Activities

1. Have each group brainstorm questions the interviewer will ask and likely answers the interviewee will give during the interview. Suggest that group members also create appropriate costumes and sets.

2. Divide the class into seven groups, each to read aloud two stanzas (the last group can read three stanzas). Have the whole class read aloud the last two stanzas. Prior to the choral reading, have students analyze their stanzas and decide on the mood they wish to convey. Review the way pitch, volume, tone of voice, and pace contribute to mood.

3. Ask your school or local librarian to make available dramatic, romantic music that suits the poem's mood. Have students work in groups, each choosing one or more stanzas to represent musically.

PREVIEWING

NONFICTION

from Commodore Perry in the Land of the Shogun
Rhoda Blumberg

PERSONAL CONNECTION

Think about a goal that you have achieved within the past year. How did you go about achieving your goal? What obstacles did you have to overcome? What strategy did you use? Briefly answer these questions in your notebook. Then, as you read this selection, consider Commodore Perry's goal and strategy.

Building Background

HISTORICAL CONNECTION

Just as individuals set goals, so do nations. In the mid-1800s, an important goal of the United States was to set up trade relations with Japan. Marco Polo had stirred curiosity about Japan in the 1200s, when he returned to Europe with tales of a land called Cipango, off the coast of China. About 1550, the Japanese began admitting Europeans to their country. By the early 1600s, however, the Japanese had grown fearful of European aggression and closed their country to foreigners. Only one port—Nagasaki—remained open, and only the Dutch and some Chinese were allowed to trade there. In this way, Japan limited its contact with Europeans for the next 200 years. During the first half of the 1800s, the United States tried to establish trade relations with Japan, but the efforts ended in failure. Then, in 1853, President Millard Fillmore decided to try once more, this time sending Commodore Perry to Japan.

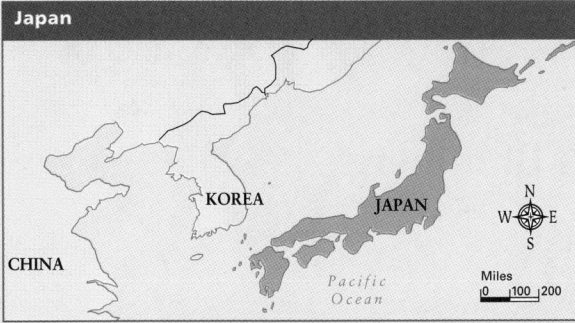

Japan

KOREA
JAPAN
CHINA
Pacific Ocean

Miles
0   100   200

Active Reading

READING CONNECTION

Visualizing Rhoda Blumberg's goal as a writer of history is to make the past seem fresh and alive. One way she achieves this goal is by taking her readers inside the minds of people involved in historic events. In this excerpt, she retells events from the perspectives of both the Japanese and Commodore Perry. To get the most out of the selection, **visualize** the details she provides—that is, picture them in your imagination. Use the details to get a clearer idea of what the Japanese and Commodore Perry were thinking and feeling.

LASERLINKS
• HISTORICAL CONNECTION

505

OVERVIEW

Objectives

- To understand and appreciate an excerpt from a biography about a naval officer and his goal
- To enrich reading by visualizing
- To identify and understand imagery
- To express understanding of the selection through a choice of writing forms, including an account, a profile, and a letter
- To extend understanding of the selection through a variety of multimodal and cross-curricular activities

Skills

READING SKILLS/ STRATEGIES
- Visualizing

THE WRITER'S STYLE
- Provocative introductions

GRAMMAR
- Subject-verb agreement in inverted sentences

LITERARY CONCEPTS
- Imagery
- Conflict

GENRE STUDY
- Nonfiction

STUDY SKILLS
- Indexes

SPEAKING, LISTENING, AND VIEWING
- Oral history

Cross-Curricular Connections

GEOGRAPHY
- Japan

SCIENCE
- Whaling

DRAMA
- Noh Play

SOCIAL STUDIES
- Shogun: the celebration

HISTORICAL CONNECTION
Perry in Japan Commodore Perry set out to open trade between the United States and Japan in 1853. These historical images show some of Perry's activities during his stay in Japan, as well as the way in which the Japanese viewed him.

Side A, Frame 49414

PRINT AND MEDIA RESOURCES

UNIT FOUR RESOURCE BOOK
Strategic Reading: Literature, p. 65
Vocabulary SkillBuilder, p. 67
Reading SkillBuilder, p. 66

GRAMMAR MINI-LESSONS
Transparencies, p. 7
Copymasters, p. 7

WRITING MINI-LESSONS
Transparencies, p. 30

ACCESS FOR STUDENTS ACQUIRING ENGLISH
Selection Summaries
Reading and Writing Support

FORMAL ASSESSMENT
Selection Test, pp. 97-98
Part Test, pp. 99–100
 Test Generator

AUDIO LIBRARY
See Reference Card

LASERLINKS
Historical Connection
Contemporary Connection

INTERNET RESOURCES
McDougal Littell Literature Center at http://www.hmco.com /mcdougal/lit

SUMMARY

Matthew Calbraith Perry was the commodore in charge of the American ships that visited Japan in 1853. His purpose was to deliver a letter to the emperor, inviting Japan to open trade relations with the United States. The shoguns had kept Japan isolated from the world for centuries. This selection tells the story of the interaction between the Japanese and Americans and how the Americans realized their goal.

Thematic Link: *High Stakes* The stakes are high as Commodore Perry attempts to open potentially lucrative trade relations with the Japanese.

Art Note

Mount Fuji and Seashore at Miho No Matsubara by **Kano Tanȳu** Tanȳu (1602–1674) was the official painter at the shogun court of Japan, and a master of many painting styles. His work was so fine the shoguns allowed him to start his own art school.

Reading the Art *How is this style of landscape painting similar to or different from other landscapes you have seen? What impression of the land do you have based on the way it is painted?*

CUSTOMIZING FOR
Students Acquiring English

• Use **ACCESS FOR STUDENTS ACQUIRING ENGLISH**, Reading and Writing Support.

• If possible, encourage students from Japanese backgrounds who are familiar with this important historical event to share more information about it.

from Commodore Perry in

Detail of *Mount Fuji and Seashore at Miho No Matsubara* (1666), Kano Tanȳu. Asian Art Museum of San Francisco, Avery Brundage Collection (B63 D7a). Photo Copyright © 1995 Asian Art Museum of San Francisco.

by Rhoda Blumberg

506 UNIT FOUR PART 2: HIGH STAKES

WORDS TO KNOW

appall (ə-pôl′) *v.* to fill with horror or alarm; shock (p. 507)

furor (fyŏŏr′ôr) *n.* a commotion or uproar (p. 509)

incessant (ĭn-sĕs′ənt) *adj.* never ceasing; constant (p. 509)

inept (ĭn-ĕpt′) *adj.* unfit for an activity; incompetent (p. 508)

mystifying (mĭs′tə-fī′ĭng) *adj.* puzzling, bewildering **mystify** *v.* (p. 508)

omen (ō′mən) *n.* an occurrence that is thought to be a sign of future events (p. 509)

replenish (rĭ-plĕn′ĭsh) *v.* to make full or complete again; resupply (p. 510)

resolve (rĭ-zŏlv′) *v.* to make a firm decision; determine (p. 511)

seclude (sĭ-klōōd′) *v.* to keep apart from others (p. 512)

turmoil (tûr′moil′) *n.* a state of great confusion and disorder; chaos (p. 508)

the Land of the Shogun

STRATEGIC READING FOR

Less Proficient Readers

Set a Purpose Ask students to describe how they might react if aliens from another planet visited the earth. Then have students read to find out how the Japanese react when they first spot the American ships.

Use **UNIT FOUR RESOURCE BOOK**, p. 65, for guidance in reading the selection.

If monsters had descended upon Japan, the effect could not have been more terrifying.

People in the fishing village of Shimoda were the first to spot four huge hulks, two streaming smoke, on the ocean's surface approaching the shore. "Giant dragons puffing smoke," cried some. "Alien[1] ships of fire," cried others. According to a folktale, smoke above water was made by the breath of clams. Only a child would believe that. Perhaps enemies knew how to push erupting volcanoes toward the Japanese homeland. Surely something horrible was happening on this day, Friday, July 8, 1853.

Fishermen pulled in their nets, grabbed their oars, and rowed to shore frantically. They had been close up and knew that these floating mysteries were foreign ships. Black ships that belched black clouds! They had never seen anything like it. They didn't even know that steamboats existed, and they were appalled by the number and size of the guns.

Barbarians from out of the blue! Will they invade, kidnap, kill, then destroy everything? What will become of the sacred Land of the Rising Sun?[2]

General alarms were sounded. Temple bells rang, and messengers raced throughout Japan to warn everyone that enemy aliens were approaching by ship.

Rumors spread that "one hundred thousand devils with white faces" were about to overrun the country. People panicked. They carried their valuables and furniture in all directions in order to hide them from invading barbarians. Women and children were locked up in their homes or sent to friends and relatives who lived inland, far from the endangered shore.

Messengers rushed to the capital of Edo (now Tokyo) to alert government officials. Edo, the

---

1. **alien:** foreign.
2. **Land of the Rising Sun:** This is a translation of the Japanese name for Japan.

> WORDS
> TO
> KNOW
>
> **appall** (ə-pôl′) v. to fill with horror or alarm; shock

507

CUSTOMIZING FOR

Gifted and Talented Students

Have students note examples of miscommunication, misconceptions, and racism in the selection as they read. Ask them to predict how these things could affect the selection's outcome.

Possible responses:

- *Page 507—"...'devils with white faces' were about to overrun the country." This racism could increase hostility and distrust.*

- *Page 511—Perry "felt that he could not trust the actions of unknown Orientals." This racism shows distrust, which could lead to even further misunderstandings.*

- *Page 511—Biddle's acceptance of an apology "was interpreted as weakness and cowardice." Misconceptions like this could lead to hostility.*

CUSTOMIZING FOR

Students Acquiring English

 Explain that the expression *from out of the blue* describes people or things that appear suddenly and without explanation.

┌──┐
Mini-Lesson ✒ The Writer's Style
└──┘

PROVOCATIVE INTRODUCTIONS Point out to students that compelling opening sentences make readers want to continue reading. This sentence is often called a "hook." Explain that because some people think of historical writing as "dry," history writers often include provocative introductions to draw the readers in. Share with students the list of techniques for generating provocative introductions.

Application Have students reread the highlighted sentence and explain why it might make them want to read farther. Have students write a different, but still engaging, opening sentence for this selection and then read it to the class.

Reteaching/Reinforcement
- Writing Handbook, anthology p. 814
- *Writing Mini-Lessons* transparencies p. 30

 The Writer's Craft

Introductions, pp. 275–277

Provocative Introductions
startling or interesting facts
vivid, detailed description
questions
incidents or anecdotes
quotations

A Kyoto was the capital of Japan from 794 to 1185. Since then it has been Japan's spiritual center. Today, Tokyo is Japan's capital, located on Japan's main island, Honshu. Three other main islands make up Japan: Hokkaido to the north of Honshu, and Kyushu and Shikoku to the south. Including other smaller islands, Japan's total area is slightly less than that of California. Japan has two mountain ranges, and several of the mountains, like the majestic Fuji, are volcanoes.

The islands of Japan are separated from mainland China, Korea, and Siberia by the Sea of Japan. Its location in the northern Pacific gives Japan—and especially its northern islands—a rather cold climate.

Active Reading: EVALUATE

B Have students analyze this passage and decide if the status and power of Shogun Ieyoshi was determined according to merit or in another way. If needed, use the following model.

Think-Aloud Model *The text says the head shogun was a weakling and inept and implies that he dedicated himself to pleasure, not governing. Therefore, he must have attained his exalted position in another way, for obviously he did not earn it by his own merit and accomplishments.*

---

world's largest city with more than one million occupants, went into a state of chaos the very day the ships were sighted. Women raced about in the streets with children in their arms. Men carried their mothers on their backs, not knowing which way to turn.

A Who could control the <u>turmoil</u>? The Emperor Komei was isolated in his royal palace at Kyoto. Although he was worshiped as a divine descendent of the sun goddess, Amaterasu, he was a powerless puppet,[3] responsible primarily for conducting religious ceremonies. During his leisure hours he was expected to study the classics and compose poetry. The Japanese referred to their emperor as "he who lives above the clouds." By law, he was not permitted to leave his heavenly palace unless he received special permission from the government. An emperor's sphere of influence was otherworldly. All down-to-earth decisions were made by shoguns who had been wielding power for more than 700 years.

The word shogun means "barbarian expelling generalissimo.[4]" How appropriate at this time! Surely the shogun would take command!

B But Shogun Ieyoshi who occupied the palace at Edo in 1853 was a weakling. No one even bothered to tell him the frightening news. Three days after the ships arrived he overheard chatter about them while enjoying a Noh[5] play that was being performed for him in his palace. The news affected him so badly that he went to bed, sick at heart.

Because the shogun was <u>inept</u>, his councillors, called the *Bakufu*, ruled the country. But accord-

After recovering from shock they ordered the great clans to prepare to battle barbarians.

ing to a Japanese reporter, "They were too alarmed to open their mouths." The Bakufu should not have been so surprised. Before reaching Japan, the American fleet had stopped at Loo Choo (now Okinawa). Japanese spies stationed there had sent word that American ships were on their way to Japan. Dutch traders had also alerted the Bakufu. But for <u>mystifying</u> reasons, the government did not take these reports seriously until the black ships arrived on July 8. After recovering from shock they ordered the great clans to prepare to battle barbarians.

Locked away from the rest of the world, using the Pacific Ocean as its moat, Japan had maintained a feudal society similar to that of Europe during the Middle Ages. There were lords (*daimyos*), knights (*samurai*), and vassals who labored in their lord's domain and paid tithes[6] to their masters.

---

3. **puppet:** a person whose actions are controlled by others.
4. **barbarian expelling generalissimo** (jĕn´ər-ə-lĭs´ə-mō´): high-ranking commander who drives out barbarians.
5. **Noh:** a traditional form of Japanese drama with music and dancing, in which the actors wear masks.
6. **tithes:** taxes.

WORDS
TO
KNOW

turmoil (tûr´moil´) *n.* a state of great confusion and disorder; chaos
inept (ĭn-ĕpt´) *adj.* unfit for an activity; incompetent
mystifying (mĭs´tə-fī´ĭng) adj. puzzling; bewildering **mystify** *v.*

508

M i n i - L e s s o n   **S t u d y   S k i l l s**

INDEXES Ask students how they would find information for a report about the shoguns. Ask them if they had a book on Japanese history, how they would determine on which pages information on the shoguns can be found. Explain to students that most nonfiction books have indexes at the back. Tell them that an index is an alphabetical list of topics that are covered in a book. Each topic listed is followed by the number of the page or pages that discuss it.

Application Have students get from the library one or more books about Japanese history. Have students use the index to identify all the topics pertaining to shoguns and then list the items covered under this topic and the pages on which the information is found. Suggest that interested students read the pages about the shoguns, note additional relevant topics, and list the page numbers that are found in the index.

The country had not been at war since it invaded Korea in 1597. That was 256 years earlier. Nevertheless, feudal lords were able to mobilize troops. Men who had never dressed for warfare worked to get rust off spears. They placed new feathers in their families' antique arrows. Tailors were pressed into service so they could fix the silk cords on ancient armor, make warriors' cloaks, and sew cotton skull-caps that would cushion the weight of heavy helmets. Seventeen thousand soldiers were readied for battle.

When the ships moved toward the land that first day, Japanese guard boats set out to surround the enemy. But they could not catch up with aliens whose ships were so magical that they steamed ahead against the wind without using sails or oars.

At five o'clock in the afternoon the foreign ships anchored a mile and a half from shore, at Edo Bay. They were less than thirty-five miles from the capital city. Beautiful cliffs, rolling green hills, and, above all, snowcapped Mount Fuji made a breathtaking scene. After dusk, beacon fires dotted the land, and there was an <u>incessant</u> toll of temple gongs.

That night a meteor with a fiery tail streaked through the sky like a rocket. An <u>omen</u> from the gods! Shrines and temples were jammed. Priests told worshipers that barbarians were about to punish them for their sins.

Four ships and 560 men of the U.S. Navy had created this <u>furor</u>. The *Mississippi* and the *Susquehanna* were steam powered. The *Plymouth* and the *Saratoga* were three-masted

Photograph of Commodore Perry.
Reproduced from the Collections of the Library of Congress.

WORDS TO KNOW	**incessant** (ĭn-sĕs'ənt) *adj.* never ceasing; constant
	omen (ō'mən) *n.* an occurrence that is thought to be a sign of future events
	furor (fyŏŏr'ôr') *n.* a commotion or uproar

509

C Make sure students understand the isolationist policy of Japan and how it influenced the reaction of the Japanese to the Americans.

• In what ways do the Japanese people show their alarm at the appearance of the American ships? *(Possible responses: People hide; temple bells sound alarms; people prepare for battle.)* Noting Relevant Details

Set a Purpose Have students read to identify Commodore Perry's goal in coming to Japan.

Critical Thinking:
MAKING JUDGMENTS

D Have students discuss why the Japanese react so negatively to the arrival of the American ships. Ask how Japan's policy of isolation might account for this reaction. *(Possible response: Japan's lack of contact with others explains the people's mistrust and fear of foreigners. In comparison to their small fishing boats, the belching fleet of steamboats might indeed look monstrous.)*

Mini-Lesson Reading Skills/Strategies

VISUALIZING Inform students that the process of forming a mental picture from a written or verbal description is called visualizing. Good readers use details supplied by the writer to picture characters, settings, and events in their mind.

Application Have students read the highlighted passage on page 509 describing the meteor. Then have students work in groups to create a painting or mural depicting the meteor. Ask students to explain how they based their illustration on information in the selection.

Reteaching/Reinforcement
• *Unit Four Resource Book*, p. 66

E In the nineteenth century, many nations hunted whales for their oil (for lighting) and baleen, often called "whalebone" (for corsets). At that time, there were no limits on whale hunting. This became a problem because whales are marine mammals, and, like many other large mammals, they bear few young and nurture them for years. Therefore, whale reproduction could not keep up with hunting pressure, and many species were hunted nearly to extinction.

In 1949, the member nations of the International Whaling Commission (IWC) voted to limit whaling. A worldwide "Save the Whales" campaign led the IWC to prohibit all whaling as of 1984. Some nations, including Norway, Japan, and Russia, continued limited whale hunting. Nevertheless, the populations of many whale species have rebounded. In 1994, the IWC created a permanent whale sanctuary in Antarctica.

Critical Thinking:
MAKING JUDGMENTS

F Ask students if they think Perry really believed his mission's main purpose was to promote peace and encourage the Japanese to give up their isolation. Have them explain their answers. *(Possible response: Probably not; more likely, the main intent was to exploit Japanese resources and enrich the American whaling industry.)*

Detail of an illustration of Commodore Perry's ships arriving in Japan (19th century), unknown artist. Yokohama (Japan) City Library.

sailing ships in tow behind the steamers. The Japanese referred to these four vessels as "The Black Ships of the Evil Men."

Commodore Matthew Calbraith Perry was in command of the squadron. He had not come to invade. He hoped to be a peacemaker who would make the isolated Empire of Japan a member of "the family of civilized nations" of the world. His mission was to unlock Japan's door. It had been slammed shut against all but a few Dutch and Chinese traders, the only ones officially allowed in for over 200 years.

Perry expected to deliver a letter from President Millard Fillmore to the Emperor of Japan, proposing "that the United States and Japan should live in friendship and have commercial intercourse with each other." The letter requested that ports be opened so that American ships could obtain coal and provisions.

America had invested seventeen million dollars in the Pacific whaling industry, and it needed Japanese ports to replenish coal and provisions for the whalers. Whale oil was essential for lighting and for lubricating machinery.

President Fillmore's letter also asked that men who had been shipwrecked on Japanese shores be treated with kindness. This point was emphasized because many American whaling ships had been wrecked off Japan's coast by violent storms, and their castaways[7] had been jailed and abused.

Perry intended to deliver the letter and sail away peacefully. He would winter in Hong

---

7. **castaways:** people who have been shipwrecked.

WORDS
TO
KNOW

replenish (rĭ-plĕn′ĭsh) v. to make full or complete again; resupply

510

Assessment ✓ **Option**

INFORMAL ASSESSMENT Assess students' understanding of the excerpt by having them rewrite this historical incident from the point of view of either a sailor aboard Perry's ship or of a Japanese villager. Have students work in groups to decide how the incident may appear when seen from the perspective of the character they've selected. Have students create an outline of what they will include in their account.

Rubric

3 Full Accomplishment Students' outline accurately reflects the sequence of events and is consistent with the viewpoint of their chosen character.

2 Substantial Accomplishment Students' outline includes most of the important events and generally is consistent with the viewpoint of their chosen character.

1 Little or Partial Accomplishment Students' outline lacks a clear sequence of events and is sometimes inconsistent with the viewpoint of their chosen character.

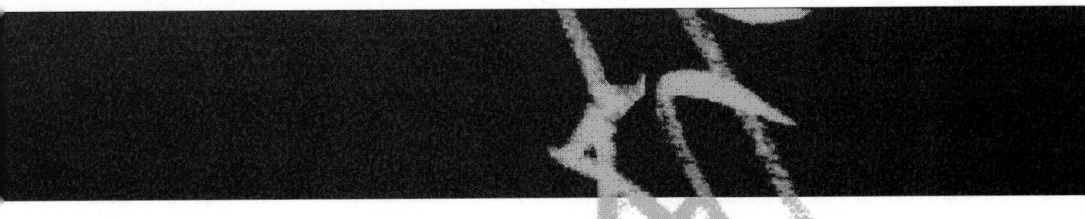

Kong. With only four ships and supplies that could last no more than one month, he would not attempt to wait for the Emperor's reply, but he planned to return in the spring—when he would have more supplies and a larger fleet.

The Commodore was determined not to use force unless attacked. But he felt that he could not trust the actions of unknown Orientals.[8] He dared not take chances, for he remembered the *Morrison,* an American ship that had sailed into Edo Bay on a peaceful mission in 1837. Its intent was to return seven Japanese castaways to their homeland. The Japanese had opened fire and forced the ship to leave.

As a precaution, Perry's squadron anchored in battle formation facing the shore. Cannons and guns were loaded. All hands took up their battle stations.

Japanese guard boats approached the moored Americans ships. Each vessel, propelled by six to eight standing oarsmen, was filled with about thirty soldiers. Fastening ropes to the ships, they tried to climb on board. Commodore Perry ordered his sailors to cut the guard boats' ropes and use pikes and cutlasses[9] to keep the Japanese away. A few tried to climb the *Mississippi's* anchor chain. A rap on the knuckles sent one soldier into the water. All of the Japanese soldiers howled and shouted angrily.

Perry's stubborn refusal to allow them on board was based on the terrible experience of another American commodore. Seven years before, in 1846, Commodore James Biddle had anchored at Edo Bay, hoping to deliver a letter to the Emperor from the United States govern-ment. The letter requested trade relations between the two countries. As a friendly gesture, Biddle allowed swarms of Japanese soldiers to come aboard. A rude soldier gave Biddle a shove that knocked him off his feet. Anxious to keep peace, Biddle graciously accepted an apology, which was interpreted as weakness and cowardice. Japanese officials mocked him, refused to deliver documents, and ordered him to leave at once. Because his orders were not to create an incident, Biddle immediately sailed away.

Perry resolved that until negotiations were successful, he would not allow more than three officials on board at a time.

A Japanese guard boat rowed close to the Commodore's flagship, the *Susquehanna.* Its men held up a scroll, written in large letters, in French, that said, "Go away! Do not dare to anchor!" Then one of the Japanese shouted in English, "I can speak Dutch." He asked to come aboard. Antón Portman, Perry's Dutch-Japanese interpreter, came on deck. He explained that the Commodore would only allow the highest officials on his ship. When

---

8. **Orientals:** an old term (now considered offensive) for Asian people.
9. **pikes and cutlasses** (kŭt′lə-səz): long spears and short curved swords.

WORDS TO KNOW	**resolve** (rĭ-zŏlv′) *v.* to make a firm decision; determine

511

J Ask students how the actions of individuals, groups, and "governments" increased the tensions and conflicts between the Americans and Japanese. *(Possible responses: Commodore Perry secluded himself in his cabin and refused to be seen by any but the most exalted Japanese official; he remained aloof and increased the conflict between the two parties; all parties displayed distrust, which led to conflict and misunderstanding.)*

Literary Concept:
CHARACTERIZATION

K Have students use descriptive words to characterize the American sailors' attitude toward the Japanese. Have students also describe how they inferred the sailors' attitude. *(Possible responses: The sailors' ridicule of the Japanese fortifications suggests an attitude that may be described as condescending, unfeeling, and superior.)*

told that there was an important person in the guard boat, he lowered a gangway ladder.

Nakajima, introduced as vice-governor of the small nearby village of Uraga, climbed up. In fact, Nakajima was not a vice-governor but merely a minor official. He was accompanied by a Dutch-speaking interpreter.

J Commodore Perry secluded himself in his cabin. He refused to be seen by a vice-governor or, indeed, by any but the most important emissaries[10] of the Emperor. Lieutenant John Contee was told to speak with Nakajima. Contee explained that the Commodore's intentions were friendly. Perry merely wished to present a letter from the President of the United States to the Emperor of Japan. Nakajima replied that the American ships must go to the port of Nagasaki, where there was a Dutch trading post so that the Dutch could act as go-betweens.

Through his lieutenant, Perry let it be known that he would never go to Nagasaki and if all guard boats didn't disperse[11] immediately there would be trouble. Nakajima went to the gangway, shouted an order, waved his fan, and all guard boats except his own departed at once. When Nakajima took his leave he promised that a higher official would see Perry the next day, Saturday, July 9.

That night, when the meteor streaked across the sky, Perry noted in his journal that this was a favorable omen: ". . . we pray God that our present attempt to bring a singular and isolated people into the family of civilized nations may succeed without resort to bloodshed."

At dawn the Americans were amazed to see a boatload of artists near the *Susquehanna*. Using fine brushes, ink stones, and rolls of rice paper, they were making sketches of the ships and any of the crew they could see. Their curiosity was obviously stronger than their fear. Within a week, pictures of the Black Ships and "hairy barbarians" were hawked in the streets and sold in shops. They were also reproduced on souvenir banners, scrolls, fans, and towels.

While these artist-reporters were acting like war correspondents, the coastline was bustling with activity. Women and children carrying baskets of dirt helped men build new fortifications. Thousands of soldiers marched to and fro while their leaders decided upon strategic battle positions. They displayed colorful banners emblazoned with their lords' arms.[12] Some trained muskets on Perry's squadron. Strips of canvas had been set up along the coast to hide these activities, but the Americans could see over them. The sailors were amused and dubbed the canvases "dungaree forts."

At seven o' clock in the morning, Kayama, so-called "governor" of Uraga, was welcomed aboard the *Susquehanna*. Actually he was not a governor but a police chief. Uraga's real governor, who did not wish to meet barbarians, gave Kayama permission to take his place. Dressed for the occasion in an embroidered silk

---

10. **emissaries** (ĕm′ĭ-sĕr′ēz): people sent to represent the interests of others.
11. **disperse:** scatter in different directions.
12. **arms:** designs symbolic of nobility, position, or achievement.

WORDS
TO
KNOW

seclude (sĭ-klōōd′) *v.* to keep apart from others

512

Mini-Lesson   **Genre Study**

NONFICTION Remind students that this selection is an excerpt from a **biography**: the story of a person's life written by another person. Tell students that biographies are often about famous people, such as Commodore Perry. Explain that while biographies contain many facts, they also include the biographer's evaluation of the subject and surrounding events. This is considered an author's bias since it reflects his or her opinion.

Application Have students work in small groups to review the selection, looking for evidence of the author's bias . Have a recorder list the group's examples. Another member can present the group's work to the class. Remind each group to give reasons to support their findings. If there is disagreement among groups, encourage students to debate whether an example reflects bias or not.

robe, a lacquered hat with padded chin straps, and clunky clogs, this little man looked comical and ill at ease, even when his Dutch interpreter introduced him as a person of great importance.

Commodore Perry would not see him. He secluded himself in his cabin again, for he rightly guessed that Kayama was not an eminent envoy[13] of the Emperor. Because he remained hidden like a holy man, the Japanese soon spoke of Perry as "The American Mikado,[14]" and called his quarters "The Abode of His High and Mighty Mysteriousness."

Commanders Franklin Buchanan and Henry Adams spoke with Kayama. The conversation was awkward because it had to be translated from English into Dutch and then into Japanese, and back again. Perry's son Oliver acted as go-between. On board as his father's secretary, he rushed to and fro with orders for Buchanan and Adams, and reports for his father.

Kayama insisted that the Americans had to go to Nagasaki. He explained that Japanese law made it impossible for a letter to be received at any other port. Perry refused to budge and threatened to deliver the letter in person at the royal palace in Edo. Frightened at the thought, Kayama promised to contact the Emperor, then timidly asked why four ships were needed in order to carry one little letter to the Emperor. "Out of respect for him," Perry retorted. (The Commodore had no way of knowing that the Shogun occupied the Edo palace, and that the Emperor was a powerless

Commodore Perry (about 1853), unknown Japanese artist. Kanagawa (Japan) Prefecture Museum.

figurehead who lived in Kyoto surrounded by the Shogun's spies.)

Kayama became even more alarmed when he noticed that small boats launched from the ships were cruising close to the mainland. He exclaimed that the Americans were violating Japanese law. The officers countered by saying that they were obeying American law. They had to survey coastal waters—a preparation in case Perry decided to land.

During the surveys one of the Americans looked at some Japanese soldiers through a telescope. The soldiers ducked, probably believing that the spyglass was a new type of gun.

Strange music came from the ships on Sunday, July 10. The crew sang hymns, accompanied by a band whose instruments were unheard of in Japan. A boatload of Japanese asked to visit, but

---

13. **eminent envoy** (ĕn'voi'): a high-ranking representative.
14. **mikado** (mĭ-kä'dō): an honorary title of the emperor of Japan.

COMMODORE PERRY IN THE LAND OF THE SHOGUN **513**

Literary Concept: IMAGERY

L Remind students that words and phrases that appeal to the reader's senses are known as imagery. Writers use details to help the reader imagine how things look, feel, smell, sound, and taste. Have students note the details that create an image of Kayama as he arrives for the meeting. Ask what senses the imagery appeals to. *(sight)* Then ask what impression of Kayama the imagery conveys. *(Possible responses: that he is funny, awkward, and clownish; not a person of great importance)*

Literary Concept: CONFLICT

M Have students discuss how Perry's refusal to budge adds to the conflict. *(Possible response: His refusal prolongs the tense period of initial contact and negotiation.)*

STRATEGIC READING FOR

Less Proficient Readers

N Make sure students understand why Perry chooses to remain in his cabin rather than see the envoy.

• What was the only kind of envoy Perry would see? *(a high official)* **Classifying**

• What was the Japanese envoy's true status? *(police chief)* **Noting Relevant Details**

Set a Purpose Have students read to find out if the Americans change their attitude toward the Japanese citizens.

CUSTOMIZING FOR

Multiple Learning Styles

O **Musical Learners** Have musically talented students compose a tune to represent the music that the Japanese might have heard coming from the ship. Ask these students to play their tune for the class.

Mini-Lesson: Speaking,  **Listening, and Viewing**

ORAL HISTORY Explain to students that many people convey their history orally by telling stories about it. In this way, a people's or nation's history is passed down through the generations.

Application Have students work in groups to write an oral history from the point of view of the Japanese telling about their encounter with the Americans. Have the entire group discuss what the oral historian will relate and emphasize. Invite one member from each group to read the history to the class.

Students Acquiring English

(3) Point out that the conjunction *thus* means "by doing so." Encourage students to use this word to connect ideas in their writing.

CUSTOMIZING FOR

Gifted and Talented Students

(P) Have students discuss why they think the Japanese and the Americans became more trusting of one another. *(Possible response: Both groups were curious about one another. After meeting, they discovered that many of their previous fears and misconceptions were unfounded.)* Then ask students what they know of current relations between Japan and the United States. Encourage students to review newspapers and journals or do on-line researching to find out more. Have them write a short then-now essay comparing and contrasting 19th century relations with today's.

STRATEGIC READING FOR

Less Proficient Readers

(Q) Have students describe how the Americans' attitude toward the Japanese changes. *(The Americans no longer fear the Japanese but are enchanted by them.)* **Summarizing**

---

they were refused admission because Sunday was the Christian day of rest.

On Monday morning surveying boats were sent farther than ever up Edo Bay. Kayama came aboard in a panic. The activities of the Americans had caused great distress in Edo, because the city's principal food supply depended upon boat traffic. Fear of the foreigners prevented supply boats from sailing.

Despite Kayama's pleas, the Americans continued to chart the coastal waters. Their survey boats came near enough to fortifications to observe that they were made of dirt and wood. There were a few cannons, but they were small and old. Most of them were 8-pounders, 200 or 300 years old, and they had not been used for a long time. The Japanese probably did not even know how to fire them. One of Perry's crew quipped that he could load all the Japanese cannons into the American 64-pound cannons and shoot them back.

Soldiers loyal to two daimyos requested permission to shoot at the Americans. Fortunately, their lords decided to hold fire, (3) thus preventing an incident that might have started a war.

Although officials were terribly alarmed, many ordinary citizens calmed down after the first day of shock. A few hailed the men in the surveying boats and offered them water and peaches. A Japanese guard boat welcomed some of the surveyors aboard. The Americans amused and fascinated their hosts by shooting Colt revolvers in the air.

Face to face, they were beginning to realize that these charming people were as courteous and hospitable as any they had ever met.

The Americans were enchanted by the kindness and friendliness of the Japanese. At one time they believed that they had sailed over the edge of world civilization and would encounter savages. Face to face, they were beginning to realize that these charming people were as courteous and hospitable as any they had ever met. They were yet to discover that Japan was a highly civilized, cultured nation. ❖

Editor's Note: On Thursday, July 14, Perry presented his documents to the emperor's representatives and then set sail for China. He returned to Japan in February 1854, with nine ships. After a few weeks, the Japanese signed the Treaty of Kanagawa. Perry had succeeded in opening the doors of trade with Japan. Today, the Japanese hold annual Black Ships festivals in Perry's honor.

Mini-Lesson Grammar

SUBJECT-VERB AGREEMENT IN INVERTED SENTENCES Point out to students that the highlighted sentence is inverted, meaning that the verb comes before the subject. Explain that even in inverted sentences the subject and the verb must agree—both must be either singular or plural.

Application Have students read the inverted sentences below and choose the correct form of either the verb or the subject.

1. The first to spot the boats (<u>was</u>/were) a person in the fishing village.
2. There were (warrior/<u>warriors</u>) dressed for battle.

3. Perry asked, "Where (<u>is</u>/are) the high-ranking Japanese envoy?"
4. Closer and closer to the shore (<u>sail</u>/sails) the American ships.

Reteaching/Reinforcement
- Grammar Handbook, anthology p. 857
- *Grammar Mini-Lessons* copymasters p. 7, transparencies p. 7

The Writer's Craft

Agreement in Inverted Sentences, p. 584

The Rise and Fall of the Shogun

Commodore Perry arrived in Japan during the Tokugawa period, also known as the Great Peace. Tokugawa Ieyasu (tō′kŏŏ-gä′wə ē-ə-yä′sōō) had become shogun in 1603 and moved to Edo (now Tokyo), where he built a castle. He passed down the shogunate to his son and established a line of succession much like that of a kingship. The Tokugawa family ruled Japan for the next 250 years.

Although the emperor was regarded as a god, the shogun was the real power in Japan, setting up rules of conduct and codes of law. Ieyasu divided Japan into about 250 provinces, each headed by a daimyo. By law, the daimyos had to swear an oath of allegiance to the shogun, to pay for repairing castles and roads, and to spend a part of every other year in Edo, serving the shogun. When returning to their own provinces, the daimyos had to leave their wives and children behind as hostages.

Tanki Yoryaku, Masahiro Mura. Woodcut illustration, The Metropolitan Museum of Art, The Bashford Dean Memorial Collection. All rights reserved, The Metropolitan Museum of Art.

Between 1612 and 1635, the shoguns also established a series of laws to isolate Japan. The Tokugawa government sought to keep Japan free from European influences. Japanese were not allowed to leave the country, nor were foreigners allowed to enter.

This isolation helped preserve a feudal society in Japan. Beneath the daimyos—the highest social class—were the samurai, the farmers, the artisans, and the merchants. The merchants controlled the flow of money by setting prices and making loans. They grew more and more powerful as their wealth increased, and by the mid-1800s they were looking forward to foreign trade.

Thus, the arrival of Commodore Perry opened the doors to a society that was changing. The shogun presented a copy of President Fillmore's letter to the emperor and turned to him for advice. From that point on, the emperor began to become more important than the shogun.

---

1. What is Commodore Perry's mission to Japan? *(to deliver a letter to the emperor)*
2. Why does Commodore Perry refuse to see the Japanese envoy? *(The envoy is not a high-ranking official.)*
3. What are the initial relations between the Americans and the Japanese like? *(Possible responses: hostile; tension-filled; lacking in trust)*
4. Do relations between the Japanese and the Americans change? If so, how? *(Possible response: Both groups get to know one another better. The Japanese become less fearful, and the Americans realize that Japan is a highly civilized, cultured nation.)*
5. What is the outcome of Perry's visit? *(He accomplishes his mission by giving the letter to the emperor's representatives. He later returns and negotiates a treaty that opens trade relations between the two countries.)*

1. What do you think the shogun's motives were when he demanded that the daimyos leave their families behind in Edo as hostages? *(Possible responses: to ensure their loyalty; to ensure their return)*
2. In what ways do you think Japanese society was already changing when Perry arrived? *(Possible responses: Lavish lifestyles made shoguns borrow money from merchants, thus the merchants were becoming more powerful; social classes below the daimyos were probably seeking the luxuries that the daimyos had.)*

Multicultural Perspectives

THE 1854 TREATY OF KANAGAWA The treaty Japan signed with the United States contained these provisions: an American diplomat would live in Japan to guarantee the better treatment of shipwrecked American sailors; the United States would be allowed trading rights in the Japanese ports of Shimoda and Hakodate. Four years later, Townsend Harris, the first U.S. diplomat to reside in Japan, negotiated a more extensive trade treaty with Japan in which foreigners were allowed to live in Japan but were subject only to

their own nation's laws. This provision is called "extraterritoriality." In that same year of 1858, The Netherlands, France, Russia, and Great Britain signed trade agreements with the Japanese, most of which also included the rights of extraterritoriality. All of the treaties signed in the 1850s were called "unequal treaties." This term refers to the fact that the treaties granted foreign countries rights that were not given to Japan in return. It was not until the 1890s, almost 40 years later, that Japan succeeded in revising the unequal treaties.

From Personal Response to Critical Analysis

1. Possible responses: The Japanese were too isolated and superstitious; Commodore Perry was too arrogant and superior.
2. Possible responses: Japanese isolationism and distrust; his own prejudice
3. Possible responses: He was justly cautious; he was too uncompromising; he was too harsh.
4. Possible responses: I would let Perry deliver the letter since we could always ignore its contents. I wouldn't let Perry deliver the letter because contact with Americans could harm our culture.
5. Possible response: Perry's goal was more important, but his strategy involved less compromise and tolerance than mine did.
6. Possible responses: Japan learned about and excelled in Western pursuits; the United States gained access to Japanese resources.

Literary Links

Ask students how the "new frontier" Perry faced compares to Louis L'Amour's "eternal frontier." *(Possible response: Both are unknown territories full of challenges.)*

Another Pathway

Have students reread Perry's journal entry on page 512 and use it and what they know about Perry's character to create an entry that Perry himself might have written.

Rubric

3 Full Accomplishment Student consistently maintains Perry's view throughout his or her entry.

2 Substantial Accomplishment Student adequately maintains Perry's view but includes extraneous material.

1 Little or Partial Accomplishment Student records primarily his or her own viewpoint, reflecting little of Perry's character.

FROM **PERSONAL RESPONSE** *TO* **CRITICAL ANALYSIS**

REFLECT 1. What are your thoughts about the Japanese and Commodore Perry? Record your impressions in your notebook, then share them with a partner.

RETHINK 2. What do you think was the greatest obstacle that Commodore Perry had to overcome in order to achieve his goal?

3. How would you evaluate Commodore Perry as a leader?
   Consider
   • what he learned from the experiences of other commanders
   • his strategy for dealing with the Japanese
   • his personal qualities

Close Textual Reading

4. What if you had been an adviser to the shogun? Would you have been in favor of or opposed to allowing Commodore Perry to deliver President Fillmore's letter to the emperor? Explain your reasons.

RELATE 5. How would you compare Commodore Perry's goal and strategy with the goal and strategy you listed for the Personal Connection on page 505?

6. Commodore Perry opened the door that isolated Japan from the outside world. In your opinion, what changes in the United States and in Japan resulted from Perry's achievement?

LITERARY CONCEPTS

Imagery consists of words that appeal to the senses. For example, the following sentence contains images that appeal to sight and hearing: "After dusk, beacon fires dotted the land, and there was an incessant toll of temple gongs." Identify other images that helped you visualize characters, places, and events in this selection.

516 UNIT FOUR PART 2: HIGH STAKES

Multimodal Learning
ANOTHER PATHWAY

This selection includes a quotation from Perry's journal, about the significance of the meteor on the night of his arrival at Edo Bay. Imagine that you are Commodore Perry. Write a journal entry that expresses your views about your goal and your impressions of Japan. Read your journal entry to the rest of the class.

QUICKWRITES

1. Imagine that you are a Japanese artist-reporter who has observed Commodore Perry's ships and crew. Write an **account** of your impressions.

2. Write a **profile** of Commodore Perry for a popular magazine. Be sure to identify the qualities that helped him achieve his goal. To get started, review the evaluation you made for question 3 under "From Personal Response to Critical Thinking."

3. Use the clues in the selection to guess what President Fillmore may have written in his letter to the emperor of Japan. Then compose your own version of the **letter,** stating Fillmore's reasons for wanting Japanese ports to be opened to Americans.

📁 **PORTFOLIO** *Save your writing. You may want to use it later as a springboard to a piece for your portfolio.*

Literary Concepts

Divide the class into groups and assign each student one page to analyze for imagery. Have students list the images they find, choose one example, and share with the group how that example helped them visualize aspects of the selection. *(Possible responses: page 507 "Giant dragons puffing smoke"; page 509 "snowcapped Mount Fuji made a breathtaking scene")*

QuickWrites

1. Have students review the description of the ships and brainstorm words a reporter unfamiliar with such ships might use.
2. Have students first outline what they want to say about Perry before writing their profiles.
3. Remind students that official letters are written in formal diplomatic language. Suggest they include persuasive statements to convince the emperor of their good intentions.

 **The Writer's Craft**

Character Sketch, pp. 54–61

Multimodal Learning

ALTERNATIVE ACTIVITIES

1. Draw a **sketch** of Perry's ships for a Japanese scroll, banner, or fan.

2. Read the rest of *Commodore Perry in the Land of the Shogun* to learn about the changes that occurred in Japan after Perry's arrival. Create a **cause-and-effect diagram** that shows the impact of Commodore Perry's achievement.

ACROSS THE CURRICULUM

Drama *Cooperative Learning* Shogun Ieyoshi was watching a Noh play when he first learned of the arrival of Perry's ships. In Noh drama, dancers present a slow, poetic dance-drama on a bare stage. Find out more about this ancient art form. Then present the arrival of Commodore Perry as a Noh play. Work with several classmates to write a simple script for the chorus, record flute and drum music, design masks and costumes, and choreograph the dance. Perform the play for your class.

ART CONNECTION

Look at the photograph of Commodore Perry on page 509 and the caricature of him on page 513. How would you describe the contrast between these two images?

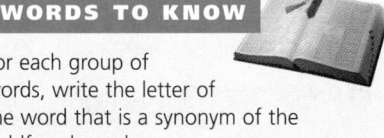
WORDS TO KNOW

For each group of words, write the letter of the word that is a synonym of the boldfaced word.

1. **incessant:** (a) continuous, (b) obnoxious, (c) blameless
2. **furor:** (a) leader, (b) danger, (c) disturbance
3. **replenish:** (a) hide, (b) donate, (c) refill
4. **omen:** (a) gesture, (b) sign, (c) injury
5. **inept:** (a) bumbling, (b) rude, (c) lost
6. **appall:** (a) amuse, (b) horrify, (c) relieve
7. **turmoil:** (a) commotion, (b) memorial, (c) harmony
8. **mystifying:** (a) clear, (b) baffling, (c) appealing
9. **resolve:** (a) decide, (b) hesitate, (c) predict
10. **seclude:** (a) entertain, (b) isolate, (c) join

RHODA BLUMBERG

Rhoda Blumberg (1917–) has referred to herself as "a compulsive researcher." As a researcher for radio programs in the 1940s, she gathered information about people with unusual stories, jobs, or talents. The material she collected provided her with ideas for magazine articles. Eventually, she decided to write nonfiction books for young people.

Blumberg loves to haunt libraries and "wade through a sea of information . . . to find out the truth about the past." Her writing not only conveys this truth but makes historic events seem as gripping and immediate as today's headlines. Several of her books have won awards.

OTHER WORKS *The Great American Gold Rush, The Truth About Dragons, The Incredible Journey of Lewis and Clark, The Remarkable Voyages of Captain Cook* Extended Reading

LASERLINKS
• *CONTEMPORARY CONNECTION*

COMMODORE PERRY IN THE LAND OF THE SHOGUN **517**

Words To Know

1. a	6. b
2. c	7. a
3. c	8. b
4. b	9. a
5. a	10. b

Reteaching/Reinforcement
• *Unit Four Resource Book,* p. 67

Across the Curriculum

Drama *Cooperative Learning* Divide the class into two groups, each to create a Noh play. In each group assign one student to research Noh plays, a second student to find appropriate music, a third to choreograph the dance, and a fourth to direct the play.

ADDITIONAL SUGGESTIONS

Social Studies *Shogun: The Celebration* Have students research and celebrate Japanese culture of the 1800s. Have them work in groups to cook Japanese food; make, paint, or find pictures of Japanese costumes; and play recordings of Japanese music. Have them decorate the room using Japanese motifs, and then share and enjoy what they've accomplished.

Art Connection

Students will most likely point to the obvious differences in realism between the photographic representation and the caricature. While Perry's photograph shows a stiff pose with an unsmiling face, the caricature exaggerates his stern expression so that he looks threatening. Remind students that a caricature is a drawing that exaggerates physical characteristics and personality traits.

CONTEMPORARY CONNECTION
The Art of Noh Drama Noh plays have a specific form that makes them unique. Students will be able to learn more about this ancient art form by watching this short documentary film.

Side A, Frame 39950

Alternative Activities

1. Have students reread the descriptions of Perry's ships and note the details the author includes. Provide students with examples of Japanese art and suggest that they mimic a "Japanese style" in their art work.

2. Ask your school or local librarian to set aside copies of this book for students to read. Encourage students to share their diagrams with the class and then lead a class discussion about the impact of Perry's achievement.

RHODA BLUMBERG

Blumberg is particularly interested in social history. She researches her subjects by examining original sources, such as manuscripts, diaries, and ships' logs. Blumberg feels this research generates new insights that enliven her books.

OVERVIEW

To gain a deeper appreciation of the selections they have read in this unit, students will explore the characteristics of a report and then create their own well-developed example in this lesson.

Objectives

- To plan a report by considering such elements as topic, thesis, examples, and organization
- To draft a report and solicit a response
- To revise, edit, and publish a report
- To reflect on the process of writing a report

Skills

LITERATURE
- Main idea

WRITING AND LANGUAGE
- Writing a thesis statement
- Using facts and statistics

GRAMMAR AND USAGE
- Formatting quotations

MEDIA LITERACY
- Reading a newspaper article
- Interpreting a map
- Watching informative programs
- Using media research sources

RESEARCH SKILLS
- KWL charts
- Creating an outline
- Crediting sources

SPEAKING, LISTENING, AND VIEWING
- Group discussion
- Peer editing and reviewing
- Reading aloud

Writing Skill:
WRITING A REPORT

A Make sure that students understand that a report is based on material from outside sources rather than on personal knowledge. Discuss these points:

- An appropriate report topic should be interesting to the writer and the audience. The topic must be narrow enough to explore in a brief report. There should be enough information available on that topic.
- A report can inform, compare and contrast, discuss cause and effect, or analyze a topic.

Media Literacy:
GATHERING IDEAS

B Science programs on television can provide excellent topics for reports. Suggest that students watch one or more of these informative programs—such as *NOVA* and *National Geographic*—to find potential topics. The Discovery Channel also offers carefully produced science programs.

WRITING FROM EXPERIENCE

WRITING A REPORT

What gives people the will to succeed? The selections in Unit Four, "Meeting Challenges," focus on characters who made extraordinary efforts to achieve a goal. What did they do to outsmart an enemy, win a sporting event, or solve a mystery?

GUIDED ASSIGNMENT

A **Write a Report of Information** Writing a report about someone who has achieved a major goal not only can help you learn about the person but might help you achieve some goals of your own. The ideas on the following pages will help you shape information about a topic into a report.

① Exploring Beyond the News

B What challenges are represented in the materials on these pages? Often articles, pictures, or maps tell you only a small part of a person's story. To learn more, you have to do research. What else would you like to know about each topic? What kinds of sources would you use to learn more?

② Brainstorm and Record Ideas

What examples of people meeting challenges have you heard or read about? In a group, brainstorm some general categories, such as

- scientific achievement
- sports
- personal triumphs
- historical events
- breakthroughs in medicine

Then discuss specific examples from each category. Where might you find information about stories that grab your interest or inspire you? Discuss your ideas with your group and record them in your notebook.

Newspaper Article

Rule-Breaking Teacher Helps Students Succeed

What makes a public school teacher quit after 14 years on the job to open her own school? How does she help "unteachable" students succeed when others can't?

In 1975, Marva Collins became frustrated with the Chicago school system's failure to teach inner-city kids. So she started her own school with $5,000 of her own money, at one point teaching out of her home. Because no one had heard of her school, she advertised by word of mouth. By working one-on-one with her students and using strict discipline, she helped them succeed. Test scores of Collins's students drastically improved, and many later succeeded in college.

Today, Collins is known as one of the country's leading educators, and her West Side Preparatory School is nationally known.

"I just feel good when I see children who develop in class right in front of me, seeing kids who were written off as failures come in here and achieve," she says.

PRINT AND MEDIA RESOURCES

UNIT FOUR RESOURCE BOOK
Prewriting, p. 71
Elaboration, p. 72
Peer Response Guide, pp. 73–74
Revising and Proofreading, p. 75
Student Model, pp. 76–78
Rubric, p. 79

GRAMMAR MINI-LESSONS
Transparencies, pp. 33–34
Copymasters, p. 43

WRITING MINI-LESSONS
Transparencies, pp. 34 and 50–61

ACCESS FOR STUDENTS ACQUIRING ENGLISH
Reading and Writing Support

FORMAL ASSESSMENT
Guidelines for Writing Assessment

LASERLINKS
Writing Springboard

Kids Deal with Loss at Camp Courage

How can scaling a wall help a child deal with the death of a loved one? The counselors at Camp Courage say that working with a partner to climb a steep wall can teach kids that people need one another when facing difficult challenges—whether the challenge is scaling a wall or dealing with the loss of a family member. The camp is one of about 50 in the country that work to meet the needs of bereaved youth.

"These kids are doing the most courageous thing that anybody can do, and that's dealing with loss," said Glenna Waxler, director of the program.

Newspaper Article

Who competes in this event? How long does it take them? More important, why do they do it?

Map
This map shows the course of the Ironman Triathlon, which is held on the island of Hawaii. How do you think people prepare for the event?

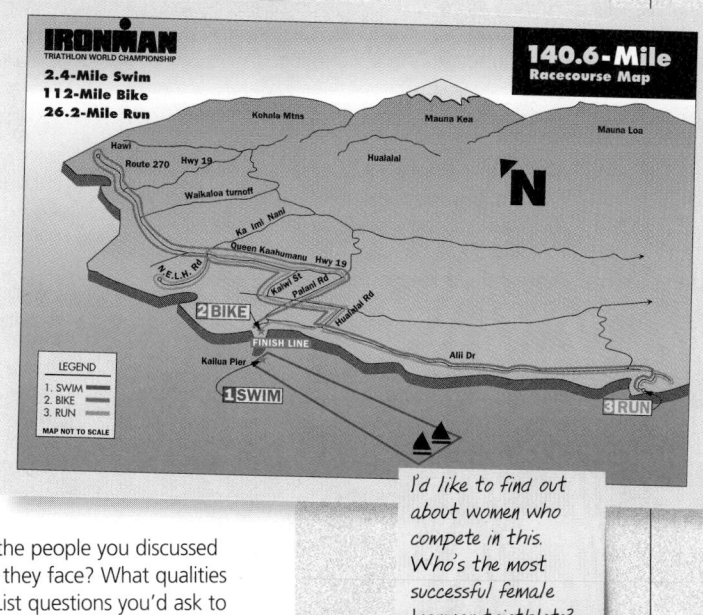

I'd like to find out about women who compete in this. Who's the most successful female Ironman triathlete?

3 QuickWrite

Take a few minutes to write about the people you discussed in your group. What challenges did they face? What qualities did each person need to succeed? List questions you'd ask to understand each person better.

Decision Point Choose one person whose story interests you the most. This is the person you'll research and write about.

→ **LASERLINKS**
• *WRITING SPRINGBOARD*

→ **WRITING COACH**

C To show students how to generate writing ideas from springboards such as articles, invite volunteers to read the articles on pages 518 and 519 to the class. Point out the handwritten comments in the margins and have students work in pairs to generate their own questions. Students familiar with sports may know about triathlons, but all students should be able to infer from the map legend that a triathlon is a race. People prepare for a triathlon by practicing swimming, biking, and running long distances.

CUSTOMIZING FOR
Less-Proficient Writers

D Inexperienced writers may have difficulty determining how much research a topic will need and the availability and location of information. Evaluate the topics these students have chosen and help them identify sources of information. You may wish to steer students toward topics for which information is readily accessible.

WRITING SPRINGBOARD
A Man and His Dog A young handicapped man shows how his dog has been trained to assist him in daily tasks.

Writing Prompt Research and report on someone who has faced a difficult challenge and found a way to achieve success. What was the challenge? What did the person do to meet the challenge?

Side B, Frame 17355

E Students who are having difficulty getting information about a topic may benefit from hearing how other students are identifying and locating sources. Arrange students in small groups to discuss their progress.

Teaching Strategy: MANAGING THE PAPER LOAD

F To help students focus their topics before they begin to write, encourage them to ask themselves the following questions:

• *Did I select an interesting topic?*
• *Is my topic sufficiently limited for a brief report?*
• *Have I prepared questions that others might ask and that I can answer in my report?*

After students have had some time to reflect on these questions, you can circulate around the room and provide immediate feedback to students who feel their topics are too broad.

Teaching Strategy:
COLLABORATIVE OPPORTUNITY

G Advanced writers who work well independently may wish to collaborate on a report topic. For instance, students working on similar topics can help each other conduct interviews. Suggest that they brainstorm and prepare questions to ask the person they intend to interview. During the interview, have partners take turns asking questions, taking notes, and operating the tape recorder.

PREWRITING

Examining Your Subject

The First Step Writing a report may seem overwhelming at first. It becomes much simpler, though, if you break the process into steps. Your first step is easy—just ask questions. Good questions help you develop a solid research plan.

❶ Get to Know Your Topic

E To better understand your topic you might want to do some preliminary reading. Read a few encyclopedia or magazine articles, and skim one or two books on the subject.

F Sometimes your reading will show you that your topic is too large to handle in a brief report. At other times, you'll find little information. In either case, you will probably have to rethink your topic a bit. The books and articles you've read may give ideas. You also may want to try clustering or brainstorming.

❷ Make a Research Plan

After you've finished your preliminary reading, write down your questions about your topic. They can serve as a guide to your research. For example, if you were writing about the Ironman Triathlon, you might ask the following questions:

• What challenges do competitors face?
• Why do athletes attempt it?
• Who has won the Ironman?
• How long do athletes train?

Gather Materials The library can be your best source of information. There you'll find

• books on specific subjects and reference books, such as encyclopedias
• magazines about a variety of topics
• newspapers
• videotapes, audiotapes, and CDs
• access to on-line information sources
• names and addresses of organizations to whom you can write for information
• names and addresses of local experts whom you can interview

Make Source Cards As you do research, keep track of sources by writing the publication information for each source on a separate index card and numbering each card. Follow the form that one student used in the source cards below. For more information about creating source cards, see page 835 of the Writing Handbook.

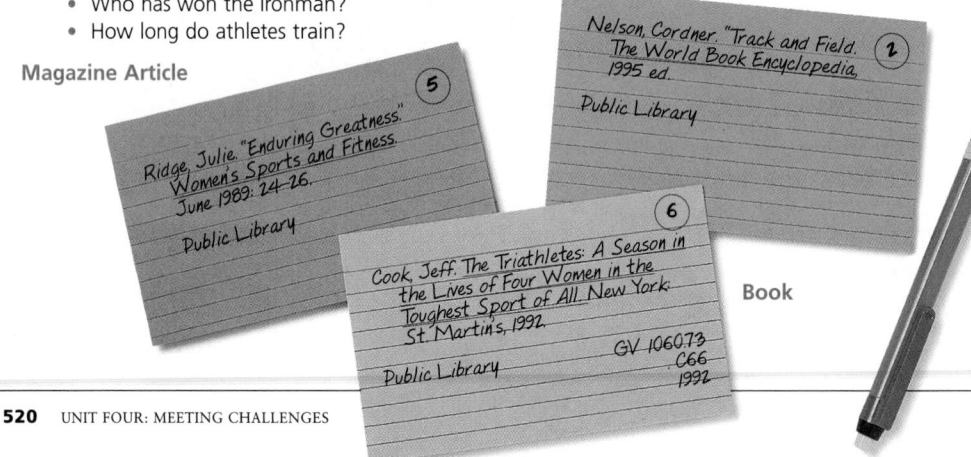

Magazine Article

Ridge, Julie. "Enduring Greatness." *Women's Sports and Fitness.* June 1989: 24-26.

Public Library
5

Cook, Jeff. *The Triathletes: A Season in the Lives of Four Women in the Toughest Sport of All.* New York: St. Martin's, 1992.

Public Library   GV 106073 .C66 1992
6

Encyclopedia Entry

Nelson, Cordner. "Track and Field." *The World Book Encyclopedia.* 1995 ed.

Public Library
1

Book

Mini-Lesson **Research Skills**

Topic: Robots		
K	W	L
Robots are mechanical devices that can move.	How are robots used? How do people feel about them? Who invented them?	

KWL CHARTS Explain to students that using a KWL chart can help them generate and organize information for their report. Describe how a KWL chart uses questions to tap prior knowledge and focus the research. Explain what KWL stands for:

K: What do I already *know* about the topic?
W: What do I *want* to *learn?*
L: What did I *learn?*

Application Have students work in small groups to fill in a KWL chart like the one shown for their topic and use it as they research and write.

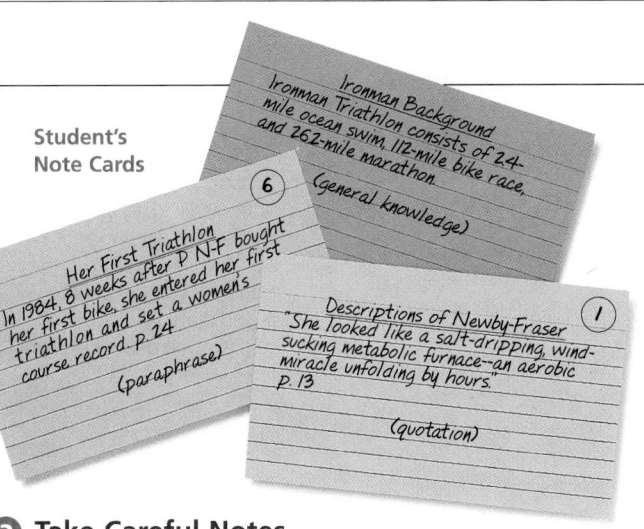

Student's Note Cards

Ironman Background
Ironman Triathlon consists of 2.4-mile ocean swim, 112-mile bike race, and 262-mile marathon.
(general knowledge)

6

Her First Triathlon
In 1984, 8 weeks after P N-F bought her first bike, she entered her first triathlon and set a women's course record p. 24
(paraphrase)

Descriptions of Newby-Fraser
"She looked like a salt-dripping, wind-sucking metabolic furnace—an aerobic miracle unfolding by hours." p. 13
(quotation)

1

③ Take Careful Notes

As you read, take careful notes. It's a good idea to record notes on cards that you can reorganize as you plan your report, as in the examples above. List each main idea and the details that support it on a separate card. Record dates and names exactly. Write the number of the source on each card. Also, include a note about whether the information is general knowledge, a paraphrase, or a direct quotation. This will remind you to credit sources when necessary. Here are some suggestions for taking notes:

* Paraphrase, or put information into your own words.
* Use abbreviations, symbols, or your own shorthand. Make sure your notes are clear enough to make sense later.
* Use quotation marks whenever you quote directly. Make sure to include the source of the quote.

No matter how good your notes are, they won't help you if you don't organize them effectively. Group related cards together and use the groupings as the basis of a rough outline. See the SkillBuilder on the right and page 836 of the Writing Handbook for information about outlining.

④ Write a Thesis Statement

Now it's time to draw some conclusions about your topic. What's the most important thing you learned about it? Your report should focus on a main idea that is supported with research. This can be written in a thesis statement, a sentence or two that tells briefly and clearly the central idea of the whole report. Try to write a thesis statement that tells readers what your report will show, prove, or explain.

SkillBuilder

 RESEARCH SKILLS

Creating an Outline

An outline helps you see where you need more information and which notes don't fit into your report. The tips below can help you create an effective outline.

* Arrange related note cards so that the ideas flow logically.
* Use the main ideas and supporting details in your note cards for the headings and subheadings of your outline.
* Feel free to change your outline as you draft your report.

APPLYING WHAT YOU'VE LEARNED
Use an outline to organize information about your topic. On a sheet of paper, write down what you think your headings and subheadings might be.

THINK & PLAN

Reflecting on Your Ideas

1. What interests you the most about your topic?
2. What are the most important ideas to include in the report?
3. What information do you still need to find out?
4. What visuals could you include to help explain different points or to make a scene clear to the reader?

Research Skills: TAKING NOTES

Ⓗ Remind students to save all their prewriting notes. Explain that as their report develops, they may wish to change direction. They can then use their notes to review earlier ideas.

Writing Skill:
USING THE COMPUTER

Ⓘ Suggest that students enter the information on their source cards in a computer file. This will allow students to organize their notes, add information, and easily call up sources.

Teaching Strategy:
STUMBLING BLOCK

Ⓙ Many students have difficulty paraphrasing effectively. Some students incorrectly believe that changing one or two words is a sufficient paraphrase. Review the examples on this page, pointing out that the writer put the main idea in his or her own words. Provide additional examples by having students work independently or in teams to paraphrase the article and map information on page 519.

SkillBuilder RESEARCH SKILLS

CREATING AN OUTLINE Share the following model outline with students:

I. Introduction
II. First main point
  A. First subpoint
    1. Details for A
    2. Details for A
  B. Second subpoint
    1. Details for B
    2. Details for B

III. Second main point
  [see II]
IV. Third main point
  [see II]
V. Conclusion

Application Remind students to indent each subdivision of the outline, capitalize the first word in each line, and avoid single subheadings.

Additional Suggestions Have students work in pairs to edit each other's outlines.

Reteaching/Reinforcement *Writing Mini-Lessons* transparencies, p. 59

 **The Writer's Craft**

Outlining, p. 668

DRAFTING

Writing Your Report

The Discovery Process So now you have pages of notes and, maybe, an outline. What next? Start writing! Simply putting words on the page and seeing how ideas are connected take you a step further toward your finished product. Sometimes you'll uncover the most interesting part of your report at the bottom of your rough draft. Let your writing be a process of discovery.

❶ Write a Rough Draft

K Try writing a paragraph for each of the main ideas on your note cards or headings in your outline. Feel free to stray from your plan if new ideas come to you as you draft. The Writing Coach can help you draft your report.

Outline: Paula Newby-Fraser

Student's Rough Draft

Ironman Triathlon

Coaching Workspace of My Report	My Comments on My Report

L They should rename the Ironman Triathlon the Ironwoman Triathlon, after Paula Newby-Fraser, who's won it seven times, more than any other athlete in Ironman history. Imagine swimming 2.4 miles, biking 112 miles, and running 26.2 miles in less than 17 hours! Every year, 1,500 athletes try to do it. Newby-Fraser does it so well that she has won the women's division of the Ironman seven times (1,2,3). The first time she competed in the Ironman, she did it just for fun, and with very little training (5).

Newby-Fraser bought her first bike just eight weeks before her first Ironman (Ridge 24). Ironman officials state that a typical Ironman triathlete trains for 7 months. Every week he or she swims 7 miles, bikes 232 miles, and runs 48 miles (Ironman Triathlon Media Guide 54). Newby-Fraser trained for only a few months and placed third. Now she trains 25 hours a week (Hamilton 33).

M In 1986, her next Ironman, Newby-Fraser set a women's course record of nine hours, 49 minutes, and fourteen seconds. It was the first year prize money was offered (Ironman Triathlon Media Guide 37).

This information would be great in the first sentence.

Double-check sources: Are distances and times correct?

Before listing wins, give biographical info to show what prepared her to be a great athlete.

WRITING SPRINGBOARD
Saving the Rhino This film is about one woman's effort to help save Africa's dwindling rhino population.

Side B, Frame 19483

Writing Prompt Research and report on an environmental challenge. Who has made efforts to face the challenge? What efforts have been made? Were they successful?

② Credit Your Sources

Whenever you use someone else's ideas or words, you need to credit the source. One way to do this is to include the source at the end of the sentence that contains information you found in your research. Put the author's last name and the page number in parentheses, as the student did in her rough draft. You'll also need to create a Works Cited list to include in your report. For more help with crediting sources, see page 837 of the Writing Handbook.

③ Analyze Your Draft

Read over what you have written. How is your report shaping up? Ask yourself questions like the following:

- Does my report do all that my thesis statement says it will?
- Can I add visuals to help readers understand the topic?
- Did I back up my main ideas with facts and statistics? For information about elaborating with facts and statistics, see the SkillBuilder on the right.

④ Rework and Share Your Draft

Now it's time to take another pass at your draft. Look for ways to get—and keep—readers interested in your topic.

Draw Your Own Conclusions Keep in mind that writing a report is not just stringing facts together. It involves thinking about the ideas of authors or people you've interviewed, interpreting facts or statistics, and sharing your conclusions.

Work on Your Introduction and Conclusion A strong introduction grabs your readers and states your main idea. Try using a question, a quotation, or an anecdote. Your conclusion might summarize the importance of your topic, give your own interpretation, or suggest ideas for future research.

 PEER RESPONSE

If you feel ready to get feedback now, try asking your peers the following questions.

- Which part of my report is most interesting? Why?
- What do you want to know more about?
- Point out any sections you found hard to follow.
- What can I do to make my report more complete?

SkillBuilder

 WRITER'S CRAFT

Using Facts and Statistics
Facts and statistics help support the main ideas of your report. **Facts** are statements that can be proved by observation, experience, or research. **Statistics** are facts that involve numbers. A graphic organizer can help you think about how you'll use facts and statistics in your report.

Main idea	Paula trains harder now.
Facts	• 1985: went weeks without training • 1995: trains 25 hrs/week

APPLYING WHAT YOU'VE LEARNED
Use a graphic organizer to link the main ideas of your report with supporting facts or statistics.

 WRITING HANDBOOK

For more information about elaboration, see page 819 of the Writing Handbook.

RETHINK & EVALUATE

Preparing to Revise

1. How can you be sure that you have complete information and accurate facts?
2. Is each fact you've included relevant to your thesis statement?
3. What facts and statistics support your main idea?

Research Skill:
USING THE COMPUTER

 N Remind students that if they have used a computer information service to locate sources, they should credit the original source (the book, magazine, or newspaper), not the name of the computer information source.

Teaching Strategy:
STUMBLING BLOCK

O Discuss with students the importance of citing original sources carefully and recording quotations accurately as they write their drafts. Completing these procedures at the drafting stage will help ensure accuracy. Also remind students to use quotation marks to indicate exactly where quoted passages begin and end.

Speaking, Listening, and Viewing:
COLLABORATIVE OPPORTUNITY

P You may wish to have students create a rough draft at home and bring it to class, along with all their notes. Then have students work in groups to read their drafts aloud and seek constructive criticism.

SkillBuilder  WRITER'S CRAFT

USING FACTS AND STATISTICS Remind students to double-check facts and statistics to make sure they are accurate. Suggest that students consult almanacs and yearbooks to get valid, current facts and statistics on topics such as government, sports, and population. Encourage them to use atlases (books of maps) for facts about highways, population, government, climates, land forms, and so on.

Periodicals (newspapers, magazines, and journals) are another good source of facts and statistics.

Application Suggest that students use a chart or idea tree format to link the main ideas with supporting facts and statistics.

Additional Suggestions Caution students to be sure that they have copied all numbers correctly. Remind them to pay special attention to decimals and percentages when they take notes.

Reteaching/Reinforcement *Writing Mini-Lessons* transparencies, p. 34

The Writer's Craft

Facts and Statistics, p. 254

Writing Skill: REVISING

Q Explain to students that, as they revise, they should pay attention to each element in turn, from overall organization to word choice. Some writers prefer to consider all the elements together, but most writers work better when they concentrate on different elements during separate stages of revision. To help students with this process, have them refer to the Standards for Evaluation on page 525 as they revise their papers.

Speaking, Listening, and Viewing: COLLABORATIVE OPPORTUNITY

R Explain to students that a writer needs to gain some distance from a draft to review it effectively. Tell students that one way to do this is to hear the draft read aloud by a peer reader. Have partners take turns reading their drafts to each other. Guide writers to listen carefully and note their responses and ideas for revision.

Teaching Strategy: MODELING

S Inexperienced writers tend to string together facts, statistics, examples, and quotations without providing their own opinions or analysis. Explain that writers must create links between ideas and explain them in their own words. Using the student model on this page, show the class how to weave source material together with their own analysis.

REVISING AND EDITING

Polishing Your Report

The Home Stretch You're almost there, but there are still some final steps to complete. First, take a careful look at your draft and consider other people's comments. Then, remember why you chose this topic. As you revise and edit your writing, ask yourself how you can communicate your interest in the topic to your readers. How can you make the information easy for them to understand?

1 Revise and Edit

As you look at your report, pretend you know nothing about your topic. Remember, you're the one who has done all the research. Your readers don't know what you know, so you have to be sure the information in your report is clear and easy to follow.

- Make sure the focus of your report is clear.
- Check every fact, name, date, and quotation for accuracy.
- Check for any missing information that might leave readers guessing.
- Credit your sources.

WOMAN OF IRON
How One Athlete Prepared for a Triathlon

Student's Final Report
Notice how the writer added details to support her main ideas.

Flores/1

Tania Flores
Mrs. Parsons
Language Arts
27 May 1997

Paula Newby-Fraser, Woman of Iron

How would you like to swim 2.4 miles in the ocean, bike 112 miles through lava beds, and run 26.2 miles in 90-degree weather in less than 17 hours? That's what 1,500 people try to do every year in the Ironman Triathlon. Paula Newby-Fraser competed in her first Ironman in 1985 and has won the event seven times since then. How did she do it? What makes her such a winning machine? Her background of athletics, her own unique formula for training, and a love of her job make her a champion.

Paula Newby-Fraser was born in 1962 in the British colony of Southern Rhodesia (now Zimbabwe). When she was two, her family moved to South Africa. Even though Newby-Fraser describes her childhood as "fairly normal," she was a dedicated athlete and dancer when she was young (Ridge 24).

Flores/4

Works Cited

Cook, Jeff. <u>The Triathletes: A Season in the Lives of Four Women in the Toughest Sport of All</u>. New York: St. Martin's, 1992.

<u>Gatorade Ironman Triathlon World Championship Media Guide</u>. The World Triathlon Corporation. 1995 ed.

Hamilton, Tish. "Tri and Mighty." <u>Rolling Stone</u>. 21 April 1994: 33–34.

Nelson, Cordner. "Track and Field." <u>The World Book Encyclopedia</u>. 1995 ed.

"The Queen of Multisport." <u>Women's Sports and Fitness</u>. March 1993: 44–45.

Ridge, Julie. "Enduring Greatness." <u>Women's Sports and Fitness</u>. June 1989: 24–29.

Svensson, Tony. "Empress of Endurance." <u>Women's Sports and Fitness</u>. March 1995: 26–27.

② Prepare Final Copy

With all of the work you've put into your research report, you want to be sure to show it in the best light. Be sure it conforms to your teacher's formatting instructions and includes a correctly punctuated Works Cited list. For more information about a Works Cited list, see page 837 of the Writing Handbook.

Standards for Evaluation

A report
- shows evidence of thoughtful and thorough research
- communicates the writer's interest in the topic
- contains facts and statistics to support general statements
- presents ideas logically
- credits sources correctly and includes a source list

SkillBuilder

GRAMMAR FROM WRITING

Formatting Quotations

Whenever you use someone else's words, use these guidelines.

- For quotations shorter than four lines, use quotation marks in the text.
- For quotations longer than four lines, indent the text ten spaces from the left margin. Do not use quotation marks.

Consider the example below.

According to one expert, Paula's training for the Ironman was "casual, at best; foolhardy, at worst" (Ridge 24).

GRAMMAR HANDBOOK

For more information about direct quotations, see page 886 of the Grammar Handbook.

Editing Checklist

- Did you double-check facts and quotations?
- Did you check the spelling of proper nouns and new words?

REFLECT & ASSESS

Evaluating the Experience

1. What was the strongest part of your report?
2. Why is it important to do careful research for a report?

📁 **PORTFOLIO** List the problem areas of your report. Put the list in your portfolio.

Teaching Strategy: MODELING

T Using this list as a model, point out that the sources are presented in alphabetical order according to the author's last name or the title of a work if an author's name is not provided. Remind students that the entries are not numbered and that the second line and all subsequent lines of each entry are indented.

Teaching Strategy: MANAGING THE PAPER LOAD

U Consider holding conferences with students who request them at this stage in the revision. Help students solve problems before they make a final copy of their report.

Writing Skill: USING THE COMPUTER

V Suggest that students use the computer to create graphics, clip art, and original art to accompany their essays. Many of the standard computer software packages include easy-to-use graphics.

PORTFOLIO

Create a student writing board to help students select writing pieces for inclusion in portfolios. Select the student advisers or have students elect members to the board.

Standards for Evaluation

Have students review their reports for the following:
Ideas and Content
- includes an introduction that hooks the reader and clearly states the topic and purpose
- presents information from several sources
- contains facts and details to support the main ideas
- concludes with a summary of main points

Structure and Form
- presents information in a logical order
- gives credit for ideas and statements of others
- includes a Work Cited list and credits sources correctly

Grammar, Usage, and Mechanics
- contains no more than two or three minor errors in grammar and usage
- contains no more than two or three minor errors in spelling, capitalization, and punctuation

---

SkillBuilder

GRAMMAR FROM WRITING

FORMATTING QUOTATIONS Remind students to use identifying tags, such as "According to one expert," and give credit for the quotation, as shown by the example "(Ridge 24)" on page 524. Tell students to place a comma after an introductory identifying tag.

Applications Have students work in pairs to review each other's papers to make sure they have correctly punctuated and indented long quotations.

Reteaching/Reinforcement *Grammar Mini-Lessons* copymasters p. 43, transparencies pp. 33-34

📁 The Writer's Craft

Using direct quotations, p. 204

UNIT REVIEW

This feature allows students to review the selections and activities in Unit Four and to assess how well they understand what they have learned. This feature provides students with several opportunities for self-assessment. You may wish to use some of the activities to assess skills such as speaking and listening or cooperative work.

Objectives

- To allow students to reflect on and assess their understanding of the theme of Unit Four—meeting challenges.
- To allow students to reflect on and assess their understanding of literary concepts such as simile, metaphor, and setting
- To provide students with the opportunity to assess and build their portfolios

REFLECTING ON THEME

OPTION 1

Have students skim the selections in this unit and the notes they took while reading them. Encourage students to jot down the ways in which the selections clarify or illuminate the meaning of Baldwin's words.

OPTION 2

Have students first skim the selections to jot down notes about each character. Encourage them to identify ways in which characters are different at the end of a selection from the way they were at the beginning. Then have students use their imaginations to identify with a particular character as they begin writing.

OPTION 3

Suggest that partners review several selections and take notes about the characters and events that they can refer to when role-playing. Remind students that their conversation should explore the qualities that enabled characters in this unit to overcome great odds.

Self-Assessment Suggest that students create a chart that lists the qualities of their personal heroes in one column and the qualities of some of the characters from the unit in a second column. Suggest that students refer to this information as they write their paragraphs.

UNIT FOUR: MEETING CHALLENGES

In the selections in this unit, you read about characters who have something special—the will to meet challenges and win. Now it's time to consider how your ideas about meeting challenges may have developed as you worked through the unit. Use one or more of the options in each of the following sections to help assess the changes.

REFLECTING ON THEME

OPTION 1 **Writing a Personal Response** At the beginning of this unit, you read a quotation from James Baldwin: "The challenge is in the moment, the time is always now." What does this quotation mean to you now that you have read the selections in the unit? Write a personal response to express your ideas, citing examples from the selections you have read and from your own experience.

OPTION 2 **Getting Inside a Character** From the selections in this unit, choose three or more characters who you think grew the most as a result of meeting personal challenges. Then write journal notes that each character might make, expressing what he or she has learned as a result of meeting a challenge.

OPTION 3 **Role-Playing** Imagine that a friend needs more self-confidence to meet a new challenge. With a partner, role-play a conversation in which you attempt to inspire your friend with the will to win. Use examples from several selections to support your points.

Consider . . .
- the characters in this unit who inspire you the most
- the challenges those characters face
- the qualities that help the characters meet challenges

Self-Assessment: Which of the characters in this unit remind you the most of your personal heroes? Write a paragraph or two, explaining your choices.

REVIEWING LITERARY CONCEPTS

OPTION 1 **Identifying Simile and Metaphor** In a simile, the word *like* or *as* is used to express a comparison, whereas a metaphor suggests a comparison without the use of either of these words. Work with a small group of classmates to identify examples of these figures of speech in the selections you have read. In a chart like the one shown, list and classify each example. Then substitute different words to create new comparisons. After you complete the chart, circle the example that you consider most striking, and explain why you find it so.

Simile and Metaphor			
Selection	**Example**	**Type**	**New Comparison**
"The Highway-man"	"The road was a ribbon of moonlight"	Metaphor	"The road was a river of shadows"

526 UNIT FOUR: MEETING CHALLENGES

OPTION 2 **Examining Setting** Setting, as you know, is the time and place of the action of a story, poem, or play. Review the selections you have read in this unit, and think about the importance of setting in each one. Which would be very different if the setting were changed? Which would be almost the same? Discuss these questions with a partner or with a small group of classmates. Then vote to choose the setting that has the greatest influence on the events in a selection.

 Self-Assessment: Besides setting, metaphor, and simile, other terms that can help you analyze fiction include minor characters, surprise ending, irony, title, and foreshadowing. In your notebook, draw a triangle. List these terms inside it, placing the one you know best at the bottom and the one you know least at the top. Then get together with a small group of classmates to compare triangles and to pool information about difficult concepts.

PORTFOLIO BUILDING

- **QuickWrites** Some of the QuickWrites assignments in this unit asked you to write profiles of characters who meet new challenges. Choose two responses in which you did an especially good job of showing what the characters are like. Then write a cover letter indicating what you did to make each character come alive. Add the responses and the note to your portfolio.

- **Writing About Literature** You have now experimented with writing a creative response to a story. Reread your response. Then write a letter to the author of the story, telling him or her how you chose to extend it and why you selected the details, characters, and dialogue that you did. Attach your letter to your creative-response essay.

- **Writing from Experience** For your report, you did research to gather information about a topic. What research skills were most helpful to you? In what other situations might you use these skills again? Write a note to answer these questions, and include the note with your report if you decide to keep it in your portfolio.

- **Personal Choice** Review all of your work for this unit—activities, graphics, and writing—and select the activity or writing assignment that

helped you most in developing your ideas about meeting challenges. Write a note explaining why the activity or assignment was so helpful. Add the note, along with the piece of writing or activity evaluation, to your portfolio.

 Self-Assessment: Review your portfolio to identify an early draft that shows you learning something important about your subject or about yourself. Reread that piece, thinking about what you might do to make it even better. List your suggestions and attach the list to the piece.

SETTING GOALS

In this unit, you read selections that deal with meeting challenges. What novels or works of nonfiction might help you explore this theme further? Browse in a bookstore or library to compile a list of several titles. Then, in your notebook, jot down the titles of any books that you would like to read on your own during the next few months.

SETTING GOALS

Encourage students to visit their local library to look for possible titles. Students can work with a librarian or use the card catalog to identify titles of works that explore the unit theme. You may wish to have students share their titles with the rest of the class.

REVIEWING LITERARY CONCEPTS

OPTION 1

You may wish to assign a different selection from this unit to each student in the group. Suggest that students also consider what each example of a simile or a metaphor contributes to their understanding of an entire piece. For a copy of the chart to distribute to the class, see *Unit Four Resource Book*, p. 83.

OPTION 2

Remind students to look for details and clues that reveal or suggest something about the setting. For example, details about customs or articles of clothing may suggest a particular time or place. Students should also consider how the setting influences the events in the plot and the decisions of the characters. You may wish to have students create charts to record and organize their ideas.

Self-Assessment By sharing what they know about the terms at the top of their triangles, students can help each other learn difficult concepts. If you wish, have students refer to the Handbook of Reading Terms and Literary Concepts (pp. 800–807) for additional information. Then have students, working alone or in pairs, review the selections to identify examples that illustrate each of the terms.

PORTFOLIO BUILDING

You may wish to help students choose options or modify the ones provided to reflect the portfolio system that they have learned. Encourage students to attach notes to their drafts and to their final products to help them monitor their progress.

Self-Assessment Suggest that students revise the early draft to apply the suggestions they have listed. Tell students that they may wish to revise this piece again after they have worked on several other pieces.

UNIT THEME

Unit Five

Not As It Seems In this unit, students will read selections that explore the contrast between appearance and reality. This unit contains two parts: Part 1, "Appearances to the Contrary," and Part 2, "Mysterious Circumstances." Selections in each part relate to the unit theme by presenting characters, situations, and objects that are not what they appear to be.

Part 1

Appearances to the Contrary In these selections the appearance of things may reveal little or nothing about their inner reality. For example, in "The Smallest Dragonboy," the main character appears small and frail but has the indomitable spirit of a hero.

Part 2

Mysterious Circumstances The selection in Part 2, "The Hound of the Baskervilles," features the famous detective Sherlock Holmes, who solves a murder by finding the truth by looking beyond what meets the eye.

Links to Unit Six

The Oral Tradition Unit Six, "Across Time and Place: The Oral Tradition," contains four selections that relate to the theme "Not As It Seems":
- "Echo and Narcissus," p. 764
- "The Force of Luck," p. 767
- "The Emperor's New Clothes," p. 775
- "Lazy Peter and His Three-Cornered Hat," p. 780

You may wish to use one or more of these selections to introduce or conclude Unit Five.

NOT AS IT
SeemS

"Appearances are often deceiving."

—AESOP Sixth-century Greek slave and fabulist

Detail of *Pearblossom Hwy., 11–18th April 1986* (1986), David Hockney.
Photographic collage, 71½" × 107". Copyright © David Hockney.

529

To help students explore the connections between the art, the quotation, and the unit theme, have them discuss the following questions:

1. What does the phrase "not as it seems" mean to you? *(Possible responses: The phrase means that people can be fooled by the appearance of other people or events. Many people form first impressions based on how things look or seem to be. Often these first impressions are false.)*

2. How apt do you think the quotation from Aesop is? Do you know of other similar sayings? *(Possible response: The quotation is very apt because appearances don't always reveal what a person or thing is really like inside. Other sayings, such as "Beauty is only skin deep" or "Don't judge a book by its cover," communicate a similar message.)*

3. In what ways do you think the artwork relates to the unit theme? *(Possible response: The artwork appears to be a single photo or painting of a landscape but actually is made up of many little photographs. In this way it suggests that things are not always what they seem to be.)*

4. What kinds of stories do you think you will read in this unit? *(Possible response: The stories will be about characters' first impressions of other people. In some of the stories I expect that characters will learn how to look beneath the surface and make new discoveries. Other characters will probably be taken in by appearances and not see the inner truth.)*

5. Describe a situation that convinced you of the danger of judging by appearances? *(Responses will vary.)*

Art Note

Pearblossom Hwy., 11–18th April 1986 **by David Hockney** In the five years David Hockney (1937–) spent with the camera, he produced nearly 400 photo-collages on various subjects, including portrait narratives and landscapes. This photo-collage is the final large-scale piece that marked the end of his experiment.

Reading the Art *Imagine that you want to describe this artwork to a friend who has not seen it. How would you describe it and the effect it creates in you?*

Selections	Reading Skills and Strategies	Literary Concepts	Writing Opportunities	Speaking, Listening, and Viewing
FICTION **The Smallest Dragonboy** Anne McCaffrey	Connecting, ML TE p. 534	Suspense, PE p. 548 Imagery, ML TE p. 533 Characterization, ML TE p. 542	Write about an impression, PE p. 531 Handbook, PE p. 548 Sequel, PE p. 548 Speech, PE p. 548 Interview, PE p. 548 Paragraph, PE p. 549 Details appealing to hearing, ML TE p. 543 Dialogue, ML TE p. 546	Performance, PE p. 548 Dialogue, ML TE p. 534 Pantomime, ML TE p. 535 Interviews, ML TE p. 540 Press conference, ML TE p. 545
FICTION **The Revolt of the Evil Fairies** Ted Poston	Making generalizations, ML TE p. 554	External and internal conflict, PE p. 557 Climax, PE p. 557 Climax, ML TE p. 556	Description, PE p. 550 Climax, PE p. 557 Interview, PE p. 557 Review, PE p. 557 Essay, PE p. 557 Paragraph, ML TE p. 553 Rewrite, ML TE p. 556	Letter, PE p. 557 Speech, PE p. 558 Skit, PE p. 558 Television news stories, PE p. 558 Reading aloud, ML TE p. 553
POETRY **The Way It Is** Gloria Oden **Without Commercials** Alice Walker		Tone, PE p. 564 Figurative language, ML TE p. 560	Description, PE p. 559 Rebuttal, PE p. 564 Letter, PE p. 564 Personal response, PE p. 564 Figurative language, ML TE p. 560 Lyric poem, ML TE p. 561 Paragraph, ML TE p. 563	Talk show, PE p. 564 Stanza, PE p. 565 Videotape, PE p. 565 Choral reading, ML TE p. 561 Dramatic reading, ML TE p. 562
FICTION **Lose Now, Pay Later** Carol Farley	Predicting, PE p. 566 Predicting, ML TE p. 570	Science fiction, PE p. 573 Setting, PE p. 573 Mood, ML TE p. 568 Point of view, ML TE p. 571	Explanation, PE p. 573 Plan, PE p. 573 Advertisement, PE p. 573 Rewrite point of view, ML TE p. 571 Sentences, ML TE p. 572	Discussion, PE p. 573 Sketch, PE p. 574 Panel discussion, PE p. 574
NONFICTION *from* **Exploring the Titanic** Robert Ballard	Fact and opinion, PE p. 576 Distinguishing fact and opinion, ML TE p. 577	Literary nonfiction, PE p. 591 Narrator, ML TE p. 586	Essay, PE p. 590 Log entry, PE p. 590 Advertisement, PE p. 590 Ballad, PE p. 590 Pamphlet, PE p. 591 Essay, ML TE p. 579 Rewrite, ML TE p. 586	Panel discussion, PE p. 591 Oral report, PE p. 591 TV interview, PE p. 591 Science display, PE p. 591 Press conference, ML TE p. 581
FICTION ON YOUR OWN **Charles** Shirley Jackson			Character sketch, TE p. 596	Performance, TE p. 595 Discussion, TE p. 597

Writing	Reading Skills and Strategies	Literary Concepts	Writing Opportunities	Speaking, Listening, and Viewing
WRITING ABOUT LITERATURE **Criticism**	Analyzing sound devices, PE pp. 598–99 Responding to literature, PE pp. 600–03	Analyzing sound devices, PE pp. 598–99 Literature elements, PE p. 600	Description, PE p. 599 Critical review, PE pp. 600–03 Using transitions to show relationships, PE p. 601	Viewing a scene, PE p. 604 Interpreting a scene, PE p. 604 Discussion, PE p. 604 Discussing issues, PE p. 605

Grammar, Usage, Mechanics, and Spelling	Multimodal Learning	Research and Study Skills	Vocabulary	
Punctuating quotations, **ML** TE p. 538 Details appealing to hearing, **ML** TE p. 543 Words ending in -ous and us, **ML** TE p. 544	Performance, PE p. 548 Model, PE p. 549 Video game, PE p. 549 Dialogue, **ML** TE p. 534 Pantomime, **ML** TE p. 535 Interviews, **ML** TE p. 540 Press conference, **ML** TE p. 545	Previewing assignments, **ML** TE p. 536	alleviate confrontation consternation desolation goad ignominious imperative oblivious prestige roster	
Capitalization of proper nouns, **ML** TE p. 552 Paragraphs and topic sentences, **ML** TE p. 553 Prefixes and base words, **ML** TE p. 555	Letter, PE p. 557 Speech, PE p. 558 Skit, PE p. 558 Television news stories, PE p. 558 Reading aloud, **ML** TE p. 553	Research segregation, PE p. 558	cite elite impromptu rationalize vanquish	
Figurative language, **ML** TE p. 560	Talk show, PE p. 564 Collage, PE p. 565 Stanza, PE p. 565 Videotape, PE p. 565 Choral reading, **ML** TE p. 561 Dramatic reading, **ML** TE p. 562	Research cosmetic surgery, PE p. 565		
Punctuating compound sentences, **ML** TE p. 569 Point of view, **ML** TE p. 571 Hard and soft g and c, **ML** TE p. 572	Discussion, PE p. 573 Sketch, PE p. 574 Designs, PE p. 574	Research calories, PE p. 574	binge cull gullible placid scam	
Elaboration, **ML** TE p. 583 Possessive plurals, **ML** TE p. 584 Words ending in -ate and -ion, **ML** TE p. 589	Log entry, PE p. 590 Panel discussion, PE p. 591 Oral report, PE p. 591 TV interview, PE p. 591 Science display, PE p. 591 Crossword puzzle, PE p. 592 Press conference, **ML** TE p. 581 Story log, **ML** TE p. 588 Performance, TE p. 595 Discussion, TE p. 597	Research the *Titanic*, PE p. 591 Research international ship regulation, PE p. 591 Research buoyancy, PE p. 591 Graphic organizers, **ML** TE p. 582 K-W-L approach, **ML** TE p. 585	accommodations dazzled eerie feverishly indefinitely	list novelty prophecy toll tribute

Grammar, Usage, Mechanics, and Spelling	Multimodal Learning	Research and Study Skills	Media Literacy
Creating emphasis with capitalization and punctuation, PE p. 599 Using transitions to show relationships, PE p. 601 Using coordinating conjunctions, PE p. 603 Run-on sentences, PE p. 603	Viewing a scene, PE p. 604 Interpreting a scene, PE p. 604 Discussion, PE p. 604 Discussing issues, PE p. 605	Analyzing literature, PE p. 600	Interpreting a scene, PE p. 604–05

Selections	Reading Skills and Strategies	Literary Concepts	Writing Opportunities	Speaking, Listening, and Viewing
DRAMA **The Hound of the Baskervilles** Sir Arthur Conan Doyle, adapted and dramatized by Tim Kelly	Reading a mystery, PE p. 607 Noting relevant details, **ML** TE p. 624	Mood, PE p. 656 Foil, PE p. 656 Suspense, **ML** TE p. 626	Speech, PE p. 655 Profile, PE p. 655 Ending, PE p. 655 Review, **ML** TE p. 654	Newspaper article, PE p. 655 Interview and oral report, PE p. 656 Poll, PE p. 656 Radio play, PE p. 656 Drama performance, **ML** TE p. 638 Scientific observation, **ML** TE p. 642 Interviews, **ML** TE p. 648

Writing	Reading Skills and Strategies	Literary Concepts	Writing Opportunities	Speaking, Listening, and Viewing
WRITING FROM EXPERIENCE **Persuasion**	Distinguishing fact and opinion, PE p. 658	Purpose, PE p. 660 Supporting details, PE p. 663	Writing an opinion paper, PE pp. 658–65 Drafting, PE pp. 662–63 Avoiding loaded adjectives, PE p. 663 Revising and publishing, PE pp. 664–65	Interviewing experts, PE p. 661 Polling, PE p. 661 Campaign, PE p. 665 Discussion group, PE p. 665

Grammar, Usage, Mechanics, and Spelling	Multimodal Learning	Research and Study Skills	Vocabulary
Dialogue in plays, **ML** TE p. 615 Sentence fragments, **ML** TE p. 631 Words ending in -ise and -ize, **ML** TE p. 635	Newspaper article, PE p. 655 Interview and oral report, PE p. 656 Poll, PE p. 656 Sketch, PE p. 656 Game, PE p. 656 Radio play, PE p. 656 Drama performance, **ML** TE p. 638 Scientific observation, **ML** TE p. 642 Interviews, **ML** TE p. 648	Research DNA fingerprinting, PE p. 656 Library catalogs, **ML** TE p. 633	accomplice exonerate bizarre implicitly captivating ominous colleague rational deception reproach dissuade surmise divulge theorize evasive

Grammar, Usage, Mechanics, and Spelling	Multimodal Learning	Research and Study Skills	Media Literacy

Avoiding loaded adjectives, PE p. 663
Making verbs agree with indefinite
  pronoun subjects, PE p. 665
	Analyzing newspaper articles, photographs,
	  and signs, PE pp. 658–59
	Interviewing experts, PE p. 661
	Polling, PE p. 661
	Campaign, PE p. 665
	Discussion group, PE p. 665
		Using news, public service, and
		  other sources, PE p. 661
			Analyzing newspaper articles,
			  photographs, and signs,
			  PE pp. 658–59

Recommended Novels

**LITERATURE CONNECTIONS WITH
SOURCEBOOK FOR TEACHERS**

The Witch of Blackbird Pond
by Elizabeth George Speare

Thematic Links Kit Tyler's life with her Puritan relatives is not as she imagined it would be when she left sunny Barbados. Her headstrong attitude keeps her at odds with the people she meets, except for Hannah, the so-called "Witch of Blackbird Pond." After Kit, too, is tried for witchcraft, she is forced to face up to the realities of her life.

About the Author Elizabeth George Speare (1908–1994) is best known for her award-winning historical fiction.

Other Works by Elizabeth George Speare *The Sign of the Beaver; The Bronze Bow; Calico Captive; Child Life in New England, 1790–1840; Life in Colonial America*

All the Weyrs of Pern
by Anne McCaffrey

Thematic Links Not all is as it seems as an exciting and dangerous plan develops to end Thread on Pern.

About the Author Anne McCaffrey (born 1926) often writes about women or children who are looking for their niche in society and must struggle against convention to succeed.

Other Works by Anne McCaffrey *Dragonsong, Dragonsinger, The Girl Who Heard Dragons, Renegades of Pern, Dragondrums*

The Shadow Guests
by Joan Aiken

Thematic Links Ghosts mysteriously appear to a young boy to ask his help in breaking a curse.

About the Author Joan Aiken (born 1924) has often been compared to Charles Dickens by critics.

Other Works by Joan Aiken *A Whisper in the Night, Go Saddle the Sea, Bridle the Wind, The Moon's Revenge*

**LITERATURE CONNECTIONS WITH
SOURCEBOOK FOR TEACHERS**

The House of Dies Drear
by Virginia Hamilton

Thematic Links When the Small family buys a house that was part of the Underground Railroad, they discover both people and places that are not as they seem.

About the Author Virginia Hamilton (born 1936) is the granddaughter of a runaway slave who bought a home near the setting of this novel. Hamilton has explored the African-American heritage in several exciting novels.

Other Works by Virginia Hamilton *Zeely, The Planet of Junior Brown, Anthony Burns: The Defeat and Triumph of a Fugitive Slave, The Time-Ago Tales of Jahdu, M.C. Higgins the Great, Sweet Whispers, Brother Rush, Many Thousand Gone: African-Americans from Slavery to Freedom, The Mystery of Drear House: The Conclusion of the Dies Drear Chronicle*

Adventures of Sherlock Holmes
by Arthur Conan Doyle

Thematic Links Mysterious circumstances are always resolved when Sherlock Holmes is on the case! This collection of adventure stories features the master detective at his cunning best.

About the Author Sir Arthur Conan Doyle (1859–1930) based the character of Sherlock Holmes on a surgeon he studied under in medical school who could tell more about a patient by a few quick glances than by a lot of questions.

Other Works by Sir Arthur Conan Doyle *The Return of Sherlock Holmes, His Last Bow: A Reminiscence of Sherlock Holmes, Memoirs of Sherlock Holmes*

For Teacher   TEACHING LITERATURE

Asher, Sandy. "Life, Live Theater, and the Lively Classroom." *ALAN Review* 21.3 (Spring 1994): 2–8.

Henly, Carolyn Powell. "Escape from the Twilight Zone: Reading and Writing with 'At Risk' Students." *ALAN Review* 19.3 (Spring 1992): 31+.

Ross, Cameron. "From the Inside Out." *English Quarterly* 25.4 (Summer 1993): 5–7.

Sanacore, Joseph. *Reading Aloud: A Neglected Strategy for Older Students* (1992): ERIC fiche ED367971.

Sandock, Frank. "Writing and Performing Original Classroom Plays." *Journal of Reading* 37.5 (February 1994): 414–15.

Recommended Readings in Cross-Curricular Areas

HISTORY

Sea Disasters
by Walter R. Brown and Norman D. Anderson (1981) Recounts eight disasters, including the sinking of the *Titanic* and the *Lusitania*. Links to Robert D. Ballard's *Exploring the Titanic.*

SOCIAL STUDIES

Big City Detective
by Jack Dautrich and Vivian Huff (1986) Uses actual case histories to describe the daily activities of an urban private eye. Links to *The Hound of the Baskervilles.*

Taking a Stand against Racism and Racial Prejudice
by Patricia and Fredrick McKissack (1990) Provides an overview of America's problems with racism and discusses what can be done when one encounters prejudice. Links to "The Revolt of the Evil Fairies."

HEALTH/SCIENCE

Nutrition
by Annette Spence (1989) Provides general information on nutrition and tips for maintaining a healthful diet. Links to Carol Farley's "Lose Now, Pay Later."

For Teacher CROSS-CURRICULAR INSTRUCTION

Cheng, Maisy, and Avi Soudack. *Anti-Racist Education: A Literature Review.* No. 205. Ontario: Toronto Board of Education, 1994.

Fawson, Parker C. "Using a Salient Characteristic Analysis Technique (SCAT) to Teach Metaphorical Comprehension." *Journal of Reading* 37.8 (May 1994): 679–80.

Gold, Muriel. "The Fictional Family: A Perspective of Many Cultures." *English Quarterly* 25.1 (1993): 26–29.

Recommended Media Resources

THE LANGUAGE OF LITERATURE

LASERLINKS
Videodisc, Gr.7
See *LaserLinks Teacher's Source Book*, pages 38–39, for an overview of Unit Five.

AUDIO LIBRARY
Unit Five: Not As It Seems
Gr. 7, Tape 12:
   Sides A & B
Gr. 7, Tape 13:
   Sides A & B

WRITING COACH
Writing Coach Software: Writing About Literature: Direct Response; Persuasive Essay

OUTSIDE RESOURCES

Films/Videos/Film Strips/Audiocassettes
The Girl Who Heard Dragons. Read by Constance Towers. Two sound cassettes. 1994. (3 hrs.)
The Giver. Read by Ron Rifkin. Four sound cassettes. (4.5 hrs.)
The Hound of the Baskervilles, videocassette, MGM Home Video, 1993.
A Wrinkle in Time. Read by Barbara Caruso. Five sound cassettes. (6.5 hrs.)

Internet Resources
Literature and Language Arts Center at http://www.hmco.com/mcdougal/lit/litcent.html

For Teacher TEACHING WITH TECHNOLOGY

Hill, Brian. *Making the Most of Video.* Technology in Language Learning Series. London: Centre for Information on Language Teaching and Research, 1989.

Carlson, Elizabeth Uzdavinis. *Teaching with Technology: "It's Just A Tool."* Annual Conference of the American Educational Research Association. Chicago. 3–7 Apr. 1991

Pina, Anthony A., and Bruce R. Harris. *Increasing Teachers' Confidence in Using Computers for Education.* Annual Meeting of the Arizona Educational Research Organization. Tucson. Nov. 1993.

Bring Some Drama to Your Classroom!

Like no other genre, drama unleashes tremendous intellectual and artistic energy in the classroom.

Drama sparks true critical thinking: What does this play mean? How can I express it on stage? How can I use my voice and gestures to interpret the play? As students prepare to read *The Hound of the Baskervilles*, introduce the following guidelines to transform your classroom into a theater of discovery.

Watch your seventh graders and it becomes apparent that Shakespeare was right—we are all players on the stage of life! As a result, putting on a play isn't as daunting as it sounds. In a nutshell, dramatic performers need to combine voice and action to bring the roles they are portraying to life. One of the basic ways actors do this is through *improvisation*—the process of presenting physical actions without rehearsal. Here's how!

IMPROVISATION

In the 1950s, improvisation developed into a dramatic form of its own. However, improvisation is primarily important as a means of developing acting skills. Share these guidelines for "improv" with your students.

- Explain that effective improvisation requires actors to concentrate on a problem to reveal their identities, the task, and the setting.
- As students prepare their improvisation, encourage them to relax as completely as they can. You may wish to lead them in some deep-breathing exercises.
- Guide students to use all five senses and a full range of body language, including posture, facial expressions, and movement.
- Have performers exaggerate the way they deal with imaginary objects. Be sure they focus on details so the audience can identify the action and understand its meaning.
- Remind performers to keep thinking of what they are doing and why. Help them react to the situation and to other people's actions.
- Caution students to remember to move the action of the improvisation forward in a logical way. For example: Show the problem, develop the action, resolve the problem.

CHARACTERIZATION

Explain to the class that characterization is the process whereby the performer internalizes the character's personality and communicates it to the audience. Characterization is the heart of acting. Here are some suggestions to help with characterization:

- Explain the importance of studying the play so performers understand the plot and the playwright's emotional and intellectual messages.
- Allow students time to research the play's setting—the time and place of the action.
- Be sure that students remember that characterization is most successful when the performer is able to communicate the character's essence through voice, mannerisms, and physical movement.
- Help students consciously select the mannerisms and physical movements that best reveal the character.
- Remind students to stay in character once a rehearsal or performance has begun. Students must project their character's actions and feelings—not their own.

MEMORIZATION

"I have to remember all those lines!" your students wail. "I can't; my brain is full." Reassure students with these helpful hints for memorization:

- Focus on the material. Tell students to turn off the TV, radio, or stereo as they memorize.
- Be sure students understand what they are memorizing. Explain that recalling something you know and understand is easier than recalling something that doesn't make sense to you.
- Memorize an entire sequence of thought, not individual words. Learn groups of closely related thoughts or ideas.
- Have students plan on spending some extra time in the beginning, when the material is unfamiliar. Remind them to review the material often to keep it fresh in their minds.

Related Reading

 Davis, Ossie. *Langston: A Play.* New York: Delacorte, 1982.

 Hamlett, Christina. *Humorous Plays for Teen-Agers.* Boston: MA: Plays, 1987.

 Kamerman, Sylvia E., ed. *The Big Book of Comedies.* Boston: MA, Plays, 1989.

Family and Community Involvement

✔ Family

All of the selections in Unit Five are connected to the theme of deceptive appearances, such as the story of an "unsinkable" ship that sinks and the true cost involved for something that appears to be free. By completing some of the following activities, your students, their families, and other community members can investigate real-life examples of deceptions and surprises.

The following Copymasters for Unit Five provide activities that students can take home and complete with a parent or other family member.

OPTION 1: READ ARTICLES ABOUT DECEPTION

- **Connection** All of the selections in Unit Five illustrate the idea that things often are not as they seem.
- **Activity** *Copymaster, page 1* Students and family members read news articles about deception and suggest strategies to avoid being deceived.

OPTION 2: WATCH A DOCUMENTARY

- **Connection** *Exploring the* Titanic provides an account of a disaster involving a supposedly "unsinkable" ship.
- **Activity** *Copymaster, page 2* Students and family members watch and discuss a documentary to learn more about the *Titanic.*

OPTION 3: WRITE AND PERFORM A SKIT

- **Connection** In *The Hound of the Baskervilles,* the famous detective Sherlock Holmes solves the mystery of the demon hound.
- **Activity** *Copymaster, page 3* Students and family members write a script for a mystery skit and stage a performance for friends and family.

✔ Community

OPTION 1
- **Connection** All of the selections in Unit Five illustrate the idea that things often are not as they seem.
- **Activity** Invite a mural artist or makeup artist to discuss with students how he or she uses art to "fool the eye."

OPTION 2
- **Connection** The poem "Without Commercials" advises the reader to be happy with his or her appearance just as it is.
- **Activity** Invite a local plastic surgeon or beautician to discuss his or her business with the class.

OPTION 3
- **Connection** In "Lose Now, Pay Later," Deb and Trinja prefer to remain ignorant about the ease of loosing weight in the slimmer machines.
- **Activity** Have the class interview a psychologist or doctor about the connection between weight and self-esteem.

OPTION 4
- **Connection** In "Revolt of the Evil Fairies," the narrator believes he has been cast for a role in the school play based on the color of his skin.
- **Activity** Ask the director of a local theater group to talk to the class about the problems and challenges of casting a play.

Part 1 Cooperative Project

Teens in the Media

Overview

Students will conduct research and surveys to analyze the current image of teenagers as portrayed by the media.

PROJECT AT A GLANCE

The selections in Unit Five, Part 1 deal with how people and things can appear to be what they are not and the importance of looking beneath the surface before rendering judgment. For this project, students will be working in small groups to investigate how the media portray teenagers and whether or not that image is correct. They will research magazine, television, newspaper, and radio advertisements to see how teens are portrayed and will conduct a survey to see if others think this image is accurate. They will also interview other teens to find how they feel about their image in the media. Groups will make a presentation of their findings for the class.

OBJECTIVES

- To analyze the various images of teens presented in the media
- To develop media awareness and critical-thinking skills
- To research various media and to interview people about the image presented by the media
- To draw conclusions about the image presented by the media
- To work cooperatively to plan and conduct a presentation that utilizes one of the mass media

SUGGESTED GROUP SIZE

4 students

MATERIALS

- Selection of magazines and newspapers, including some that are targeted for teens
- Video camera and tapes (optional)
- Television (optional)
- Tape recorder and tapes (optional)

1 Getting Started

Arranging the Project

Think about the resources available to you and about how you want to structure the project. Very likely, one will depend on the other. If you have access to video and audio equipment, students can include television and radio in their investigations and presentations. If not, they will have to write down verbatim anything they see and hear, which may not make their presentations very visually interesting. If this is the case, you might consider limiting the research to print media.

Gather a wide selection of magazines and newspapers to get students started. Be sure the collection includes some aimed at teens, some aimed at adults, some hard news, and some gossip papers. Find a few extreme examples that you can discuss later.

Arranging the Presentations

You might want to assign each group a bulletin board, or a section of one, on which to display final projects. They also might be displayed in the main hall or lobby of the school.

If you are including videotaping as part of the project, you will need a television to view parts of the presentation. Make arrangements for one well ahead of time.

2 Creating the Presentations

Introducing the Project

Explain that students will be working in groups of four to find out how the media portray teens and to draw conclusions about the accuracy of this image. They will find advertisements that use teens and will analyze those ads. They will also interview teens and adults to find out if they think that the teens in the ads represent all teens. Groups will then draw a conclusion based on the information gathered and present that conclusion and supporting arguments to the class.

Allow students time to browse through the magazines. After they have found a few examples, discuss those, along with the ones you located earlier. Have students discuss whether or not all teens look like the one(s) in the ads, whether the ad gives a negative or positive impression, and whether or not this represents an accurate picture of teens in general. You might also talk about how people not familiar with teens' interests and attitudes might view the ads and what conclusions they might draw.

Group Investigations

Divide students into groups of four. Groups will select one medium (print materials, television, radio) on which to concentrate their study, or you may assign these to avoid too much duplication. Students will research advertising in the selected medium and write a brief description of the most common type of teenager found in these ads. They will then conduct a survey of teens and adults by asking questions such as, "Teens are often portrayed in the _____ media as _____. Do you think this is a fair and/or accurate image of teens in general?"

Encourage groups to survey as many types and ages of people as they can and to keep track of the results. Caution them to use the same wording in each interview so the survey will be valid.

Groups can present their findings and their conclusions before the class. Encourage them to bring examples of the ads they used and to explain the logic behind their conclusions.

Creating a Project Description

Unless you make assignments, have each group tell you which medium they chose as soon as possible. You can then make any adjustments necessary before they begin serious work.

When groups have created a general description of teens they have found in ads, meet with them to review the descriptions before they start the next part of the project. You can help them to refine or, if necessary, revise the description to make it more useful or practical in the survey. Also hold a few brief class meetings to note any general problems groups are having with the project and to keep yourself informed of their progress.

OPTION 1: ANY GOOD NEWS? Have students look over newspapers and find the ratio of stories about negative things to stories about positive things. Have them write brief essays discussing the possible reasons behind the imbalance.

OPTION 2: OTHER TIMES, OTHER IMAGES Through old magazines and interviews, groups can research the image of teens in another era, such as the 1950s or 1970s. They can compare and contrast that image to the image teens have today.

OPTION 3: LONG-DISTANCE VIEW Students can confine their survey to those over a specific age, such as those over 60, to find out what they think teens are like today. Groups can conclude what senior citizens think of teens in general and offer support or rebuttal.

OPTION 4: CHANGE FOR THE BETTER After the initial project has been completed, hold a panel discussion among the groups. Each group should present at least one idea of how the image of teens might be improved.

As students go about the project, remind them that they should investigate all kinds of sources. In any medium they should look at advertising that is targeted at teens (teen magazines, television shows about teens, rock music radio stations) as well as ads that are targeted at other age groups to get a comprehensive picture of the teen image in the media.

③ Sharing the Presentations

This project is designed to culminate in a class presentation, but other teens in your school may be very interested to find out how others see them. If possible, arrange any written work and pictured examples in a hall or lobby bulletin board or display case. If this is impractical, display them in your classroom and invite other classes to look them over.

You might also hold a general class discussion about the results and conclusions of the project and how they may have differed from the conceptions students had before researching the subject.

 Assessing the Project

The following rubric can be used for group or individual assessment.

3 Full Accomplishment Students follow directions to create a general description of teens as portrayed by the media and use this successfully as a basis for a survey.

2 Substantial Accomplishment Students create a description and complete a survey, but the basis for one or the other is flawed.

1 Little or Partial Accomplishment Student's description and/or survey is incomplete or does not fulfill the requirements of the assignment.

For the Portfolio

Place a copy of the group's description in each student's portfolio, along with a copy of your written assessment. If possible, include any final written work from the project presentation.

Note: For other assessment options, see the *Teacher's Guide to Assessment and Portfolio Use.*

UNIT FIVE

Part 1 Lesson Planner

TIME ALLOTMENTS SHOWN ARE APPROXIMATE. DEPENDING ON YOUR GOALS AND THE NEEDS OF YOUR STUDENTS, YOU MAY WISH TO ALLOW MORE OR LESS TIME FOR CERTAIN PORTIONS OF THE LESSON.

Table of Contents	Discussion	Previewing the Selection	Reading the Selection
PART OPENER **APPEARANCES TO THE CONTRARY** **What Do You Think?** page 530	**20 MINUTES** • Reflect on the part theme		
SELECTION **The Smallest Dragonboy** page 532 CHALLENGING		**20 MINUTES** • PERSONAL CONNECTION • BACKGROUND CONNECTION • WRITING CONNECTION	**50 MINUTES** • Introduce vocabulary • Read pp. 532–47 (16 pp.)
SELECTION **The Revolt of the Evil Fairies** page 551 AVERAGE		**20 MINUTES** • PERSONAL CONNECTION • HISTORICAL CONNECTION • WRITING CONNECTION	**20 MINUTES** • Introduce vocabulary • Read pp. 551–56 (6 pp.)
SELECTIONS **The Way It Is** page 560 CHALLENGING **Without Commercials** page 562 CHALLENGING		**20 MINUTES** • PERSONAL CONNECTION • CULTURAL CONNECTION • WRITING CONNECTION	**10 MINUTES** • Read pp. 560–63 (4 pp.)
SELECTION **Lose Now, Pay Later** page 567 EASY		**20 MINUTES** • PERSONAL CONNECTION • CULTURAL CONNECTION • READING CONNECTION: Predicting	**20 MINUTES** • Introduce vocabulary • Read pp. 567–72 (6 pp.)
SELECTION *from* **Exploring the Titanic** page 577 AVERAGE		**20 MINUTES** • PERSONAL CONNECTION • HISTORICAL CONNECTION • READING CONNECTION: Fact and opinion	**50 MINUTES** • Introduce vocabulary • Read pp. 577–89 (13 pp.)
FICTION ON YOUR OWN **Charles** page 593 AVERAGE			**15 MINUTES** • Read pp. 593–97 (5 pp.)

Writing	Writer's Style	Prewriting	Drafting and Revising
WRITING ABOUT LITERATURE **Criticism**	**20 MINUTES**	**25 MINUTES**	**70 MINUTES**

Time estimates assume in-class work. You may wish to assign some of these stages as homework.

Responding to the Selection

FROM PERSONAL RESPONSE TO CRITICAL ANALYSIS	OR	ANOTHER PATHWAY	LITERARY CONCEPTS	QUICKWRITES
50 MINUTES				
• Discussion questions	OR	• Perform a script	• Suspense	• Handbook • Sequel • Interview
50 MINUTES				
• Discussion questions	OR	• Letter	• Conflict and climax	• Climax • Interview • Review • Essay
40 MINUTES				
• Discussion questions	OR	• Talk show	• Tone	• Rebuttal • Letter • Personal response
40 MINUTES				
• Discussion questions	OR	• Discussion	• Science fiction and setting	• Explanation • Plan • Advertisement
40 MINUTES				
• Discussion questions	OR	• Log entry	• Literary nonfiction	• Essay • Advertisement • Ballad

Extension Activities

	ALTERNATIVE ACTIVITIES	LITERARY LINKS	CRITIC'S CORNER	THE WRITER'S STYLE	ACROSS THE CURRICULUM	ART CONNECTION	WORDS TO KNOW	BIOGRAPHY
50 MINUTES	✔	✔			MATH	✔	✔	✔
50 MINUTES	✔		✔		SOCIAL STUDIES		✔	✔
40 MINUTES	✔	✔			SCIENCE			✔
50 MINUTES	✔	✔			HEALTH		✔	✔
50 MINUTES	✔	✔			SCIENCE		✔	✔
								✔

Publishing and Reflecting	**Grammar in Context**	**Reading the World**
30 MINUTES	15 MINUTES	30 MINUTES

UNIT FIVE PART 1

WHAT DO YOU THINK?

—— Objectives ——

The activities on this page can be used to
- introduce the theme "Appearances to the Contrary," since each activity is connected to one or more of the selections in Part 1
- create materials for personal portfolios that students can return to later for reconsideration or revision
- build an understanding of theme that students can develop as they progress through the unit

What really matters?
You may wish to have students form small groups to analyze the results of their surveys. Encourage students to consider other ways in addition to a bar graph to display the results. (See "The Revolt of the Evil Fairies," p. 550.)

What lies beyond what meets the eye?
Tell students that their sketches can be based on a real person or a fictional character about whom they have read. (See "The Smallest Dragonboy," p. 531; "The Way It Is" and "Without Commercials," p. 559; the excerpt from *Exploring the* Titanic, p. 575.)

Can you see beyond appearances?
Have students first list the points they think they should make in their conversation. Remind them that the intent of the conversation is to boost morale. (See "The Smallest Dragonboy," p. 531; and "Charles," p. 593.)

How would you create the right image?
Encourage students to think of a beauty "problem" that a new product might address. Students may wish to review some examples of current TV advertising to analyze the ways these commercials sometimes exploit a viewer's insecurities to promote a product. (See "Without Commercials," p. 559, and "Lose Now, Pay Later," p. 566.)

APPEARANCES TO THE CONTRARY

WHAT DO You THINK?

REFLECTING ON THEME

"Appearances often are deceiving"—you may have found yourself echoing Aesop's words from time to time. Things may be different from the way they seem. Someone's appearance may reveal little or nothing about the person inside. Use the activities on this page to explore your ideas about appearances.

What lies beyond what meets the eye?

Imagine that you have a pair of magical eyeglasses that enable you to see a person's true character. Write a character sketch of someone whose inner worth often goes unseen.

Can you see beyond appearances?

You, the captain of a volleyball team, notice that the opposing players tower above you and your teammates. What would you say to your teammates to give them confidence? With a group of classmates, role-play your conversation.

What really matters?

Imagine that a local hotel is sponsoring a contest to select a contestant for a national beauty pageant. Do you think the judges should judge the contestants primarily on appearance or on accomplishment? Survey a large group of classmates to discover their views on this issue, and then create a bar graph to display the results.

Survey Question: Which do you consider more important—appearance or accomplishment?

How would you create the right image?

With a small group of classmates, brainstorm ideas for a new cosmetic product. Select one of your ideas, and then plan a slick TV commercial to promote your product, making it appear better than it really is. Have a member of the group videotape the commercial to show to your classmates, or perform it live in class.

530   UNIT FIVE   PART 1: APPEARANCES TO THE CONTRARY

Cross-Curricular Connections

Social Studies Have students research the writings of early anthropologists, such as the American anthropologist Lewis Henry Morgan, who applied the theory of evolution to cultures outside Europe and North America. Students can write brief reports discussing how these anthropologists described other peoples and cultures. Ask students to consider how the anthropologists' reliance on appearance sometimes led to misunderstandings. Students can then share their reports with the class.

PARENTAL INVOLVEMENT

Invite students to work with parents or relatives to create an "Appearance and Reality" chart. Have students and their parents or relatives imagine that they are meeting each other for the first time. In one column of the chart, each person should list a first impression of the other based on appearance and conduct. Then, in the other column, each person should list one or more of the other's inner qualities that a first meeting may not reveal. Encourage students to share their charts with the class.

PREVIEWING

FICTION

The Smallest Dragonboy
Anne McCaffrey

Activating Prior Knowledge
PERSONAL CONNECTION

Think about the impressions you form of other people. What do you usually base your impressions on? What do you think other people consider when forming impressions of you or of someone else? Answer these questions in your notebook, and then compare your answers with your classmates'.

Building Background
BACKGROUND CONNECTION

In this story the main character is concerned about the impressions that others are forming of him. Above all, he hopes that he will impress one of the baby dragons that will soon hatch. In the imaginary world that Anne McCaffrey creates in this story, newly hatched dragons on the planet Pern choose their lifelong riders through a mysterious mental communication. When dragons and riders mature, they go on seek-and-destroy missions against deadly plant spores, called Thread. These spores drop from the sky and will destroy all life on Pern if they manage to touch the ground.

Photo used with permission of Windstone Editions. Copyright © 1984.

Setting a Purpose
WRITING CONNECTION

Write about a time when you formed an impression of someone or someone formed an impression of you—good or bad. Briefly explain what you think the impression was based on. Then as you read, consider the impressions that people form of the main character in this story.

When I first met Mr. Stuart, the grocer down on Brown Street, I got a bad impression of him. He was standing in front of the store yelling at a delivery man. He was very loud and angry.

OVERVIEW

Objectives

- To understand and appreciate a short story about a small boy who dreams of Impressing a baby dragon
- To enrich reading by using active reading strategies
- To identify and understand suspense
- To express understanding of the selection through a choice of writing forms, including a handbook, a sequel, a speech, and an interview
- To extend understanding of the selection through a variety of multimodal and cross-curricular activities

Skills

READING SKILLS/ STRATEGIES
- Connect

THE WRITER'S STYLE
- Descriptions of sounds

GRAMMAR
- Punctuating quotations

LITERARY CONCEPTS
- Suspense
- Imagery
- Characterization

GENRE STUDY
- Fiction: short story

SPELLING
- Words ending in -ous and -us

STUDY SKILLS
- Previewing assignments

SPEAKING, LISTENING, AND VIEWING
- Pantomime
- Interviews
- Press conference

Cross-Curricular Connections

SCIENCE
- Animal imprinting
- Design a flying dragon

MATH
- Percentages

PRINT AND MEDIA RESOURCES

UNIT FIVE RESOURCE BOOK
Strategic Reading: Literature, p. 4
Vocabulary SkillBuilder, p. 7
Reading SkillBuilder, p. 5
Spelling SkillBuilder, p. 6

GRAMMAR MINI–LESSONS
Transparencies, pp. 33–34
Copymasters, pp. 42–43

WRITING MINI–LESSONS
Transparencies, pp. 38 and 46

ACCESS FOR STUDENTS ACQUIRING ENGLISH
Selection Summaries
Reading and Writing Support

TEACHER'S GUIDE TO ASSESSMENT AND PORTFOLIO USE

FORMAL ASSESSMENT
Selection Test, pp. 101–102
Test Generator

AUDIO LIBRARY
See Reference Card

LASERLINKS
Author Background

INTERNET RESOURCES
McDougal Littell Literature Center at http://www.hmco.com /mcdougal/lit

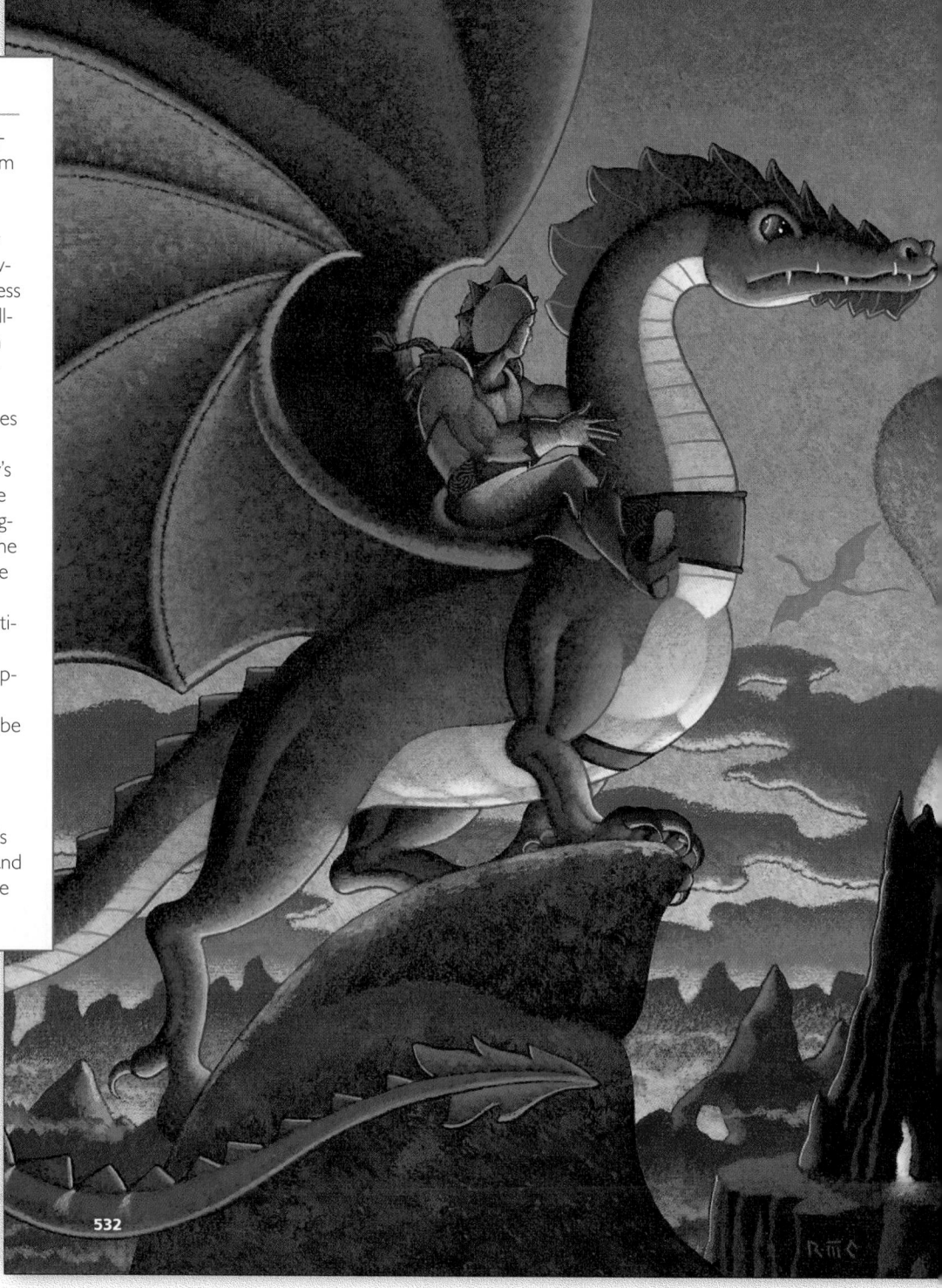

SUMMARY

In the land of Pern, riders on winged dragons fight Thread, evil creatures that fall from the sky. The only way to become a dragonrider is to Impress, or be chosen by, a newly hatched dragon. As a batch of forty dragon eggs approaches hatching time, seventy-two boys await their chance to Impress a dragon. Keevan is the youngest and smallest of the dragonboys, and this Impression will be his first. Beterli, a bully, claims a distinctively marked egg as his own. One evening during chore time, Beterli convinces Keevan that he has been eliminated from the Impression, and then snatches the boy's shovel. They fight and Keevan is injured. He finds himself laid up in bed, just as the dragon eggs are hatching. Keevan hobbles to the Hatching Ground and discovers that all the eggs have hatched. He is unaware that a bronze dragon—the rarest and most prestigious dragon of all—has rejected all the other dragonboys. As Keevan hides in disappointment, the dragon finds him and telepathically communicates that he wants to be the boy's companion for life. Keevan becomes a dragonrider.

Thematic Link: *Appearances to the Contrary* Other boys judge Keevan by his appearance. They fail to see the integrity and courage that make him a worthy candidate for the best dragon hatched.

CUSTOMIZING FOR
Students Acquiring English

- Use **ACCESS FOR STUDENTS ACQUIRING ENGLISH**, *Reading and Writing Support*.

- This science fiction story contains many coined words—such as *wingsecond, weyrleader,* and *weyrbred*—that describe the imaginary society in which it takes place. Tell students to use context clues to help them figure out meanings.

STRATEGIC READING FOR
Less-Proficient Readers

Set a Purpose Have students discuss their knowledge of dragons and then read to find out what a dragonrider is and what Keevan must do to become one.

Use **UNIT FIVE RESOURCE BOOK,** p. 4, for guidance in reading the selection.

WORDS TO KNOW

alleviate (ə-lē'vē-āt') *v.* to lessen; relieve; make more bearable (p. 542)

confrontation (kŏn'frŭn-tā'shən) *n.* the act of coming face to face, especially in a bold, unfriendly way (p. 540)

consternation (kŏn'stər-nā'shən) *n.* a sudden fear or dread that makes one feel helpless or unable to act (p. 544)

desolation (dĕs'ə-lā'shən) *n.* a feeling of being abandoned; loneliness (p. 539)

goad (gōd) *v.* to drive a person to do something; to urge on (p. 534)

ignominious (ĭg'nə-mĭn'ē-əs) *adj.* shameful; disgraceful (p. 544)

imperative (ĭm-pĕr'ə-tĭv) *adj.* absolutely necessary (p. 534)

oblivious (ə-blĭv'ē-əs) *adj.* not paying attention; unaware (p. 544)

prestige (prĕ-stēzh') *n.* widely recognized importance (p. 534)

roster (rŏs'tər) *n.* a list of names; roll (p. 538)

THE SMALLEST DRAGONBOY

By Anne McCaffrey

CUSTOMIZING FOR

Students Acquiring English

(1) Explain that *foster* indicates a family relationship that is not one of birth or legal adoption. Point out that *foster* can be used before other nouns of relationship, such as *father, child,* and *family.*

Although Keevan lengthened his walking stride as far as his legs would stretch, he couldn't quite keep up with the other candidates. He knew he would be teased again.

Just as he knew many other things that his foster mother told him he ought not to know, Keevan knew that Beterli, the most senior of the boys, set that spanking pace just to embarrass him, the smallest dragonboy. Keevan would arrive, tail fork-end of the group, breathless, chest heaving, and maybe get a stern look from the instructing wingsecond.

Dragonriders, even if they were still only hopeful candidates for the glowing eggs which were hardening on the hot sands of the Hatching Ground cavern, were expected to be punctual and prepared. Sloth[1] was not tolerated by the weyrleader of Benden Weyr. A good record was especially important now. It was very near hatching time, when the baby dragons would crack their mottled[2] shells and stagger forth to choose their lifetime companions. The very thought of that glorious moment made Keevan's breath catch in his throat. To be chosen—to be a dragonrider! To sit astride the neck of the winged beast with the jeweled eyes; to be his friend in telepathic communion[3] with him for life; to be his companion in good times and fighting extremes; to fly effortlessly over the lands of Pern! Or, thrillingly, *between* to any point anywhere on the world! Flying *between* was done on dragonback or not at all, and it was dangerous.

Keevan glanced upward, past the black mouths of the weyr caves in which grown dragons and their chosen riders lived, toward the Star Stones that crowned the ridge of the old volcano that was Benden Weyr. On the height, the blue watch-dragon, his rider mounted on his neck, stretched the great transparent pinions[4] that carried him on the winds of Pern to fight the evil Thread that fell at certain times from the sky. The many-faceted

---

1. **sloth** (slôth): laziness.
2. **mottled:** spotted or streaked with different colors.
3. **telepathic** (tĕl′ə-păth′ĭk) **communion:** a close relationship in which ideas and feelings are communicated between two minds without talking.
4. **pinions** (pĭn′yənz): wings or wing feathers.

THE SMALLEST DRAGONBOY   **533**

CUSTOMIZING FOR

Gifted and Talented Students

Have students read the selection and cite examples of the obstacles that Keevan must overcome to achieve his goal of becoming a dragonrider. Then ask students to take this information and design a "how-to" guide for potential dragonriders.

Possible responses:

• *Page 534—"People were always calling him 'babe' and shooing him away as being 'too small' or 'too young' . . ."* Keevan is young and slight.

• *Page 534—"Maybe if you run fast enough . . . you could catch a dragon. That's the only way you'll make a dragonrider!"* Keevan must face Beterli's taunting and contempt.

• *Page 542—". . . but what was pain to a dragonman?"* Keevan may suffer pain and must struggle to overcome it.

Mini-Lesson   **Literary Concepts**

REVIEWING IMAGERY Remind students that words and phrases that appeal to the reader's senses are known as imagery. Writers use details to help the reader imagine how things look, feel, smell, sound, and taste.

Application Have students reread the highlighted section on this page to identify words and phrases that appeal to their senses. Then have them suggest their own words and phrases to describe what they imagine a dragon and its rider to look like.

rainbow jewels of his eyes glistened momentarily in the greeny sun. He folded his great wings to his back, and the watch-pair resumed their statuesque pose of alertness.

Then the enticing view was obscured as Keevan passed into the Hatching Ground cavern. The sands underfoot were hot, even through heavy wher-hide boots. How the boot maker had protested having to sew so small! Keevan was forced to wonder again why being small was reprehensible. People were always calling him "babe" and shooing him away as being "too small" or "too young" for this or that. Keevan was constantly working, twice as hard as any other boy his age, to prove himself capable. What if his muscles weren't as big as Beterli's? They were just as hard. And if he couldn't overpower anyone in a wrestling match, he could outdistance everyone in a footrace.

"Maybe if you run fast enough," Beterli had jeered on the occasion when Keevan had been goaded to boast of his swiftness, "you could catch a dragon. That's the only way you'll make a dragonrider!"

"You just wait and see, Beterli, you just wait," Keevan had replied. He would have liked to wipe the contemptuous smile from Beterli's face, but the guy didn't fight fair even when the wingsecond was watching. "No one knows what Impresses a dragon!"

"They've got to be able to *find* you first, babe!"

A Yes, being the smallest candidate was not an enviable position. It was therefore imperative

that Keevan Impress a dragon in his first hatching. That would wipe the smile off every face in the cavern and accord him the respect due any dragonrider, even the smallest one.

Besides, no one knew exactly what Impressed the baby dragons as they struggled from their shells in search of their lifetime partners.

CLARIFY

 C What is Keevan hoping for?

Using a Reading Log

"I like to believe that dragons see into a man's heart," Keevan's foster mother, Mende, told him. "If they find goodness, honesty, a flexible mind, patience, courage—and you've that in quantity, dear Keevan—that's what dragons look for. I've seen many a well-grown lad left standing on the sands, Hatching Day, in favor of someone not so strong or tall or handsome. And if my memory serves me" (which it usually did—Mende knew every word of every Harper's tale worth telling, although Keevan did not interrupt her to say so), "I don't believe that F'lar, our weyrleader, was all that tall when bronze Mnementh chose him. And Mnementh was the only bronze dragon of that hatching."

 reams of Impressing a bronze were beyond Keevan's boldest reflections, although that goal dominated the thoughts of every other hopeful candidate. Green dragons were small and fast and more numerous. There was more prestige to Impressing a blue or a brown than a green. Being practical, Keevan seldom dreamed as high as a

WORDS	**goad** (gōd) *v.* to drive a person to do something; urge on
TO	**imperative** (ĭm-pĕr′ə-tĭv) *adj.* absolutely necessary
KNOW	**prestige** (prĕ-stēzh′) *n.* widely recognized importance

534

Mini-Lesson   **Reading Skills/Strategies**

ig fighting brown, like Canth, F'nor's fine
ellow, the biggest brown on all Pern. But to fly
bronze? Bronzes were almost as big as the
queen, and only they took the air when a queen
lew at mating time. A bronze rider could aspire
o become weyrleader! Well, Keevan would
onsole himself, brown riders could aspire to
become wingseconds, and that wasn't bad. He'd
ven settle for a green dragon; they were small,
out so was he. No matter! He simply had to
mpress a dragon his first time in the Hatching
Ground. Then no one in the weyr would taunt
im anymore for being so small.

"Shells," thought Keevan now, "but the
ands are hot!"

"Impression time is imminent,⁵ candidates,"
he wingsecond was saying as everyone
rowded respectfully close to him. "See the
xtent of the striations⁶ on this promising
gg." The stretch marks *were* larger than
esterday.

Everyone leaned forward and nodded
houghtfully. That particular egg was the one
Beterli had marked as his own, and no other
andidate dared, on pain of being beaten by
Beterli on the first opportunity, to approach it.
The egg was marked by a large yellowish
plotch in the shape of a dragon backwinging
o land, talons outstretched to grasp rock.
Everyone knew that bronze eggs bore distinc-
ive markings. And naturally, Beterli, who'd
been presented at eight Impressions already
and was the biggest of the candidates, had
hosen it.

"I'd say that the great opening day is almost
upon us," the wingsecond went on, and then his
ace assumed a grave expression. "As we well
know, there are only forty eggs and seventy-two
andidates. Some of you may be disappointed
on the great day. That doesn't necessarily mean

you aren't dragonrider material, just that *the*
dragon for you hasn't been shelled. You'll have
other hatchings, and it's no disgrace to be left
behind an Impression or two. Or more."

Keevan was positive that the wingsecond's
eyes rested on Beterli, who'd been stood off at
so many Impressions already. Keevan tried to
squinch down so the wingsecond wouldn't
notice him. Keevan had been reminded too
often that he was eligible to be a candidate by
one day only. He, of all the hopefuls, was most
likely to be left standing on the great day. One
more reason why he simply had to Impress at
his first hatching.

"Now move about among the eggs," the
wingsecond said. "Touch them. We don't
know that it does any good, but it certainly
doesn't do any harm."

CLARIFY

Why is Keevan afraid
that he won't Impress
a dragon?

Some of the boys
laughed nervously, but
everyone immediately
began to circulate among
the eggs. Beterli stepped
up officiously to "his"
egg, daring anyone to come near it. Keevan
smiled, because he had already touched it . . .
every inspection day . . . as the others were
leaving the Hatching Ground, when no one
could see him crouch and stroke it.

Keevan had an egg he concentrated on, too,
one drawn slightly to the far side of the others.
The shell bore a soft greenish-blue tinge with a
faint creamy swirl design. The consensus⁷ was
that this egg contained a mere green, so Keevan was rarely bothered by rivals. He was

---

5. **imminent:** about to happen.
6. **striations** (strī-ā′shənz): striped or grooved markings.
7. **consensus:** an opinion shared by most; general
   agreement.

THE SMALLEST DRAGONBOY **535**

D Have students note that Beterli has
failed at several Impressions. Ask students what they have learned and what
they can infer about Beterli's character
based on the way he's treated Keevan.
(*Possible response: He's bitter and takes
it out on Keevan.*) Then encourage students to use descriptive words to characterize Beterli. (*Possible responses:
mean, aggressive*)

Active Reading: CLARIFY

E Have students discuss what they
have already learned about Keevan.
Ask why Keevan might be under-
estimating himself. (*Possible responses:
Keevan feels that he's too young, too
little, too insignificant.*)

STRATEGIC READING FOR
Less-Proficient Readers

F Ask students the following questions to make sure they are following
the story so far.

- What is a dragonrider? (*someone who
  has a telepathic connection to a dragon
  that he rides in order to fight the
  Thread*) Restating

- How does a boy become a dragonrider? (*He is chosen by a newly
  hatched dragon.*) Summarizing

- How might stroking the egg help
  Keevan become a dragonrider? (*It's
  possible that touching the egg helps a
  person connect with the dragon inside.*)
  Relating Cause and Effect

Set a Purpose Have students continue
reading to learn what some adults propose that might prevent both Beterli
and Keevan from taking part in the
Impression.

Mini-Lesson: Speaking,   Listening, and Viewing

PANTOMIME Explain to students that pantomime
is the use of gesture, bodily movement, and facial
expressions to convey emotions or tell a story.

Application Have students work in pairs to prepare a pantomime of how the boys of Pern try to
connect with the dragon eggs. Have each pair
decide what gestures and expressions to use to
convey the scene and the boys' emotions. Suggest
that they prepare any props they may need, such as

a model or drawing of a large egg. Instruct them to
choose one student to direct the pantomime and
the other to enact it. Have students rehearse and
then present their pantomimes to the class. Then
lead a class discussion about what emotions were
conveyed through specific gestures or facial expressions. Ask students if, after viewing other pairs, they
have ideas for revising their own pantomimes.

Mini-Lesson   Study Skills

PREVIEWING ASSIGNMENTS Explain to students that it is useful to preview an assignment to get a clear understanding of what they are asked to do. When previewing assignments, students should look to see what questions are being asked of them and then create plans for completing the assignment and budgeting their time accordingly.

Application Before students carry out the activities on pages 548 and 549, you may wish to preview one of the assignments as a class. Encourage students to discuss what the assignment is asking them to do, what resources or materials they will need, and what are the most efficient means of completing the assignment. If students are working in small groups, they can preview an assignment cooperatively, making sure each member understands his or her responsibilities.

somewhat perturbed then to see Beterli wandering over to him.

"I don't know why you're allowed in this Impression, Keevan. There are enough of us without a babe," Beterli said, shaking his head.

"I'm of age." Keevan kept his voice level, telling himself not to be bothered by mere words.

"Yah!" Beterli made a show of standing on his toe tips. "You can't even see over an egg. Hatching Day, you better get in front or the dragons won't see you at all. 'Course, you could get run down that way in the mad scramble. Oh, I forget, you can run fast, can't you?"

"You'd better make sure a dragon sees *you* this time, Beterli," Keevan replied. "You're almost overage, aren't you?"

Beterli flushed and took a step forward, hand half raised. Keevan stood his ground, but if Beterli advanced one more step, he would call the wingsecond. No one fought on the Hatching Ground. Surely Beterli knew that much.

Fortunately, at that moment the wingsecond called the boys together and led them from the Hatching Ground to start on evening chores.

There were "glows" to be replenished[8] in the main kitchen caverns and sleeping cubicles, the major hallways, and the queen's apartment. Firestone sacks had to be filled against Thread attack, and black rock brought to the kitchen hearths. The boys fell to their chores, tantalized by the odors of roasting meat. The population of the weyr began to assemble for the evening meal, and the dragonriders came in from the Feeding Ground or their sweep checks.

*I*t was the time of day Keevan liked best. Once the chores were done, before dinner was served, a fellow could often get close to the dragonriders and listen to their talk. Tonight Keevan's father, K'last, was at the main dragonrider table. It puzzled Keevan how his father, a brown rider and a tall man, could be his father—because he, Keevan, was so small. It obviously never puzzled K'last when he deigned to notice his small son: "In a few more turns, you'll be as tall as I am—or taller!"

K'last was pouring Benden drink all around the table. The dragonriders were relaxing. There'd be no Thread attack for three more days, and they'd be in the mood to tell tall tales, better than Harper yarns, about impossible maneuvers they'd done a-dragonback. When Thread attack was closer, their talk would change to a discussion of tactics of evasion,[9] of going *between*, how long to suspend there until the burning but fragile Thread would freeze and crack and fall harmlessly off dragon and man. They would dispute the exact moment to feed firestone to the dragon so he'd have the best flame ready to sear[10] Thread midair and render it harmless to ground—and man—below. There was such a lot to know and understand about being a dragonrider that sometimes Keevan was overwhelmed. How would he ever be able to remember everything he ought to know at the right moment? He couldn't dare ask such a question; this would only have given additional weight to the notion that he was too young yet to be a dragonrider.

"Having older candidates makes good sense," L'vel was saying, as Keevan settled down near the table. "Why waste four to five years of a dragon's fighting prime until his rider grows up

8. **replenished:** resupplied.
9. **evasion:** the act of avoiding or escaping from.
10. *sear:* scorch or burn.

THE SMALLEST DRAGONBOY **537**

Literary Concept: IMAGERY

G Remind students that words and phrases that appeal to the reader's senses are known as imagery. Writers use details to help readers imagine how things look, feel, smell, sound, and taste. Have students identify the sense(s) that the image in this sentence appeals to. *(smell)* Encourage students to write another sentence that describes the same thing but appeals to the sense of sight.

CUSTOMIZING FOR

Multiple Learning Styles

H Spatial or Graphic Learners
Encourage students to draw or paint what they imagine a Thread attack is like. Have them show how the dragonriders repel the attack. When their artwork is completed, students can share their work with the class and talk about what imagery and details in the selection led them to portray the scene the way they did.

Mini-Lesson | **Genre Study**

FICTION Explain to students that a **short story** is a work of fiction that generally can be read in one sitting. Tell them that short stories usually focus on one or two main characters who face a single problem or conflict.

Application Have students copy the word web from the chalkboard and complete it by filling in the specific features of this short story.

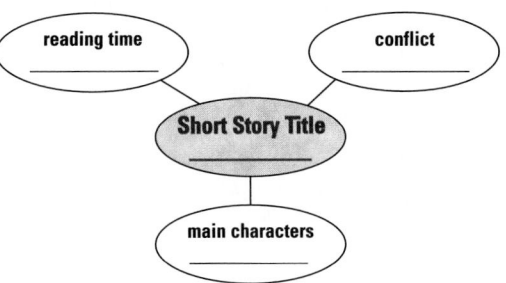

THE LANGUAGE OF LITERATURE TEACHER'S EDITION **537**

Literary Concept: SUSPENSE

I Remind students that suspense is the growing tension and excitement that readers feel as they get involved in a story. Have students discuss what is suspenseful about the fact that the dragons decide who their riders will be. (*Possible response: It raises uncertainty about whether Keevan, or any boy, can become a dragonrider.*)

STRATEGIC READING FOR

Less-Proficient Readers

J Ask students what groups of boys some adults want to drop from this Impression and why this would affect both Keevan and Beterli. (*the youngest and those who've failed in previous Impressions; Keevan is very young, and Beterli has failed several times, so it's likely they'd both be dropped*) Noting Relevant Details/Using Context Clues

Set a Purpose Have students read to find out what happens to Keevan while he fetches black rock.

enough to stand the rigors?" L'vel had Impressed a blue of Ramoth's first clutch. Most of the candidates thought L'vel was marvelous because he spoke up in front of the older riders, who awed them. "That was well enough in the Interval when you didn't need to mount the full weyr complement[11] to fight Thread. But not now. Not with more eligible candidates than ever. Let the babes wait."

"Any boy who is over twelve turns has the right to stand in the Hatching Ground," K'last replied, a slight smile on his face. He never argued or got angry. Keevan wished he were more like his father. And oh, how he wished he were a brown rider! "Only a dragon . . . each particular dragon . . . knows what he wants in a rider. We certainly can't tell. Time and again the theorists"—and K'last's smile deepened as his eyes swept those at the table— "are surprised by dragon choice. *They* never seem to make mistakes, however."

"Now, K'last, just look at the roster of this Impression. Seventy-two boys and only forty eggs. Drop off the twelve youngest, and there's still a good field for the hatchlings to choose from. Shells! There are a couple of weyrlings unable to see over a wher egg, much less a dragon! And years before they can ride Thread."

"True enough, but the weyr is scarcely under fighting strength, and if the youngest Impress, they'll be old enough to fight when the oldest of our current dragons go *between* from senility."[12]

"Half the weyrbred lads have already been through several Impressions," one of the bronze riders said then. "I'd say drop some of *them* off this time. Give the untried a chance."

"There's nothing wrong in presenting a

clutch with as wide a choice as possible," said the weyrleader, who had joined the table with Lessa, the weyrwoman.

"Has there ever been a case," she said, smiling in her odd way at the riders, "where a hatchling didn't choose?"

Her suggestion was almost heretical[13] and drew astonished gasps from everyone, including the boys.

F'lar laughed. "You say the most outrageous things, Lessa."

"Well, *has* there ever been a case where a dragon didn't choose?"

"Can't say as I recall one," K'last replied.

"Then we continue in this tradition," Lessa said firmly, as if that ended the matter.

But it didn't. The argument ranged from one table to the other all through dinner, with some favoring a weeding out of the candidates to the most likely, lopping off those who were very young or who had had multiple opportunities to Impress. All the candidates were in a swivet,[14] though such a departure from tradition would be to the advantage of many. As the evening progressed, more riders were favoring eliminating the youngest and those who'd passed four or more Impressions unchosen. Keevan felt he could bear such a dictum[15] only if Beterli was also eliminated. But this seemed less likely than that Keevan

---

11. **full . . . complement:** the entire group.
12. **senility** (sĭ-nĭl'ĭ-tē): the weakness, confusion, and memory loss that often come with old age.
13. **heretical** (hə-rĕt'ĭ-kəl): against established views or beliefs.
14. **swivet** (swĭv'ĭt): a state of strain and distress.
15. **dictum:** a formal public statement made with authority; a ruling.

WORDS
TO
KNOW   **roster** (rŏs'tər) *n.* a list of names; roll

538

Mini-Lesson   Grammar

PUNCTUATING QUOTATIONS Quotation marks show where a character's words begin and end. If a quotation is interrupted by explanatory words—such as *he said*—commas are used. Point out the quotation marks and commas in the highlighted example on this page. Explain that commas, periods, and question marks that are part of a quotation are placed inside quotation marks.

Application Have students correctly place quotation marks in the following sentences.
1. You're too small to see over an egg, Beterli sneered.

2. Has there ever been a case, she asked, in which a dragon didn't choose?
3. I must Impress a dragon this time, Keevan said.
4. Maybe touching the eggs makes the dragon choose you, Keevan said. What do you think, Beterli?

Reteaching/Reinforcement
• Grammar Handbook, anthology pp. 886–887
• *Grammar Mini-Lessons* copymasters pp. 42–43, transparencies pp. 33–34

 The Writer's Craft

Quotation Marks, pp. 648–651

would be tuffed out, since the weyr's need was for fighting dragons and riders.

CLARIFY

What are the adults arguing about?

Using a Reading Log

By the time the evening meal was over, no decision had been reached, although the weyrleader had promised to give the matter due consideration.

He might have slept on the problem, but few of the candidates did. Tempers were uncertain in the sleeping caverns next morning as the boys were routed out of their beds to carry water and black rock and cover the "glows." Mende had to call Keevan to order twice for clumsiness.

"Whatever is the matter with you, boy?" he demanded in exasperation when he tipped black rock short of the bin and sooted up the hearth.

"They're going to keep me from this Impression."

"What?" Mende stared at him. "Who?"

"You heard them talking at dinner last night. They're going to tuff the babes from the Hatching."

Mende regarded him a moment longer before touching his arm gently. "There's lots of talk around a supper table, Keevan. And it cools as soon as the supper. I've heard the same nonsense before every hatching, but nothing is ever changed."

"There's always a first time," Keevan answered, copying one of her own phrases.

"That'll be enough of that, Keevan. Finish your job. If the clutch does hatch today, we'll need full rock bins for the feast, and you won't be around to do the filling. All my fosterlings make dragonriders."

"The first time?" Keevan was bold enough to ask as he scooted off with the rockbarrow.

erhaps, Keevan thought later, if he hadn't been on that chore just when Beterli was also fetching black rock, things might have turned out differently. But he had dutifully trundled the barrow to the outdoor bunker for another load just as Beterli arrived on a similar errand.

"Heard the news, babe?" asked Beterli. He was grinning from ear to ear, and he put an unnecessary emphasis on the final insulting word.

"The eggs are cracking?" Keevan all but dropped the loaded shovel. Several anxieties flicked through his mind then: He was black with rock dust—would he have time to wash before donning the white tunic of candidacy? And if the eggs were hatching, why hadn't the candidates been recalled by the wingsecond?

"Naw! Guess again!" Beterli was much too pleased with himself.

With a sinking heart Keevan knew what the news must be, and he could only stare with intense <u>desolation</u> at the older boy.

"C'mon! Guess, babe!"

"I've no time for guessing games," Keevan managed to say with indifference. He began to shovel black rock into his barrow as fast as he could.

"I said, 'Guess.'" Beterli grabbed the shovel.

"And I said I'd no time for guessing games."

Beterli wrenched the shovel from Keevan's hands. "Guess!"

"I'll have the shovel back, Beterli." Keevan straightened up, but he didn't come up to Beterli's bulky shoulder. From somewhere,

L

WORDS TO KNOW **desolation** (dĕs′ə-la′shən) *n.* a feeling of being abandoned; loneliness

539

Active Reading: **CLARIFY**

K Have students restate the arguments presented in this section. Encourage them to discuss the various opinions presented by the arguing adults. You may wish to use the following model to give students an idea of what the adults might be thinking about:

Think-Aloud Model *I think the adults are concerned about having too many boys trying to Impress far fewer dragons. So they're arguing about dropping some boys. But I don't think they should do that because every boy should have a chance as long as he's old enough.*

Literary Concept: FORESHADOWING

L Ask students what they think the phrase *things might have turned out differently* foretells. *(Possible responses: Something tragic is about to occur; Keevan is going to do something he will regret.)*

Multicultural **Perspectives**

RITES OF PASSAGE In this story, a young person strives to achieve a goal that will signify that he has passed from childhood to adulthood. The achievement of such a goal is called a rite of passage.

Rites of passage are found in all cultures. Among Christians, confirmation is a rite of passage in which the individual is granted full membership in the spiritual community. Thirteen-year-old Jewish boys and girls study for their bar or bat mitzvah, after which their family celebrates their status as adults in the community.

The Poro is a male initiation rite practiced by the peoples of southern Liberia, Sierra Leone, and the Ivory Coast. In a series of events, masked raiders seize the boys of the village and tell their mothers they are dead. The boys are then circumcised, taught various skills needed by men, and tested. After a period of time, initiates return to the village, are given new names, and are treated as new people.

Though different, these rites of passage all test a young person's commitment and maturity and affirm that he or she deserves adult status.

(2) Help students infer that *lovey* is a term of affection.

(3) Lead students to understand that the ellipses between words indicate pauses; Keevan is hesitant to tell the weyrwoman his news. Model a hesitant tone of voice for students.

Active Reading: CONNECT

(M) Ask students if they have ever been in a situation similar to Keevan's in which they had to decide whether or not to retaliate against someone who was taunting them. Invite volunteers to relate their experiences and then have students discuss whether Keevan did the right thing by not telling on Beterli. Ask students why Keevan might have hesitated to tell on Beterli even though he dislikes him. *(Possible response: Keevan remembered that this Impression was likely to be Beterli's last chance to become a dragonrider.)*

STRATEGIC READING FOR

Less-Proficient Readers

(N) Ask students what happens to Keevan while he is fetching black rock. *(Beterli provokes a fight with him and hits him with the handle of a shovel. Keevan ends up with a broken skull and leg.)* Noting Relevant Details

Set a Purpose Have students read to find out whether Keevan gets to the Impression.

---

other boys appeared, some with barrows, some mysteriously alerted to the prospect of a <u>confrontation</u> among their numbers.

"Babes don't give orders to candidates around here, babe!"

Someone sniggered, and Keevan knew, incredibly, that he must've been dropped from the candidacy.

He yanked the shovel from Beterli's loosened grasp. Snarling, the older boy tried to regain possession, but Keevan clung with all his strength to the handle, dragged back and forth as the stronger boy jerked the shovel about.

With a sudden, unexpected movement, Beterli rammed the handle into Keevan's chest, knocking him over the barrow handles. Keevan felt a sharp, painful jab behind his left ear, an unbearable pain in his right shin, and then a painless nothingness.

(2) **M**ende's angry voice roused him, and startled, he tried to throw back the covers, thinking he'd overslept. But he couldn't move, so firmly was he tucked into his bed. And then the constriction of a bandage on his head and the dull sickishness in his leg brought back recent occurrences.

"Hatching?" he cried.

"No, lovey," said Mende, and her voice was suddenly very kind, her hand cool and gentle on his forehead. "Though there's some as won't be at any hatching again." Her voice took on a stern edge.

Keevan looked beyond her to see the weyrwoman, who was frowning with irritation.

"Keevan, will you tell me what occurred at the black-rock bunker?" Lessa asked, but her voice wasn't angry.

He remembered Beterli now and the quarrel over the shovel and . . . what had Mende said about some not being at any hatching? Much as he hated Beterli, he couldn't bring himself to tattle on Beterli and force him out of candidacy.

"Come, lad," and a note of impatience crept into the weyrwoman's voice. "I merely want to know what happened from you, too. Mende said she sent you for black rock. Beterli—and every weyrling in the cavern—seems to have been on the same errand. What happened?"

"Beterli took the shovel. I hadn't finished with it."

"There's more than one shovel. What did he *say* to you?"

"He'd heard the news."

"What news?" The weyrwoman was suddenly amused.

"That . . . that . . . there'd been changes."

"Is that what he said?"

"Not exactly."

"What did he say? C'mon, lad. I've heard from everyone else, you know."

"He said for me to guess the news."

"And you fell for that old gag?" The weyrwoman's irritation returned.

"Consider all the talk last night at supper, Lessa," said Mende. "Of course the boy would think he'd been eliminated."

"In effect, he is, with a broken skull and leg." She touched his arm, a rare gesture of sympathy in her. "Be that as it may, Keevan, you'll have other Impressions. Beterli will not. There are certain rules that must be observed by all candidates, and his conduct proves him unacceptable to the weyr."

She smiled at Mende and then left.

WORDS TO KNOW

confrontation (kŏn′frŭn-tā′shən) *n.* the act of coming face to face, especially in a bold, unfriendly way

540

Mini-Lesson: Speaking, **Listening, and Viewing**

INTERVIEWS Explain to students that interviews are an important way of getting information about a person or an event. Tell students that when acting as an interviewer, they should listen carefully to the interviewee's responses and gauge their next questions accordingly. When acting as interviewees, students should listen carefully to the interviewer's questions so they can provide appropriate and well-thought-out responses.

Application Have pairs of students enact an unrehearsed interview between Beterli and a television reporter. Suggest that the interviewer prepare possible questions to ask Beterli about how and why he started a fight that he should have known would eliminate him from the Impression. Have the student playing Beterli first outline Beterli's character and personality to use as the basis for his or her answers. Remind students that they must listen carefully to their partners in order to present appropriate questions and answers as the interview progresses.

Critical Thinking:
SYNTHESIZING

0 Encourage students to recall what Beterli did earlier in the story that was forbidden. *(fighting on the Hatching Ground)* Point out that when Beterli fought with and injured Keevan, he broke another rule and was eliminated from the Impression. Have students use the information they've gleaned from the story to brainstorm the standards of conduct that all the boys must follow if they want to be candidates at an Impression. *(Possible responses: The candidates must be punctual, energetic, honorable, fair, and considerate.)*

Active Reading: PREDICT

P Have students review what they've learned about Keevan's character and the strength of his desire to be a dragonrider. Ask students, based on what they know, if they expect Keevan to let anything stop him from being a candidate at the Impression. Make sure they support their answers. *(Possible response: no, because he is very strong-willed)*

Critical Thinking:
MAKING JUDGMENTS

Q Ask students if they think Keevan is correct in his assumption that none of the other boys have come to see him because they blame him for Beterli's elimination. Ask them if they think Mende is right about why Keevan is being left alone. *(Possible response: Neither theory is true; the others are probably too busy preparing for the Impression.)*

Critical Thinking:
SYNTHESIZING

R Ask students to think about what they've already read that may give them a clue as to why Keevan is so insistent that this is the Impression that matters. *(Possible response: Keevan is just barely old enough to be a candidate, and he is the smallest candidate. If he is chosen now, it will show that his size doesn't matter.)*

> **PREDICT**
>
> **P** How will what happened to Keevan affect his candidacy?
> *Using a Reading Log*

"I'm still a candidate?" Keevan asked urgently.

"Well, you are and you aren't, lovey," his foster mother said. "Is the numb weed working?" she asked, and when he nodded, she said, "You just rest. I'll bring you some nice broth."

At any other time in his life, Keevan would have relished such cosseting,[16] but he lay there worrying. Beterli had been dismissed. Would the others think it was his fault? But everyone was there! Beterli provoked the fight. His worry increased, because although he heard excited comings and goings in the passageway, no one tweaked back the curtain across the sleeping alcove he shared with five other boys. Surely one of them would have to come in sometime. No, they were all avoiding him. And something else was wrong. Only he didn't know what.

Mende returned with broth and beachberry bread.

"Why doesn't anyone come see me, Mende? I haven't done anything wrong, have I? I didn't ask to have Beterli tuffed out."

Q Mende soothed him, saying everyone was busy with noontime chores and no one was mad at him. They were giving him a chance to rest in quiet. The numb weed made him drowsy, and her words were fair enough. He permitted his fears to dissipate.[17] Until he heard the humming. It started low, too low to be heard. Rather he felt it in the broken shinbone and his sore head. And thought, at first, it was an effect of the numb weed. Then

the hum grew, augmented by additional sources. Two things registered suddenly in Keevan's groggy mind: The only white candidate's robe still on the pegs in the chamber was his; and dragons hummed when a clutch was being laid or being hatched. Impression! And he was flat abed.

Bitter, bitter disappointment turned the warm broth sour in his belly. Even the small voice telling him that he'd have other opportunities failed to alleviate his crushing depression. *This* was the Impression that mattered! This was his chance to show *everyone* from Mende to K'last to L'vel and even the weyrleaders that he, Keevan, was worthy of being a dragonrider.

He twisted in bed, fighting against the tears that threatened to choke him. Dragonmen don't cry! Dragonmen learn to live with pain. . . .

Pain? The leg didn't actually pain him as he rolled about on his bedding. His head felt sort of stiff from the tightness of the bandage. He sat up, an effort in itself since the numb weed made exertion difficult. He touched the splinted leg, but the knee was unhampered. He had no feeling in his bone, really. He swung himself carefully to the side of his bed and slowly stood. The room wanted to swim about him. He closed his eyes, which made the dizziness worse, and he had to clutch the bedpost.

Gingerly he took a step. The broken leg dragged. It hurt in spite of the numb weed, but what was pain to a dragonman?

No one had said he couldn't go to the

---

16. **cosseting** (kŏs'ĭt-ĭng): pampering.
17. **dissipate** (dĭs'ə-pāt'): gradually disappear.

| WORDS TO KNOW | **alleviate** (ə-lē'vē-āt') *v.* to lessen; relieve; make more bearable |

Mini-Lesson **Literary Concepts**

REVIEWING CHARACTERIZATION

Remind students that characterization includes the techniques a writer uses to create and develop characters. Explain that there are four basic methods of developing a character: 1) presenting the character's words and actions; 2) presenting the character's thoughts; 3) describing the character's appearance; 4) showing what others think about a character.

Application Have students create a chart with four columns, each headed by one of the methods of characterization, and then fill it in with details about Keevan's character.

Impression. "You are and you aren't," were Mende's exact words.

Clinging to the bedpost, he jerked off his bed shirt. Stretching his arm to the utmost, he jerked his white candidate's tunic from the peg. Jamming first one arm and then the other into the holes, he pulled it over his head. Too bad about the belt. He couldn't wait. He hobbled to the door, hung on to the curtain to steady himself. The weight on his leg was unwieldy. He'd not get very far without something to lean on. Down by the bathing pool was one of the long crook-necked poles used to retrieve clothes from the hot washing troughs. But it was down there, and he was on the level above. And there was no one nearby to come to his aid. Everyone would be in the Hatching Ground right now, eagerly waiting for the first egg to crack.

The humming increased in volume and tempo, an urgency to which Keevan responded, knowing that his time was all too limited if he was to join the ranks of the hopeful boys standing about the cracking eggs. But if he hurried down the ramp, he'd fall flat on his face.

He could, of course, go flat on his rear end, the way crawling children did. He sat down, the jar sending a stab of pain through his leg and up to the wound on the back of his head. Gritting his teeth and blinking away the tears, Keevan scrabbled down the ramp. He had to wait a moment at the bottom to catch his breath. He got to one knee, the injured leg straight out in front of him. Somehow he managed to push himself erect, though the room wanted to tip over his ears. It wasn't far to the crooked stick, but it seemed an age before he had it in his hand.

Then the humming stopped!

Keevan cried out and began to hobble frantically across the cavern, out to the bowl of the weyr. Never had the distance between the living caverns and the Hatching Ground seemed so great. Never had the weyr been so silent, breathless. As if the multitude of people and dragons watching the hatching held every breath in suspense. Not even the wind muttered down the steep sides of the bowl. The only sounds to break the stillness were Keevan's ragged breathing and the thump-thud of his stick on the hard-packed ground. Sometimes he had to hop twice on his good leg to maintain his balance. Twice he fell into the sand and had to pull himself up on the stick, his white tunic no longer spotless. Once he jarred himself so badly he couldn't get up immediately.

Then he heard the first exhalation of the crowd, the ooohs, the muted cheer, the susurrus[18] of excited whispers. An egg had cracked, and the dragon had chosen his rider. Desperation increased Keevan's hobble. Would he never reach the arching mouth of the Hatching Ground?

Another cheer and an excited spate of applause spurred Keevan to greater effort. If he didn't get there in moments, there'd be no unpaired hatchling left. Then he was actually staggering into the Hatching Ground, the sands hot on his bare feet. **T**

No one noticed his entrance or his halting progress. And Keevan could see nothing but the backs of the white-robed candidates, seventy of them ringing the area around the eggs. Then one side would surge forward or back, and there'd be a cheer. Another dragon had been Impressed. **4**

18. **susurrus** (sŏŏ-sûr′əs): a murmuring or rustling sound.

Literary Concept:
DESCRIPTION

S Remind students that a description is a picture in words of a scene, a character, or an object. A description might appeal to the reader's senses or provide detailed information about characters or events. Have students identify examples of the author's appeal to the reader's senses or her use of detail in describing Keevan's progress toward the Hatching Ground. (*Possible response: Some details show Keevan's actions and describe how he has to "scrabble" on his rear end because of his injuries. Other details appeal to the sense of touch—the reader feels Keevan's pain as he attempts to get to the Hatching Ground.*)

STRATEGIC READING FOR
Less-Proficient Readers

T Make sure that students understand how difficult it is for Keevan to make his journey to the Hatching Ground because of his injuries. Ask them what condition Keevan is in when he finally gets there. (*He's exhausted and in pain.*) **Making Inferences**

Set a Purpose Have students read to find out what happens at the Hatching Ground.

CUSTOMIZING FOR
Students Acquiring English

4 Point out that the helping verb *would* in this sentence indicates that the actions described were repeated a number of times while Keevan watched.

Mini-Lesson  **The Writer's Style**

DESCRIPTIONS OF SOUNDS Review with students how writers use details that appeal to the senses to help readers experience a character, an action, or a scene. Point out that Anne McCaffrey repeatedly describes sounds to convey what is happening at the Hatching Ground.

Application Have students identify examples of descriptions of sounds on page 543. Encourage them to explain how these descriptions add to the suspense. Then have students write three sentences that describe other sounds at the Hatching Ground.

Reteaching/Reinforcement
• Writing Handbook, anthology pp. 820–822
• *Writing Mini-Lessons* transparencies, pp. 38 and 46

The Writer's Craft

Sensory Details, p. 255

CUSTOMIZING FOR
Multiple Learning Styles

U **Linguistic Learners** Have students write a telepathic dialogue between one of the boys and the dragon that chose him. Encourage students to write dialogue that conveys the feelings of both parties.

Critical Thinking: ANALYZING

V Ask students why they think Keevan was sure that he was a failure. *(Possible response: He thought all the dragons had chosen boys and that he'd failed to Impress one.)*

CUSTOMIZING FOR
Multiple Learning Styles

W **Intrapersonal Learners** Have students write a few paragraphs describing what they think might have happened to Keevan if he had not been able to stagger to the Hatching Ground.

U Suddenly a large gap appeared in the white human wall, and Keevan had his first sight of the eggs. There didn't seem to be *any* left uncracked, and he could see the lucky boys standing beside wobble-legged dragons. He could hear the unmistakable plaintive crooning of hatchlings and their squawks of protest as they'd fall awkwardly in the sand.

V Suddenly he wished that he hadn't left his bed, that he'd stayed away from the Hatching Ground. Now everyone would see his <u>ignominious</u> failure. He scrambled now as desperately to reach the shadowy walls of the Hatching Ground as he had struggled to cross the bowl. He mustn't be seen.

He didn't notice, therefore, that the shifting group of boys remaining had begun to drift in his direction. The hard pace he had set himself and his cruel disappointment took their double toll on Keevan. He tripped and collapsed sobbing to the warm sands. He didn't see the <u>consternation</u> in the watching weyrfolk above the Hatching Ground, nor did he hear the excited whispers of speculation. He didn't know that the weyrleader and weyrwoman had dropped to the arena and were making their way toward the knot of boys slowly moving in the direction of the archway.

"Never seen anything like it," the weyrleader was saying. "Only thirty-nine riders chosen. And the bronze trying to leave the Hatching Ground without making Impression!"

"A case in point of what I said last night," the weyrwoman replied, "where a hatchling makes no choice because the right boy isn't there."

"There's only Beterli and K'last's young one missing. And there's a full wing of likely boys to choose from. . . ."

"None acceptable, apparently. Where is the creature going? He's not heading for the entrance after all. Oh, what have we there, in the shadows?"

Keevan heard with dismay the sound of voices nearing him. He tried to burrow into the sand. The mere thought of how he would be teased and taunted now was unbearable.

Don't worry! Please don't worry! The thought was urgent, but not his own.

Someone kicked sand over Keevan and butted roughly against him.

"Go away. Leave me alone!" he cried.

Why? was the injured-sounding question inserted into his mind. There was no voice, no tone, but the question was there, perfectly clear, in his head.

Incredulous, Keevan lifted his head and stared into the glowing jeweled eyes of a small bronze dragon. His wings were wet; the tips hung drooping to the sand. And he sagged in the middle on his unsteady legs, although he was making a great effort to keep erect.

Keevan dragged himself to his knees, <u>oblivious</u> to the pain of his leg. He wasn't even aware that he was ringed by the boys passed over, while thirty-one pairs of resentful eyes watched him Impress the dragon. The weyrleaders looked on, amused and surprised at the draconic[19] choice, which could not be forced. Could not be questioned. Could not be changed.

Why? asked the dragon again. *Don't you like me?* His eyes whirled with anxiety, and his tone

---

19. **draconic** (drā-kŏn′ĭk): of or having to do with a dragon.

WORDS TO KNOW	**ignominious** (ĭg′nə-mĭn′ē-əs) *adj.* shameful; disgraceful **consternation** (kŏn′stər-nā′shən) *n.* a sudden fear or dread that makes one feel helpless or unable to act **oblivious** (ə-blĭv′ē-əs) *adj.* not paying attention; unaware

544

Mini-Lesson **Spelling**

WORDS ENDING IN -OUS AND -US
Tell students that the suffix *-ous* can be added to some nouns and verbs to create adjectives. Use the examples to explain the four ways the suffix can be added. Point out that, by contrast, *-us* is not a suffix. For example, in the words *circus* and *surplus*, the ending *-us* is part of the words.

Application Have students add the suffix *-ous* to the words in parentheses to form adjectives.
1. The dragon eggs' humming was (continue).
2. Keevan's (ignominy) failure made him hide.
3. The bronze dragon's tone was (pity).
4. Keevan thought his dragon was (marvel).
5. Being a dragonrider could be (danger).

Have students look for more words that fit this pattern, in their own writing and in the things they read, and add these words to their personal word lists.

Reteaching/Reinforcement
• *Unit Five Resource Book*, p. 6

moment + -ous = momentous (no change)

nerve + -ous = nervous (drop final e)

study + -ous = studious (change y to i)

outrage + -ous = outrageous (do not drop final e if it is preceded by g)

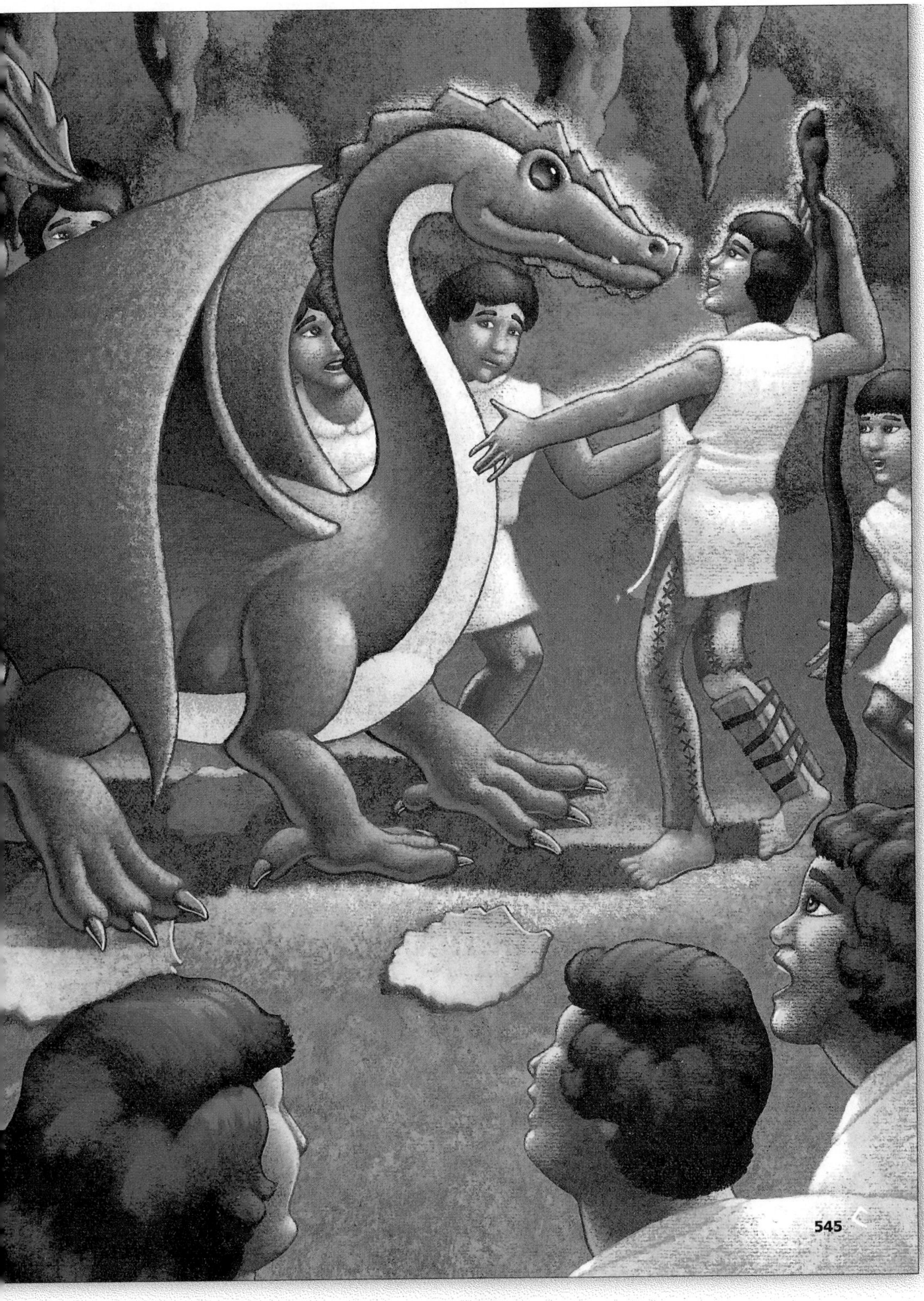

STRATEGIC READING FOR
Less-Proficient Readers

X Ask students the following questions to make sure they are following the story to this point.

- Why does one dragon seem to try to leave the Hatching Ground without having chosen a rider? *(The rider the dragon wants to choose is not among the boys present.)* **Summarizing**

- Which newly hatched dragon chooses Keevan to be its rider? *(the bronze dragon)* **Noting Relevant Details**

Set a Purpose Have students read to find out how Keevan feels about his dragon.

CUSTOMIZING FOR
Gifted and Talented Students

Y Have students discuss why the dragon asks Keevan, "Don't you like me?" *(Possible response: Keevan tried to push the dragon away, not realizing that it was the dragon trying to get his attention rather than the other boys trying to taunt him.)* Then have them discuss how self-image affects the way a person thinks other people perceive him or her.

Mini-Lesson: Speaking, Listening, and Viewing

PRESS CONFERENCE Explain to students that press conferences are often held when someone "important" has something that he or she wants the press and the media to communicate to the public.

Application Have students work in groups to enact press conferences given by the bronze dragon to tell the people of Pern why he chose Keevan as his dragonrider. In each group, choose one student to enact the role of the bronze dragon and another to act as Keevan. Have these students prepare something to say about the Impression. Have the other students act as reporters to prepare and ask questions. If possible, have one student videotape the press conference.

Interpersonal Learners Have students note how Lessa shortens Keevan's name to indicate that he has succeeded at the Impression and is now a dragonrider. Have students work in groups to think of a way to shorten their own first names, using an apostrophe, as if they were dragonriders.

STRATEGIC READING FOR
Less-Proficient Readers

AA Have students describe how both Keevan and the bronze dragon feel about having found each other and forming their lifelong relationship. *(proud and joyful)* **Restating**

COMPREHENSION CHECK

1. What is a dragonrider? *(someone who rides dragons to defend Pern)*
2. What does Beterli taunt Keevan about? *(his small size)*
3. Why is Beterli eliminated from the Impression? *(He started a fight with and injured Keevan.)*
4. What magic powers do dragons have that they probably use in choosing their dragonriders? *(They're telepathic: they can read minds.)*
5. What kind of dragon chooses Keevan? *(a bronze dragon)*

---

was so piteous that Keevan staggered forward and threw his arms around the dragon's neck, stroking his eye ridges, patting the damp, soft hide, opening the fragile-looking wings to dry them, and assuring the hatchling wordlessly over and over again that he was the most perfect, most beautiful, most beloved dragon in the entire weyr, in all the weyrs of Pern.

"What's his name, K'van?" asked Lessa, smiling warmly at the new dragonrider. K'van stared up at her for a long moment. Lessa would know as soon as he did. Lessa was the only person who could "receive" from all dragons, not only her own Ramoth. Then he gave her a radiant smile, recognizing the traditional shortening of his name that raised him forever to the rank of dragonrider.

My name is Heath, thought the dragon mildly and hiccuped in sudden urgency. *I'm hungry.*

"Dragons are born hungry," said Lessa, laughing. "F'lar, give the boy a hand. He can barely manage his own legs, much less a dragon's."

K'van remembered his stick and drew himself up. "We'll be just fine, thank you."

"You may be the smallest dragonrider ever, young K'van, but you're the bravest," said F'lar.

And Heath agreed! Pride and joy so leaped in both chests that K'van wondered if his heart would burst right out of his body. He looped an arm around Heath's neck, and the pair—the smallest dragonboy and the hatchling who wouldn't choose anybody else—walked out of the Hatching Ground together forever. ❖

Assessment Option

INFORMAL ASSESSMENT You can informally assess students' understanding of the story by having them write dialogue. Have them assume that K'van goes off to feed and care for Heath after the Impression. Ask students to write a dialogue between K'van and Heath that includes information about how dragons choose their riders and about why Heath chose Keevan.

Rubric

3 Full Accomplishment Dialogues are true to character, adhere to the story line, and sound realistic.

2 Substantial Accomplishment Dialogues are true to character, but details are insufficient or, in some cases, inaccurate.

1 Little or Partial Accomplishment Dialogues don't represent the characters or the story line correctly.

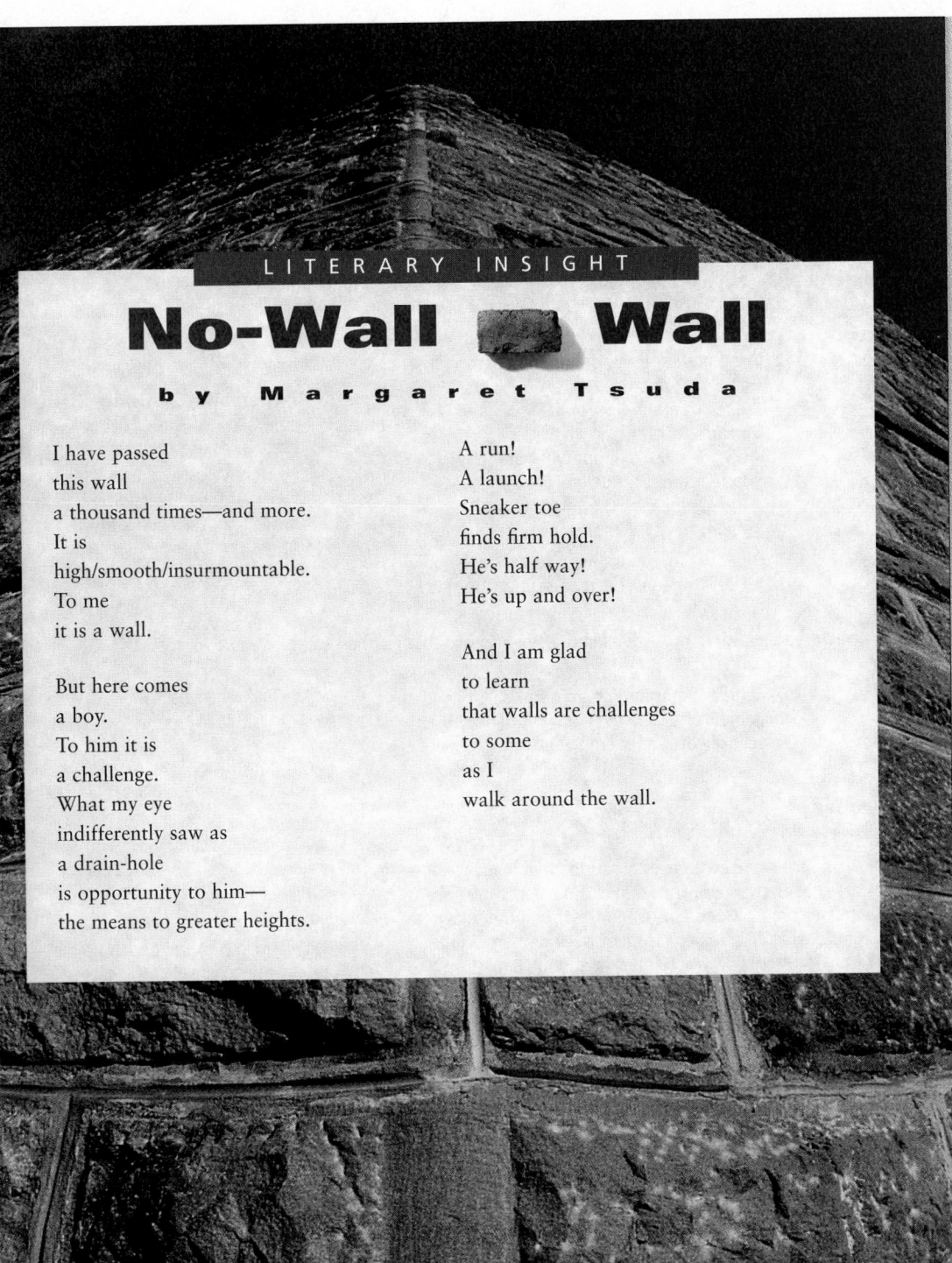

LITERARY INSIGHT

No-Wall ■ Wall

by Margaret Tsuda

I have passed
this wall
a thousand times—and more.
It is
high/smooth/insurmountable.
To me
it is a wall.

But here comes
a boy.
To him it is
a challenge.
What my eye
indifferently saw as
a drain-hole
is opportunity to him—
the means to greater heights.

A run!
A launch!
Sneaker toe
finds firm hold.
He's half way!
He's up and over!

And I am glad
to learn
that walls are challenges
to some
as I
walk around the wall.

NO-WALL WALL **547**

From Personal Response to Critical Analysis

1. Possible responses: They're very happy; they will be among the best at fighting Thread; K'van has matured a lot.

2. Possible responses: because he has courage and patience; because he has integrity; because he's honest

3. Possible responses: He might have waited until next year when Keevan would have been there; he might have died because Keevan would not have been there to feed him.

4. Possible response: K'last, because he has leadership abilities; Mende, because she appreciates a person's inner qualities.

5. Possible response: The speaker would approve of Keevan for meeting challenges and climbing his "walls."

Literary Links

Possible response: Both Nessan and Keevan are determined, honest, and brave.

Another Pathway

Cooperative Learning Encourage students to work together to determine the point of view of each character featured in the dialogue. Assign students the following roles: summarizer, to ensure that the characters' points of view are known and included; recorder, to write down the group's ideas; encourager of participation, to ensure that all members contribute ideas to the dialogue; and direction giver, to direct the performance. After the conversation is written, have each student assume a role to enact.

Rubric

3 Full Accomplishment The script accurately reflects each character's point of view and the events at the Impression.

2 Substantial Accomplishment The script accurately reflects each character, but some of the events at the Hatching Ground are not included.

1 Little or Partial Accomplishment The script includes confused characterizations and inaccurate descriptions of events at the Impression.

RESPONDING OPTIONS

FROM PERSONAL RESPONSE TO CRITICAL ANALYSIS

REFLECT 1. What are your impressions of K'van and Heath at the end of this story? In your notebook, describe or sketch your impressions.

RETHINK
Close Textual Reading

2. What do you think is the main reason that Heath chooses Keevan to be his dragonrider?

Consider
- Mende's views about what dragons look for in a candidate
- the qualities of Keevan that Heath might base his impression on

Thematic Link 3. What do you think Heath might have done if Keevan hadn't been present at the Hatching Ground?

RELATE 4. Which of the adults in the story do you think is the best role model for the candidates? Why?

5. Reread the Insight poem on page 547. What impressions of Keevan do you think the speaker of that poem might form? Why?

Multimodal Learning
ANOTHER PATHWAY
Cooperative Learning
Get together with four classmates. Imagine that K'van, Mende, K'last, F'lar, and Lessa get together after the Impression. What might they say about what happened at the Impression? Write a script for their conversation and then perform the script for the rest of the class.

LITERARY CONCEPTS

Suspense is the excitement or tension that readers feel as they get involved in a story and become eager to know the outcome. Suspense usually arises from uncertainty about what will happen next. List three or more events from the story that you found suspenseful. Rate each event using a five-point scale, with 1 being the lowest level of suspense and 5 being the highest. Discuss the events and your ratings with a partner or a small group.

LITERARY LINKS

If you have read "The Chief's Daughter" on page 259, compare Nessan's inner qualities with Keevan's.

QUICKWRITES

1. Draft a **handbook** that Lessa might prepare for dragonrider candidates.

2. How do you think life will be different for K'van than it was for Keevan? Present your ideas in an outline of a **sequel** to this story.

3. Imagine that K'van becomes weyrleader. Draft a **speech** he might give that explains how his father and foster mother have influenced his life.

4. What might a reporter ask K'van after the Impression? Draft an **interview** that might appear in the *Pern Herald*.

📁 **PORTFOLIO** Save your writing. You may want to use it later as a springboard to a piece for your portfolio.

Literary Concepts

Suggest that after students have listed suspenseful events, they explain to their partners or group members why they found each event suspenseful. Suspenseful events might include Beterli's taunting of Keevan at the black rock bunker or Keevan's struggle to reach the Hatching Ground.

QuickWrites

1. Make sure students include qualities necessary for a dragonrider. Suggest that students bind their responses into a book.

2. Explain that an outline is an organized list or a sequence of events.

3. Remind students that a speech should have an attention-getting opening and be written in a tone suitable for oral presentation.

4. Remind students that their interview should include both the questions and K'van's responses.

The Writer's Craft

Character Sketch, pp. 54–61
Short Story, p. 78–85

ALTERNATIVE ACTIVITIES

1. Create a **model** of how you imagine K'van and Heath will look as they ride through the sky.

2. Plan a **video game** in which K'van and Heath battle Thread to protect the people of Pern.

WORDS TO KNOW

EXERCISE A Answer the following questions on a sheet of paper.

1. During a **confrontation**, would people be most likley ro argue, flirt, or laugh?

2. To put yourself on a **roster**, would you use a ladder, a pencil, or a camera?

3. Is a person with **prestige** usually treated with respect, with amusement, or with scorn?

4. When you have been **oblivious** to someone's remarks, are you most likely to respond with "No way!" "Huh?" or "You bet!"

5. Would a writer be most likely to use the word *ignominious* to describe the behavior of the hero, the heroine, or the villain in a story?

6. Would a dog convey a feeling of **desolation** by growling, by howling, or by wagging its tail?

7. If it is **imperative** that you read a certain story, are you being forbidden, being encouraged, or being required to do so?

8. Which would most likely **alleviate** a person's hunger—a snack, the smell of food cooking, or a long time between meals?

9. Would a person who wanted to **goad** someone be most likely to say "Go on, chicken!" "You'll get in trouble!" or "Lucky you!"

10. Would an actor most likely convey a feeling of **consternation** by grinning, yawning, or trembling?

EXERCISE B Write a brief paragraph that summarizes the plot of "The Smallest Dragonboy." Use as many of the Words to Know as possible.

• *AUTHOR BACKGROUND*

ART CONNECTION

Review the illustrations that accompany this story. How would you compare the illustrator's impressions of the characters and events with your own?

Detail of illustration by Ray-Mel Cornelius.

ACROSS THE CURRICULUM

 Math Using the information in the story, create a word problem about the percentage of candidates who Impressed or failed to Impress hatchlings. Be prepared to explain how to solve it.

ANNE McCAFFREY

1926–

When Anne McCaffrey's brother, Kevin, was 12, a bone disease forced him to wear a painful cast. His bravery inspired his sister to write "The Smallest Dragonboy."

Nicknamed the Dragon Lady by her fans, McCaffrey writes her novels and short stories at Dragonhold, her home in County Wicklow, Ireland. Her best-known novels, *Dragonflight, Dragonsong,* and *Dragonsinger,* are set in Pern, a world with its own history, geography, and culture.

McCaffrey is the first woman to have won a Hugo Award for science fiction. She encourages "anyone to write—to dream up their own special world—as an escape or an exercise in imagination."

OTHER WORKS *Dragondrums, Dragonlady of Pern, Dragonquest, The Renegades of Pern*

Extended Reading

THE SMALLEST DRAGONBOY **549**

Alternative Activities

1. Suggest students use information they gathered in the Across the Curriculum science activity when creating Heath. Remind them that their models should depict an older K'van, not Keevan. Also remind them that the dragon's color should be bronze.

2. Review with students the objective in most games (for good guys to defeat evil or for the player to reach a goal). If possible, share with students some typical games on video. Have students write rules for their game and draw sample video screens showing what some of the game scenes might look like.

Words to Know

Exercise A

1. argue	6. howling
2. pencil	7. required
3. respect	8. a snack
4. "Huh?"	9. "Go on, chicken!"
5. villain	10. trembling

Exercise B

Paragraphs will vary. Make sure students include some Words to Know.

Reteaching/Reinforcement
• *Unit Five Resource Book,* p. 7

Art Connection

Possible responses: The illustrator's work is very realistic, whereas my impressions are more magical and fantastic. The illustrator's impressions match my impressions.

Across the Curriculum

Math Review with students the information on page 538—there are 72 boys but only 40 eggs. Students should be sure to include answers that are consistent with this information. Encourage students to test their problems by working them backwards, starting with their solutions. Students may also test their problems on friends or family members.

ADDITIONAL SUGGESTIONS

 **Science** *Design a Dragon!* Have students do research in groups to find out what kind of physical features any animal (even a mythical dragon) must have to be able to fly. Have students consult biology books and encyclopedias. Then have them sketch their own "design" for a flying dragon, labeling its physical requirements for flight. Invite students to share their sketches with the class.

ANNE McCAFFREY

Anne McCaffrey has worked as both a character actress and stage director of operas and operettas. She frequently lectures and appears as the guest of honor at science fiction conventions. About herself, she has said, "I have green eyes, silver hair, and freckles; the rest changes without notice."

AUTHOR BACKGROUND
Anne McCaffrey This author speaks about the worlds she has created and her desire to create strong characters.

Side A, Frame 42018

THE LANGUAGE OF LITERATURE   TEACHER'S EDITION   **549**

OVERVIEW

Objectives

- To understand and appreciate a short story in which the main character rebels against racial prejudice
- To identify and understand conflict
- To express understanding of the story through a choice of writing forms, including a climax, an interview, a review, and an essay
- To extend understanding of the story through a variety of multimodal and cross-curricular activities

Skills

READING SKILLS/STRATEGIES
- Making generalizations

THE WRITER'S STYLE
- Paragraphs and topic sentences

GRAMMAR
- Capitalization of proper nouns

LITERARY CONCEPTS
- Conflict
- Climax

SPELLING
- Prefixes and base words

SPEAKING, LISTENING, AND VIEWING
- Speech
- Skit

Cross-Curricular Connections

SOCIAL STUDIES
- School segregation

SCIENCE
- Skin tones

Art Note

Three Bats in the Garden by David Hockney Hockney (1937–) was an important painter in the English Pop Art movement. "Pop" was used to describe the artist's use of the popular media (comic strips, glossy magazines, television, and cinema) to convey contemporary life.

Reading the Art *What feeling do the bats give you? How does the way in which the bats are painted contribute to this feeling?*

FICTION

The Revolt of the Evil Fairies
Ted Poston

Activating Prior Knowledge
PERSONAL CONNECTION

What do you know about rebels and revolts? In social studies, you may have read about America's War of Independence or the French Revolution. Perhaps you know of individuals who got tired of being pushed around and decided to do something about the situation. What rebels from history or your own experience come to mind? Working with a small group of classmates, list several rebels and something about each one on a web like the one shown.

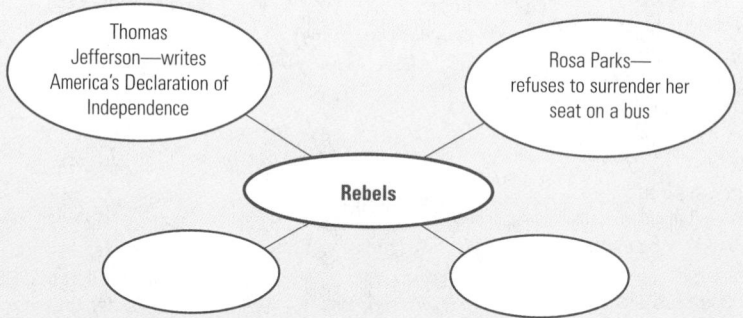

Thomas Jefferson—writes America's Declaration of Independence

Rosa Parks—refuses to surrender her seat on a bus

Rebels

Building Background
HISTORICAL CONNECTION

The **setting** of this story is a small town in the South during the early 1900s, long before the revolt known as the civil rights movement occurred. At that time, segregated schools—schools for one race only—were legal, and most African Americans experienced discrimination in one form or another. African Americans with lighter complexions generally fared better than darker-skinned ones did. Even within the African-American community, lighter-skinned blacks had greater opportunities and received more respect.

Setting a Purpose
WRITING CONNECTION

Select one of the rebels you listed for the Personal Connection. In your notebook, briefly describe this individual and the revolt that he or she triggered. Then as you read, compare this rebel with the narrator of the story.

550   UNIT FIVE   PART 1: APPEARANCES TO THE CONTRARY

PRINT AND MEDIA RESOURCES

UNIT FIVE RESOURCE BOOK
Strategic Reading: Literature, p. 11
Vocabulary SkillBuilder, p. 14
Reading SkillBuilder, p. 12
Spelling SkillBuilder, p. 13

GRAMMAR MINI–LESSONS
Transparencies, pp. 25–26
Copymasters, pp. 33–34

WRITING MINI–LESSONS
Transparencies, pp. 29–30

ACCESS FOR STUDENTS ACQUIRING ENGLISH
Selection Summaries
Reading and Writing Support

FORMAL ASSESSMENT
Selection Test, pp. 103–104
 Test Generator

 **AUDIO LIBRARY**
See Reference Card

 **LASERLINKS**
Social Studies Connection

The Revolt of the Evil Fairies

BY TED POSTON

Three Bats in the Garden (1980), David Hockney. From *L'enfant et les sortilèges*, gouache, 14" × 17". Copyright © David Hockney.

SUMMARY

The young narrator of this story is tired of being typecast in his school's annual production of Prince Charming and Sleeping Beauty. For three years in a row, he's been stuck in the role of Head Evil Fairy due to customs at his all-black school: light-skinned students play good characters and dark-skinned students play evil ones. Not getting the part of Prince Charming is especially heartbreaking for the narrator because Sarah Williams, a girl he likes, is playing the part of Sleeping Beauty. To make matters worse, the boy who plays Prince Charming, Leonardius Wright, also likes Sarah and gets to kiss her every day in rehearsal. The narrator loses his temper during the play's public performance after Leonardius raps him over the head with his sword. In the final act, the narrator punches Prince Charming and causes a fight between the Good Fairies and Evil Fairies. As punishment, he is banned from next year's production—but he doesn't care because he knows he will never get to play Prince Charming anyway.

Thematic Link: *Appearances to the Contrary* The narrator rebels when appearances, rather than acting ability, determine how roles are assigned in a school play.

CUSTOMIZING FOR
Students Acquiring English

- Use **ACCESS FOR STUDENTS ACQUIRING ENGLISH**, *Reading and Writing Support.*

- You may wish to point out that this selection focuses on different treatment given to students because of their different skin tones.

STRATEGIC READING FOR
Less-Proficient Readers

Set a Purpose Have students read to find out the role that race and skin color play in Hopkinsville.

Use **UNIT FIVE RESOURCE BOOK,** p. 11, for guidance in reading the selection.

WORDS TO KNOW

cite (sīt) *v.* to refer to or mention as an example or proof (p. 556)

elite (ĭ-lēt′) *n.* a group regarded as the best (p. 553)

impromptu (ĭm-prŏmp′tōō) *adj.* without preparation; spur-of-the-moment (p. 556)

rationalize (răsh′ə-nə-līz′) *v.* to explain or make excuses for (p. 553)

vanquish (văng′kwĭsh) *v.* to conquer; defeat (p. 553)

Ⓘ The grand dramatic offering of the Booker T. Washington Colored Grammar School was the biggest event of the year in our social life in Hopkinsville, Kentucky. It was the one occasion on which they let us use the old Cooper Opera House, and even some of the white folks came out yearly to applaud our presentation. The first two rows of the orchestra were always reserved for our white friends, and our leading colored citizens sat right behind them—with an empty row intervening,[1] of course.

Mr. Ed Smith, our local undertaker, invariably occupied a box to the left of the house and wore his cutaway coat and striped breeches. This distinctive garb was usually reserved for those rare occasions when he officiated at the funerals of our most prominent colored citizens. Mr. Thaddeus Long, our colored mailman, once rented a tuxedo and bought a box too. But nobody paid him much mind. We knew he was just showing off.

The title of our play never varied. It was always Prince Charming and the Sleeping Beauty, but no two presentations were ever the same. Miss H. Belle LaPrade, our sixth-grade teacher, rewrote the script every season, and it was never like anything you read in the storybooks.

Miss LaPrade called it "a modern morality play[2] of conflict between the forces of good and evil." And the forces of evil, of course, always came off second best.

Ⓐ The Booker T. Washington Colored Grammar School was in a state of ferment[3] from Christmas until February, for this was the period when parts were assigned. First there was the selection of the Good Fairies and the Evil Fairies. This was very important, because the Good Fairies wore white costumes and the Evil Fairies black. And strangely enough most of the Good Fairies usually turned out to be extremely light in complexion, with straight hair and white folks' features. On rare occasions a dark-skinned girl

might be lucky enough to be a Good Fairy, but not one with a speaking part.

There never was any doubt about Prince Charming and the Sleeping Beauty. They were always light-skinned. And though nobody ever discussed those things openly, it was an accepted fact that a lack of pigmentation[4] was a decided advantage in the Prince Charming and Sleeping Beauty sweepstakes.

> *It was an accepted fact that a lack of pigmentation was a decided advantage ...*

And therein lay my personal tragedy. I made the best grades in my class; I was the leading debater and the scion[5] of a respected family in the community. But I could never be Prince Charming, because I was black.

In fact, every year when they started casting our grand dramatic offering, my family started pricing black cheesecloth at Franklin's Department Store. For they knew that I would be leading the forces of darkness and skulking back in the shadows—waiting to be

---

1. **intervening:** coming between.
2. **morality play:** a drama intended to teach people right from wrong.
3. **ferment:** excited commotion.
4. **pigmentation:** dark coloring in skin.
5. **scion** (sī'ən): a descendant.

Mini-Lesson ✏ Grammar

CAPITALIZATION OF PROPER NOUNS

Proper nouns refer to specific persons, places, or things and are always capitalized. For example, Roger Jackson is the name of a person, so the first letters of his name are capitalized.

Application Have students capitalize the proper nouns in the following sentences.
1. ed smith was hopkinsville's undertaker.
2. Students were given their roles between christmas and february.
3. He fell in love with sarah, who was to play the role of sleeping beauty.
4. Rat joiner lived in the billy goat hill neighborhood.
5. The most prosperous african americans in town had formed a club called the blue vein society.

Reteaching/Reinforcement
- Grammar Handbook, anthology pp. 875–877
- *Grammar Mini-Lessons* copymasters pp. 33–34, transparencies pp. 25–26

📖 **The Writer's Craft**

Proper Nouns and Adjectives, pp. 600–601

vanquished in the third act. Mamma had experience with this sort of thing. All my brothers had finished Booker T. before me.

Not that I was alone in my disappointment. Many of my classmates felt it too. I probably just took it more to heart. Rat Joiner, for instance, could rationalize the situation. Rat was not only black; he lived on Billy Goat Hill.[6] But Rat summed it up like this:

"If you black, you black."

I should have been able to regard the matter calmly too. For our grand dramatic offering was only a reflection of our daily community life in Hopkinsville. The yallers[7] had the best of everything. They held most of the teaching jobs in Booker T. Washington Colored Grammar School. They were the Negro doctors, the lawyers, the insurance men. They even had a "Blue Vein Society,"[8] and if your dark skin obscured your throbbing pulse, you were hardly a member of the elite.

Yet I was inconsolable[9] the first time they turned me down for Prince Charming. That was the year they picked Roger Jackson. Roger was not only dumb; he stuttered. But he was light enough to pass for white, and that was apparently sufficient.

In all fairness, however, it must be admitted that Roger had other qualifications. His father owned the only colored saloon in town and was quite a power in local politics. In fact, Mr. Clinton Jackson had a lot to say about just who taught in the Booker T. Washington Colored Grammar School. So it was understandable that Roger should have been picked for Prince Charming.

My real heartbreak, however, came the year they picked Sarah Williams for Sleeping Beauty. I had been in love with Sarah since kindergarten. She had soft light hair, bluish-

Between Us (1989), Gabriel Ajayi. Wood marquetry, courtesy of the artist.

gray eyes, and a dimple which stayed in her left cheek whether she was smiling or not.

Of course Sarah never encouraged me much. She never answered any of my fervent love letters, and Rat was very scornful of my one-sided love affairs. "As long as she don't call you a black baboon," he sneered, "you'll keep on hanging around."

---

6. **Billy Goat Hill:** a very poor section of the narrator's town.
7. **yallers:** a regional term for black people with light brown, tan, or yellowish skin.
8. **"Blue Vein Society":** a reference to the Blue Vein Circle, a professional organization of light-skinned African Americans; the group was in existence from the 1890s to the 1920s.
9. **inconsolable** (ĭn´kən-sō′lə-bəl): brokenhearted; not able to be comforted.

WORDS	**vanquish** (văng′kwĭsh) v. to conquer; defeat
TO	**rationalize** (răsh′ə-nə-līz′) v. to explain or make excuses for
KNOW	**elite** (ĭ-lēt′) n. a group regarded as the best

553

Literary Concept:
CHARACTERIZATION

D Have students discuss what the narrator means when he says he took the discrimination "more to heart." Ask what this tells about his character. *(Possible response: He doesn't calmly accept injustice.)* Then ask how the narrator's character compares with that of Rat Joiner, based on his remark "If you black, you black." *(Possible response: Joiner is resigned to his situation and the treatment he receives.)*

Literary Concept: **CONFLICT**

E Ask students in what way the "daily community life in Hopkinsville" contributed to the conflict experienced by the narrator. *(Possible response: At school, the narrator experiences a conflict between his goals and the racism that prevents him from achieving them. The prejudice in the community at large spills over into the school.)*

Active Reading: **PREDICT**

F Ask students if they think the narrator's saying "it was understandable" means he will calmly accept Roger as Prince Charming. Make sure students explain their answers. *(Possible response: no, because although it may be understandable, it's still unfair)*

Art Note

Between Us by Gabriel Ajayi Gabriel Ajayi was born in Nigeria and now lives in the United States. This work is an example of marquetry—using materials such as metals, ivory, bone, and tortoise shell on wood to create a picture.

Reading the Art *What does the way in which the two figures are positioned suggest about their relationship and feelings toward each other?*

Mini-Lesson | **The Writer's Style**

PARAGRAPHS AND TOPIC SENTENCES
A paragraph is a group of related sentences that develop a single main idea or accomplish a single purpose. The main idea of the paragraph is usually summed up in one sentence, called the topic sentence. The rest of the paragraph is usually made up of sentences that support the topic sentence.

Application Have students reread the highlighted paragraph to identify the topic sentence. Have them explain how the other sentences elaborate on the main point that the topic sentence states. Then have students write their own paragraphs describing why

Sarah Williams spurns the narrator's affection. Tell students that their paragraphs must have topic sentences and other sentences that support or expand on them. Have each student read his or her paragraph aloud and have classmates identify the topic sentence.

Reteaching/Reinforcement
• Writing Handbook, anthology pp. 815–817
• *Writing Mini-Lessons* transparencies, pp. 29–30

📖 The Writer's Craft
Constructing Paragraphs, pp. 247–249

G Have students clarify why the narrator took his sister's can of Palmer's Skin Success. To help students in their explanations, you may wish to use this model:

Think-Aloud Model *To get the role of Prince Charming, the narrator knows he must have lighter skin. He probably thinks that using Palmer's Skin Success will lighten his skin and increase his chances of getting the part.*

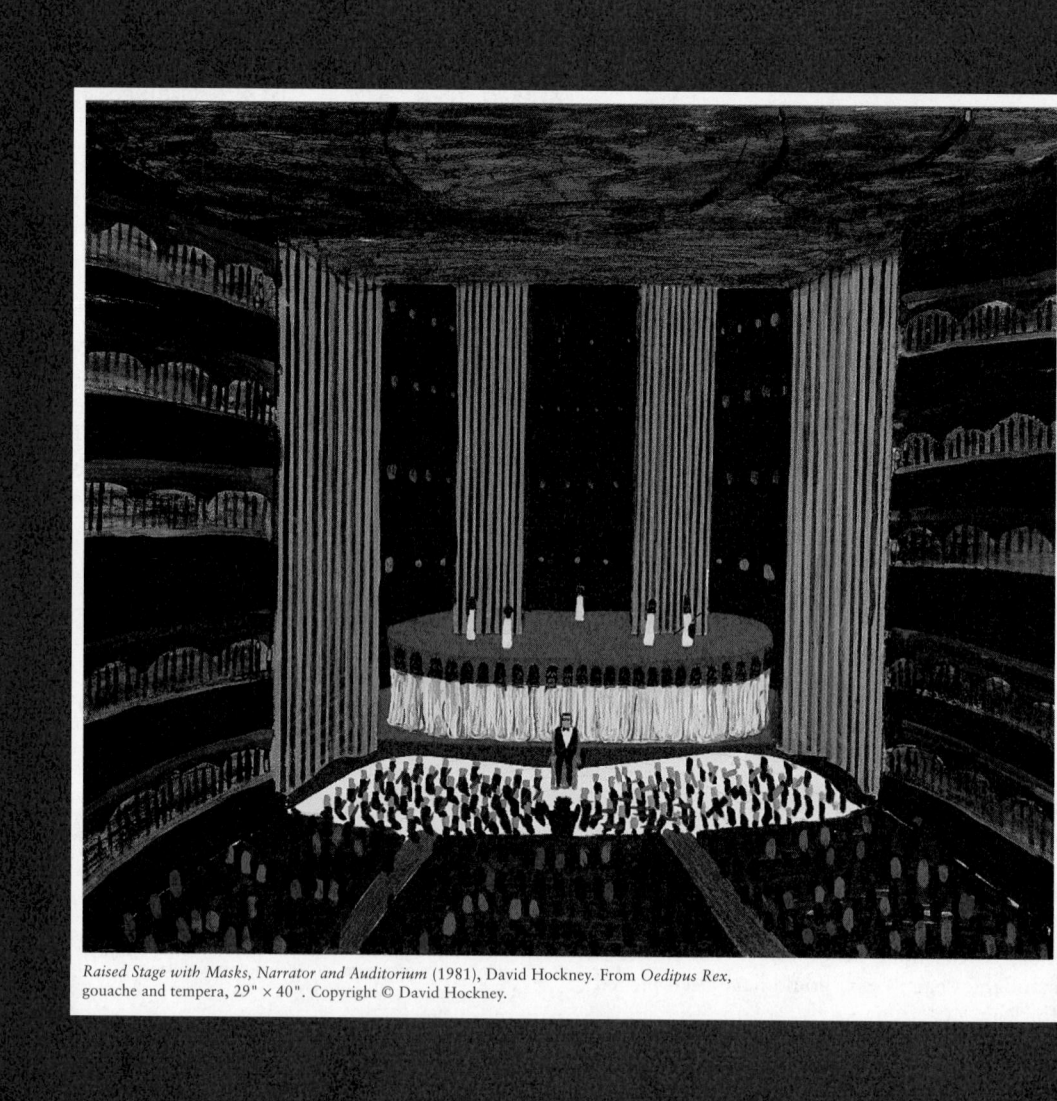

Raised Stage with Masks, Narrator and Auditorium (1981), David Hockney. From *Oedipus Rex*, gouache and tempera, 29" × 40". Copyright © David Hockney.

Mini-Lesson  **Reading Skills/Strategies**

Role/Opportunity   Skin Color

MAKING GENERALIZATIONS Explain to students that when they make generalizations, they take information they have learned and make general statements based on that information. Tell students that a generalization is an overall idea based on specific details.

Application Instruct students to gather specific details from the selection on which they will base a generalization. Have them do so by filling in a chart, like the one shown, that lists roles or opportunities available in Hopkinsville and the skin color of people who achieved them. Then have students use this information to make a generalization about the role that skin color played in determining an individual's place in the community.

Reteaching/Reinforcement
• *Unit Five Resource Book*, p. 12

After Sarah was chosen for Sleeping Beauty, I went out for the Prince Charming role with all my heart. If I had declaimed[10] boldly in previous contests, I was matchless now. If I had bothered Mamma with rehearsals at home before, I pestered her to death this time. Yes, and I purloined[11] my sister's can of Palmer's Skin Success.[12]

I knew the Prince's role from start to finish, having played the Head Evil Fairy opposite it for two seasons. And Prince Charming was one character whose lines Miss LaPrade never varied much in her many versions. But although I never admitted it, even to myself, I knew I was doomed from the start. They gave the part to Leonardius Wright. Leonardius, of course, was yaller.

The teachers sensed my resentment. They were almost apologetic. They pointed out that I had been such a splendid Head Evil Fairy for two seasons that it would be a crime to let anybody else try the role. They reminded me that Mamma wouldn't have to buy any more cheesecloth because I could use my same old costume. They insisted that the Head Evil Fairy was even more important than Prince Charming because he was the one who cast the spell on Sleeping Beauty. So what could I do but accept?

I had never liked Leonardius Wright. He was a goody-goody, and even Mamma was always throwing him up to me. But, above all, he too was in love with Sarah Williams. And now he got a chance to kiss Sarah every day in rehearsing the awakening scene.

Well, the show must go on, even for little black boys. So I threw my soul into my part and made the Head Evil Fairy a character to be remembered. When I drew back from the couch of Sleeping Beauty and slunk away into the shadows at the approach of Prince Charming, my facial expression was indeed something to behold. When I was vanquished by the shining sword of Prince Charming in the last act, I was a little hammy perhaps—but terrific!

The attendance at our grand dramatic offering that year was the best in its history. Even the white folks overflowed the two rows reserved for them, and a few were forced to sit in the intervening one. This created a delicate situation, but everybody tactfully ignored it.

The attendance at our grand dramatic offering that year was the best in its history.

When the curtain went up on the last act, the audience was in fine fettle.[13] Everything had gone well for me too—except for one spot in the second act. That was where Leonardius unexpectedly rapped me over the head with his sword as I slunk off into the shadows. That was not in the script, but Miss LaPrade quieted me down by saying it made a nice touch anyway. Rat said Leonardius did it on purpose.

---

10. **declaimed:** recited or spoken in a loud, showy way.
11. **purloined:** stole.
12. **Palmer's Skin Success:** a product supposed to lighten the skin.
13. **in fine fettle:** in good spirits.

CUSTOMIZING FOR
Gifted and Talented Students

Have students discuss whether each Evil Fairy has a personal gripe against the Good Fairy he or she is fighting. Then have students discuss the ways in which the fight represents the issue of racism.

Have students discuss their impressions of the ways in which categories of races and skin colors are created. Ask students to think about why these categories are created and the effects of these categories on people and the way they think.

Literary Concept: CLIMAX

(J) Ask students whether or not they think the death of the Evil Fairy is the story's climax. If not, ask them where the story's climax occurs. (*Possible response: It isn't the climax because it isn't a turning point. The turning point comes earlier when the narrator decides to hit Leonardius.*)

STRATEGIC READING FOR
Less-Proficient Readers

(K) Ask students to describe the unexpected occurrence in the play. (*The narrator punches Prince Charming, and a fight occurs.*) **Summarizing**

COMPREHENSION CHECK

1. Why can't the narrator be Prince Charming in the play? (*He is dark skinned.*)
2. Which students get the best roles? (*light-skinned students*)
3. How does the fight begin? (*The narrator punches Leonardius.*)
4. Why doesn't the narrator care about never being in the play again? (*He knows he can never play Prince Charming anyway.*)

The third act went on smoothly, though, until we came to the vanquishing scene. That was where I slunk from the shadows for the last time and challenged Prince Charming to mortal combat. The hero reached for his shining sword—a bit unsportsmanlike, I always thought, since Miss LaPrade consistently left the Head Evil Fairy unarmed—and then it happened!

Later I protested loudly—but in vain—that it was a case of self-defense. I pointed out that Leonardius had a mean look in his eye. I cited the impromptu rapping he had given my head in the second act. But nobody would listen. They just wouldn't believe that Leonardius really intended to brain me when he reached for his sword.

Anyway, he didn't succeed. For the minute I saw that evil gleam in his eye—or was it my own?—I cut loose with a right to the chin, and Prince Charming dropped his shining sword and staggered back. His astonishment lasted only a minute, though, for he lowered his head and came charging in, fists flailing. There was (3) nothing yellow about Leonardius but his skin.

The audience thought the scrap was something new Miss LaPrade had written in. They might have kept on thinking so if Miss LaPrade hadn't been screaming so hysterically from the sidelines. And if Rat Joiner hadn't decided that

I saw that evil gleam in his eye—or was it my own?...

this was as good a time as any to settle old scores. So he turned around and took a sock at the male Good Fairy nearest him.

When the curtain rang down, the forces of Good and Evil were locked in combat. And Sleeping Beauty was wide awake and streaking for the wings.

They rang the curtain back up fifteen minutes later, and we finished the play. I lay down and expired[14] according to specifications, but Prince Charming will probably remember my sneering corpse to his dying day. They wouldn't let me appear in the grand dramatic offering at all the next year. But I didn't care. I couldn't have been Prince Charming anyway. ❖

---

14. **expired:** died.

WORDS
TO
KNOW

cite (sīt) *v.* to refer to or mention as an example or proof
impromptu (ĭm-prŏmp'tōō) *adj.* without preparation; spur-of-the-moment

556

Mini-Lesson 🧩 **Literary Concepts**

REVIEWING CLIMAX Remind students that the climax, or turning point, is the high point of interest in the plot of a story or play. At the climax, the conflict is resolved and the outcome of the plot becomes clear.

Application Have students rewrite the ending of this story, creating a different climax. For example, the climax may be that Sarah suddenly understands the discrimination the dark-skinned students suffer under, refuses the role of Sleeping Beauty, and becomes the narrator's girlfriend. Have students brainstorm a list of possible different resolutions. Then have each student write one or two paragraphs using a new climax.

RESPONDING OPTIONS

FROM PERSONAL RESPONSE TO CRITICAL ANALYSIS

REFLECT 1. What words come to mind when you think about the narrator? List three or four words in your notebook, and then share your list with a partner.

RETHINK 2. The narrator triggers a revolt during his school's "grand dramatic offering." Do you think his punching Leonardius is justified? Give reasons for your answer.

3. How else might the narrator have handled his problems with Miss LaPrade?

4. How would you compare the narrator with Rat Joiner?

5. Did you find this story humorous? Do you think the author intended it to be so? Explain your opinion.

Consider

Close Textual Reading
• the events that occur
• the author's attitude toward the events

RELATE 6. How would you compare the rebel you described for the Personal Connection on page 550 with the narrator?

7. How do you think individuals should react when they are victims of discrimination? Support your opinion.

Multimodal Learning
ANOTHER PATHWAY

Imagine that the narrator must write a letter to the principal explaining his conduct. Compose that letter. Then choose a student to read and react to the letter as if he or she were the principal. The rest of the class should discuss the letter and the principal's reaction.

QUICKWRITES

1. This story is told from the narrator's point of view. Rewrite the **climax** of the story from Leonardius's or Miss LaPrade's point of view.

2. The school play in this story does not go quite according to the script. Write a post-performance **interview** in which a reporter for the school newspaper elicits Miss LaPrade's reaction.

3. What message do you think the author of this story conveys about appearances? Write a **review** that explores this theme.

4. Do you think the narrator achieves a victory at the end of the story? Why or why not? Draft an **essay** to support your opinion.

📁 **PORTFOLIO** Save your writing. You may want to use it later as a springboard to a piece for your portfolio.

LITERARY CONCEPTS

Conflict, as you may recall, is a struggle between opposing forces that forms the basis for the plot of a story. **External conflict** is a struggle between a character and an outside force, such as another character, society, or nature. **Internal conflict** is a struggle within a character, such as to make a decision or resolve a problem. Think about the narrator's conflicts in this story. Are they internal, external, or both? Support your views with evidence from the story.

CONCEPT REVIEW: Climax What event do you think is the climax, or turning point, of this story? Why?

THE REVOLT OF THE EVIL FAIRIES **557**

From Personal Response to Critical Analysis

1. Possible responses: defiant, smart, perceptive, confident
2. Possible responses: It is justified because racial discrimination is unjust and can result in an incredible amount of frustration and anger. It isn't justified because the discrimination wasn't Leonardius's fault and punching him doesn't solve anything.
3. Possible responses: He might have spoken to her and explained his feelings. He might have persuaded the other students to refuse to act in the play.
4. Possible response: The narrator takes action, whereas Rat Joiner accepts the status quo.
5. Possible responses: No, racial discrimination is serious and the author wanted it to be taken seriously. Yes, the author used humor—such as the unexpected turn of events on stage—to lighten a serious topic.
6. Possible responses: They both resorted to violence; one's actions were justified, but the other's were not.
7. Possible responses: They should work against it in public or change individual behavior.

Another Pathway

Make sure students think about the opinions the narrator would present and the tone of his letter.

Rubric

3 Full Accomplishment Student thoroughly explains the motivations for the narrator's conduct and maintains the narrator's point of view.

2 Substantial Accomplishment Student explores some of the narrator's reasons and for the most part reflects the narrator's point of view.

1 Little or Partial Accomplishment Student does not consistently reflect the narrator's point of view and sometimes gets off the topic.

Literary Concepts

Have groups list conflicts the narrator faces and then classify them as internal and/or external. *(Possible responses: The narrator experiences both internal and external conflicts in his struggle to be loved by Sarah and to be judged by his abilities rather than his skin color. He faces an external conflict when he fights with Leonardius.)*

Concept Review Many students will say that the fight between the narrator and Leonardius is the climax because the narrator refuses to accept injustice any longer.

QuickWrites

1. Have students determine how these characters would interpret the climax and how they would describe it.
2. Suggest that the interview include both the reporter's questions and Miss LaPrade's responses.
3. Remind students that their opinions must be supported by examples from the selection.
4. Remind students that essays argue the writer's opinion, using supporting examples.

📓 The Writer's Craft

Short Story, pp. 78–85
Supporting Opinions, pp. 144–151

Words to Know

1. c
2. b
3. a
4. d
5. c

Reteaching/Reinforcement
• *Unit Five Resource Book,* p. 14

Across the Curriculum

Social Studies *Cooperative Learning*
Students will research the 1954 Supreme Court decision *Brown* v. *Board of Education.* Group roles may include an encourager of participation, who ensures that everyone has research to do; a chief researcher, who investigates a variety of research materials; an integrator, who translates the group's findings into news stories. Students should examine what led to the Supreme Court decision, the arguments of the case, and its importance to the civil rights movement.

ADDITIONAL SUGGESTIONS

Science *The Human Rainbow* Have students do library research in biology text books and encyclopedias to find out why humans have such a range of skin colors. Suggest that they find out what colors human skin and how variations in skin color may have developed. Have students present their findings as a poster, using clippings from old magazines.

TED POSTON

After graduating from college in 1928, Poston worked for the *Amsterdam News,* an African-American weekly paper in New York City. He was fired after helping to lead a strike to unionize the paper's workers.

SOCIAL STUDIES CONNECTION
Struggle for Equality African Americans have struggled for equality in education for more than 100 years. This short film describes some of the major events of this struggle.

Side A, Frame 44287

Multimodal Learning

ALTERNATIVE ACTIVITIES

1. Suppose you were the narrator of this story. Give a **speech** to your class, explaining why discrimination is wrong. Use examples from your experiences in the "grand dramatic offerings." If possible, have another student videotape your performance.

2. Perform a **skit** for the class in which the narrator and Sarah Williams meet after the play and discuss what happened on stage.

ACROSS THE CURRICULUM

Social Studies *Cooperative Learning* What famous 1954 Supreme Court decision abolished segregation in public schools? Working with a small group of classmates, research the history of segregation in public schools, the landmark case, and some of the consequences of the Supreme Court's decision. If you have access to a computer encyclopedia program, use it as a research tool; also use documentary videos. Present your information as a series of television news stories. Videotape the stories or present them live to the rest of your classmates.

TED POSTON

Born in Hopkinsville, Kentucky, Theodore Roosevelt Poston was named after the U.S. president at that time. As a teenager, Poston began writing for his family's newspaper, which was forced to discontinue when it became too controversial. After college, Poston worked for black-owned newspapers in Pittsburgh and New York City. When he applied for a job with the *New York Post* in 1937, only two black journalists had ever worked for a white-owned daily newspaper in New York. Poston was told that the job was his if he could find a front-page story for

1906–1974

the next day's issue. He did, and he worked for the *Post* until 1972.

Poston risked his life reporting on race relations in the South. During the bus boycotts in Montgomery, Alabama, in 1955, his boss in New York asked him to phone in every night as assurance of his safety. His work earned the Heywood Broun Award of the American Newspaper Guild and several other awards in the 1950s. Poston also wrote short stories—some autobiographical—about discrimination faced by African Americans.

CRITIC'S CORNER

Ashley Green and Stephanie Hicks, two seventh-grade members of the student board, wrote that the ending is the best part of the story. Ashley liked the ending especially because the narrator "stood up for what he believed in." How would you respond to these views?

WORDS TO KNOW

Write the letter of the word or phrase that is most nearly *opposite* in meaning to the capitalized word.

1. VANQUISH: (A) overcome, (B) conquer, (C) lose, (D) defeat

2. RATIONALIZE: (A) explain away, (B) misinterpret, (C) make excuses for, (D) justify

3. ELITE: (A) worst, (B) best, (C) cream of the crop, (D) choice group

4. CITE: (A) refer to, (B) mention, (C) quote, (D) ignore

5. IMPROMPTU: (A) spur-of-the-moment, (B) unplanned, (C) rehearsed, (D) unprepared

---

• *SOCIAL STUDIES CONNECTION*

Alternative Activities

1. Have students first outline the argument they will present in their speech. Then encourage them to write an attention-getting opener for their speech. Make sure they understand that they should use simple language and clear arguments with examples suitable for oral presentation. If necessary, instruct students in the use of a video camera to tape the speeches.

2. Have students work in pairs and brainstorm what they think would happen if Sarah and the narrator were to meet this way. Then have students write the dialogue for Sarah and the narrator, being careful to reflect the author's portrayal of these characters.

PREVIEWING

POETRY

The Way It Is	Without Commercials
Gloria Oden	Alice Walker

Activating Prior Knowledge
PERSONAL CONNECTION

Think of all the television commercials you view in an average week. Many of them feature products and services that are supposed to be able to improve a person's looks. How would you describe the standard of beauty that these commercials usually promote? What effect do you think commercials can have on a viewer's attitude toward his or her appearance? In your notebook, briefly answer these questions, and then share your answers with a small group of classmates.

Building Background
CULTURAL CONNECTION

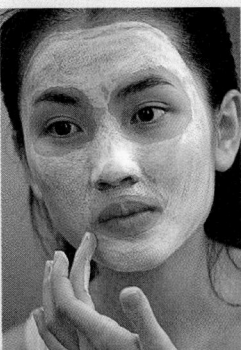

Asian woman applying green beauty mask. Copyright © Bob Thomason/Tony Stone Images.

Many people are so unhappy about their looks that they decide to change them. They dye their hair, straighten their teeth, change the color of their eyes through tinted contact lenses— or even take drastic measures. Each year, over half a million people in the United States choose to have cosmetic surgery of some kind—face lifts, hair transplants, nose reshapings, and tummy tucks, for example. Such operations are expensive. A nose reshaping may cost several thousand dollars. Still, some people spare no expense in attempting to look more like the "beautiful people" that grace their television screens.

Setting a Purpose
WRITING CONNECTION

In your opinion, what makes a person good-looking? In your notebook, describe your own standard of beauty. Then as you read these poems, consider the standard of beauty that each speaker suggests.

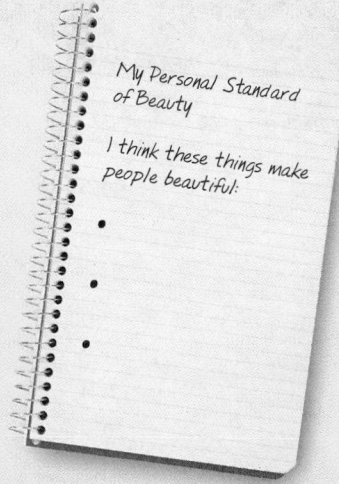

My Personal Standard of Beauty

I think these things make people beautiful:

THE WAY IT IS / WITHOUT COMMERCIALS   **559**

OVERVIEW

Objectives

- To understand and appreciate two lyric poems about standards of beauty
- To describe and understand tone
- To express understanding of the poems through a choice of writing forms, including a rebuttal, a letter, and a personal response
- To extend understanding of the poems through a variety of multimodal and cross-curricular activities

Skills

THE WRITER'S STYLE	GENRE STUDY
• Figurative language	• Poetry
LITERARY CONCEPTS	**SPEAKING, LISTENING, AND VIEWING**
• Tone	• Dramatic reading

Cross-Curricular Connections

SCIENCE	HISTORY
• Cosmetic surgery	• Changing concepts of beauty

ALTERNATIVE

Previewing

Instead of writing descriptions of their standards of beauty, students could discuss this topic with partners.

Writing Connection

Discussion Prompts *Think of beautiful people you have seen. Describe to your partner what makes these people beautiful. Then listen as your partner describes his or her idea of beauty. The following prompts may help you get started:*

- *How would you define the term beauty?*
- *Who is the most beautiful person you've seen? Why did you choose this person?*
- *What makes a person good-looking? As you read the poems, consider the standard of beauty that each speaker suggests.*

PRINT AND MEDIA RESOURCES

UNIT FIVE RESOURCE BOOK
Strategic Reading: Literature, p. 17

WRITING MINI–LESSONS
Transparencies, p. 39

ACCESS FOR STUDENTS ACQUIRING ENGLISH
Reading and Writing Support

FORMAL ASSESSMENT
Selection Test, p. 105
■ Test Generator

Art Note

Links and Lineage by Paul T. Goodnight Goodnight won the first Creative Arts Award given by the NAACP in 1988. His work, primarily depicting the African-American experience, has been shown in numerous group and solo exhibitions.

Reading the Art *How does the composition of the painting draw your eye toward the older woman? What do the people shown seem to be doing?*

THE WAY It Is

BY GLORIA ODEN

Links and Lineage (1987), Paul Goodnight. Commissioned by the Middlesex County (Massachusetts) Chapter of the Links, Inc. Copyright © 1987 Paul Goodnight.

I have always known
that had I been blonde
blue-eyed
with skin fabled white as the unicorn's[1]
5   with cheeks tinted and pearled
as May morning on the lips of a rose
such commercial virtues
could never have led me to assume myself
anywhere near as beautiful as
10   my mother
whose willow fall of black hair
—now pirate silver—
I brushed as a child
(earning five cents)
15   when shaken free from the bun
as wrapped round and pinned
it billowed in a fine mist
from her proud shoulders
to her waist.

1. **fabled white as the unicorn's:** The unicorn, an imaginary animal that looks like a horse with a horn growing from its forehead, is usually pictured as snowy white.

Mini-Lesson **The Writer's Style**

FIGURATIVE LANGUAGE Explain to students that figurative language is language that goes beyond the dictionary meanings of words. Writers use figures of speech—such as simile, metaphor, and personification—to create fresh and original descriptions. Tell students that in this poem the writer primarily uses metaphor (a comparison that does not contain the word *like* or *as*) and simile (a comparison that does contain the word *like* or *as*).

Application Have students identify the similes in the highlighted passage. Then have them write a few lines of poetry, using a simile or a metaphor to describe the appearance of someone whom they admire. Encourage volunteers to share their lines with the class.

Reteaching/Reinforcement
• *Writing Mini-Lessons* transparencies, p. 39

The Writer's Craft

Using Language Imaginatively, pp. 314–317

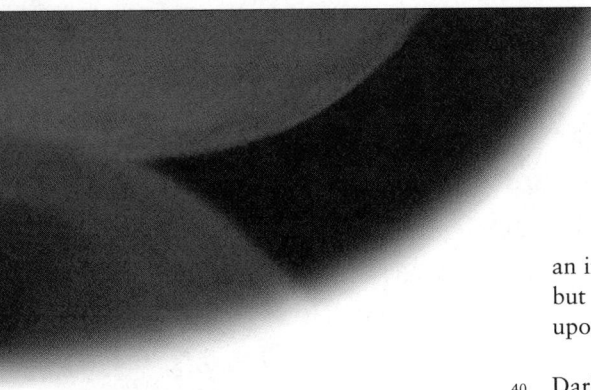

CUSTOMIZING FOR

Gifted and Talented Students

Have students note that both poems are written by African-American female poets. Ask students to discuss whether they feel the speakers of the poems express positive or negative feelings toward those having white skin. Have students support their answers with details from the poems.

20 Brown as I am, she is browner.
Walnut
like the satin leaves of the oak
that fallen overwinter in woods
where night comes quickly
25 and whose wind-peaked piles
deepen the shadows of
such seizure.

Moreover, she is tall.
At her side standing
30 I feel I am still
that scarecrow child of
yesteryear:
owl-eyed
toothed, boned, and angled
35 opposite to her
soft southern presence—

an inaudible[2] allegiance
but sweetening her attendance
upon strangers and friends.

40 Dark hair, dark skin
these are the dominant measures of
my sense of beauty
which explains possibly
why being a black girl
45 in a country of white strangers
I am so pleased with myself.

---

2. **inaudible** (ĭn-ô′də-bəl): impossible to hear.

Literary Concept:
FIGURATIVE LANGUAGE

A Ask students to identify the figure of speech and the two things that it compares. *(Possible response: a simile, which compares the color of the mother's skin to the brown of fallen oak leaves)*

Critical Thinking: SPECULATING

B Ask students to discuss what they think the speaker's feelings about herself would have been like if she were not so attached to her mother. *(Possible response: She may not have been as pleased with herself, since much of her self-esteem is due to her mother's influence.)*

FROM PERSONAL RESPONSE TO CRITICAL ANALYSIS

REFLECT
1. What images of the speaker or her mother linger in your mind? Describe or sketch the images in your notebook. Then share them with a partner.

RETHINK
2. How would you explain why the speaker is so pleased with herself?
   Consider
   • her opinion of "commercial virtues"
   • her own sense of beauty
   • how she regards her appearance

3. What words would you use to describe the speaker's relationship with her mother?

4. What advice do you think the speaker might give to parents about increasing a child's self-esteem?

THE WAY IT IS   **561**

From Personal Response to Critical Analysis

1. Possible responses: the mother's black hair, dark color, and carriage; the speaker's smallness and thinness
2. Possible responses: She sees beyond the commercial standards of beauty; she's proud because her looks are like those of her mother; black features are beautiful.
3. Possible responses: great attachment, admiration, love, adoration, respect
4. Possible response: Develop your own self-respect, and your child will develop self-esteem from your example.

Mini-Lesson   Genre Study

POETRY Review with students that poetry is a type of literature that expresses ideas and feelings in compact and imaginative language. Poets combine words in patterns to touch the reader's senses, emotions, and mind. **Lyric poems** are poems that contain language and rhythmic patterns that are often described as musical. Modern rap may be considered an example of lyric poetry.

Application Have the class perform a choral reading of one of the poems. Ask students which words or phrases they would describe as musical. Then have students write their own lyric poems, describing someone they admire. Encourage them to test the musical qualities of their words and phrases by reading them aloud. Remind them that lyric poems need not rhyme.

Literary Concept: TONE

C Tell students that a writer's attitude toward his or her subject is called tone. Ask students how they would describe the tone of the first five lines of the poem. *(Possible responses: arguing, angry, insistent)*

Literary Concept: FREE VERSE

D Remind students that poetry without regular patterns of rhyme and rhythm is called free verse. Have students read aloud several lines from this poem and discuss how they capture the sounds and rhythms of ordinary speech.

WITHOUT
Commercials

BY ALICE WALKER

C
Listen,
stop tanning yourself
and talking about
fishbelly
5 white.
The color white
is not bad at all.
There are white mornings
that bring us days.
10 Or, if you must,
tan only because
it makes you happy
to be brown,
to be able to see
15 for a summer
the whole world's
darker
face
reflected
20 in your own.

*

Stop unfolding
your eyes.
Your eyes are
beautiful.
25 Sometimes
D seeing you in the street
the fold zany[1]
and unexpected
I want to kiss
30 them

and usually
it is only
old
gorgeous
35 black people's eyes
I want
to kiss.

**

Stop trimming
your nose.
40 When you
diminish
your nose
your songs
become little
45 tinny, muted
and snub.
Better you should
have a nose
impertinent[2]
50 as a flower,
sensitive
as a root;
wise, elegant,
serious and deep.
55 A nose that
sniffs
the essence

---

1. **zany:** comical in a crazy way.
2. **impertinent** (ĭm-pûr′tn-ənt): improperly bold.

Mini-Lesson: Speaking,   Listening, and Viewing

DRAMATIC READING Remind students that in presenting a dramatic reading of a poem they enact the role of the speaker. Tell students not to stop at the end of a line or let their voices drop if the sentence continues onto the next line.

Application Have students prepare a dramatic reading of one of the two poems. Suggest that they begin by considering what they know about the speaker and reviewing what they learned about tone under Literary Concepts. Have students rehearse and then present a dramatic reading to the class.

As for me,
I have learned
to worship
the sun
90 again.
To affirm[3]
the adventures
of hair.

For we are all
95 *splendid*
descendants
of Wilderness,
Eden:
needing only
100 to see
each other
without
commercials
to believe. **E** **2**
105 Copied skillfully **F**
as Adam.

Original

as Eve.

of Earth. And knows
the message
60 of every
leaf.
        * * *
Stop bleaching
your skin
and talking
65 about
so much black
is not beautiful.
The color black
is not bad
70 at all.
There are black nights
that rock
us
in dreams.
75 Or, if you must,
bleach only
because it pleases you
to be brown,
to be able to see
80 for as long
as you can bear it
the whole world's
lighter face
reflected
85 in your own.
        * * * *

---

3. **affirm:** to declare positively; support.

WITHOUT COMMERCIALS **563**

CUSTOMIZING FOR

Students Acquiring English

② Students from some other cultures may need background information about the Biblical account of Adam and Eve.

STRATEGIC READING FOR

Less-Proficient Readers

F Help students understand that both the speakers believe in their own self-worth.

• How does each speaker learn to like her own appearance? (*The first speaker admires her mother's beauty; the second speaker believes that we are all descended from the same divine source.*) **Drawing Conclusions**

CUSTOMIZING FOR

Gifted and Talented Students

Ask each student to write a short stanza that might be added to this poem in which he or she elaborate on the poet's message about how people should feel about themselves. Encourage students to use a style similar to the poet's.

COMPREHENSION CHECK

1. From whom does the speaker of the first poem learn her standards of beauty? (*her mother*)
2. What commercial virtues does the speaker reject for herself? (*being blond, blue eyed, and white skinned*)
3. What are some things the speaker of the second poem says people should stop doing to change their appearance? (*tanning, altering their nose, bleaching their skin*)
4. What has the speaker of the second poem learned to do? (*worship the sun and "affirm the adventures of hair"*)

Assessment ✓ **Option**

INFORMAL ASSESSMENT You can informally assess students' understanding of the poems by having them write a paragraph about the influence of advertising on people's feelings about their appearance.

Rubric

3 Full Accomplishment Students clearly and convincingly describe the effects of advertising on people's feelings about their appearance.

2 Substantial Accomplishment Students provide a description that is clear but needs more details.

1 Little or Partial Accomplishment Students have difficulty describing the commercial standards of beauty and their influence on people's perceptions.

From Personal Response to Critical Analysis

1. Possible responses: sensible, inspiring, joyous, provocative
2. Possible response: Relationships might improve since each person would be valued for what he or she is, not for how well he or she matches the commercial ideal of beauty.
3. Possible response: Commercials tell you to buy things to change yourself to achieve an ideal of beauty, whereas the poet says you're fine as you are. Commercial standards are often unattainable, whereas the speaker's standards foster a deep sense of self-esteem.
4. Possible response: "Without Commercials" because its advice is universal, not based on respect for a loved one
5. Possible response: She is "Walnut/ like the satin leaves of the oak"; this simile describes brown skin as soft and beautiful.

Another Pathway

Cooperative Learning Divide the class into groups of six. Assign one student the role of the talk-show host and two students the roles of the poems' speakers. Have three students portray actors who discuss how their looks affect the kinds of roles they get. After questioning the show's guests, the host should take questions from the class acting as the audience.

Rubric

3 Full Accomplishment All students adhere to their roles and present likely arguments on standards of beauty.

2 Substantial Accomplishment Students adhere to their roles but sometimes stray from the poems' messages and subjects.

1 Little or Partial Accomplishment Students rarely stay in character, and extraneous subjects dominate the dialogues.

RESPONDING
OPTIONS

FROM **PERSONAL RESPONSE** TO **CRITICAL ANALYSIS**

REFLECT
1. In your notebook list three or four words that describe your impressions of the speaker's advice in "Without Commercials."

RETHINK
2. According to the speaker, people need "to see / each other / without / commercials." What if people did this? How do you think their relationships with others might change?

3. How would you compare the speaker's standard of beauty with the one that TV commercials promote?
   Consider
   • her advice about not changing personal appearance
   • the ideas you discussed for the Personal Connection on page 559

Close Textural Reading

RELATE
4. Imagine that a friend of yours seems too concerned about his or her looks. Which of the poems—"The Way It Is" or "Without Commercials"—might benefit your friend more? Why?

Thematic Link

5. Each poem contains vivid examples of **figurative language.** Choose an example that you consider particularly meaningful, and explain why.

LITERARY CONCEPTS

A writer's attitude toward his or her subject is called **tone.** For example, a writer's tone may be angry, bitter, admiring, or humorous, depending on how he or she feels about the subject. You can figure out the tone by examining the word choice and the kinds of statements the writer makes. How would you describe Oden's tone? How would you describe Walker's?

Multimodal Learning
ANOTHER PATHWAY

Cooperative Learning
With a group of classmates, present a talk-show program on standards of beauty. Three members should role-play the host and the speakers of the poems. Others should portray actors and actresses and members of the audience.

QUICKWRITES

1. Suppose you were a plastic surgeon or the owner of a cosmetics company. What would you say to the speaker of "Without Commercials"? Write a **rebuttal** that defends a person's right to change his or her appearance.

2. Write a **letter** to either poet expressing your opinion about the standard of beauty that her poem conveys.

3. In "Without Commercials," Alice Walker writes, "For we are all / *splendid* / descendants / of Wilderness, / Eden." Write a **personal response,** explaining what these lines mean to you.

📁 *PORTFOLIO Save your writing. You may want to use it later as a springboard to a piece for your portfolio.*

Literary Concepts

After students have determined the tone of each poem, they can brainstorm a list of other attitudes that the poets might have taken toward the subject. *(Possible responses: Oden's tone is adoring, and Walker's tone is instructive and inspiring.)*

QuickWrites

1. Remind students that a rebuttal is an argument that supports an opposing point of view.
2. Ensure that students cite examples from the poem in their letter and explain why they agree or disagree with the standard of beauty that each poet suggests.
3. Tell students that they are free to interpret these lines in terms of religion (the Bible) or as a metaphor for our common origin and worth.

 **The Writer's Craft**

Supporting Opinions, pp. 144–151
Letter Forms, p. 669
Personal Voice, pp. 312–313

ALTERNATIVE ACTIVITIES

1. Using pictures from newspapers and magazines, create a **collage** based on the theme of "Without Commercials."

2. In a space of a week, notice the number of TV commercials that attempt to motivate people to change their looks. Keep a list of the products and suggested changes in appearance. Select one of the changes and write a new **stanza** for "Without Commercials" in response to it. Read your stanza to the class.

LITERARY LINKS

In "The Revolt of the Evil Fairies," on page 550, the narrator suffers discrimination because of his dark skin. Which poem do you think he might recommend to have read aloud at his graduation ceremony? Why?

ACROSS THE CURRICULUM

 Science Research a type of cosmetic surgery listed in the Cultural Connection on page 559. Consider using a computer encyclopedia as a research tool. If possible, interview a plastic surgeon about the steps involved in the procedure, possible side effects or things that can go wrong, the cost, and the average recovery time for the patient. If the surgeon gives you permission, have a classmate videotape the interview. Show the tape to the rest of your classmates.

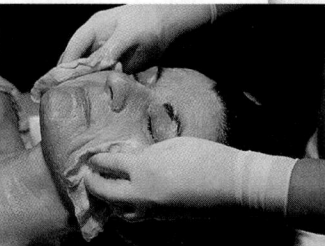

Preparation for cosmetic surgery. Copyright © 1993 S. Jezerniak/Custom Medical Stock Photo.

ALICE WALKER

1944–

When Alice Walker was eight, she was accidentally blinded in one eye by a BB-gun pellet, which left the eye badly scarred. She turned to writing as a refuge from her classmates' stares and taunts and didn't look anyone in the eye for six years. However, the injury enabled her "really to see people and things, really to notice relationships and care about how they turned out." When she was 14, the scar tissue was removed. "Almost immediately," she says, "I [became] a different person from the girl who [did] not raise her head." Newly confident, she not only began to make friends but also went on to become valedictorian of her high school class.

Walker has published novels, biographies, essays, poetry, and short stories. Probably her best-known work is *The Color Purple,* the novel that won a Pulitzer Prize and a National Book Award.
OTHER WORKS "Women," "Everyday Use"

GLORIA ODEN

1923–

Gloria Oden was born in Yonkers, New York. She received a law degree from Howard University in 1948, then she published her first book of poems in 1952. She went on to work as an editor of scientific journals, technical magazines, and college math and science textbooks. Since the 1970s she has been a professor at the University of Maryland and a visiting lecturer and poetry reader at several colleges throughout the United States. Oden is the award-winning author of two other books of poetry, additional poems and articles in anthologies and periodicals, and the script for the film "Poetry Is Alive and Well and Living in America."

Possible responses: He'd prefer Walker's poem because the speaker insists that any color is beautiful. He'd prefer Oden's poem because the speaker says that dark skin is her measure of beauty.

Science Suggest that students also look in medical books and magazine articles for information on cosmetic surgery. If they can't locate a plastic surgeon, have students contact the state board of plastic surgeons or a consumer health information service for information.

ADDITIONAL SUGGESTIONS

 History *Eye of the Beholder* Have students research how the ideal of feminine beauty has changed over time in Western culture. Suggest that they investigate art and fashion history books as well as encyclopedias. Have students present their findings as a class bulletin that includes pictures from books or magazines.

Alice Walker's work often explores the theme of hope in the midst of despair. Although her central characters are almost always black women, the impact of her writing is felt across both racial and gender boundaries.

Gloria Oden's poems have been published in prestigious literary journals. In 1984 she was awarded Townson State University's Distinguished Black Women's Award.

Alternative Activities

1. Provide students with magazines or newspapers from which they can cut out pictures. To prompt students, suggest that they create a collage around the theme "Celebrate Yourself" or one that contrasts commercial standards of beauty with the way people really look.

2. Have students create a chart they can use to record what they observe in TV commercials. Help them brainstorm practical heads and categories for the chart. At the end of the week, have students create a cumulative class chart and analyze it to determine how ads promote an unrealistic standard of beauty.

OVERVIEW

Objectives

- To understand and appreciate a science fiction story about a character who cannot resist a tempting food
- To enrich reading by using active reading strategies
- To identify and understand science fiction
- To express understanding of the story through a choice of writing forms, including an explanation, a plan, and an advertisement
- To extend understanding of the selection through a variety of multimodal and cross-curricular activities

Skills

READING SKILLS/STRATEGIES
- Predict

THE WRITER'S STYLE
- Point of view

GRAMMAR
- Punctuating compound sentences

LITERARY CONCEPTS
- Science fiction
- Mood

SPELLING
- Soft and hard g and c

SPEAKING, LISTENING, AND VIEWING
- Group discussion

Cross-Curricular Connections

HEALTH
- Calories and fat

SOCIAL STUDIES
- The Food and Drug Administration

ART
- Alien bracelets

ALTERNATIVE

Previewing

Have students choose partners and use the following prompts to preview "Lose Now, Pay Later" orally.

Personal Connection

Discussion Prompts *Define and then discuss what willpower is and how it is connected to dieting. Discuss why it's so hard to resist certain foods—particularly fats and sweets—that tend to make you gain weight. Use the following questions to start your discussion:*

- *What are your favorite foods?*

- *How much self-control do you have when it comes to resisting these foods?*

As you read the selection, think about how much self-control the main character has.

FICTION

Lose Now, Pay Later

Carol Farley

Activating Prior Knowledge / Setting a Purpose
PERSONAL CONNECTION

Is there any one food that you simply cannot resist? For example, if a freshly baked pizza with your favorite toppings were put in front of you now, would you devour it—even if you were on a diet? In your notebook, list some of your favorite foods. Which of those foods are most likely to cause you to lose self-control? On a scale like the one shown, rank them according to the level of temptation they pose. Then as you read, think about how much self-control the characters in this story have.

Food Temptation Scale

Low ———————————————————————— High

Building Background
CULTURAL CONNECTION

Resisting tempting food takes willpower; therefore, people who lack self-control can gain weight quickly. Partly for this reason, dieting has become one of our society's strongest obsessions. At any given time, more than 20 million people in the United States are on a diet. In 1992, Americans spent about 36 billion dollars on diet products and weight-loss programs. (Between 5 billion and 6 billion of those dollars were spent on fraudulent products.) Although dieters lose millions of pounds every year, about 95 percent of them regain the lost weight. To lose weight and keep it off, people must change their eating habits and must exercise regularly. However, most dieters try to lose weight rapidly, usually resulting in only a temporary victory.

Active Reading
READING CONNECTION

Predicting You probably often use the clues in a story and your own knowledge or experience to help you predict what will happen in realistic fiction. Predicting what will happen in a science fiction story like "Lose Now, Pay Later" can be a bit different, however. Science fiction stories are often set in some future time and place that exist only in a writer's imagination, so a story might mention scientific or technological equipment that doesn't really exist, or characters who possess some unusual characteristics or powers. As a reader, then, you are forced to base your predictions more upon guessing than upon your own knowledge. Using the title and the illustrations as clues, what do you predict this science fiction story will be about?

566   UNIT FIVE   PART 1: APPEARANCES TO THE CONTRARY

PRINT AND MEDIA RESOURCES

UNIT FIVE RESOURCE BOOK
Strategic Reading: Literature, p. 21
Vocabulary SkillBuilder, p. 24
Reading SkillBuilder, p. 22
Spelling SkillBuilder, p. 23

GRAMMAR MINI–LESSONS
Transparencies, p. 28
Copymasters, p. 37

WRITING MINI–LESSONS
Transparencies, p. 47

ACCESS FOR STUDENTS ACQUIRING ENGLISH
Selection Summaries
Reading and Writing Support

FORMAL ASSESSMENT
Selection Test, pp. 107–108
 Test Generator

 **AUDIO LIBRARY**
See Reference Card

LOSE NOW, PAY LATER

by Carol Farley

I think my little brother is crazy. At least I hope he is.

Because if his looney idea is right, then all of us are being

used like a flock of sheep, and that's a pretty gruesome

thought. Humans just can't be that stupid. My brother has

a dumb idea, that's all. It's just a dumb idea.

LOSE NOW, PAY LATER **567**

SUMMARY

The year is 2041, and swoodie shops are opening all over Earth. The narrator, Deb, and her best friend Trinja are among the first customers at the local swoodie shop, where machines mysteriously create free swoodies, which are similar to pudding. Soon almost everybody is lining up for swoodies—and gaining weight at an alarming rate. One day, Deb and Trinja discover a solution to their weight problem: a "slimmer" machine that removes extra weight for twenty-five yen a pound. The slimmer works instantly; afterwards customers receive a tiny blue mark for every ten pounds lost. Like the swoodie shops, slimmers become an instant success and open up in many areas. The only person skeptical about swoodies and slimmers is Deb's little brother. He thinks they may both be run by space aliens in invisible ships who are gathering up energy from human fat to use as fuel. According to his theory, swoodies, slimmers, and blue marks are part of this fat-harvesting process. Deb—with doubt in her voice—protests that people are not stupid enough to give up their freedom and dignity just so they can eat delicious treats and still stay thin. Meanwhile, her addiction to the machines provides evidence for her brother's theory.

Thematic Link: *Appearances to the Contrary* Deb and her friend believe they have found an easy way to lose weight and improve their appearance—but have they really?

CUSTOMIZING FOR

Students Acquiring English

- Use **ACCESS FOR STUDENTS ACQUIRING ENGLISH**, *Reading and Writing Support*.

- Point out that the title plays on an ad slogan: "Buy now, pay later," which encourages consumers to buy things on credit. Help students understand the two meanings of the verb *pay*: "to exchange money for" and "to be punished for."

STRATEGIC READING FOR

Less-Proficient Readers

Set a Purpose Have students read to find out what is strange about the swoodies and the slimmer.

Use **UNIT FIVE RESOURCE BOOK**, p. 21, for guidance in reading the selection.

WORDS TO KNOW

binge (bĭnj) *n.* a period of uncontrolled eating or drinking (p. 569)

cull (kŭl) *v.* to remove someone or something from the rest of a group (p. 572)

gullible (gŭl′ə-bəl) *adj.* easily fooled or tricked (p. 570)

placid (plăs′ĭd) *adj.* calm; at peace (p. 572)

scam (skăm) *n.* a dishonest business scheme; swindle (p. 570)

Art Note

Untitled (Ice Cream Dessert) by Andy Warhol Warhol (1928–1987) was one of America's most famous Pop artists. Warhol painted common, often commercial, subjects—including soup cans and celebrity portraits—in a highly realistic style.

Reading the Art *How would you describe the ice cream and desserts to a friend? Do they make you feel hungry? Why or why not?*

Literary Concept: MOOD

A Remind students that mood is the feeling that a literary work creates in the reader. Ask students what mood or atmosphere this description of the swoodies store creates. *(Possible response: The enticing aromas wafting from the store create a mood of allurement.)*

Untitled (Ice Cream Dessert) (1959), Andy Warhol. Copyright © 1996 Andy Warhol Foundation for the Visual Arts/ARS, New York.

This whole situation started about eight months ago. That's when I first knew anything about it, I mean. My best friend, Trinja, and I were shopping when we noticed a new store where an old insurance office used to be. It was a cubbyhole, really, at the far end of the mall where hardly anybody ever goes. We were there because we'd used that entrance as we came home from school.

"Swoodies!" Trinja said, pointing at the letters written across the display window. "What do you think they are, Deb?"

I stared through the glass. The place had always looked dim and dingy before, full of desks, half-dead plants, and bored-looking people; but now it was as bright and glaring as a Health Brigade Corp office. There weren't any people inside at all, but there were five or six gold-colored machines lining the walls. Signs were hung everywhere.

SWEETS PLUS GOODIES = SWOODIES, one said. Flavors were posted by each machine; peanut-butter-fudge-crunch . . . butter-rum-pecan . . . chocolate-nut-mint . . . Things like that. The biggest sign of all simply said FREE.

I have to admit that the place gave me the creeps that first time I saw it. I don't know why. It just looked so bare and bright, so empty and clean, without any people or movement. The glare almost hurt my eyes. And I guess I was suspicious about anything that was completely free. Still, though, there was a terrific aroma drifting out of there—sort of a

The biggest sign of all simply said

FREE

combination of all those flavors that were listed on the signs.

"Let's go in," Trinja said, grabbing my arm. I could see that the smell was getting to her too. She's always on a diet, so she thinks about food a lot.

"But it's so empty in there," I said, drawing away.

"They've just opened, that's all," she told me, yanking my arm again. "Besides, machines and robots run lots of the stores. Let's go inside and see what's in there."

Do you know that wonderful spurt of air that rushes out when you first open an expensive box of candy? The inside of that store smelled just like the inside of one of those boxes. For a few seconds we just stood there sniffing and grinning. My salivary glands[1] started swimming.

Trinja turned toward the nearest machine. "Coconut-almond-marshmallow." She was almost drooling. "I've got to try one, Deb." She pressed the button, and a chocolate cone dropped down, like a coffee cup from a kitcho machine. Then a mixture, similar to the look of soft ice cream, filled it. "Want to try it with me?" she asked, reaching for the cone. We both took a taste.

It was absolutely the neatest sensation I've had in my whole life. Swoodies aren't cold like

---

1. **salivary** (săl′ə-vĕr′ē) **glands:** the body organs that produce saliva.

Mini-Lesson ✦ **Literary Concepts**

REVIEWING MOOD Remind students that mood, or atmosphere, is the feeling that a literary work conveys to readers. Writers can use a variety of techniques to establish the mood—word choice, dialogue, description, and plot events. Refer students to the highlighted passage above. Emphasize the way in which the writer creates an eerie but enticing mood in this passage through the description of the swoodies store and the narrator's reaction to it.

Application Have students pretend that they will be directing a TV adaptation of this story, guiding the actors to express the mood of each scene. Then

have students work in small groups to complete charts like the one shown, listing events in the story and the mood each creates. Make sure students support their ideas with details from the selection.

Event	Mood	Details

ice cream or warm like cooked pudding, but they're a blending of both in temperature and texture. The flavor melts instantly, and your whole mouth and brain are flooded with tastes and impressions. Like that first swoodie I tried, coconut-almond-marshmallow; suddenly, as my mouth separated the individual tastes, my brain burst into memories associated with each flavor. I felt as if I were lying on a warm beach, all covered with coconut suntan oil—then I heard myself giggling and singing as a group of us roasted marshmallows around a campfire—then I relived the long-ago moments of biting into the special Christmas cookies my grandmother made with almonds when I was little.

"Wow!" Trinja looked at me, and I could see that she had just experienced the same kind of reactions. We scarfed[2] up the rest of that swoodie in just a few more bites, and we moved on to another flavor. With each one it was the same. I felt a combination of marvelous tastes and joyous thoughts. We tried every flavor before we finally staggered out into the mall again.

"I'll have to diet for a whole year now," Trinja said, patting her stomach.

"I feel like a blimp myself," I told her, but neither one of us cared. We both felt terrific. "Go ahead in there," I called to some grade-school kids who were looking at the store. "You'll love those swoodies."

"It's a publicity stunt, we think," Trinja told them. "Everything is free in there."

In no time at all the news about the swoodie shop had spread all over town. But days passed, and still everything was absolutely free. Nobody knew who the new owners were or why they were giving away their product. Nobody cared. The mall directors said a check arrived to pay for the rent, and that was all they were concerned about. The Health Brigade Corp said swoodies were absolutely safe for human consumption.

Swoodies were still being offered free a month later, but the shop owners had still not appeared. By then nobody cared. There were always long lines of people in front of the place, but the swoodies tasted so good nobody minded waiting for them. And the supply was endless. Soon more shops like the first one began opening in other places around the city, with machines running in the same quiet, efficient way. And everything was still absolutely free.

Soon all of us were gaining weight like crazy.

"It's those darn swoodies," Trinja told me as we left the mall after our daily binge. "I can't leave them alone. Each one must have a thousand calories, but I still pig out on them."

I sighed as I walked out into the sunshine. "Me too. If only there was some easy way to eat all the swoodies we want and still not gain any weight!"

The words were hardly out of my mouth when I noticed a new feature in the mall parking lot. Among all the usual heliobiles there was a tall white plastic box, sort of like those big

---

2. **scarfed:** a slang term meaning "ate eagerly."

> WORDS
> TO
> KNOW
>
> **binge** (bĭnj) *n.* a period of uncontrolled eating or drinking

569

B Tell students science fiction is based on real or imagined scientific developments and is often set in the future. Ask students what they can infer about the world of the future based on details that the author provides in this paragraph. *(Possible responses: People still suntan, roast marshmallows, have campfires, and celebrate Christmas.)*

Critical Thinking: SPECULATING

C Have students use their understanding of science fiction to speculate about who or what might own these stores, and what might be the motive for opening stores that offer free, magical desserts. *(Possible response: A sinister organization has opened these stores in an attempt to control the population.)*

Linking to Social Studies

D The present-day equivalent of the "Health Brigade Corp" is the Food and Drug Administration. Established in 1928, it is a federal agency responsible for protecting public health by ensuring the safety of the food, medicines, and cosmetics people consume and use.

CUSTOMIZING FOR
Students Acquiring English

I Point out to students that *heliobiles* don't exist now, but the author coins words for things that she imagines existing in the year 2041. You may wish to have students infer possible meanings of this word based on the prefix *helio-* (sun) and *bile* (from *mobile,* meaning "movement or transportation").

| Mini-Lesson | | Grammar |

PUNCTUATING COMPOUND SENTENCES Tell students that when two complete sentences are combined, the first period is eliminated, and the sentences are joined by a coordinating conjunction preceded by a comma. Share with students the chart that lists coordinating conjunctions.

Application Have students join the following pairs of sentences to form compound sentences.
1. I'm always on a diet. I think about pizza all the time.
2. We ate chocolate swoodies first. We ate vanilla swoodies second.

3. I was afraid to enter the slimmer. The strange lady pushed me inside.
4. I want to eat all the swoodies I can. I don't want to gain weight.
5. Nobody understands how slimmers work. Nobody cares.

Reteaching/Reinforcement
- Grammar Handbook, anthology pp. 879–880
- *Grammar Mini-Lessons* copymasters p. 37, transparencies p. 28

The Writer's Craft
Combining Complete Sentences, pp. 300–301

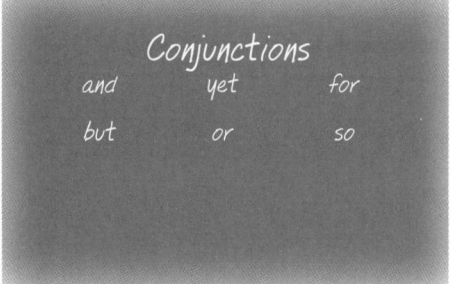

Conjunctions

| and | yet | for |
| but | or | so |

telephone booths you see in old pictures. A flashing sign near the booth said THE SLIMMER. A short, thin woman was standing beside it. She was deeply tanned, and her head was covered with a green turban almost the same color as the jumpsuit she was wearing.

Trinja looked at the sign, then glanced at the woman. "What's that mean?"

"It means that this machine can make you slimmer," the woman answered. She had a deep, strange-sounding voice. "Just step inside, and you'll lose unwanted fat."

She seemed so serious and confident that I was startled. In the old days people thought they could lose weight in a hurry, but those of us who live in 2041 aren't that <u>gullible</u>. No pills or packs or wraps or special twenty-four-hour diets can work. There isn't any easy way to get rid of fat, and that's all there is to it. I knew this booth was a <u>scam</u> or a joke of some kind, but the woman acted as if it were a perfectly respectable thing. Her seriousness sort of unnerved me. I looked into the booth half expecting someone to jump out laughing. But it was empty, stark white, and, except for some overhead grill work, it was completely smooth and bare.

"How can a thing like this make you slimmer?" I asked.

The woman shrugged. "A new process. Do you care to try? Twenty-five yen to lose one pound of body fat."

Trinja and I both burst into laughter. "And how long is it before the pound disappears?" she asked.

The woman never even cracked a smile. "Instantly. Body fat is gone instantly." She gestured to a small lever on the side nearest to her. "I regulate the power flow according to your payment."

My mouth dropped open. "But that's impossible! No exercise? No chemicals? No starving on a retreat week?"

"No." The woman folded her arms and leaned against the smooth white sides of her cubicle, as if she didn't much care whether we tried her new process or not. Trinja and I stared at each other. I was wondering if the woman had tried her machine herself—she didn't have an ounce of fat.

"You got any money?" I asked Trinja. As she was shaking her head, I was rummaging through my pack. "I've got a hundred and thirty yen."

"Five pounds then," the woman said, taking my money with one hand and setting her lever with the other. She literally pushed me into the booth, and the door slammed behind me.

At first I wanted to scream because I was so scared. The whole thing had happened too fast. I wanted to prove that this woman and her slimmer were a big joke, but suddenly I was trapped in a coffinlike structure as bare and as bright as an old microwave oven. My heart was hammering, and the hair on the back of my neck stood up straight. I opened my mouth, but before I could scream, there was a loud humming sound, and instantly the door flew open again. I saw Trinja's frightened face peering in at me.

"Are you all right, Deb? Are you okay? I guess

| WORDS TO KNOW | **gullible** (gŭl'ə-bəl) *adj.* easily fooled or tricked |
| | **scam** (skăm) *n.* a dishonest business scheme; swindle |

570

Mini-Lesson ⬦ **Reading Skills/Strategies**

ACTIVE READING: PREDICT Remind students that active readers enhance their enjoyment of a story by trying to predict what will happen based on clues the writer gives about setting, character, and action.

Application Have students discuss if they were able to predict how the story would end. Make sure students refer to specific details from the selection that they used in making their predictions.

Reteaching/Reinforcement
• *Unit Five Resource Book,* p. 22

she decided not to do anything after all. You ought to get your money back."

"Five pounds are gone," the woman said in her strange voice.

Trinja pulled me away. "I'll just bet!" she shouted back at the woman. "Somebody ought to report you and that phony machine! We might even call the Health Brigade Corp!" She leaned closer to me. "Are you really okay, Deb?"

I took a deep breath. "My jeans feel loose."

Frowning, Trinja shook her head. "It's just your imagination, that's all. What a fake! I think that woman was wacko, Debbie, really weird. The only thing slimmer after a treatment like that is your bank account. Nobody but nobody can lose weight that easily. We'll go to my house, and you can weigh yourself. You haven't lost an ounce."

But Trinja was wrong. I really *was* five pounds lighter. I know it sounds impossible, but Trinja's calshow is never wrong. The two of us hopped and howled with joy. Then we ravaged[3] her bedroom trying to find some more money. We ran all the way back to the mall, worrying all the way that the woman and her miracle machine might have disappeared. But the slimmer was still there. Within minutes Trinja had used up her three hundred yen, and she looked terrific.

"I can't believe it! I just can't believe it!" she kept saying as she notched her belt tighter. "Twelve pounds gone in seconds!"

Body fat is gone

INSTANTLY

"For safety's sake I'll have to prick your wrist, my dear," the woman said. "For every ten pounds you lose we give a tiny little mark. Nobody will ever notice it."

"It didn't even hurt," Trinja said as we walked home. And neither of us could see the tiny blue pinprick unless we looked closely. We were both so happy about the weight loss that we almost floated. All our worries and problems about calories and fat and diets were over forever.

In no time at all the slimmers were all over the city, near all the swoodie stores. They've been a real blessing. Everybody says so. Now there's hardly a fat person left on the streets. A few people have so many blue marks on their wrists that you can see them, but most have just four or five pinpricks.

Nobody really understands how these slimmers work. The attendants, all just as strange sounding as the woman in our mall, get so technical in their explanations that none of us can follow the principles they're talking about, so we don't much worry about it. The process has something to do with invisible waves that can change fat cells into energy, which then radiates away from the body.

"I don't care how the slimmers work," Trinja says happily. "Now I can eat swoodies all day

---

3. **ravaged:** attacked violently, causing severe damage.

Active Reading: CLARIFY

H Remind students that context clues are words or phrases before or after an unfamiliar word that help explain its meaning. Have students use context clues to figure out the meaning of the made-up word *calshow. (scale)* Ask them what words, phrases, or sentences suggest the meaning of the word. *("you can weigh yourself", "I really was five pounds lighter")*

Critical Thinking:
MAKING JUDGMENTS

I Encourage students to decide whether the strange woman pricks the girls' wrists really "for safety's sake." Make sure students explain and support their judgments. *(Possible response: The woman is not being honest, as suggested by her strangeness and the impossibility of what the slimmer does.)*

CUSTOMIZING FOR
Multiple Learning Styles

J **Bodily-Kinesthetic Learners**
Encourage students to enact a session at a slimmer. Have volunteers portray one of the strange attendants who run the booths. Encourage students to apply what they learned from the description of the way the strange woman acts and sounds to portray her or another attendant. Suggest that other students play the parts of likely customers.

Mini-Lesson ✒ **The Writer's Style**

POINT OF VIEW Explain to students that point of view is the vantage point, or angle, from which a story is told. Make sure students understand the difference between first-person point of view in non-fiction, where narrator and writer are the same, and first-person point of view in fiction, where one cannot assume the narrator and the writer are the same.

Application Have students reread the highlighted passage and describe how the writer re-creates the point of view of a teenage girl. Then have them rewrite this passage using the first-person point of

view of Deb's ten-year-old brother, Trevor. Students should consider what they know about Trevor specifically and ten-year-old boys in general.

Reteaching/Reinforcement
• Writing Handbook, anthology pp. 824–825
• *Writing Mini-Lessons* transparencies, p. 47

📕 **The Writer's Craft**

Point of View, pp. 318–319

long if I want, and I never gain an ounce. That's all I care about."

Everybody feels that way, I guess. We're too happy to want to upset anything by asking questions. Maybe that's why you don't hear about the swoodies or slimmers on the fax or the bodivision or read about them anywhere. Nobody understands them well enough to sound very intelligent about them. But people all over Earth are beginning to use them. My cousin in Tokyo faxed to say that they have them in her area now and people there are just as happy as we are.

Except for my brother, Trevor. He's not the least bit happy, he says. Of course, few ten-year-olds worry about weight, so he doesn't know the joy of being able to eat everything in sight and still stay thin.

"Suppose the swoodies and the slimmers are run by aliens from outer space," he says. "From lots farther than we've been able to go. Maybe they have big starships posted around Earth, and they're gathering up the energy from human fat that's sent up from the slimmers. Maybe the swoodies are here so people will get fat quicker so that there'll be more to harvest through the slimmer machines. Then they'll take the fat

back to their planet and use it as fuel."

"That's the dumbest thing I ever heard of!" Trinja has told him. "Why don't we hear about the spaceships, then? Why doesn't the Health Brigade Corp tell us to stop doing this if it isn't good for us?"

Trevor thinks he has the answers. He says the spaceships are invisible to human detection, and he says the aliens have hypnotized our leaders into being as calm and placid as we all are. The blue marks on our wrists play a big role. He says maybe after each of us has had so many blue marks, we'll be culled from the flock because our fat content won't be as good anymore.

He's crazy, isn't he? He must think we all have the brains of sheep. Ten-year-old brothers can be a real pain. He simply doesn't know people yet, that's all. Humans would never sacrifice their freedom and dignity just so they could eat and still be thin. Even aliens ought to know that.

I could quit eating swoodies and using those slimmers any time I want to.

But all those little blue marks Trinja and I have are beginning to look like delicate tattooed bracelets, and we both think they look really neat on our wrists. ❖

We'll be culled from the
FLOCK

WORDS
TO
KNOW

placid (plăs′ĭd) *adj.* calm; at peace
cull (kŭl) *v.* to remove someone or something from the rest of a group

572

Mini-Lesson ⟨TM⟩ **Spelling**

binge (soft g)
gullible (hard g)
scam (hard c)
placid (soft c)
cull (hard c)

HARD AND SOFT *g* and *c* Tell students that the letters *c* and *g* can have a hard sound (as in *cat* or in *goat*) or a soft sound (as in *cell* or in *gene*), depending on the vowel that follows them. The letter *c* is usually soft when followed by an *e* or *i*; otherwise, it's hard. The letter *g* is usually soft when followed by an *e*; otherwise, it's hard.

Application Each of the Words to Know contains a *c* or a *g*. Have students identify whether a hard or soft sound is used.

Ask students to look for more words that fit this pattern, in their own writing and in the things that they read, and to add these words to their personal word lists.

Reteaching/Reinforcement
• *Unit Five Resource Book*, p. 23

RESPONDING
OPTIONS

FROM **PERSONAL RESPONSE** TO **CRITICAL ANALYSIS**

REFLECT 1. What were you thinking as you finished reading this story? Sketch or write your thoughts in your notebook.

RETHINK 2. At the end of the story, Deb says, "Humans would never sacrifice their freedom and dignity just so they could eat and still be thin." Do you agree or disagree with her statement? Why?
Consider
- your own experiences with temptation and self-control
- the popularity of the swoodies and slimmers
- Deb's and Trinja's attitude and behavior in regard to the swoodies and slimmers

Close Textual reading

3. Do you think Deb and Trinja are justified in rejecting Trevor's theory? Why or why not?
Consider
- the title of this story
- the evidence in the story that might support Trevor's theory

Close Textual reading

RELATE 4. What do you think and how do you feel when someone offers you a "freebie" or something that you think is too good to be true? Explain.

Multimodal Learning
ANOTHER PATHWAY

Do you think people can be used or controlled like a flock of sheep, as Trevor suggests? In small groups, discuss the answer to this question. Cite evidence from the story, as well as your own experiences with temptation, instant gratification, and self-control. Have a spokesperson from each group present a summary to the rest of the class.

QUICKWRITES

1. Assume that Trevor's theory about aliens is wrong. Write your own **explanation** that accounts for the presence of the swoodies and slimmer machines.

2. Assume that Trevor's theory about aliens is right. Write the complete **plan** that the aliens are using to obtain fat from humans. Add steps to the ones that Trevor was able to guess.

3. Using the information supplied about swoodies or slimmers, write a newspaper or radio **advertisement** for them.

📁 *PORTFOLIO Save your writing. You may want to use it later as a springboard to a piece for your portfolio.*

LITERARY CONCEPTS

"Lose Now, Pay Later" is a work of science fiction. **Science fiction** stories are frequently based on possible scientific developments and are usually set in the future. Often, realistic characters with values of present-day society are projected into an imaginary world. This lets the reader examine current values in a different setting. What values of our society are reflected in this story? How do you know?

CONCEPT REVIEW: Setting Science fiction writers sometimes use imaginary terms and inventions to set their stories in the future. Find several examples of this in "Lose Now, Pay Later."

LOSE NOW, PAY LATER **573**

Words to Know

1. to cheat people
2. stomach
3. trusting
4. content
5. before

Reteaching/Reinforcement
• *Unit Five Resource Book,* p. 24

Literary Links

Possible response: In this selection, the aliens are exploiting humans' lack of willpower. The author wants us to think of the consequences before we abandon willpower. In *The Monsters Are Due on Maple Street,* the aliens exploit the human tendency to look for a scapegoat in times of trouble. The author's message is to stick together.

Across the Curriculum

Health *Cooperative Learning* Have groups of students consult health and nutrition books and CD-ROM encyclopedias for data. In each group, assign a researcher who locates sources, a student who ensures that all group members gather data, a student who helps interpret collected data, an accuracy coach who ensures that the collected data are correct, and a recorder who writes up the data and prepares the chart. Have a student integrator lead the panel discussion.

ADDITIONAL SUGGESTIONS

Art *Alien Bracelets* Have students design what the blue pinprick wrist marks look like. Encourage them to use their imaginations. For example, their designs can contain symbols, words, or a secret picture that tells the aliens when a person should be culled. Have students show their finished drawings to the class and explain their designs.

ALTERNATIVE ACTIVITIES

1. Imagine an invention that Trevor might make to prevent the slimmers from working. Draw a **sketch** of your invention and present it to the class. Explain how your invention will work.

2. Suppose you were asked to turn this story into a movie. Sketch your **designs** for some futuristic costumes, gadgets, and settings.

ACROSS THE CURRICULUM

Health *Cooperative Learning*
What is a calorie? How many calories do you have to burn to lose one pound of fat? Working in groups, find the answers to these and other questions about diet, exercise, and nutrition. Pool your findings and create a chart showing how many minutes of different kinds of exercise will burn off a set number of calories. Then conduct a panel discussion in which you answer questions from the class.

LITERARY LINKS

Assuming Trevor is right, compare and contrast this story and the play *The Monsters Are Due on Maple Street,* on page 355. What human behaviors and attitudes are the aliens in each selection exploiting? What points do you think each author is trying to make?

WORDS TO KNOW

On a sheet of paper, write answers to the following questions.

1. Is someone who runs a **scam** trying to educate people, to cheat people, or to heal people?

2. If you go on a **binge,** what is most likely to hurt afterwards—your feet, your back, or your stomach?

3. Is a **gullible** person someone who is too impatient, too trusting, or too stubborn?

4. If you are feeling **placid,** are you feeling jealous, feeling hungry, or feeling content?

5. Would someone be most likely to **cull** blueberries before, during, or after making them into jam?

CAROL FARLEY

For Carol Farley, writing is an extension of what she always loved about school. She says that her "happiest memories of school years are centered on classes I had in literature when we read fiction and talked about what we had read."

Farley has done many things besides write, however. She has taught school, picked fruit, and sold women's clothing. As an army wife, she moved 13 times in 15 years. Her varied experiences have taught her that "we all look at life from our own viewpoint,

1936–

often unaware or unconcerned about the views of others." Such concerns prompt her to write stories like "Lose Now, Pay Later" to show "that sometimes small children—like the boy in the story about the emperor's new clothes (or lack of them)—are the first to notice and report on something that is perfectly obvious."

OTHER WORKS *The Most Important Things in the World; Songs in the Night; Korea: Land of Morning Calm; Ms. Isabelle Cornell, Herself*

Extended Reading

Alternative Activities

1. Have students first outline Trevor's theory of how the slimmers work. Then have them design an "anti-slimmer" that counteracts the forces operating in the slimmer, as Trevor understands them.

2. Have students begin by reviewing the selection for details about the clothes, gadgets, and setting. Tell students they can assume that everyday objects are different in some ways from modern-day equivalents. Encourage students to let their imaginations run free.

NONFICTION

from Exploring the *Titanic*
Robert D. Ballard

Activating Prior Knowledge
PERSONAL CONNECTION

The selection you are about to read is an account of the sinking of the great ship *Titanic*, a disaster that shocked the world. What other disasters do you know about? Brainstorm with your classmates, and list the disasters on a web like the one shown. Add any details that you know about any of the disasters.

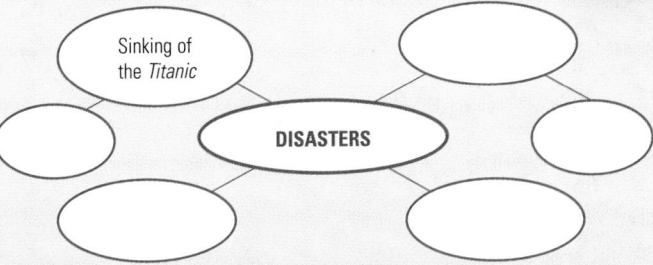

Sinking of the *Titanic*

DISASTERS

Path of Icebergs

GREENLAND

EUROPE

ICELAND

NORTH AMERICA

North Atlantic Ocean

PATH OF ICEBERGS

AVERAGE MAXIMUM LIMIT OF ICEBERGS

Titanic Sank Apr. 14, 1912 ×

N W E S

Miles
0 250 500

Activating Prior Knowledge
HISTORICAL CONNECTION

You probably already know that the *Titanic* sank because it hit an iceberg. Icebergs pose one of the greatest natural threats to ships. This is because the top of an iceberg gets smaller as it melts in the sun, but the underwater part, which is several times larger than the top, dissolves very slowly—and is nearly invisible. Every spring, a large number of icebergs travel through the sea lanes used by ocean liners. The iceberg that sank the *Titanic* was probably a North Atlantic iceberg originating in Greenland. The wreck of the *Titanic* led to the establishment of the International Ice Patrol two years later. Using ships, planes, and satellites, the patrol reports the locations of icebergs and predicts where they might be heading, in order to prevent other disasters at sea.

▶ **LASERLINKS**
• HISTORICAL CONNECTION

575

HISTORICAL CONNECTION
Discovering the *Titanic* The *Titanic* sank in the cold waters of the North Atlantic in 1912. These historical images and artworks will give students more perspective on that tragic event.

Side A, Frame 49422

Fact and Opinion

SUMMARY

On April 10, 1912, the "unsinkable" cruise liner *Titanic* began its maiden voyage from England to New York. The luxuriously furnished *Titanic* was the biggest ship in the world. Its passengers, divided among first-class, second-class, and third-class sections of the ship, included 17-year-old Jack Thayer and 12-year-old Ruth Becker. The first three days of the voyage were smooth; on the fourth day, however, the ship's radio room received repeated warnings of ice ahead. Despite the warnings, Captain Edward J. Smith kept the *Titanic* steaming full-speed ahead. Shortly before midnight, the ship collided with an iceberg, and water began pouring into a hole in the bottom half of the ship. The *Titanic*'s radio operators feverishly signaled for help, but the nearest ship had turned off its radio. The crew began lowering lifeboats into the water at 12:45 A.M. Ruth Becker was one of the lucky passengers who found a place in a lifeboat; more than fifteen hundred others remained behind. By 2:05 A.M., the ship was sinking fast. Jack Thayer jumped off the ship as it slid into the icy North Atlantic waters and pulled himself onto an overturned lifeboat. Both he and Ruth witnessed the terrible final sinking of the *Titanic* and were among the survivors rescued at dawn by a ship called the *Carpathia*.

Thematic Link: *Appearances to the Contrary* The builders, the owners, the crew, and the passengers all believed the *Titanic* was unsinkable. But on April 15, 1912, the ship struck an iceberg and sank to the bottom of the sea.

A **fact** is a statement that can be proved. An **opinion** is a statement that cannot be proved. Study these examples of fact and opinion:

Fact: Between 1880 and 1920, 23 million immigrants arrived in the United States.
Opinion: The voyage was an ordeal, but it was worth it.

You can prove the first statement by looking in a reference book or at immigration statistics. The second statement, however, you cannot prove. It expresses what someone thinks—it is an opinion, not a fact. Opinions reflect personal beliefs and are often debatable. In some kinds of writing, such as news reports, sticking to facts is crucial. In others, such as editorials, reviews, and advertisements, including opinions is important. However, those opinions must be supported by facts.

Opinions often contain **judgment words**—words that express personal feelings or beliefs. See if you can add any judgment words to the list below.

wonderful	horrible	silly	clever
exciting	boring	excellent	terrible

Decide whether each sentence below is a fact or an opinion. Explain how you made each decision.

1. Alice Walker was the daughter of sharecroppers.
2. No poet is better known than Alice Walker.
3. Few things are more important than the ability to read.
4. A love of reading made Malcolm X aware of new ideas.
5. People should accept themselves the way they are.

As you read this selection, consider how Robert Ballard's use of facts and opinions influences your reaction to the disaster. Then when you have finished reading, record some of the facts and opinions on a chart like the one below. For each opinion, list any facts that were used to support it. Two examples have been done for you.

Facts	Opinions	Support for Opinions
On May 31, 1911, the hull of the *Titanic* was launched.		
	The final size and richness of this new ship was astounding.	• 882 feet long (4 city blocks) • 9 decks (high as 11-story building)

WORDS TO KNOW

accommodations (ə-kŏm′ə-dā′shənz) *n.* a room and food, especially in hotels or on ships or trains (p. 578)

dazzled (dăz′əld) *adj.* amazed or overwhelmed by a spectacular display **dazzle** *v.* (p. 579)

eerie (îr′ē) *adj.* weird, especially in a frightening way (p. 578)

feverishly (fē′vər-ĭsh-lē) *adv.* in a highly emotional or nervous way (p. 585)

indefinitely (ĭn-dĕf′ə-nĭt-lē) *adv.* for an unlimited length of time (p. 581)

list (lĭst) *v.* to tilt; lean (p. 586)

novelty (nŏv′əl-tē) *n.* something new, original, or unusual (p. 582)

prophecy (prŏf′ĭ-sē) *n.* a prediction; foretelling of future events (p. 578)

toll (tōl) *n.* the amount of loss or destruction caused by a disaster (p. 589)

tribute (trĭb′yōōt) *n.* an action or gift that honors a deserving individual (p. 579)

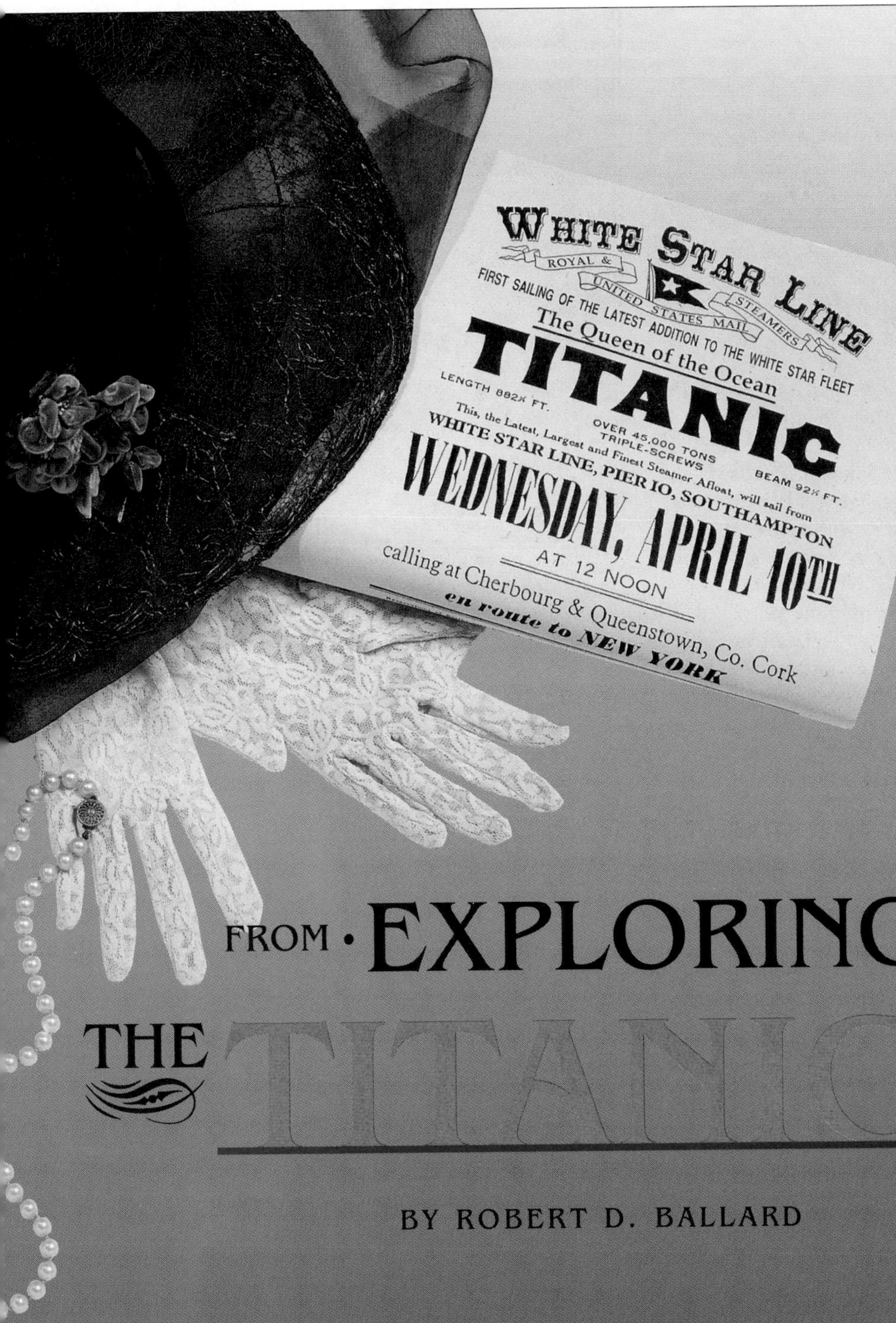

FROM · EXPLORING

THE TITANIC

BY ROBERT D. BALLARD

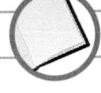

Mini-Lesson — **Reading Skills/Strategies**

DISTINGUISHING FACT AND OPINION
Remind students that a fact is a statement that can be proved. An opinion is a statement that expresses a personal belief. Students may have difficulty distinguishing facts from opinions that are supported by facts. Explain that while opinions can be supported, they cannot be proved. If necessary, review with students the Reading Connection on page 576.

Application After students finish reading the selection, they can complete the fact-and-opinion chart shown on page 576. Draw the chart on the chalkboard and invite volunteers to add to it. If there are statements that some students identify as facts and others as opinions, ask students whether the statement can be proved and, if so, how. If it can't be proved, ask if there are any signal words that indicate the statement is an opinion, not a fact.

Reteaching/Reinforcement
• *Unit Five Resource Book,* p. 28

The story of the *Titanic* began before anyone had even thought about building the great ship. In 1898, fourteen years before the *Titanic* sank, an American writer named Morgan Robertson wrote a book called *The Wreck of the Titan.*[1] In his story, the *Titan,* a passenger ship almost identical to the *Titanic,* and labeled "unsinkable," sails from England headed for New York. With many rich and famous passengers on board, the *Titan* hits an iceberg in the North Atlantic and sinks. Because there are not enough lifeboats, many lives are lost.

The story of the *Titan* predicted exactly what would happen to the *Titanic* fourteen years later. It was an <u>eerie</u> <u>prophecy</u> of terrible things to come.

In 1907, nearly ten years after *The Wreck of the Titan* was written, two men began making plans to build a real titanic ship. At a London dinner party, as they relaxed over coffee and cigars, J. Bruce Ismay, president of the White Star Line of passenger ships, and Lord Pirrie, chairman of Harland & Wolff shipbuilders, discussed a plan to build three enormous ocean liners. Their goal was to give the White Star Line a competitive edge in the Atlantic passenger trade with several gigantic ships whose <u>accommodations</u> would be the last word in comfort and elegance.

The two men certainly dreamed on a grand scale. When these floating palaces were finally

AS HER NAME BOASTED, THE *TITANIC* WAS INDEED THE BIGGEST SHIP IN THE WORLD.

built, they were so much bigger than other ships that new docks had to be built on each side of the Atlantic to service them. Four years after that London dinner party, the first of these huge liners, the *Olympic,* safely completed her maiden voyage.[2]

On May 31, 1911, the hull of the *Titanic* was launched at the Harland & Wolff shipyards in Belfast, Ireland, before a cheering crowd of 100,000. Bands played, and people came from miles around to see this great wonder of the sea. Twenty-two tons of soap, grease, and train oil were used to slide her into the water. In the words of one eyewitness, she had "a rudder as big as an elm tree . . . propellers as big as a windmill. Everything was on a nightmare scale."

For the next ten months the *Titanic* was outfitted and carefully prepared down to the last detail. The final size and richness of this new ship was astounding. She was 882 feet long, almost the length of four city blocks. With nine decks, she was as high as an eleven-story building.

Among her gigantic features, she had four huge funnels, each one big enough to drive two trains through. During construction an

---

1. *Titanic* (tī-tăn'ĭk) . . . *Titan* (tīt'n): In Greek mythology, the Titans were a race of giants. *Titanic* has come to be applied to any person or thing of great size or power.

2. **maiden voyage:** very first trip.

WORDS TO KNOW
eerie (îr'ē) *adj.* weird, especially in a frightening way
prophecy (prŏf'ĭ-sē) *n.* a prediction; foretelling of future events
accommodations (ə-kŏm'ə-dā'shənz) *n.* a room and food, especially in hotels or on ships or trains

astonishing three million rivets had been hammered into her hull. Her three enormous anchors weighed a total of thirty-one tons—the weight of twenty cars. And for her maiden voyage, she carried enough food to feed a small town for several months.

As her name boasted, the *Titanic* was indeed the biggest ship in the world. Nicknamed "the Millionaires' Special," she was also called "the Wonder Ship," "the Unsinkable Ship," and "the Last Word in Luxury" by newspapers around the world.

The command of this great ocean liner was given to the senior captain of the White Star Line, Captain Edward J. Smith. This proud, white-bearded man was a natural leader and was popular with both crew members and passengers. Most important, after thirty-eight years' service with the White Star Line, he had an excellent safety record. At the age of fifty-nine, Captain Smith was going to retire after this last trip, a perfect final <u>tribute</u> to a long and successful career.

On Wednesday, April 10, 1912, the *Titanic*'s passengers began to arrive in Southampton for the trip to New York. Ruth Becker was <u>dazzled</u> as she boarded the ship with her mother, her younger sister, and two-year-old brother, Richard. Ruth's father was a missionary in India. The rest of the family was sailing to New York to find medical help for young Richard, who had developed a serious illness in India.

The *Titanic* had two grand staircases, each five stories high and covered by a glass dome. The staircase shown was named Olympic. Joseph A. Carvalho Collection.

WORDS TO KNOW

tribute (trĭb′yo͞ot) *n.* an action or gift that honors a deserving individual
dazzled (dăz′əld) *adj.* amazed or overwhelmed by a spectacular display **dazzle** *v.*

579

Literary Concept:
LITERARY NONFICTION

 B Explain to students that writers of literary nonfiction present factual information but use many of the same techniques as fiction writers do. Ask students if this passage reflects the characteristics of literary nonfiction. *(Possible response: Yes, it provides facts about the ship's features, but it also uses vivid imagery that helps readers envision the huge ship.)*

Literary Concept: IRONY

C Remind students that irony is a contrast between what is expected and what really happens. Ask them to discuss what is ironic about the description of the captain's career. *(Possible response: Being given command of the Titanic was meant as a tribute to top off a very successful career for Captain Smith. It is ironic that on his last voyage, with a perfect safety record, Captain Smith goes down with his ship.)*

STRATEGIC READING FOR
Less-Proficient Readers

D Ask students to describe the *Titanic*. *(It was an enormous ship that was very luxurious.)* **Restating**

• What was considered special about the *Titanic*? *(Everyone thought that the ship was unsinkable.)* **Finding the Main Idea**

Set a Purpose Invite students to read through the next section to discover who some of the passengers on the *Titanic* were.

Mini-Lesson   Genre Study

NONFICTION Explain to students that literary nonfiction is writing that tells about real people, places, and events, often using narrative techniques found in fiction writing. Types of nonfiction include biographies, autobiographies, articles, and essays. Remind students that, in contrast, fiction tells an imaginary story that may or may not be based on real people and events.

Application Have students write a short essay explaining why this selection is literary nonfiction and not fiction. Students should be sure to back up their statements with specific examples from the selection.

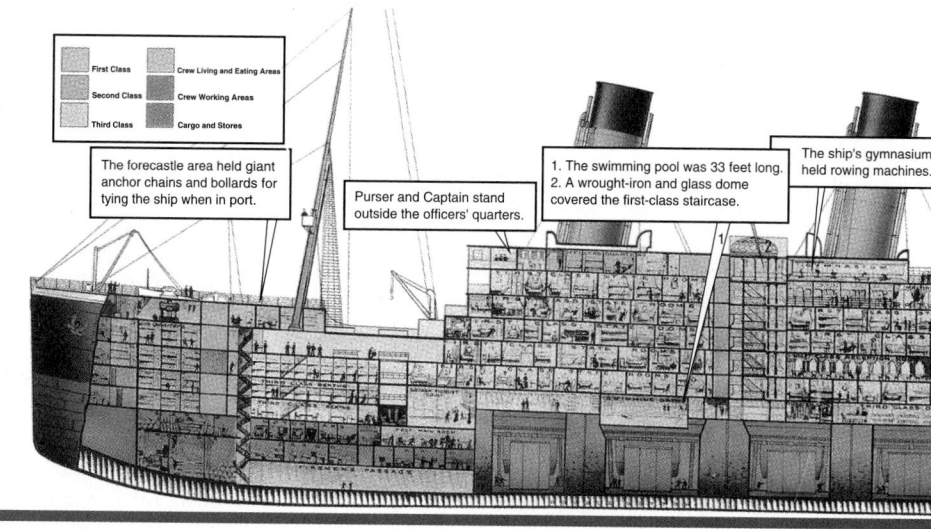

The forecastle area held giant anchor chains and bollards for tying the ship when in port.

Purser and Captain stand outside the officers' quarters.

1. The swimming pool was 33 feet long.
2. A wrought-iron and glass dome covered the first-class staircase.

The ship's gymnasium held rowing machines.

First Class   Crew Living and Eating Areas
Second Class   Crew Working Areas
Third Class   Cargo and Stores

They had booked second-class tickets on the *Titanic*.

Twelve-year-old Ruth was delighted with the ship. As she pushed her little brother about the decks in a stroller, she was impressed with what she saw. "Everything was new. New!" she recalled. "Our cabin was just like a hotel room, it was so big. The dining room was beautiful—the linens, all the bright, polished silver you can imagine."

Meanwhile, seventeen-year-old Jack Thayer from Philadelphia was trying out the soft mattress on the large bed in his cabin. The first-class rooms his family had reserved for themselves and their maid had thick carpets, carved wooden panels on the walls, and marble sinks. As his parents were getting settled in their adjoining stateroom,[3] Jack decided to explore this fantastic ship.

On A Deck, he stepped into the Verandah and Palm Court and admired the white wicker furniture and the ivy growing up the trellised walls. On the lower decks, Jack discovered the squash court,[4] the swimming pool, and the Turkish bath[5] decorated like a room in a sultan's palace. In the gymnasium, the instructor was showing passengers the latest in exercise equipment, which included a mechanical camel you could ride on, stationary bicycles, and rowing machines.

Daylight shone through the huge glass dome over the Grand Staircase as Jack went down to join his parents in the first-class reception room.

There, with the ship's band playing in the background, his father pointed out some of the other first-class passengers. "He's supposed to be the world's richest man," said his father of Colonel John Jacob Astor, who was escorting the young Mrs. Astor. He also identified Mr. and Mrs. Straus, founders of Macy's of New York, the world's largest department store. Millionaire Benjamin Guggenheim was aboard, as were Jack's parents' friends from Philadelphia, Mr. and Mrs. George Widener and their son, Harry. Mr. Widener had made a fortune building streetcars. Mr. and Mrs. William Carter were also friends of the

---

3. **stateroom:** a private cabin on a ship.
4. **squash court:** a walled court or room for playing squash, in which a rubber ball is hit off the walls.
5. **Turkish bath:** a steam bath.

580   UNIT FIVE   PART 1: APPEARANCES TO THE CONTRARY

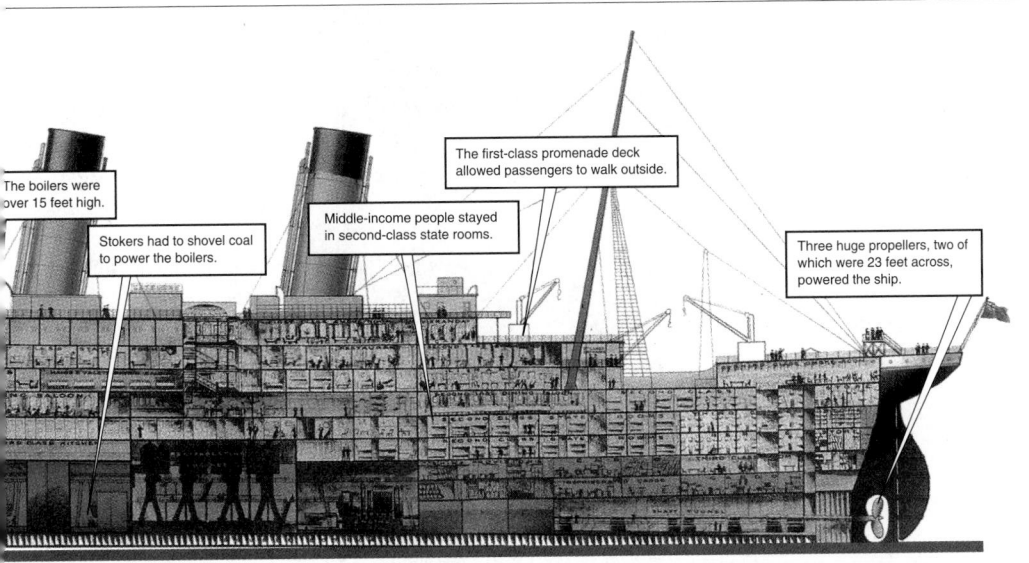

The boilers were over 15 feet high.

Stokers had to shovel coal to power the boilers.

Middle-income people stayed in second-class state rooms.

The first-class promenade deck allowed passengers to walk outside.

Three huge propellers, two of which were 23 feet across, powered the ship.

H Have students discuss their reactions to the class divisions on the *Titanic*. Encourage students who have experienced or heard about examples of class distinction to share their experiences. To prompt students, use the following model:

Think-Aloud Model *I think class divisions are wrong. We should all be treated as equals. I've heard about people who were treated badly because they had very little money or talked with a working-class accent. I don't think that's fair.*

Literary Concept:
LITERARY NONFICTION

I Remind students that literary nonfiction describes real people, places, and events. Ask them how the writer helps them imagine the launching of the Titanic. *(Possible response: by focusing on a single important detail—the size and sound of the ship's whistles)*

Linking to Science

J Speed of travel on water is measured in knots, as opposed to miles per hour. One knot is equal to the speed needed to travel one nautical mile (one minute of the arc on the earth's surface at the equator) in one hour. The word *knot* comes from the first practical tool for measuring the speed of a ship. It consisted of a chip of wood attached to a line with measured knots tied in it. A sailor could judge how fast the ship was going by throwing the chip overboard and counting how long it took the line to play out.

Thayers. Stowed in one of the holds below was a new Renault car that they were bringing back from England.

J. Bruce Ismay, president of the White Star Line, moved about the room saying hello to people. He wanted to make sure that his wealthy passengers were comfortable, that they would feel relaxed and safe aboard his floating palace.

Indeed, when Ruth Becker's mother had asked one of the second-class staff about the safety of the ship, she had been told that there was absolutely nothing to worry about. The ship had watertight compartments that would allow her to float <u>indefinitely</u>. There was much talk among the passengers about the *Titanic* being unsinkable.

In 1912, people were divided into social classes according to background, wealth, and education. Because of these class lines, the *Titanic* was rather like a big floating layer cake. The bottom layer consisted of the lowly manual workers sweating away in the heat and grime of the boiler rooms and engine rooms.

The next layer was the third-class passengers, people of many nationalities hoping to make a new start in America. After that came the second class—teachers, merchants, and professionals of moderate means like Ruth's family. Then, finally, there was the icing on the cake in first class: the rich and the aristocratic. The differences between these groups were enormous. While the wealthy brought their maids and valets[6] and mountains of luggage, most members of the crew earned such tiny salaries that it would have taken them years to save the money for a single first-class ticket.

At noon on Wednesday, April 10, the *Titanic* cast off. The whistles on her huge funnels were the biggest ever made. As she began her journey to the sea, they were heard for miles around.

Moving majestically down the River Test, and watched by a crowd that had turned out for the occasion, the *Titanic* slowly passed two ships tied up to a dock. All of a sudden, the

---

6. **valets** (vă-lāz′): gentlemen's personal servants.

WORDS TO KNOW	**indefinitely** (ĭn-dĕf′ə-nĭt-lē) *adv.* for an unlimited length of time

581

Mini-Lesson: Speaking, Listening, and Viewing

PRESS CONFERENCE Explain to students that at a press conference, one or more speakers usually deliver a statement to an audience of reporters about an event that has occurred. After the statement is read, reporters often ask the speaker questions based on the content of the statement or on their own knowledge of the situation to which it applies.

Application Invite students to role-play a press conference about the sinking of the *Titanic*. Have some students play the parts of survivors, such as Jack Thayer, Ruth Becker, Harold Bride, and possibly a representative of the White Star Line. These students should read prepared statements. Have the remaining students act as reporters who question each of the speakers.

K Ask students what they think the close call with the *New York* might bode for the rest of the voyage. *(Possible responses: People might begin to lose confidence in the* Titanic *after seeing it nearly collide with the* New York; *the* Titanic *may have other close calls during the voyage.)*

STRATEGIC READING FOR
Less-Proficient Readers

L Ask students who are the two young people whose experiences the narrator relates. *(Ruth, a 12-year-old girl, and Jack Thayer, a 17-year-old boy)*
Noting Relevant Details

• What different kinds of people made the voyage on the *Titanic*? *(wealthy people like John Jacob Astor; second-class travelers who were teachers, merchants, and other professionals; people emigrating from other countries to the United States; manual laborers who worked in the boiler and engine rooms)*
Restating

Set a Purpose Ask students to read the next section to find out what happened in the early part of the fourth night of the *Titanic's* voyage.

Linking to History

M The wireless is a radio, invented by the Italian Guglielmo Marconi in the 1890s. Marconi also invented the autoalarm, which signaled transmissions by sounding a loud alarm when radio operators were off duty. In 1912 not all ships had radios. Eventually all large ships were required by law to have wireless equipment.

CUSTOMIZING FOR
Multiple Learning Styles

N Bodily-Kinesthetic Learners
Suggest that students role-play the scene in which Bride hands Captain Smith the message about the iceberg warnings.

---

mooring ropes holding the passenger liner *New York* snapped with a series of sharp cracks like fireworks going off. The enormous pull created by the *Titanic* moving past her had broken the *New York*'s ropes and was now drawing her stern toward the *Titanic*. Jack Thayer watched in horror as the two ships came closer and closer. "It looked as though there surely would be a collision," he later wrote. "Her stern could not have been more than a yard or two from our side. It almost hit us." At the last moment, some quick action by Captain Smith and a tugboat captain nearby allowed the *Titanic* to slide past with only inches to spare.

It was not a good sign. Did it mean that the *Titanic* might be too big a ship to handle safely? Those who knew about the sea thought that such a close call at the beginning of a maiden voyage was a very bad omen.

Jack Phillips, the first wireless operator on the *Titanic*, quickly jotted down the message coming in over his headphones. "It's another iceberg warning," he said wearily to his young assistant, Harold Bride. "You'd better take it up to the bridge." Both men had been at work for hours in the *Titanic*'s radio room, trying to get caught up in sending out a large number of personal messages. In 1912, passengers on ocean liners thought it was a real <u>novelty</u> to send postcard-style messages to friends at home from the middle of the Atlantic.

Bride picked up the iceberg message and

> BESIDES, WHAT DANGER COULD A FEW PIECES OF ICE PRESENT TO AN UNSINKABLE SHIP?

stepped out onto the boat deck. It was a sunny but cold Sunday morning, the fourth day of the *Titanic's* maiden voyage. The ship was steaming at full speed across a calm sea. Harold Bride was quite pleased with himself at having landed a job on such a magnificent new ship. After all, he was only twenty-two years old and had just nine months' experience at operating a "wireless set," as a ship's radio was then called. As he entered the bridge area, he could see one of the crewmen standing behind the ship's wheel steering her course toward New York.

Captain Smith was on duty in the bridge, so Bride handed the message to him. "It's from the *Caronia*, sir. She's reporting icebergs and pack ice ahead." The captain thanked him, read the message, and then posted it on the bulletin board for other officers on watch to read. On his way back to the radio room, Bride thought the captain had seemed quite unconcerned by the message. But then again, he had been told that it was not unusual to have ice floating in the sea lanes during an April crossing. Besides, what danger could a few pieces of ice present to an unsinkable ship?

Elsewhere on board, passengers relaxed on deck chairs, reading or taking naps. Some played cards, some wrote letters, while others chatted with friends. As it was Sunday, church services had been held in the morning, the first-class service led by Captain Smith. Jack Thayer spent most of the day walking about the decks getting some fresh air with his parents.

WORDS TO KNOW **novelty** (nŏv′əl-tē) *n.* something new, original, or unusual

582

Mini-Lesson Study Skills

GRAPHIC ORGANIZERS Explain to students that one way to better understand what they read is to create a graphic organizer, which shows them at a glance information they may want to remember or reinforce. One type of graphic organizer is a time line. A time line is useful for listing events by date or time.

Application Invite students to create a time line to present events aboard the *Titanic* beginning on the fourth day of its voyage.

Two more ice warnings were received from nearby ships around lunch time. In the chaos of the radio room, Harold Bride only had time to take one of them to the bridge. The rest of the day passed quietly. Then, in the late afternoon, the temperature began to drop rapidly. Darkness approached as the bugle call announced dinner.

Jack Thayer's parents had been invited to a special dinner for Captain Smith, so Jack ate alone in the first-class dining room. After dinner, as he was having a cup of coffee, he was joined by Milton Long, another passenger going home to the States. Long was older than Jack, but in the easy-going atmosphere of shipboard travel, they struck up a conversation and talked together for an hour or so.

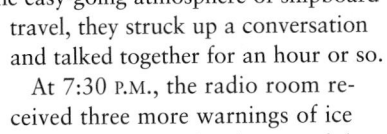

At 7:30 P.M., the radio room received three more warnings of ice about fifty miles ahead. One of them was from the steamer *Californian* reporting three large icebergs. Harold Bride took this message up to the bridge, and it was again politely received. Captain Smith was attending the dinner party being held for him when the warning was delivered. He never got to see it. Then, around 9:00 P.M., the captain excused himself and went up to the bridge. He and his officers talked about how difficult it was to spot icebergs on a calm, clear, moonless night like this with no wind to kick up white surf around them. Before going to bed, the captain ordered the lookouts to keep a sharp watch for ice.

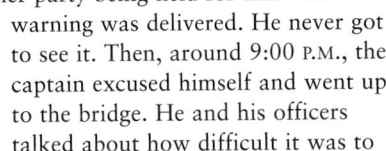

After trading travel stories with Milton Long, Jack Thayer put on his coat and walked around the deck. "It had become very much colder," he said later. "It was a brilliant, starry night. There was no moon, and I have never seen the stars shine brighter . . . sparkling like diamonds. . . . It was the kind of night that made one feel glad to be alive." At eleven

o'clock, he went below to his cabin, put on his pajamas, and got ready for bed.

In the radio room, Harold Bride was exhausted. The two operators were expected to keep the radio working twenty-four hours a day, and Bride lay down to take a much-needed nap. Phillips was so busy with the passenger messages that he actually brushed off the final ice warning of the night. It was from the *Californian*. Trapped in a field of ice, she had stopped for the night about nineteen miles north of the *Titanic*. She was so close that the message literally blasted in Phillips's ears. Annoyed by the loud interruption, he cut off the *Californian*'s radio operator with the words, "Shut up, shut up. I'm busy."

The radio room had received a total of seven ice warning messages in one day. It was quite clear that floating icebergs lay ahead of the *Titanic*. **Q**

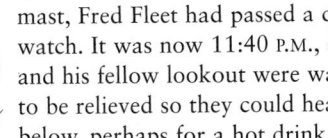

High up in the crow's nest on the forward mast, Fred Fleet had passed a quiet watch. It was now 11:40 P.M., and he and his fellow lookout were waiting to be relieved so they could head below, perhaps for a hot drink before hopping into their warm bunks. The sea was dead calm. The air was bitterly cold.

Suddenly, Fleet saw something. A huge, dark shape loomed out of the night directly ahead of the *Titanic*. An iceberg! He quickly sounded the alarm bell three times and picked up the telephone.

"What did you see?" asked the duty officer. **2**

"Iceberg right ahead," replied Fleet.

Immediately, the officer on the bridge ordered the wheel turned as far as it would go. The engine room was told to reverse the engines, while a button was pushed to close the doors to the watertight compartments in the bottom of the ship.

The lookouts in the crow's nest braced themselves for a collision. Slowly the ship started to

EXPLORING THE *TITANIC* **583**

Critical Thinking: ANALYZING

R Ask students why they think the author describes how the passengers on each of the decks react to the collision with the iceberg. *(Possible responses: so that the reader continues to identify with all of the people on board; to show the different ways that each group reacts to the disaster)*

Active Reading: EVALUATE

S Ask students if they think that the Captain and Andrews knew all along that the *Titanic* was sinkable. *(Possible response: Yes, both men knew that the ship couldn't remain afloat if more than the first four compartments were to flood, even though such an event seemed unlikely.)*

turn. It looked as though they would miss it. But it was too late. They had avoided a head-on crash, but the iceberg had struck a glancing blow along the *Titanic*'s starboard bow. Several tons of ice fell on the ship's decks as the iceberg brushed along the side of the ship and passed into the night. A few minutes later, the *Titanic* came to a stop.

Many of the passengers didn't know the ship had hit anything. Because it was so cold, almost everyone was inside, and most people had already gone to bed. Ruth Becker and her mother were awakened by the dead silence. They could no longer hear the soothing hum of the vibrating engines from below. Jack Thayer was about to step into bed when he felt himself sway ever so slightly. The engines stopped. He was startled by the sudden quiet.

Sensing trouble, Ruth's mother looked out of the door of their second-class cabin and asked a steward[7] what had happened. He told her that nothing was the matter, so Mrs. Becker went back to bed. But as she lay there, she couldn't help feeling that something was very wrong.

The *Titanic* collides with an iceberg, most of which lay hidden underwater. From *Exploring the Titanic*. Copyright © 1988, by Robert D. Ballard, Madison Press Book.

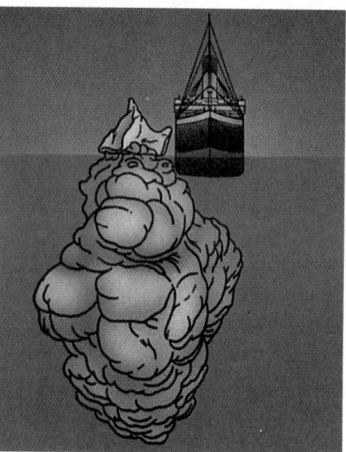

Jack heard running feet and voices in the hallway outside his first-class cabin. "I hurried into my heavy overcoat and drew on my slippers. All excited, but not thinking anything serious had occurred, I called in to my father and mother that I was going up on deck to see the fun."

On deck, Jack watched some third-class passengers playing with the ice that had landed on the forward deck as the iceberg had brushed by. Some people were throwing chunks at each other, while a few skidded about playing football with pieces of ice.

Down in the very bottom of the ship, things were very different. When the iceberg had struck, there had been a noise like a big gun going off in one of the boiler rooms. A couple of stokers[8] had been immediately hit by a jet of icy water. The noise and the shock of cold water had sent them running for safety.

Twenty minutes after the crash, things looked very bad indeed to Captain Smith. He and the ship's builder, Thomas Andrews, had made a rapid tour below decks to inspect the damage. The mail room was filling up with water, and sacks of mail were floating about. Water was also pouring into some of the forward holds and two of the boiler rooms.

Captain Smith knew that the *Titanic*'s hull was divided into a number of watertight compartments. She had been designed so that she could still float if only the first four compartments were flooded, but not any more than that. But water was pouring into the first five compartments. And when the water filled them, it would spill over into the next compartment. One by one all the remaining compartments would flood, and the ship would

---

7. **steward:** a worker on a ship who attends to the needs of the passengers.
8. **stokers:** workers who tended the boilers that powered steamships.

Mini-Lesson **Grammar**

POSSESSIVE PLURALS Remind students that to form the possessive of any singular noun, they add an apostrophe and s (for example, ship's radio). To form the possessive of a plural noun that ends in s, add an apostrophe (Millionaires' Special). To form the possessive of a plural noun that does not end in s, add an apostrophe and s (people's).

Application Ask students to replace the following underlined nouns with the correct possessive forms.

1. The <u>wireless</u> signal could not be heard aboard the *Californian.* (wireless's)

2. The <u>officer</u> concern was for his <u>passengers</u> safety. (officer's; passengers')

3. The <u>children</u> belongings were lost when the *Titanic* went down. (children's)

Reteaching/Reinforcement
- Grammar Handbook, anthology pp. 858–859
- *Grammar Mini-Lessons* copymasters p. 11, transparencies p. 9

 **The Writer's Craft**

Possessive Nouns, p. 420

eventually sink. Andrews told the captain that the ship could last an hour, an hour and a half at the most.

Harold Bride had just awakened in the radio room when Captain Smith stuck his head in the door. "Send the call for assistance," he ordered.

"What call should I send?" Phillips asked.

"The regulation international call for help. Just that." Then the captain was gone. Phillips began to send the Morse code "CQD" distress call, flashing away and joking as he did it. After all, they knew the ship was unsinkable.

Five minutes later, the captain was back. "What are you sending?" he asked.

"CQD," Phillips answered. Then Bride cut in and suggested that they try the new SOS signal that was just coming into use. They began to send out the new international call for help— it was one of the first SOS calls ever sent out from a ship in distress.

Ruth and her family had stayed in their bunks for a good fifteen minutes or so after the room steward had told them nothing was wrong. But Ruth's mother couldn't stop worrying as she heard the sound of running feet and shouting voices in the hallway. Poking her head out of the cabin, she found a steward and asked what the matter was.

"Put on your things and come at once," said the steward.

"Do we have time to dress?" she asked.

"No, madam. You have time for nothing. Put

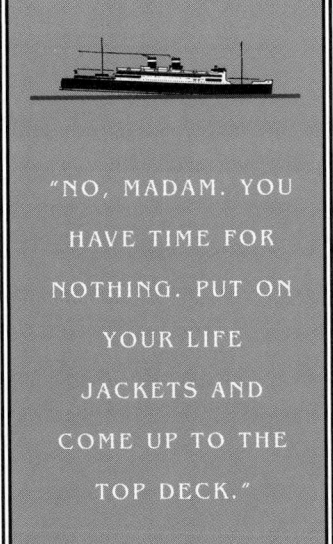

"NO, MADAM. YOU HAVE TIME FOR NOTHING. PUT ON YOUR LIFE JACKETS AND COME UP TO THE TOP DECK."

on your life jackets and come up to the top deck."

Ruth helped her mother dress the children quickly. But they only had time to throw their coats over their nightgowns and put on their shoes and stockings. In their rush, they forgot to put on their life jackets.

Just after midnight, Captain Smith ordered the lifeboats uncovered. The ship's squash court, which was thirty-two feet above the keel, was now completely flooded. Jack Thayer and his father came into the first-class lounge to try to find out exactly what the matter was. When Thomas Andrews, the ship's builder, passed by, Mr. Thayer asked him what was going on. He replied in a low voice that the ship had not much more than an hour to live. Jack and his father couldn't believe their ears.

From the bridge of the *Titanic*, a ship's lights were observed not far away, possibly the *Californian*'s. Captain Smith then ordered white distress rockets fired to get the attention of the nearby ship. They burst high in the air with a loud boom and a shower of stars. But the rockets made no difference. The mystery ship in the distance never answered.

In the radio room, Bride and Phillips now knew how serious the accident was and were feverishly sending out calls for help. A number of ships heard and responded to their calls, but most were too far away to come to the rescue in time. The closest ship they had been able to reach was the *Carpathia*, about fifty-eight miles

CUSTOMIZING FOR
Students Acquiring English

3 Explain that *eventually* is used to show that Captain Smith knew that the ship would sink, but he did now know how long it would take.

Critical Thinking: ANALYZING

T Ask students why they think the author included the information that the radio operator was joking. (*Possible responses: to show the contrast between what is really happening and what Phillips thinks is happening; to emphasize the irony of the situation*)

Active Reading: EVALUATE

U Ask students why they think the nearby ship didn't respond to the *Titanic*'s distress rockets. (*Possible responses: The other ship's crew might have also believed that the *Titanic* was unsinkable and therefore couldn't believe there was any serious trouble; the crew might have been asleep and not have seen the flares.*)

Mini-Lesson   Study Skills

KWL Explain to students that one way to organize information as they read nonfiction is to create a chart. KWL stands for:

1. what students **K**now
2. what students **W**ant to know
3. what students have **L**earned.

Share the KWL chart shown with the class.

Application Invite students to complete a KWL chart for "Exploring the *Titanic*."

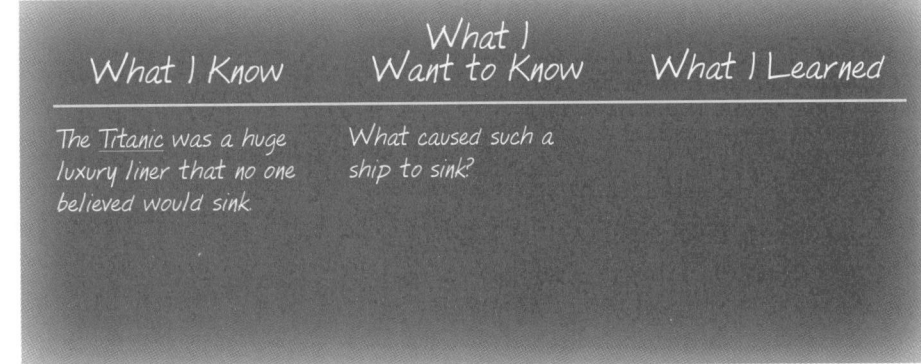

What I Know	What I Want to Know	What I Learned
The Titanic was a huge luxury liner that no one believed would sink	What caused such a ship to sink?	

V Have students describe what happened aboard the *Titanic* between 11:40 P.M. and 12:30 A.M. *(The ship collided with an iceberg, and the first five lower-deck compartments flooded. The captain ordered the wireless operators to radio for help. Some passengers didn't believe there was a problem. The captain ordered the lifeboats to be lowered away.)* Noting Sequence of Events

Set a Purpose Ask students to read to the end of the selection to see what Ruth Becker and Jack Thayer saw in the early hours of April 15.

Critical Thinking: SPECULATING

W Ask students to explain why the crew didn't fill the lifeboats with people. *(Possible responses: They still didn't believe that the ship was in danger; they were inexperienced and not prepared to respond in an emergency.)*

Active Reading: EVALUATE

X Ask students what Ruth's words suggest about what was going on. *(Possible response: The fact that no one was panicking suggests that either people were organized and not worried or that they were unaware of how serious the danger was.)*

Literary Concept: IMAGERY

Y Ask students how the words *shrieked* and *creaking* help them visualize what is going on. *(Possible responses: These words bring the scene to life; being able to "hear" these sounds makes the reader more aware of the other events that are happening.)*

away. Immediately, the *Carpathia* reported that she was racing full steam to the rescue. But could she get there in time?

Not far away, the radio operator of the *Californian* had gone to bed for the night and turned off his radio. Several officers and crewmen on the deck of the *Californian* saw rockets in the distance and reported them to their captain. The captain told them to try to contact the ship with a Morse lamp. But they received no answer to their flashed calls. No one thought to wake up the radio operator.

On board the *Titanic*, almost an hour after the crash, most of the passengers still did not realize the seriousness of the situation. But Captain Smith was a very worried man. He knew that the *Titanic* only carried lifeboats for barely half the estimated twenty-two hundred people on board. He would have to make sure his officers kept order to avoid any panic among the passengers. At 12:30 A.M. Captain Smith gave the orders to start loading the lifeboats—women and children first. Even though the *Titanic* was by now quite noticeably down at the bow and <u>listing</u> slightly to one side, many passengers still didn't want to leave the huge, brightly lit ship. The ship's band added to a  kind of party feeling as the musicians played lively tunes.

About 12:45 A.M. the first lifeboat was lowered. It could carry sixty-five

THE RADIO SIGNAL GRADUALLY GOT WEAKER AND WEAKER AS THE SHIP'S POWER FADED OUT.

people, but left with only twenty-eight aboard. Indeed, many of the first boats to leave were half empty. Ruth Becker noticed that there was no panic among the crowds of passengers milling about on the decks. "Everything was calm, everybody was orderly." But the night air was now biting cold. Ruth's mother told her to go back to their cabin to get some blankets. Ruth hurried down to the cabin and came back with several blankets in her arms. The Beckers walked toward one of the lifeboats, and a sailor picked up Ruth's brother and sister and placed them in the boat.

"That's all for this boat," he called out. "Lower away!"

"Please, those are my children!" cried Ruth's mother. "Let me go with them!"

The sailor allowed Mrs. Becker to step into the lifeboat with her two children. She then called back to Ruth to get into another lifeboat. Ruth went to the next boat and asked the officer if she could get in. He said, "Sure," picked her up, and dumped her in.

Boat No. 13 was so crowded that Ruth had to stand up. Foot by foot it was lowered down the steep side of the massive ship. The new pulleys shrieked as the ropes passed through them, creaking under the weight of the boat and its load of sixty-four people. After landing in the water, Ruth's lifeboat began to drift. Suddenly Ruth saw another lifeboat coming down right on top of them! Fearing for their

V

WORDS TO KNOW	**list** (lĭst) *v.* to tilt; lean

586

Mini-Lesson   **Literary Concepts**

POINT OF VIEW Remind students that writers of literary nonfiction use the techniques that writers of fiction use, including point of view—the perspective from which a story is told. In the first-person point of view, the narrator is one of the characters in the story and uses first-person pronouns such as *I, me, we,* or *us.* In the third-person point of view, the narrator is not in the story and uses third-person pronouns such as *he, she, it, they,* or *them.*

Application Elicit from students that this selection is written from the third-person point of view but includes quotations in the first person. Then have students rewrite the highlighted passage from the perspective of Ruth Becker as a first-person narrator.

lives, the men in charge of her boat shouted, "Stop!" to the sailors up on the deck. But the noise was so great that nobody noticed. The second lifeboat kept coming down, so close that they could actually touch the bottom of it. All of a sudden, one of the men in Ruth's boat jumped up, pulled out a knife, and cut them free of their lowering ropes. Ruth's boat pushed away from the *Titanic* just as boat No. 15 hit the water inches away from them.

Below, in the third-class decks of the ship, there was much more confusion and alarm. Most of these passengers had not yet been able to get above decks. Some of those who did finally make it out had to break down the barriers between third and first class.

 By 1:30 A.M. the bow was well down, and people were beginning to notice the slant of the decks. In the radio room, Bride and Phillips were still desperately sending out calls for help: "We are sinking fast . . . women and children in boats. We cannot last much longer." The radio signal gradually got weaker and weaker as the ship's power faded out. Out on the decks, most passengers now began to move toward the stern area, which was slowly lifting out of the water.

The last lifeboats pull away from the sinking *Titanic*, leaving approximately 1,500 people on board. Painting by Ken Marschall from *Exploring the Titanic.* Copyright © 1988, by Robert D. Ballard, Madison Press Book.

EXPLORING THE *TITANIC* **587**

Critical Thinking: ANALYZING

AA Ask students what they think the captain means when he says, "Now it's every man for himself." *(Possible response: The crew members no longer have to try to do their duty and save the passengers. It is time to save themselves.)*

Literary Concept: IMAGERY

BB Ask students how the details about the sights and sounds of the sinking ship help to bring the final terrible moments to life. *(Possible response: Through the author's use of sensory details, the reader can almost know what the survivors heard and saw and thus feel connected to them.)*

CUSTOMIZING FOR
Students Acquiring English

4 Students may be familiar with the word *terrific* as meaning "very good." Point out that "the cold was terrific" means that it was very, very cold.

CUSTOMIZING FOR
Multiple Learning Styles

CC **Musical Learners** Ask students to choose a piece of music that might accompany a silent viewing of the final moments of the *Titanic*. Have students play the music for the class and explain why they chose that piece.

CUSTOMIZING FOR
Gifted and Talented Students

DD Ask students to discuss definitions of *bravery* and *cowardice*. Invite them to look for examples of bravery and cowardice among the passengers and crew of the *Titanic*. *(Possible responses: A person who saves lives shows bravery. Someone who hides from danger shows cowardice. None of the people in the selection showed cowardice. Phillips showed bravery in working the radio until the last possible moment.)*

By 2:05 A.M. there were still over 1,500 people left on the sinking ship. All the lifeboats were now away, and a strange stillness took hold. People stood quietly on the upper decks, bunching together for warmth, trying to keep away from the side of the tilting ship.

Captain Smith now made his way to the radio room and told Harold Bride and Jack Phillips to save themselves. "Men, you have done your full duty," he told them. "You can do no more. Abandon your cabin. Now it's every man for himself." Phillips kept working the radio, hanging on until the very last moment. Suddenly Bride heard water gurgling up the deck outside the radio room. Phillips heard it, too, and cried, "Come on, let's clear out."

Near the stern, Father Thomas Byles had heard confession and given absolution[9] to over one hundred passengers. Playing to the very end, the members of the ship's brave band finally had to put down their instruments and try to save themselves. In desperation, some of the passengers and crew began to jump overboard as the water crept up the slant of the deck.

Jack Thayer stood with his friend Milton Long at the railing to keep away from the crowds. He had become separated from his father in the confusion on deck. Now Jack and his friend heard muffled thuds and explosions deep within the ship. Suddenly the *Titanic* began to slide into the water. The water rushed up at them. Thayer and Long quickly said goodbye and good luck to each other. Then they both jumped.

As he hit the water, Jack Thayer was sucked down. "The cold was terrific. The shock of the

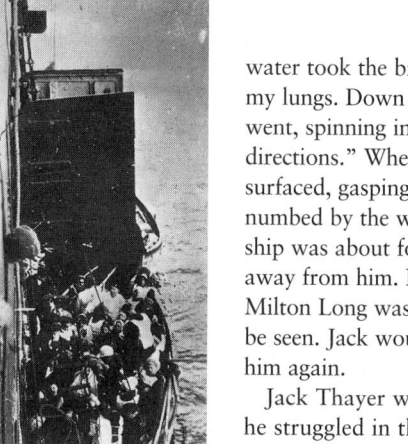

A crowded lifeboat from the *Titanic* is hoisted aboard the *Carpathia*. UPI/Bettmann.

water took the breath out of my lungs. Down and down I went, spinning in all directions." When he finally surfaced, gasping for air and numbed by the water, the ship was about forty feet away from him. His friend Milton Long was nowhere to be seen. Jack would never see him again.

Jack Thayer was lucky. As he struggled in the water, his hand came to rest on an overturned lifeboat. He grabbed hold and hung on, barely managing to pull himself up out of the water. Harold Bride had been washed overboard and now also clung to this same boat.

Both Jack and Harold witnessed the mighty ship's last desperate moments. "We could see groups of . . . people aboard, clinging in clusters or bunches, like swarming bees; only to fall in masses, pairs, or singly, as the great part of the ship . . . rose into the sky. . . ." said Thayer. "I looked upwards—we were right under the three enormous propellers. For an instant, I thought they were sure to come right down on top of us. Then . . . she slid quietly away from us into the sea."

Out in the safety of her lifeboat, Ruth Becker also witnessed the end of the *Titanic*. "I could look back and see this ship, and the decks were just lined with people looking over. Finally, as the *Titanic* sank faster, the lights died out. You could just see the stern remaining in an upright position for a couple of minutes. Then . . . it disappeared."

---

9. **heard confession . . . absolution:** Father Byles has conducted a Roman Catholic religious practice in which a priest listens to people confess their sins and then declares them forgiven.

Assessment 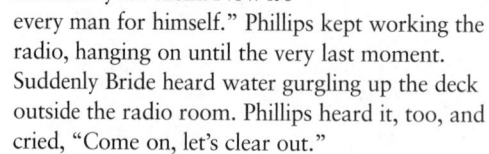 **Option**

INFORMAL ASSESSMENT You can assess students' understanding of the selection by having them create a story log that describes the sequence of events. Invite students to divide their log into time entries and summarize what happened in each time period.

Rubric

3 Full Accomplishment Students block the selection into time periods and successfully log the events that occurred.

2 Substantial Accomplishment Students identify most time periods and summarize most of the major events.

1 Little or Partial Accomplishment Students are unable to identify the time periods and/or describe a logical sequence of events.

Then, as Ruth recalled, "there fell upon the ear the most terrible noise that human beings ever listened to—the cries of hundreds of people struggling in the icy cold water, crying for help with a cry we knew could not be answered." In Thayer's words, they became "a long continuous wailing chant." Before long this ghastly wailing stopped, as the freezing water took its toll. Jack Thayer and Harold Bride and a number

Aboard the *Carpathia*, the only surviving honeymoon couple, Mr. and Mrs. George Harder, talk to Mrs. Hays, who lost her husband. The Illustrated London News Picture Library.

of other survivors clung to their overturned lifeboat, inches away from an icy death in the North Atlantic. Numb from the cold and not daring to move in case the boat sank under their weight, they prayed and waited for help. Then, as the first light of dawn crept on the horizon, a rocket was seen in the distance. The *Carpathia* had come to their rescue. ❖

HISTORICAL INSIGHT

THE CHICAGO DAILY NEWS

TITANIC, WITH 1,341 PERSONS, LIES AT BOTTOM: ONLY 868 ARE SAVED

MEN OF FAME DEAD IN DISASTER IS FEAR; LIST OF THE RESCUED

HOW WOMEN AND CHILDREN WERE SAVED.

ALL HOPE ABANDONED; HELP CAME TOO LATE; BRINGING SURVIVORS

WORDS TO KNOW   **toll** (tōl) *n.* the amount of loss or destruction caused by a disaster

589

---

1. Accept all reasonable responses.
2. Possible response: The ship should have carried enough lifeboats to accommodate all of its passengers and should not have continued its voyage after receiving warnings about icebergs.
3. Possible responses: The relaxed and unafraid behavior of people on deck was probably due more to ignorance of the danger than to bravery. The third-class passengers panicked more because they could see and hear the danger better than the first-class passengers could.
4. Possible responses: by trying to think positive thoughts; by helping others in similar situations
5. Possible response: The fact that some travelers take out insurance policies suggests that they are more cautious today.

Another Pathway

Students' log entries should reflect their understanding of how a captain with the experience and safety record of Captain Smith must have felt as the ship was going down.

Rubric

3 Full Accomplishment Student's log entry is well written and true to the characterization of Captain Smith.

2 Substantial Accomplishment Student's log entry is complete and mostly consistent with the characterization of Captain Smith.

1 Little or Partial Accomplishment Student's log entry is incomplete and inconsistent with the characterization of Captain Smith.

RESPONDING
OPTIONS

FROM PERSONAL RESPONSE TO CRITICAL ANALYSIS

REFLECT 1. What were you thinking about as you finished this selection? Jot down some notes and share them with your classmates.

RETHINK 2. In your opinion, what might have been done to prevent this disaster?

Close Textual Reading

Consider
- the reactions of the captain and crew to the ice warnings
- actions taken and not taken after the collision
- the shortage of lifeboats and lack of other safety devices

3. Evaluate the behavior of the passengers and crew as the *Titanic* was sinking.

RELATE 4. Read the headline of the Historical Insight on page 589. How do you think the survivors of a disaster such as the sinking of the *Titanic* deal with the horror of what they have lived through?

5. Are people more or less cautious about trusting new technology than they were during the time of the *Titanic*? Support your opinion with examples from the story and your own observations.

Multimodal Learning
ANOTHER PATHWAY

If Captain Smith had had the time to enter a full log entry as the ship was sinking, what do you think he would have written? Write the last entry in the captain's log and share it with your classmates.

QUICKWRITES

1. The *Titanic* was evacuated traditionally—"women and children first." Write a draft of an **essay** in which you agree or disagree with this principle.

2. Write an **advertisement** for the *Titanic*, enticing people to travel on its maiden voyage. Before you begin, look at the first page of this selection and skim the description of the ship to find details and features that you could use in your ad.

3. A **ballad** is a song or poem that tells a story. With a partner, write the lyrics to a ballad that tells the story of the *Titanic*.

📁 **PORTFOLIO** *Save your writing. You may want to use it later as a springboard to a piece for your portfolio.*

QuickWrites

1. Remind students that their essay should contain a thesis sentence that states their opinion and paragraphs that provide supporting details.
2. Remind students to select a target audience to which they want their ad to appeal.
3. If possible, play for students recordings of several ballads.

The Writer's Craft

Supporting Opinions, pp. 144–151
Advertisement, pp. 152–156

Literary Concepts

Suggest that students work in pairs to identify examples of the different types of organization used in the selection. Have them list their examples in a chart. *(Possible responses: Topic Sentence: [page 579] As her name boasted, the* Titanic *was indeed the biggest ship in the world; Chronological Order: [page 586] About 12:45 A.M. the first lifeboat was lowered. Ballard uses different types of organization to fulfill different purposes. Paragraphs that feature topic sentences supported by details work well to give the reader impressions of the* Titanic. *Ballard switches to chronological order as the ship is sinking to build suspense and drama.)*

LITERARY CONCEPTS

Literary Nonfiction provides factual information but is written to be read and experienced in much the same way you experience fiction. Writers use whatever organization works best for their purpose. In this selection, Ballard uses paragraphs organized by topic sentences to describe the *Titanic*. When the ship is sinking, he uses chronological order. Find an example of each kind of organization in the excerpt. Why do you think Ballard uses different types of organization?

LITERARY LINKS

Think about the disaster that Tennyson describes in the poem "The Charge of the Light Brigade" on page 298. What similarities and differences do you see between this disaster and the sinking of the *Titanic*?

ACROSS THE CURRICULUM

Science *Cooperative Learning* How do ships as large as the *Titanic* float and stay upright? How do sailors navigate when out of sight of land? Working in small groups, research such topics as buoyancy, displacement, stability, and equipment. Combine your research to create a hands-on science display that demonstrates scientific principles such as how the forces of gravity and buoyancy affect the stability of a vessel.

ALTERNATIVE ACTIVITIES

1. View either *The Titanic* (1953) or *A Night to Remember* (1958) with a few of your classmates. Then hold a **panel discussion** on the differences between the movie version and Ballard's account.

2. Read the rest of *Exploring the Titanic,* or refer to magazines and other resources, to find out how the sunken ship was finally discovered. Use a projector to display pictures and diagrams as you present an **oral report** to your classmates.

3. What would you want to ask Harold Bride or Jack Thayer? With a partner or a small group, stage a **TV interview** with one or more of the survivors mentioned in the selection.

4. If two ships are on a collision course, in which direction should they both alter? Does a green light mean you are seeing the port or the starboard side of a ship? Answer these and other questions by researching international regulations that help ensure safe passage for ships. Present your findings in a "Rules of the Sea" **pamphlet.**

Literary Links

Have students create a chart listing the similarities and differences between the two disasters. *(Possible responses: In both disasters, many people acted bravely and many died. The soldiers in the poem knew they were riding toward certain death, whereas many of the passengers on the* Titanic *for a time were unaware of the gravity of their situation.)*

Across the Curriculum

Science Cooperative Learning Have students assign a researcher, a direction giver, and a recorder as they begin their research tasks. Suggest that students first create a KWL chart (mini-lesson, page 585) that lists several questions they want answered about how a ship stays afloat. Remind students to use reference books such as encyclopedias, science texts, or specific texts on shipbuilding or sailing to help them find the answers to their questions.

ADDITIONAL SUGGESTIONS

Science *Where's the* Titanic? Invite students to read Robert Ballard's book, *The Discovery of the Titanic,* to learn about the special scientific equipment that was used to locate and examine the remains of the *Titanic.* Suggest that students present their findings as a poster or oral report.

Alternative Activities

1. Invite students to prepare a list of possible topics of comparison for their discussion, such as point of view, sensory details, organization, and characterization.

2. Have students create outlines to help them organize their oral reports.

3. Have students select one or more people to act as survivors and someone to act as a television interviewer or talk show host. Remind students to determine what the audience would want to know before they prepare questions to ask.

4. Suggest that students organize their pamphlet around the "most frequently asked questions" and corresponding answers. Remind them to keep their pamphlet simple and easy to read.

1. accommodations
2. novelty
3. dazzled
4. prophecy
5. eerie
6. indefinitely
7. list
8. feverishly
9. toll
10. tribute

Word Play

Students' crossword puzzles will vary. Tell students to build their crosswords by setting up a series of criss-crossing words. Remind them to write a clue for each word.

Reteaching/Reinforcement

• *Unit Five Resource Book*, p. 30

ROBERT BALLARD

As a marine geologist, Ballard helped discover volcanic vents nine thousand feet beneath the Pacific ocean near the Galápagos Islands. He played a major role in developing the Argo/Jason underwater system that was used to find the *Titanic*.

SCIENCE CONNECTION

Exploring the *Titanic* The *Titanic* sat on the ocean floor undisturbed for decades. On September 1, 1985, a robotic research vessel recorded the first view of the ship in 73 years. In this short film, students will see the *Titanic* as it appeared in the 1985 footage.

Side A, Frame 47549

WORDS TO KNOW

Review the Words to Know at the bottom of the selection pages. Then write the word that best completes each sentence.

1. In its time, the *Titanic* was the largest ship in the world, with _____ for more than 2,000 passengers.
2. It had squash courts, a swimming pool, a gymnasium, and a mechanical camel, which would have been a _____ even on land.
3. It is no wonder that everyone was _____ by the ship's size and luxury.
4. The *Titanic* was considered unsinkable, so no one would have believed a _____ that this ship's name would become a symbol for disaster.
5. The similarities between the fictional sinking of the *Titan* and the real sinking of the *Titanic* are rather _____.
6. The outside frame of the *Titanic* was divided into 16 compartments, and even if 4 were flooded, the ship could stay afloat _____.
7. When 5 of the watertight compartments were smashed by an iceberg, the water that flooded in caused the ship to _____ to one side.
8. The crew worked _____ to lower lifeboats, but there was not enough room in them for all the passengers.
9. Would the _____ of lost lives have been as high if there had been a law requiring enough lifeboats for all passengers?
10. That law and others passed because of the *Titanic* tragedy are more meaningful than any other _____ paid to the memory of the passengers and the crew.

WORD PLAY Construct a crossword puzzle using the following words: *toll, list, novelty, dazzled, tribute*. Draw the puzzle and write the clues. (Avoid using definitions or synonyms that are in the book.) Then trade puzzles with a classmate.

ROBERT D. BALLARD

1942–

Robert Ballard has been fascinated by the sea since his childhood, when he explored beaches and read about famous sailors such as Captain Cook and Admiral Byrd. As an adult, Ballard helped pay for his education in oceanography by training dolphins at a marine park. Eventually, he joined the staff at Woods Hole Oceanographic Institute in Massachusetts. There he began his search for the *Titanic*, using remote-control underwater robots. Among the first things the robot cameras saw were the empty lifeboat racks—"the last thing many of the people saw as they were looking for a lifeboat," Ballard says.

Ballard is one of the world's leading marine geologists. He has spent more time exploring the ocean depths in submarines than any other scientist has and has helped develop new systems for underwater exploration.

The explorer has now set his sights on inspiring children to learn. "We need to declare war on ignorance, and the only way is through education. I want to recruit people to study science, just as a coach recruits basketball players."

OTHER WORKS *Exploring Our Living Planet, The Discovery of the* Titanic, *The Discovery of the* Bismarck, *The Wreck of the* Isis   Extended Reading

LASERLINKS
• *SCIENCE CONNECTION*

WHAT DO YOU THINK?

Reflecting on Theme

Have students recall some of the ideas about appearances that they explored before they began reading the selections in Part One. Ask them to describe how their ideas have developed as a result of reading about the sinking of the *Titanic*.

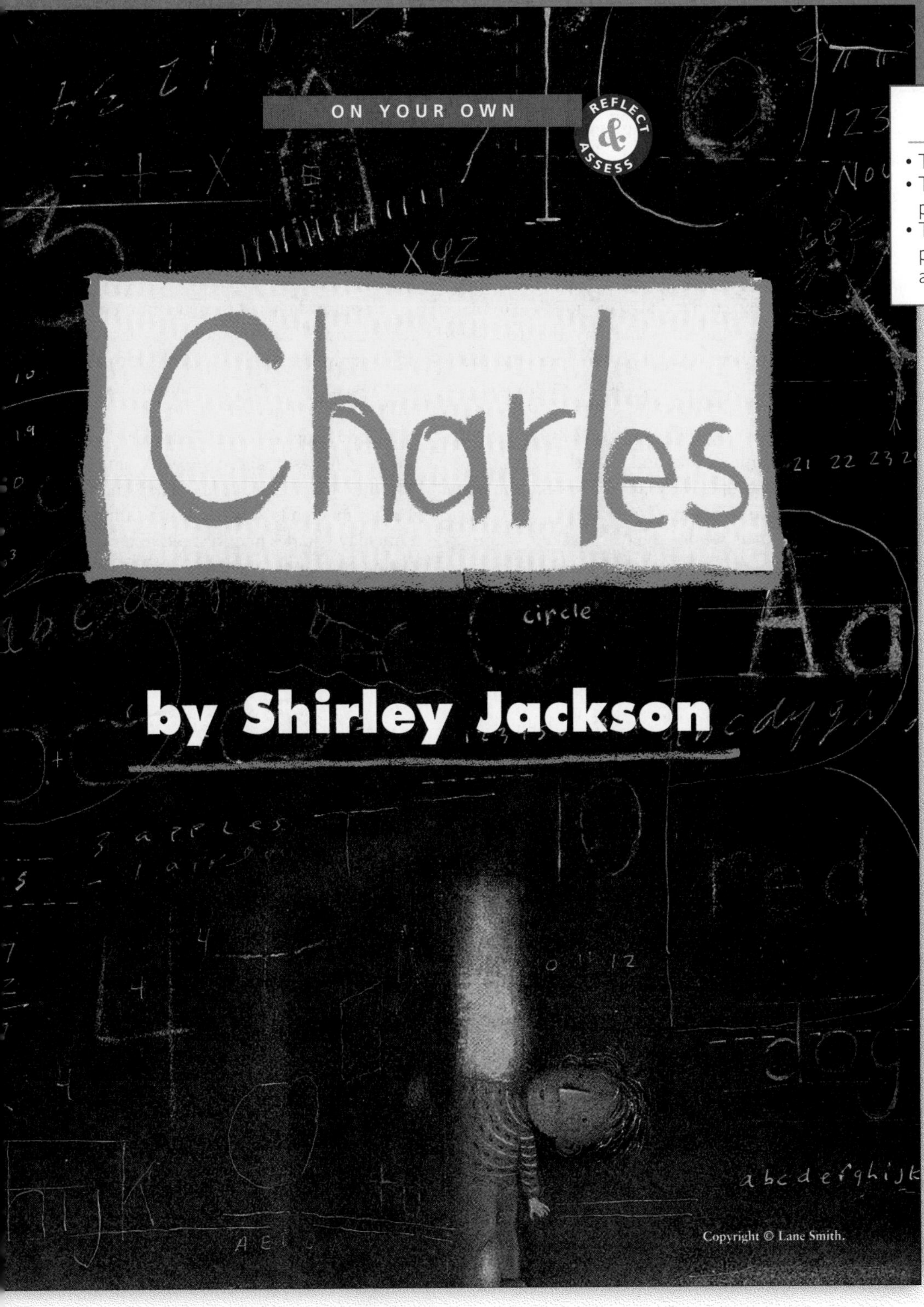

Charles

by Shirley Jackson

Copyright © Lane Smith.

Reading Pathways

- Invite students to do a choral reading, choosing parts for each person to read.

- Encourage students to read for enjoyment and discover subtle humor in the story.

- Have students read independently and write questions and comments in their journals.

- Evaluate how well students can read, interpret, discuss, and write about the selection on their own by using the Integrated Assessment for Unit Five, located in the Alternative Assessment booklet. Administer the assessment at the end of the unit after students have read all the selections and completed all the writing that was assigned.

PRINT AND MEDIA RESOURCES

UNIT FIVE RESOURCE BOOK
Strategic Reading: Literature, p. 33

FORMAL ASSESSMENT
Selection Test, p. 111
Part Test, pp. 113–114
🔲 Test Generator

ALTERNATIVE ASSESSMENT
Unit Five Integrated
  Assessment, pp. 25–30

ACCESS FOR STUDENTS ACQUIRING ENGLISH
Selection Summaries

SUMMARY

Laurie has just started kindergarten, and each day he comes home full of stories about a naughty classmate named Charles. Charles's behavior is so outrageously bad that Laurie's family often talks about it. Laurie's mother wants to meet Charles's mother, but she misses the chance when she has to skip the first Parent Teacher Association meeting. During the third and fourth weeks of school, Laurie reports that Charles is behaving much better—but Charles soon begins misbehaving again. At the next P.T.A. meeting, Laurie's mother scans the group for Charles's mother but sees no likely candidates. After the meeting, she chats with Laurie's teacher and laughingly brings up the subject of the notorious Charles. "Charles?" the teacher replies, having already hinted that Laurie is a difficult child. "We don't have any Charles in the kindergarten."

Thematic Link: *Appearances to the Contrary* When supposedly well-behaved Laurie regales his parents with tales of the mischievous Charles, they are concerned about his influence upon Laurie. His mother's surprise must be great when she finally discovers that Laurie—not the non-existent Charles —has been disrupting the kindergarten!

he day Laurie started kindergarten, he renounced[1] corduroy overalls with bibs and began wearing blue jeans with a belt. I watched him go off the first morning with the older girl next door, seeing clearly that an era of my life was ended, my sweet-voiced nursery-school tot replaced by a long-trousered, swaggering[2] character who forgot to stop at the corner and wave goodbye to me.

He came home the same way, the front door slamming open, his cap on the floor, and the voice suddenly become raucous shouting, "Isn't anybody *here*?"

At lunch he spoke insolently[3] to his father, spilled Jannie's milk, and remarked that his teacher said that we were not to take the name of the Lord in vain.

"How *was* school today?" I asked, elaborately casual.

"All right," he said.

"Did you learn anything?" his father asked.

Laurie regarded his father coldly. "I didn't learn nothing," he said.

"Anything," I said. "Didn't learn anything."

"The teacher spanked a boy, though," Laurie said, addressing his bread and butter. "For being fresh," he added with his mouth full.

"What did he do?" I asked. "Who was it?"

Laurie thought. "It was Charles," he said. "He was fresh. The teacher spanked him and made him stand in a corner. He was awfully fresh."

"What did he do?" I asked again, but Laurie slid off his chair, took a cookie, and left, while his father was still saying, "See here, young man."

The next day Laurie remarked at lunch, as soon as he sat down, "Well, Charles was bad again today." He grinned enormously and said, "Today Charles hit the teacher."

"Good heavens," I said, mindful of the Lord's name, "I suppose he got spanked again?"

"He sure did," Laurie said. "Look up," he said to his father.

"What?" his father said, looking up.

"Look down," Laurie said. "Look at my thumb. Gee, you're dumb." He began to laugh insanely.

"Why did Charles hit the teacher?" I asked quickly.

"Because she tried to make him color with red crayons," Laurie said. "Charles wanted to color with green crayons, so he hit the teacher, and she spanked him and said nobody play with Charles; but everybody did."

The third day—it was Wednesday of the first week—Charles bounced a seesaw onto the head of a little girl and made her bleed, and the teacher made him stay inside all during recess. Thursday Charles had to stand in a corner during story time because he kept pounding his

---

1. **renounced:** refused to have anything more to do with.
2. **swaggering:** walking in a showing-off way.
3. **insolently:** rudely and disrespectfully.

594   UNIT FIVE   PART 1: APPEARANCES TO THE CONTRARY

Multicultural Perspectives

KINDERGARTEN The first kindergarten was set up by Friedrich Fröbel in Blankenburg, Germany, in 1837. Although other schools had previously been established to educate young children, Fröbel was the first to call the school a *kindergarten*. Serving as a transition for children from home to more formal schooling, Fröbel used a variety of instructional materials including songs, games, stories, and specially chosen toys to work with the children.

The first kindergarten in the United States was started by Margaretha Meyer Schurz, who had studied under Fröbel in Germany. In 1856 she established a German-speaking school in her home in Watertown, Wisconsin. Elizabeth P. Peabody established an English-speaking kindergarten in Boston in 1860. Not until 1873 in St. Louis was the first public kindergarten established. At that time, the American kindergartens changed somewhat from Fröbel's original idea to include educational activities that pertained to children's own experiences in the home and their environments. They also began to teach simple handwork skills.

feet on the floor. Friday Charles was deprived of blackboard privileges because he threw chalk.

On Saturday I remarked to my husband, "Do you think kindergarten is too unsettling[4] for Laurie? All this toughness and bad grammar, and this Charles boy sounds like such a bad influence."

"It'll be all right," my husband said reassuringly. "Bound to be people like Charles in the world. Might as well meet them now as later."

On Monday Laurie came home late, full of news. "Charles," he shouted as he came up the hill; I was waiting anxiously on the front steps. "Charles," Laurie yelled all the way up the hill, "Charles was bad again."

"Come right in," I said, as soon as he came close enough. "Lunch is waiting."

"You know what Charles did?" he demanded, following me through the door. "Charles yelled so in school they sent a boy in from first grade to tell the teacher she had to make Charles keep quiet, and so Charles had to stay after school. And so all the children stayed to watch him."

"What did he do?" I asked.

"He just sat there," Laurie said, climbing into his chair at the table. "Hi, Pop, y'old dust mop."

"Charles had to stay after school today," I told my husband. "Everyone stayed with him."

"What does this Charles look like?" my husband asked Laurie. "What's his other name?"

"He's bigger than me," Laurie said, "and he doesn't ever wear a jacket."

Monday night was the first Parent-Teachers meeting, and only the fact that the baby had a cold kept me from going; I wanted passionately to meet Charles's mother. On Tuesday Laurie remarked suddenly, "Our teacher had a friend come to see her in school today."

"Charles's mother?" my husband and I asked simultaneously.

"Naaah," Laurie said scornfully. "It was a

man who came and made us do exercises; we had to touch our toes. Look." He climbed down from his chair and squatted down and touched his toes. "Like this," he said. He got solemnly back into his chair and said, picking up his fork, "Charles didn't even *do* exercises."

"That's fine," I said heartily. "Didn't Charles want to do exercises?"

"Naaah," Laurie said. "Charles was so fresh to the teacher's friend he wasn't *let* do exercises."

"Fresh again?" I said.

"He kicked the teacher's friend," Laurie said. "The teacher's friend told Charles to touch his toes like I just did, and Charles kicked him."

"What are they going to do about Charles, do you suppose?" Laurie's father asked him.

Laurie shrugged elaborately. "Throw him out of school, I guess," he said.

Wednesday and Thursday were routine; Charles yelled during story hour and hit a boy in the stomach and made him cry. On Friday Charles stayed after school again and so did all the other children.

---

4. **unsettling:** troubling; disturbing.

CHARLES **595**

Cooperative Learning
WRITING AND PERFORMING A SKIT

Divide students into two groups to create a skit about what happens *after* Laurie's mother discovers that there is no child in the kindergarten named Charles. Have one group create the dialogue and stage directions for Laurie's mother and the teacher, and the second group prepare dialogue and stage directions for the other parents (who may have been as eager to meet Laurie's mother as she was to meet "Charles's"). Have each group assign a recorder, an encourager of participation, a direction giver, and a clarifier. When each group has finished writing its skit, suggest that students choose a director to coordinate the dialogue and stage directions. Then have students perform their skit.

Teacher's Role Act as a monitor to make sure that students' dialogue and stage directions reflect Laurie's mother's realization that the real Laurie is much different from the way she has imagined him.

Rubric

3 Full Accomplishment Students quietly and efficiently work in groups and create realistic dialogue that reflects the characters being portrayed. Each assigned individual works to see that the group accomplishes its task.

2 Substantial Accomplishment Students create dialogue and stage directions for the characters but have trouble staying on task or monitoring their goal.

1 Little or Partial Accomplishment Students have difficulty projecting a possible conversation among Laurie's mother, his teacher, and other interested parents. They are unable to complete an effective dialogue.

Individual Activity

WRITING CHARACTER SKETCHES

Have students write character sketches of Charles and of Laurie. Suggest that they begin by listing character traits that they discerned from their reading. Then have them summarize the similarities and differences between the "two" characters.

Teacher's Role Suggest a structure for students to follow. For example, they might jot down details about Laurie and Charles and then draw inferences about each character's personality traits.

Rubric

3 Full Accomplishment Students develop richly detailed character sketches that show rather than merely tell what Laurie and Charles are like.

2 Substantial Accomplishment Students provide effective sketches that need a few more examples or details.

1 Little or Partial Accomplishment Students do not include enough physical description or personal qualities to make the characters seem real.

With the third week of kindergarten, Charles was an institution[5] in our family. The baby was being a Charles when she cried all afternoon. Laurie did a Charles when he filled his wagon full of mud and pulled it through the kitchen. Even my husband, when he caught his elbow in the telephone cord and pulled telephone, ash tray, and a bowl of flowers off the table, said, after the first minute, "Looks like Charles."

During the third and fourth weeks there seemed to be a reformation[6] in Charles. Laurie reported grimly at lunch on Thursday of the third week, "Charles was so good today the teacher gave him an apple."

"What?" I said, and my husband added warily, "You mean Charles?"

"Charles," Laurie said. "He gave the crayons around and he picked up the books afterward, and the teacher said he was her helper."

"What happened?" I asked incredulously.

"He was her helper; that's all," Laurie said, and shrugged.

"Can this be true, about Charles?" I asked my husband that night. "Can something like this happen?"

"Wait and see," my husband said cynically. "When you've got a Charles to deal with, this may mean he's only plotting."

He seemed to be wrong. For over a week, Charles was the teacher's helper. Each day he handed things out, and he picked things up; no one had to stay after school.

"The PTA meeting's next week again," I told my husband one evening. "I'm going to find Charles's mother there."

"Ask her what happened to Charles," my husband said. "I'd like to know."

"I'd like to know myself," I said.

On Friday of that week things were back to normal. "You know what Charles did today?" Laurie demanded at the lunch table, in a voice slightly awed.[7] "He told a little girl to say a word, and she said it; and the teacher washed her mouth out with soap, and Charles laughed."

"What word?" his father asked unwisely, and Laurie said, "I'll have to whisper it to you; it's so bad." He got down off his chair and went around to his father. His father bent his head down, and Laurie whispered joyfully. His father's eyes widened.

"Did Charles tell the little girl to say *that*?" he asked respectfully.

"She said it *twice*," Laurie said. "Charles told her to say it *twice*."

"What happened to Charles?" my husband asked.

"Nothing," Laurie said. "He was passing out the crayons."

Monday morning Charles abandoned the little girl and said the evil word himself three or four times, getting his mouth washed out with soap each time. He also threw chalk.

---

5. **institution:** a firmly established and accepted part.

6. **reformation:** an improvement in character and conduct.

7. **awed:** filled with respect, fear, and wonder.

y husband came to the door with me that evening as I set out for the PTA meeting. "Invite her over for a cup of tea after the meeting," he said. "I want to get a look at her."

"If only she's there," I said prayerfully.

"She'll be there," my husband said. "I don't see how they could hold a PTA meeting without Charles's mother."

At the meeting I sat restlessly, scanning each comfortable, matronly[8] face, trying to determine which one hid the secret of Charles. None of them looked to me haggard[9] enough. No one stood up in the meeting and apologized for the way her son had been acting. No one mentioned Charles.

After the meeting, I identified and sought out Laurie's kindergarten teacher. She had a plate with a cup of tea and a piece of chocolate cake; I had a plate with a cup of tea and a piece of marshmallow cake. We maneuvered up to one another cautiously and smiled.

"I've been so anxious to meet you," I said. "I'm Laurie's mother."

"We're all so interested in Laurie," she said.

"Well, he certainly likes kindergarten," I said. "He talks about it all the time."

"We had a little trouble adjusting, the first week or so," she said primly, "but now he's a fine little helper. With occasional lapses,[10] of course."

"Laurie usually adjusts very quickly," I said. "I suppose this time it's Charles's influence."

"Charles?"

"Yes," I said laughing, "you must have your hands full in that kindergarten, with Charles."

"Charles?" she said. "We don't have any Charles in the kindergarten." ❖

---

8. **matronly:** mature and dignified.
9. **haggard:** having a wild, worn-out look.
10. **lapses:** slips; failures.

SHIRLEY JACKSON

1919–1965

Shirley Jackson was born in San Francisco and grew up on the West Coast. After attending Syracuse University, she married the literary critic Stanley Edgar Hyman and settled with him in Vermont.

Jackson's stories have often been described as haunting, amusing, and unpredictable. Because she wrote so many stories about mysterious events, some of her friends called her the "Virginia Werewolf of Séance Fiction."

Although Jackson was best known as a master of the haunted tale, she also wrote many humorous stories, plays, and children's books. Her most hilarious books, *Life Among the Savages* (1953) and *Raising Demons* (1957), affectionately describe the personalities and escapades of her husband and four children. Since she was such a master storyteller, it is no wonder that many of her books and short stories have been adapted for television, film, and stage productions.

Jackson once remarked that she loved to write because "it's the only way I can get to sit down." She also treasured sitting down to spend time with her children, and she read to them nearly every night—but never from her own horror stories, for fear they would not be able to fall asleep. At the age of 46, Shirley Jackson died of heart failure.

OTHER WORKS "Louisa, Please Come Home," "The Lottery," *The Haunting of Hill House*

Class Discussion
SHARING IDEAS

Teacher's Role Use the following questions to engage students in a class discussion. Before you begin, you may wish to make certain students understand what the ending implies: that Charles is an imaginary person Laurie has created and that Charles's misbehavior actually describes Laurie's.

1. Why do you think Laurie creates Charles? *(Possible responses: Creating a "bad child" assures Laurie that he won't get in trouble at home; Laurie wants to test his parents' reactions to bad behavior.)*

2. Why do you think Charles's behavior at school eventually begins to improve? *(Possible responses: He grew tired of always being "bad." He had tested his teacher and schoolmates and didn't like their reactions to his misbehaving. He knew that soon his parents would discover Charles's real identity.)*

3. How do you think Laurie feels before his mother goes off to the parent-teacher meeting? *(Possible responses: scared that his mother is going to find out Charles's identity; relieved that he won't have to keep pretending about Charles)*

SHIRLEY JACKSON

Shirley Jackson is best known as a master of horror and suspense. Her brilliant story "The Lottery" depicts the dark side of quite ordinary people. Her novel *The Haunting of Hill House* (1959) earned her the prestigious Edgar Allan Poe Award for suspense horror fiction. In contrast to her disturbing horror stories, Jackson's books about the absurd and hilarious vagaries of family life reveal her humor and humanity.

OVERVIEW

In the Guided Assignment for this section, students will write a critical response to a piece of writing. By writing a critical response, students will learn to state their opinions and support them with evidence. As preparation for this assignment, The Writer's Style will help students understand how sound devices can add depth and interest to writing. In Reading the World, students will review a picture of a building to apply their skills in supporting opinions.

Objectives

- To recognize how authors use sound devices to achieve certain effects
- To add depth to writing through the use of sound devices
- To write a critical review of a piece of literature
- To express and support opinions about a controversial issue

Skills

LITERATURE
- Understanding and identifying alliteration, consonance, and onomatopoeia

WRITING AND LANGUAGE
- Using transitions to show relationships

GRAMMAR AND USAGE
- Creating emphasis with capitalization and punctuation
- Correcting run-on sentences

- Using coordinating conjunctions

MEDIA LITERACY
- Evaluating a picture of a building

SPEAKING, LISTENING, AND VIEWING
- Peer discussion
- Group conferencing
- Group discussion

CRITICAL THINKING
- Making judgments
- Synthesizing
- Analyzing
- Selecting relevant information

Teaching Strategy: MODELING
In the following models, the sound devices of alliteration and consonance add interest to the selections. Students can use these techniques in their own writing. They can also look for these techniques in the selections they read.

(A) Oden Possible response: The *w* sound is alliterative in *Walnut, woods,* and *wind.* The *s* sound is alliterative in *satin, such,* and *seizure.*

(B) Walker Possible responses: *Essence* and *message* are an example of consonance, as are *sniff* and *leaf.*

SHARING YOUR VIEWS

Have you ever finished reading a piece of literature and thought, "I've got to tell my friends to read this!" When you decide that a selection is or is not worth reading, you are doing what professional critics do: you're making an evaluation or judgment. On the following pages, you will become a better critic as you

- learn how writers emphasize the sounds of words
- evaluate some aspect of a story or poem
- explore how you evaluate opinions in everyday life

Writer's Style: Sound Devices Writers rely on the sounds of words, as well as their meanings, to give depth and interest to their writing.

Read the Literature

Try reading the excerpts aloud to hear the sound devices.

Literature Models

(A) Alliteration
Alliteration is the repetition of a sound or letter at the beginning of words. What examples of alliteration can you find in this excerpt?

> Walnut
> like the satin leaves of the oak
> that fallen overwinter in woods
> where night comes quickly
> and whose wind-peaked piles
> deepen the shadows
> of such seizure.
>
> Gloria Oden, from "The Way It Is"

(B) Consonance
Consonance is the repetition of consonant sounds within lines of poetry. What examples of consonance can you find in this excerpt?

> A nose that
> sniffs
> the essence
> of Earth. And knows
> the message
> of every
> leaf.
>
> Alice Walker, from "Without Commercials"

598 UNIT FIVE: NOT AS IT SEEMS

PRINT AND MEDIA RESOURCES

UNIT FIVE RESOURCE BOOK
The Writer's Style, p. 37
Prewriting, p. 38
Elaboration, p. 39
Peer Response Guide, pp. 40–41
Revising and Proofreading, p. 42
Student Model, p.43
Rubric, p.44

GRAMMAR MINI-LESSONS
Transparencies, pp. 2, 28, and 42
Copymasters, pp. 2 and 37

WRITING MINI-LESSONS
Transparencies, p. 33

ACCESS FOR STUDENTS ACQUIRING ENGLISH
Reading, and Writing Support

FORMAL ASSESSMENT
Guidelines for Writing Assessment

 → WRITING COACH

onnect to Life

riters use sound devices in all kinds of writing to create easing rhythms and jolts of excitement. One common vice is onomatopoeia, which uses words whose sounds ggest their meanings, such as *hiss* and *pow.* Look for omatopoeia in this excerpt from a magazine article.

agazine Article

his is pinball with a difference. u power up the little puck, hit the nch button, and flap your flippers zap the puck into the opposite al. A little red light shows where e puck is zinging around inside e game, triggering loud beeps and zzes as you score. You can play ne, but it's more fun with a friend.

from "The 1992 Toy Test"
Zillions, December 1992/January 1993

Onomatopoeia
Which words' sounds suggest their meanings? How do those words make the writing more interesting to read?

y Your Hand: Using Sound Devices

Find Sound Devices Use alliteration to describe what one of the following sounds like: school hallways between classes, a rainstorm, or traffic on a busy street.

Imitate Animals Use consonance to create a few phrases or sentences that describe the sounds and movements of a chicken, a snake, or any other animal.

Use Onomatopoeia For each thing or situation below, write a word that describes what sound you would hear.

- a snake
- a bat hitting a ball
- breaking glass
- a bursting balloon
- a barking dog

- a rock landing in water
- a speeding motorcycle
- a speeding baseball
- a singing bird
- a closing door

SkillBuilder

 GRAMMAR FROM WRITING

Creating Emphasis with Capitalization and Punctuation

Just as writers use sound devices to make their writing pleasing to the ear, they sometimes play with capitalization and punctuation to make certain words eye-catching. To emphasize certain words or phrases, writers may use nonstandard capitalization and punctuation. Capital letters, for example, can emphasize shouting or loud noises.

"JACKIE!" Maria shouted and then grabbed the hood of Jackie's sweatshirt.

In the following excerpt from Robert D. Ballard's *Exploring the Titanic,* the exclamation point creates a sense of urgency and suspense.

A huge, dark shape loomed out of the night directly ahead of the Titanic. An iceberg!

APPLYING WHAT YOU'VE LEARNED
On a separate sheet of paper, revise the following sentences. Use capitalization and punctuation to create emphasis.

1. Wow. Are these for me?
2. Hey. Don't sit there.
3. The cars hit with a loud crash. Then, crash, another car smashed into the wreck.

C "The 1992 Toy Test" Possible response: Examples of onomatopoeia include *hit, flap, zap, zinging, beeps,* and *buzzes.* They make the writing more interesting by suggesting the sounds of a pinball game.

Try Your Hand

1. Descriptions will vary but should include words that begin with similar consonants. Here is an example: The rain dripped and dropped down from the roof. It splashed and sloshed onto the soaking ground.

2. Responses will vary. Encourage students to use consonance in their descriptions. Here is a sample: The cat slept then sat around. When it purred, it fired up its throat and let out a loud sound.

3. Responses will vary. Here are some samples:
   - slither
   - crack
   - tinkle
   - pop
   - yap yap
   - plop
   - vroom
   - whoosh
   - chirp
   - click

SkillBuilder GRAMMAR FROM WRITING

CREATING EMPHASIS WITH CAPITALIZATION AND PUNCTUATION
Encourage students to understand that nonstandard capitalization should be used sparingly; otherwise, it loses its effect. Exclamation marks should also be used only in certain cases—to show surprise or add emphasis.

Application Possible responses:
1. Wow! Are these for ME?
2. HEY! Don't sit there.
3. The cars hit with a loud CRASH! Then, CRASH!

another cart smashed into the wreck.

Additional Suggestions Students can continue with these sentences:
1. And then, wham, I had the right answer.
2. The letters screamed "wet paint" in red.
3. I did not want to go to the dentist. But my mother said I must. Help.

Teaching Strategy:
STUMBLING BLOCK

D Remind students that imagery creates a picture in the reader's mind. Guide students to look for various elements, including the ones listed here, and techniques, such as the use of sentence variety and transitions, that make writing interesting and enjoyable.

Critical Thinking:
MAKING JUDGMENTS

E Students may have difficulty deciding what it is about their chosen selection that appeals to them or that they find striking. Help them to identify something about the writing that caused them to be interested in it. Remind them to review their reading logs and notebooks for descriptions of their first impressions of the selection. Encourage them to identify one element in a selection and focus only on it.

Writing Skill: DRAFTING
A THESIS STATEMENT

F Help students come up with a sentence that expresses their opinion about the selection and gives their writing a focus. Prompt them by asking them to imagine that they are describing the selection to a friend using only a single sentence. Students can begin their sentences like this: "I thought my selection was _____."

WRITING ABOUT LITERATURE

Criticism

Have you noticed that people comment on everything—from school lunches to a classmate's new haircut? How would you comment on the literature you read in this unit? One way for you to express your opinions and share them with others is by writing a critical review.

GUIDED ASSIGNMENT

Write a Critical Review On the next few pages, you'll evaluate a story or poem from Unit Five. Then you'll write a critical review focusing on one element that was most important in shaping your response.

① Prewrite and Explore

D Choose a selection from Unit Five that you felt strongly about—that you either liked or disliked. Reread the literature, jotting down comments on the use of sound devices, the imagery, the dialogue, or anything else that contributed to your opinion.

FINDING A FOCUS

Review your notes, and try to narrow your focus to one element of the literature, such as character, imagery, plot, or setting. To help yourself do this, answer these questions.

E • Which one element has the most to do with whether I like or dislike the selection?
• What personal or other reasons do I have for liking or disliking this selection?

GATHERING SUPPORT

Now that you've chosen an element to review, how will you convince others that you have sound reasons for liking or disliking it? Look through the selection for examples that can help you prove your point. You might organize your support in a cluster diagram like the one at the left.

STATING YOUR OPINION

F You may want to draft a brief statement that sums up your overall opinion of the selection. Were you mainly pleased, bored, upset, inspired

Student's Cluster Diagram

Some examples of strong imagery in "The Way It Is."

lips of a rose
wind-peaked piles
pirate silver
satin leaves
IMAGERY
owl-eyed
billowed in a fine mist
willow fall of black hair

Assessment ✓ Option

SELF-ASSESSMENT When students have completed the Gathering Support activity, they can assess their work by asking themselves the following questions:
• *Have I found more than one example for support?*
• *Does the focus accurately reflect the examples?*

• *Do I want to shift the focus to take into account other examples?*
• *Is there some order to the elements I have selected?*

---

② Make an Outline

Now that you've gathered support for your opinion, how are you going to begin your review? An informal outline is one good way to organize your ideas. You can make one in your notebook or on note cards. Some notes for the body of one student's outline are shown below.

Student's Informal Outline

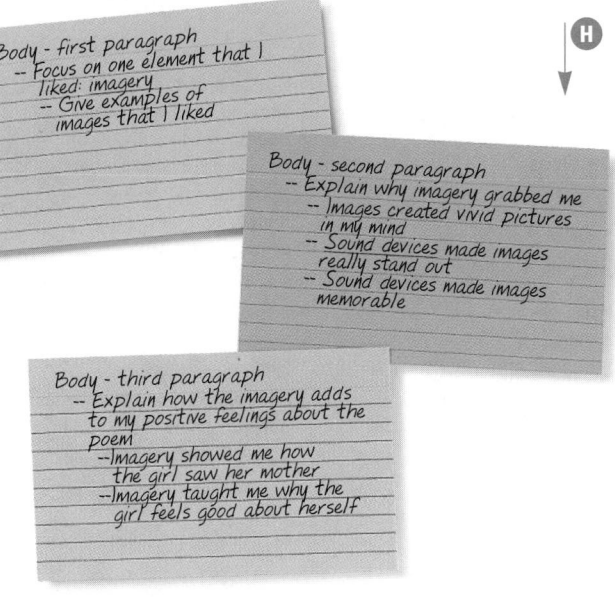

Body - first paragraph
-- Focus on one element that I liked: imagery
-- Give examples of images that I liked

Body - second paragraph
-- Explain why imagery grabbed me
-- Images created vivid pictures in my mind
-- Sound devices made images really stand out
-- Sound devices made images memorable

Body - third paragraph
-- Explain how the imagery adds to my positive feelings about the poem
-- Imagery showed me how the girl saw her mother
-- Imagery taught me why the girl feels good about herself

③ Draft and Share

You can follow your outline or organized note cards as you write your first draft. Remember, in your review tell exactly what you like or dislike, explain your reasons, and give an overall opinion. When you've finished, feel free to have another student read your writing and give you feedback.

 PEER RESPONSE

- Can you sum up in a sentence or two what you think I'm saying about the literature?
- How did you feel as you read this piece?
- Where do the ideas flow smoothly?
- Which parts, if any, were confusing?

SkillBuilder

 WRITER'S CRAFT

Using Transitions to Show Relationships

In a critical review, you express your opinions and also give reasons for them. Transitions are connecting words and phrases that show the relationship between ideas. To make your reasons clear, you can use transitions to show cause and effect. Notice the transition in the following example:

The poem "The Way It Is" has strong imagery. **For this reason,** *I think it is worth reading.*

The following are some transitions you might use to show cause-and-effect: *therefore, for this reason, thus, so, as a result, due to,* and *accordingly.*

APPLYING WHAT YOU'VE LEARNED
Fill in the blanks in the following sentences with a transition from the list above.

The sound devices really made the images stand out. . . . I still recall the sounds of phrases like "shadows of such seizure."

 The imagery added to the positive feeling I had when I read the poem. . . . I felt happy when I finished reading it.

 WRITING HANDBOOK

For more information on transitions, see pages 817–818 in the Writing Handbook.

Writing Skill: PLANNING

Ⓖ The outline provides an opportunity for students to think about their opinions and the support they have gathered. Remind students that the basic parts of an essay are the introduction, body, and conclusion. The body, which is the largest section of the essay, contains the main points students want to make. Encourage them to group each idea and its supporting examples together.

Teaching Strategy: MODELING

Ⓗ Some students may have difficulty making an outline. Encourage them to notice that each note card in the Student's Informal Outline tells what one of the paragraphs in the body of the essay will do. Lead them to discover that the evidence on each card relates to the point stated on that card. Tell them a review may have any number of points. However, advise them that one point is probably not enough, and, if they have too many points, they may want to combine some to form larger categories.

Teaching Strategy:
USING THE SKILLBUILDER

Ⓘ To help students write their drafts, you may want to teach the SkillBuilder on Using Transitions to Show Relationships at this time. It explains how transitions can make the connections between ideas clearer.

SkillBuilder  WRITER'S CRAFT

USING TRANSITIONS TO SHOW RELA-TIONSHIPS Point out to students how the transition in this example, "For this reason," links the evidence in the first sentence to the opinion that follows the transition. Explain how the other cause-and-effect transitions listed here show certain relationships. For example, the transition *therefore* can be used between evidence and a conclusion drawn from it.

Application Possible responses:

The sound devices really made the images stand out. As a result, I still recall the sounds of phrases like "shadows of such seizure."

The imagery added to the positive feeling I had when I read the poem. Thus, I felt happy when I finished reading it.

Additional Suggestions Have students continue adding transitions:

The alliteration was clever . . . it added to the fun in reading the poem.

I didn't want the poem to end . . . I was sad when it was over.

I felt like I wanted to read more by this author . . . I went to find more poems.

Reteaching/Reinforcement *Writing Mini-Lessons* transparencies p. 33

The Writer's Craft

Using transitions, pp. 271–273

J Encourage students to add more examples and to refer to their outlines to check where each example should go. Remind them to look closely at the various sound devices to see what effects these have on their reading of the selection.

Teaching Strategy: MODELING

K Discuss with students how this sample meets the Standards for Evaluation on this page. Point out that the introduction names the piece of literature and provides information as to what the poem is about. This introduction suggests that the opinions that follow will be positive. Each opinion is supported with evidence from the poem: The descriptions, imagery, and first few lines are specifically mentioned. A quotation may have been chosen instead of a paraphrase to specify the surprising twist.

Standards for Evaluation

Ideas and Content
- Gives title, author, and a brief summary of the literature.
- Gives supported evaluation of an element of the selection.
- Includes examples, quotations, and details that support the evaluation.
- Has a conclusion that clearly summarizes the evaluation.

Structure and Form
- Uses well-organized paragraphs and a clear organization.
- Includes transitional words and phrases to show relationships among ideas.

Grammar, Usage, and Mechanics
- Contains no more than two or three minor errors in grammar and usage.
- Correctly integrates quotations into the text
- Contains no more than two or three minor errors in spelling, capitalization, and punctuation.

WRITING ABOUT LITERATURE

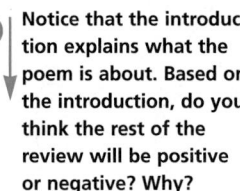

4 Revise and Edit

J Now that you are ready to revise your draft, read the story again. Can you find more support for your opinion? Does your original opinion of the selection still hold true? After you complete your final draft, think about what you discovered about poetry and the way you react to it.

Student's Final Draft

Beautiful Is "The Way It Is"

"The Way It Is" by Gloria Oden is a wonderful poem. The narrator of the poem describes how she feels about her mother and herself. Her sense of pride has everything to do with her mother. In fact, most of the poem is about the mother's beauty. The imagery is strong and unique. It drew me into the poem and helped me understand the narrator's feelings. The first few lines mention a beauty "with skin fabled white as the unicorn's," but the narrator adds a surprising line. She says, "such commercial virtues / could never have led me to assume myself / anywhere near as beautiful as / my mother."

K Notice that the introduction explains what the poem is about. Based on the introduction, do you think the rest of the review will be positive or negative? Why?

Why might the writer have chosen to quote the narrator rather than paraphrase what she said?

Standards for Evaluation

A critical review
- identifies the literature in the introduction
- gives a supported evaluation of a literature element
- states opinions clearly
- provides reasons for the opinions
- has a conclusion that presents an overall opinion of the literature

---

Assessment Option

SELF-ASSESSMENT To help students assess their own writing, have them ask themselves the following questions:
- *What is my main opinion?*
- *Have I treated each point in a separate paragraph?*
- *Does each point have supporting evidence from the poem?*
- *Does the conclusion sum up my opinion?*

Grammar in Context

Run-on Sentences If you have run-on sentences in your critical review, you will lose the reader's respect. A run-on sentence occurs when two or more sentences are written as one. This could happen because you forgot to separate sentences with a period or because you used a comma incorrectly. To correct a run-on sentence, add the proper end mark and capitalize the first letter of the second sentence.

> The imagery is strong and unique. It drew me into the poem and helped me understand the narrator's feelings. The first few lines mention a beauty "with skin fabled white as the unicorn's," *but* the narrator adds a surprising line. She says, "such commercial virtues / could never have led me to assume myself / anywhere near as beautiful as / my mother."

For more information on correcting run-ons, see the SkillBuilder on using coordinating conjunctions at the right.

Try Your Hand:
Correcting Run-on Sentences

Correct each of the following run-on sentences.

1. I remember wanting to brush my mother's hair when I was little, she never let me.
2. My mother is strong and brave she has a soft side, too.
3. I used to wish my dad was tall I also used to say he was the reason I'd never become a basketball player.
4. What do you know I learned a lesson if you try hard enough you might beat all the odds.

SkillBuilder

 GRAMMAR FROM WRITING

Using Coordinating Conjunctions

One way to correct a run-on sentence is to join the parts with a comma and a **coordinating conjunction.** The words *and, but,* and *or* are coordinating conjunctions. Adding a coordinating conjunction also shows the relationship between the parts of the sentence.

Incorrect: *We are all lovely in our own way, many people are unhappy with their features.*

Correct: *We are all lovely in our own way,* **but** *many people are unhappy with their features.*

APPLYING WHAT YOU'VE LEARNED
Correct the run-on sentences below. Try to join the sentences with a comma and a coordinating conjunction. If that method is not effective, you may add an end mark and capitalize the first word of the next sentence.

1. I am short I play basketball
2. I used to get all kinds of advice be a gymnast be a wrestler.
3. I followed my dreams look at me now.

 GRAMMAR HANDBOOK

For more information on run-on sentences, see pages 849–850 of the Grammar Handbook.

L Remind students that a complete sentence contains a subject and a verb. Stress that students cannot correct a run-on sentence by merely inserting a comma. Students must add a comma and a coordinating conjunction, a semi-colon, or a period and then begin a new sentence.

Teaching Strategy:
USING THE SKILLBUILDER

M To help students correct run-on sentences, you may want to teach the SkillBuilder on Using Coordinating Conjunctions at this time.

Try Your Hand

Responses will vary. If students have chosen to use a coordinating conjunction, check that they have used an appropriate one. Here are some sample answers:
1. I remember wanting to brush my mother's hair when I was little, but she never let me.
2. My mother is strong and brave. She has a soft side, too.
3. I used to wish my dad was tall. I also used to say he was the reason I'd never become a basketball player.
4. What do you know? I learned a lesson. If you try hard enough, you might beat all the odds.

PORTFOLIO

Invite students to write a note to themselves, indicating what they discovered about their personal tastes from writing a critical review. Have students attach the note to their final draft.

SkillBuilder GRAMMAR FROM WRITING

USING COORDINATING CONJUNCTIONS
Help students understand that changing the coordinating conjunction alters the relationship between the two ideas expressed in the main clauses.

Application Possible responses:
1. I am short, but I play basketball.
2. I used to get all kinds of advice. "Be a gymnast!" and "Be a wrestler!"
3. I followed my dreams, and look at me now!

Additional Suggestions Have students correct the following run-on sentences.
1. Now I play well I beat all the tall players.
2. They can't understand they say I have springs in my feet.
3. Secretly, I practice a lot it helps to make me more confident.

Reteaching/Reinforcement *Grammar Mini-Lessons* copymasters, pp. 2 and 37, transparencies, pp. 2, 28, and 42

The Writer's Craft

Coordinating Conjunctions, p. 546
Run-on Sentences, pp. 295 and 395–396

READING THE WORLD

On pages 600–603, students learned how to write a critical review of a work of literature. In this lesson, they can apply the skills they learned.

Critical Thinking:
MAKING JUDGMENTS

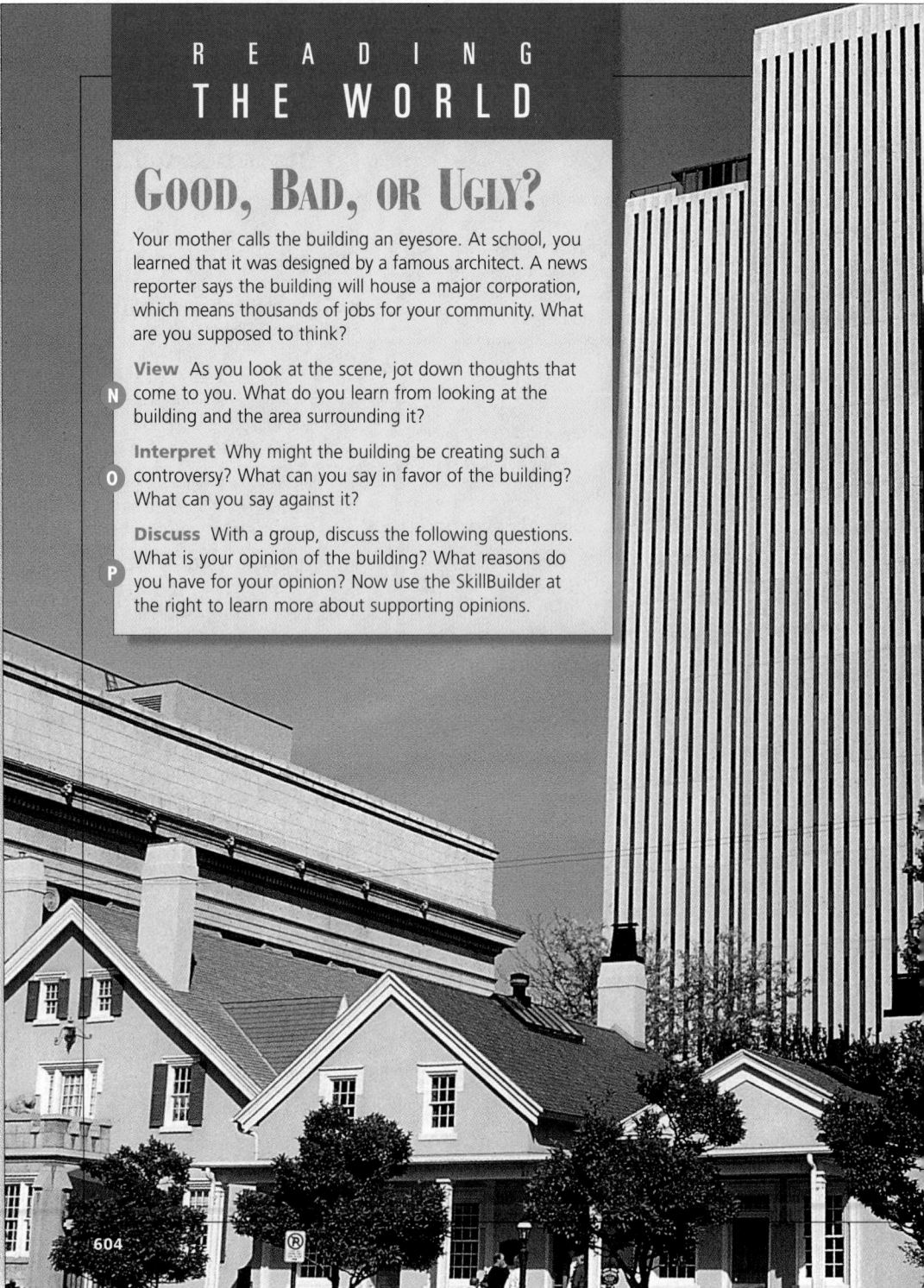

N Encourage students to note their responses to several details in the picture. Have them decide whether they like the houses in the front and whether they like the building in the back. They can consider the trees and the age of the buildings as well. Ask them how they would feel if they were living in this neighborhood. Ask them whether they would prefer the tall building to be present or not.

Media Literacy:
REVIEWING A BUILDING

O Students may speculate that the building is creating a controversy because of its size, design, or location in the neighborhood. Ask whether they like the look of the building itself or not and whether they think the building should be in a different location.

Speaking and Listening:
GROUP DISCUSSION

P Guide students to listen carefully to what others have to say about the building. You may want to require students to provide reasons to support each opinion they express.

GOOD, BAD, OR UGLY?

Your mother calls the building an eyesore. At school, you learned that it was designed by a famous architect. A news reporter says the building will house a major corporation, which means thousands of jobs for your community. What are you supposed to think?

View As you look at the scene, jot down thoughts that come to you. What do you learn from looking at the building and the area surrounding it?

Interpret Why might the building be creating such a controversy? What can you say in favor of the building? What can you say against it?

Discuss With a group, discuss the following questions. What is your opinion of the building? What reasons do you have for your opinion? Now use the SkillBuilder at the right to learn more about supporting opinions.

604

Selecting Relevant Information

Many objects and events draw mixed reviews. Be it a poem or an office building, chances are some people will like it and some people won't. As you learned in writing your critical review, it's not enough to simply like or hate something; you need to be prepared to explain why you think as you do. Answering the questions below can help you select relevant information to support your opinion.

- Have I gathered reasons, facts, and examples to support my opinion?
- Are the reasons I give to support my opinions sensible and based on facts?
- Do my facts come from a reliable source?
- How does my opinion compare with that of others familiar with the subject?
- How can I use my own experiences to support my opinion?

APPLYING WHAT YOU'VE LEARNED
Think of some other objects or events that draw mixed reviews from people. Discuss one or more of those issues in a small group. Each group member should share his or her opinion and provide support.

SkillBuilder   CRITICAL THINKING

SELECTING RELEVANT INFORMATION
You may want to explain to students that a mixed review also can be a review that shows a mixed reaction. For instance, a reviewer may like the fact that a new building will bring jobs to the community; however, the same reviewer may not like the design of the building. Such a review would show both opinions. Encourage students to understand that it is good to have a complex response to literary works and art objects.

Application Most objects and events will draw mixed reviews. Encourage groups to think about all aspects of their chosen items. For instance, students may argue that they liked a certain story, movie, or activity. Guide them to be specific about what it was that they liked. Ask them if there were any aspects they did not like.

UNIT FIVE

Part 2 Lesson Planner

TIME ALLOTMENTS SHOWN ARE APPROXIMATE. DEPENDING ON YOUR GOALS AND THE NEEDS OF YOUR STUDENTS, YOU MAY WISH TO ALLOW MORE OR LESS TIME FOR CERTAIN PORTIONS OF THE LESSON.

Table of Contents	Discussion	Previewing the Selection	Reading the Selection
PART OPENER **MYSTERIOUS CIRCUMSTANCES** **What Do You Think?** page 606	**20 MINUTES** • Reflect on the part theme		
SELECTION **The Hound of the Baskervilles** page 608 AVERAGE		**20 MINUTES** • **PERSONAL CONNECTION** • **LITERARY CONNECTION** • **READING CONNECTION:** Reading a mystery	**35 MINUTES** • Introduce vocabulary • Read pp. 608–18 (11 pp.) **20 MINUTES PER SCENE** • Read pp. 619–25 (7 pp.) • Read pp. 626–32 (7 pp.) • Read pp. 633–40 (8 pp.) • Read pp. 641–47 (7 pp.) • Read pp. 648–54 (7 pp.)

Writing	Exploring Topics	Prewriting	Drafting and Revising
WRITING FROM EXPERIENCE **Persuasion**	**30 MINUTES**	**30 MINUTES**	**80 MINUTES**

Time estimates assume in-class work. You may wish to assign some of these stages as homework.

FROM PERSONAL RESPONSE TO CRITICAL ANALYSIS		ANOTHER PATHWAY	LITERARY CONCEPTS	QUICKWRITES
	OR			

50 MINUTES

| • Discussion questions | OR | • Newspaper article | • Mood and foil | • Speech
• Profile
• Ending |

•ALTERNATIVE ACTIVITIES	•LITERARY LINKS	•CRITIC'S CORNER	•THE WRITER'S STYLE	•ACROSS THE CURRICULUM	•ART CONNECTION	•WORDS TO KNOW	•BIOGRAPHY

50 MINUTES

| ✔ | | ✔ | | SCIENCE | | ✔ | ✔ |

25 MINUTES

Part 2 Cooperative Project

A New Theme Park Attraction

Overview

Students will plan a new theme park attraction with the emphasis on the mysterious and the eerie.

PROJECT AT A GLANCE

The selection in Unit Five, Part 2 deals with the unknown in the form of an eerie "whodunit" murder mystery. For this project, students will work together to brainstorm ideas for a new theme park attraction that will epitomize all that is enigmatic and ghostly. They will draw a diagram of the attraction, specifying how and what the public will and will not see. When the diagram is complete, groups will write a scenario about taking a walk or a ride through their attraction and explain how and why their attraction would be considered mysterious and eerie. Groups will make a presentation for the class using the diagrams and scenarios. Diagrams and scenarios will then be put on display for comparison and comment by the whole class.

OBJECTIVES

- To understand how and why a person, place, thing, or situation might be considered mysterious
- To create and model a new theme park attraction that is mysterious and eerie
- To explain how the attraction fulfills the conditions of the project

SUGGESTED GROUP SIZE

3–4 students

MATERIALS

- Poster board
- Art supplies
- Theme park brochures

1 Getting Started

Arranging the Project

You might want to visit a travel agency and collect brochures on some of the most popular theme parks in your area or state, or in the country. Students are probably familiar with the names of the big parks, but many will not have actually visited them.

Gather any art supplies you think students will need. Encourage them to make their diagrams colorful and attractive. Groups will need a place to spread out while they work on the diagrams. You may have to make arrangements for them to work in the art room or elsewhere during specified hours.

Arranging the Presentations

Ideally, after groups make their presentations to the class, the diagrams and scenarios should be placed on display for all students in the school to enjoy. If possible, reserve space in the lobby display cases or hall bulletin boards.

The diagrams and scenarios should at least be placed on display in the classroom. This will allow students to inspect them in preparation for a postmortem discussion of the project.

2 Creating the Attractions

Introducing the Project

Explain that students will be working cooperatively in small groups to design a new theme park attraction. These attractions should above all be mysterious and eerie. Groups will make a complete diagram of their attraction and will write a scenario from the viewpoint of someone going through the building or taking the ride. They also will write a brief explanation justifying how and why their attraction would be considered mysterious and eerie.

Have students look over the theme park brochures you collected. If any students have visited a theme park, they might also explain what it was like in general, some of the specific attractions they saw, how they operate, and if any could be considered mysterious. Students who have seen real or fictional parks on television may also want to comment.

You might also touch on some things that people consider mysterious or eerie to get students in the mood for making some great scary attractions.

Group Investigations

Divide students into groups of three or four. They should immediately start brainstorming ideas for the attraction. These plans should include how people will view the attraction, (on foot, from a "people mover" train, from a controlled boat on water, or by some other unique method). The diagrams should not only show the path of progression but also should be labeled with everything seen by the participants. A more detailed description of the elements can be written in the scenario and mentioned in the explanation and justification of the mysteriousness of the ride.

Creating a Project Description

Meet with each group several times during the project. They can write a brief description of their attraction before beginning the diagram, and at that time you can point out any factors that may need further thought or revision. Also meet to discuss the first draft of their scenario and explanation in case they need to clarify any factors presented. You might also use a few minutes of class time to help groups overcome any obstacles they are facing.

OPTION 1: SCARY SCHOOL Students can use the school building as the basis of their attraction and unsuspecting students as participants—on paper only. Stress that all events should be nonviolent and nonthreatening to participants.

OPTION 2: MYSTERY PLAY Students can script and act out a play that involves a mystery of some sort. The solution can be left for the audience to guess, although the group should have the answer well thought out in advance. This option may require a larger number of students in each group.

OPTION 3: REAL-LIFE MYSTERIES Students can research some real-life mysteries that have never been solved. They should investigate the background of the mysteries, what people think happened, and what is being done today (if anything) to solve the mysteries. Remind students that this will require independent research, not just the repetition of information viewed on a television program.

OPTION 4: MURDER IN THE LIBRARY Several commercial murder mysteries are now available in which the players stage a "murder" and then remain in character for the audience to question as they try to solve the mystery. Some of these may be available at larger libraries, or students can write one of their own. Remind groups that they should not edit out the fun in their attractions. Encourage them to be creative and to use their imaginations.

3 Sharing the Attractions

Groups should make a presentation of their attraction before the rest of the class. This can be an abbreviated review of the scenario and explanation and a showing of the diagram. Later, put diagrams, scenarios, and explanations on display so others can review them more carefully and completely. After such review, hold a class meeting about the attractions, culminating in a vote for the most popular attraction.

 ## Assessing the Project

The following rubric can be used for group or individual assessment.

3 Full Accomplishment Students follow directions and produce a diagram of a theme park attraction that can be described as mysterious and eerie, as well as a scenario of the ride and an explanation of the elements of the ride.

2 Substantial Accomplishment Students produce a diagram, but the scenario is sketchy or the explanation lacks justification.

1 Little or Partial Accomplishment Student's diagram is incomplete or does not fulfill the requirements of the assignment.

For the Portfolio
Include a copy of your written assessment in each student's portfolio. You might also want to keep a photo of the diagram, or copies of the final scenario and/or explanation.

Note: For other assessment options, see the *Teacher's Guide to Assessment and Portfolio Use*.

Cross-Curricular Options

SOCIAL STUDIES
 Have students research superstitions from other countries and compare and contrast them with some found in the United States.

LANGUAGE ARTS
Ask students to begin with the word *mysterious* and list synonyms and other related words that they can use in a short story.

MUSIC
Students can find and record music that would be appropriate either for their theme park attraction or for mystery television, radio, or melodrama productions.

ART
Students can create a poster advertising the new theme park. They should make the poster appealing to people looking for something to do in their spare time.

Resources

Amazing Mysteries of the World by Catherine O'Neill discusses unexplained mysteries such as Big Foot, Easter Island, and UFOs.

How to Haunt a House for Halloween by Bob Friedhoffer and Harriet Brown shows how to turn any space into a scary place.

The Headless Ghost: True Tales of the Unexplained by William R. Warren features Lincoln's ghost in the White House and other famous mysteries.

The Moving Coffins: Ghosts and Hauntings around the World by David C. Knight details supernatural events from 20 countries.

UNIT FIVE **PART 2**

WHAT DO YOU THINK?

Objectives

The activities on this page can be used to
- introduce the theme "Mysterious Circumstances," since each activity is connected to the selection in Part 2
- create materials for students' personal portfolios that they can return to later for reconsideration or revision
- build an understanding of theme that students can return to and revise as they progress through the unit

How would you explain it?
Remind students that they should include only key events that help to explain the mystery. Invite students to write a draft of a mystery story based on the events they have listed.

Can you solve the puzzle?
Tell students that they first should list several words that come to mind when they think about mysteries. Students can then experiment with ways of arranging the words so that intersecting words share a letter in common. You may wish to bring in some examples of completed crosswords for students to examine.

Isn't it elementary?
Tell students that they might review the skills and traits that TV detectives often display. Encourage students to make their descriptions specific and vivid. Invite volunteers to present their completed profiles and pictures to the class.

MYSTERIOUS CIRCUMSTANCES

WHAT DO  THINK?

REFLECTING ON THEME

Some events are not easy to explain—your cat crashes into the nightstand apparently because it is fleeing from someone . . . *but only you are in the house.* Your imagination starts working, and you search for a reasonable explanation. Use the activities on this page to think about mysteries and detectives.

How would you explain it?

Suppose your cat really was fleeing from someone—or something—when it crashed into the nightstand. In your notebook, list some key events that you might include in a story that explains the mystery. Share your ideas with a partner.

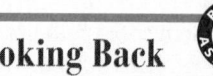

key events

Can you solve the puzzle?

Create a crossword puzzle containing words associated with mysteries, such as *crime, suspect, motive,* and *spooky.* Use your knowledge of mysteries to write a clue for each word. Photocopy the puzzle and distribute it to your classmates.

Isn't it elementary?

Imagine that you are creating a TV show about a pair of detectives. Write a profile of each detective, describing his or her personality and skills, traits, or habits. Also create a picture of each detective, either drawing it yourself or piecing it together from magazine clippings or photographs.

Looking Back

At the beginning of this unit, you thought about the difference between appearance and reality. Which of the selections in Part 1 do you think best illustrates the statement "Appearances are often deceiving"? Present your choice—and your reasons for it—in a brief speech to your classmates.

REFLECT & ASSESS

Looking Back
Students may wish to review the selections in Part 1 and summarize each briefly. From this information they can choose the selection that best illustrates Aesop's statement. Students should write their speeches before delivering them to the class, supporting their choices with examples from the selections.

COMMUNITY OUTREACH
Invite police detectives from a local precinct to the class to speak about crime solving. You may wish to have students work together in small groups to prepare questions for the speakers in advance. After the guests have spoken, have students write brief summaries of what they have learned about the importance of careful observation and investigation.

DRAMA

The Hound of the Baskervilles
Sir Arthur Conan Doyle
Adapted and dramatized by Tim Kelly

PERSONAL CONNECTION Activating Prior Knowledge

Think of some of the detectives you have read about or have seen in movies or on TV. Who are your favorite detectives? Why do you find them appealing? Record your answers in your notebook. Then, as you read this play, compare your favorite detectives with the famous Sherlock Holmes. Setting a Purpose

LITERARY CONNECTION Building Background

The Hound of the Baskervilles is a classic mystery featuring the British detective Sherlock Holmes, the most famous detective in literature. This character was created by Sir Arthur Conan Doyle in the late 1880s. Holmes is a man of science, intellect, and action—a detective who can recognize different newspaper types at a glance, make chemical analyses, and identify 140 varieties of tobacco ash. A master of observation, Holmes has trained himself to notice details that others overlook. Combining his observations with his knowledge, he uses logical reasoning to draw conclusions that often astonish other characters and readers alike.

Active Reading
READING CONNECTION

Reading a Mystery Part of the fun of reading a mystery is being a detective yourself and trying to solve the crime before the story's detective does. Good mystery writers provide readers with clues, but they also provide red herrings—information designed to throw readers off the track. As you read this play, use the evidence and your own observations to match wits with Sherlock Holmes. A chart like the one shown here can help you keep track of your observations. You may want to make a separate chart for each character in the play.

Detective Notes
Facts/clues/evidence:
Character's name/relationship:
Suspicious behavior:
Motive:
Inferences/conclusions:

 LASERLINKS
• *LITERARY CONNECTION*   **607**

OVERVIEW
Objectives

- To understand and appreciate a detective story featuring Sherlock Holmes
- To learn the skills involved in reading a mystery
- To understand mood and foil
- To express understanding of the selection through a choice of writing forms, including a speech, a profile, and a revised ending
- To extend understanding of the selection through a variety of multimodal and cross-curricular activities

---

Skills

READING SKILLS/STRATEGIES
- Noting relevant details

THE WRITER'S STYLE
- Dialogue in plays

GRAMMAR
- Sentence fragments

LITERARY CONCEPTS
- Mood
- Foil
- Suspense

GENRE STUDY
- Drama

SPELLING
- Words ending in *-ise* and *-ize*

STUDY SKILLS
- Library catalogs

SPEAKING, LISTENING, AND VIEWING
- Drama performance
- Scientific observation
- Interviews

Cross-Curricular Connections

HISTORY
- Spiritualism

MATH
- British pounds

SCIENCE
- Forensic methods
- Bogs
- Night blindness

- Warm milk
- Graphology
- Forensic science

SOCIAL STUDIES
- British class system

GEOGRAPHY
- Moors

LITERARY CONNECTION
Sherlock Holmes Sherlock Holmes was created in the late 1800s, and he soon became one of the most popular characters in the history of literature. These images show some of the early illustrations that accompanied Arthur Conan Doyle's books, sceens from movie adaptations of these detective stories, and a photograph of Conan Doyle himself.

Side A, Frame 49432

PRINT AND MEDIA RESOURCES

UNIT FIVE RESOURCE BOOK
Strategic Reading: Literature, p. 47
Vocabulary SkillBuilder, p. 50
Reading SkillBuilder, p. 48
Spelling SkillBuilder, p. 49

GRAMMAR MINI–LESSONS
Transparencies, p. 1
Copymasters, p. 1

WRITING MINI–LESSONS
Transparencies, p. 48

ACCESS FOR STUDENTS ACQUIRING ENGLISH
Selection Summaries
Reading and Writing Support

FORMAL ASSESSMENT
Selection Test, pp. 115–116
Test Generator

ALTERNATIVE ASSESSMENT
End-of-Year Integrated Assessment: Reader, pp. 31–39; Student Response Booklet, pp. 41–54

AUDIO LIBRARY
See Reference Card

LASERLINKS
Literary Connection

INTERNET RESOURCES
McDougal Littell Literature Center at http://www.hmco.com /mcdougal/lit

SUMMARY

The famous detective Sherlock Holmes and his colleague Dr. Watson are on the case at Baskerville Hall, where Sir Henry Baskerville has inherited the family fortune following his uncle Charles's mysterious death. According to an old curse, all Baskerville heirs are doomed to be killed by a monstrous beast that roams the moors—and now Sir Henry's life, too, seems to be in danger. The cast of suspicious characters includes the Barrymores, a married couple who serve at Baskerville Hall; Laura Lyons, who had an appointment with Sir Charles the night he died; and Lady Agatha, the executrix of Sir Charles's estate. Holmes determines that all these suspects are innocent and that Sir Henry's fiancée, Kathy Stapleton, is the murderer. She has trained an enormous hound to attack the Baskerville heir. Kathy's "brother" Jack is actually her husband, a Baskerville descendant who will inherit the family fortune if Sir Henry were to die childless. The police shoot the hound and arrest Kathy.

Thematic Link: *Mysterious Circumstances* Sherlock Holmes probes the mysterious curse that haunts Baskerville manor.

Art Note

***The Good Shepherd* by Henry Ossawa Tanner** Tanner (1859–1937) was the first African-American artist to acquire an international reputation in this century. The French awarded him the Cross of the Legion of Honor in 1923; after his death, the U.S. Postal Service issued a stamp in his honor.

Reading the Art *How would you describe the mood that this painting creates in you? What details help to create this mood?*

The HOUND of the BASKERVILLES

The Good Shepherd (about 1902–1903), Henry Ossawa Tanner. Oil on canvas, Jane Voorhees Zimmerli Art Museum, Rutgers, The State University of New Jersey, in memory of the deceased members of the Class of 1954 (1988.0063).

SIR ARTHUR CONAN DOYLE
ADAPTED AND DRAMATIZED BY TIM KELLY

608

WORDS TO KNOW

accomplice (ə-kŏm′plĭs) *n.* a person who knowingly helps another in a criminal act (p. 654)

bizarre (bĭ-zär′) *adj.* strange and unusual (p. 609)

captivating (kăp′tə-vā′tĭng) *adj.* attracting because of charm or beauty; fascinating **captivate** *v.* (p. 621)

colleague (kŏl′ēg′) *n.* a professional associate; partner (p. 609)

deception (dĭ-sĕp′shən) *n.* an act of deceiving; lie or trick (p. 631)

dissuade (dĭ-swād′) *v.* to persuade someone not to do something; discourage (p. 650)

divulge (dĭ-vŭlj′) *v.* to make known; reveal (p. 651)

evasive (ĭ-vā′sĭv) *adj.* avoiding straight, honest answers; not frank (p. 629)

exonerate (ĭg-zŏn′ə-rāt′) *v.* to declare innocent and free from blame (p. 654)

implicitly (ĭm-plĭs′ĭt-lē) *adv.* without doubt or reservation; unquestioningly (p. 618)

CAST OF CHARACTERS

Lady Agatha Mortimer, a medical doctor, ample, "tweedy," forceful

Perkins, a young maid

Watson, Holmes' colleague

Sherlock Holmes, a famed private investigator interested in bizarre cases, a master at detection

Mrs. Barrymore, the housekeeper

Sir Henry, a young nobleman, heir to a fortune and a curse

Barrymore, a butler, slightly sinister, but capable

Kathy Stapleton, a vivacious young woman

Jack, her brother, given to emotional outbursts

Laura Lyons, a capable young woman with a dangerous secret

Act One
SCENE 1

Setting: *A large sitting room in Baskerville Hall, a manor house[1] located on the English moor.[2] It's a melancholy room with the scent of age and tradition in every corner. Stage right there's a fireplace with a chair on each side. Above the fireplace there's a portrait of Sir Hugo Baskerville, an 18th-century aristocrat, brutal, cruel, insensitive. Upstage center is an entry hall that leads into other parts of the house, with exits right and left, with a few steps in view, left, if possible, to indicate a stairway to the upper floors. On each side of the entry, in the room, there are bookshelves or, perhaps, tables with books,*

---

1. **manor house:** the main house on a large estate.
2. **moor:** an area of open, rolling, often marshy land.

WORDS TO KNOW

colleague (kŏl′ēg′) *n.* a professional associate; partner
bizarre (bĭ-zär′) *adj.* strange and unusual

609

WORDS TO KNOW

ominous (ŏm′ə-nəs) *adj.* threatening harm or evil (p. 651)

rational (răsh′ə-nəl) *adj.* capable of reasoning; sensible (p. 612)

reproach (rĭ-prōch′) *n.* to accuse or blame (p. 646)

surmise (sər-mīz′) *v.* to form an opinion or conclusion without much evidence; guess (p. 612)

theorize (thē′ə-rīz′) *v.* to form an idea or opinion; guess (p. 632)

610

Literary Note

C Although this adaptation of the story is set in the present, it retains much of the tone and style of the original, which is set in 1899. Although modern conveniences, such as a car, are mentioned, the characters behave more like the original Victorian characters than like modern-day people.

Cultural Note

D The fictional Agatha Mortimer, like the real Conan Doyle, received a title of nobility. Peerages, or titles of nobility, are granted by the English king or queen on the recommendation of the prime minister. Life peerages are created for achievement and are valid for only the life of the honoree; hereditary peerages pass on to the peer's closest male heir.

Literary Concept:
STAGE DIRECTIONS

E Explain to students that the italicized words in parentheses are called stage directions. Be sure that students understand that stage directions are for the actors, directors, and stage crew—and, of course, readers of the script. Then point out the stage directions in this passage and ask students to explain their function. *(Possible responses: They tell how the actress playing Lady Agatha should move and appear.)*

Critical Thinking: ANALYZING

F Have students analyze Lady Agatha's greeting and explain what it suggests about her opinion of Holmes and Watson. *(Possible response: She believes the situation is bad at Baskerville Hall but that Holmes and Watson are capable of setting things right.)*

---

statuary, candlesticks or lamps, etc. Stage left are French doors that open out to the moor surrounding Baskerville Hall. Down left there is a writing desk that faces the wall with a chair in front of it. Down right center there is a chaise lounge or a small sofa. Down left center there is a fine chair with a small side table on the upstage side. Additional stage dressing will greatly enhance the stage picture; rugs, books, wall tapestries, et al.;[3] *but about everything hangs a heavy aura of the past—as if the room were about to be turned into a museum. The set is also suited to drapes.*

C Time: *Present. Early afternoon.*

D At Rise: *Lady Agatha Mortimer, a rather ample woman dressed in tweeds, is seated at the desk poring over some document. She is quite aware of the contents and reads to reacquaint herself with certain facts.*

Lady Agatha. "Of the origin of the hound of the Baskervilles there have been many statements, yet as I come in a direct line from Hugo Baskerville, and as I had the story from my own father, who also had it from his, I have set it down with all belief that it occurred even as is here set forth . . ."

(Perkins, *a maid, enters up center, from right.*)

Perkins. He's still not back, Lady Agatha. No sign of him from the upstairs windows, either.

E **Lady Agatha** (*turns, worried*). You shouldn't have allowed him to go, Perkins.

Perkins. It's not my place to stop Sir Henry if he wants to go out.

Lady Agatha. He doesn't know the moor as we do. You know how treacherous it can be.

Perkins. Indeed, I do, m'am. Only yesterday another pony went under the mud at Grimpen Mire.[4]

Lady Agatha. A false step there is sure death.

Perkins. Anyhow, Barrymore's gone to fetch him back.

Lady Agatha. Good. (*Stands, moves center.*) I'm expecting a Dr. Watson and a Mr. Holmes shortly. Show them in the minute they arrive.

Perkins. I will, m'am. Will you be wanting tea?

Lady Agatha. Yes. For four. Sir Henry will be joining us, I trust.

(Perkins *exits.* Dr. John Watson *enters through the open French doors, exuberant and hale.*)

Watson. Ah, there you are, Lady Agatha. Not late, am I?

Lady Agatha. (*She moves to him. They shake hands.*) You'll never know how thankful I am for your presence, Watson. (*looks left*) Where is Mr. Holmes?

Watson. He'll be along shortly.

Lady Agatha (*indicates sofa*). I've arranged for tea.

Watson (*crosses, sits*). I hope you won't take offense, but you do seem distraught.[5] Not

---

3. **et al.:** and others (an abbreviation of the Latin words *et alii*).

4. **mire:** an area of wet, soggy, muddy ground (also called a bog).

5. **distraught:** very troubled.

like you at all. There's one thing I always remember about you from those days we worked together at the hospital. Nerves of steel and a disposition to match.

Lady Agatha. Thank you, Watson. I appreciate that. To tell the truth I have been on edge. Desperate, some might say.

Watson. Desperate?

Lady Agatha. When I heard you and Mr. Holmes were on holiday nearby, I wasted no time getting in touch.

Watson. Not exactly a holiday. Holmes has always been fascinated by the grim charm of this locale, especially the traces of the prehistoric people who lived here.

Lady Agatha. You mean the stone huts dotting the moors. They do give one the feeling of another time.

Watson. Downright creepy if you ask me.

Lady Agatha. I wouldn't be at all surprised to see a skin-clad hairy man crawl out from one of those huts.

Watson. Doing what may I ask?

Lady Agatha. Fitting a flint-tipped arrow on to the string of his bow.

Watson. I'm not given much to flights of fancy. Imagination is more in Holmes' line.

Lady Agatha. I'm looking forward to meeting him.

Holmes. (*He enters via the French doors.*) And so you shall, Lady Agatha.

Lady Agatha. (*They shake hands.*) A very great pleasure for me, Mr. Holmes.

Holmes. Kind of you to say so. I trust you enjoyed your walk around the excavations at Grimpen Mire. The south section, I believe.

Lady Agatha. How do you know I've been there?

Holmes. You left your walking stick outside. The tip is coated with a reddish clay that is found only in that area.

Lady Agatha. You live up to your reputation.

Holmes. Judging from the consistency of the clay you were there within the last three hours.

Lady Agatha. Bravo.

Holmes. I would be cautious if you take your schnauzer there. They have a tendency to move impulsively. Miniature, I should imagine.

Lady Agatha. How do you know I even have a dog?

Holmes. Teeth marks on the walking stick. Obviously the dog is in the habit of carrying it from time to time. The jaw, as indicated by the space between the marks, is not large.

G Ask students what they learn about Lady Agatha from Watson's remarks. (*Possible responses: Lady Agatha has "nerves of steel and a disposition to match," meaning she is usually steady and courageous, but she now appears worried and distraught.*)

CUSTOMIZING FOR

Students Acquiring English

I Encourage students to guess what *prehistoric people* are (*ancient inhabitants*); if necessary, remind them that the prefix *pre-* means "before."

Literary Concept: DRAMA

H Ask students why the playwright has Holmes enter the scene at this point and in this way—through the French doors. (*Possible response: Holmes's entrance generates excitement, especially because he enters just as Lady Agatha mentions him to Watson.*)

Critical Thinking:
MAKING JUDGMENTS

I Explore with students what Holmes's remarks in this passage suggest about his character. Then have students decide if he has the makings of a good detective. (*Possible responses: He is extremely analytical, intelligent, observant, and rational. These are important skills for a good detective.*)

Literary Concept: FOIL

J Explain to students that a foil is a character who provides a striking contrast to the main character. A foil helps make the personal qualities of the main character more apparent. Ask students to explain how Watson is a foil to Holmes in this passage. *(Possible responses: Watson refers to Holmes as an inhuman machine because of Holmes's sharp powers of observation, making Holmes seem all the more imaginative and brilliant. The contrast between Watson's treatment of Lady Agatha and Holmes's treatment emphasizes Holmes's logical nature.)*

CUSTOMIZING FOR
Students Acquiring English

2 You may want to point out that *Elementary* is used to indicate that Holmes regards his deductions about the dog to be very simple—to him, the details were obvious. *Elementary* is probably the one word most English-speakers associate with the detective.

Linking to History

K Between 1850 and 1900, occultism took the form of spiritualism, the belief that the spirits of the dead can communicate with the living through people known as mediums. By 1916, Conan Doyle himself had become convinced that communication with the dead was possible. In fact, he devoted the rest of his life to lecturing on and writing about spiritualism, spending more than a quarter of a million dollars of his own money on this endeavor.

Active Reading: CLARIFY

L Ask students to explain how the village girl escaped. *(Possible response: by climbing out her window and descending the wall, holding onto the ivy)*

That and—(*He plucks a bit of hair from* Lady Agatha's *tweeds.*) this small puff of silver-gray dog fur leads me to <u>surmise</u>—a miniature schnauzer.

J Watson. You really are an automaton, Holmes. A calculating machine. There is something positively inhuman about you at times.

Lady Agatha. (*She sits down left center.*) You take my breath away, Mr. Holmes.

2 Holmes. Elementary.

Watson. You said you needed our help.

Lady Agatha. I do.

Holmes (*moves center*). Does your request, in some way, concern itself with the recent demise of Sir Charles Baskerville?

Lady Agatha. It does.

Watson. London papers said it was a heart attack.

Holmes. An elderly gentleman, if I recall correctly.

Lady Agatha. Over eighty.

Holmes. You suspect foul play.

Lady Agatha. What makes you say that?

Holmes. You would hardly have called upon my services if the situation were not grave.

Lady Agatha. I have always considered myself a <u>rational</u> woman. Watson can vouch for that.

K Watson. Absolutely.

Lady Agatha. I've never taken the occult[6] seriously.

Watson. The occult?

Lady Agatha. (*She stands, crosses to desk, picks up document.*) Perhaps this will explain. (*She steps back, hands the document to* Holmes.)

Holmes (*scans it*). Early eighteenth century, unless it's a forgery.

Lady Agatha. It's no forgery.

Watson. What is it?

Holmes. I'm not unfamiliar with the contents. (*to* Watson) It purports to describe the origin of the curse of the Baskervilles.

Watson. Curse?

Holmes. Come, come, Watson. Common knowledge.

Watson. May be common knowledge to you, but not to me.

(Lady Agatha *crosses to fireplace, studies the portrait of Sir Hugo.*)

Holmes (*studying the document*). The exact date is 1742. (*recalls the legend*) Sir Hugo Baskerville was a villain, a coarse man given to excesses of intemperance[7] and rage. He came to love, if that word can be used with his sort, a village girl. He kidnapped her, kept her prisoner in this house, while night after night he and his foul companions reveled below, probably in this very room.

(Watson *looks around as if he expected Sir Hugo to materialize.*)

Lady Agatha (*looking at portrait*). He has much to answer for.

Holmes. One night, with the aid of the stout ivy outside her window, she made her escape.

Watson. Good for her.

Holmes. There's more to it than that, Watson. Sir Hugo gave chase over the moor, his companions-in-drink riding at his heels. He outdistanced them. (*checks the document again*) Sir Hugo's companions found him on the moor. By the two great stones.

---

6. **the occult:** supernatural matters.

7. **intemperance** (ĭn-tĕm′pər-əns): lack of self-control, especially in drinking alcohol.

WORDS TO KNOW	**surmise** (sər-mīz′) *v.* to form an opinion or conclusion without much evidence; guess
	rational (răsh′ə-nəl) *adj.* capable of reasoning; sensible

612

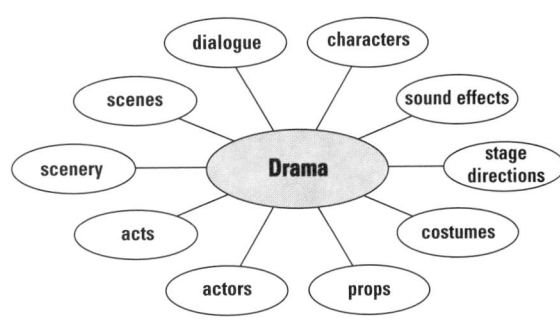

Illustration by Sergio Martinez. From Children's Classics Edition of *The Hound of the Baskervilles* by Sir Arthur Conan Doyle. Copyright © 1992 Crown Publishers, Inc., reprinted by permission of Crown Publishers, Inc.

613

Mini-Lesson **Genre Study**

DRAMA On the chalkboard, draw the web shown, and use it to discuss the elements of a drama:
- meant to be performed
- tells a story through dialogue and the characters' actions
- may contain stage directions to suggest how the actors should move and speak
- may divide the action into acts and scenes

Application Have students copy the web and add examples from *The Hound of the Baskervilles* to illustrate each item.

dialogue · characters · sound effects · stage directions · costumes · props · actors · acts · scenery · scenes · **Drama**

Literary Note

 Sidney Paget, the artist who illustrated the original Sherlock Holmes stories, is credited with helping to establish the image of Sherlock Holmes that stands today. He made Holmes more handsome than Conan Doyle intended and also introduced the famous deerstalker cap, which is used as a design motif on these pages. Conan Doyle gave the detective a "close-fitting cloth cap" in one story and an "ear-flapped traveling cap" in another. The deerstalker cap appears in only eight of the stories; in the rest of the illustrations, Holmes is shown wearing toppers, felt hats, bowlers, and straw boaters.

Literary Concept: SUSPENSE

N Describe how the playwright provides exposition, or background information the audience needs to understand the characters, setting, and mystery. Then have students explain what details in the exposition create suspense. (*Possible response: The mysterious deaths and violent imagery create tension and anticipation.*)

Critical Thinking: HYPOTHESIZING

O Ask students why this detail about Barrymore might be relevant to the story. (*Possible response: Barrymore's discovery of Sir Charles's body makes him a suspect in his murder.*)

Lady Agatha. You can see them from the windows. They marked the door to some long-forgotten temple.

Watson. I have seen them, frightening things in the moonlight.

Holmes. When they came on the spot, the village girl had expired. Fallen dead of fear and fatigue.

Watson. And Sir Hugo?

Holmes. He was by her side. Also dead. But that wasn't what terrified the friends that found him.

Watson. What did?

Holmes. (*He hands him the document; indicates a passage.*) Read it for yourself.

Watson. ". . . and plucking at his throat, there stood a foul thing, a great black beast, shaped like a hound, yet larger than any hound that ever mortal eye has rested upon. And even as they looked the thing tore the throat out of Hugo Baskerville."

Lady Agatha. Many of the family have been unhappy in their deaths. Sudden, bloody, mysterious.

Watson. Surely you don't believe this mumbo-jumbo?

Holmes (*takes back the document*). It is obvious the Baskerville who wrote the account did. (*reads*) "I counsel you by way of caution to forbear from crossing the moor in those dark hours when the powers of evil are exalted."[8]

Watson (*scoffs*). Powers of evil, indeed. It's a fairy tale.

Lady Agatha. Sir Charles believed in the curse.

Holmes. As I recall, Sir Charles was only in residence for a few years.

Lady Agatha. That is correct. His business interests, mainly those in South Africa, kept him away.

Holmes. Who looked after Baskerville Hall?

Lady Agatha. The Barrymores. A married couple. He acts as butler, she as housekeeper.

Holmes. Still in service here?

Lady Agatha. Oh, yes. It was Barrymore who found the body. It was Sir Charles' habit each night to take a walk before retiring.

Holmes. But never onto the moor.

Lady Agatha. Never.

Watson. Because of that silly legend?

Holmes. Watson, please. Do continue, Lady Agatha.

Lady Agatha. The night of his death he went out as usual. He never returned.

---

8. **exalted:** strengthened; more powerful.

Holmes. No sign of violence on the body?

Lady Agatha. None.

Watson. At his advanced age he probably passed on from cardiac exhaustion.

Lady Agatha. Exactly.

Holmes. Who performed the police autopsy?

Lady Agatha. I did.

Holmes. The coroner's jury[9] accepted the medical evidence?

Lady Agatha. There was no reason not to.

Holmes. Lady Agatha, it is not what you're saying that I find of interest, rather what you're not saying.

Lady Agatha. If you weren't a private investigator, Mr. Holmes, I would suspect you of being a psychic.

Holmes. (*He goes to the desk, sets down the document.* Lady Agatha *moves center.*) Why not come directly to the point?

Lady Agatha. I believe Sir Charles was . . . "frightened to death."

Holmes. Proof?

Lady Agatha. Within the last few months it became increasingly plain to me that Sir Charles' nervous system was strained to the breaking point.

Holmes. I asked for proof. Facts.

Lady Agatha. The expression on his face was one of sheer terror.

Watson. Easily explained by a muscle spasm.

Lady Agatha. There was one false statement made by Barrymore at the inquest.

Holmes. Oh?

Lady Agatha. He said there were no tracks on the ground round the body.

Holmes. You said a "false" statement.

Lady Agatha. Perhaps Barrymore didn't see what I saw.

Watson. Which was?

Lady Agatha. My motive for withholding it from the coroner's inquiry is that a person of science shrinks from placing one's self in a position of seeming to endorse a popular superstition.

Holmes. In other words you did see footprints.

Lady Agatha. Yes. A distance off, but fresh and clear.

Watson. Why conceal the fact?

Lady Agatha. I have already explained my reason.

Holmes. The footprints. A man's or a woman's?

Lady Agatha. (*She pauses. Her voice drops low.*) They were the footprints of a gigantic hound. **Q**

(Watson *and* Holmes *exchange a guarded look.* Mrs. Barrymore, *a severe sort of woman, enters up center from left.*)

Mrs. Barrymore. Beg pardon, Lady Agatha. It's Sir Henry. I saw him from upstairs. He's cutting across the moor now.

Lady Agatha. Thank heaven.

Holmes. You're the housekeeper, I take it.

Mrs. Barrymore. Yes, sir. Mrs. Barrymore.

Holmes. How long have you been in service at Baskerville Hall?

(Mrs. Barrymore *looks to* Lady Agatha, *bewildered by the questions.*)

Lady Agatha. It's quite all right, Mrs. Barrymore. This is Mr. Sherlock Holmes.

Mrs. Barrymore. I've been in service here most of my life. **R**

---

9. **coroner's jury:** a jury appointed to look into a death that does not seem to be due to natural causes; its investigation is called an inquest.

THE HOUND OF THE BASKERVILLES **615**

CUSTOMIZING FOR
Students Acquiring English

(3) Explain that a *psychic* is a person who is believed to be sensitive to forces beyond the material world.

Active Reading: EVALUATE

P Have students evaluate Lady Agatha's validity as a witness. You may wish to share the following model with students:

Think-Aloud Model *I remember from the cast of characters that Lady Agatha is a doctor, so she would be familiar with death—even murder. Also, Watson described her as having "nerves of steel and a disposition to match." I think she is cool under pressure and a reliable witness.*

Literary Concept: MOOD

Q Have students describe the mood and the details that help create it. (*Possible responses: The mood is terrifying and eerie. It is created by Lady Agatha's pause, drop in voice, and mentioning of the hound.*)

STRATEGIC READING FOR
Less-Proficient Readers

R Ask students the following questions to make sure they are following the story so far.

• Why have Holmes and Watson come to Baskerville Hall? (*Lady Agatha has summoned them to investigate the mystery of Sir Charles's death.*) **Summarizing**

• According to the newspapers, what was the cause of Sir Charles's death? (*a heart attack*) **Noting Relevant Details**

• What is the curse of the Baskervilles? (*Members of the Baskerville family die suddenly, violently, and mysteriously.*) **Summarizing**

Set a Purpose Have students read to find out about the warning Sir Henry receives, how he reacts, and what Holmes instructs Sir Henry not to do.

Mini-Lesson **The Writer's Style**

DIALOGUE IN PLAYS Explain to students that writers use dialogue—the words that characters speak aloud—in stories, poems, plays, essays, and letters. In plays, dialogue moves the action along, makes the story more interesting, and helps readers understand the characters by showing what they are thinking and feeling.

Application Direct students to reread the dialogue on page 615 to see how it suggests what each character is like. Have students record their inferences on a chart like the one shown.

Reteaching/Reinforcement
• *Writing Mini-Lessons,* transparencies, p. 48

The Writer's Craft

Creating Dialogue, pp. 320–322

Character	Dialogue	Character Traits Inferred

Holmes. Then you know the moor.

Mrs. Barrymore. I grew up on the moor, Mr. Holmes.

Lady Agatha. Mrs. Barrymore and her husband know more about Baskerville Hall than anyone in the county.

Mrs. Barrymore. If you have no other questions, sir, I'll see to my duties.

Holmes. I have no other questions at this time. (Mrs. Barrymore *nods and exits up center, turns right.*) Remarkable woman. Reminds me of Aimee Small, the noted axe murderess of Charing Cross.

Sir Henry. (*He enters via the French doors. A good-looking young man.*) Ah, I see you've finally caught him in your net, Lady Agatha.

Lady Agatha. Henry, you mustn't wander over the countryside until you know more of the place.

Sir Henry. Nonsense. I stuck to the paths and the light was excellent. I was visiting with Kathy.

Lady Agatha. (*She moves behind the sofa.*) I sent Barrymore to go and look for you.

Sir Henry (*moves center, extends his hand to Watson*). It's a pleasure for me, Mr. Holmes.

Watson (*stands, shakes*). Thank you, but I'm not Holmes. I'm John Watson, M.D., a former colleague of Lady Agatha's. (*He nods to Holmes at desk.*)

Sir Henry. You'll forgive me. (*He moves down center. Holmes meets him halfway. They shake.*)

Holmes. I take it from the timbre of your accent that you've spent some time in America, Sir Henry.

Sir Henry. The States and Canada. I only recently returned. If it hadn't been for my uncle's death, I'd still be there.

Watson. Surely you don't believe the balderdash

Lady Agatha has been spouting. (*turns to Lady Agatha, apologetic*) I beg your pardon, my dear.

Holmes. Watson has never been noted for an abundance of tact. (Watson *pouts, sits on the sofa.*) Do you share Lady Agatha's doubts about your uncle's death?

Sir Henry. I haven't made up my mind.

Lady Agatha. Show him the letter.

Holmes. Letter?

Sir Henry. (*He sits down left center, takes out a wallet and from it plucks a folded piece of stationery.*) This arrived one morning at my London hotel. (*He hands it to Holmes who unfolds it.*)

Holmes. Words cut from the London *Times* and gummed to the paper.

Watson. Rather an old-fashioned gambit,[10] eh, Holmes?

Holmes. Arsenic[11] is old-fashioned too, Watson, but it does the trick.

Lady Agatha. How can you tell it's the *Times*?

Holmes. *Times* print is entirely distinctive. These words could have been taken from nothing else. (*reads aloud*) "As you value your life or your reason keep away from the moor."

Watson (*to Lady Agatha*). Nothing supernatural about that.

Holmes. It might have been sent by someone who was convinced that Sir Charles' death was . . . "unearthly."

Watson. Who?

Holmes. Someone trying to frighten Sir Henry from Baskerville Hall. No envelope, no stamp?

---

10. **gambit:** clever trick; ploy.

11. **arsenic:** a kind of poison.

Sir Henry. I found it tucked under the door of my room.

Holmes. You intend to remain in residence here, Sir Henry?

Sir Henry. There is no man on earth, or devil in hell who can prevent me from staying in my own home.

Holmes. I take that as a final answer?

Sir Henry. Absolutely.

Holmes. Then you did well to seek me out, Lady Agatha. May I keep this? (*the letter*)

Sir Henry. Of course.

Holmes (*to* Lady Agatha). Anything found near the body?

Lady Agatha. The stub of Sir Charles' cigar. Two stubs actually, and a great deal of cigar ash.

Holmes (*ponders this*). Curious. (*quick*) There is no other claimant on the estate, I presume?

Lady Agatha. There were three brothers. Sir Charles was the elder. The second died young.

Sir Henry. That was my father.

Holmes. And the third?

Lady Agatha. Rodger Baskerville. A black sheep.[12] Fled to Central America and died there of tropical fever.

Holmes. Supposing that anything happened to our young friend here—you'll forgive the unpleasant hypothesis—who would then inherit?

Lady Agatha. Since Rodger died unmarried, the estate would descend to James Desmond.

Sir Henry. A distant cousin.

Watson. Is there any other kind? (*He chuckles.*)

Holmes. Watson, please. (Watson *pouts*.)

Sir Henry. He's a clergyman in the village of Tracey Coombes.

Holmes. Quite close, actually.

Sir Henry. It's a short drive.

Holmes. Who profited by Sir Charles' will?

Lady Agatha. There were many significant sums to individuals and a large number of charities.

Sir Henry. He was a generous man.

Holmes (*impatient*). Yes, yes.

Sir Henry. The Barrymores each received five thousand pounds.

Watson (*impressed*). He was generous.

Holmes. Did they know they would receive this sum?

---

12. **black sheep:** a person considered less respectable than the rest of his or her family.

Linking to Science

W Many of the investigative methods that Conan Doyle described in his Sherlock Holmes stories are now commonplace in today's forensic labs. For example, police now realize the importance of the study of tobacco ash. Today, every laboratory has a complete set of tables giving the appearance and composition of various ashes. Standard detective methods now include studying poisons, handwriting, stains, dust, footprints, traces of wheels, the shape and position of wounds, and the theory of cryptograms.

Critical Thinking:
HYPOTHESIZING

X Have students guess why Holmes is questioning Sir Henry and Lady Agatha about other members of the Baskerville family. (*Possible responses: He suspects that Sir Henry profited by Sir Charles's murder; he wants to make sure that there is no hidden heir who has a motive for murder.*)

Active Reading: EVALUATE

Y Ask students why Holmes is so curious about who will inherit the estate. (*Possible response: Holmes is trying to establish a motive for the murder. Greed and personal gain are common reasons for murder.*)

Lady Agatha. Sir Charles was fond of talking about the provisions of his will.

Holmes. Unwise.

Lady Agatha. I hope you won't suspect everyone who profited. After all, Sir Charles left me ten thousand.

Watson. (*He gives a long, low whistle. Holmes freezes him with a stare. He swallows hard.*) Sorry.

Lady Agatha. You will take the case, Mr. Holmes?

Holmes (*lost in thought*). Hmmmmm?

Lady Agatha. You will take the case.

Holmes (*brisk*). Out of the question.

Lady Agatha. But you must.

Sir Henry. We've been counting on you, Mr. Holmes.

Holmes. I'm due in Bristol sometime tomorrow, then I must spend a few days in London.

Sir Henry. If it's a question of money—

Holmes. My professional charges are on a fixed scale. I do not vary them, except when I remit them altogether.

Watson. Holmes, surely you can let other matters wait.

Holmes. You know my methods. (*to Lady Agatha and Sir Henry*) I will do my best to settle my prior obligations as quickly as possible. In the meantime, I shall leave Watson here to look out for you, Sir Henry.

Sir Henry. Whatever you think best.

Holmes. Please follow his advice. I trust him implicitly. (*to Watson*) You will communicate anything of interest to me in London.

Watson. (*He is delighted with the "assignment."*) You can depend on it.

Holmes. On one point I must demand complete fidelity.[13]

Sir Henry. What is it?

Holmes. Under no circumstances must you venture onto the moor at night. I can't impress the importance of this enough.

Lady Agatha. Then you do believe the legend?

Holmes. You understand, Watson?

Watson. I do.

Holmes (*moves for open doors*). There's something in the air that disturbs me.

Sir Henry. The air? What's in the air, Mr. Holmes?

Holmes (*turns back*). The scent of murder, Sir Henry. *Murder.* (Holmes *exits. The others look after him and, then, nervously to each other.*)

CURTAIN

---

13. **fidelity:** faithful obedience.

WORDS
TO
KNOW   **implicitly** (ĭm-plĭs′ĭt-lē) *adv.* without doubt or reservation; unquestioningly

618

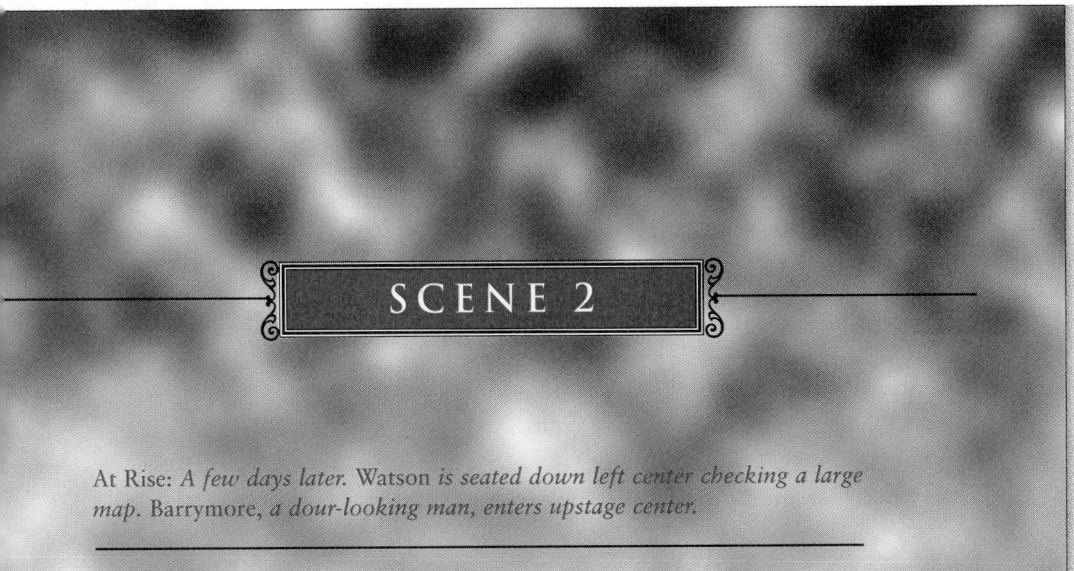

SCENE 2

At Rise: A few days later. Watson *is seated down left center checking a large map.* Barrymore, *a dour-looking man, enters upstage center.*

Barrymore. You wanted to see me, Dr. Watson?

Watson (*turns*). Ah, Barrymore. Yes. I don't know quite how to put this.

Barrymore (*doesn't understand*). Sir?

Watson. I mean, I'm not altogether sure of what I heard. (Barrymore *looks puzzled.*) Last night, close to midnight, did you hear the sound of a woman sobbing?

Barrymore. I did not.

Watson. Hmmmm.

Barrymore. Perhaps it was the wind. The wind racing on the moor can make all sorts of strange noises.

Watson. The sound was most certainly in the house, not on the moor. I thought, perhaps, it might have been Mrs. Barrymore.

Barrymore. We share the same room, Doctor. If my wife were crying I would have known.

Watson. Could it have been Perkins?

Barrymore. Highly unlikely. Perkins seldom spends the night. She lives with her family on the Grimpen Mire road.

Watson. (*He is certain of what he heard, but realizes he isn't going to get anywhere with* Barrymore.) You may be right. The wind racing on the moor.

Barrymore. I'll be going into the village later this afternoon, Doctor Watson. Is there anything I might get for you?

Watson. No, thank you, Barrymore. I'll be going in myself.

Barrymore. Very good, sir. (*turns to exit*)

Watson. One moment, Barrymore.

Barrymore (*faces* Watson). Sir?

Watson. You've been in service here for quite some time.

Barrymore. My father was the caretaker. My family has looked after the Hall for four generations.

Watson. In that case, you know the families that inhabit the moor.

Barrymore. I do.

Watson (*back to the map*). I see the cottage that belongs to Lady Agatha, and Baskerville Hall

THE HOUND OF THE BASKERVILLES **619**

Active Reading: QUESTION

CC Ask students to question why Watson has summoned Barrymore, based on the information in the stage directions and their prior knowledge of Barrymore and his position. If students are having difficulty asking questions, you may wish to use the following model:

Think-Aloud Model *I see from these stage directions that Watson is studying a map. I remember that Barrymore is the butler and has been working for Sir Charles and his family for many years. Maybe he knows the area very well. Is Watson going to question Barrymore about the area surrounding Baskerville Hall?*

Critical Thinking:
MAKING JUDGMENTS

DD Invite students to explain why Barrymore told Watson he didn't hear the noise. Ask students if they think he is telling the truth. (*Possible responses: Barrymore may really not have heard the noise. Or he may be covering for his wife. As a butler, he may feel that discretion is his best course.*)

Literary Concept:
CHARACTERIZATION

EE Direct students to study these stage directions. Then ask students what they can infer about Watson based on what they have learned. (*Possible response: The stage directions clearly indicate that Watson is certain he heard a noise. He is a trained professional scientist working with the world's best detective, so he is probably an accurate observer.*)

Active Reading: EVALUATE

FF Ask students to evaluate the relevance of these details to the plot, based on what they have learned thus far about the mystery of the curse of the Baskervilles. *(Possible responses: This information may be designed to throw readers off the track because Frankland is not mentioned in the cast of characters; this is an important plot detail because it mentions one of Sir Charles's neighbors who may know something about his murder.)*

Critical Thinking: CLASSIFYING

GG Have students classify Mr. Stapleton's character based on what they learn about him in this passage. *(Possible responses: Chasing butterflies implies that he is harmless and slightly daffy, or that he is serious and scholarly.)*

CUSTOMIZING FOR

Multiple Learning Styles

HH **Bodily-Kinesthetic Learners** Invite students to explain what Barrymore's body language in this scene suggests about his feelings about Watson's questions. Ask students to offer some reasons why Barrymore might be reluctant to talk about Mr. Frankland's daughter, Laura. Have students work in pairs to act out this scene and demonstrate their conclusions to the class.

clearly marked, but who lives here . . . (*indicates*) northeast of the great rocks?

Barrymore. That would be the house of Mr. Frankland.

Watson (*recalls the name*). Frankland? An elderly man, choleric,[14] with a beard.

Barrymore. You've met him then, Doctor Watson?

Watson. Bumped into at the post office. Disagreeable sort.

Barrymore (*steps downstage*). His passion is for the British law.

Watson. Sues people, they tell me.

Barrymore. He's spent a considerable fortune in litigation. Mr. Frankland fights for the mere pleasure of fighting. He's ready to take up either side of a question as long as he can have his day in court.

Watson. I know the sort. (*indicates*) And this cottage?

Barrymore. Mr. Stapleton and his sister.

Watson. Ah, Sir Henry's friend. What's she like?

Barrymore. Quite lively.

Watson. And her brother?

Barrymore. I've only met him on one occasion. On the moor. Chasing butterflies.

Watson. Butterflies?

Barrymore (*confirms*). Butterflies.

Watson (*clarifying*). So what we have close by are the homes of the Stapletons, Lady Agatha and Mr. Frankland.

Barrymore. There are other cottages on the moor, but they're in bad repair, quite unlivable.

Watson. If you don't mind me saying so, Barrymore, things are a bit backward in this region.

Barrymore. Sir Charles was doing his best to remedy the situation, that's why his death was such a loss.

Watson. Mr. Frankland lives alone?

Barrymore. He does now.

Watson. No family?

Barrymore. He has a daughter.

Watson. Where is she? (*laughter from outside*)

Barrymore (*moves up center, looks out the open French doors*). That would be Sir Henry.

Watson. What about Mr. Frankland's daughter?

Barrymore (*still looking off*). Miss Stapleton is with him.

---

14. **choleric** (kŏl´ə-rĭk): bad-tempered.

Watson. Never mind about Miss Stapleton. I asked you about Mr. Frankland's daughter.

Barrymore (*anxious to avoid the topic*). Her name was Laura.

Watson. Why are you making such a mystery out of it?

Sir Henry. (*He enters, calling over his shoulder.*) Never mind the flowers. I want a bit of lunch.

Watson. You look as if you've been enjoying yourself.

Sir Henry. Kathy took me on a tour of the old huts. The moor is riddled with old mine shafts, too. I didn't know that. (*Barrymore clears his throat.*) What is it, Barrymore?

Barrymore. I wonder if I might have a word with you, Sir Henry.

Sir Henry. Certainly, what is it? (*Barrymore looks to* Watson, *meaning he wants to speak in private.*)

Watson (*stands*). I'll go and introduce myself to your young friend.

Sir Henry. We won't be long. (*Watson exits via French doors. Sir Henry moves down left.*) Well?

Barrymore. My wife and I will be happy, Sir Henry, to stay with you until you have made fresh arrangements.

Sir Henry. What is that supposed to mean?

Barrymore. Under the new conditions this house will require considerable staff.

Sir Henry. I wish I understood what you're driving at. What "new conditions"?

Barrymore. I only meant that Sir Charles led a retired life and we were able to look after his wants. You would, naturally, wish to have more company, and so you will need changes in your household.

Sir Henry. I'm quite comfortable with you and your wife. Isn't Perkins of some help?

Barrymore. She's a village girl, sir. Not terribly bright. Not accustomed to service. So few are these days.

Sir Henry. What you're really saying is that you and your wife wish to leave.

Barrymore. Only when it is convenient for you, sir.

Sir Henry. This is bad news. I'm sorry to begin my life here by breaking an old family connection.

Barrymore. My wife and I were both attached to Sir Charles. His death gave us a shock.

Sir Henry. It didn't exactly give me a sense of security, Barrymore.

Barrymore. No, sir. But, we fear we'll never again be easy in our minds at Baskerville Hall.

Sir Henry. What do you intend to do?

Barrymore. We shall establish ourselves in some business. Sir Charles' generosity has given us the means to do so.

Sir Henry. I won't try to stop you. We'll talk about this later.

Barrymore. Yes, sir. (*Barrymore exits upstage center. Sir Henry is unhappy.*)

Kathy. (*She sticks her head in from the outside.*) Is it safe?

Sir Henry. Barrymore's left, if that's what you mean.

Kathy (*calls over her shoulder*). Come along, Doctor. The coast is clear. (*She sweeps in. She is an attractive young woman, vital, alert and altogether* captivating. *She carries flowers.*) We ought to put these in water.

Sir Henry. I'll ring for Perkins. (*He moves to some bell rope on the wall.* Kathy *moves to the sofa, sits.* Watson *enters.*)

Kathy. (*The flowers.*) They don't last long. It's a pity.

WORDS TO KNOW **captivating** (kăp'tə-vā'tĭng) *adj.* attractive because of charm or beauty; fascinating **captivate** *v.*

621

Active Reading: CLARIFY

II Have students explain what Barrymore is hinting about in this passage. (*Possible response: Barrymore is saying that he and his wife want to leave their jobs as servants in Baskerville Hall.*)

Critical Thinking: ANALYZING

JJ Ask students to analyze Barrymore's motive for departure. (*Possible responses: He is guilty and wants to escape the scene of the crime as quickly as possible; he is upset by the murder and fears that his own life is in danger; he now has the money to give up being a servant.*)

Literary Concept: STAGE DIRECTIONS

KK Have students analyze these stage directions to explain what they suggest about Kathy's character. (*Possible response: Her body language, as described in the stage directions, shows that she is confident, self-assured, and in command.*)

Active Reading: QUESTION

 Discuss any questions students have about the characters at this point in the selection. *(Possible response: What is someone as pretty, vibrant, and young as Kathy really doing living in such an isolated place?)*

Linking to Social Studies

Although this dramatization is set in the present, Conan Doyle set this story in 1899. Thus the characters reflect the class divisions of British society in the nineteenth and early twentieth centuries. An individual's social class was determined by birth far more than by economic status or achievement. It was extremely difficult to cross class lines. Kathy's dismissive remark about the Barrymores is an example of accepted behavior toward those in a lower class.

Active Reading: EVALUATE

Ask students why the information in this passage might be relevant to the plot. *(Possible response: The fact that there is no way the people in Baskerville Hall can call for assistance may foreshadow a future crisis. It also provides a sense of isolation and entrapment and helps create a feeling of tension and suspense.)*

STRATEGIC READING FOR
Less-Proficient Readers

Ask students why Kathy and Jack have come to live on the moor. You may need to point out that *capital* means money invested to generate an income. *(Their school failed, and they have no money left.)* **Noting Relevant Details/Relating Cause and Effect**

Set a Purpose Have students read to find out what makes Watson start to believe in the curse.

Sir Henry. Yes, it is. The moor needs color.

Kathy (*holds up the bouquet*). Aren't they lovely, Doctor?

Watson. (*He moves to the sofa. The sly rogue.*) They are when you hold them, my dear.

Kathy. Did you hear that, Henry? The Doctor knows how to dispense compliments as well as pills.

Watson. What was all the mystery with Barrymore?

Sir Henry (*steps center*). The Barrymores want to leave.

Watson. What?

Sir Henry. That's what he tells me.

Kathy. I thought the Barrymores came with the wallpaper. (Watson *laughs*.)

Sir Henry. So did I.

Kathy. That will present a problem. Villagers don't like to work on the moor.

Watson. One can hardly blame them. I'm grateful Baskerville Hall has modern plumbing, but I'd feel more at home if it had a telephone.

Kathy. There are no phones on the moor. Only the village.

Watson. That sense of isolation doesn't trouble you?

Sir Henry. Nothing troubles Kathy. (*He sits beside her.*)

Kathy. That's not true. Especially when the mist is thick. It frightens me. (Sir Henry *takes her hand. They smile.*)

Watson. (*He moves center.*) The moor is a rather odd place to find such a lovely creature.

Sir Henry. I quite agree.

Watson (*half-flirting*). I can't help but wonder why such a vital young woman wants to tuck herself away in this corner of England.

Kathy. It wasn't exactly by choice. My brother and I had a school in the north country. I'm afraid the fates were against us.

Watson. How so?

Kathy. A serious epidemic broke out in the school. Two of the lads never recovered.

Watson. Bad luck, indeeed.

Kathy. (Sir Henry *pats her hand protectively.*) Our capital was used up and poor Jack was devastated. He hasn't recovered yet. Still, the moor is perfect for him.

Watson. Why?

Kathy. He has an avid interest in botany and zoology. He keeps his mind occupied and expenses are minimal. We have books, we have our studies, and we have—(*smiles at* Sir Henry) interesting neighbors. (Perkins *enters up center from right.*)

Sir Henry (*takes flowers from* Kathy). Put this in water, will you, Perkins.

Perkins (*steps down*). Yes, sir.

Kathy. No, just bring a vase. I'll arrange them myself.

Perkins. Yes, miss. (*She steps to* Watson, *loud whisper.*) It's been seen again, Doctor.

Watson. What?

Perkins. The hound.

Watson (*doesn't wish to question her with* Kathy *and* Sir Henry *listening*). We'll talk later, Perkins. Go along.

Perkins. Yes, sir.

Sir Henry (*stands*). Wait.

Watson. Let me deal with this, Sir Henry.

Sir Henry. There's no sense in trying to protect my sensibilities,[15] Doctor. What did you mean "the hound"?

Perkins. It's only that Doctor Watson asked me to report anything I heard in the village.

Sir Henry. What did you hear?

Perkins. It's not what I heard, Sir Henry. It's what Mr. Blake saw and heard.

Sir Henry. Blake?

Kathy. The greengrocer. The man's a dolt.

Watson. Well, well, what did he see and hear?

Perkins. He was on his bicycle, and he heard a long, low moan sweep over the moor.

Kathy. I've heard it once or twice myself.

Sir Henry. WHAT!

Kathy (*grins*). The bogs make odd noises. It's the mud settling or the water rising, or something.

Perkins. That's not what Mr. Blake said.

Kathy. My own guess would be a bittern booming.

Watson. Good gracious. What's that?

Kathy. A very rare bird, practically extinct in England now, but all things are possible on the moor. I wouldn't be at all surprised that what Mr. Blake heard is the cry of the last of the bitterns.

Sir Henry. That'll be all, Perkins.

Perkins (*pouts that they don't believe her*). Yes, Sir Henry. (*She exits up center, turns right.*)

Sir Henry. Seems all the servants are in something of a mood.

Watson. I was trying to get Barrymore to tell me about old Frankland's daughter. He pointedly avoided the subject.

Sir Henry. He's not one for gossip.

Kathy. It's a rather sad situation. She married an artist named Lyons, who came sketching on the moor. He proved to be a blackguard[16] and deserted her. Her father refused to have anything to do with her, because she married without his consent.

Watson. I wonder why Barrymore couldn't have told me as much.

Kathy. When you've been here a while, you'll realize these people are clannish and protective of one another.

Watson. If you'll excuse me, I want to have a word or two with Mrs. Barrymore. (*He exits up center, turns left.*)

Sir Henry. I seem to have come into an inheritance with a vengeance.[17]

Kathy. I wouldn't pay attention to village chatter. They're a superstitious lot.

Sir Henry. The hound is the pet story of my family.

Kathy. That's a bad joke, Henry.

Sir Henry. I've heard of the beast ever since I was in the nursery. I never thought of taking it seriously.

---

15. **sensibilities:** feelings.
16. **blackguard:** wicked person; villain.
17. **with a vengeance:** in an excessive degree.

 Invite students to state Kathy's motivation in describing the strange happenings at Baskerville Hall as having a "sane, rational explanation." *(Possible responses: She likes Sir Henry and doesn't want to upset him; she is a sensible person; she is guilty of the murder and wants to deflect attention from herself.)*

Active Reading: EVALUATE

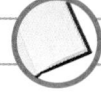 Ask students to explain why they think Jack is so upset when he sees Sir Henry kissing Kathy. Have students evaluate whether this is an important detail in the mystery and explain their reasoning. *(Possible responses: Jack thinks that Sir Henry is taking advantage of Kathy; Jack is nervous and high-strung and given to inappropriate emotional outbursts. The severity of Jack's reaction suggests that this is a key plot detail.)*

CUSTOMIZING FOR
Students Acquiring English

(5) Point out that *Who do you think you are?* is not a literal question. Explain that it is an expression used when the speaker thinks another person is behaving arrogantly.

Kathy. You're not thinking of doing so now?

Sir Henry. This business with my uncle confuses me. The whole thing seems boiling up in my head, and I can't get it clear yet.

Kathy. There's a sane, rational explanation for everything that's happened. *(She reaches into some pocket and produces something wrapped in tissue paper. She holds it out proudly.)* Here. For you. *(He takes the paper, unwraps, and displays a handsome pocket watch.)* I couldn't resist it.

Sir Henry. It's a beauty.

Kathy. I saw the watch in the jeweler's window. The letter "B" is engraved on the back.

Sir Henry. You're too generous. You won't save money giving gifts to me.

Kathy. This gift is "special."

Sir Henry. Then I must secure something "extra" special for you. I thought I'd find no one on this desolate moor but rustics and eccentrics.[18] *(He pulls her to her feet.)*

Kathy. I'm on the moor.

Sir Henry. You're no eccentric, and far from being a rustic. *(He kisses her as . . . Jack Stapleton, Kathy's brother, enters via the French door. He's a nervous young man, given to emotional outbursts. He carries a butterfly net.)*

Jack *(furious).* I'll thank you to keep your attentions from my sister, Sir Henry!

Kathy *(steps away from Sir Henry).* Jack, what's the matter with you?!

Jack. I'll deal with you later.

Kathy. Stop it!

Sir Henry. You're behaving badly aren't you, Stapleton?

Jack. How I'm behaving is my own concern.

Kathy *(distressed).* What's the matter with you?

Jack. Just because you're rich and have a title you think you can do as you want.

Kathy *(close to tears).* I'm not going to stay and listen to you.

Jack. Rich and powerful—you're all the same.

(Kathy, in tears, runs onto the moor.)

Sir Henry. Kathy!

Jack *(a step in closer).* You stay away from her. She's not for you.

Sir Henry. It's no concern of yours. I shall see her as often as she permits it.

(Watson returns, stands up center, listening.)

Jack. Then I'll see that she doesn't permit it.

Sir Henry. Who do you think you are? (5)

Jack. I won't warn you again. Stay away from

---

18. **rustics and eccentrics** (ĭk-sĕn'trĭks): simple country people and people who behave oddly.

Mini-Lesson **Reading Skills/Strategies**

NOTING RELEVANT DETAILS Explain to students that details are small pieces of information about a topic. Be sure students understand that details serve many purposes, such as describing a character, telling more about the plot, or backing up an important point. Tell students that details can be relevant or irrelevant. Explain that relevant details directly relate to the topic; irrelevant details, in contrast, are off the topic. Tell students that mystery writers may include some irrelevant details to throw readers off the track and maintain suspense.

Application Have students create charts that track some of the details about the characters in the play. Students should classify each detail as relevant or irrelevant based on whether or not it provides evidence about the characters' innocence or guilt.

Reteaching/Reinforcement
• *Unit Five Resource Book,* p. 48

Kathy. (*He turns, exits. Sir Henry moves to the French doors.*)

Sir Henry. And I'll thank you to stay away from Baskerville Hall!

Watson. What was all that?

Sir Henry. Stapleton. The man's a lunatic. Came in here in a rage when he saw Kathy and me together. My feelings towards his sister are nothing for me to be ashamed of. He drove her away in tears. Why should he object to me?

Watson. Perhaps he's on the verge of some sort of breakdown. Remember, he hasn't been well.

Sir Henry (*moves stage left*). He's liable to do Kathy some harm.

Watson. Be careful.

Sir Henry . I'm not afraid of Stapleton and his bad temper.

(Sir Henry *follows after the pair. Watson steps into the room, moves to the French doors, looks off as* Perkins *returns, a vase in her hand.*)

Perkins. Here's the vase and water, Miss. (*She looks around.*) Where's Miss Kathy, Doctor Watson?

Watson. Gone.

Perkins. What about the flowers?

Watson (*turns*). On the sofa there.

Perkins. (*She sees them, crosses to the sofa, picks them up and crosses to the mantle, arranges them, talking as she goes.*) I wasn't allowed to finish, sir.

Watson. Hmmmm?

Perkins. About Mr. Blake. He didn't only hear the hound.

Watson. Oh?

Perkins. He saw it.

Watson. (*He moves center.*) When?

Perkins. Last night, sir.

Watson. How did he describe it?

Perkins. More like a great dark shape than anything else, moving so fast Mr. Blake feared for his own life.

Watson. If it were only a great dark shape how could he be sure of what he saw?

Perkins. Because its eyes were fiery red and it was breathing flame. (*guarded*) Do you believe him, Doctor Watson?

Watson (*pauses, then*). Yes, Perkins, I'm sorry to say I do.

Perkins. (*She is surprised.*) Why, sir?

Watson. Because I, myself, got a glimpse of what he saw. Last night—on the moor.

Perkins (*wide-eyed*). The hound of the Baskervilles?

Watson. No, Perkins—a hound of hell.

CURTAIN

Literary Concept: SUSPENSE

VV Ask students why the playwright ends the scene this way. (*Possible responses: The "cliff-hanger" ending creates great suspense that holds the audience's interest.*)

STRATEGIC READING FOR

Less-Proficient Readers

WW Review with students Watson's opinion of the curse on the Baskervilles.

• How does Watson react at first to tales of a curse? (*Being a scientist, he doesn't believe in a curse.*) **Making Generalizations**

• What happens to change Watson's mind? (*He saw some sort of frightening creature on the moor.*) **Noting Relevant Details**

Set a Purpose Have students read to discover new evidence regarding the death of Sir Charles Baskerville.

In March of 1901, Conan Doyle went on a vacation with his friend Fletcher Robinson, who told him the legend of a ghostly hound associated with Robinson's birthplace in Dartmoor, Devonshire. Intrigued, Conan Doyle visited Dartmoor himself. Upon his return, Conan Doyle began writing what he called "a real creeper" of a novel about the eerie legend. Later, he decided to include Sherlock Holmes in the novel.

Illustration by Sergio Martinez. From Children's Classics Edition of *The Hound of the Baskervilles* by Sir Arthur Conan Doyle. Copyright © 1992 Crown Publishers, Inc., reprinted by permission of Crown Publishers, Inc.

626

Mini-Lesson  Literary Concepts

REVIEWING SUSPENSE Remind students that suspense is the feeling of growing tension and excitement felt by a reader. Tell students that writers create suspense by raising questions in the reader's minds about what might happen in the plot.

Application Have students review the play and identify points in the story where they felt suspense. Then have students work in pairs to make a line graph, listing important events on the horizontal line and numbers from 1 to 10 on the vertical line. Students should place a dot on the graph above each event to reflect the degree of excitement they felt, with 1 for some excitement and 10 for extreme tension.

A ┃ SCENE 3 ┃

B At Rise: *Later in the week. Night. Sound of wind howling on the moor. Stage remains empty for a few moments. Barrymore,* cautious, *enters up center. He looks around as if he half-expected someone to pop up any second. He looks to the portrait, speaks with a hint of sarcasm.*

Barrymore. Good evening to you, Sir Hugo. (*He suppresses a chuckle, dims the lights, so the room is in shadows. He moves to the French doors, with a flashlight in hand. He points it onto the moor, snaps it on . . . and off . . . and on . . . and off . . .*)

Sir Henry's Voice. Doctor Watson, are you back? (*Nervous,* Barrymore *moves down to the desk and quickly puts the flashlight into some drawer.*)

Sir Henry. (*He enters up center from right.*) What's happened to the lights?

Barrymore. I'll put them on at once, Sir Henry. (*He does so, efficient, the perfect butler.*)

Sir Henry. So, it's you, Barrymore.

Barrymore. Yes, sir.

Sir Henry. What were you doing in here in the dark?

Barrymore. The dark, Sir Henry?

Sir Henry. You have an annoying habit of repeating things.

Barrymore. Actually, sir . . . well, the truth is . . . uh,—I'm afraid I fell asleep. (*indicates down left center chair*)

Sir Henry. That's most unlike you.

Barrymore. I suffer from headaches, sir. I felt a bit faint. I thought if I rested for a moment, I'd feel better. When I awoke the dark had settled in.

Sir Henry. (*He, again, isn't buying the explanation but decides not to press the matter for the time being.*) If you say so. I was looking for the *Weekly Journal.*

Barrymore. My wife has it, sir. It came with yesterday's post.

Sir Henry. I would like to see it.

Barrymore. At once, Sir Henry. (*He exits up center, turns right.*) ⑥

Active Reading: CLARIFY

B Have students describe the mood of this scene, based on what they learn in the stage directions. *(Possible response: The sound of the wind "howling on the moor" helps establish an eerie, frightening mood.)*

Critical Thinking: HYPOTHESIZING

C Ask students to guess what Barrymore is doing, based on his actions in this passage. Then invite students to share their thoughts on Barrymore's guilt or innocence in the murder of Sir Charles. *(Possible responses: Barrymore is trying to frighten or signal someone on the moor. Barrymore may be the murderer because he had much to gain from Sir Charles's death, is eager to leave the house, and is acting in a suspicious manner.)*

CUSTOMIZING FOR

Students Acquiring English

⑥ Explain that *at once* means "immediately, right away."

(Sir Henry *takes the pocket watch from his jacket, looks at it fondly. He moves to sofa, sits holding the watch to his ear. It's not working. He frowns, begins to wind it. While this is going on, the wind rises and a face appears at the French doors, an evil face with a bristling beard. Suddenly,* Sir Henry *stiffens, aware that he is not alone. The "face" outside the room puts a hand to the door, opens it . . . quietly. A man steps into the room, staring at the heir. His clothes are ragged and his hair is matted. He looks wild and, quite possibly, mad.)*

Sir Henry (*without turning, wary*). Who . . . who's there . . . ? (*Like a frightened animal, the man darts back outside.* Sir Henry *jumps to his feet, turns. He sees there is no one, but his instincts tell him otherwise.*) Who is it? (*Silence. He moves stage left. Wind up. He notices the opened door.*) Watson, that you out there?

Perkins. (*She, fast, enters up center, from right, with a tray hosting a mug and pitcher. Cheery.*) Here's your *Weekly Journal,* Sir Henry.

Sir Henry (*startled*). WHAT!

Perkins (*gives a startled gasp*). Sir Henry, there's no need to jump at me.

Sir Henry (*another look through the panes*). Oh, it's you, Perkins. I didn't mean to bark.

Perkins. I thought you might like some warm milk, so I've brought a pitcher and a mug. (*She moves to the mantle or some table, right, and puts the tray down.*)

Sir Henry (*closes door*). That was thoughtful. How is it you're still here?

Perkins. The mist rolled in too fast for me. I never cross the moor on nights like this. I sleep in the small room at the far end of the west wing.

Sir Henry. Have you done that recently?

Perkins (*doesn't understand*). Sir?

Sir Henry (*moves center*). Have you stayed over in the last few weeks?

Perkins. Once.

Sir Henry. I wonder, Perkins, did you hear anyone—crying?

Perkins. Crying? I don't think so. I'm a sound sleeper. Of course, at that end of the house one might as well be in a tomb. The walls are that thick.

Sir Henry (*rubs his arms as if he were cold*). Tomb is exactly what this place feels like at times.

Perkins. Would you like me to light the fire?

Sir Henry. I'll take care of it.

Perkins. Very good, Sir Henry.

Watson. (*He enters up center, from right.*) It's a miserable night out.

Sir Henry. Did you walk back from the village?

Watson. I did.

Perkins. I hope you carried a torch, Doctor Watson.

Watson. Certainly not. I have excellent night sight. Comes from eating carrots. You should try it, Perkins.

Perkins. Can't abide carrots, Doctor Watson. I don't like the sound of the crunch. (*She exits up center.*)

Watson (*moves down center*). These villagers are everything Kathy Stapleton said they were. Imagine. Not liking the sound of a carrot's crunch. Silly creature. (*He sits on the sofa.*)

Sir Henry. What news from Holmes?

Watson. It's positively infuriating.

Sir Henry. How so?

Watson. Everytime I call London I get his answering machine.

Sir Henry. Surely, he's back in London by now.

Watson. Let's hope so. If I don't get him tomor-

row, or hear from him, I think a brief holiday would do us both some good.

Sir Henry. You mean a trip to London.

Watson. You'll have to go with me. I couldn't leave you here alone.

Sir Henry. I appreciate everything you're doing, but I'm not ready for a London outing. Whatever it is that's terrifying Baskerville Hall, I intend to stick it out.

Watson. In that case, I'll remain here also.

Sir Henry. Did you see anyone outside the house?

Watson. When?

Sir Henry. On your way back. (*He crosses to the pitcher, pours himself a mug.*)

Watson. Can't see a thing. The mist from the moors is thicker than guilt. Can't imagine why Lady Agatha favors the place.

Sir Henry. Bit like Kathy and her brother. She lost almost everything in bad investments a few years back.

Watson. I didn't know that. Yet, she's the sort that belongs out of the big city. I never felt she was comfortable with the rush.

Sir Henry (*holds up the mug*). Warm milk. Don't suppose you'd care for a mug?

Watson. Milk? No, no. Why did you ask what you did? If I had seen anyone outside the house?

Sir Henry. I heard something at the French doors. They were opened.

Watson. (*He moves quickly to the doors, checks them.*) They're closed now.

Sir Henry. I closed them.

Watson. Was there anyone else in the room?

Sir Henry. Barrymore was in here just before I came downstairs. In the dark. Said he fell asleep.

Watson. He's an odd one.

Sir Henry. I'm inclined to agree with you. I don't know what he was doing in this room, but I certainly don't believe he was sleeping.

Watson. He's <u>evasive</u> with my questions, yet the Barrymores and Lady Agatha were the only witnesses the night your poor uncle met his death. It's clear to me that so long as there are none of the family at Baskerville Hall, Barrymore has a mighty fine home and nothing to do. (*Watson is aware that someone is standing out of sight in the entry hall, left. He signals Sir Henry to be quiet.*) No need to eavesdrop in the shadows, Barrymore. Come out where we can see you.

(*Long pause. Sir Henry and Watson turn up center—Mrs. Barrymore comes into view.*)

Sir Henry. Mrs. Barrymore, do you make a habit of listening in on other people's conversation?

Mrs. Barrymore. No, Sir Henry, I do not.

Watson. Would you care to explain your extraordinary behavior?

Mrs. Barrymore. You're thinking ill of my husband.

Watson. What if we are?

Mrs. Barrymore. He's a loyal retainer.[19] As I am. He would never do anything to harm you in any way, Sir Henry.

Watson. There's cold comfort in that. (*Mrs. Barrymore takes a charred piece of stationery from some pocket.*) What have you there?

Mrs. Barrymore. I should have spoken out before, but it was long after the inquest that I found it. I've never breathed a word about it to anyone. Not even to my husband. (*weak*) I wonder—may I sit down. I'm not feeling at my best.

Sir Henry. Certainly.

---

19. **retainer:** servant.

WORDS
TO
KNOW

evasive (ĭ-vā′sĭv) *adj.* avoiding straight, honest answers; not frank

629

Literary Concept: SIMILE

G Remind students that a simile conveys a comparison by means of the word *like* or *as.* Have students identify the simile in this passage and explain how it enhances the mood. (*Possible response: "The mist from the moors is thicker than guilt" is a simile. It reinforces the air of mystery.*)

Linking to Science

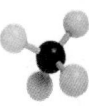

H Warm milk is a traditional treatment for insomnia. Recent scientific studies have confirmed the wisdom of using this folk remedy. Drinking milk increases the body's level of serotonin, a protein that helps the body fall asleep. In addition, the calcium in milk is thought to encourage drowsiness. The milk works equally well warm or cold, but the warmth adds a psychological advantage.

Active Reading: PREDICT

I Invite students to explain why Watson suspects that Barrymore is eavesdropping. Then invite students to predict which character is hiding. (*Possible responses: Watson suspects Barrymore because the butler has been acting suspiciously; further, he is always around the house.*)

Cultural Note

J Today's moral climate is very different from that of the turn of the century, when Conan Doyle wrote this story. Then, for example, it was improper for unmarried men and women to meet without a suitable chaperone. A respectable man would never place a woman in a potentially compromising situation, and a respectable woman zealously guarded her reputation.

STRATEGIC READING FOR
Less-Proficient Readers

K Make sure that students recognize the new information about the night Sir Charles died by asking the following questions.

- What new evidence about Sir Charles's murder has been found? *(A letter making an appointment with Sir Charles for the night he was killed)* Noting Relevant Details

- Who found it? *(Mrs. Barrymore)* Noting Relevant Details

- On which character does this evidence cast suspicion? *(Laura Lyons)* Noting Relevant Details

Set a Purpose Have students read to find out how Holmes describes the atmosphere at Baskerville Hall and what he does with the flashlight he finds.

Literary Concept: SUSPENSE

L Have students analyze how the playwright creates suspense in this passage. *(Possible response: Tension results from the mystery over the intruder's identity and the potential for danger.)*

Mrs. Barrymore. (*She moves down left center, sits. She hands the paper to* Watson.) I know why Sir Charles was on the moor.

Sir Henry. Well?

Mrs. Barrymore. He was to meet a woman.

Sir Henry. I don't believe it.

Mrs. Barrymore. The letter came the morning of your uncle's death. From the village of Tracey Coombes.

Watson. How long have you known this paper existed?

Mrs. Barrymore. Only a few weeks ago I was cleaning out Sir Charles' study. It hadn't been touched since his death. I found the ashes of a burned letter in the back of the grate. Most of it was charred to pieces, but one little slip, the end of the page, hung together. (*She points to the paper in* Watson's *hand.*)

Watson (*reads*). "Please, please, as you are a gentleman, burn this letter, and be by the gate on the moor at ten o'clock."

Sir Henry. How can you be sure this is the same letter that arrived that morning?

Mrs. Barrymore. There was a silver trim on the border of the envelope. The same trim is on the bottom of the notepaper Doctor Watson holds.

Sir Henry. What's the woman's name?

Watson. No name.

Mrs. Barrymore. Only the initials. "L.L."

Sir Henry. I can't understand why you would want to conceal this information.

Mrs. Barrymore. Well, sir, we were both of us devoted to Sir Charles, as well might be considering all that he'd done for us. To rake this up couldn't help our poor master, and it's well to go carefully when there's a lady in the case.

Watson. In other words you thought this communication would somehow compromise[20] Sir Charles' reputation?

Mrs. Barrymore (*nods, stands*). I hope I've done the right thing at last.

Watson. You have.

Mrs. Barrymore. If you have no more questions—

Watson. Later, perhaps.

(*She moves up center, turns to look at the portrait.*)

Sir Henry. What is it?

Mrs. Barrymore. I was thinking how the evil legacy of Sir Hugo hangs on. It would have been better if he'd never been born. (*She nods, exits up center.*)

Watson. Little late to worry about that. (*the letter*) What do you make of this? L.L.

Sir Henry. Laura Lyons.

Watson. Old Frankland's daughter? Of course!

Sir Henry (*looks to doors*). There is someone out there!

Watson. Outside the house?

Sir Henry. Yes. (*Quick,* Sir Henry *moves to the fireplace and seizes a poker.*)

Watson. No need for that, Sir Henry. I have a revolver. (Watson *dips into his pocket and produces a small pistol. Both move for the French doors. A shape materializes outside the room, quickly opens the French doors, slips inside with force and assurance—*Sherlock Holmes.)

Holmes. No need for weaponry, gentlemen. Your intruder is an ally.

Watson. Holmes!

Sir Henry. We thought you were in London.

Holmes. Which is exactly what I wanted you to think. (Sir Henry *returns the poker to the fire-*

---

20. **compromise:** to open to suspicion or disgrace.

place, stands stage right.) I think you'd be more comfortable seated, Watson. I'd appreciate it if you'd point that revolver in another direction. (Watson *pockets the gun, sits on the sofa.*)

Sir Henry. I never was more glad to see anyone in my life.

Watson. Where have you been?

Holmes. On the moor.

Watson. Since when?

Holmes. Since the day Lady Agatha invited us for tea.

Sir Henry. Then you've never left?

Holmes. That is correct.

Watson (*pouts*). You might have trusted me to keep your confidence.

Holmes. My dear fellow, you have been invaluable to me in this as in many other cases. In your kindness you might have brought me out some comfort or other, and an unnecessary risk would be run.

Watson. You underestimate me, Holmes.

Holmes. Never. I know, my dear Watson, that you share my love of all that is bizarre and outside the conventions and humdrum[21] of everyday life. I trust you've kept notes, jotted everything down.

Watson. I have.

Holmes. Splendid.

Watson. I still don't see the need for your deception.

Holmes. Had I remained with you and Sir Henry, my point of view would have been the same as yours. My presence would have warned the menace to be on its guard. In one disguise or another I have moved about freely.

Sir Henry. What did you learn on the moor?

Holmes. Considerable.

Watson. That doesn't tell us much.

Sir Henry. What's after me? Human or supernatural? Flesh and blood, or the devil?

Holmes. For the time being I'm afraid I will have to hold that question in abeyance.

Sir Henry. Why do you avoid answering me?

Holmes. In a modest way I have combated evil, but to take on the Father of Evil himself would, perhaps, be too ambitious a task. (*quick, precise, professional*) Now, Sir Henry, did you see anyone in this room earlier? In the dark? ⑧

Sir Henry. Yes.

Holmes. Who?

Sir Henry. Barrymore.

Holmes. You mean *Mrs.* Barrymore, don't you?

Sir Henry. No. It was Barrymore.

Holmes. Sir Henry, have you been conscious of a "presence" somewhere in the house from time to time?

Sir Henry. I have.

Watson. The place has an eerie quality about it. Perfectly natural reaction.

Holmes. I think I can prove you wrong, Watson. Did Barrymore have a flashlight with him? ⓞ

Sir Henry. I'm sure he didn't.

Holmes. Did you disturb him when you entered the room?

Sir Henry. I think I did.

(Watson *and* Sir Henry *exchange a perplexed glance.* Holmes *looks from corner to corner. His eyes hit the desk.*)

21. **conventions and humdrum:** ordinary customs, routines, and talk.

WORDS TO KNOW	**deception** (dǐ-sĕp′shən) *n.* an act of deceiving; lie or trick

631

Mini-Lesson **Grammar**

SENTENCE FRAGMENTS Explain that a sentence fragment is a group of words that does not express a complete idea. A sentence fragment leaves out the subject, the verb, or sometimes both. Write on the chalkboard the examples shown and explain why each is a fragment. Explain that while writers of plays sometimes use fragments to make dialogue sound realistic, other kinds of writing usually require complete sentences.

Application Have students change each of these fragments from page 631 into sentences.

1. On the moor. (*I have been on the moor.*)
2. Since when? (*Since when have you been there?*)
3. Considerable. (*I learned a considerable amount.*)
4. Splendid. (*I think that is splendid.*)

Reteaching/Reinforcement
- Grammar Handbook, anthology p. 848
- *Grammar Mini-Lessons* copymasters, p. 1, transparencies, p. 1

 The Writer's Craft

Correcting Problem Sentences, pp. 294–295

Fragments

died on the moors	missing a subject
Laura Lyons	missing a verb
near the house	missing subject and verb

Active Reading: CLARIFY

P Have students explain what Holmes means here. Guide them to identify who has an "unimaginative mind." *(Possible response: Holmes is referring to Barrymore and his inability to hide the flashlight in a less obvious place when taken by surprise.)*

Literary Concept: DRAMA

Q Have students explain what effect the division of a play into acts and scenes has on its content, especially the end of each scene or act. *(Possible responses: By dividing plays into acts and scenes, playwrights can focus on one aspect of the narrative at a time. Divisions allow for easier time or place transitions. In a mystery, divisions allow playwrights to build certain scenes or acts to a peak of suspense.)*

STRATEGIC READING FOR
Less-Proficient Readers

R Ask students the following questions to make sure they are following the story so far.

- According to Holmes, what is surrounding Baskerville Hall? *(evil)* **Noting Relevant Details**

- What does Holmes do with the flashlight he finds in the desk drawer? *(He uses it to mimic the signal Barrymore used, to which someone responds.)* **Summarizing**

Set a Purpose Have students read to learn about the relationships among Sir Henry, Jack, and Kathy and what the three agree to do.

P **Holmes.** Ah, the desk! The perfect hiding place for the unimaginative mind taken unaware.

Sir Henry. Mr. Holmes, I know the contents of that desk. There's no flashlight there.

Holmes. (*He marches to the desk, goes through a drawer and, then, another.*) It is a capital mistake, Sir Henry, to <u>theorize</u> before you have all the evidence. (*He pulls out the flashlight.*) Eureka![22]

Watson. So Barrymore had a flashlight. What does that signify?

Holmes. I expected better of you, Watson. Think, man.

Sir Henry. You mean he was searching for something in the room. In the dark. He didn't want to be discovered.

Holmes. No, Sir Henry, what he was after was not in this room. (*points*) It was out there. On the moor. (*rush of wind*) Watson, the lights. (*Watson stands, moves to dim the lighting. Again, the room is cloistered in eerie shadows.*) Come close, Sir Henry. I shall now demonstrate that my time on the moor was put to good use. (*Sir Henry moves behind Holmes at the French doors; Watson follows.*) Keep your eyes focused on the near clump of rocks.

Watson. How can we? The mist has blocked out everything.

Holmes. Not quite. (*He repeats the business Barrymore did earlier. He snaps the flashlight on and off . . . on and off . . . on and off . . .*)

Watson. What are you doing?

Holmes. I should think that's fairly obvious.

Sir Henry. You're signaling someone.

Watson. Who?

Holmes. That is only one part of the puzzle.

Sir Henry. Look! There's a light out there.

Watson. They're answering your signal, Holmes.

Holmes. No, Watson, not my signal.

Sir Henry. (*Angry, Sir Henry storms back to the fireplace, picks up the poker.*) I've had enough of it. Who or whatever is out there means to do me harm. I intend to put a stop to it. (*He takes a step in.* Holmes *moves center to stop him.*)

Holmes. No, Sir Henry. That is precisely what they wish you to do. Remember my warning—you must not venture onto the moor at night.

Sir Henry. What's out there, Mr. Holmes? You know, don't you?

Holmes. There is more evil surrounding Baskerville Hall than I have ever encountered before.

(*Sound of "Something" on the moor—vague, distant.*)

Watson. Listen!

Sir Henry. It can't be—

Holmes. I fear it is. The horror that killed Sir Charles is prowling the moor once again.

(*Sir Henry stands motionless, terrified. Watson, in fear and wondering, continues to stare out into the mist. Again, the howl of the hound—louder and more chilling than before, like a cursed soul that can find no rest. What's left of the room's stage lighting dims quickly, leaving the trio in near silhouette. Another howl . . .*)

CURTAIN—END OF ACT ONE

---

22. **eureka** (yŏŏ-rē′kə): an exclamation used to express joy at a discovery (from a Greek word meaning "I have found").

WORDS
TO   **theorize** (thē′ə-rīz′) *v.* to form an idea or opinion; guess
KNOW

632

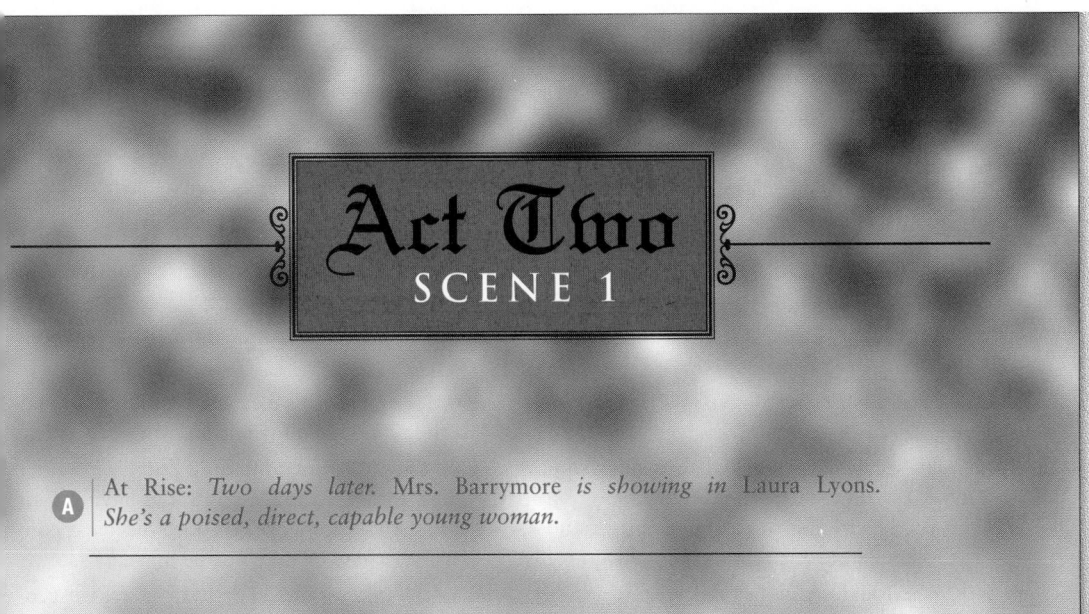

Act Two
SCENE 1

A **At Rise:** *Two days later.* Mrs. Barrymore *is showing in* Laura Lyons. *She's a poised, direct, capable young woman.*

Mrs. Barrymore. If you'll come in here, my dear, and wait. (*She indicates the sofa. Laura crosses to it, sits.*) I'll tell Mr. Holmes you're here.

Laura. You might also tell him my time is as valuable as his. I would prefer not to be kept waiting.

Mrs. Barrymore. (*She is taken aback by the severity of Laura's tone.*) I'll tell him. (*She exits up center, turns left. Laura sits a moment, impatient. Looks at the portrait, stands, moves to it, studies Sir Hugo's visage.*)

Jack. (*He enters via the French doors.*) I saw you driving by the cottage. I thought you might stop in.

Laura (*turns*). I planned to on my way back.

Jack. You really shouldn't take that old car of yours on these dirt roads. They're fit for nothing but pony carts.

Laura. I wouldn't do it at night.

Jack. You could skid into the mire.

Laura. You do worry about me, don't you?

Jack. When you let me.

Laura. You must be on good terms with Sir Henry.

Jack. What makes you think that?

Laura. The way you walk into his home.

Jack. The moor is free and easy about such things.

Laura. Nothing's easy on the moor, Jack.

Jack (*moves behind down left center chair*). Come to pay your respects to Sir Henry?

Laura. Why should I? I'm no longer a neighbor of Baskerville Hall.

Jack. Then why are you here?

Holmes. (*He enters up center, from left.*) Perhaps I can answer that, Mr. Stapleton. I called Mrs. Lyons and asked for this meeting. (*to Laura*) There was no need to trouble yourself. I planned to see you in Tracey Coombes.

THE HOUND OF THE BASKERVILLES **633**

Literary Concept:
STAGE DIRECTIONS

A Have students form impressions of Laura Lyons based on the information provided in the stage directions.

CUSTOMIZING FOR
Students Acquiring English

I Help students use context clues to figure out the meaning of *visage* in these stage directions. (*The clues* portrait *and* Sir Hugo's *suggest that* visage *means "face."*)

Critical Thinking:
HYPOTHESIZING

B Guide students to figure out the relationship between Laura and Jack, based on their conversation in this passage. (*Possible responses: They are good friends, as shown by Jack's interest in Laura's safety. They are lovers. They are neighbors united against a common enemy, Holmes.*)

Mini-Lesson **Study Skills**

LIBRARY CATALOGS Tell students that the easiest way to find material in a library is to use a catalog. Explain that library catalogs list the books and other materials that the library owns. Be sure that students understand that there are several kinds of catalog systems in use. One of the most common types is the card catalog, a file of individual cards usually kept in drawers in a cabinet. Each card gives information about a book in the library, and each book is represented by at least three cards in the catalog. These cards are arranged in alphabetical order according to the book's title, author, or subject. Many libraries now catalog their collections using computers; information also can be accessed by a book's title, author, or subject.

Application Direct students to use either a card or computer catalog in the library to find books about forensic science they can use to complete the Science Connection on page 656.

Multiple Learning Styles

C **Interpersonal Learners** Invite students to analyze this scene. Have them explain how Holmes manages to place the hostile suspect, Laura Lyons, at ease and thus gather as much information as possible from her. Guide students to consider the stage directions as well as the dialogue in their analysis.

Literary Concept: MOTIVATION

D Ask students to explain why Laura doesn't answer Holmes directly. Direct students to consider her reasons for concealing information from Holmes. *(Possible responses: Laura is concerned that anything she says to Holmes may incriminate her in Sir Charles's murder. She distrusts Holmes and is careful not to give him any ammunition to use against her.)*

Linking to Math

E The pound is the British unit of money. In recent years, the pound has been worth $1.60 to $1.80. In the original setting, 1899, the pound had considerably greater buying power.

Laura. I'll be spending some time with a friend, so I thought I would save you the trouble.

C **Holmes.** A friend here on the moor, you mean?

Laura. Lady Agatha.

Holmes. My associate, Doctor Watson, is at her cottage now. I had no idea she was that social.

Laura. Perhaps I should have made an appointment.

Holmes. Not at all. Your arrival is most opportune. (*to* Jack) Sorry I haven't taken you up on your invitation to view your insect collection, Stapleton. A situation I hope to remedy.

Jack. You'll find my collection quite special.

Holmes. Mr. Stapleton and I met on the moor not long ago. He was in pursuit of a Grizzled Skipper butterfly.

Jack. It escaped my net.

Holmes. Pity. Are you waiting to see Sir Henry?

Jack. My sister and I, yes.

Holmes. Might try the potting shed. He and Barrymore were there earlier.

Jack. Will you give me a ride back when you leave?

Laura. Happy to.

Jack. I have only a few things to say to Sir Henry. I won't be long. (*He exits left.*)

Holmes. Old friends?

D **Laura.** Mr. Stapleton has been exceedingly . . . helpful.

Holmes. Won't you sit down?

Laura. (*She returns to the sofa.*) There's a great deal of excitement in the village.

Holmes (*moves down center*). Oh?

Laura. The police have traced a dangerous convict to the moor. Apparently, he escaped from Princetown prison some time ago.

Holmes. That would be Selden, the Notting Hill murderer.

Laura. You're well informed, Mr. Holmes.

Holmes. In some circles there's considerable doubt as to his sanity.

Laura. Sane or insane, the farmers here about don't like it.

Holmes. I understand they get a hundred pounds if they can give information.

Laura. The chance of a hundred pounds is a poor thing compared to the chance of having your throat cut. Surely, we're not to discuss a convict who may or may not be insane.

Holmes. I understand you had the pleasure of knowing Sir Charles.

Laura. (*She cools. She doesn't care for the drift of the conversation.*) Yes.

Holmes. And I've had the pleasure of knowing your father.

Laura. I don't know what you're driving at, Mr. Holmes. There is nothing in common between my father and me. I owe him nothing, and his friends are not mine. If it were not for Sir Charles and some other kind hearts I might have starved for all that my father cared.

Holmes. Did you correspond with Sir Charles?

Laura. Why are you asking these questions?

Holmes. I assure you, Mrs. Lyons, they are necessary.

Laura (*gives in*). I wrote to him once or twice to thank him for his kindness.

Holmes. Kindness? Would you care to explain?

Laura. I've already explained as much. He contributed money so I could set up a small shop in Tracey Coombes.

Holmes. Have you the dates of those letters?

Laura. Dates? No.

Holmes. Did you ever write to Sir Charles asking him to meet you?

Laura (*nervous*). That's an odd question.

Holmes. I intend to repeat it. (*insists*) Did you ever write to Sir Charles asking him to meet you?

Laura. No.

Holmes. Not on the day of his death?

Laura. No.

Holmes. Surely your memory deceives. I could even quote a passage of your communication. It ran, "Please, please, as you are a gentleman, burn this letter, and be at the gate by ten o'clock."

Laura. Then he didn't do as I asked.

Holmes. You do Sir Charles an injustice. He did burn the letter. Most of it, in any case.

Laura. All right. I wrote it. I wished him to assist me further. I thought that if I had an inter-view I could gain his help, so I asked him to meet me.

Holmes. At an hour when the moor is deserted and dark.

Laura. The hour seemed unimportant.

Holmes. You asked him to meet you *outside* the house.

Laura. What does it matter? I never went.

Holmes. Why?

Laura. A private matter. It concerns only me.

Holmes. Why deny you wrote the letter?

Laura. Obvious, I should think. Gossip.

Holmes. You admit you made an appointment with Sir Charles at the hour and place he met his death.

Laura. I do.

Holmes. Yet you deny you kept the appointment.

Laura. Yes. (*She sits like a block of ice.*)

Holmes. Is that all you wish to tell me?

Laura. Mr. Holmes, that is all I am going to tell you. (*She stands.*) I'll wait for Mr. Stapleton in the car. (*She exits up center, turns right.*)

Holmes (*to himself*). Remarkable woman. Not to the manner born,[23] but giving an excellent imitation. (*sniffs*)

Kathy. (*She enters via the French doors, watches.*) You're a bloodhound in the true sense of the word, Mr. Holmes.

Holmes. There are seventy-five perfumes, which it is very necessary that a criminal expert be able to distinguish from each other. Mrs. Lyons favors none of them.

Kathy (*moves into the room*). How did you find her?

---

23. **not to the manner born:** not accustomed to a particular lifestyle since birth.

Active Reading: PREDICT

F Have students predict what Holmes plans to reveal with this line of questioning. Guide students to make their guesses based on information they have already learned in the play, especially the clues that Holmes has gathered. (*Possible response: Holmes will verify that Laura Lyons is the "L.L." who wrote the letter to Sir Charles.*)

Critical Thinking: MAKING JUDGMENTS

G Ask students if they agree with Laura's apparent decision to withhold information from Holmes. Have students form two groups and debate this issue. (*Possible responses: She should withhold information because she doesn't know anything about Holmes and how he will use her confession. She should tell Holmes the entire truth to help him solve the mystery of Sir Charles's murder.*)

Literary Concept: PLOT

H Discuss with students how Laura's letter to Sir Charles, the time and place of their appointment, Laura's lie, and Laura's hostility make her a very strong suspect in the murder. Then explore with students some reasons why the author would produce such a strong suspect at this point in the plot. (*Possible responses: to build suspense; to show who is guilty; to divert our attention from the real killer*)

Mini-Lesson Spelling

WORDS ENDING IN -ISE AND -IZE Write *theory + ize = theorize* on the board. Point out that *-ize* is a suffix used to form verbs that mean "to make or become." Then write *despise* on the board and underline *-ise*. Explain that *-ise* is usually part of the base word itself rather than a suffix added to a word.

Application Read aloud the following words from the selection and have students spell them correctly.

1. memorize
2. apologize
3. compromise
4. supervise
5. burglarize
6. surprise
7. advertise
8. criticize
9. sympathize
10. surmise

Ask students to look for more words that fit this pattern, in their own writing and in the things that they read, and to add these words to their personal word lists.

Reteaching/Reinforcement
• *Unit Five Resource Book,* p. 49

Active Reading: EVALUATE

I Have students evaluate the writer's purpose in mentioning the shoe to decide if it is an important clue in solving the mystery. Encourage students to support their conclusions with evidence from the text. *(Possible responses: It must be important because it gets so much attention on this page. It is irrelevant because it is not linked to anything else that has happened in the play so far.)*

Critical Thinking:
HYPOTHESIZING

J Invite students to guess what Jack is going to say, based on what they have learned about his character and his actions. *(Possible responses: He is going to confess to the murder, reveal a secret about Kathy, or apologize to Sir Henry for his prior rude behavior.)*

CUSTOMIZING FOR
Students Acquiring English

2 Tell students that *cowed*, in the stage directions, indicates that Kathy backs down from Jack.

Active Reading: EVALUATE

K Have students evaluate Jack's request to Sir Henry. Guide students to decide if the request is valid and tell why or why not. *(Possible responses: It is valid because it gives the couple a reasonable length of time to decide if their feelings are true. It is not valid because Jack does not know how Sir Henry and Kathy already feel about each other. Perceptive students might suggest that Jack has another reason for delaying the marriage.)*

Holmes. I didn't. She found me. I must say she isn't quite what I expected.

Kathy. What did you expect?

Holmes. Someone less sure of herself.

Sir Henry. (*He enters up center carrying a shoe. To* Kathy.) I saw you walking over the moor from my window.

Kathy. It's Jack. He has something to say. He went looking for you.

Holmes. I'm afraid I misdirected him to the potting shed.

Kathy. (*She moves to the French doors, calls out.*) Jack! (*to others*) He's already on his way back.

Holmes. The shoe doesn't fit properly?

Sir Henry. It fits, but there's only one.

Holmes. Where is its companion?

Sir Henry. Haven't the slightest idea. (*He puts it on the floor, by the sofa.*)

Jack. (*He enters left, stands awkwardly.*) I should have returned long before this, Sir Henry.

Sir Henry (*distant*). You have something to say to me?

Jack. I do. (*He looks at* Holmes.) It's rather personal.

Sir Henry. Anything you have to say to me, you may say in front of Mr. Holmes.

Holmes. My presence isn't required.

Jack. Thank you, Mr. Holmes. And you will come and see my collection. I'm anxious for your reaction.

Holmes. You may count on it. (Holmes *exits up center, turns left.*)

Kathy. My brother wants to apologize for his temper.

Jack. (*He turns on her, his words harsh, biting.*) I prefer to speak for myself!

Kathy (*cowed*). I didn't mean to speak for you, Jack.

Jack. Then don't. (*Softer tone to* Sir Henry.) You must understand the thought of losing my sister was hard for me. She's all I have for family. I suspected your motives, that you were simply using your title and position to impress her.

Sir Henry. Nothing could have been further from my intent.

Jack. I know that—now.

Sir Henry. I must tell you, Stapleton, that I have every intention of marrying your sister. She's told you?

Jack. She has. I will withdraw all opposition if you promise to wait three months until you are completely sure that marriage is what you truly want. I've seen one unhappy marriage on the moor. I've no desire to see another. My sister's happiness is my only concern.

Sir Henry. Kathy is no Laura Lyons and I'm no idle painter of pastoral scenes.

Jack. Then we are agreed? Three months?

Sir Henry (*nods assent*). What must be must be. Three months. (Jack *extends his hand. They shake.*)

Kathy. Wonderful.

Jack. Will you be riding back with Laura and me, Kathy?

Kathy. I'll walk back.

Jack. I'm not sure that's wise. That convict might be lurking.

Sir Henry. I'll see that Kathy gets home without incident.

---

636   UNIT FIVE   PART 2: MYSTERIOUS CIRCUMSTANCES

Illustration by Sergio Martinez. From Children's Classics Edition of *The Hound of the Baskervilles* by Sir Arthur Conan Doyle. Copyright © 1992 Crown Publishers, Inc., reprinted by permission of Crown Publishers, Inc.

637

L Review with students the relationships among Jack, Kathy, and Sir Henry.

- How are Jack and Kathy related? *(They are brother and sister.)* **Noting Relevant Details**

- What is the relationship between Sir Henry and Kathy? *(They are in love and want to get married.)* **Making Inferences/Noting Relevant Details**

- To what plan do these three characters agree? *(Sir Henry and Kathy will be married after waiting three months.)* **Summarizing**

Set a Purpose Have students read to discover the identity of the strange man seen at the windows of Baskerville Hall.

Literary Note

Sherlock Holmes fans have organized fan clubs in numerous countries, including Australia, Burma, Denmark, Germany, Holland, Sweden, Japan, and the United States. In this country, the clubs are known as "scion societies" and name themselves after the stories or details in them, such as the "Hounds of the Baskervilles" of Chicago. In addition, there are magazines devoted entirely to Sherlockian scholarship, including the *Baker Street Journal* and the *Sherlock Holmes Journal.*

Critical Thinking: SYNTHESIZING

M Have students use what they know about Kathy to analyze her reply in this passage. Then have students explain why they think she avoids the question. *(Possible responses: She is ashamed to admit that she is afraid of Jack. She does not think the issue is any of Sir Henry's concern. She is hiding something from Sir Henry.)*

Literary Concept: MOOD

N Ask students what mood or feeling Sir Henry's remarks create here. Then explore with students why the author creates this particular mood at this point in the play. *(Possible response: Sir Henry's remarks create a frightening mood and serve to bring the play back to its main purpose— to entertain by creating a mood of mystery, fear, and terror.)*

Jack. Thank you, Sir Henry. I wonder—would you dine with us at the cottage tomorrow evening?

Sir Henry. Delighted.

Jack. I'll go find Laura. (*He exits via the French doors.* Kathy *moves to* Sir Henry, *elated.*)

Sir Henry. I'm not so sure I like that provision of three months. If it will make things easier with your brother, I'm not going to argue.

Kathy. I knew he'd come around.

Sir Henry (*sits down left center*). Kathy, have you always been afraid of your brother?

Kathy. Yes, I think I have.

Sir Henry. He's never harmed you in any way?

Kathy (*avoids the question*). I was surprised to find Laura was here.

Sir Henry. So was Mr. Holmes, I think.

Perkins. (*She enters up center.*) Mrs. Barrymore said you were looking for me, sir.

Sir Henry (*points to the shoe*). I can't find my other shoe.

Perkins (*crosses, picks it up*). Aren't these the shoes you gave me yesterday for polish?

Sir Henry. Barrymore brought them back to my room last night. When I went to put them on

just now, I could find only one.

Perkins. I can't imagine where the other one is, sir.

Sir Henry. My favorite pair.

Perkins. I'll turn the place upside down.

Sir Henry. No need to do that. Just see if you can locate the mate.

Perkins. I'll try, Sir Henry. I can't imagine what's become of it. Will you be staying for tea, Miss?

Kathy (*grins*). If Sir Henry has no objection.

Sir Henry. You'll be seeing a great deal of Miss Stapleton around Baskerville Hall in the coming weeks, Perkins.

Perkins. That will be nice, sir. Especially if the Barrymores leave. I wouldn't like being the only woman here. I scare easily. (*She exits up center, turns right.*)

Kathy. Are they really leaving?

Sir Henry. Not immediately. Can't say I blame them. Kathy, you do understand the danger? The curse of the Baskervilles. Oh, I try to pretend everything is perfectly normal, and act according but I know there's a sword hanging over my head, ready to drop at any minute.

Kathy. Henry, whatever this thing is, we'll defeat it together. Mr. Holmes will let no harm come to you. You've got to believe that.

Sir Henry. I try.

Kathy. I'll see if I can't arrange a nice bouquet for the tray. The wildflowers are almost done for this time of the year.

Sir Henry. Don't be long. (Kathy *exits left, onto the moor, almost colliding with* Barrymore.)

Barrymore. I beg your pardon, Miss Stapleton.

Kathy. No harm done.

Barrymore. (*He waits until* Kathy *is outside, then enters.*) I've taken an inventory of everything in the potting shed, Sir Henry. You'll be needing some new tools.

Mini-Lesson: Speaking, Listening, and Viewing

DRAMA PERFORMANCE Explain that *The Hound of the Baskervilles* is an ideal play for students to perform for friends and family. You may wish to show students a filmed version of the play so that they can get a visual understanding of some of the elements of stagecraft. Then share with students the word web and use it to explain the tasks involved in staging a play.

Application According to his or her interests and learning style, assign each student a role in a class production of the selection. In addition to acting, students can direct; prepare scenery, lighting, costumes, and playbills; create or find background music and sound effects; or videotape the performance.

Sir Henry. You haven't been entirely honest with me, have you, Barrymore? (*moves down left*)

Barrymore. About the inventory?

Sir Henry. No.

Barrymore. I'm afraid I don't understand, sir.

Sir Henry. Your family has lived with mine for generations under this roof, and here I find you in some dark plot against me.

Barrymore. I assure you, Sir Henry, you have no reason to think such a thing.

Sir Henry. Haven't I?

Mrs. Barrymore. (*She enters up center, from right.*) Beg pardon, Sir Henry, Perkins says there's something amiss with one of your shoes. (*She senses the tension in the room, looks to her husband.*) What's wrong?

Barrymore. Sir Henry believes I engage in some dark plot against him.

Sir Henry. I'm not fooled by your tricks with the flashlight at the window. (*Mrs. Barrymore is startled, suppresses a gasp.*) Sit down, Mrs. Barrymore. You look unwell.

Mrs. Barrymore (*moves to sofa, sits*). No, no, sir. You misunderstand. No plot against you.

Sir Henry. (*He stands, moves up center, calls off.*) Mr. Holmes! Mr. Holmes! (*He turns back, steps center.*)

Barrymore (*to his wife*). We have to go. This is the end of it. You can pack our things.

Mrs. Barrymore. I've brought us to this. It's my doing, Sir Henry. All mine. My husband has done nothing except for my sake and because I asked him.

Sir Henry. What does that mean?

Barrymore. My wife is speaking the truth. If there was a plot it was not against you.

Mrs. Barrymore. My unhappy brother is starving on the moor.

Barrymore. We couldn't let him perish. (*Holmes enters up center from left.*)

Sir Henry. You mean your brother is—

Barrymore. The escaped convict, sir.

Holmes (*annoyed*). Sir Henry, I expressly asked that you leave this matter to me. I told you you had nothing to fear from the light on the moor.

Sir Henry. I think, Mr. Holmes, it's time I took a hand in all this.

Holmes. That would be a most unwise maneuver.

Mrs. Barrymore. Selden is my younger brother. We humored him when he was a lad and gave him his own way in everything. When he grew older he fell in with a bad lot, the devil was in him. From crime to crime he sank lower and lower.

Barrymore. He's quite mad.

Mrs. Barrymore. Don't say that.

Barrymore. He came here for help.

Mrs. Barrymore. Dragged himself here one night, starving. I couldn't refuse to help him.

Sir Henry. Haven't you overstepped yourself, Mr. Holmes? Selden is a wanted criminal. Dangerous.

Holmes. I assure you, Sir Henry, Selden is dangerous to no one but himself. His mind most certainly is deranged, but in a childlike manner. He is not the same man as when he murdered. My guess would be drug damage. I've seen cases like this before. Selden will end his days as little more than a vegetable—passive, frightened, disoriented. (*Mrs. Barrymore cries, takes out a handkerchief.*) No harm will come to him, Mrs. Barrymore. If he's in danger of apprehension I have instructed him to come immediately to Baskerville Hall.

Barrymore. You've talked to him?

Holmes. He has been on the moor for some

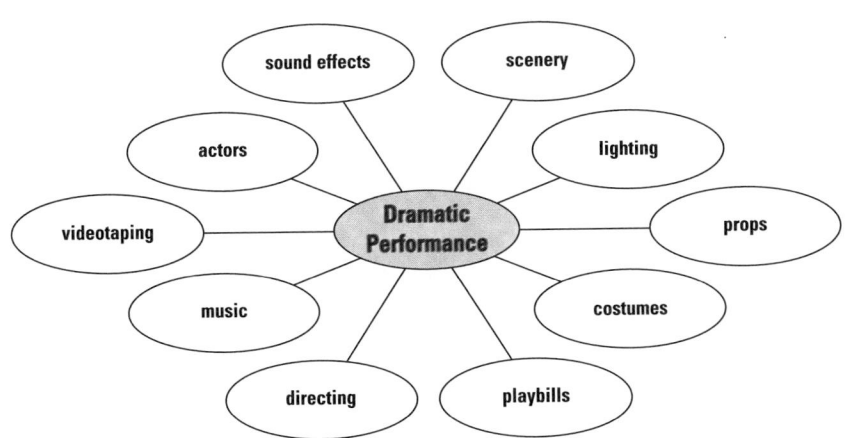

Critical Thinking:
HYPOTHESIZING

S Invite students to guess how Selden might have helped Holmes. *(Possible responses: Selden gave Holmes clues about the identity of the murderer, the nature of the hound, or the background of the Baskerville curse.)*

Literary Concept: **PLOT**

T Ask students if they think the letter was really written by Lady Agatha and why or why not. If so, ask them why she would warn Sir Henry. If not, ask them why someone else would write the letter and sign it with Lady Agatha's name. *(Possible responses: Lady Agatha wrote it because she knows the identity of the murderer and wants to warn Sir Henry. Someone else is trying to delay the investigation, scare Sir Henry into leaving Baskerville Hall, or frame Lady Agatha.)*

STRATEGIC READING FOR
Less-Proficient Readers

U Ask students what the letter sent to sir Henry says. *(It is signed "Lady Agatha," and it warns Sir Henry to leave Baskerville Hall that night.)* **Summarizing**

Set a Purpose Have students read to find out what Lady Agatha has not told Holmes and Watson about Sir Charles Baskerville's will.

S weeks, and he has proved invaluable to me, a fact I shall relay to the authorities. (*Perkins enters up center holding an envelope.*)

Sir Henry. What is it, Perkins?

Perkins. I found this under the door, sir. In the kitchen. I heard someone outside, but when I looked I couldn't see anyone.

Sir Henry. Let me have it.

Holmes. One moment, Sir Henry. Are you in the custom of receiving mail in this manner?

Sir Henry. Under the kitchen door? Certainly not.

Holmes. Give me the letter, Perkins. (*She looks to Sir Henry,* he nods. Perkins *hands the letter to Holmes. He takes it and moves, down, to the desk, picks up a magnifying glass. All watch.*) Curious.

Sir Henry. What is it?

Holmes. Unless I'm mistaken this is the same stationery used for your London warning. (Holmes *opens the letter.*)

Sir Henry. What . . . what's the message?

Holmes (*reads*). "If you value your life, leave Baskerville Hall tonight. There'll be no further warning."

Sir Henry. The words clipped from a newspaper and stuck to the page?

Holmes. Not this time. It's handwritten and it's signed. (*all tense*)

Mrs. Barrymore. Signed?

Holmes. Signed . . . Lady Agatha Mortimer. (*The others exchange astonished looks with one another. Holmes* studies the page with the magnifying glass.) Interesting.

CURTAIN

SCENE 2

V
At Rise: That evening. The mist is on the moor and, once again, the lighting in the room causes shadows and an atmosphere of foreboding.[24] Holmes is standing in front of the portrait. Voices up center, from right.

Watson's Voice. We'll soon discover the mystery, Lady Agatha.

Lady Agatha's Voice. I trust so. It's a nuisance being called away at this hour.

Watson. (*He and* Lady Agatha *enter up center.*) There you are, Holmes.

Holmes (*turns*). I see Barrymore reached you. Good of you to come, Lady Agatha.

Lady Agatha. (*She crosses down, sits down left center.*) He said it was urgent.

Holmes. It is.

Watson. Dash it, Holmes, we hadn't even sat down to dinner.

Holmes. My apologies.

Watson. I'm famished.

Holmes. You make too much of food, Watson. You should follow my example. I am perfectly content with a roast beef sandwich and a cryptogram.[25]

Watson. Unfortunately, I can't eat cryptograms. Besides, it wasn't a roast beef sandwich. It was steak and kidney pie. My favorite. Lady Agatha was expecting a guest, too. I was looking forward to company.

Holmes. Laura Lyons.

Lady Agatha. She hadn't arrived by the time Barrymore called.

Holmes. Odd. She left Baskerville Hall some hours ago.

Lady Agatha. Not alone? They suspect that escaped convict is still on the moor.

Holmes. Stapleton was with her.

Lady Agatha. He knows the moor as well as anyone.

---

24. **foreboding:** a feeling that something bad is about to happen.

25. **cryptogram** (krĭp′tə-grăm′): something written in code; a word puzzle.

Active Reading: CLARIFY

V Guide students to use context clues to clarify that *at rise* means "at the beginning of the play" or, more literally, "when the curtain rises." Then have students use the stage directions to clarify the mood of this scene. (*Possible responses: suspenseful, tense, fearful*)

CUSTOMIZING FOR

Students Acquiring English

4 Point out that *Dash it* is an exclamation used in British English to express annoyance or anger. A corresponding American English expression is *Darn it.*

Literary Concept: PLOT

W Have students explore the tone of Watson's dialogue. Then discuss with the class why the author has Watson complaining about his missed dinner at this point in the play. (*Possible responses: The tone is humorous, light, comic. This shift in tone relieves the grim mood.*)

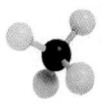 Ask students what motive Holmes might have had for coming to Baskerville Hall. *(Possible response: He wanted the thrill of investigating the Baskerville curse.)*

Linking to Science

Graphology is the study and analysis of handwriting to discover the writer's character traits. In theory, there are more than 20 different handwriting elements, such as degree of slant, height of letters, and space between lines, that reveal the writer's personality. The field of scientific handwriting analysis, in contrast, is designed to determine the authenticity of a signature or important document such as a will.

Active Reading: EVALUATE

Z Have students evaluate Holmes's statement about the signature not being important. Ask students if they agree or disagree with his comment and to support their responses. *(Possible responses: I agree that the signature is not really important in the end because it's just a way for the murderer to try and throw off Holmes's investigation; I disagree because Holmes might be able to find out who the murderer is by analyzing the forged signature.)*

CUSTOMIZING FOR
Students Acquiring English

5 In the stage directions, *sotto* refers to *sotto voce*, a term that indicates the line is to be spoken softly, as if Watson is talking to himself.

Watson. No one knows this area as well as you, Lady Agatha.

Lady Agatha. You've discovered something of importance, haven't you, Mr. Holmes? That's why you sent Barrymore.

Watson. Holmes, I think your holiday to this part of the country was carefully planned. I don't think you were interested in those smelly old huts at all. I think you were only interested in Baskerville Hall.

Holmes. (*He crosses behind the sofa, hands the letter to* Watson, *indicates* Lady Agatha.) Watson, if you'd be so kind. (*He takes the letter and hands it to* Lady Agatha.)

Lady Agatha (*reads, then*). Outrageous.

Holmes. I take it you disown authorship?

Lady Agatha. "If you value your life, leave Baskerville Hall tonight. There'll be no further warning." Why, whoever signed my name hasn't the remotest idea of my handwriting style.

Holmes. I suspected as much. Are you familiar with your guest's handwriting?

Lady Agatha. Watson here has a bold hand.

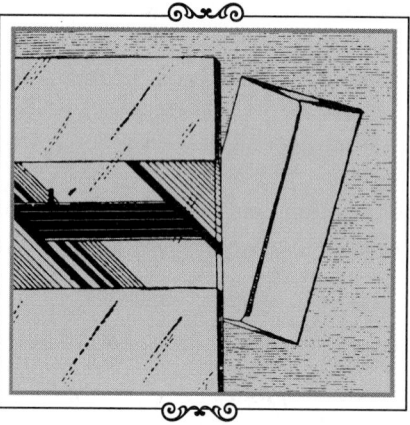

Holmes. I wasn't referring to Doctor Watson. I meant Laura Lyons.

Lady Agatha. I am quite familiar with her penmanship. (*positive*) Laura did not write this message.

Watson. Why would anyone sign Lady Agatha's name, and not even make an attempt at a good forgery?

Holmes. To delay investigation, possibly. I don't think the signature is important. The writer was intent in pressing the warning. The net draws tighter.

Watson. It settles one issue.

Holmes. Which is?

Watson. There's no supernatural force behind this ugly business.

Holmes. Then how do you account for the beast you described to me—dripping with a bluish flame, eyes ringed with fire?

Watson (*frowns*). I'd forgotten about him.

Holmes. I haven't.

Lady Agatha. The moor plays tricks, Doctor Watson. You saw something you mistook for the specter.[26]

Watson. You've certainly changed your tune. I know what I saw.

Holmes. In that case are we to surmise your spectral beast can also wield pen and ink?

Watson. You're being rude, Holmes. (Watson *is offended, moves to the desk, sits.*)

Holmes. No need to take offense.

Watson (*still pouting, sotto*). Positively rude.

Lady Agatha. I take it you have suspicions about Laura?

---

26. **specter:** ghostly figure.

Mini-Lesson: Speaking,  **Listening, and Viewing**

SCIENTIFIC OBSERVATION Tell students that Holmes is a master of scientific observation. Explain that scientists, like detectives, are careful to make accurate observations. Outline for students the following steps to help ensure they make accurate scientific observations:

1. Examine the entire object or situation, using your sense of sight.
2. Look carefully for details.
3. Use other senses to make additional observations.
4. Write down everything you observe.

Application Invite students to test their own powers of observation. Have students spend a few minutes observing their classroom setting and taking notes about its details. Then divide students into pairs. Have one partner close his or her eyes and listen while the other partner describes something in the classroom. The first partner must then guess what object is being described. If necessary, the second partner can provide additional clues. Then have partners switch roles. Encourage students to use details that appeal to a variety of senses.

Holmes. Suspicions about many things. Were you aware she was in correspondence with Sir Charles?

Lady Agatha. No.

Holmes. Were you aware that Barrymore was in London the exact time Sir Henry received the first warning?

Lady Agatha. Barrymore never leaves the moor.

Holmes. You are mistaken. I have it on authority that he left Baskerville Hall during Sir Henry's London stay.

Watson. What authority?

Holmes. A gentleman on the moor.

Watson. You mean Jack Stapleton?

Lady Agatha. You'll be casting your doubts on me next, Mr. Holmes. (*stands*) You don't think I had a hand in this?

Holmes. You did leave out one extremely revealing fact when you first called upon my assistance.

Lady Agatha. I told you everything.

Holmes. Everything?

Lady Agatha. I'm not in the habit of lying.

Holmes. You neglected to mention one salient point. You are executrix[27] of Sir Charles' estate.

Lady Agatha. (*She stiffens, calmly—*) What if I am?

Holmes. In the event any misfortune should befall Sir Henry, who has yet to make a will, you would be in a most enviable situation.

Watson. You go too far, Holmes.

Holmes. On the contrary, I don't go far enough.

Lady Agatha. Not telling you was an oversight on my part, nothing more.

Holmes. Indeed.

Lady Agatha. You know of my bad financial situation.

Holmes. Thanks to Watson here.

Lady Agatha (*turns to* Watson). He always did have a rather large mouth.

Watson (*livid*). I protest.

(*Sound of the hound—distant, vague.*)

Holmes. Quiet.

Perkins. (*She enters up center, from right.*) Mr. Holmes, have you seen Sir Henry about?

Holmes. Sssssh!

(Perkins *stands motionless. No one moves—then—the howl of the hound—loud, incessant, bloodchilling.*)

Lady Agatha. It's close to the house.

Holmes (*to Perkins*). What about Sir Henry?

Perkins. He's not in his room.

Watson. Where could he have got to?

Holmes. The hound! Come, Watson! We may be too late! (*He moves fast to the French doors, opens them, exits into the night,* Watson *right behind him.*)

Perkins (*alarmed*). What is it? What's wrong?

Lady Agatha. Get Barrymore.

Perkins. Barrymore?

Lady Agatha. Stop asking so many questions. Do as you're told. Be quick about it.

Perkins. Yes, m'am. (*She runs out.*)

(Lady Agatha *moves to the French doors, looks out. Howl of the hound again. Worried, she backs into the room. She looks at the letter in her hand, thinks. She moves to the fireplace, takes a matchbox from the mantle and prepares to burn the letter as, quickly,* Mrs. Barrymore *enters.*)

Mrs. Barrymore. Perkins whimpered something about the hound and Sir Henry. (*sees* Lady Agatha) What are you doing?

---

27. **executrix** (ĭg-zĕk′yə-trĭks′): a woman appointed to carry out the directions in a will.

Literary Note

The Sherlock Holmes stories have inspired a number of imitations, parodies, and tributes. Among the best known are Nicholas Meyer's *The Seven-Percent Solution,* Vincent Starrett's "The Unique Hamlet," and John Kendrick Bangs's "Shylock Holmes" stories. Even Conan Doyle got into the act, writing a parody of his own Holmes stories, called "How Watson Learned the Trick."

Illustration by Sergio Martinez. From Children's Classics Edition of *The Hound of the Baskervilles* by Sir Arthur Conan Doyle. Copyright © 1992 Crown Publishers, Inc., reprinted by permission of Crown Publishers, Inc.

644

Lady Agatha (*pockets the letter, lies*). I was going to light the fire. It's not important now. We need your husband. Where is he?

Mrs. Barrymore. Perkins is fetching him. (*looks about the empty room*) Where are Mr. Holmes and Doctor Watson?

Lady Agatha. (*She moves behind sofa.*) They've gone onto the moor.

Mrs. Barrymore (*distraught, fearing for her brother*). They're not going to do him any harm? (*moves to French doors*) Mr. Holmes promised to protect him.

Lady Agatha. Who are you talking about?

Mrs. Barrymore. He's like a child now. He wouldn't hurt anyone.

(Barrymore *enters up center, hurriedly.*)

Lady Agatha. They'll need help, Barrymore . . . Mr. Holmes. Watson. They've gone after Sir Henry. He's out there.

Barrymore. Sir Henry never goes on the moor at night.

Lady Agatha. Don't waste time.

Mrs. Barrymore. Get the strong light. In the hall chest. (*He exits up center.*) They mustn't harm him.

Lady Agatha. Why should they want to do harm to Sir Henry? You don't talk sense, woman.

Mrs. Barrymore. Not Sir Henry. My brother. He's been out there for weeks.

Lady Agatha. Brother?

Mrs. Barrymore (*moves back into room*). Selden, the Notting Hill murderer.

Lady Agatha. The escaped convict who has the countryside terrified?

Mrs. Barrymore. Yes.

Lady Agatha (*aghast*). You've known he's been out there? And you've said nothing!

Mrs. Barrymore. Mister Holmes said he would help him.

Lady Agatha. It isn't your brother they went after. It's the hound.

Mrs. Barrymore. (*She, emotionally exhausted, sits down left center.*) This place is cursed. I never wanted to believe that, but it's true.

Lady Agatha. Stop talking rubbish. I'd better see if there's need for me.

Mrs. Barrymore. No, don't leave me.

Lady Agatha. I'll get a sedative for you.

Barrymore. (*He enters holding the flashlight. He holds it up.*) It has a good beam to cut the fog.

Watson. (*He enters via French doors. He looks exhausted, defeated.*) I'm afraid that will be of no help.

Lady Agatha (*wary*). Sir Henry?

Watson (*a pause, then*). Dead.

(General reaction. Watson *moves down to the desk, pours himself a drink from a decanter.*)

Lady Agatha. Impossible!

(Barrymores *are struck dumb. Positions at this point as follows:* Watson *at the desk,* Mrs. Barrymore *in the chair down left center,* Barrymore *up center,* Lady Agatha *in front of sofa.*)

Watson. If that were only true. (*grim*) I've never heard screams like that from any man or woman. (Lady Agatha *sits on sofa, numb.*) The beast had bitten and clawed and chewed.

Mrs. Barrymore. Doctor Watson, please.

Watson. You'll have to excuse my nerves. I've never encountered anything like this before. The supernatural is quite beyond me.

Barrymore. What could have possessed him to go onto the moor after all the warnings?

Watson. I don't know. He tried to flee, but the creature was too swift.

EE Ask students to discuss what might motivate a person to tell a lie. Then have students evaluate Lady Agatha's decision to lie to Mrs. Barrymore.

Active Reading: CLARIFY

FF Ask students to use the dialogue and stage directions in this passage to identify the character Mrs. Barrymore is talking about. (*Possible response: The details "distraught, fearing for her brother" and "He's like a child now" suggest she means her brother, Selden, the criminal.*)

Literary Concept: SUSPENSE

GG Invite students to isolate the details in this passage that help create suspense. (*Possible responses: the description of the dying man's screams and the mutilated body*)

Literary Concept:
CHARACTERIZATION

HH Have students describe what this passage reveals about Holmes's character. Remind students to use the stage directions as well as the dialogue as they draw conclusions. *(Possible responses: He is cool and in command in emergencies; he is not repulsed by brutal murders.)*

Active Reading: CLARIFY

II Ask students to clarify who was attacked and killed by the hound on the moor. *(Selden, Mrs. Barrymore's brother)*

CUSTOMIZING FOR
Multiple Learning Styles

II **Linguistic Learners** Invite students to write and deliver a eulogy for Selden's funeral.

Lady Agatha. Uncle and nephew—murdered. One frightened to death by the sight of the beast.

Watson. The other driven to his end in his flight to escape from it. I'll be along in a moment. Give him a hand will you, Barrymore?

Lady Agatha. Better bring the body in here.

Holmes. (*He enters, cold, precise, efficient.*) That won't be necessary.

Lady Agatha. There can be no mistake? He's dead.

Holmes. There is no mistake.

Mrs. Barrymore. Poor, poor Sir Henry.

Holmes. I'm afraid your sympathy is misplaced. You will have to prepare yourself for another shock.

Barrymore. How do you mean, sir?

Holmes. In his distress, Watson neglected to wait for my complete report. True, the man is dead. But he is a man with a beard.

Mrs. Barrymore. Beard?

Holmes. I regret having to bring you this information.

Mrs. Barrymore. My brother, isn't it?

Holmes. Yes.

Watson. Why would the hound attack Selden?

Holmes. He attacked a scent. Selden was wearing one of Sir Henry's hunting jackets.

Barrymore. I can explain. A woman from the church committee asked if we had anything we might donate for a bazaar. Sir Henry gave some of his old clothes, among other things.

Mrs. Barrymore. They were warm and comfortable. I thought—why should others have them, when my brother was cold and in rags on the moor.

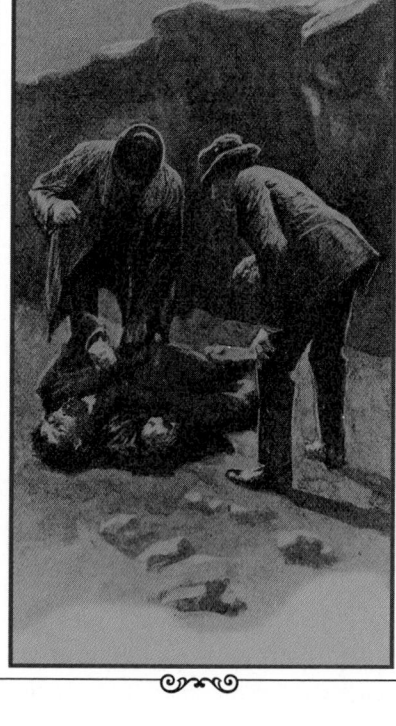

Holmes. You have no need to <u>reproach</u> yourself.

Mrs. Barrymore (*fatalistic*). Perhaps it's for the best. I only wish he didn't die so horribly.

Sir Henry. (*He enters up center.*) Perkins found me. Said I was wanted.

(*All react.*)

Watson. Where have you been?

Lady Agatha. We feared for your life.

Watson. You promised never to go onto the moor at night.

Sir Henry. I was in the potting shed. Any prohibition against that, Mister Holmes?

WORDS
TO
KNOW

reproach (rĭ-prōch′) *n.* to accuse or blame

646

Holmes. None.

Sir Henry. Why do you all look so strange?

Barrymore. It's my wife's brother, sir. Selden.

Watson. Savaged by the beast.

Sir Henry (*in wonder*). Then the curse doesn't only concern the Baskervilles.

Holmes. I wish that were true.

Sir Henry. What connection does Selden have to me?

Mrs. Barrymore. He was wearing your hunting jacket, sir.

Barrymore. The one you donated to the church sale.

Holmes. The hound had your scent.

Sir Henry. How could he get my scent in the first place?

Lady Agatha. When you deal with the supernatural, ordinary explanations are worthless.

Holmes. I'm afraid I can't agree.

Lady Agatha. What choice have you?

Holmes. An investigator needs facts, not legend or rumors. This has not been a satisfactory case.

Sir Henry (*desperate*). Can't you promise any hope?

Holmes. I can promise you something far more startling than hope.

Sir Henry. What?

Holmes. By tomorrow, Sir Henry, the curse of the Baskervilles will either be broken. Or—

Mrs. Barrymore. Or?

Lady Agatha. Or?

Holmes. Someone in this room will be dead. (*Lights fade quickly, as—*)

CURTAIN

Active Reading: EVALUATE

KK Ask students if they think this detail about the jacket is relevant to the mystery. Guide students to support their conclusions with specific details from the play. (*Possible responses: It is extremely relevant, because it suggests that the dog was specifically trained to attack Sir Henry. This means that someone is determined to kill Sir Henry. The detail is not relevant because Selden was killed by supernatural forces.*)

Critical Thinking: ANALYZING

LL Have students explain why they think Lady Agatha attributes Selden's death to supernatural forces. (*Possible responses: She truly believes that Selden was killed by a hound from hell. She wants to hide her own involvement in the murder. She wants to shield someone else from implication in the murder.*)

STRATEGIC READING FOR
Less-Proficient Readers

MM Review with students the events that have occurred on the moor.

• What happens to Mrs. Barrymore's brother Selden? (*He is brutally killed on the moors.*) **Noting Relevant Details**

• What was Selden wearing when he died? (*one of Sir Henry's hunting jackets*) **Noting Relevant Details**

Set a Purpose Have students read to discover new information about Jack and Kathy.

Have students analyze the stage directions to discover what mood is established. Then challenge students to explain what the storm that is building might symbolize. *(Possible responses: The stage directions create a suspenseful, tense mood. The storm that is building in the natural world suggests that the relationships among the characters in the drama might undergo a sudden and destructive change.)*

CUSTOMIZING FOR
Multiple Learning Styles

Bodily-Kinesthetic Learners
Explain that anxiety is a common cause of stress-related disorders such as muscle tension, an upset stomach, or headaches. Encourage students to find out about exercises that can be used to relieve tension. Many people find mild stretching or breathing exercises relaxing. Invite students to share their exercises with the class. Then have the class assess the success of the method.

SCENE 3

 At Rise: *The following evening. A storm is building . . . distant thunder.* Sir Henry *is busy at the writing desk.* Watson *stands by the fireplace, which sends out a warming glow.*

Sir Henry. Makes me feel strange. Sitting here writing all this down.

Watson. One should always keep his affairs in order, Sir Henry.

Sir Henry. No argument there. Only I've never been concerned about a will before. My own will, that is.

Watson. You'll feel better for it.

Sir Henry. Will I?

Watson. Count on it. Can't imagine why Holmes went to see Lady Agatha this afternoon. Yesterday, he practically accused her of being implicated.[28]

Sir Henry. At least we're done with that ghastly business with Selden.

Watson. You're dining with the Stapletons this evening.

Sir Henry. Unless Mr. Holmes brings up some new objection. (*the writing*) Somehow I feel this will is a prelude to my— (*He breaks off, not wanting to say the word "death."*)

Watson. Trust Holmes.

Sir Henry. I do intellectually. Emotionally I'm tight as a knot inside.

Barrymore. (*He, wearing a raincoat, carrying suitcase and hat, appears up center.*) We are leaving now, sir.

(Mrs. Barrymore *appears behind her husband. They step in the room.*)

Sir Henry (*stands, moves to them*). There's nothing I can do to change your minds?

Barrymore. I'm afraid not, Sir Henry. I think it best my wife and I started a new life elsewhere.

Sir Henry. I understand. (*extends his hand*) Goodbye, Barrymore, and good luck.

Barrymore. Thank you, Sir Henry.

Sir Henry (*shakes hands with* Mrs. Barrymore). Goodbye, Mrs. Barrymore.

Mrs. Barrymore (*nods*). Sir Henry.

---

28. **implicated:** involved in a crime.

Mini-Lesson: Speaking, Listening, and Viewing

INTERVIEWS Discuss with the class how Sherlock Holmes listens intently when questioning or interviewing potential suspects. Teach students these rules for taking part in interviews:
- Use body language to project an image of control and confidence.
- Make eye contact often and pay attention.
- Speak clearly and audibly.
- Take time to think over your questions or answers before speaking.
- Listen closely to the interviewer or interviewee. If you don't understand the question or response,

ask the individual to repeat or rephrase it.
- Stay on the topic. Avoid digressing into irrelevant details.

Application Invite students to work in groups of three to role-play the interviewing of suspects in *The Hound of the Baskervilles.* Suggest that students take turns playing Sherlock Holmes, Dr. Watson, and one of the suspects in the play. Caution students to stay in character during the interview, listen carefully, and apply the rules listed above.

Sir Henry. You will write and let me know how things are going?

Barrymore. Yes, sir. (*to his wife*) We don't want to miss the train. Goodbye, Doctor Watson.

Watson. Goodbye. Luck to both of you.

(*The* Barrymores *exit up center, turn right.*)

Sir Henry. They'll be all right. They did well by my uncle's will.

Watson. Handsomely. Still, I've never trusted Barrymore. (*thinks*) I didn't know there was a train at this hour.

Sir Henry (*snaps*). Train? Train? What does a train matter? (*calms down*) Forgive me. I'm . . . I'm tense . . .

Watson. I can well believe it. You've been under a terrible strain, and Holmes is up in his room with his foul-smelling tobacco. He says this is a six-pipe case.

Laura. (*She enters up center from right.*) I'm sorry to intrude like this. Mrs. Barrymore said I should come right in. I'm Mrs. Lyons. Mr. Frankland's daughter.

Sir Henry. I've heard of you. (Laura *doesn't know how she should take this remark.*) This is Doctor Watson.

Laura (*nods*). Oh, yes. Lady Agatha's comrade. She speaks highly of you.

Watson. Sorry we didn't meet the other evening. Won't you sit down?

Laura. (*She crosses to sofa, sits.*) I must see Mr. Holmes. It's important.

Watson. I'll get him.

Laura. Thank you.

(Watson *exits up center, turns left.*)

Sir Henry. Aren't you afraid to cross the moor?

Laura. I understood they captured the convict.

Sir Henry. That's true.

Laura. You mean—the storm?

Sir Henry. I mean the hound.

Laura. It isn't the other world that will hurt one, Sir Henry. It's the living.

Sir Henry. I believe I heard Mr. Holmes say you were from the village of Tracey Coombes.

Laura. I have a small shop.

Sir Henry. I have a distant relative living there.

Laura. I've heard of no Baskervilles in the area.

Sir Henry. No, the name is Desmond. An elderly clergyman. Could I get you something? I fear I'm understaffed at the moment. The maid leaves before dark and the Barrymores have deserted.

Laura. I saw the suitcases in their grip.

Sir Henry. Place won't be the same without them.

Laura. I want you to know, Sir Henry, that I had the utmost respect for your uncle. He was kind, generous, and most thoughtful. His death . . . disturbed me.

THE HOUND OF THE BASKERVILLES **649**

RR Help students clarify the relationship between Jack and Kathy by asking the following questions:

- How do Jack and Kathy claim to be related? *(as brother and sister)*

- How are they actually related? *(as husband and wife)*

Set a Purpose Have students finish reading the play to discover the solution to the mystery.

Active Reading: CONNECT

SS Invite volunteers to tell about times when people they know have made excuses for a friend or allowed a friend to take advantage of them. Have students explore the reasons why people act this way and use these reasons to explain Laura's behavior. *(Possible response: Close friends or people in love sometimes do things that they know are wrong or ill-advised because of their feelings for the other person. That is what Laura did here.)*

Critical Thinking:
MAKING JUDGMENTS

TT Ask students if they believe Laura's excuse. Guide students to support their opinions with details from the play. *(Possible response: Yes, because she came to see Holmes on her own and so far seems to have told the truth. No, because she withheld this information and so may be withholding additional evidence.)*

Holmes. (*He enters up right.*) I expected to see you earlier than this, Mrs. Lyons.

Laura. You knew I'd return?

Holmes. I hoped you would.

Sir Henry. You'll probably want privacy.

Holmes. I think you'd best stay, Sir Henry. What Mrs. Lyons is about to reveal concerns you.

(Watson *enters up center, stands left.*)

Sir Henry. Me?

Holmes. Your uncle, to be precise.

Laura. You anticipate.[29]

Holmes. I am a flawless judge of character, Mrs. Lyons. You did not impress me as the sort of female who could live comfortably with a serious lie.

Sir Henry. What are you driving at?

Laura. (Holmes *looks to her—pointedly.*) It is true I wrote the letter to Sir Charles . . .

Holmes. On the instigation[30] of another.

(Laura, *troubled.*)

Sir Henry. What other?

Laura. I . . . I . . .

Holmes. I know what you communicated in our earlier interview, and also what you've withheld in connection with this matter. I regard this case as one of murder and the evidence may implicate not only your friend Jack Stapleton, but his wife as well.

Laura (*stands, startled*). His wife!

Sir Henry. Wife? What are you saying?

Holmes. The person who has passed for his sister is really his wife.

Watson. I don't believe it.

Laura. Nor I. He's *not* a married man.

Holmes. Kathy unwittingly revealed the ruse[31]

when she told Watson of the school she and her "brother" ran in the north country. (*fishes out photograph*) I made inquiries and one of the employees of the school sent on this photograph. (*hands it to* Sir Henry) Four years ago it was taken. I think you will recognize the couple—Mr. and Mrs. Stapleton. The employee has written the identification on the back.

Laura. Let me see that. (*She takes it from* Sir Henry, *turns it over.*) It's true.

Holmes. Stapleton asked you to write the letter to entice Sir Charles out of the house.

Laura. (*She nods, still staring at the photograph.*) He . . . he promised to marry me once my problems were settled.

Sir Henry. Now I know why Kathy lives in fear of her "brother."

Watson. That's why he went into a rage when he saw you and Kathy close together. He couldn't control the instincts of a jealous husband.

Laura. I swear to you when I wrote the letter I never dreamed of any harm to the old gentleman. He had been a good friend.

Holmes. I presume the reason Stapleton gave was that you would receive help from Sir Charles for the legal expense connected with your divorce.

Laura. Yes. Jack said he couldn't help because he himself was penniless.

Holmes. After you sent the letter he <u>dissuaded</u> you from keeping the appointment.

Laura. Yes.

---

29. **You anticipate:** You're imagining what I'm going to say before I say it.

30. **instigation:** urging.

31. **ruse** (roōs): a trick or plan for fooling someone.

WORDS
TO
KNOW   **dissuade** (dǐ-swād′) *v.* to persuade someone not to do something; discourage

650

Holmes. Then you heard nothing until you read of Sir Charles' death.

Laura. He said the death was a mysterious one, and that I should certainly be suspected if the facts came out. He frightened me into remaining silent.

Holmes. I think, on the whole, you've had a fortunate escape. You had him in your power and he knew it, and yet you are alive.

Laura. I couldn't remain silent any longer.

Holmes. The line between fear and love is often a thin one. As you have been honest with me, I shall be honest with you. You are still in danger.

Sir Henry. He's likely to hurt Kathy.

Holmes. Not if everything falls into place. Time is the essential element. Watson, you will escort Mrs. Lyons to Lady Agatha's cottage.

Laura. I can take care of myself.

Holmes. You heard me, Watson.

Watson. Come along, my dear. You can trust my protection. (*He opens the French doors. Laura looks once more at the photograph, returns it to Holmes.*)

Laura. I was right, y'know. Nothing's easy on the moor. (*She exits, Watson follows.*)

Sir Henry. You must really be worried for her safety?

Holmes. Hang her safety. I merely want some guarantee she won't warn Stapleton.

Sir Henry (*worried*). We must help Kathy.

Holmes. You will do exactly as I instruct.

Sir Henry. I'm ready.

Holmes. You will walk to Stapleton Cottage, and enjoy your dinner.

Sir Henry. You're not serious? I'm not sure I can face Jack Stapleton.

Holmes. That is precisely what you must do. You will <u>divulge</u> the path you will take on your return. Clear?

Sir Henry. Where will you be?

Holmes. Nearby. Leave within the hour. (*He steps into the night. Sir Henry is taken aback by Holmes' abrupt departure. He crosses to the French doors.*)

Sir Henry. Wait a minute, Mr. Holmes! (*calls after him*) Holmes! (*Thunder. Sir Henry reluctantly closes the door. He looks about the room feeling a sense of isolation. He moves up center.*) Barrymore! Barrymore! (*Suddenly it dawns that the Barrymores have departed. He forces a smile.*) Better get hold of myself. They're all gone. (*He takes out the pocket watch, checks the hour.*) Wait one hour. (*He pockets the watch, moves to the desk, sits, picks up a pen, his eyes drift to something atop the desk. He picks it up. It's the manuscript of the legend. He can't resist, picks it up, reads. Thunder.*) "Of the origin of the Hound of the Baskervilles there have been many statements . . . know then that in the time of the Great Rebellion . . . this Manor of Baskerville was held by Hugo of that name . . ."

(*The lights flicker from the storm. From outside the house—that unmistakable wail of the accursed—the hound! Sir Henry startles alert. He gets up, frozen to the spot, his eyes betraying terror. He listens. Again—the bay,[32] hair-raising, nerve-shattering, <u>ominous</u>! A pause and, then, the laugh of a woman from up center. Bewildered, Sir Henry turns. A moment passes and then Kathy enters, right.*)

Kathy. Good evening, Henry.

---

32. **bay:** barking or howling.

| WORDS TO KNOW | **divulge** (dĭ-vŭlj′) *v.* to make known; reveal |
| | **ominous** (ŏm′ə-nəs) *adj.* threatening harm or evil |

651

Critical Thinking: HYPOTHESIZING

UU Ask students to guess what other reasons Holmes might have had for asking Watson to escort Laura to Lady Agatha's cottage. Guide students to build on what they learned about Laura's relationship to Jack. (*Possible response: Holmes might be worried that Laura will warn Jack that Holmes is after him.*)

Critical Thinking: ANALYZING

VV Ask students why Holmes insists that Sir Henry eat dinner with Kathy and Jack as planned. (*Possible responses: Holmes does not want to alert Kathy and Jack that he knows they are guilty; he wants to trap them in the act of trying to harm Sir Henry.*)

Literary Concept: PLOT

WW Remind students that plots have an exposition, complications, a climax, and a resolution. Have students identify this part of the plot and support their answer. (*Possible response: It is the climax, the highest point of interest or suspense, because it is where we find out the identity of the murderer.*)

XX Ask students what they can infer about Kathy's character from the stage directions. *(Possible response: From the words* cynical, cold, bloodless, *you can infer that Kathy is involved in the plot to murder Sir Henry.)*

Active Reading: CLARIFY

YY Have students explain why Kathy murdered Sir Charles and plotted to murder Sir Henry. *(Possible response: With both men dead, Kathy's husband becomes the sole Baskerville heir, and she can share in his wealth.)*

Literary Concept: PLOT

ZZ Guide students to explain how they know that this scene is the resolution of the plot. *(Possible response: All the unanswered questions—such as the reason why Sir Henry's shoe was stolen—are explained.)*

Sir Henry (*amazed*). Kathy . . . ?

Kathy. (*She grins, her words are cynical, cold, bloodless.*) Yes. Kathy. Sweet, endearing, innocent.

Sir Henry. What's wrong with you? I told Holmes I was afraid for your life. He knows you're married to Stapleton.

Kathy. Does he? I'll have to deal with that in time.

Sir Henry. You . . . (*getting the picture*) You and Stapleton plotted all this together!

Kathy. Jack? Don't be a fool. He's weak. Never did a thing that I wasn't right there behind him, pushing, insisting. It was all my idea.

Sir Henry. I . . . I don't understand . . .

Kathy. He's the son of Rodger Baskerville, the younger brother of Sir Charles, the one who fled to South America and "supposedly" died unmarried. Now everything will be Jack's and that means—mine.

Sir Henry (*devastated*). He's my cousin . . .

(*Another wail from the hound. Sir Henry reacts. Kathy grins.*)

Kathy. It's outside the front door. Chained. I waited until the house was empty, 'til the moor was dark.

Sir Henry. What . . . what is it?

Kathy. You'll soon see. He's starved. I keep him that way. I'm going to release him.

Sir Henry. No!

Kathy. You have only one chance. Onto the moor, Henry! Run, run, run. Outrace him if you can! It's your only hope! Run!

(*Confused, frantic, Sir Henry moves for the French door. Sound of gunfire from off right. Kathy turns to the sound. Holmes enters from the moor.*)

Holmes. That would be for the hound, Mrs. Stapleton.

Kathy (*wild-eyed*). What's happened to him!

Holmes. I suspect the police have killed the doomed animal. I was able to persuade the wardens and others searching for Selden to remain in the area for one more night.

Kathy (*bitter*). Jack warned you, didn't he?

Holmes. You weren't quite as sure of him as you thought.

Kathy. You haven't won yet, Mr. Holmes. There's always Grimpen Mire! (*She runs out up center, then turns right.*)

Sir Henry. Kathy!

Holmes. You needn't worry, Sir Henry. Her melodramatic gesture is wasted. The house is completely surrounded.

Sir Henry. How did you know she wouldn't be at the cottage?

Holmes. An able assist from Lady Agatha. Earlier this evening she tracked Kathy to where the hound was secreted in an abandoned mine. Later, when it was dark, she observed Kathy moving not to the cottage, but to this house.

Sir Henry. Then there really was a hound.

Holmes. An enormous dog. Gigantic. Part mastiff, part Great Dane.

Sir Henry. But the glow?

Holmes. Phosphorus.[33] Your missing shoe would supply the scent.

Sir Henry. And Stapleton did try to save my life?

Holmes. In his clumsy fashion. Selden told me that Stapleton, too, was off the moor during your London stay. Also he gave himself away with that handwritten warning. I recognized the scrawl as the same found on the catalog

---

33. **phosphorus** (fŏs′fər-əs): a chemical element that burns slowly when exposed to air, giving off a weak light.

652 UNIT FIVE PART 2: MYSTERIOUS CIRCUMSTANCES

Illustration by Sergio Martinez. From Children's Classics Edition of *The Hound of the Baskervilles* by Sir Arthur Conan Doyle. Copyright © 1992 Crown Publishers, Inc., reprinted by permission of Crown Publishers, Inc.

Have students improvise a scene not included in the play—for example, one involving Kathy and Jack as they discuss their plans to murder Sir Henry. Students can perform their scene for the class and explain what it adds to their understanding of these characters.

653

Literary Concept: FOIL

A Ask students how Watson functions as a foil for Holmes in this scene. *(Possible response: Watson had no idea that Kathy was the murderer. His befuddlement underscores Holmes's brilliance.)*

CUSTOMIZING FOR
Students Acquiring English

(6) Point out to students that the word *things* is used here to mean "belongings."

STRATEGIC READING FOR
Less-Proficient Readers

B Have students summarize who the murderer was and what the motive was. *(Kathy was the murderer. She wanted her husband Jack, a Baskerville heir, to inherit the Baskerville fortune.)*
Summarizing

COMPREHENSION CHECK

1. Who asks Holmes and Watson to come to Baskerville Hall? *(Lady Agatha)*
2. What mystery is Holmes investigating? *(the death of Sir Charles Baskerville)*
3. What happens to Mrs. Barrymore's brother? *(He is killed by the hound.)*
4. What is the real relationship between Kathy and Jack Stapleton? *(They are husband and wife.)*
5. What is the hound of the Baskervilles? *(a dog Kathy has trained to kill Sir Henry)*

---

cards he uses for his butterfly collection.

Watson. (*He comes hurrying in with* Lady Agatha, *from outside.*) Holmes, the police have stopped everyone on the moor.

Holmes. A safety precaution. They'll pick up Jack Stapleton at the cottage and— (*sound of whistles in distance*) Kathy has been apprehended, judging from those whistles.

A **Watson** (*befuddled*). Kathy? What's she got to do with it?

Sir Henry. How could he possibly hope to claim the inheritance?

Holmes. Any number of ways. He could claim it from South America, establish identity before the British authorities there. Or, he might adopt an elaborate disguise during the short time he needed to be in London. He might hire an <u>accomplice</u> to impersonate him, retaining[34] a claim on some portion of the income.

Lady Agatha. I was so afraid you suspected me, I thought of burning the warning with my name on it.

Holmes. Don't worry about that. I am the last and highest court of appeal in detection, and I <u>exonerate</u> you.

Watson (*pouts*). Bit pompous, Holmes.

Sir Henry. Kathy had no feeling for me at all.

Holmes. If it's any consolation, Sir Henry, the most winning woman I ever knew was hanged for poisoning three little children for their insurance money. Come Watson, no time to waste if we're to catch that late train.

Watson. Now? This minute?

Holmes. There was a most interesting message from Mrs. Hudson.[35] A retired officer from the Palace Guard is being blackmailed by some devilishly clever ruse. I suspect an organized ring with connections in Detroit.

Watson. But my things, my clothes?

Holmes. Lady Agatha, if you'll be so kind as to see that Perkins packs everything and sends it off to Baker Street.

Lady Agatha. First thing in the morning.

Holmes (*moves to French doors*). Come along, Watson. The game is afoot! (*He's out like a shot.*)

Watson. (*He moves to follow, sighs.*) The man has no mercy.

(Sir Henry *picks up the document that relates the legend and tears it in two.* Lady Agatha *waves goodbye as the curtains close.*)

Lady Agatha. Come back anytime. You're always welcome.

END OF PLAY

---

34. **retaining:** keeping; holding on to.
35. **Mrs. Hudson:** Holmes's housekeeper.

WORDS TO KNOW	**accomplice** (ə-kŏm′plĭs) *n.* a person who knowingly helps another in a criminal act
	exonerate (ĭg-zŏn′ə-rāt′) *v.* to declare innocent and free from blame

654

Assessment ✓ Option

SELF-ASSESSMENT To help students assess their understanding of the selection, invite them to write a review of *The Hound of the Baskervilles*. Have them respond to the following questions in their reviews:
- Which parts of the play do you like best? Why?
- Which parts do you remember best?
- Which characters seem most realistic?
- If you could interview Conan Doyle about the play, what would you ask him?

RESPONDING OPTIONS

FROM PERSONAL RESPONSE TO CRITICAL ANALYSIS

REFLECT

1. What are your impressions at the end of this play? Jot them down in your notebook before sharing them with the class.

RETHINK

2. At what point in the play—if any—did you have enough evidence to solve the murder? (Use the chart or charts you created for Reading Connection on page 607 to help you remember.) Were you surprised by the identity of the criminal? Why or why not?

3. Which details that you listed on your chart or charts turned out to be genuine clues, and which turned out to be red herrings?

4. How would you evaluate Sherlock Holmes as a detective?

Close Textual Reading

Consider
- his knowledge and background
- his questions, attitudes, and actions
- how he arrives at the deductions he makes
- what Watson says and thinks of him
- his treatment of Selden

5. Besides Holmes, which character or characters in this play do you consider most resourceful? Explain your choice or choices.

6. What, if anything, might Kathy Stapleton have done differently to commit the perfect crime?

RELATE

7. How does Holmes compare with the detectives you listed for the Personal Connection on page 607?

Thematic Link

8. Consider the methods that real-life detectives use to solve mysteries today. Which of their techniques do you think would be most effective in solving a mystery like the "curse of the Baskervilles"? Explain your answer.

Multimodal Learning

ANOTHER PATHWAY

Work with a group of classmates to write a newspaper article about the mysterious events of the Baskerville case—as well as the arrest of the culprits, thanks to the detective work of Sherlock Holmes. Be sure to include all the important details your readers will need in order to understand what happened. Read your article to the rest of the class.

QUICKWRITES

1. Write a **speech** that Watson might deliver at a banquet or a roast (a humorous tribute) honoring Sherlock Holmes.

2. Choose one of the characters in this play and write a **profile** of him or her for a popular entertainment magazine.

3. If you were writing a play about the Baskerville case, which character would you make the murderer of Sir Charles? Use your Reading Connection chart or charts to rewrite the play's **ending.** Identify the culprit, and explain how and why the character committed the crime.

📁 *PORTFOLIO Save your writing. You may want to use it later as a springboard to a piece for your portfolio.*

THE HOUND OF THE BASKERVILLES **655**

From Personal Response to Critical Analysis

1. Possible responses: Holmes is a brilliant detective, and Watson is a supportive friend.
2. Possible responses: When Laura Lyons revealed her relationship to Jack in Scene 3; when Kathy cornered Sir Henry later in the same scene. I was surprised that Kathy was the murderer; Jack Stapleton, Barrymore, and Laura Lyons all seemed to be more likely suspects.
3. Possible responses: Genuine clues included the warning letters, missing shoe, and Jack's butterfly hobby. Red herrings included the flashlight, the supposed curse of the Baskervilles, and the engraved pocket watch Kathy gives Sir Henry.
4. Possible responses: He is a brilliant detective who has extraordinary powers of observation and deduction; he is skillful at his profession because he can see beyond appearances and has a deep understanding of human nature.
5. Possible response: Lady Agatha, because she tracked Kathy to where the hound was hidden, a key clue in solving the mystery
6. Possible responses: She might have killed Laura to prevent her betrayal of Jack; she might have hidden the hound in a more secluded place.
7. Possible responses: He is more intelligent and more skilled in the art of deduction; he is their equal as a detective but not as warm and sympathetic as a person.
8. Possible responses: identifying fingerprints, tapping telephones to overhear conversations

Another Pathway

Cooperative Learning Assign each group a recorder to draft the article, a direction giver to keep the group focused, and a voice monitor for volume control.

Rubric

3 Full Accomplishment Students include all the key details and organize them effectively.

2 Substantial Accomplishment Students include most of the key details in the article.

1 Little or Partial Accomplishment Key plot details are missing or poorly organized.

QuickWrites

1. Suggest that students first make an outline to organize their information. Tell students to include details from the play and to try to capture Watson's "voice" as they draft the speech.
2. Suggest that students read some profiles in popular magazines to get the flavor of their style.
3. Remind students that their new ending must take into account the details of the play to make sense.

 **The Writer's Craft**

Feature Article, pp. 208–210

THE LANGUAGE OF LITERATURE **TEACHER'S EDITION 655**

Ask students which detective they admire more, Sherlock Holmes in *The Hound of the Baskervilles* or the detective in "A Retrieved Reformation." Why? *(Possible responses: Sherlock Holmes, because he stays detached from the suspects; Ben Price, because he seems more human than Holmes)*

SCIENCE CONNECTION

Have students conduct their research in small groups. Suggest that each group appoint a summarizer to restate the group's conclusion and a generator to spark additional avenues of discovery. Guide each group to prepare written questions before the interview and to be sure to obtain in advance the subject's permission to tape-record the interview.

ADDITIONAL SUGGESTIONS

Geography *More about Moors* Have students use a map of England to locate Dartmoor and other moors of southwestern England. Then have them research the conditions on the moor—what makes the land boggy and why fog forms so easily—and present their research as an oral report.

LITERARY CONCEPTS

A **mood** is a feeling or atmosphere that a work conveys to a reader. Descriptive words, setting, dialogue, and characters' actions can all contribute to a work's mood. How would you describe the mood of this play? What techniques does the writer use to establish it?

A **foil** is a character who provides a striking contrast to a main character. Foils help draw attention to certain qualities in the main character. Do you think Watson serves as a good foil to Sherlock Holmes? Why or why not? Which aspects of Holmes's personality does Watson highlight?

ACROSS THE CURRICULM

Science If Sherlock Holmes were a detective in today's world, he would have many new and exciting sleuthing tools at his disposal. Perhaps one of the newest and most controversial of those tools is DNA fingerprinting. Perform some sleuthing of your own and find out what you can about that forensic science. If you can, conduct and tape an interview with a local science professor, lawyer, or law-enforcement official to find out how scientists and policemen use DNA fingerprinting to identify suspects and what controversies surround DNA fingerprinting. Present your findings to the class in an oral presentation.

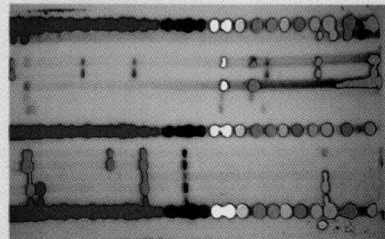

CRITIC'S CORNER

Sir Arthur Conan Doyle has been criticized for not always giving readers the clues that Holmes has seen. Is this true in *The Hound of the Baskervilles*? Use your Reading Connection chart or charts to support your response.

Multimodal Learning

ALTERNATIVE ACTIVITIES

1. With the rest of the class, watch the 1939 movie version of *The Hound of the Baskervilles*, starring Basil Rathbone. Jot down the differences you notice between the movie and Tim Kelly's adaptation. After discussing the differences with your classmates, conduct a **poll** of the class to determine which version they prefer and why they prefer it.

2. Use your imagination and the description given in the play to make a **sketch** of *The Hound of the Baskervilles*.

3. Imagine that it is your job to create a new board game based on *The Hound of the Baskervilles*. Design the **game** and write directions reflecting details from the play.

4. With some of your classmates, produce *The Hound of the Baskervilles* as a **radio play,** complete with sound effects. Some students can read parts, and others can find creative ways to produce the sound effects. Choose appropriate background music to capture the mood and highlight the suspense. Rehearse your performance, then tape it for other classes.

656   UNIT FIVE   PART 2: MYSTERIOUS CIRCUMSTANCES

Invite students to work together in small groups to identify techniques the writer used to set the drama's mood. Groups will most likely describe the mood as tense, frightening, terrifying, and suspenseful. They should also note that the writer established the mood through word choice, dialogue, description, and plot events.

Watson is an ideal foil to Holmes because his average powers of observation and analysis contrast with Holmes's extraordinary skills in these areas.

Alternative Activities

1. Guide students to prepare a detailed poll and carefully tabulate the responses. Suggest that students show their results on a graphic organizer such as a pie chart or bar graph.

2. Encourage students to reread relevant portions of the play to gather specific details about the hound and the effect it creates.

3. Suggest that students design their game for a specific audience, such as seventh graders.

4. In preparation, have students listen to a famous radio play, such as Orson Welles's *War of the Worlds.*

WORDS TO KNOW

EXERCISE A On a sheet of paper, answer the following questions.

1. Does a dog sound most **ominous** when it whines, when it howls, or when it growls?

2. Would a criminal's **accomplice** be the criminal's victim, the criminal's assistant, or the criminal's judge?

3. If you know something **implicitly,** are you nervous about it, sure about it, or afraid of it?

4. Would a woman's **colleague** be her coworker, her professor, or her doctor?

5. When judges **exonerate** accused people, will the people then be put on trial, be set free, or be sent to jail?

EXERCISE B For each phrase in the left-hand column, write the letter of the synonymous rhyming phrase in the right-hand column.

1. a really weird automobile	a. to reproach the coach
2. to enthusiastically divulge a secret	b. terrifying lying
3. to criticize the sports instructor	c. to reveal with zeal
4. a time of rational royal rule	d. a bizarre car
5. to discourage the servant	e. to arise and surmise
6. enchanting spins on ice	f. a sane reign
7. an evasive house designer	g. to guess to excess
8. a frightening deception	h. to dissuade the maid
9. to theorize too much	i. an indirect architect
10. to stand up and jump to a conclusion	j. captivating skating

SIR ARTHUR CONAN DOYLE

Sir Arthur Conan Doyle was an athlete, a scholar, a doctor, a reporter, and a political activist. He is best known, however, as the creator of Sherlock Holmes, the world's most famous fictional detective. Born in Edinburgh, Scotland, Doyle received a medical degree in 1881 and spent the next few months working as a ship's doctor. During the Boer War, he served in a military hospital in South Africa. In 1902, he was knighted for writing a pamphlet that defended the British cause in that war.

While he was in medical school, Doyle published his first story. He produced his first novel featuring Sherlock Holmes—*A Study in Scarlet*—in 1887. As Doyle's literary reputation grew, his medical career diminished. Although he tired of writing stories about Holmes and tried to kill the detective off, public outcry forced Doyle to revive him.

1859–1930

In addition to numerous historical and political works and other works of fiction, Doyle wrote a total of 4 novels and 56 short stories about Sherlock Holmes between 1887 and 1927. The popularity of the Holmes stories made him the highest-paid writer in the world at that time. He claimed to have modeled the character of Holmes after Dr. Joseph Bell, one of his medical-school professors.

While on a golfing holiday with a friend, Doyle heard the legend of a ghostly hound. Upon returning from his holiday, he began writing what he called "a real creeper" of a novel based on that legend. *The Hound of the Baskervilles* became one of his best-known works. Over the years, it and Doyle's other stories about Sherlock Holmes have been adapted as plays, motion pictures, radio programs, and television series.

OTHER WORKS *The Adventures of Sherlock Holmes, The Memoirs of Sherlock Holmes*

Extended Reading

THE HOUND OF THE BASKERVILLES **657**

SIR ARTHUR CONAN DOYLE

Conan Doyle said that he wrote his first detective story because in all the detective fiction he had read, the solution of the mystery depended on the detective having a flash of intuition. Conan Doyle said that he wanted to "reduce this fascinating but unorganized business to something nearer to an exact science."

WHAT DO YOU THINK?

Reflecting on Theme

Have students look back at the crossword puzzle they created before reading *The Hound of the Baskervilles*. Ask them to consider how their thinking about mysteries has developed as a result of reading this play. Then invite students to revise their puzzles—adding words and clues that they now associate with mysteries—to reflect their new ideas.

OVERVIEW

To gain a deeper appreciation of the selections they have read in this unit, students will explore the characteristics of an opinion paper and then create their own well-developed example in this lesson.

Objectives

- To plan an opinion paper by considering such elements as purpose, support, and organization
- To draft an opinion paper and solicit a response
- To revise, edit, and publish an opinion paper
- To reflect on the process of writing an opinion paper

Skills

LITERATURE
- Using details

WRITING AND LANGUAGE
- Distinguishing between facts and opinions
- Considering purpose
- Organizing ideas
- Avoiding loaded adjectives

GRAMMAR AND USAGE
- Making verbs agree with indefinite pronoun subjects

MEDIA LITERACY
- Interpreting a newspaper article

- Analyzing photographs
- Researching with media resources

RESEARCH SKILLS
- Using Government Documents

SPEAKING, LISTENING, AND VIEWING
- Interviewing
- Role-playing
- Debating
- Reading aloud
- Group evaluating
- Giving a speech

Teaching Strategy: STUMBLING BLOCK

A Be sure that students understand that facts are statements that can be proved by direct observation or outside sources; opinions are statements that cannot be proved. Opinions usually reflect personal beliefs and are often debatable.

Teaching Strategy: MODELING

B Have students discuss the magazine article and how stereotypes caused Stanley Joseph, from first grade on, to deny his Haitian heritage.

WRITING FROM EXPERIENCE

WRITING TO EXPRESS

Have you ever made a quick judgment that was entirely wrong or unfair? As you saw in Unit Five, "Not As It Seems," people often judge others unfairly based on nothing more than how the person looks or the country he or she is from. This type of judgment is called stereotyping.

GUIDED ASSIGNMENT
Write an Opinion Paper In this lesson you will decide whether a certain person or group has been represented or treated fairly and write a paper explaining your opinion.

1 Distinguish Fact from Opinion

A Prejudice and stereotyping are sometimes hard to spot. In the sign on the far right, the tone is friendly, but is the message? What does the sign say about the storeowner's view of students? Do you think the view is based on fact or on a stereotype? What stereotype is shown in the magazine article? What stereotype is questioned in the photograph?

2 Write Your Response

The items on this page either make a judgment about a group of people or make you question your own judgment. Ask yourself the questions below.

- Which item causes you to react most strongly?
- Do you agree or disagree with its message? Why?
- Do you have specific reasons, or do you just have an emotional reaction?

Jot down your opinion and a few reasons for it.

Magazine Article
B What effects did the stereotypes about Stanley Joseph's ethnic background have on him?

An Immigrant's Story

Listen to an immigrant's tale, and two themes keep returning: hardship and dreams. Stanley Joseph, 18, was an infant when his family left Haiti.

When I was in first grade I realized that being Haitian was the worst thing that could happen to anybody. If other kids found out, they'd beat you up. The stereotype of Haitians is that they are stupid, ugly, and they just came off the boat. I didn't like that, so from first grade I always said I was American.

• • • • • • • • •

I finished high school. I'm going to college. I'd love to sing in an opera some day. Ever since I was a child I've loved opera. Some people say that we Haitians are snobbish because we have such big dreams, but you shouldn't live on dreams if you're not going to chase them.

Lisa Margonelli, from "A Hard Road to Travel"
Scholastic Update

PRINT AND MEDIA RESOURCES

UNIT FIVE RESOURCE BOOK
Prewriting, p. 53
Elaboration, p. 54
Peer Response Guide, pp. 55–56
Revising and Proofreading, p. 57
Student Model, p. 58
Rubric, p. 59

GRAMMAR MINI-LESSONS
Transparencies, p. 6
Copymasters, p. 6

WRITING MINI-LESSONS
Transparencies, pp. 26, 28–29, 34, and 37

ACCESS FOR STUDENTS ACQUIRING ENGLISH
Reading and Writing Support

FORMAL ASSESSMENT
Guidelines for Writing Assessment

 LASERLINKS
Writing Springboard

  WRITING COACH

News Photograph

I wonder if people realize that most homeless people aren't bums.

Sign in Store Window

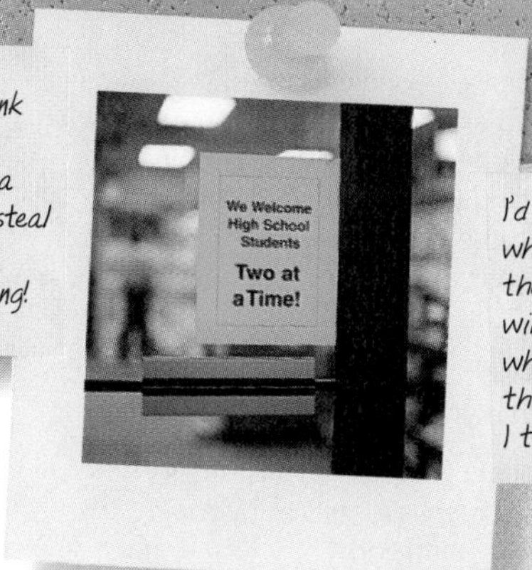

Do they think that just because I'm a student I'll steal something? They're wrong!

I'd like to ask why they put the sign in the window. I wonder what other kids think of the sign. I think it stinks.

We Welcome High School Students

Two at a Time!

3 Explore Other Ideas

Can you think of a time when a person you know or have read about was represented unfairly or judged on the basis of a stereotype? What have you heard about such groups as boys, girls, people with disabilities, or senior citizens? What about less obvious groups, like overweight people, athletes, or brainy people?

Decision Point Choose one stereotype, either from these pages or from somewhere else, to investigate and write about.

◉➤ **LASERLINKS**
  • *WRITING SPRINGBOARD*

▭➤ **WRITING COACH**

WRITING FROM EXPERIENCE   **659**

◉ **WRITING SPRINGBOARD**
  It's Not Fair Manuel, a young Hispanic teenager, reflects on prejudice against Hispanic people.

Side B, Frame 22562

Writing Prompt Describe an incident in which you or someone you know was treated unfairly. Explain why you think the treatment was unfair and what should be done to correct the situation.

C Guide students to use the springboards on pages 658 and 659 to spark ideas. Arrange the class into three groups and have each group prepare a debate on one of the issues. Allow the groups time to prepare and then have them present their debates to the class. Encourage the audience to jot down writing topics that arise from the debates.

Teaching Strategy: MODELING

D You can use the following model or one of your own to show students another way to use the springboard to gather writing ideas:

Think-Aloud Model *This sign about students not being allowed to shop in groups makes me think of the Jim Crow laws. They were used in the South before the 1960s to exclude African Americans from shops, parks, and other places. This sign also makes me think of unwritten laws that excluded Jewish people in the 1940s and 1950s. Either of those ideas might make good topics.*

PREWRITING

Scratching the Surface

Stereotype or Facts? You've chosen a stereotype or unfair judgment that you want to explore and write about. You can use your first reaction as a basis for research. Then you'll start shaping your findings into a well-stated opinion that is supported by facts.

1 Examine Your Opinion

People often do not realize that they are making unfair judgments about other people. Their stereotypes are based on ignorance, misinformation, or even fear.

E Look again at the brief opinion you wrote. Was it based on fact or on feelings? As you do research, the answer to this question may become clearer to you.

2 Think About Your Purpose

Why did you react so strongly to the stereotype you chose to explore? What do you hope to accomplish by presenting your opinion? Understanding your feelings will help you find the purpose of your paper. For example, you might want to

F • argue against a stereotype
• explain the basis for a stereotype
• show the stereotype's effect on people

One student wanted to argue against the stereotype that all teens are thieves by conducting a pro-teen campaign.

3 Consider the Sources

Understanding a stereotype is the first step t arguing that it's wrong. Try asking yourself the questions below.

• Why was a stereotype used—to be funny, to hurt someone, to cause change?
• Do people really believe the stereotype?
• What was the tone? Was it angry? fearful
• What is the basis of the stereotype—fact, misinformation, lack of experience, or fear?
• What effect would the stereotype have on others?

Based on the answers to these questions, what might be some ways you could argue against the stereotype?

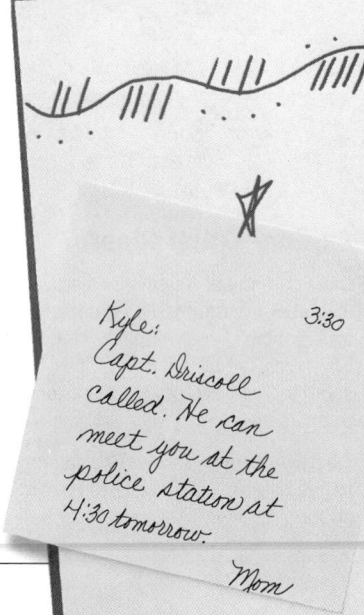

Kyle:
Capt. Driscoll called. He can meet you at the police station at 4:30 tomorrow.
3:30
Mom

Mini-Lesson: Speaking, Listening, and Viewing

INTERVIEWING Remind students that interviews can be useful ways to gather information for an opinion paper. Then share these guidelines for planning and conducting an interview:

Planning Stage:
1. Contact the person to be interviewed. Set up a time and place to meet, or arrange to conduct the interview by telephone.
2. Do some background reading on the person or topic. Learn as much as possible beforehand so you can ask useful questions.
3. Write a list of questions.

4. If the subject agrees, consider tape-recording the interview.

Interview Stage:
1. Speak slowly and clearly. Use standard English and make sure the person understands each question before you go on.
2. Listen carefully and take accurate notes.
3. Ask follow-up questions to clarify anything you don't understand.

Application Encourage students to follow these practical steps as they conduct interviews to gather information.

4 Gather Information

It's one thing to think someone else's opinion is wrong or unfair. It's another thing to prove that it is. You'll want to gather as many facts as possible to show how reality differs from the stereotype. Sources might include

- editorials and public-service announcements
- census data
- news and human-interest stories
- your own observation
- interviews of the group being stereotyped and the source of the stereotype
- a poll of people in your school or community

The example below shows how the student set up a chart to compare the stereotype about teens with reality.

Student's Compare-Contrast Chart

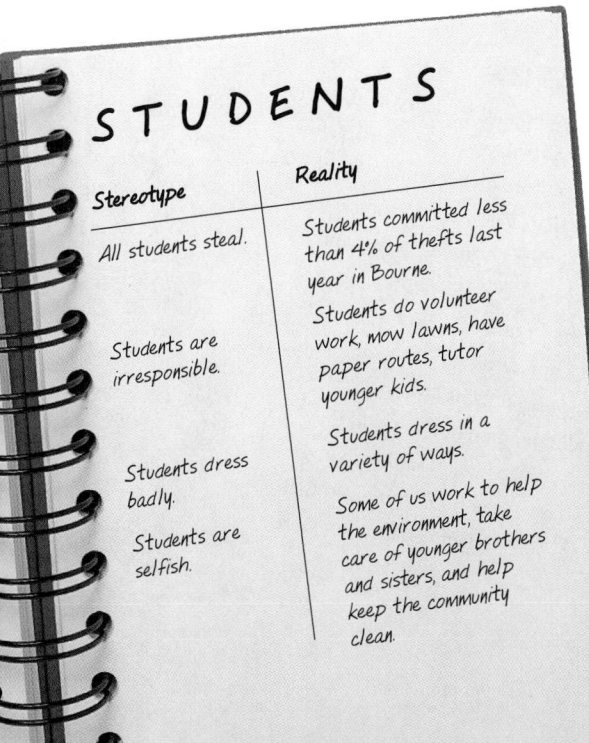

STUDENTS

Stereotype	Reality
All students steal.	Students committed less than 4% of thefts last year in Bourne.
Students are irresponsible.	Students do volunteer work, mow lawns, have paper routes, tutor younger kids.
Students dress badly.	Students dress in a variety of ways.
Students are selfish.	Some of us work to help the environment, take care of younger brothers and sisters, and help keep the community clean.

H

THINK & PLAN

Reflecting on Your Ideas

1. How can you state your opinion more clearly?
2. How has your research changed your opinion?
3. What additional information do you need?
4. Which facts best support your opinion?

Research Skills: USING GOVERNMENT DOCUMENTS

G Tell students that the United States government is the largest publisher in the world. Government documents contain census data, speeches, statistics, public service announcements, and a wealth of additional information. Explain that some of the government documents are in print form, but much of the material is on computer databases. Encourage students to use this easily available and reliable reference source.

Teaching Strategy: MODELING

H Explain to students that if their writing involves examples of the similarities and differences between several things, a compare-and-contrast chart can help them organize their ideas. Be sure students understand that they can customize a compare-and-contrast chart to fit their needs.

Mini-Lesson: Speaking, **Listening, and Viewing**

ROLE-PLAYING In addition to using the mini-lesson on the bottom of page 660 to teach interview skills, you may wish to have students role-play their interviews beforehand. Partners can take turns assuming the roles of interviewer and subject. Have students tape-record the interview to check their volume, diction, and pace. Encourage students to make any necessary adjustments in their interview techniques.

Application Encourage students to search for interview subjects who hold differing viewpoints. Suggest that students speak with teachers, parents, classmates, and community members to gather a list of suitable subjects for an interview. Students may also wish to consult with service organizations such as Rotary and religious groups for ideas.

Additional Suggestions Remind students to send a written thank-you letter to anyone they interviewed to thank the person for his or her contribution.

Writing Skill:
USING THE COMPUTER

① Encourage students to draft their opinion papers on a computer. Explore with students how the computer allows writers to express their ideas quickly and to revise their work easily. If students do draft on the computer, guide them to use The Writing Coach, which gives writers useful and easy guidelines for the drafting stage. You may also want to suggest that students who work on computers copy their writing into several documents. Explain that this allows them to experiment with different ways to organize their material.

CUSTOMIZING FOR
Less-Proficient Writers

① The actual process of writing a draft may pose special problems, especially for students with learning disabilities. You might want to offer these students the option of first creating their opinion papers as a speech. Have students use a tape recorder to explore and store their prewriting ideas and to save much of the research they locate. Then have students use the tape recorder for drafting. When students are satisfied with their draft, suggest that they transcribe their tape to produce a written version of their essay.

DRAFTING

Expressing Your Ideas

Just a Beginning Take a careful look at your notes. Which facts should you include in your report? You don't have to use every fact you gathered, just the ones that best support your opinion and will interest readers most.

❶ Write a Discovery Draft

Try beginning your paper by stating your opinion in a sentence or by telling an anecdote that makes your point. Then give reasons to support your position. Or, just begin by freewriting and watching the idea develop as you write. Your notes can also help you remember important details.

Student's Discovery Draft

I guess I want to say that students are not all bad OR all good—we're all different!

Not All Students Are Shoplifters

It seems that some business owners in town think all students steal. More than one store has a sign in the window saying no more than 2 students could go in. ~~What's going on?~~ I guess some store owners think we all steal. Later I wondered, *why* would they think that? I don't steal and none of my friends do, either. He shouldn't assume that we are all punks and shoplifters. It's not fair!

Then I thought, maybe more kids steal than I think do. So I went to the police station to find out. According to Capt. Driscoll, less than 4% of shoplifters caught in the past two years were students.

I talked to 8 different store owners, and only three of them said they've caught students stealing in their store. And one person said the kid was from another town! Mrs. Gardner, who owns the bookstore, said that sometimes she gets nervous when a bunch of students go into her store.

We spend money in their stores. Don't they want our business?

I think I'll write a letter to Thirteen magazine Speak Out!

add quotes from interviews

662

WRITING SPRINGBOARD
Nobody Gets Cut Young people discuss their school's no-cuts policy, which allows students to participate in teams without worrying about getting cut.

Side B, Frame 24050

Writing Prompt After viewing this film, think about a policy at your school that you think is helpful to students or a policy that is unfair. Write an essay about the policy and explain why it is helpful or unfair.

Support Your Opinion

However you choose to introduce your topic, be sure to state your opinion clearly at the start. Then try to put each of your reasons into a separate paragraph, with the supporting facts, examples, and other details. Begin a new paragraph for each main reason you give to support your opinion. Try to make sure that all the details in a paragraph are related.

Organize Your Ideas

If your purpose is to attack what you feel is an unfair image of someone, thoughtful organization will help you make your point. Below is one way to organize your paper.

- First, present the stereotype.
- Next, state your opinion about it.
- Then, you can either explain why people have this image and show why they're wrong, or show the harmful effects of the stereotype.
- Finally, you can call for a change or suggest some action. Sometimes just sharing your opinion can have an effect on people.

Share Your Work

Once you are happy with your draft, put it aside for a few hours or even a day. Then reread it.

 PEER RESPONSE

You might also ask someone else to respond to your draft. If you wish, ask your peer readers the following questions.

- How would you restate my opinion in a sentence or two?
- What other ideas can you add to support my opinion?
- Do you agree or disagree with my opinion? Why?
- Which of my reasons are strongest? weakest?

Writing Skill: REVISING

N Suggest that students who wrote their drafts by hand try writing their changes and additions on separate slips of paper. Show students how to tape these slips of paper over the old copy or at the side and bottom of the page. Explain that attaching the slips with tape allows the writer access to both the original and revised versions. Also, remind students to use the Standards for Evaluation as they revise their papers.

Teaching Strategy: MODELING

O As a class, compare the student's final opinion paper to the initial draft on page 662. Explore how the writer used his own comments to revise and improve the paper. Discuss how the writer sharpened the focus, added quotations from interviews for support, eliminated irrelevant sentences, and used paragraphs to organize ideas. Then discuss the question in the side column. The writer supports the argument with a fact about the portrayal of teens in the media and a statistic about the amount of volunteer work they do.

REVISING & EDITING

Finalizing Your Paper

A Checklist for Success Revising and editing your report can be a messy job. It helps to make a checklist of your common mistakes and to check your draft against it. As you revise, try writing changes on self-stick notes or on separate pieces of paper. Attach them over the old text or at the sides or bottom of the page so that your revisions will be easier to follow.

1 Revise and Edit

You have a strong opinion, you've supported it with research, and you've written a solid draft. Don't get into trouble by letting mistakes distract the reader.

- Fix any problems mentioned by your peers.
- Check whether your opinion is supported by facts.
- Make sure your introduction and conclusion are effective.

Student's Final Opinion Essay

> Kyle Stevens
> 357 Pine Street
> Bourne, MA 02553
>
> Speak Out!
> Thirteen Magazine
> 1452 Keystone Ave.
> Indianapolis, IN 46033

> 357 Pine Street
> Bourne, MA 02553
> May 28, 1997
>
> Speak Out!
> Thirteen Magazine
> 1452 Keystone Ave.
> Indianapolis, IN 46033
>
> Dear Thirteen Magazine:
> Some stores in my town allow only two students inside at a time. It seems that some adults are lumping every student they meet with an image of teens that they've gotten from newspapers or TV, which is an image of rowdy troublemakers. It's not fair! We're all different. Some of us might be bad, but most of us are good.
> "You kids mess up the books and magazines and then leave," says the owner of the bookstore. However, my parents taught me to clean up after myself, and so did my friends' parents. Neither I nor my friends have ever stolen anything.
> According to Thelma Rodriguez, director of County Volunteer Services, teens performed 30 percent of the the volunteer work at local hospitals and rest homes.
>
> 1

Why do you think th[e] student wrote to th[is] particular magazine[?]

What facts does [the] student use to ar[gue] against the stereo[type] about teenagers?

	Singular	
another	either	no one
anybody	everybody	nobody
anyone	everyone	one
anything	everything	somebody
each	neither	someone

	Plural		
both	few	many	several

664

GO TEENS!
How teenagers help the community

- A "Te...
- Numb...
- Build...
- Subje...
- "Oth...

★TEN★
Great Things Teens Did Last Year

1. Planted ten trees in the town square
2. Tutored 27 younger students in math, science, and reading
3. Shoveled the driveways of the elderly and disabled
4. Collected 300 lb. of newspaper to be recycled
5. Petitioned City Hall to create a new tot lot, and won
6. Sang holiday songs at rest homes
7. Collected $428 for the homeless
8. Baby-sat for 20 families
9. Raised $1,000 for cancer research in a walk-a-thon
10. Raked leaves

❷ Share Your Work

One way to share your ideas is to create a campaign, which might include a letter and pamphlet like those shown on these pages. The campaign could include pamphlets, buttons, and bumper stickers. Others ideas include

- a class newspaper editorial page
- a class discussion group
- a letter to the editor of your local newspaper

Standards for Evaluation

An opinion paper
- has a strong introduction that engages the reader
- clearly states the writer's opinion
- provides strong, well-supported reasons for ideas
- has a strong conclusion

SkillBuilder

 **GRAMMAR FROM WRITING**

Making Verbs Agree with Indefinite Pronoun Subjects

Some indefinite pronouns, such as *all, most, none,* and *some,* can be singular or plural, depending on their meaning in a sentence. Your verbs should agree in number with indefinite pronoun subjects. See the examples below.

Singular	All of the candy was stolen.
Plural	Most of the merchants distrust students.

GRAMMAR HANDBOOK

See Grammar Handbook page 853 about pronoun subjects.

Editing Checklist

- Is your opinion stated clearly?
- Did you support your ideas?
- Do subjects and verbs agree?

REFLECT & ASSESS

Evaluating the Experience

1. What did you learn about stereotypes?
2. How did your opinion change or develop as you wrote?
3. What did you do in your writing that you want to try again?

 PORTFOLIO Write a note about how the research process shaped your opinion. Slip it into your portfolio.

Speaking, Listening, and Viewing:
GIVING A SPEECH

P Invite students to present their papers as a speech. Guide students to practice their speech with a partner or a tape recorder until they are confident about their delivery. As they prepare, students should concentrate on pacing, eye contact, diction, volume, body language, and gestures. You may wish to invite families and community members to hear students' views on important issues of the day.

PORTFOLIO

Suggest that students write a brief note to themselves that identifies the techniques that they found most helpful in gathering information. Have students attach the note to their opinion papers.

Guidelines for Evaluation

Ideas and Content
- States clearly the issue and the writer's opinion.
- Supports ideas with observations, facts, or expert opinions.
- Presents ideas logically.
- Concludes by summing up reasons, making a recommendation, or asking readers to rethink their opinion.

Structure and Form
- Uses well-organized paragraphs and a clear organization.
- Includes transitional words and phrases to show relationships among ideas.
- Uses a variety of sentence structures.

Grammar, Usage, and Mechanics
- Contains no more than two or three minor errors in grammar and usage.
- Contains no more than two or three minor errors in spelling, capitalization, and punctuation.

SkillBuilder **GRAMMAR FROM WRITING**

MAKING VERBS AGREE WITH INDEFINITE PRONOUN SUBJECTS Remind students that an indefinite pronoun is one that does not refer to a particular person or thing. Singular indefinite pronouns are used with singular verbs; plural indefinite pronouns are used with plural verbs. Review the list of singular and plural indefinite pronouns shown at the bottom of page 664..

Application Have students review their opinion papers to make sure that each indefinite pronoun and its verb agree in number.

Reteaching/Reinforcement *Grammar Mini-Lessons* copymasters, p. 6, transparencies, p. 6

The Writer's Craft

Agreement with Indefinite Pronouns, p. 588

UNIT REVIEW

This feature allows students to reflect on the selections and activities in Unit Five and to assess how well they understand what they have learned. Although this feature provides students with several opportunities for self-assessment, you may wish to use some of the activities to informally assess specific skills—such as speaking and listening or cooperative work.

Objectives

- To allow students to reflect on and assess their understanding of the Unit 5 theme—Not As It Seems
- To allow students to reflect on and assess their understanding of literary concepts, especially suspense and foil characters
- To provide students with the opportunity to assess and build their portfolios

REFLECTING ON THEME

OPTION 1

Encourage students also to review the notes they took while reading or discussing the selections. You may wish to have each group concentrate on a single selection, identifying several situations to which its message might apply.

OPTION 2

Ask students to review particular selections and to jot down their impressions of the characters they feel illustrate the expression. Encourage students to write brief outlines to help organize their thoughts and ideas, including details from the selections and their own experiences.

OPTION 3

You may choose to have students work in pairs or in small groups. Encourage them to skim the selections in this unit, jotting down their evaluations of each character. Suggest that students use these notes to complete their charts. After they have completed the activity, you may wish to have students discuss their charts with other students. For a copy of the chart to distribute to the class, see *Unit Five Resource Book,* p. 60.

REFLECT & ASSESS

UNIT FIVE: NOT AS IT SEEMS

In this unit you explored the differences between the way things appear and the way they really are. As a result of your reading, writing, and discussions, you probably have formed some new ideas and have rethought other ideas. Choose one or more of the following options in each section to assess how your thinking has changed.

REFLECTING ON THEME

OPTION 1 Making Connections Review the selections in this unit and jot down the message or messages that you got from each one. Which of these messages best apply to situations that young people often encounter? Discuss this question with a small group of classmates, supporting your views by relating the messages to situations from real life.

OPTION 2 Writing an Essay When you think about the expression "appearances often are deceiving," which characters from this unit come to mind? Which characters from your own experiences do you recall? Write an essay that explores the meaning of this expression, using characters from this unit and from real life as examples.

OPTION 3 Evaluating Characters In many of the selections in this unit, characters judge other people or situations. Some characters base their judgments primarily on appearances; others look beyond appearances to the truth hidden within. Review the characters in the selections you have read. Then create a chart like the one shown, and sort the characters into two groups, based on whether or not a character can see beyond appearances. Next to each character's name, jot down evidence from the selection to support your evaluation. After you have completed the chart, identify the character who you think is most perceptive in his or her judgments.

CHARACTERS

Bases Judgments on Appearances	Looks Beyond Appearances
	Mende in "The Smallest Dragonboy" appreciates Keevan's inner qualities, such as courage.

 Self-Assessment: Which of the selections in this unit do you think had the most influence on your ideas about appearances and reality? Write a letter to the author, describing this influence.

REVIEWING LITERARY CONCEPTS

OPTION 1 Experiencing Suspense Suspense, as you know, is the excitement or tension that readers feel as they get involved in a story and become eager to learn the outcome. Work with a partner to review the stories and the play in this unit. Which of these selections do you think generates the greatest suspense? Which generates the least? Consider the selection that you regard as least suspenseful. How might you change the plot to heighten the suspense? Jot down notes for a plot that would be more suspenseful.

666   UNIT FIVE: NOT AS IT SEEMS

 Self-Assessment In order to help students write their letters, have them note what they have learned about appearances from each of the selections and then determine which selection affected them the most. Encourage them to include several details from a selection in their letters to the author.

OPTION 2 **Examining Foil Characters** As you have learned, a **foil** is a character who provides a striking contrast to a main character. In your notebook, list several foils in novels and short stories that you have read and in movies or TV programs that you have seen. Then consider the selections in this unit and list each foil character. Identify the selection in which a foil character helped you the most in forming your opinion of the main character. Finally, draw sketches that reflect the characters' different personalities.

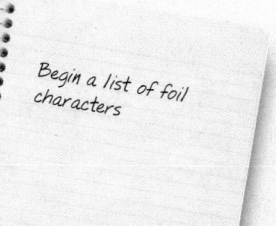

Begin a list of foil characters

 Self-Assessment: Recall the other literary terms that were introduced or reviewed in this unit—conflict, climax, tone, science fiction, setting, literary nonfiction, and mood. Identify the term that you consider most difficult to understand. Learn more about the term by referring to the Handbook of Reading Terms and Literary Concepts. Then explain the term to a small group of classmates, using examples from your outside reading to illustrate the definition.

PORTFOLIO BUILDING

- **QuickWrites** Review the writing assignments that required you to support an opinion. Select the response that you think presents your strongest arguments. Write a note analyzing why these arguments are so strong. Attach the note to the QuickWrite, and add both to your portfolio.

- **Writing About Literature** In your critical review, you had the chance to examine and evaluate an element of a story or poem. Reread your review. Then write a note listing several careers in which the skills you learned in writing a critical review might be useful. Attach the note to your critical review.

- **Writing from Experience** You expressed your opinion about an issue that has meaning for you in your opinion paper. Sometimes posters can be a good way to get people to see your side of an issue. Make a poster sketch that conveys one of the reasons you presented in your opinion paper. Add the sketch and your opinion paper to your portfolio.

- **Personal Choice** Review all the writing and group activities that you completed while working through this unit. Which ones do you think helped you the most to explore the contrast between appearance and reality? Select one piece of writing and one evaluation, and attach to them a note explaining how they helped your thinking evolve. Add both to your portfolio.

 Self-Assessment: At this point, you probably have revised some early pieces of writing based on peer comments and suggestions. Select a piece that you think improved greatly as a result of revision, and attach a note explaining how you used peer comments to strengthen it.

SETTING GOALS

This unit featured a full-length play, a long work of nonfiction, poems, and short stories. Which type of literature do you find most challenging to read and write about? Why? What skills do you see yourself developing as you read and write about more examples of this type? Write a note to yourself, answering these questions.

REFLECT & ASSESS **667**

REVIEWING LITERARY CONCEPTS

O P T I O N   1

Make sure that partners support their decisions regarding the degree of suspense with details from each selection. You may also wish to have students create before-and-after diagrams of the plot, showing the change in events and the heightening of the suspense.

O P T I O N   2

You may wish to have students skim the selections in this unit and create charts that list the foil characters and their contrasting qualities. Encourage students to consider the ways in which the author presents their chosen foil character. Students can then jot down the qualities of this character that they want to depict in their sketches.

Self-Assessment You may wish to have volunteers teach selected terms to the entire class, giving them an opportunity to share their enthusiasm about stories they have read on their own.

PORTFOLIO BUILDING

You may wish to help students choose options or modify the ones shown based on the portfolio system that you have established for the class. Encourage students to consider including drafts, as well as final products, so that they can gauge their development at different stages of the writing process.

Self-Assessment Have students identify the changes and revisions they made to a piece of writing in response to peer comments. Encourage them to jot down their thoughts about the best ways to use peer comments while revising a work.

SETTING GOALS

Ask students to try to be as specific as they can in describing why they find a genre to be especially challenging and in listing the skills they intend to develop.

UNIT SIX

UNIT OVERVIEW

In Unit Six, "Across Time and Place: The Oral Tradition," students will read a variety of myths, fables, folk tales, and legends from the oral tradition of many cultures. This unit contains five sections, each linked to a previous unit in this book:

Links to Unit One: On the Threshold
- Prometheus
- The People Could Fly
- The Fitting of the Slipper

Links to Unit Two: Life's Lessons
- The Wolf in Sheep's Clothing
- The Travelers and the Purse
- The Old Grandfather and His Little Grandson
- Phaëthon
- Gombei and the Wild Ducks

Links to Unit Three: Stepping Forward
- How Odin Lost His Eye
- Where the Girl Saved Her Brother
- Waters of Gold

Links to Unit Four: Meeting Challenges
- The Arrow and the Lamp: The Story of Psyche
- Pumpkin Seed and the Snake
- Kelfala's Secret Something

Links to Unit Five: Not As It Seems
- Echo and Narcissus
- The Force of Luck
- The Emperor's New Clothes
- Lazy Peter and His Three-Cornered Hat

You may wish to begin or end Units One through Five with theme-related selections from Unit Six, or you may choose to present the selections from Unit Six as a separate unit.

Discovering the Oral Tradition

Use the following prompts to help students recognize the meaning of the oral tradition.
- What does the term *oral tradition* mean to you? *(Possible responses: stories that were originally told orally and later written down; stories that have been passed down from generation to generation; myths and legends from specific cultures)*
- Brenda Wong Aoki is a storyteller. What function do you think she and other storytellers serve today? *(Possible responses: They help preserve and pass on ideals and values of a heritage and culture.)*
- How does the quotation from storyteller Brenda Wong Aoki apply to the oral tradition? *(Possible responses: The quotation shows how stories that are part of the oral tradition have been passed on from generation to generation, teaching essential truths about the human condition.)*
- On the basis of the unit title and quotation, what types of selections do you imagine will be in this unit? *(Possible responses: legends, myths, folk tales, folklore from many countries)*

Across Time and Place

The Oral Tradition

"I feel the energy of the earth coming up through my feet and all these thousands of ancestors around me. I am not just a separate voice crying out. I have a responsibility to the earth and to my ancestors to tell the truth. The truth is where I'm moved in my heart."

Brenda Wong Aoki

Brenda Wong Aoki lives in California, where she keeps the ancient traditions of her ancestors alive through storytelling.

668

669

Introducing Storytelling

To help students understand how stories are embellished and changed as they pass through generations of tellers, invite students to work in small groups to create modern-day endings for traditional fairy tales. Start by having the class brainstorm a list of fairy tales such as "Snow White," "Cinderella," "Beauty and the Beast," "Rumpelstiltskin," "Hansel and Gretel," and "Little Red Riding Hood." Then have each group select one of the stories, review the plot, and retell it, changing the ending. After everyone has finished working, invite groups to share their stories with the class. Encourage group members to jump in and revise the story as it is being retold. Discuss how the stories change as different people retell them, adding or subtracting various details. Explore how some of the changes make the stories more dramatic, rhythmic, and easier to retell. Link this demonstration to the stories that students are about to read in this unit.

Art Note

Point out to students that Brenda Wong Aoki's clothing recalls the traditional Japanese *kimono*, a wrapped dress held in place with a wide sash called an *obi*. Also be sure that students notice that Ms. Aoki is wearing a hair ornament and carrying a decorated fan, an accessory that she uses as a prop to enhance her storytelling.

Reading the Art *Like Brenda Wong Aoki, storytellers around the world wear clothing that reflects their heritage and the background of the stories they are retelling. Skilled storytellers often also include props, such as fans and simple musical instruments. How would you explain what the storyteller's clothing and accessories might add to the audience's experience of the story?*

Mini-Lesson: Speaking, Listening, and Viewing

STORYTELLING IN THE CLASSROOM
Since storytelling is a dramatic experience, you may wish to modify your classroom environment to enhance the speaking, listening, and viewing dimensions of storytelling. Use one or more of the following suggestions:

- Have students sit in a circle rather than in rows.
- Close the shades and dim the lights.
- Provide a box of props that you or students can use when telling stories.
- Encourage students to create simple sound effects as they tell the stories.
- Tape-record the stories so students can listen to themselves performing and can later modify their presentations.

Selections	Reading Skills and Strategies	Literary Concepts	Writing Opportunities	Speaking, Listening, and Viewing
LINKS TO UNIT ONE **Prometheus** **The People Could Fly** **The Fitting of the Slipper**	Analyzing values and customs, PE p. 675 Recognizing cultural values, PE p. 675 Analyzing characters' thresholds, PE p. 675 Questioning, (ML) TE p. 685	Alliteration, (ML) TE p. 678 Figurative language, (ML) TE p. 682 Characterization, (ML) TE p. 686 Sensory details, (ML) TE p. 689 Humor, (ML) TE p. 694	Script, PE p. 698 Sentence, (ML) TE p. 682 Rewrite sensory details, (ML) TE p. 689	Dramatize a tale, PE p. 698 Oral report, PE p. 698 Interviews, PE p. 699 Video and discussion, PE p. 699 Role-playing, (ML) TE p. 676 Reading aloud, (ML) TE p. 678 Storytelling, (ML) TE pp. 680, 688 Discussion, (ML) TE p. 685 Dialect, (ML) TE p. 687 Retelling, (ML) TE p. 690 Pantomime, (ML) TE p. 693 Dramatic scene, (ML) TE p. 696
LINKS TO UNIT TWO **The Wolf in Sheep's Clothing** **The Travelers and the Purse** **The Old Grandfather and His Little Grandson** **Phaëthon** **Gombei and the Wild Ducks**	Analyzing lessons, PE p. 701 Recognizing relevance, PE p. 701 Recognizing cultural values, PE p. 701 Connecting, (ML) TE p. 711	Imagery, (ML) TE p. 710	Comparison, PE p. 715	Talk show, PE p. 714 Audio-visual display, PE p. 714 Survey, PE p. 715 Interview, PE p. 715 Oral report, PE p. 715 Role-playing a debate, PE p. 715 Reader's theater, PE p. 715 Storytelling, (ML) TE p. 702 Reader's theater, (ML) TE p. 707
LINKS TO UNIT THREE **How Odin Lost His Eye** **Where the Girl Saved Her Brother** **Waters of Gold**	Recognizing cultural values, PE p. 717 Identifying admired behaviors, PE p. 717 Analyzing risks, PE p. 717 Making judgments, (ML) TE p. 729	Topic sentences and supporting details, (ML) TE p. 722	Speech, PE p. 732 Paragraph, (ML) TE p. 722	Present an award, PE p. 732 Travel brochure, PE p. 732 Role-playing, PE p. 733 Mime or dance, PE p. 733 Storytelling, (ML) TE p. 726 Group discussion, (ML) TE p. 728

Writing	Reading Skills and Strategies	Literary Concepts	Writing Opportunities	Speaking, Listening, and Viewing
WRITING ABOUT LITERATURE **Creative Response**	Responding to literature, PE pp. 736–39	Details, PE p. 735 Characters, PE p. 736	Add details, PE p. 735 Revise, PE p. 735 Rewrite, PE p. 735 Fable, PE pp. 736–39	Telling stories, PE p. 737 Viewing photographs, PE p. 741 Interpreting photographs, PE p. 741 Discussion, PE p. 741 Gestures and facial expressions, PE p. 741

Grammar, Usage, Mechanics, and Spelling	Multimodal Learning	Research and Study Skills	Vocabulary
The prefix -ex, (ML) TE p. 677 Alliteration, (ML) TE p. 678 Sensory details, (ML) TE p. 689 Past participles, (ML) TE p. 691	Dramatize a tale, PE p. 698 Oral report, PE p. 698 Interviews, PE p. 699 Display, PE p. 699 Venn diagram, PE p. 699 Video and discussion, PE p. 699 Role-playing, (ML) TE p. 676 Reading aloud, (ML) TE p. 678 Storytelling, (ML) TE pp. 680, 688 Discussion, (ML) TE p. 685 Dialect, (ML) TE p. 687 Retelling, (ML) TE p. 690 Pantomime, (ML) TE p. 693 Dramatic scene, (ML) TE p. 696	Research the Underground Railroad, PE p. 698 Research fire, PE p. 699	aptitude brandish comprehension endow explicit humility implore pretense receding wrathful
Chronological order, (ML) TE p. 704 Doubling final consonants, (ML) TE p. 709 Subject-verb agreement, (ML) TE p. 712	Talk show, PE p. 714 Audio-visual display, PE p. 714 K-W-L chart, PE p. 715 Survey, PE p. 715 Interview, PE p. 715 Oral report, PE p. 715 Role-playing a debate, PE p. 715 Graph, PE p. 715 Readers theater, PE p. 715 Storytelling, (ML) TE p. 702 Readers theater, (ML) TE p. 707	Research the sun, PE p. 714 Research the needs of the elderly, PE p. 715	abode acknowledge dreary plummet
Words with j, ge, and dge, (ML) TE p. 719 Topic sentence and supporting details, (ML) TE p. 722 Cause-and-effect transitions, (ML) TE p. 725 Who and Whom, (ML) TE p. 727	Present an award, PE p. 732 Travel brochure, PE p. 732 Sequence chart, PE p. 732 Picture, PE p. 733 Calendar, PE p. 733 Graphic, PE p. 733 Mime or dance, PE p. 733 Storytelling, (ML) TE p. 726 Group discussion, (ML) TE p. 728	Research China, Montana, or Scandinavia, PE p. 732 Research the Battles of the Rosebud, the Little Bighorn, and Wounded Knee, PE p. 732	jostling perilously render smugly

Grammar, Usage, Mechanics, and Spelling	Multimodal Learning	Research and Study Skills	Media Literacy
Using adjectives and adverb phrases, PE p. 735 Distinguishing between compound verbs and compound sentences, PE p. 739	Telling stories, PE p. 737 Viewing photographs, PE p. 741 Interpreting photographs, PE p. 741 Discussion, PE p. 741 Gestures and facial expressions, PE p. 741		Interpreting photographs, PE pp. 740–41

Skills Trace: Links to Units 4–5   ML DENOTES MINI-LESSON IN TEACHER'S EDITION

Selections	Reading Skills and Strategies	Literary Concepts	Writing Opportunities	Speaking, Listening, and Viewing
LINKS TO UNIT FOUR **The Arrow and the Lamp: The Story of Psyche** **Pumpkin Seed and the Snake** **Kelfala's Secret Something**	Analyzing virtuous behavior, PE p. 743 Recognizing negative behavior, PE p. 743 Evaluating cultural messages, PE p. 743 Evaluating characters' challenges, PE p. 743 Classifying, ML TE p. 747	Personification, ML TE p. 745 Conflict, ML TE p. 750	Rewrite a tale, PE p. 760 Cookbook, PE p. 760 Letter, PE p. 761	Publish new tales, PE p. 760 International festival, PE p. 760 Music, PE p. 760 Draw pictures, PE p. 760 Create a pa ndau, PE p. 761 Interview, PE p. 761 Language phrase book, PE p. 761 Examine artwork, PE p. 761 Oral report, PE p. 761 Dramatic reading, ML TE p. 744 Choral reading, ML TE p. 755 Interview, ML TE p. 757
LINKS TO UNIT FIVE **Echo and Narcissus** **The Force of Luck** **The Emperor's New Clothes** **Lazy Peter and His Three-Cornered Hat**	Comparing cultural values and customs, PE p. 763 Analyzing appearances, PE p. 762 Analyzing characters, PE p. 762 Evaluating characters' lessons, PE p. 763 Connecting, ML TE p. 768	Dialogue, ML TE p. 776	Booklet, PE p. 785 Summary, PE p. 785 Multiple-choice test, ML TE p. 771	Character evaluation, PE p. 784 Oral report, PE p. 785 Diagram, PE p. 785 Investigate advertising, PE p. 785 Booklet, PE p. 785 Contest, PE p. 785 Films and videos, ML TE p. 769 Retelling, ML TE p. 773 Press conference, ML TE p. 777

Writing	Reading Skills and Strategies	Literary Concepts	Writing Opportunities	Speaking, Listening, and Viewing
WRITING FROM EXPERIENCE **Informative Exposition**	Connecting, PE p. 786 Comparing and contrasting, PE pp. 786–93	Story elements, PE p. 789	Writing a compare-and-contrast essay, PE pp. 786–93 Drafting, PE pp. 790–91 Writing an effective introduction, PE p. 791 Revising and publishing, PE pp. 792–93	Retelling, PE p. 787 Interviews, PE p. 788

Grammar, Usage, Mechanics, and Spelling	Multimodal Learning	Research and Study Skills	Vocabulary
Personification, ML TE p. 745 Silent letters, ML TE p. 748 Demonstrative adjectives, ML TE p. 752	Publish new tales, PE p. 760 International festival, PE p. 760 Music, PE p. 760 Draw pictures, PE p. 760 Create a pa ndau, PE p. 761 Interview, PE p. 761 Language phrase book, PE p. 761 Examine artwork, PE p. 761 Oral report, PE p. 761 Dramatic reading, ML TE p. 744 Choral reading, ML TE p. 755 Interview ML TE p. 757	Research recipes, PE p. 760 Research music, PE p. 760 Research Hmong pa ndau, PE p. 761 Research Swahili, PE p. 761 Research art, PE p. 761 Research the Hmong, PE p. 761	doomed retort tread wretched
Punctuating compound sentences, ML TE p. 765 The prefixes *com-* and *in-*, ML TE p. 770 Dialogue in fiction, ML TE p. 776	Character evaluation, PE p. 784 Oral report, PE p. 785 Diagram, PE p. 785 Investigate advertising, PE p. 785 Booklet, PE p. 785 Contest, PE p. 785 Films and videos, ML TE p. 769 Retelling, ML TE p. 773 Press conference, ML TE p. 777 Storyboard, ML TE p. 782	Research Puerto Rico, Greece, and Denmark, PE p. 784 Research echoes, PE p. 785 Research natural phenomena, PE p. 785 Taking objective tests: multiple-choice questions, ML TE p. 771 Memorizing, ML TE p. 775	anguish bartering benefactor console contend crafty distinguish haggle induce intact outset pathetic priceless rogue squander unsound writhe

Grammar, Usage, Mechanics, and Spelling	Multimodal Learning	Research and Study Skills	Media Literacy
Using transitions, PE p. 791 Using irregular comparatives and superlatives, PE p. 793	Analyzing toys, folk tales, book excerpts, and newspaper articles, PE pp. 786–87 Retelling, PE p. 787 Interviews, PE p. 788 Story map, PE p. 789	Reference books and museums, PE p. 788 On-line services, PE p. 788 Interviews, PE p. 788	Analyzing toys, folk tales, book excerpts, and newspaper articles, PE pp. 786–87 On-line services, PE p. 788

Recommended Collections

Celtic Fairy Tales
by Joseph Jacobs

Thematic Links A classic collection of Celtic fairy tales.
About the Author Joseph Jacobs (1854–1916) is best known for his books for children and his research into folklore.
Other Works by Joseph Jacobs *English Fairy Tales, Indian Fairy Tales, Aesop's Fables, The Book of Wonder Voyages, European Folk and Fairy Tales*

Eighty Fairy Tales
by Hans Christian Andersen

Thematic Links A collection of Andersen's best-loved tales.
About the Author Hans Christian Andersen (1805–1875) is best known for his folk and fairy tales.
Other Works by Hans Christian Andersen *Danish Fairy Legends and Tales, Stories and Fairy Tales, The Dream of Little Tuk and Other Tales*

Noodlehead Stories from Around the World
by M. A. Jagendorf, ed.

Thematic Links A collection of 65 funny folk tales from 36 countries.
About the Author M. A. Jagendorf (1888–1981) was primarily a folklorist, although he did spend some time in New York theaters as an agent, director, and producer.
Other Works by M. A. Jagendorf *In the Days of the Han; Fairyland and Footlights; Sand in the Bag and Other Folk Stories of Ohio, Indiana, and Illinois*

Further Tales of Uncle Remus
by Julius Lester

Thematic Links This book is the third volume in Lester's series of the Uncle Remus stories. These tales feature Uncle Remus, an aging African-American man, telling stories about the deep South, most of them depicting amusing antics of animal characters with human qualities.
About the Author Julius Lester (born 1939) connects his interest in folklore to his experiences of long summer evenings spent listening to his father and his father's friends telling stories.
Other Works by Julius Lester *The Tales of Uncle Remus, More Tales of Uncle Remus, This Strange New Feeling, To Be a Slave*

Greek Myths
by Olivia Coolidge

Thematic Links This collection includes 27 well-known myths retold by Coolidge.
About the Author Olivia Coolidge (born 1908) is best known for her young adult biographies.
Other Works by Olivia Coolidge *The Golden Days of Greece, The Maid of Artemis, Men of Athens*

For Teacher TEACHING LITERATURE

Collins, Rives B. "Storytelling: Water from Another Time." *Drama Theatre Teacher* 5.2 (Winter 1993): 4–12.

Calkins, Lucy McCormick, and Shelley Harwayne. *Living Between the Lines.* Portsmouth, NH: Heinemann Educational Books, 1991.

Serafin, Anne M. "African Literature: An Overview." *English Journal* 84.3 (March 1995): 49–59.

Recommended Readings in Cross-Curricular Areas

SOCIAL STUDIES

Kenya . . . in Pictures
published by Lerner (1988)
This concise pictorial guide describes the history, geography, and people of Kenya. Links to Adjai Robinson's "Kelfala's Secret Something."

Red Star and Green Dragon: Looking at New China
by Lila Perl (1983)
Concentrates on modern Chinese life with a brief discussion of Chinese history. Links to Laurence Yep's "Waters of Gold."

Cinderella
collected by Judy Sierra (1992)
Versions of the classic tale from different cultures are presented. Links to William J. Brooke's "The Fitting of the Slipper."

LANGUAGE ARTS

The Illustrated Dictionary of Greek and Roman Mythology
by Michael Stapleton (1986)
Discusses the historical importance of Greek and Roman mythology, as well as names and places. Links to the Greek and Roman myths in this unit.

For Teacher　CROSS-CURRICULAR INSTRUCTION

Athanases, Steven A., et al. "Fostering Empathy and Finding Common Ground in Multiethnic Classes." *English Journal* 84.3 (March 1995): 25–34.

Gudmundsdoffir, Sigrun. "Story-Maker, Story-Teller: Narrative Structures in Curriculum." *Journal of Curriculum Studies* 23.3 (May-June 1991): 207–18.

Reissman, Rose. *The Evolving Multicultural Classroom.* Alexandria, VA: Association for Supervision and Curriculum Development, 1994.

Seeley, Virginia, ed., et al. *Plains Native American Literature. Multicultural Literature Collection.* Englewood Cliffs, NJ: Globe Book Co., 1993.

Recommended Media Resources

THE LANGUAGE OF LITERATURE

LASERLINKS
Videodisc, Gr.7
See *LaserLinks Teacher's Source Book,* page 43, for information about Unit 6.

AUDIO LIBRARY
Unit Six: Across Time and Place
Gr. 7, Tape 14: Sides A & B
Gr. 7, Tape 15: Sides A & B
Gr. 7, Tape 16: Sides A & B

WRITING COACH
Writing Coach Software: Writing About Literature: Direct Response; Compare-and-Contrast Essay

OUTSIDE RESOURCES

Films/Videos/Film Strips/Audiocassettes
Why the Dog Chases the Cat. Read by David Holt and Bill Mooney. One sound cassette. 1994. (60 min.)
Hans Christian Andersen, videocassette, RKO Radio Pictures, 1952.
The Rainbow People. Read by George Guidall. Chinese folk tales. Three sound cassettes. (4 hrs.)
Wonderful World of Brothers Grimm, videocassette, live action film, 1962. (134 min.)

Internet Resources
Literature and Language Arts Center at http://www.hmco.com/mcdougal/lit/litcent.html

For Teacher　TEACHING WITH TECHNOLOGY

Bender, Robert M. "Creating Communities on the Internet: Electronic Discussion Lists in the Classroom." *Computers in Libraries* 15 (May 1995) 38–43.

Educational Technology. Educational Technology Publications, Inc., 720 Palisade Avenue, Englewood Cliffs, NJ 07632.

Ely, Donald P. *Trends in Educational Technology.* Syracuse, NY: Information Resources Publications, 1992.

It's a Small World, After All

> Today, the coin of the realm is diversity, not homogeneity. We all use our previous set of experiences — social, familial, community, cultural — to filter new experiences.

Everyone learns from previous experiences, and those experiences are embedded in culture. We can greatly enhance learning by considering those previous experiences and using them as bridges between cultures. As students read the tales in Unit Six, use this essay to help them recognize and affirm cultural diversity in their own classroom.

You may wish to start by presenting your students with a common vocabulary to use as they explore folk tales, fables, myths, and legends—the very fabric of multicultural education.

THE LANGUAGE OF FOLKLORE

Open the discussion by explaining that folklore refers to the stories, songs, and poems that have been handed down from generation to generation through the oral tradition, or by word of mouth. Since folklore was originally spoken rather than written, the words have been changed over the years. This is why students might have seen several different versions of the same familiar story.

Explain that the oral tradition also created a unique intimacy between storyteller and audience. No doubt the audience's comments strongly affected the content of the stories. As a result, the stories expressed the wishes, hopes, and fears of many people, not just the concerns of a particular writer. These stories dealt with universal human dilemmas that span differences in age, culture, and geography. Be sure that students understand that there are many different versions of each work, and the original authors are no longer known.

Folklore includes folk tales, fables, fairy tales, myths, trickster tales, legends, and tall tales. Explain each kind of folklore so that students can see how they are the same as and different from each other.

- *Folk tales* are stories that entertain readers or listeners. They are not meant to be taken as truthful. Usually, the characters are farmers or laborers. They are shown to have better values than their more wealthy, powerful neighbors.
- *Fables* are brief stories that teach a lesson through a moral, a principle of right and wrong. Most fables have animal characters that behave like people.
- *Fairy tales* are about fanciful characters with unbelievable abilities. Characters include giants, monsters, dragons, fairies, trolls, gnomes, evil beings, and kindly godmothers. Events include transformations, wishes, things happening in threes, superhuman strength or abilities, talking animals, and trickery.
- *Myths* are stories set in ancient days that explain natural events. Greek and Roman myths tell of gods and goddesses. Creation myths explain how the earth was formed. Myths are the earliest of all known stories. Some Greek myths, for example, are more than 3,000 years old.
- *Trickster tales* describe incidents in which clever people or animals take advantage of foolish people or animals. Trickster tales are well-known in Native American and African American folklore.
- *Legends* are stories that often describe real historical figures in imaginary, larger-than-life situations.
- *Tall tales* combine fact and fiction. They describe exaggerated, ridiculous incidents in a serious way. The main characters show courage, cleverness, strength, and imagination.

THE VALUE OF CULTURAL DIVERSITY

Explain to students that the folklore of many cultures keeps the past alive, helps young people understand the history and beliefs of their society, teaches moral lessons and qualities valued by the society, and warns against negative qualities. When heard over and over, these tales serve not only to entertain but also to transmit the values and wisdom of different cultures and to provide a deep well of vivid images that become part of an individual's imagination and even of his or her everyday language.

Speaking of folklore, author Meridel LeSuer once said, "These are stories that never die, that are carried like seed into a new country." Help pass these cultural seeds along to your students.

Related Reading

Anaya, Rudolfo. *Bless Me, Ultima: A Novel.* TSQ Publications, 1972.

D'Aulaire, Ingri and Edgar. *Book of Greek Myths.* New York: Doubleday, 1962.

Presilla, Maricel E. *Feliz Nochebuena Feliz Navidad.* New York: Henry Holt, 1994.

Family and Community Involvement

Family

From myths intended to answer questions about the world to legends based on facts, the selections in Unit Six are meant to be told aloud and are connected to the common theme of the oral tradition. By completing some of the following activities, your students, their families, and other community members can make important connections outside the classroom as they explore other examples of the oral tradition.

The following Copymasters for Unit Six provide activities that students can take home and complete with a parent or other family member.

OPTION 1: PERFORM A STORY

- **Connection** All of the selections in Unit Six illustrate the theme of the oral tradition.
- **Activity** *Copymaster, page 1* Students and family members read a favorite story aloud and act it out.

OPTION 2: TELL A STORY

- **Connection** A young girl is forced to marry a snake in "Pumpkin Seed and the Snake."
- **Activity** *Copymaster, page 2* Students and family members tell a story about a snake as they build the story one sentence at a time.

OPTION 3: INTERVIEW STORYTELLERS

- **Connection** The stories "Lazy Peter and His Three-Cornered Hat" and "The Old Grandfather and His Little Grandson" teach lessons about human behavior.
- **Activity** *Copymaster, page 3* Students interview family members about lessons they have taught or learned and record these stories for retelling.

Community

OPTION 1

- **Connection** All of the selections in Unit Six illustrate the theme of the oral tradition.
- **Activity** Encourage students to organize and participate in "story hours" for peers and younger children at local libraries and bookstores.

OPTION 2

- **Connection** In "Where the Girl Saved Her Brother," a young Cheyenne girl shows great bravery at the Battle of the Rosebud.
- **Activity** Invite a member of the local historical society or an expert in Native American history to discuss the earliest native inhabitants of your region.

OPTION 3

- **Connection** Crafty weavers create "invisible" fabric in the tale "The Emperor's New Clothes."
- **Activity** Take the class on a field trip to a weaving shop to see how fabric is created on a loom or to a clothing factory to see how clothes are manufactured. Or invite members of a local sewing circle or quilting bee to share and demonstrate their craft.

OPTION 4

- **Connection** The selections in this unit all originated in different parts of the world.
- **Activity** Ask a local bookseller or librarian to bring in a collection of children's books that includes folk tales, myths, legends, and fables from around the world.

Cooperative Project

Storytelling Festival

Overview

Students will plan a program of stories to be told during a storytelling festival.

PROJECT AT A GLANCE

The selections in Unit Six emphasize how storytelling acts as a means of preserving cultural heritage and passes on oral histories and traditions. For this project, students will work together in small groups to plan a Storytelling Festival in which each member of the group will tell a story. Groups will collaborate on the selection of stories as well as the props and/or costumes, rehearsing together so others can help with the interpretation of the story and characterization for the narrator. The stories will be told either in a festival or in front of the class.

OBJECTIVES

- To learn about the importance and use of folklore and story-telling
- To work collaboratively with a small group to prepare a program of stories
- To develop storytelling skills by recognizing what keeps an audience interested
- To develop listening and speaking skills by participating in a story-telling festival

SUGGESTED GROUP SIZE
5–6 students

MATERIALS
- Video camera and tapes (optional)
- Old clothing or items to be used as props (optional)
- Art materials to decorate presentation area (optional)

1 Getting Started

Arranging the Project

Decide how far you would like to take this project. If you are going for an actual festival with an invited audience, you will need to reserve a date in the auditorium or other appropriate room, as well as some rehearsal time for the groups to practice. If you plan to decorate the area, think about how you will do it and start gathering sheets for backdrops that groups can paint. Decide if you will get costumes, or if they will be the responsibility of individual groups.

If you see this as a project culminating in a class presentation, you will still need to consider if you want costumes, and props, but other than that you will only need to arrange a bit of furniture on the given day.

If you would like to invite a storyteller to talk to the class, now is the time to locate one and schedule a time.

Arranging the Festival

Storytelling demands an audience. If you think students are ready to tell stories before a real audience, try to arrange a true Storytelling Festival. Have the event in a public room in the school and invite not only other students but administrators and families as well. Many storytelling events feature storytellers in different rooms or areas recounting their tales concurrently. The audience is free to walk around until they find an interesting tale to enjoy. If this is too unstructured for you or your students, plan a program where one story follows another. You will have to monitor the length of each story to maintain the audience's interest.

2 Creating the Festival

Introducing the Project

Explain that students will be working cooperatively to plan and present a program of stories. During this program, each member of the group will tell a story. Groups will decide together which stories will be told, perhaps selecting a particular culture to represent or theme to follow. Groups will rehearse together, relying on each other to help with interpretation and to give suggestions that would make each story more enjoyable. The project will culminate in a public performance in front of the class or an invited audience. At this time, explain exactly what you expect in the way of props, costumes, and settings so that students can begin work as necessary.

Discuss what makes a story interesting to an audience. You might point out that the character of the narrator has a great deal of influence on how the audience responds to the story. If possible, you might want to ask a professional storyteller to speak to the class about ways he or she keeps the audience interested.

Consider giving groups a time limit for their performance. This may be given on a per-story basis (about five minutes) or as a cumulative amount of time. Groups may have to edit stories to fit the time limit.

Group Investigations

Divide students into groups of five or six. Groups should work together to decide a theme for their stories and then to research stories to consider. The final selection of stories should be a group decision. The group should work together to edit the stories into a final form that will fit in the time allowed and should assign each story to a group member. Members can rehearse individually, then meet again as a group to help one another with interpretation and characterization. Groups should determine the order in which they would like to tell the stories.

Creating a Project Description

When groups have finalized their list of stories, meet with them to check the list for coherency in theme or culture. As groups work to edit the stories, meet again to offer suggestions and help them decide which elements of the story are necessary and which are expendable. Stress that the oral tradition entails personal interpretation each time the tale is related, so students can add their own touch as long as the basic story and lesson remain intact.

OPTION 1: PANTOMIME OR DANCE Students can plan an interpretive pantomime or dance to go along with a story. While the narrator relates the story, the mime or dance can go on in front of or next to the narrator.

OPTION 2: PUPPET SHOW Students can create hand puppets and act out stories through puppetry. They should also research the origins of puppetry to better understand the art form. In this case, students might want to choose stories to present to a class of young children.

OPTION 3: PRESERVE THE PERFORMANCES If possible, you might want to capture the storytellers on video to preserve the performances for other classes and for your own review. Arrange for a school media person or volunteer parent to assist with the taping.

OPTION 4: A PARALLEL WORLD Students can write a new version of an old tale, substituting the modern era for the old. Remind students that all references in the tale must be modernized, not just a few selected items. During the progression of the project, keep students focused on the fact that storytelling should be fun for both the teller and the listening audience. Encourage storytellers to consider the dramatic elements of their performance.

3 Sharing the Performances

If possible, arrange for students to tell their stories to more than just their peers. Invite families and teachers, as well as other students. If this is not an option, you might consider inviting a few school officials to join you for the class session.

If you are able to videotape the storytelling, you can share the performances by circulating the tapes around school.

Assessing the Project

The following rubric can be used for group or individual assessment.

3 Full Accomplishment Students follow directions and select, edit, and perform stories for an audience.

2 Substantial Accomplishment Students select, edit, and perform stories for an audience, but the selections are unrelated or not easily followed by the audience.

1 Little or Partial Accomplishment Students do not complete the project to the point of performing, or the performance does not fulfill the requirements of the assignment.

For the Portfolio
You may want to keep a copy of each group's original story selections and performance assignments in each student's portfolio, along with a written copy of your group performance assessment.

Note: For other assessment options, see the *Teacher's Guide to Assessment and Portfolio Use.*

Cross-Curricular Options

SOCIAL STUDIES

Ask students to research one historical figure who has become a legend. They can give a talk describing the legendary aspects of this person's life.

SCIENCE

Students can contrast mythological explanations of natural phenomena with scientific explanations. Discussion might center on whether or not the explanations have anything in common.

MUSIC
Students can study the musical characteristics of folk ballads and discuss the link between those characteristics (e.g., repetition, simplicity) and those of the oral tradition.

ART
Students can study the ways different cultures have used myths and legends in the visual arts, perhaps focusing on famous or interesting examples.

Resources

Best-Loved Folktales of the World edited by Joanna Cole provides 200 tales, arranged geographically.

Favorite Folktales from Around the World edited by Jane Yolen features 160 tales, from the Brothers Grimm to Native American legends.

Tall Tale America: A Legendary History of Our Humorous Heroes by Walter Blair includes legends such as Johnny Appleseed, Pecos Bill, and Davy Crockett.

UNIT SIX

Lesson Planner: Links to Units 1–3

TIME ALLOTMENTS SHOWN ARE APPROXIMATE. DEPENDING ON YOUR GOALS AND THE NEEDS OF YOUR STUDENTS, YOU MAY WISH TO ALLOW MORE OR LESS TIME FOR CERTAIN PORTIONS OF THE LESSON.

Table of Contents	Discussion	Previewing the Selections	Reading the Selections
PART OPENER **Across Time and Place: The Oral Tradition** page 668	**30 MINUTES** • Discuss storytellers past and present • Review the history of storytelling		
LINKS TO UNIT ONE **Prometheus** page 676 AVERAGE **The People Could Fly** page 680 AVERAGE **The Fitting of the Slipper** page 684 AVERAGE		**10 MINUTES** • GREECE • UNITED STATES • CHINA	**50 MINUTES** • Introduce vocabulary • Read pp. 676–79 (4 pp.) • Read pp. 680–83 (4 pp.) • Read pp. 684–97 (14 pp.)
LINKS TO UNIT TWO **The Wolf in Sheep's Clothing** page 702 EASY **The Travelers and the Purse** page 703 EASY **The Old Grandfather and His Little Grandson** page 704 EASY **Phaëthon** page 706 CHALLENGING **Gombei and the Wild Ducks** page 709 AVERAGE		**10 MINUTES** • GREECE • RUSSIA • JAPAN	**50 MINUTES** • Introduce vocabulary • Read pp. 702–03 (2 pp.) • Read pp. 704–05 (2 pp.) • Read pp. 706–08 (3 pp.) • Read pp. 709–13 (5 pp.)
LINKS TO UNIT THREE **How Odin Lost His Eye** page 718 AVERAGE **Where the Girl Saved Her Brother** page 721 AVERAGE **Waters of Gold** page 725 EASY		**10 MINUTES** • SCANDINAVIA • UNITED STATES • CHINA	**40 MINUTES** • Introduce vocabulary • Read pp. 718–20 (3 pp.) • Read pp. 721–24 (4 pp.) • Read pp. 725–31 (7 pp.)

Writing	Writer's Style	Prewriting	Drafting and Revising
WRITING ABOUT LITERATURE **Creative Response**	**30 MINUTES**	**20 MINUTES**	**80 MINUTES**

Time estimates assume in-class work. You may wish to assign some of these stages as homework.

- LITERATURE CONNECTION
- CROSS-CURRICULAR CONNECTIONS
- CULTURAL CONNECTIONS

90 MINUTES

- Dramatize a tale

SOCIAL STUDIES
- Explore the Underground Railroad

SCIENCE
- Investigate fire

- Compare/contrast characters
- Compare Cinderella tales

90 MINUTES

- Hold a talk show

SCIENCE
- Create a science exhibit

SOCIAL STUDIES
- Examine the needs of the elderly

- Compare characters or themes
- Hold a debate
- Create a graph
- Write a modern fable

90 MINUTES

- Present an award

GEOGRAPHY
- Design a travel brochure

SOCIAL STUDIES
- Complete a sequence chart

- Make an illustrated calendar
- Role-play a meeting
- Draw or paint a picture
- Perform a mime or dance
- Compare/contrast mythical gods

Publishing and Reflecting	Grammar in Context	Reading the World
30 MINUTES	10 MINUTES	30 MINUTES

UNIT SIX

BRENDA WONG AOKI:
Brenda Wong Aoki Tells "The Twilight Crane" Professional storyteller Brenda Wong Aoki likes to tell the Japanese myth "The Twilight Crane" because it conveys ideas shared by many cultures. In Aoki's words, "The essence of the story is that the greatest gift in the world is life itself." She explains, "Relationships are sustained when we give part of ourselves away to someone else. Our co-dependence with others, our connections to others is what life is about. When those ties are broken, part of us dies."

Trained as a performer in the ancient Japanese tradition of Noh drama, Aoki approaches stories from the perspective of movement first. "Most people in the world do not speak English," she says. "The movements I make during a performance are symbolic movements, a way of communicating meaning that originated in Noh drama. In the telling of 'The Twilight Crane' the fan is only a prop; it is the movements that help tell the story," she explains.

Side B, Frame 35533

STORYTELLERS PAST AND PRESENT

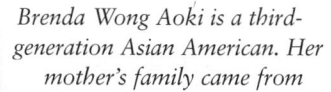

BRENDA WONG AOKI

A Present Day Storyteller Speaks

Brenda Wong Aoki is a third-generation Asian American. Her mother's family came from Canton, China. Her father's family came from Japan. In telling her stories, Brenda draws on this blend of cultures.

When I was about three or four, my grandfather lived in Chinatown in San Francisco. He worked at the Tonga Room in the famous Fairmont Hotel. My grandpa and his friends would sit in the kitchen and "talk story." They'd tell stories from the old country. In this way they would find comfort in the new land. For immigrants, storytelling is a crucial way to remember their native culture. Most of my stories come from China and Japan; a few come from Hawaii. The reasons Pacific Rim people tell stories are similar to the reasons people of other cultures do. Some stories are myths that explain things, like the creation of humans. Some stories show what is bad and what is good. Some stories are meant to pass on news. In Japan, this was the job of the *rakugo*—the itinerant (traveling) storyteller. He brought information from place to place. Storytellers also add their own perspectives to stories in order to teach lessons or give people strategies for living.

One of the favorite types of Japanese story is the *obake*, or ghost story, which was used to strengthen the spirits of the samurai warriors. The warriors would light 100 candles and tell ghost stories. When a warrior finished his story, a candle would be blown out. As the night grew darker, the stories grew scarier. Only cowards would leave.

Japanese belief is that there are spirits of our departed loved ones all around us. When I'm telling stories, I try to be truthful to this belief. I feel the energy of the earth coming up through my feet and all these thousands of ancestors around me. I am

An Ancient storyteller
Brenda Wong Aoki practices an art
form that dates back to the distant
past. For centuries, storytellers have
shared tales that convey timeless truths.

not just a separate voice crying out. I have a
responsibility to the earth and to my ancestors
to tell the truth. The truth is where I'm moved
in my heart.

Stories stand the test of time because they
have universal truths in them. You may look at
a story when you're young and see it as a story
of courage. Then, as you get older, you see
how the story can mean something else.
I remember a story of a Japanese
woodcarver. He says that he
looks at a tree and, if the tree
says "bear" to him, he chips
away every-thing that is not
bear. To me it is the same
way with a story. I listen to
a story over and over. I
chip away at it until I get
to its essential core.

The soul of an artist is
the most important thing. In
telling stories we are weaving
a beautiful tapestry. It's not just
the story. It's family, friends, and
the spirits of our dear departed
loved ones. This is why I sculpt a
story until I get to the emotional
truth, the human truth. It is this
truth that makes a bridge of
understanding between peoples.

A decorated fan is an
important prop that
many storytellers use
to suggest an action or
to express an emotion.

Sometimes
storytellers wear
costumes to suggest
a particular place
or time.

LASERLINKS
• Brenda Wong Aoki: *Twilight Crane*

STORYTELLERS PAST AND PRESENT **671**

Ⓐ Brenda Wong Aoki says she "chips
away" at a story until she gets to its
"essential core." Ask students what
they think the "core" of a story might
be and how a storyteller knows when
it has been reached. *(Possible responses:
The "core" is the essential truth that the
story conveys, the timeless message that
applies to people in all ages and cultures.
The core may consists of the wishes,
hopes, and fears of many people rather
than the concerns of a particular writer. A
storyteller might use audience response
to gauge when the core has been
reached.)*

Linking to Social Studies

People who study folklore
have found startling similarities
among the stories told by
peoples as diverse as
Australian Aborigines, Indian Buddhists,
Christians, and Native Americans.
Scholars suggest two theories to
explain these similarities. One theory is
that the themes and concerns of these
stories are universal. Almost every culture searches for explanations of natural phenomena, how the world began,
how the world will or may end, and
how people should act and relate. As
storytellers grapple with these concerns, common elements emerge in
the tales from diverse cultures: rites of
passage, journeys or spiritual quests,
earthly or heavenly paradises, heavenly
paradises, and many others. The second
theory suggests that as cultures interact
through conquest, travel, trade, and
intermarriage, stories from different
cultures are shared and get changed in
the retelling.

Mini-Lesson: Speaking, **Listening, and Viewing**

FAMILY HISTORIES Explain to students that
every culture has its own fables, folk tales, legends,
and myths that come from the oral tradition.
Similarly, individual families have their own cherished
stories as well. Usually, these stories are versions of
important or funny family events that are told and
retold and passed down from one generation to
the next.

Application Have students work in small groups
to share some of the stories told in their families.
You may also wish to invite students to tape-record
their stories. Then place the tapes in an "oral history"
section of the classroom for students to enjoy in
their free time.

STRATEGIC READING FOR
Less-Proficient Readers

Because of the intermix of words and pictures, less-proficient readers may have difficulties interpreting the time line. Guide students to read the events in sequence from the earliest to the last. Be sure that students understand the abbreviations A.D. and B.C.

To check students' understanding of the time line, ask the following questions:

- What Asian countries are included in the time line? *(China, Vietnam, and Japan; Students may also include Russia, since eastern parts of Russia may be considered part of Asia.)*
- Which events took place in North America? *(Indian civilizations in Mexico, the colonization of Puerto Rico, the Underground Railroad, Battle of Little Bighorn)*

Literary Concept:
TYPES OF LITERATURE

A Help students distinguish among the four types of literature in the oral tradition. Ask which type teaches lessons about human behavior and concludes with a moral. *(fables)* Ask students to contrast the main purpose of myths and folk tales. *(Possible response: Myths offer answers to basic questions about the world, while folk tales are told primarily to entertain.)* Then point out the fact that athletes often tell stories about coaches who have inspired them. Ask students which type of literature such stories represent. *(a legend)*

KEEPING THE PAST ALIVE

Storytellers like Brenda Wong Aoki represent a tradition that goes back to the dawn of history. In every culture, people told stories. Some of these stories took on a life of their own, outliving their storytellers and passing from one generation to the next. Through them, the past spoke to the present. Through them, the values of a culture stayed alive. These stories make up what is called the oral tradition. The chart below lists the types of stories in the oral tradition—myths, folk tales, legends, and fables—their distinct features and their common elements. The time line introduces each culture represented in this unit, listing one or more stories from its oral tradition and a "fascinating fact" from its history.

MYTHS
- *attempt to answer basic questions about the world*
- *are considered truthful by their originators*

FOLK TALES
- *are told primarily for entertainment*
- *feature human beings or humanlike animals*

COMMON ELEMENTS
A
- keep the past alive
- teach lessons about human behavior
- reveal the values of the society

FABLES
- *are short tales that illustrate morals*
- *have characters that are animals*

LEGENDS
- *are considered factual by those who tell them*
- *may be based on facts*
- *are usually set in the past*

KENYA

Kelfala's Secret
Something 754

. . .

about **1000** B.C.
People from other parts of Africa begin to settle in Kenya.

GREECE

Prometheus. 676
Aesop's Fables. 702
Phaëthon 706
The Arrow and
the Lamp 744
Echo and Narcissus. . 764

. . .

about **477–431** B.C.
Greek civilization reaches its pinnacle.

CHINA

Waters of Gold 725
The Fitting of
the Slipper 684

. . .

about **500** B.C. *The philosopher Confucius develops a moral system that influences China for more than 2000 years.*

Mini-Lesson *int* **Genre Study**

LITERATURE IN THE ORAL TRADITION
On the chalkboard, draw the web shown and then explain that stories from the oral tradition have the following characteristics:

- They are passed down by word of mouth within a culture.
- They reflect such types of literature as legends, folk tales, myths, and fables.
- They reveal the values of a particular culture.

Application Invite students to copy the web into their notebooks. As students read the selections in this unit, they can classify each according to the type of literature that it exemplifies. Suggest that students write the titles directly on the web, as examples of each category.

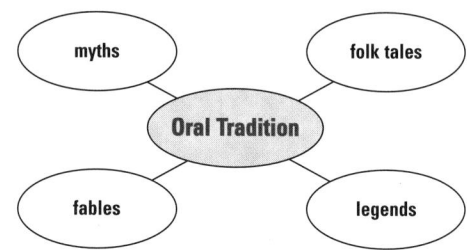

myths   folk tales

Oral Tradition

fables   legends

B

C

KEEPING THE PAST ALIVE **673**

Critical Thinking:
HYPOTHESIZING

B Direct students to study the entry about slaves escaping to freedom via the Underground Railroad. Then invite students to speculate about how stories from these people might have been passed across cultures. *(Possible response: The escaping slaves from the South carried their stories to their new homes in the North and Canada.)*

Critical Thinking:
SPECULATING

C Point out that the time line stops at A.D. 1876. Ask students to speculate about what types of stories from the oral tradition might be developed today. *(Possible responses: Legends about great sports heroes such as Mickey Mantle, myths about dramatic events such as earthquakes, and fables that teach lessons about 20th-century problems such as conservation.)*

Literary Note

In 1812, Jakob and Wilhelm Grimm published the first volume of *Kinder-und Hausmärchen,* translated as *Grimms' Fairy Tales. Märchen* is a German word that refers to a folk tale set in an unnamed, distant place in the past where magical events can occur. A second volume of the Grimms' work, which was published a few years later, increased the total collection of tales to 211. Both volumes were widely translated. The popularity of the Grimms' work was influential in encouraging scholars from other countries and cultures to collect, publish, and preserve their own folk tales and other folk literature as well.

Mini-Lesson ● **Study Skills**

INTERPRETING GRAPHICS Explain that some graphic devices are especially well suited for exploring ideas. Others are useful for organizing ideas. For example, a time line organizes events by showing the order in which they happen, from first to last. Mention that the events in a story or the steps in a process can be organized on a time line.

Application Divide the class into two groups. Have each group research several of the cultures represented in this unit and identify other "fascinating facts" to add to the time line.

OVERVIEW

Objectives

- To understand and appreciate a myth, a folk tale, and a modern retelling of a folk tale about taking risks
- To appreciate the culture and history of Greece and of the United States
- To extend understanding of the selections through a variety of multimodal and cross-curricular activities

Skills

READING SKILLS/ STRATEGIES
- Questioning

THE WRITER'S STYLE
- Alliteration
- Sensory details

GRAMMAR
- Past participles

LITERARY CONCEPTS
- Figurative language
- Characterization
- Humor

GENRE STUDY
- Folk tales

SPELLING
- The prefix ex-

SPEAKING, LISTENING, AND VIEWING
- Role-playing
- Storytelling
- Dialect
- Pantomime
- Dramatic scene

Cross-Curricular Connections

SOCIAL STUDIES
- Underground Railroad
- Slave tales

GEOGRAPHY
- Caucasus Mountains

SCIENCE
- Fire

Reading Pathways

- Select one or several students to read each story aloud to the entire class or to small groups of students. Assign this reading in advance so that the readers can incorporate into their presentations some of the techniques used by professional storytellers. Have students listen carefully to the tales without following along in their texts.
- Read each tale aloud to the class, pausing at key points to discuss how elements of the tale inform students about the history or customs of the culture. Have students compare these customs with those of their own culture. Have them record their responses and observations in their notebooks.
- After students have read the tales once, have them read each tale again to identify such structural elements as main characters, minor characters, conflict, setting, and plot. Then ask students to identify similarities and differences between these tales and the selections in the related unit. For example, they can compare the risks taken by characters such as Prometheus in the Greek myth and Jimmy Valentine in "A Retrieved Reformation."

LINKS TO UNIT ONE

On the Threshold

Activating Prior Knowledge

To be on the threshold is to be on the brink of a new decision, discovery, or experience. The tales you are about to read, show, as do the selections in Unit One, what happens when characters take risks and cross thresholds.

Building Background

UNITED STATES

The People Could Fly

retold by Virginia Hamilton

"The People Could Fly" is an African-American slave tale. Slave tales developed among the various peoples who were captured in Africa and transported to America. Most slaves were not allowed to speak their own language or learn how to read or write English, so they passed down much of their culture and experience orally. Tales such as "The People Could Fly" provided slaves comfort and hope and preserved the history of their lives and the legends of their African homelands. Virginia Hamilton's style imitates the dialect that a storyteller might have used in retelling this story.

PRINT AND MEDIA RESOURCES

UNIT SIX RESOURCE BOOK
Strategic Reading: Literature, p. 4
Vocabulary SkillBuilder, p. 7
Reading SkillBuilder, p. 5
Spelling SkillBuilder, p. 6

GRAMMAR MINI–LESSONS
Transparencies, p. 18
Copymasters, p. 25

WRITING MINI–LESSONS
Transparencies, pp. 34 and 38

ACCESS FOR STUDENTS ACQUIRING ENGLISH
Selection Summaries
Reading and Writing Support

TEACHER'S GUIDE TO ASSESS-MENT AND PORTFOLIO USE

FORMAL ASSESSMENT
Selection Test, pp. 117-118
 Test Generator

 **AUDIO LIBRARY**
See Reference Card

 **INTERNET RESOURCES**
McDougal Littell Literature Center at http://www.hmco.com /mcdougal/lit

Building Background

The Fitting of the Slipper
a Cinderella tale by William J. Brooke

"The Fitting of the Slipper" retells the story of "Cinderella," the best-known folk tale in the world. The tale probably originated in China, but versions of it are found in many cultures. Two of the common motifs, or repeated features, in Cinderella tales are the ill treatment of the heroine and the proof of her identity by a shoe that fits only her foot. In this version of the tale, William J. Brooke adds some new twists to the familiar story, challenging readers to re-examine what happens when people from different worlds risk crossing a threshold.

SUMMARY

Prometheus Prometheus, a young giant called a Titan, continually asks the god Zeus why he has not given fire to humans. "He will grow big and poisoned with pride and fancy himself a god," Zeus replies. Not satisfied with this answer, Prometheus himself brings fire to humans in their caves and teaches them how to use it. Soon people are building houses, ships, and chariots; forging metal into tools and weapons; carrying torches and cooking food. Zeus is furious when he discovers what Prometheus has done. He orders that the Titan be chained to a mountaintop, where two vultures pluck at his liver until Heracles rescues him many centuries later. As for humans, Zeus's revenge is to watch them destroy themselves with their new skills.

Building Background

GREECE

Prometheus
retold by Bernard Evslin

In many Greek myths, characters overstep bounds or ignore warnings from the gods. The myth "Prometheus" (prə-mē'thē-əs) tells about a Greek Titan who takes a risk to help improve the lives of humans—even though he has been warned not to do so. Prometheus and his brother Epimetheus (ĕp'ə-mē'thē-əs) were the only Titans who sided with Zeus in his battle against his father Cronus (krō'nəs) to become supreme ruler. After Zeus' victory, he ordered Prometheus to create humans. As you will see, Prometheus and Zeus disagree about how to treat these new beings.

Setting a Purpose

AS YOU READ . . .

Examine the values and customs presented.

Determine which behaviors and traits are rewarded in a particular culture.

Consider what is gained or lost when characters cross a threshold.

WORDS TO KNOW

aptitude (ăp'tĭ-tōōd') *n.* a natural ability (p. 677)
brandish (brăn'dĭsh) *v.* to wave something (such as a weapon) in a threatening manner (p. 689)
comprehension (kŏm'prĭ-hĕn'shən) *n.* awareness and understanding (p. 689)
endow (ĕn-dou') *v.* to provide with a quality or a talent (p. 677)
explicit (ĭk-splĭs'ĭt) *adj.* plain; straightforward (p. 677)

humility (hyōō-mĭl'ĭ-tē) *n.* the quality of showing an awareness of one's faults; lack of pride (p. 677)
implore (ĭm-plôr') *v.* to beg (p. 685)
pretense (prē'tĕns') *n.* the act of pretending; a false appearance or action meant to trick someone (p. 685)
receding (rĭ-sēd'ĭng) *adj.* becoming fainter or more distant **recede** *v.* (p. 695)
wrathful (răth'fəl) *adj.* extremely angry (p. 690)

PROMETHEUS

retold by Bernard Evslin

Mini-Lesson: Speaking, Listening, and Viewing

ROLE-PLAYING Explain to students that role-playing is one technique they can use to better understand characters in a story. Tell students that before role-playing a character or a scene from a story, they should first review the story to look for details or to make inferences about a character's personality and motivation. Point out that having such information will enhance their performance.

Application Have students work in pairs to role-play the scene in which Heracles frees Prometheus after centuries of torture. Encourage partners to discuss what they know about Prometheus and what they imagine Heracles might be like. Also encourage them to outline or prepare a script for a dialogue they imagine the two characters might have.

Prometheus was a young Titan,[1] no great admirer of Zeus. Although he knew the great lord of the sky hated <u>explicit</u> questions, he did not hesitate to beard[2] him when there was something he wanted to know.

One morning he came to Zeus and said, "O Thunderer, I do not understand your design. You have caused the race of man to appear on earth, but you keep him in ignorance and darkness."

"Perhaps you had better leave the race of man to me," said Zeus. "What you call ignorance is innocence. What you call darkness is the shadow of my decree. Man is happy now. And he is so framed that he will remain happy unless someone persuades him that he is unhappy. Let us not speak of this again."

But Prometheus said, "Look at him. Look below. He crouches in caves. He is at the mercy of beast and weather. He eats his meat raw. If you mean something by this, enlighten me with your wisdom. Tell me why you refuse to give man the gift of fire."

Zeus answered, "Do you not know, Prometheus, that every gift brings a penalty? This is the way the Fates[3] weave destiny—by which gods also must abide. Man does not have fire, true, nor the crafts which fire teaches. On the other hand, he does not know disease, warfare, old age, or that inward pest called worry. He is happy, I say, happy without fire. And so he shall remain."

"Happy as beasts are happy," said Prometheus. "Of what use to make a separate race

called man and <u>endow</u> him with little fur, some wit, and a curious charm of unpredictability? If he must live like this, why separate him from the beasts at all?"

"He has another quality," said Zeus, "the capacity for worship. An <u>aptitude</u> for admiring our power, being puzzled by our riddles and amazed by our caprice.[4] That is why he was made."

"Enough, Prometheus! I have been patient with you, but do not try me too far."

"Would not fire, and the graces he can put on with fire, make him more interesting?"

"More interesting, perhaps, but infinitely more dangerous. For there is this in man too: a vaunting pride that needs little sustenance[5] to make it swell to giant size. Improve his lot, ② and he will forget that which makes him pleasing—his sense of worship, his <u>humility</u>. He will grow big and poisoned with pride and fancy himself a god, and before we know it, ③ we shall see him storming Olympus. Enough, Prometheus! I have been patient with you, but

---

1. **Titan:** in Greek mythology, one of a family of giants who were overthrown by the family of Zeus.
2. **beard:** to confront.
3. **Fates:** in Greek mythology, the three goddesses who decide the course of people's lives.
4. **caprice** (kə-prēs´): the quality of acting without planning or thinking beforehand.
5. **sustenance** (sŭs´tə-nəns): nourishment; assistance.

Detail of illustration by Robert Baxter from *Prometheus and the Story of Fire* by I. M. Richardson. Copyright © 1983 Troll Associates. Reprinted with permission of the publisher.

WORDS TO KNOW

explicit (ĭk-splĭs´ĭt) *adj.* plain; straightforward
endow (ĕn-dou´) *v.* to provide with a quality or a talent
aptitude (ăp´tĭ-tōōd´) *n.* natural ability
humility (hyōō-mĭl´ĭ-tē) *n.* lack of pride

677

CUSTOMIZING FOR
Gifted and Talented Students

Ask students to discuss Zeus's statement, "What you call ignorance is innocence.... Man is happy now. And... he will remain happy unless someone persuades him that he is unhappy." Invite students to compare the lives of the humans before and after they receive fire. Ask students whether they agree with Zeus that ignorance is innocence and therefore happiness. *(Possible response: After Prometheus gives the humans fire, their lives are more challenging but richer. Ignorance is never happiness because knowledge provides choices.)*

CUSTOMIZING FOR
Multiple Learning Styles

A **Spatial or Graphic Learners** Invite students to draw a picture of the all-powerful Zeus. Suggest that they begin by deciding what physical characteristics to portray to suggest his power.

Critical Thinking: HYPOTHESIZE
B Ask students why they think that Zeus hates explicit questions. *(Possible responses: He does not like his authority to be challenged; he might be afraid someone will ask him a question he can't answer; he doesn't want to have to explain his actions to anyone.)*

CUSTOMIZING FOR
Students Acquiring English

① Explain that the word *man* is traditionally used to refer to the entire human race, including men, women, and children.

② If students need help understanding the sentence "Improve his lot, and he will forget that which makes him pleasing," point out that the sentence is an implied conditional. Invite them to paraphrase the sentence by using *if*. *(If a man's situation is improved, he will become vain and proud.)*

③ Explain that Olympus is the mythical home of the Greek gods.

Mini-Lesson   Spelling

THE PREFIX EX- Explain that the prefix *ex*-remains *ex*- when added to roots that begin with *p, t,* or *c* (as in *explicit*); that it changes to *ef*- when added to roots that begin with *f* (as in *effort*); and that it changes to *-e* before all other consonants (as in *elevate*).

Application Ask students to spell the following words that begin with the prefix *ex*-.
1. ex + treme (*extreme*)
2. ex + scape (*escape*)
3. ex + vaporate (*evaporate*)
4. ex + tinct (*extinct*)
5. ex + pensive (*expensive*)

6. ex + fective (*effective*)
7. ex + terior (*exterior*)
8. ex + pire (*expire*)
9. ex + ficient (*efficient*)
10. ex + cuse (*excuse*)

Ask students to look for more words that fit this pattern, in their own writing and in things that they read, and to add these words to their personal word lists.

Reteaching/Reinforcement
• *Unit Six Resource Book,* p. 6

do not try me too far. Go now and trouble me no more with your speculations."

Prometheus was not satisfied. All that night he lay awake making plans. Then he left his couch at dawn and, standing tiptoe on Olympus, stretched his arm to the eastern horizon where the first faint flames of the sun were flickering. In his hand he held a reed filled with a dry fiber; he thrust it into the sunrise until a spark smoldered. Then he put the reed in his tunic and came down from the mountain.

At first men were frightened by the gift. It was so hot, so quick; it bit sharply when you touched it and for pure spite made the shadows dance. They thanked Prometheus and asked him to take it away. But he took the haunch[6] of a newly killed deer and held it over the fire. And when the meat began to sear and sputter, filling the cave with its rich smells, the people felt themselves melting with hunger and flung themselves on the meat and devoured it greedily, burning their tongues.

C "This that I have brought you is called 'fire,'" Prometheus said. "It is an ill-natured spirit, a little brother of the sun, but if you handle it carefully, it can change your whole life. It is very greedy; you must feed it twigs, but only until it becomes a proper size. Then you must stop, or it will eat everything in sight—and you too. If it escapes, use this magic: water. It fears the water spirit, and if you touch it with water, it will fly away until you need it again."

He left the fire burning in the first cave, with children staring at it wide-eyed, and then went to every cave in the land.

Then one day Zeus looked down from the mountain and was amazed. Everything had changed. Man had come out of his cave. Zeus saw woodmen's huts, farmhouses, villages, walled towns, even a castle or two. He saw men cooking their food,

"Let them destroy themselves with their new skills. This will make a long, twisted game, interesting to watch. . . . My first business is with Prometheus."

carrying torches to light their way at night. He saw forges[7] blazing, men beating out ploughs, keels, swords, spears. They were making ships and raising white wings of sails and daring to use the fury of the winds for their journeys. They were wearing helmets, riding out in chariots to do battle, like the gods themselves.

Zeus was full of rage. He seized his largest thunderbolt. "So they want fire," he said to himself. "I'll give them fire—more than they can use. I'll turn their miserable little ball of earth into a cinder." But then another thought came to him, and he lowered his arm. "No," he said to himself, "I shall have vengeance—and entertainment too. Let them destroy themselves with their new skills. This will make a long, twisted game, interesting to watch. I'll attend to them later. My first business is with Prometheus."

He called his giant guards and had them seize Prometheus, drag him off to the Caucasus,[8] and there bind him to a mountain peak with great

---

6. **haunch:** the hip and leg of an animal.
7. **forges:** places where metal is heated and hammered into shape.
8. **Caucasus** (kô′kə-səs): a mountainous region in southeastern Europe.

Mini-Lesson **The Writer's Style**

ALLITERATION Explain to students that alliteration is the repetition of a consonant sound at the beginning of words. Tell them that it can link words, create a mood, or add emphasis.

Application Ask groups of students to find examples of alliteration using the consonants *f* and *s* in the highlighted paragraph on this page. Invite students to read the paragraph aloud and then discuss within their group the ways alliteration adds emphasis or mood to the passage.

Reteaching/Reinforcement

The Writer's Craft

Alliteration, p. 317

chains specially forged by Hephaestus[9]—chains which even a Titan in agony could not break. And when the friend of man was bound to the mountain, Zeus sent two vultures to hover about him forever, tearing at his belly and eating his liver.

Men knew a terrible thing was happening on the mountain, but they did not know what. But the wind shrieked like a giant in torment and sometimes like fierce birds.

Many centuries he lay there—until another hero was born brave enough to defy the gods. He climbed to the peak in the Caucasus and struck the shackles[10] from Prometheus and killed the vultures. His name was Heracles.[11] ❖

9. **Hephaestus** (hĭ-fĕs′təs): in Greek mythology, the god of fire and metalworking.

10. **shackles:** metal bonds for holding the ankles or wrists of a prisoner.

11. **Heracles** (hĕr′ə-klēz): another name for Hercules, a son of Zeus who was famous for his great strength and courage in Greek and Roman mythology.

Illustration by Robert Baxter from *Prometheus and the Story of Fire* by I. M. Richardson. Copyright © 1983 Troll Associates. Reprinted with permission of the publisher.

BERNARD EVSLIN

1922–1993

When Bernard Evslin's wife asked him for advice on how she could interest her students in mythology, he wrote his own retelling of a Greek myth. The students loved his story and asked for more. Evslin went on to write more than 30 books for young people, including *The Greek Gods; Heroes, Gods, and Monsters of the Greek Myths; The Green Hero,* which was nominated for a National Book Award; and *Hercules,* which received the Washington Irving Children's Book Choice Award.

In addition to mythologies and histories, Evslin also wrote award-winning television films and documentaries and two plays. More than 6 million copies of his works are in print.

OTHER WORKS *The Epics of Achilles and Ulysses, Heraclea: A Legend of Warrior Women, Jason and the Argonauts*

PROMETHEUS **679**

From Personal Response to Critical Analysis

1. Do you think Zeus is a good ruler? Explain your answer. *(Possible response: no, because he treats humans like animals and seeks revenge)*

2. Do you think Prometheus is a hero? *(Possible responses: yes, because he defies the gods to follow his own beliefs; yes, because he is willing to risk his life for humans)*

3. Why do you think that Prometheus risks the wrath of Zeus by giving humans the gift of fire? *(Possible response: Prometheus feels strongly that humans need this gift to reach their potential.)*

4. Do you think Prometheus got satisfaction from the risk he took? *(Possible responses: Yes, he has the satisfaction of knowing he improved the lives of humans. No, the terrible punishment overwhelms any sense of satisfaction.)*

5. What do you do when you disagree with an authority figure? How do you resolve your conflict? *(Possible response: I listen to the other person's opinions and then calmly express my own.)*

COMPREHENSION CHECK

1. Why did Zeus make man? *(to worship the gods, admire their power, be puzzled by their riddles, and be amazed by their caprice)*

2. Why does Prometheus give fire to humans? *(He believes that humans should have all of the benefits fire allows, such as cooking and creating warmth.)*

3. What is the magic that will stop fire if it tries to escape? *(water)*

4. How does fire change the lives of humans? *(It helps them make tools, build houses and towns, cook food, and take risks such as exploring the seas.)*

The People Could Fly

retold by Virginia Hamilton

SUMMARY

The People Could Fly This poetic folk tale tells about Africans who long ago had the power to fly. Captured and sent across the sea on slave ships, they had to leave their wings behind. In their misery, most forgot they could fly, although they still had the power. One slave who possessed the magic was an old man named Toby. He worked in the fields alongside Sarah, a woman who at one time had had wings. When an overseer cruelly whipped Sarah and her baby, Toby told her the magic words and she flew to freedom with her child. The next day, Toby spoke the magic words to fellow slaves exhausted by the heat, and they flew away like blackbirds. The master wanted to kill him, but Toby just laughed and flew away with the others, while the slaves who could not fly watched longingly from the ground. Eventually, these slaves escaped to freedom on foot and told their children about the people who could fly, and so the story has been passed down for generations.

Art Note

***The People Could Fly* by Leo and Diane Dillon** Leo and Diane Dillon often illustrate literary classics. This illustration for the book *The People Could Fly* gives the impression that flying is quite normal. Note how the people's bodies are angled to show lifting.

Reading the Art *How do the illustrators convey a sense of flight? Use details from the artwork to explain your answer.*

CUSTOMIZING FOR
Students Acquiring English

This selection contains many features of informal spoken English; it is written in the language of oral storytelling. Ask students to identify these features of spoken English. Some examples include the dropped *g* on *-ing* verbs (*climbin'*, *flappin'*) and the tag question *don't you know.*

STRATEGIC READING FOR
Less-Proficient Readers

Set a Purpose Ask students to read to find out how slaves become free and who helps them.

Mini-Lesson: Speaking, **Listening, and Viewing**

STORYTELLING Explain to students that to be effective storytellers, they should try to
- focus on details that bring characters and scenes to life
- use strong descriptive words that create vivid images
- concentrate (An audience will lose interest if a storyteller's focus begins to wander.)
- slow down and speed up as appropriate
- practice

Application Divide the class into three groups. Invite each group to choose a familiar story, such as a fairy tale or legend. Have group members write down the main points of their chosen story. Then ask them to take turns telling a part of the story. Have each storyteller end his or her part with "And then . . ." to get the next person started. Remind students to apply the suggestions for effective storytelling.

They say the people could fly. Say that long ago in Africa, some of the people knew magic. And they would walk up on the air like climbin' up on a gate. And they flew like blackbirds over the fields. Black, shiny wings flappin' against the blue up there.

Then, many of the people were captured for Slavery. The ones that could fly shed their wings. They couldn't take their wings across the water on the slave ships. Too crowded, don't you know.

The folks were full of misery, then. Got sick with the up and down of the sea. So they forgot about flyin' when they could no longer breathe the sweet scent of Africa.

Say the people who could fly kept their power, although they shed their wings. They kept their secret magic in the land of slavery. They looked the same as the other people from Africa who had been coming over, who had dark skin. Say you couldn't tell anymore one who could fly from one who couldn't.

One such who could was an old man, call him Toby. And standin' tall, yet afraid, was a young woman who once had wings. Call her Sarah. Now Sarah carried a babe tied to her back. She trembled to be so hard worked and scorned.

The slaves labored in the fields from sunup to sundown. The owner of the slaves callin' himself their Master. Say he was a hard lump of clay. A hard, glinty coal. A hard rock pile, wouldn't be moved. His Overseer[1] on horse-

back pointed out the slaves who were slowin' down. So the one called Driver cracked his whip over the slow ones to make them move faster. That whip was a slice-open cut of pain. So they did move faster. Had to.

Sarah hoed and chopped the row as the babe on her back slept.

Say the child grew hungry. That babe started up bawling too loud. Sarah couldn't stop to feed it. Couldn't stop to soothe and quiet it down. She let it cry. She didn't want to. She had no heart to croon[2] to it.

"Keep that thing quiet," called the Overseer. He pointed his finger at the babe. The woman scrunched low. The Driver cracked his whip across the babe anyhow. The babe hollered like any hurt child, and the woman fell to the earth.

The old man that was there, Toby, came and helped her to her feet.

"I must go soon," she told him.

"Soon," he said.

Sarah couldn't stand up straight any longer. She was too weak. The sun burned her face. The babe cried and cried, "Pity me, oh, pity me," say it sounded like. Sarah was so sad and starvin', she sat down in the row.

"Get up, you black cow," called the Overseer. He pointed his hand, and the Driver's whip snarled around Sarah's legs. Her sack dress tore into rags. Her legs bled onto the earth. She couldn't get up.

---

1. **Overseer:** a person who directs the work of others; supervisor.
2. **croon:** to sing softly.

THE PEOPLE COULD FLY **681**

CUSTOMIZING FOR
Students Acquiring English

(I) The writer uses many sentence fragments and starts some sentences with *and*. Students may be confused by the sentences that begin with *say*. Point out that this is short for *they say*, which reminds the reader that this story has been handed down orally.

Literary Concept:
FIGURATIVE LANGUAGE

A Remind students that a metaphor is a figure of speech that compares two things directly, without using *like* or *as*. Ask students to identify the metaphors used to describe the Master. (*a hard lump of clay; a hard, glinty coal; a hard rock pile*)

CUSTOMIZING FOR
Multiple Learning Styles

B Bodily-Kinesthetic Learners Ask students to find and list sensory details here that appeal to touch. (*cut of pain, chopped, baby on her back, soothe and quiet it, scrunched low, cracked his whip, fell*)

Active Reading: EVALUATE

C Ask students what they think Sarah means when she tells Toby she "must go soon." To give students an idea of how they might respond, use the following model:

Think-Aloud Model *The description of the abuse heaped on Sarah is so horrible that my first thought is that she is going to die. Then I thought that maybe she was planning to run away and that Toby might help her. I am eager to find out how she gets away and saves herself and her baby from all that cruelty.*

Multicultural Perspectives

SLAVE TALES Outwitting a master, as Sarah and Toby do, is a common theme in African-American oral literature. A trickster, often named Jack or John, generally outsmarts the master with his cunning wit and ingenuity. Animals also often appear as trickster characters. While masters of slaves attempted to get rid of slaves' tribal languages and customs, they saw these animal stories as harmless, apparently not understanding the connection between the victories of the tricksters and the hopes and desires of the

storytellers. Many of these animal characters—lions, leopards, tigers, and monkeys—come from African folk tales, while others were transformed into North American equivalents. For instance, the African jackal, hare, and tortoise became the American fox, rabbit, and turtle, respectively. Perhaps the best-known trickster animal character is Brer Rabbit. His uncanny ability to get the better of bigger and stronger animals made him a popular hero in slave tales.

D Explain that in this selection and in "Waiting" the main characters are waiting for something to happen before they act. Have students compare and contrast the characters' situations and the things that they are waiting for. *(Possible response: In "Waiting," Henrietta suffers her sister's derision and cruelty until she has the chance to excel and feels the power that is uniquely hers. In this selection, Sarah, Toby, and the other slaves who can fly endure cruelty and punishment until they can take it no longer and fly off to find freedom. In both cases, the power inside the characters is far greater than the power of their oppressors.)*

CUSTOMIZING FOR
Multiple Learning Styles

E **Bodily-Kinesthetic Learners** Invite students to create a dance that reflects the events described in these paragraphs. Encourage them to choose music to accompany their dance.

Critical Thinking: ANALYZING

F Ask students what they think the narrator means when she says, "The words of ancient Africa once heard are never remembered completely." *(Possible responses: The words are only symbols for much deeper feelings of freedom; the feelings are more important than the words; the words are magical.)*

CUSTOMIZING FOR
Students Acquiring English

2 Invite students to speculate about why the narrator says *"the one callin' himself Master"* instead of simply saying *"the Master."* (Possible response: No person is really master of another.)

Active Reading: CLARIFY

G Ask students what they think the narrator means when she describes the ancient words as "a dark promise." *(Possible responses: The promise is so deep and secret that few people are aware of it; it is a promise of freedom that few people allow themselves to think about; it is a promise of hope.)*

Toby was there where there was no one to help her and the babe.

D "Now, before it's too late," panted Sarah. "Now, Father!"

"Yes, Daughter, the time is come," Toby answered. "Go, as you know how to go!"

He raised his arms, holding them out to her. *"Kum . . . yali, kum buba tambe,"* and more magic words, said so quickly, they sounded like whispers and sighs.

E The young woman lifted one foot on the air. Then the other. She flew clumsily at first, with the child now held tightly in her arms. Then she felt the magic, the African mystery. Say she rose just as free as a bird. As light as a feather.

The Overseer rode after her, hollerin'. Sarah flew over the fences. She flew over the woods. Tall trees could not snag her. Nor could the Overseer. She flew like an eagle now, until she was gone from sight. No one dared speak about it. Couldn't believe it. But it was, because they that was there saw that it was.

Say the next day was dead hot in the fields. A young man slave fell from the heat. The Driver come and whipped him. Toby come over and spoke words to the fallen one. The words of **F** ancient Africa once heard are never remembered completely. The young man forgot them as soon as he heard them. They went way inside him. He got up and rolled over on the air. He rode it awhile. And he flew away.

Another and another fell from the heat. Toby was there. He cried out to the

> There was a great outcryin'. The bent backs straightened up. Old and young who were called slaves and could fly joined hands.

fallen and reached his arms out to them. *"Kum kunka yali, kum . . . tambe!"* Whispers and sighs. And they too rose on the air. They rode the hot breezes. The ones flyin' were black and shinin' sticks, wheelin' above the head of the Overseer. They crossed the rows, the fields, the fences, the streams, and were away.

"Seize the old man!" cried the Overseer. "I heard him say the magic *words*. Seize him!"

The one callin' himself Master come runnin'. The Driver got his whip ready to curl around old Toby and tie him up. The slave owner took his hip gun from its place. He meant to kill old black Toby.

But Toby just laughed. Say he threw back his head and said, "Hee, hee! Don't you know who I am? Don't you know some of us in this field?" He said it to their faces. "We are ones who fly!"

And he sighed the ancient words that were a dark promise. He said them all around to the others in the field under the whip, ". . . *buba yali . . . buba tambe . . .*"

There was a great outcryin'. The bent backs straightened up. Old and young who were called slaves and could fly joined hands. Say like they

---

Mini-Lesson   🧩   **Literary Concepts**

REVIEWING FIGURATIVE LANGUAGE
Figurative language goes beyond the dictionary meanings of words to create fresh and original descriptions. In a figurative expression, the words are not literally true, and one thing may be described in terms of another. A metaphor, for example, states that one thing is something else. A simile compares two things, using words such as *like*, *as*, or *resembles*. Personification gives human characteristics to something that is not human.

Application Have partners identify examples of figurative language in the highlighted passage on this

page. Then ask partners to add another sentence that uses figurative language to describe Sarah's flight to freedom.

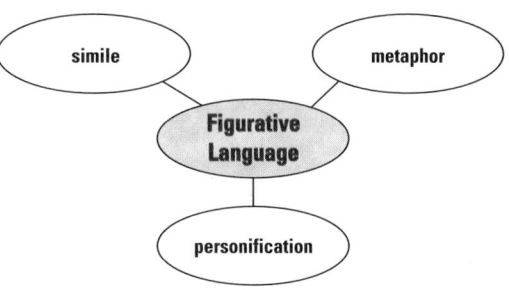

---

would ring-sing. But they didn't shuffle in a circle. They didn't sing. They rose on the air. They flew in a flock that was black against the heavenly blue. Black crows or black shadows. It didn't matter, they went so high. Way above the plantation, way over the slavery land. Say they flew away to *Free-dom*.

And the old man, old Toby, flew behind them, takin' care of them. He wasn't cryin'. He wasn't laughin'. He was the seer. His gaze fell on the plantation where the slaves who could not fly waited.

"Take us with you!" Their looks spoke it, but they were afraid to shout it. Toby couldn't take them with him. Hadn't the time to teach them to fly. They must wait for a chance to run.

"Goodie-bye!" the old man called Toby spoke to them, poor souls! And he was flyin' gone.

So they say. The Overseer told it. The one called Master said it was a lie, a trick of the light. The Driver kept his mouth shut.

The slaves who could not fly told about the people who could fly to their children. When they were free. When they sat close before the fire in the free land, they told it. They did so love firelight and *Free-dom*, and tellin'.

They say that the children of the ones who could not fly told their children. And now, me, I have told it to you. ❖

VIRGINIA HAMILTON

A gifted storyteller and distinguished author, Virginia Hamilton grew up listening to the stories told by her relatives on their small farm in Ohio. Her mother's side of the family is descended from a fugitive slave who settled in the Ohio Valley, and her great-grandmother is said to have been a conductor on the Underground Railroad. Much of Hamilton's work—which includes realistic fiction, fantasies, biographies, and folk tales—has been influenced by the stories she heard as a child.

As a writing major in college, Hamilton composed short stories. Later, she expanded one of her children's stories into her first novel, *Zeely*. Her novel *M.C. Higgins, the Great* was the first book to win both a Newbery Medal and a National Book Award.

1936–

In *The People Could Fly: American Black Folktales* and in other collections, Hamilton retells myths and folk tales from her own African-American heritage. She says that "folk tales were once a creative way for an oppressed people to express their fears and hopes to one another" and that these tales "are part of the American tradition and part of the history of our country."

OTHER WORKS *The House of Dies Drear, Anthony Burns: The Defeat and Triumph of a Fugitive Slave, In the Beginning: Creation Stories from Around the World, Many Thousand Gone: African Americans from Slavery to Freedom, Drylongso, The All Jahdu Storybook*

THE PEOPLE COULD FLY **683**

CUSTOMIZING FOR

Gifted and Talented Students

Virginia Hamilton, the author of this folk tale, once wrote that she learned "to manage feelings in terms of stories." Ask students to explain what they think she meant and what feelings she might have learned to manage through this story. *(Possible response: She learned to harness emotions by applying them to storytelling. The feelings might be the deep and dark rage of oppression or the hope that freedom offers.)*

From Personal Response to Critical Analysis

1. How did you feel as you read the end of the folk tale? Write your ideas in your notebook. *(Responses will vary.)*
2. Do you think that Sarah would have remembered her magic if Toby had not been there? Explain your answer. *(Possible responses: yes, since she had it inside her; no, because she was so overwhelmed by physical fatigue and battering)*
3. Why might this story appeal to all audiences, not just to those descended from African-American slaves? *(Possible response: It is beautifully written and offers hope for anyone who is feeling oppressed by an unfair or cruel authority.)*

COMPREHENSION CHECK

1. What special power did some of the people in Africa have? *(the power to fly)*
2. Why were these people captured? *(to be brought to America as slaves)*
3. What does the Driver do to Sarah and her baby? *(whips them)*
4. How does Sarah escape from the cruel treatment she receives? *(Toby whispers the magic words to her, and she flies away to freedom.)*

CUSTOMIZING FOR
Students Acquiring English

This story is a retelling of the fairy tale "Cinderella," with which some students acquiring English may not be familiar. You may want to provide them with an outline of the plot of "Cinderella" before they read "The Fitting of the Slipper."

CUSTOMIZING FOR
Gifted and Talented Students

Ask students to make notes, as they read, of the ways that the words *fit* and *fitting* are used throughout the story and to explain why the use of these words changes.

Possible responses:

Page 685—"This is not fitting."

Page 692—"It was my intention to try the fit of the slipper on all ladies of respectable houses."

Page 693—"If the slipper fits, I want you."

Page 693—"You don't want the slipper to fit nobody."

Page 693—"To prove that no one is fitting."

Page 694—"It may not fit."

Page 695—"The slipper didn't fit. It didn't near fit."

Page 697—"It isn't fitting."

Page 697—"And the first step of all the many they took together smashed the glass slipper past all fitting."

The use of the words changes because what is considered fitting changes as the events unfold.

STRATEGIC READING FOR
Less-Proficient Readers

Set a Purpose Ask students to read the first part of the story to learn where the Prince finds himself when he runs out of the room.

The Fitting
of the Slipper

by William J. Brooke

684   UNIT SIX: THE ORAL TRADITION

"Please," <u>implored</u> the Prince, stepping back in some distress, "this is not fitting."

"Not yet, but it will in a minute," she muttered between clenched teeth.

"No, I mean it is not right."

She looked at the slipper in confusion for a moment. Then she took it off her right foot and began jamming it onto her left. "You might have said something sooner," she grumbled. "Your Highness," she added, remembering that she hoped to marry the Prince and must not snap at him until after the wedding.

She wore the daintiest little socklets, creamy white lawns with tiny red flowers strewn across them. They would have been enchanting but for the red that blossomed between the flowers as she tried to put herself in the royal shoe by any means available.

"I thank you for trying," the Prince began to say as he gestured for his Lord Chamberlain to retrieve the slipper.

She swung her foot away from him on the <u>pretense</u> of getting a better angle of entry. "No trouble, no trouble, just I've been on my feet all day and they're a bit swollen." She shoved a finger behind her heel and tried to force her way in.

The Prince stared, appalled. "This cannot go on," he sighed to his Lord Chamberlain, who knelt at the woman's feet.

"It can! It can!" she said, redoubling her efforts as she saw her chances slipping away. "It's almost on now." Four toes had found a lodging place, and she seemed perfectly determined to abandon the last to make its own way in the world.

"No! No!" He pushed forward and grabbed the slipper from her. A smear of red appeared on his snowy-white garments. "I am on a mission of romance. I am seeking love and finding naught[1] but greed and grotesque self-mutilation."[2]

he pursed up her mouth like a prune and said, "Well, I never heard of a shoe size being a sound basis for matrimony, but if Your Highness chooses to place his future on that footing, I don't suppose he can blame anyone for trying to cut a few corners."

"Silence, woman," the Lord Chamberlain snapped automatically, but he looked as if he probably agreed with her.

"You do not understand," the Prince sighed. He stood open-mouthed, as if looking for words, then shook his head. "You did not see her. You do not know the feeling of . . . Oh, what is the use?"

The Lord Chamberlain tried to take control. "If Your Highness will step outside, we have three more houses to visit in this street."

"No! No more! No more feet, no more blood, no more women who wish only to crush me beneath their heels! I cannot bear it!"

And with that he clutched the bloody slipper to his bosom and swept out the door.

Only it was the wrong door, and he found himself in a dark little hallway instead of on the street where the royal retinue[3] waited. The door behind him started to open again, and he knew it would be the Lord Chamberlain.

---

1. **naught** (nôt): nothing.
2. **grotesque** (grō-těsk´) **self-mutilation:** horrible injuries done to oneself.
3. **retinue** (rět´n-ōō´): a group of attendants or servants.

WORDS TO KNOW	**implore** (ĭm-plôr´) v. to beg **pretense** (prē´těns´) n. the act of pretending; a false appearance or action meant to trick someone

685

Mini-Lesson Reading Skills/Strategies

QUESTIONING Being an active reader means asking questions as one reads. Tell them that one way to do this is to stop at various points and ask *who, what, where, when,* and *why* questions about the events and characters. Draw these five "W" questions on the chalkboard as shown.

Application Have students work in groups of five. Each group member should write one question about "The Fitting of the Slipper," using one of the five "W" questions. One student can write down all five questions on a single sheet of paper. Have groups exchange questions and answer them.

Reteaching/Reinforcement
• *Unit Six Resource Book,* p. 5

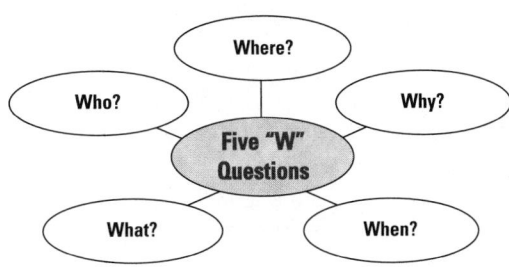

③ Students may be confused by this use of the word *suit*. Instead of the more common uses of this word—to refer to clothing or a legal action—*suit* here means a request, as in asking for a favor.

Literary Concept:
CHARACTERIZATION

C Explain that the Prince carries on a fantasy dialogue with himself about what he wishes he could say. Then ask students to discuss what the private dialogue tells them about the Prince's character. *(Possible response: that he wishes he could be a little bit naughty and say something outrageous instead of doing the right thing all the time)*

Active Reading: EVALUATE

D Ask students why they think the Prince is so interested in the texture of the door. Prompt students by using this model:

Think-Aloud Model *At first, I wondered why the author placed so much emphasis on the Prince's feelings about the door. Then I realized that the Prince probably always has doors opened for him. Because he is in this unfamiliar place, he may be marveling at a new, although simple, discovery.*

Critical Thinking: ANALYZING

E Ask students to analyze what the smooth, featureless slipper and the rugged, knotty door might symbolize. *(Possible response: The door symbolizes real life, with all its flaws and roughness. The slipper represents romance and fantasy life, where everything is smooth, flawless, and unreal.)*

"You are not to open that door on pain of . . ." The only punishment he could think of at the moment was decapitation,[4] and that seemed excessive. ". . . Of my severe displeasure," he finished, rather lamely. The door closed again and he was alone.

Before anything else could happen, he slipped down the hall and through another door. He was not sure where he was going or what he wanted, but he knew that he wanted to be away from what was behind him. He closed the door and dropped a bar into place. He listened for any movement, but there was none. He was alone.

For a moment the Prince was so thrilled to be by himself that he paid no attention to his surroundings. He took a deep breath and listened. There was nothing. No one asking, "Is Your Highness ready to meet with your ministers?" No one imploring, "If Your Highness would only listen to my suit . . ." No one hinting, "Would Your Highness care to dine now?" Strange that it always sounded as if he were being asked his pleasure when in fact he was being told to do this or that right away. For being a Highness and a Majesty, he was always being bossed around by someone or other. The only time he was left alone was when he went to the bathroom. And even then it wasn't long before there would be a discreet knock and "Does Your Majesty wish to review the troops now?" Sometimes he would imagine himself replying, "Why, certainly, My Majesty always likes to review the troops with his pants around his ankles. It is a little hard to walk, but it sets a

③

Whenever he got that sort of thought, he would blush and say . . . "This is not fitting."

good example for the recruits." But he knew he would never say anything remotely like that. And whenever he got that sort of thought, he would blush and say to himself, "This is not fitting." Then he would hurry up and be more obedient than ever.

For he knew he should be grateful for his wealth and position and that he owed it all to the love and goodwill of his people, and it was his responsibility and blah blah blah. Sometimes he felt that a very wicked Prince lived inside him and would leap out and take over if he gave it the least chance. But he had never given it that chance. Until now.

For a while he just listened to the quiet. It was dark and shadowy with only a little fire at the far end of the room, and he could not see very much. But he could hear lots of lovely silence, and when he put out his hand he could feel the rough wood of the door. It felt wonderful to him, all uneven and knotted and slivery, and it squirmed with lovely deep-red shadows in the flicker of the fire. He could feel the glass slipper in his other hand. That was what he was used to in his life, everything smooth and silky and featureless. He held it up and looked at its crystalline transparency, beautiful and perfect and boring. In sheer delight, he ran his hand across the rough landscape of the door.

And gave a howl as a big splinter slid into his palm.

He stuck the glass slipper under one arm and tried to ease the pain with his other hand. Then

---

4. **decapitation:** the act of cutting off someone's head.

Mini-Lesson   **Literary Concepts**

REVIEWING CHARACTERIZATION Explain that characterization refers to the techniques writers use to create and develop characters. There are four basic methods of developing a character: (1) presenting the character's words and actions, (2) presenting the character's thoughts, (3) describing the character's appearance, and (4) showing what others think about the character.

Application Invite students to look for examples of each method of characterization used to develop the characters of the Prince and Ella in the story.

Suggest that they record examples on a web like the one shown.

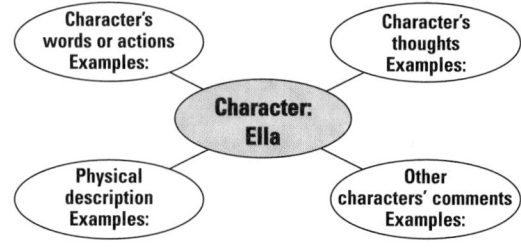

he froze and caught his breath again to listen.

Something had moved at the far end of the room. Near the fire, but in the shadows. In fact, one of the shadows itself.

He peered as hard as he could, but the harder he looked, the less he saw. When he moved his eyes, blue images of the fire danced in the dark. Even when he shut his eyes, the blue fire flitted about until he wasn't sure whether his eyes were open or closed.

He held his breath as tight as he could. But he noticed now that the breath he held was full of smells. They were kitchen smells, and to anyone who had grown up in a snug little cottage, they would have been comforting and comfortable smells. To someone like the Prince, though, who had grown up perfumed and scented and protected, they smelled like a wild beast in its lair.

He found himself wishing he had at least one of his guards or even a fawning courtier with him. Stories he had been told as a child came back to him, tales of witches and demons and unspeakable stews boiling on heathen hearths.

He had not thought of those stories in many years. They had been told him by an old peasant woman who had been his wet nurse when he was tiny. The infant Prince cried whenever she left him, and the Royal Nurse could not abide a squalling child, even if it was a Princeling. So the old woman had been allowed to stay until the child was old enough to learn that neither listening to silly stories nor crying was part of his responsibilities toward his people. One day he noticed he had not seen the old woman for a while. Eventually he forgot to notice when he never saw her again. He had outgrown her stories and her warm, soft hugs and her wet kisses.

ow he wondered how he had forgotten her. Her memory made the room a lovely warm haven again. Even the smells seemed to belong to her, and they comforted him like the low murmur of music from a distant place.

Suddenly a bent and twisted shadow stepped in front of the fire. The Prince gasped and grabbed for the door and gave out another howl when the splinter slid in a little deeper. The shadow pushed something into the fire. There was a little burst of light as a twig caught, and then the shadow turned and thrust it at him, bright-blazing and shadow-twisting.

The Prince fell back against the door in absolute terror. He could see nothing past the light but a filthy hand, a coarse sleeve, and the dark bent shape beyond.

They were frozen like that for a moment of silence. Then the shape gave a low sigh in a rough woman's voice. "Aaow. You am come then. I can't believe you really come."

There was something familiar about the voice, and the Prince straightened up to try to see. The shape abruptly dropped to its knees, and the light lowered. "Your 'Ighness! I'm forgettin' me place! 'Ere is me all dirty an' bent over with scrubbin' an' stickin' the fire right in yer face like I 'ad any right at all. Please say yer fergivin' of me!"

The Prince stared down over the flame at the wild, tangled hair and dirt-laden face, as if searching a dark thicket for a wounded boar. But instead of a ravening beast, that face held eyes bright and darting as twin harts[5] startled by the hunt. He was still frightened, but it was different now. And she sounded somehow familiar. . . .

---

5. **harts:** male deer.

THE FITTING OF THE SLIPPER   **687**

Mini-Lesson: Speaking, Listening, and Viewing

DIALECT Explain to students that the dialect a character speaks often tells readers a lot about that character. Remind students that dialect refers to language spoken in a particular place by a certain group or class of people. Therefore, a character's dialect might tell readers something about the region the character comes from, his or her economic background, and perhaps his or her age.

Application Invite a volunteer to read aloud the highlighted passage on this page. Then ask students what Ella's dialect tells them about her. Have students discuss how storytellers can use dialect to enhance their oral tales.

STRATEGIC READING FOR
Less-Proficient Readers

F Ask students where the Prince is and why this is an unusual place for him. (*He is in the kitchen. It's unusual because he has servants to cook for him, so he never goes into the kitchen.*) **Making Inferences**

Set a Purpose Invite students to read on to find out why the Prince tells a lie to his Lord Chamberlain.

Active Reading: EVALUATE

G Ask students why they think the Prince is so terrified by the shadows and the "filthy hand" that he sees in the room. (*Possible responses: He has no idea how to deal with anything unexpected; he doesn't feel safe and has no idea how to defend himself.*)

CUSTOMIZING FOR
Multiple Learning Styles

H **Musical Learners** Invite students to choose background music to play during the reading of the woman's dialogue with the Prince. Have them describe and explain their choices.

CUSTOMIZING FOR
Students Acquiring English

4 If students find the woman's dialect difficult to read, point out that the apostrophes represent dropped letters. For example, the woman drops the initial *h* from *Highness, here,* and *had.*

Literary Concept: FIGURATIVE LANGUAGE

I Explain to students that a simile is a comparison between two things using *like* or *as.* Have them describe what the woman's eyes looked like based on the simile. (*Possible responses: alert, lively, wary*)

Active Reading: PREDICT

J Point out that the woman's voice sounds familiar to the Prince. Have students predict who the woman will prove to be. (*Possible responses: the Prince's nurse; the woman whose foot fits the slipper*)

 Remind students that even though the Prince is nervous about having the woman pierce him with a needle, he finds himself giggling. Ask students what they think this reaction reveals about the Prince. (Possible responses: It suggests that he is excited at the prospect of being where he is not supposed to be; it reflects his conflict between his duties and his desires.)

he silence stretched out, with him looking thoughtfully down at her and her looking up at him with a question and a hope that belied[6] dirt and rags. Then he blinked and pulled himself together.

"I believe that you have the most awful grammar that I have ever heard," he finally said.

She didn't reply but slowly lowered her eyes from his.

"I do not mean that as an insult. It is actually quite interesting to me. Everyone makes such a point of being precisely correct with me, it is rather refreshing to hear someone jabbering away." She stiffened at that. "Well, I do not really mean 'jabbering,' just . . ."

Her eyes, which had veiled themselves, suddenly widened with concern. "Yer 'urt! Why din't you tell me?" She was staring at the blood on his clothes.

"Oh, that is not my blood," he said. "That came from this." He held out the slipper. She looked hard at the glass shoe and then raised eyes filled with some terrible emotion.

He found it impossible to meet those pain-filled eyes, so he held out his hand. "I do have a slight injury, however—a splinter from your door."

She took his hand without a word and led him to the fire. She pulled a rough chair close to it and seated him, respectfully but firmly. Then she knelt before him, studying his hand in the firelight. She glanced up to see that he was ready, then seized the splinter and pulled it out.

It actually hurt rather a lot, but he was determined not to show it. "Thank you, my good woman." He wasn't sure if she was a woman or a girl. Even close to the fire, the layers of dirt and ragged clothes hid her almost completely.

He started to rise, but she took his hand again and examined it. "Not all out," she pronounced, and hurried away to a dark corner where she sorted through the contents of a box with a great clanking of metal and wood.

"Actually, it feels much better, and perhaps I will wait for the Court Surgeon." But she was back then with a long, sharp darning needle, which caught the light like a dagger. She thrust its point into the fire and waited silently for it to heat up. The Prince felt distinctly ill at ease.

There was a faint scraping in the hall outside and a low tap on the door. The voice of the Lord Chamberlain sounded deliberately unconcerned, as though pretending that nothing was out of the ordinary. "Is Your Majesty ready to proceed to the next house?"

The Prince looked nervously at the needle, which was beginning to glow red at its tip, and at the girl whose shoulders tightened at the voice. He wondered what the Lord Chamberlain would think if he knew he was closeted with a strange serving girl who was about to apply a red-hot point to the royal person. The thought almost made him giggle.

"Perhaps Your Highness does not realize the lateness . . ."

"My Highness is perfectly capable of telling time. Even now I am looking at a clock above the mantel. I shall come out when I am ready."

"Very good, Your Majesty." After a moment, the steps scraped away down the hall again.

She looked at him warily. "We got no clock in 'ere."

He looked abashed. "I know. It was a lie."

"You lie a lot, then, do ya?"

---

6. **belied:** showed to be false.

Mini-Lesson   Genre Study

FOLK TALES Tell students that one common element of folk tales is a happy ending, which usually involves the main character's finding his or her true love. Point out that this person often is not the sort of person the main character expects to fall in love with. For example, the Prince's Cinderella is ragged and dirty, Beauty's Prince is a hideous beast, and the Frog Prince isn't even human at the start of the story. Tell students that in these stories, and in many others, true love triumphs over all obstacles.

Application Have students discuss what "happily ever after" would be like for some of the folk tale characters in this unit. Ask students whether they think the characters will be completely happy. Then have students form small groups and take turns telling stories that extend a well-known folk tale (or fairy tale) of their choosing. Just how "happily" the characters live is up to each story teller.

"Never! I just . . . It wasn't me, it was . . ."

"Was what?"

Something made him blurt it out before he could think. "The Wicked Prince who lives inside me and tries to get out." He held his breath. He had never told anyone about the Wicked Prince.

She didn't laugh. "The Wicked Prince 'oo tries to get out. Well, I guess 'e succeeded this time, din't 'e? Don't seem to 'ave done much damage. Maybe you should let 'im out more often. Maybe 'e woun't be so wicked if 'e just got a breath o' fresh air every onc't in a while." She smiled. And her smile cut right through the dirt like a spray of clear, crisp spring water and made him smile back.

"Let's see if we can' cut 'im some air 'oles right now." She wiped the glowing needle on a rag and <u>brandished</u> it in the air with a piratical grin.

The Prince lost his smile. "Perhaps I should be going. There is a great deal of . . ."

She didn't answer but knelt before him, grabbed his hand, and turned her back to him so that his arm was immobilized under her own, pressed against her side. It took only a moment, she was so quick, and he was left with the curious feeling of being completely defenseless and completely protected at the same time. She plunged the needle in swiftly and deftly. He tried not to think of the pain, and after a moment he didn't. His face was very close to her shoulder, and all along the inside of his arm he was touching her. He could feel roundness and softness beneath the coarse fabrics. He could smell her smell, which was the scent that rises from under the earth after rainfall. And in the play of the firelight on her cheek he felt he could see beneath the dirt to some kind of shining essence that . . .

"I said, 'All finished.' "

He realized it was not the first time she had spoken. Yet she had not moved from where he half leaned against her, just waited for his pleasure. He sat back, embarrassed, and she turned and seated herself on the floor beside the fire.

"Not too bad? Yer 'and," she added when he showed no sign of <u>comprehension</u>.

"Oh! Oh, that. Fine. No pain at all. I am sorry that I am a little dreamy, but I was thinking of my old Nurse Reba. You make me think of her."

"Well, I don't know if I want to remind you of any old nurse."

"Not that you are old. I mean, I do not know if you are old. I mean, what is your name?"

She smiled to show that there was no offense. "Ella, Yer 'Ighness."

"Ella," he repeated. "A good . . . plain name. Fitting for a . . ."

"A good, plain girl?" she suggested.

"A good and faithful servant," he finished, trying to make it sound like a hearty compliment.

"Actually, I'm more in the line of poor relation than yer outright 'ouse'old servant."

> He held his breath. He had never told anyone about the Wicked Prince.

WORDS TO KNOW

brandish (brăn'dĭsh) v. to wave something (such as a weapon) in a threatening manner

comprehension (kŏm'prĭ-hĕn'shən) n. awareness and understanding

689

STRATEGIC READING FOR
Less-Proficient Readers

L Ask students what lie the Prince tells his Lord Chamberlain and why he tells it. (*He says he is looking at a clock, but there is none. He tells the lie to make the Lord Chamberlain leave him alone for a while.*)

Set a Purpose Have students read on to learn the woman's position in the household.

Critical Thinking:
SPECULATING

M Have students speculate about why the woman doesn't laugh when the Prince tells her about the "Wicked Prince." (*Possible response: She takes him seriously and may see the "Wicked Prince" as the first glimmer of the "real" Prince.*)

Active Reading: CLARIFY

N Ask students what realization the Prince comes to about the strange woman. (*He realizes that she is "real" flesh and blood and that under her dirt there is beauty and "some kind of shining essence."*)

Literary Links

O Ask students to discuss the similarities and the differences between Ernie in "A Crush" and Ella in this story. (*Possible responses: Ernie and Ella both approach their situations with no pretenses. They are completely themselves and remain true to themselves no matter what happens. Their honesty affects the lives of the people around them. They are different in that Ernie is mentally retarded.*)

Mini-Lesson  **The Writer's Style**

SENSORY DETAILS Explain that when writers describe the way something looks, sounds, smells, tastes, or feels, they are providing sensory details. These details help readers to better imagine the characters, scenes, or events in the story.

Application Ask students to create new sentences from the following, using rich sensory details. Remind them to appeal to as many of the senses as possible.

1. The woman was dressed in rags, and her face was dirty. She looked startled.

2. The door was rough, and the Prince got a splinter when he went to open it.

3. Ella reminded the Prince of his nurse from a long time ago.

4. It was dark, and the Prince could not see the woman's face in the shadows.

Reteaching/Reinforcement
- *Writing Handbook,* anthology p. 819
- *Writing Mini-Lessons* transparencies, pp. 34 and 38

The Writer's Craft

Sensory Details, p. 255

STRATEGIC READING FOR
Less-Proficient Readers

P Ask students who the woman is that the Prince has encountered. *(Ella, the daughter of the house, whose step-mother has made her a servant)* Noting Relevant Details

Set a Purpose Ask students to read on to find out where the Prince met the woman before.

CUSTOMIZING FOR
Students Acquiring English

(5) Help students understand that Ella's statement "It 'asn't been as bad as 'ow it might seem" suggests that she is happy with her life even though it seems it might be difficult.

(6) Point out that when the Prince refers to himself as "we," he is using the royal "we," a linguistic convention that allows members of royalty to distinguish themselves from common people. As a member of royalty, a person can use the plural pronoun because he or she speaks for the nation. After an uncomfortable situation, the Prince uses the royal "we" in an attempt to recover his dignity.

Active Reading: CLARIFY

Q Have students explain the cause of the Prince's anger and wrathful expression. *(Possible response: He is angry about the way the woman speaks of Ella.)*

"Ah, I see. A cousin of the house whose own family fell on hard times?"

She looked sadly at the walls around her. "This 'ouse is the 'ouse of me father."

The Prince couldn't take it in. "Your father? You are the daughter of this house? But this is a substantial⁷ house, so why are you . . ." He gestured mutely at their surroundings.

P "Me mother died when I was a tiny one. Me father married agin an' 'ad two more daughters an' no more 'appiness afore 'e went to join me mother. Since then, this room 'as been me 'ome."

 he Prince didn't know what to say. He felt deeply ashamed that he had ever felt ill-treated in his royal position.

(5) Ella felt his pity and hastened to add, "It 'asn't been as bad as 'ow it might seem. There's good in anything if you know where to look for it."

The Prince felt deeply uncomfortable. He decided it was time to return to his duties. He tried to find something cheerful to say. "I am (6) quite sure you are right. And we thank you for your good service to your Prince. Now we must be going, for there is much of importance to be done."

He started for the door, but she was in front of him suddenly, eyes flashing. " 'Much of importance to be done.' More customers to try on, ya mean."

"What!" he exclaimed, drawing himself up into a state of outraged dignity. "How dare you judge your betters! You should remember your place!"

She fell instantly into a deep and clumsy

curtsy. "Fergive me, Yer 'Ighness. I just want the best for you."

He was sorry for her but determined to be dignified. "It is all right, my girl. It was really our fault for encouraging you in a way we should never have done. You have your Prince's gratitude and his kind thoughts."

She held her face in shadow and spoke low. "I just wanted you to know as 'ow I wasn't just what I seemed."

"Of course. Thank you and farewell." He strode to the door.

He was starting to lift the bar when he was stopped by a gentle rap at the door. He sighed resignedly and said, "Yes, my Lord Chamberlain?"

But it was the voice of the older woman who had greeted them at the door. "If Your Highness please, my other daughter is still waiting to try her fortune. Or if Your Highness wishes to stay by the fire awhile, I wonder if you might send Cinderella out so she can get to her chores."

The Prince looked at Ella. She had slunk back into the corner by the fire, merging into the shadows from which she had appeared. "Cinderella?" he called through the door. She raised her eyes to him then, but he could not read them in the dark.

"Yes," called back the woman. "Cinderella, our kitchen maid." She laughed. "Unless Your Highness was figuring to try the slipper on her as well."

The Prince hurled the bar into a corner and threw the door open. The woman fell into a deep curtsy at his <u>wrathful</u> expression. "Your

---

7. **substantial:** large.

WORDS
TO
KNOW **wrathful** (răth′fəl) *adj.* extremely angry

690

Illustration by Tom Curry.

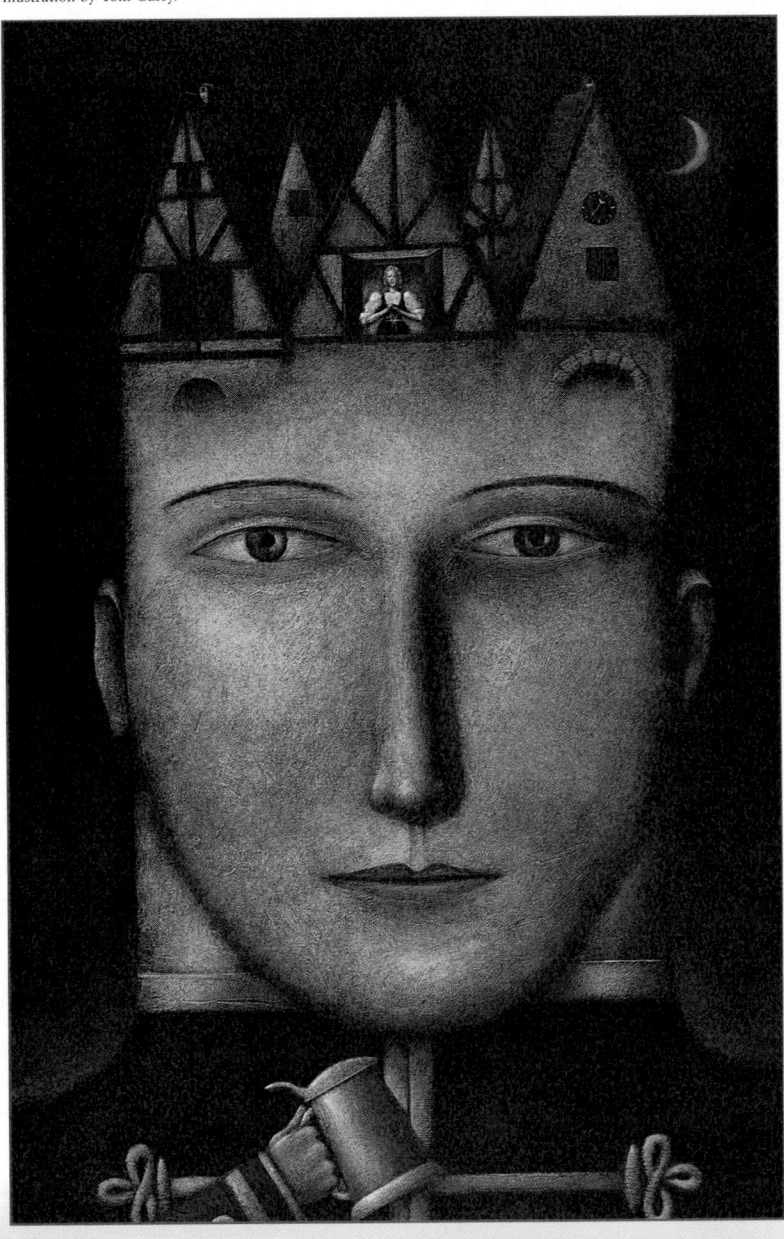

Mini-Lesson Grammar

PAST PARTICIPLES Tenses are made from the three principal parts of verbs: the present, the past, and the past participle. With regular verbs, such as *drop* and *like*, the past tense is formed by the addition of *-ed* or *-d,* and the past tense and the past participle are spelled the same. Irregular verbs do not use *-d* or *-ed* to form the past tense or the past participle. In some cases, as with *bring*, the past tense and the past participle are the same. In others, such as *take* and *find*, the past participle is different from the present and the past tenses.

Application Ask students to substitute a help-ing verb and a past participle for the existing verb in each of the following sentences:
1. The Prince saw Ella in the shadows. *(has seen, had seen)*
2. Ella hoped the Prince would love her. *(had hoped)*
3. The fairy godmother gives Ella one night of beauty and glamour. *(has given, had given)*
4. The Prince and Ella talk about fantasy and reality. *(have talked, had talked)*

Present	Past	Past Participle
drop	dropped	(has) dropped
like	liked	(has) liked
bring	brought	(has) brought
take	took	(has) taken
find	found	(has) found

Reteaching/Reinforcement
• Grammar Handbook, anthology pp. 871–872
• *Grammar Mini-Lessons* copymasters p. 25, transparencies p. 18

 The Writer's Craft

Principal Parts, p. 477

Critical Thinking: ANALYZING

R Ask students why they think the Prince really wants to try the slipper on Ella. *(Possible responses: He wants to repay her for her kindness and the way she made him feel. He probably does not think she is the woman he is searching for but wants to anger her stepmother.)*

Highness!" she gasped, not at all sure what she had done.

"Yes," he said after a moment. "You are quite right. Please rise." She did so, uncertainly. "It was my intention to try the fit of the slipper on all the ladies of respectable houses. So of course I shall try it on Ella. If there is time, I shall do the same for your other daughter."

The woman was speechless for a moment. "Ella! A lady?"

The Prince silenced her with a look. "She has treated us as a lady should treat her liege⁸ and as others have not. Await us without." He closed the door on the woman's white, startled face.

R The Prince was furious but also delighted. It was the sort of thing the Wicked Prince would have urged him to do, and yet it seemed entirely in keeping with royal behavior. He might find a way to reconcile himself⁹ yet.

He turned to the shadow that was frozen by the fire. "All right, my girl, come over here and try this . . ." He stopped in surprise as she burst past him and tried to get out the door. He reached past her and slammed it.

"No, no!" she cried, fleeing into shadow. "Please, my Prince, don't make me do it!"

"Come, girl, do not be silly. Stop it! The sooner you do it, the sooner we are done. Come, that is a good girl."

She came to him slowly, unwillingly.

"If Yer 'Ighness insists . . ."

"I do. I command it."

"Then I must tell Yer 'Ighness somethin' afore I try on that shoe."

"What is it, girl?"

"It's my shoe."

The Prince blinked. "What?"

"It's my shoe. It fell off o' me when I was runnin' . . ."

"What! Listen, girl. I am doing this out of the goodness of my heart, and you are wasting my time. Just put your foot . . ."

" 'Me birthright for yer name,' " she said, and his breath caught in his throat. " 'If I stay another moment, I'll lose everything.' "

"How do you know that?" he gasped out. He grabbed her shoulders and shook her. "I have told no one except my father our last words to each other. How do you know them?"

She broke away from him and stood up proudly. "I know 'cause I was there!"

"But you . . . you . . . Look at you!"

She did not lower her eyes. "I clean up better than you'd expect."

"But you jabber away like a trained bird and dart about like a ferret! *She* spoke so precisely and moved with a stateliness that shamed the court!"

"You try 'avin' a conversation without usin' any 'H' words an' see 'ow precise you sound. An' if you want stateliness, just you 'op up onto a pair o' glass 'eels. Believe me, it's either stately or fall down in them things."

"Your gown! Your coach! Whence came they?"

"Well, whence they come was a friend o' mine. A person o' some power, I might add. An'

> "She was beauty beyond beauty. . . . I do not expect you to understand."

---

8. **liege** (lēj): lord.

9. **reconcile himself:** make his two parts into one whole person again.

don't ask to meet 'er, 'cause she operates on 'er own schedule and only shows up when I need 'er. An' she's the one as decides when that is, 'owever much me own opinion may disagree."

The Prince sat in the chair and began to rub his temples. "You do not understand what I am feeling. You cannot be the person. And yet you know things you could not if you were not."

She stood behind him. "Why can't I be 'er?"

"You would not ask if you had seen her."

She began to rub his neck and shoulders. "Tell me about 'er."

He knew it was an unpardonable liberty, both her touch and her request, but the warmth and the shadowy darkness and the smells gave him a sense that ordinary rules had been suspended.

And her closeness.

"She was beauty beyond beauty. She moved like a spirit slipping the bonds of earth. She was light in my eyes and light in my arms. Each moment with her was molten gold, slipping away all the faster the harder I clutched to hold it. And with the stroke of twelve, the dream was broken and I fell back to earth. I do not expect you to understand."

he massaged his neck in silence while they stared into the fire. Her hands were rough and firm and knowing. He felt unfathomable[10] content. "You was so tall an' so 'andsome," she said from the darkness at his back. "When we danced, you 'eld me like a big dog with a egg in 'is mouth, like if you chose you could of crushed me in a second. Which you couldn't of, you know." And she gave his neck a teasing little slap. "But it was good to be treated fragile, even if I wasn't. You was so strong an' gentle. The music was playin' just for us, an' there was

colors everywhere, but I couldn't see nothin' but you. It was the best night I'll ever 'ave."

Her hands were still upon his shoulders. They waited in silence. Finally he spoke into the fire. "If you feel that way, try on the slipper."

She let her hands drop. "No. You'd 'ave to marry me, an' that ain't what you want."

He turned in the chair and took her hands. "If the slipper fits, I want you."

"No. You don't want the slipper to fit nobody."

"That is mad. Why do you think I am going through the whole kingdom on my knees to every woman who wants to try her foot at winning a prince?"

She smiled. "It's actually yer Lord Chamberlain 'oo is on 'is knees."

"Figuratively on my knees. Why am I doing it? Tell me."

She shrugged. "To prove that no one is fitting." He started to object, but she silenced him. "You don't know that, but it's true. If you found 'er, she might turn out to be real.

"You feel sorry for me, but I feel sorry for you. Our night was like a beautiful dream for me, too, but I can wake up an' get on with it. I've got me little kitchen an' me work and I can be 'appy. And if me stepmother someday needs to make a connection with a rich 'ouse, she'll clean me up an' marry me off to some stupid, ugly oaf of a merchant's son. And I'll be 'appy 'cause I'll keep me 'ouse tidy an' me kitchen cozy and afore I goes to sleep, I'll think a secret thought about me Prince. And I'll sleep smilin'.

"But I can see *you* in twenty years. You'll be King an' they'll 'ave married you off to someone or other 'oo you only see at dinnertime. An' you'll drink too much wine an' shed

---

10. **unfathomable:** more than can be measured.

Active Reading: EVALUATE

T Point out that the author uses the sentence fragment "And her closeness" as a single paragraph. Ask students why he chose to do this and what the fragment means. You may wish to use the following model:

Think-Aloud Model *It is unusual to find a sentence fragment like that just stuck in between two longer paragraphs. I have a feeling that the author wants to emphasize that the Prince was moved by the physical closeness of Ella. He is enjoying being this close to another human being. This sentence fragment tells me that he is probably attracted to Ella.*

**Critical Thinking:
HYPOTHESIZING**

U Have students interpret what Ella means when she says that the Prince "don't want the slipper to fit nobody." *(Possible response: She means that he is trying to find someone who doesn't exist; he is looking for a fantasy person, and no one can really be what he wishes.)*

Mini-Lesson: Speaking, Listening, and Viewing

PANTOMIME Explain to students that a pantomime is a performance without words. Point out that mimes tell a story by using only bodily movements, gestures, and facial expressions to convey both the events of the plot and the feelings of the characters.

Application Have students work alone or in pairs to pantomime an action from the story. Possibilities include the first woman's attempt to fit into the glass slipper, the Prince's escape and entry into the kitchen, and the way Ella describes walking on glass slippers.

Active Reading: CONNECT

V Encourage students to talk about unrealistic expectations they have had about a person or a situation. Have them tell whether they were disappointed once they discovered that their expectations were not realistic.

STRATEGIC READING FOR

Less-Proficient Readers

W Ask students what Ella predicts may happen when she tries on the slipper. *(It may not fit.)* Summarizing

Set a Purpose Ask students to read to the end of the selection to find out whether Ella's prediction comes true.

a tear for what might 'ave been. An' you could 'ave been a good King, but you won't be, 'cause you won't want to get down an' dirty yourself in what's real an' common. You'll just be thinkin' about yer dream Princess. It'll be sad, but it'll be better than if you found 'er an' married 'er an' discovered that 'er breath smelt bad in the mornin' just like real people."

He had sat down again as she talked. "What's wrong with wanting to live a dream?" he mused into the fire.

"In a dream, you got to play by its rules, an' there's more nightmares than sweet dreams in my experience. In real life, you got a chance to make yer own rules, especially if yer a prince to start off with." She stroked his hair. "Forget yer dream Princess. Be the King you can be. Think kindly of me now an' then, but don't let me 'old ya back. There's a beauty in what's real, too."

He sat silent a moment. She gave him a little push to get him moving. He stood and slowly moved to the door. "Don't forget this." She picked up the slipper, saw it was stained, and dipped it in a bucket of water and dried it on her skirts. "Good as new. Drink me a toast out of it now and agin. Onc't a year. No more."

He nodded, took it, and turned to the door. He put his hand on the latch, then leaned his head against the rough wood. "I have to know," he said.

She gave a sigh. "Are ya sure?"

"Yes. As sure as I am of anything." He turned and knelt to place the slipper before her.

She started to lift her foot, then set it down. "There's one thing you ought to know afore I try it on."

"And that is?"

She rolled her eyes up for a minute, then looked back to him. "It may not fit."

From his kneeling position, he slowly slumped down into a sprawl on the floor. He cradled his head in his hands. "What are you doing to me?"

"Just tryin' to be honest with ya."

"But you knew our last words. It *must* have been you."

"Everybody in the kingdom knows your last words."

"That's impossible! I told no one but my father. He would never have repeated it to anyone."

"Yer sure nobody could 'ave over'eard?"

"There was no one else there!"

he counted off on her fingers. "Nobody 'cept for six guards, three table servants, two butlers an' one old falconer 'oo pretended 'e needed the King's advice about where to tie the pigeons for the next 'unt just so's 'e could 'ear the story for 'isself. Twelve people. Eleven versions of the story was all over the kingdom within twenty-four hours, an' the twelfth was a day late only 'cause one of the guards had laryngitis."

The Prince knit his brow. "I never noticed them."

She nodded. "You wouldn't 'ave paid them much mind."

"And that is how you knew what I said."

"No, I knew 'cause I was there. I'm just sayin' you 'aven't been quite as secret as you thought."

"Then why will the slipper not fit you?"

"Might not fit," she corrected. "Because it

Mini-Lesson 🧩 Literary Concepts

REVIEWING HUMOR Storytellers often add humor to their tales. A common technique for injecting humor is the use of exaggeration. Some storytellers use many details in a passage to give the impression of exaggeration, even when they are telling the truth.

Application Ask students to read the highlighted passage on this page and to identify the details Ella uses to describe the scene. Ask them how the contrast between her version and the Prince's version adds to the humor of the story.

was got by magic. See, the person I mentioned 'oo got me me gown and all was me fairy godmother. She did the coach out of a punkin an' the 'orses out o' mice an' so on. So I don't know if me foot really fit in that glass shoe or if that was more of 'er doin'."

He rose from the floor and stood before her, looking deep into her eyes. He spoke softly.

"That is the most ridiculous story I have ever heard."

She nodded. "I guess I'd 'ave to agree with ya. Bein' true is no excuse for bein' ridiculous."

He laughed. "But I do not care." He thought a moment. "I don't care. I have felt more in the last hour with you than I have felt in all the rest of my life. Except for one night. And I can live with that one night as a golden, receding memory if I know that I can have every day with you. I love you, Cinderella."

> "I have felt more in the last hour with you than I have felt in all the rest of my life."

She was troubled even as she felt the stirring of hope. "I don't like that name."

"But it is a part of your life, and I must have it. I want to know all of you." He smiled with a contentment he had never known. "Marry me, Cinderella."

She burst into tears then. "No, no! It can't be. Look at me! Listen to me!"

"That's all I want to do. That and hold you forever." He longed to touch her, but he waited.

She dried her tears on a sleeve and tried to laugh, but it was a desperate sort of attempt. "I'll say yes, 'cause there's no way I could say no." He stepped toward her. "But first—I'll try on the slipper."

He stepped away from her, and his brow was furrowed. "You don't have to do that. I don't care."

"Not now, maybe. But in five years or ten years, you'd start regrettin' it. An' regret is the only thing that love can't cure. So gimme that slipper. What's the worst that could 'appen?"

Hollow-eyed, he looked at her. "It might fit," he whispered.

She started at that but looked him straight in the face and said, "Give it to me."

He set the slipper in front of her, then straightened. She touched her hand to his face and knelt to the fitting.

They stood, then, face to face. And there was so much hope and joy and fear and pain that neither one could have said which of them was feeling what.

"Look," she said. He tried not to, but he couldn't help it.

The slipper didn't fit.

It didn't near fit.

He raised his eyes to hers and saw the hope in them change to a terrible fear.

"It isn't fitting," he said. "It is not fitting." She cringed. The Wicked Prince was out for good.

"It isn't fitting that a Princess dance on her wedding night in shoes that do not fit her."

Her face was crumpling. He could do nothing but go on.

"I shall have to summon the royal glass blower."

Her eyes flashed the question at him.

695

Critical Thinking: ANALYZING

X Ask students why they think the Prince believes the worst thing that can happen is that the shoe will fit. *(Possible response: By now he is beginning to understand that it is not the person that needs to fit the shoe— it is the shoe that needs to fit the person. He doesn't want it to fit because then he must face the reality of the situation.)*

Active Reading: CLARIFY

Y Point out that just before Ella steps into the slipper, there is much "hope and joy and fear and pain" between her and the Prince. Ask students to what each of these emotions refers. *(Possible responses: Ella's hope that the shoe will fit and the Prince will love her as she loves him; the Prince's joy in realizing that no matter what, he loves Ella; Ella's fear of having her hopes dashed; Ella's pain in realizing the possibility of rejection.)*

Critical Thinking: HYPOTHESIZING

Z Have students hypothesize about what might have happened had the slipper fit. *(Possible responses: Both Ella and the Prince might have been relieved to have the slipper fit because then the Prince would have been sure that Ella was the one he danced with at the ball. The outcome wouldn't have been any different because the Prince ceases to care whether Ella was the woman at the ball—he loves her for herself.)*

Gifted and Talented Students

AA Ask students to identify the lesson presented in "The Fitting of the Slipper" that can be applied to real life. *(Possible responses: Romantic expectations have nothing to do with reality; happiness comes from being true to oneself; beauty lies within; first impressions are not always right; things that appear to be flawless, such as the slipper, may be boring and without character.)*

Critical Thinking:
SYNTHESIZING

BB Remind students that the usual ending of a fairy tale is "And they lived happily ever after." Ask students how the last sentence in this story compares with the traditional ending. Elicit from them what they think is the importance of smashing the glass slipper. *(Possible response: The glass slipper represents flawless perfection. By taking steps together and smashing the glass slipper, the couple are not being taken in by the romance that the glass slipper represented. This ending is more realistic than the traditional ending but still suggests that the couple will live happily together.)*

STRATEGIC READING FOR

Less-Proficient Readers

CC Ask students what happens when Ella tries on the glass slipper. *(It doesn't fit.)* **Restating**

Copyright © Pierre Pratt.

Mini-Lesson: Speaking, **Listening, and Viewing**

DRAMATIC SCENE Explain to students that in contemporary films, the story often ends with a suggestion about what might happen next. This allows filmmakers to continue the narrative in a sequel. Point out that although this story has the typical happy ending, there is a hint of adjustments to come in the highlighted paragraph on page 697: Ella will have to adjust to life in the royal court.

Application Have students work in groups to write and perform a sequel scene in which Ella is introduced to the Prince's parents. Remind students that Ella's dialogue must be written in her dialect, not in the formal English used by the Prince and his parents. Characters must include Ella, the Prince, the King, and the Queen. Students may include other characters, such as a court jester, the Lord Chamberlain, or Ella's stepmother. If possible, have students videotape their performances.

"To make you shoes that fit. The shoe must fit the foot. It's madness to try to make the foot fit the shoe."

She kicked it off and stepped close, and they stood a moment, savoring together the bittersweet of the last instant of aloneness they would ever know.

Then he swept her up into his arms, so strong yet gentle, as if he feared to crush her, which he couldn't have.

And the first step of all the many they took together smashed the glass slipper past all fitting. ❖

1. Which version of the Cinderella story do you like better, the traditional version or this one? Why? Write your thoughts in your notebook. *(Responses will vary.)*

2. By the end of the story, what do you think the night of the ball symbolizes for the Prince? *(Possible response: one special night that can't be repeated every day)*

3. Why do you think the Prince didn't notice that the servants were nearby when he told his father about his encounter at the ball? *(Possible response: He was used to ignoring the servants and not taking them seriously as human beings.)*

4. Do you agree with the Prince when he says, "It's madness to try to make the foot fit the shoe"? Explain. *(Possible response: yes, because you experience only unhappiness when you try to force reality to fit an unrealistic dream)*

WILLIAM J. BROOKE

1946–

Born in Washington, D.C., William J. Brooke now lives in New York City, where he and his wife work as singers and actors. "Theater has always been my first love," he says. Brooke acted extensively in high school and college. In New York, he has performed leading roles with all the major Gilbert and Sullivan companies. Brooke has also sung in operas and has written musical reviews that have been performed off-Broadway and in theaters in the United States and Canada.

Brooke says he approaches his writing with the instincts of an actor and singer: "The dialogue must be speakable, and the prose must be rhythmic and musical. I enjoy creating character 'business'—the gestures or ways of moving that I would use if playing the characters on stage—and incorporating it in the story."

OTHER WORKS *Untold Tales, A Brush with Magic*

THE FITTING OF THE SLIPPER **697**

COMPREHENSION CHECK
1. How does the Prince find Ella? *(by accident when he opens a door)*
2. Who is the "Wicked Prince"? *(another side to the Prince that he feels lives inside him)*
3. Why does Ella take out a long needle while she is talking to the Prince? *(to remove his splinter)*
4. What happens when Ella tries on the glass slipper? *(It doesn't fit.)*

Dramatize a Tale Divide the class into teams and suggest that team members devise a fair procedure for determining who will work as writers, actors, directors, and members of the stage crew. Help students determine how to divide the tales into scenes for their dramatization by making the following suggestions:

"Prometheus"

Scene 1: The Disagreement (Zeus and Prometheus disagree about giving fire to humans.)

Scene 2: The Delivery (Prometheus delivers fire to humans.)

Scene 3: The Wrath of Zeus (Zeus chains Prometheus to the mountaintop.)

"The People Could Fly"

Scene 1: The Journey (Africans are taken from Africa and transported by ship to America.)

Scene 2: The Field (Sarah, Toby, and others work in the field and are abused by the Overseer.)

Scene 3: The Flight (Flying slaves take off.)

"The Fitting of the Slipper"

Scene 1: The House (The Prince tries the slipper on Ella's stepsister.)

Scene 2: The Escape (The Prince runs out through the wrong door.)

Scene 3: The Meeting (Ella and the Prince meet and talk.)

Scene 4: If the Shoe Fits (The Prince tries the slipper on Ella; they decide to marry.)

Rubric

3 Full Accomplishment Students work cooperatively to dramatize one of the folk tales. The presentation is well organized and flows from one scene to another.

2 Substantial Accomplishment Students work cooperatively to present a dramatization, but it is somewhat disorganized in terms of presenting the events in the story.

1 Little or Partial Accomplishment Students have difficulty working cooperatively and presenting a coherent dramatization.

RESPONDING
OPTIONS

LITERATURE CONNECTION PROJECT 1 Multimodal Activity

Dramatize a Tale Perform as a play one of the tales you just read. Begin by listing the characters, dividing the tale into scenes, and choosing parts. To involve as many students as possible, choose a different cast for each scene. Then form teams to adapt the tale into a script and to work on costumes, sets, music, and props. Refer to these suggestions as you carry out this project.

Writers Identify the cast of characters and, if necessary, ask your teacher how to structure the story into scenes. List the events in outline form before writing a script for the tale. Decide if you will need a narrator to comment on events and to link the scenes together.

Actors After memorizing your part, work on bringing your character to life. Emphasize the words that you consider important. Use gestures, facial expressions, and movements and vary the pitch and volume of your voice to convey the character's qualities, ideas, and feelings.

Stage crew (set/costumes/props/music) Skim the script and list the costumes and props you will need. Decide what music would enhance the mood, such as African vocal or instrumental music or spirituals for "The People Could Fly."

SOCIAL STUDIES CONNECTION PROJECT 2 Multimodal Activity

Explore the past Tales such as "The People Could Fly" expressed the wishes of slaves who had only their imaginations to set them free. Other slaves, however, actually were able to run away while in the fields or under cover of darkness, sometimes using code words along the way, such as "Come fly away!"

Find out more about how slaves actually escaped from slavery. Research the secret network of escape routes called the Underground Railroad. First, brainstorm questions about the topic and record them in a web like the one shown. Use books, encyclopedias, and computer databases to find out details. Then present your findings in a group oral report.

Why was it called that?

What was it?

When was it in operation?

What were the risks?

The Underground Railroad

How was it organized?

Where/How did slaves travel?

Who was involved?

How many slaves escaped?

Explore the Past Have students work in small groups. Have them assign roles of researchers, elaborator, recorder, and integrator. Suggest that the recorder prepare a web on poster paper and then fill in data as the researchers gather them. Encourage students to use their web as a graphic aid during their oral presentation.

Rubric

3 Full Accomplishment Students gather and report pertinent information. The presentation is clear and concise, and the main ideas are supported by relevant details.

2 Substantial Accomplishment Students research and write a report but have some difficulty presenting it orally.

1 Little or Partial Accomplishment Students have difficulty translating their research into an oral report; their main ideas are not supported by relevant details.

Investigate Fire Divide the class into three groups. Have one group conduct interviews with people who work with fire, a second group research the chemical and physical aspects of fire, and a third group research the wide variety of manufacturing processes that require the use of fire. When students have completed their research, assign a facilitator in each group to help decide how the group will present its findings in a coherent display. Provide needed supplies, such as poster paper, markers, and video playback equipment.

Rubric

3 Full Accomplishment Students gather ample information on fire and translate it into a coherent visual display.

2 Substantial Accomplishment Students conduct adequate research but have difficulty determining the best way to present and display their findings.

1 Little or Partial Accomplishment Students are unable to translate their research into a coherent presentation for display.

SCIENCE CONNECTION PROJECT 3 Multimodal Activity

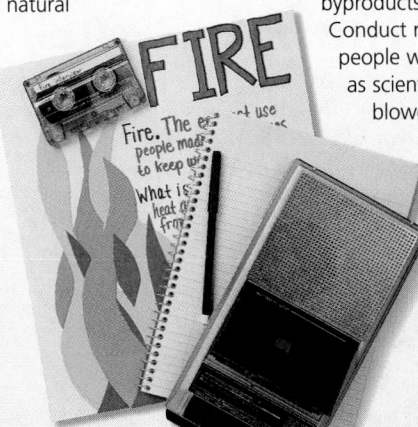

Investigate fire Myths, such as "Prometheus," attempted to explain the origin of mysterious natural forces, such as fire. Myths from nearly every culture contain some account of how fire first came to humans. Primitive peoples regarded fire as "a gift from the gods" because it was essential for survival. Modern people explain the mystery of fire scientifically.

Find out more about fire. What are its elements and properties? How is it produced? What are its byproducts? How is it controlled? Conduct research and interviews with people who study or work with fire, such as scientists, firefighters, welders, glass blowers, and mill or refinery workers. Construct a display featuring pictures, charts, slides, videos, or other graphics, that show the properties, uses, and dangers of fire.

ACROSS CULTURES MINI-PROJECTS   Multimodal Activities

Create a graphic Choose a pair of characters, one character from the tales you've just read and one from Unit One. For example, you might choose Toby and Malcolm X, Cinderella and Dolores, or the Prince and Jimmy Valentine. Compare the two characters' similarities and differences. Draw a Venn diagram like the one shown. In the overlapping area, list the qualities that the characters have in common. Outside this area, list the qualities that are unique to each character.

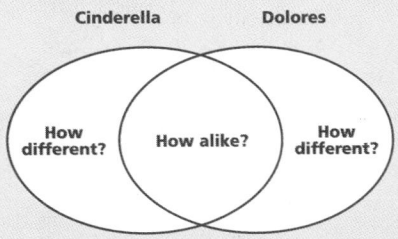

Cinderella   Dolores

How different?   How alike?   How different?

Watch a video View Walt Disney's *Cinderella* and then compare it with "The Fitting of the Slipper" and other versions of "Cinderella" that you have read or have seen. How is the heroine portrayed in each version? What assumptions or attitudes does Brooke's version challenge? Discuss your comparisons with your classmates.

Extended Social Studies Reading

MORE ABOUT THE CULTURES

- *The Black Americans: A History in Their Own Words* by Milton Meltzer
- *Now Is Your Time! The African-American Struggle for Freedom* by Walter Dean Myers
- *The Golden Days of Greece* by Olivia E. Coolidge

LINKS TO UNIT ONE **699**

Create a Graphic Have the class compile a list of characters from which students can choose pairs for comparison. Then suggest that individual students list all of the character traits they can for each character they want to compare. Have them fit those traits into the Venn diagram.

Watch a Video Suggest that students create a chart to help them answer each of the questions posed. For example, after students have watched the video, have them list the characteristics of Cinderella. Then have them list Ella's characteristics.

OVERVIEW

Objectives

- To understand and appreciate two fables, two folk tales, and a myth about life's lessons
- To appreciate the cultures of Greece, Japan, and Russia
- To extend understanding of the selections through a variety of multimodal and cross-curricular activities

Skills

READING SKILLS/ STRATEGIES
- Connecting

THE WRITER'S STYLE
- Chronological order

GRAMMAR
- Subject-verb agreement

LITERARY CONCEPTS
- Imagery

SPELLING
- Doubling final consonants

SPEAKING, LISTENING, AND VIEWING
- Storytelling
- Readers Theater

Cross-Curricular Connections

SOCIAL STUDIES
- Needs of the elderly

SCIENCE
- Constellations
- Ducks
- The sun

Reading Pathways

- Select one or several students to read each tale aloud to the entire class or to small groups of students. Assign this reading in advance so that the readers can incorporate into their presentations some of the techniques used by professional storytellers. Have students listen carefully to the tales without following along in their texts.
- Read each tale aloud to the class, pausing at key points to discuss how elements of the tale inform students about the customs of the culture. Have students compare these customs with those of their own culture. Have them record their responses and observations in their notebooks.
- After students have read the tales once, have them read each tale again to identify such structural elements as main characters, minor characters, conflict, setting, and plot. Then ask students to identify similarities and differences between these tales and the selections in the related unit. For example, they can compare the lesson learned by Ebenezer Scrooge in *A Christmas Carol* and that learned by Gombei in "Gombei and the Wild Ducks."

LINKS TO UNIT TWO

Life's Lessons

Activating Prior Knowledge

The characters you read about in Unit Two—for example, Casey, Roger, and Ebenezer Scrooge—all learn lessons through mistakes and failures. Similarly, the characters in the tales you are about to read learn some of life's hard lessons.

Building Background

GREECE

The Wolf in Sheep's Clothing
The Travelers and the Purse

by Aesop

These fables are attributed to Aesop, a Greek slave who lived around the sixth century B.C. Aesop's fables are brief stories that convey a lesson about life and that usually conclude with a moral that offers useful advice. Some of the fables probably are ancient stories that Aesop retold, popularized, and passed down to succeeding generations. In many fables, animal characters—such as the tortoise and the hare—represent human qualities.

Building Background

GREECE

Phaëthon

retold by Moira Kerr and John Bennett

Greek myths are stories about gods, goddesses, and heroes. These stories attempt to explain natural events or to answer basic questions about the world. In this myth, one of the characters is Apollo, the god of the sun, music, and healing. This myth explores several issues important to the ancient Greeks, such as the problem of human limitations.

700   UNIT SIX: THE ORAL TRADITION

PRINT AND MEDIA RESOURCES

UNIT SIX RESOURCE BOOK
Strategic Reading: Literature, p. 11
Vocabulary SkillBuilder, p. 14
Reading SkillBuilder, p. 12
Spelling SkillBuilder, p. 13

GRAMMAR MINI-LESSONS
Transparencies, pp. 3–6
Copymasters, pp. 3–6

WRITING MINI-LESSONS
Transparencies, p. 33

ACCESS FOR STUDENTS ACQUIRING ENGLISH
Selection Summaries
Reading and Writing Support

FORMAL ASSESSMENT
Selection Test, pp. 119–120
 Test Generator

📼 **AUDIO LIBRARY**
See Reference Card

💻 **INTERNET RESOURCES**
McDougal Littell Literature Center at http://www.hmco.com /mcdougal/lit

---

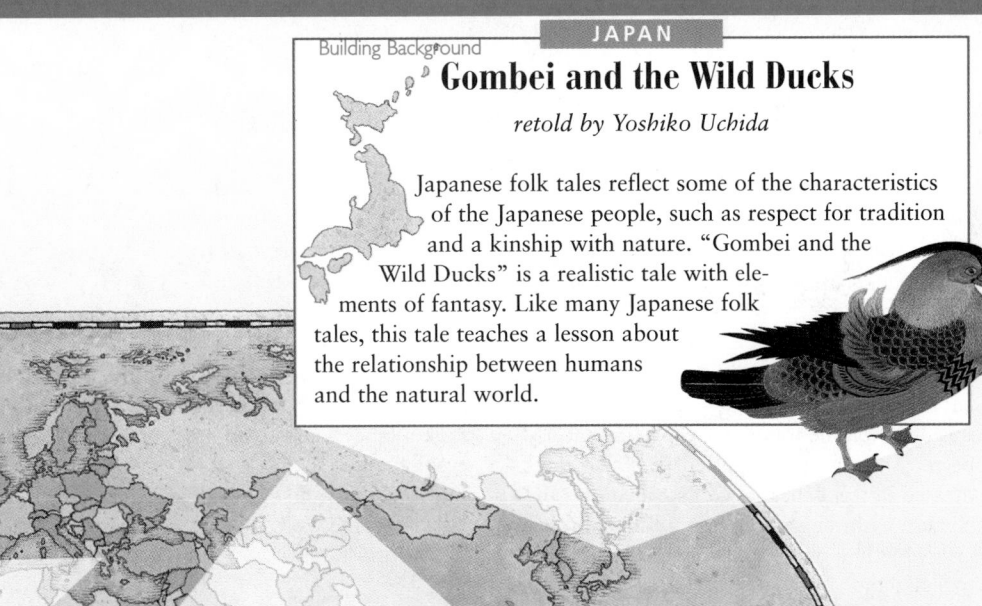

Building Background

Gombei and the Wild Ducks

retold by Yoshiko Uchida

Japanese folk tales reflect some of the characteristics of the Japanese people, such as respect for tradition and a kinship with nature. "Gombei and the Wild Ducks" is a realistic tale with elements of fantasy. Like many Japanese folk tales, this tale teaches a lesson about the relationship between humans and the natural world.

SUMMARY

The Wolf in Sheep's Clothing This fable tells of a wolf who slips into a pasture disguised as a sheep and carries off a lamb. When the wolf tries his trick again, a shepherd mistakes him for a sheep and slaughters him. The moral: Evildoers are often harmed by their own tricks.

The Travelers and the Purse A man finds a well-filled purse and refuses to share it with his traveling companion—until an armed mob shouting "Stop, thief!" bears down on him. *Suddenly* he is anxious to share responsibility for the purse, but his traveling mate declines. The moral: Don't expect to share your misfortune unless you are also willing to share your good fortune.

Building Background

The Old Grandfather and His Little Grandson

retold by Leo Tolstoy

A Russian aristocrat, Leo Tolstoy came to regard peasants as sources of wisdom. He retold many of the tales that he first heard in peasants' huts. For centuries in Russia, the peasants had farmed the land as serfs, or slaves. In 1861, the serfs were freed. This tale tells how a peasant couple learns a powerful lesson.

Setting a Purpose
AS YOU READ . . .

Think about the lessons that the tales teach.

Decide which lessons are most relevant today.

Consider what the lessons reveal about the values of the culture.

LINKS TO UNIT TWO **701**

WORDS TO KNOW

abode (ə-bōd´) *n.* a home (p. 707)
acknowledge (ăk-nŏl´ĭj) *v.* to recognize the status or rights of (p. 707)

dreary (drîr´ē) *adj.* gloomy; cheerless; depressing (p. 710)
plummet (plŭm´ĭt) *v.* to fall suddenly (p. 711)

TWO FABLES BY AESOP

Ⓘ THE *Wolf* IN SHEEP'S CLOTHING

A certain wolf could not get enough to eat because of the watchfulness of the shepherds. But one night he found a sheep skin that had been cast aside and forgotten. The next day, dressed in the skin, the wolf strolled into the pasture with the sheep. Soon a little lamb was following him about and was quickly led away

Ⓐ to slaughter.

That evening the wolf entered the fold with the flock. But it happened that the shepherd took a fancy for mutton broth that very evening and, picking up a knife, went to the fold. There the first he laid hands on and killed was the wolf. ❖

THE EVILDOER OFTEN COMES TO HARM THROUGH HIS OWN DECEIT.

Copyright © Charles Santore.

Mini-Lesson: Speaking, Listening, and Viewing

STORYTELLING Explain to students that when they tell or retell a story, they make it their own by using their own style of presentation. Point out that vocal intonation, hand and facial gestures, and pacing are techniques that storytellers develop and practice. Tell them that every time a story is retold, it changes slightly to reflect the personality of the speaker.

Application Have students work in groups. Ask two members of each group to retell each of Aesop's fables. Tell the other group members to jot down the ways the fable changes as it is told by a new storyteller. Then invite two more group members to retell the fables. Ask students to evaluate how the fables change with each retelling.

Illustration Copyright © 1988 Robert Rayevsky. From dedication page of *Belling the Cat and Other Aesop's Fables* by Tom Paxton. By permission of Morrow Junior Books, a division of William Morrow and Company, Inc.

THE TRAVELERS AND THE PURSE

Literary Links

A Have students compare how unsuspecting characters are lured into a trap in this fable and in "Hollywood and the Pits." Invite students to write a moral that could apply to both stories. *(Possible response: In the fable, a lamb is lured to its death by a wolf. In "Hollywood and the Pits," predators are lured to their death by other animals that are trapped in the tar pits. A moral might be "Keep your eyes open" or "Things are not always what they seem.")*

Two men were traveling in company along the road when one of them picked up a well-filled purse.

"How lucky I am!" he said. "I have found a purse. Judging by its weight it must be full of gold."

"Do not say '*I* have found a purse,'" said his companion. "Say rather '*We* have found a purse' and 'How lucky *we* are.' Travelers ought to share alike the fortunes or misfortunes of the road."

"No, no," replied the other angrily. "*I* found

it and *I* am going to keep it."

Just then they heard a shout of "Stop, thief!" and looking around saw a mob of people armed with clubs coming down the road.

The man who had found the purse fell into a panic.

"We are lost if they find the purse on us," he cried.

"No, no," replied the other. "You would not say 'we' before, so now stick to your 'I.' Say '*I* am lost.'" ❖

B

WE CANNOT EXPECT ANYONE TO SHARE OUR MISFORTUNES UNLESS WE ARE WILLING TO SHARE OUR GOOD FORTUNE ALSO.

AESOP

Little is known about Aesop, the world's most famous writer of fables. Some historians think he may have been an African slave who worked on Samos, an island off eastern Greece. The number of fables he actually wrote also remains a mystery.

One account of Aesop's life is as eventful as one of his fables. According to this story, Aesop's second master granted him his freedom in appreciation of his wit. After telling stories throughout Greece and Egypt, Aesop was appointed an ambassador by King

620-560 B.C.

Croesus. On diplomatic missions, Aesop often told fables to advise, instruct, or clinch an argument. Most of the time, his skill with words enabled him to wriggle out of trouble. His luck, however, ran out in Delphi, where he was sent to distribute money due to the citizens. Aesop found them so greedy that he returned the money to Croesus instead.

As Aesop prepared to leave Delphi, someone hid a golden bowl in his baggage. Aesop was arrested for theft, condemned by the court, and pushed off a cliff.

STRATEGIC READING FOR
Less-Proficient Readers

B Ask students to restate the morals of the fables in their own words. *(When you set out to deceive, you lose. You have to share both the good and the bad.)*
Finding the Main Idea

From Personal Response to Critical Analysis

1. Do you think that the morals of Aesop's fables are universally true? Why or why not? Write your ideas in your notebook. *(Responses will vary.)*
2. For what purpose do you think Aesop told the fables? *(Possible responses: to deliver messages about what he considered universal truths; to describe human behavior and its consequences)*
3. Do you think that someone should share money if he or she finds it while with another person? *(Possible response: Yes, if the money is found while in the company of another, it should be shared equally.)*

COMPREHENSION CHECK

1. Why does the wolf dress in sheep's clothing? *(to get close to the sheep and eat them)*
2. What eventually happens to the wolf? *(He is mistaken for a sheep and is slaughtered by the shepherd.)*
3. Why does the traveler's companion criticize his friend? *(because the friend doesn't want to share the money he found)*
4. Why are the people armed with clubs? *(because they are going after a thief)*
5. Why does the companion urge his friend to "stick to your 'I'"? *(because he used "I" when he wanted to keep the money but uses "we" when he wants to share his bad luck)*

Hermit by Mikhail Vasilievich Nesterov

Hermit is among the first pieces Mikhail Vasilievich Nesterov painted in a series that shows people, such as hermits and monks, who live a life of solitude. Nestorov is famous for his rich, poetic style and for his ability to capture a feeling on canvas.

Reading the Art *What does this painting suggest about the old man?*

CUSTOMIZING FOR

Students Acquiring English

(I) Call students' attention to the word *toothless,* and invite them to tell what the suffix *-less* means. *(without)*

STRATEGIC READING FOR

Less-Proficient Readers

Set a Purpose Have students read to find out how the way in which the grandfather is treated changes.

Critical Thinking:
SPECULATING

Ⓐ Ask students why they think the grandfather doesn't speak up when he is treated poorly. *(Possible responses: He may feel a sense of shame, which keeps him from speaking; he wants to avoid a battle with his son and daughter-in-law.)*

THE OLD
GRANDFATHER
AND HIS LITTLE
GRANDSON

Hermit (1888), Mikhail Vasilievich Nesterov. Oil on canvas, 91 ¥ 84 cm. The State Russian Museum, St. Petersburg, Russia.

704 UNIT SIX: THE ORAL TRADITION

Mini-Lesson **The Writer's Style**

CHRONOLOGICAL ORDER Explain that writers use transitional words that show time—such as *before, last, yesterday, one day, after, next, later,* and *then*—to indicate the order of events in a selection.

Application Ask students to look for transitional words that show time in "The Grandfather and His Little Grandson." Have them reread the story and mentally remove these words. Then have them explain how the inclusion of the transitional words helps clarify the sequence of events in the story.

Reteaching/Reinforcement
• Writing Handbook, anthology p. 817
• *Writing Mini-Lessons* transparencies, p. 33

The Writer's Craft

Using Transitions, pp. 271–272

BY LEO TOLSTOY

The grandfather had become very old. His legs would not carry him, his eyes could not see, his ears could not hear, and he was toothless. When he ate, bits of food sometimes dropped out of his mouth. His son and his son's wife no longer allowed him to eat with them at the table. He had to eat his meals in the corner near the stove.

One day they gave him his food in a bowl. He tried to move the bowl closer; it fell to the floor and broke. His daughter-in-law scolded him. She told him that he spoiled everything in the house and broke their dishes, and she said that from now on he would get his food in a wooden dish. The old man sighed and said nothing.

A few days later, the old man's son and his wife were sitting in their hut, resting and watching their little boy playing on the floor. They saw him putting together something out of small pieces of wood. His father asked him, "What are you making, Misha?"

The little grandson said, "I'm making a wooden bucket. When you and Mamma get old, I'll feed you out of this wooden dish."

The young peasant and his wife looked at each other, and tears filled their eyes. They were ashamed because they had treated the old grandfather so meanly, and from that day they again let the old man eat with them at the table and took better care of him. ❖

LEO TOLSTOY

1828–1910

The most famous of Russian writers, Count Leo Tolstoy is best known for two masterpieces: *War and Peace* tells of Russia during Napoleon's invasion in 1812, and *Anna Karenina* depicts a woman who is destroyed by love.

Born to a wealthy family in Russia, Tolstoy was orphaned at the age of nine. He was raised by relatives and educated by tutors. He married in 1862, and at first his married life was happy. Soon, however, Tolstoy felt torn between his responsibilities as a landowner and his desire to live a simple, moral life. He no longer believed aristocrats should have as much

land, money, and power as he had. He experienced a religious conversion that changed his life. He tried to give away his wealth and live like a peasant, making his own shoes and shirts and praising the virtues of physical labor.

At the age of 82, Tolstoy turned over his entire estate to his family and secretly ran away, supposedly seeking freedom from worldly concerns. He died a few days later at a railroad station in a small town.

OTHER WORKS *Great Short Works of Leo Tolstoy; The Death of Ivan Ilyich; Childhood, Boyhood, and Youth*

SUMMARY

The Old Grandfather and His Little Grandson In this simply told Russian tale, a grandfather lives with his son and daughter-in-law. The old man is blind, deaf, toothless, and unable to walk. The couple banish him from the supper table for dribbling food and force him to eat from a wooden bowl after he breaks a dish. One day the son and his wife see their little boy making a wooden bucket. He tells his parents, "When you and Mamma get old, I'll feed you out of this wooden dish." Ashamed, the couple allow the grandfather back at the table and begin treating him humanely.

STRATEGIC READING FOR
Less-Proficient Readers

B Have students describe how the way in which the grandfather is treated changes. *(At first, he is ill-treated and is made to eat in the corner from a wooden dish. Later, he is invited to eat with the family and is better cared for.)* **Comparing and Contrasting**

Literary Links

C Ask students to compare the lesson learned by the son and his wife with the one learned by Ebenezer Scrooge in *A Christmas Carol*. Ask students what is similar about the way the son, his wife, and Ebenezer Scrooge learn their lesson. *(Possible response: All the characters learn to treat people with greater kindness. The characters learn their lesson by "seeing" a bleak future for themselves if they don't mend their ways.)*

From Personal Response to Critical Analysis

1. What are your thoughts about this story? Jot down your ideas in your notebook. *(Responses will vary.)*
2. Why do you think the son and his wife put the grandfather in the corner? *(Possible responses: The grandfather is disrupting their orderly life; he is helpless, and they are frustrated by that; his habits make them both feel uncomfortable.)*
3. What other title do you think would be appropriate for this story? *(Possible response: "A Son Learns a Lesson.")*

COMPREHENSION CHECK

1. Who are the characters in this story? *(the son, his wife, the grandfather, and the little grandson)*
2. Why is the grandfather no longer allowed to eat at the table? *(He drops food from his mouth while eating.)*
3. What do the son and his wife do about the grandfather's behavior? *(They make him sit in a corner and eat from a wooden dish.)*
4. What does the grandson do that changes the behavior of the son and his wife? *(He makes a wooden dish for his parents to eat from when they get old.)*

The Fall of Phaëthon by Peter Paul Rubens Flemish painter Peter Paul Rubens (1577–1640) was also a diplomat. His diplomatic travels to Spain and Italy allowed him to study the works of other artists such as Titian, Carracci, and Caravaggio. Rubens's paintings often are scenes depicting religious or mythical events. He is noted for his ability to create rich, sensual surfaces.

Reading the Art *What adjectives would you use to describe this painting?*

STRATEGIC READING FOR
Less-Proficient Readers

Set a Purpose Ask students to read to find out what happens to Phaëthon when he rides his father's chariot.

Literary Concept:
FIGURATIVE LANGUAGE

A Remind students that similes and metaphors are two kinds of figurative language. Tell them that a simile is a comparison using *like* or *as* and that a metaphor compares two things directly, without using *like* or *as*. Ask students which type of comparison is used to describe the columns of Apollo's house. *(a simile)* Then ask them to what the columns are compared. *(fire)*

CUSTOMIZING FOR
Multiple Learning Styles

Linguistic Learners Ask students to write a poem that tells the story of Phaëthon and Apollo. Remind them to use highly descriptive words and to include the main ideas of the story.

EDITOR'S NOTE
With the permission of the author or copyright holder, potentially offensive material has been deleted from the selection.

PHAËTHON

The Fall of Phaethon (about 1637), Peter Paul Rubens. Oil sketch on wood, The Granger Collection, New York.

RETOLD BY MOIRA KERR AND JOHN BENNETT

One day the fair youth Phaëthon,[1] whose father was the sun god, Apollo, was taunted about his parentage by Epaphus,[2] a youth of the same age whose father was the mighty Zeus.

Stung with shame, Phaëthon reported the insults to his mother, Clymene.[3]

"I am unable to answer them. If my father is really a god, as you have told me, give me proof of my noble birth, and let me take my place in heaven."

Clymene was moved.

"It would not take you long to visit your father's dwelling place. If you wish to do so, go and question the sun himself, for Apollo is indeed your father."

Apollo's <u>abode</u> was a lofty palace of glittering gold and bronze. Its towering columns, supporting a roof of polished ivory, shone like fire. Its double doors reflected the light from their silver surfaces.

After climbing the steep approach, Clymene's son was ushered into the presence of his father, who was dressed in a purple robe and was sitting on a throne of shining emeralds. But Phaëthon could not approach too close, for he could not bear the blinding light.

"What do you want in this citadel,[4] Phaëthon, my son? Son, I call you, for you are one whom any parent would be proud to <u>acknowledge</u>."

"To prove that I am indeed your son, give me evidence."

"To remove any doubt from your mind, Phaëthon, make any request you wish, and you shall have it from me."

Instantly the lad asked to be allowed for one day to drive his father's sun chariot across the sky.

The words were scarcely spoken when Apollo regretted his oath. A mortal may, perhaps, break his word, but not so a god who had sworn by the waters of the Styx.[5] Apollo knew that the request meant death for a mortal, and he used every argument to dissuade his son from a venture that was suicide.

"You cannot possibly keep the horses under control. I, a god, can scarcely manage them. Even Zeus himself couldn't drive the chariot. The heavens are dangerous. You will have to keep to the path, past the horns of the hostile Bull, past the Thracian Archer and the paws of the raging Lion, past the Scorpion's cruel pincers and the clutching claws of the Crab.[6] Release me from my promise. Ask anything else and I shall grant it."

But Phaëthon, full of confidence, would not change his mind, and the reluctant Apollo had the swift Hours[7] yoke his team, lead the four fire-breathing steeds from the stable, and fasten on the jingling harness.

No sooner had the proud youth leaped into the chariot and taken the reins in his hands than the horses knew they had not the firm

---

1. **Phaëthon** (fā′ə-thŏn′).
2. **Epaphus** (ĕp′ə-fəs): in Greek mythology, the son of Zeus and the mortal woman Io.
3. **Clymene** (klĭm′ə-nē).
4. **citadel:** a fortress.
5. **Styx** (stĭks): in Greek mythology, the river around Hades, which is the kingdom of the dead. When the dead enter Hades, a ferry takes them across the river.
6. **Bull . . . Crab:** the constellations known as Taurus (the Bull), Sagittarius (the Thracian Archer), Leo (the Lion), Scorpio (the Scorpion), and Cancer (the Crab).
7. **Hours:** servants of Apollo.

WORDS TO KNOW	**abode** (ə-bōd′) *n.* a home
	acknowledge (ăk-nŏl′ĭj) *v.* to recognize the status or rights of

707

Mini-Lesson: Speaking, Listening, and Viewing

READERS THEATER Explain to students that Readers Theater is a performance that requires no props, no costumes, and no memorization—the performers read their parts while sitting on chairs before an audience. Point out that participating in Readers Theater can help students deepen their understanding of a story.

Application Have students work together to prepare and perform a Readers Theater version of "Phaëthon." Divide the story into brief scenes, and assign small groups to write a script. Encourage groups either to use a narrator for expository parts or to turn the exposition into dialogue. You may wish to assign one group to direct and record the performance.

hands of their master to guide them. Feeling their burden was too light, off they raced, out of control. The lad was panic-stricken. He did not know the path, he did not even know the names of the horses, and he was not able to manage the horses, even had he known. He could only cling helplessly to the sides of the swaying chariot as it plunged hither and thither through the sky.

For the first time, the cold stars of the Northern Plough grew hot, and the Serpent[8] which lay close to the icy pole was roused to fury as it sweltered in the heat. Phaëthon's terror mounted as he sighted the Scorpion and the other monstrous beasts sprawling over the face of the high heavens. Then the horses went plunging downward towards the earth. The heat of the sun's rays seared[9] the ground, destroying vegetation and drying up rivers and seas. Great cities perished, and whole nations were reduced to ashes. So close did the chariot come to Africa that Libya became a desert. . . .

Everywhere the ground gaped open, and great beams of light descended even to Tartarus,[10] frightening the king of the underworld and his queen. Three times did Poseidon[11] try to emerge above the waters, but the fiery air was too much for him.

It was then that the alarmed Zeus had to interfere, or the whole world would have perished in flame. Mounting to the highest point of heaven, he let fly a powerful thunderbolt against the young charioteer, which dashed the luckless Phaëthon to earth.

His body fell into the Po River, and the Italian nymphs[12] buried it on the bank. On a rock, they set this inscription:

~~HERE PHAËTHON LIES: HIS FATHER'S CAR HE TRIED— THOUGH PROVED TOO WEAK, HE GREATLY DARING DIED.~~

---

8. **Northern Plough** (plou) . . . **Serpent:** the constellations known as the Big Dipper and Draco.
9. **seared:** burned; scorched.
10. **Tartarus** (tär′tər-əs): in Greek mythology, another name for Hades.
11. **Poseidon** (pō-sīd′n): in Greek mythology, the god of the sea.
12. **nymphs** (nĭmfs): beautiful young women

MOIRA KERR

Born in Canada, Moira Kerr (1938–) taught for several years in Toronto. When her students did not enjoy the versions of the myths they were reading, she began writing her own retellings. She and the artist John Bennett collaborated on an illustrated book called *Myth*.

Kerr, who now works as a psychologist in Oklahoma, says, "Much of my interest in life has been exploring the deep wisdom which lies within all of us."

GOMBEI
AND THE WILD DUCKS

Moonlight on the River Sheba (about 1830–1844), Ando Hiroshige. Musée Guimet, Paris, Giraudon/Art Resource, New York.

RETOLD BY YOSHIKO UCHIDA

GOMBEI AND THE WILD DUCKS **709**

SUMMARY

Gombei and the Wild Ducks Gombei, a Japanese trapper, lives beside a marsh that attracts wild ducks. For years, he has snared only one duck a day, but laziness prompts him to set rope traps for a hundred ducks at one time. After ninety-nine ducks step into the traps, Gombei holds onto their ropes and waits for the hundredth. Suddenly, the ducks fly away and lift Gombei high into the air. Losing his grip on the rope, he starts to fall— and then discovers he has become a wild duck himself. Powerless to turn himself back into a man, Gombei swoops into a marsh and searches for food. There he is quickly ensnared by the same kind of rope trap he set. Now that he is the hunted instead of the hunter, Gombei weeps tears of regret for his former cruelty. His falling tears dissolve the ropes and restore his human state. Vowing never to trap again, Gombei becomes a farmer who gives his produce to living creatures—especially the wild ducks that flock to his marsh.

STRATEGIC READING FOR
Less-Proficient Readers

Set a Purpose Ask students to read to find out what convinces Gombei that his shortcut is wrong.

CUSTOMIZING FOR
Gifted And Talented Students

Explain that many folk tales are created to illustrate a lesson that is timeless and universal. Although students may not be familiar with hunting or wild ducks, they can look for the lesson of this folk tale and apply it to their lives. Invite students to look for similarities between themselves and Gombei. When they have finished the story, they can come up with a single sentence that reflects the universal lesson learned by Gombei. (*Possible response: Treat all creatures as you would like to be treated.*)

Mini-Lesson **Spelling**

DOUBLING FINAL CONSONANTS Explain that in VAC words—words that have a single <u>v</u>owel in an <u>a</u>ccented final syllable with one final <u>c</u>onsonant—the final consonant of the base word is doubled when adding a suffix. Point out to students the accented syllables in the following words:

> plum′met-ed   hap′pen-ed
> com-mit′ted   per-mit′ted
> con′fer-ence

Application Have students add -ed to the following verbs. Remind them to check the accented syllable in order to determine whether or not to double the final consonant.

1. murmur (*murmured*)
2. differ (*differed*)
3. prefer (*preferred*)
4. orbit (*orbited*)
5. admit (*admitted*)
6. transmit (*transmitted*)
7. gallop (*galloped*)
8. refer (*referred*)

Ask students to look for more words that fit this pattern, in their own writing and in things that they read, and to add these words to their personal word lists.

Reteaching/Reinforcement
• *Unit Six Resource Book,* p. 13

CUSTOMIZING FOR

Students Acquiring English

(I) If possible, invite Japanese-speaking students to model the pronunciation of *Gombei*.

Critical Thinking:
HYPOTHESIZING

(A) Ask students to speculate as to why Gombei hadn't thought of a shortcut before. *(Possible responses: because he had been taught by his father to set only one trap at a time; because he didn't have a need for more ducks before)*

Active Reading: CONNECT

(B) Ask students whether they have ever sought a shortcut to a time-consuming job. Invite them to relate any consequences they experienced as a result of their shortcut. To give students an idea of how they might respond, use the following model:

Think-Aloud Model *I once was putting together a chair from a kit. The directions called for using wood glue as well as screws to join two pieces of the chair. I decided to forget the glue and just put in the screws. About three months later, a friend sat in the chair and it fell apart underneath him! I learned never to substitute a shortcut when it comes to following directions!*

(I) Once long ago, in a small village in Japan, there lived a man whose name was Gombei.[1] He lived very close to a wooded marsh where wild ducks came each winter to play in the water for many long hours. Even when the wind was cold and the marsh waters were frozen, the ducks came in great clusters, for they liked Gombei's marsh, and they often stayed to sleep on the ice.

Just as his father had done before him, Gombei made his living by trapping the wild ducks with simple loops of rope. When a duck stepped into a loop, Gombei simply pulled the rope tight and the duck was caught. And like his father before him, Gombei never trapped more than one duck each day.

"After all, the poor creatures come to the marsh never suspecting that they will be caught," Gombei's father had said. "It would be too cruel to trap more than one at a time."

And so for all the years that Gombei trapped, he never caught more than one duck a day.

One cold winter morning, however, Gombei woke up with a <u>dreary</u> ache in his bones. "I am growing too old to work so hard, and there is no reason to continue as my father did for so many years," he said to himself. "If I caught one hundred ducks all at once, I could loaf for ninety-nine days without working at all."

(A) Gombei wondered why he hadn't done this sooner. "It is a brilliant idea," he thought.

The very next morning, he hurried out to the marsh and discovered that its waters were frozen. "Very good! A fine day for trapping," he murmured, and quickly he laid a hundred (B) traps on the icy surface. The sun had not yet

come up, and the sky was full of dark clouds. Gombei knelt behind a tree and clutched the ends of the hundred rope traps as he shivered and waited for the ducks to come.

Slowly the sky grew lighter, and Gombei could see some ducks flying toward his marsh. He held his breath and watched eagerly as they swooped down onto the ice. They did not see his traps at all and gabbled noisily as they searched for food. One by one as the ducks stepped into his traps, Gombei tightened his hold on the ropes.

"One—two—three—" he counted, and in no time at all, he had ninety-nine ducks in his traps. The day had not even dawned, and already his work was done for the next ninety-nine days. Gombei grinned at his cleverness and thought of the days and weeks ahead during which he could loaf.

"One more," he said patiently, "just one more duck and I will have a hundred."

The last duck, however, was the hardest of all to catch. Gombei waited and waited, but still there was no duck in his last trap. Soon the sky grew bright, for the sun had appeared at the rim of the wooded hills, and suddenly a shaft of light scattered a rainbow of sparkling colors over the ice. The startled ducks uttered a shrill cry, and almost as one they fluttered up into the sky, each trailing a length of rope from its legs.

Gombei was so startled by their sudden flight he didn't let go of the ropes he held in his hands. Before he could even call for help, he found himself swooshed up into the cold winter sky as

---

1. **Gombei** (gōm′bā).

WORDS
TO   **dreary** (drîr′ē) *adj.* gloomy; cheerless; depressing
KNOW

710

Mini-Lesson   **Literary Concepts**

REVIEWING IMAGERY Explain that words and phrases appealing to a reader's senses are known as imagery. Tell students that writers use imagery to help the reader imagine how things look, feel, smell, sound, and taste.

Application Ask students to brainstorm a list of words that describe the way things sound (for example, *loud, squeaking*) and feel (*rough, hot*). Then have them use these or other words to describe how they think the wild ducks sounded to Gombei and how the marsh water felt to the ducks when they landed.

the ninety-nine wild ducks soared upward, pulling him along at the end of their traps.

"Stop! Let me down!" Gombei shouted, but the ducks soared on and on. Higher and higher they flew, over rivers and fields and hills, and beyond distant villages that Gombei had never seen before.

"Help! Save me!" Gombei called frantically, but there was no one to hear him high up in the sky.

Gombei was so frightened his face turned white and then green, but all he could do was hold on with all his strength to the ninety-nine pieces of rope. If he let go now, all would be over. He glanced down and then quickly clamped his eyes shut. The land below was whirling about like a toy top.

"Somebody! Help!" he shouted once more, but the only sound that came back to him was the steady flap-flap, flap-flap of the wild ducks' wings.

Soon one hand began to slip, a little at first and then a little more. He was losing his grip on the ropes! Slowly Gombei felt the ropes slide from his numb fingers, and finally he was unable to hold on any longer. He closed his eyes tight and murmured a quick prayer as he plummeted pell-mell[2] down to earth. The wild ducks, not knowing what had happened, flew on, trailing their ropes behind like ribbons in the sky.

As Gombei tumbled toward the ground, however, a very strange thing began to take place. First he sprouted a bill, and then feathers and wings, and then a tail and webbed feet.

Flowers and Birds (about 1560–1590), Kanō Eitoku. Detail of a painted sliding door in the Juko-in Temple, Kyoto, Japan. Photo courtesy of Shogakukan Inc., Tokyo.

HE LIVED VERY CLOSE TO A WOODED MARSH WHERE WILD DUCKS CAME EACH WINTER TO PLAY IN THE WATER FOR MANY LONG HOURS.

---

2. **pell-mell:** in confusion and disorder.

WORDS TO KNOW   **plummet** (plŭm'ĭt) *v.* to fall suddenly

711

Literary Concept:
ONOMATOPOEIA

C Ask students what purpose the use of "flap-flap, flap-flap" serves. *(Possible response: It imitates the sound of the ducks' wings, making the experience more real for the reader.)*

Linking to Science

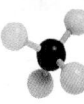 **D** Ducks are found in wetlands throughout the world. They are related to geese and swans but have shorter wings and wider bills. Each duck has a gland near its tail that secretes a waxy oil that the duck rubs on its feathers. This oil helps to protect the animal from very cold water. Ducks migrate during the winter and, like many other birds, exhibit homing behavior, which helps them return to the same wetland area each spring.

Art Note

***Flowers and Birds* by Kanō Eitoku**
Reading the Art *When you look at this detail from a painting, to what is your eye drawn? In what way do you think the artist draws you into the scene?*

| Mini-Lesson | Reading Skills/Strategies |

CONNECTING Tell students that one way to become an active reader is to try to connect with the characters one reads about. Point out that by identifying with a character's situation, the reader becomes more involved in the story and can deepen his or her appreciation of it.

Application Ask students to record, on a chart like the one shown, any connections between Gombei and themselves. Suggest that they include descriptions of Gombei's experiences and of similar experiences they have had.

Reteaching/Reinforcement
• *Unit Six Resource Book*, p. 12

| Experience | Gombei | Me |
| Not wanting to do all the work | | |

Reading the Art *What do you find most appealing about this art? Compare this work with the painting on page 711. How are the two works similar? How are they different? Explain.*

CUSTOMIZING FOR
Multiple Learning Styles

E **Bodily-Kinesthetic Learners** Ask students to act out Gombei's transformation from man to duck. Prompt them to consider all of their senses and to ask themselves what a duck would sound like and look like. Also ask them to imagine what its feathers would feel like. Suggest that they use their responses to these prompts to help them prepare their portrayal.

CUSTOMIZING FOR
Students Acquiring English

2 Explain that *If I am to be* is a formal, old-fashioned way of saying "If I am going to be."

3 Point out that *Oh me* is an old-fashioned exclamation of despair. You may wish to model Gombei's wailing *Oh-h-h-h me* for students.

Literary Links

F Point out that Gombei is given a second chance when he discovers the error of his ways. Ask students who else they have read about in Unit Two that was given a second chance. *(Possible response: Ebenezer Scrooge in* A Christmas Carol *and Roger in "Thank You M'am.")*

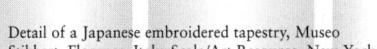

Detail of a Japanese embroidered tapestry, Museo Stibbert, Florence, Italy, Scala/Art Resource, New York.

"IF I AM TO BE A WILD DUCK, I MUST LIVE LIKE ONE," HE THOUGHT, AND HE HEADED SLOWLY TOWARD THE WATERS OF A MARSH HE SAW GLISTENING IN THE SUN.

E By the time he was almost down to earth, he looked just like the creatures he had been trying to trap. Gombei wondered if he were having a bad dream. But no, he was flying and flapping his wings, and when he tried to call out, the only sound that came from him was the call of the wild duck. He had indeed become a wild duck himself. Gombei fluttered about frantically, trying to think and feel like a duck instead of a man. At last, he decided there was only one thing to do.

2 "If I am to be a wild duck, I must live like one," he thought, and he headed slowly toward the waters of a marsh he saw glistening in the sun. He was so hungry he simply had to find something to eat, for he had not even had breakfast yet. He swooped down to the marsh and looked about hungrily. But as he waddled about thinking only of his empty stomach, he suddenly felt a tug at his leg. He pulled and he pulled, but he could not get away. Then he looked down, and there, wound around his leg, was the very same kind of rope trap that he set each day for the wild ducks of his marsh.

"I wasn't harming anything. All I wanted was some food," he cried. But the man who had set the trap could not understand what Gombei was trying to say. He had been trapped like a wild animal, and soon he would be plucked and eaten.

3 "Oh-h-h-h me," Gombei wailed, "now I know how terrible it is for even one wild duck to be trapped, and only this morning I was trying to trap a hundred poor birds. I am a wicked and greedy man," he thought, "and I deserve to be punished for being so cruel."

F As Gombei wept, the tears trickled down his body and touched the rope that was wound

712 UNIT SIX: THE ORAL TRADITION

Mini-Lesson **Grammar**

SUBJECT-VERB AGREEMENT A verb must agree in number with its subject. A subject and verb agree in number when both are singular or both are plural. Compound subjects and indefinite pronouns used as subjects also must agree with their verbs.

Application Write the following sentences on the chalkboard. Then invite students to circle the correct form of the verb.

1. Gombei (was/were) frightened when the birds flew off.
2. The birds (<u>do</u>/does) not understand why they (<u>are</u>/is) being trapped.
3. Gombei and his father (was/<u>were</u>) both trappers.
4. After becoming a duck and then a human again, Gombei (<u>didn't</u>/don't) want to be a trapper of ducks anymore.
5. A hundred ducks (<u>soar</u>/soars) into the sky.

Reteaching/Reinforcement
• Grammar Handbook, anthology pp. 851–852
• *Grammar Mini-Lessons* copymasters, pp. 3–6, transparencies, pp. 3–6

 The Writer's Craft

Agreement, pp. 578–580

tightly about his leg. The moment they did, a wonderful thing happened. The rope that was so secure suddenly fell apart, and Gombei was no longer caught in the trap.

"I'm free! I'm free!" Gombei shouted, and this time he wept tears of joy. "How good it is to be free and alive! How grateful I am to have another chance," he cried.

As the tears rolled down his face and then his body, another strange and marvelous thing happened. First his feathers began to disappear, and then his bill, and then his tail and his webbed feet. Finally he was no longer a duck but had become a human being once more.

"I'm not a duck! I'm a man again," Gombei called out gleefully. He felt his arms to be sure they were no longer wings. Yes, there were his fingers and his hands. He felt his nose to be sure it was no longer a duck's bill, and he looked down in astonishment at the clothes that had reappeared on his body. Then he ran down the road as fast as his two human legs would carry him and hurried home to his own village by the wooded marsh.

"Never again will I ever trap another living thing," Gombei vowed when he reached home safely. Then he went to his cupboard and threw out all his rope traps and burned them into ash.

"From this moment on, I shall become a farmer," he said. "I will till the soil and grow rice and wheat and food for all the living creatures of the land." And Gombei did exactly that for the rest of his days.

As for the wild ducks, they came in ever-increasing numbers, for now they found grain and feed instead of traps laid upon the ice, and they knew that in the sheltered waters of Gombei's marsh they would always be safe. ❖

G

H

YOSHIKO UCHIDA

1921–1992

Yoshiko Uchida's mother often read Japanese folk tales to her when she was a child. At the age of ten, Uchida was writing stories of her own on brown wrapping paper, which she bound into booklets. After war broke out between Japan and the United States in 1941, she and her family were sent to an internment camp along with thousands of other Japanese Americans. Uchida was eventually allowed to leave the camp to do graduate work at Smith College. In 1952 she received a fellowship to go to Japan and collect folk tales. Her travels in Japan deepened her respect for her ancestors' culture and fostered her pride in being a Japanese American.

Uchida wrote numerous books about Japanese culture, including the award-winning *Journey to Topaz* —which recounts her experiences at the internment camp in Utah—and its sequel, *Journey Home.* Uchida once said, "Although all my books have been about the Japanese people, my hope is that they will enlarge and enrich the reader's understanding, not only of the Japanese and the Japanese Americans, but of the human condition. I think it's important for each of us to take pride in our special heritage, but we must never lose our sense of connection with the community of man."

OTHER WORKS *A Jar of Dreams, The Best Bad Thing, The Happiest Ending, The Dancing Kettle and Other Japanese Folk Tales*

COMPREHENSION CHECK

1. What did Gombei's father tell him about trapping ducks? *(He told him to trap one at a time because trapping more would be cruel.)*
2. Why does Gombei want to trap 100 ducks all at once? *(He wants to use a shortcut so that he can loaf for 99 days.)*
3. What happens to Gombei when the ducks fly off? *(He is so startled he doesn't let go of the ropes and is carried off by the ducks.)*
4. What convinces Gombei that it is terrible to trap ducks? *(He turns into a duck and gets trapped himself.)*
5. What change of occupation does Gombei make? *(from trapper to farmer)*

CUSTOMIZING FOR
Students Acquiring English

④ Call students' attention to the exclamation *How good it is to be free and alive!* You may wish to point out that in modern spoken English, this exclamation would be worded "It's so good to be free and alive!"

Literary Links

Ⓖ Ask students what Mrs. Jones in "Thank You M'am" would think of Gombei's decision at the end of "Gombei and the Wild Ducks." *(Possible response: Because she provided food for Roger and took care of him, Mrs. Jones would approve of Gombei's decision to do the right thing for the rest of his days and help all living creatures.)*

STRATEGIC READING FOR
Less-Proficient Readers

Ⓗ Ask students to summarize what happened to Gombei that convinced him that his shortcut was a bad idea. *(Gombei was carried away by ducks, became a duck himself, and experienced what it was like to be trapped.)*
Summarizing

From Personal Response to Critical Analysis

1. What is the lesson taught in "Gombei and the Wild Ducks"? *(Possible response: Put yourself in someone else's position so you can understand how he or she feels and behave accordingly.)*
2. How would you evaluate the importance of the lesson Gombei learns? *(Answers will vary.)*
3. Do you think that Gombei was clever or lazy when he devised a plan to simplify his work? Explain your answer. *(Possible responses: He was clever in trying to devise a new way to do his work in less time; he was lazy because all he wanted to do was loaf for 99 days.)*

Literature Connection

Hold a Talk Show Have a volunteer familiar with talk shows summarize a typical talk-show format. As the show progresses, have each character tell his or her "story," state the lesson learned, and explain how the experience changed his or her life. Then invite the audience to brainstorm other ways the characters might have reacted to their experiences or lessons learned. For example, have them talk about what might have happened to Gombei had he not heeded the lesson offered to him. Encourage students to have fun with this project and to be dramatic as they present their stories.

Rubric

3 Full Accomplishment Students retell events in the stories and identify the important lessons learned. They accurately portray the characters, capturing their important personality traits.

2 Substantial Accomplishment Students mimic a talk-show format but have difficulty incorporating the lessons learned in the stories.

1 Little or Partial Accomplishment Students have difficulty mimicking a talk-show format, describing the lessons learned, and portraying the characters.

LITERATURE CONNECTION PROJECT 1 Multimodal Activity

Hold a talk show As a class, hold a talk show on the topic "What is the most important lesson about life that people should learn?" First list the characters in the selections you have read and describe the lesson that each one learns. Then choose students to role-play a host or hostess of a talk show and the characters in the selections who will appear as guests on the show. During the talk show, each character should explain the importance of the lesson he or she learned. The rest of the class can portray a TV audience and direct questions to the characters and to the host or hostess. If possible, have a classmate videotape the show.

SCIENCE CONNECTION PROJECT 3 Multimodal Activity

Create a science exhibit In the Greek myth "Phaëthon," four fire-breathing horses gallop across the heavens with Apollo's sun chariot, scorching the earth and endangering life on our planet. Working in pairs or in a small group, compile a list of facts that solar astronomers have discovered about the sun, including its size, distance from the earth, approximate temperatures at the center and at the surface, composition, diameter, and movement. Find out how much closer the sun would need to be to destroy all life on Earth. Consult books, magazines, encyclopedias, and CD-ROMs to find information. If possible, visit a planetarium and talk to an astronomer. Then make an audio-visual display to share your sun facts with the rest of the class.

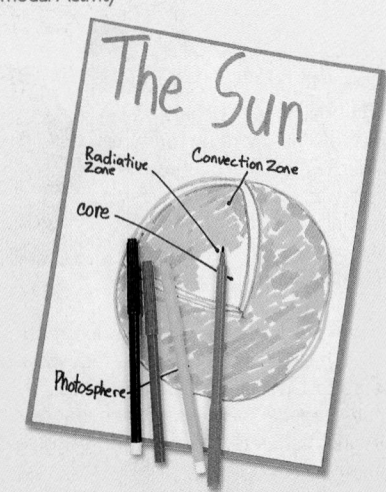

Science Connection

Create a Science Exhibit Suggest that students begin by making a list of questions they want to have answered. Students may want to add music to their audiovisual display. Encourage students to describe aspects of the sun in terms of familiar things—for example, the size of the sun in relation to the size of the earth.

Rubric

3 Full Accomplishment Students gather pertinent information and present facts in an original format.

2 Substantial Accomplishment Students find some information about the sun but have difficulty creating an audiovisual display.

1 Little or Partial Accomplishment Students have difficulty gathering facts about the sun and cannot create an audiovisual display.

SOCIAL STUDIES CONNECTION PROJECT 3   Multimodal Activity

Examine the needs of the elderly When the couple in the "The Old Grandfather and His Little Grandson" realize that they too will grow old, their attitude toward the grandfather changes. What do you know about elderly people and their special needs? Create a K-W-L chart like the one shown. In the "K" column, write down what you know about elderly people; in the "W" column, list some of the questions you have about them. Then work in one of the following groups to complete the "L" column of your chart.

Group 1: Researchers To find answers to questions in the "W" column, check magazine and newspaper articles, books, pamphlets at senior citizen centers, videos, and if possible, a computer database or encyclopedia.

Group 2: Surveyors Find out what other people in your community consider to be the special needs of the elderly. Survey several people in your family, school, and neighborhood.

Group 3: Interviewers Interview some elderly people to find out about their problems, needs, and recommendations. Prepare your questions in advance. With the permission of the people you interview, tape-record or have a classmate videotape each interview.

Group 4: Presenters After all the groups have finished their tasks, they should compile their findings. Each group should then choose someone to present an oral report to the rest of the class, and choose a format that is appropriate. For example, the surveyors could present their findings in graphs or charts, or the interviewers could play a portion or portions of each interview.

K	W	L
What We Know	What We Want to Find Out	What We Learned

ACROSS CULTURES MINI-PROJECTS   Multimodal Activities

Make connections Compare a character or a theme from one of the selections in Unit Two with a character or a theme from one of the selections you have just read. For example, you may compare Ebenezer Scrooge with Gombei or Teruo with Phaëthon, or you may compare the theme of the myth "Phaëthon" with the theme of the poem "Into the Sun."

Have a debate With a partner, role-play a debate between Gombei at the end of the story and a modern hunter on the topic of hunting animals for food and sport. Are there advantages and disadvantages to both kinds of hunting?

Create a graph that illustrates how the percentage of Americans over the age of 65 has increased from 1900 to the present.

Write a modern fable Imitating Aesop's style, draft a brief story that conveys a lesson about life. Select classmates to enact the characters you create. Then perform the fable in a Reader's Theater presentation.

Extended Social Studies Reading

MORE ABOUT THE CULTURES

- *Japanese Culture: A Short History* by Paul H. Varley
- *The Rise of the Greeks* by Michael Grant
- *Life in Ancient Greece* by Pierre Miquel
- *Master Puppeteer* by Katherine Paterson
- *Peter the Great* by Diane Stanley
- *The Buddhist World* by Anne Bancroft

LINKS TO UNIT TWO   **715**

Social Studies Connection

Examine the Needs of the Elderly Suggest that the surveyors also talk to people involved with organizations that provide services to the elderly. Encourage students to include in their presentations their own opinions about whether the needs of the elderly are being properly met in their community.

Rubric

3 Full Accomplishment Students are thorough in gathering data and answer their own questions. They create an original format for their presentation.

2 Substantial Accomplishment Students generate questions about the needs of the elderly but have some difficulty locating answers and creating a format for presenting their oral report.

1 Little or Partial Accomplishment Students have difficulty posing questions about the needs of the elderly. They need a lot of support to gather information or present their findings orally.

Across Cultures

Make Connections Have students list in a chart the information about each character or theme. Suggest that students also compare the events the characters experience and the lessons they learn.

Have a Debate Remind students to convey the likely opinions of Gombei and a modern hunter, not their own opinions. Have them list possible advantages and disadvantages before role-playing.

Create a Graph Suggest that students present their data in the form of a time line, pie chart, or bar graph.

Write a Modern Fable Before students draft a story, have them brainstorm a list of lessons about life, from which they can select one lesson. Remind them that Aesop's fables contain many characters that are animals. Encourage students to use costumes and props in their performance.

OVERVIEW

Objectives

- To understand and appreciate a legend, a myth, and a folk tale about characters who come forward in a time of need and change the course of events
- To appreciate the values of Native American, Chinese, and Scandinavian cultures
- To extend understanding of the selections through a variety of multimodal and cross-curricular activities

Skills

READING SKILLS/ STRATEGIES
- Making judgments

THE WRITER'S STYLE
- Topic sentences and supporting details
- Cause-and-effect transitions

GRAMMAR
- *Who* and *whom*

SPELLING
- Words with *j, ge,* and *dge*

SPEAKING, LISTENING, AND VIEWING
- Storytelling
- Group discussions

Cross-Curricular Connections

HISTORY
- The Sioux
- Reservations
- Gold

SOCIAL STUDIES
- Norse mythology
- Commemorative stamp

- Chinese literature

GEOGRAPHY
- Travel brochure

SCIENCE
- Water and mosquitoes

Reading Pathways

- Invite several students to read each story aloud to the class or to small groups. Assign the presentation in advance to allow readers time to incorporate some of the techniques used by professional storytellers. Have the audience listen to the stories without following along in their texts.
- Read the stories aloud to the class, pausing at key points to discuss how elements of the story inform students about the customs of the cultures. Have students compare these customs with those of their own cultures and regions.
- After students have read the stories, they can identify structural elements such as characters, conflict, setting, and plot. Then have students identify similarities and differences between these tales and the selections in the related unit. For example, have students compare the courage shown by Buffalo Calf Road Woman in "Where the Girl Saved Her Brother" with that shown by Nessan in "The Chief's Daughter."

LINKS TO UNIT THREE

Stepping Forward

In Unit Three you read about characters who showed courage or who experienced inner change. The tales you are about to read present characters from different cultures who have the courage to take risks.

UNITED STATES

Where the Girl Saved Her Brother

retold by Rachel Strange Owl

This Native American legend has its origins in an important historical event—the Battle of the Rosebud, which took place in southeastern Montana on June 17, 1876. In that battle, Sioux warriors defeated General Crook's troops. The U. S. Army then sent a force led by Lieutenant Colonel George Custer against the Sioux. This legend tells of a Cheyenne woman whose actions are said to have contributed to Native American victories in two battles, the Battle of the Rosebud and the Battle of Little Bighorn.

716 UNIT SIX: THE ORAL TRADITION

PRINT AND MEDIA RESOURCES

UNIT SIX RESOURCE BOOK
Strategic Reading: Literature, p. 17
Vocabulary SkillBuilder, p. 20
Reading SkillBuilder, p. 18
Spelling SkillBuilder, p. 19

GRAMMAR MINI-LESSONS
Copymasters, p. 17

WRITING MINI-LESSONS
Transparencies, pp. 29–33

ACCESS FOR STUDENTS ACQUIRING ENGLISH
Selection Summaries
Reading and Writing Support

FORMAL ASSESSMENT
Selection Test, pp. 121–122
■ Test Generator

AUDIO LIBRARY
See Reference Card

INTERNET RESOURCES
McDougal Littell Literature Center at http://www.hmco.com /mcdougal/lit

How Odin Lost His Eye

retold by Catharine F. Sellew

Scandinavia is the name given to a group of countries in northern Europe that includes Norway, Sweden, and Denmark. In these countries, much of the land away from the sea is covered with snow. According to Norse (Scandinavian) mythology, the giant tree that supports all creation has three roots. One of the roots extends to a misty underworld. Another goes to Asgard (ăs′gärd), the heavenly realm where the gods dwell. The third root reaches Jotunheim (yō′tən-hīm′), the icy realm of the frost giants. From his throne in Asgard, Odin, the mightiest Norse god, keeps watch on all the lands of creation.

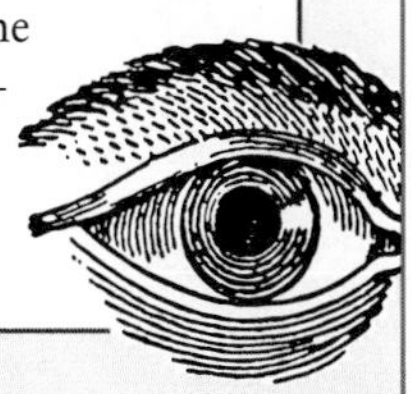

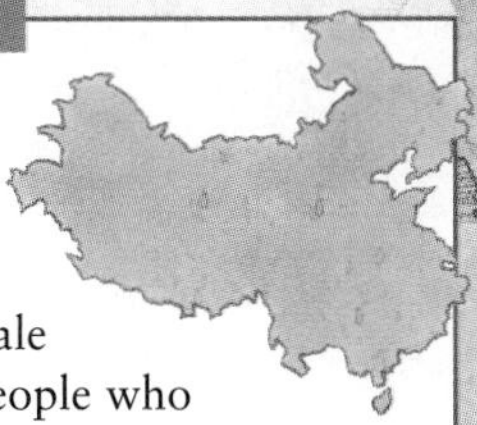

Waters of Gold

retold by Laurence Yep

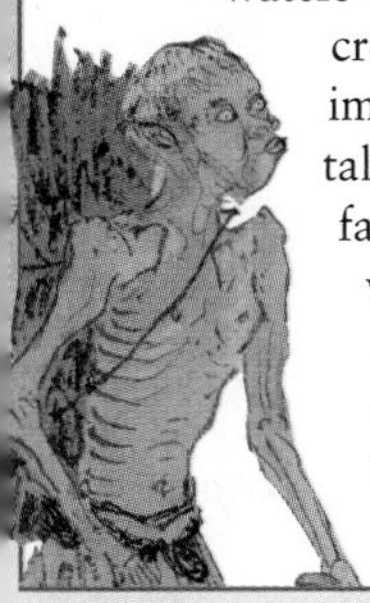

"Waters of Gold" is a folk tale created by Chinese people who immigrated to the United States. These tales helped immigrants and their families remember their culture and values. Many of these tales concern human relationships. Some have elements of magic and reflect the belief that ordinary people may experience extraordinary things.

AS YOU READ . . .

Notice the unique cultural values presented.

Identify the attitudes and behaviors that are admired and those that are not.

Consider the risks the characters take.

LINKS TO UNIT THREE **717**

SUMMARY

How Odin Lost His Eye This Norse myth tells about Odin, king of gods and creator of the world. Having made men and women, he wants to protect them from evil frost giants, who bring cold and ice to the earth. Odin leaves his throne and descends to earth to learn more about the frost giants. He visits a well whose surface reflects images of the past and future—but only to those who have sipped its water. The old man in charge of the well, Mimir, warns Odin that he will have to pay a great price in order to drink the water. Odin resolves to make any sacrifice necessary to save humankind. When the old man asks for one of Odin's eyes, the god immediately plucks it out and hands it over. He then drinks deeply of the water and sees that the future holds much sorrow and death, redeemed by glorious promise at the end. As for his eye, it settles at the bottom of Mimir's well as a reminder of Odin's great sacrifice.

WORDS TO KNOW

jostling (jŏs′lĭng) *n.* roughly bumping, pushing, or shoving **jostle** *v.* (p. 730)

perilously (pĕr′ə-ləs-lē) *adv.* dangerously (p. 730)

render (rĕn′dər) *v.* to cause to be; make (p. 722)

smugly (smŭg′lē) *adv.* in a self-satisfied way (p. 726)

HOW ODIN LOST HIS EYE

RETOLD BY CATHARINE F. SELLEW

Odin astride Sleipnir. Illumination from *Poetic Edda* in a 13th-century Icelandic manuscript, The Granger Collection, New York.

A Once when the world was still very young, Odin sat on his throne in the most beautiful palace in Asgard. His throne was so high that he could see over all three parts of the world from where he sat. On his head he wore a helmet shaped like an eagle. On his shoulders perched two black ravens called Memory and Thought. And at his feet crouched two snarling wolves.

The great king gazed thoughtfully down on the earth below him. He had made the green land that stretched out before his eyes. With the help of the other gods he had made men and women who lived on that earth. And he felt truly like the All-father he was called.

The fair elves had promised they would help his children of the earth. The elves were the tiny people who lived between heaven and earth. They were so small that they could flit about doing their work unseen. Odin knew that they were the artists who painted the flowers and made the beds for the streams. They took care of all the bees and the butterflies. And it was the elves who brought the gentle rain and sunshine to the earth.

Even the ugly dwarfs, who lived in the heart of the mountains, agreed to help. They forged[1] iron and metals, made tools and weapons. They dug gold and silver and beautiful jewels out of the earth. Sometimes they even cut the grain and ground the flour for the farmers on the earth.

All seemed to be going well. Odin found it hard to think of evil times. But he knew that the frost giants were only waiting for a chance to bring trouble to his children. They were the ones who brought cold and ice to the world and shook the earth in anger. They hated Odin and all the work of the gods.

And from high on his throne Odin looked down beyond the earth deep into the gloomy land of his enemies. He saw dark figures of huge men moving about. They looked like evil shadows. He, the king of the gods, must have more wisdom. It was not enough just to see his enemies. He must know more about them.

So Odin wrapped his tall figure in a blue cloak. Down from his throne he climbed. Down the broad rainbow bridge he strode and across the green earth till he came to one of the roots of the great evergreen tree. There, close by the tree, was a well full of clear water. Its surface was so still it was like a mirror. In it one could see pictures of things that had happened and things that were going to happen.

But beside the well sat an old man. His face was lined with the troubles of the world. His name was Mimir, which means "memory." No one, not even the great Odin, could see the pictures in the well unless he first drank some of its water. Only Mimir could give the magic drink.

"Aged Mimir," Odin said to the old man, "you who hold the knowledge of the past and future in your magic waters, let me have but one sip. Then I can know enough to protect the men and women of the earth from the hate of the giants."

Mimir looked kindly at Odin, but he did not smile. Although he spoke softly, his voice was so deep it reminded Odin of the distant roar of the ocean.

"The price of one drink from this well is not cheap," Mimir said. "And once you have drunk and gazed into the mirror of life, you may wish you had not. For sorrow and death as well as joy are pictured there. Think again before you ask to drink."

But once the king of the gods had made up his mind, nothing could change it. He was not afraid to look upon sorrow and death.

"What is your price, aged Mimir?" Odin asked.

"You are great and good, Odin," answered Mimir. "You have worked hard to make the world. Only those who know hard work may drink from my well. However, that is not enough. What have you given up that is very dear to you? What have you sacrificed? The price of a drink must be a great sacrifice. Are you still willing to pay the price?"

What could the king of the gods sacrifice? What was most dear to him? Odin thought of his handsome son, Balder, whom he loved most in the world. To give up his son would be like giving up life and all that was wonderful around him. Odin stood silent before Mimir.

---

1. **forged:** heated and hammered into shape.

CUSTOMIZING FOR

Students Acquiring English

(1) Explain that *fair* is used here to mean "beautiful."

(2) Explain that *aged* means "old" and model its pronunciation. Point out that the word is used respectfully here.

Critical Thinking: ANALYZING

B Have students explain why the frost giants might be the villains in a Scandinavian legend. Then invite students to identify possible villains in legends from other climatic regions, such as those from the Caribbean islands. *(Possible response: The frost kings represent the cold— the great threat in northern climates. In the Caribbean, for example, hurricanes or heat waves might be the villains.)*

Active Reading: EVALUATE

C Ask students if they think Odin would be a good leader, based on this passage. *(Possible response: Yes, because he is wise, courageous, and farseeing.)*

Active Reading: PREDICT

D Invite students to predict what they think Odin will sacrifice and have them explain why. *(Possible response: He will sacrifice his son because it is the greatest sacrifice he can make.)*

Cultural Note

E Norse mythology includes an account of the end of the world. There will be a great battle between the giants and the gods. Everyone will be killed, and the earth will be destroyed by fire. Then the earth will be reborn, cleansed of evil and treachery, and will endure forever.

Mini-Lesson **TM** **Spelling**

WORDS WITH J, GE, AND DGE Tell students that the *j* sound can be spelled *j* (as in *justice*), *ge* (as in *urge*), and *dge* (as in *judge*). The letter *j* occurs at the beginning and in the middle of words. The letters *ge* occur at the ends of words. The letters *dge* are used only in one-syllable words with short vowels.

Application Have students spell the following words as you recite them.
1. conjunction
2. rejoice
3. huge
4. bridge

5. jewels
6. courage
7. ledge
8. marriage
9. journal
10. oblige

Ask students to look for more words that fit this pattern, in their own writing and in things that they read, and to add these words to their personal word lists.

Reteaching/Reinforcement
• *Unit Six Resource Book*, p. 19

Literary Links

F Remind students Nessan was willing to die for Dara in "The Chief's Daughter." Ask students if they think Nessan's sacrifice was greater than or less than Odin's and have them explain their answer. *(Possible responses: Odin's was less because he did not have to offer his life; Odin's was greater because he lost half his vision.)*

STRATEGIC READING FOR

Less-Proficient Readers

G Ask students to describe how Odin loses his eye. *(He sacrifices it for a look at the future.)* Summarizing

From Personal Response to Critical Analysis

1. Draw a sketch of Odin that shows your feelings about him. *(Sketches will vary.)*

2. How would you have responded to this story if Odin had sacrificed Balder? *(Possible responses: anger, pain, and admiration because the sacrifice was so great)*

3. Odin wants to drink the magic waters so he can protect the people from the giants. Do you think he will be able to protect the people? *(Possible response: yes, because he is a wise leader, much admired by Mimir)*

4. Think back to what you learned about the oral tradition in the beginning of this unit. How does this story fit with that tradition? *(Possible responses: It was passed down from generation to generation; it reveals the values of a specific culture.)*

---

③ Indeed that would be a high price!

Then Mimir spoke again. He had read Odin's thoughts.

"No, I am not asking for your dear son. The Fates[2] say his life must be short, but he has time yet to live and bring happiness to the gods and the world. I ask for one of your eyes."

Odin put his hands up to his bright blue eyes. Those two eyes had gazed across the world from his high throne in the shining city of the gods. His eyes had taught him what was good and beautiful, what was evil and ugly. But those eyes had also seen his children, the men and women of the earth, struggling against the hate of the giants. One eye was a small sacrifice to win knowledge of how to help them. And without another thought, Odin plucked out one of his blue eyes and handed it to Mimir.

Then Mimir smiled and gave Odin a horn full of the waters of his well.

"Drink deeply, brave king, so you may see all that you wish in the mirror of life."

Odin lifted the horn to his lips and drank. Then he knelt by the edge of the well and watched the pictures passing across its still and silent surface. When he stood up again, he sighed, for it was as Mimir had said. He had seen sorrow and death as well as joy. It was only the glorious promise at the end that gave him courage to go on.

So Odin, the great king of the gods, became one-eyed. If you can find Mimir's well, you will see Odin's blue eye resting on the bottom. It is there to remind men and women of the great sacrifice he made for them. ❖

---

2. **Fates:** goddesses who decide the course of people's lives.

CATHARINE F. SELLEW

As a child, Catharine Sellew loved to listen as her mother read myths. Sellew later studied mythology and published a collection of Greek myths, *Adventures with the Gods.*

1922–1982

She then retold Norse myths in *Adventures with the Giants* and *Adventures with the Heroes.* She also retold stories from the Old Testament and wrote a novel for teenagers, entitled *Torchlight.*

COMPREHENSION CHECK

1. According to this legend, who created the world and its people? *(Odin and the other gods)*

2. Who hates Odin and the work of the gods? *(the frost giants)*

3. Why does Odin go to Mimir's well? *(to protect the people of the earth from the frost giants, their enemies)*

4. What does Odin sacrifice for a drink from the well? *(one of his eyes)*

5. What gives Odin the courage to go on after he has drunk from the well? *(the glorious promise he sees at the end of the world)*

WHERE THE GIRL SAVED HER BROTHER

RETOLD BY RACHEL STRANGE OWL

Illustration by Linda Benson/Artworks New York.

SUMMARY

Where the Girl Saved Her Brother This legend tells of the Battle of the Rosebud, fought in Montana in 1876 between Native Americans and U.S. soldiers. At issue was the Native Americans' right to keep their land and way of life. Many tribes united for the battle, including the Sioux and Cheyenne. Among the brave Cheyenne warriors were a girl named Buffalo Calf Road Woman and her brother, Chief Comes-in-Sight. Soon after the fight started, soldiers killed Chief Comes-in-Sight's horse and surrounded the young warrior. Letting out a shrill war cry, Buffalo Calf Road Woman rode into the thick of battle and rescued her brother. As they safely dodged bullets and arrows, warriors whooped and even soldiers cheered her. General Crook, leader of the U.S. troops, retreated rather than face such fearless warriors. Buffalo Calf Road Woman's act of bravery earned her the highest honors, and the Cheyenne have ever since referred to the Battle of the Rosebud as "Where the Girl Saved Her Brother."

Almost exactly a hundred years ago, in the summer of 1876, the two greatest battles between soldiers and Indians were fought on the plains of Montana. The first fight was called the Battle of the Rosebud. The second battle, which was fought a week later, was called the Battle of the Little Bighorn, where General Custer was defeated and killed. The Cheyennes call the Battle of the Rosebud the fight "Where the Girl Saved Her Brother." Let me tell you why.

But first let me explain what is meant when an Indian says, "I have counted coup."[1] "Counting coup" is gaining war honors. The Indians think that it is easy to kill an enemy by shooting him from ambush. This brings no

---

1. coup (ko͞o).

STRATEGIC READING FOR

Less-Proficient Readers

Set a Purpose Have students read to discover why the Cheyennes call the Battle of the Rosebud the fight "Where the Girl Saved Her Brother."

Linking to History

A In 1875, the U.S. government ordered the Sioux onto a reservation. In 1876, after the Sioux had refused to move, U.S. troops attacked what they thought was the village of Crazy Horse, the Sioux leader. In retaliation, Crazy Horse led Sioux and Cheyenne warriors in battle against Custer, wiping out his entire command.

Multicultural Perspectives

RESERVATIONS In the 1800s, the U.S. government tried to justify moving Native Americans off their land. The government representatives claimed they needed the land for expansion of the railroad and for pioneers settling in the area. Today, some Native-American groups are demanding that their lands be returned to them.

The narrator of this legend expresses the view of many Native Americans in describing the reservations as "prisons." Many Native Americans, both in the past and the present, have resented the way the government forced them off their land and altered their way of life.

B honor. It is not counting coup. But to ride up to an enemy, or walk up to him while he is still alive, unwounded and armed, and then to hit him with your feathered coup stick, or touch him with your hand, this brings honor and earns you eagle feathers. This is counting coup. To steal horses in a daring raid can also be counting coup. But one of the greatest honors is to be gained by dashing with your horse into the midst of your enemies to rescue a friend, surrounded and unhorsed, to take him up behind you and gallop out again, saving his life by risking your own. That is counting coup indeed, counting big coup.

Well, a hundred years ago, the white men wanted the Indians to go into prisons called "reservations," to give up their freedom to roam and hunt buffalo, to give up being Indians. Some gave in tamely and went to live behind the barbed wire of the agencies,[2] but others did not.

Those who went to the reservations to live like white men were called "friendlies." Those who would not go were called "hostiles." They were not hostile, really. They did not want to fight. All they wanted was to be left alone to live the Indian way, which was a good way. But the soldiers would not let them. They decided to make a great surround and catch all "hostiles," kill those who resisted, and bring the others back as prisoners to the agencies. Three columns of soldiers entered the last stretch of land left to the red man. They were led by Generals Crook, Custer, and Terry. Crook had the most

ONE OF THE GREATEST HONORS IS TO BE GAINED BY DASHING WITH YOUR HORSE INTO THE MIDST OF YOUR ENEMIES TO RESCUE A FRIEND, . . . SAVING HIS LIFE BY RISKING YOUR OWN.

men with him, about two thousand. He also had cannon and Indian scouts to guide him. At the Rosebud he met the united Sioux and Cheyenne warriors.

The Indians had danced the sacred Sun Dance. The great Sioux chief Sitting Bull had been granted a vision telling him that the soldiers would be defeated. The warriors were in high spirits. Some men belonging to famous warrior societies had vowed to fight until they were killed, singing their death songs, throwing their lives away, as it was called. They painted their faces for war. They put on their finest outfits so that, if they were killed, their enemies should say, "This must have been a great fighter or chief. See how nobly he lies there."

The old chiefs instructed the young men how to act. The medicine men prepared the charms for the fighters, putting gopher dust on their hair or painting their horses with hailstone designs. This was to <u>render</u> them invisible to their foes or to make them bullet-proof. Brave Wolf had the most admired medicine—a mounted hawk that he fastened to the back of his head. Brave Wolf always rode into battle blowing on his eagle-bone whistle—and once the fight started, the hawk came alive and whistled too.

---

2. **agencies:** reservations.

WORDS
TO
KNOW

render (rĕn′dər) *v.* to cause to be; make

Mini-Lesson  The Writer's Style

TOPIC SENTENCES AND SUPPORTING DETAILS Explain that one good way to achieve unity in a paragraph is to state the main idea in a topic sentence. Stress how the topic sentence helps the reader stay focused on the key idea. Be sure that students understand that the topic sentence can fall anywhere in a paragraph, although it is often first. Describe how writers use supporting details to back up the topic sentence. Use the web to explain different kinds of supporting details writers can use.

Application Have students use their imaginations to write a paragraph describing a young Cheyenne

warrior's impression of Buffalo Calf Road Woman's act of bravery. Have students read their writing to the class, and have the audience identify the topic sentence and supporting details.

Reteaching/Reinforcement
- Writing Handbook, anthology pp. 815–817
- *Writing Mini-Lessons* transparencies, pp. 29–32

The Writer's Craft

Constructing Paragraphs, pp. 249–250

facts
statistics
examples
Supporting Details
dialogue
sensory information

Many proud tribes were there besides the Cheyenne—the Hunkpapa, the Miniconjou, the Oglala, the Burned Thighs, the Two Kettles—and many famous chiefs and brave warriors—Two Moons, White Bull, Dirty Moccasins, Little Hawk, Yellow Eagle, Lame White Man. Among the Sioux was the great Crazy Horse, and Sitting Bull—their holy man, still weak from his flesh offerings made at the Sun Dance—and the fierce Rain-in-the-Face. Who can count them all, and what a fine sight they were!

Those who earned the right to wear war bonnets were singing, lifting them up. Three times they stopped in their singing, and the fourth time they put the bonnets on their heads, letting the streamers fly and trail behind them. How good it must have been to see this! What would I give to have been there!

Crazy Horse of the Oglala shouted his famous war cry, "A good day to die, and a good day to fight. Cowards to the rear, brave hearts—follow me!"

The fight started. Many brave deeds were done, many coups counted. The battle swayed to and fro. More than anybody else's, this was the Cheyenne's fight. This was their day. Among them was a brave young girl, Buffalo Calf Road Woman, who rode proudly at the side of her husband, Black Coyote. Her brother, Chief Comes-in-Sight, was in the

THE SOLDIERS WERE FIRING AT HER, AND THEIR CROW SCOUTS WERE SHOOTING ARROWS AT HER HORSE—BUT IT MOVED TOO FAST. . . . THEN SHE TURNED HER HORSE AND RACED UP THE HILL.

battle too. She looked for him and at last saw him. His horse had been killed from under him. He was surrounded. Soldiers were aiming their rifles at him. Their white Crow scouts[3] circled around him, waiting for an opportunity to count cheap coups upon him. But he fought them with bravery and skill.

Buffalo Calf Road Woman uttered a shrill, high-pitched war cry. She raced her pony right into the midst of the battle, into the midst of the enemy. She made the spine-chilling, trilling, warbling sound of the Indian woman encouraging her man during a fight. Chief Comes-in-Sight jumped up on her horse behind his sister. Buffalo Calf Road Woman laughed with joy and with the excitement of battle. Buffalo Calf Road Woman sang while she was doing this. The soldiers were firing at her, and their Crow scouts were shooting arrows at her horse—but it moved too fast for her or Chief Comes-in-Sight to be hit. Then she turned her horse and raced up the hill from which the old chiefs and the medicine men watched the battle. The Sioux and Cheyenne saw what was being done. And then the white soldiers saw it too. They all stopped fighting and just looked at that brave girl saving her brother's life. The warriors raised their arms and set up a mighty shout—a long, trilling, undulating[4] war cry that made one's hairs stand on end. And even some of the soldiers threw their caps in the air

---

3. **white Crow scouts:** The Crow are Native Americans, but here they are called white because they are traitors, working for the white soldiers.

4. **undulating** (ŭn′jə-lā′tĭng): having wavelike variations in loudness or pitch.

F The great chief Crazy Horse was pictured on a 1982 postage stamp. This was the first time in America's history that a government agency paid such an honor to someone who had fought against the U.S. Army. Crazy Horse was never photographed, so an artist's conception of his appearance was used for the stamp.

Critical Thinking: SYNTHESIZING

G Have students analyze this passage and combine their analyses with what they already have read to infer Crazy Horse's philosophy of war. *(Possible responses: He believes that it is better to die a hero in battle than to live as a coward; he believes that there are good days and bad days to fight, possibly determined by visions from the spirits.)*

CUSTOMIZING FOR
Gifted and Talented Students

After students finish the story, they can retell it from the viewpoint of a U.S. soldier. Remind them that such a retelling would probably emphasize the bravery of the U.S. soldiers and downplay the bravery of the Native Americans.

(1) Point out that *He was to have joined up with Custer* is a more formal way of saying "He was supposed to (or "He had planned to") join up with Custer."

(2) Invite students to work in groups to compare and contrast their ideas of fairy tales and legends. *(Possible response: Legends are based on facts.)*

Literary Concept: CHARACTER

(H) Ask students what words they would use to describe Buffalo Calf Road Woman. *(Possible responses: brave, caring, self-sacrificing, loyal, fierce, proud)*

(1) Ask students to explain why the Battle of the Rosebud is called "Where the Girl Saved Her Brother." *(because the girl who saved her brother counted the biggest coup of the battle)* Using Context Clues

From Personal Response to Critical Analysis

1. What is your favorite part of the story? Why? Write your ideas in your notebook. *(Responses will vary.)*

2. A legend may be based on a real person or event. What parts of this story could be true? What parts seem imaginary? *(Possible responses: True parts include the battle itself and details about its cause; imaginary parts may include specific details such as Brave Wolf's hawk coming to life.)*

3. Why do you think the story of Buffalo Calf Road Woman continues to be told more than 100 years after the event? *(Possible response: It is an inspirational legend that make Sioux and Cheyenne listeners proud of their heritage.)*

and shouted "Hurrah" in honor of Buffalo Calf Road Woman.

The battle was still young. Not many men had been killed on either side, but the white general was thinking, "If their women fight like this, what will their warriors be like? Even if I win, I will lose half my men." And so General Crook retreated a hundred miles or so. He was to have joined up with Custer, Old Yellow Hair, but when Custer had to fight the same Cheyennes and Sioux again a week later, Crook was far away and Custer's army was wiped out. So Buffalo Calf Road Woman in a way contributed to the winning of that famous battle too.

Many who saw what she had done thought that she had counted the biggest coup—not taking life but giving it. That is why the Indians call the Battle of the Rosebud "Where the Girl Saved Her Brother."

The spot where Buffalo Calf Road Woman counted coup has long since been plowed under. A ranch now covers it. But the memory of her deed lives on—and will live on as long as there are Indians. This is not a fairy tale, but it is a legend. ❖

RACHEL STRANGE OWL

Rachel Strange Owl, a Cheyenne Indian, lives on the Northern Cheyenne Lame Deer Reservation in Montana. In the early 1970s she told the legend "Where the Girl Saved Her Brother" to Richard Erdoes, a collector of Native American myths and legends. She first heard the

1947–

story, which is based on actual events, from her mother.

Today Strange Owl lives on the reservation with her husband and several of her seven children. She supervises artists who bead high-fashion clothes with Cheyenne and Cree designs.

COMPREHENSION CHECK

1. What is counting coup? *(gaining war honors)*

2. Where do the white men want the Native Americans in this legend to move to? *(reservations)*

3. Why do the "hostiles" refuse to move? *(They want to live their own way.)*

4. How does Buffalo Calf Road Woman rescue her brother? *(She rides into the battle with a loud war cry. He jumps on her horse, and they ride away.)*

5. What effect do her actions have on the enemy? *(The enemy retreats.)*

Waters of Gold

RETOLD BY LAURENCE YEP

A Spring Morning at Yen-ling-t'an (Chekiang) (Qing dynasty, China, 1642–1715), Wang Yuan-ch'i. Handscroll, ink and color on paper, 38 cm × 304.7 cm, courtesy of Museum of Fine Arts, Boston, Keith McLeod Fund (56.10). Photo Copyright © 1995 Museum of Fine Arts, Boston, all rights reserved.

Many years ago, there lived a woman whom everyone called Auntie Lily. She was Auntie by blood to half the county and Auntie to the other half by friendship. As she liked to say, "There's a bit of Heaven in each of us." As a result, she was always helping people out.

Because of her many kind acts, she knew so many people that she couldn't go ten steps without meeting someone who wanted to chat. So it would take her half the day to go to the village well and back to her home.

Eventually, though, she helped so many people that she had no more money. She had to sell

WATERS OF GOLD **725**

SUMMARY

Waters of Gold Auntie Lily is famous throughout her village for her generosity, but this very quality has left her penniless. She is forced to sell her property to her neighbor, a rich old woman who charges Lily rent to live in her former house. One day, a filthy beggar enters the village and begs for water to wash his feet. Everybody refuses him except Auntie Lily. After washing his feet in the bucket she provides, the beggar tells her to keep the used water beside her bed overnight. The next morning, the bucket is filled with gold. As soon as the rich neighbor hears the news, she regrets her own meanness toward the beggar. She drags him to her house when he reappears and forces him to wash his feet. Told to leave the bucket of water beside her bed overnight, she plunges her hand in it the next morning—only to be bitten by snakes, lizards, and ants. The old woman grows sick, and Auntie Lily nurses her. "Kindness comes with no price," she teaches the old woman. When a leper comes to the village, only Auntie Lily and her neighbor show him hospitality. The grateful leper—brother to the beggar—cures the old woman, and she remains kind for the rest of her life.

STRATEGIC READING FOR
Less-Proficient Readers

Set a Purpose Have students read to find out how Auntie Lily helps the beggar.

Mini-Lesson The Writer's Style

CAUSE-AND-EFFECT TRANSITIONS
Remind students that transitions are connecting words that let readers know how the details in a paragraph are related. Elicit from students that transitions show different relationships, such as comparison, contrast, spatial order, order of importance, and cause and effect. Use the transitions shown to present some common cause-and-effect transitions. Tell students that placing the causes before the effects is an especially clear method of organization.

Application Direct students to find two cause-and-effect transitions in the highlighted paragraph on page 725. Then have students identify the details concerning the causes and effects in this paragraph.

Reteaching/Reinforcement
• *Writing Handbook*, anthology pp. 817–818
• *Writing Mini-Lessons* transparencies, p. 33

 **The Writer's Craft**

Using Transitions, pp. 271–273

> *Cause-and-Effect Transitions*
> accordingly   due to   since
> as a result   for this reason   so
> because   if . . . then   therefore
> consequently   owing to   thus

Literary Concept:
FIGURATIVE LANGUAGE

A Have students identify the metaphors and simile in this passage. Then guide students to explain why these are effective descriptions. *(Possible responses: The metaphors are "a trash heap" and "a walking pig wallow." The simile is "as muddy and matted as a bird's nest." They create vivid images of the beggar's shabby state.)*

Literary Links

B Have students compare the rich neighbor in this story with the prejudiced people in "The Noble Experiment." *(Possible response: Both the rich woman and the prejudiced people are biased, shortsighted, and narrow-minded.)*

Literary Concept: CHARACTER

C Explore with students the reasons why the rich woman refuses the beggar and Auntie Lily accepts him. Have students make a Venn diagram to show how these two characters are similar and different. *(Possible responses: Both women live in the same village. The rich woman is selfish; Auntie Lily is selfless.)*

---

her fields and even her house to her neighbor, a rich old woman. "If you'd helped yourself instead of others, you wouldn't have to do this," the neighbor said smugly. "Where are all those other people when you need them?"

"That isn't why I helped them," Auntie Lily said firmly. She wound up having to pay rent for the house she had once owned. She supported herself by her embroidery; but since her eyes were going bad, she could not do very much.

One day an old beggar entered the village. He was a ragbag of a man—a trash heap, a walking pig wallow. It was impossible to tell what color or what shape his clothes had once been, and his hair was as muddy and matted as a bird's nest. As he shuffled through the village gates, he called out, "Water for my feet. Please, water for my feet. One little bowl of water—that's all I ask."

Everyone ignored him, pretending to concentrate on their chores instead. One man went on replacing the shaft of his hoe. A woman swept her courtyard. Another woman fed her hens.

The beggar went to each in turn, but they all showed their backs to him.

After calling out a little while longer, the

> As he shuffled through the
> village gates, he called out,
> "Water for my feet. Please,
> water for my feet."

---

beggar went to the nearest home, which happened to belong to the rich old woman. When he banged at her door, he left the dirty outline of his knuckles on the clean wood. And when the rich woman opened her door, his smell nearly took her breath away.

Now it so happened that she had been chopping vegetables when the beggar had knocked. When the beggar repeated his request, she raised her cleaver menacingly. "What good would one bowl of water be? You'd need a whole river to wash you clean. Go away."

"A thousand pardons," the old beggar said, and shambled on to the next house.

Though Auntie Lily had to hold her nose, she asked politely, "Yes?"

"I'd like a bowl of water to wash my feet." And the beggar pointed one grimy finger toward them.

Her rich neighbor had stayed in her doorway to watch the beggar. She scolded Auntie Lily now. "It's all your fault those beggars come into the village. They know they can count on a free meal."

It was an old debate between them, so Auntie Lily simply said, "Any of us can have bad luck."

"Garbage," the rich old woman declared, "is garbage. They must have done something bad, or Heaven wouldn't have let them become beggars."

Auntie Lily turned to the beggar. "I may be joining you on the road someday. Wait here."

Much to the neighbor's distress, Auntie Lily went inside and poured water from a large jar in her kitchen into a bucket. Carrying it in both hands, she brought it outside to the beggar and set it down.

WORDS
TO
KNOW   **smugly** (smŭg'lē) *adv.* in a self-satisfied way

726

| **Mini-Lesson: Speaking,** | **Listening, and Viewing** |

STORYTELLING Explain to students that in addition to passing on traditional myths and legends, ancient storytellers also served as "journalists" by passing on current information. These ancient storytellers walked from village to village relaying news about births, deaths, big hunts, celebrations, and so on. To make their stories more dramatic, the storytellers often incorporated personal details they knew about the people.

Application Arrange students in small groups and have each group select one of three stories grouped here. Direct each student to pick a different character in the story. Make sure that everyone in the group has a role. Next, have each student analyze the character's actions and assume his or her personality. Finally, have each group member tell the chosen story to the rest of the group from the character's perspective, using the first-person pronoun *I*.

The beggar stood on one leg, just like a crane, while he washed one callused, leathery sole over the bucket. "You can put mud on any other part of me, but if my feet are clean, then I feel clean."

As he fussily continued to cleanse his feet, Auntie Lily asked kindly, "Are you hungry? I don't have much, but what I have I'm willing to share."

The beggar shook his head. "I've stayed longer in this village than I have in any other. Heaven is my roof, and the whole world my house."

Auntie Lily stared at him, wondering what she would look like after a few years on the road. "Are you very tired? Have you been on the road for very long?"

"No, the road is on me," the beggar said, and held up his hands from his dirty sides. "But thank you. You're the first person to ask. And you're the first person to give me some water. So place the bucket of water by your bed tonight and do not look into it till tomorrow morning."

As the beggar shuffled out of the village again, Auntie Lily stared down doubtfully at the bucket of what was now muddy water. Then, even though she felt foolish, she picked it up again.

"You're not really going to take that scummy water inside?" laughed the rich neighbor. "It'll probably breed mosquitoes."

"It seemed important to him," she answered. "I'll humor him."

"Humoring people," snapped the neighbor, "has got you one step from begging yourself."

Detail of *Beggars and Street Characters* (1516), Zhou Chen. Album leaves; ink and colors on paper. Honolulu (Hawaii) Academy of Arts, gift of Mrs. Carter Galt, 1956 (2239.1).

WATERS OF GOLD **727**

Art Note

Detail of Beggars and Street Characters **by Zhou Chen** Zhou Chen painted this depiction of a beggar in the early 16th century.

Reading the Art *How would you compare the subject of this painting with your image of the beggar in the story?*

Active Reading: EVALUATE

D Invite students to evaluate Auntie Lily's character based on this passage. *(Possible response: She is exceedingly kind, generous, and considerate.)*

STRATEGIC READING FOR

Less-Proficient Readers

E Ask students how Auntie Lily befriends the beggar. *(She provides water so he can wash his feet. She also offers him food.)* Summarizing

Set a Purpose Have students read to find out how Auntie Lily is rewarded for her kindness.

CUSTOMIZING FOR

Students Acquiring English

3 Make sure that students understand the idiomatic meaning of *on the road* ("in the process of traveling") and the humor that arises when the beggar rearranges these words to make a pun. *No, the road is on me* is a reference to the dirt he has picked up as he has traveled.

Linking to Science

 **F** Water does not literally breed mosquitoes. However, female mosquitoes lay their eggs only in water. Common sites include woodland pools, marshes, swamps, and rain barrels. Mosquitoes can be dangerous because many species inject infectious microorganisms when they bite. As a result, mosquitoes can transmit such diseases as malaria, yellow fever, and dengue fever.

Mini-Lesson Grammar

WHO AND WHOM A pronoun is a word that is used to take the place of a noun. Pronouns have subject (*I*) , object (*me*), and possessive (*my, mine*) forms. The pronouns *who* and *whom* are often confused. Explain that *who* is the subject form; *whom* is the object form. Tell students that in spoken English, *who* is used in place of *whom* so often that *whom* sounds stilted. Nonetheless, *whom* is still used in formal speaking and writing.

Application Have students select the correct pronoun in each of the following sentences.

1. (Who, Whom) wouldn't want to wake up to a bucket filled with gold?

2. To (who, whom) will the beggar next appear?
3. (Who, Whom) will be the lucky winner then?
4. (Who, Whom) do you see as the best person in the story?
5. (Who, Whom) is the central figure in this story?

Reteaching/Reinforcement
• Grammar Handbook, anthology pp. 364–365
• *Grammar Mini-Lessons* copymasters p. 17, transparencies p. 10

The Writer's Craft

Who and Whom. p. 541

Active Reading: PREDICT

G Remind students that this is a folk tale, so mysterious and magical things can happen. Then invite students to predict what they think will happen to the bucket of water. *(Possible response: There will be gold in the water.)*

Literary Concept: PLOT

H Ask students to explain who the beggar might be and why he has transformed the dirty water into a fortune. *(Possible responses: He must be a person who possesses magical powers, perhaps a magician or a holy man. He transforms the water to reward Auntie Lily for her goodness and kindness.)*

Linking to History

I Gold, one of the few metals that can be found in pure form, has been prized by people since prehistoric times. Gold mining dates to the time of the ancient Etruscan, Minoan, Assyrian, and Egyptian cultures. Gold is the most malleable of all the metals, which means it can be easily hammered into different shapes. An ingot measuring 2 cubic inches—about the size of a matchbox—can be beaten or rolled into enough gold leaf to cover a tennis court.

STRATEGIC READING FOR

Less-Proficient Readers

J Ask students how the beggar rewards Auntie Lily. *(The water she gave him turns into gold.)* **Relating Cause and Effect**

Set a Purpose Have students read to find out what happens the next time the beggar appears.

G However, Auntie Lily carried the bucket inside anyway. Setting it down near her sleeping mat, she covered the mouth of the bucket with an old, cracked plate so she wouldn't peek into it by mistake, and then she got so caught up in embroidering a pair of slippers that she forgot all about the beggar and his bucket of water.

She sewed until twilight, when it was too dark to use her needle. Then, because she had no money for oil or candles, she went to sleep.

The next morning Auntie Lily rose and stretched the aches out of her back. She sighed. "The older I get, the harder it is to get up in the morning."

She was always saying something like that, but she had never stayed on her sleeping mat— even when she was sick. Thinking of all that day's chores, she decided to water the herbs she had growing on one side of her house.

Her eyes fell upon the beggar's bucket with its covering plate. "No sense using fresh water when that will do as well. After all, dirt's dirt to a plant."

Squatting down, she picked up the bucket and was surprised at how heavy it was. "I must have filled it fuller than I thought," she grunted.

She staggered out of the house and over to the side where rows of little green herbs grew. "Here you go," she said to her plants. "Drink deep."

Taking off the plate, she upended the bucket; but instead of muddy brown water, there was a flash of reflected light and a clinking sound as gold coins rained down upon her plants.

H Auntie Lily set the bucket down hastily and crouched, not trusting her weak eyes. However, where some of her herbs had been, there was now a small mound of gold coins. She squinted in disbelief and rubbed her aching eyes and stared again; but the gold was still there.

She turned to the bucket. There was even more gold inside. Scooping up coins by the handful, she freed her little plants and made sure that the stalks weren't too bent.

Then she sat gazing at her bucket full of gold until a farmer walked by. "Tell me I'm not dreaming," she called to him.

The farmer yawned and came over with his hoe over his shoulder. "I wish I were dreaming, because that would mean I'm still in bed instead of having to go off to work."

Auntie Lily gathered up a handful of gold coins and let it fall in a tinkling, golden shower back into the bucket. "And this is real?"

The farmer's jaw dropped. He picked up one coin with his free hand and bit into it. He flipped it back in with the other coins. "It's as real as me, Auntie. But where did you ever get that?"

So Auntie Lily told him. And as others woke up and stepped outside, Auntie told them as well, for she still could not believe her luck and wanted them to confirm that the gold was truly gold. In no time at all, there was a small crowd around her.

If the bucket had been filled with ordinary copper cash, that would have been more money than any of them had ever seen. In their wildest dreams, they had never expected to see that much gold. Auntie Lily stared at the bucket uncomfortably. "I keep thinking it's going to disappear the next moment."

The farmer, who had been standing there all this time, shook his head. "If it hasn't disappeared by now, I don't think it will. What are you going to do with it, Auntie?"

728 UNIT SIX: THE ORAL TRADITION

Mini-Lesson: Speaking,  **Listening, and Viewing**

GROUP DISCUSSIONS Explain to students that they use critical skills before, during, and after listening to any speaker in a group discussion. Provide students with these listening guidelines:

• *Before the discussion, keep an open mind and prepare yourself. Think about the purpose and likely focus of the discussion. Also consider what you already know about the discussion topic.*

• *While you listen, concentrate on each speaker's words.*

• *After you listen, ask questions about the discussion. Repeat the speaker's words in your questions to help you check your understanding. Listen to the answers, and then evaluate the discussion.*

Application Have students make a listening checklist to use as they listen to the storytelling presentations in the Mini-Lesson on page 726. Instruct students to list at least five items that will help them become more active listeners.

Auntie Lily stared at the bucket, and suddenly she came to a decision. Stretching out a hand, she picked up a gold coin. "I'm going to buy back my house, and I'm going to get back my land."

The farmer knew the fields. "Those old things? You could buy a valley full of prime land with half that bucket. And a palace with the other half."

"I want what I sweated for." Asking the farmer to guard her bucket, Auntie Lily closed her hand around the gold coin. Then, as the crowd parted before her, she made her way over to her neighbor.

Now the rich old woman liked to sleep late; but all the noise had woken her up, so she was just getting dressed when Auntie knocked. The old woman yanked her door open as she buttoned the last button of her coat. "Who started the riot? Can't a person get a good night's sleep?"

With some satisfaction, Auntie Lily held up the gold coin. "Will this buy back my house and land?"

"Where did you get that?" the old woman demanded.

"Will it buy them back?" Auntie Lily repeated.

The rich old woman snatched the coin out of Auntie Lily's hand and bit into it just as the farmer had. "It's real," the old woman said in astonishment.

"Will it?" Auntie asked again.

"Yes, yes, yes," the old woman said crabbily. "But where did you ever get that much gold?"

When Auntie Lily told her the story and showed her the bucket of gold, the rich old woman stood moving her mouth like a fish out of water. Clasping her hands together, she shut

her eyes and moaned in genuine pain. "And I sent him away. What a fool I am. What a fool." And the old woman beat her head with her fists.

That very afternoon, the beggar—the ragbag, the trash heap, the walking pig wallow—shuffled once more through the village gates with feet as dirty as before. As he went, he croaked, "Water for my feet. Please, water for my feet. One little bowl of water—that's all I ask."

This time, people dropped whatever they were doing when they heard his plea. Hoes, brooms, and pots were flung down, hens and pigs were kicked out of the way as everyone hurried to fill a bucket with water. There was a small riot by the village well as everyone fought to get water at the same time. Still others rushed out with buckets filled from the jars in their houses.

"Here, use my water," one man shouted, holding up a tub.

A woman shoved in front of him with a

> *That very afternoon, the beggar—the ragbag, the trash heap, the walking pig wallow—shuffled once more through the village gates with feet as dirty as before.*

Literary Concept: CHARACTER

K Explore with students how Auntie Lily reacts to her extraordinary good fortune. Then ask students what her reaction reveals about her character. (*Possible response: Her decision to buy back only that which she feels is rightfully hers reveals that she is level-headed and not greedy.*)

Active Reading: PREDICT

L Have students predict what they think might happen next in the plot, based on the rich old woman's reaction to Auntie Lily's good fortune. If students need help responding, prompt them with the following model.

Think-Aloud Model *I know the old woman is greedy and selfish. Her reactions to Aunt Lily's story—moving her mouth like a fish, clasping her hands, shutting her eyes, moaning in pain—suggest that she will try very hard to find the beggar and make him give her a fortune as well.*

Critical Thinking: HYPOTHESIZING

M Ask students to explain what the townspeople are doing. Then invite students to hypothesize how the beggar will react to their plans. (*Possible responses: They are all trying to be nice to the beggar so he will give them a fortune too. He will probably not give them gold because their actions now are based on greed, not kindness.*)

Mini-Lesson ⬦ **Reading Skills/Strategies**

MAKING JUDGMENTS Remind students that when they make judgments, they form opinions about characters and events. By making judgments, readers can better understand what happens in a story and why. Encourage students to make judgments as they read by asking themselves questions about a character's actions or reactions and then deciding how they feel about what happens in the story.

Application Have students evaluate Auntie Lily's actions in the highlighted paragraphs on page 728. Students should list the action taken, the result of the action, and what they think about the character after reading each paragraph.

Reteaching/Reinforcement
• *Unit Six Resource Book*, p. 18

Literary Links

N Invite students to compare and contrast the townspeople here to the neighbors in *The Monsters Are Due on Maple Street*. (*Possible response: Both sets of characters show unkind behavior, but the people in this story also are greedy.*)

CUSTOMIZING FOR

Students Acquiring English

4 Point out that the word *vultures* is used to refer to greedy people who prey on other people.

STRATEGIC READING FOR

Less-Proficient Readers

0 Have students discuss the following questions to contrast the beggar's two visits to the town.

• How do people respond to the beggar this time? Why? (*They are eager to befriend him because they know about the gold.*) **Making Inferences**

• Who "wins" the chance to help the beggar? (*the rich old woman*) **Noting Relevant Details**

• How are these characters' actions different from their actions the first time they saw the beggar? (*The first time they turned away from the beggar, but now they welcome him.*) **Comparing and Contrasting**

Set a Purpose Have students read to see how the rich woman's life changes.

Literary Concept: IRONY

P Invite students to explain the irony in this passage. (*Possible response: It is ironic that the rich old woman was expecting gold but got biting creatures instead.*)

Literary Concept: MORAL

Q Point out that Auntie Lily's words act as the story's moral. Then invite students to write a new moral for this story, based on the characters and events. (*Possible response: Goodness is its own reward.*)

bucket in her arms. "No, no, use mine. It's purer."

N They surrounded the old beggar, pleading with him to use their water, and in the process of <u>jostling</u> one another, they splashed a good deal of water on one another and came <u>perilously</u> close to drowning the beggar. The rich old woman, Auntie Lily's neighbor, charged to the rescue.

4 "Out of the way, you vultures," the rich old woman roared. "You're going to trample him." Using her elbows, her feet, and in one case even her teeth, the old woman fought her way through the mob.

No longer caring if she soiled her hands, the old woman seized the beggar by the arm. "This way, you poor, misunderstood creature."

Fighting off her neighbors with one hand and keeping her grip on the beggar with the other, the old woman hauled him inside her house. Barring the door against the rest of the village, she ignored all the fists and feet thumping on her door and all the shouts.

"I really wasn't myself yesterday, because I had been up the night before tending a sick friend. This is what I meant to do." She fetched a fresh new towel and an even newer bucket and forced the beggar to wash his feet.

When he was done, he handed her the now filthy towel. "Dirt's dirt, and garbage is garbage," he said.

However, the greedy old woman didn't recognize her own words. She was too busy trying to remember what else Auntie Lily had done. "Won't you have something to eat? Have you traveled very far? Are you tired?" **0** she asked, all in the same breath.

The old beggar went to the door and waited patiently while she unbarred it. As he shuffled outside, he instructed her to leave the bucket of water by her bed but not to look into it until the morning.

That night, the greedy old woman couldn't sleep as she imagined the heap of shiny gold that would be waiting for her tomorrow. She waited impatiently for the sun to rise and got up as soon as she heard the first rooster crow.

Hurrying to the bucket, she plunged her hands inside expecting to bring up handfuls of gold. Instead, she gave a cry as dozens of little things bit her, for the bucket was filled not with gold but with snakes, lizards, and ants.

The greedy old woman fell sick—some said from her bites, some claimed from sheer frustration. Auntie Lily herself came to nurse her neighbor. "Take this to heart: Kindness comes with no price."

> *Hurrying to the bucket,*
> *she plunged her hands*
> *inside expecting to bring*
> *up handfuls of gold.*

WORDS TO KNOW	**jostling** (jŏs′lĭng) *n.* roughly bumping, pushing, or shoving **jostle** *v.* **perilously** (pĕr′ə-ləs-lē) *adv.* dangerously

730

Multicultural 🌐 **Perspectives**

CHINESE LITERATURE There are two clear-cut traditions in Chinese literature: the literary and the vernacular. Both traditions can be traced back more than 2,000 years. The literary tradition began with poetry and grew to include drama, fiction, history, and popular stories. The vernacular tradition includes folk tales. Although as time-honored as works in the literary tradition, these folk stories were long considered beneath literary consideration. The scholar-officials, who were the arbiters of literary standards, had ruled that such colloquial tales as "Waters of Gold" were neither sufficiently polished nor stylized for academic acceptance. It was not until the 20th century that folk literature gained the full acceptance and appreciation of the Chinese literary establishment.

The old woman was so ashamed that she did, indeed, take the lesson to heart. Though she remained sick, she was kind to whoever came to her door.

One day, a leper came into the village. Everyone hid for fear of the terrible disease. Doors slammed and shutters banged down over windows, and soon the village seemed deserted.

Only Auntie Lily and her neighbor stepped out of their houses. "Are you hungry?" Auntie Lily asked.

"Are you thirsty?" the neighbor asked. "I'll make you a cup of tea."

The leper thanked Auntie Lily and then turned to the neighbor as if to express his gratitude as well; but he stopped and studied her. "You're looking poorly, my dear woman. Can I help?"

With a tired smile, the rich old woman explained what had happened. When she was finished, the leper stood thoughtfully for a moment. "You're not the same woman as before: You're as kind as Auntie Lily, and you aren't greedy anymore. So take this humble gift from my brother, the old beggar."

With that, the leper limped out of the village; and as he left, the illness fell away from the old woman like an old, discarded cloak. But though the old woman was healthy again, she stayed as kind as Auntie Lily and used her own money as well and wisely as Auntie Lily used the waters of gold. ❖

LAURENCE YEP

1948–

When Laurence Yep was a college freshman, he published his first short story. When he was 25, he published his first book. Two years later he wrote his second book, *Dragonwings*, which won a number of awards, including a Newbery Honor Award. Yep has written 2 plays and over 17 books, many of which reflect his Chinese heritage.

Since Yep is a third-generation Chinese American, some of his novels—such as *Child of the* *Owl* and *Sea Glass*—focus on Chinese-American characters who are caught between two cultures. Yep says that his books are popular among teenagers because "I'm always pursuing the theme of being an outsider—an alien—and many teenagers feel they're aliens."

OTHER WORKS *Tongues of Jade, The Rainbow People, The Serpent's Children, Mountain Light*

Cultural Note
Tales such as this one served to educate Chinese Americans about the China they had left or perhaps had never seen. More important, the tales also taught listeners how a true Chinese person was supposed to behave according to the values of the society.

CUSTOMIZING FOR

Gifted and Talented Students

R Have students explain what the "waters of gold" might symbolize. *(Possible responses: physical and spiritual riches; a great fortune and a great goodness of heart)*

STRATEGIC READING FOR

Less-Proficient Readers

S Ask students to explain how and why the rich old lady changes. *(She becomes genuinely kind because of Auntie Lily's kindness and the lesson she learns from the beggar.)* **Relating Cause and Effect**

From Personal Response to Critical Analysis

1. How do you feel about the ending of this story? Write your ideas in your notebook. *(Responses will vary.)*
2. How would you explain why the old woman continues to be kind even after she has regained her health? *(Possible response: Her personality has really changed as a result of the lesson she has learned.)*
3. Do you think that kindness really comes with no price? Explain your answer. *(Possible responses: no, because people always want something in return; yes, because some people are genuinely kind and selfless)*

COMPREHENSION CHECK
1. How does Auntie Lily lose all her money? *(She spends it on helping people.)*
2. How does Auntie Lily support herself? *(by her embroidery)*
3. What happens to the bucket of dirty water that Auntie Lily places next to her bed? *(The water turns to gold.)*
4. What happens when the rich old woman plunges her hands into the bucket of dirty water? *(She is bitten by snakes, lizards, and ants.)*
5. What gift does the leper give the rich old lady? *(the gift of health)*

Present an award Assign each group a recorder to write the heroic qualities the character possesses. You may wish to divide the group into a team to draft the speech and a team to edit and revise it. In addition to selecting a group member to give the speech, groups may choose to select a member to portray the recipient of the award, who can give an acceptance speech.

Rubric

3 Full Accomplishment Students cite specific heroic qualities the character evinces to justify the award. The speech is well organized, persuasive, and detailed.

2 Substantial Accomplishment Students cite the character's heroic qualities and present an organized speech.

1 Little or Partial Accomplishment Students are unable to identify heroic qualities or have difficulty giving a speech.

Geography Connection

Design a travel brochure Suggest that groups divide the research tasks by subject, so that one student researches climate, another researches tourist attractions, and so on. An alternative way to divide tasks is by source, with one student using encyclopedias, another using on-line sources, and so on.

Rubric

3 Full Accomplishment The travel brochure is attractive, inviting, and complete.

2 Substantial Accomplishment The brochure has adequate facts but is not very enticing.

1 Little or Partial Accomplishment The brochure does not contain sufficient information and is not inviting.

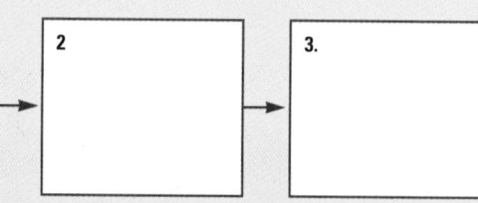

RESPONDING
OPTIONS

LITERATURE CONNECTION PROJECT 1 — Multimodal Activity

Present an award Working with a small group of classmates, design and present an award to the character in these tales that you consider most heroic—Odin, Buffalo Calf Road Woman, or Auntie Lily. Follow these guidelines as you carry out this project.

- Choose your character and then brainstorm some heroic qualities he or she has demonstrated. Have a member of the group list the qualities. Cite examples from the selection.

- Use the list to draft a speech that nominates the character for the award. Then design the award.

- Select one person in your group to give the speech and present the award in front of the class.

GEOGRAPHY CONNECTION PROJECT 2 — Multimodal Activity

Design a travel brochure The stories in this part of Unit Six originated in three different places: China, Montana, and Scandinavia. Choose one of these places to investigate. Then work with a group of classmates to design a travel brochure advertising the place. Include information about climate during different seasons, major tourist attractions, lodging, and airlines that fly there. Use maps, atlases, travel guides, encyclopedias, and on-line computer resources to find information. When you finish, display your brochure with those created by other groups. Have students vote on which brochure best attracts them to visit a particular place.

SOCIAL STUDIES CONNECTION PROJECT 3 — Multimodal Activity

Complete a sequence chart The Battles of the Rosebud and the Little Bighorn were part of a period of warfare between the U.S. Army and the Sioux. Research the events that led up to the Battle of the Rosebud, the Battle of the Little Bighorn, and the battle—or massacre—at Wounded Knee. Complete a sequence chart like the one shown here to record the sequence of events.

1. Treaties: U.S. government guarantees land between Missouri River and Oregon Territory to Native Americans.	→	2.	→	3.

Social Studies Connection

Complete a sequence chart Guide students to consult authoritative reference books on the events before the battles. Such reference sources include print or computer encyclopedias, history texts, and on-line computer resources. If available, students may wish to contact local Native-American organizations for other bibliographic suggestions. Before they begin to construct their flow charts, suggest that students synthesize what they have read by making a list of key events to include in their charts.

Rubric

3 Full Accomplishment The chart correctly records, in chronological order, the key events that led up to the battles.

2 Substantial Accomplishment The chart includes most of the events, but some events are missing or out of order.

1 Little or Partial Accomplishment The chart does not show the main events in order.

ACROSS CULTURES MINI-PROJECTS Multimodal Activities

Make an illustrated calendar Find out which days of the week are named for Norse gods and goddesses, which are named for the sun and the moon, and which is named for a Roman god. Use an encyclopedia or other reference books to gather information about Norse and Roman myths. Then paint an accompanying picture or symbol to represent each day of the week.

Role-play a meeting Working with a partner, role-play a meeting between Buffalo Calf Road Woman and either Grandpa from "The Medicine Bag" (page 285) or Chief Dan George, the author of "I Am a Native of North America" (page 343). What would Grandpa or Chief Dan George tell Buffalo Calf Road Woman and her brother, Chief Comes-in-Sight, about life on a reservation and about relations between whites and Native Americans? Drawing upon details from the selections, act out your meeting for the rest of the class.

Draw or paint a picture Imagine and depict one of the future scenes that Odin might have viewed in Mimir's well. Your picture might depict something that you think might happen in your own future or in the future of the world.

Perform a mime or dance With a group of classmates, select one of these three tales and create a mime or dance based on it to perform for the class. Since your audience is already familiar with the plot and characters of the tale, concentrate on expressing the emotions of each scene. Use simple costumes appropriate to the culture you are representing.

Create a graphic Compare and contrast the Norse god Odin and the Greek god Prometheus by making a chart like the one shown. What qualities do you think were valued most by the ancient Greeks? by the Norse?

	Description	Attitude	Sacrifices	Courage
Odin				
Prometheus				

Extended Social Studies Reading

MORE ABOUT THE CULTURES

- *Strange Footprints on the Land: Vikings in America* by Richard B. Lyttle
- *War Clouds in the West: Indians and Cavalrymen, 1860–1890* by Albert Marrin
- *Indian Legacy: Native American Influences on World Life and Culture* by Hermina Poatgieter
- *The Great Wall of China* by Leonard Everett Fisher
- *See Inside an Ancient Chinese Town* by Penelope Hughes-Stanton

LINKS TO UNIT THREE   **733**

Make an Illustrated Calendar Suggest that students consult an almanac, encyclopedia, or history of language text for information about the days of the week. Monday comes from the Anglo-Saxon term *monandaeg*, which means moon's day. Tuesday, Wednesday, Thursday, and Friday are named for the Norse gods and goddess Tyr, Woden/Odin, Thor, and Freya, respectively. Saturday is named for the Roman god Saturn. Sunday is named for the sun. Students familiar with other languages may know of days of the week named after other gods. For instance, in French *mardi* and *mercredi*—Tuesday and Wednesday in English—are named after the Roman gods Mars and Mercury, respectively.

Role-Play a Meeting Suggest that students start by writing a script of the meeting. Encourage students to consult pages 322 in *The Writer's Craft* for guidelines for writing dialogue and to include specific details. Then have students rehearse their role-playing until they are confident about the quality of their performance.

Draw or Paint a Picture Guide students to use the medium that best captures the mood of the scene. Possibilities include paints, acrylics, markers, colored pencils, and pen and ink. Encourage students to review illustrated books of Norse mythology to get ideas about setting and costume details. Finished pictures might show a scene that logically extends the story.

Perform a Mime or Dance Suggest that students also include background music to help set the mood for their interpretative dance or mime.

Create a Graphic Encourage students to include specific details, examples, and facts from the stories to make their comparisons vivid. If necessary, help students make inferences about the qualities most valued by the ancient Greeks and Norse.

OVERVIEW

In the Guided Assignment for this section, students will write a fable that teaches a lesson about contemporary life. By doing so, they will learn more about fables and also will practice writing a story. As preparation for this assignment, The Writer's Style will help students use adjective and adverb phrases and compound sentences to tell stories with a variety of sentence types. In Reading the World, students will interpret an oral storyteller's gestures to understand the significance of body language.

Objectives

- To recognize that good writers vary sentence types to create a variety of rhythms
- To make writing more effective and entertaining by varying sentence structure
- To write a modern fable that teaches a lesson
- To analyze facial and body language in real-world situations

Skills

LITERATURE
- Identifying different sentence types

WRITING AND LANGUAGE
- Adding sentence variety

GRAMMAR AND USAGE
- Using adjective and adverb phrases
- Distinguishing between compound verbs and compound sentences

MEDIA LITERACY
- Interpreting body language

SPEAKING, LISTENING, AND VIEWING
- Revising with a peer
- Peer discussion
- Group conferencing

CRITICAL THINKING
- Interpreting gestures and expressions

Teaching Strategy: MODELING

In the following models, the authors use various sentence structures to make sure their writing captures and holds their readers' attention.

(A) Tolstoy Possible responses: The second to last sentence may reflect the way the daughter-in-law lectures the old man or the fact that she feels annoyed by him. The last sentence is short and simple. It shows the old man's quiet and stoic reaction.

(B) Sellew The first sentence opener draws attention to the world being like a person and "very young." The third, fourth, and fifth openers draw readers' attention to the various parts of Odin's body: his head, his shoulders, and his feet.

STORYTELLING

People enjoy hearing and telling stories. As you read the stories in this unit, were you able to imagine them being told by storytellers? How would you tell the stories yourself? In the following pages you will

- see how sentence variety can add interest to a story
- write and tell a fable based on one you've just read
- apply your storytelling skills to a real-life situation

Writer's Style: Varying Sentence Types Good writers create rhythms in their stories by varying the kinds of sentences they use, the length of their sentences, and the sentence beginnings and endings.

Read the Literature

Notice how the writers of these excerpts vary their sentences.

Literature Models

(A) Sentence Length
Look at the last two sentences of this passage. How does the length of each sentence reflect what is happening?

> One day they gave him his food in a bowl. He tried to move the bowl closer; it fell to the floor and broke. His daughter-in-law scolded him. She told him that he spoiled everything in the house and broke their dishes, and she said that from now on he would get his food in a wooden dish. The old man sighed and said nothing.
>
> Leo Tolstoy
> from "The Old Grandfather and His Little Grandson"

(B) Sentence Openers
Writers begin some sentences by calling attention to certain details. What details do the openers of the first, third, fourth, and fifth sentences emphasize?

> Once when the world was still very young, Odin sat on his throne in the most beautiful palace in Asgard. His throne was so high that he could see over all three parts of the world from where he sat. On his head he wore a helmet shaped like an eagle. On his shoulders perched two black ravens called Memory and Thought. And at his feet crouched two snarling wolves.
>
> Catharine F. Sellew
> from "How Odin Lost His Eye"

734 UNIT SIX: THE ORAL TRADITION

PRINT AND MEDIA RESOURCES

UNIT SIX RESOURCE BOOK
Writer's Style, p. 23
Prewriting, p. 24
Elaboration, p. 25
Peer Response Guide, pp. 26–27
Revising and Proofreading, p. 28
Student Model, p. 29
Rubric, p. 30

GRAMMAR MINI-LESSONS
Transparencies, pp. 12, 28, 44 and 47
Copymasters, pp. 19 and 37

WRITING MINI-LESSONS
Transparencies, p. 42

ACCESS FOR STUDENTS ACQUIRING ENGLISH
Reading and Writing Support

FORMAL ASSESSMENT
Guidelines for Writing Assessment

 WRITING COACH

Connect to Life

Writers can also use a variety of declarative, interrogative, imperative, and exclamatory sentences to engage the reader. Similarly,
when people speak, they use different kinds of sentences to
express their feelings and hold listeners' interest.

Quotation

"I'd hear them scolding their kids and
fighting their husbands and I'd say,
'Gosh! Why don't you go after the
people that have you living like this?
Why don't you go after the growers
that have you tired from working out
in the fields at low wages and keep us
poor all the time? Let's go after them!
They're the cause of our misery!'"

Jessie Lopez De La Cruz
quoted in *Moving the Mountain*
by Ellen Cantarow

Kinds of Sentences
Notice the exclama-
tory, interrogative,
and imperative
sentences. What do
they tell you about
how the speaker
was feeling?

Try Your Hand: Adding Sentence Variety

1. Adding Details Add a sentence opener to each sentence.
An example of a sentence with an opener is shown below.
Example: *Feeling cold and hungry, the child went to bed.*

- . . . they gave him food in a bucket.
- . . . he settled down by the fire to rest.

2. Revise Your Writing Look through your writing portfolio
and choose a piece that you think needs greater sentence
variety. Revise the piece, using the techniques you've learned.

3. Work Together With a partner, rewrite the paragraph below
so that it is not dull and repetitive. You can vary the sentence
openers as well as the kinds and lengths of sentences.

The girl went outside. She hurried across the yard.
She hurried toward the creek. She splashed in each
puddle she passed. She reached the creek. Water had
leaked into her boots. Her pants were muddy.

SkillBuilder

G → GRAMMAR FROM WRITING

**Using Adjective and
Adverb Phrases**
An **adjective phrase** modifies a
noun or pronoun.

In a rage, the daughter-in-law
scolded him.

An **adverb phrase** modifies a
verb, an adjective, or an adverb.

His bowl fell to the floor.

For the sake of emphasis or variety, you may sometimes want to
begin a sentence with an adjective or adverb phrase. For example, if many of your sentences
start with the subject, you could
add interest by moving an adjective or adverb phrase to the
beginning of a sentence.

The bowl hit the floor **with
a crash.**

With a crash, *the bowl hit
the floor.*

APPLYING WHAT YOU'VE LEARNED
Revise the following paragraph.
Create variety by moving one or
two adjective or adverb phrases
to the beginnings of sentences.

*The daughter began cleaning in
a rush of angry energy. She
grew angrier and angrier as she
worked. Finally, she began
yelling at her father. The old
man cowered in fear. The little
grandson on the verge of tears
watched his mother.*

WRITING ABOUT LITERATURE **735**

**Teaching Strategy:
STUMBLING BLOCK**

C Students are likely to pass quickly
over the list of types of sentences without noting their differences. A declarative sentence is a statement of fact and
is used when making an observation or
assertion. An interrogative sentence
asks a question. An imperative sentence
gives a command. An exclamatory sentence expresses strong emotion, such
as a feeling of surprise or amazement.

Teaching Strategy: MODELING

D Possible responses: Even though
three sentences have exclamation
marks, only the first and last sentences
are exclamatory sentences. They
express the speaker's surprise at the
women's behavior and outrage at the
growers. The two interrogative sentences, identified by the question
marks, show the speaker wanting to
ask why the workers don't redirect
their anger. The imperative sentence,
"Let's go after them!" urges the women
to go after the growers.

Try Your Hand

1. Sentence openers will vary. Here are
some examples:
   - After getting angry with him, they
gave him food in a bucket.
   - Feeling weary, they settled down
by the fire to rest.
2. Revisions will vary. Students should
add sentence variety by using
openers and by varying sentence
structure.
3. Rewrites will vary. Here is a sample:
The girl went outside and hurried
across the yard toward the creek.
Why did she have to splash in every
puddle as she passed? When she
reached the creek, water had leaked
into her boots. Her pants were
muddy all over!

SkillBuilder  **GRAMMAR FROM WRITING**

**USING ADJECTIVE AND ADVERB
PHRASES** Draw students' attention to the fact
that beginning a sentence with an adjective or
adverb phrase is an effective way to add variety to
a paragraph, especially when many of its sentences
start with the subject.

Application Possible response: In a rush of angry
energy, the daughter began cleaning. She grew angrier and angrier as she worked. Finally, she began
yelling at her father. The old man cowered in fear.

On the verge of tears, the grandson watched his
mother. He wished she would stop yelling.

Additional Suggestions Have students continue
by revising the following paragraph.

They went out on a warm summer night. It was
going to be fun at the fairground. She was ready
with money to spend. She could see all the lights
as they walked down the steep hill. They all walked
faster and faster.

Reteaching/Reinforcement
Grammar Mini-Lessons copymasters p. 19,
transparencies pp. 12 and 44.

 The Writer's Craft

Using Prepositional Phrases, p. 543

Teaching Strategy:
STUMBLING BLOCK

E Students may have difficulty deciding what kind of lesson is appropriate.
Help them to list lessons that they
have read about or have learned from
their own experiences. Examples of
lessons might include respecting others,
not judging other people by appearances, trusting your own ideas instead
of following others, or thinking before
acting.

Writing Skill:
DEVELOPING CHARACTER

F Tell students that fables usually
have one main character who learns
the lesson. This character often has
some sort of personal or moral fault
that the fable shows needs to be corrected. Often, another character leads
the main character into trouble
because of that main character's fault.
Other characters can help the main
character see the fault and want to
correct it.

Creative Response

For ages, storytellers have been using stories to teach
lessons. Why are these folk tales and fables such effective
teaching tools? You can find out by creating a fable of
your own. In the process, you'll develop a greater appreciation for the fables and discover the power of storytelling.

GUIDED ASSIGNMENT

Write a Modern Fable On the next few pages, you will
write a fable that teaches a lesson. After you've written
your fable, you will tell it aloud to members of your class.

❶ Prewrite and Explore

Fables, such as "The Old Grandfather and
His Little Grandson," are very short tales
that present a clear, often directly stated,
moral—a principle of right and wrong
behavior. With a partner review the fable
by Leo Tolstoy on page 704. If you wish,
take turns telling it aloud. Ask yourself these
questions:

- What lesson does the fable teach?
- What qualities do the characters show?

Student's Note Cards

PLAYING WITH IDEAS

In your own life, you have learned lessons
that you could turn into fables. Here's how
you can start planning a fable of your own:

E • First, decide on a lesson to teach.
- Next, think of characters that would represent the traits you want to show.
F • Finally, consider situations and events that
  could be used to illustrate your lesson.

You might organize your plans on note cards
like the ones below.

> Lesson
> If you try to be someone you are not, you
> will discover that you are better off
> being yourself.

> Characters
> Bird: unhappy with his plain looks and
>   simple song
> 1st Shopkeeper: fair
> 2nd Shopkeeper: greedy
> Bird's friends and family: happy to be
>   plain and simple

> Situations and Events
> Event 1: Bird flies to city.
> Event 2: In the city the bird sells his feathe
>   for a new look and a new song.
> Event 3: Bird can't fly because he traded
>   his feathers for heavy clothes.
> Event 4: Bird's friends and family tell him
>   that they loved him the way he was.

736

Assessment Option

SELF-ASSESSMENT After students have
finished Playing with Ideas, they can assess their
plans. Students can ask themselves the following
questions:
- *What lesson am I trying to teach?*
- *Do I have a variety of characters?*
- *Do I have a main character or characters who will
  learn the lesson?*

- *Are the characters individual and vivid?*
- *Are the events sequenced to make a clear story?*
- *Do I need additional events to make the story
  clearer or more logically structured?*

➋ Write a Discovery Draft

As you draft your fable, use your note cards as a guide and allow your ideas to flow freely. Keep in mind these tips:

• If you don't know where to start, try setting the scene.
• Don't worry about writing too much or too little. You can add or take away anything later.

Student's Discovery Draft

This bird felt bad because he looked so plain. The bird flew from his nest one morning. He flew very far. The sun began to rise. The bird kept flying. He flew all the way to the city.

How can I make my fable sound more like the fables I've read?

The shopkeeper wanted some of the bird's black feathers. He offered to trade his ribbons and buttons for 20 feathers. The bird agreed.

This would be a great place to add dialogue!

➌ Share Your Work

When you like your draft well enough to share it, stop writing and ask a classmate to read and comment on your fable. Sometimes a partner can give you suggestions that you haven't thought of yourself.

 PEER RESPONSE

• What was the lesson of my fable?
• What positive or negative traits did the characters have?
• Which parts did you like best? Why did you like them?

SkillBuilder

 SPEAKING & LISTENING

G **Telling Stories**
Just as the fables of long ago were passed along orally, you can share your fable in a story-telling session. Read on for several storytelling tips.

Preparing the material

• Mark words, phrases, or sentences that you want to emphasize.
• Decide where you will use a loud or forceful tone and where you'll speak softly.
• Mark places where you might use gestures, props, costumes, or music.
• Try out a variety of techniques to see what you like and what you don't.

Presenting the fable

• Telling a story is better than reading it. If you have time, memorize your fable.
• Speak more quickly when the action heats up. Slow down to increase suspense. Pause for dramatic effect.
• Try to look at members of your audience.
• Use facial expressions and gestures for emphasis.

H **APPLYING WHAT YOU'VE LEARNED**
Tell your story to a partner or a small group. Then use the suggestions in this column to evaluate how well you presented your fable. Discuss what else you can do before telling your story to a larger audience.

WRITING ABOUT LITERATURE **737**

Writing Skill: ELABORATION

G The Discovery Draft provides an opportunity for students to develop ideas and sort through the information they have gathered. Students can draft their fables by elaborating on each event listed on their note cards. They can add details about characters and scenes, narrate how a character gets from one place to another, or show, step by step, how a character does something important. All these types of elaboration should help make their writing clear and entertaining.

Teaching Strategy:
COLLABORATIVE OPPORTUNITY

H Encourage students to write questions—either in the margin or on a separate piece of paper—about other students' essays as they read. Questions can be about points they like and think could be expanded or about parts that are obscure and need clarifying.

Mini-Lesson: Speaking, Listening, and Viewing

TELLING STORIES Encourage students to practice telling stories, exploring a variety of techniques. If students cannot memorize all of their stories, have them try to memorize the more important or exciting sections.

Application Readers and listeners can evaluate the fable by referring to the list of suggestions. Encourage students to give constructive criticism that indicates both what was well written or read and what could be improved. Students then can use these comments to discuss what can be done to improve the story.

Additional Suggestions When students have received the suggestions, they can read on to learn how to revise the story. They can mark more words, phrases, or sentences that they want to emphasize or read aloud in some special way.

Critical Thinking: ANALYZING

I To evaluate and revise their modern fables, students should use a variety of sentence structures and adjective or adverb phrases where appropriate.

Teaching Strategy: MODELING

J Use the model of a final draft to show students the various elements that make a good fable. Discuss with them how this sample meets the Standards for Evaluation. Encourage students to decide the best way to read the story aloud. Students may decide that it is best to raise their voices when the shopkeeper speaks or when an important action occurs, such as when the bird plucks the feathers out. They may lower their voices or pause to enhance suspense—for example, after they have described the bird's flight in the first paragraph. Also, students may want to use gestures to emphasize the distance the bird travels, such as drawing an arm through the air. Or they may use props such as a box of buttons and ribbons to show the variety of materials that may have been available to the bird.

Standards for Evaluation

Ideas and Content
• develops central characters and events
• contains characters that show positive or negative traits
• is written in lively, colorful language
• illustrates a principle of right and wrong behavior

Structure and Form
• demonstrates proper and effective paragraphing
• includes transitional words and phrases to show relationships among ideas
• includes sentences with a variety of structure

Grammar, Usage, and Mechanics
• contains no more than two or three minor errors in grammar and usage
• contains no more than two or three minor errors in spelling, capitalization, and punctuation

---

WRITING ABOUT LITERATURE

④ Revise and Prepare

I As you revise your fable for clarity and sentence variety, you should also prepare to tell it aloud. You've thought about voice, gestures, and expressions. Now consider a few final details. Do you think you have enough dialogue? Are your ideas easy to understand? Have you used descriptive language?

J Student's Final Draft

The Unhappy Bird

In a place far away lived a bird who was unhappy with his plain feathers and simple song. So early one morning the bird flew from his nest. He flew over forests, hills, and rivers. He flew all the way to the city.

In the city was a store that sold buttons and ribbons of every color. The bird went to the store, and he filled his beak with ribbons and buttons. Sadly, he had no money.

The shopkeeper said, "Well, I need feathers. If you give me 20 feathers, I'll give you those ribbons and buttons." So with his own beak, the bird plucked 20 feathers from his back. Then the shopkeeper put the ribbons on the bird and sewed the buttons to his wings.

If you were telling this fable, when would you raise your voice? When would you lower it? What gestures might you use?

Where would you pause for dramatic effect? What props or special effects might you use?

Standards for Evaluation

An effective fable
• develops central characters and events
• contains characters that show positive or negative traits
• is written in lively, colorful language
• shows variety in its sentence structure
• illustrates a principle of right and wrong behavior

738 UNIT SIX: THE ORAL TRADITION

A s s e s s m e n t ✓ O p t i o n

SELF-ASSESSMENT To help students assess and revise their own writing and storytelling, have them consider the following questions:
• *What is the main lesson I want to teach?*
• *Will readers and listeners understand the main lesson?*

• *Did I use vivid details to make the story come alive for readers and listeners?*
• *Did I use a variety of sentence styles?*
• *Did I vary my voice appropriately when I read the story aloud?*

Grammar in Context

Compound Sentences One way to vary the length and type of your sentences is to combine two or more simple sentences into a compound sentence. The following compound sentences are from the fable "The Old Grandfather and His Little Grandson."

> He tried to move the bowl closer; it fell to the floor and broke.

> The young peasant and his wife looked at each other, and tears filled their eyes.

 The parts of a compound sentence can be joined by a semi-colon or by a comma and a coordinating conjunction such as *and*, *but*, or *or*.

The writer of the model below used compound sentences instead of short, repetitive sentences in her fable.

 In the city was a store that sold buttons and ribbons of every color. The bird went to the store*s. ,and* He filled his beak with ribbons and buttons. Sadly, he had no money.

Try Your Hand: Combining Sentences

On a separate sheet of paper, combine the simple sentences to make compound sentences.

1. Children learn from their elders. They can teach their elders too.
2. The boy in the story acted like his parents. He taught them a lesson.
3. They realized their mistake. They changed their ways.
4. The whole family grew closer. Life was sweet.

SkillBuilder

 GRAMMAR FROM WRITING

Distinguishing Between Compound Verbs and Compound Sentences

The following excerpt from "The Old Grandfather and His Little Grandson" is a simple sentence with a compound verb.

The old man sighed and said nothing.

Notice that the two parts of the verb, *sighed* and *said*, are joined by the conjunction *and*. No punctuation comes between the parts of a compound verb.

What two simple sentences make up the following compound sentence?

The old man sighed, and he said nothing.

APPLYING WHAT YOU'VE LEARNED
Rewrite each sentence below, correcting punctuation errors.

1. The little grandson clapped his hands and he danced.
2. The grandfather clapped but he couldn't dance.
3. The grandfather got up, and walked outside.

GRAMMAR HANDBOOK

For more information on compound sentences, see page 879 of the Grammar Handbook.

CUSTOMIZING FOR
Students Acquiring English

K Some students may have difficulty creating compound sentences. Encourage them to revise their own writing by noticing which simple sentences are related. Tell them they can use any of the coordinating conjunctions to write compound sentences, but they should notice how each one functions. *And* is used to add a piece of information. *But* indicates a change where the second part of the sentence qualifies the first. *Or* expresses a choice between the two items. Tell them that other coordinating conjunctions are: *so, for, yet,* and *nor.*

Teaching Strategy:
USING THE SKILLBUILDER

L You may want to teach the SkillBuilder on Distinguishing Between Compound Verbs and Compound Sentences at this time. It will help students use commas correctly when they revise their writing.

Try Your Hand

Possible responses:

1. Children learn from their elders, but they can teach their elders too.
2. The boy in the story acted like his parents, and he taught them a lesson.
3. They realized their mistake, so they changed their ways.
4. The whole family grew closer, and life was sweet.

PORTFOLIO

Invite students to write a note to themselves identifying methods they used to achieve sentence variety. Have students attach the note to the final draft of their modern fable.

SkillBuilder   G   GRAMMAR FROM WRITING

DISTINGUISHING BETWEEN COMPOUND VERBS AND COMPOUND SENTENCES Point out that a coordinating conjunction can be used to link two simple sentences. Encourage them to check whether a comma is necessary by making sure the parts on both sides of the conjunction are complete sentences.

Application Answers:
1. The little grandson clapped his hands, and he danced.
2. The grandfather clapped, but he couldn't dance.
3. The grandfather got up and walked outside.

Additional Suggestions Encourage students to practice by correcting these sentences:
1. The little grandson watched him go, and followed him outside.
2. The old man was sitting on a bench and the boy went up to him.
3. He wanted to help his grandfather but he couldn't.

Reteaching/Reinforcement
Grammar Mini-Lessons copymasters p. 37, transparencies p. 28

 The Writer's Craft

Compound Verbs, p. 384
Compound Sentences, pp. 556–557

READING THE WORLD

On pages 734–739, students learned to write a modern fable and then read it aloud. In this lesson, they will learn about interpreting gestures and expressions that storytellers use.

Critical Thinking: ANALYZING

M Students should notice the variety of facial expressions that Brenda Wong Aoki uses. Her gestures include small and subtle ones—like placing her arms on her hips—or large, expansive ones—like raising her arms in the air. Sometimes, she holds her body tall and upright. Other times, she leans forward.

Media Literacy: INTERPRETING BODY LANGUAGE

N Have students look closely at each image. Emotions students may see include joy, surprise, and suspense. Aoki could be telling a story about a variety of events. On the top right, some big and surprising action may have taken place. On the bottom left, perhaps she is describing a character moving forward or traveling somewhere.

Speaking and Listening: GROUP DISCUSSION

O Have students work in groups to interpret Brenda Wong Aoki's facial expressions and gestures. Tell them that there is no one "correct" interpretation. However, students should base their inferences on what they observe. Encourage them to imagine how they would feel if they were making the same gestures and facial expressions.

READING THE WORLD

WATCHING A STORY

Your experience with oral storytelling has taught you that the expressions on your face, the hand gestures you use, and the way you hold your body all send a message. Professional storytellers, like Brenda Wong Aoki, are masters at using both verbal and body language.

View What expressions are on Brenda Wong Aoki's face? What gestures is she using? How is she holding her body?

Interpret What emotion do you see in each photo? What could be happening at each point in her story? Do you think her voice is loud or soft?

Discuss Share your ideas with a few classmates. Why did you each interpret the photos as you did? The SkillBuilder at the right tells you more about reading gestures and expressions.

SkillBuilder

 CRITICAL THINKING

Interpreting Gestures and Expressions

People give off signals in their gestures and expressions. Whether you're watching a story-teller or talking with a friend, you are called upon to read gestures and expressions. A smile is an easy expression to read. A pout is pretty easy too. But what does it mean when a person fidgets with a piece of jewelry or chews on a pen cap?

When you learn to read gestures and expressions, you will better understand the people you talk to and see on the street.

APPLYING WHAT YOU'VE LEARNED

1. You need to borrow five dollars from a friend. As you approach him, you notice that he's scowling, his hands are stuffed in his pockets, and he's pacing back and forth in front of his locker. Is now a good time to ask for a favor? How do you know?

2. With a partner, try out gestures and facial expressions to convey each of the following emotions: disappointment, worry, triumph, grief, nervousness, boredom, enthusiasm, rage, exhaustion.

READING THE WORLD **741**

SkillBuilder **CRITICAL THINKING**

INTERPRETING GESTURES AND EXPRESSIONS Help students realize that they interpret gestures and expressions—often even subtle ones—every day. Students may recognize that fidgeting is a sign of nervousness. They also may recognize that people chew on pen caps when they are distracted or thinking. Remind them, however, that gestures can vary according to different cultures. For instance, people in certain cultures may use expansive gestures while talking.

Application Possible responses:
1. It is probably not a good time to ask him for a favor. He seems annoyed and angry.
2. Students can use a variety of techniques, combining gestures and facial expressions to show the emotions.

UNIT SIX

Lesson Planner: Links to Units 4–5

TIME ALLOTMENTS SHOWN ARE APPROXIMATE. DEPENDING ON YOUR GOALS AND THE NEEDS OF YOUR STUDENTS, YOU MAY WISH TO ALLOW MORE OR LESS TIME FOR CERTAIN PORTIONS OF THE LESSON.

Table of Contents	Discussion	Previewing the Selections	Reading the Selections

LINKS TO UNIT FOUR

The Arrow and the Lamp: The Story of Psyche
page 744 AVERAGE

Pumpkin Seed and the Snake
page 750 EASY

Kelfala's Secret Something
page 754 AVERAGE

		10 MINUTES	**50 MINUTES**
		• GREECE	• Introduce vocabulary
		• SOUTHEAST ASIA	• Read pp. 744–49 (6 pp.)
		• KENYA	• Read pp. 750–53 (4 pp.)
			• Read pp. 754–59 (6 pp.)

LINKS TO UNIT FIVE

Echo and Narcissus
page 764 AVERAGE

The Force of Luck
page 767 AVERAGE

The Emperor's New Clothes
page 775 AVERAGE

Lazy Peter and His Three-Cornered Hat
page 780 AVERAGE

		10 MINUTES	**60 MINUTES**
		• GREECE	• Introduce vocabulary
		• MEXICO	• Read pp. 764–66 (3 pp.)
		• DENMARK	• Read pp. 767–74 (8 pp.)
		• PUERTO RICO	• Read pp. 775–79 (5 pp.)
			• Read pp. 780–83 (4 pp.)

Writing	Exploring Topics	Prewriting	Drafting and Revising

WRITING FROM EXPERIENCE

Informative Exposition

	25 MINUTES	**35 MINUTES**	**70 MINUTES**

Time estimates assume in-class work. You may wish to assign some of these stages as homework.

• LITERATURE CONNECTION	**• CROSS-CURRICULAR CONNECTIONS**	**• CULTURAL CONNECTIONS**

90 MINUTES

• Publish a collection of tales	**SOCIAL STUDIES** • Hold an international festival **ART** • Create a pa ndau	• Write a letter • Create a language phrase book • Examine a different artwork • Present a report on the Hmong

90 MINUTES

• Evaluate characters	**GEOGRAPHY** • Explore geography **SCIENCE** • Research echoes	• Find the "threes" in tales • Investigate deceptive advertising • Explain Greek myths • Hold a contest

Publishing and Reflecting

20 MINUTES

OVERVIEW

Objectives

- To understand and appreciate a myth and two folk tales about characters who take on challenges
- To appreciate the cultures of Kenya, Vietnam, and ancient Greece
- To extend understanding of the selections through a variety of multimodal and cross-curricular activities

Skills

READING SKILLS/ STRATEGIES
- Classifying

THE WRITER'S STYLE
- Personification

LITERARY CONCEPTS
- Conflict

GRAMMAR
- Demonstrative adjectives

SPELLING
- Silent letters

SPEAKING, LISTENING, AND VIEWING
- Dramatic reading
- Choral reading
- Interviews

Cross-Curricular Connections

SOCIAL STUDIES
- Ancient gods
- Hmong culture
- International festival

SCIENCE
- Snakes

LANGUAGE
- The word *Psyche*

Reading Pathways

- Select one or several students to read each tale aloud to the entire class or to small groups of students. Assign this reading in advance so that the readers can incorporate into their presentations some of the techniques used by professional storytellers. Have the audience listen carefully to the tales without following along in their texts.

- Read the tales aloud to the class, pausing at key points to discuss how elements of the tale inform students about the customs of the cultures. Have students compare these customs with those of their own culture and region. Have students record their responses and observations in their notebooks.

- After students have read the tales once, they can read them again to identify structural elements such as main characters, minor characters, conflict, setting, and plot. Then have students identify similarities and differences between these tales and the selections in the related unit. For example, have students compare the challenges that Psyche faces with the ones that Mark Armitage meets in "The Serial Garden."

LINKS TO UNIT FOUR

Meeting Challenges

Activating Prior Knowledge

Often when a challenge is great, so too are the rewards for success and the penalties for failure. In the tales you are about to read, which link to Unit Four, characters meet challenges that test their inner strength.

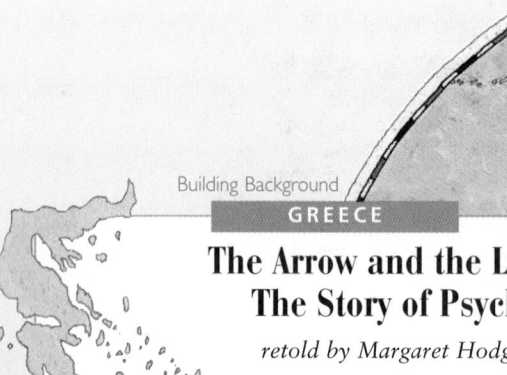

Building Background

GREECE

The Arrow and the Lamp: The Story of Psyche

retold by Margaret Hodges

The ancient Greeks believed that the gods controlled people's fates. Therefore, if someone or something angered the gods, there could be quite a price to pay. In this myth, Psyche (sī′kē), a mortal woman, responds with courage and love as she is challenged by the goddess Aphrodite (ăf′rə-dī′tē).

742 UNIT SIX: THE ORAL TRADITION

PRINT AND MEDIA RESOURCES

UNIT SIX RESOURCE BOOK
Strategic Reading: Literature, p. 31
Vocabulary SkillBuilder, p. 34
Reading SkillBuilder, p. 32
Spelling SkillBuilder, p. 33

GRAMMAR MINI–LESSONS
Transparencies, p. 14
Copymasters, p. 22

WRITING MINI–LESSONS
Transparencies, p. 39

ACCESS FOR STUDENTS ACQUIRING ENGLISH
Selection Summaries
Reading and Writing Support

FORMAL ASSESSMENT
Selection Test, pp. 123–124
 Test Generator

 AUDIO LIBRARY
See Reference Card

INTERNET RESOURCES
McDougal Littell Literature Center at http://www.hmco.com /mcdougal/lit

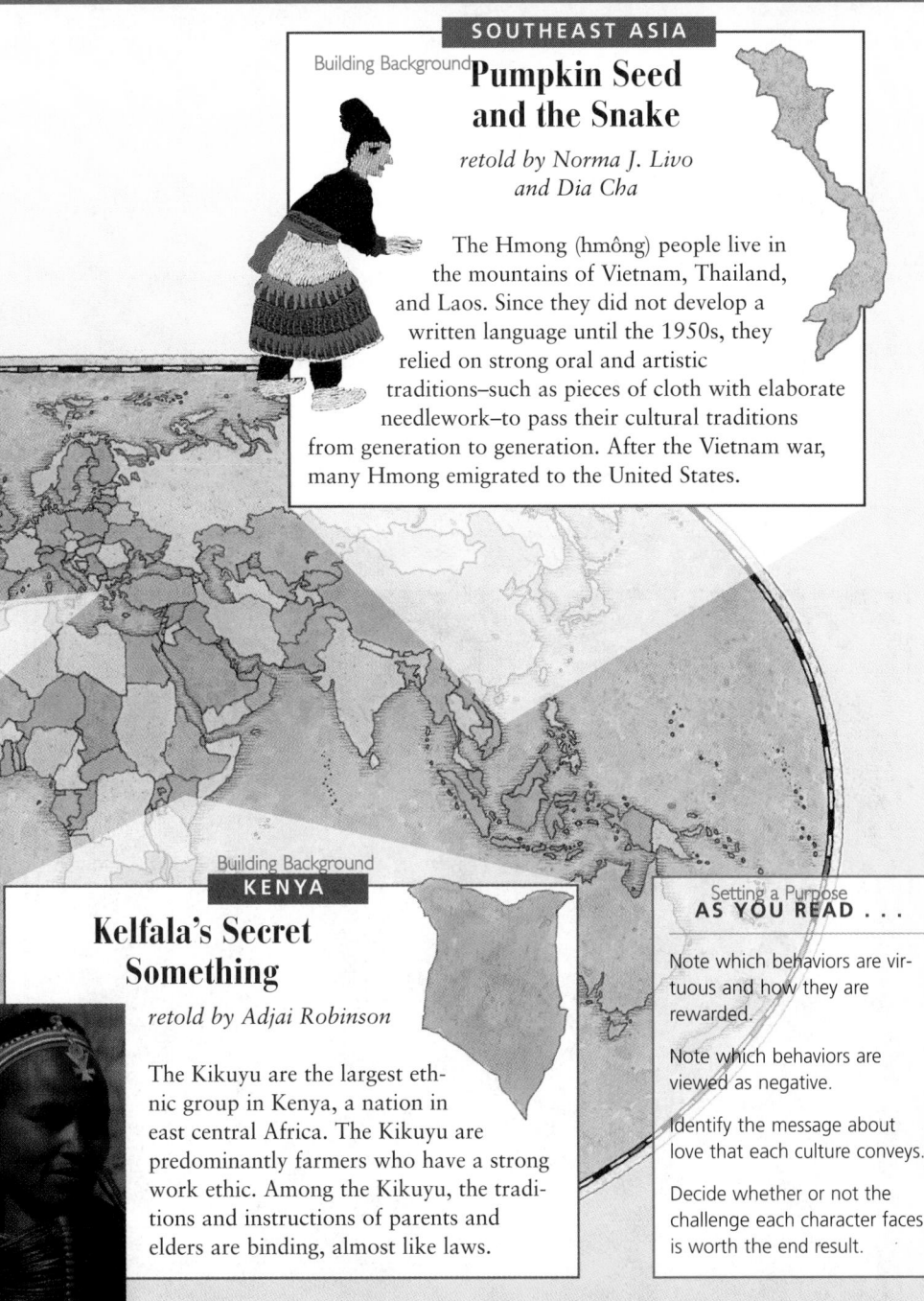

Building Background

Pumpkin Seed and the Snake

retold by Norma J. Livo and Dia Cha

The Hmong (hmông) people live in the mountains of Vietnam, Thailand, and Laos. Since they did not develop a written language until the 1950s, they relied on strong oral and artistic traditions–such as pieces of cloth with elaborate needlework–to pass their cultural traditions from generation to generation. After the Vietnam war, many Hmong emigrated to the United States.

Building Background

KENYA

Kelfala's Secret Something

retold by Adjai Robinson

The Kikuyu are the largest ethnic group in Kenya, a nation in east central Africa. The Kikuyu are predominantly farmers who have a strong work ethic. Among the Kikuyu, the traditions and instructions of parents and elders are binding, almost like laws.

Setting a Purpose
AS YOU READ . . .

Note which behaviors are virtuous and how they are rewarded.

Note which behaviors are viewed as negative.

Identify the message about love that each culture conveys.

Decide whether or not the challenge each character faces is worth the end result.

LINKS TO UNIT FOUR **743**

SUMMARY

The Arrow and the Lamp: The Story of Psyche The Greek maiden Psyche is so beautiful that people call her the new Aphrodite. The real Aphrodite, goddess of love and beauty, is furious at the comparison. She instructs her son Eros to wound Psyche with an arrow and make her love a cruel, ugly man. Instead the young god accidentally wounds himself with his arrow and falls in love with Psyche. He sends her to a dazzling palace in a secret valley, where he visits her every night but instructs her never to look at him. When Psyche grows lonely for human company, Eros sends her sisters to the palace. Jealous of Psyche's riches, they hint that her husband must be a monster. That night, Psyche peeks at sleeping Eros; he awakes and scolds her for distrusting him, then vanishes along with the palace. Psyche roams the world fruitlessly searching for her husband, finally begging Aphrodite for help. The double-crossing goddess gives Psyche three impossible tasks, which she accomplishes with the help of the natural world. Hoping to be rid of Psyche forever, Aphrodite sends her to the underworld to gather beauty from Queen Persephone. When Psyche tries to borrow some of Persephone's beauty, Psyche falls into a deep sleep. Eros rescues her and carries her off to Mount Olympus. There she is granted the status of goddess and lives eternally as Eros's wife.

WORDS TO KNOW

doomed (dōōmd) *adj.* condemned beforehand to a bad fate or disaster **doom** *v.*(p. 745)
retort (rĭ-tôrt′) *v.* to respond to a comment, such as an insult or argument, with a reply of the

same type, often quick, sharp, or witty (p. 759)
tread (trĕd) *v.* to walk on, in, or along (p. 757)
wretched (rĕch′ĭd) *adj.* deserving contempt; inferior (p. 747)

The ARROW and the LAMP: The Story of PSYCHE

retold by Margaret Hodges

Cupid Delivering Psyche (about 1871), Sir Edward Burne-Jones. Graves Art Gallery, Sheffield, England, Bridgeman/Art Resource, New York.

Mini-Lesson: Speaking, Listening, and Viewing

DRAMATIC READING Explain to students that in a dramatic reading, actors sit or stand on a bare stage. They hold their scripts rather than memorize them. There are no props, scenery, or costumes. Be sure that students understand that this means the performers hold the audience's attention through voice, expression, and body language. Go through these guidelines for a dramatic reading:
• *Prepare thoroughly before the reading. Know which parts of the reading call for humor, excitement, suspense, and so on.*

• *Speak up so the audience can hear you clearly. Project your voice so that it reaches the back of the room.*
• *Use your voice to show emotion. For example, to show tension, try raising the volume of your voice and increasing the pace of your delivery.*

Application Invite students to stage a dramatic reading of "The Arrow and the Lamp: The Story of Psyche." Direct students to follow the guidelines detailed above.

Once a king and a queen had three daughters. All three were beautiful, but the youngest, Psyche,[1] was different. Her sisters were content to know what they were told. Psyche always wanted to know more. She was so lovely that men called her a new Aphrodite,[2] a young goddess of love and beauty, but no man dared to marry a goddess. So while the two older sisters found husbands and went away to live in their own homes, Psyche stayed on alone with her father and mother.

Now all might have been well if golden, sweet-smiling Aphrodite had not heard of Psyche. The goddess came up out of the sea to find out whether men were really leaving her temples empty and silent and throwing flowers in the streets where Psyche walked. And when Aphrodite saw that it was true, she no longer smiled. She was furious, and she said to herself, "This girl is mortal. Beautiful she may be, but like all mortals she will die, and until she dies, she must never have a happy day. I shall see to that."

Then she called her favorite child, Eros,[3] and he came flying to her. This young god, as fair as his mother, had golden wings on which he moved swiftly and unseen on his mysterious errands, often doing mischief. He carried a golden bow and a quiver filled with arrows.

"Go to this girl, this Psyche," said Aphrodite. "Wound her with one of your arrows. Pour bitterness on her lips. Then find her the vilest husband in the world—mean, bad tempered, ugly—and make her fall in love with him."

There were two springs of water in Aphrodite's garden—one bitter, the other sweet. Carrying water from both springs, Eros flew off, invisible.

He found Psyche asleep. Her beauty moved him to pity, but, obeying his mother's command, he poured bitter water on her lips and touched her side with one of his arrows. Psyche felt the pain and opened her eyes. She could not see Eros, but as he looked into her eyes, the arrow trembled in his hand, and by chance he wounded himself. He poured a little of the sweet water on her forehead and flew away.

Still no lovers came to ask for Psyche's hand in marriage, so the king and the queen, guessing that their daughter had somehow angered one of the gods, asked an oracle[4] to look into the future and tell them what could be done to find a husband for her.

The oracle answered with frightening words: "Dress your daughter for her funeral. She will never marry a mortal man but will be the bride of a creature with wings, feared even by the gods. Take Psyche to the stony top of the mountain that looks down on your city, and leave her there alone to meet her fate."

When they heard this prophecy, all the people wept with Psyche's father and mother. But Psyche said, "Tears will not help me. I was <u>doomed</u> from the moment when you called me the new Aphrodite. It must be Aphrodite herself whom I have angered. Obey the oracle before the goddess punishes all of you. I alone must bear her anger."

Psyche led the way to the mountaintop and said good-bye to her weeping parents and the

---

1. **Psyche** (sī′kē).
2. **Aphrodite** (ăf′rə-dī′tē).
3. **Eros** (ĕr′ŏs′).
4. **oracle:** in ancient Greece, a priest who people believed could consult the gods in order to foretell the future.

WORDS TO KNOW	**doomed** (do͞omd) *adj.* condemned beforehand to a bad fate or to disaster **doom** *v.*

745

Linking to Languages

A *Psyche* is the Greek word for "soul." From this root comes many words we use today, including *psychology* (the study of the mind), *psychiatrist* (a healer of disorders of the mind), and *psychoanalysis* (a technique for analyzing thinking).

Cultural Note

B The poet Hesiod derived the name *Aphrodite* from the Greek word *aphros*, which means "foam." According to the myth he relates, she was born fully grown from sea foam. The Roman name of Aphrodite is Venus.

Active Reading: CLARIFY

C Ask students why Aphrodite is angry with Psyche. *(Possible responses: Aphrodite is jealous that Psyche, a human, is just as beautiful as a goddess; Aphrodite is furious that people are adoring Psyche instead of worshipping her, Aphrodite.)*

CUSTOMIZING FOR

Students Acquiring English

I You may want to point out that Eros, the god of love, is also known in English as Cupid.

Critical Thinking: HYPOTHESIZING

D Explain that, according to the myth, anyone wounded by one of Eros's arrows falls in love with the next person he or she sees. Ask students why they think the Greeks pictured falling in love this way. *(Possible responses: because love can come suddenly, like an arrow shot from a bow; because love can hurt; because falling in love sometimes seems unintentional)*

M i n i - L e s s o n   **T h e W r i t e r ' s S t y l e**

PERSONIFICATION Explain to students that personification is a type of figurative language that gives human qualities to nonhuman things such as animals, objects, and ideas. Point out that mythology often contains many examples of personification, such as animals or plants that speak or act as humans.

Application Have students explain why each of the following sentences from this story is an example of personification.

1. "...she heard the whispering of the reeds that grew along the shore...."

2. "But the reeds whispered, 'Do not give up.'"
3. "Psyche heard the waters roaring, 'Beware!'"

Reteaching/Reinforcement
• *Writing Mini-Lessons* transparencies, p. 39

The Writer's Craft

Personification, pp. 315–316

"Light the lamp and look at him. *If he is a monster, kill him . . ."*

crowd of folk who had sadly followed her. When all were gone, she sat down, trembling and afraid, to wait. But no monster husband came. Instead, the warm west wind began to blow and, raising her gently in the air, carried her down the far side of the mountain to a green and flowering meadow in a hidden valley.

Psyche fell peacefully asleep in the soft grass. When she woke, she saw a grove of tall trees watered by a clear stream. In the grove stood a marvelous palace, its golden pillars topped with a roof of carved sandalwood and ivory.

She entered through the open doorway, wondering at the light that flashed from silver walls. Surely only a god could have made such a palace! Psyche passed from room to room, walking on floors made of precious stones, until she came to a marble pool filled with scented water.

Then a voice spoke to her: "Lady, all of this is yours. Ask for whatever you like." Unseen hands led her to the bath and afterward clothed her in a robe of fine silk. A table appeared, spread with delicious food, and Psyche ate and drank while invisible servants waited on her and the air was filled with the sound of sweet voices singing.

When darkness fell, Psyche found a bed ready for her and lay down to rest. But in the night she woke, feeling the presence of someone standing beside her bed, and she was full of fear. Then a voice said, "Do not be afraid, Psyche. I am the husband you have been waiting for. Trust me. No harm will come to you. Only do not try to see me." Psyche's husband stayed with her all night long, but before daylight he was gone.

For some months Psyche lived in the palace, surrounded by beauty and comfort. The unseen servants answered all her wishes, and when her unseen husband came at night, he was always kind. She began to long for the sound of his voice and very soon fell deeply in love with him. Still, the days seemed empty and she often felt lonely.

One night her husband said to her, "Psyche, your sisters are looking for you. If you hear them calling, do not answer."

Psyche promised to obey, but she wished more and more to see a face. The clear waters of the pool reflected only her own face, and the palace now seemed like a prison. At last her husband found her weeping and, taking her in his arms, said, "Well, my love, have your wish, even if it brings trouble. The west wind shall carry your sisters here." And Psyche thanked him with grateful kisses.

The next day she heard her sisters calling to her from the mountaintop, and she called back to them. Then the west wind carried them down into the valley, and when they found Psyche safe and well, they embraced her joyfully. But their joy turned to jealousy as she showed them her palace and they saw how she was dressed and waited on like a queen.

When Psyche confessed that she had never seen her husband, they spoiled her happiness by planting suspicions in her mind: "If your husband will not let you see him, he must be the monster that the oracle said you would marry. He is only biding his time until he is ready to kill you. Take our advice. The next time he comes, have a lamp and a sharp knife hidden at your side. When he is asleep, light the lamp and look at him. If he is a monster, kill him while there is yet time."

The west wind carried the sisters away as safely as they had come, but Psyche was tormented by what they had said. At last she

Multicultural Perspectives

ANCIENT GODS Around the eighth century B.C., the poet Hesiod collected the Greek myths that are well known today. Seven centuries later, the poet Ovid adapted these myths into the Roman culture. As a result, the gods and goddesses in the myths have both Greek and Roman names. The following chart lists common Greek and Roman characters:

Greek	Roman	Title
Zeus	Jupiter, Jove	Supreme Ruler
Poseidon	Neptune	God of the Sea
Persephone	Proserpine	Maiden of Spring
Aphrodite	Venus	Goddess of Love, Beauty
Eros	Cupid	God of Love
Hades	Pluto, Dis	God of the Underworld
Athena	Minerva	Goddess of Wisdom
Apollo	Apollo	Sun God
Hermes	Mercury	Messenger of the Gods
Artemis	Diana	Goddess of the Moon
Ares	Mars	God of War

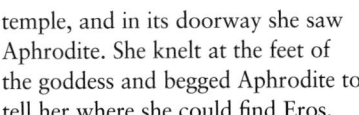
"*Golden sheep are grazing. Bring* ———————— *me a strand of their fleece.*"

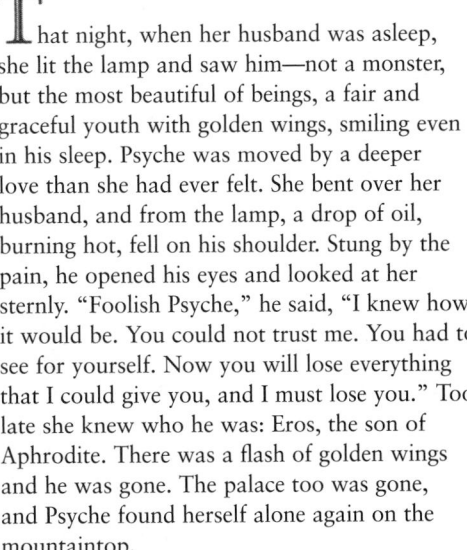

filled a little lamp with oil and found a sharp knife, both of which she hid beside her bed.

That night, when her husband was asleep, she lit the lamp and saw him—not a monster, but the most beautiful of beings, a fair and graceful youth with golden wings, smiling even in his sleep. Psyche was moved by a deeper love than she had ever felt. She bent over her husband, and from the lamp, a drop of oil, burning hot, fell on his shoulder. Stung by the pain, he opened his eyes and looked at her sternly. "Foolish Psyche," he said, "I knew how it would be. You could not trust me. You had to see for yourself. Now you will lose everything that I could give you, and I must lose you." Too late she knew who he was: Eros, the son of Aphrodite. There was a flash of golden wings and he was gone. The palace too was gone, and Psyche found herself alone again on the mountaintop.

Psyche was determined to find her lost husband, but although she walked all the roads of the world, she could not discover where he was. He had flown to one of his mother's many palaces, sick at heart and feverish with the burning pain of the oil from Psyche's lamp. Aphrodite was angrier than she had ever been. "You are meant to make mortals fall in love, not to fall in love yourself," she said. "However, you will soon be well and will forget all about that girl." She locked him into a chamber, and there he lay.

As Psyche searched for Eros, she came at last to a faraway river that flowed from a high waterfall. At the edge of the river stood a

temple, and in its doorway she saw Aphrodite. She knelt at the feet of the goddess and begged Aphrodite to tell her where she could find Eros. But Aphrodite, jealous of her beauty, answered with a false smile, "I will give Eros back to you if you will do something for me." And when Psyche eagerly agreed, the goddess led her into the temple and showed her a room filled with a great heap of grains: corn and barley, poppy seed, lentils, and beans, all mixed together. "Anyone as ugly as you is fit only to work," Aphrodite said scornfully. "Sort all of these grains into separate piles, and have it done by evening."

When the goddess had left her, Psyche sat down and began to cry. The task was impossible. But as she sat there weeping, she saw a procession of little ants coming out of the earth and running to her rescue. They attacked the heap of grains and carried each kind to a separate pile, never stopping until the work was done. Then they vanished into the earth.

When Aphrodite returned in the evening, she found Psyche sitting with folded hands. All the work was finished. "You do not deceive me, <u>wretched</u> girl," cried the goddess. "Someone has helped you. Tomorrow you must work alone, but your task is easy. Across the river is a field where golden sheep are grazing. Bring me a strand of their fleece."

At dawn Psyche went to the river and stepped into the water. But as she did so, she heard the whispering of the reeds that grew along the shore: "Psyche, the sheep are wild rams, as fierce as the sun's rays. They will batter you with their stony foreheads and pierce you with their sharp horns."

| WORDS TO KNOW | **wretched** (rĕch′ĭd) *adj.* deserving contempt; inferior |

747

Active Reading: EVALUATE

H Ask students whether they think that Psyche's fate is fair. Guide students to base their answers on the details in the story and on their prior knowledge. *(Possible responses: yes, because Eros had asked her to trust him and she betrayed him; no, because Eros did not tell her what would happen if she ever tried to see him; no, because she cannot be expected to live forever with someone she cannot see)*

Cultural Note

I In other myths and folk tales, such as the Greek myth of Orpheus and Eurydice and the Scandinavian folk tale "East of the Sun, West of the Moon," the main characters share Psyche's plight; they promise not to look at their beloved, they break their promise, and they lose their love. Students may know other tales, such as "Pandora's Box," in which curiosity gets a character into deep trouble.

STRATEGIC READING FOR
Less-Proficient Readers

J Ask students what Psyche does that causes her husband to go away. *(Although she was told not to look at him, she sneaks a look while he is sleeping. He awakens and must leave.)*
Relating Cause and Effect

Set a Purpose Have students read to find out the four tasks that Aphrodite gives Psyche.

CUSTOMIZING FOR
Students Acquiring English

2 Point out that the phrase *You are meant to* means "You are supposed to."

Mini-Lesson **Reading Skills/Strategies**

CLASSIFYING Point out to students that active readers often classify, or group together, characters or events in a story. For example, the characters in this story can be classified as gods or mortals.

Application Have students classify aspects of Psyche's experiences in the palace as realistic or fanciful. For example, the food and clothing are realistic, but the invisible servants that provide them are fanciful.

Reteaching/Reinforcement
• *Unit Six Resource Book,* p. 32

"*Go . . . and ask Queen Persephone to*  *fill this box with . . . her beauty.*"

Psyche was ready to sink down into the river, despairing. But the reeds whispered, "Do not give up. Be patient. Things will change. Wait until the sun sinks. Then the rams sleep, and you can easily gather a strand of their golden fleece from the bushes along the edge of the field." Psyche obeyed and in the evening gave the shining fleece to Aphrodite.

K The goddess was enraged. She could not bear to find Psyche still alive. "Tomorrow you must work again," she said. She gave Psyche a crystal jar and pointed to the waterfall that plunged from the mountain peak. "That is where the river Styx comes from Hades,[5] the land of death. Bring me water from the top of the waterfall," she ordered. She thought to herself, "The girl will never return. It is a just punishment for stealing my son's love."

Psyche made her way to the foot of the mountain and climbed the steep and rugged path—up, up, on and on, fearing every moment that she would fall and be dashed to pieces. At last she reached the topmost crag, a rough and slippery rock, and saw that the torrent of water poured out of a cavern guarded by dragons with unwinking eyes. Psyche heard the waters roaring, "Beware!" and stood as if turned to stone by fear. Then, from high in the air above her, there flew down an eagle, the messenger of Zeus, king of the gods. The eagle took the crystal jar in its claws and swooped past the dragons. It hovered at the top of the waterfall until the jar was filled to the brim, then brought it back to Psyche.

That night Aphrodite could hardly believe her eyes when she saw Psyche alive and well, bearing the jar of water in her hands. "I have

obeyed all your commands," said Psyche. "I beg you to give me my husband."

"I have only one more task for you," said Aphrodite with a bitter smile. "If you accomplish this, Eros shall be yours forever. Go to the world of the dead and ask Queen Persephone[6] to fill this box with some of her beauty." "For," she thought to herself, "no mortal comes back from Hades."

Psyche took the box. She knew now that Aphrodite wished nothing less than her death, and she climbed a high tower, ready to leap to the ground and so be taken at once to the land of the dead, never to return. But as she looked out from the top of the windy tower, a voice echoed from its walls: "Psyche, do not lose hope. There is a way to accomplish the last of your labors. Near at hand you will find a cave. A path leads through it to the river Styx. Carry two coins in your mouth to pay the ferryman who will row you across the river to Hades and back again. A three-headed dog guards the palace of Hades. Take two barley cakes for the dog. Give him one when you enter, the other when you leave."

Psyche found the cave and followed the dark path that led through it into the secret places of the earth. When she came to the river Styx, the ferryman took one of the coins from her mouth and rowed her across. When the fierce three-headed dog of Hades barked at her, she silenced

---

5. **Styx** (stĭks) . . . **Hades** (hā′dēz): in Greek mythology, Styx is a river that borders Hades, the kingdom of the dead. The ruler of the kingdom of the dead was also called Hades.

6. **Persephone** (pər-sĕf′ə-nē): in Greek mythology, Hades kidnapped Persephone from the earth and forced her to marry him. Persephone's mother, Demeter, persuaded Hades to allow Persephone to spend part of each year on earth.

748   UNIT SIX: THE ORAL TRADITION

Mini-Lesson ⟨TM⟩ Spelling

him with a barley cake and went on to the jeweled palace of Hades. There Queen Persephone came to greet her. And when Psyche saw that gentle face, she knew why even Aphrodite wanted to have some of its beauty. The goddess took the box and put something into it, saying in a voice both soft and kind, "Do not open this, my child. It is not for you."

Gratefully, Psyche took the box and ran from the palace. She gave her last cake to the three-headed dog, her last coin to the ferryman, and hurried up the path. But as she stepped out under the open sky, she thought, "My husband once said that I was beautiful. He may no longer think so, after all my labors. Perhaps I should keep a little of Persephone's beauty for myself." She opened the box. At once a deep sleep came over her, and she lay as if dead.

But even from afar, Eros saw her. He had recovered from his hurt, and his love for her was so strong that he burst open the locked door of

his chamber and flew to her, tenderly wiping away the spell of sleep. He closed the box and gave it back to her. Then, with Psyche in his arms, he flew upward. As they neared the top of Mount Olympus,[7] the heavenly radiance shone brighter and brighter, and in the center of the light Psyche saw Zeus, the father of light. He called Aphrodite and all the other gods and goddesses together and spoke to them: "See this mortal girl whom Eros loves. No mortal can have Persephone's beauty, but Psyche has brought some of that beauty to us. So give her the food and drink of gods, and let her be one of us, never to die, never to be separated again from her love."

Finally, even Aphrodite said it should be so. Then from Psyche's shoulders delicate wings, like those of a butterfly, unfolded. And mortals, seeing butterflies in summer fields, remember Psyche and her love. ❖

---

7. **Mount Olympus:** in Greek mythology, the home of the gods.

MARGARET HODGES

Margaret Hodges (1911–) has been writing or telling stories for most of her life. She published her first works in grade school and studied English and acting in college. In some of her earlier books, she told "real-life stories based on the adventures and misadventures of [her] three sons." She later began writing myths, legends, and folk tales.

For 11 years, Hodges appeared as a storyteller on the television program *Tell Me a Story.* She says, "The art of storytelling thrilled me because I saw it as the best way to . . . bring marvelous old tales to listeners of all ages."

A retired professor of library science, Hodges has published more than 35 books. She has often done research and found inspiration for her stories during her travels.

THE ARROW AND THE LAMP **749**

CUSTOMIZING FOR

Gifted and Talented Students

N Invite students to retell the myth from the viewpoint of Aphrodite or Psyche. Then have students explain how certain details in the myth change depending on the point of view.

STRATEGIC READING FOR

Less-Proficient Readers

O Ask students what happens to Psyche and Eros. *(They are reunited, and Psyche becomes one of the gods.)*
Summarizing

From Personal Response to Critical Analysis

1. What is your reaction to this myth? Write your thoughts in a notebook. *(Responses will vary.)*
2. How would you compare Aphrodite and Psyche? *(Possible responses: Aphrodite is powerful and immortal but also jealous and petty. Psyche is curious and mistrustful but also brave and determined.)*
3. Why do you think the gods finally accept Psyche as Eros' wife? *(Possible responses: because she brings them some of Persephone's beauty; because they know she really loves Eros)*
4. Do you think Psyche has earned her reward? Explain. *(Possible response: yes, by suffering and showing determination to win her husband back; no, because she couldn't have completed Aphrodite's tasks without help)*

COMPREHENSION CHECK

1. What does Aphrodite order Eros to do? *(wound Psyche with one of his arrows, pour bitterness on her lips, and find her a vile husband)*
2. Where do Psyche's parents take her to die? *(the mountaintop)*
3. What does Psyche find when she awakens? *(a beautiful palace)*
4. Why does Psyche lose Eros? *(because she lights a lamp and looks at him after he has warned her not to look)*
5. How does Psyche succeed with the tasks Aphrodite set for her? *(Ants help her sort the grain, reeds tell her how to get the fleece, Zeus sends an eagle to help her get water, and a voice from the tower walls tells her how to reach Persephone.)*

SUMMARY

Pumpkin Seed and the Snake A widow and her two daughters named Pumpkin Vine and Pumpkin Seed come upon a boulder in their garden. The widow says to herself that if someone can remove the rock, she will let him marry one of her daughters. When the rock disappears the next day, the widow says she was only joking. This happens two more times. After the widow makes her promise a fourth time, a snake says he will remove the rock if she promises not to lie anymore. The widow agrees, and the snake throws the rock into a river and follows her home. When the daughters hear what has happened, they at first refuse to open the door. Finally, when the mother whispers that she will kill the snake when it falls asleep, Pumpkin Seed agrees to marry it. That night, when the widow discovers a handsome young man—instead of the snake—sleeping beside Pumpkin Seed, she cannot kill him. In the morning, however, the snake has reappeared. Pumpkin Seed must go with the snake to his home. On their way, they come to a stream. The snake tells Pumpkin Seed that when he has gone off to take a bath, she will see colorful bubbles pouring down the stream. He tells her she should not play with the green ones. While he is gone, she scoops up the green bubbles. They turn into twisting snakes that stick to her hands. Moments later, a handsome young man appears, and reveals that he is her husband. When he blows on her hands, the snakes fall off and disappear. Then Pumpkin Seed and her husband go home and live happily ever after.

STRATEGIC READING FOR
Less-Proficient Readers

Set a Purpose Invite students to brainstorm a list of qualities people often look for in a mate and rank them from most to least important. Ask students to read to find out whom Pumpkin Seed marries.

Use **UNIT SIX RESOURCE BOOK**, p. 31, for guidance in reading the selection.

Literary Concept: FOLK TALE

A Ask students how the language of the opening shows the influence of the oral tradition. (*Possible response: It is simple, rhythmic, and easy to understand. This would make it easy to remember and retell.*)

PUMPKIN SEED AND THE SNAKE

RETOLD BY NORMA J. LIVO AND DIA CHA

Once long ago, in another time and place, in a small village, there lived a widow and her two daughters. The older daughter was named Pumpkin Vine and the younger one was named Pumpkin Seed.

The family had a garden near the river. They had to work hard to prepare the field for the coming growing season. But they had a problem, because in the middle of the garden was a huge boulder. One day as she was working around the rock, the widow said to herself, "If someone could remove this rock from the middle of my garden I would let him marry one of my daughters."

At the end of the day, the family went home. The next day, the three women went back to work in the garden and found that the rock was gone! The widow started to laugh and said out loud, "I was only joking. I wouldn't allow either of my daughters to marry whoever

---

Mini-Lesson — **Literary Concepts**

REVIEWING CONFLICT Remind students that conflict is the struggle between two opposing forces and that characters can experience internal and external conflicts. Internal conflicts occur when the struggle is within a character. External conflicts occur when the character struggles against some outside person or force. Explain how conflicts advance the plot and engage the reader's interest. You may wish to have students recall some of the conflicts the characters in Unit 4, such as Rikki-tikki-tavi, had.

Application Have students work in small groups to identify the conflicts in "Pumpkin Seed and the Snake." Suggest that they track the conflicts on a chart like the one shown.

Character	Type of Conflict	Resolution
the widow		
Pumpkin Seed		
the snake		

"IF SOMEONE COULD REMOVE THIS ROCK FROM THE MIDDLE OF MY GARDEN I WOULD LET HIM MARRY ONE OF MY DAUGHTERS."

removed that rock." The widow thought that was the last of the giant rock. But the next day when the widow and her daughters went back to the field to work, there was the rock, in its original place in the middle of the garden.

Once more the widow said to herself, "If someone would take this rock from the middle of the field I would let him marry one of my daughters."

The next day the rock was gone again, but the widow said, "I did not mean it. I wouldn't allow either of my daughters to marry whoever removed that rock," as she laughed.

The next morning the rock was back in its spot, and the widow again promised one of her daughters in marriage to the person who could remove the rock.

Just like the other times, the rock disappeared from the field and the widow again teased, "I did not mean it. I wouldn't allow either of my daughters to marry the person who moved the rock."

The next morning the widow went to the field alone and found the rock back in its place. Giggling a little, the widow whispered, "If someone would take this rock from the middle of the field I would let him marry one of my daughters."

This time, a snake that was nearby said, "If you promise not to lie anymore I will remove the rock."

The widow was so startled that she promised not to lie anymore. The snake slithered from the

edge of the garden, placed his tail around the rock, and threw it into the river. Since the widow's two daughters hadn't come to the field with her, the snake followed the widow home.

When they got home the widow called from outside to her daughters. She told them what had happened and said that one of them would have to marry the snake. Pumpkin Vine and Pumpkin Seed didn't want to marry the snake. They refused to open the door and let the snake into the house.

The snake and the widow waited and waited until it was dark, but the girls wouldn't open the door. Then the mother whispered through the door to her daughters, "I will kill the snake when he falls asleep." Even though her mother had said this would work, Pumpkin Vine, being the older one, still refused to open the door. It was very dark outside by this time. Pumpkin Seed, on the other hand, thought that things would go as easily as her mother said, so she opened the door.

When the snake got into the house, Pumpkin Vine and Pumpkin Seed were frightened by its huge size and ugly shininess. Pumpkin Vine protested bitterly when her mother asked her to marry the snake. The widow finally convinced Pumpkin Seed to marry the snake. The snake followed Pumpkin Seed wherever she went. It curled up beside her feet when she sat down. When she went to bed, the snake slid into her bed and coiled up beside her.

E

F

PUMPKIN SEED AND THE SNAKE **751**

Multicultural Perspectives

HMONG CULTURE "Pumpkin Seed and the Snake" comes from the culture of the Hmong people of Southeast Asia. The Hmong see many animals as possessing symbolic power. The snake, central to this story, is a key symbol. For example, a snake entering the house is a sign that someone in the family may soon die. A bird flying into the house also is an evil portent. Bears and tigers are especially feared. People's souls are thought to be imprisoned in tigers under special circumstances. A magic soul-tiger is recognized by its five toes; real tigers

have only four toes. Elephants are considered a good sign, greatly respected for their strength. The Hmong avoid saying anything bad about these creatures to make sure they do not come and damage the family's property. The rooster is believed to awaken the sun in the morning; the crab shields the opening to the sky that allows floods to cover the earth. Tortoises bring advice from the spirit world to the living.

752 THE LANGUAGE OF LITERATURE

Literary Concept: SUSPENSE

G Ask students to describe the effect of the widow's repeated attempts and failures to kill the snake. *(The repetition and delay build excitement and suspense, stimulating readers' interest in finding out what will happen.)*

Literary Note

H Nearly all cultures have folk stories that involve a dramatic transformation from animal to human. Among the best known is "Beauty and the Beast." Water is often an important element in transformation stories. In Chinese folklore, enchanted men also turn up as frogs, and beautiful young women appear as plants.

Literary Links

I Invite students to compare and contrast the snake in this story with the cobras Nag and Nagaina in "Rikki-tikki-tavi." *(Possible response: The snake in this story is helpful and protective, whereas Nag and Nagaina are utterly evil.)*

Active Reading: EVALUATE

J Have students evaluate Pumpkin Seed's actions in this passage. Ask students why they think she disobeys the snake and what the consequences might be. *(Possible responses: She disobeys out of curiosity and excitement. Her actions might prevent the snake's transformation into a man.)*

IT WAS NOT AN UGLY SNAKE SLEEPING BESIDE PUMPKIN SEED, BUT THE MOST HANDSOME YOUNG MAN THAT SHE HAD EVER SEEN.

That night, with a sharp knife in one hand and a candle in the other, the widow crept into Pumpkin Seed's bedroom to kill the snake. But she discovered it was not an ugly snake sleeping beside Pumpkin Seed, but the most handsome young man that she had ever seen. She couldn't kill him.

G The next day when Pumpkin Seed woke up, the snake was still alive. She cried and demanded to know why her mother hadn't kept her promise and killed it. "I'll kill the snake tonight, Pumpkin Seed. Please trust me," begged the widow.

That night, the snake again slid into Pumpkin Seed's bed and coiled up beside her. The widow came into the room with her sharp knife and the candle and crept up to the bed to kill the snake. Again, though, instead of an ugly snake sleeping beside Pumpkin Seed, it was the handsome young man. Once more, she just couldn't kill him.

The next morning Pumpkin Seed woke up and there the snake was in her bed, still alive. She cried and cried and demanded to know why her mother hadn't killed it. "I'll kill the snake tonight, Pumpkin Seed. Please give me one more chance. Please trust me," pleaded the widow.

When the sun rose the next morning bright and warm, Pumpkin Seed woke up and there was the snake—still alive. Now Pumpkin Seed

had no choice. She had to go with the snake to his home. On the way they came to a lovely clear stream. "Pumpkin Seed, I will go take a bath over behind the rocks. You wait here while I am gone." "All right," Pumpkin Seed agreed.

"When I am gone, you will see lots of colorful bubbles pouring down the stream. You must not touch the green bubbles. You can play with the white and yellow ones, but do not touch the green bubbles," warned the snake. Pumpkin Seed nodded in agreement.

The snake had been gone for a while when, sure enough, Pumpkin Seed noticed a variety of colored bubbles floating down the stream. She stood in delighted amazement as the bright, glittering bubbles traveled smoothly down the clear water. She eagerly pulled out some of the yellow bubbles. To her surprise the bubbles turned into gold jewels in her hands. Then she gathered some white bubbles, and they turned into silver jewels. Pumpkin Seed was so happy. She had never had such beautiful riches. She gaily put them on her neck, her wrists, her ears, and her fingers.

As she was admiring them, she thought, "Why shouldn't I have some of the green bubbles?" So she reached down and scooped up some green bubbles, and before her startled eyes they turned

---

Mini-Lesson ✏ Grammar

DEMONSTRATIVE ADJECTIVES Write the words *this, that, these,* and *those* on the chalkboard. Explain that when used as modifiers, these words are called demonstrative adjectives. They must agree in number with the noun they modify: *this* and *that* modify singular nouns; *these* and *those* modify plural nouns. Then present on the chalkboard the examples shown.

Application Have students select the correct demonstrative adjectives in the following sentences.
1. We read (<u>this</u>/these) story about a snake.
2. (Those/<u>This</u>) kind of story is a folk tale.
3. (<u>These</u>/that) stories involve magical events.
4. The storytellers passed (that/<u>these</u>) tales from generation to generation.

Reteaching/Reinforcement
• Grammar Handbook, anthology p. 869
• *Grammar Mini-Lessons* copymasters p. 22, transparencies p. 14

📕 **The Writer's Craft**

Demonstrative Adjectives, p. 506

Singular
I like this folk tale.

Did you read that story?

Plural
These stories are great!

Those stories are better.

THE YOUNG MAN SMILED AND SAID, "I AM YOUR HUSBAND...."

into twisting snakes in her hands. They even stuck all over her hands. She frantically tried to remove the snakes, but they wouldn't come off.

A moment later a young, handsome man came toward her, and she quickly hid her wriggling hands behind her back. "Why are you hiding your hands?" asked the man.

Her voice quivered as she told him, "Oh, my husband is a snake. He went up the stream to bathe and he told me to keep my hands like this."

The young man smiled and said, "I am your husband. . . ." Pumpkin Seed interrupted him. "No, you can't be!"

The man smiled and said, "Look at this!" He raised his arm and showed her the remaining snakeskin in his armpit. She believed him when she saw the skin and felt ashamed when she showed him her hands.

But he simply blew on her hands and the snakes fell off and disappeared like magic. Then they went home and lived happily for the rest of their lives. ❖

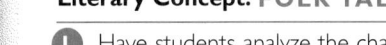

NORMA J. LIVO

Raised in Appalachia, Norma Livo (1929–) says she grew up with her mother's "folklorish" stories and her father's "tall tales, music, and ballads full of mischief," so "no matter what side of the family got together, music and storytelling were important."

When one of Livo's sons was diagnosed as having a learning disability, she returned to school to learn how to help him. She received a doctorate in education and began using her own stories and her children's to teach her son to read. Livo introduced storytelling into elementary and secondary classrooms and began teaching a storytelling course at the University of Colorado.

Livo writes books about the storytelling process and records the folklore of other cultures. She worked with Dia Cha, a Hmong immigrant, to retell "Pumpkin Seed and the Snake" and other tales, collected in *Folk Stories of the Hmong: Peoples of Laos, Thailand, and Vietnam.*

PUMPKIN SEED AND THE SNAKE **753**

SUMMARY

Kelfala's Secret Something Kelfala is the village clown, but he is seriously in love with the local beauty, Wambuna. Kelfala and Wambuna used to play together as children; now she will not even speak to him. The much-courted Wambuna has good reason to be silent, for tradition decrees she must marry the first man she talks to. Kelfala, trying to coax her into speaking, pulls out every trick in his bag of humor without success. Finally he comes up with a plan. He dresses and paints himself foolishly, then follows Wambuna to her farm. While she is busy weeding, he slips a Gituyu—an animal not even a dog would eat—onto the firestone where her yams are cooking. Then Kelfala laughs so loudly that he unintentionally lures his friends Shortie Bumpie and Longie Tallie out of the bush. As Wambuna joins in their laughter, Kelfala points out the Gituyu roasting in the fire. "A Gituyu! It cannot be!" she cries out, at which Kelfala proclaims her his wife. Immediately his friends point out that Wambuna talked to *all* of them—and so all three qualify as husbands. Unsuccessful but undiscouraged, Kelfala begins plotting a new strategy to win Wambuna's hand.

From *Samburu* by Nigel Pavitt.
Copyright © 1992 Nigel Pavitt,
reprinted by permission of
Henry Holt and Co., Inc.

RETOLD BY ADJAI ROBINSON

754

LISTEN, CHILDREN,

DO YOU KNOW THE

GITUYU? IT IS SUCH

AN ANIMAL THAT IN

KENYA IT IS SAID

THAT EVEN THE DOGS

WILL NOT EAT ITS

MEAT FOR SUPPER,

NOR THE HYENA, NOR

EVEN THE WILDCAT—

AND NEVER THE

POOREST OF PEOPLE.

THAT IS TRADITION.

THIS YOU MUST KNOW.

Literary Concept: PLOT

B Ask students why a storyteller might begin a tale this way. (*Possible responses: to introduce an important idea or theme, to interest listeners right away by providing an intriguing detail*)

Critical Thinking: ANALYZING

C Point out to students that the word *tradition* was also mentioned at the end of the first paragraph. Have students explain what they can infer from the repetition of this word. (*Possible responses: Traditions are important to the people in the story; the plot of the story depends on repetition.*)

CUSTOMIZING FOR
Students Acquiring English

I Point out that *clown*, as used here, refers to a person who enjoys making other people laugh.

Cultural Note

D The majority of Kenya's population is rural and contains both nomadic and settled groups. Women are the primary caretakers of children. They also participate in the planting and harvesting of crops. Increasingly, more people—especially young men—are migrating to urban areas of Kenya to find work. This migration has affected women's roles in their societies by forcing them to take on more of the field work for which the young men were responsible. Women living in urban areas tend to marry later and have fewer children than their rural counterparts.

But the story . . .

On the steep slopes of the Kilimanjaro[1] stood a tiny village of very hardy people. Mountain climbers were they all, and their gardens of tea and pyrethrum[2] and coffee were as dear to their hearts as the cap of snow shielding the head of their father mountain. The men and women had strong hands and great mountain strides. They were a happy people with warm hearts. And they were a people faithful to their traditions.

The young fellow, Kelfala, was one of these. Kelfala, the clown. People used to say that he was funny from the time he entered his mother's womb. He could make a thousand and one faces with his one fleshy face. His lips, he could twist and curl, and even if you wanted to hiss, your hissing would turn to laughing. If you listened to Kelfala's stories, I tell you, you would see and hear all the animals in the forest in this one Kelfala. And he sprang surprises as fast as he spinned yarns, on everything around.

Kelfala, the clown, was like his grandfather before him. He was funny. He was clever. Oh, he was a charming darling. It seemed that nothing or no one could resist Kelfala.

No one, except the beautiful Wambuna. She would not even turn his way.

Before, as children, these two had played together, laughed together, teased together. But Wambuna had gone into the girl's society, as all girls of the village do. There, the old women had taught her how to wash and care for

---

1. **Kilimanjaro** (kĭl′ə-mən-jär′ō): the highest mountain in Africa.
2. **pyrethrum** (pī-rē′thrəm): a showy flowering plant.

KELFALA'S SECRET SOMETHING   **755**

Mini-Lesson: Speaking,   Listening, and Viewing

CHORAL READING Remind students that the stories in this unit are part of the oral tradition. As such, they were first passed on by word of mouth rather than through the written word. Explain to students that storytellers often use body language as well as words to express emotion. The storyteller's hands, face, posture, and movements all help convey the feeling behind the words. For example, a facial expression of a quick double take can convey humor.

Application Arrange students in small groups and have each group prepare a choral reading of a substantial passage from "Kelfala's Secret Something." Direct groups to use body language as well as volume, pitch, and tone in their presentation. You may wish to tape record the presentations so students can listen to their readings later.

E Ask students why people might have a tradition like this one. Discuss what purposes it might serve. (*Possible responses: It keeps young men and women apart; it lets parents have much more involvement in the choice of their child's mate.*)

Literary Concept: NARRATOR

F Ask students how the narrator of this story tries to draw readers in and engage their sympathy for the characters and their problems. (*Possible response: The narrator addresses readers directly and asks them questions, suggests that readers would feel the way the characters do, and alerts readers to what is important.*)

Literary Links

G Invite students to compare the tone of this story with the tone of "Amigo Brothers." If necessary, remind students that tone is the writer's attitude toward his or her subject. (*Possible response: The tone of this story is much lighter and more humorous than the serious tone of "Amigo Brothers."*)

STRATEGIC READING FOR
Less-Proficient Readers

H Ask students how Kelfala plans to get Wambuna to marry him. (*He plans to get her to talk to him.*) Summarizing

Set a Purpose Have students read to find out how Kelfala's "secret something" gets Wambuna to speak.

---

babies, how to prepare leaves and herbs for simple cures, how to sing the village songs, how to cook meats and yams and vegetables. Her roasted peanuts were always brown and tasty. And, if you ate her sauces, you would lick your fingers as if you were going to bite them, too. Her graces were admired even by other young girls. And when she came out,[3] she was given the oath: that from that time on, if she talked to any man outside her family, she was bound to marry him. That was tradition.

Kelfala would sit in the bush and watch this darling Wambuna. Her skin was as smooth as a mirror. Her mahogany-brown arms swayed gracefully by her sides, keeping time with her swaying hips. When she laughed, she showed ivory-white teeth. And just a smile from Wambuna sent warm thrills through clownish Kelfala. Her head, she carried erect, and the rings sat on her neck like rows of diamonds on a crown. The more Kelfala watched, the more he wanted Wambuna for his own.

But she had an endless stream of suitors. (If you could have seen her, you would not mind even being last, as long as you were in line.) Some of these young men went to her father to ask for Wambuna. That was tradition. But many had heard his loud "No-No" and tried to trick Wambuna, instead. But do you think she talked to the young men around? Well! You wait and see.

Always, they paid their visits to her at the garden, always when the elders were having their rest from the hot midday sun.

"Wambuna, let me get you water from the stream."

"Ay'ee, Wambuna, I hit my toe against a stone. It is gushing out blood!"

"Wambuna, your plants are not growing at all. You are so lazy. Yambuyi's plants are better than yours, lazy you!"

From *Samburu* by Nigel Pavitt. Copyright © 1992 Nigel Pavitt, reprinted by permission of Henry Holt and Co., Inc.

"Wambuna, hear your father? He is snoring so hard under this hot sun, he has driven all the animals away!"

But Wambuna's lips were sealed, and all this teasing and coaxing only kept her lips tighter. She would not even raise her head to smile. She worked in silence, and if she talked at all, she only whispered kind things to her plants.

Now, Kelfala joined the line, too. And—tradition or not—he would not risk the father's "No-No." Why? He, Kelfala, the clown?

---

3. **when . . . out:** when she was officially regarded as having reached adulthood.

Multicultural Perspectives

MARRIAGE An arranged marriage—one in which the parents select a mate for their child—was the accepted form of marriage in many countries for centuries. In prerevolutionary China, for example, a bride and groom often met for the first time on their wedding day. In some African, Indian, and other societies, parents still arrange their chil-dren's marriages. Arranged marriages are the custom in the society that forms the backdrop of "Kelfala's Secret Something." That is why some suitors ask Wambuna's father for permission to marry his daughter. Her only other option is to marry the first man outside her own family to whom she speaks.

Kelfala, who could coax words and laughter out of trees? He would get Wambuna to speak!

He tried his hippopotamus face, to get her to shout in fear. He turned into a leopard, springing into Wambuna's path when she was alone, so she would cry for help. He hid behind a clump of trees and became Wambuna's mother, asking questions and questions and questions that needed answers.

But Wambuna's lips were sealed.

The stream of suitors grew smaller, like the village stream itself, shrinking and shrinking in the dry season when the rains have stopped. But Kelfala did not give up. Finally, he confided in two friends that he had a something that would win Wambuna for him. A secret something. (He did not tell them what.)

For two weeks Kelfala and his two friends, Shortie Bumpie and Longie Tallie, trailed Wambuna and her family as they went to the farm. Then Kelfala's day came. They spied Wambuna going alone to the farm with her basket balanced on her head. He and Shortie Bumpie and Longie Tallie set out behind her, *kunye, kunye, kunye* as if they were <u>treading</u> on hot coals. They stood behind the trees and bushes, unseen by anyone but themselves, and waited.

On this day, Kelfala had put on his best dress. But if you had seen him, you would think that he was the most unlikely suitor for a young girl. His dress was rags and tatters. He had rubbed grease all over his body, mud on his head, and funny chalk marks on his face. He also had painted his front teeth with red-black clay.

The birds were twitting happily as they caught worms on the dewy grass. Nearby the stream was flowing by, its waters dazzling in the early morning sunlight. From time to time Kelfala opened his sack, touched his something, and smiled to himself.

Wambuna started working hard and fast. Indeed, she was racing the sun. By the time the sun got halfway on its journey, she hoped to have gotten to the end of hers. She only stopped her work for a moment, went to the stream with her calabash[4] for water, then returned and kindled a fire. She took some yams from her little basket, put them on the hot coals, and returned to her plants. She was weeding the new grasses on her tea beds.

Kelfala's opportunity had come. Soon, Kelfala, the clown, Kelfala, the funny one, would be married to the most beautiful, the most gentle, the mildest lady on Kilimanjaro. At least, that is what Kelfala thought.

Kelfala spied here, there, and everywhere from his hiding, stepped out into the open, and hopped and skipped to the fireplace. Out of his sack he pulled his something and placed it on the hot coals beside Wambuna's yams. Then he squatted on the largest firestone and poled the red-hot coals. Shoving Wambuna's yams aside, he uttered a throaty chuckle, which he quickly trapped with his hands. He glanced again at the fireplace, and like a cock ready to peck at the yams, he tittered quietly to himself. But again he quickly stopped himself.

But only for a moment, for suddenly more chuckles escaped, and Kelfala howled like a ruffled owl. He hooted the monkeys out of the treetops. He rolled himself into a ball as he

L

---

4. **calabash** (kăl′ə-băsh′): the dried, hollowed-out shell of a gourd, used as a bowl.

WORDS TO KNOW

tread (trĕd) *v.* to walk on, in, or along

757

Literary Concept: CHARACTER

I Ask students why they think Kelfala behaves as he does. (*Possible response: He thinks that this behavior will make Wambuna speak, and he will be able to win her.*) Then ask students what Kelfala's behavior here reveals about his personality. (*Possible responses: He is very self-confident; he is sure that he can charm anyone.*)

Critical Thinking: ANALYZING

J Have students explain why the storyteller selected these names for Kelfala's friends. (*Possible responses: because they create humor, which suits the story's amusing, light tone*)

Active Reading: PREDICT

K Invite students to predict what plan Kelfala will carry out to win Wambuna. Encourage students to base their guesses on what they already know about the characters and setting. (*Possible responses: He is going to do something outrageous and silly because he is a clown.*)

Literary Concept: SUSPENSE

L Ask students to describe how suspense builds in this part of the story. (*Possible responses: The details of Kelfala's plan are revealed slowly, keeping the meaning of Kelfala's actions a secret; it implies that soon Kelfala and Wambuna will be married.*)

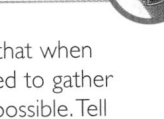

Mini-Lesson: Speaking, Listening, and Viewing

INTERVIEWS Explain to students that when they write articles or reports, they need to gather information from as many sources as possible. Tell the class that one way to gather information is to conduct a personal interview. Present these guidelines:

• *Before the interview, think carefully about what you want to find out. Define your purpose and prepare your questions. This way you can focus on listening during the interview rather than on thinking up questions.*

• *During the interview, listen carefully and avoid distractions. If possible, tape-record the interview so you can listen to the responses later as often as needed..*

• *After the interview, listen to the recording and make your notes. Isolate the main ideas and supporting details.*

Application Have students use these skills to conduct an interview as they complete the Across Cultures Mini-Projects on creating a language phrase book or presenting a report, on page 761.

(2) Point out that *the bush came alive* is not meant literally; instead, it means that the bush started moving and sounds came from behind it when Kelfala's friends began laughing.

Active Reading: CLARIFY

M To clarify the meaning of *a Gituyu*, have students review the opening paragraph of the story. Ask students to speculate why they think no person or animal is willing to eat this creature's meat. *(Possible response: It tastes dreadful or smells bad.)*

STRATEGIC READING FOR
Less-Proficient Readers

N Ask students how Kelfala gets Wambuna to speak. *(He places a Gituyu next to the yams she is cooking. This is the animal nobody will eat, so Wambuna is very surprised.)* Relating Cause and Effect

Set a Purpose Have students read to see whether Kelfala gets to marry Wambuna.

Literary Concept: REPETITION

O Ask students how repetition affects the tone in this passage of the story. Ask what it conveys about Kelfala's character. *(Possible responses: It makes the tone very playful; it helps convey Kelfala's excitement and glee at the apparent success of his plan.)*

---

rolled and rolled with laughter. Kelfala, the laughing clown. He laughed and he laughed and he laughed.

(2) Now, the bush came alive. Shortie Bumpie and Longie Tallie poked their heads out to see what was happening. At first they twitched their faces and cocked their ears. But as Kelfala rolled on and on, and the laughter rolled on and on, it dragged the two young men with it.

Wambuna—who had to poke her fire—tried to sneak past the hooting trio, but the loud roars quickly sank into *her* bones. Oh, how silly those three idle friends! Kelfala, that clown Kelfala! But as she watched them, her grin turned into a broad smile, *her* smile turned into a shy laugh, and without realizing it, she became one of the howling trio. She was all fits of laughter. Oh! How the tears ran down Wambuna's eyes.

All four laughed and laughed, laughed and laughed and laughed.

When all at once Kelfala stood, with arms akimbo[5] and stomach shot forward, and pointed to Wambuna's fireplace.

"A beautiful girl like you," he laughed, **M** "proud as the cotton tree and the greatest cook in the village, you, you roast a Gituyu with your yams!"

Wambuna turned around.

There by the giant firestone, on the ashes, was Kelfala's something. A shrunken, old, burnt Gituyu!

Wambuna caught her breath, looked from Kelfala to his friends, and cried out between tears and laughter. "A Gituyu! It cannot be. It **N** cannot . . ."

But, at that Kelfala threw up his arms. "Aha! You have spoken to Kelfala. Kelfala, the

great, Kelfala, the clown! Kelfala, the cunning one. Kelfala, the proud husband of a proud wife!"

"Wait a minute, Kelfala," one of his friends said. "Kelfala, I tell you now, she doesn't belong to you."

"Oh, no, you Shortie Bumpie? The trick was mine, see?" and with that, Kelfala hopped.

"The plan was mine, see?" and with that, Kelfala skipped.

---

5. **akimbo** (ə-kĭm′bō): with hands on hips, and elbows bent outward.

AS SHE WATCHED THEM, HER GRIN TURNED INTO A BROAD SMILE, *HER* SMILE TURNED INTO A SHY LAUGH, AND WITHOUT REALIZING IT, SHE BECAME ONE OF THE HOWLING TRIO.

M u l t i c u l t u r a l **P e r s p e c t i v e s**

POLYGYNY *Polygyny* is the term used to describe the custom of having more than one wife at a time. *Polyandry* refers to the practice of having more than one husband at a time. *Polygamy*, which comes from a Greek word that means "many marriages," can refer to either gender.

Like many other peoples of Africa, the Kikuyu traditionally practiced polygyny. Having more than one wife was a mark of wealth and status. In such cir-

cumstances the children had a *maitu munyinyi,* or "small mother," as well as their *maitu,* or biological mother.

In most countries, polygamy is prohibited by law. For instance, China and Turkey—where polygyny was once customary—now have legislation outlawing this practice. In the United States, Congress passed legislation against polygamy in 1862.

"The secret was mine, see?" and with that, he jumped.

"The Gituyu was mine, see? My secret something! And the laughter was mine, see, I started it." And with that, he laughed and laughed and laughed . . .

Wambuna stood, amazed, but she soon found support in Shortie Bumpie and Longie Tallie.

"I know that a man has had three wives, but never on this whole mountain has ever a woman shared three husbands," retorted Shortie Bumpie.

"Yes, Kelfala, this girl either belongs to all of us . . . or none of us," cried the other friend.

You could see Kelfala's heart heaving.

"What did you say? You, Longie Tallie?"

Wambuna lifted her eyes.

"Yes," Longie Tallie went on. "Wambuna laughed at you. She cried at you. She mumbled, she grumbled at you. She laughed-cried. She laughed-mumbled-cried at you. But she talked to all three of us!"

Wambuna pressed her lips together in a quiet, sly smile and looked into Kelfala's eyes. Then she walked back to her plants with her head raised up like a large pink rose in early spring.

Kelfala just looked, his head bowed like a weeping willow. But then, he tapped his bag and grinned. "Today is only for today. There is still tomorrow. There will always be another secret."

That was tradition, too. ❖

ADJAI ROBINSON

1932–

Growing up in the African country of Sierra Leone, Adjai Robinson listened to storytellers recount wonderful tales. Later he began to record folk tales and became a storyteller on the radio.

Robinson came to the United States to lead workshops about African folklore and to attend Columbia University. In 1975, he moved to Nigeria to become principal education officer at the Nigeria Teachers Institute. Robinson has since published a number of children's books. About his books, he has said, "Each book that I have written for boys and girls is also a book I have written for myself. . . . since, if I don't find the story exciting or interesting or funny, . . . I don't think boys and girls will either."

OTHER WORKS *Singing Tales of Africa, Femi and Old Grandaddie, Kasho and the Twin Flutes*

WORDS TO KNOW

retort (rĭ-tôrt′) *v.* respond to a comment, such as an insult or argument, with a reply of the same type, often quick, sharp, or witty

759

COMPREHENSION CHECK

1. What is Kelfala like? *(He is funny and a great storyteller.)*
2. Why won't Wambuna talk to a man who is not a member of her family? *(She would have to marry him if she spoke to him.)*
3. What does Kelfala place on the hot coals besides Wambuna's yams? *(a Gituyu)*
4. Why does Wambuna speak? *(She is surprised to see the Gituyu with her yams.)*
5. Why doesn't Wambuna have to marry Kelfala? *(She spoke to his friends at the same time. Since she can't marry three men, she marries none of them.)*

Publish a new collection of tales
Suggest that writers begin by listing aspects of the story that they intend to rewrite.

Editors/proofreaders may wish to create a checklist to help them target specific aspects of the story for editing. Suggest that editors/proofreaders check for sentence fragments, errors in subject/verb agreement, and spelling errors. Encourage illustrators to use different media (pencils, chalk, watercolor, cutouts, and so on).

Rubric

3 Full Accomplishment The finished story presents a clever twist on the original tale, illustrations that reflect the changes to the original story, and represents the work of the entire group.

2 Substantial Accomplishment The completed story contains a twist on plot, character, or setting. The entire group contributes to the story.

1 Little or Partial Accomplishment The completed story does not substantially change the original tale.

RESPONDING
OPTIONS

LITERATURE CONNECTION PROJECT 1   Multimodal Activity

Publish a new collection of tales With a small group of classmates, choose a tale in this part of Unit Six and rewrite it with your own twist. For example, you might choose to rewrite the ending, to set the story in modern times or in your own neighborhood, to include characters from other stories, or to change the actions or the gender of one or more characters. Here are some suggestions for carrying out this project:

Writers Work together to rewrite the whole story, or have one writer begin the story and another develop the plot, and still another finish it.

Editors/Proofreaders Read the story silently and then aloud. Check for inconsistencies within the story and for parts that are unclear or that need more details. Then consult with the writers to make changes that will improve the tale. After making the necessary changes, proofread the completed story carefully, correcting any spelling, grammar, or punctuation errors. Finally, make a clean copy of your tale.

Illustrators Draw pictures to illustrate the changes that have been made to the original tale. Share your new story and illustrations with the rest of the class.

SOCIAL STUDIES CONNECTION PROJECT 2   Multimodal Activity

Hold an international festival Work with your class to put on an International Festival that includes art, music, and food from the Kikuyu, Hmong, or Greek cultures—or any of the other cultures represented in Unit Six. Choose one of these areas to work on:

Food Find recipes for and prepare dishes from the culture or region of your choice. You may want to find recipes for Hmong dishes by consulting Thai or Vietnamese cookbooks. Kikuyu recipes may appear in cookbooks from Kenya or other parts of Africa. Compile the recipes into a cookbook to share with your classmates.

Music From your local library, borrow recordings of African, Greek, or Southeast Asian music to play during the festival. You also may want to make, draw, or bring in instruments such as drums, rattles, flutes, and thumb pianos from Africa; gongs and cymbals from Southeast Asia; or harps and lyres from Greece.

Decorations Draw pictures of the art, architecture, or landscape of a particular country or region to hang on the walls. If possible, bring in examples of art and crafts from the different regions.

760   UNIT SIX: THE ORAL TRADITION

Hold an international festival As a class, select the culture or cultures to be represented in the International Festival. Then arrange students in small groups to research the food, music, or decorations from the culture. Encourage students to consult with people from that cultural group as well as research print sources. Students may wish to contact the Parent-Teacher Organization, Chamber of Commerce, local branches of service organizations such as Rotary, and religious groups to find people from these cultures who would like to share their heritage.

Rubric

3 Full Accomplishment Students find detailed, accurate, and verifiable information on one area of the country's culture.

2 Substantial Accomplishment Students find information about one aspect of the culture, but the results may lack details.

1 Little or Partial Accomplishment Students have not found accurate, verifiable information about the culture.

ART CONNECTION PROJECT 3 — Multimodal Activity

Create your own pa ndau The Hmong have depicted their history, folk tales, and culture on pa ndau (păn-dou'), which are pieces of cloth with elaborate needlework. Pa ndau art can include appliqué, reverse appliqué, cross-stitches, chain stitches, batik, and embroidery. The stitching or appliqué was traditionally done on a deep blue cotton background.

Find pictures or examples of Hmong pa ndau art. Then choose a story from this part of Unit Six—or use the tale you rewrote for the Literature Connection—and create a pa ndau story cloth for it. Working with your classmates, first sketch scenes from the story on paper. Then use fabric paint or one of the techniques mentioned to

make the characters, actions, and scenery come to life on the cloth. Display the pa ndau and use it to retell the story to a younger class.

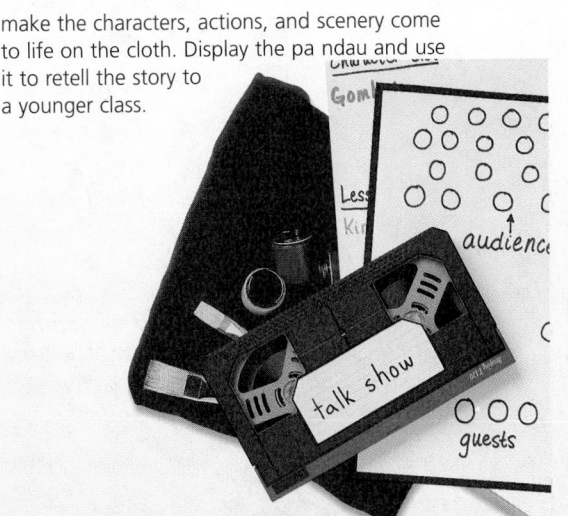

ACROSS CULTURES MINI-PROJECTS — Multimodal Activities

Write a Letter Choose a character from one of these tales and write a letter to him or her explaining why you admire or disapprove of his or her behavior. Post the letter on a bulletin board with other classmates' letters.

Create a language phrase book Find out more about Swahili, Kenya's national language, or the language of any other culture represented in this unit. Use library resources such as dictionaries, phrase books, and textbooks, and, if possible, interview people who speak the language. On your own or with a few classmates, create a guide—complete with pronunciations and definitions—for a number of common words and phrases in that language. Teach some of the words and phrases to the class.

Examine different artwork Aphrodite and Eros—Venus and Cupid in Roman mythology—have been popular subjects for artists and writers in ancient as well as in modern times. Look in art history books and other sources for reproductions of art such as sculptures and paintings that depict these gods and goddesses of love. Display the

reproductions for the class, and compare the depiction of the god or goddess in the artwork with the depiction in the myth.

Present a report The Hmong are some of the most recent immigrants to the United States. Find out about their history and the challenges they face in adjusting to a new culture while trying to preserve their own. Look for stories about the Hmong in magazines and newspapers. Present an oral report on the Hmong to your classmates.

Extended Social Studies Reading

MORE ABOUT THE CULTURES

- *Grandmother's Path, Grandfather's Way: Hmong Preservation Project: Oral Lore—Generation to Generation* by Vang Lue and Judy Lewis
- *The Land I Lost: Adventures of a Boy in Viet Nam* by Huynh Quang Nhuong
- *The Land and the People of Kenya* by Michael Maren
- *Ancient Greece* by Tessa Board

Create your own pa ndau Keep the groups small—no more than three students per group—to make it easier for students to agree on a design and execute it. Suggest that students find out more about traditional stitching techniques from a homemakers' organization, craft books and magazines, and home and career skills teachers. Suggest that students who wish to try stitching use a large needle and sturdy all-cotton thread, as these are easiest to manipulate. Fabric paints stain clothing, so caution students to wear old clothing or a smock to cover their school clothes when they are working with these paints. In addition, you may wish to guide students to create a flowchart for their story before they sketch scenes. Suggest that students select dramatic, important scenes that will tell the story with the greatest visual impact.

Rubric

3 Full Accomplishment Students create a pa ndau story cloth that accurately retells a story in Unit 6 or the tale they rewrote for the Literature Connection.

2 Substantial Accomplishment The pa ndau story cloth accurately retells the folk tale but lacks some drama or visual appeal.

1 Little or Partial Accomplishment The story cloth does not retell the events in sequence.

Across Cultures Mini-Projects

Write a letter Suggest that students select a character about whom they have strong positive or negative feelings.

Create a language phrase book Caution students that many languages have regional variations or dialects. As a result, tell students to be sure to check each entry in at least two sources to make sure that the spelling, definition, and punctuation are correct.

Examine different artwork You may wish to review all the artwork that students find to make sure that it is suitable for display in class.

Present a report Students can also consult almanacs and government documents for information about the Hmong culture. Encourage students to try to find one or more Hmong immigrants who would consent to an interview. Students can tape-record the interview, with the subject's approval, and share it with the class.

OVERVIEW

Objectives

- To understand and appreciate a myth and three folk tales about the contrast between appearance and reality
- To appreciate the cultures of ancient Greece, Mexico, Denmark, and Puerto Rico
- To extend understanding of the selections through a variety of multimodal and cross-curricular activities

Skills

READING SKILLS/ STRATEGIES
- Connecting

THE WRITER'S STYLE
- Dialogue in fiction

GRAMMAR
- Punctuating compound sentences

SPELLING
- The prefixes *com-* and *in-*

STUDY SKILLS
- Multiple-choice questions
- Memorizing

SPEAKING, LISTENING, AND VIEWING
- Role-playing
- Films and videos
- Retelling
- Press conference

Cross-Curricular Activities

SOCIAL STUDIES
- Southwestern culture
- Millers
- Fabrics
- Trickster tales

GEOGRAPHY
- Features of Puerto Rico, Greece, and Denmark

SCIENCE
- Diamonds
- Echoes

Reading Pathways

- Select one or several students to read each tale aloud to the entire class or to small groups of students. Assign this reading in advance so that the readers can incorporate into their presentations some of the techniques used by professional storytellers. Have the audience listen carefully to the tales without following along in their texts.
- Read the tales aloud to the class, pausing at key points to discuss how elements of each tale inform students about the customs of a particular culture. Have students compare these customs with those of their own culture, recording their responses and observations in their notebooks.
- After students have read the tales once, have them read them again to identify structural elements such as main characters, minor characters, conflict, setting, and plot. Then have students identify similarities and differences between these tales and the selections in Unit Five. For example, have students compare the trickery in "Lazy Peter and His Three-Cornered Hat" with that in "Lose Now, Pay Later."

PREVIEWING

LINKS TO UNIT FIVE

Not As It Seems

Activating Prior Knowledge
Things aren't always what they seem. A person or situation that appears one way at first glance may appear very different upon closer inspection. In the tales you are about to read, which link to Unit Five, the contrast between appearance and reality is important.

Building Background
MEXICO

The Force of Luck
retold by Rudolfo A. Anaya

This tale comes from an area of the U.S. Southwest that formerly belonged to Mexico. This area reflects a mixture of cultures that includes Spanish, Mexican, and Native American. The main character in this tale works at a grain mill, where he grinds corn and wheat. In many Hispanic tales, millers serve as symbols of honest hard labor.

Building Background
PUERTO RICO

Lazy Peter and His Three-Cornered Hat
retold by Ricardo E. Alegría

"Lazy Peter and His Three-Cornered Hat" is a trickster tale that comes from Puerto Rico. The folklore of Puerto Rico has roots in Asia, Arabia, Spain, and West Africa. Although trickster tales reflect an admiration for cleverness, the tricksters themselves are not depicted as heroic but as what they really are—con artists.

762   UNIT SIX: THE ORAL TRADITION

PRINT AND MEDIA RESOURCES

UNIT SIX RESOURCE BOOK
Strategic Reading: Literature, p. 37
Vocabulary SkillBuilder, p. 40
Reading SkillBuilder, p. 38
Spelling SkillBuilder, p. 39

GRAMMAR MINI–LESSONS
Transparencies, p. 28
Copymasters, p. 37

WRITING MINI–LESSONS
Transparencies, pp. 48

ACCESS FOR STUDENTS ACQUIRING ENGLISH
Selection Summaries
Reading and Writing Support

FORMAL ASSESSMENT
Selection Test, pp. 125–126
Unit Six test, pp. 126–127
 Test Generator

ALTERNATIVE ASSESSMENT
End-of-Year Integrated Assessment
  Reader, pp. 31–39
  Student Response Booklet, pp. 41–54

📼 **AUDIO LIBRARY**
See Reference Card

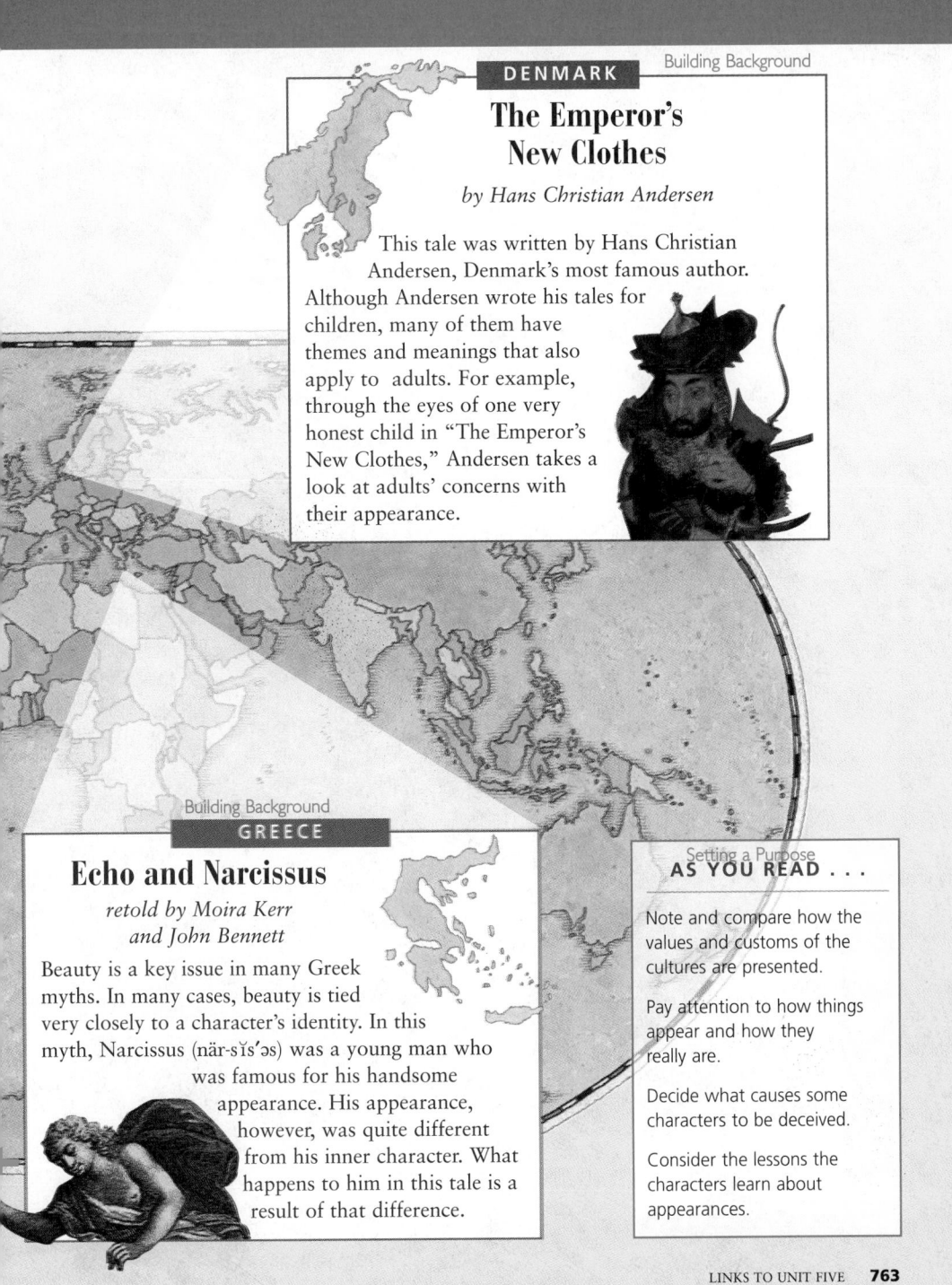

DENMARK

The Emperor's New Clothes

by Hans Christian Andersen

This tale was written by Hans Christian Andersen, Denmark's most famous author. Although Andersen wrote his tales for children, many of them have themes and meanings that also apply to adults. For example, through the eyes of one very honest child in "The Emperor's New Clothes," Andersen takes a look at adults' concerns with their appearance.

GREECE

Echo and Narcissus

retold by Moira Kerr and John Bennett

Beauty is a key issue in many Greek myths. In many cases, beauty is tied very closely to a character's identity. In this myth, Narcissus (när-sĭs′əs) was a young man who was famous for his handsome appearance. His appearance, however, was quite different from his inner character. What happens to him in this tale is a result of that difference.

Setting a Purpose
AS YOU READ . . .

Note and compare how the values and customs of the cultures are presented.

Pay attention to how things appear and how they really are.

Decide what causes some characters to be deceived.

Consider the lessons the characters learn about appearances.

LINKS TO UNIT FIVE **763**

WORDS TO KNOW

anguish (ăng′gwĭsh) *n.* great physical or mental suffering, as from grief or pain (p. 769)
bartering (bär′tər-ing) *n.* trading by exchange of goods or services without using money **barter** *v.* (p. 772)
benefactor (bĕn′ə-făk′tər) *n.* a person who provides money or help (p. 772)
console (kən-sōl′) *v.* to comfort (p. 769)
contend (kən-tĕnd′) *v.* to argue (p. 768)
crafty (krăf′tē) *adj.* skillfully tricky; sly (p. 777)

distinguish (dĭ-stĭng′gwĭsh) *v.* to observe or show the difference in; separate and classify (p. 776)
haggle (hăg′əl) *v.* to argue about terms or price; bargain (p. 782)
induce (ĭn-dōōs′) *v.* to persuade (p. 778)
intact (ĭn-tăkt′) *adj.* whole and undamaged with nothing missing (p. 774)
outset (out′sĕt′) *n.* beginning (p. 776)
pathetic (pə-thĕt′ĭk) *adj.* arousing pity or sympa-

thy; pitiful (p. 766)
priceless (prīs′lĭs) *adj.* too valuable to be measured by price (p. 783)
rogue (rōg) *n.* a rascal (p. 778)
squander (skwŏn′dər) *v.* to spend carelessly (p. 769)
unsound (ŭn-sound′) *adj.* not free from fault or weakness; not sensible; inaccurate (p. 782)
writhe (rīth) *v.* to twist or turn in distress or embarrassment; squirm (p. 779)

ECHO

SUMMARY

Echo and Narcissus Echo falls in love with handsome Narcissus, but he mocks Echo. Shamed, she hides and wastes away. Narcissus continues to break hearts until the gods punish him by having him fall in love with his own reflection in a pool. Unable to tear himself away from it, he withers away into a flower.

Art Note

Narcissus enchanted by his reflection
French engraving, 18th century
Reading the Art *Study the art and its title. What do you think they convey about Narcissus's personality? How do you think Narcissus would describe himself? How would you describe him?*

CUSTOMIZING FOR
Students Acquiring English

• Use **ACCESS FOR STUDENTS ACQUIRING ENGLISH,** *Reading and Writing Support.*

• Some students may find Echo's dialogue confusing. Make sure they understand the curse Hera has put on Echo and how it affects her speech.

• In addition to these boxes, you may wish to use the suggestions under Strategic Reading for Less-Proficient Readers.

STRATEGIC READING FOR
Less-Proficient Readers

Set a Purpose Invite students to describe how a vain and conceited person acts. Discuss why such people are disagreeable to others. Then ask students to read to find out how Narcissus is punished for his conceit and egotism.

• Use **UNIT SIX RESOURCE BOOK,** p. 37, for guidance in reading the selection.

CUSTOMIZING FOR
Gifted and Talented Students

You may want to give students the related words *narcissist* and *narcissism*—words whose meaning reflects the selfishness and vanity Narcissus displays in this myth. Then invite students to identify the mysteries of nature that this myth explains. *(Possible responses: It explains what an echo is; it tells how narcissus flowers came to be.)*

Detail of Narcissus enchanted by his reflection. French engraving from an 18th century edition of Ovid's *Metamorphoses*, The Granger Collection, New York.

764   UNIT SIX: THE ORAL TRADITION

Mini-Lesson: Speaking, Listening, and Viewing

ROLE-PLAYING Explain to students that role-playing characters from the stories helps them to understand the characters. Point out that successful role-playing is based on inferences made about a character's traits and motivations.

Application Have students work in pairs and role-play the dialogue between Narcissus and Echo.

Challenge students playing Narcissus to convey his vanity, and challenge those playing Echo to convey her shyness and frustration because of Hera's curse. Encourage students to embellish upon the dialogue already provided.

NARCISSUS

RETOLD BY MOIRA KERR AND JOHN BENNETT

Not many men, or even gods, were as handsome as young Narcissus. So fair was he that almost everyone who saw him fell in love with him that very moment.

One day, as Narcissus roamed the forests with his hunting companions, he was spied by the watchful eye of the nymph[1] Echo. She had once been a great chatterer, ready to talk to any passerby on any subject at any time, and on several occasions she had detained the goddess Hera[2] with hours of casual talk, just as Hera was on the point of stumbling upon Zeus with one of his illicit[3] loves. Eventually Hera grew so annoyed that she put a curse on Echo, and from that time on the unfortunate nymph could say nothing but the last few words that she had heard.

Trembling, Echo followed Narcissus through the trees. She longed to go closer to him, to gaze upon the beauty of his face, but she feared that he would laugh at her silly speech. Before long, Narcissus wandered away from his companions, and when he realized he was lost, he called in panic, "Is there anybody here?"

"Here!" called Echo.

Mystified by this reply, Narcissus shouted, "Come!"

"Come!" shouted Echo.

Narcissus was convinced that someone was playing tricks on him.

"Why are you avoiding me?" he called. The only answer he heard was his own question repeated from the woods.

"Come here, and let us meet!" pleaded Narcissus.

"Let us meet!" Echo answered, delighted.

She overcame her shyness and crept from her hiding place to approach Narcissus. But he, satisfied now that he had solved the mystery of

---

1. **nymph** (nĭmf): in Greek mythology, a godlike being that appears as a beautiful young woman in a natural setting.

2. **Hera** (hîr′ə): in Greek mythology, the wife of Zeus.

3. **illicit** (ĭ-lĭs′ĭt): forbidden; not allowed by custom.

Mini-Lesson ✏ Grammar

PUNCTUATING COMPOUND SENTENCES Remind students that a compound sentence consists of two or more simple sentences joined together. Tell students that the parts of a compound sentence are joined either by a comma and a coordinating conjunction (*and, but, or, for, so*) or by a semicolon (;). Draw on the chalkboard the examples shown.

Application Have students correct these compound sentences by adding a comma and conjunction or a semicolon.

1. Echo longed to go closer to him she feared that he would laugh at her silly speech.

2. She overcame her shyness she crept from her hiding place to approach Narcissus.

3. Echo's youth and beauty vanished her body withered away.

4. His heart trembled from the sight he could not tear himself away from it.

Reteaching/Reinforcement
- Grammar Handbook, anthology pp. 879–880
- *Grammar Mini-Lessons* copymasters, p. 37, transparencies, p. 28

 The Writer's Craft

Compound Sentences, p. 559

Compound Sentences

Echo loved Narcissus, but he mocked her.

Echo loved Narcissus; he mocked her.

E According to some accounts, it was Nemesis, the goddess of vengeance, who decided on Narcissus's punishment. Nemesis helped people get even with those who had wronged them because she was responsible for maintaining the balance of good and evil in the world. Today, the word *nemesis* means "a person or force that torments or defeats someone."

CUSTOMIZING FOR

Students Acquiring English

2 If possible, show students a picture of a narcissus.

STRATEGIC READING FOR

Less-Proficient Readers

F Ask students to explain how Narcissus is punished. *(He is made to fall in love with his own reflection.)*
Restating

From Personal Response to Critical Analysis

1. In your journal describe your impressions of Echo and Narcissus. *(Possible responses: Narcissus is vain and insensitive; Echo is pathetic and vulnerable.)*

2. How do you think Narcissus's identity is related to his appearance? *(Possible responses: His beauty is the one thing that everyone notices about him; his beauty makes him lack compassion for others.)*

3. Myth can have more than one purpose. How would you explain the purposes of this myth? *(Possible responses: to warn against foolishness and idle chatter; to emphasize the danger of being vain; to explain the origin of echoes and the narcissus flower)*

the voice, roughly pushed her away and ran.

"I would die before I would have you near me!" he shouted mockingly over his shoulder.

Helpless, Echo had to call after him, "I would have you near me!"

The nymph was so embarrassed and ashamed that she hid herself in a dark cave and never came into the air and sunlight again. Her youth and beauty withered away, and her body became so shrunken and tiny that eventually she vanished altogether. All that was left was the <u>pathetic</u> voice which still roams the world, anxious to talk, yet able only to repeat what others say.

Poor Echo was not the only one to be treated brutally by Narcissus. He had played with many hearts, and at last one of those he had scorned

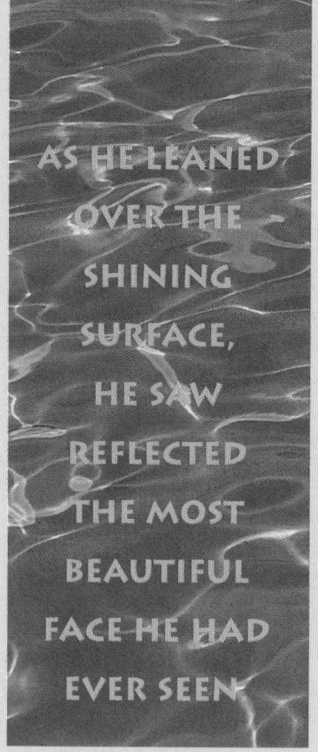

AS HE LEANED OVER THE SHINING SURFACE, HE SAW REFLECTED THE MOST BEAUTIFUL FACE HE HAD EVER SEEN

prayed to the gods that Narcissus would some day find himself scorned by one he loved. The prayer was heard and granted.

Tired and thirsty from his hunting, Narcissus threw himself down beside a still, clear pool to drink. As he leaned over the shining surface, he saw reflected the most beautiful face he had ever seen. His heart trembled at the sight, and he could not tear himself away from it—his own image.

For a long time Narcissus remained there beside the pool, never raising his eyes from the surface, and from time to time murmuring words of love. At last his body withered away and became the stem of a flower, and his head the lovely gold and white blossom which still looks into quiet pools and is called the narcissus. ❖

MOIRA KERR

For a biography of Moira Kerr, see page 708.

| WORDS TO KNOW | **pathetic** (pə-thĕt'ĭk) *adj.* arousing pity or sympathy; pitiful |

766

COMPREHENSION CHECK

1. What curse does Hera put on Echo? *(Echo can only repeat what she has heard.)*

2. Why does Hera put this curse on Echo? *(Hera is annoyed at Echo for talking too much.)*

3. Why does Echo hide in a cave and wither away? *(She has been rejected by Narcissus.)*

4. With whom does Narcissus finally fall in love? *(with himself)*

5. What happens to Narcissus at the end of the myth? *(His body withers away, and he becomes a flower.)*

The Force of Luck

LUCK

Roadside Conference (1953), Archibald J. Motley, Jr. Oil on canvas, 16¾" × 11", Atlanta University Collection of Afro-American Art at Clark Atlanta University.

retold by Rudolfo A. Anaya

767

SUMMARY

The Force of Luck What makes a man rich—luck or money? Two wealthy friends are debating this question. Finally, one tries to settle it by giving a poor but honest miller two hundred dollars. Unfortunately, the miller is cursed with bad luck. He loses most of the money to a hawk that flies off with his bag. Three months later, the wealthy friends return to see what has happened. Hearing the miller's hard-luck story, the man who believes in money gives out another two hundred dollars. This time, the miller hides the money in a bran jar, but loses it all when his wife trades the jar for clay. When the wealthy friends come around again, the money man doubts the miller's second hard-luck story. He gives out no more cash, but his friend tosses the miller a worthless piece of lead, which he passes along to a fisherman to weigh down his nets. In return, the miller receives a fish that has a diamond in its stomach, making him and his wife rich. Some time later, the two wealthy friends pass through, and the miller eagerly shows them his new mill and cottage. During the tour, they coincidentally find the money the hawk stole and the money in the bran jar. In this way, the miller proves his honesty, and the friends' original question has an obvious answer.

Art Note

Roadside Conference by Archibald J. Motley, Jr. This picture was painted in 1953 when Motley, an African-American artist, lived in Mexico. His work often portrayed ordinary people going about everyday activities.

Reading the Art *Look at how the artist has depicted his subjects. Why do you think he chose this style? What impression do you have of these two men? Explain.*

STRATEGIC READING FOR
Less-Proficient Readers

Set a Purpose Discuss the things or qualities that people need to be successful. Then have students debate what makes a person more successful: luck or money. Have students read to find out how the miller gets—and loses—a large amount of money.

Multicultural ● **Perspectives**

SOUTHWESTERN CULTURE The area of the American Southwest in which this tale originated was influenced by two cultures with roots in Spain. The older culture is Spanish, primarily found in northern New Mexico and southern Colorado. Centuries ago, settlers from Spain brought their traditions and beliefs to the New World .

The more recent culture is that of Mexican Americans. This culture is concentrated mostly along the border between Mexico and the United States. Mexican cultural values are strong in this area, in part because successive waves of Mexican immigrants have brought Mexican culture back into the lives of third- and fourth-generation Mexican Americans.

A A miller is someone who grinds grains such as wheat or rye into flour. In most technologically advanced countries today, grain is ground by machines. However, it is still ground by hand in less advanced places in the world.

CUSTOMIZING FOR

Students Acquiring English

I Point out that the idiomatic expression *make ends meet* means "have enough money for living expenses."

Literary Concept: FOLK TALE

B Point out that the author has already explained what the argument is about in the first paragraph. Ask students why the author repeats the entire point again. *(Possible response: Repetition is part of the style of a folk tale. It makes the story easy to remember, which is important for stories that were transmitted through the oral tradition. Repetition also serves to remind listeners of details they may have forgotten.)*

Active Reading: CONNECT

C Ask students to relate any experiences they have had after being given a gift of money. Have them describe how they came to a decision about what to spend their money on.

Once two wealthy friends got into a heated argument. One said that it was money which made a man prosperous, and the other maintained that it wasn't money, but luck, which made the man. They argued for some time and finally decided that if only they could find an honorable man, then perhaps they could prove their respective points of view.

One day while they were passing through a small village they came upon a miller who was grinding corn and wheat. They paused to ask the man how he ran his business. The miller replied that he worked for a master and that he earned only four bits[1] a day, and with that he had to support a family of five.

The friends were surprised. "Do you mean to tell us you can maintain a family of five on only fifteen dollars a month?" one asked.

"I live modestly to make ends meet," the humble miller replied.

The two friends privately agreed that if they put this man to a test, perhaps they could resolve their argument.

"I am going to make you an offer," one of them said to the miller. "I will give you two hundred dollars, and you may do whatever you want with the money."

"But why would you give me this money when you've just met me?" the miller asked.

"Well, my good man, my friend and I have a long-standing argument. He <u>contends</u> that it is luck which elevates a man to high position, and I say it is money. By giving you this money, perhaps we can settle our argument. Here, take it, and do with it what you want!"

So the poor miller took the money and spent the rest of the day thinking about the strange meeting which had presented him with more money than he had ever seen. What could he possibly do with all this money? Be that as it

may, he had the money in his pocket, and he could do with it whatever he wanted.

When the day's work was done, the miller decided the first thing he would do would be to buy food for his family. He took out ten dollars and wrapped the rest of the money in a cloth and put the bundle in his bag. Then he went to the market and bought supplies and a good piece of meat to take home.

On the way home he was attacked by a hawk that had smelled the meat which the miller carried. The miller fought off the bird, but in the struggle he lost the bundle of money. Before the miller knew what was happening the hawk grabbed the bag and flew away with it. When he realized what had happened he fell into deep thought.

"Ah," he moaned, "wouldn't it have been better to let that hungry bird have the meat! I could have bought a lot more meat with the money he took. Alas, now I'm in the same poverty as before! And worse, because now those two men will say I am a thief! I should have thought carefully and bought nothing. Yes, I should have gone straight home, and this wouldn't have happened!"

So he gathered what was left of his provisions and continued home, and when he arrived he told his family the entire story.

When he was finished telling his story his wife said, "It has been our lot to be poor, but have faith in God and maybe someday our luck will change."

The next day the miller got up and went to work as usual. He wondered what the two men would say about his story. But since he had never been a man of money he soon forgot the entire matter.

Three months after he had lost the money to

---

1. **four bits:** a slang term for fifty cents.

WORDS
TO
KNOW

contend (kən-těnd′) *v.* to argue

768

Mini-Lesson   **Reading Skills/Strategies**

ACTIVE READING: CONNECT Ask students if they have ever read a story and said to themselves, "I remember what I did in a situation like that." Explain that if they had that experience, then they were using the active reading skill of connecting. Remind students that active readers become involved in what they read. Tell students that when readers connect with the text, they are thinking of similarities between what is described in the story and what they have experienced, heard about, or read. This will help them better identify with characters and their situations.

Application Have students create a Venn diagram like the one shown to compare and contrast their own personality traits, values, and experiences with the miller's.

Reteaching/Reinforcement
• *Unit Six Resource Book,* p. 38

the miller   **Similarities**   me

the hawk, it happened that the two wealthy men returned to the village. As soon as they saw the miller they approached him to ask if his luck had changed. When the miller saw them he felt ashamed and afraid that they would think that he had squandered the money on worthless things. But he decided to tell them the truth, and as soon as they had greeted each other he told his story. The men believed him. In fact, the one who insisted that it was money and not luck which made a man prosper took out another two hundred dollars and gave it to the miller.

"Let's try again," he said, "and let's see what happens this time."

The miller didn't know what to think. "Kind sir, maybe it would be better if you put this money in the hands of another man," he said.

"No," the man insisted, "I want to give it to you because you are an honest man, and if we are going to settle our argument you have to take the money!"

The miller thanked them and promised to do his best. Then as soon as the two men left he began to think what to do with the money so that it wouldn't disappear as it had the first time. The thing to do was to take the money straight home. He took out ten dollars, wrapped the rest in a cloth, and headed home.

When he arrived his wife wasn't at home. At first he didn't know what to do with the money. He went to the pantry, where he had stored a large earthenware jar filled with bran. That was as safe a place as any to hide the money, he thought, so he emptied out the grain and put the bundle of money at the bottom of the jar, then covered it up with the grain. Satisfied that the money was safe, he returned to work.

That afternoon when he arrived home from work he was greeted by his wife.

"Look, my husband, today I bought some good clay with which to whitewash² the entire house."

"And how did you buy the clay if we don't have any money?" he asked.

"Well, the man who was selling the clay was willing to trade for jewelry, money, or anything of value," she said. "The only thing we had of value was the jar full of bran, so I traded it for the clay. Isn't it wonderful? I think we have enough clay to whitewash these two rooms!"

The man groaned and pulled his hair.

"Oh, you crazy woman! What have you done? We're ruined again!"

"But why?" she asked, unable to understand his anguish.

"Today I met the same two friends who gave me the two hundred dollars three months ago," he explained. "And after I told them how I lost the money they gave me another two hundred. And I, to make sure the money was safe, came home and hid it inside the jar of bran—the same jar you have traded for dirt! Now we're as poor as we were before! And what am I going to tell the two men? They'll think I'm a liar and a thief for sure!"

"Let them think what they want," his wife said calmly. "We will only have in our lives what the good Lord wants us to have. It is our lot to be poor until God wills it otherwise."

So the miller was consoled, and the next day he went to work as usual. Time came and went, and one day the two wealthy friends returned to ask the miller how he had done with the second two hundred dollars. When

---

2. **whitewash:** to paint something white.

WORDS TO KNOW	**squander** (skwŏn'dər) *v.* to spend carelessly
	anguish (ăng'gwĭsh) *n.* great physical or mental suffering, as from grief or pain
	console (kən-sōl') *v.* to comfort

769

Literary Concept: THEME

D Folk tales often contrast the noble poor with the greedy rich. Ask students if they think such a contrast is being drawn in this tale, and have them explain their answers. (*Possible responses: yes, because the rich men are using the honest miller as a pawn to settle a petty argument between themselves; no, because the rich men are honest with the miller, and he needs the money the men give him*)

Active Reading: EVALUATE

E Ask students to evaluate the wisdom in the miller's choice of a hiding place for the money. (*Possible response: His choice of a hiding place is not wise, because food like bran is likely to be used at any time.*)

STRATEGIC READING FOR
Less-Proficient Readers

F Use the following questions to help students review the ups and downs of the miller's life:

• How does the miller get and then lose $200 the first time? (*Two strangers give it to him. A hawk steals it.*) **Noting Relevant Details**

• How does he get and lose money the second time? (*The same men give him money, which he hides in a jar of grain. His wife then trades the grain to a neighbor.*) **Noting Relevant Details**

Set a Purpose Have students read to find out whether the miller becomes successful.

CUSTOMIZING FOR
Students Acquiring English

2 Explain that *wills*, as used here, is a verb that means "determines, makes happen."

Mini-Lesson: Speaking, Listening, and Viewing

FILMS AND VIDEOS Discuss with students how viewing films and videos can be a useful way to learn about how folklore reflects cultural values and concerns. Invite students to brainstorm some films and videos that have helped them learn more about another culture. Then present students with these guidelines for viewing a film or video:

• *Ask yourself questions about what is happening on the screen. Explore possible reasons for what is going on and how the characters can help you understand the plot.*

• *Make mental notes about words or statements that confuse you, but don't get sidetracked. Things may get clearer later in the film.*

• *Try to figure out what will happen next and how the film will end.*

Application Have students use the guidelines above as they view *Chicano from the Southwest,* a movie in which a boy struggles to keep his traditions while growing up in the city (Britannica Video, 1992). Then have the class discuss what they learned about cultural values from the movie.

Literary Concept: CONFLICT

G Ask students how each man's opinion of the miller reflects his side of the argument about luck and money. *(Possible responses: The "money man" doesn't trust the miller, because according to his argument, the miller should be prospering. The "luck man" wants to trust the miller because the miller's bad luck supports his point—that luck is the key to prosperity.)*

CUSTOMIZING FOR
Students Acquiring English

3 If necessary, remind students that the suffix *-less* means "without." Then ask students to find and define two words in these paragraphs that contain this suffix. *(luckless, "without luck"; worthless, "without worth")*

Literary Concept: FOLKLORE

H Point out that events often happen in sets of three in folk tales. The first two events are similar to set readers up for the third, crucial event. Ask students how this story follows the traditional folklore pattern. *(Possible response: The miller got three gifts from the rich men—two identical sums of money, which he lost, and a worthless lump of lead. According to the pattern, the lead should turn out to be valuable or important to the story's climax and resolution.)*

Active Reading: PREDICT

I Invite students to predict what the "piece of glass" might turn out to be. *(Possible responses: a valuable jewel; a magic stone)*

---

the poor miller saw them he was afraid they would accuse him of being a liar and a spendthrift.[3] But he decided to be truthful, and as soon as they had greeted each other he told them what had happened to the money.

"That is why poor men remain honest," the man who had given him the money said. "Because they don't have money they can't get into trouble. But I find your stories hard to believe. I think you gambled and lost the money. That's why you're telling us these wild stories."

G "Either way," he continued, "I still believe that it is money and not luck which makes a man prosper."

"Well, you certainly didn't prove your point by giving the money to this poor miller," his **3** friend reminded him. "Good evening, you luckless man," he said to the miller.

"Thank you, friends," the miller said.

"Oh, by the way, here is a worthless piece of lead I've been carrying around. Maybe you can use it for something," said the man who believed in luck. Then the two men left, still debating their points of view on life.

H Since the lead was practically worthless, the miller thought nothing of it and put it in his jacket pocket. He forgot all about it until he arrived home. When he threw his jacket on a chair he heard a thump, and he remembered the piece of lead. He took it out of the pocket and threw it under the table. Later that night after the family had eaten and gone to bed, they heard a knock at the door.

"Who is it? What do you want?" the miller asked.

"It's me, your neighbor," a voice answered. The miller recognized the fisherman's wife. "My husband sent me to ask you if you have any lead you can spare. He is going fishing tomorrow, and he needs the lead to weight down the nets."

The miller remembered the lead he had

---

thrown under the table. He got up, found it, and gave it to the woman.

"Thank you very much, neighbor," the woman said. "I promise you the first fish my husband catches will be yours."

"Think nothing of it," the miller said and returned to bed. The next day he got up and went to work without thinking any more of the incident. But in the afternoon when he returned home he found his wife cooking a big fish for dinner.

"Since when are we so well off we can afford fish for supper?" he asked his wife.

"Don't you remember that our neighbor promised us the first fish her husband caught?" his wife reminded him. "Well, this was the fish he caught the first time he threw his net. So it's ours, and it's a beauty. But you should have been here when I gutted him! I found a large piece of glass in his stomach!"

"And what did you do with it?"

"Oh, I gave it to the children to play with," she shrugged.

When the miller saw the piece of glass he noticed it shone so brightly it appeared to illuminate the room, but because he knew nothing about jewels he didn't realize its value and left it to the children. But the bright glass was such a novelty that the children were soon fighting over it and raising a terrible fuss.

Now it so happened that the miller and his wife had other neighbors who were jewelers. The following morning when the miller had gone to work, the jeweler's wife visited the miller's wife to complain about all the noise her children had made.

"We couldn't get any sleep last night," she moaned.

"I know, and I'm sorry, but you know how it is with a large family," the miller's wife

---

3. **spendthrift:** a person who wastes money.

Mini-Lesson  Spelling

THE PREFIXES *COM-* AND *IN-* Explain to students that the prefix *com-* is used before roots beginning with *b, m,* and *p*. This prefix is spelled *col-* when joined to the letter *l* and *con-* before all other letters. The prefix *in-* has four forms: *im-* before words beginning with *m* or *p; il-* before words beginning with *l; ir-* before words beginning with *r;* and *in-* before all other letters.

Application Have students create new words by adding prefixes.

1. com + sole
2. com + tend
3. com + plicated
4. com + bination
5. com + mend
6. in + tact
7. in + regular
8. in + balance
9. in + mature
10. in + logical

Ask students to look for more words that fit this pattern, in their own writing and in things that they read, and to add these words to their personal word lists.

Reteaching/Reinforcement
• *Unit Six Resource Book,* p. 39

Mujer con Pescados [Woman with fish] (1980), Francisco Zuniga. Lithograph, 21⅞" × 29½", edition of 135, courtesy of Brewster Gallery, New York.

Art Note

Mujer con Pescados by Francisco Zuniga Born in Costa Rica, artist Francisco Zuniga (1912–) has made his home in Mexico since 1936. This portrayal of a woman with a basket of fish, painted in 1980, is typical of his work and has a startling presence.

Reading the Art *What adjectives would you use to describe the woman in the painting? Explain your choices.*

Active Reading: EVALUATE

J Ask students if they trust the jeweler's wife. Guide students to base their conclusions on the text and the story's theme. *(Possible response: The jeweler's wife contrasts with the poor but honest miller: She seems greedy and thus appears untrustworthy.)*

Linking to Science

 **K** Diamonds, the hardest natural substance known, are also among the most highly valued. The largest known diamond is the Cullinan, discovered in South Africa in 1905. Before cutting, it weighed 1.37 pounds—3,016 carats. The diamond was cut into 105 gems, the largest being the Star of Africa, which is 530.2 carats. It is the largest cut diamond in existence, and it is now set in the British royal scepter.

explained. "Yesterday we found a beautiful piece of glass, and I gave it to my youngest one to play with, and when the others tried to take it from him he raised a storm."

The jeweler's wife took interest. "Won't you show me that piece of glass?" she asked.

"But of course. Here it is."

"Ah, yes, it's a pretty piece of glass. Where did you find it?"

"Our neighbor gave us a fish yesterday, and when I was cleaning it I found the glass in its stomach."

"Why don't you let me take it home for just a moment. You see, I have one just like it, and I want to compare them."

"Yes, why not? Take it," answered the miller's wife.

So the jeweler's wife ran off with the glass to show it to her husband. When the jeweler saw the glass, he instantly knew it was one of the finest diamonds he had ever seen.

"It's a diamond!" he exclaimed.

"I thought so," his wife nodded eagerly. "What shall we do?"

"Go tell the neighbor we'll give her fifty dollars for it, but don't tell her it's a diamond!"

"No, no," his wife chuckled, "of course not." She ran to her neighbor's house. "Ah, yes, we have one exactly like this," she told the miller's wife. "My husband is willing to

K

Mini-Lesson **Study Skills**

TAKING OBJECTIVE TESTS: MULTIPLE CHOICE QUESTIONS Remind students that objective tests can contain true/false, matching, and multiple-choice questions. Present these suggestions for answering multiple-choice questions:

• *Read all the choices first and eliminate obviously incorrect answers.*

• *Pay particular attention to choices that read "none of the above" or "all of the above."*

• *Choose the most complete or most accurate answer.*

Application Have students work on their own to create a ten-question multiple-choice test on "The Force of Luck." Then ask students to exchange tests with a classmate and use the suggestions above to help them answer their partners' test questions. When finished, partners can exchange tests again to check answers.

buy it for fifty dollars—only so we can have a pair, you understand."

"I can't sell it," the miller's wife answered. "You will have to wait until my husband returns from work."

That evening when the miller came home from work his wife told him about the offer the jeweler had made for the piece of glass.

"But why would they offer fifty dollars for a worthless piece of glass?" the miller wondered aloud. Before his wife could answer, they were interrupted by the jeweler's wife.

"What do you say, neighbor, will you take fifty dollars for the glass?" she asked.

"No, that's not enough," the miller said cautiously. "Offer more."

"I'll give you fifty thousand!" the jeweler's wife blurted out.

"A little bit more," the miller replied.

"Impossible!" the jeweler's wife cried. "I can't offer any more without consulting my husband." She ran off to tell her husband how the <u>bartering</u> was going, and he told her he was prepared to pay a hundred thousand dollars to acquire the diamond.

He handed her seventy-five thousand dollars and said, "Take this and tell him that tomorrow, as soon as I open my shop, he'll have the rest."

When the miller heard the offer and saw the money he couldn't believe his eyes. He imagined the jeweler's wife was jesting with him, but it was a true offer, and he received the hundred thousand dollars for the diamond. The miller had never seen so much money, but he still didn't quite trust the jeweler.

"I don't know about this money," he confided to his wife. "Maybe the jeweler plans to accuse us of robbing him and thus get it back."

"Oh no," his wife assured him, "the money is ours. We sold the diamond fair and square—

we didn't rob anyone."

"I think I'll still go to work tomorrow," the miller said. "Who knows, something might happen and the money will disappear, then we would be without money and work. Then how would we live?"

So he went to work the next day, and all day he thought about how he could use the money. When he returned home that afternoon, his wife asked him what he had decided to do with their new fortune.

"I think I will start my own mill," he answered, "like the one I operate for my master. Once I set up my business we'll see how our luck changes."

The next day he set about buying everything he needed to establish his mill and to build a new home. Soon he had everything going.

Six months had passed, more or less, since he had seen the two men who had given him the four hundred dollars and the piece of lead. He was eager to see them again and to tell them how the piece of lead had changed his luck and made him wealthy.

Time passed and the miller prospered. His business grew, and he even built a summer cottage where he could take his family on vacation. He had many employees who worked for him. One day while he was at his store he saw his two <u>benefactors</u> riding by. He rushed out into the street to greet them and ask them to come in. He was overjoyed to see them, and he was happy to see that they admired his store.

"Tell us the truth," the man who had given him the four hundred dollars said. "You used that money to set up this business."

The miller swore he hadn't, and he told them how he had given the piece of lead to his neigh-

| WORDS TO KNOW | **bartering** (bär′tər) *n.* arguing over a price; bargaining **barter** *v.* |
| | **benefactor** (bĕn′e-făk′tər) *n.* a person who provides money or help |

772

bor and how the fisherman had in return given him a fish with a very large diamond in its stomach. And he told them how he had sold the diamond.

"And that's how I acquired this business and many other things I want to show you," he said. "But it's time to eat. Let's eat first, then I'll show you everything I have now."

The men agreed, but one of them still doubted the miller's story. So they ate, and then the miller had three horses saddled, and they rode out to see his summer home. The cabin was on the other side of the river, where the mountains were cool and beautiful. When they arrived the men admired the place very much. It was such a peaceful place that they rode all afternoon through the forest. During their ride they came upon a tall pine tree.

"What is that on top of the tree?" one of them asked.

"That's the nest of a hawk," the miller replied.

"I have never seen one; I would like to take a closer look at it!"

"Of course," the miller said, and he ordered a servant to climb the tree and bring down the nest so his friend could see how it was built. When the hawk's nest was on the ground they examined it carefully. They noticed that there was a cloth bag at the bottom of the nest. When the miller saw the bag he immediately knew that it was the very same bag he had lost to the hawk which fought him for the piece of meat years ago.

Cargador al pie de la escalera [Porter at the foot of the stairway] (1956), Diego Rivera. Watercolor on rice paper, 15¼" × 10¾". Photo courtesy of Christie's, New York.

"You won't believe me, friends, but this is the very same bag in which I put the first two hundred dollars you gave me," he told them.

"If it's the same bag," the man who had doubted him said, "then the money you said the hawk took should be there."

"No doubt about that," the miller said. "Let's see what we find."

THE FORCE OF LUCK   **773**

Mini-Lesson: Speaking, Listening, and Viewing

RETELLING Remind students that "The Force of Luck" was originally passed down by word of mouth from one generation to the next. Explain to students that anyone who retells a story interprets it. Tell students that there are three goals to keep in mind when retelling a story: summarizing it accurately, expressing your interpretation, and entertaining your audience. Discuss these steps in the process:

1. Think about the selection you want to retell. Review and summarize the material beforehand. Concentrate on summarizing the key information.

2. Use your voice to express the story. For example, to emphasize certain words or passages, change the way you say them (volume, tone, and so on).

3. Use body language effectively to reinforce your words.

Application Have students work in pairs to retell "The Force of Luck." Encourage students to apply the steps above and to limit their presentations to three minutes.

S Ask students to predict how the story will end. *(Possible response: The miller and the two wealthy men will prove that luck is more important than wealth in achieving success.)*

CUSTOMIZING FOR

Gifted and Talented Students

T Ask students whether they think the miller earns his rewards and deserves his prosperity. *(Possible responses: yes, because he earned his wealth by investing wisely and working hard; no, because his wealth resulted from a stroke of luck)*

STRATEGIC READING FOR

Less-Proficient Readers

U Ask students how the men become convinced that the miller is honest. *(They find the money they gave him where the miller claimed to have lost it.)* Noting Relevant Details

From Personal Response to Critical Analysis

1. How would you describe the miller? Write your description in your notebook. *(Possible responses: honest, hard-working, humble)*

2. Who or what do you think is primarily responsible for the miller's success? Why? *(Possible responses: Luck is primarily responsible because the miller's success is the result of a series of unexpected occurrences. Hard work is primarily responsible because the miller made the most of his money.)*

3. What values do you think this story teaches? *(Possible responses: that patience and honesty are rewarded; that people should seize the opportunities life offers; that success requires hard work, money, and luck)*

The three of them examined the old, weather-beaten bag. Although it was full of holes and crumbling, when they tore it apart they found the money <u>intact</u>. The two men remembered what the miller had told them, and they agreed he was an honest and honorable man. Still, the man who had given him the money wasn't satisfied. He wondered what had really happened to the second two hundred he had given the miller.

They spent the rest of the day riding in the mountains and returned very late to the house.

As he unsaddled their horses, the servant in charge of grooming and feeding the horses suddenly realized that he had no grain for them. He ran to the barn and checked, but there was no grain for the hungry horses. So he ran to the neighbor's granary, and there he was able to buy a large clay jar of bran. He carried the jar home and emptied the bran into a bucket to wet it before he fed it to the horses. When he got to the bottom of the jar he noticed a large lump which turned out to be a rag-covered package. He examined it and felt something inside. He immediately went to give it to his master, who had been eating dinner.

"Master," he said, "look at this package which I found in an earthenware jar of grain which I just bought from our neighbor!"

The three men carefully unraveled the cloth and found the other one hundred and ninety dollars which the miller had told them he had lost. That is how the miller proved to his friends that he was truly an honest man.

And they had to decide for themselves whether it had been luck or money which had made the miller a wealthy man! ❖

RUDOLFO A. ANAYA

Rudolfo Anaya (1937–) says, "In New Mexico everyone tells stories; it is a creative pastime." Anaya is an American author of Mexican heritage. His writing is inspired by his cultural background and his fascination with the oral tradition of Spanish folk tales.

Anaya was born in Pastura, New Mexico. His family has lived in New Mexico for several genera-tions. Currently a professor at the University of New Mexico, Anaya has given readings from his work throughout the Southwest and, in 1980, at the White House. Anaya has won many awards for his fiction and nonfiction, which draw on New Mexico's Hispanic past.

OTHER WORKS *Bless Me, Ultima; Heart of Aztlan; Tortuga; The Silence of the Llano: Short Stories*

WORDS
TO
KNOW

774

intact (ĭn-tăkt′) *adj.* whole and undamaged with nothing missing

COMPREHENSION CHECK

1. What issue are the two wealthy men try-ing to settle when they meet the poor miller? *(whether it is luck or money that brings prosperity)*

2. What are the first two gifts the wealthy men give to the miller? *(They give him two gifts of $200 each.)*

3. What is the third and last gift? *(a piece of lead)*

4. What does the miller's wife find in the fish's stomach? *(a diamond)*

5. What business does the miller set up? *(his own mill)*

THE Emperor's NEW Clothes

BY HANS CHRISTIAN ANDERSEN

775

SUMMARY

The Emperor's New Clothes The emperor in this tale is a vain clotheshorse, easily tricked by two swindlers who offer to weave him the most beautiful cloth imaginable. The cloth supposedly has the unique quality of being invisible to people who are dull-witted or unfit for their posts. The emperor pays the hucksters in advance and gives them gold and silk thread for their task. Pocketing the profits, they begin an elaborate charade of weaving imaginary cloth on real looms. From courtiers on up to the emperor himself, people are afraid to say they cannot see the cloth. The swindlers pretend to make the clothes and then to put them on the naked emperor. He marches nude through the street while the public—fearful of seeming stupid—say good things about what he is wearing. Finally a child speaks the truth: "But he has got nothing on!" and the crowd takes up the cry. The embarrassed emperor continues the royal procession as if nothing has happened—proving that he is indeed foolish and unfit for his post.

STRATEGIC READING FOR

Less-Proficient Readers

Set a Purpose Ask students to explain the old saying, "Clothes make the man." Discuss with the class how people are often judged by their appearance—and the advantages and disadvantages of this practice. Then ask students to read this story to find out what new clothes the Emperor wears.

CUSTOMIZING FOR

Gifted and Talented Students

Have students create two new titles for this selection and explain their titles to the class.

Mini-Lesson **Study Skills**

MEMORIZING Remind students that learning about a topic often involves committing it to memory. Suggest students apply the following guidelines to help them memorize:

1. Read the information several times, both silently and aloud.
2. Break up long passages into shorter sections, which are easier to remember.
3. Have a partner help you by prompting and quizzing you.
4. Review the information several times each day until you commit it to memory.

Application Have students memorize a favorite passage from one of the tales in this unit or from a selection in Unit Five. Suggest they work alone and in pairs to apply these guidelines.

Literary Concept: CHARACTER

A Have students compare the Emperor with Narcissus from the myth "Echo and Narcissus." *(Possible responses: Both characters are excessively concerned with their appearance. This obsession leads both characters to neglect other aspects of life.)*

Active Reading: CONNECT

B Invite students to discuss some of the advantages and disadvantages of being able to tell instantly who is wise and who is foolish. *(Possible responses: An advantage is that knowing who is wise helps you know whom to trust. A disadvantage is that such labeling leads to stereotyping and possible mistreatment of others.)*

CUSTOMIZING FOR
Students Acquiring English

I Students may not be familiar with this unusual use of the word *stuff* ("fabric"). Encourage them to use context clues to infer the meaning.

Critical Thinking: ANALYZING

C Ask students what the minister's reaction to the "cloth" reveals about him. *(Possible responses: He lacks self-confidence; he doesn't trust his own judgment.)*

A **M**any years ago there was an emperor who was so excessively fond of new clothes that he spent all his money on them. He cared nothing about his soldiers, nor for the theater, nor for driving in the woods except for the sake of showing off his new clothes. He had a costume for every hour in the day. Instead of saying as one does about any other king or emperor, "He is in his council chamber," the people here always said, "The emperor is in his dressing room."

Life was very gay in the great town where he lived. Hosts of strangers came to visit it every day, and among them one day were two swindlers. They gave themselves out as weavers and said that they knew how to weave the most beautiful fabrics imaginable. Not only were the colors and patterns unusually fine, but the clothes that were made of this cloth had the peculiar quality of becoming invisible to every person who was not fit for the office he held, or who was impossibly dull.

"Those must be splendid clothes," thought the emperor. "By wearing them I should be able to discover which men in my kingdom are unfitted for their posts. I shall distinguish the wise men from the fools. Yes, I certainly must order some of that stuff to be woven for me."

B He paid the two swindlers a lot of money in advance, so that they might begin their work at once.

They did put up two looms and pretended to weave, but they had nothing whatever upon their shuttles. At the outset they asked for a quantity of the finest silk and the purest gold thread, all of which they put into their own bags while they worked away at the empty looms far into the night.

"I should like to know how those weavers are getting on with their cloth," thought the emperor, but he felt a little queer when he reflected that anyone who was stupid or unfit for his post would not be able to see it. He certainly thought that he need have no fears for himself, but still he thought he would send somebody else first to see how it was getting on. Everybody in the town knew what wonderful power the stuff possessed, and everyone was anxious to see how stupid his neighbor was.

"I will send my faithful old minister to the weavers," thought the emperor. "He will be best able to see how the stuff looks, for he is a clever man, and no one fulfills his duties better than he does."

So the good old minister went into the room where the two swindlers sat working at the empty loom.

"Heaven help us," thought the old minister, opening his eyes very wide. "Why, I can't see a thing!" But he took care not to say so.

Both the swindlers begged him to be good enough to step a little nearer and asked if he did not think it a good pattern and beautiful coloring. They pointed to the empty loom. The poor old minister stared as hard as he could, but he could not see anything, for of course there was nothing to see.

"Good heavens," thought he. "Is it possible that I am a fool? I have never thought so, and nobody must know it. Am I not fit for my post? It will never do to say that I cannot see the stuff."

"Well, sir, you don't say anything about the stuff," said the one who was pretending to weave.

"Oh, it is beautiful—quite charming," said the minister, looking through his spectacles. "Such a pattern and such colors! I will certainly tell the emperor that the stuff pleases

| WORDS TO KNOW | **distinguish** (dǐ-stǐng'gwǐsh) *v.* to observe or show the difference in; separate and classify |
| | **outset** (out'sĕt') *n.* beginning |

776

Mini-Lesson  **The Writer's Style**

DIALOGUE IN FICTION Using the dialogue on this page as an example, explain to students that effective dialogue accomplishes several aims. It moves the plot along, it adds interest to the story, and it shows the reader how the characters speak—sometimes by including informal language and slang. Explain that a character's words give the reader a clue to his or her personality.

Application Invite students to use the dialogue in this tale to interpret the characters. Have students complete the following chart in their notebooks by jotting down a passage of dialogue that illustrates each of the traits listed.

Reteaching/Reinforcement
• Writing Handbook, anthology p. 815
• *Writing Mini-Lessons* transparencies, p. 48

 **The Writer's Craft**

Dialogue in Fiction, pp. 320–321

Name	Traits	Dialogue
Emperor	vain	
Tailors	dishonest	
Minister	self-serving	
Child	honest	

me very much."

"We are delighted to hear you say so," said the swindlers, and then they named all the colors and described the peculiar pattern. The old minister paid great attention to what they said, so as to be able to repeat it when he got home to the emperor.

Then the swindlers went on to demand more money, more silk, and more gold, to be able to proceed with the weaving. But they put it all into their own pockets. Not a single strand was ever put into the loom, but they went on as before, weaving at the empty loom.

The emperor soon sent another faithful official to see how the stuff was getting on and if it would soon be ready. The same thing happened to him as to the minister. He looked and looked, but as there was only the empty loom, he could see nothing at all.

"Is not this a beautiful piece of stuff?" said both the swindlers, showing and explaining the beautiful pattern and colors which were not there to be seen.

"I know I am no fool," thought the man, "so it must be that I am unfit for my good post. It is very strange, though. However, one must not let it appear." So he praised the stuff he did not see and assured them of his delight in the beautiful colors and the originality of the design.

"It is absolutely charming," he said to the emperor. Everybody in the town was talking about this splendid stuff.

King Saul (1952), Jack Levine. Oil on panel, 13¾" × 11", collection of John and Joanne Payson. Photo courtesy of Midtown Payson Galleries, New York.

Now the emperor thought he would like to see it while it was still on the loom. So, accompanied by a number of selected courtiers, among whom were the two faithful officials who had already seen the imaginary stuff, he went to visit the <u>crafty</u> impostors, who were working away as hard as ever they could at the empty loom.

777

Art Note

King Saul **by Jack Levine** American painter Jack Levine uses vivid colors to portray the king and a dark gray-blue background to serve as an effective foil to the figure. Levine also adapts the Oriental system of perspective, which uses an upward movement to convey the sense of moving backward into the pictorial space.

Reading the Art *Based on details in the painting, decide whether this is a person you would want to meet and explain why or why not.*

Active Reading: EVALUATE

D Ask students to share their opinions of the swindlers and the emperor's courtiers. Ask which of these characters they consider more deserving of blame. Have them support their opinions with specific references to the story. *(Possible responses: The emperor and his courtiers are more deserving of blame because they are foolish and dishonest; the swindlers are more deserving of blame because they carry out the hoax that exploits the insecurity of the emperor and his courtiers.)*

Literary Concept: IRONY

E Invite volunteers to explain how the cloth actually does reveal who is foolish and unfit for office. Then ask students to explain how this is ironic. *(Possible response: By believing the swindlers' absurd story and by being too cowardly to admit that they can't see the fabric, the minister and the faithful official show that they are foolish, dishonest, and unfit for holding office. This is ironic because the nonexistent fabric actually lives up to the false claims of the swindlers.)*

Mini-Lesson: Speaking,  Listening, and Viewing

PRESS CONFERENCE Explain to students that officials often hold press conferences to convey important information to the media. This information can concern key issues in such areas as commerce, education, or economics. Speakers at press conferences sometimes attempt to recast embarrassing incidents in a more flattering light. Reporters, in contrast, usually try to ask questions that reveal the truth about the incident.

Application Invite students to work in small groups to hold a press conference explaining how the emperor was duped by the "tailors." Have half the students in each group act as the emperor's speakers and have the rest act as reporters asking questions. Guide the speakers to recast the emperor's actions in the best possible light; guide the reporters to stick to the facts of the story to reveal the truth. You may wish to videotape the press conferences so that the participants can watch their performances.

Literary Concept: THEME

(F) Point out that although Andersen wrote his stories for children, they also appeal to adults because of their insights. Challenge students to explain the subjects of Andersen's satire. *(Possible responses: people who maintain their status in society by acting dishonestly; people who tell a boss anything he or she wants to hear)*

Literary Concept: IRONY

(G) Ask students to explain the irony of the emperor giving the two rogues these awards. *(Possible responses: One would expect the thieves to be punished, not rewarded; the thieves are scoundrels, not gentlemen.)*

Active Reading: CONNECT

(H) Invite students to share real-life examples of people going along with something that was wrong or ill-advised simply because speaking out would draw unwelcome attention to themselves. *(Possible response: people not speaking out when bullies attack someone)*

---

(2) "It is magnificent," said both the trusted officials. "Only see, Your Majesty, what a design! What colors!" And they pointed to the empty loom, for they each thought no doubt the others could see the stuff.

(F) "What?" thought the emperor. "I see nothing at all. This is terrible! Am I a fool? Am I not fit to be emperor? Why, nothing worse could happen to me!"

"Oh, it is beautiful," said the emperor. "It has my highest approval." And he nodded his satisfaction as he gazed at the empty loom. Nothing would induce him to say that he could not see anything.

The whole suite[1] gazed and gazed but saw nothing more than all the others. However, they all exclaimed with His Majesty, "It is very beautiful." And they advised him to wear a suit made of this wonderful cloth on the occasion of a great procession which was just about to take place. "Magnificent! Gorgeous! Excellent!" went from mouth to mouth. They were all equally delighted with it. The emperor gave each of the rogues an order of knighthood to be worn in their buttonholes and the title of "Gentleman Weaver."

(G) The swindlers sat up the whole night before the day on which the procession was to take place, burning sixteen candles, so that people might see how anxious they were to get the emperor's new clothes ready. They pretended to take the stuff off the loom. They cut it out in the air with a huge pair of scissors, and they stitched away with needles without any thread in them. At last they said, "Now the emperor's new clothes are ready."

The emperor with his grandest courtiers went to them himself, and both swindlers raised one arm in the air, as if they were holding something. They said, "See, these are the trousers. This is the coat. Here is the mantle,"[2] and so on. "It is as light as a spider's web. One might think one had nothing on, but that is the very beauty of it."

"Yes," said all the courtiers, but they could not see anything, for there was nothing to see.

"Will Your Imperial Majesty be graciously pleased to take off your clothes?" said the impostors. "Then we may put on the new ones, right here before the great mirror."

The emperor took off all his clothes, and the impostors pretended to give him one article of dress after the other of the new ones which they had pretended to make. They pretended to fasten something around his waist and to tie on something. This was the train, and the emperor turned round and round in front of the mirror.

"How well His Majesty looks in the new clothes! How becoming they are!" cried all the people round. "What a design, and what colors! They are most gorgeous robes."

"The canopy is waiting outside which is to be carried over Your Majesty in the procession," said the master of the ceremonies.

"Well, I am quite ready," said the emperor. "Don't the clothes fit well?" Then he turned round again in front of the mirror, so that he should seem to be looking at his grand things.

The chamberlains who were to carry the train stooped and pretended to lift it from the ground with both hands, and they walked along with their hands in the air. They dared not let it appear that they could not see anything.

---

1. **suite** (swēt): a group of attendants or servants.
2. **mantle:** a royal robe.

| WORDS
TO
KNOW | **induce** (ĭn-dōos′) *v.* to persuade
rogue (rōg) *n.* a rascal |

778

 Multicultural Perspectives

FABRICS The fabric in "The Emperor's New Clothes" is imaginary, but some real fabrics and their origins are described here:

• **Denim** comes from the French phrase *serge de Nîmes* (serge of Nîmes). Blue jeans, thought to have been invented in 1850 by Levi Strauss, a sail maker, take their name from *gene (or jene) fustian,* a heavy twilled cotton cloth first made in Genoa, Italy.

• **Poplin** takes it name from the town where it was made, Avignon, a *papalino* or papal city. From *papalino* came *poplin.*

• **Tweed** was named by error. In 1832, a Scottish weaver offered London merchant James Locke some twilled (diagonally ribbed) fabric. The Scotsman spelled *twilled* in its Scottish form, *tweeled.* Locke misread the word as *tweed,* and the name stuck.

hen the emperor walked along in the procession under the gorgeous canopy, and everybody in the streets and at the windows exclaimed, "How beautiful the emperor's new clothes are! What a splendid train! And they fit to perfection!" Nobody would let it appear that he could see nothing, for then he would not be fit for his post, or else he was a fool.

None of the emperor's clothes had been so successful.

"But he has got nothing on," said a little child.

"Oh, listen to the innocent," said its father. And one person whispered to the other what the child had said. "He has nothing on—a child says he has nothing on!"

"But he has nothing on!" at last cried all the people.

The emperor <u>writhed</u>, for he knew it was true. But he thought, "The procession must go on now." So he held himself stiffer than ever, and the chamberlains held up the invisible train. ❖

HANS CHRISTIAN ANDERSEN

1805–1875

At the age of 14, Hans Christian Andersen, the son of a poor washerwoman and a shoemaker, went to Copenhagen, the capital of Denmark, hoping to win fame in the theater. He failed as an actor, a dancer, and a singer before he finally found patrons who arranged for his education.

Later, Andersen turned to writing. In 1835 he published an inexpensive booklet called *Tales Told for Children*. His tales became immensely popular, gaining him fame across Europe. Andersen wrote 168 tales in all, including "The Princess and the Pea" and "The Ugly Duckling."

Interestingly, Andersen never thought highly of his tales, perhaps because he always hoped his success would come in the theater. Ironically, he had no particular liking for children.

OTHER WORKS *The Fairy Tale of My Life*, "The Little Mermaid," "The Snow Queen," "The Nightingale," "The Little Match Girl," "The Wild Swans"

WORDS TO KNOW

writhe (rīth) *v.* to twist or turn in distress or embarrassment; squirm

779

THE LANGUAGE OF LITERATURE TEACHER'S EDITION **779**

CUSTOMIZING FOR

Gifted and Talented Students

I Ask students why the child's exclamation at the procession is the climax of the story. *(Possible response: Readers have been waiting for someone to acknowledge that the emperor's new clothes aren't real; all the events have led up to this moment of exposing the fraud.)* Then have students write a new climax for the story.

Critical Thinking:
HYPOTHESIZING

J Have students speculate on why the crowd so quickly accepts the truth of the child's statement. *(Possible responses: It is a relief to hear the truth; the people are fed up with the emperor's vanity and glad to see him embarrassed.)*

STRATEGIC READING FOR

Less-Proficient Readers

K Ask students what new clothes the emperor wears in the procession. *(none; he is naked)* **Noting Relevant Details**

From Personal Response to Critical Analysis

1. What is your reaction to the story's ending? Jot down your thoughts in your notebook. *(Responses will vary.)*
2. Why do you think it takes a child to tell the truth about the emperor's clothes? *(Possible responses: The child is too young to know that he should pretend; the child does not have to worry about his reputation or position.)*
3. Why do you think the emperor and his court continue their procession, even after the truth is revealed? *(Possible response: They would look even more foolish if they acknowledged the truth.)*

COMPREHENSION CHECK
1. What is the emperor's main interest? *(wearing fine clothing)*
2. What special properties do the weavers say that their cloth has? *(It is invisible to incompetents and fools.)*
3. How do the weavers make people believe that they are really weaving cloth? *(by pantomiming the weaving and talking about the colors and patterns as if they were real)*
4. Why do the emperor and his courtiers praise the clothes? *(They don't want people to think they are incompetent or unfit for office.)*
5. Who points out that the emperor has nothing on? *(a child)*

SUMMARY

Lazy Peter and His Three-Cornered Hat Lazy Peter is a lazy rascal who prefers trickery to honest labor. In this adventure, he visits a village during a country fair and, using his three-cornered hat as bait, sets up an elaborate scheme. First, Peter entrusts a bag of money to the owner of a stand, asking that the money be returned to him when he appears with one corner of his hat turned down. Using two more bags of money, Peter makes similar arrangements with the local druggist and priest. Then he targets a rich, greedy farmer at the fair. First he arouses the farmer's interest in the "magic" hat, explaining that all he has to do is turn down a corner of it and people give him money. Next comes the demonstration: Peter adjusts his hat and approaches the stand owner, who—as prearranged—hands over the bag of money. The impressed farmer offers to buy the hat for 10,000 pesos. The farmer begins to hesitate and asks for further demonstrations, but Peter thoroughly convinces him by getting money from the druggist and the priest. By now, the price has risen to 10,000 pesos and the farmer's horse—all of which he gladly exchanges for the magic hat. As Peter escapes from the town, the farmer tries the hat trick on various merchants and quickly discovers he has been tricked.

Art Note

***Carnival in Huejotzingo* by Diego Rivera**
Rivera (1886–1957) was a pioneer of an art style called Cubism, a defender of art for art's sake, a leader in the Mexican Mural Renaissance, and a champion of the worker.

Reading the Art *How would you describe the impressions that this painting gives you?*

STRATEGIC READING FOR
Less-Proficient Readers

Set a Purpose Explore with students a variety of stories in the news about swindlers and con artists. Talk about some of the different ways they trick their victims. Then ask students to read this story to find out how Lazy Peter tricks the farmer.

Lazy Peter and His

Carnival in Huejotzingo (1942), Diego Rivera. Watercolor on paper, 5 ¼″ × 3 ½″, Courtesy of Sotheby's, New York.

Multicultural Perspectives

TRICKSTER TALES Humorous trickster tales are an important subgenre of folk tales. Sometimes, the trickster is in conflict with a bully. The question of justice and balance of power forms the basis of these tales. As a result, they often comment on the rights of the everyday person. For example, in the African tale "A Tug-of-War," the clever turtle wins over two larger animals by resorting to deception. Readers side with him because he shows that large, powerful creatures need not always triumph over the weak and powerless. In the American Indian tale

"The Theft of Fire," the trickster-hero Manbozho steals fire from a powerful older man who has hoarded all the fire for himself. Stories like this reinforce a belief in justice.

In other tales, the trickster gets burned by his own cleverness. "The Rubber Man" (Africa) and "Anansi Play with Fire, Anansi Get Burned" (Caribbean) are two tales that hold up the trickster as an object lesson. In these, the trickster is a greedy fool. He is so eager to get his way that he humiliates himself.

Three-Cornered Hat

RETOLD BY RICARDO E. ALEGRÍA

This is the story of Lazy Peter, a shameless rascal of a fellow who went from village to village making mischief.

 One day Lazy Peter learned that a fair was being held in a certain village. He knew that a large crowd of country people would be there selling horses, cows, and other farm animals and that a large amount of money would change hands. Peter, as usual, needed money, but it was not his custom to work for it. So he set out for the village, wearing a red three-cornered hat.

The first thing he did was to stop at a stand and leave a big bag of money with the owner, asking him to keep it safely until he returned for it. Peter told the man that when he returned for the bag of money, one corner of his hat would be turned down, and that was how the owner of the stand would know him. The man promised to do this, and Peter thanked him. Then he went to the drugstore in the village and gave the druggist another bag of money, asking him to keep it until he returned with one corner of his hat turned up. The druggist agreed, and Peter left. He went to the church and asked the priest to keep another bag of money and to return it to him only when he came back with one corner of his hat twisted to the side. The priest said fine, he would do this.

Having disposed of three bags of money, Peter

went to the edge of the village where the farmers were buying and selling horses and cattle. He stood and watched for a while until he decided that one of the farmers must be very rich indeed, for he had sold all of his horses and cows. Moreover, the man seemed to be a miser who was never satisfied but wanted always more and more money. This was Peter's man! He stopped beside him. It was raining; and instead of keeping his hat on to protect his head, he took it off and wrapped it carefully in his cape, as though it were very valuable. It puzzled the farmer to see Peter stand there with the rain falling on his head and his hat wrapped in his cape.

After a while he asked, "Why do you take better care of your hat than of your head?"

Peter saw that the farmer had swallowed the bait, and smiling to himself, he said that the hat was the most valuable thing in all the world and that was why he took care to protect it from the rain. The farmer's curiosity increased at this reply, and he asked Peter what was so valuable about a red three-cornered hat. Peter told him that the hat worked for him; thanks to it, he never had to work for a living because whenever he put the hat on with one of the corners turned over, people just handed him any money he asked for.

The farmer was amazed and very interested in what Peter said. As money-getting was his greatest ambition, he told Peter that he couldn't

LAZY PETER AND HIS THREE-CORNERED HAT **781**

CUSTOMIZING FOR
Gifted and Talented Students

Share with students the adage "A fool and his money are soon parted." This adage suggests that victims of scams are gullible and deserve what happens to them. Challenge students to debate this issue. Make sure students support their arguments.

Literary Concept: HUMOR

A Ask students what "it was not his custom to work for it" means. *(Possible responses: Peter is lazy; Peter gets his money in some underhanded way.)* Ask students why they think the author uses the word *custom* to express his idea. *(Possible responses: It makes Peter's laziness seem funny, as if it were just a lifestyle choice; it presents laziness as a charming shortcoming.)*

Critical Thinking: ANALYZING

B Ask students why Peter is so sure that the farmer is his "man." Guide students to analyze why Peter has picked out this particular person. *(Possible responses: The man seems wealthy, stingy, and greedy—a perfect mark.)*

Literary Links

C Ask students how they think Sherlock Holmes from "The Hound of the Baskervilles" would react to Lazy Peter. *(Possible responses: He would admire Lazy Peter's ability to judge people; he would despise him for taking advantage of others.)*

Linking to History

 **D** Today, hats aren't a key fashion accessory, but that was not always the case. For example, mobs of curious Londoners crowded around James Heatherington when he first wore his tall, shiny "topper" hat in 1797. Women fainted; one boy had his arm broken in the mob. Heatherington was fined the enormous sum of 50 pounds for disturbing the peace, but top hats later became required headgear at many social events.

I Help students infer from the context that *astonishment* means "great surprise."

Literary Concept:
CHARACTERIZATION

E Ask students how the author shows Peter's cleverness. *(Possible response: Peter's actions show that he is clever. By making the hat seem unobtainable, Peter makes the farmer want it all the more. This way, he hopes to increase the amount the farmer is willing to pay for it.)*

Literary Note

F Sets of three are often found in folk tales. An event might be repeated three times, or three similar characters or objects might be featured. In this selection, Peter plays the same trick with the hat and bag of money three times. Examples of other well-known stories that contain sets of three include "Goldilocks and the Three Bears" and "The Three Little Pigs."

G Challenge these students to explain what Lazy Peter and the farmer might symbolize. *(Possible responses: Peter might symbolize trickery and the farmer foolishness and greed.)*

believe a word of it until he saw the hat work with his own eyes. Peter assured him that he could do this, for he, Peter, was hungry, and the hat was about to start working, since he had no money with which to buy food.

With this, Peter took out his three-cornered hat, turned one corner down, put it on his head, and told the farmer to come along and watch the hat work. Peter took the farmer to the stand. The minute the owner looked up, he handed over the bag of money Peter had left with him. The farmer stood with his mouth open in astonishment. He didn't know what to make of it. But of one thing he was sure—he had to have that hat!

Peter smiled and asked if he was satisfied, and the farmer said yes, he was. Then he asked Peter if he would sell the hat. This was just what Lazy Peter wanted, but he said no, he was not interested in selling the hat because with it, he never had to work and he always had money. The farmer said he thought that was <u>unsound</u> reasoning because thieves could easily steal a hat, and wouldn't it be safer to invest in a farm with cattle? So they talked, and Peter pretended to be impressed with the farmer's arguments. Finally he said yes, that he saw the point, and if the farmer would make him a good offer, he would sell the hat. The farmer, who had made up his mind to have the hat at any price, offered a thousand pesos. Peter laughed aloud and said he could make as much as that by just putting his hat on two or three times.

As they continued <u>haggling</u> over the price, the farmer grew more and more determined to have that hat, until, finally, he offered all he had realized from the sale of his horses and cows—ten thousand pesos in gold. Peter still pretended not to be interested, but he chuckled to himself,

thinking of the trick he was about to play on the farmer. All right, he said, it was a deal. Then the farmer grew cautious and told Peter that before he handed over the ten thousand pesos, he would like to see the hat work again. Peter said that was fair enough. He put on the hat with one of the corners turned up and went with the farmer to the drugstore. The moment the druggist saw the turned-up corner, he handed over the money Peter had left with him. At this the farmer was convinced and very eager to set the hat to work for himself. He took out a bag containing ten thousand pesos in gold and was about to hand it to Peter when he had a change of heart and thought better of it. He asked Peter please to excuse him, but he had to see the hat work just once more before he could part with his gold. Peter said that that was fair enough, but now he would have to ask the farmer to give him the fine horse he was riding as well as the ten thousand pesos in gold. The farmer's interest in the hat revived, and he said it was a bargain!

Lazy Peter put on his hat again, doubled over one of the corners, and told the farmer that since he still seemed to have doubts, this time he could watch the hat work in the church. The farmer was delighted with this, his doubts were stilled, and he fairly beamed thinking of all the money he was going to make once that hat was his.

They entered the church. The priest was hearing confession, but when he saw Peter with his hat, he said, "Wait here, my son," and he went to the sacristy[1] and returned with the bag of money Peter had left with him. Peter thanked the priest, then knelt and asked for a blessing before he left. The farmer had seen everything and was fully convinced of the hat's magic powers. As soon as they left the church, he gave

---

1. **sacristy** (săk'rĭ-stē): in a church, a room where sacred objects are stored.

WORDS TO KNOW | **unsound** (ŭn-sound') *adj.* not free from fault or weakness; not sensible; inaccurate
haggle (hăg'əl) *v.* to argue about terms or price; bargain

782

Assessment **Option**

INFORMAL ASSESSMENT

Storyboard To assess students' understanding of the story, have them create a storyboard for "Lazy Peter and his Three-Cornered Hat." Explain that a storyboard is a series of drawings that show the main events in the story's plot. Invite students to add captions or dialogue balloons to their drawings.

Rubric

3 Full Accomplishment Student creates a series of drawings that highlight the story's main events in the correct chronological order.

2 Substantial Accomplishment Student's storyboard covers most of the main events of the story but may also include less relevant details.

1 Little or Partial Accomplishment Student's storyboard does not depict key events and/or depicts events out of chronological sequence.

Peter the ten thousand pesos in gold and told him to take the horse also. Peter tied the bag of pesos to the saddle, gave the hat to the farmer, begging him to take good care of it, spurred his horse, and galloped out of town.

As soon as he was alone, the farmer burst out laughing at the thought of the trick he had played on Lazy Peter. A hat such as this was priceless! He couldn't wait to try it. He put it on with one corner turned up and entered the butcher shop. The butcher looked at the hat, which was very handsome indeed, but said nothing. The farmer turned around, then walked up and down until the butcher asked him what he wanted. The farmer said he was waiting for the bag of money. The butcher laughed aloud and asked if he was crazy. The farmer thought that there must be something wrong with the way he had folded the hat. He took it off and doubled another corner down. But this had no effect on the butcher. So he decided to try it out some other place. He went to the mayor of the town.

The mayor, to be sure, looked at the hat but did nothing. The farmer grew desperate and decided to go to the druggist who had given Peter a bag of money. He entered and stood with the hat on. The druggist looked at him but did nothing.

The farmer became very nervous. He began to suspect that there was something very wrong. He shouted at the druggist, "Stop looking at me and hand over the bag of money!"

The druggist said he owed him nothing, and what bag of money was he talking about, anyway? As the farmer continued to shout about a bag of money and a magic hat, the druggist called the police. When they arrived, he told them that the farmer had gone out of his mind and kept demanding a bag of money. The police questioned the farmer, and he told them about the magic hat he had bought from Lazy Peter. When he heard the story, the druggist explained that Peter had left a bag of money, asking that it be returned when he appeared with a corner of his hat turned up. The owner of the stand and the priest told the same story. And I am telling you the farmer was so angry that he tore the hat to shreds and walked home. ❖

RICARDO E. ALEGRÍA

Ricardo Enrique Alegría is not only an avid collector of folk tales but also an anthropologist and historian. For many years, Alegría was a professor of history at the University of Puerto Rico. He has served as the director of the Institute of Puerto Rican Culture and the archaeological museum and research center at the University of Puerto Rico. He has

1921–

written many books and articles on the history and folklore of Puerto Rico and has a special interest in the Indians who first inhabited the West Indies.
OTHER WORKS *The Three Wishes, History of the Indians of Puerto Rico, Ball Courts and Ceremonial Plazas in the West Indies*

WORDS
TO
KNOW

priceless (prīs′lĭs) *adj.* too valuable to be measured by price

783

Active Reading: PREDICT

H Invite students to predict what will happen to the farmer at the end of the story. *(Possible responses: He will be furious when he discovers that he has been tricked; he will be embarrassed by his own greed.)*

**Literary Concept:
CHARACTERIZATION**

I Ask students how the author conveys the farmer's character in this passage. *(Possible response: by revealing what the farmer feels and showing what he says)*

STRATEGIC READING FOR

Less-Proficient Readers

J Have students explain how Lazy Peter was able to trick the farmer. *(Peter spotted the farmer's weakness—greed—and exploited it.)*

From Personal Response to Critical Analysis

1. What is your reaction to the story's ending? Write your ideas in your notebook. *(Responses will vary.)*
2. Do you feel sorry for the farmer? Why or why not? *(Possible responses: yes, because losing everything he has is a worse fate than he deserves; no, because he is greedy and tries to trick Peter out of what he thinks is a priceless item)*
3. What lesson or moral do you see in this story? *(Possible response: Greedy people are easily tricked by their own avarice.)*

COMPREHENSION CHECK
1. How many bags of money does Peter entrust to others? *(three)*
2. Why does Peter select that particular farmer as his victim? *(The farmer is rich and seems to be a greedy miser.)*
3. Why does the farmer want Peter's hat? *(He has seen a man hand Peter a bag of money and concludes that Peter's hat caused him to do so.)*
4. What happens when the farmer wears the hat? *(No one gives him any money; he gets very upset.)*
5. What is the outcome of Lazy Peter's trick? *(The farmer tears up the hat, and Peter ends up with all the farmer's money.)*

Evaluate the characters One member of each group should write the ratings as the group determines them. As students debate each character's rating, have them offer evidence from the story to support their views. After all groups report their findings, the class may wish to average the ratings for each character.

Rubric

3 Full Accomplishment Students rank the level of justice for each important character in the four tales in this cluster. The rankings are supported by explanations that include details from the stories and a clear value system.

2 Substantial Accomplishment Students rate the level of justice for each character in the tales in this cluster, but the rankings may lack detailed explanations.

I Little or Partial Accomplishment Group members are unable to agree on a rating for the level of justice each character receives; the explanations are unclear or illogical. There is little evidence from the stories to support the rankings.

RESPONDING
OPTIONS

LITERATURE CONNECTION PROJECT 1   Multimodal Activity

Evaluate the characters Do you think the characters in the tales you have just read get what they deserve in the end? In small groups, rate the level of justice for each important character. Make a chart like the one shown, with 1 representing the most unfair treatment and 5 representing the fairest. Write a brief explanation for why you rated each character the way you did. Then have one member of the group read the ratings and explanations to the rest of the class.

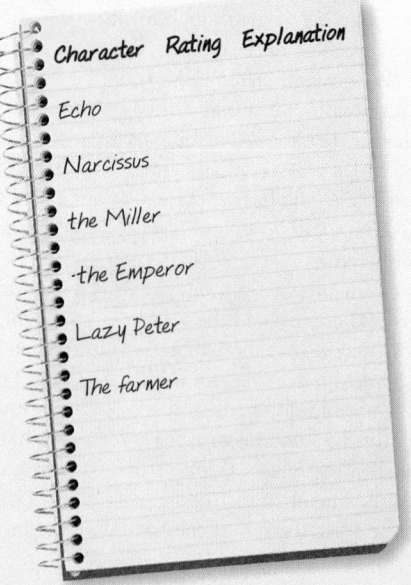

Character   Rating   Explanation

Echo

Narcissus

the Miller

the Emperor

Lazy Peter

The farmer

GEOGRAPHY CONNECTION PROJECT 2   Multimodal Activity

Explore geography While Puerto Rico is a single island, Greece and Denmark each consist of a peninsula and numerous islands. Denmark has 482 islands, and Greece has more than 2,000. Compare and contrast Puerto Rico, Greece, and Denmark in terms of climate, elevation, size in square miles, and population. Find out more about the geographical features of these places by referring to encyclopedias, atlases, travel books, other nonfiction books, and videos. Consider searching the Internet or using other computer sources for additional information.

	Puerto Rico	Greece	Denmark
Climate			
Elevation			
Size			
Population			

Explore geography Since there is a great deal of material to research in this project, suggest that students take notes on index cards while they work. Explain that doing so will enable them to extract the key points as they read, and then they can arrange the information logically when it comes time to write their reports. Remind students to carefully note the source of each statistic. You may wish to teach students how to prepare a Works Cited page. Consult pages 193, 197, and 202 in *The Writer's Craft* for guidelines.

Rubric

3 Full Accomplishment Students compare and contrast Puerto Rico, Greece, and Denmark in terms of climate, elevation, size in square miles, and population. All statistics are current, accurate, and well organized on a chart. Sources are clearly noted.

2 Substantial Accomplishment Students compare and contrast Puerto Rico, Greece, and Denmark in terms of climate, elevation, size in square miles, and population. Not all statistics are well organized or current.

I Little or Partial Accomplishment Students do not compare and contrast all three countries; information is missing or inaccurate.

SCIENCE CONNECTION PROJECT 3 Multimodal Activity

Research echoes In very different ways, myth and science both attempt to explain various natural phenomena. Whereas myths offer imaginative stories, science offers theories and facts as explanations. Research the scientific explanation of echoes. Find out the ideal conditions for hearing echoes and how to use the speed of sound waves to calculate the time it takes to hear them repeat a sound. Find out what devices are used to measure echoes and how they work. Describe how certain animals use echoes to detect objects. Share your findings in an oral report that includes illustrations and demonstrations of scientific principles.

ACROSS CULTURES MINI-PROJECTS Multimodal Activities

Find the "threes" Events often happen in "threes" in folk tales—three tricks, three gifts, three wishes, or three visits. Use the diagram to record the events in threes in the tales below. Then add examples from other stories—such as "The Three Little Pigs"—that involve the use of three. Share your tales with the rest of the class.

	1st event	2nd event	3rd event
Lazy Peter			
Force of Luck			
Other tale			

Investigate deceptive advertising Like the rogues who deceived the emperor with their beautiful but invisible clothes, modern advertisers sometimes use trickery to sell products and services. Working with a small group, identify examples of newspaper or magazine ads that misrepresent products or services. Clip the ads and write explanations that expose their trickery. Post your findings on the board.

Explain other Greek myths Find other Greek myths that explain natural events or phenomena, and research the scientific explanation for each one. Write a brief summary of the explanation and then collect all the summaries into a booklet. Create a cover and share the booklet with students in other classes.

Hold a contest See who can find the most advertising logos that contain symbols and names from mythology. Look for them in the yellow pages of telephone books, in newspaper and magazine ads, and on labels for products. Write a brief summary that explains why a company would want people to associate each mythological name with its particular product.

Extended Social Studies Reading

MORE ABOUT THE CULTURES
- *The Greeks* by Roy Burrell
- *The Olympians* by Leonard Everett Fisher
- *Mexican American Folklore* by John O. West
- *Puerto Rico Mio: Four Decades of Change* by Jack Delano
- *The Hispanic Americans* by Milton Meltzer

LINKS TO UNIT FIVE **785**

Research echoes Suggest that students first get an overview of the topic by reading an encyclopedia article. Invite students to use either print or CD-ROM encyclopedias. Then have students consult more detailed sources, such as science textbooks, science magazines, and on-line sources such as the Internet. Remind students to prepare visual aids that clarify technical aspects of their oral reports.

Rubric

3 Full Accomplishment The oral report clearly and accurately describes the scientific explanation of echoes. The illustrations and demonstrations reinforce the text.

2 Substantial Accomplishment The oral report describes the scientific explanation of echoes, but some aspects of the explanation may not be clear. The illustrations and demonstrations only partially help illuminate the explanation.

1 Little or Partial Accomplishment Students are unable to describe the scientific explanation of echoes. The oral report is poorly organized and lacks specific details, illustrations, and demonstrations.

Across Cultures

Find the "threes" Suggest that students skim additional folk tales for facts rather than read every word. Guide students to consult collections of folk tales from different countries to get the widest and most interesting selection of stories.

Investigate deceptive advertising You may wish to review logical fallacies such as straw man, circular reasoning, and propaganda to help students spot deception in both the text and pictures of several advertisements.

Explain other Greek myths Recommend that students avoid abridged editions of the Greek myths. Suggest that students use science books, technical magazine and newspaper articles, and encyclopedias to find explanations of the scientific phenomena.

Hold a contest Suggest that students first skim the table of contents of a complete book of Greek myths to familiarize themselves with the names of all the gods and goddesses who appear in the myths.

OVERVIEW

To gain a deeper appreciation of the selections they have read in this unit, students will explore the characteristics of a compare-and-contrast essay and then create their own well-developed example in this lesson.

Objectives

- To plan a compare-and-contrast essay by exploring similarities and differences and discovering ways to organize ideas
- To draft a compare-and-contrast essay and solicit a response
- To revise, edit, and publish a compare-and-contrast essay
- To reflect on the process of writing a compare-and-contrast essay

Skills

LITERATURE
- Interpreting folk tales
- Analyzing story elements such as setting, conflict, characters, and theme

WRITING AND LANGUAGE
- Organizing information clearly
- Writing an effective introduction
- Using transitions

GRAMMAR AND USAGE
- Using irregular comparatives and superlatives

MEDIA LITERACY
- Analyzing newspaper articles

CRITICAL THINKING
- Analyzing story elements

RESEARCH SKILLS
- Using the computer

SPEAKING, LISTENING, AND VIEWING
- Conferencing
- Reading aloud
- Storytelling

CUSTOMIZING FOR
Students Acquiring English

Ⓐ This writing assignment offers students an ideal opportunity to share stories from their native cultures. Invite volunteers to brainstorm a list of folk tales and to retell their favorites to the class.

WRITING FROM EXPERIENCE

WRITING TO EXPLAIN

Was "The Pumpkin Seed and the Snake" a little bit like "The Frog Prince"? Did "The Fitting of the Slipper" have anything in common with another popular story? Fairy tales often describe experiences so common that you find similar tales in many cultures. Sometimes, variations of the story are retold in the same culture from generation to generation.

GUIDED ASSIGNMENT
Write a Compare-and-Contrast Essay The following pages will help you compare and contrast a folk tale to a similar story or to another version of the tale.

Toy Based on Movie Character

❶ Making Connections

Look at the items on these pages. They are all variations of the Cinderella story. How are they alike? How are they different? Can you think of other books or tales from your own culture that are similar?

Ⓐ ❷ **What Story Will You Explore?**

In a group, brainstorm stories that might have many different versions. Your list might include fairy tales, such as "The Ugly Duckling," "Beauty and the Beast," and "Peter Pan," or other types of tales. Choose one to explore.

Folk Tale

The Rough-Face Girl
RAFE MARTIN · DAVID SHANNON

This story shows the main character as resourceful and determined.

786   UNIT SIX: THE ORAL TRADITION

PRINT AND MEDIA RESOURCES

UNIT SIX RESOURCE BOOK
Prewriting, p. 43
Elaboration, p. 44
Peer Response Guide, pp. 45–46
Revising and Proofreading, p. 47
Student Model, pp. 48–49
Rubric, p. 50

GRAMMAR MINI-LESSONS
Transparencies, p. 13
Copymasters, p. 20

WRITING MINI-LESSONS
Transparencies, pp. 10–11 and 33–35

ACCESS FOR STUDENTS ACQUIRING ENGLISH
Reading and Writing Support

FORMAL ASSESSMENT
Guidelines for Writing Assessment

 **LASERLINKS**
Writing Springboard

  ▶ WRITING COACH

Book Excerpt

Newspaper Article
Why do you think some
people would call this a
modern Cinderella story?

The 21st Century Princess

Back when she was a student at Harvard, Masako Owada introduced some of her friends to a card game called Emperor. The various players drew titles from emperor to commoner. Funny thing was that Owada always managed to win: when she played she always turned out to be empress.

Who says that cards do not deal the hand of fate? Owada seems to have the world at her feet. On June 9, 1993, she married Crown Prince Naruhito, who will be the next Emperor of Japan, the world's oldest monarchy.

Martha Duffy
adapted from "The 21st Century Princess"
Time magazine

Cinderella

There was once a man who took for his second wife the most haughty, stuck-up woman you ever saw. She had two daughters of her own, just like her in everything. The husband for his part had a young daughter, but she was gentle and sweet-natured, taking after her mother, who had been the best person in the world.

The wedding was barely over when the stepmother let her temper show; she couldn't bear the young girl's goodness, for it made her own daughters seem even more hateful. She gave her the vilest household chores: it was she who cleaned the dishes and the stairs, she who scrubbed Madam's chamber, and the chambers of those little madams, her stepsisters; she slept at the top of the house in an attic, on a shabby mattress, while her sisters had luxurious boudoirs, with beds of the latest fashion, and mirrors in which they could study themselves from head to toe. The poor girl suffered it all patiently and didn't dare complain to her father, who would have scolded her, because he was completely under the woman's sway.

Charles Perrault

from *The Complete Fairy Tales of Charles Perrault*

In this story, Cinderella is turned into a dazzling beauty by her godmother's magic.

③ Oral Communication

Once you've chosen a story to explore, try retelling it to a partner or group. If you can't recall all the details, ask others to add them for you.

▶ **LASERLINKS**
• WRITING SPRINGBOARD
💻 **WRITING COACH**

WRITING FROM EXPERIENCE   **787**

Teaching Strategy: MODELING

B Ask students to name the characteristics that they expect in a Cinderella story. Possibilities include:
• A beautiful and kind heroine is mistreated.
• Fate intervenes to help the heroine escape from a miserable situation.
• A prince falls in love with her and chooses her to be his wife.

Then have the class read the newspaper article to discover how "The 21st Century Princess" is a variation of the Cinderella story. If necessary, prompt students with questions such as the following: Was Masako Owada mistreated? Do you think fate was primarily responsible for her royal marriage? Encourage students to list other stories—such as "Jack and the Beanstalk"—that might have modern variations.

**Teaching Strategy:
STUMBLING BLOCK**

C Students might have difficulty recalling some of the details of their story. Suggest that they refer to anthologies of folk tales to gather details about the story they have chosen to retell. Then have students construct a time line, listing the events in the plot in chronological order. Encourage students to refer to this time line as they prepare their retelling of their story. Also suggest that listeners jot down parts of the story that are not clear so that storytellers can clarify these parts before selecting a companion tale.

💿 **WRITING SPRINGBOARD**
Between Two Cultures In these interviews with teenagers whose life experiences span two cultures, students will hear about the positive and negative aspects of being bicultural.

Side B, Frame 27393

Writing Prompt Using this film as a starting point, gather information about another culture that interests you. Your resources could include encyclopedia entries, newspaper reports, or stories told by individuals. Write a compare-and-contrast essay about some aspect of that culture that you find different from your own.

D Increasingly, material can be located through the use of a computer as well as through reference books in print. Explain that material available to computer users is called a database. Tell the class that computer-assisted research can be divided into two categories: material they can find on their own and material that a reference librarian can help them find. Explain that many school libraries have the following databases that might provide information for this assignment:

Reader's Guide Index Abstracts
Humanities Index
Newspaper Abstracts

Writing Skill: USING
GRAPHIC ORGANIZERS

E Students may find a Venn diagram a useful tool for exploring similarities and differences. Explain that to make a Venn diagram, they draw two overlapping circles. Then they write the characteristics that are common to both stories in the overlapping area and the characteristics that are unique to each story outside this area. On the board, model how you would use a Venn diagram to show the comparisons and contrasts presented in the student's chart. See the example at the bottom of this page.

PREWRITING

Sorting Through Your Ideas

The Same, but Different What was it about one story that reminded you of another? Are parts of the two stories based on a similar theme? Comparing and contrasting can help you go deeper than the actual words on the page.

❶ Find a Match for Your Story

Try using different sources to find a similar story from another culture. Sources include

- books, such as anthologies of folk tales from different cultures
- interviews with family or friends about favorite folk tales from another culture
- on-line information services
- the local cultural center or museum for exhibits about different cultures
- professional storytellers, who can be knowledgeable about folk tales from around the world.

D

Student's Compare-
and-Contrast Chart

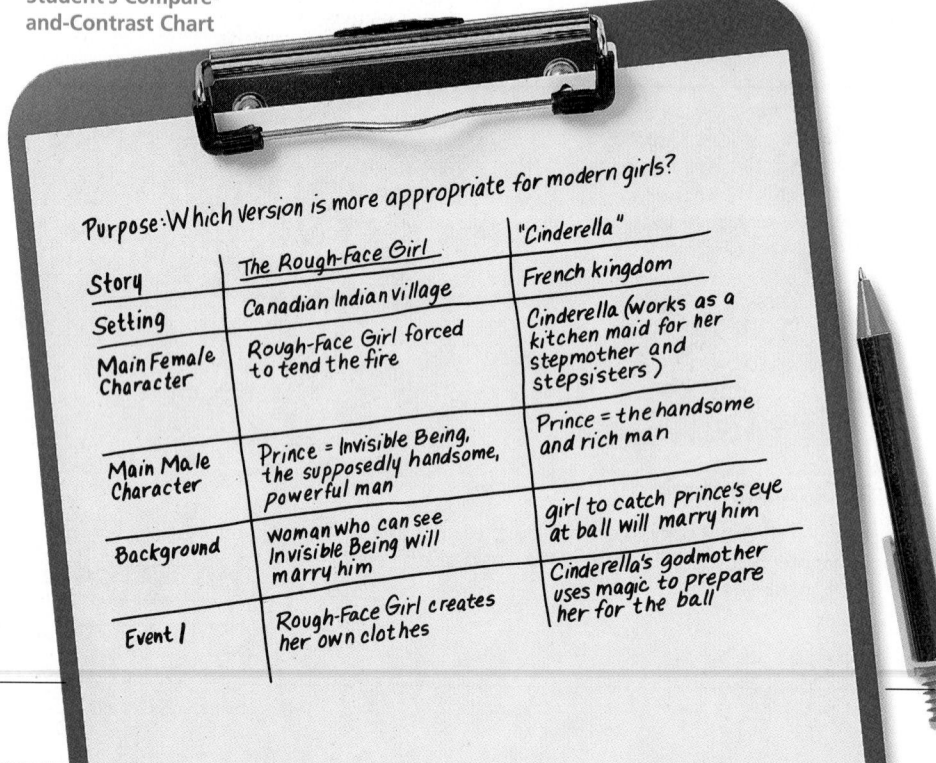

Purpose: Which version is more appropriate for modern girls?

Story	The Rough-Face Girl	"Cinderella"
Setting	Canadian Indian village	French kingdom
Main Female Character	Rough-Face Girl forced to tend the fire	Cinderella (works as a kitchen maid for her stepmother and stepsisters)
Main Male Character	Prince = Invisible Being, the supposedly handsome, powerful man	Prince = the handsome and rich man
Background	Woman who can see Invisible Being will marry him	girl to catch Prince's eye at ball will marry him
Event 1	Rough-Face Girl creates her own clothes	Cinderella's godmother uses magic to prepare her for the ball

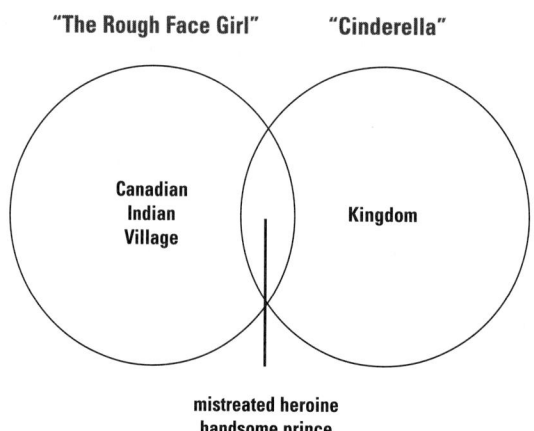

"The Rough Face Girl"   "Cinderella"

Canadian Indian Village

Kingdom

mistreated heroine
handsome prince

② Choose Features to Compare

What do you want to learn by making your comparison? Are you curious about the differences between the tales? Do you want to learn about the culture of one story? Perhaps you want to urge a friend to read the story by comparing it to one he or she already knows. Knowing your purpose will help you choose features to discuss in your essay.

As you do your comparison, consider the characters, the events, and the theme of each story. For help, see the SkillBuilder at the right.

③ List Similarities and Differences

For each story, list the main features, such as characters, events, and themes. How are they alike? How are they different?

You can use a chart like the one on the previous page to compare and contrast story features. Divide a piece of paper into three columns. In column one, list the features you will compare. In columns two and three, describe specific examples from each story.

④ Organize Your Thoughts

There are two ways you can organize your compare-and-contrast essay, either subject by subject or feature by feature. The charts below show both ways to compare "Cinderella" with *The Rough-Face Girl*.

STUDENT'S COMPARE-AND-CONTRAST PATTERNS

Subject by Subject

1. "Cinderella"
   * location
   * main character
   * turning point

2. *The Rough-Face Girl*
   * location
   * main character
   * turning point

Feature by Feature

1. Location
   * "Cinderella"
   * *The Rough-Face Girl*

2. Main Character
   * "Cinderella"
   * *The Rough-Face Girl*

3. Turning Point
   * "Cinderella"
   * *The Rough-Face Girl*

SkillBuilder

◯● CRITICAL THINKING

Analyzing Story Elements

When comparing and contrasting two stories or folk tales, it often helps to examine each one in terms of story elements, such as characters, setting, plot, and theme. For example, the information on page 788 can be grouped in the following way.

Characters: Rough-Face Girl, Invisible Being, mean older sisters;

Cinderella, prince, mean stepsisters

Setting: Indian village; kingdom

Theme: Beauty comes from within; good wins over evil

APPLYING WHAT YOU'VE LEARNED
Think of your two stories in terms of story elements. For each story, try to create a story map and then compare and contrast the story elements.

THINK & PLAN

Reflecting on Your Ideas

1. What have you learned by comparing and contrasting the two stories?
2. How will you use the information in your essay?
3. Who do you think will be interested in hearing your ideas?
4. How might you present your ideas?

Teaching Strategy: MODELING

F Have students review the Student's Compare-and-Contrast chart shown on page 788. Encourage students to suggest additional story elements that they might list.

Writing Skill: USING THE COMPUTER

G Students can use computers to organize material and show patterns like the ones on this page. Some writing programs tailored to the needs of middle school students offer outline formats that can be shortened or expanded by the deletion or addition of subheads. The writer can keep deleted subheads available for possible inclusion later. Encourage students to use such writing programs when organizing information about their folk tales.

CUSTOMIZING FOR
Less-Proficient Writers

H If students have trouble organizing their ideas, suggest they write each item on an index card. The ability to move the cards around, arrange them differently, and easily eliminate items often facilitates students' work.

SkillBuilder ◯ CRITICAL THINKING

ANALYZING STORY ELEMENTS Explain to students that in addition to selecting narrative elements—such as conflict, characters, setting, and plot—they can consider elements of style, such as figurative language, irony, humor, and mood. Have students work in groups to define these elements and to identify examples of them. If needed, suggest that students refer to the Handbook of Reading Terms and Literary Concepts (on pages 800–807) for definitions.

Application Encourage students to explore a variety of story maps as they arrange their story elements. Guide students to select the graphic organizer that best suits their details.

Writing Skill: OUTLINING

1 Explain that writers use outlines in different ways. Some writers use them to plan the drafting process; others use them to check the organization of a completed draft. Writers also use different types of outlines for different writing tasks. Some writers find topic outlines helpful, whereas others prefer a sentence outline. Tell students that each writer must discover the outlining strategies that work the best for a particular purpose and audience.

Writing Skill: USING THE COMPUTER

J Point out that this draft was prepared on a computer. Some writers are somewhat reluctant to give up their pens and papers for computers. Encourage students to use The Writing Coach, which provides drafting guidelines. You may also wish to provide this quick overview of basic word-processing terms:

cursor: a movable indicator that shows where copy can be entered or changed

delete: cut, erase

insert: add

cut and paste: move material

save: record on a disk

scroll: look up or down the screen

search: find a specific word or group of words on the screen

DRAFTING

Putting Ideas on Paper

Thoughts into Words Once you have collected your information, you can begin putting your ideas together on paper. Some people begin by organizing material into an outline. This often helps you to organize your thoughts subject by subject or feature by feature. Other people just start writing. Experiment with both approaches. The method shown here is one way you can begin.

1 Write a Rough Draft

As you compare the two stories, ask what the comparison shows. What do the differences and similarities tell you about the cultures? Which version is more meaningful or effective? Why?

The Writing Coach can give you step-by-step help in drafting a compare-and-contrast essay.

J | **Student's Rough Draft**

Compare-and-Contrast Essay

My Rough Draft

If you liked the story "Cinderella," you'll love *The Rough-Face Girl,* a Native American version of it. Both stories deal with a girl leaving a horrible situation and marrying a prince. One story shows a character who is helped by someone, and the other shows a character who helps herself.

The Rough-Face Girl lives with her father and two mean sisters who force her to tend the fire day and night. She is badly scarred from the fire and looks ugly. In "Cinderella," the main character is forced to work as a kitchen maid and so her beauty is hidden under dirt and raggedy clothes. The Invisible Being lives in the Indian village. All the girls want to marry him. But only the girl who can see him will be able to marry him. In the kingdom of "Cinderella," there's a handsome prince who will marry the most beautiful girl at the ball. In both stories, the main male character rescues the main female character.

Because her sisters took all the nice clothes, the Rough-Face Girl pieces together an outfit to wear for her visit to the Invisible Being. Cinderella, on the other hand, is helped by her godmother, who creates a beautiful gown and carriage out of magic.

Peer Reviewer's Comments
My Rough Draft

Say more about each feature. For example, I'd like to know more about the Invisible Being. KM

Additional comment: I'm finding it hard to follow your organization. You jump from story to story and feature to feature.

790 UNIT SIX: THE ORAL TRADITION

WRITING SPRINGBOARD
Dances from Around the World
Every culture celebrates with dance. This short film shows a variety of dances from cultures around the world. In it, students will see some of the many forms that dance can take.

Side B, Frame 31986

Writing Prompt Write a compare-and-contrast essay about celebrations or ceremonies from two different cultures. Describe the two ways of celebrating and include a discussion of the form the celebrations take. Use as many examples as possible to support your ideas.

2 **Analyze Your Draft**

Ask yourself the following questions.

- How do I introduce the subjects I am comparing?
- Does my essay show both the similarities and differences?
- Would my comparison be clearer if I organized the information differently?
- What format would best suit my audience?

3 **Rework Your Comparison and Share**

Keep the following suggestions in mind as you rework your draft.

Introduction Introduce the two subjects you are comparing in the beginning of your essay. Tell why you are comparing the two stories. Try to make readers curious about the comparison you plan to show so that they will read on.

Check Your Organization Check to be sure that you use the same pattern of organization from beginning to end.

 Use Transitions Use transition words such as *both, also,* and *similarly* to draw attention to similarities. Use *but, instead,* and *on the other hand* to signal differences.

Consider Illustrations Consider using illustrations, such as drawings of the main characters from each story or your compare-and-contrast chart, to get your point across.

Polish Your Conclusion What did you learn about your subjects? Your conclusion should focus on your discoveries.

PEER RESPONSE

Consider asking a peer reviewer questions like the following.

- What do you think I am trying to show with the comparison I'm making?
- What similarities or differences did you find the most interesting? the least interesting?
- Did any other comparisons come to mind as you read my draft? What other features might I have included?

SkillBuilder

 WRITER'S CRAFT

Writing an Effective Introduction

A good compare-and-contrast essay has an attention-getting introduction. You might start with a question or quotation, or you might talk about your own reaction to the stories. Remember that your introduction should clearly state what two subjects you are comparing and why you are comparing them.

APPLYING WHAT YOU'VE LEARNED
Read your introduction to a friend. Ask whether it makes him or her want to continue reading. If it doesn't, ask for suggestions to improve it.

 WRITING HANDBOOK

For more ideas for creating a good introduction, see page 814 of the Writing Handbook.

RETHINK & EVALUATE

Preparing to Revise

1. How can you make sure you accomplish what you set out to do with this comparison?
2. Is your information organized clearly and effectively?
3. Are there any important similarities or differences you would like to add?

WRITING FROM EXPERIENCE **791**

Teaching Strategy: MANAGING THE PAPER LOAD

K Conferencing with students at this stage in the writing process can help them strengthen the organization, development, and style of their drafts. As students analyze their drafts, they can isolate the area that presents the most difficulty for them. Focus the conference on that area. Then have students work in small groups to identify any other problems before revising their drafts.

Teaching Strategy: STUMBLING BLOCK

L Students might have difficulty generating a complete list of transitions useful for compare-and-contrast essays. Write the following list on the board for them to use:

Transitions that signal	
similarities	**differences**
both	but
also	instead
neither	however
in addition	yet
similarly	unlike
likewise	on the other hand

Speaking, Listening, and Viewing: COLLABORATIVE OPPORTUNITY

M Have partners read each other's papers and then create simple compare-and-contrast charts, showing the main points in the paper they have read. Partners can switch papers and reevaluate their work with a fresh eye.

SkillBuilder **WRITER'S CRAFT**

WRITING AN EFFECTIVE INTRODUCTION Remind students that they can use a personal anecdote, a statistic, a description, a quotation, a bit of dialogue, or an example to begin their compare-and-contrast essay in an interesting way. Invite volunteers to share the openings they used. Write these on the chalkboard. Have the rest of the class critique each opening, offering praise as well as suggestions for revision.

Application Have partners identify the method the writer used in the introduction. Direct partners to try other methods until they settle on one that works best for their purpose and audience.

Additional Suggestions To make students aware of the wide variety of introductory strategies, ask them to bring in articles from newspapers and magazines. Discuss each introductory paragraph and its appropriateness for the subject, audience, and purpose.

Reteaching/Reinforcement

 The Writer's Craft

Introductions, pp. 275–277

Teaching Strategy: MODELING

N Invite a volunteer to read the model essay aloud. Explore the paper's organization by listing the main points on the board. Then have students identify the transitions that the writer used (*however, both,* and *on the other hand*).

Then help students understand that the first half of the second paragraph identifies similarities between the two stories and is organized feature-by-feature. The second half of the paragraph presents the differences between the two heroines and is organized subject-by-subject. Students should discuss the advantages and disadvantages of this method of organization.

Writing Skill: REVISING

O If students are drafting their papers on a computer, remind them to save all drafts under separate titles on the disk in order to prevent material from being lost or written over. You may wish to demonstrate this process before students start writing by using titles such as story1.doc, story2.doc, story3.doc, and so on. Be sure that students use the Standards for Evaluation as they revise their papers.

REVISING AND PUBLISHING

Adding the Final Touches

One Last Look Use the guidelines on these pages to help you improve your essay before you share it with others. Also, think of the format you are using to present your essay. Do you need to make any last-minute changes to make the format work better?

Student's Final Essay

Two Cinderellas

Most people know the story of Cinderella, the housemaid who is changed into a beauty and marries the handsome prince. This story has been repeated in many cultures around the world. For example, *The Rough-Face Girl*, a Native American folk tale retold by Rafe Martin, has many features in common with "Cinderella." However, because of its heroine, girls of the 1990s might prefer *The Rough-Face Girl* to "Cinderella."

Both stories have similar characters, plots, and endings. Both girls have trouble at home. Both girls are beautiful on the inside, if not on the outside. Both girls end up being exactly what the prince is looking for in a wife. Most importantly, both girls are rescued by a man and live happily ever after. However, in "Cinderella," the girl's looks win the prince. The story does not tell very much about what she thinks or what she does. In *The Rough-Face Girl*, on the other hand, the main character is wise and resourceful as well as kind.

The message of "Cinderella" seems to be "Beauty and kindness win over cruelty and selfishness." The message of *The Rough-Face Girl* seems to be "Be resourceful, kind, and true to your dreams, and you will succeed." If I were to choose a role model from either story, I would choose the Rough-Face Girl.

Two Cinderellas

---

❶ Revise and Edit

How well have you compared and contrasted the two stories you chose? Put your essay aside for a few days and then take a careful look at it.

- Use the SkillBuilder on page 793 to check whether you've used correct comparative and superlative forms.
- See how one student developed her discussion of each feature to improve her essay.
- Refer to the Standards for Evaluation to be sure your essay clearly states the subjects being compared and shows how they are alike and different.

What words does the writer use to signal the similarities and differences between her subjects?

How has the writer organized her essay? Is it effective?

② Share Your Work

One student decided to include some drawings of what she thinks the main character of each story looks like. You might consider including visuals like these with your compare-and-contrast essay.

Dark skin and hair represent beauty standard of Native American society

Rough-Face Girl uses scraps and found objects to make a dress

Invisible Being loves her for her inner beauty and goodness

Her wisdom and faith make her the only one to see Invisible Being

The Rough-Face Girl

Fairy godmother uses magic to make her beautiful

Blonde hair and blue eyes represent beauty standard of French society

Her beauty dazzles prince

Prince uses glass slipper to find his bride

Cinderella

P

SkillBuilder

⟳ GRAMMAR FROM WRITING

Using Irregular Comparatives and Superlatives
Some forms of comparative and superlative adjectives and adverbs are irregular. Look at the examples below.

bad	worse	worst
good well	better	best
much many	more	most

Use a dictionary for help if you are unsure of which form to use.

📘 GRAMMAR HANDBOOK

For more help with comparatives and superlatives, see page 867 of the Grammar Handbook.

Editing Checklist:
- Did you use correct comparative and superlative forms?
- Did you signal new ideas with transitions?
- Did you punctuate correctly?

REFLECT & ASSESS

Evaluating the Experience

1. What did you learn about folklore by comparing and contrasting your subjects?
2. How well did your form of organization work? What might have worked better?

📁 **PORTFOLIO** Write your answer to question 1 and include it in your portfolio.

Speaking, Listening, and Viewing: STORYTELLING

P Suggest that students read the folk tales they compared and contrasted and their essays to an audience of younger students. You may wish to speak to a teacher in your school to arrange to have a class of younger students come for these presentations. No matter what the audience, remind readers to vary their pitch, volume, and pacing as they read aloud.

PORTFOLIO

Invite students to write a note to themselves indicating what they learned about organizing information. Have students attach the note to the final draft of their compare-and-contrast essay.

SkillBuilder ⟳ GRAMMAR FROM WRITING

USING IRREGULAR COMPARATIVES AND SUPERLATIVES Remind students that when adjectives and adverbs are used in comparisons, they have special forms. Short adjectives and adverbs change their forms by adding *-er* for the comparative (a comparison between two things) and *-est* for the superlative (a comparison among three or more things). Longer adjectives and most adverbs use the word *more* or the word *less* for the comparative and the word *most* or the word *least* for the superlative. Then mention that the comparative and superlative forms of irregular adjectives and adverbs are totally different words.

Application Have students replace each comparative with the correct superlative form.
1. My dog is the (better) dog in the world.
2. Yesterday was the (worse) day so far this winter.
3. We just made the (more) cookies of any group at the bake sale.

Reteaching/Reinforcement
Grammar Mini-Lessons copymasters p. 20, transparencies p. 13.

📕 The Writer's Craft

Adjectives in Comparisons, pp. 501–502
Adverbs in Comparisons, p. 520

This feature allows students to reflect on the selections, activities, and projects that they have completed while working through Unit Six and to assess how well they understand what they have learned. This feature provides students with several options for self-assessment. You may wish to use some of these options to informally assess skills such as speaking and listening or cooperative work.

Objectives

- To allow students to reflect on and assess their understanding of the selections and the cultures they represent
- To allow students to reflect on and assess their understanding of literary genres such as myths and folk tales
- To provide students with the opportunity to review and build their portfolios

REFLECTING ON THEME

OPTION 1

Encourage students to reread the selections that contain characters that impressed them strongly. As they do so, students should jot down notes about the characters and the types of behavior that a particular culture rewards or punishes. Students can use these notes to write the dialogue for their scripts.

OPTION 2

Have students jot down their responses to the prompts provided for this activity. Make sure students include specific examples from the selections in their personal responses.

OPTION 3

Before students discuss their impressions with a group of classmates, they can create charts that list the characters they admire and the reasons why. Students can then refer to the information on their charts during their discussions.

 **Self-Assessment** In order to help students get started, you might encourage them to make a before-and-after chart in which to jot down notes about what they learned about a particular culture from reading a selection.

REFLECT & ASSESS

UNIT SIX: THE ORAL TRADITION

This unit provides a rich mixture of stories that reflect cultures from many parts of the world. Now that you have read the selections, it's time to reflect on your growth as a reader and a writer. Choose one or more of the following options in each section to help assess how your thinking has developed.

REFLECTING ON THEME

OPTION 1 **Writing a Script** From two or more stories in this unit, choose the characters that made the strongest impression on you. What type of behavior does each character's culture reward or reject? Jot down your ideas in your notebook. Then use them to write a brief script in which the characters meet and discuss their experiences and the standards of conduct that their cultures uphold.

OPTION 2 **Personal Response** According to the storyteller Brenda Wong Aoki, "Stories stand the test of time because they have universal truths in them." What do you think this statement means? Write a draft of a personal response, explaining your ideas and supporting them with several examples from the stories in this unit.

Consider . . .
- how you would define a universal truth
- the stories that meant the most to you, and why
- the messages about life that these stories convey

OPTION 3 **Discussion** As you read these stories, some of the characters may have triggered strong reactions in you—positive or negative. Which characters do you admire the most, and why? Which one do you think would make the best role model, and why? With a small group of classmates, discuss these questions.

Self-Assessment: Choose two or more selections that increased your understanding of particular cultures in important ways. Write a paragraph or two, describing what you learned.

REVIEWING LITERARY CONCEPTS

OPTION 1 **Examining Myths** As you have learned, myths are traditional stories that deal with basic questions about the world. Work with a partner to review the myths that you have read in this unit. Then in a chart like the one shown, list each myth, the question that you think it attempts to answer, and one or more cultural values it reveals to you. After you have completed the chart, choose the myth that you think conveys the most important values.

Myth	Question	Cultural Values
"Prometheus"	How did humans obtain fire?	courage, self-sacrifice, endurance

OPTION 2 **Evaluating Folk Tales** Like myths, folk tales teach important lessons about human behavior. Review the folk tales that you have read in this unit, and jot down a sentence or two about each, describing the lesson it teaches. Then evaluate the lessons according to their importance for young people today. Share your evaluations with a group of classmates.

Self-Assessment: As you analyzed the stories in this unit, you probably applied several literary terms that you learned from your study of fiction and drama. Which terms do you think are particularly useful for reading literature from the oral tradition? In your notebook, list the terms in the order of their usefulness to you, with the most useful term at the top.

PORTFOLIO BUILDING

- **Literature Connection** Review any writing you did in response to the Literature Connection projects. Choose the response that you think helped you the most in getting inside the mind of a character in these stories. Then write a cover note, showing how writing the response helped you to understand a character better. Add the response and the note to your portfolio.

- **Writing About Literature** Earlier in this unit, you wrote a fable, or a short story that teaches a moral. Imagine that a first-grade teacher asks you to turn your fable into a children's book. What might you change to make the story and its lesson clearer for a younger audience? What pictures might you draw to help explain your story? Write a note to answer these questions, and attach it to your fable.

- **Writing from Experience** In your compare-and-contrast essay, you examined the similarities and differences between two subjects. Did your views about the subjects change as a result of writing about them? If so, how? Do you now like one subject better than the other, or do you still like both subjects equally? Write a note, explaining your answers, and include the note with your essay if you choose to keep it in your portfolio.

- **Personal Choice** Review all of your work for this unit—activities, graphics, and writing—and select

the piece of writing or the project that helped you experience a culture most deeply. Write a note explaining what you gained from doing the writing or completing the project. Attach the note to the piece of writing or the evaluation, and add both to your portfolio.

Self-Assessment: At this point, you may be completing your portfolio for this school year. Look back through all your pieces, and identify the ones that helped you the most in developing your skills. Write a note, reviewing your portfolio and explaining how these pieces helped you grow as a reader and a writer.

SETTING GOALS

In this unit you read stories from many different cultures. Which cultures stir your curiosity the most? Which customs, beliefs, and values would you like to explore more thoroughly? In your notebook, list one or more cultures and identify one or more characteristics that you want to learn more about. Then jot down a few strategies you might use to uncover the information you want.

REFLECT AND ASSESS **795**

REVIEWING LITERARY CONCEPTS

OPTION 1

Encourage partners to fill in their chart as they review the selections in this unit. You may wish to have partners compare their chart with the ones completed by other pairs of students. Make sure that students provide examples to support their choice of the myth that conveys the most important values. For a copy of the chart to distribute to the class, see *Unit Six Resource Book*, p. 53.

OPTION 2

You may wish to have students make a chart that lists the title of each folk tale and the most important lesson it conveys. Students can then share their charts with classmates. Make sure students consider the ways that these lessons might apply to the experiences of young people today.

 Self-Assessment This activity provides students with an opportunity to assess how well they can use literary concepts on their own. You may also wish to have students compare their list with a partner's.

PORTFOLIO BUILDING

You may wish to help students choose options or modify the ones that are provided. Encourage students to compare recent drafts and evaluations with ones that they completed earlier in the school year.

 Self-Assessment Suggest that students identify one or more pieces that they strengthened as a result of revision. Have students identify some changes they made and consider what they learned in the process.

SETTING GOALS

Have students identify the selections that had the most impact on them and the cultures they found most intriguing. Remind students to list practical suggestions for learning more about these cultures, such as locating reference books in the library, using a computer on-line service, or contacting a cultural center in the nearby area.

Student Resource Bank

797

Words to Know: Access Guide

A
abode, 707
abundance, 224
accommodations, 578
accomplice, 654
acknowledge, 707
aggrievedly, 421
alleviate, 542
anguish, 769
antagonism, 361
antidote, 436
anxious, 263
apathy, 40
appall, 507
apparatus, 492
aptitude, 677
arresting, 47
articulate, 65
assiduously, 29

B
balk, 29
barrage, 405
barren, 152
bartering, 772
beckon, 89
bedlam, 411
benefactor, 772
bewildered, 157
binge, 569
bizarre, 609
bleak, 98
brandish, 689
brashness, 465
brooding, 209

C
captivating, 621
cavorting, 461
chaos, 430
charitable, 234
cherish, 18
cite, 556
clambering, 267
clamor, 458
colleague, 609
combatant, 209
comeback, 185
compassionate, 124
comprehension, 689
compulsory, 29
concussion, 490
confines, 292
confound, 102

confrontation, 540
consolation, 396
console, 769
consternation, 544
contempt, 461
contend, 768
contorted, 366
convalescing, 422
cower, 389
crafty, 777
crux, 124
cull, 572
cunningly, 396
currency, 231
cynical, 277

D
dazzled, 579
deception, 631
defiant, 361
deliberation, 186
descendant, 289
desolation, 539
destitute, 224
devastating, 436
din, 57
disarm, 184
discreetly, 21
dispel, 409
displaced, 160
dissuade, 650
distinguish, 776
divulge, 651
dominant, 40
doomed, 745
drawl, 88
dreary, 710

E
eerie, 578
elaborate, 478
elite, 553
eloquence, 276
elusive, 30
emerge, 225
eminent, 29
emulate, 65
endow, 677
enfeebled, 123
ensuing, 185
essence, 103
evading, 411
evasive, 629
excavated, 158

exonerate, 654
explicit, 677

F
fatigue, 288
feign, 67
feint, 411
fervent, 57
feverishly, 585
finale, 242
flamboyant, 40
flourishing, 475
flustered, 359
forage, 428
frail, 150
furor, 509

G
game, 411
gaudy, 420
glistening, 157
goad, 534
grovel, 163
gullible, 570

H
haggle, 782
harmonize, 183
harried, 103
headland, 262
hover, 265
humility, 677

I
idiosyncrasy, 365
ignominious, 544
impaled, 16
imperative, 534
impetus, 438
implicitly, 618
implore, 685
impoverished, 57
impromptu, 556
improvise, 408
incalculable, 427
incessant, 509
incorporate, 438
incredulous, 278
incriminate, 363
indefinitely, 581
indifference, 463
indignantly, 189
indomitable, 60
induce, 778
inept, 508

infuriatingly, 49
inquisitive, 184
inscription, 90
insinuation, 278
intact, 774
integrated, 277
intense, 360
intricate, 105
invalid, 99
irate, 464

J
jaunty, 476
jostling, 730

K
kindred, 262

L
legacy, 123
legitimate, 364
liberation, 89
list, 586
lithe, 459
loathsome, 479

M
malignant, 481
migrant, 210
mimicry, 459
mistrust, 151
mortal, 228
multitude, 436
mystifying, 508

N
novelty, 582

O
oblivious, 544
obsess, 157
omen, 509
ominous, 651
optimistic, 360
outset, 776

P
painstaking, 65
passive, 99
pathetic, 766
pensively, 406
perilously, 730
perpetual, 408
persistent, 360
placid, 572
pledge, 231

plummet, 711
plush, 157
poring, 157
presentable, 151
prestige, 534
pretense, 685
priceless , 783
priority, 210
prominent, 209
prophecy, 578
provision, 224

Q
quarantine, 42

R
rational, 612
rationalize, 553
reassurance, 227
receding, 695
refuge, 464
rehabilitate, 29
rehabilitation, 66
reluctantly, 288
render, 722
replenish, 510

reproach, 646
resilient, 493
resolve, 511
retaliate, 276
retort, 759
retribution, 30
revive, 387
rogue, 778
roster, 538
rummage, 123

S
sanction, 102
sanctuary, 103
saunter, 47
savor, 493
scam, 570
scheme, 88
scouring, 262
scuffle, 267
scuttle, 396
seclude, 512
shrewdly, 276
skewing, 160
smugly, 726
solitude, 222

speculating, 278
spree, 188
squander, 769
stupefying, 46
submissive, 40
subterranean, 161
suede, 151
suitor, 17
sullen, 263
summon, 227
surmise, 612
surplus, 224
susceptible, 427
swarthy, 17

T
tactic, 458
tantalizing, 423
taunt, 280
teeming, 60
temperament, 183
thatch, 262
theorize, 632
toll, 589
transaction, 186
transform, 221

tread, 757
tribute, 579
tumultuously, 493
turmoil, 508

U
ultimate, 280
unbridled, 408
unobtrusively, 32
unperceived, 33
unseemly, 288
unsound, 782

V
vanquish, 553
vigil, 417
vigor, 47
virtuous, 29

W
wan, 417
waver, 270
welfare, 228
wily, 103
wrathful, 690
wretched, 747

Pronunciation Key

Symbol	Examples	Symbol	Examples	Symbol	Examples
ă	at, gas	m	man, seem	v	van, save
ā	ape, day	n	night, mitten	w	web, twice
ä	father, barn	ng	sing, anger	y	yard, lawyer
âr	fair, dare	ŏ	odd, not	z	zoo, reason
b	bell, table	ō	open, road, grow	zh	treasure, garage
ch	chin, lunch	ô	awful, bought, horse	ə	awake, even, pencil,
d	dig, bored	oi	coin, boy		pilot, focus
ĕ	egg, ten	ŏŏ	look, full	ər	perform, letter
ē	evil, see, meal	ōō	root, glue, through		
f	fall, laugh, phrase	ou	out, cow		**Sounds in Foreign Words**
g	gold, big	p	pig, cap	KH	*German* ich, auch;
h	hit, inhale	r	rose, star		*Scottish* loch
hw	white, everywhere	s	sit, face	N	*French* entre, bon, fin
ĭ	inch, fit	sh	she, mash	œ	*French* feu, cœur;
ī	idle, my, tried	t	tap, hopped		*German* schön
îr	dear, here	th	thing, with	ü	*French* utile, rue;
j	jar, gem, badge	*th*	then, other		*German* grün
k	keep, cat, luck	ŭ	up, nut		
l	load, rattle	ûr	fur, earn, bird, worm		

Stress Marks

′ This mark indicates that the preceding syllable receives the primary stress. For example, in the word *language*, the first syllable is stressed: lăng′gwĭj.

′ This mark is used only in words in which more than one syllable is stressed. It indicates that the preceding syllable is stressed, but somewhat more weakly than the syllable receiving the primary stress. In the word *literature*, for example, the first syllable receives the primary stress, and the last syllable receives a weaker stress: lĭt′ər-ə-chŏŏr′.

Adapted from *The American Heritage Dictionary of the English Language, Third Edition*; Copyright © 1992 by Houghton Mifflin Company. Used with the permission of Houghton Mifflin Company.

Reading Terms and Literary Concepts

Act An act is a major section of a play. Each act may be further divided into smaller sections, called **scenes.** *The Monsters Are Due on Maple Street* has two acts.

Alliteration Alliteration is a repetition of a sound or letter at the beginning of words. Writers use alliteration to emphasize particular words and to give their writing a musical quality. Note the repetition of the c sound in this line from "The Highwayman":

> Over the cobbles he clattered and clashed . . .

Analysis Analysis is a process of breaking something down into its elements so that they can be examined individually. When you analyze a literary work, you examine its parts in order to understand how they work together in the work as a whole.

Author's Purpose An author's purpose is his or her reason for creating a particular work. The purpose may be to entertain, to explain or inform, to express an opinion, or to persuade readers to do or believe something. An author may have more than one purpose for writing, but usually one is the most important.

Autobiography An autobiography is a form of nonfiction in which a person tells the story of his or her own life. "The Noble Experiment" from Jackie Robinson's *I Never Had It Made* is an example of autobiography.

Biography A biography is the story of a person's life, written by someone else. The subjects of biographies are often famous people, as in William Jay Jacobs's "Eleanor Roosevelt."

Cast of Characters In the script of a play, a cast of characters is a list of all the characters in the play, usually in order of appearance. This list is usually found at the beginning of the script.

Cause and Effect Two events are related as cause and effect when one event brings about the other. The event that happens first is the cause; the one that follows is the effect. This statement from "The Noble Experiment" shows a cause-and-effect relationship: "He pointed out that I couldn't play for a few days anyhow because of my bum arm."

Character A character is a person, an animal, or an imaginary creature that takes part in the action of a literary work. Generally, a work focuses on one or more **main characters,** but it may also include less important characters, called **minor characters.** Characters who change little, if at all, are called **static characters.** Characters who change significantly are called **dynamic characters.**

Characterization Characterization includes all the techniques writers use to create and develop characters. There are four basic methods of developing a character: (1) presenting the character's words and actions, (2) presenting the character's thoughts, (3) describing the character's appearance, and (4) showing what others think about the character.

Chronological Order Chronological order is the order in which events happen in time. In the biography "Eleanor Roosevelt," the events of Roosevelt's life are told in chronological order, beginning with her birth and ending with her death.

Clarifying The process of pausing while reading to review previous events in a work and to check one's understanding is called clarifying. Readers stop to reflect on what they know, to make inferences about what is happening, and to better understand what they are reading.

Climax In the plot of a story or play, the climax (or turning point) is the point of maximum interest. At the climax, the conflict is resolved and the outcome of the plot becomes clear. The climax of "The Smallest Dragonboy," for example, occurs when Keevan impresses the dragon at the hatching.

See also **Conflict** and **Plot.**

Comparison The process of identifying similarities is called comparison. In "All Summer in a Day," for example, Margot is compared to "an old photograph dusted from an album, whitened away" because both Margot and the photograph are pale and fragile.

Conflict Conflict is a struggle between opposing forces. In an **external conflict,** such as the battle between Rikki and the cobras in "Rikki-tikki-tavi," a character struggles against another character or against some outside force. **Internal conflict,** on the other hand, is a struggle is within a character. In "The Medicine Bag," Martin experiences internal conflict when he is caught between feelings of love and shame for his grandfather.

Connecting A reader's process of relating the content of a literary work to his or her own knowledge and experience is called connecting. In "Charles," for example, Laurie's description of Charles's antics at school may lead readers to recall similar events from their own schooling.

Connotation A word's connotations are the ideas and feelings associated with the word, as opposed to its dictionary definition. For example, the word *mother,* in addition to its basic meaning ("a female parent"), has connotations of love, warmth, and security.

Context Clues Unfamiliar words are often surrounded by words or phrases—called context clues—that help readers understand their meaning. A context clue may be a definition, a synonym, an example, a comparison or contrast, or any other expression that enables readers to infer the word's meaning.

Contrast The process of pointing out differences between things is called contrast. In "Last Cover," for example, the narrator contrasts himself with his brother Colin when he says, "I was following in my father's footsteps, true to form, but Colin threatened to break the family tradition. . . ."

Denotation A word's denotation is its dictionary definition.

See also **Connotation.**

Description Description is the process by which a writer creates a picture in readers' imaginations. A good description includes details that enable readers to visualize a scene, a character, or an object.

Dialect A dialect is a form of language that is spoken in a certain place or by a certain class of people. Dialects of a language may differ from one another in pronunciation, vocabulary, and grammar. In the excerpt from *Boy: Tales of Childhood,* Mrs. Pratchett speaks the dialect of the British working class: "Let's 'ave a look at some of them titchy ones."

Dialogue The words that characters speak aloud are called dialogue. In most literary works, dialogue is set off with quotation marks. In play scripts, however, each character's dialogue simply follows his or her name, without being indicated by quotation marks.

Drama A drama, or play, is a form of literature meant to be performed by actors before an audience. In drama, the characters' dialogue and actions tell the story.

Drawing Conclusions Combining several pieces of information to make an inference is called drawing a conclusion. A reader's conclusions may be based on the details presented in a literary work, on his or her previous inferences, or on a combination of these.

See also **Inference.**

Essay An essay is a short work of nonfiction that deals with a single subject. Some essays, such as "Homeless," emphasize personal feelings. Others, such as "The Eternal Frontier," are written primarily to convey information.

Evaluating Evaluating is the process of judging the worth of something or someone. A work of literature, or any of its parts, may be evaluated in terms of its entertainment, its believability, its originality, or its emotional power.

Exaggeration An extreme overstating of an idea is called exaggeration—as when Andrew in "What I Want to Be When I Grow Up" vows that he won't speak to anyone over the age of 18 for at least a month.

Exposition Exposition, which is usually found at the beginning of a story or play, serves to introduce the main characters, to describe the setting, and sometimes to establish the conflict. In "The War of the Wall," for example, the first three paragraphs provide most of the exposition.

See also **Plot.**

External Conflict. *See* **Conflict.**

Fable A fable is a brief story that teaches a lesson about human nature. In many fables, animals act and speak like human beings. Usually, a fable—like "The Wolf in Sheep's Clothing," for example—concludes with a moral.

Fact and Opinion A fact is a statement that can be proved, such as "April has 30 days." An opinion, in contrast, is a statement that cannot be proved, such as "April is the nicest month of the year." Opinions usually reflect personal beliefs and are often debatable.

Fantasy A fantasy is a story that takes place in an unreal, imaginary world, such as Pern in "The Smallest Dragonboy." Fantasies often involve magic or characters with superhuman powers.

Fiction Fiction is prose writing that tells an imaginary story. The writer of a fictional work may invent all the events and characters in it or may base parts of the story on real people or events.

See also **Novel** *and* **Short Story.**

Figurative Language Authors use figurative language to create fresh and original descriptions. Figurative expressions, while not literally true, help readers picture ordinary things in new ways. In many, one thing is described in terms of another—as when the speaker of "Barter" compares music to "a curve of gold."

See also **Metaphor, Personification** *and* **Simile.**

Flashback In a literary work, a flashback is an interruption of the action to present a scene that took place at an earlier time. In "Last Cover," for example, a flashback is used to show how Colin found Bandit.

Foil A character who provides a striking contrast to a main character is called a foil. The foil helps make the main character's qualities apparent to the reader. For example, Rat Joiner is the narrator's foil in "The Revolt of the Evil Fairies."

Folklore The traditions, customs, and stories that are passed down within a culture are known as its folklore. Folklore includes various types of literature, such as legends, folk tales, myths, and fables.

Folk Tale A folk tale is a story that has been passed from generation to generation by word of mouth. Folk tales may be set in the distant past and involve supernatural events, and the characters in them may be animals, people, or superhuman beings. "The Force of Luck" is an example of a folk tale.

Foreshadowing Foreshadowing occurs when a writer provides hints that suggest future events in a story. In "The Chief's Daughter," for example, Nessan says to Dara, "You would not have been even a prisoner, if I had not pleaded for you. They meant to sacrifice you to the Black Mother; you know that, don't you?" Her comments foreshadow her future rescue of Dara, when her people again plan to kill him as a sacrifice.

Form A literary work's form is its structure or organization. The form of a poem includes the arrangement of words and lines on the page. Some poems follow predictable patterns, with the same number of syllables in each line and the same number of lines in each stanza. Other poems, like E. E. Cummings's "Old Age Sticks," have irregular forms.

Free Verse Poetry without regular patterns of rhyme and rhythm is called free verse. Some poets use free verse to capture the sounds and rhythms of ordinary speech. "74th Street" is an example of a poem written in free verse.

Generalization A generalization is a broad statement about an entire group, such as "Novels take longer to read than short stories." Not all generalizations are true. Some are too broad or not supported by sufficient evidence, like the statement "All seventh graders are tall."

Genre A type or category of literature is called a genre. The main literary genres are fiction, nonfiction, poetry, and drama.

Imagery Imagery consists of words and phrases that appeal to readers' senses. Writers use sensory details to help readers imagine how things look, feel, smell, sound, and taste. Note the imagery in these lines from "It Happened in Montgomery":

The news slushed through the littered streets
Slipped into the crowded churches,
Slimmered onto the unmagnolied side of town
While the men talked and talked and talked.

Inference An inference is a logical guess or conclusion based on evidence. For example, in "The Emperor's New Clothes" the emperor is described as "so excessively fond of new clothes that he spent all his money on them. He cared nothing about his soldiers. . . ." From this description and their own knowledge, readers can infer that the emperor is superficial, vain, and self-centered.

Internal Conflict. See **Conflict.**

Irony Irony is a contrast between what is expected and what actually exists or happens. For example, most readers of "A Man Who Had No Eyes" believe that the successful and prosperous Mr. Parsons is sighted, only to discover at the end that he is blind.

Jargon Jargon is a specialized vocabulary used by members of a particular profession.

Legend A legend is a story handed down from the past about a specific person—usually someone of heroic accomplishments. Legends usually have some basis in historical fact. "Where the Girl Saved Her Brother" is an example of a legend.

Main Idea A main idea is a writer's principal message. It may be the central idea of an entire work or a thought expressed in the topic sentence of a paragraph. (The term *main idea* is usually used in discussions of nonfiction.)

Metaphor A metaphor is a comparison of two things that have some quality in common. Unlike a simile, a metaphor does not contain the word *like* or *as;* instead, it says that one thing *is* another. In the following sentence from "All Summer in a Day," a metaphor is used to convey the quietness of Margot's speech: "If she spoke at all, her voice would be a ghost."

Minor Character. *See* **Character.**

Mood A mood, or atmosphere, is a feeling that a literary work conveys to readers. Writers use a variety of techniques—including word choice, dialogue, description, and plot complications—to establish moods. In "All Summer in a Day," for example, Ray Bradbury creates a mood of tension and anticipation.

Moral A moral is a lesson that a story teaches. Morals are often stated directly at the end of fables.

Motivation A character's motivation is the reason why he or she acts, feels, or thinks in a certain way. For example, in "Say It with Flowers," a desire to be honest is part of Teruo's motivation. Motivations may be stated directly, or they may be implied.

Myth A myth is a traditional story, usually of unknown authorship, that deals with basic questions about the universe. Gods and heroes often figure prominently in myths, which may attempt to explain such things as the origin of the world, mysteries of nature, or social customs. "Phaëthon" is an example of a myth.

Narrative A narrative is writing that tells a story. The events in a narrative may be real, or they may be imaginary. Narratives that deal with real events include biographies and autobiographies. Fictional narratives include myths, short stories, novels, and narrative poems.

Narrative Poetry Poetry that tells a story is called narrative poetry. Like fiction, narrative poetry contains characters, settings, plots, and themes. It may also contain such elements of poetry as rhyme, rhythm, imagery, and figurative language. "The Highwayman" is an example of a narrative poem.

Narrator The narrator is the teller of a story.

See also **Point of View.**

Nonfiction Writing that tells about real people, places, and events is called nonfiction. Writers of nonfiction often get their information from both **primary sources** (original, firsthand accounts) and **secondary sources** (descriptions based on primary sources). **Informative nonfiction** is written mainly to provide factual information. A work of **literary nonfiction,** on the other hand, reads like a work of fiction—although it too provides factual information.

See also **Autobiography, Biography,** *and* **Essay.**

Novel A novel is a work of fiction that is longer and more complex than a short story. A novel's setting, plot, characters, and theme are usually developed in greater detail than a short story's.

Onomatopoeia Onomatopoeia is the use of words whose sound suggests their meaning—like *whir, buzz, pop,* and *sizzle.* In "The Highwayman," the onomatopoeic *tlot-tlot* is used to imitate the clopping of a horse's hoofs on a road.

Personification The giving of human qualities to an animal, object, or idea is known as personification. In "Rikki-tikki-tavi," for example, the mongoose and the cobras are personified, conversing as if they were human.

Persuasion Persuasion is a type of writing that is meant to sway readers' feelings, beliefs, or actions. Persuasion normally appeals to both the mind and the heart of its readers.

Play. *See* **Drama.**

Plot A story's plot is the sequence of related events that make up the story. In a typical plot, an **exposition** introduces the characters and establishes the main conflict. Complications arise as the characters try to resolve the conflict. Eventually, the plot builds toward a **climax,** the point of greatest interest or suspense. In the **resolution**—the final stage of the plot—loose ends are tied up and the story is brought to a close.

Poetry Poetry is a type of literature in which ideas and feelings are expressed in compact, imaginative, and musical language. Poets arrange words in ways intended to touch readers' senses, emotions, and minds. Most poems are written in lines, which may contain regular patterns of rhyme and rhythm. These lines may, in turn, be grouped in stanzas.

Point of View Every story is told from a particular point of view, or perspective. When a story is told from the **first-person** point of view, the narrator is a character in the story and uses first-person pronouns, such as *I, me, we,* and *us.* In a story told from a **third-person** point of view, on the other hand, the narrator is not a character; he or she uses third-person pronouns, such as *he, she, it, they,* and *them.*

The **third-person omniscient** (all-knowing) point of view allows the narrator to relate the thoughts and feelings of several, if not all, the story's characters. The narrator of "The Emperor's New Clothes," for example, reveals the thoughts and feelings of the emperor's officials as well as the emperor himself. In the **third-person limited** point of view, the narrator is allowed inside the mind of only one character—as in "The Smallest Dragonboy," in which the focus is limited to Keevan's thoughts and feelings.

Predicting Using what you know to guess what may happen is called predicting. Good readers gather information as they read and combine that information with prior knowledge to predict upcoming events in a story.

Prose Prose is the ordinary form of spoken and written language—that is, it is language that lacks the special features of poetry.

Questioning The process of raising questions while reading is called questioning. Good readers ask questions in an effort to understand characters and events, looking for answers as they continue to read.

Repetition Repetition is a use of any element of language—a sound, a word, a phrase, a gram-matical structure—more than once. Writers use repetition to stress ideas and to create memorable sound effects, as in these lines from "The Charge of the Light Brigade":

> Theirs not to make reply,
>
> Theirs not to reason why,
>
> Theirs but to do and die

See also **Alliteration** *and* **Rhyme.**

Resolution. *See* **Plot.**

Rhyme Rhyme is a repetition of sounds at the end of words. Words rhyme when their accented vowels and all the letters that follow have identical sounds. *Dog* and *log* rhyme, as do *letter* and *better.*

The most common form of rhyme in poetry is **end rhyme,** where the rhyming words occur at the end of lines. Rhyme that occurs within a line is called **internal rhyme.**

Rhythm The rhythm of a line of poetry is the pattern of stressed and unstressed syllables in the line. When this pattern is repeated throughout a poem, the poem is said to have a regular beat. Note the rhythm in these lines from "If I Can Stop One Heart from Breaking" (the mark ´ indicates a stressed syllable; the mark ˘, an unstressed syllable):

> If I can stop one Heart from breaking
>
> I shall not live in vain

Scanning Scanning is the process of searching through writing for a particular fact or piece of information. When you scan, your eyes sweep across a page, looking for key words that may lead you to the information you want.

Scene In a play, a scene is a section presenting events that occur in one place at one time. Each scene presents an episode of the play's plot. For example, in *A Christmas Carol,* Scene 1 shows what occurs in Scrooge's shop, and Scene 2 shows what occurs at Scrooge's home.

Science Fiction Science fiction is fiction based on real or imagined scientific developments. Science fiction stories are often set in imaginary places and in the future. "Lose Now, Pay Later" is an example of science fiction.

Setting The setting of a story, poem, or play is the time and place of the action. Elements of setting may include geographic location, historical period (past, present, or future), the season of the year, the time of day, and the beliefs, customs, and standards of a society. The influence of setting on characters' decisions and actions may vary from work to work.

Short Story A short story is a brief work of fiction that can usually be read in a single sitting. A short story generally focuses on one or two main characters and on a single conflict.

Simile A simile is a comparison of two things that have some quality in common. In a simile, the comparison is conveyed by means of the word *like* or *as*. Note the simile in this sentence from *Boy: Tales of Childhood:* "What is left looks rather like a gigantic black pancake."

Skimming Skimming is the process of reading quickly to identify the main idea of, or to get an overview of, a work or passage. It involves reading the title, the headings, the words in special type, and the first sentence of each paragraph, as well as any charts, graphs, and time lines that accompany the writing.

Sound Effects

See **Alliteration, Onomatopoeia, Repetition, Rhyme,** *and* **Rhythm.**

Speaker In a poem, the speaker is the voice that talks to the reader—like the narrator in a work of fiction. Frequently, recognizing the speaker's attitude is a key to understanding a poem's meaning. In some poems, such as "There Is No Word for Goodbye," the speaker expresses the feelings of the poet. In others, the speaker's attitude and the poet's may not be the same.

Stage Directions In the script of a play, the instructions to the actors, director, and stage crew are called stage directions. They may suggest scenery, lighting, music, sound effects, and ways for actors to move and speak. In the plays in this book, stage directions appear in italic type and are enclosed in parentheses.

Stanza A group of lines within a poem is called a stanza. A stanza is like a paragraph in a work of prose. "The Charge of the Light Brigade," for example, contains six stanzas.

Stereotype A stereotype is a generalization about a group of people, in which individual differences are disregarded. Stereotypes may lead to unfair judgments of individuals on the basis of race, ethnic background, or physical appearance.

Structure The structure of a work of literature is the way in which it is put together. In poetry, structure involves the arrangement of words and lines to produce a desired effect. One structural unit in poetry is the stanza. In prose, structure involves the arrangement of such elements as sentences, paragraphs, and events. "Hollywood and the Pits," for example, has the overall structure of a first-person narrative that is interrupted occasionally by passages of nonfiction written from the third-person point of view.

Style A style is a manner of writing; it involves *how* something is said rather than *what* is said. The excerpt from *Boy: Tales of Childhood,* for example, has a playful style that relies on exaggeration, humor, and colorful words. Many elements contribute to style, including word choice, sentence length, tone, and figurative language.

Summarizing Summarizing is telling the main ideas of a piece of writing briefly in one's own words, omitting unimportant details.

Surprise Ending An unexpected plot twist at the end of a story is called a surprise ending. "A Retrieved Reformation" is an example of a story with a surprise ending.

Suspense Suspense is a feeling of growing tension and excitement felt by a reader. Writers create suspense by raising questions in readers' minds about what might happen. For example, in "A Retrieved Reformation," a suspenseful moment occurs when Agatha is trapped inside the bank vault and readers wonder whether she will suffocate.

Symbol A symbol is a person, a place, an object, or an action that stands for something beyond itself. The bald eagle, for example, is a symbol of the United States.

Literary symbols acquire meaning from the context of the works in which they appear. In "Into the Sun," for instance, the multicolored wild horse might represent any risky opportunity that could lead to self-fulfillment.

Teleplay A play written for television is called a teleplay. In a teleplay, the stage directions usually include camera instructions. *The Monsters Are Due on Maple Street* is an example of a teleplay.

Theme A theme is the message about life or human nature that is conveyed by a literary work. A work may have more than one theme, and in many cases readers must infer the writer's message. One way to infer a fictional work's theme is to decide what general statement could be supported by the experiences of the main character. For example, a theme of "The Christmas Hunt" might be that a child can begin to grow up by taking responsibility for his or her actions.

Title The title of a piece of writing is the name that is attached to it. A title often refers to an important aspect of the work to which it is attached. For example, the title "The War of the Wall" refers to Lou and the narrator's extended conflict with the "painter lady."

Tone The tone of a work is the writer's attitude toward his or her subject. Words such as *amused, objective,* and *angry* can be used to describe different tones. The tone of "Formula," for example, might be described as dreamy or escapist.

Visualizing The process of forming a mental picture based on a written description is called visualizing. Good readers use the details supplied by writers to picture characters, settings, and events in their minds.

1 The Writing Process

The writing process consists of four stages: prewriting, drafting, revising and editing, and publishing and reflecting. As the graphic to the right shows, these stages are not steps that you must complete in a set order. Rather, you may return to any one at any time in your writing process, using feedback from your readers along the way.

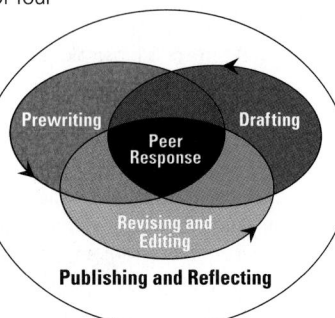

1.1 Prewriting

In the prewriting stage, you explore your ideas and discover what you want to write about.

Choosing a Topic

Ideas for writing can come from just about anywhere: experiences, memories, conversations, dreams, or imaginings. The following techniques can help you to generate ideas for writing and to choose a writing topic you care about.

Personal Techniques
Make a list of people, places, and activities that have had an effect on you.
Ask who, what, when, where, and why about an important event.
Ask what-if questions about everyday life.
Browse through magazines, newspapers, and on-line bulletin boards for ideas.

Sharing Techniques
With a group, brainstorm a topic by trying to come up with as many ideas as you can. Do not stop to evaluate your ideas for at least five minutes.
With a group, discuss a topic in depth, sharing your questions and ideas.

Writing Techniques
Use a word or picture as a starting point for freewriting.
Freewrite for a short time and then circle the ideas you would like to explore.
Pick a topic and list all the related ideas that occur to you.

Graphic Techniques
Create a time line of memorable events in your life.
Make a cluster diagram of subtopics related to a general topic.

Determining Your Purpose

At some time during your writing process, you need to consider your purpose, or general reason, for writing. For example, your purpose may be one of the following: to express yourself, to entertain, to explain, to describe, to analyze, or to persuade. To clarify your purpose, ask yourself questions like these:

- Why did I choose to write about my topic?
- What aspects of the topic mean the most to me?
- What do I want others to think or feel after they read my writing?

Identifying Your Audience

Knowing who will read your writing can help you clarify your purpose, focus your topic, and choose the details and tone that will best communicate your ideas. As you think about your readers, ask yourself questions like these:

- What does my audience already know about my topic?
- What will they be most interested in?
- What language is most appropriate for this audience?

1.2   Drafting

In the drafting stage, you put your ideas on paper and allow them to develop and change as you write.

There's no right or wrong way to draft. Sometimes you might be adventuresome and just dive right into your writing. At other times, you might draft slowly, planning carefully beforehand. You can combine aspects of these approaches to suit yourself and your writing projects.

 LINK TO LITERATURE

Inspiration for your writing can come from everyday events. Shirley Jackson's story "Charles," on page 593—a humorous account of a child's difficult but amusing introduction to kindergarten—is based on her own experience as a parent.

 LINK TO LITERATURE

Roald Dahl—the author of *Boy: Tales of Childhood,* on page 473—understood the importance of identifying his audience. According to Dahl, "Children are a great discipline because they are highly critical. . . . And if you think a child is getting bored, you must think up something that jolts it [the child] back. Something that tickles."

Discovery drafting is a good approach when you've gathered some information on your topic or have a rough idea for writing but are not quite sure how you feel about your subject or what exactly you want to say. You just plunge into your draft and let your ideas lead you where they will. After finishing a discovery draft, you may decide to start another draft, do more prewriting, or revise your first draft.

Planned drafting may work better for reports and other kinds of formal writing. Try thinking through a writing plan or making an outline before you begin drafting. Then, as you write, you can develop your ideas and fill in the details.

1.3   Using Peer Response

The suggestions and comments your peers or classmates make about your writing are called peer response.

Talking with peers about your writing can help you discover what you want to say or how well you have communicated your ideas. You can ask a peer reader for help at any point in the writing process. For example, your peers can help you develop a topic, narrow your focus, discover confusing passages, or organize your writing.

Questions for Your Peer Readers

You can help your peer readers provide you with the most useful kinds of feedback by following these guidelines:

- Tell readers where you are in the writing process. Are you still trying out ideas, or have you completed a draft?
- Ask questions that will help you get specific information about your writing. Open-ended questions that require more than yes-or-no answers are more likely to give you information you can use as you revise.
- Give your readers plenty of time to respond thoughtfully to your writing.
- Encourage your readers to be honest when they respond to your work. It's OK if you don't agree with them—you always get to decide which changes to make.

The chart on the following page explains different peer-response techniques you might use when you're ready to share your work with others.

WRITING TIP

Besides using friends as peer readers, consider asking for responses from people you don't know well. Someone who doesn't know you may approach your writing with a fresh perspective.

Technique	When to Use It	Questions to Ask
Sharing	Use this when you are just exploring ideas or when you want to celebrate the completion of a piece of writing by sharing it with another person.	Will you please read or listen to my writing without criticizing it or making suggestions afterward?
Summarizing	Use this when you want to know if your main idea or goals are clear to readers.	What do you think I'm trying to say? What's my main idea?
Telling	Use this to find out which parts of your writing are affecting readers the way you want and which parts are confusing.	What did you think or feel as you read my words? Which passage were you reading when you had that response?
Replying	Use this when you want to get some new ideas to use in your writing.	What are your ideas about my topic? What do you think about what I have said in my piece?
Identifying	Use this when you want to identify the strengths and weaknesses of your writing.	Where do you like the wording? Where can it be improved? Does the organization make sense? What parts were confusing?

Tips for Being a Peer Reader

Remember these guidelines when you act as a peer reader:

- Respect the writer's feelings.
- Make sure you understand what kind of feedback the writer is looking for before you respond, and then limit your comments accordingly.
- Use "I" statements, such as "I like . . .," "I think . . .," and "It would help me if. . . ." Remember that your impressions and opinions may not be the same as someone else's.

1.4   Revising and Editing

In the revising and editing stage, you improve your draft, choose the words that best express your ideas, and proofread for mistakes in spelling, grammar, usage, and punctuation.

 WRITING TIP

You may want to ask peer readers questions if their comments are not clear or helpful to you. For example, if a reader says "This part is confusing," you can probe to find out why. Ask, What are you confused about? What do you think might make it clearer?

When you finish a draft, take a break before rereading it. The break will help you distance yourself from your writing and allow you to evaluate it more objectively. You may decide to make several drafts, in which you change direction or even start over, before you're ready to revise and polish a piece of writing.

For help with identifying and correcting problems that are listed in the Proofreading Checklist, see the Grammar Handbook, pages 848–887.

The changes you make in your writing during this stage usually fall into three categories: revising for ideas, revising for form, and editing to correct mistakes. Use the questions and suggestions that follow to help you assess problems in your draft and determine what kinds of changes would improve it.

Revising for Ideas

- Have I discovered the main idea or focus of my writing? Have I expressed it clearly in my draft?
- Have I accomplished my purpose?
- Do my readers have all the information they need, or would adding more details help?
- Are any of my ideas unnecessary?

Revising for Form and Language

- Is my writing unified? Are all the ideas directly related to my main idea or focus?
- Is my writing organized well? Are the relationships among ideas clear?
- Is my writing coherent? Is the flow of sentences and paragraphs smooth and logical?

Editing to Improve Your Writing

When you are satisfied with your draft, proofread and edit it, correcting any mistakes you might have made in spelling, grammar, usage, and punctuation. You may want to proofread your writing several times, looking for different types of mistakes each time. The following checklist may help you proofread your work.

Proofreading Checklist	
Sentence Structure and Agreement	Are there any run-on sentences or sentence fragments? Do all verbs agree with their subjects? Do all pronouns agree with their antecedents? Are verb tenses correct and consistent?
Forms of Words	Do adverbs and adjectives modify the appropriate words? Are all forms of *be* and other irregular verbs used correctly? Are pronouns used correctly? Are comparative and superlative forms of adjectives correct?
Capitalization, Punctuation, and Spelling	Is any punctuation mark missing or not needed? Are all words spelled correctly? Are all proper nouns, all proper adjectives, and the first words of all sentences capitalized?

Use the proofreading symbols shown below to mark your draft with the changes that you need to make. See the Grammar Handbook for models in which these symbols are used.

Proofreading Symbols	
∧ Add letters or words.	/ Make a capital letter lowercase.
⊙ Add a period.	¶ Begin a new paragraph.
≡ Capitalize a letter.	– or ⌴ Take out letters or words.
⌒ Close up space.	∼ Switch the positions of letters, words, or punctuation marks.
∧ Add a comma.	

1.5 Publishing and Reflecting

After you've completed a writing project, consider sharing it with a wider audience—even when you've produced it for a class assignment. Reflecting on your writing process is another good way to bring closure to a writing project.

Creative Publishing Ideas

Following are some ideas for publishing and sharing your writing.

- Display your writing on a school bulletin board.
- Working with other students in your class, create an anthology, or collection, of stories, poems, plays, and other writing.
- Give a dramatic reading of your work for another class or group.
- Submit your writing to a local newspaper or a magazine that publishes student writing.
- Enter your work in a writing contest.
- Go on line with your writing by posting it on an electronic bulletin board or sending it to others via e-mail.
- Create a multimedia presentation and share it with classmates.

Reflecting on Your Writing

Think about your writing process and consider whether you'd like to add your writing to your portfolio. You might write yourself a note answering questions like these and attach it to your work:

- What did I learn about myself and my subject?
- Which parts of the writing process did I most and least enjoy?
- As I wrote, what was my biggest problem? How did I solve it?
- What did I learn that I can use the next time I write?

 WRITING TIP

If you create an anthology with your classmates, consider basing it on a theme that all of the writing relates to. Also, you could create artwork to illustrate your anthology or invite an art class to illustrate it.

Building Blocks of Good Writing

2.1 Introductions

A good introduction catches your reader's interest and often presents the main idea of your writing. To introduce your writing effectively, try one of the following methods.

Share a Fact

Beginning with an interesting fact can make your reader think, I'd like to learn more about that. In the example below, the unusual facts about bats can capture the reader's interest.

> Bats may seem like a nuisance, but not as much as the 99 pounds of insects a colony of bats can eat in one night. Despite their ugly faces and all the scary stories about them, bats are very important and useful animals.

Present a Description

A vivid description sets a mood and brings a scene to life. The details below set the scene for a discussion about pollution.

> The temperature is 15 degrees. Drifts of snow hide picnic tables and swings. In the middle of the park, however, steam rises from a lake where Canada geese swim. It sounds beautiful, but the water is warm because it has been heated by a chemical plant upriver. In fact, the geese should have migrated south by now.

Ask a Question

Beginning with a question can make your reader want to read on to find out the answer. Note how the introduction that follows invites the reader to learn more about how the invention of plastics changed the world of recreation.

WRITING TIP

Writing the introduction does not need to be your first task when you begin a writing project. Instead, begin with any part of your piece that you feel ready to write. Once your ideas come into better focus, you'll probably get a good idea about how to introduce your piece.

> What do billiard balls and movie film have in common? It was in an effort to find a substitute for ivory billiard balls that John Hyatt created celluloid. This plastic substance was also used to make the first movies.

Relate an Incident

An engaging narrative that includes sensory details or dialogue can help catch your reader's attention. The example below uses an incident to introduce a science report.

> When I was younger, my friends and I would rub balloons in our hair and make them stick to our clothes. Someone once said, "I get a charge out of this," not knowing that we were really generating static electricity.

Use Dialogue

As you can see from the example above, quoting a person's words can be an effective beginning to a piece of writing. You can also write dialogue to draw the reader into your piece, as shown in the opening to a personal narrative below.

> "Are you scared?" asked my little sister, Shilo.
> "Of a little thunder and lightning? Of course not."
> Just as lightning struck the tree in front of our apartment, I admitted, "OK, maybe a little."
> Our parents had been delayed by the storm, and Shilo and I were home alone.

2.2 Paragraphs

A paragraph is made up of sentences that work together to develop an idea or accomplish a purpose. Whether or not it contains a topic sentence stating the main idea, a good paragraph must have both unity and coherence.

 WRITING TIP

When writing dialogue, be sure to start a new paragraph every time the speaker changes, as in the example at the left. For help with punctuation and capitalization in quotations, see page 886 of the Grammar Handbook.

A topic sentence makes the main idea or purpose of a paragraph clear to your reader. A topic sentence can appear anywhere in a paragraph, but when it is the first sentence, it can capture the reader's attention and clearly suggest what will follow.

> *Flying a hot-air balloon looks fun, but it requires a good mathematician to fly one safely.* Since a balloon is controlled by heating and cooling the air inside the balloon, the pilot must know the temperature of the air outside it and how high he or she plans to fly in order to calculate the maximum weight the balloon can carry. If the pilot doesn't do the math correctly, the balloon could crash.

Unity

A paragraph has unity if every sentence in it supports the same main idea or purpose. One way to achieve unity in a paragraph is to state the main idea in a topic sentence and be sure that all the other sentences support that idea, as in the example above. You can create unity in a paragraph without using a topic sentence, however. Decide on a goal for your paragraph and make sure that each sentence supports that goal. Sentences should logically flow from one to the next, as shown in the narrative paragraph below.

> Our Spelunkers' Club members entered the cave through a narrow opening in the face of the cliff. Once inside, we waited until our eyes had grown accustomed to the darkness. Then we proceeded farther into the cave, walking single file over the slippery floor and grabbing at the damp walls for support when we felt that we were losing our footing.

Coherence

In a coherent paragraph, details are presented in a clear, sensible order. The following paragraph is coherent because the writer connects the sentences by repeating important words from one sentence to the next.

LINK TO LITERATURE

Notice the use of strong topic sentences in "The Noble Experiment" by Jackie Robinson, as told to Alfred Duckett. For example, on page 276 the first paragraph begins, "Winning his directors' approval was almost insignificant in contrast to the task which now lay ahead of the Dodger president." The rest of the paragraph then explains that task in detail.

WRITING TIP

When you are revising your writing, be sure to delete any details that do not relate to the main idea of each paragraph. If a paragraph contains two main ideas, you may break it into two separate paragraphs.

We constantly use and reuse the water that comes from our faucets. Because we contaminate that water faster than nature can purify it, we need water purification plants. Most purification processes have two stages. In the first stage, solid wastes settle in large tanks. In the second stage, oxygen is pumped through the water to cause the growth of bacteria and organisms that destroy most of the remaining waste.

2.3   Transitions

Transitions are words that show the connections between details, such as relationships in time and space, order of importance, causes and effects, and similarities or differences.

Chronological Order

Some transitions help to clarify the order in which events take place. To arrange details chronologically, as in the example below, use transitional words such as *first, second, always, then, next, later, soon, before, finally, after, earlier, afterward,* and *tomorrow.*

Long *before* mountain bikes were made, bicycles were much less comfortable. The *first* cycle, which actually had four wheels, was made in 1645 and had to be walked. *Later,* two-wheeled cycles with pedals were called boneshakers because of their bumpy ride.

Spatial Order

Transitional words and phrases such as *in front, behind, next to, nearest, lowest, above, below, underneath, to the left,* and *in the middle* can help show where items are located. The following example uses spatial transitions to describe a theater.

The audience entered the theater *from the back.* The stage was *in front,* and fire exits were located *to the right and left* of the stage.

 LINK TO LITERATURE

Notice how William Jay Jacobs uses transitions in "Eleanor Roosevelt." On page 210, he uses *also, above all,* and *similarly* to make smooth transitions between paragraphs about Roosevelt's accomplishments when she was the First Lady.

Degree

Transitions such as *mainly, strongest, weakest, first, second, most important, least important, worst,* and *best* rank order of details or show degree of importance, as in the model below.

> *At best,* the canoeing trip would mean not hearing my little brother and sister squabbling over the TV. *At the very worst,* I could expect to be living in wet clothes for two weeks.

Compare and Contrast

Words and phrases such as *similarly, likewise, also, like, as, neither . . . nor,* and *either . . . or* show similarity, or likeness, between details. *However, by contrast, yet, but, unlike, instead, whereas,* and *while* show contrast, or difference. Note the use of both types of transitions in the model below.

> *While* my local public library is a quieter place to study *than* home, I don't always get much done at the library. I'm so used to the cheerful chatter of my baby brother that, *by contrast,* the stillness of the library makes me sleepy.

Cause and Effect

To show that details are linked in a cause-and-effect relationship, use transitional words and phrases such as *since, because, thus, therefore, so, due to, for this reason,* and *as a result.* Transitions in the following example explain the cause-and-effect relationship between the weather and the school calendar.

> *Because* we missed seven days of school *as a result* of snowstorms, the school year will be extended. *Therefore,* we will be in school until June 17.

WRITING TIP

When you begin a sentence with a transition such as *most important, therefore, nevertheless, still,* or *instead,* set the transition off with a comma.

2.4 Elaboration

To develop the main idea of a paragraph or a longer piece, you need to provide elaboration, or details, so that your readers aren't left with unanswered questions.

Facts and Statistics

A fact is a statement that can be proved, while a statistic is a fact stated in numbers. As in the model below, the facts and statistics you use should strongly support the statements you make.

> The Statue of Liberty, one of the most popular monuments in the United States, is expensive to maintain. From 1983 to 1986, it cost $66 million to renovate the copper-covered 151-foot-tall statue.

Sensory Details

By showing how something looks, sounds, smells, tastes, and feels, sensory details like the ones in the model below can help your readers more fully experience your subject.

> I was so nervous during my math test last week. Chewing on my pencil left my mouth feeling dry and flaky. My palms were sweating so much, they left stains on the pages. The ticking of the clock seemed like the beating of a drum inside my head.

Incidents

Describing a brief incident can help to explain or develop an idea. The writer of the model below includes an incident to help describe being afraid of heights.

> People who are afraid of heights tend to panic even in perfectly safe situations. When my friend Jennifer and I rode to the top floor of a shopping mall, I enjoyed the view from the glass-enclosed elevator, but Jennifer's face was pale and her hands trembled.

WRITING TIP

Facts and statistics are especially useful in supporting opinions. Be sure that you double-check in your original sources the accuracy of all facts and statistics you cite.

LINK TO LITERATURE

Notice on page 57 the use of examples in the selection from Russell Freedman's *Immigrant Kids.* When the writer states that none of the immigrants forgot their first glimpse of the Statue of Liberty, he elaborates by using the example of immigrant Edward Corsi's first impression.

Examples

The model below shows how using an example can help support or clarify an idea. A well-chosen example often can be more effective than a lengthy explanation.

> The origins of today's professional sporting events can be traced to ancient games from countries all over the world. For example, hockey is believed to have come from an old Dutch game called *kolf*, played on the ice with a ball and crooked sticks.

Quotations

Choose quotations that clearly support your points and be sure that you copy each quotation word for word. Remember to always credit the source.

> In Ted Poston's "The Revolt of the Evil Fairies," the narrator understands that unspoken prejudice denies some students the opportunity to play the leading role in a school play. The narrator says, "And though nobody ever discussed those things openly, it was an accepted fact that a lack of pigmentation was a decided advantage in the Prince Charming . . . sweepstakes."

2.5　Description

Descriptive writing conveys images and impressions of a person, a place, an event, or a thing.

Descriptive writing appears almost everywhere, from cookbooks to poems. You might use a description to introduce a character in a narrative or to create a strong closing to a persuasive essay. Whatever your purpose and wherever you use description, the following guidelines for good descriptive writing will help you.

Include Plenty of Details

Vivid sensory details help the reader feel like an on-the-scene observer of the subject. The sensory details of the following scene appeal to the senses of sight, hearing, smell, touch, and even taste.

> Red and gold pennants welcomed us to the fairgrounds, where the delicious aroma of popcorn mingled with the pungent odor of the animals. Food vendors hawked their wares, and the tinny music of the carousel filled the air. Munching on roasted peanuts, we took our seats on the rough benches of the judging arena.

Organize Your Details

Details that are presented in a logical order help the reader form a mental picture of the subject. Descriptive details may be organized chronologically, spatially, by order of importance, or by order of impression.

> As I stepped into my grandmother's front hall, a whirl of sweet and salty odors overwhelmed me. Peeking around the corner, I witnessed a parade of pies, breads, and salads stretching across every inch of counter space.

Show, Don't Tell

Instead of just telling about a subject in a general way, provide details and quotations that expand and support what you want to say and that enable your readers to share your experience. The following example just tells and doesn't show.

> I was proud of myself when the local paper published my article.

The paragraph below uses descriptive details to show how proud the writer felt.

> I've delivered newspapers since I was eight, but last Thursday, for the first time, the newspaper printed an article I had written for a contest. I bought a pad of sticky notes and left messages for my customers: "Check out page B7. Enjoy the paper today." I thought about signing the article, but I decided that would be too much.

 LINK TO LITERATURE

Note on page 417 the organization of details describing Miss Pride's shop of Joan Aiken's "The Serial Garden." The narrator begins with the shop window as seen from the outside, then describes the interior of the store, and finally shows the reader Miss Pride herself.

LINK TO LITERATURE

On page 481, in *Boy: Tales of Childhood*, Roald Dahl uses a simile—a comparison using *like* or *as*—to create a vivid description. To describe his friends and himself as they prepare to play a prank, he says, "We felt *like* a gang of desperados setting out to rob a train or blow up the sheriff's office."

Use Precise Language

To create a clear image in your reader's mind, use vivid and precise words. Instead of using general nouns, verbs, and adjectives (*building, walk, sad*), use specific ones (*high-rise, saunter, glum*). Notice what happens when vague, general words are replaced with precise words, as in the example below.

> The bus was stuck in traffic.
>
> The crowded school bus inched along in bumper-to-bumper rush-hour traffic.

2.6 Conclusions

A conclusion should leave readers with a strong final impression. Try any of the following approaches for concluding a piece of writing.

Restate the Main Idea

Close by returning to your central idea and stating it in a new way. If possible, link the beginning of your conclusion with the information you have presented, as the model below shows.

> As these arguments show, planting a tree on Arbor Day is more than just a pleasant symbolic act. It also makes your neighborhood a more attractive place and sets an example for others to follow. Planting one tree will make a difference in the environment that goes well beyond this one day.

Ask a Question

Try asking a question that sums up what you have said and gives readers something to think about. The following example from a piece of persuasive writing ends with a question that suggests a course of action.

> If tutoring a younger student in writing, reading, or math can help you do better in these subjects yourself, shouldn't you take advantage of the opportunities to tutor at Western Elementary School?

Make a Recommendation

When you are writing to persuade, you can use your conclusion to tell readers what you want them to do. The conclusion below recommends learning a foreign language.

> Since learning a foreign language gives you a chance to expand your world view and make new friends, register for one of the introductory courses that start next fall.

End with the Last Event

If you're telling a story, you may end with the last thing that happens. Here, the ending includes an important moment for the narrator.

> As I raced down the basketball court in the final seconds of the game, I felt as alone as I did on all those nights practicing by myself in the driveway. My perfect lay-up drew yells from the crowd, but I was cheering for myself on the inside.

Generalize About Your Information

The model below concludes by making a general statement about the importance of the subject.

> In Toshio Mori's story "Say It with Flowers," Teruo decides that keeping his honesty is more important than keeping his job. His willingness to make a statement about right and wrong teaches a lesson from which we can all benefit.

 LINK TO LITERATURE

Note on page 311 the conclusion of the excerpt from Ellen M. Dolan's *Susan Butcher and the Iditarod Trail*. Dolan ends by describing the statue honoring Balto and the other sled dogs that relayed vials of serum from Nenana to Nome, Alaska.

3 Narrative Writing

Narrative writing tells a story. If you write a story from your imagination, it is called a fictional narrative. A true story about actual events is called a nonfictional narrative.

Writing Standards

Good narrative writing

▶ includes descriptive details and dialogue to develop the characters, setting, and plot

▶ has a clear beginning, middle, and end

▶ maintains a consistent tone and point of view

▶ uses language that is appropriate for the audience

▶ demonstrates the significance of the events or ideas

Key Techniques of Narrative Writing

Define the Conflict

The conflict of a narrative is the problem that the main character faces. The conflict below involves the struggle of a character against himself and his newfound values.

Example
The bikes were lined up in a row, beautiful, shiny, and bright. He ran his hand over the handlebars and felt his face flush with embarrassment. How could he spend all the stranger's money on a fancy bike that he didn't really need?

Clearly Organize the Events

Choose the important events and explain them in an order that is easy to understand. In a fictional narrative, this series of events is the story's plot.

Example
- kind stranger gives Roger money he doesn't really deserve
- Roger goes to buy fancy new bike with the money
- salesperson accuses him of not having the money to buy the bike
- Roger decides not to buy the bike and leaves to find the stranger

Depict Characters Vividly

Use vivid details to show your readers what your characters look like, what they say, and what they think.

Example
The salesperson strolled the show-room carpet like a rich prince walking the halls of his castle. He said nothing, but his pacing made the boy slightly nervous.

Organizing Narrative Writing

One way to organize a piece of narrative writing is to arrange the events in chronological order, as shown in Option 1 below.

Option 1

Example

Focus on Events	
• Introduce characters and setting	Roger walked into the store where he had seen the fancy new bikes.
• Show event 1	"Can I help you?" the salesperson asked, his voice showing interest in a sale. Roger mumbled and pointed toward the bikes against the wall.
• Show event 2	As his hand glided over the handlebars on the bike, he barely heard the salesperson ask if he even had the money for the new bike.
• End, perhaps showing the significance of the events	Roger's hand flashed dollar bills, but he let go of the bike. He ran for the door, knowing he had to find the old woman who had given him the money.

Chronological order is the most common way to organize a narrative. However, you may wish to focus more directly on character, as shown in Option 2, or conflict, as shown in Option 3.

Option 2

Focus on Character
• Introduce the main character
• Describe the conflict the character faces
• Relate the events and the changes the character goes through as a result of the conflict
• Present the final change or new understanding

Option 3

Focus on Conflict
• Present the characters and setting
• Introduce the conflict
• Describe the events that develop from the initial conflict
• Show the struggle of the main character with the conflict
• Resolve the conflict

WRITING TIP

Introductions Try hooking your reader's interest by opening a story with an exciting event or some attention-grabbing dialogue. After your introduction, you may need to go back in time and relate the incidents that led up to the opening event.

Explanatory Writing

Explanatory writing is writing that informs and explains. For example, you can use it to tell how to cook spaghetti, to explore the origins of the universe, or to compare two pieces of literature.

Types of Explanatory Writing

Analysis

Analysis explains how something works, how it is defined, or what its parts are.

Example
The Africanized honeybee is a new insect nuisance that has the potential to affect agriculture, recreation, and the environment.

Compare and Contrast

Compare-and-contrast writing explores the similarities and differences between two or more subjects.

Example
While the domestic honeybee has been bred for good honey production and gentleness, the Africanized bee is a "wild" bee that is quick-tempered and uncomfortable around animals and people.

Problem-Solution

Problem-solution writing examines a problem and proposes a solution to it.

Example
The best way to protect yourself against the stings of the Africanized bee is to understand how it behaves and react accordingly.

Cause and Effect

Cause-and-effect writing explains why something happened, why certain conditions exist, or what resulted from an action or a condition.

Example
If the Africanized bees drive out or breed into domesticated honeybee colonies, commercial beekeepers in the United States could be forced out of business.

4.1   Compare and Contrast

Compare-and-contrast writing explores the similarities and differences between two or more subjects.

Organizing Compare-and-Contrast Writing

When you compare and contrast subjects, you can organize your information in different ways. Two of your options are shown below.

Option 1

Feature by Feature	Example
Feature 1	Similarities in appearance
• Subject A	Domestic honeybees are about five-eighths of an inch long.
• Subject B	Africanized bees, contrary to rumor, are about the same size.
Feature 2	Differences in temperament
• Subject A	Domestic honeybees are bred to be gentle.
• Subject B	The Africanized bee is a "wild" bee that is quick-tempered around animals and people.

Option 2

Subject by Subject	Example
Subject A	Domestic honeybees
• Feature 1	Domestic honeybees are about five-eighths of an inch long.
• Feature 2	Domestic honeybees are bred to be gentle.
Subject B	Africanized bees
• Feature 1	Africanized bees are also about five-eighths of an inch long.
• Feature 2	The Africanized honeybee is a "wild" bee that is quick-tempered around people and animals.

Writing Standards

Good compare-and-contrast writing

▶ clearly states the subjects being compared and shows how they are alike and different

▶ is easy to follow, using either feature-by-feature or subject-by-subject organization

▶ uses transitions to signal similarities and differences

▶ ends with a conclusion that explains the decision made or creates a new understanding of the subjects compared

 WRITING TIP

A Venn diagram can help you explore the similarities and differences between two subjects. You might even consider using a Venn diagram in your final paper.

WRITING TIP

See page 817 of the Writing Handbook for information on using transitions in your compare-and-contrast writing.

WRITING HANDBOOK   **827**

🕐 ▬ **WRITING TIP** ▬

You may want to include in your essay a diagram or chart that shows the cause-and-effect relationship explained in your writing.

🕐 ▬ **WRITING TIP** ▬

You must test cause-and-effect relationships as you work. First, be sure that the first event you mention comes before the second event in time. Next, be sure that the effect you state could not have happened without the cause you state.

4.2   Cause and Effect

Cause-and-effect writing explains why something happened, why certain conditions exist, or what resulted from an action or a condition.

Organizing Cause-and-Effect Writing

Your organization will depend on your topic and purpose for writing. If your focus is on explaining the effects of an event, start by stating the cause and then explain the effects (Option 1). If you want to explain the causes of an event like the threat of Africanized bees to commercial beekeeping, first state the effect and then examine its causes (Option 2). Sometimes you'll want to describe a chain of cause-and-effect relationships (Option 3) to explore a topic such as the myths about the Africanized honeybee.

Option 1   **Example**

Cause to Effect
Cause
• Effect 1
• Effect 2
• Effect 3

Africanized bees began migrating to the United States from South America in the 1950s.

"Wild" Africanized bees have injured people at outdoor recreation events.

Africanized bees have threatened domestic beekeeping.

Africanized bees have upset the balance of the ecosystem.

Option 2

Effect to Cause
Effect
• Cause 1
• Cause 2
• Cause 3

Option 3

Cause-and-Effect Chain
Cause
↓
effect (cause)
↓
effect (cause)
↓
effect (cause)

828   WRITING HANDBOOK

4.3 Problem-Solution

Problem-solution writing clearly states a problem, analyzes the problem, and proposes a solution to the problem.

Organizing Problem-Solution Writing

Your organization will depend on the goal of your problem-solution piece, your intended audience, and the specific problem you choose to address. The organizational methods outlined below are effective for different kinds of problem-solution writing.

Option 1

Simple Problem-Solution

- Description of problem
- Why it needs to be solved
- Recommended solution
- Explanation of solution
- Conclusion

Example

Africanized bees have migrated to the United States since the 1950s.

Africanized bees threaten commercial beekeepers and are a danger to people and animals.

We should study the Africanized bees' behavior and try to keep them out of commercial hives.

Understanding the bees' behavior will protect humans; keeping the bees out of hives will maintain the gentle domestic breed.

Scientists need to work on this problem.

Option 2

Deciding Between Solutions

- **Description of problem**
- **Solution A**
  - Pros
  - Cons
- **Solution B**
  - Pros
  - Cons
- **Recommendation**

Example

Africanized bees have migrated to the United States since the 1950s.

Individuals and state government agencies need to address the threat of Africanized bees.

This will reduce the dangers of Africanized bees for commerce, people, and animals.

This solution doesn't stop the flow of Africanized bees into the United States.

We need to develop a pesticide to control the flow of Africanized bees into the United States.

WRITING TIP

Anticipate possible objections to your solution. You can strengthen your arguments by responding to the objections in a clear, reasonable way.

Writing Standards
A good analysis
▸ has a strong introduction and conclusion
▸ clearly states the subject and explains its parts
▸ uses a specific organizing structure
▸ uses transitions to connect thoughts
▸ uses language and details appropriate for the audience

4.4 Analysis

In an analysis you try to help your readers understand a subject by explaining how it works, how it is defined, or what its parts are.

The details you include will depend upon the kind of analysis you're writing.

- A **process analysis** should provide background information, such as definitions of terms and a list of needed equipment, and then explain each important step or stage in the process. For example, you might explain the steps for making a beehive or the stages of a bee's life.
- A **definition** should include the most important characteristics of the subject. To define a kind of bee, you might include such characteristics as scientific name, life cycle, and life function.
- A **parts analysis** should describe each part, group, or type that make up the subject. For example, you might analyze the parts of a bee's body or the main types of bees.

Organizing Your Analysis

Organize your details in a logical order appropriate for the kind of analysis you're writing. A process analysis is usually organized chronologically, with steps or stages in the order they occur.

Option 1   **Example**

Process Analysis

Introduce topic → Simple precautions can make your home safe from the Africanized honeybee.

Background information → The Africanized honeybee's reputation as a "killer" bee is exaggerated, but the bee can be a threat to your safety.

Explain steps

- Step 1 → Make your home "beeproof" by filling nesting sites such as holes in trees and walls.

- Step 2 → Look for active hives around your home, but do not remove a hive yourself. If you find active hives, contact a beekeeper to remove them.

- Step 3 → Watch for new hives in the spring and fall, when bees "swarm" to establish new colonies.

You can organize the details in a definition or a parts analysis in order of importance or impression. Characteristics in the following definition are organized from most to least obvious.

Option 2	Example
Definition	Africanized honeybees are also known as South American "killer bees."
Introduce term	
General definition	Africanized honeybees are crosses between domestic bees and aggressive African bees.
Explain qualities	The bees look like domestic honeybees but their behavior is different.
• Quality 1	
• Quality 2	The aggressiveness of the African bee ancestors is a dominant quality in the hybrid bees.
• Quality 3	The Africanized bee is not comfortable around animals or humans.
	An individual who threatens the bees may receive hundreds of stings and even die.

In the following parts analysis, different products of beekeeping are ordered from the most important to the least important.

Option 3	Example
Parts Analysis	Beekeeping is a productive industry.
Introduce subject	Many products come from beekeeping.
Explain how subject can be broken into parts	The primary product is honey, and the United States produces 250 million pounds each year.
• Part 1	
• Part 2	Other products are beeswax and royal jelly.
• Part 3	Honeybees pollinate more than 90 cultivated crops, affecting about every third bite of food that people eat.

WRITING TIP

Introductions You may want to begin with a vivid description of the subject to capture the reader's attention. For example, a description of swarming Africanized bees could introduce the process analysis on how to "beeproof" a home.

WRITING TIP

Conclusions Try ending an analysis by stating the importance of the subject to the reader. The parts analysis of beekeeping could conclude with a quick summary of all the different ways in which honeybees and beekeeping affect people in positive ways.

5 Persuasive Writing

Persuasive Writing

Persuasive writing allows you to use the power of language to inform and influence others.

Writing Standards

Good persuasive writing

▸ has a strong introduction

▸ clearly states the issue and the writer's position

▸ presents ideas logically

▸ answers opposing viewpoints

▸ ends with a strong argument or summary or a call for action

Key Techniques of Persuasive Writing

State Your Opinion

Taking a stand on an issue and clearly stating your opinion are essential to every piece of persuasive writing you do.

Example
Everyone should read "Waters of Gold." It teaches the importance of helping others and not expecting a reward for your kindness.

Know Your Audience

Knowing who will read your writing will help you decide what information you need to share and what tone you should use to communicate your message. In the example below, the writer has chosen an informal tone that is appropriate for a class newspaper.

Example
Do you ever feel that you could do more to help others? I just read a Chinese folk tale about a woman who shared all that she had in order to help others in need.

Support Your Opinion

Using reasons, examples, facts, statistics, and anecdotes to support your opinion will show your audience why you feel the way you do. Below, the writer gives a reason to support her opinion.

Example
We should all do what we can to help others. Knowing that we have done something worthwhile makes us feel good. Kind deeds are their own reward.

Organizing Persuasive Writing

In persuasive writing, you need to gather information to support your opinions. Here are some ways you can organize material to convince your audience.

Option 1

Reasons for Your Opinion

Your opinion
- Reason 1
- Reason 2
- Reason 3

Example

Everyone should read "Waters of Gold." It teaches the importance of helping others and not expecting a reward for your kindness.

It offers a model of behavior in the actions of Auntie Lily, who expects nothing for her kindness but is rewarded with a pail full of gold.

It makes an important moral point when a character is punished for pretending to be kind when she is actually greedy.

In real life, you probably won't be given gold for doing something kind, but reading the story will remind you of the value of good deeds.

Depending on the purpose and form of your writing, you may want to show the weaknesses of other opinions as you explain the strength of your own. Two options for organizing writing that includes more than just your side of the issue are shown below.

Option 2

Why Your Opinion Is Stronger

Your opinion
- your reasons

Other opinion
- evidence refuting reasons for other opinion and showing strengths of your opinion

Option 3

Why Another Opinion Is Weaker

Other opinion
- reasons

Your opinion
- reasons supporting your opinion and pointing out the weaknesses of the other side

Remember: Effective support for your opinion is often organized from the weakest argument to the strongest.

 LINK TO LITERATURE

The examples at the left are based on "Waters of Gold," a folk tale retold by Laurence Yep. The main character in the story, Auntie Lily, teaches others around her that "kindness comes with no price."

 WRITING TIP

Introductions Start a persuasive piece with a question, a surprising fact, or an anecdote to capture your readers' interest and make them want to keep reading.

 WRITING TIP

Conclusions The ending of a persuasive piece is often the part that sticks in a reader's mind. Your conclusion might summarize the two sides of an issue, restate your position, invite readers to make up their own minds, or call for some action.

Research Report Writing

In research report writing, you can find answers to questions about a topic. Your writing organizes information from various sources and presents it to your readers as a unified and coherent whole.

Key Techniques of Research Report Writing

Clarify Your Thesis

Your thesis statement explains to your reader what question your report will answer. In the example below, the writer's thesis statement answers the question "What did Eleanor Roosevelt do that made her such an important First Lady?"

Example

Eleanor Roosevelt's active participation in political and social issues changed the role of future First Ladies and offered a new vision for the roles of women in general.

Document Your Sources

You need to document, or credit, the sources where you find your information. In the example below, the writer uses a quotation and documents the source.

Example

Eleanor Roosevelt was tireless in her work. A joke in Washington was that President Roosevelt prayed every night, "Dear God, please make Eleanor a little tired" (Goodwin 41).

Support Your Ideas

You need to support your ideas with details and facts from reliable sources. In the example below, the writer uses a detail to explain how Eleanor Roosevelt helped women.

Example

To encourage newspapers to hire women, Eleanor Roosevelt did not allow men at her White House press conferences (Toor 63).

Finding and Evaluating Sources

Begin your research by looking for information about your topic in books, magazines, newspapers, and computer databases. In addition to using your library's card or computer catalog, look up your subject in indexes, such as the *Readers' Guide to Periodical Literature* or the *New York Times Index*. The bibliographies in books that you find during your research may also lead to additional sources. The following checklist will help you evaluate the reliability of the sources you find.

Checklist for Evaluating Your Sources	
Authoritative	Someone who has written several books or articles on your subject or whose work has been published in a well-respected newspaper or journal may be considered an authority.
Up-to-date	Check the publication date to see if the source reflects the most current research on your subject.
Respected	In general, tabloid newspapers and popular-interest magazines are not reliable sources. If you have questions about whether you are using a respected source, ask your librarian.

LINK TO LITERATURE

Your reading can inspire ideas for research topics. For example, after reading William Jay Jacobs's essay "Eleanor Roosevelt," on page 203, you may be interested in learning more about her. Jacobs's essay mentions some of Roosevelt's activity during World War II; the models in this section reflect more in-depth research of those activities.

Making Source Cards

For each source you find, record the bibliographic information on a separate index card. You will need this information to give credit to the sources in your paper. The samples at the right show how to make source cards for encyclopedia entries, magazine articles, and books. You will use the source number on each card to identify the notes you take during your research.

Taking Notes

As you find material that suits the purpose of your report, record each piece of information on a separate note card. You will probably use all three of the note-taking methods listed on the following page.

Encyclopedia Entry

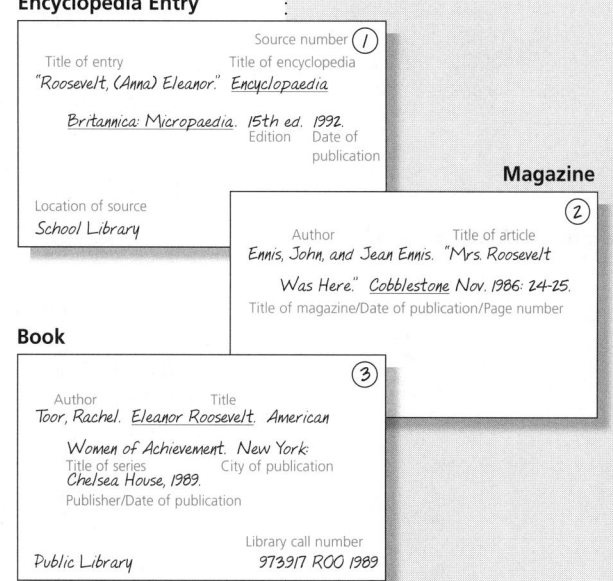

Source number ①
Title of entry · Title of encyclopedia
"Roosevelt, (Anna) Eleanor." *Encyclopaedia*

Britannica: Micropaedia. 15th ed. 1992.
Edition · Date of publication

Location of source
School Library

Magazine

②
Author · Title of article
Ennis, John, and Jean Ennis. "Mrs. Roosevelt

Was Here." *Cobblestone* Nov. 1986: 24-25.
Title of magazine/Date of publication/Page number

Book

③
Author · Title
Toor, Rachel. *Eleanor Roosevelt. American*

Women of Achievement. New York:
Title of series · City of publication
Chelsea House, 1989.
Publisher/Date of publication

Library call number
Public Library · 973.917 ROO 1989

Main idea
Source number ③
Visiting soldiers
During her 23,000-mile Pacific trip during
WWII, Eleanor Roosevelt visited over 400,000
soldiers at camps and hospitals on 17 different
islands. 82
Page number

(Paraphrase)
Type of note

- Paraphrase, or restate in your own words, the main ideas and supporting details from a passage.
- Summarize, or rephrase the original material in fewer words, trying to capture the key ideas.
- Quote, or copy the original text word for word, if you think the author's own words best clarify a particular point. Use quotation marks to signal the beginning and the end of the quotation.

Writing a Thesis Statement

A thesis statement in a research report defines the main idea, or overall purpose, of your report. A clear one-sentence answer to your main question will result in a good thesis statement.

Question: What did Eleanor Roosevelt do that made her such an important First Lady in American history?

Thesis Statement: Eleanor Roosevelt's active participation in political and social issues changed the role for future First Ladies and offered a new vision for the roles of women in general.

Making an Outline

To organize your report, group your note cards into main ideas and arrange them in a logical order. With your notes, make a topic outline, beginning with a shortened version of your thesis statement. Key ideas are listed after Roman numerals, and sub-points are listed after uppercase letters and Arabic numerals, as in the following example.

LINK TO LITERATURE

Note on page 208 William Jay Jacobs's use of a quotation in "Eleanor Roosevelt." The three periods (. . .) indicate an ellipsis, the leaving out of words from the quoted source. You can eliminate words that are unnecessary for your report as long as you do not alter the author's original meaning.

WRITING TIP

Use the same form for items of the same rank in your outline. For example, if A is a noun, then B and C should be nouns.

Eleanor Roosevelt: A First Among First Ladies
Introduction—Eleanor Roosevelt changed role of First Lady
and of all women
I. Background information about Eleanor Roosevelt
II. Her new vision for the role of the First Lady
A. Press conferences
B. Travel overseas
1. Visiting soldiers during WWII
2. Reporting to the War Department
C. Fight against injustices
III. Her contributions to women's rights

Documenting Your Sources

When you quote one of your sources or write in your own words information you have found in a source, you need to credit that source, using parenthetical documentation.

Guidelines for Parenthetical Documentation	
Work by One Author	Put the author's last name and the page reference in parentheses: **(Toor 29)**. If you mention the author's name in the sentence, put only the page reference in parentheses: **(29)**.
Work by Two or Three Authors	Put the authors' last names and the page reference in parentheses: **(Ennis and Ennis 24)**.
Work by More Than Three Authors	Give the first author's last name followed by *et al.*, and the page reference: **(Herzberg et al. 15)**.
Work with No Author Given	Give the title or a shortened version and the page reference: **("Roosevelt" 172)**.
One of Two or More Works by Same Author	Give the author's last name, the title or a shortened version, and the page reference: **(Roosevelt, This I Remember 59)**.

Creating a Works Cited Page

At the end of your research report, you need to include a Works Cited page. Any source that you have cited in your report needs to be listed alphabetically by the author's last name. If no author is given, use the editor's last name or the title of the work. Note the guidelines for spacing and punctuation on the model page.

WRITING TIP

Plagiarism Presenting someone else's writing or ideas as your own is plagiarism. To avoid plagiarism, you need to credit sources as noted at the left. However, if a piece of information is common knowledge—available in several sources—you do not need to credit the source. To see an example of parenthetical documentation, see the essay on page 524.

Student's last name   Page number

½"

Flores   14

Center heading   1"

Works Cited

1"—Ennis, John, and Jean Ennis. "Mrs. Roosevelt Was Here."

Cobblestone Nov. 1986: 24-25.

Goodwin, Doris Kearns. "The Home Front." The New   —1"—

Yorker 15 Aug. 1994: 38-61.

"Roosevelt, (Anna) Eleanor." Encyclopaedia Britannica:

Micropaedia. 15th ed. 1992.

Roosevelt, Eleanor. The Autobiography of Eleanor

Roosevelt. New York: De Capo, 1992.

Indent additional lines ½"

Double-space between all lines

2 spaces after periods

Getting Information Electronically

1

Electronic resources provide you with a convenient and efficient way to gather information.

1.1 On-line Resources

When you use your computer to communicate with another computer or with another person using a computer, you are working "on-line." On-line resources include commercial information services and information available on the Internet.

Commercial Information Services

You can subscribe to various services that offer information such as the following:

- up-to-date news, weather, and sports reports
- access to encyclopedias, magazines, newspapers, dictionaries, almanacs, and databases (collections of information)
- electronic mail (e-mail) to and from other users
- forums, or ongoing electronic conversations among users interested in a particular topic

Internet

The Internet is a vast network of computers. News services, libraries, universities, researchers, organizations, and government agencies use the Internet to communicate and to distribute information. The Internet includes two key features:

- **World Wide Web,** which provides you with information on particular subjects and links you to related topics and resources (such as the Web pages shown at the left)
- **Electronic mail** (e-mail), which allows you to communicate with other e-mail users worldwide

1.2 CD-ROM

A CD-ROM (compact disc–read-only memory) stores data that may include text, sound, photographs, and video.

Almost any kind of information can be found on CD-ROMs, which you can use at the library or purchase, including

- encyclopedias, almanacs, and indexes
- other reference books on a variety of subjects
- news reports from newspapers, magazines, television, or radio
- museum art collections
- back issues of magazines
- literature collections

1.3 Library Computer Services

Many libraries offer computerized catalogs and a variety of other electronic resources.

Computerized Catalogs

You may search for a book in a library by typing the title, author, subject, or key words into a computer terminal. For example, if you ask for titles by Avi, you'll see a screen like the one at the right. Then you can find out more about one title, including its call number and whether it is on the shelf or checked out. When a particular work is not available, you may be able to search the catalogs of other libraries.

Other Electronic Resources

In addition to computerized catalogs, many libraries offer electronic versions of books or other reference materials. They may also have a variety of indexes on CD-ROM, which allow you to search for magazine or newspaper articles on any topic you choose. Ask your librarian for assistance in using these resources.

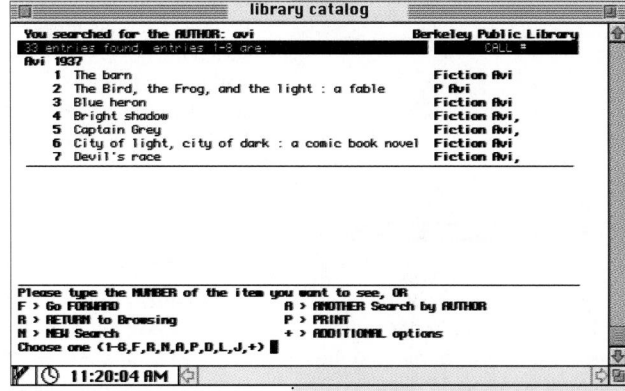

MULTIMEDIA HANDBOOK **839**

2 Word Processing

- Computer
- Word-processing program
- Printer

Word-processing programs allow you to draft, revise, edit, and format your writing and to produce neat, professional-looking papers. They also allow you to share your writing with others.

2.1 Revising and Editing

Improving the quality of your writing becomes easier when you use a word-processing program to revise and edit.

Revising a Document

Most word-processing programs allow you to make the following kinds of changes:

- add or delete words
- move text from one location in your document to another
- undo a change you have made in the text
- save a document with a new name, allowing you to keep old drafts for reference
- view more than one document at a time, so you can copy text from one document and add it to another

Editing a Document

Many word-processing programs have the following features to help you catch errors and polish your writing:

- The **spell checker** automatically finds misspelled words and suggests possible corrections.
- The **grammar checker** spots possible grammatical errors and suggests ways you might correct them.
- The **thesaurus** suggests synonyms for a word you want to replace.
- The **dictionary** will give you the definitions of words so you can be sure you have used words correctly.
- The **search and replace** feature searches your whole document and corrects every occurrence of something you want to change, such as a misspelled name.

WRITING TIP

Even if you use a spell checker, you should still proofread your draft carefully to make sure you've used the right words. For example, you may have used *there* or *they're* when you meant to use *their*.

2.2 Formatting Your Work

Format is the layout and appearance of your writing on the page. You may choose your formatting options before or after you write.

Formatting Type

You may want to make changes in the typeface, type size, and type style of the words in your document. For each of these, your word-processing program will most likely have several options to choose from. These options allow you to

- change the typeface to create a different look for the words in your document
- change the type size of the entire document or of just the headings of sections in the paper
- change the type style when necessary; for example, use italics or underline for the titles of books and magazines

Typeface	Size	Style
Geneva	7-point Times	*Italic*
Times	10-point Times	**Bold**
Chicago	12-point Times	<u>Underline</u>
`Courier`	14-point Times	

Formatting Pages

Not only can you change the way individual words look; you can also change the way they are arranged on the page. Some of the formatting decisions you make will depend on how you plan to use a printout of a draft or on the guidelines of an assignment.

- Set the line spacing, or the amount of space you need between lines of text. Double spacing is commonly used for final drafts.

Centered

Things to Buy

Our class voted to buy the following items with money we raised from our magazine sale:

Bigger fish tank $48.95
Microscope $65.00
Class library books $50.00
Total $163.95

Left-aligned

Right-aligned

- Set the margins, or the amount of white space around the edges of your text. A one-inch margin on all sides is commonly used for final drafts.
- Create a header for the top of the page or a footer for the bottom if you want to include such information as your name, the date, or the page number on every page.
- Determine the alignment of your text. The screen at the left shows your options.

WRITING TIP

Keep your format simple. Your goal is to create not only an attractive document but also one that is easy to read. Your readers will have difficulty if you change the type formatting frequently.

TECHNOLOGY TIP

Some word-processing programs or other software packages provide preset templates, or patterns, for writing outlines, memos, letters, newsletters, or invitations. If you use one of these templates, you will not need to adjust the formatting.

Some word-processing programs, such as the Writing Coach software referred to in this book, allow you to leave notes for your peer readers in the side column or in a separate text box. If you wish, leave those areas blank so your readers can write comments or questions.

2.3 Working Collaboratively

Computers allow you to share your writing electronically. Send a copy of your work to someone via e-mail or put it in someone's drop box if your computer is linked to other computers on a network. Then use the feedback of your peers to help you improve the quality of your writing.

Peer Editing on a Computer

The writer and the reader can both benefit from the convenience of peer editing "on screen," or at the computer.

- Be sure to save your current draft and then make a copy of it for each of your peer readers.
- You might have each peer reader enter his or her comments in a different typeface or type style from the one you used for your text.
- Ask each of your readers to include his or her initials in the file name.
- If your computer allows you to open more than one file at a time, open each reviewer's file and refer to the files as you revise your draft.

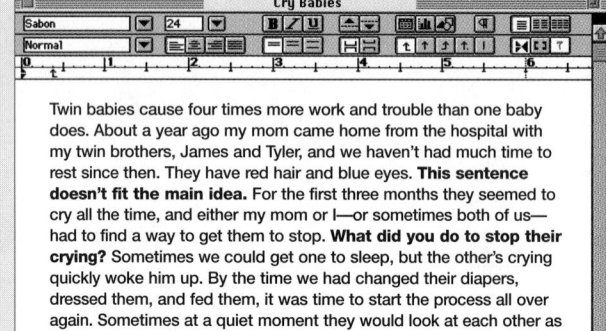

Twin babies cause four times more work and trouble than one baby does. About a year ago my mom came home from the hospital with my twin brothers, James and Tyler, and we haven't had much time to rest since then. They have red hair and blue eyes. **This sentence doesn't fit the main idea.** For the first three months they seemed to cry all the time, and either my mom or I—or sometimes both of us—had to find a way to get them to stop. **What did you do to stop their crying?** Sometimes we could get one to sleep, but the other's crying quickly woke him up. By the time we had changed their diapers, dressed them, and fed them, it was time to start the process all over again. Sometimes at a quiet moment they would look at each other as if to say, "Whose turn is it to cry this time?" **Aren't there good things too? You could add something about these.**

Peer Editing on a Printout

Some peer readers prefer to respond to a draft on paper rather than on the computer.

- Double-space or triple-space your document so that your peer editor can make suggestions between the lines.
- Leave extra-wide margins to give your readers room to note their reactions and questions as they read.
- Print out your draft and photocopy it if you want to share it with more than one reader.

Using Visuals

3

Tables, graphs, diagrams, and pictures often communicate information more effectively than words alone do. Many computer programs allow you to create visuals to use with written text.

3.1 When to Use Visuals

Use visuals in your work to illustrate complex concepts and processes or to make a page look more interesting.

Although you should not expect a visual to do all the work of written text, combining words and pictures or graphics can increase the understanding and enjoyment of your writing. Many computer programs allow you to create and insert graphs, tables, time lines, diagrams, and flow charts into your document. An art program allows you to create border designs for a title page or to draw an unusual character or setting for narrative or descriptive writing. You may also be able to add clip art, or premade pictures, to your document. Clip art can be used to illustrate an idea or concept in your writing or to make your writing more appealing for young readers.

3.2 Kinds of Visuals

The visuals you choose will depend on the type of information you want to present to your readers.

Tables

Tables allow you to arrange facts or numbers into rows and columns so that your reader can compare information more easily. In many word-processing programs, you can create a table by choosing the number of vertical columns and horizontal rows you need and then entering information in each box, as the illustration shows.

WHAT YOU'LL NEED

- A graphics program to create visuals
- Access to clip-art files from a CD-ROM, a computer disk, or an on-line service

TECHNOLOGY TIP

A spreadsheet program provides you with a preset table for your statistics and performs any necessary calculations.

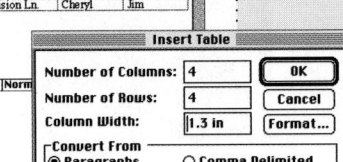

Graphs and Charts

You can sometimes use a graph or chart to help communicate complex information in a clear visual image. For example, you could use a line graph to show how a trend changes over time, a bar graph to compare statistics from different years, or a pie chart, like the one at the right, to compare percentages. You might want to explore ways of displaying data in more than one visual format before deciding which will work best for you.

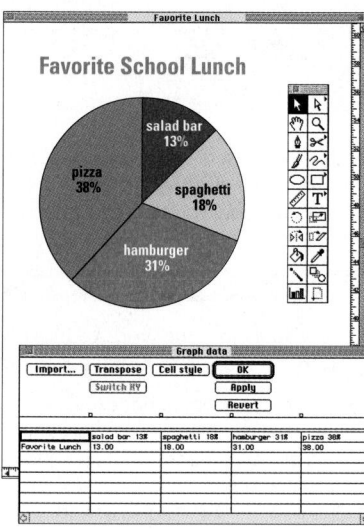

Other Visuals

Art and design programs allow you to create visuals for your writing. Many programs include the following features:

- drawing tools that allow you to draw, color, and shade pictures
- clip art that you can copy or change with drawing tools
- page borders that you can use to decorate title pages, brochures, or invitations, such as the one shown at the left
- text options that allow you to combine words with your illustrations
- tools for making geometric shapes in flow charts, time lines, and diagrams that show a process or sequence of events

844 MULTIMEDIA HANDBOOK

Creating a Multimedia Presentation

4

A multimedia presentation is a combination of text, sound, and visuals such as photographs, videos, and animation. Your audience reads, hears, and sees your presentation at a computer, following different "paths" you create to lead the user through the information you have gathered.

4.1 Features of Multimedia Programs

To start planning your multimedia presentation, you need to know what options are available to you. You can combine sound, photos, videos, and animation to enhance any text you write about your topic.

Sound

Including sound in your presentation can help your audience understand information in your written text. For example, the user may be able to listen and learn from

- the pronunciation of an unfamiliar or foreign word
- a speech
- a recorded news interview
- a musical selection
- a dramatic reading of a work of literature

Photos and Videos

Photographs and live-action videos can make your subject come alive for the user. Here are some examples:

- videotaped news coverage of a historical event
- videos of music, dance, or theater performances
- charts and diagrams
- photos of an artist's work
- photos or video of a geographical setting that is important to the written text

WHAT YOU'LL NEED

- Individual programs to create and edit the text, graphics, sound, and videos you will use
- A multimedia authoring program that allows you to combine these elements and create links between the screens

Animation

Many graphics programs allow you to add animation, or movement, to the visuals in your presentation. Animated figures add to the user's enjoyment and understanding of what you present. You can use animation to illustrate

- what happens in a story
- the steps in a process
- changes in a chart, graph, or diagram
- how your user can explore information in your presentation

4.2 Planning Your Presentation

To create a multimedia presentation, first choose your topic and decide what you want to include. Then plan how you want your user to move through your presentation.

Imagine that you are creating a multimedia presentation about the 1980 volcanic eruption of Mount Saint Helens in the state of Washington. You know you want to include the following items:

- text describing the 1980 volcanic eruption of Mount Saint Helens
- animated diagram showing what happens when a volcano erupts
- photo of the eruption
- recorded interviews with people affected by the eruption
- video of rescue work and cleanup after the eruption
- photo of Mount Saint Helens today, showing how much vegetation has grown back
- text about current volcano research

You can choose one of the following ways to organize your presentation:

- step by step with only one path, or order, in which the user can see and hear the information
- a branching path that allows users to make some choices about what they will see and hear, and in what order

A flow chart can help you figure out the path a user can take through your presentation. Each box in the flow chart on the following page represents something about Mount Saint Helens for the audience to read, see, or hear. The arrows on the flow chart show a branching path the user can follow.

Whenever boxes branch in more than one direction, it means that the user can choose which item to see or hear first.

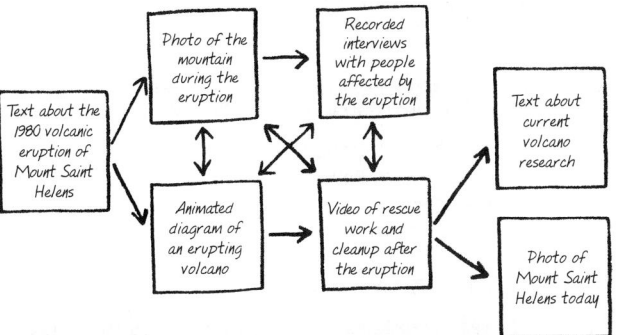

4.3 Guiding Your User

Your user will need directions to follow the path you have planned for your multimedia presentation.

Most multimedia authoring programs allow you to create screens that include text or audio directions that guide the user from one part of your presentation to the next. In the example below, the user can choose between several paths, and directions on the screen explain how to make the choice.

If you need help creating your multimedia presentation, ask your school's technology adviser. You may also be able to get help from your classmates or your software manual.

WRITING TIP

You usually need permission from the person or organization that owns the copyright on materials if you want to copy them. You do not need permission, however, if you are not making money from your presentation, if you use it only for educational purposes, and if you use only a small percentage of the original material.

Navigational buttons take the user back and forth, one screen at a time.

The user clicks on a button to select any of these options.

This screen shows a picture of Mount Saint Helens.

Writing Complete Sentences

1

1.1 Sentence Fragments

A sentence fragment is a group of words that does not express a complete thought. It may be missing a subject, a predicate, or both. A sentence fragment makes you wonder *What is this about?* or *What happened?*

Missing Subject or Predicate

You can correct a sentence fragment by adding the missing subject or predicate to complete the thought.

> *The Monsters Are Due on Maple Street* is a spooky tale.
> It
> ∧ Tells about ordinary neighbors turning into a mob.
>   *sometimes get violent*
> Fearful people ∧.

Phrase and Subordinate-Clause Fragments

When the fragment is a phrase or a subordinate clause, you may join the fragment to an existing sentence.

> Under normal circumstances, The conflicts neighbors
> have with one another are easy to ignore. However,
> these unresolved problems can suddenly become huge,
> When a crisis threatens.

APPLY WHAT YOU'VE LEARNED

Rewrite this paragraph, correcting the sentence fragments.

[1]In *The Monsters Are Due on Maple Street.* **[2]**Normal social bonds were broken. **[3]**The small amount of community feeling that existed on Maple Street. **[4]**Was quickly destroyed. **[5]**A sense of community is necessary. **[6]**If people are to live together safely and happily. **[7]**The earliest human communities came into being. **[8]**When the need for safety arose. **[9]**Neighbors in a community.

[10]Give one another practical and emotional support. **[11]**They work to resolve. **[12]**Problems among members rather than ignoring conflict. **[13]**Even neighbors who live close together. **[14]**Do not necessarily share similar values. **[15]**Is essential in building a strong, stable community. **[16]**A true community. **[17]**Might have been able to stand up to the outside threat posed in this teleplay. **[18]**Without community Maple Street.

1.2 Run-on Sentences

A run-on sentence consists of two or more sentences written incorrectly as one. A run-on sentence occurs because the writer either used no end mark or used a comma instead of a period to end the first complete thought. A run-on sentence may confuse readers because it does not show where one thought ends and the next begins.

Forming Separate Sentences

One way to correct a run-on sentence is to form two separate sentences. Use a period or other end punctuation after the first sentence, and capitalize the first letter of the next sentence.

> In "The Chief's Daughter" a girl named Nessan does what she knows is right she must, however, be ready to pay a high price. Nessan takes responsibility for her own actions she shows great courage.

  LINK TO LITERATURE

In "The Chief's Daughter" Rosemary Sutcliff writes long sentences that sometimes look like run-ons. These sentences might look complicated, but they are actually clear and easy to understand. Sutcliff's logical grouping of thoughts and careful use of punctuation guarantee clarity.

Forming Compound Sentences

You can also correct a run-on sentence by rewriting it to form a compound sentence. One way to do this is by using a comma and a coordinating conjunction.

Never join simple sentences with a comma alone, or a run-on sentence will result. You need a comma followed by a conjunction such as *and, but,* or *or* to hold the sentences together.

> Nessan's decision saved Dara's life, *and* it also restored the village's water supply.

You may use a semicolon to join two ideas that are closely related.

In addition, you can correct a run-on sentence by using a semicolon and a conjunctive adverb. Commonly used conjunctive adverbs are *however, therefore, nevertheless,* and *besides.*

> Nessan chose not to take the easy way out, she refused to let anyone else suffer for choices she had made. She faced her fear, *besides,* she learned more about her elders.

1.2 Run-on Sentences

Answers will vary. See typical answers below.

1 In "The Chief's Daughter" Irish raiders come to Wales; they steal cattle and take people as slaves. **2** This story reflects real archaeological discoveries about life back then. Researchers think the raiding was caused by several factors. **3** First, people could travel freely; they had learned to cross small stretches of water and to ride on horseback. **4** It was easy for them to invade other people's territories; however, it was dangerous. **5** Second, populations were increasing; therefore, the best land was always taken. **6** People had to clear new land for crops and pasture for animals. Thousands of years earlier, people had used flint axes to cut down forests to make space for farms. **7** At the time of the story, people had begun to use other land that was not well suited for agriculture, and they had to abandon it when it no longer produced enough food. **8** It was easier to raid than to find enough good land to cultivate; therefore, the raiders probably thought they had no choice.

APPLY WHAT YOU'VE LEARNED

Rewrite this paragraph, correcting the run-on sentences.

1In "The Chief's Daughter" Irish raiders come to Wales they steal cattle and take people as slaves. **2**This story reflects real archaeological discoveries about life back then, researchers think the raiding was caused by several factors. **3**First, people could travel freely they had learned to cross small stretches of water and to ride on horseback. **4**It was easy for them to invade other people's territories it was dangerous. **5**Second, populations were increasing, the best land was always taken. **6**People had to clear new land for crops and pasture for animals, thousands of years earlier, people had used flint axes to cut down forests to make space for farms. **7**At the time of the story, people had begun to use other land that was not well suited for agriculture they had to abandon it when it no longer produced enough food. **8**It was easier to raid than to find enough good land to cultivate the raiders probably thought they had no choice.

Making Subjects and Verbs Agree

2

2.1 Simple and Compound Subjects

A verb must agree in number with its subject. *Number* refers to whether a word is singular or plural. When a word refers to one thing, it is singular. When a word refers to more than one thing, it is plural.

Agreement with Simple Subjects

Use a singular verb with a singular subject.

When the subject is a singular noun, you use the singular form of the verb. The present-tense singular form of a regular verb usually ends in *-s* or *-es*.

> In "Lose Now, Pay Later" Deb use her money to pay
> for a weight-loss treatment. Her brother warn her about
> another payment.

Use a plural verb with a plural subject.

> Deb's friends knows nothing about the future.

Agreement with Compound Subjects

Use a plural verb with a compound subject whose parts are joined by *and*, regardless of the number of each part.

> Deb and her friend discovers a sweet shop that provides
> delicious desserts called swoodies.

REVISING TIP

To find the subject of a sentence, first find the verb. Then ask *who* or *what* performs the action of the verb. Say the subject and the verb together to see if they agree.

GRAMMAR HANDBOOK **851**

When the parts of a compound subject are joined by *or* or *nor*, make the verb agree in number with the part that is closer to it.

Usually *or* and *nor* appear with their correlatives *either* and *neither*.

Neither Deb nor her brother know^s for sure who is running the dessert machines or the slimmers. They argue about whether a smart human or some scheming aliens controls them.

2.1 Simple and Compound Subjects

1. provide
2. open
3. use
4. gets
5. consists
6. become
7. research
8. learn
9. discovers
10. prove
11. lose
12. involve

APPLY WHAT YOU'VE LEARNED

Write the correct form of the verb given in parentheses.

1. In the science fiction story "Lose Now, Pay Later," shops (provide, provides) free desserts that tempt people to eat them and gain weight.
2. Instant weight-loss machines mysteriously (opens, open) soon after.
3. In real life the people who invest in shops and machines (use, uses) the science called marketing.
4. Neither the buyers nor the seller (get, gets) results without marketing.
5. A market (consist, consists) of possible customers for a product or service.
6. In the story Deb and her friend (becomes, become) part of this group.
7. In real life the investors (researches, research) the market.
8. The investors (learn, learns) a lot about what people like best.
9. Either they or their researcher also (discovers, discover) the best prices for products and services.
10. If the investors' predictions (prove, proves) wrong, people might not use the product or service.
11. Then the investors (lose, loses) their money.
12. Investments and experiments always (involve, involves) risk.

2.2 Pronoun Subjects

When a pronoun is used as a subject, the verb must agree with it in number.

Agreement with Personal Pronouns

When the subject is a singular personal pronoun, use a singular verb. When the subject is a plural personal pronoun, use a plural verb.

Even though *I* and *you* are singular, they take the plural form of the verb.

> In the excerpt from *Commodore Perry in the Land of the Shogun*, Perry seems like a smart diplomat. He are ~~are~~ *is* more than just a ship's captain, I thinks.

When *he, she,* or *it* is the part of the subject closer to the verb in a compound subject containing *or* or *nor*, use a singular verb. When a pronoun is a part of a compound subject containing *and*, use a plural verb.

> When the commodore and his battleships enters Edo Bay, neither the Americans nor he hesitate *s* in the mission.

Agreement with Indefinite Pronouns

When the subject is a singular indefinite pronoun, use the singular form of the verb.

The following are singular indefinite pronouns: *another, either, nobody, anybody, everybody, somebody, no one, anyone, everyone, someone, one, nothing, anything, everything, something, each,* and *neither*.

> Everybody agree *s* that Perry played a dangerous game, one of great risk to Japanese citizens.

LINK TO LITERATURE

Notice how the agreement of pronoun subjects with verbs in the excerpt from Rhoda Blumberg's *Commodore Perry in the Land of the Shogun,* pages 506–514, makes it easy for her to discuss complex events. Correct grammatical construction gives readers a clear view of the incidents the author describes.

When the subject is a plural indefinite pronoun *(both, few, many,* or *several)*, use the plural form of the verb.

> Few ignores the meaning of huge gunboats entering a foreign harbor. Many agrees that this act is an aggressive one.

The indefinite pronouns *some, all, any, none,* and *most* can be either singular or plural. When the pronoun refers to one thing, use a singular verb. When the pronoun refers to several things, use a plural verb.

> Some wonders whether the United States ever has the right to pressure another nation as Perry did. All of the evidence show, however, that he was determined to avoid battle if he could.

2.2 Pronoun Subjects

1. learns
2. think
3. remember
4. were
5. were
6. seem
7. disagree
8. seem
9. appear
10. show

APPLY WHAT YOU'VE LEARNED

Write the correct form of the verb given in parentheses.

1. In *Commodore Perry in the Land of the Shogun* one (learn, learns) how Matthew Perry was ahead of his time.
2. Among students of history, some (thinks, think) that his success in Japan set the tone for later U.S. foreign policy.
3. Most (remember, remembers), however, that the Japanese knew the fate of the Chinese in 1842 in the Opium War.
4. Neither they nor the Chinese (was, were) able to resist the advanced weapons of the Western nations.
5. Actually, the Japanese and Perry (was, were) quite likely to forge an agreement without violence.
6. Of the parties to this conflict, both (seem, seems) to have acted wisely.
7. Few (disagrees, disagree) about what Perry wanted: he and others urged the United States to compete with European powers in the Pacific.
8. He and they (seem, seems) to have thought alike.
9. All (appear, appears) to have agreed on the importance of gaining Pacific island bases for commercial and naval ships.
10. European and American leaders felt it was important that they (show, shows) strength in the region.

2.3 Common Agreement Problems

Several other situations can cause problems in subject-verb agreement.

Agreement with Irregular Verbs

Use the singular forms of the irregular verbs *do, be,* and *have* with singular subjects. Use the plural forms of these verbs with plural subjects.

	Do	Be	Have
Singular Subjects	I do you do the dog does it does each doesn't	I am/was you are/were Joe is/was he isn't/wasn't either is/was	I have you have Pat hasn't she has anybody has
Plural Subjects	we do dogs do they do many don't	we are/were boys are/were they are/were both are/were	we have girls have they haven't few have

The selection "Eleanor Roosevelt" do^es much to show the struggle of a dynamic first lady, and it ~~have~~ *has* some insights into her success. Eleanor ~~are~~ *is* a splendid achiever; she ~~have~~ *has* qualities that anyone can cultivate.

Interrupting Words

Be sure the verb agrees with its subject when a word or words come between them.

Sometimes one or more words come between the subject and the verb. The interrupter does not affect the number of the subject.

Eleanor, moreover, encourage^s the hiring of female reporters by closing her press conferences to men.

 REVISING TIP

Look carefully at words that come before the verb to find the subject. Remember that the subject may not be the noun or pronoun closest to the verb.

In the section of "Eleanor Roosevelt" that appears on page 205, notice how William Jay Jacobs makes subjects and verbs agree in spite of words or phrases that separate them. This skill allows him to add more information to each sentence and to vary the rhythm of the sentences.

Interrupting Phrases

Be certain that the verb agrees with its subject when a phrase comes between them.

The subject of a verb is never found in a prepositional phrase, which may follow the subject and come before the verb.

> Eleanor, in spite of several tragedies in her life, triumph[S] over adversity.
>
> This woman of many talents rank[S] high in the list of great Americans.

Phrases beginning with *including, as well as, along with,* and *in addition to* are not part of the subject.

> Her mother's coldness, as well as her father's alcoholism, create[S] a challenging situation for a young child.
>
> Eleanor's strong will, along with her other outstanding qualities, make[S] her a wonderful role model.

The subject of the verb is never found in an appositive, which may follow the subject and come before the verb.

> Eleanor, one of several self-trained diplomats, help[S] create the United Nations after World War II.
>
> Her assistants, a dedicated group, still sings her praises.

Inverted Sentences

When the subject comes after the verb, be sure the verb agrees with the subject in number.

A sentence in which the subject follows the verb is called an inverted sentence. Questions are usually in inverted form, as are sentences beginning with *here, there,* and *where.* (*Where are the reporters? There is a press conference today.*)

> Where do^es Eleanor find the courage to overcome her
> shyness? How do^es she grow during her life? Does other
> first ladies follow her example? There is^are many more
> questions we would like answered about the great lady,
> Eleanor Roosevelt.

 REVISING TIP

To check subject-verb agreement in inverted sentences, place the subject before the verb. For example, change *there are many duties* to *many duties are there* to check agreement.

APPLY WHAT YOU'VE LEARNED

Write the correct form of each verb given in parentheses.

1. Readers, while examining "Eleanor Roosevelt," (learn, learns) about the powerful influence that a father can have on his daughter.
2. Eleanor's father, in spite of his faults, (seem, seems) to have helped her feel unconditionally loved.
3. However, Eleanor's mother, in addition to the rest of the family, (was, were) relatively cold to her and filled her with self-doubt.
4. There (was, were) a sort of second mother to Eleanor, who lived near London.
5. How (is, are) Eleanor's early years related to her later achievements?
6. Joseph Lash, one of her biographers, (note, notes) that her childhood loneliness helped her understand all people who were left out.
7. Her heredity, as far as Eleanor was concerned, (appear, appears) to explain her great energy.
8. Looking back, she calmly recalls, "I think I (have, has) a good deal of my uncle Theodore in me. . . ."
9. What do you think (was, were) her greatest achievement?
10. *Presidential Wives,* one of several books by Paul Boller, (remind, reminds) us of the vitality of women like Eleanor.

2.3 Common Agreement Problems

1. learn
2. seems
3. was
4. was
5. are
6. notes
7. appears
8. have
9. was
10. reminds

3 Using Nouns and Pronouns

LINK TO LITERATURE

In "The Charge of the Light Brigade" on page 298, Tennyson does what many poets do. He changes words, including noun plurals, to make his lines rhyme and to give them the correct number of syllables. In the third stanza he uses "shell" for "shells," and in the fifth stanza he uses "horse and hero" for "horses and heroes."

REVISING TIP

The plurals of many musical terms that end in *o* preceded by a consonant are formed by adding -*s*. These nouns include *tempos* and *concertos*.

3.1 Plural and Possessive Nouns

Nouns refer to people, places, things, and ideas. Nouns are plural when they refer to more than one person, place, thing, or idea. Possessive nouns show who or what owns something.

Plural Nouns

Follow these guidelines to form noun plurals.

Nouns	To Form Plural	Examples
Most nouns	add -*s*	jaw—jaws
Most nouns that end in *s, sh, ch, x,* or *z*	add -*es*	fox—foxes flash—flashes
Most nouns that end in *ay, ey, oy,* or *uy*	add -*s*	delay—delays valley—valleys
Most nouns that end in a consonant and *y*	change *y* to *i* and add -*es*	cavalry—cavalries casualty—casualties
Most nouns that end in *o*	add -*s*	alto—altos arroyo—arroyos soprano—sopranos
Some nouns that end in a consonant and *o*	add -*es*	echo—echoes hero—heroes tomato—tomatoes
Most nouns that end in *f* or *fe*	change *f* to *v* and add -*es* or -*s*	sheaf—sheaves knife—knives *but* belief—beliefs

Some nouns use the same spelling in both singular and plural: *series, fish, sheep, cannon.* Some noun plurals use an irregular form that doesn't follow any rule: *teeth, geese.*

In "The Charge of the Light Brigade" the ~~heros~~ *heroes* endured hideous ~~vollies~~ *volleys* and ~~flashs~~ *flashes* of exploding shell*s*. Those whose ~~lifes~~ *lives* were spared would never forget their brush with death.

Possessive Nouns

Follow these guidelines to form possessive nouns.

Nouns	To Form Possessive	Examples
Singular nouns	add apostrophe and -*s*	league—league's
Plural nouns ending in *s*	add apostrophe	fields—fields' brigades—brigades'
Plural nouns not ending in *s*	add apostrophe and -*s*	children—children's oxen—oxen's

The poet showed the men*'s* plight—and their horse*'s*— as they fell that day. These soldiers were victims of carefully placed artillery and of their leader*s'* mistakes.

APPLY WHAT YOU'VE LEARNED

Write the correct noun given in parentheses.

1 "The Charge of the Light Brigade" describes the massacre of cavalry by artillery (volleys, vollies) during the Crimean War. **2** The Crimean War involved several nations because each side had (allies, allys, allies'). **3** This (war's, wars') toll was extreme. **4** About half a million (mens, men) died in it. **5** The (brigades, brigades', brigade's) mission was to ride straight into the (artillery's, artilleries) line of fire. **6** Cavalry were soldiers on horseback, armed only with (sabers, saber's). **7** (Swords', Sword's) hilts often were brass, and some protected the entire hand. **8** (Artillery, Artillerie) during this war consisted mostly of bronze cannons on two-wheeled carts. **9** Wind force and direction affected the (cannonball's, cannonballs') paths. **10** Cavalry were overcome by guns because their (weapon's, weapons') use was limited to hand-to-hand combat. **11** The (heroes, heros) of this charge were the 600 who obeyed orders.

REVISING TIP

The dictionary usually lists the plural form of a noun if the plural form is irregular or if there is more than one plural form. Dictionary listings are especially helpful for nouns that end in *o*, *f*, and *fe*.

REVISING TIP

Be careful when placing apostrophes in possessive plural nouns. A misplaced apostrophe changes the word's meaning. For example, *boy's* refers to possession by one boy, but *boys'* refers to possession by more than one boy.

3.1 Plural and Possessive Nouns

1. volleys
2. allies
3. war's
4. men
5. brigade's; artillery's
6. sabers
7. Swords'
8. Artillery
9. cannonballs'
10. weapons'
11. heroes

A personal pronoun is a pronoun that can be used in the first, second, or third person. A personal pronoun has three forms: the subject form, the object form, and the possessive form.

Subject Pronouns

Use the subject form of a pronoun when it is the subject of a sentence or the subject of a clause. *I, you, he, she, it, we,* and *they* are subject pronouns.

Using the correct pronoun form is seldom a problem when the sentence has just one pronoun. Problems can arise, however, when a noun and a pronoun or two pronouns are used in a compound subject or compound object. To see if you are using the correct pronoun form, read the sentence, using only one pronoun.

> "A Christmas Carol" tells the familiar tale of Scrooge.
> *He*
> ~~Him~~ and the three Spirits of Christmas stage a drama.
> Afterward, Scrooge's cold heart is transformed.

Use the subject form of a pronoun when it follows a linking verb as a predicate pronoun.

You often hear the object form used in casual conversation as a predicate pronoun. ("It is him.") For this reason, the subject form may sound awkward to you, though it is preferred for more formal writing.

> The Spirits showed Scrooge what his future would be
> *he*
> like. It was ~~him~~, however, who made important changes
> that night in his outlook.

Object Pronouns

Use the object form of a pronoun when it is the object of a sentence, the object of a clause, or the object of a preposition. *Me, you, him, her, it, us,* and *them* are object pronouns.

> The events of Scrooge's Christmas Eve changed ~~he~~ *him* for
> the better. The next day, Scrooge's new approach to the
> Cratchit family worked wonders for ~~they~~ *them*.

Possessive Pronouns

Never use an apostrophe in a possessive pronoun. *My, mine, your, yours, his, her, hers, its, our, ours, their,* and *theirs* are possessive pronouns.

Writers often confuse the possessive pronouns *its, your,* and *their* with the contractions *it's, you're,* and *they're.* Remember that the pairs are spelled differently and that they have different meanings.

> Scrooge thanked the Spirits for ~~they're~~ *their* help. Then, on
> Christmas morning, he sent a turkey to the Cratchits.
> To him, ~~it's~~ *its* price was small for the joy it would give.

APPLY WHAT YOU'VE LEARNED

Write the correct pronoun form given in parentheses.

1Charles Dickens wrote *A Christmas Carol* in 1843, when (he, him) was 31 years old. **2**This work of (him, his) was written in only a few weeks. **3**In 1836 he was a famous writer; that year (he, him) and Catherine Hogarth were married. **4**(He, Him) was famous enough to tour America in 1842. **5**Did you know that it was (him, he) who wrote other novels about Christmas? **6**All of (they're, their) dates of composition are from the 1840s. **7**(They, Them) include the rest of the books mentioned here, such as *The Chimes,* published in 1844. **8**The next year saw another Christmas book of (his, him), *The Cricket on the Hearth.* **9**The year following, *The Battle of Life* took (it's, its) place among his titles. **10**Finally, *The Haunted Man,* an 1848 effort, was (him, his). **11**These books are said to be part of the first phase of (his', his) works. **12**(Them, They) have rather serious themes mixed with some humor. **13**When Thackeray, a fellow writer, reviewed *A Christmas Carol,* he said that (its, it's) publication was a national benefit.

3.2 Pronoun Forms

1. he
2. his
3. he
4. He
5. he
6. their
7. They
8. his
9. its
10. his
11. his
12. They
13. its

An antecedent is the noun or pronoun to which a personal pronoun refers. The antecedent usually precedes the pronoun.

Pronoun and Antecedent Agreement

A pronoun must agree with its antecedent in
- number—singular or plural
- person—first, second, or third
- gender—male or female

Use a singular pronoun to refer to a singular antecedent; use a plural pronoun to refer to a plural antecedent.

Do not allow interrupting words to determine the number of the personal pronoun.

> In "The Medicine Bag" Martin let his fear of ridicule
>
> and embarrassment influence him. If he had ignored
>
> ~~them~~, *it* he could have felt more at ease with his Teton
>
> Sioux great-grandfather.

If the antecedent is a noun that could be either male or female, use *he* or *she* (*him* or *her, his* or *her*) or reword the sentence to avoid the need for a singular pronoun.

> Each one of Cheryl's friends got to visit Grandpa, and
> *he or she*
> ~~they~~ excitedly told ~~their~~ *his or her* other friends about him.
> Or
> *All*
> ~~Each one~~ of Cheryl's friends got to visit Grandpa, and
> they excitedly told their other friends about him.

Be sure that the antecedent of a pronoun is clear.

In most cases, do not use a pronoun to refer to an entire idea or clause. Writing is much clearer if the exact reference is repeated.

LINK TO LITERATURE

In "The Medicine Bag," starting on page 285, Virginia Driving Hawk Sneve writes as a teenage boy, Martin. Her use of language is casual. Still, the pronouns she uses agree with their antecedents. The agreement keeps her story easy to understand.

One of Martin's worries was what his friends would

think of Grandpa. ~~They~~ *Martin's concerns* were hard for him to ignore

because ~~he~~ *his Grandpa* looked so old and different.

When Grandpa came to Martin's home, ~~he~~ *Martin* learned to

be truly proud of his Sioux heritage. This *pride* was one of

the most important things ~~he~~ *Grandpa* had to teach him.

Indefinite Pronouns as Antecedents

When a singular indefinite pronoun is the antecedent, use
he or she (him or her, his or her) **or rewrite the sentence to**
avoid the need for a singular pronoun.

Everybody liked Grandpa, and ~~they~~ *he or she* showed it by the

respect and attention ~~they~~ *he or she* paid him.

Or

~~Everybody~~ *Many* liked Grandpa, and they showed it by the

respect and attention they paid him.

Indefinite Pronouns				
Singular	another anybody anyone anything	each either	everybody everyone everything	neither nobody no one nothing one	somebody someone something
Plural	both	few	many	several	
Singular or Plural	all	any	most	none	some

REVISING TIP

To avoid vague pronoun reference, do not use *this* or
that alone to start a clause.
Instead, include a word that
clarifies what *this* or *that*
refers to—*this experience,
this situation, that concept.*

REVISING TIP

Avoid the indefinite use of
you and *they*.

At home, sometimes ~~they~~ *family members*

used Sioux words.

Martin thought ~~you~~ *a person*

always should be able to

tell what someone was

like by the way ~~they~~ *he or she*

looked.

3.3 Pronoun Antecedents

Answers will vary. See typical answers below.

1 In "The Medicine Bag" Martin and his great-grandfather gave each other gifts as the great-grandfather was dying of old age. **2** The Sioux and some other settlers originally lived on the Great Plains, and these people were buffalo hunters. **3** A hunter would offer prayers before killing buffalo, and he would apologize to the animals. **4** All said that they only killed buffalo so their families could have food and skins for clothing and shelter. **5** These people said that eventually everyone would die and he or she would become part of the earth. **6** The hunters thanked the Chief Animal Spirit for allowing the creatures to be killed, and killing them was seen as a sacred act. **7** Back then, each hunter saw the links between himself and the physical and spiritual worlds. **8** The Sioux considered people, animals, and plants their relatives. **9** Everything in the universe was kin, so everything deserved respect. **10** The Sioux were reverent toward living things, and this reverence seems strange for hunters.

APPLY WHAT YOU'VE LEARNED

Rewrite this paragraph to make the pronoun reference clear.

¹In "The Medicine Bag" Martin and his great-grandfather gave each other gifts as he was dying of old age. **²**The Sioux and some other settlers originally lived on the Great Plains, and they were buffalo hunters. **³**A hunter would offer prayers before killing buffalo, and they would apologize to them. **⁴**Everybody said that they only killed them so their families could have food and skins for clothing and shelter. **⁵**It says that even-tually everyone would die and they would become part of the earth. **⁶**The hunters thanked the Chief Animal Spirit for allowing the creatures to be killed, and it was seen as a sacred act. **⁷**Back then, each hunter saw the links between themselves and the physical and spiritual worlds. **⁸**The Sioux considered people, animals, and plants their relatives. **⁹**Everything in the universe was kin, so they deserved respect. **¹⁰**The Sioux were reverent toward living things, and it seems strange for hunters.

3.4 Pronoun Usage

The form that a pronoun takes is always determined by its function within its own clause or sentence.

Who and *Whom*

Use *who* or *whoever* as the subject of a clause or sentence.

In *The Hound of the Baskervilles* whom at the manor was most likely to commit murder?

Use *whom* as the direct or indirect object of a verb or verbal and as the object of a preposition.

People often use *who* for *whom* when speaking informally. However, in written English the pronouns should be used correctly.

To who did Watson attach the greatest suspicion at first? When Holmes disagreed with him, Watson questioned his decision, saying, "I am to interview *who*?"

REVISING TIP

Whom should replace *who* in both sentences in the second example:
To whom—object of the preposition
To interview whom—object of the infinitive *to interview*

In trying to determine the correct pronoun form, ignore interrupters that come between the subject and the verb.

> Whom in your estimation has the best reason to try to
>
> arrange Sir Henry's death?

Pronouns in Contractions

Do not confuse the contractions *it's, they're, who's,* and *you're* with possessive pronouns that sound the same—*its, their, whose,* and *your*.

> Whenever the hound is heard, some of the characters
>
> wonder whether maybe their wrong. Maybe the beast
>
> is supernatural! Whose to know for certain?

Pronouns with Nouns

Determine the correct form of the pronoun in phrases such as *we girls* and *us boys* by dropping the noun and saying the sentence without the noun that follows the pronoun.

> I do believe that a mystery is best when us readers are
>
> kept in suspense until the story's end.

APPLY WHAT YOU'VE LEARNED

Write the correct pronoun given in parentheses.

1(Who, Whom) in *The Hound of the Baskervilles* most enjoyed a walk on the moor? **2**(Whomever, Whoever) best understands a moor should define it for us. **3**Kate proclaims, "A moor is a vast expanse of open land where heather and sphagnum moss grow, and (whom, who) should know better than I?" **4**To (who, whom) is the moor's lovely bilberry most familiar? **5**Those (who, whom) ignore the bog are missing a great deal. **6**(Their, They're) missing sedges, peat-creating mosses, and algae. **7**Like scientists, you might find typical bog water so acidic that (your, you're) unlikely to see animals in it. **8**(Its, It's) amazing how much sphagnum reduces the oxygen content of bogs!

3.4 Pronoun Usage

1. Who
2. Whoever
3. who
4. whom
5. who
6. They're
7. you're
8. It's

Using Modifiers Effectively

4.1 Adjective or Adverb?

Use an adjective to modify a noun or a pronoun. Use an adverb to modify a verb, an adjective, or another adverb.

> The traditional Japanese family regards reserve just as
> high*ly* as respect. "Koden" is about the relationship
> between a young woman and her ~~pretty~~ *rather* stern father. He
> changes ~~real~~ *very* suddenly after a family funeral.

Use an adjective after a linking verb to describe the subject.

Remember that in addition to forms of the verb *be*, the following are linking verbs: *become, seem, appear, look, sound, feel, taste, grow,* and *smell*.

> Sensing her father's disapproval of her, the narrator feels
> badly. Her father seemed differently by the end of the story.

REVISING TIP

Always determine first which word is being modified. For example, in the first sentence of the example to the right, *regards* is the word being modified; because *regards* is a verb, its modifier must be an adverb.

APPLY WHAT YOU'VE LEARNED

Write the correct modifier in each pair.

¹*Koden* is only one Japanese gift-giving custom observed (regular, regularly) in this country. **²**In California (particular, particularly), the Japanese community is (real, really) strong. **³**The bereaved family (usual, usually) has thank-you letters printed (professional, professionally). **⁴**A modest gift is sent (respectful, respectfully) to each person who has presented *koden*. **⁵***Oseibo*, at year-end, and *o-chugen*, at about midyear, are other (traditional, traditionally) gift-giving times. **⁶**The gifts are always wrapped (real, really) simply and are often opened in private. **⁷**Another (interesting, interestingly) Japanese-American tradition is *omiyage*, a gift to a host or hostess. **⁸**To enter another's home empty-handed would appear very (rude, rudely).

4.1 Adjective or Adverb?

1. regularly
2. particularly; really
3. usually; professionally
4. respectfully
5. traditional
6. really
7. interesting
8. rude

4.2 Comparisons and Negatives

Comparative and Superlative Adjectives

Use the comparative form of an adjective when comparing two things.

Comparative adjectives are formed by adding -er to short adjectives (*small—smaller*) or by using the word *more* with longer adjectives (*horrible—more horrible*).

> The author of *Immigrant Kids* states that traveling
>
> across the Atlantic Ocean in days past was much
>
> *more*
> ^uncomfortabler than flying is today.

Use the superlative form when comparing three or more things.

The superlative is formed by adding -est to short adjectives (*tall—tallest*) or by using the word *most* with longer adjectives (*interesting—most interesting*).

> Obtaining passage, traveling steerage, or passing
>
> *most difficult*
> through customs: which was difficultest?
> ^

The comparative and superlative forms of some adjectives are irregular.

Adjective	Comparative	Superlative
good	better	best
well	better	best
bad	worse	worst
ill	worse	worst
little	less *or* lesser	least
much	more	most
many	more	most
far	farther *or* further	farthest *or* furthest

REVISING TIP

When comparing something with everything else of its kind, do not leave out the word *other*. (*Kim is shorter than any* **other** *member of her family.*)

Comparative and Superlative Adverbs

When comparing two actions, use the comparative form of an adverb, which is formed by adding -er or the word more.

European immigrants, ~~frequenter~~ *more frequently* than not, entered the United States frightened and exhausted.

When comparing more than two actions, use the superlative form of an adverb, which is formed by adding -est or by using the word most.

Of the several ports of entry, European immigrants entered through Ellis Island ~~more~~ *most* often.

Double Negatives

To avoid double negatives, use only one negative word in a clause.

Besides *not* and *no*, the following are negative words: *never, nobody, none, no one, nothing,* and *nowhere.*

Most immigrants ~~didn't~~ never regret*ted* their decision to move to a new country.

Do not use both *-er* and *more* or *-est* and *most.*

The ship was the most famous~~est~~ of the time. It traveled ~~more~~ faster than most others.

APPLY WHAT YOU'VE LEARNED

Write the correct modifier in each pair.

¹More than 60 years after Ellis Island opened as the (larger, largest) port of entry to this country, it was abandoned. ²In the 1980s the facilities underwent the (greatest, most greatest) restoration ever. ³The National Park Service helped supervise but did not try to find (any, no) funding sources. ⁴The Statue of Liberty–Ellis Island Restoration Project (activelier, more actively) solicited contributions. ⁵In 1990 there was a (grand, grandly) reopening of the main building. ⁶The museum and examination rooms remind us that our immigration process used to be (worse, worser). ⁷Which films, objects, and oral histories (more vividly, most vividly) record our past?

4.2 Comparisons and Negatives

1. largest
2. greatest
3. any
4. more actively
5. grand
6. worse
7. most vividly

The following terms are frequently misused in spoken English, but they should be used correctly in written English.

Them and Those

Them is always a pronoun and never a modifier for a noun. **Those** is a pronoun when it stands alone. It is an adjective when followed by a noun.

> In "Hollywood and the Pits" Lee describes ~~them~~ *those*
> frustrations that led her to the LaBrea Tar Pits.

Bad and Badly

Always use *bad* as an adjective, whether before a noun or after a linking verb. *Badly* should generally be used to modify an action verb.

> Lee's mother asked whether Lee had done bad*ly* at the
> audition. She felt bad~~ly~~ when the girl lost an acting job.

This, That, These, and Those

Whether used as adjectives or pronouns, **this** and **these** refer to people and things that are nearby, and **that** and **those** refer to people and things that are farther away.

> Working at the La Brea Tar Pits, Lee found ~~that~~ *this* work
> more satisfying than ~~this~~ *that* glamorous acting career. She
> sympathized with ~~these~~ *those* mammals of long ago that had
> been trapped in the sticky mire.

REVISING TIP

Avoid the use of *here* with *this* and *these*; also, do not use *there* with *that* and *those*.

I was surprised by this ~~here~~ story. Those ~~there~~ pits in Hollywood amaze me.

Good and Well

Good is always an adjective, never an adverb. Use *well* as either an adjective or an adverb, depending on the sentence.

When used as an adjective, *well* usually refers to a person's health. As an adverb, *well* modifies an action verb. In the expression "feeling good," *good* refers to being happy or pleased.

> The writer and her sister sang, danced, and acted good. [*well*]
>
> Their mother felt well about their success. [*good*]

Few and Little, Fewer and Less

Few refers to numbers of things that can be counted; *little* refers to amounts or quantities. *Fewer* is used when comparing numbers of things; *less* is used when comparing amounts or quantities.

> As Lee grew older, she got less jobs. [*fewer*] She received few [*less*] satisfaction from auditions and fewer [*less*] sense of accomplishment in her acting career.

---

1. those
2. Fewer; little
3. good
4. Those
5. bad; good
6. badly; this
7. Few
8. Those; well

APPLY WHAT YOU'VE LEARNED

Write the modifier from each pair that fits the meaning of the sentence.

[1]The La Brea Tar Pits referred to in "Hollywood and the Pits" are only one of (those, them) tourist attractions found near Los Angeles. [2](Fewer, Less) people visit La Brea than Hollywood, for example, because most people have (few, little) interest in fossil remains. [3]Hollywood became important because early filmmakers thought that its weather was (good, well) for their industry. [4](Those, Them) rainy days when they could not work were rare. [5]Movies convince the world that America is (bad, badly) or (good, well). [6]Americans should respond (bad, badly) to films that present (this, that) country inaccurately. [7](Few, Little) foreign moviegoers get a realistic picture of our country from such films. [8](Them, Those) people who produce films (good, well) should get patrons' support.

Using Verbs Correctly

5

Verb tense shows the time of an action or a condition. Writers sometimes cause confusion when they use different verb tenses in describing actions that occur at the same time.

Consistent Use of Tenses

When two or more actions occur at the same time or in sequence, use the same verb tense to describe the actions.

> In "The Eternal Frontier" Louis L'Amour writes about
> outer space. He considered the effect of space-age tech-
> nology on our daily lives.

A shift in tense is necessary when two events occur at different times or out of sequence. The tenses of the verbs should clearly indicate that one action precedes the other.

> We once ~~have~~ found adventure in the discovery of new
> lands. Now we ~~will~~ receive transmissions from places
> that in the past we only imagine.

Tense	Verb Form
Present	open/opens
Past	opened
Future	will/shall open
Present perfect	have/has opened
Past perfect	had opened
Future perfect	will/shall have opened

REVISING TIP

In telling a story, be careful not to shift tenses so often that the reader has difficulty keeping the sequence of events straight.

LINK TO LITERATURE

In "The Eternal Frontier" L'Amour uses the present tense to relate the challenges that we meet in this day and age. However, notice on page 437 how he switches to the past tense to tell of past achievements. Returning to the present allows readers to imagine a future in which they are very much involved.

1. deals
2. began
3. have grown
4. began
5. have come
6. is
7. have sprung

(a x) → **REVISING TIP**

Louis L'Amour moves from the past through the present to the future, backward and forward, to show how space-age discoveries affect our daily lives. When using this technique, be careful to use verb tenses that make your intentions clear.

Past Tense and the Past Participle

The simple past form of a verb can always stand alone. The past participle of the following irregular verbs should always be used with a helping verb.

Present Tense	Past Tense	Past Participle
be (is/are)	was/were	(have, had) been
begin	began	(have, had) begun
break	broke	(have, had) broken
bring	brought	(have, had) brought
choose	chose	(have, had) chosen
come	came	(have, had) come
do	did	(have, had) done
drink	drank	(have, had) drunk
eat	ate	(have, had) eaten
fall	fell	(have, had) fallen
freeze	froze	(have, had) frozen
give	gave	(have, had) given
go	went	(have, had) gone
lose	lost	(have, had) lost
grow	grew	(have, had) grown

Some developments—electricity, radio, television, and the automobile—~~begun~~ *began* before the space age. These developments have ~~gave~~ *given* space pioneers new tools to work with.

APPLY WHAT YOU'VE LEARNED

Write the correct verb tense for each sentence.

[1]"The Eternal Frontier" (deals, dealt, will deal) with the opportunities that the space age offers. [2]Some medical developments (are beginning, began, begun) with the space age—for example, laparoscopy and robotics. [3]Both of these areas (grow, grew, have grown) to advance the field of surgery dramatically. [4]In 1993 a "robotic assistant" (begin, began, has begun) helping in surgery. [5]People also (come, have came, have come) to expect simpler procedures because of these new techniques. [6]Laser surgery (is, have been, will be) another procedure that avoids cutting into tissue. [7]Such techniques (spring, sprang, have sprung) from technology developed for space exploration.

5.2 Commonly Confused Verbs

The following verb pairs are easily confused.

Let and Leave

Let means "to allow or permit." **Leave** means "to depart" or "to allow something to remain where it is."

> Rudyard Kipling, who wrote "Rikki-tikki-tavi," often
> ~~left~~ *let* animal characters tell his stories.

Lie and Lay

Lie means "to rest in a flat position." **Lay** means "to put or place."

> When Rikki-tikki revived after being washed out of his
> burrow, he was ~~laying~~ *lying* in the middle of a path.

REVISING TIP

If you're uncertain about which verb to use, check to see whether the verb has an object. The verbs *lie, sit,* and *rise* never have objects.

Sit and Set

Sit means "to be in a seated position." **Set** means "to put or place."

> He ~~set~~ *sat* on the shoulder of the little boy, who imme-
> diately ~~sat~~ *set* a piece of meat before the playful mongoose.

Rise and Raise

Rise means "to move upward." **Raise** means "to move something upward."

> Nag the cobra just ~~raised~~ *rose* up, ~~rising~~ *raising* his head threateningly.

Learn and Teach

Learn means "to gain knowledge or skill." *Teach* means "to help someone learn."

> The mongoose learned the snake to fear something—
> but too late for Nag to benefit from the knowledge.

(taught marked above "learned")

Here are the principal parts of these troublesome verb pairs.

Present Tense	Past Tense	Past Participle
let	let	(have, had) let
leave	left	(have, had) left
lie	lay	(have, had) lain
lay	laid	(have, had) laid
sit	sat	(have, had) sat
set	set	(have, had) set
rise	rose	(have, had) risen
raise	raised	(have, had) raised
learn	learned	(have, had) learned
teach	taught	(have, had) taught

APPLY WHAT YOU'VE LEARNED

Choose the correct verb from each pair of words.

1Rudyard Kipling's tale "Rikki-tikki-tavi" (learns, teaches) readers many facts about the cobra and its natural enemy, the mongoose. **2**Most snakes (lay, lie) hidden to avoid people and animals much of the time. **3**The cobra, however, (raises, rises) to seek out its victim. **4**(Letting, Leaving) a cobra alone is no protection either. **5**An unintentional disturbance can (set, sit) one against you. **6**Both male and female, while protecting their eggs, for example, will (raise, rise) up against any approaching intruder. **7**The venom of the cobra is a deadly nerve- and muscle-paralyzing substance that (lets, leaves) a human being dead in minutes.

5.2 Commonly Confused Verbs

1. teaches
2. lie
3. rises
4. Leaving
5. set
6. rise
7. leaves

Correcting Capitalization

6.1   Proper Nouns and Adjectives

A common noun names a whole class of persons, places, things, or ideas. A proper noun names a particular person, place, thing, or idea. A proper adjective is an adjective formed from a proper noun. All proper nouns and proper adjectives are capitalized.

Names and Personal Titles

Capitalize the name and title of a person.

Also capitalize the initials and abbreviations of titles that stand for those names. *Thomas Alva Edison, T. A. Edison, Governor James Thompson,* and *Mr. Aaron Copland* are capitalized correctly.

> In *The Autobiography of Malcolm X,* malcolm x tells
> how his desire to write letters—to elijah muhammad,
> for example—inspired him to study.

Capitalize a word referring to a family relationship when it is used as someone's name *(Uncle Al)* but not when it is used to identify a person *(Jill's uncle).*

> If the people he mentions—ella and reginald—had been
> Aunt and Uncle instead of Sister and Brother, he might
> have called them aunt ella and uncle reginald.

LINK TO LITERATURE

Notice throughout the excerpt from *The Autobiography of Malcolm X,* on page 63, how references to specific people and places conjure up images as you read. Specific names help you visualize the scenes that Malcolm X pictures. The author's use of proper nouns (*Bimbi* and *Norfolk Prison Colony*) helps make the story more believable.

REVISING TIP

Do not capitalize personal titles used as common nouns. (*We met the* **mayor**.)

Languages, Nationalities, Religious Terms

Capitalize the names of languages and nationalities as well as religious names and terms.

Capitalize languages and nationalities, such as *French, Gaelic, Chinese,* and *Tagalog.* Capitalize religious names and terms, such as *Allah, Jehovah, the Bible,* and *the Koran.*

This famous african american was a muslim, so he must have read the koran.

School Subjects

Capitalize the name of a specific school course (*Civics 101, General Science*). Do not capitalize a general reference to a school subject (*social studies, algebra, art*).

Malcolm X read about History and Religion, but at first he could have used courses such as penmanship 101 or beginning english.

Organizations, Institutions

Capitalize the important words in the official names of organizations and institutions (*Congress, Duke University*).

Do not capitalize words that refer to kinds of organizations or institutions (*college, hospital, museums*) or words that refer to specific organizations but are not their official names (*to the museum*).

He began reading in charlestown prison but really explored in depth the Library at norfolk prison colony.

REVISING TIP

Do not capitalize minor words in a proper noun that is made up of several words (*Field Museum **of** Natural History*).

Geographical Names, Events, Time Periods

Capitalize geographical names, as well as the names of events, historical periods and documents, holidays, and months and days, but not the names of seasons or directions.

Names	Examples
Continents	Africa, South America
Bodies of water	Pacific Ocean, Lake Charles, Amazon River
Political units	Maine, Japan, Brasília
Sections of a country	the South, Middle Atlantic States
Public areas	the Loop, Boston Commons
Roads and structures	Park Avenue, Hoover Dam, Chrysler Building
Historical events	the War of 1812, the Emancipation Proclamation
Documents	Magna Carta, the Treaty of Paris
Periods of history	the Middle Ages, Reconstruction
Holidays	Arbor Day, New Year's Day
Months and days	May, Sunday
Seasons	summer, autumn
Directions	north, south

As Malcolm X studied the dictionary, he learned about the *aardvark*, a termite-eating mammal from africa. He read constantly—Summer, Winter, Spring, and Fall—in the library and in his cell.

 REVISING TIP

Do not capitalize a reference that does not use the full name of a place, event, or period. (*The Empire State Building was once the tallest* **building** *in the world.*)

APPLY WHAT YOU'VE LEARNED

Write the correct forms of the words given in parentheses.

[1]Like (malcolm X, Malcolm X), Jawaharlal Nehru, first (prime minister, Prime Minister) of India, used prison for serious reading and writing. [2]While imprisoned, (nehru, Nehru), too, used letter writing to improve his communication skills. [3]His letters to his daughter, Indira, later (prime minister, Prime Minister) Ghandi, were the basis for a book on (world history, World History). [4]In prison, too, Nehru completed his (autobiography, Autobiography). [5]A Brahmin from (kashmir, Kashmir), he was educated at (harrow school, Harrow School) and (cambridge university, Cambridge University) in England. [6]He was as eloquent in (english, English) as in (hindi, Hindi).

6.1 Proper Nouns and Adjectives

1. Malcolm X; prime minister
2. Nehru
3. Prime Minister; world history
4. autobiography
5. Kashmir; Harrow School; Cambridge University
6. English; Hindi

Titles need to follow certain capitalization rules.

Poems, Stories, Articles

Capitalize the first word, the last word, and all other important words in the title of a poem, a story, or an article. Enclose the title in quotation marks.

Walt Whitman's poem ˅song of ̲myself ̲ ˅celebrates his humanity and the joy of living in a glorious world.

Books, Plays, Magazines, Newspapers, Films

Capitalize the first word, the last word, and all other important words in the title of a book, play or musical, magazine, newspaper, or film. Underline or italicize the title to set it off.

Within a title, don't capitalize articles, conjunctions, and prepositions of fewer than five letters.

It appeared in his book <u>leaves of grass</u>, whose unconventional form and apparent immodesty shocked readers.

APPLY WHAT YOU'VE LEARNED

Rewrite this paragraph, correcting punctuation and capitalization of titles.

[1]Some of Walt Whitman's first published poems appeared in the small book leaves of grass. [2]Others—such as those about the Civil War—beat! beat! drums!, when lilacs last in the dooryard bloom'd, and o captain! my captain!—appeared in the collection drum-taps. [3]Whitman was also a journalist: founder of the freeman, editor-printer of the long islander, editor of the Brooklyn daily eagle and the Brooklyn times, and reporter or writer for numerous other newspapers. [4]Some of his short stories were published in popular magazines such as the democratic review. [5]Others—for example, the half-breed—appeared in collections. [6]Whitman even wrote a novel: franklin evans. [7]Some collections of his works include the complete writings of walt whitman and the uncollected poetry and prose of walt whitman.

6.2 Titles of Created Works

1 Some of Walt Whitman's first published poems appeared in the small book *Leaves of Grass.* **2** Others—such as those about the Civil War—"Beat! Beat! Drums!," "When Lilacs Last in the Dooryard Bloom'd," and "O Captain! My Captain!"—appeared in the collection *Drum-Taps.* **3** Whitman was also a journalist: founder of *The Freeman,* editor-printer of *The Long Islander,* editor of the *Brooklyn Daily Eagle* and the *Brooklyn Times,* and reporter or writer for numerous other newspapers. **4** Some of his short stories were published in popular magazines such as *The Democratic Review.* **5** Others—for example, "The Half-Breed"—appeared in collections. **6** Whitman even wrote a novel: *Franklin Evans.* **7** Some collections of his works include *The Complete Writings of Walt Whitman* and *The Uncollected Poetry and Prose of Walt Whitman.*

Correcting Punctuation

7

7.1 Compound Sentences

Punctuation helps organize longer sentences that have several clauses.

Commas in Compound Sentences

Use a comma before the conjunction that joins the clauses of a compound sentence.

> In "Where the Girl Saved Her Brother" author Rachel Strange Owl describes the Battle of the Rosebud∧and she also talks about the Battle of the Little Bighorn.

Semicolons in Compound Sentences

Use a semicolon between the clauses of a compound sentence when no conjunction is used. Use a semicolon before, and a comma after, a conjunctive adverb that joins the clauses of a compound sentence.

Conjunctive adverbs include *therefore, however, then, nevertheless, consequently,* and *besides.*

> The Cheyennes took pride in winning war honors∧they called their brave deeds "counting coup." Actions performed without risk did not count as coup∧however∧Cheyennes had many opportunities for bravery.

LINK TO LITERATURE

Notice on pages 722–723 of "Where the Girl Saved Her Brother" how Rachel Strange Owl uses compound and complex sentences. She combines ideas and merges pieces of information in a way that shows their relation to one another.

REVISING TIP

Even when clauses are connected by a coordinating conjunction, you should use a semicolon between them if one or both clauses contain a comma. (*Two battles involving soldiers and Indians, Little Bighorn and Rosebud, stand out in American history; but they ended differently.*)

1 Buffalo Calf Woman was a brave Native American warrior, but she was not the only such woman in history. 2 Both Awashonks and Wetamoo were brave Wampanoag women, and both fought in Rhode Island in the 1670s. 3 Awashonks ruled the Saconnet band in the Little Compton area of Rhode Island; she became leader when her husband died. 4 She fought with King Philip against the British; however, she switched allegiance to the colonists. 5 Wetamoo was from near Tiverton; she became chief after her father. 6 She commanded her braves for King Philip; thus, she died on the battlefield. 7 The colonists beheaded King Philip and her; their heads were publicly displayed.

APPLY WHAT YOU'VE LEARNED

Rewrite these sentences, adding commas and semicolons where necessary.

[1]Buffalo Calf Woman was a brave Native American warrior but she was not the only such woman in history. [2]Both Awashonks and Wetamoo were brave Wampanoag women and both fought in Rhode Island in the 1670s. [3]Awashonks ruled the Saconnet band in the Little Compton area of Rhode Island she became leader when her husband died. [4]She fought with King Philip against the British however she switched allegiance to the colonists. [5]Wetamoo was from near Tiverton she became chief after her father. [6]She commanded her braves for King Philip thus she died on the battlefield. [7]The colonists beheaded King Philip and her their heads were publicly displayed.

7.2 Elements Set Off in a Sentence

Most elements that are not essential to a sentence are set off by commas to highlight the main idea of the sentence.

Introductory Words

Use a comma to separate an introductory word from the rest of the sentence.

> Certainly ∧ "The Old Grandfather and His Little Grandson" by Leo Tolstoy teaches an important lesson.

Use a comma to separate an introductory phrase from the rest of the sentence.

Use a comma to set off more than one introductory prepositional phrase but not for a single prepositional phrase in most cases.

> In this tale of family life ∧ we see the effect our conduct has. At home, ∧ our actions are a powerful teacher.

Interrupters

Use commas to set off a word that interrupts the flow of a sentence.

The parents, fortunately, were ashamed when they realized what they were teaching their son. They thought about their behavior, therefore, and decided to improve their conduct.

Use commas to set off a group of words that interrupts the flow of a sentence.

Misha noticed his parents treating his grandfather badly and, to his parents' surprise, started to make a wooden bucket for them.

Nouns of Address

Use commas to set off a noun in direct address at the beginning of a sentence.

"Father, your table manners are an embarrassment. Please eat in the corner," the father might have said.

Use commas to set off a noun in direct address in the middle of a sentence.

The boy's mother asked, "What are you making, Misha, from those pieces of wood?"

Appositives

Set off with commas an appositive phrase that is not necessary to the meaning of the sentence,

The following sentence could be understood without the words set off by commas.

> The father, the old man's son, scolded the grandfather.

Do not set off with commas an appositive phrase that is necessary to the meaning of the sentence.

The following sentence could not be understood without the words set off by commas:

> Misha, the child, was showing what Misha, the man, would be like.

For Clarity

Use a comma to prevent misreading or misunderstanding.

> While the old man was eating bits of food that would sometimes drop out of his mouth disgusted the couple.

Ⓠ **REVISING TIP**

Sometimes if a comma is missing, a reader may group parts of a sentence in more than one way. A comma separates the parts so they can be read in only one way.

APPLY WHAT YOU'VE LEARNED

Rewrite these sentences. Add or delete commas where necessary.

[1]In our part of the world aged parents were once expected to live with their children. [2]Today a variety of lifestyles are available to senior citizens, and the variety is increasing. [3]Many however still live in familiar surroundings. [4]They may rent or own senior-citizen housing either house or apartment. [5]In spite of these options according to the latest census more than 67 percent of seniors still live in family homes. [6]Some people of course are able to live independently. [7]These people can get help nursing or housekeeping care. [8]Would you believe Willard that not even 1 percent live in traditional nursing homes? [9]People may go in as couples or singly. [10]In 1992 9,773 more elderly people lived in this country than did in 1980.

7.2 Elements Set Off in a Sentence

1 In our part of the world, aged parents were once expected to live with their children. 2 Today, a variety of lifestyles are available to senior citizens, and the variety is increasing all the time. 3 Many, however, still live in familiar surroundings. 4 They may rent or own senior-citizen housing, either house or apartment. 5 In spite of these options, according to the latest census, more than 67 percent of seniors still live in family homes. 6 Some people, of course, are able to live independently. 7 These people can get help, nursing or housekeeping care. 8 Would you believe, Willard, that not even 1 percent live in traditional nursing homes? 9 People may go in as couples or singly. 10 In 1992, 9,773 more elderly people lived in this country than did in 1980.

7.3 Elements in a Series

Commas should be used to separate three or more items in a series and to separate adjectives preceding a noun.

Subjects, Predicates, and Other Elements

Use a comma after every item except the last in a series of three or more items.

Subjects or predicates may occur in series.

> In "The Highwayman" the highwayman himself, the landlord's daughter, and the soldiers are the main characters. The soldiers come to the inn, lay a trap there, and tie up the robber's sweetheart.

Predicate adjectives often occur in series.

> The robber's sweetheart is brave, faithful, and self-sacrificing. The entire poem by Alfred Noyes is romantic, atmospheric, and exciting.

Adverbs and prepositional phrases may also occur in series.

> The bold highwayman approaches the inn confidently, eagerly, but quietly. The highwayman came riding at midnight, in the silence, and by moonlight.

 REVISING TIP

Note in the example that a comma followed by a conjunction precedes the last element in the series. That comma is always used.

7.3 Elements in a Series

1. The poem "The Highwayman" speaks of a time when wagons, stagecoaches, and carriages were the main means of transportation.

2. The design of these vehicles had changed little from the Middle Ages through the 17th, 18th, and 19th centuries.

3. Those who preyed on travelers could find wealthy, unprotected victims by lying in wait on the roads.

4. The dashing, daring, dangerous highwaymen held great appeal for many.

5. We often find today's robbers less charming, more frightening, and more dangerous.

6. Stagecoaches traveled in stages, stopped at scheduled points, and changed horses at each stop.

7. Can you visualize the highwayman's big, powerful black charger?

Two or More Adjectives

In most sentences, use a comma after each adjective except the last of two or more adjectives that precede a noun.

If you can reverse the order of adjectives without changing the meaning or if you can use *and* between them, separate the two adjectives with a comma.

> The beautiful black-eyed daughter was braiding a dark, red loveknot into her lovely long hair.

APPLY WHAT YOU'VE LEARNED

Rewrite each sentence, inserting commas where they are needed.

1. The poem "The Highwayman" speaks of a time when wagons stagecoaches and carriages were the main means of transportation.
2. The design of these vehicles had changed little from the Middle Ages through the 17th 18th and 19th centuries.
3. Those who preyed on travelers could find wealthy unprotected victims by lying in wait on the roads.
4. The dashing daring dangerous highwaymen held great appeal for many.
5. We often find today's robbers less charming more frightening and often more dangerous.
6. Stagecoaches traveled in stages stopped at scheduled points and changed horses at each stop.
7. Can you visualize the highwayman's big powerful black charger?

7.4 Dates, Addresses, and Letters

Punctuation in dates, addresses, and letters makes information easy to understand.

Dates

Use a comma between the day of the month and the year. If the date falls in the middle of a sentence, use another comma after the year.

> The sailing recorded in "Exploring the *Titanic*," took place on April 10, 1912, amidst great fanfare.

884 GRAMMAR HANDBOOK

Cities

Use a comma to separate a city from its state or country. If the city and state or country fall in mid-sentence, use a comma after the state or country too.

> The hull of the ship was launched in Belfast͵Ireland͵ before thousands of spectators and several bands.

Parts of a Letter

Use a comma after the greeting and after the closing in a letter.

> Dear Mother͵
>
> You cannot imagine how gorgeous the *Titanic* is. Our stateroom seems straight out of the Grand Hotel!
>
> Affectionately͵
>
> Millicent

APPLY WHAT YOU'VE LEARNED

Rewrite the following sentences, correcting the comma errors.

1. Like the wreck of the *Titanic,* the *Hindenburg* disaster of May 6 1937 was the result of a simple accident.
2. The *Hindenburg* was a showpiece in its time, traveling between Germany and Lakehurst New Jersey for a year before it was destroyed.
3. Research at the library in Chicago Illinois revealed that the airship was named for Paul von Hindenburg, a German military leader and president.
4. The hydrogen-filled *Hindenburg* crashed in Lakehurst New Jersey when the gas caught fire.
5. On September 14 1996 I first read about the *Hindenburg* tragedy, in which 35 people met their doom.
6. I wonder whether passengers could send messages home as they traveled:
   Dear Will
   This is my most exciting trip ever! I only wish you could be here too.
   Sincerely
   Maya

---

1. Like the wreck of the *Titanic,* the Hindenburg disaster of May 6, 1937, was the result of a simple accident.
2. The *Hindenburg* was a showpiece in its time, traveling between Germany and Lakehurst, New Jersey, for a year before it was destroyed.
3. Research at the library in Chicago, Illinois, revealed that the airship was named for Paul von Hindenburg, a German military leader and president.
4. The hydrogen-filled *Hindenburg* crashed in Lakehurst, New Jersey, when the gas caught fire.
5. On September 14, 1996, I first read about the *Hindenburg* tragedy, in which 35 people met their doom.
6. I wonder whether passengers could send messages home as they traveled:

   Dear Will,

   This is my most exciting trip ever! I only wish you could be here too.

   Sincerely,

   Maya

Quotation marks let readers know exactly who said what. Incorrectly placed or missing quotation marks cause confusion.

Quotation Marks

Use quotation marks at the beginning and the end of direct quotations and to set off titles of short works.

> In Langston Hughes's ˇThank You, M'am,ˇ Roger replies simply,ˇYes'm,ˇ to some of the woman's questions. He replies,ˇNo'm,ˇ to others.

Capitalize the first word of a direct quotation, especially in a piece of dialogue.

> The woman replies, "Um-hum," to Roger's apology.

End Punctuation

Place periods inside quotation marks. Place question marks and exclamation points inside quotation marks if they belong to the quotation; place them outside if they do not belong to the quotation. Place semicolons outside quotation marks.

> The boy asks, "You gonna take me to jail"?
>
> The woman replies, "Not with that face"!
>
> Offered food, he says, "That will be fine;" then he eats.

REVISING TIP

If quoted words are from a written source and are not complete sentences, they can begin with a lowercase letter. (*Mark Twain said that cauliflower was "nothing but cabbage with a college education."*)

Use a comma to end a quotation that is a complete sentence but is followed by explanatory words.

> "I wanted a pair of blue suede shoes," said the boy.

Divided Quotations

Capitalize the first word of the second part of a direct quotation if it begins a new sentence.

> "Well, you didn't have to snatch *my* pocketbook," Mrs. Jones replied. "you could of asked me."

Do not capitalize the first word of the second part of a divided quotation if it does not begin a new sentence.

> "I have done things, too, which I would not tell you, son," she explained quietly, "Neither tell God, if he didn't already know."

 ▶ **REVISING TIP**

Should the first word of the second part of a divided quotation be capitalized? Imagine the quotation without the explanatory words. If a capital letter would not be used, then do not use one in the divided quotation.

APPLY WHAT YOU'VE LEARNED

Rewrite this paragraph, inserting appropriate punctuation and capitalization.

1Langston Hughes once wrote children should be born without parents. **2**His difficult childhood may have been the inspiration for one of his best-loved poems, titled dreams. **3**It begins with the line hold fast to dreams; it is short, so I have memorized it.

4You may know it the teacher said. I have seen the first stanza printed on T-shirts. **5**My soul has grown deep like the rivers Hughes says in The Negro Speaks of Rivers. **6**How happy he would have been at his memorial service to hear his favorite Ellington song, Do Nothing 'Til You Hear from Me! **7**Have you read any stories by Hughes other than Thank You, M'am?

7.5 Quotations

1 Langston Hughes once wrote, "Children should be born without parents." **2** His difficult childhood may have been the inspiration for one of his best-loved poems, titled "Dreams." **3** It begins with the line "Hold fast to dreams"; it is short, so I have memorized it. **4** "You may know it," the teacher said. "I have seen the first stanza printed on T-shirts." **5** "My soul has grown deep like the rivers," Hughes says in "The Negro Speaks of Rivers." **6** How happy he would have been at his memorial service to hear his favorite Ellington song, "Do Nothing 'Til You Hear from Me"! **7** Have you read any stories by Hughes other than "Thank You, M'am"?

Grammar Glossary

This glossary contains various terms you need to understand when you use the Grammar Handbook. Used as a reference source, this glossary will help you explore grammar concepts and how they relate to one another.

 A

Adjective An adjective modifies, or describes, a noun or a pronoun. (*good* friend, *lonesome* me)

A **predicate adjective** follows a linking verb and describes the subject. (She is *pretty*.)

A **proper adjective** is formed from a proper noun. (*Irish* stew)

The **comparative** form of an adjective compares two things. (*more agreeable, stranger*)

The **superlative** form of an adjective compares three or more things. (*most agreeable, strangest*)

What Adjectives Tell	Examples
How many	*some* books *most* students
What kind	*famous* poets *strange* planet
Which one(s)	*that* door *these* folders

Adverb An adverb modifies a verb, an adjective, or another adverb. (Stan walked *slowly*.)

The **comparative** form of an adverb compares two actions. (*more surprisingly, faster*)

The **superlative** form of an adverb compares three or more actions. (*most surprisingly, fastest*)

What Adverbs Tell	Examples
How	sing *sweetly* cough *loudly*
When	*Then* the band stopped. *later* in the day
Where	They looked *down*. *There* we rested.
To what extent	I was *too* tired. The story was *quite* long.

Agreement Sentence parts that correspond with one another are said to be in agreement.

In **pronoun-antecedent agreement,** a pronoun and the word it refers to are the same in number, gender, and person. (The *boy* ate *his* lunch. The *boys* ate *their* lunch.)

In **subject-verb agreement,** the subject and the verb in a sentence are the same in number. (*We like* summer. *She likes* apples.)

Antecedent An antecedent is the noun or pronoun to which a pronoun refers. (If *Mae* loses *her* books, *she* will be sorry. *I* ate *my* pear.)

Appositive An appositive is a noun or phrase that explains one or more words in a sentence. (Juan, *my best friend*, lives next door.)

Article Articles are the special adjectives *a, an,* and *the*.

The **definite article** (the word *the*) is used with a noun that refers to a specific thing. (*the* plane)

An **indefinite article** is used with a noun that does not refer to a particular example of a thing. (*a* bird)

 C

Clause A clause is a group of words that contains a verb and its subject. (*She arrived*)

A **main (independent) clause** can stand by itself as a sentence.

A **subordinate (dependent) clause** does not express a complete thought and cannot stand by itself as a sentence.

Clause	Example
Main (independent)	The hikers set out
Subordinate (dependent)	before the sun had risen.

Collective noun. *See* **Noun.**

Common noun. *See* **Noun.**

Complete predicate The complete predicate of a sentence consists of the main verb plus any words that modify or complete the verb's meaning. (The apples *covered the ground under the tree.*)

Complete subject The complete subject of a sentence consists of the subject noun or pronoun plus any words that modify or describe it. (*A large boulder* lay in the field.)

Complex sentence A complex sentence contains one main clause and one or more subordinate clauses. (*If I remember, I'll call you.*)

Compound sentence A compound sentence consists of two or more independent clauses. (*Sue will play, and the rest of us will cheer.*)

Compound sentence part A sentence element that consists of two or more subjects, predicates, objects, or other parts is compound. (*Lee* and *Vi* played. Al *swims* and *runs.* Jay owns a *cat* and a *dog.*)

Conjunction A conjunction is a word that links other words or groups of words.

A *coordinating conjunction* connects related words, groups of words, or sentences. (*and, but, or*)

A *correlative conjunction* is one of a pair of conjunctions that work together to connect sentence parts. (*either . . . or, neither . . . nor*)

A *subordinating conjunction* introduces a subordinate clause. (*unless, while, if*)

Conjunctive adverb A conjunctive adverb joins the clauses of a compound sentence. (*however, therefore, besides*)

Contraction A contraction is formed by joining two words and substituting an apostrophe for letters left out of one of the words. (*isn't*)

Coordinating conjunction. *See* **Conjunction.**

Correlative conjunction. *See* **Conjunction.**

 D

Demonstrative pronoun. *See* **Pronoun.**

Dependent clause. *See* **Clause.**

Direct object A direct object receives the action of a verb. (Jean baked a *cake.*)

Double negative A double negative is an incorrect use of two negative words when only one is needed. (*Scarcely no one* came to the party.)

 E

End mark An end mark is any of the several punctuation marks that can end a sentence. See the punctuation chart on page 891.

 F

Fragment. *See* **Sentence fragment.**

Future tense. *See* **Verb tense.**

 G

Gerund A gerund is a verbal that ends in *-ing* and functions as a noun. (*Playing* soccer is fun.)

 H

Helping verb. *See* **Verb.**

 I

Indefinite pronoun. *See* **Pronoun.**

Independent clause. *See* **Clause.**

Indirect object An indirect object tells to or for whom (sometimes to or for what) something is done. (He gave *Verdell* the schedule.)

Infinitive An infinitive is a verbal that begins with the word *to;* the two words create a phrase. (*to know*)

Intensive pronoun. *See* **Pronoun.**

Interjection An interjection is a word or phrase used to express strong feeling. (*Ah!*)

Interrogative pronoun. *See* **Pronoun.**

Inverted sentence An inverted sentence is one in which the subject comes after the verb. (*What is the answer? Down came the rain.*)

Irregular verb. *See* **Verb.**

 L

Linking verb. *See* **Verb.**

 M

Main clause. *See* **Clause.**

Main verb. *See* **Verb.**

Modifier A modifier makes another word more precise. Modifiers most often are adjectives or adverbs. (*happy* occasion, played *quietly*)

 N

Noun A noun names a person, a place, a thing, or an idea. (*Mark, stadium, tree, goodness*)

An *abstract noun* names an idea, a quality, or a feeling. (*joy*)

A *collective noun* names a group of things. (*crowd*)

A *common noun* is the general name of a person, a place, a thing, or an idea. (*boy, hill, dinner, ambition*)

A *compound noun* contains two or more words. (*raindrop, sweatshirt, mother-in-law*)

A *noun of direct address* is the name of a person being directly spoken to. (*Ed,* please help me.)

A *possessive noun* shows who or what owns something. (*Edna's* coat, the *book's* cover)

A *predicate noun* follows a linking verb and renames the subject. (She is our favorite *aunt.*)

A **proper noun** names a particular person, place, or thing. (*Al Kaline, New Jersey, Statue of Liberty*)

Number A word is **singular** in number if it refers to just one person, place, thing, idea, or action, and **plural** in number if it refers to more than one person, place, thing, idea, or action. (The words *he, farmer,* and *eats* are singular. The words *they, farmers,* and *eat* are plural.)

Object of a preposition The object of a preposition is the noun or pronoun after the preposition. (The practice started with a warmup *drill*.)

Object of a verb The object of a verb receives the action of the verb. (Meg peeled *potatoes*.)

Participle A participle is often used as part of a verb phrase. (have *owned*) It can also be used as a verbal that functions as an adjective. (the *sinking* sun)

The **present participle** is formed by adding *-ing* to the present tense of a verb. (*Opening* her eyes, she saw the surprise.)

The **past participle** of a regular verb is formed by adding *-d* or *-ed* to the present tense. The past participle of irregular verbs does not follow this pattern. (The *startled* goslings ran to the *grown* geese.)

Past tense. *See* **Verb tense.**

Perfect tenses. *See* **Verb tense.**

Person A pronoun's person depends on whom the pronoun refers to.

A **first-person** pronoun refers to the person speaking. (*We* danced.)

A **second-person** pronoun refers to the person spoken to. (*You* came.)

A **third-person** pronoun refers to some other person(s) or thing(s) being spoken of. (*He* helped.)

Personal pronoun. *See* **Pronoun.**

Phrase A phrase is a group of related words that does not contain a verb and its subject. (*speaking of friends*)

Possessive A noun or pronoun that is possessive shows ownership. (*Maude's* story, *my* uncle)

Possessive noun. *See* **Noun.**

Possessive pronoun. *See* **Pronoun.**

Predicate The predicate of a sentence tells what the subject is or does. (The race *starts at the corner.*)

Predicate adjective. *See* **Adjective.**

Predicate noun. *See* **Noun.**

Predicate pronoun. *See* **Pronoun.**

Preposition A preposition relates a word to another part of the sentence or to the sentence as a whole. (Jo waited *for* an answer.)

Prepositional phrase A prepositional phrase consists of a preposition, its object, and the object's modifiers. (message *from a friend*)

Present tense. *See* **Verb tense.**

Pronoun A pronoun replaces a noun or another pronoun. Some pronouns allow a writer or speaker to avoid repeating a particular noun. Other pronouns let a writer refer to unknown or unidentified persons or things.

A **demonstrative pronoun** singles out one or more persons or things. (*That* is the game.)

An **indefinite pronoun** refers to an unidentified person or thing. (*Anybody* could have made a mistake.)

An **intensive pronoun** emphasizes a noun or pronoun. (Nick *himself* carried all the boxes.)

An **interrogative pronoun** asks a question. (*What* is the answer?)

A **personal pronoun** refers to the first, second, or third person. (*I* ran. *You* go. *She* saw.)

A **possessive pronoun** shows ownership. (*Your* gift is in the mail. These gloves are *hers*.)

A **predicate pronoun** follows a linking verb and renames the subject. (The winner was *she*.)

A **reflexive pronoun** reflects an action back on the subject of the sentence. (Cal injured *himself*.)

A **relative pronoun** relates a subordinate clause to the word it modifies in the main clause. (You gave the answer *that* we expected)

Pronoun-antecedent agreement. *See* **Agreement.**

Pronoun forms

The **subject form of a pronoun** is used when the pronoun is the subject of a clause or follows a linking verb as a predicate pronoun. (*I* won. The speaker was *he*.)

The **object form of a pronoun** is used when the pronoun is the direct or indirect object of a verb or the object of a preposition or verbal. (Give *them* to *him*.)

Proper adjective. *See* **Adjective.**

Proper noun. *See* **Noun.**

Punctuation Punctuation clarifies the structure of sentences. See the chart at the bottom of page 891.

Reflexive pronoun. *See* **Pronoun.**

Regular verb. *See* **Verb.**

Relative pronoun. *See* **Pronoun.**

Run-on sentence A run-on sentence consists of two or more sentences written incorrectly as one. (*It was cold everyone said so.*)

Sentence A sentence expresses a complete thought. The chart below shows the four kinds of sentences.

Kind of Sentence	Example
Declarative (statement)	Everyone is here.
Exclamatory (strong feeling)	You did it!
Imperative (request, command)	Open the windows.
Interrogative (question)	What is the answer?

Sentence fragment A sentence fragment is a group of words that is only part of a sentence. (*If you try, arriving on time*)

Subject The subject is the part of a sentence that tells whom or what the sentence is about. (*Lois* knows the answer.)

Subject-verb agreement. *See* **Agreement.**

Subordinate clause. *See* **Clause.**

Verb A verb expresses an action, a condition, or a state of being.

When the subject of a sentence performs the action, the verb is **active.** (Estelle *skated.*) When the subject receives the action or expresses the result of the action, the verb is **passive.** (A visitor *was announced.*)

A **helping verb** is used with the main verb; together they make up a verb phrase. (*had* spoken)

A **linking verb** expresses a state of being or connects the subject with a word or words that describe the subject. (The breeze *feels* good.)

A **main verb** describes action or state of being; it may have one or more helping verbs. (can be *seen.*)

The past tense and past participle of a **regular verb** are formed by adding *-d* or *-ed.* (*open, opened*) An **irregular verb** does not follow this pattern. (*sing, sang, sung*)

Verbal A verbal is formed from a verb and acts as a noun, an adjec-

tive, or an adverb. *See* **Gerund; Infinitive; Participle.**

Verb phrase A verb phrase consists of a main verb and one or more helping verbs. (*might have ordered*)

Verb tense Verb tense shows the time of an action or a state of being.

The **present tense** places an action or condition in the present. (She *speaks* to her pets.)

The **past tense** places an action or condition in the past. (I *ran.*)

The **future tense** places an action or condition in the future. (They *will stop.*)

The **present perfect tense** describes an action that was completed in an indefinite past time or that began in the past and continues in the present. (*has happened, have dropped*)

The **past perfect tense** describes one action that happened before another action in the past. (*had seen, had believed*)

The **future perfect tense** describes a future event that will be finished before another future action begins. (*will have noticed*)

Punctuation	Uses	Examples	
Apostrophe (')	Shows possession Forms a contraction	Pedro's house They'll come.	Allen's shoes The door's open.
Colon (:)	Introduces a list or long quotation	these colors: red, green, and black	
Comma (,)	Separates ideas Separates modifiers Separates items in series	I arrived early, and I set up the chairs. the beautiful, rare jewels She bought bread, fruit, and meat.	
Exclamation point (!)	Ends an exclamatory sentence	Have a wonderful time!	
Hyphen (-)	Joins words in some compound nouns	father-in-law, sergeant-at-arms	
Period (.)	Ends a declarative sentence Indicates most abbreviations	The rainbow suddenly appeared. yd. Dr. Ave. Mrs. Oct.	
Question mark (?)	Ends an interrogative sentence	Can you draw?	
Semicolon (;)	Joins some compound sentences Separates items in series that contain commas	Gene left school early; he went straight home. Bruce saw a bright, young cardinal; a tiny, fluttering hummingbird; and a large, noisy crow.	

Index of Fine Art

INDEX OF FINE ART **893**

Index of Skills

Literary Concepts

Author's purpose, 121, 800
Autobiography, 53, 63, 68, 283, 800
Ballad, 487
Biographer, 53
Biography, 53, 75, 214, 800
Cast of characters, 216, 800
Character, 13, 51, 53, 153, 216, 248, 800
 contrasting, 37
 evaluating, 666
 dynamic/static, 15
 foil, 656, 667
 main/minor, 13, 51, 400
Characterization, 340, 380, 486, 800
Climax, 14, 35, 190, 557, 801
Complications (plot), 14
Conflict, 13–14, 93, 106, 248, 801
 external and internal, 153, 557, 801
Connotation, 801
Denotation, 801
Description, 271
Dialect, 83, 93, 486, 801
Dialogue, 216, 369, 381, 801
Diary, 53
Drama, 216–217, 802
 act, 217, 800
 characters, 216
 dialogue, 216, 369
 Noh play, 517
 plot, 216
 resolution, 217
 scene, 217, 805
 scenery/props, 216
 script, 216
 setting, 216, 217
 sound effects, 218
 stage directions, 216, 217, 218, 355, 806
 teleplay, 355, 807
Essay, 53–54, 126, 802
 biographical, 75
 formal, 54
 informal (personal), 54, 126
 personal response, 76, 77
Exaggeration, 802
Exposition, 13–14, 295, 802
Fable. *See* Folklore.
Fiction, 13–14, 802. *See also* Folklore.
 fantasy, 415, 802
 mystery, 607
 novel, 13, 804
 science fiction, 415, 573, 806

short story, 13, 246, 248
Figurative language, 109, 175, 201, 802
 extended metaphor, 353
 metaphor, 109, 175, 353, 495
 personification, 109, 385
 simile, 109, 175, 201, 271, 353, 495
Figure of speech. *See* Figurative language.
Flashback, 803
Foil, 656, 667, 803
Folklore, 802
 fable, 672, 700, 763, 802
 folk tale, 672, 675, 700, 717, 762, 802
 legend, 672, 716, 803
 myth, 672, 675, 700, 717, 804
 trickster tale, 762
Foreshadowing, 471, 803
Form, 108, 803
Genre, 803
Humor, 329, 433
Hyperbole, 146
Imagery, 109, 119, 172–173, 516, 803
Irony, 433, 803
Jargon, 803
Journal, 53
Legend. *See* Folklore.
Lyric poetry, 198
Memoir, 53
Metaphor, 109, 175, 526, 803
Mood, 225, 656, 804
Moral, of a fable, 700, 804
Motif, 675
Motivation, 26, 27, 283, 804
Myth. *See* Folklore.
Narrative, 804, 824
Narrative poetry, 141, 503, 804
Narrator, 24, 165, 250, 804
Nonfiction, 53–54, 804
 article, 35
 autobiography, 53, 63, 68, 283
 biography, 53, 75
 diary/journal, 53
 essay, 53–54, 126, 802
 informative, 53, 61
 letters, 53, 68, 93
 literary, 53, 590
 memoir, 53, 68
 personal essay, 54, 126
Novel, 13, 805
Oral tradition, 674, 743
Personal narrative, 92
Personification, 804
Play. *See* Drama.

Plot, 13–14, 35, 53, 804
    climax, 14, 35
    complications, 14
    conflict, 13, 53, 106, 248
    in drama, 216, 217
    exposition, 13–14
    foreshadowing, 471
    narrative, 824
    resolution, 14
    short story, 248
    surprise ending, 413
    theme, 13, 14
Poetry, 108–109, 113, 805
    alliteration, 800
    figures of speech, 109
    form, 108
    free verse, 108, 196, 803
    imagery, 109, 119, 198
    lines, 108
    lyric poem, 198
    narrative, 141, 298, 804
    onomatopoeia, 805
    rhyme, 108, 113, 141, 145, 805
    rhythm, 108, 141, 145, 503
    sound devices, 108, 141
    speaker, 110, 806
    stanza, 108, 145, 806
    style, 146
    theme, 109
    tone, 564
    understanding, 109
    word choice, 109, 119, 199
Point of view, 24, 93, 805
    first person, 24, 53, 93, 805
    third person, 24, 93, 165, 805
Prose, 806
Repetition, 108, 113, 201, 805
Resolution, 14, 217
Rhyme, 108, 113, 141, 805
    end rhyme, 113, 145, 805
    internal rhyme, 145, 805
    in narrative poetry, 141
Rhyme scheme, 113
Rhythm, 108, 298, 503, 599, 805
    narrative poetry, 141, 298
    poetry, 108, 503
Sensory details/language, 75, 131, 198
Setting, 13, 53, 106, 248, 266, 400, 527, 573, 806
Short story, 13, 806
Simile, 109, 526, 806
Slang words, 26
Sound devices, 141, 599
    alliteration, 598, 599
    consonance, 598, 599
    onomatopoeia, 503, 599
    poetry, 108, 141
    repetition, 108, 113, 201
Speaker, in poetry, 110

Standard language, 486. *See also* Dialect; Slang words.
Stanza, 108, 145
Stereotypes, 658, 806
Structure, 806
Style, 51, 74, 146, 806
Surprise ending, 413, 806
Suspense, 14, 548, 807
Symbol, 83, 807
Techniques, 74, 385
Theme, 13, 14, 109, 136, 243, 254, 369, 380, 526, 794, 807
Title, 190, 439, 807
Tone, 564, 807
Word choice, 109, 119, 199

Reading and Critical Thinking

Active reading, strategies for, 6
Advertising, 178
Analyzing, 24, 35, 50, 51, 68, 81, 95, 106, 113, 117, 119, 126, 145, 153, 165, 190, 194, 196, 199, 201, 214, 225, 232, 238, 243, 271, 283, 295, 301, 329, 340, 348, 353, 400, 413, 432, 435, 439, 486, 495, 516, 548, 557, 564, 573, 575, 590, 655, 698
Application
    ideas to literature, 74, 259, 789
    literature to life, 24, 61, 62, 63, 68, 384
Associations, 178, 179
Author's purpose, 24, 121, 126, 165
Brainstorming, 27, 63, 180, 374, 384, 385, 400, 439, 495, 518, 530, 575, 698, 786
Categorizing, 15, 24, 131, 181, 245
Cause and effect, 148, 218, 232, 800
Chronological order, 203, 801
Clarifying, 6, 7, 9, 40, 44, 186, 391, 394, 534, 535, 539, 801
Classifying details, 131
Compare and contrast, 6, 27, 36, 37, 50, 51, 68, 69, 81, 107, 115, 126, 136, 145, 165, 232, 243, 244, 271, 296, 302, 329, 330, 341, 351, 353, 413, 432, 439, 471, 486, 488, 496, 503, 516, 557, 564, 574, 591, 661, 699, 763, 788, 789, 801. *See also* Similarities and differences.
Connecting, 1, 83, 109, 110, 111, 126, 128, 145, 179, 199, 201, 321, 351, 380, 660, 801
    through art, 25, 94, 113, 202
    background connection, 15, 37, 55, 63, 95, 115, 121
    cultural connection, 147, 331, 342, 786
    historical connection, 55, 141, 155
    personal connection, 15, 24, 26, 35, 37, 55, 61, 63, 95, 115, 119, 121, 141, 147, 181, 225, 232, 235, 285, 298, 333, 353, 355, 402, 432, 455, 470, 486, 488, 495, 503, 505, 516, 531, 566, 573
    through reading, 14, 15, 26, 55, 83, 95, 110, 115, 121, 155, 193, 298, 384, 454, 550
Context, 98, 801
Context clues. *See entry in* Vocabulary Skills *index.*
Cooperative learning. *See* Working in Groups *in the* Speaking, Listening, and Viewing *index.*

Grammar, Usage, and Mechanics

Writing Skills, Modes, and Formats

Visualizing, 172–173, 194, 314, 505
Word choice, 35
Word processing, 840
Writing about literature, 74
    character analysis, 214, 340, 413
    character sketch, 50, 340
    comparing and contrasting characters, 107, 153, 191, 218, 341, 550
    comparing and contrasting plots, 218
    comparing and contrasting stories, 191, 433, 471, 496, 504, 786–792
    critical review, 271, 557, 600–603
    extending the story, 191, 271, 446, 448, 548
    interpretive essay, 316
    literary analysis, 243, 271
    personal response, 76–78, 353, 434, 590
    responding as a character, 153, 191, 249, 295, 301, 314, 340, 348, 400, 432, 486, 516, 548, 557
    responding to a character, 76, 196, 225, 243
    responding to imagery, 172–173, 201
    responding to plot, 190, 225, 298
    responding to setting, 225, 272
    responding to speaker, 196, 199, 350
    responding to theme, 193, 243, 384, 454
    responding to tone, 564
Writing activities, 126–130
Writing process, 808–813. *See also* Drafting; Gathering information; Prewriting; Proofreading; Publishing; Reflecting on your writing; Revising
    self-evaluation, 78, 135, 379, 450, 525, 602
    writing with computers, 68, 146, 840

Vocabulary Skills

Analogies, 69
Antonyms, 26, 166, 245, 349, 434, 558
Connotation, 109, 119, 165, 199, 414, 663
Context clues, 26, 27, 36, 52, 62, 83, 94, 95, 107, 127, 154, 192, 215, 272, 297, 371, 414, 453, 472, 487, 496, 592, 801
    inferences, 62, 260, 319
Crossword puzzle, 592, 606
Definitions, 50, 126, 154, 297, 349, 371, 401, 413, 414, 434, 487, 549, 574, 657
Denotation, 297, 349, 371, 401, 487, 549
Dialect, 83, 93
Dictionaries, 27, 371, 374, 375
Dictionary study, 69
Figurative language, 109, 175
Figures of speech. *See* Figurative language.
Homophones, 432
Hyperbole, 146
Idioms, 487
Imagery, 109, 119, 172–173
Inference, 260
Signal words, 203

Slang words, 27, 93. *See also* Dialect.
Spell checker, 840
Synonyms, 26, 107, 125, 157, 166, 173, 245, 284, 349, 440, 517, 657
Thesaurus, 374, 840
Word problem, 549

Research and Study Skills

Atlases, 784
Bartlett's *Familiar Quotations*, 374
CD-ROM, 839
Card catalog, 835
Catalogs, computerized, 835, 839
Computer
    on-line databases, 127, 838
    on-line searching, 197
    research indexes, 835
Dictionaries, 27, 35, 370, 375, 840
    specialized, 27, 68
Dictionary study, 69
Documentary video, 558
E-mail, 838
Electronic resources, 839
Encyclopedias
    CD-ROM, 36, 215, 272, 471, 487, 496, 558
    computer, 565
    general, 520, 698, 784
    on-line, 36, 197, 487, 496
Indexes, research, 835
Information services, 838
Internet, 784, 838
Interviewing, 51, 62, 191, 302, 330, 414, 565, 656, 661
Journals, 130
Letters, 61, 130
Library, 520
    computer services, 838–839
    using the, 835–836
Maps, 51
Memorabilia, 51, 130
New York Times Index, 835
Note-taking, 835–836
On-line resources, 127, 197, 370, 838, 839
Oral history, 302
Photo albums, 130
Quotations, 374
Readers' Guide to Periodical Literature, 835
Reference books, 191, 374, 520
Research activities
    Alcoholics Anonymous, 330
    Athabaskan people, 120
    Better Business Bureau, 191
    boxing, 414
    calorie, 574
    carols and caroling, 244
    child development, 25

Speaking, Listening, and Viewing Skills

Index of Titles and Authors

Page numbers that appear in italics refer to biographical information.

Acknowledgments *(continued)*

Random House, Inc.: Excerpt from *The Autobiography of Malcolm X* by Malcolm X, with the assistance of Alex Haley; Copyright © 1964 by Alex Haley and Malcolm X, renewed © 1965 by Alex Haley and Betty Shabazz. Reprinted by permission of Random House, Inc.

Marian Reiner, Literary Agent: "Aardvark," from *Nine Black Poets* by Julia Fields. Reprinted by permission of Marian Reiner for the author.

Bilingual Press/Editorial Bilingüe: "The Scholarship Jacket," from *Nosotras: Latina Literature Today* by Marta Salinas. By permission of Bilingual Press/Editorial Bilingüe.

Toni Cade Bambara: "The War of the Wall" by Toni Cade Bambara. By permission of the author.

Lawrence Hill Books: "Last Cover," from *The Best Nature Stories of Paul Annixter* by Paul Annixter; Copyright © 1974 Paul and Jane Annixter. By permission of the publisher, Lawrence Hill Books, New York, NY.

M. Catherine Costello, literary executor for Mary TallMountain Circle: "There Is No Word for Goodbye" from *The Light on the Tent Wall* by Mary TallMountain, published by the University of California American Indian Studies Center, 1990.

Arte Publico Press: "Graduation Morning," from *Chants* by Pat Mora. Reprinted with permission from the publisher of *Chants*, Arte Publico Press—University of Houston, 1985.

Random House, Inc.: Excerpt from *Living Out Loud* by Anna Quindlen; Copyright © 1987 by Anna Quindlen. By permission of Random House, Inc.

Susan Bergholz Literary Services: "Bums in the Attic," from *The House on Mango Street* by Sandra Cisneros; Copyright © 1984 by Sandra Cisneros, published by Vintage Books, a division of Random House, Inc., New York.

Unit Two

Harold Ober Associates, Inc.: "Thank You M'am," from *The Langston Hughes Reader* by Langston Hughes; Copyright © 1958 by Langston Hughes, renewed 1986 by George Houston Bass. Reprinted by permission of Harold Ober Associates, Incorporated.

Fifi Oscard Agency, Inc.: "Hollywood and the Pits" by Cherylene Lee, from *American Dragons: Twenty-Five Asian American Voices*, edited by Laurence Yep. Copyright © 1992 by Cherylene Lee. By permission of Fifi Oscard Agency, Inc.

Viking Penguin: "A Conversation with My Dogs," from *What the Dogs Have Taught Me* by Merrill Markoe; Copyright © 1992 by Merrill Markoe. Used by permission of Viking Penguin, a division of Penguin Books USA Inc.

HarperCollins Publishers, Inc.: All lines from "Dog Around the Block," from *The Fox of Peapack* by E. B. White; Copyright 1930 by E. B. White, renewed © 1958 by E. B. White. This poem originally appeared in *The New Yorker*. Reprinted by permission of HarperCollins Publishers, Inc.

Caxton Printers, Ltd.: "Say It with Flowers," from *Yokohama, California* by Toshio Mori. By permission of The Caxton Printers, Ltd., Caldwell, Idaho 83605.

Liveright Publishing Corporation: "old age sticks," from *Complete Poems, 1904–1962* by E. E. Cummings, Edited by George J. Firmage; Copyright © 1958, 1986, 1991 by the Trustees for the E. E. Cummings Trust. By permission of Liveright Publishing Corporation.

Phil W. Petrie: "It Happened in Montgomery," from *The Magic of Black Poetry* by Phil W. Petrie. Reprinted by permission of Phil W. Petrie, Sr.

William Morrow & Company, Inc.: "Choices," from *Cotton Candy on a Rainy Day* by Nikki Giovanni; Copyright © 1978 by Nikki Giovanni. By permission of William Morrow & Company, Inc.

Macmillan Publishing Company: "Barter," from *Selected Poems of Sara Teasdale* (New York: Macmillan, 1937). Reprinted with the permission of Macmillan Publishing Company, a division of Simon & Schuster, Inc.

Saturday Review: "Ride a Wild Horse," by Hannah Kahn from *Saturday Review,* March, 1953; Copyright 1953 by Saturday Review. By permission of Saturday Review.

Atheneum Books for Young Readers: Excerpt from "Eleanor Roosevelt," from *Great Lives: Human Rights* by William Jay Jacobs; Copyright © 1990 by William Jay Jacobs. Reprinted and recorded with the permission of Atheneum Books for Young Readers, an imprint of Simon & Schuster, Inc.

Simon & Schuster, Inc.: Excerpt from *No Ordinary Time* by Doris Kearns Goodwin; Copyright © 1994 by Doris Kearns Goodwin. Reprinted by permission of Simon & Schuster, Inc.

University of Minnesota Press: *A Christmas Carol* by Charles Dickens, adapted by Fred Gaines, from *Five Plays from the Children's Theatre Company of Minneapolis,* published by the University of Minnesota Press. Copyright © 1975 by Fred Gaines.

Sports Illustrated for Kids: Excerpt from "The Worst Day I Ever Had," by Adonal Foyle, from *Sports Illustrated for Kids,* July, 1995: Copyright © 1995 by Time Inc. Reprinted by permission of Sports Illustrated for Kids. All rights reserved.

Unit Three

Murray Pollinger: "The Chief's Daughter," from *Heather, Oak and Olive* by Rosemary Sutcliff; Published by Dutton & Co., Inc. By permission of Murray Pollinger, Literary Agent.

Jackie Robinson Foundation: Excerpt from *I Never Had It Made* by Jackie Robinson, as told to Alfred Duckett. By permission of Rachel Robinson.

Doubleday: Excerpt from *The Quality of Courage* by Mickey Mantle; Copyright © 1964 by Bedford S. Wynne, Trustee of four separate trusts for the benefit of Mickey Elven Mantle, David Harold Mantle, Billy Giles Mantle, and Danny Murl Mantle. Used by permission of Doubleday, a division of Bantam Doubleday Dell Publishing Group, Inc.

Virginia Driving Hawk Sneve: "The Medicine Bag" by Virginia Driving Hawk Sneve, first printed in *Boys' Life,* March 1975. Reprinted with permission of the author.

Walker and Company: Excerpt from *Susan Butcher and the Iditarod Trail* by Ellen M. Dolan; Copyright © 1993 by Ellen M. Dolan. Reprinted by permission of Walker and Company, 435 Hudson Street, New York, NY 10014. All rights reserved.

Little, Brown and Company and Thistledown Press Ltd.: "What I Want to Be When I Grow Up," from *Paradise Cafe and Other Stories* by Martha Brooks; Copyright © 1988 by Martha Brooks. By permission of Little, Brown and Company and Thistledown Press Ltd.

Judith Nihei: "Koden" by Judith Nihei, from *American Dragons: Twenty-Five Asian American Voices,* edited by Laurence Yep. Reprinted by permission of the author.

Hancock House Publishers, Ltd.: Excerpt from *My Heart Soars* by Chief Dan George and Helmut Hirnschall, published by Hancock House Publishers, 1431 Harrison Avenue, Blaine, WA 98231.

Wylie, Aitken & Stone: "The Time We Climbed Snake Mountain," from *Voices of the Rainbow: Contemporary Poetry by American Indians* by Leslie Marmon Silko; Copyright © by Leslie Marmon Silko. By permission of Wylie, Aitken & Stone.

T. D. Allen: "Direction" by Alonzo Lopez, from *The Whispering Wind: Poetry by Young American Indians,* edited by T. D. Allen; published by Doubleday. Used by permission of the author.

The Rod Serling Trust: *The Monsters Are Due on Maple Street* by Rod Serling; Copyright © 1960 by Rod Serling, © 1988 by Carolyn Serling, Jody Serling and Anne Serling. Reprinted by permission of the Rod Serling Trust.

Unit Four

Alfred A. Knopf, Inc.: Excerpt from *Stories from El Barrio* by Piri Thomas; Copyright © 1978 by Piri Thomas. Reprinted by permission of Alfred A. Knopf, Inc., a division of Random House, Inc.

Brandt & Brandt Literary Agents, Inc., and A. M. Heath, Ltd.: "The Serial Garden" from *Armitage, Armitage, Fly Away Home* by Joan Aiken; Copyright © 1966 by Macmillan & Co., Ltd. Reprinted by permission of Brandt & Brandt Literary Agents, Inc., and A. M. Heath, Ltd.

Bantam Books: "The Eternal Frontier," from *Frontier* by Louis L'Amour. Copyright © 1984 by Louis L'Amour Enterprises, Inc. By permission of Bantam Books, a division of Bantam Doubleday Dell Publishing Group, Inc.

Scholastic, Inc.: "Hockey" by Scott Blaine. Reprinted by permission of Scholastic, Inc.

Marian Reiner, Literary Agent: "The Women's 400 Meters," from *The Sidewalk Racer and Other Poems of Sports and Motion* by Lillian Morrison; Copyright © 1965, 1967, 1968, 1977 by Lillian Morrison. Reprinted with permission of Marian Reiner for the author.

"74th Street," from *The Malibu and Other Poems* by Myra Cohn Livingston; Copyright © 1972 by Myra Cohn Livingston. Reprinted by permission of Marian Reiner for the author.

Naomi Washington for the Estate of Margaret Danner: "I'll Walk the Tightrope" by Margaret Danner. Reprinted by permission of Naomi Washington for the estate of the author.

Samuel W. Allen: "To Satch" by Samuel W. Allen; Copyright © by Samuel W. Allen. Reprinted by permission of the author.

Estate of Borden Deal: "The Christmas Hunt" by Borden Deal, first appeared in *The Saturday Evening Post.* By permission of the Estate of Borden Deal.

Organization of American States: "Formula" by Ana Maria Iza, from *Américas,* a bimonthly magazine published in English and Spanish by the General Secretariat of the Organization of American States.

Farrar, Straus & Giroux, Inc., and Murray Pollinger: "The Bicycle and the Sweet-Shop," "The Great Mouse Plot," and "Mr. Coombes" from *Boy: Tales of Childhood* by Roald Dahl; Copyright © 1984 by Roald Dahl. By permission of Farrar, Straus & Giroux, Inc. and Murray Pollinger.

Don Congdon Associates, Inc.: "All Summer in a Day," by Ray Bradbury; Copyright © 1954, renewed 1982 by Ray Bradbury. Reprinted by permission of Don Congdon Associates, Inc.

Harcourt Brace & Company and Penguin Books, Ltd.: "What Do We Do with a Variation?" from *When I Dance* by James Berry; Copyright © 1991, 1988 by James Berry. Reprinted by permission of Harcourt Brace & Company and Penguin Books, Ltd.

Hugh Noyes: "The Highwayman," by Alfred Noyes. Reprinted by permission of Hugh Noyes, for the Trustees of the Literary Estate of Alfred Noyes.

William Morrow & Company, Inc.: Excerpt from *Commodore Perry in the Land of the Shogun* by Rhoda Blumberg; Copyright © 1985 by Rhoda Blumberg. Reprinted by permission of Lothrop, Lee & Shepard Books, a division of William Morrow & Company, Inc.

Unit Five

Virginia Kidd, Literary Agent for Anne McCaffrey: "The Smallest Dragonboy," by Anne McCaffrey; Copyright © 1973 by Anne McCaffrey; first appeared in *Science Fiction Tales*. Reprinted by permission of the author and the author's agent, Virginia Kidd.

Margaret Tsuda: "No-Wall Wall," from *Urban River* by Margaret Tsuda. Discovery Books, HCR 01, Box 343, Owls Head, NY 12969.

Estate of Ted Poston: "The Revolt of the Evil Fairies," from *The Dark Side of Hopkinsville* by Ted Poston; Copyright © 1991 by the University of Georgia Press, Athens, Georgia.

Gloria Oden: "The Way It Is," from *Poetry Is Alive and Well and Living in America* by Gloria Oden. Reprinted by permission of the author.

Harcourt Brace & Company: "Without Commercials," from *Horses Make a Landscape Look More Beautiful*; Copyright © 1984 by Alice Walker. Reprinted by permission of Harcourt Brace & Company.

GRM Associates, Inc.: "Lose Now, Pay Later," from *2041: Twelve Short Stories About the Future of Science* by Carol Farley; Copyright © 1991 by Carol Farley. Reprinted by permission of GRM Associates, Inc., Agents for Carol Farley.

Scholastic Inc.: Excerpts from *Exploring the Titanic* by Robert D. Ballard; Copyright © 1988 by Robert D. Ballard. Reprinted by permission of Scholastic Inc.

Farrar, Straus & Giroux, Inc.: "Charles," from *The Lottery* by Shirley Jackson; Copyright 1948, 1949 by Shirley Jackson, renewed © 1976, 1977 by Laurence Hyman, Barry Hyman, Mrs. Sarah Webster and Mrs. Joanne Schnurer. Reprinted by permission of Farrar, Straus & Giroux, Inc.

Samuel French, Inc.: "The Hound of the Baskervilles" adapted by Tim Kelly; Copyright © 1976 by Tim Kelly. CAUTION: Professionals and amateurs are hereby warned that *The Hound of the Baskervilles* being fully protected under the copyright laws of the United States of America, the British Commonwealth countries, including Canada, and other countries of the Copyright Union, is subject to a royalty. All rights, including professional, amateur, motion picture, recitation, public reading, radio, television and cable broadcasting, and the rights of translation into foreign languages, are strictly reserved. Any inquiry regarding the availability of performance rights, or the purchase of individual copies of the authorized acting edition, must be directed to Samuel French Inc., 45 West 25 Street, New York, NY 10010 with other locations in Hollywood, CA, and Toronto, Canada.

Unit Six

Scholastic Inc.: Excerpt from *Heroes, Gods and Monsters of Greek Myths* by Bernard Evslin; Copyright © 1966, 1977 by Scholastic Inc. Reprinted by permission of Scholastic Inc.

Alfred A. Knopf, Inc.: Excerpt from *The People Could Fly: American Black Folktales* by Virginia Hamilton. Reprinted by permission of Alfred A. Knopf, Inc., a division of Random House, Inc.

HarperCollins Publishers: "The Fitting of the Slipper," from *A Telling of the*

Tales by William J. Brooke; Text Copyright © 1990 by William J. Brooke. Reprinted by permission of HarperCollins Publishers.

Copp Clark Pitman Ltd.: "Phaëthon," from *Myth* by Moira Kerr and John Bennett; Copyright © 1966, Copp Clark Pitman Ltd. Used by permission of the publisher.

Mary Jane Perna for the Estate of Yoshiko Uchida: "Gombei and the Wild Ducks" by Yoshiko Uchida. Reprinted by permission of the Estate of Yoshiko Uchida.

Little, Brown and Company: "How Odin Lost His Eye," from *Adventures with the Giants* by Catherine F. Sellew; Copyright 1950 by Catherine Sellew Hinchman, renewed © 1978. *The Arrow and the Lamp: The Story of Psyche* retold by Margaret Hodges; Copyright © 1989 by Margaret Hodges. By permission of Little, Brown and Company.

Pantheon Books: Excerpt from *The Sound of Flutes and Other Indian Legends* by Richard Erdoes; Text Copyright © 1976 by Richard Erdoes. Reprinted by permission of Pantheon Books, a division of Random House, Inc.

HarperCollins Publishers: "Waters of Gold," from *Tongues of Jade* by Laurence Yep; Text Copyright © 1991 by Laurence Yep. Reprinted by permission of HarperCollins Publishers.

Libraries Unlimited, Inc.: "Pumpkin Seed and the Snake," from *Folk Stories of the Hmong* by Norma Livo and Dia Cha; Copyright © 1991 by Libraries Unlimited, Inc. By permission of Libraries Unlimited, Inc.

The Putnam Publishing Group: "Kelfala's Secret Something," from *Three African Tales* by Adjai Robinson; Copyright © 1979 by Adjai Robinson. Reprinted with the permission of The Putnam Publishing Group.

Copp Clark Pitman Ltd.: "Echo and Narcissus," from *Myth* by Moira Kerr and John Bennett; Copyright © 1966, Copp Clark Pitman Ltd. Used by permission of the publisher.

Museum of New Mexico Press: "La suerte: The Force of Luck" by Rudolfo A. Anaya; Copyright © 1980. Reprinted with the permission of the Museum of New Mexico Press, from *Cuentos: Tales from the Hispanic Southwest* by Jose Griego y Maestas and Rudolfo Anaya.

Ricardo E. Alegría: "Lazy Peter and His Three-Cornered Hat," from *The Three Wishes* by Ricardo E. Alegría. Reprinted by permission of the author.

Art Credits

Commissioned Art and Photography
2 *top*, 76 *bottom*, 128, 129, 134, 135, 172, 173, 174 *top*, 176, 248, 249, 372–374, 378, 379, 446, 448 *top*, 449, 450, 525, 598, 600 *top*, 659 *center*, 662, 664, 734–739, 786 *top*, 787 *right* Allan Landau.
4–5, 23, 25, 51, 70, 74, 75, 76 *top*, 78, 84, 130–131, 155, 174 *bottom*, 178–179, 187, 191, 223, 246–247, 250–253, 261, 274, 294, 312–316, 332–333, 336–338, 341, 354, 375–376, 409, 412, 416, 418, 422, 429, 431, 441–445 *skates*, 448 *bottom*, 474–485, 498, 501–502, 518–524, 547, 551–552, 555–556, 563, 568–572, 577, 583, 586–588, 597, 600 *bottom*, 601–602, 658–661, 665, 698–699, 714, 733, 742, 743 *top*, 746, 748, 750, 752, 760–761, 767, 773, 785 786 *bottom*, 787 *left*, 788, 792–793 Sharon Hoogstraten.
286, 288, 292–294 Ruta Daugavietis. 303, 306–308, 310, 386–398, 668–669, 674–675, 700–701, 716–717, 742–743, 762–763 *maps* John Sandford. 532–534, 536, 541, 543, 545 Ray-Mel Cornelius. 575 *diagram* Jason O'Malley. 669–670

Gordon Lewis. **671** Richard Waldrep. **684, 697** Pierre Pratt.

All other maps: Robert Voights.

The editors have made every effort to trace the ownership of all copyrighted art and photography found in this book and to make full acknowledgment for their use. Omissions brought to our attention will be corrected in a subsequent edition.

Author Photographs and Portraits
26 Margaret Miller. **36, 302, 401, 657** Stock Montage. **62** Copyright © 1988 Chicago Tribune Co., all rights reserved. **69, 114, 154, 504, 703, 705, 779** The Granger Collection, New York. **94, 558** Schomburg Center for Research in Black Culture, The New York Public Library, Astor, Lenox and Tilden Foundations. **120** *left* Lance Woodruff; *right* Arte Publico Press. **127** Courtesy of the *New York Times*. **146** Harvard University Archives. **171, 440, 597** AP/Wide World Photos, Inc. **192** Stephen V. Mori. **197** Copyright © Nancy Crampton. **202, 371** UPI/Bettmann. **245** Culver Pictures. **284** Courtesy of the *Chicago Defender*. **354** Moorland-Spingarn Research Center, Howard University. **442** Copyright © 1987 Elizabeth Gilliland. **487** Copyright © Sophie Baker. **496, 549** Jay Kay Klein. **565** Jim Marshall. **592** Barbara Nitke. **683** Cox Studios. **713** Copyright © June Finfer, Filmedia, Chicago. **724** Courtesy of Richard Forbes. **731** Photo by K. Yep.

Miscellaneous Art Credits
xii *Reverie* (1989), Frank Webb. Pastel, 12″ × 8″, collection of Barbara Webb. **xiv** *The Tribesman* (1982), Hubert Shuptrine. Montgomery (Alabama) Museum of Art, Blount Collection. Copyright © 1982 Hubert Shuptrine, all rights reserved. **xvi** Detail of *Mount Fuji and Seashore at Miho No Matsubara* (1966), Kano Tanyū. Asian Art Museum of San Francisco, Avery Brundage Collection (B63 D7a). Photo Copyright © 1995 Asian Art Museum of San Francisco. **xix** Illustration by Sergio Martinez. From Children's Classics Edition of *The Hound of the Baskervilles* by Sir Arthur Conan Doyle. Copyright © 1992 Crown Publishers, Inc., reprinted by permission. **xxi** Narcissus enchanted by his reflection. French engraving from an 18th-century edition of Ovid's *Metamorphoses*, The Granger Collection, New York. **xxiv–1** *Sanary* (1952), Ellsworth Kelly. Oil on wood, 51½″ × 60″, (EK 48). **2** *center left* Copyright © 1995 Jay Freis/Image Bank; *center right* Copyright © Chris Noble/Tony Stone Images; *bottom* Copyright © T. Nakajima/Photonica. **3** *top* Copyright © 1993 Jim Cummins/FPG International Corp. **12** Copyright © Don Smetzer/Tony Stone Images. **38** Cupak/Mauritius/H. Armstrong Roberts. **51** *map* Copyright © American Map Corporation. **80–81** AP/Wide World Photos, Inc. **82** Copyright © Melanie Carr/Zephyr Pictures. **93** *Mural* (1980), Judy Jamerson, Church St. Mission High School, San Francisco. Copyright © Judy Jamerson. **129** *right* Copyright © 1982 The Far Side cartoon by Gary Larson is reprinted by permission of Chronicle Features, San Francisco, California, all rights reserved. **130** *center left* Copyright © Julie Habel/Westlight. **156, 164** Courtesy of the George C. Page Museum. **158–161, 163** Copyright © Craig Aurness/Westlight. **178–179** Copyright © 1995 National Fluid Milk Processor Promotion Board. **201** Copyright © Martin Wendler/Photo Researchers. **214** Jacket art and design Copyright © 1994 Wendell Minor. Published by Clarion Books. **247** *center* Copyright © Manny Millan; **263** *background* Copyright © Toni Schneiders/H. Armstrong Roberts. **318–319** Copyright © Joel Sternfeld, Courtesy Pace/MacGill Gallery, New York. **323, 325–326** Details of *The Subway* (1976), Red Grooms. Set design from *Ruckus*

Grooms. Set design from *Ruckus Manhattan*. Mixed media, 9′ × 18′7″ × 37′2″, courtesy of Marlborough Gallery, New York. Copyright © 1995 Artists Rights Society (ARS), New York. **344–346,** Detail of *The Birth of Ikce Wicasa* (1990), Colleen Cutschall. Courtesy of Art Gallery of Southwestern Manitoba, Canada. **351** Copyright © 1995 Peter Miller/Panoramic Images, Chicago. **352** Copyright © M. Barrett/H. Armstrong Roberts. **356, 368** Copyright © Archive Photos. **357, 364** Illustrations by Paul Rátz de Tagyos. **372** *bottom* Copyright © 1939 Turner Entertainment Co., all rights reserved. **373** *center* AP/Wide World Photos, Inc. **374** *top* Courtesy of Houghton Mifflin Company; *bottom* Courtesy of Little, Brown and Company. **379** *drugs* Copyright © Charles Thatcher/Tony Stone Images; *garbage* Copyright © Peter Cade/Tony Stone Images; *mask* Copyright © David Chambers/Tony Stone Images; *graffiti* Copyright © Hugh Sitton/Tony Stone Images; *firefighters* Copyright © Gary Irving/Tony Stone Images; *mom* Copyright © Timothy Shonnard/Tony Stone Images; *climber* Copyright © Dugald Bremner/Tony Stone Images; *police officer* Copyright © Robert E. Daemmrich/Tony Stone Images. **386** Copyright © Allen Garns/Stockworks. **400** Copyright © Harry Engels/Photo Researchers, Inc. **401** Copyright © John Mitchell/Photo Researchers, Inc. **403, 412** Copyright © G. Bliss/Masterfile. **433** *Lily Pool*, detail by Ruth Sanderson. **436–437** Copyright © John Lurner/Tony Stone Images. **438** Science Source/Photo Researchers, Inc. **441–445** *hockey players* Copyright © Calvin Nicholls/Masterfile; *runners* Copyright © David Madison/Tony Stone Images; *acrobat* Illustration by Sally Wern. Copyright © 1990 Howard Merrell & Partners Advertising, Raleigh, North Carolina; *Satchel Paige* UPI/ Bettmann. **452–453** Photo by Peter Ackerman, courtesy of Asbury Park Press. **454** Copyright © Warren Bolster/Tony Stone Images, Inc. **491–492** *background* Copyright © 1994 Thomas Wiewandt. **492** *foreground* Detail of *Wee Maureen* (1926), Robert Henri. Oil on canvas, 24″ × 20″, courtesy of the Museum of American Art of the Pennsylvania Academy of the Fine Arts, Philadelphia, gift of Mrs. Herbert Cameron Morris. **501–502** Illustrations by Charles Mikolaycak. Copyright © 1995 Carole Kismaric Mikolaycak. **506, 508, 511, 514** Japanese calligraphy courtesy of Buddhist Temple of Chicago. **506–511** *top* Copyright © 1985 Larry West/FPG International Corp. **518** *center* Courtesy of Westside Preparatory School, Chicago. **519** *top, Chicago Tribune* photo by Bob Langer. **524** *inset* Copyright © Mike Powell/Allsport. **547** Copyright © 1991 David Doody/FPG International Corp. **551** Reproduced from the collections of the Library of Congress. **561** Copyright © Randy Wells/Tony Stone Images. **561** Copyright © IFA/West Stock. **562–563** Copyright © Vera Storman/Tony Stone Images. **566** Copyright © 1991 Barry Seidman. **567** Illustration by Laura Tedeschi. Copyright © Stock Illustration Source, Inc. **569** *Untitled (Ice Cream Dessert)* (1959), Andy Warhol. Copyright © 1996 Andy Warhol Foundation for the Visual Arts/ARS, New York. **570** *Untitled (Ice Cream Dessert)* (1959), Andy Warhol. Copyright © 1996 Andy Warhol Foundation for the Visual Arts/ARS, New York. **571** *Untitled (Ice Cream Dessert)* (1959), Andy Warhol. Copyright © 1996 Andy Warhol Foundation for the Visual Arts/ARS, New York. **572** *Untitled (Ice Cream Dessert)* (1959), Andy Warhol. Copyright © 1996 Andy Warhol Foundation for the Visual Arts/ARS, New York. **580–581** From *Exploring the Titanic*. Copyright © 1988 by Robert D. Ballard, a Madison Press Book. **594** Copyright © Bob Conge. **604–605** Copyright © Craig J. Brown/Gamma Liaison. **607** Copyright © The Secretary to Sherlock Holmes, London. **611, 614, 617, 627, 634, 646** Illustration by Sydney Paget. From *The Strand* Magazine, photos courtesy of The Newberry Library. **659** *top* Copyright © William Viggiano. **672** *top* Photo by Carl Purcell; *middle* The Bettmann Archive; *bottom* The Granger Collection, New York. **673** *top center, bottom left* The

Bettmann Archive; *bottom center* The Granger Collection, New York; *top left* Odyssey/Frerck/Chicago; *top right* Sovfoto; *middle left* Copyright © Tom Wagner/Odyssey/Chicago; *middle right* La Casa del Libro, San Juan, Puerto Rico; *bottom right* Copyright © Jerry Jacka Photography. **674** Illustration by Leo and Diane Dillon, from *The People Could Fly* by Virginia Hamilton. Illustration Copyright © 1985 Leo and Diane Dillon. Reprinted by permission of Alfred A. Knopf, Inc. **675** *top* Illustration by Tom Curry; *bottom* Detail of an illustration by Robert Baxter from *Prometheus and the Story of Fire* by I. M. Richardson. Copyright © 1983 Troll Associates. Reprinted with permission of the publisher. **676** Detail of an illustration by Robert Baxter from *Prometheus and the Story of Fire* by I. M. Richardson. Copyright © 1983 Troll Associates. Reprinted with permission of the publisher; *background* Copyright © 1994 Randy Faris/Westlight. **700** *top* Detail Copyright © Charles Santore. **701** *top* Detail of a Japanese embroidered tapestry, Museo Stibbert, Florence, Italy, Scala/Art Resource, New York; *bottom* Detail of *Hermit* (1888), Mikhail Vasilievich Nesterov. Oil on canvas, 91 × 84 cm. The State Russian Museum, St. Petersburg, Russia. **716** Detail of an illustration by Linda Benson/Artworks New York. **717** Detail of *Beggars and Street Characters* (1516), Zhou Chen. Album leaves; ink and colors on paper. Honolulu (Hawaii) Academy of Arts, gift of Mrs. Carter Galt, 1956 (2239.1). **740–741** Copyright © Tom Raymond. **743** *top* Courtesy of Adrienne McGrath; *bottom* From *Samburu* by Nigel Pavitt. Copyright © 1992 Nigel Pavitt, reprinted by permission of Henry Holt and Co., Inc. **747** Copyright © Arthur C. Smith III/Grant Heilman Photography, Inc. **750, 752** Courtesy of Adrienne McGrath. **762** *left* Detail of *Mujer con Pesacados* [Woman with fish] (1980), Francisco Zuniga. Lithograph, $21\frac{7}{8}'' \times 29\frac{1}{2}''$, edition of 135, courtesy of Brewster Gallery, New York; *right* Detail of *Carnival in Huejotzingo* (1942), Diego Rivera. Watercolor on paper, $5\frac{5}{8}'' \times 3\frac{3}{4}''$, Sotheby's, New York. **763** *top* Detail of *King Saul* (1952), Jack Levine. Oil on panel, $13\frac{3}{4}'' \times 11''$, collection of John and Joanne Payson. Photo courtesy of Midtown Payson Galleries, New York; *bottom* Narcissus enchanted by his reflection. Detail of French engraving from an 18th-century edition of Ovid's *Metamorphoses,* The Granger Collection, New York. **764, 766, 780** Copyright © Japack/Leo de Wys Inc. **786** *top* Disney Character © The Walt Disney Company; *bottom* Cover illustration by David Shannon, reprinted by permission of G. P. Putnam's Sons from *The Rough-Face Girl* by Rafe Martin. Illustrations Copyright © 1992 David Shannon. **824** Copyright © William Means/Tony Stone Images. **826** Copyright © Peter Poulides/Tony Stone Images. **832** Copyright © D. E. Cox/Tony Stone Images. **834** Victor de Palma/Black Star. **838** Netscape, Netscape Navigator and the Netscape Communications Corporation Logo are trademarks of Netscape Communications Corporation; *center* NASA. **841–843** Screen shots reprinted with permission from Microsoft Corporation. **844** Used with express permission. Adobe and Adobe Illustrator are trademarks of Adobe Systems Incorporated. **845** Photo by James Lee. Copyright © Earth Images. **847** Photo by Steven Muir. Copyright © Earth Images

Teacher Review Panels *(continued)*

Bonnie Garrett, Davis Middle School, Compton School District

Sally Jackson, Madrona Middle School, Torrance Unified School District

Sharon Kerson, Los Angeles Center for Enriched Studies, Los Angeles Unified School District

Gail Kidd, Center Middle School, Azusa School District

Corey Lay, ESL Department Chairperson, Chester Nimitz Middle School, Los Angeles Unified School District

Myra LeBendig, Forshay Learning Center, Los Angeles Unified School District

Dan Manske, Elmhurst Middle School, Oakland Unified School District

Joe Olague, Language Arts Department Chairperson, Alder Middle School, Fontana School District

Pat Salo, 6th Grade Village Leader, Hidden Valley Middle School, Escondido Elementary School District

FLORIDA

Judi Briant, English Department Chairperson, Armwood High School, Hillsborough County School District

Beth Johnson, Polk County English Supervisor, Polk County School District

Sharon Johnston, Learning Resource Specialist, Evans High School, Orange County School District

Eileen Jones, English Department Chairperson, Spanish River High School, Palm Beach County School District

Jan McClure, Winter Park High School Orange County School District

Wanza Murray, English Department Chairperson (retired), Vero Beach Senior High School, Indian River City School District

Shirley Nichols, Language Arts Curriculum Specialist Supervisor, Marion County School District

Debbie Nostro, Ocoee Middle School, Orange County School District

Barbara Quinaz, Assistant Principal, Horace Mann Middle School, Dade County School District

OHIO

Joseph Bako, English Department Chairperson, Carl Shuler Middle School, Cleveland City School District

Deb Delisle, Language Arts Department Chairperson, Ballard Brady Middle School, Orange School District

Ellen Geisler, English/Language Arts Department Chairperson, Mentor Senior High School, Mentor School District

Dr. Mary Gove, English Department Chairperson, Shaw High School, East Cleveland School District

Loraine Hammack, Executive Teacher of the English Department, Beachwood High School, Beachwood City School District

Sue Nelson, Shaw High School, East Cleveland School District

Mary Jane Reed, English Department Chairperson, Solon High School, Solon City School District

Nancy Strauch, English Department Chairperson, Nordonia High School, Nordonia Hills City School Dictrict

Ruth Vukovich, Hubbard High School, Hubbard Exempted Village School District

TEXAS

Anita Arnold, English Department Chairperson, Thomas Jefferson High School, San Antonio Independent School District

Gilbert Barraza, J.M. Hanks High School, Ysleta School District

Sandi Capps, Dwight D. Eisenhower High School, Alding Independent School District

Judy Chapman, English Department Chairperson, Lawrence D. Bell High School, Hurst-Euless-Bedford School District

Pat Fox, Grapevine High School, Grapevine-Colley School District

LaVerne Johnson, McAllen Memorial High School, McAllen Independent School District

Donna Matsumura, W.H. Adamson High School, Dallas Independent School District

Ruby Mayes, Waltrip High School, Houston Independent School District

Mary McFarland, Amarillo High School, Amarillo Independent School District

Adrienne Thrasher, A.N. McCallum High School, Austin Independent School Distric

Manuscript Reviewers *(continued)*

Maryann Lyons, Literacy Specialist, Mentor teacher, San Francisco Unified School District, San Francisco, California

Karis MacDonnell, Ed.D., Dario Middle School, Miami, Florida

Bonnie J. Mansell, Downey Adult School, Downey, California

Martha Mitchell, Memorial Middle School, Orlando, Florida

Nancy Nachman, Landmark High School, Jacksonville, Florida

Karen Williams Perry, English Department Chairperson, Kennedy Jr. High School, Lisle, Illinois

Julia Pferdehirt, free-lance writer, former Special Education teacher, Middleton, Wisconsin

Phyllis Stewart Rude, English Department Head, Mears Jr./Sr. High School, Anchorage, Alaska

Leo Schubert, Bettendorf Middle School, Bettendorf, Iowa

Gertrude H. Vannoy, Curriculum Liaison Specialist, Gifted and Horizon teacher, Meany Middle School, Seattle, Washington

Richard Wagner, Language Arts Curriculum Coordinator, Paradise Valley School District, Phoenix, Arizona

Stephen J. Zadravec, Newmarket Jr./Sr. High School, Newmarket, New Hampshire